Selections from
the Work of

CHARLES DICKENS

CHARLES DICKENS
FOUR NOVELS

The Adventures of Oliver Twist
or The Parish Boy's Progress

A Christmas Carol

A Tale of Two Cities

Great Expectations

Introduction by Ernest Hilbert, PhD

CANTERBURY CLASSICS
San Diego

©2011 Canterbury Classics/Baker & Taylor Publishing Group

All correspondence concerning the content of this book should be
addressed to   Canterbury Classics
                      10350 Barnes Canyon Road, Suite 100
                      San Diego, CA 92121

Library of Congress Cataloging-in-Publication Data

Dickens, Charles, 1812-1870.
  [Novels. Selections]
  Charles Dickens : four novels / introduction by Ernest Hilbert.
    p. cm.
  ISBN-13: 978-1-60710-312-7
  ISBN-10: 1-60710-312-5
  I. Hilbert, Ernest, 1970- II. Title.
  PR4552 2011
  823'.8—dc22

                                        2011013998

PRINTED IN CHINA

1 2 3 4 5 15 14 13 12 11

Contents

Selections from
the Work of

CHARLES DICKENS

Introduction

Charles Dickens was the greatest novelist of the Victorian era and perhaps the most famous English novelist of all time. He once went so far as to describe himself as "an amazing man," and it is true that he was exceedingly gifted. In fact, his creative powers were matched only by his ambition. He is undoubtedly the most "English" of authors after William Shakespeare, meticulously capturing the lives, locales, and affairs of his native land at a time of remarkable societal change. He invented characters that seem to leap off the page. They live on in our imaginations long after the last leaf is turned. His popularity and influence were not only unmatched in his day but absolutely groundbreaking, altering the very essence of the novel. Aside from amusing his readers—something he never failed to do—Dickens had a real impact on the world around him. Energized by ideas of social reform, he was both a humanistic novelist and a true humanitarian. He supported the abolition of slavery and founded a home for "fallen" women, Urania College in London, with the help of heiress Angela Burdett Coutts. Novels such as *Oliver Twist* are works of fierce social commentary that helped to alter public opinion, thus steering the course of legislative reform. As novelist Jane Smiley wrote in her biography of the author, Dickens "never forgot that his fame gave him an unusual opportunity to comment upon and influence political events."

Born into a family of modest means in 1812, when Napoleon still ruled over much of Europe, Dickens would be greeted with unprecedented accomplishment as a novelist in a century that saw the British Empire attain its greatest reach, spanning the globe and dominating international commerce. The Industrial Revolution swung into full force in England, producing magnificent wealth but also horrendous and even harmful conditions for workers. The Victorian era roughly coincided with the Pax Britannica, or Peace of Britain—the era between Wellington's triumph over Napoleon at Waterloo in 1815 and the first shots of World War I in 1914—when Britain remained free of the threat of outside invasion. Railways and popular newspapers changed the very fabric of daily life for the English, and the Elementary Education Act of 1870 promised literacy for all. It was an era of rapid political and scientific adjustment unseen in earlier centuries: Charles Darwin embarked on his groundbreaking scientific travels on the HMS *Beagle* in 1831, and Karl Marx and Friedrich Engels published *The Communist Manifesto* in 1848 (Marx moved to London the following year and remained there for the rest of his life).

With the first of the Reform Acts (measures to enfranchise new voters) in 1832 and Queen Victoria's ascension to the throne five years later, the Victorian era began in earnest, bringing with it a bewildering combination of affluence and deprivation, progress and reaction. London swelled as agrarian workers poured in to find work, growing from roughly one million inhabitants in 1800 to more than six million by the end of the century. Buildings were black with soot from coal-fire stoves, and streets were filthy. Raw sewage spewed into the river Thames, which flows directly through the city. In fact, Dickens's London would appear to us a sprawling third-world city, crammed with beggars, plagued by crime, and fouled by pollution. Graveyards overflowed, and bodies were buried on top of one another. Contemporary accounts describe the stench as horrific. As Dickens biographer Peter Ackroyd has written, "If a late twentieth-century person were suddenly to find himself in a tavern or house of the period, he would be literally sick—sick with the smells, sick with the food, sick with the atmosphere around him."

From Rags to Riches

Charles's father, John Dickens, worked for a time as a clerk in the Royal Navy Pay Office in Portsmouth, briefly affording his family a comfortable life. As a boy, Charles read the episodic adventure novels of Tobias Smollett and Henry Fielding, which later inspired his own style of writing. He retained fond memories of early boyhood, but such times would not last. As Michael Slater has written, "During the first six years of Dickens's life his parents moved house no fewer than five times and it seems likely that this restlessness affected Dickens in his later life when he seemed to have some sort of need for constant changes of environment." Sadly, his father's penchant for living beyond his means ended in his arrest and consignment to Marshalsea debtor's prison in London. The rest of the family eventually joined him there with the exception of Charles, who was sent to live with a family friend in the Camden Town section of North London.

What may be the most influential event of the author's life occurred at this time. Dickens enjoyed his education at William Giles's School in Chatham, but after his father's imprisonment he was obliged to begin work at the tender age of twelve in order to help support his family. He was dispatched to Warren's Blacking Warehouse, where he worked grueling ten-hour days applying labels to bottles of boot polish. Dickens described the factory to his friend John Forster, author of *The Life of Charles Dickens*, the first of many biographies of the author:

> It was a crazy, tumble-down old house, abutting of course on the river, and literally overrun with rats. Its wainscoted rooms, and its rotten floors and staircase, and the old grey rats swarming down in the cellars, and the sound of their squeaking and scuffling coming up the stairs at all times, and the dirt and decay of the place, rise up visibly before me, as if I were there again.

To make matters worse, the young Dickens was displayed to passersby in a window, a cruel parody of his later aspiration to appear on the stage. The extraordinarily bright boy was crushed by this experience, and there is little doubt it sparked his lifelong commitment to the reform of working conditions for the poor. It would also inspire him to write about the underprivileged—laborers, servants, beggars, thieves—who rarely figured in the literature of the age, remaining entirely invisible as they had in novels of a previous generation, such as those of Jane Austen. Dickens might have spent years in the factory if not for two strokes of fate: the death of his paternal grandmother, who left a modest sum to his father, and the passage by Parliament of the Insolvent Debtors Act, which allowed the Dickens family to leave Marshalsea and relieve young Charles from his position at Warren's Blacking. Dickens enrolled in Wellington House Academy in North London, but his mother, Elizabeth Dickens, contemplated sending young Charles back to the blacking factory. He later wrote: "I never afterwards forgot, I never shall forget, I never can forget, that my mother was warm for my being sent back." It is very likely that Charles never fully forgave his father's spendthrift ways or his mother's willingness to see her son sent to work for the family at such a young age.

In 1827, Dickens's mother partly redeemed herself when she helped to place him as a law clerk at the firm of Ellis and Blackmore. This busy and demanding post soon led to another as a court stenographer. His experience with the firm provided him with material he would use again and again in his novels. All three full-length novels in this volume contain famous courtroom scenes: Oliver Twist faints from illness before a judge when accused of the theft of a book actually stolen by the Artful Dodger; Charles Darnay is falsely accused of spying for the French in *A Tale of Two Cities*; and the stern lawyer Mr. Jaggers and his charming clerk John Wemmick play pivotal roles in *Great Expectations*. Even the short novel *A Christmas Carol* can be read as an indictment and eventual acquittal of its central figure, Ebenezer Scrooge, on charges of hard-heartedness. Dickens would have also witnessed grisly hangings at Newgate Prison, near the Old Bailey, the central courtrooms of London. All four novels end with an execution of one kind or another: *Oliver Twist* with that of the child-exploiter Fagin at Newgate; *A Tale of Two Cities* with that of Sydney Carton in the Place du Revolution; *Great Expectations* with that of Magwitch, who dies in prison before he may be hanged; and even *A Christmas Carol* contains an execution of sorts, when Scrooge is shown his own cold, unvisited grave by the ghost of Christmas Yet to Come.

The Early Achievements

In 1833, at the age of 21, Dickens published his first story in the *Monthly Magazine* and began work as a journalist, covering parliamentary debates and election campaigns for the *Morning Chronicle*, another experience that would serve him well as a novelist. He began composing "sketches" of scenes and characters from his daily routines. These would be collected into his first book, *Sketches by Boz*, in 1836 ("Boz" was his occasional pen name). Around this time, Dickens entertained thoughts of a possible career as an actor. As fate would have it, he took ill on the day of his audition at the Lyceum Theatre and failed to appear. Afterward, he settled on a career as a novelist, though he never entirely surrendered dreams of the stage.

Dickens truly enjoyed acting. It was in his blood. He appeared in amateur theatricals throughout his life, always to encouraging reviews. He enjoyed mimicry and performed wildly entertaining impressions for friends. When crafting his novels, he stood before a mirror to sound out voices and test facial expressions. This goes some way to explaining his amazing ability to create such lifelike characters. In fact, outside of Shakespeare, it is hard to think of an English writer who generated such an astonishing array of characters from all social ranks and circumstances. He sometimes wrote for the stage, though his plays were never met with the enthusiasm that attended his novels, and they are largely forgotten. Later in life, he became a popular public reader of his own novels, assuming voices and acting out whole scenes single-handedly. For example, Jane Smiley writes that he gave a reading "in Bradford that attracted 3,700 people, followed by another in London. He read *A Christmas Carol* each time and used the story and the time of year and the occasions to promote the sort of openhearted generosity that had always been important to him. . . . It was one thing [for Dickens] to act in a play or a farce, in character and often speaking the words of another author. It was quite different to say his own words, passing through the personae of characters he himself had created, giving voice and action to his own inner life." His tours of England, Scotland, Ireland, and America earned substantial sums of money for his family and a variety of causes he championed.

In 1836, Dickens married Catherine Hogarth. Together they reared ten children and spent many years in what most believe to be domestic contentment, though by the end they split acrimoniously, much to the chagrin of both Dickens's friends and the public at large. Family life was important for Dickens, and he suffered terribly as his marriage came apart. One can feel the unquenchable desire for domestic happiness throughout his novels: The orphan Oliver seeking the protection and love he was denied in the workhouse; Doctor Alexandre Manette released from years of imprisonment to his daughter's care; young Pip struggling to create the semblance of a family with his cruel sister and avuncular brother-in-law; and even Scrooge, as he yearningly peers in on the humble Christmas feast of his clerk Bob Cratchit.

Dickens was a flamboyant dresser, a bit of a dandy, and was a favorite at parties, where his exuberant personality held sway. From a young age he found himself constantly in demand as the celebrated writer of the day. He kept a pet raven, named Grip, which he had stuffed upon its death (after King George IV stuffed his pet giraffe, such morbid practices became all the rage in England). Grip appeared as a talking raven in Dickens's 1841 novel *Barnaby Rudge*, and many believe this inspired Edgar Allan Poe to pen his famous poem "The Raven" in 1845. (Grip, surely the most famous raven of his or any other time, now resides at the Free Library of Philadelphia.) Dickens enjoyed great adulation from his fiercely devoted readers. He packed large auditoriums on his reading tours and was cheered on the streets of New York City. He became a household name, as did many of his most famous characters.

Although earlier publishing contracts failed to satisfy him financially, fame allowed Dickens to dictate his own terms, and he eventually became quite wealthy from his novels. He owned many properties and traveled widely, constantly in need of a change of scenery. He was, in some ways, one of the first modern celebrities. His fame was spectacular, his followers almost hysterical for a glimpse of the man himself. He was an artist, but also very much a man of the world. Perhaps his proudest possession, one imbued with great symbolic significance, was Gads Hill Place in Higham, Kent. When Dickens was a young boy, his father pointed to the country home, probably at random, and told him that if he worked hard he could someday own a home just like it. When Dickens saw it for sale in 1856, he could not resist. He purchased it and soon added much-needed bookcases. He entertained equally famous friends there, including Hans Christian Andersen and Henry Wadsworth Longfellow. It served as a tangible emblem of artistic and financial success—things craved by the man who once toiled in a blacking factory.

A Prolific Career

Over the course of his life, Dickens published fifteen novels (the last, *The Mystery of Edwin Drood*, was left unfinished upon his death, so we will never know "who did it") along with five shorter Christmas novels, including *A Christmas Carol*. He also found time to edit several periodicals—*Master Humphrey's Clock* (1840–41), *Household Words*

(1850–59), and *All the Year Round* (1859–70)—as well as compile nonfiction volumes such as *American Notes* (1843) and *Pictures from Italy* (1846). His novels appeared in serial form before book publication, either in periodicals or, more often, as individual chapters for sale at newsstands. Interest in a story line could be gauged by how well each chapter sold. Typically, sales increased over time as word of enticing plots spread and curiosity mounted. This represented a new way of selling as well as a new way of telling. Readers were gripped by a story that was still being written. Dickens changed story lines based on audience reactions, since he himself did not yet know how a story would progress or what fate a character might meet, even as the whole of London was abuzz with a novel's early chapters. Installments regularly ended in cliff-hanger fashion, leaving his fans eager for more. It is said that American readers waited on the docks for boats carrying new installments of *The Old Curiosity Shop*, on one occasion pleading to know "is Little Nell dead?"

With great success, though, came disappointments. Dickens's private life was under terrible scrutiny at all times, especially after he finally separated from his wife. He learned that pirated copies of his work were sold without his permission, particularly in America, where he, as a British subject, was not protected. Also, the strain of touring and the frantic pace of writing against deadlines began to take a toll on his health. Strained almost to the point of breaking, Dickens embarked on a series of self-proclaimed "farewell" readings for his fans in the late 1860s. In 1870, while working on his last novel at his beloved Gads Hill, he suffered a stroke and died. He was interred at Poets' Corner in Westminster Abbey alongside the likes of Geoffrey Chaucer, John Dryden, and Samuel Johnson.

An Advocate for the Poor

Dickens's legacy is keenly felt today. His books are as popular as ever, and they have never gone out of print. Countless movies and television series have been adapted from them. Dickens festivals are held around the world. He may be the only novelist to have an amusement park based on his works. Dickens World in Chatham, where Dickens lived parts of his life, is a privately funded theme park that boasts Europe's longest indoor ride, the Great Expectations boat trip. Other attractions include the Haunted House of Ebenezer Scrooge and Fagin's Den, a play area (watch out, Oliver!). Dickens has only grown in popularity in the last century and a half, even appearing as a selection of Oprah Winfrey's book club, and there is no sign his fame will diminish anytime soon.

Oliver Twist is a novel of injustice, compassion, and charity. It is Dickens's second, begun when he was only 25. It was his first true best-seller, appearing in monthly installments between February 1837 and April 1839. It is a severe critique of English society and law (most notably the Poor Law, which provided meager provisions for orphans), packed with sarcasm, bleak humor, and, of course, plenty of action and suspense. It was the first major English novel told from the perspective of a child. Readers thrilled with fear for Oliver, an orphan raised in a workhouse, where inmates have grown accustomed to ritual deprivation and abuse. Oliver's plaintive request for a second meager helping of gruel, "Please, sir, I want some more," is surely one of the most resonant lines in any novel. The simple request, made on behalf of another boy, incites disbelief and then rage on the part of his well-fed keepers, who lend him out as an apprentice to the undertaker Mr.

Sowerberry, who in turn lends him out as an extra "mourner" for children's funerals. Mrs. Sowerberry, the undertaker's wife, takes an instant dislike to Oliver and proceeds to all but starve him. After Oliver is goaded into a rage by taunts from a fellow apprentice, he is beaten by the hypocritical Mr. Bumble, a parish beadle, and runs away to London, where he is taken in by the evil Fagin. A professional thief and fencer, Fagin lures homeless boys into a sinister facsimile of family life, where they are cared for, to a point, in return for serving as pickpockets and lookouts for Fagin's criminal syndicate. Other boys in Fagin's "family," including the Artful Dodger, attempt, unsuccessfully, to attract Oliver to their criminal ways:

> What was Oliver's horror and alarm as he stood a few paces off, looking on with his eyelids as wide open as they would possibly go, to see the Dodger plunge his hand into the old gentleman's pocket, and draw from thence a handkerchief! To see him hand the same to Charley Bates; and finally to behold them, both, running away round the corner at full speed.

When the other boys steal the handkerchief of the gentleman Mr. Brownlow, Oliver, though an innocent bystander, is chased and captured. Sent before a judge, Oliver faints from exhaustion but is acquitted by eyewitness testimony. Mr. Brownlow, who believes Oliver to be innocent, takes him home, where he cares for the orphan with help from his housekeeper, Mrs. Bedwin. Throughout the novel, Oliver is torn between these two families, that of the evil Fagin and his murderous accomplice Bill Sikes on the one hand, and that of the gentle and charitable Mr. Brownlow and Mrs. Bedwin on the other.

Oliver Twist mixes dynamic realism not common to English readers of the time with unpitying lampoons of the types of men who would exploit the young, such as the fatuous Mr. Bumble. Dickens's terrifying descriptions of the conniving Fagin and Sikes excited readers like nothing that had come before, and when Dickens later reenacted Sikes's brutal murder of his moll Nancy, audiences reacted with shock but were drawn irresistibly to hear it again:

> She staggered and fell: nearly blinded with the blood that rained down from a deep gash in her forehead; but raising herself, with difficulty, on her knees, drew from her bosom a white handkerchief—Rose Maylie's own—and holding it up, in her folded hands, as high towards Heaven as her feeble strength would allow, breathed one prayer for mercy to her Maker.

> It was a ghastly figure to look upon. The murderer staggering backward to the wall, and shutting out the sight with his hand, seized a heavy club and struck her down.

The novel's portrayal of life in London's slums and workhouses shocked readers no less than Nancy's murder, laying bare the appalling conditions of the poor to a middle class audience that had little knowledge of such things. The battle played out for possession of Oliver, the naive orphan, is actually a battle for the soul of England itself, waged between those who would corrupt and exploit and those who sought to enlighten and improve.

The Spirit of Christmas

A Christmas Carol, a fable of redemption, is the first of five short Christmas novels Dickens published annually in the 1840s, though it is the only one that remains familiar to most readers today. It was published six years into Queen Victoria's reign and was extremely popular at the time (pirating, a common practice in the era, began directly after publication; Dickens, protected under British copyright law, pursued the pirates with cases in the Court of Chancery; after one victory, Dickens exclaimed, "The pirates are beaten flat!"). In fact, its popularity has never waned. *A Christmas Carol* is a departure from Dickens's customary realistic style and can be best understood as a parable dressed as a ghost story. The slim novel did much to revive the celebration of Christmas in both England and America, though the trend it spurred along was already underway. There was a common nostalgia for Christmas in the Victorian age, roused by Prince Albert's introduction of the Christmas tree from Germany in 1841 (he was born to the German family of Saxe-Coburg-Saalfeld) and the Christmas card in 1843, along with the publication of several collections of Christmas carols, such as William B. Sandys's *Selection of Christmas Carols, Ancient and Modern* (1833). As peculiar as the yuletide ghost story might seem, it fully expresses Dickens's characteristic sympathy for the poor and his disdain for those who seek to take advantage of them.

Dickens wrote *A Christmas Carol* in a mere six weeks, in order to have it ready for the season (his publisher, Chapman & Hall, rushed it out on December 19, 1843). He divided it into five "staves," or musical stanzas, in keeping with its title, describing the spiritual journey of Ebenezer Scrooge from callous miser to a warmhearted benefactor. Scrooge is one of Dickens's most famous characters: To this day the word "Scrooge" conjures the image of a person lacking Christmas spirit. Scrooge's love of money and marked lack of interest in others make him persona non grata right from the start:

> Nobody ever stopped him in the street to say, with gladsome looks, "My dear Scrooge, how are you? when will you come see me?" No beggars implored him to bestow a trifle, no children asked him what it was o'clock, no man or woman ever once in all his life inquired the way to such and such a place, of Scrooge. Even the blindmen's dogs appeared to know him; and when they saw him coming on, would tug their owners into doorways and up courts.

Even dogs avoid the man. Amazingly, Scrooge prefers it that way: "But what did Scrooge care? It was the very thing he liked." After refusing his nephew's invitation to Christmas dinner, and only reluctantly releasing his dutiful employee Bob Cratchit for one day's holiday leave, Scrooge returns home alone to be greeted by the first of four ghosts that haunt him that night. His business partner, Jacob Marley, who worked himself to death years before, appears first as a warning face on Scrooge's door knocker and then in full after Scrooge locks himself inside. Marley's ghost drags a chain of clerical instruments behind him even in death:

> The same face: the very same. Marley in his pigtail, usual waistcoat, tights and boots; the tassels on the latter bristling, like his pigtail, and his coat-skirts, and the hair upon his head. The chain he drew was clasped about his middle.

It was long, and wound about him like a tail; and it was made (for Scrooge observed it closely) of cash-boxes, keys, padlocks, ledgers, deeds, and heavy purses wrought in steel. His body was transparent; so that Scrooge, observing him, and looking through his waistcoat, could see the two buttons on his coat behind.

Even this dreadful scene contains some of Dickens's trademark comic sparkle: "Scrooge had often heard it said that Marley had no bowels, but he had never believed it until now."

Marley tells Scrooge that he will be visited by three ghosts upon the stroke of one: "'Without their visits,' said the Ghost, 'you cannot hope to shun the path I tread,'" the path, that is, of the wandering dead. The first ghost, Christmas Past, transports Scrooge from his bed to scenes of his youth, when, as a young man, he was tender, hopeful, and kind, before he dedicated himself completely to work. Scrooge begins his positive transformation almost immediately, regretting that there "was a boy singing a Christmas Carol at my door last night. I should like to have given him something." The second ghost, Christmas Present, sweeps Scrooge off to witness how others celebrate Christmas (stopping at a miner's shack, briefly on a ship at sea, and at a lighthouse), including his impoverished employee Bob Cratchit, whose crippled son, Tiny Tim, strains to enjoy the holiday with his family, declaring, "God bless us every one." The third spirit, the Ghost of Christmas Yet to Come, is a "mysterious presence" that fills Scrooge "with a solemn dread." The grim form presents Scrooge with his own forlorn and unvisited grave. This final vision, of an unredeemed death and squandered life, convinces Scrooge to change, and he beseeches the spirit to "assure me that I yet may change these shadows you have shown me, by an altered life."

Transformed at last, Scrooge wakes to learn only a single night has passed and that it is Christmas morning. He sends a prize turkey as an anonymous gift to Bob Cratchit's family and spends Christmas day in the affectionate company of his nephew's family. *A Christmas Carol* ends on a jubilant chord, drawing the reader in as well: "It was always said of him, that he knew how to keep Christmas well, if any man alive possessed the knowledge. May that be truly said of us, and all of us! And so, as Tiny Tim observed, God bless Us, Every One!"

A Student of Revolution

A Tale of Two Cities is a historical epic of loyalty, sacrifice, and revenge. It begins and ends with two of the most famous passages in all of English literature. To properly summon the sense of uncertainty heralded by the French Revolution, Dickens starts with a series of baffling paradoxes that nonetheless define both the age and the unbridgeable divide between Paris and London, the two cities of the title:

It was the best of times, it was the worst of times, it was the age of wisdom, it was the age of foolishness, it was the epoch of belief, it was the epoch of incredulity, it was the season of Light, it was the season of Darkness, it was the spring of hope, it was the winter of despair, we had everything before us, we had nothing before us, we were all going direct to Heaven, we were all going direct the other way . . .

The novel concludes with the heroic and consoling words of Sydney Carton, who sacrifices himself to the guillotine in order to permit Charles Darnay, a blameless man, to escape Paris and return to London with his family. Redeeming his otherwise depraved and parasitical life, Carton whispers in "a tender and a faltering voice" that "it is a far, far better thing that I do, than I have ever done; it is a far, far better rest that I go to than I have ever known."

The powerful drama of these passages matches the grand historical tone of the entire novel. *A Tale of Two Cities* is one of only two historical novels written by Dickens (the other is *Barnaby Rudge*, published in book form in 1841, another tale of mobs and riots, set during the anti-Catholic Gordon Riots). The sense of tension and unease begins right from the start, on the road from London to Dover, where passengers embark for France:

> The Dover mail was in its usual genial position that the guard suspected the passengers, the passengers suspected one another and the guard, they all suspected everybody else, and the coachman was sure of nothing but the horses.

Not long after, across the channel, in front of Madame DeFarge's St. Antoine Wine Shop in Paris, a wine cask "tumbled out with a run, the hoops had burst, and it lay on the stones just outside the door of the wine-shop, shattered like a walnut-shell," an accident which inaugurates a mad sprawl by passersby, who fall to their knees to lap the wine from the cobblestones. This symbolically bloody omen is emphasized when "one tall joker so besmirched, his head more out of a long squalid bag of a nightcap than in it, scrawled upon a wall with his finger dipped in muddy wine-lees—BLOOD."

A Tale of Two Cities is one of the most popular novels of all time, and it elated Victorian readers no less than their twentieth-century counterparts. Although moments of high melodrama may occasionally strike modern readers as unnecessarily sentimental, the descriptions of mob violence are among the finest of their kind. An ominous mood permeates the novel, and one fully comprehends the sense of looming disaster felt by those who lived through the French Revolution on both sides of the English Channel. Dickens based some of the scenes on Thomas Carlyle's 1837 book *The French Revolution: A History*, but he populates the historical landscape with his uniquely human characters. Dickens's descriptions of societal disorder and political hysteria in a city beset by spies, traitors, informants, tyrants, and assassins are no less fresh today than they were when he wrote them in the mid-nineteenth century.

Dickens was almost certainly moved by sympathy for the poor and exploited of Paris—no less than he was for those of London—yet he does not advocate revolution, certainly not of the chaotic and bloody variety that detonated in France. He preferred reasonable movement toward parliamentary reform over time. He was a humanitarian, after all, and his compassion is realized through the strength of his characters, distinct and memorable individuals who stand out from mobs and crowds. Throughout *A Tale of Two Cities*, Dickens views the revolutionary fervor and accompanying violence as a peculiarly French condition. Although much of the English monarchy's once-absolute power had been dissipated by the 1688 Glorious Revolution, which shifted large powers to Parliament, the French aristocracy knew no checks on its power until it was annihilated at the hands of revolutionaries. Though Dickens instinctively sympathizes with the French peasantry, subject to hardships, shortages, and arbitrary abuses—including imprisonment and murder—at the hands of the Ancien Régime, he seems similarly chilled by the rampant paranoia and unquenchable lust for revenge exhibited by the mobs that seize control of the city.

The guillotine itself is brought to life. Carlyle saw it as a function of the crazed new state: "The Guillotine, we find, gets always a quicker motion, as other things are quickening. The Guillotine, by its speed of going, will give index of the general velocity of the Republic." Dickens lavishes even greater, and more detailed, attention to the deadly instrument:

> Every day, through the stony streets, the tumbrels now jolted heavily, filled
> with Condemned. Lovely girls; bright women, brown-haired, black-haired,
> and grey; youths; stalwart men and old; gentle born and peasant born; all
> red wine for La Guillotine, all daily brought into light from the dark cellars
> of the loathsome prisons, and carried to her through the streets to slake her
> devouring thirst. Liberty, equality, fraternity, or death;—the last, much the
> easiest to bestow, O Guillotine!

There is something oddly theatrical about the bloodshed that unfolds on the streets of Paris. The assault upon the Bastille, and its liberation, seem more symbolic than anything else, given that only seven prisoners were held within. Likewise, the daily passage of the tumbrels, carts that carried the condemned, and the grisly beheadings in the Place du Revolution, attended by audiences eager for a show—many of whom reserved seats— seems bizarrely staged by the revolutionaries.

The Master of Character Development

As with all of his novels, Dickens created minor characters for *A Tale of Two Cities* every bit as striking as the principal ones. It is hard to forget the morbid endeavors of Jerry Cruncher, messenger for Tellson's Bank, who steals off to ply his second trade as a resurrection man, or body snatcher, exhuming recently interred corpses to sell to medical students, a highly illegal but much-demanded trade. Equally memorable is the stout, ruddy Englishwoman Mrs. Pross, who proudly declares, "I am a Briton," as she bravely stands off against the menacing Madame DeFarge, refusing to back down even at the threat of death.

Yet it is the primary characters who drive the story. The frail Dr. Manette is the central victim of the novel. Cast into the Bastille by a *letter de cachet*—an anonymous denunciation by a nobleman—he spends eighteen torturous years secretly imprisoned in solitary confinement, which deranges him to such an extent that he forgets who he is and replies only "105 North Tower" when asked his name. His daughter, Lucie—a figure so pure as to challenge credulity—rescues him when he is "recalled to life" after being released from the prison where it was believed he had died. With help from the Englishman Jarvis Lorry of Tellson's Bank, Lucie brings Dr. Manette to London and nurses him to some semblance of mental health, where he takes his place at the center of a loving family in SoHo (London, sometimes populated by spies and riffraff, remained infinitely safer than the Paris of Robespierre's Reign of Terror). The Manettes embody quiet family life, the basis of a moderately ordered civil society, one rendered impossible across the channel by ancient oppression and radical retribution.

Gentle Lucie's foil is the frightening Madame DeFarge, who plots rebellion and assassination from the St. Antoine Wine Shop. Driven mad with hatred for decadent French aristocracy, Madame DeFarge becomes a cold-blooded and utterly unreasonable angel of death, bent on endless slaughter. It becomes impossible to pity her, despite the terrors once inflicted upon her and her family. Charles Darnay, though he turned his back on his demonic uncle, Marquis St. Evrémonde, is eventually sentenced to death in Paris for his family name and his uncle's crimes against the peasantry. The last-minute swap in the cell before the execution has become one of the most enduring moments in the novel: Darnay, an innocent man, escapes the insatiable "justice" of the revolution through deception, and Syndey Carton, through the ultimate sacrifice, finally finds meaning.

The Prince of Perception

Great Expectations is a novel of aspiration, remorse, and friendship. It first appeared in installments in the magazine *All the Year Round* in 1860 and 1861, and it is one of Dickens's most mature novels, reflecting a level of sophistication and subtlety sometimes lacking in earlier works. Like *Oliver Twist*, it begins with a young orphan, Pip, although *Great Expectations*, unlike *Oliver Twist*, proceeds to follow Pip's growth into adulthood, tracing his efforts to meet the "great expectations" placed upon him. The opening scene gives us Pip, a boy of seven, visiting the grave of his parents on Christmas Eve. He is suddenly seized by the monstrous escaped convict Magwitch, who demands that Pip pilfer scraps of food and drink from his home for him:

> A fearful man, all in coarse grey, with a great iron on his leg. A man with no hat, and with broken shoes, and with an old rag tied round his head. A man who had been soaked in water, and smothered in mud, and lamed by stones, and cut by flints, and stung by nettles, and torn by briars; who limped, and shivered, and glared and growled; and whose teeth chattered in his head as he seized me by the chin.

Magwitch is one of the great villains of Dickens's novels, but he is also the most complex, as readers discover later in the novel. Magwitch is eventually recaptured and returned to the prison ship where he is jailed off the coast, but Pip has been inducted into an adult world of suspicion and fear from which he is never again entirely free.

The genial Pip is raised by his bad-tempered adult sister and Joe Gargery, a gentle giant of a man, a village blacksmith who works a forge adjoined to the family home. Pip's miserable life in the parish is interrupted when his uncle, the pompous Mr. Pumblechook, is asked by the mysterious and wealthy Miss Havisham to locate a suitable young boy to spend time with her. The spinster Miss Havisham dwells in a decayed mansion that was "of old brick, and dismal, and had a great many iron bars to it. Some of the windows had been walled up; of those that remained, all the lower were rustily barred." She lives with an equally mysterious young woman, the imperious and beautiful Estella. Miss Havisham, wearing a stained wedding gown, lives in suspended time, her clocks all stopped at twenty minutes to nine, the moment when, as a young woman, she was jilted by her lover:

I saw that the dress had been put upon the rounded figure of a young woman, and that the figure upon which it now hung loose, had shrunk to skin and bone. Once, I had been taken to see some ghastly waxwork at the Fair, representing I know not what impossible personage lying in state. Once, I had been taken to one of our old marsh churches to see a skeleton in the ashes of a rich dress, that had been dug out of a vault under the church pavement. Now, waxwork and skeleton seemed to have dark eyes that moved and looked at me. I should have cried out, if I could.

The room remains as it stood that day, eerily prepared for a wedding celebration that never took place: "It was spacious, and I dare say had once been handsome, but every discernible thing in it was covered with dust and mould, and dropping to pieces." Pip continues to visit Miss Havisham in her ghostly chambers and receives payment for his company. In the course of his visits, he falls in love with Miss Havisham's adopted daughter, Estella, who expresses no feeling at all for him in return. When Pip is inexplicably given a lavish allowance by an anonymous benefactor (he naturally suspects Miss Havisham), he moves to London to educate himself and become a gentleman, to fulfill the "great expectations" of the novel's title.

From here, the stage is set for an examination of Pip's development into manhood, through folly and humiliation, battling sensations of guilt while pursuing elusive love and struggling against enemies on the streets of London. Pip's ambivalence and feelings of shame are something new in a Dickens novel, and they add to the already considerable intricacy of the work. *Great Expectations* is part coming-of-age story, part mystery, part morality tale, part love story, part thriller, though no one of these features ultimately defines it. Unlike most Dickens novels, *Great Expectations* challenges readers' expectations. It does not present a battle between clearly defined forces of good and evil, and it refuses to serve up a triumphant ending in which noble figures are rewarded and villains sent off to die. In other words, it rather unsettlingly resembles real life.

Charles Dickens's characters, so powerfully rooted in their times and places, are, at the same time, universal and timeless, by turns instructive, comical, and enlightening. They offer useful lessons and are, in fact, nothing less than enduring meditations on humanity. They teach us a great deal about nineteenth-century England, its conflicts and concerns, its people and persuasions, but we are always surprised to find something of ourselves in his characters as well. Charles Dickens remains a favorite with both critics and readers, an unusual circumstance for a classic author. His fame survived his own era, while countless other authors, many of whom were celebrated and greatly admired in their day, have disappeared entirely from our shelves. The best Dickens novels stand shoulder to shoulder with the finest works of literature from any era. Perhaps no more proof of this is needed than the simple fact that we continue take pleasure in his works a century and a half after they first moved and delighted eager readers on the foggy streets of Queen Victoria's London.

Ernest Hilbert, PhD
Philadelphia, Pennsylvania
January 11, 2011

The Adventures of Oliver Twist

or The Parish Boy's Progress

CHAPTER I

*Treats of the Place Where Oliver Twist Was Born and
of the Circumstances Attending His Birth*

Among other public buildings in a certain town, which for many reasons it will be prudent to refrain from mentioning, and to which I will assign no fictitious name, there is one anciently common to most towns, great or small: to wit, a workhouse; and in this workhouse was born; on a day and date which I need not trouble myself to repeat, inasmuch as it can be of no possible consequence to the reader, in this stage of the business at all events; the item of mortality whose name is prefixed to the head of this chapter.

For a long time after it was ushered into this world of sorrow and trouble, by the parish surgeon, it remained a matter of considerable doubt whether the child would survive to bear any name at all; in which case it is somewhat more than probable that these memoirs would never have appeared; or, if they had, that being comprised within a couple of pages, they would have possessed the inestimable merit of being the most concise and faithful specimen of biography, extant in the literature of any age or country.

Although I am not disposed to maintain that the being born in a workhouse, is in itself the most fortunate and enviable circumstance that can possibly befall a human being, I do mean to say that in this particular instance, it was the best thing for Oliver Twist that could by possibility have occurred. The fact is, that there was considerable difficulty in inducing Oliver to take upon himself the office of respiration,—a troublesome practice, but one which custom has rendered necessary to our easy existence; and for some time he lay gasping on a little flock mattress, rather unequally poised between this world and the next: the balance being decidedly in favour of the latter. Now, if, during this brief period, Oliver had been surrounded by careful grandmothers, anxious aunts, experienced nurses, and doctors of profound wisdom, he would most inevitably and indubitably have been killed in no time. There being nobody by, however, but a pauper old woman, who was rendered rather misty by an unwonted allowance of beer; and a parish surgeon who did such matters by contract; Oliver and Nature fought out the point between them. The result was, that, after a few struggles, Oliver breathed, sneezed, and proceeded to advertise to the inmates of the workhouse the fact of a new burden having been imposed upon the parish, by setting up as loud a cry as could reasonably have been expected from a male infant who had not been possessed of that very useful appendage, a voice, for a much longer space of time than three minutes and a quarter.

As Oliver gave this first proof of the free and proper action of his lungs, the patchwork coverlet which was carelessly flung over the iron bedstead, rustled; the pale face of a young woman was raised feebly from the pillow; and a faint voice imperfectly articulated the words, "Let me see the child, and die."

The surgeon had been sitting with his face turned towards the fire: giving the palms of his hands a warm and a rub alternately. As the young woman spoke, he rose, and advancing to the bed's head, said, with more kindness than might have been expected of him:

"Oh, you must not talk about dying yet."

"Lor bless her dear heart, no!" interposed the nurse, hastily depositing in her pocket a green glass bottle, the contents of which she had been tasting in a corner with evident satisfaction.

"Lor bless her dear heart, when she has lived as long as I have, sir, and had thirteen children of her own, and all on 'em dead except two, and them in the wurkus with me, she'll know better than to take on in that way, bless her dear heart! Think what it is to be a mother, there's a dear young lamb do."

Apparently this consolatory perspective of a mother's prospects failed in producing its due effect. The patient shook her head, and stretched out her hand towards the child.

The surgeon deposited it in her arms. She imprinted her cold white lips passionately on its forehead; passed her hands over her face; gazed wildly round; shuddered; fell back—and died. They chafed her breast, hands, and temples; but the blood had stopped forever. They talked of hope and comfort. They had been strangers too long.

"It's all over, Mrs. Thingummy!" said the surgeon at last.

"Ah, poor dear, so it is!" said the nurse, picking up the cork of the green bottle, which had fallen out on the pillow, as she stooped to take up the child. "Poor dear!"

"You needn't mind sending up to me, if the child cries, nurse," said the surgeon, putting on his gloves with great deliberation. "It's very likely it will be troublesome. Give it a little gruel if it is." He put on his hat, and, pausing by the bed-side on his way to the door, added, "She was a good-looking girl, too; where did she come from?"

"She was brought here last night," replied the old woman, "by the overseer's order. She was found lying in the street. She had walked some distance, for her shoes were worn to pieces; but where she came from, or where she was going to, nobody knows."

The surgeon leaned over the body, and raised the left hand. "The old story," he said, shaking his head: "no wedding-ring, I see. Ah! Good-night!"

The medical gentleman walked away to dinner; and the nurse, having once more applied herself to the green bottle, sat down on a low chair before the fire, and proceeded to dress the infant.

What an excellent example of the power of dress, young Oliver Twist was! Wrapped in the blanket which had hitherto formed his only covering, he might have been the child of a nobleman or a beggar; it would have been hard for the haughtiest stranger to have assigned him his proper station in society. But now that he was enveloped in the old calico robes which had grown yellow in the same service, he was badged and ticketed, and fell into his place at once—a parish child—the orphan of a workhouse—the humble, half-starved drudge—to be cuffed and buffeted through the world—despised by all, and pitied by none.

Oliver cried lustily. If he could have known that he was an orphan, left to the tender mercies of church-wardens and overseers, perhaps he would have cried the louder.

CHAPTER II

Treats of Oliver Twist's Growth, Education, and Board

For the next eight or ten months, Oliver was the victim of a systematic course of treachery and deception. He was brought up by hand. The hungry and destitute situation of the infant orphan was duly reported by the workhouse authorities to the parish authorities. The parish authorities inquired with dignity of the workhouse authorities, whether there was no female then domiciled in "the house" who was in a situation to impart to Oliver Twist, the consolation and nourishment of which he stood in need. The workhouse authorities replied with humility, that there was not. Upon this, the parish authorities magnanimously and humanely resolved, that Oliver should be "farmed," or, in other words, that he should be dispatched to a branch-workhouse some three miles off, where twenty or thirty other juvenile offenders against the poor-laws, rolled about the floor all day, without the inconvenience of too much food or too much clothing, under the parental superintendence of an elderly female, who received the culprits at and for the consideration of sevenpence-halfpenny per small head per week. Sevenpence-halfpenny's worth per week is a good round diet for a child; a great deal may be got for sevenpence-halfpenny, quite enough to overload its stomach, and make it uncomfortable. The elderly female was a woman of wisdom and experience; she knew what was good for children; and she had a very accurate perception of what was good for herself. So, she appropriated the greater part of the weekly stipend to her own use, and consigned the rising parochial generation to even a shorter allowance than was originally provided for them. Thereby finding in the lowest depth a deeper still; and proving herself a very great experimental philosopher.

Everybody knows the story of another experimental philosopher who had a great theory about a horse being able to live without eating, and who demonstrated it so well, that he had got his own horse down to a straw a day, and would unquestionably have rendered him a very spirited and rampacious animal on nothing at all, if he had not died, four-and-twenty hours before he was to have had his first comfortable bait of air. Unfortunately for, the experimental philosophy of the female to whose protecting care Oliver Twist was delivered over, a similar result usually attended the operation of her system; for at the very moment when the child had contrived to exist upon the smallest possible portion of the weakest possible food, it did perversely happen in eight and a half cases out of ten, either that it sickened from want and cold, or fell into the fire from neglect, or got half-smothered by accident; in any one of which cases, the miserable little being was usually summoned into another world, and there gathered to the fathers it had never known in this.

Occasionally, when there was some more than usually interesting inquest upon a parish child who had been overlooked in turning up a bedstead, or inadvertently scalded to death when there happened to be a washing—though the latter accident was very scarce, anything approaching to a washing being of rare occurrence in the farm—the jury would take it into their heads to ask troublesome questions, or the parishioners would rebelliously affix their signatures to a remonstrance. But these impertinences were speedily checked by the evidence of the surgeon, and the testimony of the beadle; the former of whom had always opened the body and found nothing inside (which was very probable indeed), and the latter of whom invariably swore whatever the parish wanted; which was very self-devotional. Besides, the board made periodical pilgrimages to the farm, and always sent the beadle the day before, to say they were going. The children were neat and clean to behold, when they went; and what more would the people have!

It cannot be expected that this system of farming would produce any very extraordinary or luxuriant crop. Oliver Twist's ninth birthday found him a pale thin child, somewhat diminutive in stature, and decidedly small in circumference. But nature or inheritance had implanted a good sturdy spirit in Oliver's breast. It had had plenty of room to expand, thanks to the spare diet of the establishment; and perhaps to this circumstance may be attributed his having any ninth birth-day at all. Be this as it may, however, it was his ninth birthday; and he was keeping it in the coal-cellar with a select party of two other young gentleman, who, after participating with him in a sound thrashing, had been locked up for atrociously presuming to be hungry, when Mrs. Mann, the good lady of the house, was unexpectedly startled by the apparition of Mr. Bumble, the beadle, striving to undo the wicket of the garden-gate.

"Goodness gracious! Is that you, Mr. Bumble, sir?" said Mrs. Mann, thrusting her head out of the window in well-affected ecstasies of joy. "(Susan, take Oliver and them two brats upstairs, and wash 'em directly.)—My heart alive! Mr. Bumble, how glad I am to see you, sure-ly!"

Now, Mr. Bumble was a fat man, and a choleric; so, instead of responding to this open-hearted salutation in a kindred spirit, he gave the little wicket a tremendous shake, and then bestowed upon it a kick which could have emanated from no leg but a beadle's.

"Lor, only think," said Mrs. Mann, running out,—for the three boys had been removed by this time,—"only think of that! That I should have forgotten that the gate was bolted on the inside, on account of them dear children! Walk in sir; walk in, pray, Mr. Bumble, do, sir."

Although this invitation was accompanied with a curtsey that might have softened the heart of a church-warden, it by no means mollified the beadle.

"Do you think this respectful or proper conduct, Mrs. Mann," inquired Mr. Bumble, grasping his cane, "to keep the parish officers a waiting at your garden-gate, when they come here upon porochial business with the porochial orphans? Are you aweer, Mrs. Mann, that you are, as I may say, a porochial delegate, and a stipendiary?"

"I'm sure Mr. Bumble, that I was only a telling one or two of the dear children as is so fond of you, that it was you a coming," replied Mrs. Mann with great humility.

Mr. Bumble had a great idea of his oratorical powers and his importance. He had displayed the one, and vindicated the other. He relaxed.

"Well, well, Mrs. Mann," he replied in a calmer tone; "it may be as you say; it may be. Lead the way in, Mrs. Mann, for I come on business, and have something to say."

Mrs. Mann ushered the beadle into a small parlour with a brick floor; placed a seat for him; and officiously deposited his cocked hat and cane on the table before him. Mr. Bumble wiped from his forehead the perspiration which his walk had engendered, glanced complacently at the cocked hat, and smiled. Yes, he smiled. Beadles are but men: and Mr. Bumble smiled.

"Now don't you be offended at what I'm a going to say," observed Mrs. Mann, with captivating sweetness. "You've had a long walk, you know, or I wouldn't mention it. Now, will you take a little drop of somethink, Mr. Bumble?"

"Not a drop. Nor a drop," said Mr. Bumble, waving his right hand in a dignified, but placid manner.

"I think you will," said Mrs. Mann, who had noticed the tone of the refusal, and the gesture that had accompanied it. "Just a leetle drop, with a little cold water, and a lump of sugar."

Mr. Bumble coughed.

"Now, just a leetle drop," said Mrs. Mann persuasively.

"What is it?" inquired the beadle.

"Why, it's what I'm obliged to keep a little of in the house, to put into the blessed infants' Daffy, when they ain't well, Mr. Bumble," replied Mrs. Mann as she opened a corner cupboard, and took down a bottle and glass. "It's gin. I'll not deceive you, Mr. B. It's gin."

"Do you give the children Daffy, Mrs. Mann?" inquired Bumble, following with his eyes the interesting process of mixing.

"Ah, bless 'em, that I do, dear as it is," replied the nurse. "I couldn't see 'em suffer before my very eyes, you know sir."

"No"; said Mr. Bumble approvingly; "no, you could not. You are a humane woman, Mrs. Mann." (Here she set down the glass.) "I shall take a early opportunity of mentioning it to the board, Mrs. Mann." (He drew it towards him.) "You feel as a mother, Mrs. Mann." (He stirred the gin-and-water.) "I—I drink your health with cheerfulness, Mrs. Mann"; and he swallowed half of it.

"And now about business," said the beadle, taking out a leathern pocket-book. "The child that was half-baptized Oliver Twist, is nine year old to-day."

"Bless him!" interposed Mrs. Mann, inflaming her left eye with the corner of her apron.

"And notwithstanding a offered reward of ten pound, which was afterwards increased to twenty pound. Notwithstanding the most superlative, and, I may say, supernat'ral exertions on the part of this parish," said Bumble, "we have never been able to discover who is his father, or what was his mother's settlement, name, or condition."

Mrs. Mann raised her hands in astonishment; but added, after a moment's reflection, "How comes he to have any name at all, then?"

The beadle drew himself up with great pride, and said, "I inwented it."

"You, Mr. Bumble!"

"I, Mrs. Mann. We name our fondlings in alphabetical order. The last was a S,—Swubble, I named him. This was a T,—Twist, I named him. The next one comes will be Unwin, and the next Vilkins. I have got names ready made to the end of the alphabet, and all the way through it again, when we come to Z."

"Why, you're quite a literary character, sir!" said Mrs. Mann.

"Well, well," said the beadle, evidently gratified with the compliment; "perhaps I may be. Perhaps I may be, Mrs. Mann." He finished the gin-and-water, and added, "Oliver being now too old to remain here, the board have determined to have him back into the house. I have come out myself to take him there. So let me see him at once."

"I'll fetch him directly," said Mrs. Mann, leaving the room for that purpose. Oliver, having had by this time as much of the outer coat of dirt which encrusted his face and hands, removed, as could be scrubbed off in one washing, was led into the room by his benevolent protectress.

"Make a bow to the gentleman, Oliver," said Mrs. Mann.

Oliver made a bow, which was divided between the beadle on the chair, and the cocked hat on the table.

"Will you go along with me, Oliver?" said Mr. Bumble, in a majestic voice.

Oliver was about to say that he would go along with anybody with great readiness, when, glancing upward, he caught sight of Mrs. Mann, who had got behind the beadle's chair, and was shaking her fist at him with a furious countenance. He took the hint at once, for the fist had been too often impressed upon his body not to be deeply impressed upon his recollection.

"Will she go with me?" inquired poor Oliver.

"No, she can't," replied Mr. Bumble. "But she'll come and see you sometimes."

This was no very great consolation to the child. Young as he was, however, he had sense enough to make a feint of feeling great regret at going away. It was no very difficult matter for the boy to call tears into his eyes. Hunger and recent ill-usage are great assistants if you want to cry; and Oliver cried very naturally indeed. Mrs. Mann gave him a thousand embraces, and what Oliver wanted a great deal more, a piece of bread and butter, less he should seem too hungry when he got to the workhouse. With the slice of bread in his hand, and the little brown-cloth parish cap on his head, Oliver was then led away by Mr. Bumble from the wretched home where one kind word or look had never lighted the gloom of his infant years. And yet he burst into an agony of childish grief, as the cottage-gate closed after him. Wretched as were the little companions in misery he was leaving behind, they were the only friends he had ever known; and a sense of his loneliness in the great wide world, sank into the child's heart for the first time.

Mr. Bumble walked on with long strides; little Oliver, firmly grasping his gold-laced cuff, trotted beside him, inquiring at the end of every quarter of a mile whether they were "nearly there." To these interrogations Mr. Bumble returned very brief and snappish replies; for the temporary blandness which gin-and-water awakens in some bosoms had by this time evaporated; and he was once again a beadle.

Oliver had not been within the walls of the workhouse a quarter of an hour, and had scarcely completed the demolition of a second slice of bread, when Mr. Bumble, who had handed him over to the care of an old woman, returned; and, telling him it was a board night, informed him that the board had said he was to appear before it forthwith.

Not having a very clearly defined notion of what a live board was, Oliver was rather astounded by this intelligence, and was not quite certain whether he ought to laugh or cry. He had no time to think about the matter, however; for Mr. Bumble gave him a tap on the head, with his cane, to wake him up: and another on the back to make him lively: and bidding him to follow, conducted him into a large white-washed room, where eight or ten fat gentlemen were sitting round a table. At the top of the table, seated in an arm-chair rather higher than the rest, was a particularly fat gentleman with a very round, red face.

"Bow to the board," said Bumble. Oliver brushed away two or three tears that were lingering in his eyes; and seeing no board but the table, fortunately bowed to that.

"What's your name, boy?" said the gentleman in the high chair.

Oliver was frightened at the sight of so many gentlemen, which made him tremble: and the beadle gave him another tap behind, which made him cry. These two causes made him answer in a very low and hesitating voice; whereupon a gentleman in a white waistcoat said he was a fool. Which was a capital way of raising his spirits, and putting him quite at his ease.

"Boy," said the gentleman in the high chair, "listen to me. You know you're an orphan, I suppose?"

"What's that, sir?" inquired poor Oliver.

"The boy is a fool—I thought he was," said the gentleman in the white waistcoat.

"Hush!" said the gentleman who had spoken first. "You know you've got no father or mother, and that you were brought up by the parish, don't you?"

"Yes, sir," replied Oliver, weeping bitterly.

"What are you crying for?" inquired the gentleman in the white waistcoat. And to be sure it was very extraordinary. What could the boy be crying for?

"I hope you say your prayers every night," said another gentleman in a gruff voice; "and pray for the people who feed you, and take care of you—like a Christian."

"Yes, sir," stammered the boy. The gentleman who spoke last was unconsciously right. It would have been very like a Christian, and a marvellously good Christian too, if Oliver had prayed for the people who fed and took care of him. But he hadn't, because nobody had taught him.

"Well! You have come here to be educated, and taught a useful trade," said the red-faced gentleman in the high chair.

"So you'll begin to pick oakum to-morrow morning at six o'clock," added the surly one in the white waistcoat.

For the combination of both these blessings in the one simple process of picking oakum, Oliver bowed low by the direction of the beadle, and was then hurried away to a large ward; where, on a rough, hard bed, he sobbed himself to sleep. What a novel illustration of the tender laws of England! They let the paupers go to sleep!

Poor Oliver! He little thought, as he lay sleeping in happy unconsciousness of all around him, that the board had that very day arrived at a decision which would exercise the most material influence over all his future fortunes. But they had. And this was it:

The members of this board were very sage, deep, philosophical men; and when they came to turn their attention to the workhouse, they found out at once, what ordinary folks would never have discovered—the poor people liked it! It was a regular place of public entertainment for the poorer classes; a tavern where there was nothing to pay; a public breakfast, dinner, tea, and supper all the year round; a brick and mortar elysium, where it was all play and no work. "Oho!" said the board, looking very knowing; "we are the fellows to set this to rights; we'll stop it all, in no time." So, they established the rule, that all poor people should have the alternative (for they would compel nobody, not they), of being starved by a gradual process in the house, or by a quick one out of it. With this view, they contracted with the water-works to lay on an unlimited supply of water; and with a corn-factor to supply periodically small quantities of oatmeal; and issued three meals of thin gruel a day, with an onion twice a week, and half a roll of Sundays. They made a great many other wise and humane regulations, having reference to the ladies, which it is not necessary to repeat; kindly undertook to divorce poor married people, in consequence of the great expense of a suit in Doctors' Commons; and, instead of compelling a man to support his family, as they had theretofore done, took his family away from him, and made him a bachelor! There is no saying how many applicants for relief, under these last two heads, might have started up in all classes of society, if it had not been coupled with the workhouse; but the board were long-headed men, and had provided for this difficulty. The relief was inseparable from the workhouse and the gruel; and that frightened people.

For the first six months after Oliver Twist was removed, the system was in full operation. It was rather expensive at first, in consequence of the increase in the undertaker's bill, and the necessity of taking in the clothes of all the paupers, which fluttered loosely on their wasted, shrunken forms, after a week or two's gruel. But the number of workhouse inmates got thin as well as the paupers; and the board were in ecstasies.

The room in which the boys were fed, was a large stone hall, with a copper at one end: out of which the master, dressed in an apron for the purpose, and assisted by one or two women, ladled the gruel at mealtimes. Of this festive composition each boy had one porringer, and no more—except on occasions of great public rejoicing, when he had two ounces and a quarter of bread besides.

The bowls never wanted washing. The boys polished them with their spoons till they shone again; and when they had performed this operation (which never took very long, the spoons being nearly as large as the bowls), they would sit staring at the copper, with such eager eyes, as if they could have devoured the very bricks of which it was composed; employing themselves, meanwhile, in sucking their fingers most assiduously, with the view of catching up any stray splashes of gruel that might have been cast thereon. Boys have generally excellent appetites. Oliver Twist and his companions suffered the tortures of slow starvation for three months: at last they got so voracious and wild with hunger, that one boy, who was tall for his age, and hadn't been used to that sort of thing (for his father had kept a small cook-shop), hinted darkly to his companions, that unless he had another basin of gruel per diem, he was afraid he might some night happen to eat the boy who slept next him, who happened to be a weakly youth of tender age. He had a wild, hungry eye; and they implicitly believed him. A council was held; lots were cast who should walk up to the master after supper that evening, and ask for more; and it fell to Oliver Twist.

The evening arrived; the boys took their places. The master, in his cook's uniform, stationed himself at the copper; his pauper assistants ranged themselves behind him; the gruel was served out; and a long grace was said over the short commons. The gruel disappeared; the boys whispered each other, and winked at Oliver; while his next neighbors nudged him. Child as he was, he was desperate with hunger, and reckless with misery. He rose from the table; and advancing to the master, basin and spoon in hand, said: somewhat alarmed at his own temerity:

"Please, sir, I want some more."

The master was a fat, healthy man; but he turned very pale. He gazed in stupefied astonishment on the small rebel for some seconds, and then clung for support to the copper. The assistants were paralysed with wonder; the boys with fear.

"What!" said the master at length, in a faint voice.

"Please, sir," replied Oliver, "I want some more."

The master aimed a blow at Oliver's head with the ladle; pinioned him in his arm; and shrieked aloud for the beadle.

The board were sitting in solemn conclave, when Mr. Bumble rushed into the room in great excitement, and addressing the gentleman in the high chair, said,

"Mr. Limbkins, I beg your pardon, sir! Oliver Twist has asked for more!"

There was a general start. Horror was depicted on every countenance.

"For more!" said Mr. Limbkins. "Compose yourself, Bumble, and answer me distinctly. Do I understand that he asked for more, after he had eaten the supper allotted by the dietary?"

"He did, sir," replied Bumble.

"That boy will be hung," said the gentleman in the white waistcoat. "I know that boy will be hung."

Nobody controverted the prophetic gentleman's opinion. An animated discussion took place. Oliver was ordered into instant confinement; and a bill was next morning pasted on the outside of the gate, offering a reward of five pounds to anybody who would take Oliver Twist off the hands of the parish. In other words, five pounds and Oliver Twist were offered to any man or woman who wanted an apprentice to any trade, business, or calling.

"I never was more convinced of anything in my life," said the gentleman in the white waistcoat, as he knocked at the gate and read the bill next morning: "I never was more convinced of anything in my life, than I am that that boy will come to be hung."

As I purpose to show in the sequel whether the white waistcoated gentleman was right or not, I should perhaps mar the interest of this narrative (supposing it to possess any at all), if I ventured to hint just yet, whether the life of Oliver Twist had this violent termination or no.

CHAPTER III

Relates How Oliver Twist Was Very Near Getting a Place Which Would Not Have Been a Sinecure

For a week after the commission of the impious and profane offence of asking for more, Oliver remained a close prisoner in the dark and solitary room to which he had been consigned by the wisdom and mercy of the board. It appears, at first sight not unreasonable to suppose, that, if he had entertained a becoming feeling of respect for the prediction of the gentleman in the white waistcoat, he would have established that sage individual's prophetic character, once and for ever, by tying one end of his pocket-handkerchief to a hook in the wall, and attaching himself to the other. To the performance of this feat, however, there was one obstacle: namely, that pocket-handkerchiefs being decided articles of luxury, had been, for all future times and ages, removed from the noses of paupers by the express order of the board, in council assembled: solemnly given and pronounced under their hands and seals. There was a still greater obstacle in Oliver's youth and childishness. He only cried bitterly all day; and, when the long, dismal night came on, spread his little hands before his eyes to shut out the darkness, and crouching in the corner, tried to sleep: ever and anon waking with a start and tremble, and drawing himself closer and closer to the wall, as if to feel even its cold hard surface were a protection in the gloom and loneliness which surrounded him.

Let it not be supposed by the enemies of "the system," that, during the period of his solitary incarceration, Oliver was denied the benefit of exercise, the pleasure of society, or the advantages of religious consolation. As for exercise, it was nice cold weather, and he was allowed to perform his ablutions every morning under the pump, in a stone yard, in the presence of Mr. Bumble, who prevented his catching cold, and caused a tingling sensation to pervade his frame, by repeated applications of the cane. As for society, he was carried every other day into the hall where the boys dined, and there sociably flogged as a public warning and example. And so for from being denied the advantages of religious consolation, he was kicked into the same apartment every evening at prayer-time, and there permitted to listen to, and console his mind with, a general supplication of the boys, containing a special clause, therein inserted by authority of the board, in which they entreated to be made good, virtuous, contented, and obedient, and to be guarded from the sins and vices of Oliver Twist: whom the supplication distinctly set forth to be under the exclusive patronage and protection of the powers of wickedness, and an article direct from the manufactory of the very Devil himself.

It chanced one morning, while Oliver's affairs were in this auspicious and comfortable state, that Mr. Gamfield, chimney-sweep, went his way down the High Street, deeply cogitating in his mind his ways and means of paying certain arrears of rent, for which his landlord had become rather pressing. Mr. Gamfield's most sanguine estimate of his finances could not raise them within full five pounds of the desired amount; and, in a species of arithmetical desperation, he was alternately cudgelling his brains and his donkey, when passing the workhouse, his eyes encountered the bill on the gate.

"Wo—o!" said Mr. Gamfield to the donkey.

The donkey was in a state of profound abstraction: wondering, probably, whether he was destined to be regaled with a cabbage-stalk or two when he had disposed of the two sacks of soot with which the little cart was laden; so, without noticing the word of command, he jogged onward.

Mr. Gamfield growled a fierce imprecation on the donkey generally, but more particularly on his eyes; and, running after him, bestowed a blow on his head, which would inevitably have beaten in any skull but a donkey's. Then, catching hold of the bridle, he gave his jaw a sharp wrench, by way of gentle reminder that he was not his own master; and by these means turned him round. He then gave him another blow on the head, just to stun him till he came back again. Having completed these arrangements, he walked up to the gate, to read the bill.

The gentleman with the white waistcoat was standing at the gate with his hands behind him, after having delivered himself of some profound sentiments in the board-room. Having witnessed the little dispute between Mr. Gamfield and the donkey, he smiled joyously when that person came up to read the bill, for he saw at once that Mr. Gamfield was exactly the sort of master Oliver Twist wanted. Mr. Gamfield smiled, too, as he perused the document; for five pounds was just the sum he had been wishing for; and, as to the boy with which it was encumbered, Mr. Gamfield, knowing what the dietary of the workhouse was, well knew he would be a nice small pattern, just the very thing for register stoves. So, he spelt the bill through again, from beginning to end; and then, touching his fur cap in token of humility, accosted the gentleman in the white waistcoat.

"This here boy, sir, wot the parish wants to 'prentis," said Mr. Gamfield.

"Ay, my man," said the gentleman in the white waistcoat, with a condescending smile. "What of him?"

"If the parish vould like him to learn a right pleasant trade, in a good 'spectable chimbley-sweepin' bisness," said Mr. Gamfield, "I wants a 'prentis, and I am ready to take him."

"Walk in," said the gentleman in the white waistcoat. Mr. Gamfield having lingered behind, to give the donkey another blow on the head, and another wrench of the jaw, as a caution not to run away in his absence, followed the gentleman with the white waistcoat into the room where Oliver had first seen him.

"It's a nasty trade," said Mr. Limbkins, when Gamfield had again stated his wish.

"Young boys have been smothered in chimneys before now," said another gentleman.

"That's acause they damped the straw afore they lit it in the chimbley to make 'em come down again," said Gamfield; "that's all smoke, and no blaze; vereas smoke ain't o' no use at all in making a boy come down, for it only sinds him to sleep, and that's wot he likes. Boys is wery obstinit, and wery lazy, Gen'l'men, and there's nothink like a good hot blaze to make 'em come down vith a run. It's humane too, gen'l'men, acause, even if they've stuck in the chimbley, roasting their feet makes 'em struggle to hextricate theirselves."

The gentleman in the white waistcoat appeared very much amused by this explanation; but his mirth was speedily checked by a look from Mr. Limbkins. The board then proceeded to converse among themselves for a few minutes, but in so low a tone, that the words "saving of expenditure," "looked well in the accounts," "have a printed report published," were alone audible. These only chanced to be heard, indeed, or account of their being very frequently repeated with great emphasis.

At length the whispering ceased; and the members of the board, having resumed their seats and their solemnity, Mr. Limbkins said:

"We have considered your proposition, and we don't approve of it."

"Not at all," said the gentleman in the white waistcoat.

"Decidedly not," added the other members.

As Mr. Gamfield did happen to labour under the slight imputation of having bruised three or four boys to death already, it occurred to him that the board had, perhaps, in some unaccountable freak, taken it into their heads that this extraneous circumstance ought to influence their proceedings. It was very unlike their general mode of doing business, if they had; but still, as he had no particular wish to revive the rumour, he twisted his cap in his hands, and walked slowly from the table.

"So you won't let me have him, gen'l'men?" said Mr. Gamfield, pausing near the door.

"No," replied Mr. Limbkins; "at least, as it's a nasty business, we think you ought to take something less than the premium we offered."

Mr. Gamfield's countenance brightened, as, with a quick step, he returned to the table, and said,

"What'll you give, gen'l'men? Come! Don't be too hard on a poor man. What'll you give?"

"I should say, three pound ten was plenty," said Mr. Limbkins.

"Ten shillings too much," said the gentleman in the white waistcoat.

"Come!" said Gamfield; "say four pound, gen'l'men. Say four pound, and you've got rid of him for good and all. There!"

"Three pound ten," repeated Mr. Limbkins, firmly.

"Come! I'll split the diff'erence, gen'l'men," urged Gamfield. "Three pound fifteen."

"Not a farthing more," was the firm reply of Mr. Limbkins.

"You're desperate hard upon me, gen'l'men," said Gamfield, wavering.

"Pooh! pooh! nonsense!" said the gentleman in the white waistcoat. "He'd be cheap with nothing at all, as a premium. Take him, you silly fellow! He's just the boy for you. He wants the stick, now and then: it'll do him good; and his board needn't come very expensive, for he hasn't been overfed since he was born. Ha! ha! ha!"

Mr. Gamfield gave an arch look at the faces round the table, and, observing a smile on all of them, gradually broke into a smile himself. The bargain was made. Mr. Bumble, was at once instructed that Oliver Twist and his indentures were to be conveyed before the magistrate, for signature and approval, that very afternoon.

In pursuance of this determination, little Oliver, to his excessive astonishment, was released from bondage, and ordered to put himself into a clean shirt. He had hardly achieved this very unusual gymnastic performance, when Mr. Bumble brought him, with his own hands, a basin of gruel, and the holiday allowance of two ounces and a quarter of bread. At this tremendous sight, Oliver began to cry very piteously: thinking, not unnaturally, that the board must have determined to kill him for some useful purpose, or they never would have begun to fatten him up in that way.

"Don't make your eyes red, Oliver, but eat your food and be thankful," said Mr. Bumble, in a tone of impressive pomposity. "You're a going to be made a 'prentice of, Oliver."

"A prentice, sir!" said the child, trembling.

"Yes, Oliver," said Mr. Bumble. "The kind and blessed gentleman which is so many parents to you, Oliver, when you have none of your own: are a going to 'prentice' you: and to set you up in life, and make a man of you: although the expense to the parish is three pound ten!—three pound ten, Oliver!—seventy shillins—one hundred and forty sixpences!—and all for a naughty orphan which nobody can't love."

As Mr. Bumble paused to take breath, after delivering this address in an awful voice, the tears rolled down the poor child's face, and he sobbed bitterly.

"Come," said Mr. Bumble, somewhat less pompously, for it was gratifying to his feelings to observe the effect his eloquence had produced; "Come, Oliver! Wipe your eyes with the cuffs of your jacket, and don't cry into your gruel; that's a very foolish action, Oliver." It certainly was, for there was quite enough water in it already.

On their way to the magistrate, Mr. Bumble instructed Oliver that all he would have to do, would be to look very happy, and say, when the gentleman asked him if he wanted to be apprenticed, that he should like it very much indeed; both of which injunctions Oliver promised to obey: the rather as Mr. Bumble threw in a gentle hint, that if he failed in either particular, there was no telling what would be done to him. When they arrived at the office, he was shut up in a little room by himself, and admonished by Mr. Bumble to stay there, until he came back to fetch him.

There the boy remained, with a palpitating heart, for half an hour. At the expiration of which time Mr. Bumble thrust in his head, unadorned with the cocked hat, and said aloud:

"Now, Oliver, my dear, come to the gentleman." As Mr. Bumble said this, he put on a grim and threatening look, and added, in a low voice, "Mind what I told you, you young rascal!"

Oliver stared innocently in Mr. Bumble's face at this somewhat contradictory style of address; but that gentleman prevented his offering any remark thereupon, by leading him at once into an adjoining room: the door of which was open. It was a large room, with a great window. Behind a desk, sat two old gentleman with powdered heads: one of whom was reading the newspaper; while the other was perusing, with the aid of a pair of tortoise-shell spectacles, a small piece of parchment which lay before him. Mr. Limbkins was standing in front of the desk on one side; and Mr. Gamfield, with a partially washed face, on the other; while two or three bluff-looking men, in top-boots, were lounging about.

The old gentleman with the spectacles gradually dozed off, over the little bit of parchment; and there was a short pause, after Oliver had been stationed by Mr. Bumble in front of the desk.

"This is the boy, your worship," said Mr. Bumble.

The old gentleman who was reading the newspaper raised his head for a moment, and pulled the other old gentleman by the sleeve; whereupon, the last-mentioned old gentleman woke up.

"Oh, is this the boy?" said the old gentleman.

"This is him, sir," replied Mr. Bumble. "Bow to the magistrate, my dear."

Oliver roused himself, and made his best obeisance. He had been wondering, with his eyes fixed on the magistrates' powder, whether all boards were born with that white stuff on their heads, and were boards from thenceforth on that account.

"Well," said the old gentleman, "I suppose he's fond of chimney-sweeping?"

"He doats on it, your worship," replied Bumble; giving Oliver a sly pinch, to intimate that he had better not say he didn't.

"And he will be a sweep, will he?" inquired the old gentleman.

"If we was to bind him to any other trade to-morrow, he'd run away simultaneous, your worship," replied Bumble.

"And this man that's to be his master—you, sir—you'll treat him well, and feed him, and do all that sort of thing, will you?" said the old gentleman.

"When I says I will, I means I will," replied Mr. Gamfield doggedly.

"You're a rough speaker, my friend, but you look an honest, open-hearted man," said the old gentleman: turning his spectacles in the direction of the candidate for Oliver's premium, whose villainous countenance was a regular stamped receipt for cruelty. But the magistrate was half blind and half childish, so he couldn't reasonably be expected to discern what other people did.

"I hope I am, sir," said Mr. Gamfield, with an ugly leer.

"I have no doubt you are, my friend," replied the old gentleman: fixing his spectacles more firmly on his nose, and looking about him for the inkstand.

It was the critical moment of Oliver's fate. If the inkstand had been where the old gentleman thought it was, he would have dipped his pen into it, and signed the indentures, and Oliver would have been straightway hurried off. But, as it chanced to be immediately under his nose, it followed, as a matter of course, that he looked all over his desk for it, without finding it; and happening in the course of his search to look straight before him, his gaze encountered the pale and terrified face of Oliver Twist: who, despite all the admonitory looks and pinches of Bumble, was regarding the repulsive countenance of his future master, with a mingled expression of horror and fear, too palpable to be mistaken, even by a half-blind magistrate.

The old gentleman stopped, laid down his pen, and looked from Oliver to Mr. Limbkins; who attempted to take snuff with a cheerful and unconcerned aspect.

"My boy!" said the old gentleman, "you look pale and alarmed. What is the matter?"

"Stand a little away from him, Beadle," said the other magistrate: laying aside the paper, and leaning forward with an expression of interest. "Now, boy, tell us what's the matter: don't be afraid."

Oliver fell on his knees, and clasping his hands together, prayed that they would order him back to the dark room—that they would starve him—beat him—kill him if they pleased—rather than send him away with that dreadful man.

"Well!" said Mr. Bumble, raising his hands and eyes with most impressive solemnity. "Well! of all the artful and designing orphans that ever I see, Oliver, you are one of the most bare-facedest."

"Hold your tongue, Beadle," said the second old gentleman, when Mr. Bumble had given vent to this compound adjective.

"I beg your worship's pardon," said Mr. Bumble, incredulous of having heard aright. "Did your worship speak to me?"

"Yes. Hold your tongue."

Mr. Bumble was stupefied with astonishment. A beadle ordered to hold his tongue! A moral revolution!

The old gentleman in the tortoise-shell spectacles looked at his companion, he nodded significantly.

"We refuse to sanction these indentures," said the old gentleman: tossing aside the piece of parchment as he spoke.

"I hope," stammered Mr. Limbkins: "I hope the magistrates will not form the opinion that the authorities have been guilty of any improper conduct, on the unsupported testimony of a child."

"The magistrates are not called upon to pronounce any opinion on the matter," said the second old gentleman sharply. "Take the boy back to the workhouse, and treat him kindly. He seems to want it."

That same evening, the gentleman in the white waistcoat most positively and decidedly affirmed, not only that Oliver would be hung, but that he would be drawn and quartered into the bargain. Mr. Bumble shook his head with gloomy mystery, and said he wished he might come to good; whereunto Mr. Gamfield replied, that he wished he might come to him; which, although he agreed with the beadle in most matters, would seem to be a wish of a totally opposite description.

The next morning, the public were once informed that Oliver Twist was again To Let, and that five pounds would be paid to anybody who would take possession of him.

CHAPTER IV

Oliver, Being Offered Another Place, Makes
His First Entry Into Public Life

In great families, when an advantageous place cannot be obtained, either in possession, reversion, remainder, or expectancy, for the young man who is growing up, it is a very general custom to send him to sea. The board, in imitation of so wise and salutary an example, took counsel together on the expediency of shipping off Oliver Twist, in some small trading vessel bound to a good unhealthy port. This suggested itself as the very best thing that could possibly be done with him: the probability being, that the skipper would flog him to death, in a playful mood, some day after dinner, or would knock his brains out with an iron bar; both pastimes being, as is pretty generally known, very favourite and common recreations among gentleman of that class. The more the case presented itself to the board, in this point of view, the more manifold the advantages of the step appeared; so, they came to the conclusion that the only way of providing for Oliver effectually, was to send him to sea without delay.

Mr. Bumble had been despatched to make various preliminary inquiries, with the view of finding out some captain or other who wanted a cabin-boy without any friends; and was returning to the workhouse to communicate the result of his mission; when he encountered at the gate, no less a person than Mr. Sowerberry, the parochial undertaker.

Mr. Sowerberry was a tall gaunt, large-jointed man, attired in a suit of threadbare black, with darned cotton stockings of the same colour, and shoes to answer. His features were not naturally intended to wear a smiling aspect, but he was in general rather given to professional jocosity. His step was elastic, and his face betokened inward pleasantry, as he advanced to Mr. Bumble, and shook him cordially by the hand.

"I have taken the measure of the two women that died last night, Mr. Bumble," said the undertaker.

"You'll make your fortune, Mr. Sowerberry," said the beadle, as he thrust his thumb and forefinger into the proffered snuff-box of the undertaker: which was an ingenious little model of a patent coffin. "I say you'll make your fortune, Mr. Sowerberry," repeated Mr. Bumble, tapping the undertaker on the shoulder, in a friendly manner, with his cane.

"Think so?" said the undertaker in a tone which half admitted and half disputed the probability of the event. "The prices allowed by the board are very small, Mr. Bumble."

"So are the coffins," replied the beadle: with precisely as near an approach to a laugh as a great official ought to indulge in.

Mr. Sowerberry was much tickled at this: as of course he ought to be; and laughed a long time without cessation. "Well, well, Mr. Bumble," he said at length, "there's no denying that, since the new system of feeding has come in, the coffins are something narrower and more shallow than they used to be; but we must have some profit, Mr.

Bumble. Well-seasoned timber is an expensive article, sir; and all the iron handles come, by canal, from Birmingham."

"Well, well," said Mr. Bumble, "every trade has its drawbacks. A fair profit is, of course, allowable."

"Of course, of course," replied the undertaker; "and if I don't get a profit upon this or that particular article, why, I make it up in the long-run, you see—he! he! he!"

"Just so," said Mr. Bumble.

"Though I must say," continued the undertaker, resuming the current of observations which the beadle had interrupted: "though I must say, Mr. Bumble, that I have to contend against one very great disadvantage: which is, that all the stout people go off the quickest. The people who have been better off, and have paid rates for many years, are the first to sink when they come into the house; and let me tell you, Mr. Bumble, that three or four inches over one's calculation makes a great hole in one's profits: especially when one has a family to provide for, sir."

As Mr. Sowerberry said this, with the becoming indignation of an ill-used man; and as Mr. Bumble felt that it rather tended to convey a reflection on the honour of the parish; the latter gentleman thought it advisable to change the subject. Oliver Twist being uppermost in his mind, he made him his theme.

"By the bye," said Mr. Bumble, "you don't know anybody who wants a boy, do you? A porochial 'prentis, who is at present a dead-weight; a millstone, as I may say, round the porochial throat? Liberal terms, Mr. Sowerberry, liberal terms?" As Mr. Bumble spoke, he raised his cane to the bill above him, and gave three distinct raps upon the words "five pounds": which were printed thereon in Roman capitals of gigantic size.

"Gadso!" said the undertaker: taking Mr. Bumble by the gilt-edged lappel of his official coat; "that's just the very thing I wanted to speak to you about. You know— dear me, what a very elegant button this is, Mr. Bumble! I never noticed it before."

"Yes, I think it rather pretty," said the beadle, glancing proudly downwards at the large brass buttons which embellished his coat. "The die is the same as the porochial seal—the Good Samaritan healing the sick and bruised man. The board presented it to me on Newyear's morning, Mr. Sowerberry. I put it on, I remember, for the first time, to attend the inquest on that reduced tradesman, who died in a doorway at midnight."

"I recollect," said the undertaker. "The jury brought it in, 'Died from exposure to the cold, and want of the common necessaries of life,' didn't they?"

Mr. Bumble nodded.

"And they made it a special verdict, I think," said the undertaker, "by adding some words to the effect, that if the relieving officer had—"

"Tush! Foolery!" interposed the beadle. "If the board attended to all the nonsense that ignorant jurymen talk, they'd have enough to do."

"Very true," said the undertaker; "they would indeed."

"Juries," said Mr. Bumble, grasping his cane tightly, as was his wont when working into a passion: "juries is ineddicated, vulgar, grovelling wretches."

"So they are," said the undertaker.

"They haven't no more philosophy nor political economy about 'em than that," said the beadle, snapping his fingers contemptuously.

"No more they have," acquiesced the undertaker.

"I despise 'em," said the beadle, growing very red in the face.

"So do I," rejoined the undertaker.

"And I only wish we'd a jury of the independent sort, in the house for a week or two," said the beadle; "the rules and regulations of the board would soon bring their spirit down for 'em."

"Let 'em alone for that," replied the undertaker. So saying, he smiled, approvingly: to calm the rising wrath of the indignant parish officer.

Mr Bumble lifted off his cocked hat; took a handkerchief from the inside of the crown; wiped from his forehead the perspiration which his rage had engendered; fixed the cocked hat on again; and, turning to the undertaker, said in a calmer voice:

"Well; what about the boy?"

"Oh!" replied the undertaker; "why, you know, Mr. Bumble, I pay a good deal towards the poor's rates."

"Hem!" said Mr. Bumble. "Well?"

"Well," replied the undertaker, "I was thinking that if I pay so much towards 'em, I've a right to get as much out of 'em as I can, Mr. Bumble; and so—I think I'll take the boy myself."

Mr. Bumble grasped the undertaker by the arm, and led him into the building. Mr. Sowerberry was closeted with the board for five minutes; and it was arranged that Oliver should go to him that evening "upon liking"—a phrase which means, in the case of a parish apprentice, that if the master find, upon a short trial, that he can get enough work out of a boy without putting too much food into him, he shall have him for a term of years, to do what he likes with.

When little Oliver was taken before "the gentlemen" that evening; and informed that he was to go, that night, as general house-lad to a coffin-maker's; and that if he complained of his situation, or ever came back to the parish again, he would be sent to sea, there to be drowned, or knocked on the head, as the case might be, he evinced so little emotion, that they by common consent pronounced him a hardened young rascal, and ordered Mr. Bumble to remove him forthwith.

Now, although it was very natural that the board, of all people in the world, should feel in a great state of virtuous astonishment and horror at the smallest tokens of want of feeling on the part of anybody, they were rather out, in this particular instance. The simple fact was, that Oliver, instead of possessing too little feeling, possessed rather too much; and was in a fair way of being reduced, for life, to a state of brutal stupidity and sullenness by the ill usage he had received. He heard the news of his destination, in perfect silence; and, having had his luggage put into his hand—which was not very difficult to carry, inasmuch as it was all comprised within the limits of a brown paper parcel, about half a foot square by three inches deep—he pulled his cap over his eyes; and once more attaching himself to Mr. Bumble's coat cuff, was led away by that dignitary to a new scene of suffering.

For some time, Mr. Bumble drew Oliver along, without notice or remark; for the beadle carried his head very erect, as a beadle always should: and, it being a windy day, little Oliver was completely enshrouded by the skirts of Mr. Bumble's coat as they blew open, and disclosed to great advantage his flapped waistcoat and drab plush knee-breeches. As they drew near to their destination, however, Mr. Bumble thought it expedient to look down, and see that the boy was in good order for inspection by his new master: which he accordingly did, with a fit and becoming air of gracious patronage.

"Oliver!" said Mr. Bumble.

"Yes, sir," replied Oliver, in a low, tremulous voice.

"Pull that cap off your eyes, and hold up your head, sir."

Although Oliver did as he was desired, at once; and passed the back of his unoccupied hand briskly across his eyes, he left a tear in them when he looked up at his conductor. As Mr. Bumble gazed sternly upon him, it rolled down his cheek. It was followed by another, and another. The child made a strong effort, but it was an unsuccessful one. Withdrawing his other hand from Mr. Bumble's he covered his face with both; and wept until the tears sprung out from between his chin and bony fingers.

"Well!" exclaimed Mr. Bumble, stopping short, and darting at his little charge a look of intense malignity. "Well! Of all the ungratefullest, and worst-disposed boys as ever I see, Oliver, you are the—"

"No, no, sir," sobbed Oliver, clinging to the hand which held the well-known cane; "no, no, sir; I will be good indeed; indeed, indeed I will, sir! I am a very little boy, sir; and it is so—so—"

"So what?" inquired Mr. Bumble in amazement.

"So lonely, sir! So very lonely!" cried the child. "Everybody hates me. Oh! sir, don't, don't pray be cross to me!" The child beat his hand upon his heart; and looked in his companion's face, with tears of real agony.

Mr. Bumble regarded Oliver's piteous and helpless look, with some astonishment, for a few seconds; hemmed three or four times in a husky manner; and after muttering something about "that troublesome cough," bade Oliver dry his eyes and be a good boy. Then once more taking his hand, he walked on with him in silence.

The undertaker, who had just put up the shutters of his shop, was making some entries in his day-book by the light of a most appropriate dismal candle, when Mr. Bumble entered.

"Aha!" said the undertaker; looking up from the book, and pausing in the middle of a word; "is that you, Bumble?"

"No one else, Mr. Sowerberry," replied the beadle. "Here! I've brought the boy." Oliver made a bow.

"Oh! that's the boy, is it?" said the undertaker: raising the candle above his head, to get a better view of Oliver. "Mrs. Sowerberry, will you have the goodness to come here a moment, my dear?"

Mrs. Sowerberry emerged from a little room behind the shop, and presented the form of a short, then, squeezed-up woman, with a vixenish countenance.

"My dear," said Mr. Sowerberry, deferentially, "this is the boy from the workhouse that I told you of." Oliver bowed again.

"Dear me!" said the undertaker's wife, "he's very small."

"Why, he is rather small," replied Mr. Bumble: looking at Oliver as if it were his fault that he was no bigger; "he is small. There's no denying it. But he'll grow, Mrs. Sowerberry—he'll grow."

"Ah! I dare say he will," replied the lady pettishly, "on our victuals and our drink. I see no saving in parish children, not I; for they always cost more to keep, than they're worth. However, men always think they know best. There! Get downstairs, little bag o' bones." With this, the undertaker's wife opened a side door, and pushed Oliver down a steep flight of stairs into a stone cell, damp and dark: forming the ante-room to the coal-cellar, and denominated "kitchen"; wherein sat a slatternly girl, in shoes down at heel, and blue worsted stockings very much out of repair.

"Here, Charlotte," said Mr. Sowerberry, who had followed Oliver down, "give this boy some of the cold bits that were put by for Trip. He hasn't come home since the morning, so he may go without 'em. I dare say the boy isn't too dainty to eat 'em—are you, boy?"

Oliver, whose eyes had glistened at the mention of meat, and who was trembling with eagerness to devour it, replied in the negative; and a plateful of coarse broken victuals was set before him.

I wish some well-fed philosopher, whose meat and drink turn to gall within him; whose blood is ice, whose heart is iron; could have seen Oliver Twist clutching at the dainty viands that the dog had neglected. I wish he could have witnessed the horrible avidity with which Oliver tore the bits asunder with all the ferocity of famine. There is only one thing I should like better; and that would be to see the Philosopher making the same sort of meal himself, with the same relish.

"Well," said the undertaker's wife, when Oliver had finished his supper: which she had regarded in silent horror, and with fearful auguries of his future appetite: "have you done?"

There being nothing eatable within his reach, Oliver replied in the affirmative.

"Then come with me," said Mrs. Sowerberry: taking up a dim and dirty lamp, and leading the way upstairs; "your bed's under the counter. You don't mind sleeping among the coffins, I suppose? But it doesn't much matter whether you do or don't, for you can't sleep anywhere else. Come; don't keep me here all night!"

Oliver lingered no longer, but meekly followed his new mistress.

CHAPTER V

Oliver Mingles With New Associates. Going to a Funeral for the First Time, He Forms an Unfavourable Notion of His Master's Business

Oliver, being left to himself in the undertaker's shop, set the lamp down on a workman's bench, and gazed timidly about him with a feeling of awe and dread, which many people a good deal older than he will be at no loss to understand. An unfinished coffin on black tressels, which stood in the middle of the shop, looked so gloomy and death-like that a cold tremble came over him, every time his eyes wandered in the direction of the dismal object: from which he almost expected to see some frightful form slowly rear its head, to drive him mad with terror. Against the wall were ranged, in regular array, a long row of elm boards cut in the same shape: looking in the dim light, like high-shouldered ghosts with their hands in their breeches pockets. Coffin-plates, elm-chips, bright-headed nails, and shreds of black cloth, lay scattered on the floor; and the wall behind the counter was ornamented with a lively representation of two mutes in very stiff neckcloths, on duty at a large private door, with a hearse drawn by four black steeds, approaching in the distance. The shop was close and hot. The atmosphere seemed tainted with the smell of coffins. The recess beneath the counter in which his flock mattress was thrust, looked like a grave.

Nor were these the only dismal feelings which depressed Oliver. He was alone in a strange place; and we all know how chilled and desolate the best of us will sometimes feel in such a situation. The boy had no friends to care for, or to care for him. The regret of no recent separation was fresh in his mind; the absence of no loved and well-remembered face sank heavily into his heart.

But his heart was heavy, notwithstanding; and he wished, as he crept into his narrow bed, that that were his coffin, and that he could be lain in a calm and lasting sleep in the churchyard ground, with the tall grass waving gently above his head, and the sound of the old deep bell to soothe him in his sleep.

Oliver was awakened in the morning, by a loud kicking at the outside of the shop-door: which, before he could huddle on his clothes, was repeated, in an angry and impetuous manner, about twenty-five times. When he began to undo the chain, the legs desisted, and a voice began.

"Open the door, will yer?" cried the voice which belonged to the legs which had kicked at the door.

"I will, directly, sir," replied Oliver: undoing the chain, and turning the key.

"I suppose yer the new boy, ain't yer?" said the voice through the key-hole.

"Yes, sir," replied Oliver.

"How old are yer?" inquired the voice.

"Ten, sir," replied Oliver.

"Then I'll whop yer when I get in," said the voice; "you just see if I don't, that's all, my work'us brat!" and having made this obliging promise, the voice began to whistle.

Oliver had been too often subjected to the process to which the very expressive monosyllable just recorded bears reference, to entertain the smallest doubt that the owner of the voice, whoever he might be, would redeem his pledge, most honourably. He drew back the bolts with a trembling hand, and opened the door.

For a second or two, Oliver glanced up the street, and down the street, and over the way: impressed with the belief that the unknown, who had addressed him through the key-hole, had walked a few paces off, to warm himself; for nobody did he see but a big charity-boy, sitting on a post in front of the house, eating a slice of bread and butter: which he cut into wedges, the size of his mouth, with a clasp-knife, and then consumed with great dexterity.

"I beg your pardon, sir," said Oliver at length: seeing that no other visitor made his appearance; "did you knock?"

"I kicked," replied the charity-boy.

"Did you want a coffin, sir?" inquired Oliver, innocently.

At this, the charity-boy looked monstrous fierce; and said that Oliver would want one before long, if he cut jokes with his superiors in that way.

"Yer don't know who I am, I suppose, Work'us?" said the charity-boy, in continuation: descending from the top of the post, meanwhile, with edifying gravity.

"No, sir," rejoined Oliver.

"I'm Mister Noah Claypole," said the charity-boy, "and you're under me. Take down the shutters, yer idle young ruffian!" With this, Mr. Claypole administered a kick to Oliver, and entered the shop with a dignified air, which did him great credit. It is difficult for a large-headed, small-eyed youth, of lumbering make and heavy countenance, to look dignified under any circumstances; but it is more especially so, when superadded to these personal attractions are a red nose and yellow smalls.

Oliver, having taken down the shutters, and broken a pane of glass in his effort to stagger away beneath the weight of the first one to a small court at the side of the house in which they were kept during the day, was graciously assisted by Noah: who having consoled him with the assurance that "he'd catch it," condescended to help him. Mr. Sowerberry came down soon after. Shortly afterwards, Mrs. Sowerberry appeared. Oliver having "caught it," in fulfilment of Noah's prediction, followed that young gentleman down the stairs to breakfast.

"Come near the fire, Noah," said Charlotte. "I saved a nice little bit of bacon for you from master's breakfast. Oliver, shut that door at Mister Noah's back, and take them bits that I've put out on the cover of the bread-pan. There's your tea; take it away to that box, and drink it there, and make haste, for they'll want you to mind the shop. D'ye hear?"

"D'ye hear, Work'us?" said Noah Claypole.

"Lor, Noah!" said Charlotte, "what a rum creature you are! Why don't you let the boy alone?"

"Let him alone!" said Noah. "Why everybody lets him alone enough, for the matter of that. Neither his father nor his mother will ever interfere with him. All his relations let him have his own way pretty well. Eh, Charlotte? He! he! he!"

"Oh, you queer soul!" said Charlotte, bursting into a hearty laugh, in which she was joined by Noah; after which they both looked scornfully at poor Oliver Twist, as he sat shivering on the box in the coldest corner of the room, and ate the stale pieces which had been specially reserved for him.

Noah was a charity-boy, but not a workhouse orphan. No chance-child was he, for he could trace his genealogy all the way back to his parents, who lived hard by; his mother being a washerwoman, and his father a drunken soldier, discharged with a wooden leg, and a diurnal pension of twopence-halfpenny and an unstateable fraction. The shop-boys in the neighbourhood had long been in the habit of branding Noah in the public streets, with the ignominious epithets of "leathers," "charity," and the like; and Noah had bourne them without reply. But, now that fortune had cast in his way a nameless orphan, at whom even the meanest could point the finger of scorn, he retorted on him with interest. This affords charming food for contemplation. It shows us what a beautiful thing human nature may be made to be; and how impartially the same amiable qualities are developed in the finest lord and the dirtiest charity-boy.

Oliver had been sojourning at the undertaker's some three weeks or a month. Mr. and Mrs. Sowerberry—the shop being shut up—were taking their supper in the little back-parlour, when Mr. Sowerberry, after several deferential glances at his wife, said,

"My dear—" He was going to say more; but, Mrs. Sowerberry looking up, with a peculiarly unpropitious aspect, he stopped short.

"Well," said Mrs. Sowerberry, sharply.

"Nothing, my dear, nothing," said Mr. Sowerberry.

"Ugh, you brute!" said Mrs. Sowerberry.

"Not at all, my dear," said Mr. Sowerberry humbly. "I thought you didn't want to hear, my dear. I was only going to say—"

"Oh, don't tell me what you were going to say," interposed Mrs. Sowerberry. "I am nobody; don't consult me, pray. I don't want to intrude upon your secrets." As Mrs. Sowerberry said this, she gave an hysterical laugh, which threatened violent consequences.

"But, my dear," said Sowerberry, "I want to ask your advice."

"No, no, don't ask mine," replied Mrs. Sowerberry, in an affecting manner: "ask somebody else's." Here, there was another hysterical laugh, which frightened Mr. Sowerberry very much. This is a very common and much-approved matrimonial course of treatment, which is often very effective. It at once reduced Mr. Sowerberry to begging, as a special favour, to be allowed to say what Mrs. Sowerberry was most curious to hear. After a short duration, the permission was most graciously conceded.

"It's only about young Twist, my dear," said Mr. Sowerberry. "A very good-looking boy, that, my dear."

"He need be, for he eats enough," observed the lady.

"There's an expression of melancholy in his face, my dear," resumed Mr. Sowerberry, "which is very interesting. He would make a delightful mute, my love."

Mrs. Sowerberry looked up with an expression of considerable wonderment. Mr. Sowerberry remarked it and, without allowing time for any observation on the good lady's part, proceeded.

"I don't mean a regular mute to attend grown-up people, my dear, but only for children's practice. It would be very new to have a mute in proportion, my dear. You may depend upon it, it would have a superb effect."

Mrs. Sowerberry, who had a good deal of taste in the undertaking way, was much struck by the novelty of this idea; but, as it would have been compromising her dignity to have said so, under existing circumstances, she merely inquired, with much sharpness, why such an obvious suggestion had not presented itself to her husband's mind before? Mr. Sowerberry rightly construed this, as an acquiescence in his proposition; it was speedily determined, therefore, that Oliver should be at once initiated into the mysteries of the trade; and, with this view, that he should accompany his master on the very next occasion of his services being required.

The occasion was not long in coming. Half an hour after breakfast next morning, Mr. Bumble entered the shop; and supporting his cane against the counter, drew forth his large leathern pocket-book: from which he selected a small scrap of paper, which he handed over to Sowerberry.

"Aha!" said the undertaker, glancing over it with a lively countenance; "an order for a coffin, eh?"

"For a coffin first, and a porochial funeral afterwards," replied Mr. Bumble, fastening the strap of the leathern pocket-book: which, like himself, was very corpulent.

"Bayton," said the undertaker, looking from the scrap of paper to Mr. Bumble. "I never heard the name before."

Bumble shook his head, as he replied, "Obstinate people, Mr. Sowerberry; very obstinate. Proud, too, I'm afraid, sir."

"Proud, eh?" exclaimed Mr. Sowerberry with a sneer. "Come, that's too much."

"Oh, it's sickening," replied the beadle. "Antimonial, Mr. Sowerberry!"

"So it is," acquiesced the undertaker.

"We only heard of the family the night before last," said the beadle; "and we shouldn't have known anything about them, then, only a woman who lodges in the same house made an application to the porochial committee for them to send the porochial surgeon to see a woman as was very bad. He had gone out to dinner; but his 'prentice (which is a very clever lad) sent 'em some medicine in a blacking-bottle, offhand."

"Ah, there's promptness," said the undertaker.

"Promptness, indeed!" replied the beadle. "But what's the consequence; what's the ungrateful behaviour of these rebels, sir? Why, the husband sends back word that the medicine won't suit his wife's complaint, and so she shan't take it—says she shan't take it, sir! Good, strong, wholesome medicine, as was given with great success to two Irish labourers and a coal-heaver, only a week before—sent 'em for nothing, with a blackin'-bottle in,—and he sends back word that she shan't take it, sir!"

As the atrocity presented itself to Mr. Bumble's mind in full force, he struck the counter sharply with his cane, and became flushed with indignation.

"Well," said the undertaker, "I ne—ver—did—"

"Never did, sir!" ejaculated the beadle. "No, nor nobody never did; but now she's dead, we've got to bury her; and that's the direction; and the sooner it's done, the better."

Thus saying, Mr. Bumble put on his cocked hat wrong side first, in a fever of parochial excitement; and flounced out of the shop.

"Why, he was so angry, Oliver, that he forgot even to ask after you!" said Mr. Sowerberry, looking after the beadle as he strode down the street.

"Yes, sir," replied Oliver, who had carefully kept himself out of sight, during the interview; and who was shaking from head to foot at the mere recollection of the sound of Mr. Bumble's voice.

He needn't haven taken the trouble to shrink from Mr. Bumble's glance, however; for that functionary, on whom the prediction of the gentleman in the white waistcoat had made a very strong impression, thought that now the undertaker had got Oliver upon trial the subject was better avoided, until such time as he should be firmly bound for seven years, and all danger of his being returned upon the hands of the parish should be thus effectually and legally overcome.

"Well," said Mr. Sowerberry, taking up his hat, "the sooner this job is done, the better. Noah, look after the shop. Oliver, put on your cap, and come with me." Oliver obeyed, and followed his master on his professional mission.

They walked on, for some time, through the most crowded and densely inhabited part of the town; and then, striking down a narrow street more dirty and miserable than any they had yet passed through, paused to look for the house which was the object of their search. The houses on either side were high and large, but very old, and tenanted by people of the poorest class: as their neglected appearance would have sufficiently denoted, without the concurrent testimony afforded by the squalid looks of the few men and women who, with folded arms and bodies half doubled, occasionally skulked along. A great many of the tenements had shop-fronts; but these were fast closed, and mouldering away; only the upper rooms being inhabited. Some houses which had become insecure from age and decay, were prevented from falling into the street, by huge beams of wood reared against the walls, and firmly planted in the road; but even these crazy dens seemed to have been selected as the nightly haunts of some houseless wretches, for many of the rough boards which supplied the place of door and window, were wrenched from their positions, to afford an aperture wide enough for the passage of a human body. The kennel was stagnant and filthy. The very rats, which here and there lay putrefying in its rottenness, were hideous with famine.

There was neither knocker nor bell-handle at the open door where Oliver and his master stopped; so, groping his way cautiously through the dark passage, and bidding Oliver keep close to him and not be afraid the undertaker mounted to the top of the first flight of stairs. Stumbling against a door on the landing, he rapped at it with his knuckles.

It was opened by a young girl of thirteen or fourteen. The undertaker at once saw enough of what the room contained, to know it was the apartment to which he had been directed. He stepped in; Oliver followed him.

There was no fire in the room; but a man was crouching, mechanically, over the empty stove. An old woman, too, had drawn a low stool to the cold hearth, and was sitting beside him. There were some ragged children in another corner; and in a small recess, opposite the door, there lay upon the ground, something covered with an old blanket. Oliver shuddered as he cast his eyes toward the place, and crept involuntarily closer to his master; for though it was covered up, the boy felt that it was a corpse.

The man's face was thin and very pale; his hair and beard were grizzly; his eyes were bloodshot. The old woman's face was wrinkled; her two remaining teeth protruded over her under lip; and her eyes were bright and piercing. Oliver was afraid to look at either her or the man. They seemed so like the rats he had seen outside.

"Nobody shall go near her," said the man, starting fiercely up, as the undertaker approached the recess. "Keep back! Damn you, keep back, if you've a life to lose!"

"Nonsense, my good man," said the undertaker, who was pretty well used to misery in all its shapes. "Nonsense!"

"I tell you," said the man: clenching his hands, and stamping furiously on the floor,—"I tell you I won't have her put into the ground. She couldn't rest there. The worms would worry her—not eat her—she is so worn away."

The undertaker offered no reply to this raving; but producing a tape from his pocket, knelt down for a moment by the side of the body.

"Ah!" said the man: bursting into tears, and sinking on his knees at the feet of the dead woman; "kneel down, kneel down—kneel round her, every one of you, and mark my words! I say she was starved to death. I never knew how bad she was, till the fever came upon her; and then her bones were starting through the skin. There was neither fire nor candle; she died in the dark—in the dark! She couldn't even see her children's faces, though we heard her gasping out their names. I begged for her in the streets: and they sent me to prison. When I came back, she was dying; and all the blood in my heart has dried up, for they starved her to death. I swear it before the God that saw it! They starved her!" He twined his hands in his hair; and, with a loud scream, rolled grovelling upon the floor: his eyes fixed, and the foam covering his lips.

The terrified children cried bitterly; but the old woman, who had hitherto remained as quiet as if she had been wholly deaf to all that passed, menaced them into silence. Having unloosened the cravat of the man who still remained extended on the ground, she tottered towards the undertaker.

"She was my daughter," said the old woman, nodding her head in the direction of the corpse; and speaking with an idiotic leer, more ghastly than even the presence of death in such a place. "Lord, Lord! Well, it is strange that I who gave birth to her, and was a woman then, should be alive and merry now, and she lying there: so cold and stiff! Lord, Lord!—to think of it; it's as good as a play—as good as a play!"

As the wretched creature mumbled and chuckled in her hideous merriment, the undertaker turned to go away.

"Stop, stop!" said the old woman in a loud whisper. "Will she be buried to-morrow, or next day, or to-night? I laid her out; and I must walk, you know. Send me a large cloak: a good warm one: for it is bitter cold. We should have cake and wine, too, before we go! Never mind; send some bread—only a loaf of bread and a cup of water. Shall we have some bread, dear?" she said eagerly: catching at the undertaker's coat, as he once more moved towards the door.

"Yes, yes," said the undertaker, "Of course. Anything you like!" He disengaged himself from the old woman's grasp; and, drawing Oliver after him, hurried away.

The next day, (the family having been meanwhile relieved with a half-quartern loaf and a piece of cheese, left with them by Mr. Bumble himself,) Oliver and his master returned to the miserable abode; where Mr. Bumble had already arrived, accompanied by four men from the workhouse, who were to act as bearers. An old black cloak had been thrown over the rags of the old woman and the man; and the bare coffin having been screwed down, was hoisted on the shoulders of the bearers, and carried into the street.

"Now, you must put your best leg foremost, old lady!" whispered Sowerberry in the old woman's ear; "we are rather late; and it won't do, to keep the clergyman waiting. Move on, my men,—as quick as you like!"

Thus directed, the bearers trotted on under their light burden; and the two mourners kept as near them, as they could. Mr. Bumble and Sowerberry walked at a good smart pace in front; and Oliver, whose legs were not so long as his master's, ran by the side.

There was not so great a necessity for hurrying as Mr. Sowerberry had anticipated, however; for when they reached the obscure corner of the churchyard in which the nettles grew, and where the parish graves were made, the clergyman had not arrived; and the clerk, who was sitting by the vestry-room fire, seemed to think it by no means improbable that it might be an hour or so, before he came. So, they put the bier on the brink of the grave; and the two mourners waited patiently in the damp clay, with a cold rain drizzling down, while the ragged boys whom the spectacle had attracted into the churchyard played a noisy game at hide-and-seek among the tombstones, or varied their amusements by jumping backwards and forwards over the coffin. Mr. Sowerberry and Bumble, being personal friends of the clerk, sat by the fire with him, and read the paper.

At length, after a lapse of something more than an hour, Mr. Bumble, and Sowerberry, and the clerk, were seen running towards the grave. Immediately afterwards, the clergyman appeared: putting on his surplice as he came along. Mr. Bumble then thrashed a boy or two, to keep up appearances; and the reverend gentleman, having read as much of the burial service as could be compressed into four minutes, gave his surplice to the clerk, and walked away again.

"Now, Bill!" said Sowerberry to the grave-digger. "Fill up!"

It was no very difficult task, for the grave was so full, that the uppermost coffin was within a few feet of the surface. The grave-digger shovelled in the earth; stamped it loosely down with his feet: shouldered his spade; and walked off, followed by the boys, who murmured very loud complaints at the fun being over so soon.

"Come, my good fellow!" said Bumble, tapping the man on the back. "They want to shut up the yard."

The man who had never once moved, since he had taken his station by the grave side, started, raised his head, stared at the person who had addressed him, walked forward for a few paces; and fell down in a swoon. The crazy old woman was too much occupied in bewailing the loss of her cloak (which the undertaker had taken off), to pay him any attention; so they threw a can of cold water over him; and when he came to, saw him safely out of the churchyard, locked the gate, and departed on their different ways.

"Well, Oliver," said Sowerberry, as they walked home, "how do you like it?"

"Pretty well, thank you, sir" replied Oliver, with considerable hesitation. "Not very much, sir."

"Ah, you'll get used to it in time, Oliver," said Sowerberry. "Nothing when you are used to it, my boy."

Oliver wondered, in his own mind, whether it had taken a very long time to get Mr. Sowerberry used to it. But he thought it better not to ask the question; and walked back to the shop: thinking over all he had seen and heard.

CHAPTER VI

Oliver, Being Goaded by the Taunts of Noah, Rouses Into Action, and Rather Astonishes Him

The month's trial over, Oliver was formally apprenticed. It was a nice sickly season just at this time. In commercial phrase, coffins were looking up; and, in the course of a few weeks, Oliver acquired a great deal of experience. The success of Mr. Sowerberry's ingenious speculation, exceeded even his most sanguine hopes. The oldest inhabitants recollected no period at which measles had been so prevalent, or so fatal to infant existence; and many were the mournful processions which little Oliver headed, in a hat-band reaching down to his knees, to the indescribable admiration and emotion of all the mothers in the town. As Oliver accompanied his master in most of his adult expeditions too, in order that he might acquire that equanimity of demeanour and full command of nerve which was essential to a finished undertaker, he had many opportunities of observing the beautiful resignation and fortitude with which some strong-minded people bear their trials and losses.

For instance; when Sowerberry had an order for the burial of some rich old lady or gentleman, who was surrounded by a great number of nephews and nieces, who had been perfectly inconsolable during the previous illness, and whose grief had been wholly irrepressible even on the most public occasions, they would be as happy among themselves as need be—quite cheerful and contented—conversing together with as much freedom and gaiety, as if nothing whatever had happened to disturb them. Husbands, too, bore the loss of their wives with the most heroic calmness. Wives, again, put on weeds for their husbands, as if, so far from grieving in the garb of sorrow, they had made up their minds to render it as becoming and attractive as possible. It was observable, too, that ladies and gentlemen who were in passions of anguish during the ceremony of interment, recovered almost as soon as they reached home, and became quite composed before the tea-drinking was over. All this was very pleasant and improving to see; and Oliver beheld it with great admiration.

That Oliver Twist was moved to resignation by the example of these good people, I cannot, although I am his biographer, undertake to affirm with any degree of confidence; but I can most distinctly say, that for many months he continued meekly to submit to the domination and ill-treatment of Noah Claypole: who used him far worse than before, now that his jealousy was roused by seeing the new boy promoted to the black stick and hatband, while he, the old one, remained stationary in the muffin-cap and leathers. Charlotte treated him ill, because Noah did; and Mrs. Sowerberry was his decided enemy, because Mr. Sowerberry was disposed to be his friend; so, between these three on one side, and a glut of funerals on the other, Oliver was not altogether as comfortable as the hungry pig was, when he was shut up, by mistake, in the grain department of a brewery.

And now, I come to a very important passage in Oliver's history; for I have to record an act, slight and unimportant perhaps in appearance, but which indirectly produced a material change in all his future prospects and proceedings.

One day, Oliver and Noah had descended into the kitchen at the usual dinner-hour, to banquet upon a small joint of mutton—a pound and a half of the worst end of the neck—when Charlotte being called out of the way, there ensued a brief interval of time, which Noah Claypole, being hungry and vicious, considered he could not possibly devote to a worthier purpose than aggravating and tantalising young Oliver Twist.

Intent upon this innocent amusement, Noah put his feet on the table-cloth; and pulled Oliver's hair; and twitched his ears; and expressed his opinion that he was a "sneak"; and furthermore announced his intention of coming to see him hanged, whenever that desirable event should take place; and entered upon various topics of petty annoyance, like a malicious and ill-conditioned charity-boy as he was. But, making Oliver cry, Noah attempted to be more facetious still; and in his attempt, did what many sometimes do to this day, when they want to be funny. He got rather personal.

"Work'us," said Noah, "how's your mother?"

"She's dead," replied Oliver; "don't you say anything about her to me!"

Oliver's colour rose as he said this; he breathed quickly; and there was a curious working of the mouth and nostrils, which Mr. Claypole thought must be the immediate precursor of a violent fit of crying. Under this impression he returned to the charge.

"What did she die of, Work'us?" said Noah.

"Of a broken heart, some of our old nurses told me," replied Oliver: more as if he were talking to himself, than answering Noah. "I think I know what it must be to die of that!"

"Tol de rol lol lol, right fol lairy, Work'us," said Noah, as a tear rolled down Oliver's cheek. "What's set you a snivelling now?"

"Not you," replied Oliver, sharply. "There; that's enough. Don't say anything more to me about her; you'd better not!"

"Better not!" exclaimed Noah. "Well! Better not! Work'us, don't be impudent. Your mother, too! She was a nice 'un she was. Oh, Lor!" And here, Noah nodded his head expressively; and curled up as much of his small red nose as muscular action could collect together, for the occasion.

"Yer know, Work'us," continued Noah, emboldened by Oliver's silence, and speaking in a jeering tone of affected pity: of all tones the most annoying: "Yer know, Work'us, it can't be helped now; and of course yer couldn't help it then; and I am very sorry for it; and I'm sure we all are, and pity yer very much. But yer must know, Work'us, yer mother was a regular right-down bad 'un."

"What did you say?" inquired Oliver, looking up very quickly.

"A regular right-down bad 'un, Work'us," replied Noah, coolly. "And it's a great deal better, Work'us, that she died when she did, or else she'd have been hard labouring in Bridewell, or transported, or hung; which is more likely than either, isn't it?"

Crimson with fury, Oliver started up; overthrew the chair and table; seized Noah by the throat; shook him, in the violence of his rage, till his teeth chattered in his head; and collecting his whole force into one heavy blow, felled him to the ground.

A minute ago, the boy had looked the quiet child, mild, dejected creature that harsh treatment had made him. But his spirit was roused at last; the cruel insult to his dead mother had set his blood on fire. His breast heaved; his attitude was erect; his eye bright and vivid; his whole person changed, as he stood glaring over the cowardly tormentor who now lay crouching at his feet; and defied him with an energy he had never known before.

"He'll murder me!" blubbered Noah. "Charlotte! missis! Here's the new boy a murdering of me! Help! help! Oliver's gone mad! Char—lotte!"

Noah's shouts were responded to, by a loud scream from Charlotte, and a louder from Mrs. Sowerberry; the former of whom rushed into the kitchen by a side-door, while the latter paused on the staircase till she was quite certain that it was consistent with the preservation of human life, to come further down.

"Oh, you little wretch!" screamed Charlotte: seizing Oliver with her utmost force, which was about equal to that of a moderately strong man in particularly good training. "Oh, you little un-grate-ful, mur-de-rous, hor-rid villain!" And between every syllable, Charlotte gave Oliver a blow with all her might: accompanying it with a scream, for the benefit of society.

Charlotte's fist was by no means a light one; but, lest it should not be effectual in calming Oliver's wrath, Mrs. Sowerberry plunged into the kitchen, and assisted to hold him with one hand, while she scratched his face with the other. In this favourable position of affairs, Noah rose from the ground, and pommelled him behind.

This was rather too violent exercise to last long. When they were all wearied out, and could tear and beat no longer, they dragged Oliver, struggling and shouting, but nothing daunted, into the dust-cellar, and there locked him up. This being done, Mrs. Sowerberry sunk into a chair, and burst into tears.

"Bless her, she's going off!" said Charlotte. "A glass of water, Noah, dear. Make haste!"

"Oh! Charlotte," said Mrs. Sowerberry: speaking as well as she could, through a deficiency of breath, and a sufficiency of cold water, which Noah had poured over her head and shoulders. "Oh! Charlotte, what a mercy we have not all been murdered in our beds!"

"Ah! mercy indeed, ma'am," was the reply. I only hope this'll teach master not to have any more of these dreadful creatures, that are born to be murderers and robbers from their very cradle. Poor Noah! He was all but killed, ma'am, when I come in."

"Poor fellow!" said Mrs. Sowerberry: looking piteously on the charity-boy.

Noah, whose top waistcoat-button might have been somewhere on a level with the crown of Oliver's head, rubbed his eyes with the inside of his wrists while this commiseration was bestowed upon him, and performed some affecting tears and sniffs.

"What's to be done!" exclaimed Mrs. Sowerberry. "Your master's not at home; there's not a man in the house, and he'll kick that door down in ten minutes." Oliver's vigorous plunges against the bit of timber in question, rendered this occurance highly probable.

"Dear, dear! I don't know, ma'am," said Charlotte, "unless we send for the police-officers."

"Or the millingtary," suggested Mr. Claypole.

"No, no," said Mrs. Sowerberry: bethinking herself of Oliver's old friend. "Run to Mr. Bumble, Noah, and tell him to come here directly, and not to lose a minute; never mind your cap! Make haste! You can hold a knife to that black eye, as you run along. It'll keep the swelling down."

Noah stopped to make no reply, but started off at his fullest speed; and very much it astonished the people who were out walking, to see a charity-boy tearing through the streets pell-mell, with no cap on his head, and a clasp-knife at his eye.

CHAPTER VII

Oliver Continues Refractory

Noah Claypole ran along the streets at his swiftest pace, and paused not once for breath, until he reached the workhouse-gate. Having rested here, for a minute or so, to collect a good burst of sobs and an imposing show of tears and terror, he knocked loudly at the wicket; and presented such a rueful face to the aged pauper who opened it, that even he, who saw nothing but rueful faces about him at the best of times, started back in astonishment.

"Why, what's the matter with the boy!" said the old pauper.

"Mr. Bumble! Mr. Bumble!" cried Noah, with well-affected dismay: and in tones so loud and agitated, that they not only caught the ear of Mr. Bumble himself, who happened to be hard by, but alarmed him so much that he rushed into the yard without his cocked hat,—which is a very curious and remarkable circumstance: as showing that even a beadle, acted upon a sudden and powerful impulse, may be afflicted with a momentary visitation of loss of self-possession, and forgetfulness of personal dignity.

"Oh, Mr. Bumble, sir!" said Noah: "Oliver, sir,—Oliver has—"

"What? What?" interposed Mr. Bumble: with a gleam of pleasure in his metallic eyes. "Not run away; he hasn't run away, has he, Noah?"

"No, sir, no. Not run away, sir, but he's turned wicious," replied Noah. "He tried to murder me, sir; and then he tried to murder Charlotte; and then missis. Oh! what dreadful pain it is! Such agony, please, sir!" And here, Noah writhed and twisted his body into an extensive variety of eel-like positions; thereby giving Mr. Bumble to understand that, from the violent and sanguinary onset of Oliver Twist, he had sustained severe internal injury and damage, from which he was at that moment suffering the acutest torture.

When Noah saw that the intelligence he communicated perfectly paralysed Mr. Bumble, he imparted additional effect thereunto, by bewailing his dreadful wounds ten times louder than before; and when he observed a gentleman in a white waistcoat crossing the yard, he was more tragic in his lamentations than ever: rightly conceiving it highly expedient to attract the notice, and rouse the indignation, of the gentleman aforesaid.

The gentleman's notice was very soon attracted; for he had not walked three paces, when he turned angrily round, and inquired what that young cur was howling for, and why Mr. Bumble did not favour him with something which would render the series of vocular exclamations so designated, an involuntary process?

"It's a poor boy from the free-school, sir," replied Mr. Bumble, "who has been nearly murdered—all but murdered, sir,—by young Twist."

"By Jove!" exclaimed the gentleman in the white waistcoat, stopping short. "I knew it! I felt a strange presentiment from the very first, that that audacious young savage would come to be hung!"

"He has likewise attempted, sir, to murder the female servant," said Mr. Bumble, with a face of ashy paleness.

"And his missis," interposed Mr. Claypole.

"And his master, too, I think you said, Noah?" added Mr. Bumble.

"No! he's out, or he would have murdered him," replied Noah. "He said he wanted to."

"Ah! Said he wanted to, did he, my boy?" inquired the gentleman in the white waistcoat.

"Yes, sir," replied Noah. "And please, sir, missis wants to know whether Mr. Bumble can spare time to step up there, directly, and flog him—'cause master's out."

"Certainly, my boy; certainly," said the gentleman in the white waistcoat: smiling benignly, and patting Noah's head, which was about three inches higher than his own. "You're a good boy—a very good boy. Here's a penny for you. Bumble, just step up to Sowerberry's with your cane, and see what's best to be done. Don't spare him, Bumble."

"No, I will not, sir," replied the beadle. And the cocked hat and cane having been, by this time, adjusted to their owner's satisfaction, Mr. Bumble and Noah Claypole betook themselves with all speed to the undertaker's shop.

Here the position of affairs had not at all improved. Sowerberry had not yet returned, and Oliver continued to kick, with undiminished vigour, at the cellar-door. The accounts of his ferocity as related by Mrs. Sowerberry and Charlotte, were of so startling a nature, that Mr. Bumble judged it prudent to parley, before opening the door. With this view he gave a kick at the outside, by way of prelude; and, then, applying his mouth to the keyhole, said, in a deep and impressive tone:

"Oliver!"

"Come; you let me out!" replied Oliver, from the inside.

"Do you know this here voice, Oliver?" said Mr. Bumble.

"Yes," replied Oliver.

"Ain't you afraid of it, sir? Ain't you a-trembling while I speak, sir?" said Mr. Bumble.

"No!" replied Oliver, boldly.

An answer so different from the one he had expected to elicit, and was in the habit of receiving, staggered Mr. Bumble not a little. He stepped back from the keyhole; drew himself up to his full height; and looked from one to another of the three bystanders, in mute astonishment.

"Oh, you know, Mr. Bumble, he must be mad," said Mrs. Sowerberry.

"No boy in half his senses could venture to speak so to you."

"It's not Madness, ma'am," replied Mr. Bumble, after a few moments of deep meditation. "It's Meat."

"What?" exclaimed Mrs. Sowerberry.

"Meat, ma'am, meat," replied Bumble, with stern emphasis. "You've over-fed him, ma'am. You've raised a artificial soul and spirit in him, ma'am unbecoming a person of his condition: as the board, Mrs. Sowerberry, who are practical philosophers, will tell you. What have paupers to do with soul or spirit? It's quite enough that we let 'em have live bodies. If you had kept the boy on gruel, ma'am, this would never have happened."

"Dear, dear!" ejaculated Mrs. Sowerberry, piously raising her eyes to the kitchen ceiling: "this comes of being liberal!"

The liberality of Mrs. Sowerberry to Oliver, had consisted of a profuse bestowal upon him of all the dirty odds and ends which nobody else would eat; so there was a great deal of meekness and self-devotion in her voluntarily remaining under Mr. Bumble's heavy accusation. Of which, to do her justice, she was wholly innocent, in thought, word, or deed.

"Ah!" said Mr. Bumble, when the lady brought her eyes down to earth again; "the only thing that can be done now, that I know of, is to leave him in the cellar for a day or so, till he's a little starved down; and then to take him out, and keep him on gruel all through the apprenticeship. He comes of a bad family. Excitable natures, Mrs. Sowerberry! Both the nurse and doctor said, that that mother of his made her way here, against difficulties and pain that would have killed any well-disposed woman, weeks before."

At this point of Mr. Bumble's discourse, Oliver, just hearing enough to know that some allusion was being made to his mother, recommenced kicking, with a violence that rendered every other sound inaudible. Sowerberry returned at this juncture. Oliver's offence having been explained to him, with such exaggerations as the ladies thought best calculated to rouse his ire, he unlocked the cellar-door in a twinkling, and dragged his rebellious apprentice out, by the collar.

Oliver's clothes had been torn in the beating he had received; his face was bruised and scratched; and his hair scattered over his forehead. The angry flush had not disappeared, however; and when he was pulled out of his prison, he scowled boldly on Noah, and looked quite undismayed.

"Now, you are a nice young fellow, ain't you?" said Sowerberry; giving Oliver a shake, and a box on the ear.

"He called my mother names," replied Oliver.

"Well, and what if he did, you little ungrateful wretch?" said Mrs. Sowerberry. "She deserved what he said, and worse."

"She didn't" said Oliver.

"She did," said Mrs. Sowerberry.

"It's a lie!" said Oliver.

Mrs. Sowerberry burst into a flood of tears.

This flood of tears left Mr. Sowerberry no alternative. If he had hesitated for one instant to punish Oliver most severely, it must be quite clear to every experienced reader that he would have been, according to all precedents in disputes of matrimony established, a brute, an unnatural husband, an insulting creature, a base imitation of a man, and various other agreeable characters too numerous for recital within the limits of this chapter. To do him justice, he was, as far as his power went—it was not very extensive—kindly disposed towards the boy; perhaps, because it was his interest to be so; perhaps, because his wife disliked him. The flood of tears, however, left him no resource; so he at once gave him a drubbing, which satisfied even Mrs. Sowerberry herself, and rendered Mr. Bumble's subsequent application of the parochial cane, rather unnecessary. For the rest of the day, he was shut up in the back kitchen, in company with a pump and a slice of bread; and at night, Mrs. Sowerberry, after making various remarks outside the door, by no means complimentary to the memory of his mother, looked into the room, and, amidst the jeers and pointings of Noah and Charlotte, ordered him upstairs to his dismal bed.

It was not until he was left alone in the silence and stillness of the gloomy workshop of the undertaker, that Oliver gave way to the feelings which the day's treatment may be supposed likely to have awakened in a mere child. He had listened to their taunts with a look of contempt; he had borne the lash without a cry: for he felt that pride swelling in his heart which would have kept down a shriek to the last, though they had roasted him alive. But now, when there were none to see or hear him, he fell upon his knees on the floor; and, hiding his face in his hands, wept such tears as, God send for the credit of our nature, few so young may ever have cause to pour out before him!

For a long time, Oliver remained motionless in this attitude. The candle was burning low in the socket when he rose to his feet. Having gazed cautiously round him, and listened intently, he gently undid the fastenings of the door, and looked abroad.

It was a cold, dark night. The stars seemed, to the boy's eyes, farther from the earth than he had ever seen them before; there was no wind; and the sombre shadows thrown by the trees upon the ground, looked sepulchral and death-like, from being so still. He softly reclosed the door. Having availed himself of the expiring light of the candle to tie up in a handkerchief the few articles of wearing apparel he had, sat himself down upon a bench, to wait for morning.

With the first ray of light that struggled through the crevices in the shutters, Oliver arose, and again unbarred the door. One timid look around—one moment's pause of hesitation—he had closed it behind him, and was in the open street.

He looked to the right and to the left, uncertain whither to fly.

He remembered to have seen the waggons, as they went out, toiling up the hill. He took the same route; and arriving at a footpath across the fields: which he knew, after some distance, led out again into the road; struck into it, and walked quickly on.

Along this same footpath, Oliver well-remembered he had trotted beside Mr. Bumble, when he first carried him to the workhouse from the farm. His way lay directly in front of the cottage. His heart beat quickly when he bethought himself of this; and he half resolved to turn back. He had come a long way though, and should lose a great deal of time by doing so. Besides, it was so early that there was very little fear of his being seen; so he walked on.

He reached the house. There was no appearance of its inmates stirring at that early hour. Oliver stopped, and peeped into the garden. A child was weeding one of the little beds; as he stopped, he raised his pale face and disclosed the features of one of his former companions. Oliver felt glad to see him, before he went; for, though younger than himself, he had been his little friend and playmate. They had been beaten, and starved, and shut up together, many and many a time.

"Hush, Dick!" said Oliver, as the boy ran to the gate, and thrust his thin arm between the rails to greet him. "Is any one up?"

"Nobody but me," replied the child.

"You musn't say you saw me, Dick," said Oliver. "I am running away. They beat and ill-use me, Dick; and I am going to seek my fortune, some long way off. I don't know where. How pale you are!"

"I heard the doctor tell them I was dying," replied the child with a faint smile. "I am very glad to see you, dear; but don't stop, don't stop!"

"Yes, yes, I will, to say good-b'ye to you," replied Oliver. "I shall see you again, Dick. I know I shall! You will be well and happy!"

"I hope so," replied the child. "After I am dead, but not before. I know the doctor must be right, Oliver, because I dream so much of Heaven, and Angels, and kind faces that I never see when I am awake. Kiss me," said the child, climbing up the low gate, and flinging his little arms round Oliver's neck. "Good-b'ye, dear! God bless you!"

The blessing was from a young child's lips, but it was the first that Oliver had ever heard invoked upon his head; and through the struggles and sufferings, and troubles and changes, of his after life, he never once forgot it.

CHAPTER VIII

Oliver Walks to London. He Encounters on the Road a Strange Sort of Young Gentleman

Oliver reached the stile at which the by-path terminated; and once more gained the high-road. It was eight o'clock now. Though he was nearly five miles away from the town, he ran, and hid behind the hedges, by turns, till noon: fearing that he might be pursued and overtaken. Then he sat down to rest by the side of the milestone, and began to think, for the first time, where he had better go and try to live.

The stone by which he was seated, bore, in large characters, an intimation that it was just seventy miles from that spot to London. The name awakened a new train of ideas in the boy's mind.

London!—that great place!—nobody—not even Mr. Bumble—could ever find him there! He had often heard the old men in the workhouse, too, say that no lad of spirit need want in London; and that there were ways of living in that vast city, which those who had been bred up in country parts had no idea of. It was the very place for a homeless boy, who must die in the streets unless some one helped him. As these things passed through his thoughts, he jumped upon his feet, and again walked forward.

He had diminished the distance between himself and London by full four miles more, before he recollected how much he must undergo ere he could hope to reach his place of destination. As this consideration forced itself upon him, he slackened his pace a little, and meditated upon his means of getting there. He had a crust of bread, a coarse shirt, and two pairs of stockings, in his bundle. He had a penny too—a gift of Sowerberry's after some funeral in which he had acquitted himself more than ordinarily well—in his pocket. "A clean shirt," thought Oliver, "is a very comfortable thing; and so are two pairs of darned stockings; and so is a penny; but they are small helps to a sixty-five miles' walk in winter time." But Oliver's thoughts, like those of most other people, although they were extremely ready and active to point out his difficulties, were wholly at a loss to suggest any feasible mode of surmounting them; so, after a good deal of thinking to no particular purpose, he changed his little bundle over to the other shoulder, and trudged on.

Oliver walked twenty miles that day; and all that time tasted nothing but the crust of dry bread, and a few draughts of water, which he begged at the cottage-doors by the road-side. When the night came, he turned into a meadow; and, creeping close under a hay-rick, determined to lie there, till morning. He felt frightened at first, for the wind moaned dismally over the empty fields: and he was cold and hungry, and more alone than he had ever felt before. Being very tired with his walk, however, he soon fell asleep and forgot his troubles.

He felt cold and stiff, when he got up next morning, and so hungry that he was obliged to exchange the penny for a small loaf, in the very first village through which he passed. He had walked no more than twelve miles, when night closed in again. His feet were sore, and his legs so weak that they trembled beneath him. Another night passed in the bleak damp air, made him worse; when he set forward on his journey next morning he could hardly crawl along.

He waited at the bottom of a steep hill till a stage-coach came up, and then begged of the outside passengers; but there were very few who took any notice of him: and even those told him to wait till they got to the top of the hill, and then let them see how far he could run for a halfpenny. Poor Oliver tried to keep up with the coach a little way, but was unable to do it, by reason of his fatigue and sore feet. When the outsides saw this, they put their halfpence back into their pockets again, declaring that he was an idle young dog, and didn't deserve anything; and the coach rattled away and left only a cloud of dust behind.

In some villages, large painted boards were fixed up: warning all persons who begged within the district, that they would be sent to jail. This frightened Oliver very much, and made him glad to get out of those villages with all possible expedition. In others, he would stand about the inn-yards, and look mournfully at every one who passed: a proceeding which generally terminated in the landlady's ordering one of the post-boys who were lounging about, to drive that strange boy out of the place, for she was sure he had come to steal something. If he begged at a farmer's house, ten to one but they threatened to set the dog on him; and when he showed his nose in a shop, they talked about the beadle—which brought Oliver's heart into his mouth,—very often the only thing he had there, for many hours together.

In fact, if it had not been for a good-hearted turnpike-man, and a benevolent old lady, Oliver's troubles would have been shortened by the very same process which had put an end to his mother's; in other words, he would most assuredly have fallen dead upon the king's highway. But the turnpike-man gave him a meal of bread and cheese; and the old lady, who had a shipwrecked grandson wandering barefoot in some distant part of the earth, took pity upon the poor orphan, and gave him what little she could afford—and more—with such kind and gentle words, and such tears of sympathy and compassion, that they sank deeper into Oliver's soul, than all the sufferings he had ever undergone.

Early on the seventh morning after he had left his native place, Oliver limped slowly into the little town of Barnet. The window-shutters were closed; the street was empty; not a soul had awakened to the business of the day. The sun was rising in all its splendid beauty; but the light only served to show the boy his own lonesomeness and desolation, as he sat, with bleeding feet and covered with dust, upon a door-step.

By degrees, the shutters were opened; the window-blinds were drawn up; and people began passing to and fro. Some few stopped to gaze at Oliver for a moment or two, or turned round to stare at him as they hurried by; but none relieved him, or troubled themselves to inquire how he came there. He had no heart to beg. And there he sat.

He had been crouching on the step for some time: wondering at the great number of public-houses (every other house in Barnet was a tavern, large or small), gazing listlessly at the coaches as they passed through, and thinking how strange it seemed that they could do, with ease, in a few hours, what it had taken him a whole week of courage and determination beyond his years to accomplish: when he was roused by observing that a boy, who had passed him carelessly some minutes before, had returned, and was now surveying him most earnestly from the opposite side of the way. He took little heed of this at first; but the boy remained in the same attitude of close observation so long, that Oliver raised his head, and returned his steady look. Upon this, the boy crossed over; and walking close up to Oliver, said,

"Hullo, my covey! What's the row?"

The boy who addressed this inquiry to the young wayfarer, was about his own age: but one of the queerest looking boys that Oliver had even seen. He was a snub-nosed, flat-browed, common-faced boy enough; and as dirty a juvenile as one would wish to see; but he had about him all the airs and manners of a man. He was short of his age: with rather bow-legs, and little, sharp, ugly eyes. His hat was stuck on the top of his head so lightly, that it threatened to fall off every moment—and would have done so, very often, if the wearer had not had a knack of every now and then giving his head a sudden twitch, which brought it back to its old place again. He wore a man's coat, which reached nearly to his heels. He had turned the cuffs back, half-way up his arm, to get his hands out of the sleeves: apparently with the ultimate view of thrusting them into the pockets of his corduroy trousers; for there he kept them. He was, altogether, as roystering and swaggering a young gentleman as ever stood four feet six, or something less, in the bluchers.

"Hullo, my covey! What's the row?" said this strange young gentleman to Oliver.

"I am very hungry and tired," replied Oliver: the tears standing in his eyes as he spoke. "I have walked a long way. I have been walking these seven days."

"Walking for sivin days!" said the young gentleman. "Oh, I see. Beak's order, eh? But," he added, noticing Oliver's look of surprise, "I suppose you don't know what a beak is, my flash com-pan-i-on."

Oliver mildly replied, that he had always heard a bird's mouth described by the term in question.

"My eyes, how green!" exclaimed the young gentleman. "Why, a beak's a madgst'rate; and when you walk by a beak's order, it's not straight forerd, but always agoing up, and niver a coming down agin. Was you never on the mill?"

"What mill?" inquired Oliver.

"What mill! Why, the mill—the mill as takes up so little room that it'll work inside a Stone Jug; and always goes better when the wind's low with people, than when it's high; acos then they can't get workmen. But come," said the young gentleman; "you want grub, and you shall have it. I'm at low-water-mark myself—only one bob and a magpie; but, as far as it goes, I'll fork out and stump. Up with you on your pins. There! Now then! 'Morrice!"

Assisting Oliver to rise, the young gentleman took him to an adjacent chandler's shop, where he purchased a sufficiency of ready-dressed ham and a half-quartern loaf, or, as he himself expressed it, "a fourpenny bran!" the ham being kept clean and preserved from dust, by the ingenious expedient of making a hole in the loaf by pulling out a portion of the crumb, and stuffing it therein. Taking the bread under his arm, the young gentleman turned into a small public-house, and led the way to a tap-room in the rear of the premises. Here, a pot of beer was brought in, by direction of the mysterious youth; and Oliver, falling to, at his new friend's bidding, made a long and hearty meal, during the progress of which the strange boy eyed him from time to time with great attention.

"Going to London?" said the strange boy, when Oliver had at length concluded.

"Yes."

"Got any lodgings?"

"No."

"Money?"

"No."

The strange boy whistled; and put his arms into his pockets, as far as the big coat-sleeves would let them go.

"Do you live in London?" inquired Oliver.

"Yes. I do, when I'm at home," replied the boy. "I suppose you want some place to sleep in to-night, don't you?"

"I do, indeed," answered Oliver. "I have not slept under a roof since I left the country."

"Don't fret your eyelids on that score," said the young gentleman. "I've got to be in London to-night; and I know a 'spectable old gentleman as lives there, wot'll give you lodgings for nothink, and never ask for the change—that is, if any genelman he knows interduces you. And don't he know me? Oh, no! Not in the least! By no means. Certainly not!"

The young gentleman smiled, as if to intimate that the latter fragments of discourse were playfully ironical; and finished the beer as he did so.

This unexpected offer of shelter was too tempting to be resisted; especially as it was immediately followed up, by the assurance that the old gentleman referred to, would doubtless provide Oliver with a comfortable place, without loss of time. This led to a more friendly and confidential dialogue; from which Oliver discovered that his friend's name was Jack Dawkins, and that he was a peculiar pet and protege of the elderly gentleman before mentioned.

Mr. Dawkin's appearance did not say a vast deal in favour of the comforts which his patron's interest obtained for those whom he took under his protection; but, as he had a rather flighty and dissolute mode of conversing, and furthermore avowed that among his intimate friends he was better known by the sobriquet of "The Artful Dodger," Oliver concluded that, being of a dissipated and careless turn, the moral precepts of his benefactor had hitherto been thrown away upon him. Under this impression, he secretly resolved to cultivate the good opinion of the old gentleman as quickly as possible; and, if he found the Dodger incorrigible, as he more than half suspected he should, to decline the honour of his farther acquaintance.

As John Dawkins objected to their entering London before nightfall, it was nearly eleven o'clock when they reached the turnpike at Islington. They crossed from the Angel into St. John's Road; struck down the small street which terminates at Sadler's Wells Theatre; through Exmouth Street and Coppice Row; down the little court by the side of the workhouse; across the classic ground which once bore the name of Hockley-in-the-Hole; thence into Little Saffron Hill; and so into Saffron Hill the Great: along which the Dodger scudded at a rapid pace, directing Oliver to follow close at his heels.

Although Oliver had enough to occupy his attention in keeping sight of his leader, he could not help bestowing a few hasty glances on either side of the way, as he passed along. A dirtier or more wretched place he had never seen. The street was very narrow and muddy, and the air was impregnated with filthy odours.

There were a good many small shops; but the only stock in trade appeared to be heaps of children, who, even at that time of night, were crawling in and out at the doors, or screaming from the inside. The sole places that seemed to prosper amid the general blight of the place, were the public-houses; and in them, the lowest orders of Irish were wrangling with might and main. Covered ways and yards, which here and there diverged from the main street, disclosed little knots of houses, where drunken men and women were positively wallowing in filth; and from several of the door-ways, great ill-looking fellows were cautiously emerging, bound, to all appearance, on no very well-disposed or harmless errands.

Oliver was just considering whether he hadn't better run away, when they reached the bottom of the hill. His conductor, catching him by the arm, pushed open the door of a house near Field Lane; and drawing him into the passage, closed it behind them.

"Now, then!" cried a voice from below, in reply to a whistle from the Dodger.

"Plummy and slam!" was the reply.

This seemed to be some watchword or signal that all was right; for the light of a feeble candle gleamed on the wall at the remote end of the passage; and a man's face peeped out, from where a balustrade of the old kitchen staircase had been broken away.

"There's two on you," said the man, thrusting the candle farther out, and shielding his eyes with his hand. "Who's the t'other one?"

"A new pal," replied Jack Dawkins, pulling Oliver forward.

"Where did he come from?"

"Greenland. Is Fagin upstairs?"

"Yes, he's a sortin' the wipes. Up with you!" The candle was drawn back, and the face disappeared.

Oliver, groping his way with one hand, and having the other firmly grasped by his companion, ascended with much difficulty the dark and broken stairs: which his conductor mounted with an ease and expedition that showed he was well acquainted with them.

He threw open the door of a back-room, and drew Oliver in after him.

The walls and ceiling of the room were perfectly black with age and dirt. There was a deal table before the fire: upon which were a candle, stuck in a ginger-beer bottle, two or three pewter pots, a loaf and butter, and a plate. In a frying-pan, which was on the fire, and which was secured to the mantelshelf by a string, some sausages were cooking; and standing over them, with a toasting-fork in his hand, was a very old shrivelled Jew, whose villainous-looking and repulsive face was obscured by a quantity of matted red hair. He was dressed in a greasy flannel gown, with his throat bare; and seemed to be dividing his attention between the frying-pan and the clothes-horse, over which a great number of silk handkerchiefs were hanging. Several rough beds made of old sacks, were huddled side by side on the floor. Seated round the table were four or five boys, none older than the Dodger, smoking long clay pipes, and drinking spirits with the air of middle-aged men. These all crowded about their associate as he whispered a few words to the Jew; and then turned round and grinned at Oliver. So did the Jew himself, toasting-fork in hand.

"This is him, Fagin," said Jack Dawkins, "My friend Oliver Twist."

The Jew grinned; and, making a low obeisance to Oliver, took him by the hand, and hoped he should have the honour of his intimate acquaintance. Upon this, the young gentleman with the pipes came round him, and shook both his hands very hard—especially the one in which he held his little bundle. One young gentleman was very anxious to hang up his cap for him; and another was so obliging as to put his hands in his pockets, in order that, as he was very tired, he might not have the trouble of emptying them, himself, when he went to bed. These civilities would probably be extended much farther, but for a liberal exercise of the Jew's toasting-fork on the heads and shoulders of the affectionate youths who offered them.

"We are very glad to see you, Oliver, very," said the Jew. "Dodger, take off the sausages; and draw a tub near the fire for Oliver. Ah, you're a-staring at the pocket-handkerchiefs! eh, my dear. There are a good many of 'em, ain't there? We've just looked 'em out, ready for the wash; that's all, Oliver; that's all. Ha! ha! ha!"

The latter part of this speech, was hailed by a boisterous shout from all the hopeful pupils of the merry old gentleman. In the midst of which they went to supper.

Oliver ate his share, and the Jew then mixed him a glass of hot gin-and-water: telling him he must drink it off directly, because another gentleman wanted the tumbler. Oliver did as he was desired. Immediately afterwards he felt himself gently lifted on to one of the sacks; and then he sunk into a deep sleep.

CHAPTER IX

Containing Further Particulars Concerning the Pleasant Old Gentleman, and His Hopeful Pupils

It was late next morning when Oliver awoke, from a sound, long sleep. There was no other person in the room but the old Jew, who was boiling some coffee in a saucepan for breakfast, and whistling softly to himself as he stirred it round and round, with an iron spoon. He would stop every now and then to listen when there was the least noise below: and when he had satisfied himself, he would go on whistling and stirring again, as before.

Although Oliver had roused himself from sleep, he was not thoroughly awake. There is a drowsy state, between sleeping and waking, when you dream more in five minutes with your eyes half open, and yourself half conscious of everything that is passing around you, than you would in five nights with your eyes fast closed, and your senses wrapt in perfect unconsciousness. At such time, a mortal knows just enough of what his mind is doing, to form some glimmering conception of its mighty powers, its bounding from earth and spurning time and space, when freed from the restraint of its corporeal associate.

Oliver was precisely in this condition. He saw the Jew with his half-closed eyes; heard his low whistling; and recognised the sound of the spoon grating against the saucepan's sides: and yet the self-same senses were mentally engaged, at the same time, in busy action with almost everybody he had ever known.

When the coffee was done, the Jew drew the saucepan to the hob. Standing, then in an irresolute attitude for a few minutes, as if he did not well know how to employ himself, he turned round and looked at Oliver, and called him by his name. He did not answer, and was to all appearances asleep.

After satisfying himself upon this head, the Jew stepped gently to the door: which he fastened. He then drew forth: as it seemed to Oliver, from some trap in the floor: a small box, which he placed carefully on the table. His eyes glistened as he raised the lid, and looked in. Dragging an old chair to the table, he sat down; and took from it a magnificent gold watch, sparkling with jewels.

"Aha!" said the Jew, shrugging up his shoulders, and distorting every feature with a hideous grin. "Clever dogs! Clever dogs! Staunch to the last! Never told the old parson where they were. Never poached upon old Fagin! And why should they? It wouldn't have loosened the knot, or kept the drop up, a minute longer. No, no, no! Fine fellows! Fine fellows!"

With these, and other muttered reflections of the like nature, the Jew once more deposited the watch in its place of safety. At least half a dozen more were severally drawn forth from the same box, and surveyed with equal pleasure; besides rings, brooches, bracelets, and other articles of jewellery, of such magnificent materials, and costly workmanship, that Oliver had no idea, even of their names.

Having replaced these trinkets, the Jew took out another: so small that it lay in the palm of his hand. There seemed to be some very minute inscription on it; for the Jew laid it flat upon the table, and shading it with his hand, pored over it, long and earnestly. At length he put it down, as if despairing of success; and, leaning back in his chair, muttered:

"What a fine thing capital punishment is! Dead men never repent; dead men never bring awkward stories to light. Ah, it's a fine thing for the trade! Five of 'em strung up in a row, and none left to play booty, or turn white-livered!"

As the Jew uttered these words, his bright dark eyes, which had been staring vacantly before him, fell on Oliver's face; the boy's eyes were fixed on his in mute curiousity; and although the recognition was only for an instant—for the briefest space of time that can possibly be conceived—it was enough to show the old man that he had been observed.

He closed the lid of the box with a loud crash; and, laying his hand on a bread knife which was on the table, started furiously up. He trembled very much though; for, even in his terror, Oliver could see that the knife quivered in the air.

"What's that?" said the Jew. "What do you watch me for? Why are you awake? What have you seen? Speak out, boy! Quick—quick! for your life."

"I wasn't able to sleep any longer, sir," replied Oliver, meekly. "I am very sorry if I have disturbed you, sir."

"You were not awake an hour ago?" said the Jew, scowling fiercely on the boy.

"No! No, indeed!" replied Oliver.

"Are you sure?" cried the Jew: with a still fiercer look than before: and a threatening attitude.

"Upon my word I was not, sir," replied Oliver, earnestly. "I was not, indeed, sir."

"Tush, tush, my dear!" said the Jew, abruptly resuming his old manner, and playing with the knife a little, before he laid it down; as if to induce the belief that he had caught it up, in mere sport. "Of course I know that, my dear. I only tried to frighten you. You're a brave boy. Ha! ha! you're a brave boy, Oliver." The Jew rubbed his hands with a chuckle, but glanced uneasily at the box, notwithstanding.

"Did you see any of these pretty things, my dear?" said the Jew, laying his hand upon it after a short pause.

"Yes, sir," replied Oliver.

"Ah!" said the Jew, turning rather pale. "They—they're mine, Oliver; my little property. All I have to live upon, in my old age. The folks call me a miser, my dear. Only a miser; that's all."

Oliver thought the old gentleman must be a decided miser to live in such a dirty place, with so many watches; but, thinking that perhaps his fondness for the Dodger and the other boys, cost him a good deal of money, he only cast a deferential look at the Jew, and asked if he might get up.

"Certainly, my dear, certainly," replied the old gentleman. "Stay. There's a pitcher of water in the corner by the door. Bring it here; and I'll give you a basin to wash in, my dear."

Oliver got up; walked across the room; and stooped for an instant to raise the pitcher. When he turned his head, the box was gone.

He had scarcely washed himself, and made everything tidy, by emptying the basin out of the window, agreeably to the Jew's directions, when the Dodger returned: accompanied by a very sprightly young friend, whom Oliver had seen smoking on the previous night, and who was now formally introduced to him as Charley Bates. The four sat down, to breakfast, on the coffee, and some hot rolls and ham which the Dodger had brought home in the crown of his hat.

"Well," said the Jew, glancing slyly at Oliver, and addressing himself to the Dodger, "I hope you've been at work this morning, my dears?"

"Hard," replied the Dodger.

"As nails," added Charley Bates.

"Good boys, good boys!" said the Jew. "What have you got, Dodger?"

"A couple of pocket-books," replied that young gentleman.

"Lined?" inquired the Jew, with eagerness.

"Pretty well," replied the Dodger, producing two pocket-books; one green, and the other red.

"Not so heavy as they might be," said the Jew, after looking at the insides carefully; "but very neat and nicely made. Ingenious workman, ain't he, Oliver?"

"Very indeed, sir," said Oliver. At which Mr. Charles Bates laughed uproariously; very much to the amazement of Oliver, who saw nothing to laugh at, in anything that had passed.

"And what have you got, my dear?" said Fagin to Charley Bates.

"Wipes," replied Master Bates; at the same time producing four pocket-handkerchiefs.

"Well," said the Jew, inspecting them closely; "they're very good ones, very. You haven't marked them well, though, Charley; so the marks shall be picked out with a needle, and we'll teach Oliver how to do it. Shall us, Oliver, eh? Ha! ha! ha!"

"If you please, sir," said Oliver.

"You'd like to be able to make pocket-handkerchiefs as easy as Charley Bates, wouldn't you, my dear?" said the Jew.

"Very much, indeed, if you'll teach me, sir," replied Oliver.

Master Bates saw something so exquisitely ludicrous in this reply, that he burst into another laugh; which laugh, meeting the coffee he was drinking, and carrying it down some wrong channel, very nearly terminated in his premature suffocation.

"He is so jolly green!" said Charley when he recovered, as an apology to the company for his unpolite behaviour.

The Dodger said nothing, but he smoothed Oliver's hair over his eyes, and said he'd know better, by and by; upon which the old gentleman, observing Oliver's colour mounting, changed the subject by asking whether there had been much of a crowd at the execution that morning? This made him wonder more and more; for it was plain from the replies of the two boys that they had both been there; and Oliver naturally wondered how they could possibly have found time to be so very industrious.

When the breakfast was cleared away; the merry old gentleman and the two boys played at a very curious and uncommon game, which was performed in this way. The merry old gentleman, placing a snuff-box in one pocket of his trousers, a note-case in the other, and a watch in his waistcoat pocket, with a guard-chain round his neck, and sticking a mock diamond pin in his shirt: buttoned his coat tight round him, and putting his spectacle-case and handkerchief in his pockets, trotted up and down the room with a stick, in imitation of the manner in which old gentlemen walk about the streets any hour in the day. Sometimes he stopped at the fire-place, and sometimes at the door, making believe that he was staring with all his might into shop-windows. At such times, he would look constantly round him, for fear of thieves, and would keep slapping all his pockets in turn, to see that he hadn't lost anything, in such a very funny and natural manner, that Oliver laughed till the tears ran down his face. All this time, the two boys followed him closely about: getting out of his sight, so nimbly, every time he turned round, that it was impossible to follow their motions. At last, the Dodger trod upon his toes, or ran upon his boot accidently, while Charley Bates stumbled up against him behind; and in that one moment they took from him, with the most extraordinary rapidity, snuff-box, note-case, watch-guard, chain, shirt-pin, pocket-handkerchief, even the spectacle-case. If the old gentleman felt a hand in any one of his pockets, he cried out where it was; and then the game began all over again.

When this game had been played a great many times, a couple of young ladies called to see the young gentleman; one of whom was named Bet, and the other Nancy. They wore a good deal of hair, not very neatly turned up behind, and were rather untidy about the shoes and stockings. They were not exactly pretty, perhaps; but they had a great deal of colour in their faces, and looked quite stout and hearty. Being remarkably free and agreeable in their manners, Oliver thought them very nice girls indeed. As there is no doubt they were.

The visitors stopped a long time. Spirits were produced, in consequence of one of the young ladies complaining of a coldness in her inside; and the conversation took a very convivial and improving turn. At length, Charley Bates expressed his opinion that it was time to pad the hoof. This, it occurred to Oliver, must be French for going out; for directly afterwards, the Dodger, and Charley, and the two young ladies, went away together, having been kindly furnished by the amiable old Jew with money to spend.

"There, my dear," said Fagin. "That's a pleasant life, isn't it? They have gone out for the day."

"Have they done work, sir?" inquired Oliver.

"Yes," said the Jew; "that is, unless they should unexpectedly come across any, when they are out; and they won't neglect it, if they do, my dear, depend upon it. Make 'em your models, my dear. Make 'em your models," tapping the fire-shovel on the hearth to add force to his words; "do everything they bid you, and take their advice in all matters—especially the Dodger's, my dear. He'll be a great man himself, and will make you one too, if you take pattern by him.—Is my handkerchief hanging out of my pocket, my dear?" said the Jew, stopping short.

"Yes, sir," said Oliver.

"See if you can take it out, without my feeling it; as you saw them do, when we were at play this morning."

Oliver held up the bottom of the pocket with one hand, as he had seen the Dodger hold it, and drew the handkerchief lightly out of it with the other.

"Is it gone?" cried the Jew.

"Here it is, sir," said Oliver, showing it in his hand.

"You're a clever boy, my dear," said the playful old gentleman, patting Oliver on the head approvingly. "I never saw a sharper lad. Here's a shilling for you. If you go on, in this way, you'll be the greatest man of the time. And now come here, and I'll show you how to take the marks out of the handkerchiefs."

Oliver wondered what picking the old gentleman's pocket in play, had to do with his chances of being a great man. But, thinking that the Jew, being so much his senior, must know best, he followed him quietly to the table, and was soon deeply involved in his new study.

CHAPTER X

Oliver Becomes Better Acquainted With the Characters of His New Associates; and Purchases Experience at a High Price. Being a Short, but Very Important Chapter, in This History

For many days, Oliver remained in the Jew's room, picking the marks out of the pocket-handkerchief, (of which a great number were brought home,) and sometimes taking part in the game already described: which the two boys and the Jew played, regularly, every morning. At length, he began to languish for fresh air, and took many occasions of earnestly entreating the old gentleman to allow him to go out to work with his two companions.

Oliver was rendered the more anxious to be actively employed, by what he had seen of the stern morality of the old gentleman's character. Whenever the Dodger or Charley Bates came home at night, empty-handed, he would expatiate with great vehemence on the misery of idle and lazy habits; and would enforce upon them the necessity of an active life, by sending them supperless to bed. On one occasion, indeed, he even went so far as to knock them both down a flight of stairs; but this was carrying out his virtuous precepts to an unusual extent.

At length, one morning, Oliver obtained the permission he had so eagerly sought. There had been no handkerchiefs to work upon, for two or three days, and the dinners had been rather meagre. Perhaps these were reasons for the old gentleman's giving his assent; but, whether they were or no, he told Oliver he might go, and placed him under the joint guardianship of Charley Bates, and his friend the Dodger.

The three boys sallied out; the Dodger with his coat-sleeves tucked up, and his hat cocked, as usual; Master Bates sauntering along with his hands in his pockets; and Oliver between them, wondering where they were going, and what branch of manufacture he would be instructed in, first.

The pace at which they went, was such a very lazy, ill-looking saunter, that Oliver soon began to think his companions were going to deceive the old gentleman, by not going to work at all. The Dodger had a vicious propensity, too, of pulling the caps from the heads of small boys and tossing them down areas; while Charley Bates exhibited some very loose notions concerning the rights of property, by pilfering divers apples and onions from the stalls at the kennel sides, and thrusting them into pockets which were so surprisingly capacious, that they seemed to undermine his whole suit of clothes in every direction. These things looked so bad, that Oliver was on the point of declaring his intention of seeking his way back, in the best way he could; when his thoughts were suddenly directed into another channel, by a very mysterious change of behaviour on the part of the Dodger.

They were just emerging from a narrow court not far from the open square in Clerkenwell, which is yet called, by some strange perversion of terms, "The Green': when the Dodger made a sudden stop; and, laying his finger on his lip, drew his companions back again, with the greatest caution and circumspection.

"What's the matter?" demanded Oliver.

"Hush!" replied the Dodger. "Do you see that old cove at the book-stall?"

"The old gentleman over the way?" said Oliver. "Yes, I see him."

"He'll do," said the Dodger.

"A prime plant," observed Master Charley Bates.

Oliver looked from one to the other, with the greatest surprise; but he was not permitted to make any inquiries; for the two boys walked stealthily across the road, and slunk close behind the old gentleman towards whom his attention had been directed. Oliver walked a few paces after them; and, not knowing whether to advance or retire, stood looking on in silent amazement.

The old gentleman was a very respectable-looking personage, with a powdered head and gold spectacles. He was dressed in a bottle-green coat with a black velvet collar; wore white trousers; and carried a smart bamboo cane under his arm. He had taken up a book from the stall, and there he stood, reading away, as hard as if he were in his elbow-chair, in his own study. It is very possible that he fancied himself there, indeed; for it was plain, from his abstraction, that he saw not the book-stall, nor the street, nor the boys, nor, in short, anything but the book itself: which he was reading straight through: turning over the leaf when he got to the bottom of a page, beginning at the top line of the next one, and going regularly on, with the greatest interest and eagerness.

What was Oliver's horror and alarm as he stood a few paces off, looking on with his eyelids as wide open as they would possibly go, to see the Dodger plunge his hand into the old gentleman's pocket, and draw from thence a handkerchief! To see him hand the same to Charley Bates; and finally to behold them, both running away round the corner at full speed!

In an instant the whole mystery of the handkerchiefs, and the watches, and the jewels, and the Jew, rushed upon the boy's mind.

He stood, for a moment, with the blood so tingling through all his veins from terror, that he felt as if he were in a burning fire; then, confused and frightened, he took to his heels; and, not knowing what he did, made off as fast as he could lay his feet to the ground.

This was all done in a minute's space. In the very instant when Oliver began to run, the old gentleman, putting his hand to his pocket, and missing his handkerchief, turned sharp round. Seeing the boy scudding away at such a rapid pace, he very naturally concluded him to be the depredator; and shouting "Stop thief!" with all his might, made off after him, book in hand.

But the old gentleman was not the only person who raised the hue-and-cry. The Dodger and Master Bates, unwilling to attract public attention by running down the open street, had merely retired into the very first doorway round the corner. They no sooner heard the cry, and saw Oliver running, than, guessing exactly how the matter stood, they issued forth with great promptitude; and, shouting "Stop thief!" too, joined in the pursuit like good citizens.

Although Oliver had been brought up by philosophers, he was not theoretically acquainted with the beautiful axiom that self-preservation is the first law of nature. If he had been, perhaps he would have been prepared for this. Not being prepared, however, it alarmed him the more; so away he went like the wind, with the old gentleman and the two boys roaring and shouting behind him.

"Stop thief! Stop thief!" There is a magic in the sound. The tradesman leaves his counter, and the car-man his waggon; the butcher throws down his tray; the baker his basket; the milkman his pail; the errand-boy his parcels; the school-boy his marbles; the paviour his pickaxe; the child his battledore. Away they run, pell-mell, helter-skelter, slap-dash: tearing, yelling, screaming, knocking down the passengers as they turn the corners, rousing up the dogs, and astonishing the fowls: and streets, squares, and courts, re-echo with the sound.

"Stop thief! Stop thief!" The cry is taken up by a hundred voices, and the crowd accumulate at every turning. Away they fly, splashing through the mud, and rattling along the pavements: up go the windows, out run the people, onward bear the mob, a whole audience desert Punch in the very thickest of the plot, and, joining the rushing throng, swell the shout, and lend fresh vigour to the cry, "Stop thief! Stop thief!"

"Stop thief! Stop thief!" There is a passion for hunting something deeply implanted in the human breast. One wretched breathless child, panting with exhaustion; terror in his looks; agony in his eyes; large drops of perspiration streaming down his face; strains every nerve to make head upon his pursuers; and as they follow on his track, and gain upon him every instant, they hail his decreasing strength with joy. "Stop thief!" Ay, stop him for God's sake, were it only in mercy!

Stopped at last! A clever blow. He is down upon the pavement; and the crowd eagerly gather round him: each new comer, jostling and struggling with the others to catch a glimpse. "Stand aside!" "Give him a little air!" "Nonsense! he don't deserve it." "Where's the gentleman?" "Here his is, coming down the street." "Make room there for the gentleman!" "Is this the boy, sir!" "Yes."

Oliver lay, covered with mud and dust, and bleeding from the mouth, looking wildly round upon the heap of faces that surrounded him, when the old gentleman was officiously dragged and pushed into the circle by the foremost of the pursuers.

"Yes," said the gentleman, "I am afraid it is the boy."

"Afraid!" murmured the crowd. "That's a good 'un!"

"Poor fellow!" said the gentleman, "he has hurt himself."

"I did that, sir," said a great lubberly fellow, stepping forward; "and preciously I cut my knuckle agin' his mouth. I stopped him, sir."

The follow touched his hat with a grin, expecting something for his pains; but, the old gentleman, eyeing him with an expression of dislike, look anxiously round, as if he contemplated running away himself: which it is very possible he might have attempted to do, and thus have afforded another chase, had not a police officer (who is generally the last person to arrive in such cases) at that moment made his way through the crowd, and seized Oliver by the collar.

"Come, get up," said the man, roughly.

"It wasn't me indeed, sir. Indeed, indeed, it was two other boys," said Oliver, clasping his hands passionately, and looking round. "They are here somewhere."

"Oh no, they ain't," said the officer. He meant this to be ironical, but it was true besides; for the Dodger and Charley Bates had filed off down the first convenient court they came to.

"Come, get up!"

"Don't hurt him," said the old gentleman, compassionately.

"Oh no, I won't hurt him," replied the officer, tearing his jacket half off his back, in proof thereof. "Come, I know you; it won't do. Will you stand upon your legs, you young devil?"

Oliver, who could hardly stand, made a shift to raise himself on his feet, and was at once lugged along the streets by the jacket-collar, at a rapid pace. The gentleman walked on with them by the officer's side; and as many of the crowd as could achieve the feat, got a little ahead, and stared back at Oliver from time to time. The boys shouted in triumph; and on they went.

CHAPTER XI

Treats of Mr. Fang the Police Magistrate; and Furnishes a Slight Specimen of His Mode of Administering Justice

The offence had been committed within the district, and indeed in the immediate neighborhood of, a very notorious metropolitan police office. The crowd had only the satisfaction of accompanying Oliver through two or three streets, and down a place called Mutton Hill, when he was led beneath a low archway, and up a dirty court, into this dispensary of summary justice, by the back way. It was a small paved yard into which they turned; and here they encountered a stout man with a bunch of whiskers on his face, and a bunch of keys in his hand.

"What's the matter now?" said the man carelessly.

"A young fogle-hunter," replied the man who had Oliver in charge.

"Are you the party that's been robbed, sir?" inquired the man with the keys.

"Yes, I am," replied the old gentleman; "but I am not sure that this boy actually took the handkerchief. I—I would rather not press the case."

"Must go before the magistrate now, sir," replied the man. "His worship will be disengaged in half a minute. Now, young gallows!"

This was an invitation for Oliver to enter through a door which he unlocked as he spoke, and which led into a stone cell. Here he was searched; and nothing being found upon him, locked up.

This cell was in shape and size something like an area cellar, only not so light. It was most intolerably dirty; for it was Monday morning; and it had been tenanted by six drunken people, who had been locked up, elsewhere, since Saturday night. But this is little. In our station-houses, men and women are every night confined on the most trivial charges—the word is worth noting—in dungeons, compared with which, those in Newgate, occupied by the most atrocious felons, tried, found guilty, and under sentence of death, are palaces. Let any one who doubts this, compare the two.

The old gentleman looked almost as rueful as Oliver when the key grated in the lock. He turned with a sigh to the book, which had been the innocent cause of all this disturbance.

"There is something in that boy's face," said the old gentleman to himself as he walked slowly away, tapping his chin with the cover of the book, in a thoughtful manner; "something that touches and interests me. Can he be innocent? He looked like—Bye the bye," exclaimed the old gentleman, halting very abruptly, and staring up into the sky, "Bless my soul!—where have I seen something like that look before?"

After musing for some minutes, the old gentleman walked, with the same meditative face, into a back anteroom opening from the yard; and there, retiring into a corner, called up before his mind's eye a vast amphitheatre of faces over which a dusky curtain had hung for many years. "No," said the old gentleman, shaking his head; "it must be imagination."

He wandered over them again. He had called them into view, and it was not easy to replace the shroud that had so long concealed them. There were the faces of friends, and foes, and of many that had been almost strangers peering intrusively from the crowd; there were the faces of young and blooming girls that were now old women; there were faces that the grave had changed and closed upon, but which the mind, superior to its power, still dressed in their old freshness and beauty, calling back the lustre of the eyes, the brightness of the smile, the beaming of the soul through its mask of clay, and whispering of beauty beyond the tomb, changed but to be heightened, and taken from earth only to be set up as a light, to shed a soft and gentle glow upon the path to Heaven.

But the old gentleman could recall no one countenance of which Oliver's features bore a trace. So, he heaved a sigh over the recollections he awakened; and being, happily for himself, an absent old gentleman, buried them again in the pages of the musty book.

He was roused by a touch on the shoulder, and a request from the man with the keys to follow him into the office. He closed his book hastily; and was at once ushered into the imposing presence of the renowned Mr. Fang.

The office was a front parlour, with a panelled wall. Mr. Fang sat behind a bar, at the upper end; and on one side the door was a sort of wooden pen in which poor little Oliver was already deposited; trembling very much at the awfulness of the scene.

Mr. Fang was a lean, long-backed, stiff-necked, middle-sized man, with no great quantity of hair, and what he had, growing on the back and sides of his head. His face was stern, and much flushed. If he were really not in the habit of drinking rather more than was exactly good for him, he might have brought action against his countenance for libel, and have recovered heavy damages.

The old gentleman bowed respectfully; and advancing to the magistrate's desk, said, suiting the action to the word, "That is my name and address, sir." He then withdrew a pace or two; and, with another polite and gentlemanly inclination of the head, waited to be questioned.

Now, it so happened that Mr. Fang was at that moment perusing a leading article in a newspaper of the morning, adverting to some recent decision of his, and commending him, for the three hundred and fiftieth time, to the special and particular notice of the Secretary of State for the Home Department. He was out of temper; and he looked up with an angry scowl.

"Who are you?" said Mr. Fang.

The old gentleman pointed, with some surprise, to his card.

"Officer!" said Mr. Fang, tossing the card contemptuously away with the newspaper. "Who is this fellow?"

"My name, sir," said the old gentleman, speaking like a gentleman, "my name, sir, is Brownlow. Permit me to inquire the name of the magistrate who offers a gratuitous and unprovoked insult to a respectable person, under the protection of the bench.' Saying this, Mr. Brownlow looked around the office as if in search of some person who would afford him the required information.

"Officer!" said Mr. Fang, throwing the paper on one side, "what's this fellow charged with?"

"He's not charged at all, your worship," replied the officer. "He appears against this boy, your worship."

His worship knew this perfectly well; but it was a good annoyance, and a safe one.

"Appears against the boy, does he?" said Mr. Fang, surveying Mr. Brownlow contemptuously from head to foot. "Swear him!"

"Before I am sworn, I must beg to say one word," said Mr. Brownlow; "and that is, that I really never, without actual experience, could have believed—"

"Hold your tongue, sir!" said Mr. Fang, peremptorily.

"I will not, sir!" replied the old gentleman.

"Hold your tongue this instant, or I'll have you turned out of the office!" said Mr. Fang. "You're an insolent impertinent fellow. How dare you bully a magistrate!"

"What!" exclaimed the old gentleman, reddening.

"Swear this person!" said Fang to the clerk. "I'll not hear another word. Swear him."

Mr. Brownlow's indignation was greatly roused; but reflecting perhaps, that he might only injure the boy by giving vent to it, he suppressed his feelings and submitted to be sworn at once.

"Now," said Fang, "what's the charge against this boy? What have you got to say, sir?"

"I was standing at a bookstall—" Mr. Brownlow began.

"Hold your tongue, sir," said Mr. Fang. "Policeman! Where's the policeman? Here, swear this policeman. Now, policeman, what is this?"

The policeman, with becoming humility, related how he had taken the charge; how he had searched Oliver, and found nothing on his person; and how that was all he knew about it.

"Are there any witnesses?" inquired Mr. Fang.

"None, your worship," replied the policeman.

Mr. Fang sat silent for some minutes, and then, turning round to the prosecutor, said in a towering passion.

"Do you mean to state what your complaint against this boy is, man, or do you not? You have been sworn. Now, if you stand there, refusing to give evidence, I'll punish you for disrespect to the bench; I will, by—"

By what, or by whom, nobody knows, for the clerk and jailor coughed very loud, just at the right moment; and the former dropped a heavy book upon the floor, thus preventing the word from being heard—accidently, of course.

With many interruptions, and repeated insults, Mr. Brownlow contrived to state his case; observing that, in the surprise of the moment, he had run after the boy because he had saw him running away; and expressing his hope that, if the magistrate should believe him, although not actually the thief, to be connected with the thieves, he would deal as leniently with him as justice would allow.

"He has been hurt already," said the old gentleman in conclusion. "And I fear," he added, with great energy, looking towards the bar, "I really fear that he is ill."

"Oh! yes, I dare say!" said Mr. Fang, with a sneer. "Come, none of your tricks here, you young vagabond; they won't do. What's your name?"

Oliver tried to reply but his tongue failed him. He was deadly pale; and the whole place seemed turning round and round.

"What's your name, you hardened scoundrel?" demanded Mr. Fang. "Officer, what's his name?"

This was addressed to a bluff old fellow, in a striped waistcoat, who was standing by the bar. He bent over Oliver, and repeated the inquiry; but finding him really incapable of understanding the question; and knowing that his not replying would only infuriate the magistrate the more, and add to the severity of his sentence; he hazarded a guess.

"He says his name's Tom White, your worship," said the kind-hearted thief-taker.

"Oh, he won't speak out, won't he?" said Fang. "Very well, very well. Where does he live?"

"Where he can, your worship," replied the officer; again pretending to receive Oliver's answer.

"Has he any parents?" inquired Mr. Fang.

"He says they died in his infancy, your worship," replied the officer: hazarding the usual reply.

At this point of the inquiry, Oliver raised his head; and, looking round with imploring eyes, murmured a feeble prayer for a draught of water.

"Stuff and nonsense!" said Mr. Fang: "don't try to make a fool of me."

"I think he really is ill, your worship," remonstrated the officer.

"I know better," said Mr. Fang.

"Take care of him, officer," said the old gentleman, raising his hands instinctively; "he'll fall down."

"Stand away, officer," cried Fang; "let him, if he likes."

Oliver availed himself of the kind permission, and fell to the floor in a fainting fit. The men in the office looked at each other, but no one dared to stir.

"I knew he was shamming," said Fang, as if this were incontestable proof of the fact. "Let him lie there; he'll soon be tired of that."

"How do you propose to deal with the case, sir?" inquired the clerk in a low voice.

"Summarily," replied Mr. Fang. "He stands committed for three months—hard labour of course. Clear the office."

The door was opened for this purpose, and a couple of men were preparing to carry the insensible boy to his cell; when an elderly man of decent but poor appearance, clad in an old suit of black, rushed hastily into the office, and advanced towards the bench.

"Stop, stop! don't take him away! For Heaven's sake stop a moment!" cried the new comer, breathless with haste.

Although the presiding Genii in such an office as this, exercise a summary and arbitrary power over the liberties, the good name, the character, almost the lives, of Her Majesty's subjects, expecially of the poorer class; and although, within such walls, enough fantastic tricks are daily played to make the angels blind with weeping; they are closed to the public, save through the medium of the daily press. [Footnote: Or were virtually, then.] Mr. Fang was consequently not a little indignant to see an unbidden guest enter in such irreverent disorder.

"What is this? Who is this? Turn this man out. Clear the office!" cried Mr. Fang.

"I will speak," cried the man; "I will not be turned out. I saw it all. I keep the bookstall. I demand to be sworn. I will not be put down. Mr. Fang, you must hear me. You must not refuse, sir."

· The man was right. His manner was determined; and the matter was growing rather too serious to be hushed up.

"Swear the man," growled Mr. Fang, with a very ill grace. "Now, man, what have you got to say?"

"This," said the man: "I saw three boys: two others and the prisoner here: loitering on the opposite side of the way, when this gentleman was reading. The robbery was committed by another boy. I saw it done; and I saw that this boy was perfectly amazed and stupified by it." Having by this time recovered a little breath, the worthy bookstall keeper proceeded to relate, in a more coherent manner the exact circumstances of the robbery.

"Why didn't you come here before?" said Fang, after a pause.

"I hadn't a soul to mind the shop," replied the man. "Everybody who could have helped me, had joined in the pursuit. I could get nobody till five minutes ago; and I've run here all the way."

"The prosecutor was reading, was he?" inquired Fang, after another pause.

"Yes," replied the man. "The very book he has in his hand."

"Oh, that book, eh?" said Fang. "Is it paid for?"

"No, it is not," replied the man, with a smile.

"Dear me, I forgot all about it!" exclaimed the absent old gentleman, innocently.

"A nice person to prefer a charge against a poor boy!" said Fang, with a comical effort to look humane. "I consider, sir, that you have obtained possession of that book, under very suspicious and disreputable circumstances; and you may think yourself very fortunate that the owner of the property declines to prosecute. Let this be a lesson to you, my man, or the law will overtake you yet. The boy is discharged. Clear the office!"

"D—n me!" cried the old gentleman, bursting out with the rage he had kept down so long, "d—n me! I'll—"

"Clear the office!" said the magistrate. "Officers, do you hear? Clear the office!"

The mandate was obeyed; and the indignant Mr. Brownlow was conveyed out, with the book in one hand, and the bamboo cane in the other: in a perfect phrenzy of rage and defiance. He reached the yard; and his passion vanished in a moment. Little Oliver Twist lay on his back on the pavement, with his shirt unbuttoned, and his temples bathed with water; his face a deadly white; and a cold tremble convulsing his whole frame.

"Poor boy, poor boy!" said Mr. Brownlow, bending over him. "Call a coach, somebody, pray. Directly!"

A coach was obtained, and Oliver having been carefully laid on the seat, the old gentleman got in and sat himself on the other.

"May I accompany you?" said the book-stall keeper, looking in.

"Bless me, yes, my dear sir," said Mr. Brownlow quickly. "I forgot you. Dear, dear! I have this unhappy book still! Jump in. Poor fellow! There's no time to lose."

The book-stall keeper got into the coach; and away they drove.

CHAPTER XII

*In Which Oliver Is Taken Better Care of Than He Ever Was Before.
And in Which the Narrative Reverts to the Merry Old Gentleman
and His Youthful Friends*

The coach rattled away, over nearly the same ground as that which Oliver had traversed when he first entered London in company with the Dodger; and, turning a different way when it reached the Angel at Islington, stopped at length before a neat house, in a quiet shady street near Pentonville. Here, a bed was prepared, without loss of time, in which Mr. Brownlow saw his young charge carefully and comfortably deposited; and here, he was tended with a kindness and solicitude that knew no bounds.

But, for many days, Oliver remained insensible to all the goodness of his new friends. The sun rose and sank, and rose and sank again, and many times after that; and still the boy lay stretched on his uneasy bed, dwindling away beneath the dry and wasting heat of fever. The worm does not work more surely on the dead body, than does this slow creeping fire upon the living frame.

Weak, and thin, and pallid, he awoke at last from what seemed to have been a long and troubled dream. Feebly raising himself in the bed, with his head resting on his trembling arm, he looked anxiously around.

"What room is this? Where have I been brought to?" said Oliver. "This is not the place I went to sleep in."

He uttered these words in a feeble voice, being very faint and weak; but they were overheard at once. The curtain at the bed's head was hastily drawn back, and a motherly old lady, very neatly and precisely dressed, rose as she undrew it, from an arm-chair close by, in which she had been sitting at needle-work.

"Hush, my dear," said the old lady softly. "You must be very quiet, or you will be ill again; and you have been very bad,—as bad as bad could be, pretty nigh. Lie down again; there's a dear!" With those words, the old lady very gently placed Oliver's head upon the pillow; and, smoothing back his hair from his forehead, looked so kindly and loving in his face, that he could not help placing his little withered hand in hers, and drawing it round his neck.

"Save us!" said the old lady, with tears in her eyes. "What a grateful little dear it is. Pretty creetur! What would his mother feel if she had sat by him as I have, and could see him now!"

"Perhaps she does see me," whispered Oliver, folding his hands together; "perhaps she has sat by me. I almost feel as if she had."

"That was the fever, my dear," said the old lady mildly.

"I suppose it was," replied Oliver, "because heaven is a long way off; and they are too happy there, to come down to the bedside of a poor boy. But if she knew I was ill, she must have pitied me, even there; for she was very ill herself before she died. She can't know anything about me though," added Oliver after a moment's silence. "If she had seen me hurt, it would have made her sorrowful; and her face has always looked sweet and happy, when I have dreamed of her."

The old lady made no reply to this; but wiping her eyes first, and her spectacles, which lay on the counterpane, afterwards, as if they were part and parcel of those features, brought some cool stuff for Oliver to drink; and then, patting him on the cheek, told him he must lie very quiet, or he would be ill again.

So, Oliver kept very still; partly because he was anxious to obey the kind old lady in all things; and partly, to tell the truth, because he was completely exhausted with what he had already said. He soon fell into a gentle doze, from which he was awakened by the light of a candle: which, being brought near the bed, showed him a gentleman with a very large and loud-ticking gold watch in his hand, who felt his pulse, and said he was a great deal better.

"You are a great deal better, are you not, my dear?" said the gentleman.

"Yes, thank you, sir," replied Oliver.

"Yes, I know you are," said the gentleman: "You're hungry too, an't you?"

"No, sir," answered Oliver.

"Hem!" said the gentleman. "No, I know you're not. He is not hungry, Mrs. Bedwin," said the gentleman: looking very wise.

The old lady made a respectful inclination of the head, which seemed to say that she thought the doctor was a very clever man. The doctor appeared much of the same opinion himself.

"You feel sleepy, don't you, my dear?" said the doctor.

"No, sir," replied Oliver.

"No," said the doctor, with a very shrewd and satisfied look. "You're not sleepy. Nor thirsty. Are you?"

"Yes, sir, rather thirsty," answered Oliver.

"Just as I expected, Mrs. Bedwin," said the doctor. "It's very natural that he should be thirsty. You may give him a little tea, ma'am, and some dry toast without any butter. Don't keep him too warm, ma'am; but be careful that you don't let him be too cold; will you have the goodness?"

The old lady dropped a curtsey. The doctor, after tasting the cool stuff, and expressing a qualified approval of it, hurried away: his boots creaking in a very important and wealthy manner as he went downstairs.

Oliver dozed off again, soon after this; when he awoke, it was nearly twelve o'clock. The old lady tenderly bade him good-night shortly afterwards, and left him in charge of a fat old woman who had just come: bringing with her, in a little bundle, a small Prayer Book and a large nightcap. Putting the latter on her head and the former on the table, the old woman, after telling Oliver that she had come to sit up with him, drew her chair close to the fire and went off into a series of short naps, chequered at frequent intervals with sundry tumblings forward, and divers moans and chokings. These, however, had no worse effect than causing her to rub her nose very hard, and then fall asleep again.

And thus the night crept slowly on. Oliver lay awake for some time, counting the little circles of light which the reflection of the rushlight-shade threw upon the ceiling; or tracing with his languid eyes the intricate pattern of the paper on the wall. The darkness and the deep stillness of the room were very solemn; as they brought into the boy's mind the thought that death had been hovering there, for many days and nights, and might yet fill it with the gloom and dread of his awful presence, he turned his face upon the pillow, and fervently prayed to Heaven.

Gradually, he fell into that deep tranquil sleep which ease from recent suffering alone imparts; that calm and peaceful rest which it is pain to wake from. Who, if this were death, would be roused again to all the struggles and turmoils of life; to all its cares for the present; its anxieties for the future; more than all, its weary recollections of the past!

It had been bright day, for hours, when Oliver opened his eyes; he felt cheerful and happy. The crisis of the disease was safely past. He belonged to the world again.

In three days' time he was able to sit in an easy-chair, well propped up with pillows; and, as he was still too weak to walk, Mrs. Bedwin had him carried downstairs into the little housekeeper's room, which belonged to her. Having him set, here, by the fire-side, the good old lady sat herself down too; and, being in a state of considerable delight at seeing him so much better, forthwith began to cry most violently.

"Never mind me, my dear," said the old lady; "I'm only having a regular good cry. There; it's all over now; and I'm quite comfortable."

"You're very, very kind to me, ma'am," said Oliver.

"Well, never you mind that, my dear," said the old lady; "that's got nothing to do with your broth; and it's full time you had it; for the doctor says Mr. Brownlow may come in to see you this morning; and we must get up our best looks, because the better we look, the more he'll be pleased." And with this, the old lady applied herself to warming up, in a little saucepan, a basin full of broth: strong enough, Oliver thought, to furnish an ample dinner, when reduced to the regulation strength, for three hundred and fifty paupers, at the lowest computation.

"Are you fond of pictures, dear?" inquired the old lady, seeing that Oliver had fixed his eyes, most intently, on a portrait which hung against the wall; just opposite his chair.

"I don't quite know, ma'am," said Oliver, without taking his eyes from the canvas; "I have seen so few that I hardly know. What a beautiful, mild face that lady's is!"

"Ah!" said the old lady, "painters always make ladies out prettier than they are, or they wouldn't get any custom, child. The man that invented the machine for taking likenesses might have known that would never succeed; it's a deal too honest. A deal," said the old lady, laughing very heartily at her own acuteness.

"Is—is that a likeness, ma'am?" said Oliver.

"Yes," said the old lady, looking up for a moment from the broth; "that's a portrait."

"Whose, ma'am?" asked Oliver.

"Why, really, my dear, I don't know," answered the old lady in a good-humoured manner. "It's not a likeness of anybody that you or I know, I expect. It seems to strike your fancy, dear."

"It is so pretty," replied Oliver.

"Why, sure you're not afraid of it?" said the old lady: observing in great surprise, the look of awe with which the child regarded the painting.

"Oh no, no," returned Oliver quickly; "but the eyes look so sorrowful; and where I sit, they seem fixed upon me. It makes my heart beat," added Oliver in a low voice, "as if it was alive, and wanted to speak to me, but couldn't."

"Lord save us!" exclaimed the old lady, starting; "don't talk in that way, child. You're weak and nervous after your illness. Let me wheel your chair round to the other side; and then you won't see it. There!" said the old lady, suiting the action to the word; "you don't see it now, at all events."

Oliver did see it in his mind's eye as distinctly as if he had not altered his position; but he thought it better not to worry the kind old lady; so he smiled gently when she looked at him; and Mrs. Bedwin, satisfied that he felt more comfortable, salted and broke bits of toasted bread into the broth, with all the bustle befitting so solemn a preparation. Oliver got through it with extraordinary expedition. He had scarcely swallowed the last spoonful, when there came a soft rap at the door. "Come in," said the old lady; and in walked Mr. Brownlow.

Now, the old gentleman came in as brisk as need be; but, he had no sooner raised his spectacles on his forehead, and thrust his hands behind the skirts of his dressing-gown to take a good long look at Oliver, than his countenance underwent a very great variety of odd contortions. Oliver looked very worn and shadowy from sickness, and made an ineffectual attempt to stand up, out of respect to his benefactor, which terminated in his sinking back into the chair again; and the fact is, if the truth must be told, that Mr. Brownlow's heart, being large enough for any six ordinary old gentlemen of humane disposition, forced a supply of tears into his eyes, by some hydraulic process which we are not sufficiently philosophical to be in a condition to explain.

"Poor boy, poor boy!" said Mr. Brownlow, clearing his throat. "I'm rather hoarse this morning, Mrs. Bedwin. I'm afraid I have caught cold."

"I hope not, sir," said Mrs. Bedwin. "Everything you have had, has been well aired, sir."

"I don't know, Bedwin. I don't know," said Mr. Brownlow; "I rather think I had a damp napkin at dinner-time yesterday; but never mind that. How do you feel, my dear?"

"Very happy, sir," replied Oliver. "And very grateful indeed, sir, for your goodness to me."

"Good by," said Mr. Brownlow, stoutly. "Have you given him any nourishment, Bedwin? Any slops, eh?"

"He has just had a basin of beautiful strong broth, sir," replied Mrs. Bedwin: drawing herself up slightly, and laying strong emphasis on the last word: to intimate that between slops, and broth will compounded, there existed no affinity or connection whatsoever.

"Ugh!" said Mr. Brownlow, with a slight shudder; "a couple of glasses of port wine would have done him a great deal more good. Wouldn't they, Tom White, eh?"

"My name is Oliver, sir," replied the little invalid: with a look of great astonishment.

"Oliver," said Mr. Brownlow; "Oliver what? Oliver White, eh?"

"No, sir, Twist, Oliver Twist."

"Queer name!" said the old gentleman. "What made you tell the magistrate your name was White?"

"I never told him so, sir," returned Oliver in amazement.

This sounded so like a falsehood, that the old gentleman looked somewhat sternly in Oliver's face. It was impossible to doubt him; there was truth in every one of its thin and sharpened lineaments.

"Some mistake," said Mr. Brownlow. But, although his motive for looking steadily at Oliver no longer existed, the old idea of the resemblance between his features and some familiar face came upon him so strongly, that he could not withdraw his gaze.

"I hope you are not angry with me, sir?" said Oliver, raising his eyes beseechingly.

"No, no," replied the old gentleman. "Why! what's this? Bedwin, look there!"

As he spoke, he pointed hastily to the picture over Oliver's head, and then to the boy's face. There was its living copy. The eyes, the head, the mouth; every feature was the same. The expression was, for the instant, so precisely alike, that the minutest line seemed copied with startling accuracy!

Oliver knew not the cause of this sudden exclamation; for, not being strong enough to bear the start it gave him, he fainted away. A weakness on his part, which affords the narrative an opportunity of relieving the reader from suspense, in behalf of the two young pupils of the Merry Old Gentleman; and of recording—

That when the Dodger, and his accomplished friend Master Bates, joined in the hue-and-cry which was raised at Oliver's heels, in consequence of their executing an illegal conveyance of Mr. Brownlow's personal property, as has been already described, they were actuated by a very laudable and becoming regard for themselves; and forasmuch as the freedom of the subject and the liberty of the individual are among the first and proudest boasts of a true-hearted Englishman, so, I need hardly beg the reader to observe, that this action should tend to exalt them in the opinion of all public and patriotic men, in almost as great a degree as this strong proof of their anxiety for their own preservation and safety goes to corroborate and confirm the little code of laws which certain profound and sound-judging philosophers have laid down as the main-springs of all Nature's deeds and actions: the said philosophers very wisely reducing the good lady's proceedings to matters of maxim and theory: and, by a very neat and pretty compliment to her exalted wisdom and understanding, putting entirely out of sight any considerations of heart, or generous impulse and feeling. For, these are matters totally beneath a female who is acknowledged by universal admission to be far above the numerous little foibles and weaknesses of her sex.

If I wanted any further proof of the strictly philosophical nature of the conduct of these young gentlemen in their very delicate predicament, I should at once find it in the fact (also recorded in a foregoing part of this narrative), of their quitting the pursuit, when the general attention was fixed upon Oliver; and making immediately for their home by the shortest possible cut. Although I do not mean to assert that it is usually the practice of renowned and learned sages, to shorten the road to any great conclusion (their course indeed being rather to lengthen the distance, by various circumlocutions and discursive staggerings, like unto those in which drunken men under the pressure of a too mighty flow of ideas, are prone to indulge); still, I do mean to say, and do say distinctly, that it is the invariable practice of many mighty philosophers, in carrying out their theories, to evince great wisdom and foresight in providing against every possible contingency which can be supposed at all likely to affect themselves. Thus, to do a great right, you may do a little wrong; and you may take any means which the end to be attained, will justify; the amount of the right, or the amount of the wrong, or indeed the distinction between the two, being left entirely to the philosopher concerned, to be settled and determined by his clear, comprehensive, and impartial view of his own particular case.

It was not until the two boys had scoured, with great rapidity, through a most intricate maze of narrow streets and courts, that they ventured to halt beneath a low and dark archway. Having remained silent here, just long enough to recover breath to speak, Master Bates uttered an exclamation of amusement and delight; and, bursting into an uncontrollable fit of laughter, flung himself upon a doorstep, and rolled thereon in a transport of mirth.

"What's the matter?" inquired the Dodger.

"Ha! ha! ha!" roared Charley Bates.

"Hold your noise," remonstrated the Dodger, looking cautiously round. "Do you want to be grabbed, stupid?"

"I can't help it," said Charley, "I can't help it! To see him splitting away at that pace, and cutting round the corners, and knocking up again' the posts, and starting on again as if he was made of iron as well as them, and me with the wipe in my pocket, singing out arter him—oh, my eye!" The vivid imagination of Master Bates presented the scene before him in too strong colours. As he arrived at this apostrophe, he again rolled upon the door-step, and laughed louder than before.

"What'll Fagin say?" inquired the Dodger; taking advantage of the next interval of breathlessness on the part of his friend to propound the question.

"What?" repeated Charley Bates.

"Ah, what?" said the Dodger.

"Why, what should he say?" inquired Charley: stopping rather suddenly in his merriment; for the Dodger's manner was impressive. "What should he say?"

Mr. Dawkins whistled for a couple of minutes; then, taking off his hat, scratched his head, and nodded thrice.

"What do you mean?" said Charley.

"Toor rul lol loo, gammon and spinnage, the frog he wouldn't, and high cockolorum," said the Dodger: with a slight sneer on his intellectual countenance.

This was explanatory, but not satisfactory. Master Bates felt it so; and again said, "What do you mean?"

The Dodger made no reply; but putting his hat on again, and gathering the skirts of his long-tailed coat under his arm, thrust his tongue into his cheek, slapped the bridge of his nose some half-dozen times in a familiar but expressive manner, and turning on his heel, slunk down the court. Master Bates followed, with a thoughtful countenance.

The noise of footsteps on the creaking stairs, a few minutes after the occurrence of this conversation, roused the merry old gentleman as he sat over the fire with a saveloy and a small loaf in his hand; a pocket-knife in his right; and a pewter pot on the trivet. There was a rascally smile on his white face as he turned round, and looking sharply out from under his thick red eyebrows, bent his ear towards the door, and listened.

"Why, how's this?" muttered the Jew: changing countenance; "only two of 'em? Where's the third? They can't have got into trouble. Hark!"

The footsteps approached nearer; they reached the landing. The door was slowly opened; and the Dodger and Charley Bates entered, closing it behind them.

CHAPTER XIII

Some New Acquaintances Are Introduced to the Intelligent Reader,
Connected With Whom Various Pleasant Matters Are Related,
Appertaining to This History

"Where's Oliver?" said the Jew, rising with a menacing look. "Where's the boy?"

The young thieves eyed their preceptor as if they were alarmed at his violence; and looked uneasily at each other. But they made no reply.

"What's become of the boy?" said the Jew, seizing the Dodger tightly by the collar, and threatening him with horrid imprecations. "Speak out, or I'll throttle you!"

Mr. Fagin looked so very much in earnest, that Charley Bates, who deemed it prudent in all cases to be on the safe side, and who conceived it by no means improbable that it might be his turn to be throttled second, dropped upon his knees, and raised a loud, well-sustained, and continuous roar—something between a mad bull and a speaking trumpet.

"Will you speak?" thundered the Jew: shaking the Dodger so much that his keeping in the big coat at all, seemed perfectly miraculous.

"Why, the traps have got him, and that's all about it," said the Dodger, sullenly. "Come, let go o' me, will you!" And, swinging himself, at one jerk, clean out of the big coat, which he left in the Jew's hands, the Dodger snatched up the toasting fork, and made a pass at the merry old gentleman's waistcoat; which, if it had taken effect, would have let a little more merriment out than could have been easily replaced.

The Jew stepped back in this emergency, with more agility than could have been anticipated in a man of his apparent decrepitude; and, seizing up the pot, prepared to hurl it at his assailant's head. But Charley Bates, at this moment, calling his attention by a perfectly terrific howl, he suddenly altered its destination, and flung it full at that young gentleman.

"Why, what the blazes is in the wind now!" growled a deep voice. "Who pitched that 'ere at me? It's well it's the beer, and not the pot, as hit me, or I'd have settled somebody. I might have know'd, as nobody but an infernal, rich, plundering, thundering old Jew could afford to throw away any drink but water—and not that, unless he done the River Company every quarter. Wot's it all about, Fagin? D—me, if my neck-handkercher an't lined with beer! Come in, you sneaking warmint; wot are you stopping outside for, as if you was ashamed of your master! Come in!"

The man who growled out these words, was a stoutly-built fellow of about five-and-thirty, in a black velveteen coat, very soiled drab breeches, lace-up half boots, and grey cotton stockings which inclosed a bulky pair of legs, with large swelling calves;—the kind of legs, which in such costume, always look in an unfinished and incomplete state without a set of fetters to garnish them. He had a brown hat on his head, and a dirty belcher handkerchief round his neck: with the long frayed ends of which he smeared the beer from his face as he spoke. He disclosed, when he had done so, a broad heavy countenance with a beard of three days' growth, and two scowling eyes; one of which displayed various parti-coloured symptoms of having been recently damaged by a blow.

"Come in, d'ye hear?" growled this engaging ruffian.

A white shaggy dog, with his face scratched and torn in twenty different places, skulked into the room.

"Why didn't you come in afore?" said the man. "You're getting too proud to own me afore company, are you? Lie down!"

This command was accompanied with a kick, which sent the animal to the other end of the room. He appeared well used to it, however; for he coiled himself up in a corner very quietly, without uttering a sound, and winking his very ill-looking eyes twenty times in a minute, appeared to occupy himself in taking a survey of the apartment.

"What are you up to? Ill-treating the boys, you covetous, avaricious, in-sa-ti-a-ble old fence?" said the man, seating himself deliberately. "I wonder they don't murder you! I would if I was them. If I'd been your 'prentice, I'd have done it long ago, and—no, I couldn't have sold you afterwards, for you're fit for nothing but keeping as a curiousity of ugliness in a glass bottle, and I suppose they don't blow glass bottles large enough."

"Hush! hush! Mr. Sikes," said the Jew, trembling; "don't speak so loud!"

"None of your mistering," replied the ruffian; "you always mean mischief when you come that. You know my name: out with it! I shan't disgrace it when the time comes."

"Well, well, then—Bill Sikes," said the Jew, with abject humility. "You seem out of humour, Bill."

"Perhaps I am," replied Sikes; "I should think you was rather out of sorts too, unless you mean as little harm when you throw pewter pots about, as you do when you blab and—"

"Are you mad?" said the Jew, catching the man by the sleeve, and pointing towards the boys.

Mr. Sikes contented himself with tying an imaginary knot under his left ear, and jerking his head over on the right shoulder; a piece of dumb show which the Jew appeared to understand perfectly. He then, in cant terms, with which his whole conversation was plentifully besprinkled, but which would be quite unintelligible if they were recorded here, demanded a glass of liquor.

"And mind you don't poison it," said Mr. Sikes, laying his hat upon the table.

This was said in jest; but if the speaker could have seen the evil leer with which the Jew bit his pale lip as he turned round to the cupboard, he might have thought the caution not wholly unnecessary, or the wish (at all events) to improve upon the distiller's ingenuity not very far from the old gentleman's merry heart.

After swallowing two of three glasses of spirits, Mr. Sikes condescended to take some notice of the young gentlemen; which gracious act led to a conversation, in which the cause and manner of Oliver's capture were circumstantially detailed, with such alterations and improvements on the truth, as to the Dodger appeared most advisable under the circumstances.

"I'm afraid," said the Jew, "that he may say something which will get us into trouble."

"That's very likely," returned Sikes with a malicious grin. "You're blowed upon, Fagin."

"And I'm afraid, you see," added the Jew, speaking as if he had not noticed the interruption; and regarding the other closely as he did so,—"I'm afraid that, if the game was up with us, it might be up with a good many more, and that it would come out rather worse for you than it would for me, my dear."

The man started, and turned round upon the Jew. But the old gentleman's shoulders were shrugged up to his ears; and his eyes were vacantly staring on the opposite wall.

There was a long pause. Every member of the respectable coterie appeared plunged in his own reflections; not excepting the dog, who by a certain malicious licking of his lips seemed to be meditating an attack upon the legs of the first gentleman or lady he might encounter in the streets when he went out.

"Somebody must find out wot's been done at the office," said Mr. Sikes in a much lower tone than he had taken since he came in.

The Jew nodded assent.

"If he hasn't peached, and is committed, there's no fear till he comes out again," said Mr. Sikes, "and then he must be taken care on. You must get hold of him somehow."

Again the Jew nodded.

The prudence of this line of action, indeed, was obvious; but, unfortunately, there was one very strong objection to its being adopted. This was, that the Dodger, and Charley Bates, and Fagin, and Mr. William Sikes, happened, one and all, to entertain a violent and deeply-rooted antipathy to going near a police-office on any ground or pretext whatever.

How long they might have sat and looked at each other, in a state of uncertainty not the most pleasant of its kind, it is difficult to guess. It is not necessary to make any guesses on the subject, however; for the sudden entrance of the two young ladies whom Oliver had seen on a former occasion, caused the conversation to flow afresh.

"The very thing!" said the Jew. "Bet will go; won't you, my dear?"

"Wheres?" inquired the young lady.

"Only just up to the office, my dear," said the Jew coaxingly.

It is due to the young lady to say that she did not positively affirm that she would not, but that she merely expressed an emphatic and earnest desire to be "blessed" if she would; a polite and delicate evasion of the request, which shows the young lady to have been possessed of that natural good breeding which cannot bear to inflict upon a fellow-creature, the pain of a direct and pointed refusal.

The Jew's countenance fell. He turned from this young lady, who was gaily, not to say gorgeously attired, in a red gown, green boots, and yellow curl-papers, to the other female.

"Nancy, my dear," said the Jew in a soothing manner, "what do YOU say?"

"That it won't do; so it's no use a-trying it on, Fagin," replied Nancy.

"What do you mean by that?" said Mr. Sikes, looking up in a surly manner.

"What I say, Bill," replied the lady collectedly.

"Why, you're just the very person for it," reasoned Mr. Sikes: "nobody about here knows anything of you."

"And as I don't want 'em to, neither," replied Nancy in the same composed manner, "it's rather more no than yes with me, Bill."

"She'll go, Fagin," said Sikes.

"No, she won't, Fagin," said Nancy.

"Yes, she will, Fagin," said Sikes.

And Mr. Sikes was right. By dint of alternate threats, promises, and bribes, the lady in question was ultimately prevailed upon to undertake the commission. She was not, indeed, withheld by the same considerations as her agreeable friend; for, having recently removed into the neighborhood of Field Lane from the remote but genteel suburb of Ratcliffe, she was not under the same apprehension of being recognised by any of her numerous acquaintances.

Accordingly, with a clean white apron tied over her gown, and her curl-papers tucked up under a straw bonnet,—both articles of dress being provided from the Jew's inexhaustible stock,—Miss Nancy prepared to issue forth on her errand.

"Stop a minute, my dear," said the Jew, producing, a little covered basket. "Carry that in one hand. It looks more respectable, my dear."

"Give her a door-key to carry in her t'other one, Fagin," said Sikes; "it looks real and genivine like."

"Yes, yes, my dear, so it does," said the Jew, hanging a large street-door key on the forefinger of the young lady's right hand.

"There; very good! Very good indeed, my dear!" said the Jew, rubbing his hands.

"Oh, my brother! My poor, dear, sweet, innocent little brother!" exclaimed Nancy, bursting into tears, and wringing the little basket and the street-door key in an agony of distress. "What has become of him! Where have they taken him to! Oh, do have pity, and tell me what's been done with the dear boy, gentlemen; do, gentlemen, if you please, gentlemen!"

Having uttered those words in a most lamentable and heart-broken tone: to the immeasurable delight of her hearers: Miss Nancy paused, winked to the company, nodded smilingly round, and disappeared.

"Ah, she's a clever girl, my dears," said the Jew, turning round to his young friends, and shaking his head gravely, as if in mute admonition to them to follow the bright example they had just beheld.

"She's a honour to her sex," said Mr. Sikes, filling his glass, and smiting the table with his enormous fist. "Here's her health, and wishing they was all like her!"

While these, and many other encomiums, were being passed on the accomplished Nancy, that young lady made the best of her way to the police-office; whither, notwithstanding a little natural timidity consequent upon walking through the streets alone and unprotected, she arrived in perfect safety shortly afterwards.

Entering by the back way, she tapped softly with the key at one of the cell-doors, and listened. There was no sound within: so she coughed and listened again. Still there was no reply: so she spoke.

"Nolly, dear?" murmured Nancy in a gentle voice; "Nolly?"

There was nobody inside but a miserable shoeless criminal, who had been taken up for playing the flute, and who, the offence against society having been clearly proved, had been very properly committed by Mr. Fang to the House of Correction for one month; with the appropriate and amusing remark that since he had so much breath to spare, it would be more wholesomely expended on the treadmill than in a musical instrument. He made no answer: being occupied mentally bewailing the loss of the flute, which had been confiscated for the use of the county: so Nancy passed on to the next cell, and knocked there.

"Well!" cried a faint and feeble voice.

"Is there a little boy here?" inquired Nancy, with a preliminary sob.

"No," replied the voice; "God forbid."

This was a vagrant of sixty-five, who was going to prison for not playing the flute; or, in other words, for begging in the streets, and doing nothing for his livelihood. In the next cell was another man, who was going to the same prison for hawking tin saucepans without license; thereby doing something for his living, in defiance of the Stamp-office.

But, as neither of these criminals answered to the name of Oliver, or knew anything about him, Nancy made straight up to the bluff officer in the striped waistcoat; and with the most piteous wailings and lamentations, rendered more piteous by a prompt and efficient use of the street-door key and the little basket, demanded her own dear brother.

"I haven't got him, my dear," said the old man.

"Where is he?" screamed Nancy, in a distracted manner.

"Why, the gentleman's got him," replied the officer.

"What gentleman! Oh, gracious heavens! What gentleman?" exclaimed Nancy.

In reply to this incoherent questioning, the old man informed the deeply affected sister that Oliver had been taken ill in the office, and discharged in consequence of a witness having proved the robbery to have been committed by another boy, not in custody; and that the prosecutor had carried him away, in an insensible condition, to his own residence: of and concerning which, all the informant knew was, that it was somewhere in Pentonville, he having heard that word mentioned in the directions to the coachman.

In a dreadful state of doubt and uncertainty, the agonised young woman staggered to the gate, and then, exchanging her faltering walk for a swift run, returned by the most devious and complicated route she could think of, to the domicile of the Jew.

Mr. Bill Sikes no sooner heard the account of the expedition delivered, than he very hastily called up the white dog, and, putting on his hat, expeditiously departed: without devoting any time to the formality of wishing the company good-morning.

"We must know where he is, my dears; he must be found," said the Jew greatly excited. "Charley, do nothing but skulk about, till you bring home some news of him! Nancy, my dear, I must have him found. I trust to you, my dear,—to you and the Artful for everything! Stay, stay," added the Jew, unlocking a drawer with a shaking hand; "there's money, my dears. I shall shut up this shop to-night. You'll know where to find me! Don't stop here a minute. Not an instant, my dears!"

With these words, he pushed them from the room: and carefully double-locking and barring the door behind them, drew from its place of concealment the box which he had unintentionally disclosed to Oliver. Then, he hastily proceeded to dispose the watches and jewellery beneath his clothing.

A rap at the door startled him in this occupation. "Who's there?" he cried in a shrill tone.

"Me!" replied the voice of the Dodger, through the key-hole.

"What now?" cried the Jew impatiently.

"Is he to be kidnapped to the other ken, Nancy says?" inquired the Dodger.

"Yes," replied the Jew, "wherever she lays hands on him. Find him, find him out, that's all. I shall know what to do next; never fear."

The boy murmured a reply of intelligence: and hurried downstairs after his companions.

"He has not peached so far," said the Jew as he pursued his occupation. "If he means to blab us among his new friends, we may stop his mouth yet."

CHAPTER XIV

Comprising Further Particulars of Oliver's Stay at Mr. Brownlow's,
With the Remarkable Prediction Which One Mr. Grimwig Uttered
Concerning Him, When He Went Out on an Errand

Oliver soon recovering from the fainting-fit into which Mr. Brownlow's abrupt exclamation had thrown him, the subject of the picture was carefully avoided, both by the old gentleman and Mrs. Bedwin, in the conversation that ensued: which indeed bore no reference to Oliver's history or prospects, but was confined to such topics as might amuse without exciting him. He was still too weak to get up to breakfast; but, when he came down into the housekeeper's room next day, his first act was to cast an eager glance at the wall, in the hope of again looking on the face of the beautiful lady. His expectations were disappointed, however, for the picture had been removed.

"Ah!" said the housekeeper, watching the direction of Oliver's eyes. "It is gone, you see."

"I see it is ma'am," replied Oliver. "Why have they taken it away?"

"It has been taken down, child, because Mr. Brownlow said, that as it seemed to worry you, perhaps it might prevent your getting well, you know," rejoined the old lady.

"Oh, no, indeed. It didn't worry me, ma'am," said Oliver. "I liked to see it. I quite loved it."

"Well, well!" said the old lady, good-humouredly; "you get well as fast as ever you can, dear, and it shall be hung up again. There! I promise you that! Now, let us talk about something else."

This was all the information Oliver could obtain about the picture at that time. As the old lady had been so kind to him in his illness, he endeavoured to think no more of the subject just then; so he listened attentively to a great many stories she told him, about an amiable and handsome daughter of hers, who was married to an amiable and handsome man, and lived in the country; and about a son, who was clerk to a merchant in the West Indies; and who was, also, such a good young man, and wrote such dutiful letters home four times a-year, that it brought the tears into her eyes to talk about them. When the old lady had expatiated, a long time, on the excellences of her children, and the merits of her kind good husband besides, who had been dead and gone, poor dear soul! just six-and-twenty years, it was time to have tea. After tea she began to teach Oliver cribbage: which he learnt as quickly as she could teach: and at which game they played, with great interest and gravity, until it was time for the invalid to have some warm wine and water, with a slice of dry toast, and then to go cosily to bed.

They were happy days, those of Oliver's recovery. Everything was so quiet, and neat, and orderly; everybody so kind and gentle; that after the noise and turbulence in the midst of which he had always lived, it seemed like Heaven itself. He was no sooner strong enough to put his clothes on, properly, than Mr. Brownlow caused a complete new suit, and a new cap, and a new pair of shoes, to be provided for him. As Oliver was told that he might do what he liked with the old clothes, he gave them to a servant who had been very kind to him, and asked her to sell them to a Jew, and keep the money for herself. This she very readily did; and, as Oliver looked out of the parlour window, and saw the Jew roll them up in his bag and walk away, he felt quite delighted to think that they were safely gone, and that there was now no possible danger of his ever being able to wear them again. They were sad rags, to tell the truth; and Oliver had never had a new suit before.

One evening, about a week after the affair of the picture, as he was sitting talking to Mrs. Bedwin, there came a message down from Mr. Brownlow, that if Oliver Twist felt pretty well, he should like to see him in his study, and talk to him a little while.

"Bless us, and save us! Wash your hands, and let me part your hair nicely for you, child," said Mrs. Bedwin. "Dear heart alive! If we had known he would have asked for you, we would have put you a clean collar on, and made you as smart as sixpence!"

Oliver did as the old lady bade him; and, although she lamented grievously, meanwhile, that there was not even time to crimp the little frill that bordered his shirt-collar; he looked so delicate and handsome, despite that important personal advantage, that she went so far as to say: looking at him with great complacency from head to foot, that she really didn't think it would have been possible, on the longest notice, to have made much difference in him for the better.

Thus encouraged, Oliver tapped at the study door. On Mr. Brownlow calling to him to come in, he found himself in a little back room, quite full of books, with a window, looking into some pleasant little gardens. There was a table drawn up before the window, at which Mr. Brownlow was seated reading. When he saw Oliver, he pushed the book away from him, and told him to come near the table, and sit down. Oliver complied; marvelling where the people could be found to read such a great number of books as seemed to be written to make the world wiser. Which is still a marvel to more experienced people than Oliver Twist, every day of their lives.

"There are a good many books, are there not, my boy?" said Mr. Brownlow, observing the curiosity with which Oliver surveyed the shelves that reached from the floor to the ceiling.

"A great number, sir," replied Oliver. "I never saw so many."

"You shall read them, if you behave well," said the old gentleman kindly; "and you will like that, better than looking at the outsides,—that is, some cases; because there are books of which the backs and covers are by far the best parts."

"I suppose they are those heavy ones, sir," said Oliver, pointing to some large quartos, with a good deal of gilding about the binding.

"Not always those," said the old gentleman, patting Oliver on the head, and smiling as he did so; "there are other equally heavy ones, though of a much smaller size. How should you like to grow up a clever man, and write books, eh?"

"I think I would rather read them, sir," replied Oliver.

"What! wouldn't you like to be a book-writer?" said the old gentleman.

Oliver considered a little while; and at last said, he should think it would be a much better thing to be a book-seller; upon which the old gentleman laughed heartily, and declared he had said a very good thing. Which Oliver felt glad to have done, though he by no means knew what it was.

"Well, well," said the old gentleman, composing his features. "Don't be afraid! We won't make an author of you, while there's an honest trade to be learnt, or brick-making to turn to."

"Thank you, sir," said Oliver. At the earnest manner of his reply, the old gentleman laughed again; and said something about a curious instinct, which Oliver, not understanding, paid no very great attention to.

"Now," said Mr. Brownlow, speaking if possible in a kinder, but at the same time in a much more serious manner, than Oliver had ever known him assume yet, "I want you to pay great attention, my boy, to what I am going to say. I shall talk to you without any reserve; because I am sure you are well able to understand me, as many older persons would be."

"Oh, don't tell you are going to send me away, sir, pray!" exclaimed Oliver, alarmed at the serious tone of the old gentleman's commencement! "Don't turn me out of doors to wander in the streets again. Let me stay here, and be a servant. Don't send me back to the wretched place I came from. Have mercy upon a poor boy, sir!"

"My dear child," said the old gentleman, moved by the warmth of Oliver's sudden appeal; "you need not be afraid of my deserting you, unless you give me cause."

"I never, never will, sir," interposed Oliver.

"I hope not," rejoined the old gentleman. "I do not think you ever will. I have been deceived, before, in the objects whom I have endeavoured to benefit; but I feel strongly disposed to trust you, nevertheless; and I am more interested in your behalf than I can well account for, even to myself. The persons on whom I have bestowed my dearest love, lie deep in their graves; but, although the happiness and delight of my life lie buried there too, I have not made a coffin of my heart, and sealed it up, forever, on my best affections. Deep affliction has but strengthened and refined them."

As the old gentleman said this in a low voice: more to himself than to his companion: and as he remained silent for a short time afterwards: Oliver sat quite still.

"Well, well!" said the old gentleman at length, in a more cheerful tone, "I only say this, because you have a young heart; and knowing that I have suffered great pain and sorrow, you will be more careful, perhaps, not to wound me again. You say you are an orphan, without a friend in the world; all the inquiries I have been able to make, confirm the statement. Let me hear your story; where you come from; who brought you up; and how you got into the company in which I found you. Speak the truth, and you shall not be friendless while I live."

Oliver's sobs checked his utterance for some minutes; when he was on the point of beginning to relate how he had been brought up at the farm, and carried to the workhouse by Mr. Bumble, a peculiarly impatient little double-knock was heard at the street-door: and the servant, running upstairs, announced Mr. Grimwig.

"Is he coming up?" inquired Mr. Brownlow.

"Yes, sir," replied the servant. "He asked if there were any muffins in the house; and, when I told him yes, he said he had come to tea."

Mr. Brownlow smiled; and, turning to Oliver, said that Mr. Grimwig was an old friend of his, and he must not mind his being a little rough in his manners; for he was a worthy creature at bottom, as he had reason to know.

"Shall I go downstairs, sir?" inquired Oliver.

"No," replied Mr. Brownlow, "I would rather you remained here."

At this moment, there walked into the room: supporting himself by a thick stick: a stout old gentleman, rather lame in one leg, who was dressed in a blue coat, striped waistcoat, nankeen breeches and gaiters, and a broad-brimmed white hat, with the sides turned up with green. A very small-plaited shirt frill stuck out from his waistcoat; and a very long steel watch-chain, with nothing but a key at the end, dangled loosely below it. The ends of his white neckerchief were twisted into a ball about the size of an orange; the variety of shapes into which his countenance was twisted, defy description. He had a manner of screwing his head on one side when he spoke; and of looking out of the corners of his eyes at the same time: which irresistibly reminded the beholder of a parrot. In this attitude, he fixed himself, the moment he made his appearance; and, holding out a small piece of orange-peel at arm's length, exclaimed, in a growling, discontented voice.

"Look here! do you see this! Isn't it a most wonderful and extraordinary thing that I can't call at a man's house but I find a piece of this poor surgeon's friend on the staircase? I've been lamed with orange-peel once, and I know orange-peel will be my death, or I'll be content to eat my own head, sir!"

This was the handsome offer with which Mr. Grimwig backed and confirmed nearly every assertion he made; and it was the more singular in his case, because, even admitting for the sake of argument, the possibility of scientific improvements being brought to that pass which will enable a gentleman to eat his own head in the event of his being so disposed, Mr. Grimwig's head was such a particularly large one, that the most sanguine man alive could hardly entertain a hope of being able to get through it at a sitting—to put entirely out of the question, a very thick coating of powder.

"I'll eat my head, sir," repeated Mr. Grimwig, striking his stick upon the ground. "Hallo! what's that!" looking at Oliver, and retreating a pace or two.

"This is young Oliver Twist, whom we were speaking about," said Mr. Brownlow.

Oliver bowed.

"You don't mean to say that's the boy who had the fever, I hope?" said Mr. Grimwig, recoiling a little more. "Wait a minute! Don't speak! Stop—" continued Mr. Grimwig, abruptly, losing all dread of the fever in his triumph at the discovery; "that's the boy who had the orange! If that's not the boy, sir, who had the orange, and threw this bit of peel upon the staircase, I'll eat my head, and his too."

"No, no, he has not had one," said Mr. Brownlow, laughing. "Come! Put down your hat; and speak to my young friend."

"I feel strongly on this subject, sir," said the irritable old gentleman, drawing off his gloves. "There's always more or less orange-peel on the pavement in our street; and I know it's put there by the surgeon's boy at the corner. A young woman stumbled over a bit last night, and fell against my garden-railings; directly she got up I saw her look towards his infernal red lamp with the pantomime-light. "Don't go to him," I called out of the window, "he's an assassin! A man-trap!" So he is. If he is not—' Here the irascible old gentleman gave a great knock on the ground with his stick; which was always understood, by his friends, to imply the customary offer, whenever it was not expressed in words. Then, still keeping his stick in his hand, he sat down; and, opening a double eye-glass, which he wore attached to a broad black riband, took a view of Oliver: who, seeing that he was the object of inspection, coloured, and bowed again.

"That's the boy, is it?" said Mr. Grimwig, at length.

"That's the boy," replied Mr. Brownlow.

"How are you, boy?" said Mr. Grimwig.

"A great deal better, thank you, sir," replied Oliver.

Mr. Brownlow, seeming to apprehend that his singular friend was about to say something disagreeable, asked Oliver to step downstairs and tell Mrs. Bedwin they were ready for tea; which, as he did not half like the visitor's manner, he was very happy to do.

"He is a nice-looking boy, is he not?" inquired Mr. Brownlow.

"I don't know," replied Mr. Grimwig, pettishly.

"Don't know?"

"No. I don't know. I never see any difference in boys. I only knew two sort of boys. Mealy boys, and beef-faced boys."

"And which is Oliver?"

"Mealy. I know a friend who has a beef-faced boy; a fine boy, they call him; with a round head, and red cheeks, and glaring eyes; a horrid boy; with a body and limbs that appear to be swelling out of the seams of his blue clothes; with the voice of a pilot, and the appetite of a wolf. I know him! The wretch!"

"Come," said Mr. Brownlow, "these are not the characteristics of young Oliver Twist; so he needn't excite your wrath."

"They are not," replied Mr. Grimwig. "He may have worse."

Here, Mr. Brownlow coughed impatiently; which appeared to afford Mr. Grimwig the most exquisite delight.

"He may have worse, I say," repeated Mr. Grimwig. "Where does he come from! Who is he? What is he? He has had a fever. What of that? Fevers are not peculiar to good people; are they? Bad people have fevers sometimes; haven't they, eh? I knew a man who was hung in Jamaica for murdering his master. He had had a fever six times; he wasn't recommended to mercy on that account. Pooh! nonsense!"

Now, the fact was, that in the inmost recesses of his own heart, Mr. Grimwig was strongly disposed to admit that Oliver's appearance and manner were unusually prepossessing; but he had a strong appetite for contradiction, sharpened on this occasion by the finding of the orange-peel; and, inwardly determining that no man should dictate to him whether a boy was well-looking or not, he had resolved, from the first, to oppose his friend. When Mr. Brownlow admitted that on no one point of inquiry could he yet return a satisfactory answer; and that he had postponed any investigation into Oliver's previous history until he thought the boy was strong enough to hear it; Mr. Grimwig chuckled maliciously. And he demanded, with a sneer, whether the housekeeper was in the habit of counting the plate at night; because if she didn't find a table-spoon or two missing some sunshiny morning, why, he would be content to—and so forth.

All this, Mr. Brownlow, although himself somewhat of an impetuous gentleman: knowing his friend's peculiarities, bore with great good humour; as Mr. Grimwig, at tea, was graciously pleased to express his entire approval of the muffins, matters went on very smoothly; and Oliver, who made one of the party, began to feel more at his ease than he had yet done in the fierce old gentleman's presence.

"And when are you going to hear a full, true, and particular account of the life and adventures of Oliver Twist?" asked Grimwig of Mr. Brownlow, at the conclusion of the meal; looking sideways at Oliver, as he resumed his subject.

"To-morrow morning," replied Mr. Brownlow. "I would rather he was alone with me at the time. Come up to me to-morrow morning at ten o'clock, my dear."

"Yes, sir," replied Oliver. He answered with some hesitation, because he was confused by Mr. Grimwig's looking so hard at him.

"I'll tell you what," whispered that gentleman to Mr. Brownlow; "he won't come up to you to-morrow morning. I saw him hesitate. He is deceiving you, my good friend."

"I'll swear he is not," replied Mr. Brownlow, warmly.

"If he is not," said Mr. Grimwig, "I'll—' and down went the stick.

"I'll answer for that boy's truth with my life!" said Mr. Brownlow, knocking the table.

"And I for his falsehood with my head!" rejoined Mr. Grimwig, knocking the table also.

"We shall see," said Mr. Brownlow, checking his rising anger.

"We will," replied Mr. Grimwig, with a provoking smile; "we will."

As fate would have it, Mrs. Bedwin chanced to bring in, at this moment, a small parcel of books, which Mr. Brownlow had that morning purchased of the identical bookstall-keeper, who has already figured in this history; having laid them on the table, she prepared to leave the room.

"Stop the boy, Mrs. Bedwin!" said Mr. Brownlow; "there is something to go back."

"He has gone, sir," replied Mrs. Bedwin.

"Call after him," said Mr. Brownlow; "it's particular. He is a poor man, and they are not paid for. There are some books to be taken back, too."

The street-door was opened. Oliver ran one way; and the girl ran another; and Mrs. Bedwin stood on the step and screamed for the boy; but there was no boy in sight. Oliver and the girl returned, in a breathless state, to report that there were no tidings of him.

"Dear me, I am very sorry for that," exclaimed Mr. Brownlow; "I particularly wished those books to be returned to-night."

"Send Oliver with them," said Mr. Grimwig, with an ironical smile; "he will be sure to deliver them safely, you know."

"Yes; do let me take them, if you please, sir," said Oliver. "I'll run all the way, sir."

The old gentleman was just going to say that Oliver should not go out on any account; when a most malicious cough from Mr. Grimwig determined him that he should; and that, by his prompt discharge of the commission, he should prove to him the injustice of his suspicions: on this head at least: at once.

"You shall go, my dear," said the old gentleman. "The books are on a chair by my table. Fetch them down."

Oliver, delighted to be of use, brought down the books under his arm in a great bustle; and waited, cap in hand, to hear what message he was to take.

"You are to say," said Mr. Brownlow, glancing steadily at Grimwig; "you are to say that you have brought those books back; and that you have come to pay the four pound ten I owe him. This is a five-pound note, so you will have to bring me back, ten shillings change."

"I won't be ten minutes, sir," said Oliver, eagerly. Having buttoned up the bank-note in his jacket pocket, and placed the books carefully under his arm, he made a respectful bow, and left the room. Mrs. Bedwin followed him to the street-door, giving him many directions about the nearest way, and the name of the bookseller, and the name of the street: all of which Oliver said he clearly understood. Having superadded many injunctions to be sure and not take cold, the old lady at length permitted him to depart.

"Bless his sweet face!" said the old lady, looking after him. "I can't bear, somehow, to let him go out of my sight."

At this moment, Oliver looked gaily round, and nodded before he turned the corner. The old lady smilingly returned his salutation, and, closing the door, went back to her own room.

"Let me see; he'll be back in twenty minutes, at the longest," said Mr. Brownlow, pulling out his watch, and placing it on the table. "It will be dark by that time."

"Oh! you really expect him to come back, do you?" inquired Mr. Grimwig.

"Don't you?" asked Mr. Brownlow, smiling.

The spirit of contradiction was strong in Mr. Grimwig's breast, at the moment; and it was rendered stronger by his friend's confident smile.

"No," he said, smiting the table with his fist, "I do not. The boy has a new suit of clothes on his back, a set of valuable books under his arm, and a five-pound note in his pocket. He'll join his old friends the thieves, and laugh at you. If ever that boy returns to this house, sir, I'll eat my head."

With these words he drew his chair closer to the table; and there the two friends sat, in silent expectation, with the watch between them.

It is worthy of remark, as illustrating the importance we attach to our own judgments, and the pride with which we put forth our most rash and hasty conclusions, that, although Mr. Grimwig was not by any means a bad-hearted man, and though he would have been unfeignedly sorry to see his respected friend duped and deceived, he really did most earnestly and strongly hope at that moment, that Oliver Twist might not come back.

It grew so dark, that the figures on the dial-plate were scarcely discernible; but there the two old gentlemen continued to sit, in silence, with the watch between them.

CHAPTER XV

*Showing How Very Fond of Oliver Twist, the Merry Old Jew
and Miss Nancy Were*

In the obscure parlour of a low public-house, in the filthiest part of Little Saffron Hill; a dark and gloomy den, where a flaring gas-light burnt all day in the winter-time; and where no ray of sun ever shone in the summer: there sat, brooding over a little pewter measure and a small glass, strongly impregnated with the smell of liquor, a man in a velveteen coat, drab shorts, half-boots and stockings, whom even by that dim light no experienced agent of the police would have hesitated to recognise as Mr. William Sikes. At his feet, sat a white-coated, red-eyed dog; who occupied himself, alternately, in winking at his master with both eyes at the same time; and in licking a large, fresh cut on one side of his mouth, which appeared to be the result of some recent conflict.

"Keep quiet, you warmint! Keep quiet!" said Mr. Sikes, suddenly breaking silence. Whether his meditations were so intense as to be disturbed by the dog's winking, or whether his feelings were so wrought upon by his reflections that they required all the relief derivable from kicking an unoffending animal to allay them, is matter for argument and consideration. Whatever was the cause, the effect was a kick and a curse, bestowed upon the dog simultaneously.

Dogs are not generally apt to revenge injuries inflicted upon them by their masters; but Mr. Sikes's dog, having faults of temper in common with his owner, and labouring, perhaps, at this moment, under a powerful sense of injury, made no more ado but at once fixed his teeth in one of the half-boots. Having given in a hearty shake, he retired, growling, under a form; just escaping the pewter measure which Mr. Sikes levelled at his head.

"You would, would you?" said Sikes, seizing the poker in one hand, and deliberately opening with the other a large clasp-knife, which he drew from his pocket. "Come here, you born devil! Come here! D'ye hear?"

The dog no doubt heard; because Mr. Sikes spoke in the very harshest key of a very harsh voice; but, appearing to entertain some unaccountable objection to having his throat cut, he remained where he was, and growled more fiercely than before: at the same time grasping the end of the poker between his teeth, and biting at it like a wild beast.

This resistance only infuriated Mr. Sikes the more; who, dropping on his knees, began to assail the animal most furiously. The dog jumped from right to left, and from left to right; snapping, growling, and barking; the man thrust and swore, and struck and blasphemed; and the struggle was reaching a most critical point for one or other; when, the door suddenly opening, the dog darted out: leaving Bill Sikes with the poker and the clasp-knife in his hands.

There must always be two parties to a quarrel, says the old adage. Mr. Sikes, being disappointed of the dog's participation, at once transferred his share in the quarrel to the new comer.

"What the devil do you come in between me and my dog for?" said Sikes, with a fierce gesture.

"I didn't know, my dear, I didn't know," replied Fagin, humbly; for the Jew was the new comer.

"Didn't know, you white-livered thief!" growled Sikes. "Couldn't you hear the noise?"

"Not a sound of it, as I'm a living man, Bill," replied the Jew.

"Oh no! You hear nothing, you don't," retorted Sikes with a fierce sneer. "Sneaking in and out, so as nobody hears how you come or go! I wish you had been the dog, Fagin, half a minute ago."

"Why?" inquired the Jew with a forced smile.

"Cause the government, as cares for the lives of such men as you, as haven't half the pluck of curs, lets a man kill a dog how he likes," replied Sikes, shutting up the knife with a very expressive look; "that's why."

The Jew rubbed his hands; and, sitting down at the table, affected to laugh at the pleasantry of his friend. He was obviously very ill at ease, however.

"Grin away," said Sikes, replacing the poker, and surveying him with savage contempt; "grin away. You'll never have the laugh at me, though, unless it's behind a nightcap. I've got the upper hand over you, Fagin; and, d——me, I'll keep it. There! If I go, you go; so take care of me."

"Well, well, my dear," said the Jew, "I know all that; we—we—have a mutual interest, Bill,—a mutual interest."

"Humph," said Sikes, as if he thought the interest lay rather more on the Jew's side than on his. "Well, what have you got to say to me?"

"It's all passed safe through the melting-pot," replied Fagin, "and this is your share. It's rather more than it ought to be, my dear; but as I know you'll do me a good turn another time, and—"

"Stow that gammon," interposed the robber, impatiently. "Where is it? Hand over!"

"Yes, yes, Bill; give me time, give me time," replied the Jew, soothingly. "Here it is! All safe!" As he spoke, he drew forth an old cotton handkerchief from his breast; and untying a large knot in one corner, produced a small brown-paper packet. Sikes, snatching it from him, hastily opened it; and proceeded to count the sovereigns it contained.

"This is all, is it?" inquired Sikes.

"All," replied the Jew.

"You haven't opened the parcel and swallowed one or two as you come along, have you?" inquired Sikes, suspiciously. "Don't put on an injured look at the question; you've done it many a time. Jerk the tinkler."

These words, in plain English, conveyed an injunction to ring the bell. It was answered by another Jew: younger than Fagin, but nearly as vile and repulsive in appearance.

Bill Sikes merely pointed to the empty measure. The Jew, perfectly understanding the hint, retired to fill it: previously exchanging a remarkable look with Fagin, who raised his eyes for an instant, as if in expectation of it, and shook his head in reply; so slightly that the action would have been almost imperceptible to an observant third person. It was lost upon Sikes, who was stooping at the moment to tie the boot-lace which the dog had torn. Possibly, if he had observed the brief interchange of signals, he might have thought that it boded no good to him.

"Is anybody here, Barney?" inquired Fagin; speaking, now that that Sikes was looking on, without raising his eyes from the ground.

"Dot a shoul," replied Barney; whose words: whether they came from the heart or not: made their way through the nose.

"Nobody?" inquired Fagin, in a tone of surprise: which perhaps might mean that Barney was at liberty to tell the truth.

"Dobody but Biss Dadsy," replied Barney.

"Nancy!" exclaimed Sikes. "Where? Strike me blind, if I don't honour that 'ere girl, for her native talents."

"She's bid havid a plate of boiled beef id the bar," replied Barney.

"Send her here," said Sikes, pouring out a glass of liquor. "Send her here."

Barney looked timidly at Fagin, as if for permission; the Jew remaining silent, and not lifting his eyes from the ground, he retired; and presently returned, ushering in Nancy; who was decorated with the bonnet, apron, basket, and street-door key, complete.

"You are on the scent, are you, Nancy?" inquired Sikes, proffering the glass.

"Yes, I am, Bill," replied the young lady, disposing of its contents; "and tired enough of it I am, too. The young brat's been ill and confined to the crib; and——"

"Ah, Nancy, dear!" said Fagin, looking up.

Now, whether a peculiar contraction of the Jew's red eye-brows, and a half closing of his deeply-set eyes, warned Miss Nancy that she was disposed to be too communicative, is not a matter of much importance. The fact is all we need care for here; and the fact is, that she suddenly checked herself, and with several gracious smiles upon Mr. Sikes, turned the conversation to other matters. In about ten minutes' time, Mr. Fagin was seized with a fit of coughing; upon which Nancy pulled her shawl over her shoulders, and declared it was time to go. Mr. Sikes, finding that he was walking a short part of her way himself, expressed his intention of accompanying her; they went away together, followed, at a little distant, by the dog, who slunk out of a back-yard as soon as his master was out of sight.

The Jew thrust his head out of the room door when Sikes had left it; looked after him as we walked up the dark passage; shook his clenched fist; muttered a deep curse;

and then, with a horrible grin, reseated himself at the table; where he was soon deeply absorbed in the interesting pages of the Hue-and-Cry.

Meanwhile, Oliver Twist, little dreaming that he was within so very short a distance of the merry old gentleman, was on his way to the book-stall. When he got into Clerkenwell, he accidently turned down a by-street which was not exactly in his way; but not discovering his mistake until he had got half-way down it, and knowing it must lead in the right direction, he did not think it worth while to turn back; and so marched on, as quickly as he could, with the books under his arm.

He was walking along, thinking how happy and contented he ought to feel; and how much he would give for only one look at poor little Dick, who, starved and beaten, might be weeping bitterly at that very moment; when he was startled by a young woman screaming out very loud. "Oh, my dear brother!" And he had hardly looked up, to see what the matter was, when he was stopped by having a pair of arms thrown tight round his neck.

"Don't," cried Oliver, struggling. "Let go of me. Who is it? What are you stopping me for?"

The only reply to this, was a great number of loud lamentations from the young woman who had embraced him; and who had a little basket and a street-door key in her hand.

"Oh my gracious!" said the young woman, "I have found him! Oh! Oliver! Oliver! Oh you naughty boy, to make me suffer such distress on your account! Come home, dear, come. Oh, I've found him. Thank gracious goodness heavins, I've found him!" With these incoherent exclamations, the young woman burst into another fit of crying, and got so dreadfully hysterical, that a couple of women who came up at the moment asked a butcher's boy with a shiny head of hair anointed with suet, who was also looking on, whether he didn't think he had better run for the doctor. To which, the butcher's boy: who appeared of a lounging, not to say indolent disposition: replied, that he thought not.

"Oh, no, no, never mind," said the young woman, grasping Oliver's hand; "I'm better now. Come home directly, you cruel boy! Come!"

"Oh, ma'am," replied the young woman, "he ran away, near a month ago, from his parents, who are hard-working and respectable people; and went and joined a set of thieves and bad characters; and almost broke his mother's heart."

"Young wretch!" said one woman.

"Go home, do, you little brute," said the other.

"I am not," replied Oliver, greatly alarmed. "I don't know her. I haven't any sister, or father and mother either. I'm an orphan; I live at Pentonville."

"Only hear him, how he braves it out!" cried the young woman.

"Why, it's Nancy!" exclaimed Oliver; who now saw her face for the first time; and started back, in irrepressible astonishment.

"You see he knows me!" cried Nancy, appealing to the bystanders. "He can't help himself. Make him come home, there's good people, or he'll kill his dear mother and father, and break my heart!"

"What the devil's this?" said a man, bursting out of a beer-shop, with a white dog at his heels; "young Oliver! Come home to your poor mother, you young dog! Come home directly."

"I don't belong to them. I don't know them. Help! help!" cried Oliver, struggling in the man's powerful grasp.

"Help!" repeated the man. "Yes; I'll help you, you young rascal! What books are these? You've been a stealing 'em, have you? Give 'em here.' With these words, the man tore the volumes from his grasp, and struck him on the head.

"That's right!" cried a looker-on, from a garret-window. "That's the only way of bringing him to his senses!"

"To be sure!" cried a sleepy-faced carpenter, casting an approving look at the garret-window.

"It'll do him good!" said the two women.

"And he shall have it, too!" rejoined the man, administering another blow, and seizing Oliver by the collar. "Come on, you young villain! Here, Bull's-eye, mind him, boy! Mind him!"

Weak with recent illness; stupified by the blows and the suddenness of the attack; terrified by the fierce growling of the dog, and the brutality of the man; overpowered by the conviction of the bystanders that he really was the hardened little wretch he was described to be; what could one poor child do! Darkness had set in; it was a low neighborhood; no help was near; resistance was useless. In another moment he was dragged into a labyrinth of dark narrow courts, and was forced along them at a pace which rendered the few cries he dared to give utterance to, unintelligible. It was of little moment, indeed, whether they were intelligible or no; for there was nobody to care for them, had they been ever so plain.

* * * * *

The gas-lamps were lighted; Mrs. Bedwin was waiting anxiously at the open door; the servant had run up the street twenty times to see if there were any traces of Oliver; and still the two old gentlemen sat, perseveringly, in the dark parlour, with the watch between them.

CHAPTER XVI

Relates What Became of Oliver Twist, After He Had Been Claimed by Nancy

The narrow streets and courts, at length, terminated in a large open space; scattered about which, were pens for beasts, and other indications of a cattle-market. Sikes slackened his pace when they reached this spot: the girl being quite unable to support any longer, the rapid rate at which they had hitherto walked. Turning to Oliver, he roughly commanded him to take hold of Nancy's hand.

"Do you hear?" growled Sikes, as Oliver hesitated, and looked round.

They were in a dark corner, quite out of the track of passengers.

Oliver saw, but too plainly, that resistance would be of no avail. He held out his hand, which Nancy clasped tight in hers.

"Give me the other," said Sikes, seizing Oliver's unoccupied hand. "Here, Bull's-Eye!"

The dog looked up, and growled.

"See here, boy!" said Sikes, putting his other hand to Oliver's throat; "if he speaks ever so soft a word, hold him! D'ye mind!"

The dog growled again; and licking his lips, eyed Oliver as if he were anxious to attach himself to his windpipe without delay.

"He's as willing as a Christian, strike me blind if he isn't!" said Sikes, regarding the animal with a kind of grim and ferocious approval. "Now, you know what you've got to expect, master, so call away as quick as you like; the dog will soon stop that game. Get on, young'un!"

Bull's-eye wagged his tail in acknowledgment of this unusually endearing form of speech; and, giving vent to another admonitory growl for the benefit of Oliver, led the way onward.

It was Smithfield that they were crossing, although it might have been Grosvenor Square, for anything Oliver knew to the contrary. The night was dark and foggy. The lights in the shops could scarcely struggle through the heavy mist, which thickened every moment and shrouded the streets and houses in gloom; rendering the strange place still stranger in Oliver's eyes; and making his uncertainty the more dismal and depressing.

They had hurried on a few paces, when a deep church-bell struck the hour. With its first stroke, his two conductors stopped, and turned their heads in the direction whence the sound proceeded.

"Eight o' clock, Bill," said Nancy, when the bell ceased.

"What's the good of telling me that; I can hear it, can't I!" replied Sikes.

"I wonder whether THEY can hear it," said Nancy.

"Of course they can," replied Sikes. "It was Bartlemy time when I was shopped; and there warn't a penny trumpet in the fair, as I couldn't hear the squeaking on. Arter I was locked up for the night, the row and din outside made the thundering old jail so silent, that I could almost have beat my brains out against the iron plates of the door."

"Poor fellow!" said Nancy, who still had her face turned towards the quarter in which the bell had sounded. "Oh, Bill, such fine young chaps as them!"

"Yes; that's all you women think of," answered Sikes. "Fine young chaps! Well, they're as good as dead, so it don't much matter."

With this consolation, Mr. Sikes appeared to repress a rising tendency to jealousy, and, clasping Oliver's wrist more firmly, told him to step out again.

"Wait a minute!" said the girl: "I wouldn't hurry by, if it was you that was coming out to be hung, the next time eight o'clock struck, Bill. I'd walk round and round the place till I dropped, if the snow was on the ground, and I hadn't a shawl to cover me."

"And what good would that do?" inquired the unsentimental Mr. Sikes. "Unless you could pitch over a file and twenty yards of good stout rope, you might as well be walking fifty mile off, or not walking at all, for all the good it would do me. Come on, and don't stand preaching there."

The girl burst into a laugh; drew her shawl more closely round her; and they walked away. But Oliver felt her hand tremble, and, looking up in her face as they passed a gas-lamp, saw that it had turned a deadly white.

They walked on, by little-frequented and dirty ways, for a full half-hour: meeting very few people, and those appearing from their looks to hold much the same position in society as Mr. Sikes himself. At length they turned into a very filthy narrow street, nearly full of old-clothes shops; the dog running forward, as if conscious that there was no further occasion for his keeping on guard, stopped before the door of a shop that was closed and apparently untenanted; the house was in a ruinous condition, and on the door was nailed a board, intimating that it was to let: which looked as if it had hung there for many years.

"All right," cried Sikes, glancing cautiously about.

Nancy stooped below the shutters, and Oliver heard the sound of a bell. They crossed to the opposite side of the street, and stood for a few moments under a lamp. A noise, as if a sash window were gently raised, was heard; and soon afterwards the door softly opened. Mr. Sikes then seized the terrified boy by the collar with very little ceremony; and all three were quickly inside the house.

The passage was perfectly dark. They waited, while the person who had let them in, chained and barred the door.

"Anybody here?" inquired Sikes.

"No," replied a voice, which Oliver thought he had heard before.

"Is the old 'un here?" asked the robber.

"Yes," replied the voice, "and precious down in the mouth he has been. Won't he be glad to see you? Oh, no!"

The style of this reply, as well as the voice which delivered it, seemed familiar to Oliver's ears: but it was impossible to distinguish even the form of the speaker in the darkness.

"Let's have a glim," said Sikes, "or we shall go breaking our necks, or treading on the dog. Look after your legs if you do!"

"Stand still a moment, and I'll get you one," replied the voice. The receding footsteps of the speaker were heard; and, in another minute, the form of Mr. John Dawkins, otherwise the Artful Dodger, appeared. He bore in his right hand a tallow candle stuck in the end of a cleft stick.

The young gentleman did not stop to bestow any other mark of recognition upon Oliver than a humourous grin; but, turning away, beckoned the visitors to follow him down a flight of stairs. They crossed an empty kitchen; and, opening the door of a low earthy-smelling room, which seemed to have been built in a small back-yard, were received with a shout of laughter.

"Oh, my wig, my wig!" cried Master Charles Bates, from whose lungs the laughter had proceeded: "here he is! oh, cry, here he is! Oh, Fagin, look at him! Fagin, do look at him! I can't bear it; it is such a jolly game, I cant' bear it. Hold me, somebody, while I laugh it out."

With this irrepressible ebullition of mirth, Master Bates laid himself flat on the floor: and kicked convulsively for five minutes, in an ectasy of facetious joy. Then jumping to his feet, he snatched the cleft stick from the Dodger; and, advancing to Oliver, viewed him round and round; while the Jew, taking off his nightcap, made a great number of low bows to the bewildered boy. The Artful, meantime, who was of a rather saturnine disposition, and seldom gave way to merriment when it interfered with business, rifled Oliver's pockets with steady assiduity.

"Look at his togs, Fagin!" said Charley, putting the light so close to his new jacket as nearly to set him on fire. "Look at his togs! Superfine cloth, and the heavy swell cut! Oh, my eye, what a game! And his books, too! Nothing but a gentleman, Fagin!"

"Delighted to see you looking so well, my dear," said the Jew, bowing with mock humility. "The Artful shall give you another suit, my dear, for fear you should spoil that Sunday one. Why didn't you write, my dear, and say you were coming? We'd have got something warm for supper."

At his, Master Bates roared again: so loud, that Fagin himself relaxed, and even the Dodger smiled; but as the Artful drew forth the five-pound note at that instant, it is doubtful whether the sally of the discovery awakened his merriment.

"Hallo, what's that?" inquired Sikes, stepping forward as the Jew seized the note. "That's mine, Fagin."

"No, no, my dear," said the Jew. "Mine, Bill, mine. You shall have the books."

"If that ain't mine!" said Bill Sikes, putting on his hat with a determined air; "mine and Nancy's that is; I'll take the boy back again."

The Jew started. Oliver started too, though from a very different cause; for he hoped that the dispute might really end in his being taken back.

"Come! Hand over, will you?" said Sikes.

"This is hardly fair, Bill; hardly fair, is it, Nancy?" inquired the Jew.

"Fair, or not fair," retorted Sikes, "hand over, I tell you! Do you think Nancy and me has got nothing else to do with our precious time but to spend it in scouting arter, and kidnapping, every young boy as gets grabbed through you? Give it here, you avaricious old skeleton, give it here!"

With this gentle remonstrance, Mr. Sikes plucked the note from between the Jew's finger and thumb; and looking the old man coolly in the face, folded it up small, and tied it in his neckerchief.

"That's for our share of the trouble," said Sikes; "and not half enough, neither. You may keep the books, if you're fond of reading. If you ain't, sell 'em."

"They're very pretty," said Charley Bates: who, with sundry grimaces, had been affecting to read one of the volumes in question; "beautiful writing, isn't is, Oliver?" At sight of the dismayed look with which Oliver regarded his tormentors, Master Bates, who was blessed with a lively sense of the ludicrous, fell into another ectasy, more boisterous than the first.

"They belong to the old gentleman," said Oliver, wringing his hands; "to the good, kind, old gentleman who took me into his house, and had me nursed, when I was near dying of the fever. Oh, pray send them back; send him back the books and money. Keep me here all my life long; but pray, pray send them back. He'll think I stole them; the old lady: all of them who were so kind to me: will think I stole them. Oh, do have mercy upon me, and send them back!"

With these words, which were uttered with all the energy of passionate grief, Oliver fell upon his knees at the Jew's feet; and beat his hands together, in perfect desperation.

"The boy's right," remarked Fagin, looking covertly round, and knitting his shaggy eyebrows into a hard knot. "You're right, Oliver, you're right; they WILL think you have stolen 'em. Ha! ha!" chuckled the Jew, rubbing his hands, "it couldn't have happened better, if we had chosen our time!"

"Of course it couldn't," replied Sikes; "I know'd that, directly I see him coming through Clerkenwell, with the books under his arm. It's all right enough. They're soft-hearted psalm-singers, or they wouldn't have taken him in at all; and they'll ask no questions after him, fear they should be obliged to prosecute, and so get him lagged. He's safe enough."

Oliver had looked from one to the other, while these words were being spoken, as if he were bewildered, and could scarcely understand what passed; but when Bill Sikes concluded, he jumped suddenly to his feet, and tore wildly from the room: uttering shrieks for help, which made the bare old house echo to the roof.

"Keep back the dog, Bill!" cried Nancy, springing before the door, and closing it, as the Jew and his two pupils darted out in pursuit. "Keep back the dog; he'll tear the boy to pieces."

"Serve him right!" cried Sikes, struggling to disengage himself from the girl's grasp. "Stand off from me, or I'll split your head against the wall."

"I don't care for that, Bill, I don't care for that," screamed the girl, struggling violently with the man, "the child shan't be torn down by the dog, unless you kill me first."

"Shan't he!" said Sikes, setting his teeth. "I'll soon do that, if you don't keep off."

The housebreaker flung the girl from him to the further end of the room, just as the Jew and the two boys returned, dragging Oliver among them.

"What's the matter here!" said Fagin, looking round.

"The girl's gone mad, I think," replied Sikes, savagely.

"No, she hasn't," said Nancy, pale and breathless from the scuffle; "no, she hasn't, Fagin; don't think it."

"Then keep quiet, will you?" said the Jew, with a threatening look.

"No, I won't do that, neither," replied Nancy, speaking very loud. "Come! What do you think of that?"

Mr. Fagin was sufficiently well acquainted with the manners and customs of that particular species of humanity to which Nancy belonged, to feel tolerably certain that it would be rather unsafe to prolong any conversation with her, at present. With the view of diverting the attention of the company, he turned to Oliver.

"So you wanted to get away, my dear, did you?" said the Jew, taking up a jagged and knotted club which law in a corner of the fireplace; "eh?"

Oliver made no reply. But he watched the Jew's motions, and breathed quickly.

"Wanted to get assistance; called for the police; did you?" sneered the Jew, catching the boy by the arm. "We'll cure you of that, my young master."

The Jew inflicted a smart blow on Oliver's shoulders with the club; and was raising it for a second, when the girl, rushing forward, wrested it from his hand. She flung it into the fire, with a force that brought some of the glowing coals whirling out into the room.

"I won't stand by and see it done, Fagin," cried the girl. "You've got the boy, and what more would you have?—Let him be—let him be—or I shall put that mark on some of you, that will bring me to the gallows before my time."

The girl stamped her foot violently on the floor as she vented this threat; and with her lips compressed, and her hands clenched, looked alternately at the Jew and the other robber: her face quite colourless from the passion of rage into which she had gradually worked herself.

"Why, Nancy!" said the Jew, in a soothing tone; after a pause, during which he and Mr. Sikes had stared at one another in a disconcerted manner; "you,—you're more clever than ever to-night. Ha! ha! my dear, you are acting beautifully."

"Am I!" said the girl. "Take care I don't overdo it. You will be the worse for it, Fagin, if I do; and so I tell you in good time to keep clear of me."

There is something about a roused woman: especially if she add to all her other strong passions, the fierce impulses of recklessness and despair; which few men like to provoke. The Jew saw that it would be hopeless to affect any further mistake regarding the reality of Miss Nancy's rage; and, shrinking involuntarily back a few paces, cast a glance, half imploring and half cowardly, at Sikes: as if to hint that he was the fittest person to pursue the dialogue.

Mr. Sikes, thus mutely appealed to; and possibly feeling his personal pride and influence interested in the immediate reduction of Miss Nancy to reason; gave utterance to about a couple of score of curses and threats, the rapid production of which reflected great credit on the fertility of his invention. As they produced no visible effect on the object against whom they were discharged, however, he resorted to more tangible arguments.

"What do you mean by this?" said Sikes; backing the inquiry with a very common imprecation concerning the most beautiful of human features: which, if it were heard above, only once out of every fifty thousand times that it is uttered below, would render blindness as common a disorder as measles: "what do you mean by it? Burn my body! Do you know who you are, and what you are?"

"Oh, yes, I know all about it," replied the girl, laughing hysterically; and shaking her head from side to side, with a poor assumption of indifference.

"Well, then, keep quiet," rejoined Sikes, with a growl like that he was accustomed to use when addressing his dog, "or I'll quiet you for a good long time to come."

The girl laughed again: even less composedly than before; and, darting a hasty look at Sikes, turned her face aside, and bit her lip till the blood came.

"You're a nice one," added Sikes, as he surveyed her with a contemptuous air, "to take up the humane and gen—teel side! A pretty subject for the child, as you call him, to make a friend of!"

"God Almighty help me, I am!" cried the girl passionately; "and I wish I had been struck dead in the street, or had changed places with them we passed so near to-night, before I had lent a hand in bringing him here. He's a thief, a liar, a devil, all that's bad, from this night forth. Isn't that enough for the old wretch, without blows?"

"Come, come, Sikes," said the Jew appealing to him in a remonstratory tone, and motioning towards the boys, who were eagerly attentive to all that passed; "we must have civil words; civil words, Bill."

"Civil words!" cried the girl, whose passion was frightful to see. "Civil words, you villain! Yes, you deserve 'em from me. I thieved for you when I was a child not half as old as this!" pointing to Oliver. "I have been in the same trade, and in the same service, for twelve years since. Don't you know it? Speak out! Don't you know it?"

"Well, well," replied the Jew, with an attempt at pacification; "and, if you have, it's your living!"

"Aye, it is!" returned the girl; not speaking, but pouring out the words in one continuous and vehement scream. "It is my living; and the cold, wet, dirty streets are my home; and you're the wretch that drove me to them long ago, and that'll keep me there, day and night, day and night, till I die!"

"I shall do you a mischief!" interposed the Jew, goaded by these reproaches; "a mischief worse than that, if you say much more!"

The girl said nothing more; but, tearing her hair and dress in a transport of passion, made such a rush at the Jew as would probably have left signal marks of her revenge upon him, had not her wrists been seized by Sikes at the right moment; upon which, she made a few ineffectual struggles, and fainted.

"She's all right now," said Sikes, laying her down in a corner. "She's uncommon strong in the arms, when she's up in this way."

The Jew wiped his forehead: and smiled, as if it were a relief to have the disturbance over; but neither he, nor Sikes, nor the dog, nor the boys, seemed to consider it in any other light than a common occurance incidental to business.

"It's the worst of having to do with women," said the Jew, replacing his club; "but they're clever, and we can't get on, in our line, without 'em. Charley, show Oliver to bed."

"I suppose he'd better not wear his best clothes tomorrow, Fagin, had he?" inquired Charley Bates.

"Certainly not," replied the Jew, reciprocating the grin with which Charley put the question.

Master Bates, apparently much delighted with his commission, took the cleft stick: and led Oliver into an adjacent kitchen, where there were two or three of the beds on which he had slept before; and here, with many uncontrollable bursts of laughter, he produced the identical old suit of clothes which Oliver had so much congratulated himself upon leaving off at Mr. Brownlow's; and the accidental display of which, to Fagin, by the Jew who purchased them, had been the very first clue received, of his whereabout.

"Put off the smart ones," said Charley, "and I'll give 'em to Fagin to take care of. What fun it is!"

Poor Oliver unwillingly complied. Master Bates rolling up the new clothes under his arm, departed from the room, leaving Oliver in the dark, and locking the door behind him.

The noise of Charley's laughter, and the voice of Miss Betsy, who opportunely arrived to throw water over her friend, and perform other feminine offices for the promotion of her recovery, might have kept many people awake under more happy circumstances than those in which Oliver was placed. But he was sick and weary; and he soon fell sound asleep.

CHAPTER XVII

Oliver's Destiny Continuing Unpropitious, Brings a Great Man to London to Injure His Reputation

It is the custom on the stage, in all good murderous melodramas, to present the tragic and the comic scenes, in as regular alternation, as the layers of red and white in a side of streaky bacon. The hero sinks upon his straw bed, weighed down by fetters and misfortunes; in the next scene, his faithful but unconscious squire regales the audience with a comic song. We behold, with throbbing bosoms, the heroine in the grasp of a proud and ruthless baron: her virtue and her life alike in danger, drawing forth her dagger to preserve the one at the cost of the other; and just as our expectations are wrought up to the highest pitch, a whistle is heard, and we are straightway transported to the great hall of the castle; where a grey-headed seneschal sings a funny chorus with a funnier body of vassals, who are free of all sorts of places, from church vaults to palaces, and roam about in company, carolling perpetually.

Such changes appear absurd; but they are not so unnatural as they would seem at first sight. The transitions in real life from well-spread boards to death-beds, and from mourning-weeds to holiday garments, are not a whit less startling; only, there, we are busy actors, instead of passive lookers-on, which makes a vast difference. The actors in the mimic life of the theatre, are blind to violent transitions and abrupt impulses of passion or feeling, which, presented before the eyes of mere spectators, are at once condemned as outrageous and preposterous.

As sudden shiftings of the scene, and rapid changes of time and place, are not only sanctioned in books by long usage, but are by many considered as the great art of authorship: an author's skill in his craft being, by such critics, chiefly estimated with relation to the dilemmas in which he leaves his characters at the end of every chapter: this brief introduction to the present one may perhaps be deemed unnecessary. If so, let it be considered a delicate intimation on the part of the historian that he is going back to the town in which Oliver Twist was born; the reader taking it for granted that there are good and substantial reasons for making the journey, or he would not be invited to proceed upon such an expedition.

Mr. Bumble emerged at early morning from the workhouse-gate, and walked with portly carriage and commanding steps, up the High Street. He was in the full bloom and pride of beadlehood; his cocked hat and coat were dazzling in the morning sun; he clutched his cane with the vigorous tenacity of health and power. Mr. Bumble always carried his head high; but this morning it was higher than usual. There was an abstraction in his eye, an elevation in his air, which might have warned an observant stranger that thoughts were passing in the beadle's mind, too great for utterance.

Mr. Bumble stopped not to converse with the small shopkeepers and others who spoke to him, deferentially, as he passed along. He merely returned their salutations with a wave of his hand, and relaxed not in his dignified pace, until he reached the farm where Mrs. Mann tended the infant paupers with parochial care.

"Drat that beadle!" said Mrs. Mann, hearing the well-known shaking at the garden-gate. "If it isn't him at this time in the morning! Lauk, Mr. Bumble, only think of its being you! Well, dear me, it IS a pleasure, this is! Come into the parlour, sir, please."

The first sentence was addressed to Susan; and the exclamations of delight were uttered to Mr. Bumble: as the good lady unlocked the garden-gate: and showed him, with great attention and respect, into the house.

"Mrs. Mann," said Mr. Bumble; not sitting upon, or dropping himself into a seat, as any common jackanapes would: but letting himself gradually and slowly down into a chair; "Mrs. Mann, ma'am, good morning."

"Well, and good morning to you, sir," replied Mrs. Mann, with many smiles; "and hoping you find yourself well, sir!"

"So-so, Mrs. Mann," replied the beadle. "A porochial life is not a bed of roses, Mrs. Mann."

"Ah, that it isn't indeed, Mr. Bumble," rejoined the lady. And all the infant paupers might have chorussed the rejoinder with great propriety, if they had heard it.

"A porochial life, ma'am," continued Mr. Bumble, striking the table with his cane, "is a life of worrit, and vexation, and hardihood; but all public characters, as I may say, must suffer prosecution."

Mrs. Mann, not very well knowing what the beadle meant, raised her hands with a look of sympathy, and sighed.

"Ah! You may well sigh, Mrs. Mann!" said the beadle.

Finding she had done right, Mrs. Mann sighed again: evidently to the satisfaction of the public character: who, repressing a complacent smile by looking sternly at his cocked hat, said,

"Mrs. Mann, I am going to London."

"Lauk, Mr. Bumble!" cried Mrs. Mann, starting back.

"To London, ma'am," resumed the inflexible beadle, "by coach. I and two paupers, Mrs. Mann! A legal action is a coming on, about a settlement; and the board has appointed me—me, Mrs. Mann—to dispose to the matter before the quarter-sessions at Clerkinwell. And I very much question," added Mr. Bumble, drawing himself up, "whether the Clerkinwell Sessions will not find themselves in the wrong box before they have done with me."

"Oh! you mustn't be too hard upon them, sir," said Mrs. Mann, coaxingly.

"The Clerkinwell Sessions have brought it upon themselves, ma'am," replied Mr. Bumble; "and if the Clerkinwell Sessions find that they come off rather worse than they expected, the Clerkinwell Sessions have only themselves to thank."

There was so much determination and depth of purpose about the menacing manner in which Mr. Bumble delivered himself of these words, that Mrs. Mann appeared quite awed by them. At length she said,

"You're going by coach, sir? I thought it was always usual to send them paupers in carts."

"That's when they're ill, Mrs. Mann," said the beadle. "We put the sick paupers into open carts in the rainy weather, to prevent their taking cold."

"Oh!" said Mrs. Mann.

"The opposition coach contracts for these two; and takes them cheap," said Mr. Bumble. "They are both in a very low state, and we find it would come two pound cheaper to move 'em than to bury 'em—that is, if we can throw 'em upon another parish, which I think we shall be able to do, if they don't die upon the road to spite us. Ha! ha! ha!"

When Mr. Bumble had laughed a little while, his eyes again encountered the cocked hat; and he became grave.

"We are forgetting business, ma'am," said the beadle; "here is your porochial stipend for the month."

Mr. Bumble produced some silver money rolled up in paper, from his pocket-book; and requested a receipt: which Mrs. Mann wrote.

"It's very much blotted, sir," said the farmer of infants; "but it's formal enough, I dare say. Thank you, Mr. Bumble, sir, I am very much obliged to you, I'm sure."

Mr. Bumble nodded, blandly, in acknowledgment of Mrs. Mann's curtsey; and inquired how the children were.

"Bless their dear little hearts!" said Mrs. Mann with emotion, "they're as well as can be, the dears! Of course, except the two that died last week. And little Dick."

"Isn't that boy no better?" inquired Mr. Bumble.

Mrs. Mann shook her head.

"He's a ill-conditioned, wicious, bad-disposed porochial child that," said Mr. Bumble angrily. "Where is he?"

"I'll bring him to you in one minute, sir," replied Mrs. Mann. "Here, you Dick!"

After some calling, Dick was discovered. Having had his face put under the pump, and dried upon Mrs. Mann's gown, he was led into the awful presence of Mr. Bumble, the beadle.

The child was pale and thin; his cheeks were sunken; and his eyes large and bright. The scanty parish dress, the livery of his misery, hung loosely on his feeble body; and his young limbs had wasted away, like those of an old man.

Such was the little being who stood trembling beneath Mr. Bumble's glance; not daring to lift his eyes from the floor; and dreading even to hear the beadle's voice.

"Can't you look at the gentleman, you obstinate boy?" said Mrs. Mann.

The child meekly raised his eyes, and encountered those of Mr. Bumble.

"What's the matter with you, porochial Dick?" inquired Mr. Bumble, with well-timed jocularity.

"Nothing, sir," replied the child faintly.

"I should think not," said Mrs. Mann, who had of course laughed very much at Mr. Bumble's humour.

"You want for nothing, I'm sure."

"I should like—' faltered the child.

"Hey-day!" interposed Mr. Mann, "I suppose you're going to say that you DO want for something, now? Why, you little wretch—"

"Stop, Mrs. Mann, stop!" said the beadle, raising his hand with a show of authority. "Like what, sir, eh?"

"I should like," faltered the child, "if somebody that can write, would put a few words down for me on a piece of paper, and fold it up and seal it, and keep it for me, after I am laid in the ground."

"Why, what does the boy mean?" exclaimed Mr. Bumble, on whom the earnest manner and wan aspect of the child had made some impression: accustomed as he was to such things. "What do you mean, sir?"

"I should like," said the child, "to leave my dear love to poor Oliver Twist; and to let him know how often I have sat by myself and cried to think of his wandering about in the dark nights with nobody to help him. And I should like to tell him," said the child pressing his small hands together, and speaking with great fervour, "that I was glad to die when I was very young; for, perhaps, if I had lived to be a man, and had grown old, my little sister who is in Heaven, might forget me, or be unlike me; and it would be so much happier if we were both children there together."

Mr. Bumble surveyed the little speaker, from head to foot, with indescribable astonishment; and, turning to his companion, said, "They're all in one story, Mrs. Mann. That out-dacious Oliver had demogalized them all!"

"I couldn't have believed it, sir' said Mrs Mann, holding up her hands, and looking malignantly at Dick. "I never see such a hardened little wretch!"

"Take him away, ma'am!" said Mr. Bumble imperiously. "This must be stated to the board, Mrs. Mann.

"I hope the gentleman will understand that it isn't my fault, sir?" said Mrs. Mann, whimpering pathetically.

"They shall understand that, ma'am; they shall be acquainted with the true state of the case," said Mr. Bumble. "There; take him away, I can't bear the sight on him."

Dick was immediately taken away, and locked up in the coal-cellar. Mr. Bumble shortly afterwards took himself off, to prepare for his journey.

At six o'clock next morning, Mr. Bumble: having exchanged his cocked hat for a round one, and encased his person in a blue great-coat with a cape to it: took his place on the outside of the coach, accompanied by the criminals whose settlement was disputed; with whom, in due course of time, he arrived in London.

He experienced no other crosses on the way, than those which originated in the perverse behaviour of the two paupers, who persisted in shivering, and complaining of the cold, in a manner which, Mr. Bumble declared, caused his teeth to chatter in his head, and made him feel quite uncomfortable; although he had a great-coat on.

Having disposed of these evil-minded persons for the night, Mr. Bumble sat himself down in the house at which the coach stopped; and took a temperate dinner of steaks, oyster sauce, and porter. Putting a glass of hot gin-and-water on the chimney-piece, he drew his chair to the fire; and, with sundry moral reflections on the too-prevalent sin of discontent and complaining, composed himself to read the paper.

The very first paragraph upon which Mr. Bumble's eye rested, was the following advertisement.

"FIVE GUINEAS REWARD"

"Whereas a young boy, named Oliver Twist, absconded, or was enticed, on Thursday evening last, from his home, at Pentonville; and has not since been heard of. The above reward will be paid to any person who will give such information as will lead to the discovery of the said Oliver Twist, or tend to throw any light upon his previous history, in which the advertiser is, for many reasons, warmly interested."

And then followed a full description of Oliver's dress, person, appearance, and disappearance: with the name and address of Mr. Brownlow at full length.

Mr. Bumble opened his eyes; read the advertisement, slowly and carefully, three several times; and in something more than five minutes was on his way to Pentonville: having actually, in his excitement, left the glass of hot gin-and-water, untasted.

"Is Mr. Brownlow at home?" inquired Mr. Bumble of the girl who opened the door.

To this inquiry the girl returned the not uncommon, but rather evasive reply of "I don't know; where do you come from?"

Mr. Bumble no sooner uttered Oliver's name, in explanation of his errand, than Mrs. Bedwin, who had been listening at the parlour door, hastened into the passage in a breathless state.

"Come in, come in," said the old lady: "I knew we should hear of him. Poor dear! I knew we should! I was certain of it. Bless his heart! I said so all along."

Having heard this, the worthy old lady hurried back into the parlour again; and seating herself on a sofa, burst into tears. The girl, who was not quite so susceptible, had run upstairs meanwhile; and now returned with a request that Mr. Bumble would follow her immediately: which he did.

He was shown into the little back study, where sat Mr. Brownlow and his friend Mr. Grimwig, with decanters and glasses before them. The latter gentleman at once burst into the exclamation:

"A beadle. A parish beadle, or I'll eat my head."

"Pray don't interrupt just now," said Mr. Brownlow. "Take a seat, will you?"

Mr. Bumble sat himself down; quite confounded by the oddity of Mr. Grimwig's manner. Mr. Brownlow moved the lamp, so as to obtain an uninterrupted view of the beadle's countenance; and said, with a little impatience,

"Now, sir, you come in consequence of having seen the advertisement?"

"Yes, sir," said Mr. Bumble.

"And you ARE a beadle, are you not?" inquired Mr. Grimwig.

"I am a porochial beadle, gentlemen," rejoined Mr. Bumble proudly.

"Of course," observed Mr. Grimwig aside to his friend, "I knew he was. A beadle all over!"

Mr. Brownlow gently shook his head to impose silence on his friend, and resumed:

"Do you know where this poor boy is now?"

"No more than nobody," replied Mr. Bumble.

"Well, what DO you know of him?" inquired the old gentleman. "Speak out, my friend, if you have anything to say. What DO you know of him?"

"You don't happen to know any good of him, do you?" said Mr. Grimwig, caustically; after an attentive perusal of Mr. Bumble's features.

Mr. Bumble, catching at the inquiry very quickly, shook his head with portentous solemnity.

"You see?" said Mr. Grimwig, looking triumphantly at Mr. Brownlow.

Mr. Brownlow looked apprehensively at Mr. Bumble's pursed-up countenance; and requested him to communicate what he knew regarding Oliver, in as few words as possible.

Mr. Bumble put down his hat; unbuttoned his coat; folded his arms; inclined his head in a retrospective manner; and, after a few moments' reflection, commenced his story.

It would be tedious if given in the beadle's words: occupying, as it did, some twenty minutes in the telling; but the sum and substance of it was, that Oliver was a foundling, born of low and vicious parents. That he had, from his birth, displayed no better qualities than treachery, ingratitude, and malice. That he had terminated his brief career in the place of his birth, by making a sanguinary and cowardly attack on an unoffending lad, and running away in the night-time from his master's house. In proof of his really being the person he represented himself, Mr. Bumble laid upon the table the papers he had brought to town. Folding his arms again, he then awaited Mr. Brownlow's observations.

"I fear it is all too true," said the old gentleman sorrowfully, after looking over the papers. "This is not much for your intelligence; but I would gladly have given you treble the money, if it had been favourable to the boy."

It is not improbable that if Mr. Bumble had been possessed of this information at an earlier period of the interview, he might have imparted a very different colouring to his little history. It was too late to do it now, however; so he shook his head gravely, and, pocketing the five guineas, withdrew.

Mr. Brownlow paced the room to and fro for some minutes; evidently so much disturbed by the beadle's tale, that even Mr. Grimwig forbore to vex him further.

At length he stopped, and rang the bell violently.

"Mrs. Bedwin," said Mr. Brownlow, when the housekeeper appeared; "that boy, Oliver, is an imposter."

"It can't be, sir. It cannot be," said the old lady energetically.

"I tell you he is," retorted the old gentleman. "What do you mean by can't be? We have just heard a full account of him from his birth; and he has been a thorough-paced little villain, all his life."

"I never will believe it, sir," replied the old lady, firmly. "Never!"

"You old women never believe anything but quack-doctors, and lying story-books," growled Mr. Grimwig. "I knew it all along. Why didn't you take my advise in the beginning; you would if he hadn't had a fever, I suppose, eh? He was interesting, wasn't he? Interesting! Bah!" And Mr. Grimwig poked the fire with a flourish.

"He was a dear, grateful, gentle child, sir," retorted Mrs. Bedwin, indignantly. "I know what children are, sir; and have done these forty years; and people who can't say the same, shouldn't say anything about them. That's my opinion!"

This was a hard hit at Mr. Grimwig, who was a bachelor. As it extorted nothing from that gentleman but a smile, the old lady tossed her head, and smoothed down her apron preparatory to another speech, when she was stopped by Mr. Brownlow.

"Silence!" said the old gentleman, feigning an anger he was far from feeling. "Never let me hear the boy's name again. I rang to tell you that. Never. Never, on any pretence, mind! You may leave the room, Mrs. Bedwin. Remember! I am in earnest."

There were sad hearts at Mr. Brownlow's that night.

Oliver's heart sank within him, when he thought of his good friends; it was well for him that he could not know what they had heard, or it might have broken outright.

CHAPTER XVIII

How Oliver Passed His Time in the Improving Society of His Reputable Friends

About noon next day, when the Dodger and Master Bates had gone out to pursue their customary avocations, Mr. Fagin took the opportunity of reading Oliver a long lecture on the crying sin of ingratitude; of which he clearly demonstrated he had been guilty, to no ordinary extent, in wilfully absenting himself from the society of his anxious friends; and, still more, in endeavouring to escape from them after so much trouble and expense had been incurred in his recovery. Mr. Fagin laid great stress on the fact of his having taken Oliver in, and cherished him, when, without his timely aid, he might have perished with hunger; and he related the dismal and affecting history of a young lad whom, in his philanthropy, he had succoured under parallel circumstances, but who, proving unworthy of his confidence and evincing a desire to communicate with the police, had unfortunately come to be hanged at the Old Bailey one morning. Mr. Fagin did not seek to conceal his share in the catastrophe, but lamented with tears in his eyes that the wrong-headed and treacherous behaviour of the young person in question, had rendered it necessary that he should become the victim of certain evidence for the crown: which, if it were not precisely true, was indispensably necessary for the safety of him (Mr. Fagin) and a few select friends.

Mr. Fagin concluded by drawing a rather disagreeable picture of the discomforts of hanging; and, with great friendliness and politeness of manner, expressed his anxious hopes that he might never be obliged to submit Oliver Twist to that unpleasant operation.

Little Oliver's blood ran cold, as he listened to the Jew's words, and imperfectly comprehended the dark threats conveyed in them. That it was possible even for justice itself to confound the innocent with the guilty when they were in accidental companionship, he knew already; and that deeply-laid plans for the destruction of inconveniently knowing or over-communicative persons, had been really devised and carried out by the Jew on more occasions than one, he thought by no means unlikely, when he recollected the general nature of the altercations between that gentleman and Mr. Sikes: which seemed to bear reference to some foregone conspiracy of the kind. As he glanced timidly up, and met the Jew's searching look, he felt that his pale face and trembling limbs were neither unnoticed nor unrelished by that wary old gentleman.

The Jew, smiling hideously, patted Oliver on the head, and said, that if he kept himself quiet, and applied himself to business, he saw they would be very good friends yet. Then, taking his hat, and covering himself with an old patched great-coat, he went out, and locked the room-door behind him.

And so Oliver remained all that day, and for the greater part of many subsequent days, seeing nobody, between early morning and midnight, and left during the long hours to commune with his own thoughts. Which, never failing to revert to his kind friends, and the opinion they must long ago have formed of him, were sad indeed.

After the lapse of a week or so, the Jew left the room-door unlocked; and he was at liberty to wander about the house.

It was a very dirty place. The rooms upstairs had great high wooden chimney-pieces and large doors, with panelled walls and cornices to the ceiling; which, although they were black with neglect and dust, were ornamented in various ways. From all of these tokens Oliver concluded that a long time ago, before the old Jew was born, it had belonged to better people, and had perhaps been quite gay and handsome: dismal and dreary as it looked now.

Spiders had built their webs in the angles of the walls and ceilings; and sometimes, when Oliver walked softly into a room, the mice would scamper across the floor, and run back terrified to their holes. With these exceptions, there was neither sight nor sound of any living thing; and often, when it grew dark, and he was tired of wandering from room to room, he would crouch in the corner of the passage by the street-door, to be as near living people as he could; and would remain there, listening and counting the hours, until the Jew or the boys returned.

In all the rooms, the mouldering shutters were fast closed: the bars which held them were screwed tight into the wood; the only light which was admitted, stealing its way through round holes at the top: which made the rooms more gloomy, and filled them with strange shadows. There was a back-garret window with rusty bars outside, which had no shutter; and out of this, Oliver often gazed with a melancholy face for hours together; but nothing was to be descried from it but a confused and crowded mass of housetops, blackened chimneys, and gable-ends. Sometimes, indeed, a grizzly head might be seen, peering over the parapet-wall of a distant house; but it was quickly withdrawn again; and as the window of Oliver's observatory was nailed down, and dimmed with the rain and smoke of years, it was as much as he could do to make out the forms of the different objects beyond, without making any attempt to be seen or heard,—which he had as much chance of being, as if he had lived inside the ball of St. Paul's Cathedral.

One afternoon, the Dodger and Master Bates being engaged out that evening, the first-named young gentleman took it into his head to evince some anxiety regarding the decoration of his person (to do him justice, this was by no means an habitual weakness with him); and, with this end and aim, he condescendingly commanded Oliver to assist him in his toilet, straightway.

Oliver was but too glad to make himself useful; too happy to have some faces, however bad, to look upon; too desirous to conciliate those about him when he could honestly do so; to throw any objection in the way of this proposal. So he at once expressed his readiness; and, kneeling on the floor, while the Dodger sat upon the table so that he could take his foot in his laps, he applied himself to a process which Mr. Dawkins designated as "japanning his trotter-cases." The phrase, rendered into plain English, signifieth, cleaning his boots.

Whether it was the sense of freedom and independence which a rational animal may be supposed to feel when he sits on a table in an easy attitude smoking a pipe, swinging one leg carelessly to and fro, and having his boots cleaned all the time, without even the past trouble of having taken them off, or the prospective misery of putting them on, to disturb his reflections; or whether it was the goodness of the tobacco that soothed the feelings of the Dodger, or the mildness of the beer that mollified his thoughts; he was evidently tinctured, for the nonce, with a spice of romance and enthusiasm, foreign to his general nature. He looked down on Oliver, with a thoughtful countenance, for a brief space; and then, raising his head, and heaving a gentle sign, said, half in abstraction, and half to Master Bates:

"What a pity it is he isn't a prig!"

"Ah!" said Master Charles Bates; "he don't know what's good for him."

The Dodger sighed again, and resumed his pipe: as did Charley Bates. They both smoked, for some seconds, in silence.

"I suppose you don't even know what a prig is?" said the Dodger mournfully.

"I think I know that," replied Oliver, looking up. "It's a the—; you're one, are you not?" inquired Oliver, checking himself.

"I am," replied the Dodger. "I'd scorn to be anything else." Mr. Dawkins gave his hat a ferocious cock, after delivering this sentiment, and looked at Master Bates, as if to denote that he would feel obliged by his saying anything to the contrary.

"I am," repeated the Dodger. "So's Charley. So's Fagin. So's Sikes. So's Nancy. So's Bet. So we all are, down to the dog. And he's the downiest one of the lot!"

"And the least given to peaching," added Charley Bates.

"He wouldn't so much as bark in a witness-box, for fear of committing himself; no, not if you tied him up in one, and left him there without wittles for a fortnight," said the Dodger.

"Not a bit of it," observed Charley.

"He's a rum dog. Don't he look fierce at any strange cove that laughs or sings when he's in company!" pursued the Dodger. "Won't he growl at all, when he hears a fiddle playing! And don't he hate other dogs as ain't of his breed! Oh, no!"

"He's an out-and-out Christian," said Charley.

This was merely intended as a tribute to the animal's abilities, but it was an appropriate remark in another sense, if Master Bates had only known it; for there are a good many ladies and gentlemen, claiming to be out-and-out Christians, between whom, and Mr. Sikes' dog, there exist strong and singular points of resemblance.

"Well, well," said the Dodger, recurring to the point from which they had strayed: with that mindfulness of his profession which influenced all his proceedings. "This hasn't go anything to do with young Green here."

"No more it has," said Charley. "Why don't you put yourself under Fagin, Oliver?"

"And make your fortun' out of hand?" added the Dodger, with a grin.

"And so be able to retire on your property, and do the gen-teel: as I mean to, in the very next leap-year but four that ever comes, and the forty-second Tuesday in Trinity-week," said Charley Bates.

"I don't like it," rejoined Oliver, timidly; "I wish they would let me go. I—I—would rather go."

"And Fagin would RATHER not!" rejoined Charley.

Oliver knew this too well; but thinking it might be dangerous to express his feelings more openly, he only sighed, and went on with his boot-cleaning.

"Go!" exclaimed the Dodger. "Why, where's your spirit? Don't you take any pride out of yourself? Would you go and be dependent on your friends?"

"Oh, blow that!" said Master Bates: drawing two or three silk handkerchiefs from his pocket, and tossing them into a cupboard, "that's too mean; that is."

"I couldn't do it," said the Dodger, with an air of haughty disgust.

"You can leave your friends, though," said Oliver with a half smile; "and let them be punished for what you did."

"That," rejoined the Dodger, with a wave of his pipe, "That was all out of consideration for Fagin, 'cause the traps know that we work together, and he might have got into trouble if we hadn't made our lucky; that was the move, wasn't it, Charley?"

Master Bates nodded assent, and would have spoken, but the recollection of Oliver's flight came so suddenly upon him, that the smoke he was inhaling got entangled with a laugh, and went up into his head, and down into his throat: and brought on a fit of coughing and stamping, about five minutes long.

"Look here!" said the Dodger, drawing forth a handful of shillings and halfpence. "Here's a jolly life! What's the odds where it comes from? Here, catch hold; there's plenty more where they were took from. You won't, won't you? Oh, you precious flat!"

"It's naughty, ain't it, Oliver?" inquired Charley Bates. "He'll come to be scragged, won't he?"

"I don't know what that means," replied Oliver.

"Something in this way, old feller," said Charly. As he said it, Master Bates caught up an end of his neckerchief; and, holding it erect in the air, dropped his head on his shoulder, and jerked a curious sound through his teeth; thereby indicating, by a lively pantomimic representation, that scragging and hanging were one and the same thing.

"That's what it means," said Charley. "Look how he stares, Jack! I never did see such prime company as that 'ere boy; he'll be the death of me, I know he will." Master Charley Bates, having laughed heartily again, resumed his pipe with tears in his eyes.

"You've been brought up bad," said the Dodger, surveying his boots with much satisfaction when Oliver had polished them. "Fagin will make something of you, though, or you'll be the first he ever had that turned out unprofitable. You'd better begin at once; for you'll come to the trade long before you think of it; and you're only losing time, Oliver."

Master Bates backed this advice with sundry moral admonitions of his own: which, being exhausted, he and his friend Mr. Dawkins launched into a glowing description of the numerous pleasures incidental to the life they led, interspersed with a variety of hints to Oliver that the best thing he could do, would be to secure Fagin's favour without more delay, by the means which they themselves had employed to gain it.

"And always put this in your pipe, Nolly," said the Dodger, as the Jew was heard unlocking the door above, "if you don't take fogels and tickers—"

"What's the good of talking in that way?" interposed Master Bates; "he don't know what you mean."

"If you don't take pocket-handkechers and watches," said the Dodger, reducing his conversation to the level of Oliver's capacity, "some other cove will; so that the coves that lose 'em will be all the worse, and you'll be all the worse, too, and nobody half a ha'p'orth the better, except the chaps wot gets them—and you've just as good a right to them as they have."

"To be sure, to be sure!" said the Jew, who had entered unseen by Oliver. "It all lies in a nutshell my dear; in a nutshell, take the Dodger's word for it. Ha! ha! ha! He understands the catechism of his trade."

The old man rubbed his hands gleefully together, as he corroborated the Dodger's reasoning in these terms; and chuckled with delight at his pupil's proficiency.

The conversation proceeded no farther at this time, for the Jew had returned home accompanied by Miss Betsy, and a gentleman whom Oliver had never seen before, but who was accosted by the Dodger as Tom Chitling; and who, having lingered on the stairs to exchange a few gallantries with the lady, now made his appearance.

Mr. Chitling was older in years than the Dodger: having perhaps numbered eighteen winters; but there was a degree of deference in his deportment towards that young gentleman which seemed to indicate that he felt himself conscious of a slight inferiority in point of genius and professional aquirements. He had small twinkling eyes, and a pock-marked face; wore a fur cap, a dark corduroy jacket, greasy fustian trousers, and an apron. His wardrobe was, in truth, rather out of repair; but he excused himself to the company by stating that his "time" was only out an hour before; and that, in consequence of having worn the regimentals for six weeks past, he had not been able to bestow any attention on his private clothes. Mr. Chitling added, with strong marks of irritation, that the new way of fumigating clothes up yonder was infernal unconstitutional, for it burnt holes in them, and there was no remedy against the County. The same remark he considered to apply to the regulation mode of cutting the hair: which he held to be decidedly unlawful. Mr. Chitling wound up his observations by stating that he had not touched a drop of anything for forty-two moral long hard-working days; and that he "wished he might be busted if he warn't as dry as a lime-basket."

"Where do you think the gentleman has come from, Oliver?" inquired the Jew, with a grin, as the other boys put a bottle of spirits on the table.

"I—I—don't know, sir," replied Oliver.

"Who's that?" inquired Tom Chitling, casting a contemptuous look at Oliver.

"A young friend of mine, my dear," replied the Jew.

"He's in luck, then," said the young man, with a meaning look at Fagin. "Never mind where I came from, young 'un; you'll find your way there, soon enough, I'll bet a crown!"

At this sally, the boys laughed. After some more jokes on the same subject, they exchanged a few short whispers with Fagin; and withdrew.

After some words apart between the last comer and Fagin, they drew their chairs towards the fire; and the Jew, telling Oliver to come and sit by him, led the conversation to the topics most calculated to interest his hearers. These were, the great advantages of the trade, the proficiency of the Dodger, the amiability of Charley Bates, and the liberality of the Jew himself. At length these subjects displayed signs of being thoroughly exhausted; and Mr. Chitling did the same: for the house of correction becomes fatiguing after a week or two. Miss Betsy accordingly withdrew; and left the party to their repose.

From this day, Oliver was seldom left alone; but was placed in almost constant communication with the two boys, who played the old game with the Jew every day: whether for their own improvement or Oliver's, Mr. Fagin best knew. At other times the old man would tell them stories of robberies he had committed in his younger days: mixed up with so much that was droll and curious, that Oliver could not help laughing heartily, and showing that he was amused in spite of all his better feelings.

In short, the wily old Jew had the boy in his toils. Having prepared his mind, by solitude and gloom, to prefer any society to the companionship of his own sad thoughts in such a dreary place, he was now slowly instilling into his soul the poison which he hoped would blacken it, and change its hue for ever.

CHAPTER XIX

In Which a Notable Plan Is Discussed and Determined On

It was a chill, damp, windy night, when the Jew: buttoning his great-coat tight round his shrivelled body, and pulling the collar up over his ears so as completely to obscure the lower part of his face: emerged from his den. He paused on the step as the door was locked and chained behind him; and having listened while the boys made all secure, and until their retreating footsteps were no longer audible, slunk down the street as quickly as he could.

The house to which Oliver had been conveyed, was in the neighborhood of Whitechapel. The Jew stopped for an instant at the corner of the street; and, glancing suspiciously round, crossed the road, and struck off in the direction of the Spitalfields.

The mud lay thick upon the stones, and a black mist hung over the streets; the rain fell sluggishly down, and everything felt cold and clammy to the touch. It seemed just the night when it befitted such a being as the Jew to be abroad. As he glided stealthily along, creeping beneath the shelter of the walls and doorways, the hideous old man seemed like some loathsome reptile, engendered in the slime and darkness through which he moved: crawling forth, by night, in search of some rich offal for a meal.

He kept on his course, through many winding and narrow ways, until he reached Bethnal Green; then, turning suddenly off to the left, he soon became involved in a maze of the mean and dirty streets which abound in that close and densely-populated quarter.

The Jew was evidently too familiar with the ground he traversed to be at all bewildered, either by the darkness of the night, or the intricacies of the way. He hurried through several alleys and streets, and at length turned into one, lighted only by a single lamp at the farther end. At the door of a house in this street, he knocked; having exchanged a few muttered words with the person who opened it, he walked upstairs.

A dog growled as he touched the handle of a room-door; and a man's voice demanded who was there.

"Only me, Bill; only me, my dear," said the Jew looking in.

"Bring in your body then," said Sikes. "Lie down, you stupid brute! Don't you know the devil when he's got a great-coat on?"

Apparently, the dog had been somewhat deceived by Mr. Fagin's outer garment; for as the Jew unbuttoned it, and threw it over the back of a chair, he retired to the corner from which he had risen: wagging his tail as he went, to show that he was as well satisfied as it was in his nature to be.

"Well!" said Sikes.

"Well, my dear," replied the Jew.—"Ah! Nancy."

The latter recognition was uttered with just enough of embarrassment to imply a doubt of its reception; for Mr. Fagin and his young friend had not met, since she had interfered in behalf of Oliver. All doubts upon the subject, if he had any, were speedily removed by the young lady's behaviour. She took her feet off the fender, pushed back her chair, and bade Fagin draw up his, without saying more about it: for it was a cold night, and no mistake.

"It is cold, Nancy dear," said the Jew, as he warmed his skinny hands over the fire. "It seems to go right through one," added the old man, touching his side.

"It must be a piercer, if it finds its way through your heart," said Mr. Sikes. "Give him something to drink, Nancy. Burn my body, make haste! It's enough to turn a man ill, to see his lean old carcase shivering in that way, like a ugly ghost just rose from the grave."

Nancy quickly brought a bottle from a cupboard, in which there were many: which, to judge from the diversity of their appearance, were filled with several kinds of liquids. Sikes pouring out a glass of brandy, bade the Jew drink it off.

"Quite enough, quite, thankye, Bill," replied the Jew, putting down the glass after just setting his lips to it.

"What! You're afraid of our getting the better of you, are you?" inquired Sikes, fixing his eyes on the Jew. "Ugh!"

With a hoarse grunt of contempt, Mr. Sikes seized the glass, and threw the remainder of its contents into the ashes: as a preparatory ceremony to filling it again for himself: which he did at once.

The Jew glanced round the room, as his companion tossed down the second glassful; not in curiosity, for he had seen it often before; but in a restless and suspicious manner habitual to him. It was a meanly furnished apartment, with nothing but the contents of the closet to induce the belief that its occupier was anything but a working man; and with no more suspicious articles displayed to view than two or three heavy bludgeons which stood in a corner, and a "life-preserver" that hung over the chimney-piece.

"There," said Sikes, smacking his lips. "Now I'm ready."

"For business?" inquired the Jew.

"For business," replied Sikes; "so say what you've got to say."

"About the crib at Chertsey, Bill?" said the Jew, drawing his chair forward, and speaking in a very low voice.

"Yes. Wot about it?" inquired Sikes.

"Ah! you know what I mean, my dear," said the Jew. "He knows what I mean, Nancy; don't he?"

"No, he don't," sneered Mr. Sikes. "Or he won't, and that's the same thing. Speak out, and call things by their right names; don't sit there, winking and blinking, and talking to me in hints, as if you warn't the very first that thought about the robbery. Wot d'ye mean?"

"Hush, Bill, hush!" said the Jew, who had in vain attempted to stop this burst of indignation; "somebody will hear us, my dear. Somebody will hear us."

"Let 'em hear!" said Sikes; "I don't care.' But as Mr. Sikes DID care, on reflection, he dropped his voice as he said the words, and grew calmer.

"There, there," said the Jew, coaxingly. "It was only my caution, nothing more. Now, my dear, about that crib at Chertsey; when is it to be done, Bill, eh? When is it to be done? Such plate, my dear, such plate!" said the Jew: rubbing his hands, and elevating his eyebrows in a rapture of anticipation.

"Not at all," replied Sikes coldly.

"Not to be done at all!" echoed the Jew, leaning back in his chair.

"No, not at all," rejoined Sikes. "At least it can't be a put-up job, as we expected."

"Then it hasn't been properly gone about," said the Jew, turning pale with anger. "Don't tell me!"

"But I will tell you," retorted Sikes. "Who are you that's not to be told? I tell you that Toby Crackit has been hanging about the place for a fortnight, and he can't get one of the servants in line."

"Do you mean to tell me, Bill," said the Jew: softening as the other grew heated: "that neither of the two men in the house can be got over?"

"Yes, I do mean to tell you so," replied Sikes. "The old lady has had 'em these twenty years; and if you were to give 'em five hundred pound, they wouldn't be in it."

"But do you mean to say, my dear," remonstrated the Jew, "that the women can't be got over?"

"Not a bit of it," replied Sikes.

"Not by flash Toby Crackit?" said the Jew incredulously. "Think what women are, Bill,"

"No; not even by flash Toby Crackit," replied Sikes. "He says he's worn sham whiskers, and a canary waistcoat, the whole blessed time he's been loitering down there, and it's all of no use."

"He should have tried mustachios and a pair of military trousers, my dear," said the Jew.

"So he did," rejoined Sikes, "and they warn't of no more use than the other plant."

The Jew looked blank at this information. After ruminating for some minutes with his chin sunk on his breast, he raised his head and said, with a deep sigh, that if flash Toby Crackit reported aright, he feared the game was up.

"And yet," said the old man, dropping his hands on his knees, "it's a sad thing, my dear, to lose so much when we had set our hearts upon it."

"So it is," said Mr. Sikes. "Worse luck!"

A long silence ensued; during which the Jew was plunged in deep thought, with his face wrinkled into an expression of villainy perfectly demoniacal. Sikes eyed him furtively from time to time. Nancy, apparently fearful of irritating the housebreaker, sat with her eyes fixed upon the fire, as if she had been deaf to all that passed.

"Fagin," said Sikes, abruptly breaking the stillness that prevailed; "is it worth fifty shiners extra, if it's safely done from the outside?"

"Yes," said the Jew, as suddenly rousing himself.

"Is it a bargain?" inquired Sikes.

"Yes, my dear, yes," rejoined the Jew; his eyes glistening, and every muscle in his face working, with the excitement that the inquiry had awakened.

"Then," said Sikes, thrusting aside the Jew's hand, with some disdain, "let it come off as soon as you like. Toby and me were over the garden-wall the night afore last, sounding the panels of the door and shutters. The crib's barred up at night like a jail; but there's one part we can crack, safe and softly."

"Which is that, Bill?" asked the Jew eagerly.

"Why," whispered Sikes, "as you cross the lawn—"

"Yes?" said the Jew, bending his head forward, with his eyes almost starting out of it.

"Umph!" cried Sikes, stopping short, as the girl, scarcely moving her head, looked suddenly round, and pointed for an instant to the Jew's face. "Never mind which part it is. You can't do it without me, I know; but it's best to be on the safe side when one deals with you."

"As you like, my dear, as you like" replied the Jew. "Is there no help wanted, but yours and Toby's?"

"None," said Sikes. "Cept a centre-bit and a boy. The first we've both got; the second you must find us."

"A boy!" exclaimed the Jew. "Oh! then it's a panel, eh?"

"Never mind wot it is!" replied Sikes. "I want a boy, and he musn't be a big 'un. Lord!" said Mr. Sikes, reflectively, "if I'd only got that young boy of Ned, the chimbley-sweeper's! He kept him small on purpose, and let him out by the job. But the father gets lagged; and then the Juvenile Delinquent Society comes, and takes the boy away from a trade where he was earning money, teaches him to read and write, and in time makes a 'prentice of him. And so they go on," said Mr. Sikes, his wrath rising with the recollection of his wrongs, "so they go on; and, if they'd got money enough (which it's a Providence they haven't,) we shouldn't have half a dozen boys left in the whole trade, in a year or two."

"No more we should," acquiesced the Jew, who had been considering during this speech, and had only caught the last sentence. "Bill!"

"What now?" inquired Sikes.

The Jew nodded his head towards Nancy, who was still gazing at the fire; and intimated, by a sign, that he would have her told to leave the room. Sikes shrugged his shoulders impatiently, as if he thought the precaution unnecessary; but complied, nevertheless, by requesting Miss Nancy to fetch him a jug of beer.

"You don't want any beer," said Nancy, folding her arms, and retaining her seat very composedly.

"I tell you I do!" replied Sikes.

"Nonsense," rejoined the girl coolly, "Go on, Fagin. I know what he's going to say, Bill; he needn't mind me."

The Jew still hesitated. Sikes looked from one to the other in some surprise.

"Why, you don't mind the old girl, do you, Fagin?" he asked at length. "You've known her long enough to trust her, or the Devil's in it. She ain't one to blab. Are you Nancy?"

"I should think not!" replied the young lady: drawing her chair up to the table, and putting her elbows upon it.

"No, no, my dear, I know you're not," said the Jew; "but—" and again the old man paused.

"But wot?" inquired Sikes.

"I didn't know whether she mightn't p'r'aps be out of sorts, you know, my dear, as she was the other night," replied the Jew.

At this confession, Miss Nancy burst into a loud laugh; and, swallowing a glass of brandy, shook her head with an air of defiance, and burst into sundry exclamations of "Keep the game a-going!" "Never say die!" and the like. These seemed to have the effect of re-assuring both gentlemen; for the Jew nodded his head with a satisfied air, and resumed his seat: as did Mr. Sikes likewise.

"Now, Fagin," said Nancy with a laugh. "Tell Bill at once, about Oliver!"

"Ha! you're a clever one, my dear: the sharpest girl I ever saw!" said the Jew, patting her on the neck. "It WAS about Oliver I was going to speak, sure enough. Ha! ha! ha!"

"What about him?" demanded Sikes.

"He's the boy for you, my dear," replied the Jew in a hoarse whisper; laying his finger on the side of his nose, and grinning frightfully.

"He!" exclaimed. Sikes.

"Have him, Bill!" said Nancy. "I would, if I was in your place. He mayn't be so much up, as any of the others; but that's not what you want, if he's only to open a door for you. Depend upon it he's a safe one, Bill."

"I know he is," rejoined Fagin. "He's been in good training these last few weeks, and it's time he began to work for his bread. Besides, the others are all too big."

"Well, he is just the size I want," said Mr. Sikes, ruminating.

"And will do everything you want, Bill, my dear," interposed the Jew; "he can't help himself. That is, if you frighten him enough."

"Frighten him!" echoed Sikes. "It'll be no sham frightening, mind you. If there's anything queer about him when we once get into the work; in for a penny, in for a pound. You won't see him alive again, Fagin. Think of that, before you send him. Mark my words!" said the robber, poising a crowbar, which he had drawn from under the bedstead.

"I've thought of it all," said the Jew with energy. "I've—I've had my eye upon him, my dears, close—close. Once let him feel that he is one of us; once fill his mind with the idea that he has been a thief; and he's ours! Ours for his life. Oho! It couldn't have come about better! The old man crossed his arms upon his breast; and, drawing his head and shoulders into a heap, literally hugged himself for joy.

"Ours!" said Sikes. "Yours, you mean."

"Perhaps I do, my dear," said the Jew, with a shrill chuckle. "Mine, if you like, Bill."

"And wot," said Sikes, scowling fiercely on his agreeable friend, "wot makes you take so much pains about one chalk-faced kid, when you know there are fifty boys snoozing about Common Garden every night, as you might pick and choose from?"

"Because they're of no use to me, my dear," replied the Jew, with some confusion, "not worth the taking. Their looks convict 'em when they get into trouble, and I lose 'em all. With this boy, properly managed, my dears, I could do what I couldn't with twenty of them. Besides," said the Jew, recovering his self-possession, "he has us now if he could only give us leg-bail again; and he must be in the same boat with us. Never mind how he came there; it's quite enough for my power over him that he was in a robbery; that's all I want. Now, how much better this is, than being obliged to put the poor leetle boy out of the way—which would be dangerous, and we should lose by it besides."

"When is it to be done?" asked Nancy, stopping some turbulent exclamation on the part of Mr. Sikes, expressive of the disgust with which he received Fagin's affectation of humanity.

"Ah, to be sure," said the Jew; "when is it to be done, Bill?"

"I planned with Toby, the night arter to-morrow," rejoined Sikes in a surly voice, "if he heerd nothing from me to the contrairy."

"Good," said the Jew; "there's no moon."

"No," rejoined Sikes.

"It's all arranged about bringing off the swag, is it?" asked the Jew.

Sikes nodded.

"And about—"

"Oh, ah, it's all planned," rejoined Sikes, interrupting him. "Never mind particulars. You'd better bring the boy here to-morrow night. I shall get off the stone an hour arter daybreak. Then you hold your tongue, and keep the melting-pot ready, and that's all you'll have to do."

After some discussion, in which all three took an active part, it was decided that Nancy should repair to the Jew's next evening when the night had set in, and bring Oliver away with her; Fagin craftily observing, that, if he evinced any disinclination to the task, he would be more willing to accompany the girl who had so recently interfered in his behalf, than anybody else. It was also solemnly arranged that poor Oliver should, for the purposes of the contemplated expedition, be unreservedly consigned to the care and custody of Mr. William Sikes; and further, that the said Sikes should deal with him as he thought fit; and should not be held responsible by the Jew for any mischance or evil that might be necessary to visit him: it being understood that, to render the compact in this respect binding, any representations made by Mr. Sikes on his return should be required to be confirmed and corroborated, in all important particulars, by the testimony of flash Toby Crackit.

These preliminaries adjusted, Mr. Sikes proceeded to drink brandy at a furious rate, and to flourish the crowbar in an alarming manner; yelling forth, at the same time, most unmusical snatches of song, mingled with wild execrations. At length, in a fit of professional enthusiasm, he insisted upon producing his box of housebreaking tools: which he had no sooner stumbled in with, and opened for the purpose of explaining the nature and properties of the various implements it contained, and the peculiar beauties of their construction, than he fell over the box upon the floor, and went to sleep where he fell.

"Good-night, Nancy," said the Jew, muffling himself up as before.

"Good-night."

Their eyes met, and the Jew scrutinised her, narrowly. There was no flinching about the girl. She was as true and earnest in the matter as Toby Crackit himself could be.

The Jew again bade her good-night, and, bestowing a sly kick upon the prostrate form of Mr. Sikes while her back was turned, groped downstairs.

"Always the way!" muttered the Jew to himself as he turned homeward. "The worst of these women is, that a very little thing serves to call up some long-forgotten feeling; and, the best of them is, that it never lasts. Ha! ha! The man against the child, for a bag of gold!"

Beguiling the time with these pleasant reflections, Mr. Fagin wended his way, through mud and mire, to his gloomy abode: where the Dodger was sitting up, impatiently awaiting his return.

"Is Oliver a-bed? I want to speak to him," was his first remark as they descended the stairs.

"Hours ago," replied the Dodger, throwing open a door. "Here he is!"

The boy was lying, fast asleep, on a rude bed upon the floor; so pale with anxiety, and sadness, and the closeness of his prison, that he looked like death; not death as it shows in shroud and coffin, but in the guise it wears when life has just departed; when a young and gentle spirit has, but an instant, fled to Heaven, and the gross air of the world has not had time to breathe upon the changing dust it hallowed.

"Not now," said the Jew, turning softly away. "To-morrow. To-morrow."

CHAPTER XX

Wherein Oliver Is Delivered Over to Mr. William Sikes

W hen Oliver awoke in the morning, he was a good deal surprised to find that a new pair of shoes, with strong thick soles, had been placed at his bedside; and that his old shoes had been removed. At first, he was pleased with the discovery: hoping that it might be the forerunner of his release; but such thoughts were quickly dispelled, on his sitting down to breakfast along with the Jew, who told him, in a tone and manner which increased his alarm, that he was to be taken to the residence of Bill Sikes that night.

"To—to—stop there, sir?" asked Oliver, anxiously.

"No, no, my dear. Not to stop there," replied the Jew. "We shouldn't like to lose you. Don't be afraid, Oliver, you shall come back to us again. Ha! ha! ha! We won't be so cruel as to send you away, my dear. Oh no, no!"

The old man, who was stooping over the fire toasting a piece of bread, looked round as he bantered Oliver thus; and chuckled as if to show that he knew he would still be very glad to get away if he could.

"I suppose," said the Jew, fixing his eyes on Oliver, "you want to know what you're going to Bill's for——eh, my dear?"

Oliver coloured, involuntarily, to find that the old thief had been reading his thoughts; but boldly said, Yes, he did want to know.

"Why, do you think?" inquired Fagin, parrying the question.

"Indeed I don't know, sir," replied Oliver.

"Bah!" said the Jew, turning away with a disappointed countenance from a close perusal of the boy's face. "Wait till Bill tells you, then."

The Jew seemed much vexed by Oliver's not expressing any greater curiosity on the subject; but the truth is, that, although Oliver felt very anxious, he was too much confused by the earnest cunning of Fagin's looks, and his own speculations, to make any further inquiries just then. He had no other opportunity: for the Jew remained very surly and silent till night: when he prepared to go abroad.

"You may burn a candle," said the Jew, putting one upon the table. "And here's a book for you to read, till they come to fetch you. Good-night!"

"Good-night!" replied Oliver, softly.

The Jew walked to the door: looking over his shoulder at the boy as he went. Suddenly stopping, he called him by his name.

Oliver looked up; the Jew, pointing to the candle, motioned him to light it. He did so; and, as he placed the candlestick upon the table, saw that the Jew was gazing fixedly at him, with lowering and contracted brows, from the dark end of the room.

"Take heed, Oliver! take heed!" said the old man, shaking his right hand before him in a warning manner. "He's a rough man, and thinks nothing of blood when his own is up. Whatever falls out, say nothing; and do what he bids you. Mind!" Placing a strong emphasis on the last word, he suffered his features gradually to resolve themselves into a ghastly grin, and, nodding his head, left the room.

Oliver leaned his head upon his hand when the old man disappeared, and pondered, with a trembling heart, on the words he had just heard. The more he thought of the Jew's admonition, the more he was at a loss to divine its real purpose and meaning.

He could think of no bad object to be attained by sending him to Sikes, which would not be equally well answered by his remaining with Fagin; and after meditating for a long time, concluded that he had been selected to perform some ordinary menial offices for the housebreaker, until another boy, better suited for his purpose could be engaged. He was too well accustomed to suffering, and had suffered too much where he was, to bewail the prospect of change very severely. He remained lost in thought for some minutes; and then, with a heavy sigh, snuffed the candle, and, taking up the book which the Jew had left with him, began to read.

He turned over the leaves. Carelessly at first; but, lighting on a passage which attracted his attention, he soon became intent upon the volume. It was a history of the lives and trials of great criminals; and the pages were soiled and thumbed with use. Here, he read of dreadful crimes that made the blood run cold; of secret murders that had been committed by the lonely wayside; of bodies hidden from the eye of man in deep pits and wells: which would not keep them down, deep as they were, but had yielded them up at last, after many years, and so maddened the murderers with the sight, that in their horror they had confessed their guilt, and yelled for the gibbet to end their agony. Here, too, he read of men who, lying in their beds at dead of night, had been tempted (so they said) and led on, by their own bad thoughts, to such dreadful bloodshed as it made the flesh creep, and the limbs quail, to think of. The terrible descriptions were so real and vivid, that the sallow pages seemed to turn red with gore; and the words upon them, to be sounded in his ears, as if they were whispered, in hollow murmurs, by the spirits of the dead.

In a paroxysm of fear, the boy closed the book, and thrust it from him. Then, falling upon his knees, he prayed Heaven to spare him from such deeds; and rather to will that he should die at once, than be reserved for crimes, so fearful and appalling. By degrees, he grew more calm, and besought, in a low and broken voice, that he might be rescued from his present dangers; and that if any aid were to be raised up for a poor outcast boy who had never known the love of friends or kindred, it might come to him now, when, desolate and deserted, he stood alone in the midst of wickedness and guilt.

He had concluded his prayer, but still remained with his head buried in his hands, when a rustling noise aroused him.

"What's that!" he cried, starting up, and catching sight of a figure standing by the door. "Who's there?"

"Me. Only me," replied a tremulous voice.

Oliver raised the candle above his head: and looked towards the door. It was Nancy.

"Put down the light," said the girl, turning away her head. "It hurts my eyes."

Oliver saw that she was very pale, and gently inquired if she were ill. The girl threw herself into a chair, with her back towards him: and wrung her hands; but made no reply.

"God forgive me!" she cried after a while, "I never thought of this."

"Has anything happened?" asked Oliver. "Can I help you? I will if I can. I will, indeed."

She rocked herself to and fro; caught her throat; and, uttering a gurgling sound, gasped for breath.

"Nancy!" cried Oliver, "What is it?"

The girl beat her hands upon her knees, and her feet upon the ground; and, suddenly stopping, drew her shawl close round her: and shivered with cold.

Oliver stirred the fire. Drawing her chair close to it, she sat there, for a little time, without speaking; but at length she raised her head, and looked round.

"I don't know what comes over me sometimes," said she, affecting to busy herself in arranging her dress; "it's this damp dirty room, I think. Now, Nolly, dear, are you ready?"

"Am I to go with you?" asked Oliver.

"Yes. I have come from Bill," replied the girl. "You are to go with me."

"What for?" asked Oliver, recoiling.

"What for?" echoed the girl, raising her eyes, and averting them again, the moment they encountered the boy's face. "Oh! For no harm."

"I don't believe it," said Oliver: who had watched her closely.

"Have it your own way," rejoined the girl, affecting to laugh. "For no good, then."

Oliver could see that he had some power over the girl's better feelings, and, for an instant, thought of appealing to her compassion for his helpless state. But, then, the thought darted across his mind that it was barely eleven o'clock; and that many people were still in the streets: of whom surely some might be found to give credence to his tale. As the reflection occured to him, he stepped forward: and said, somewhat hastily, that he was ready.

Neither his brief consideration, nor its purport, was lost on his companion. She eyed him narrowly, while he spoke; and cast upon him a look of intelligence which sufficiently showed that she guessed what had been passing in his thoughts.

"Hush!" said the girl, stooping over him, and pointing to the door as she looked cautiously round. "You can't help yourself. I have tried hard for you, but all to no purpose. You are hedged round and round. If ever you are to get loose from here, this is not the time."

Struck by the energy of her manner, Oliver looked up in her face with great surprise. She seemed to speak the truth; her countenance was white and agitated; and she trembled with very earnestness.

"I have saved you from being ill-used once, and I will again, and I do now," continued the girl aloud; "for those who would have fetched you, if I had not, would have been far more rough than me. I have promised for your being quiet and silent; if you are not, you will only do harm to yourself and me too, and perhaps be my death. See here! I have borne all this for you already, as true as God sees me show it."

She pointed, hastily, to some livid bruises on her neck and arms; and continued, with great rapidity:

"Remember this! And don't let me suffer more for you, just now. If I could help you, I would; but I have not the power. They don't mean to harm you; whatever they make you do, is no fault of yours. Hush! Every word from you is a blow for me. Give me your hand. Make haste! Your hand!"

She caught the hand which Oliver instinctively placed in hers, and, blowing out the light, drew him after her up the stairs. The door was opened, quickly, by some one shrouded in the darkness, and was as quickly closed, when they had passed out. A hackney-cabriolet was in waiting; with the same vehemence which she had exhibited in addressing Oliver, the girl pulled him in with her, and drew the curtains close. The driver wanted no directions, but lashed his horse into full speed, without the delay of an instant.

The girl still held Oliver fast by the hand, and continued to pour into his ear, the warnings and assurances she had already imparted. All was so quick and hurried, that he had scarcely time to recollect where he was, or how he came there, when the carriage stopped at the house to which the Jew's steps had been directed on the previous evening.

For one brief moment, Oliver cast a hurried glance along the empty street, and a cry for help hung upon his lips. But the girl's voice was in his ear, beseeching him in such tones of agony to remember her, that he had not the heart to utter it. While he hesitated, the opportunity was gone; he was already in the house, and the door was shut.

"This way," said the girl, releasing her hold for the first time. "Bill!"

"Hallo!" replied Sikes: appearing at the head of the stairs, with a candle. "Oh! That's the time of day. Come on!"

This was a very strong expression of approbation, an uncommonly hearty welcome, from a person of Mr. Sikes' temperament. Nancy, appearing much gratified thereby, saluted him cordially.

"Bull's-eye's gone home with Tom," observed Sikes, as he lighted them up. "He'd have been in the way."

"That's right," rejoined Nancy.

"So you've got the kid," said Sikes when they had all reached the room: closing the door as he spoke.

"Yes, here he is," replied Nancy.

"Did he come quiet?" inquired Sikes.

"Like a lamb," rejoined Nancy.

"I'm glad to hear it," said Sikes, looking grimly at Oliver; "for the sake of his young carcase: as would otherways have suffered for it. Come here, young 'un; and let me read you a lectur', which is as well got over at once."

Thus addressing his new pupil, Mr. Sikes pulled off Oliver's cap and threw it into a corner; and then, taking him by the shoulder, sat himself down by the table, and stood the boy in front of him.

"Now, first: do you know wot this is?" inquired Sikes, taking up a pocket-pistol which lay on the table.

Oliver replied in the affirmative.

"Well, then, look here," continued Sikes. "This is powder; that 'ere's a bullet; and this is a little bit of a old hat for waddin'."

Oliver murmured his comprehension of the different bodies referred to; and Mr. Sikes proceeded to load the pistol, with great nicety and deliberation.

"Now it's loaded," said Mr. Sikes, when he had finished.

"Yes, I see it is, sir," replied Oliver.

"Well," said the robber, grasping Oliver's wrist, and putting the barrel so close to his temple that they touched; at which moment the boy could not repress a start; "if you speak a word when you're out o'doors with me, except when I speak to you, that loading will be in your head without notice. So, if you do make up your mind to speak without leave, say your prayers first."

Having bestowed a scowl upon the object of this warning, to increase its effect, Mr. Sikes continued.

"As near as I know, there isn't anybody as would be asking very partickler arter you, if you was disposed of; so I needn't take this devil-and-all of trouble to explain matters to you, if it warn't for your own good. D'ye hear me?"

"The short and the long of what you mean," said Nancy: speaking very emphatically, and slightly frowning at Oliver as if to bespeak his serious attention to her words: "is, that if you're crossed by him in this job you have on hand, you'll prevent his ever telling tales afterwards, by shooting him through the head, and will take your chance of swinging for it, as you do for a great many other things in the way of business, every month of your life."

"That's it!" observed Mr. Sikes, approvingly; "women can always put things in fewest words.—Except when it's blowing up; and then they lengthens it out. And now that he's thoroughly up to it, let's have some supper, and get a snooze before starting."

In pursuance of this request, Nancy quickly laid the cloth; disappearing for a few minutes, she presently returned with a pot of porter and a dish of sheep's heads: which gave occasion to several pleasant witticisms on the part of Mr. Sikes, founded upon the singular coincidence of "jemmies" being a can name, common to them, and also to an ingenious implement much used in his profession. Indeed, the worthy gentleman, stimulated perhaps by the immediate prospect of being on active service, was in great spirits and good humour; in proof whereof, it may be here remarked, that he humourously drank all the beer at a draught, and did not utter, on a rough calculation, more than four-score oaths during the whole progress of the meal.

Supper being ended—it may be easily conceived that Oliver had no great appetite for it—Mr. Sikes disposed of a couple of glasses of spirits and water, and threw himself on the bed; ordering Nancy, with many imprecations in case of failure, to call him at five precisely. Oliver stretched himself in his clothes, by command of the same authority, on a mattress upon the floor; and the girl, mending the fire, sat before it, in readiness to rouse them at the appointed time.

For a long time Oliver lay awake, thinking it not impossible that Nancy might seek that opportunity of whispering some further advice; but the girl sat brooding over the fire, without moving, save now and then to trim the light. Weary with watching and anxiety, he at length fell asleep.

When he awoke, the table was covered with tea-things, and Sikes was thrusting various articles into the pockets of his great-coat, which hung over the back of a chair. Nancy was busily engaged in preparing breakfast. It was not yet daylight; for the candle was still burning, and it was quite dark outside. A sharp rain, too, was beating against the window-panes; and the sky looked black and cloudy.

"Now, then!" growled Sikes, as Oliver started up; "half-past five! Look sharp, or you'll get no breakfast; for it's late as it is."

Oliver was not long in making his toilet; having taken some breakfast, he replied to a surly inquiry from Sikes, by saying that he was quite ready.

Nancy, scarcely looking at the boy, threw him a handkerchief to tie round his throat; Sikes gave him a large rough cape to button over his shoulders. Thus attired, he gave his hand to the robber, who, merely pausing to show him with a menacing gesture that he had that same pistol in a side-pocket of his great-coat, clasped it firmly in his, and, exchanging a farewell with Nancy, led him away.

Oliver turned, for an instant, when they reached the door, in the hope of meeting a look from the girl. But she had resumed her old seat in front of the fire, and sat, perfectly motionless before it.

CHAPTER XXI

The Expedition

It was a cheerless morning when they got into the street; blowing and raining hard; and the clouds looking dull and stormy. The night had been very wet: large pools of water had collected in the road: and the kennels were overflowing. There was a faint glimmering of the coming day in the sky; but it rather aggravated than relieved the gloom of the scene: the sombre light only serving to pale that which the street lamps afforded, without shedding any warmer or brighter tints upon the wet house-tops, and dreary streets. There appeared to be nobody stirring in that quarter of the town; the windows of the houses were all closely shut; and the streets through which they passed, were noiseless and empty.

By the time they had turned into the Bethnal Green Road, the day had fairly begun to break. Many of the lamps were already extinguished; a few country waggons were slowly toiling on, towards London; now and then, a stage-coach, covered with mud, rattled briskly by: the driver bestowing, as he passed, an admonitory lash upon the heavy waggoner who, by keeping on the wrong side of the road, had endangered his arriving at the office, a quarter of a minute after his time. The public-houses, with gas-lights burning inside, were already open. By degrees, other shops began to be unclosed, and a few scattered people were met with. Then, came straggling groups of labourers going to their work; then, men and women with fish-baskets on their heads; donkey-carts laden with vegetables; chaise-carts filled with live-stock or whole carcasses of meat; milk-women with pails; an unbroken concourse of people, trudging out with various supplies to the eastern suburbs of the town. As they approached the City, the noise and traffic gradually increased; when they threaded the streets between Shoreditch and Smithfield, it had swelled into a roar of sound and bustle. It was as light as it was likely to be, till night came on again, and the busy morning of half the London population had begun.

Turning down Sun Street and Crown Street, and crossing Finsbury square, Mr. Sikes struck, by way of Chiswell Street, into Barbican: thence into Long Lane, and so into Smithfield; from which latter place arose a tumult of discordant sounds that filled Oliver Twist with amazement.

It was market-morning. The ground was covered, nearly ankle-deep, with filth and mire; a thick steam, perpetually rising from the reeking bodies of the cattle, and mingling with the fog, which seemed to rest upon the chimney-tops, hung heavily above. All the pens in the centre of the large area, and as many temporary pens as could be crowded into the vacant space, were filled with sheep; tied up to posts by the gutter side were long lines of beasts and oxen, three or four deep. Countrymen, butchers, drovers, hawkers, boys, thieves, idlers, and vagabonds of every low grade, were mingled together in a mass; the whistling of drovers, the barking dogs, the bellowing and plunging of the oxen, the bleating of sheep, the grunting and squeaking of pigs, the cries of hawkers, the shouts, oaths, and quarrelling on all sides; the ringing of bells and roar of voices, that issued from every public-house; the crowding, pushing, driving, beating, whooping and yelling; the hideous and discordant dim that resounded from every corner of the market; and the unwashed, unshaven, squalid, and dirty figures constantly running to and fro, and bursting in and out of the throng; rendered it a stunning and bewildering scene, which quite confounded the senses.

Mr. Sikes, dragging Oliver after him, elbowed his way through the thickest of the crowd, and bestowed very little attention on the numerous sights and sounds, which so astonished the boy. He nodded, twice or thrice, to a passing friend; and, resisting as many invitations to take a morning dram, pressed steadily onward, until they were clear of the turmoil, and had made their way through Hosier Lane into Holborn.

"Now, young 'un!" said Sikes, looking up at the clock of St. Andrew's Church, "hard upon seven! you must step out. Come, don't lag behind already, Lazy-legs!"

Mr. Sikes accompanied this speech with a jerk at his little companion's wrist; Oliver, quickening his pace into a kind of trot between a fast walk and a run, kept up with the rapid strides of the house-breaker as well as he could.

They held their course at this rate, until they had passed Hyde Park corner, and were on their way to Kensington: when Sikes relaxed his pace, until an empty cart which was at some little distance behind, came up. Seeing "Hounslow" written on it, he asked the driver with as much civility as he could assume, if he would give them a lift as far as Isleworth.

"Jump up," said the man. "Is that your boy?"

"Yes; he's my boy," replied Sikes, looking hard at Oliver, and putting his hand abstractedly into the pocket where the pistol was.

"Your father walks rather too quick for you, don't he, my man?" inquired the driver: seeing that Oliver was out of breath.

"Not a bit of it," replied Sikes, interposing. "He's used to it. Here, take hold of my hand, Ned. In with you!"

Thus addressing Oliver, he helped him into the cart; and the driver, pointing to a heap of sacks, told him to lie down there, and rest himself.

As they passed the different mile-stones, Oliver wondered, more and more, where his companion meant to take him. Kensington, Hammersmith, Chiswick, Kew Bridge, Brentford, were all passed; and yet they went on as steadily as if they had only just begun their journey. At length, they came to a public-house called the Coach and Horses; a little way beyond which, another road appeared to run off. And here, the cart stopped.

Sikes dismounted with great precipitation, holding Oliver by the hand all the while; and lifting him down directly, bestowed a furious look upon him, and rapped the side-pocket with his fist, in a significant manner.

"Good-bye, boy," said the man.

"He's sulky," replied Sikes, giving him a shake; "he's sulky. A young dog! Don't mind him."

"Not I!" rejoined the other, getting into his cart. "It's a fine day, after all.' And he drove away.

Sikes waited until he had fairly gone; and then, telling Oliver he might look about him if he wanted, once again led him onward on his journey.

They turned round to the left, a short way past the public-house; and then, taking a right-hand road, walked on for a long time: passing many large gardens and gentlemen's houses on both sides of the way, and stopping for nothing but a little beer, until they reached a town. Here against the wall of a house, Oliver saw written up in pretty large letters, "Hampton." They lingered about, in the fields, for some hours. At length they came back into the town; and, turning into an old public-house with a defaced sign-board, ordered some dinner by the kitchen fire.

The kitchen was an old, low-roofed room; with a great beam across the middle of the ceiling, and benches, with high backs to them, by the fire; on which were seated several rough men in smock-frocks, drinking and smoking. They took no notice of Oliver; and very little of Sikes; and, as Sikes took very little notice of them, he and his young comrade sat in a corner by themselves, without being much troubled by their company.

They had some cold meat for dinner, and sat so long after it, while Mr. Sikes indulged himself with three or four pipes, that Oliver began to feel quite certain they were not going any further. Being much tired with the walk, and getting up so early, he dozed a little at first; then, quite overpowered by fatigue and the fumes of the tobacco, fell asleep.

It was quite dark when he was awakened by a push from Sikes. Rousing himself sufficiently to sit up and look about him, he found that worthy in close fellowship and communication with a labouring man, over a pint of ale.

"So, you're going on to Lower Halliford, are you?" inquired Sikes.

"Yes, I am," replied the man, who seemed a little the worse—or better, as the case might be—for drinking; and not slow about it neither. My horse hasn't got a load behind him going back, as he had coming up in the mornin'; and he won't be long a-doing of it. Here's luck to him. Ecod! he's a good 'un!"

"Could you give my boy and me a lift as far as there?" demanded Sikes, pushing the ale towards his new friend.

"If you're going directly, I can," replied the man, looking out of the pot. "Are you going to Halliford?"

"Going on to Shepperton," replied Sikes.

"I'm your man, as far as I go," replied the other. "Is all paid, Becky?"

"Yes, the other gentleman's paid," replied the girl.

"I say!" said the man, with tipsy gravity; "that won't do, you know."

"Why not?" rejoined Sikes. "You're a-going to accommodate us, and wot's to prevent my standing treat for a pint or so, in return?"

The stranger reflected upon this argument, with a very profound face; having done so, he seized Sikes by the hand: and declared he was a real good fellow. To which Mr. Sikes replied, he was joking; as, if he had been sober, there would have been strong reason to suppose he was.

After the exchange of a few more compliments, they bade the company good-night, and went out; the girl gathering up the pots and glasses as they did so, and lounging out to the door, with her hands full, to see the party start.

The horse, whose health had been drunk in his absence, was standing outside: ready harnessed to the cart. Oliver and Sikes got in without any further ceremony; and the man to whom he belonged, having lingered for a minute or two "to bear him up," and to defy the hostler and the world to produce his equal, mounted also. Then, the hostler was told to give the horse his head; and, his head being given him, he made a very unpleasant use of it: tossing it into the air with great disdain, and running into the parlour windows over the way; after performing those feats, and supporting himself for a short time on his hind-legs, he started off at great speed, and rattled out of the town right gallantly.

The night was very dark. A damp mist rose from the river, and the marshy ground about; and spread itself over the dreary fields. It was piercing cold, too; all was gloomy and black. Not a word was spoken; for the driver had grown sleepy; and Sikes was in no mood to lead him into conversation. Oliver sat huddled together, in a corner of the cart; bewildered with alarm and apprehension; and figuring strange objects in the gaunt trees, whose branches waved grimly to and fro, as if in some fantastic joy at the desolation of the scene.

As they passed Sunbury Church, the clock struck seven. There was a light in the ferry-house window opposite: which streamed across the road, and threw into more sombre shadow a dark yew-tree with graves beneath it. There was a dull sound of falling water not far off; and the leaves of the old tree stirred gently in the night wind. It seemed like quiet music for the repose of the dead.

Sunbury was passed through, and they came again into the lonely road. Two or three miles more, and the cart stopped. Sikes alighted, took Oliver by the hand, and they once again walked on.

They turned into no house at Shepperton, as the weary boy had expected; but still kept walking on, in mud and darkness, through gloomy lanes and over cold open wastes, until they came within sight of the lights of a town at no great distance. On looking intently forward, Oliver saw that the water was just below them, and that they were coming to the foot of a bridge.

Sikes kept straight on, until they were close upon the bridge; then turned suddenly down a bank upon the left.

"The water!" thought Oliver, turning sick with fear. "He has brought me to this lonely place to murder me!"

He was about to throw himself on the ground, and make one struggle for his young life, when he saw that they stood before a solitary house: all ruinous and decayed. There was a window on each side of the dilapidated entrance; and one story above; but no light was visible. The house was dark, dismantled: and the all appearance, uninhabited.

Sikes, with Oliver's hand still in his, softly approached the low porch, and raised the latch. The door yielded to the pressure, and they passed in together.

CHAPTER XXII

The Burglary

"Hallo!" cried a loud, hoarse voice, as soon as they set foot in the passage.

"Don't make such a row," said Sikes, bolting the door. "Show a glim, Toby."

"Aha! my pal!" cried the same voice. "A glim, Barney, a glim! Show the gentleman in, Barney; wake up first, if convenient."

The speaker appeared to throw a boot-jack, or some such article, at the person he addressed, to rouse him from his slumbers: for the noise of a wooden body, falling violently, was heard; and then an indistinct muttering, as of a man between sleep and awake.

"Do you hear?" cried the same voice. "There's Bill Sikes in the passage with nobody to do the civil to him; and you sleeping there, as if you took laudanum with your meals, and nothing stronger. Are you any fresher now, or do you want the iron candlestick to wake you thoroughly?"

A pair of slipshod feet shuffled, hastily, across the bare floor of the room, as this interrogatory was put; and there issued, from a door on the right hand; first, a feeble candle: and next, the form of the same individual who has been heretofore described as labouring under the infirmity of speaking through his nose, and officiating as waiter at the public-house on Saffron Hill.

"Bister Sikes!" exclaimed Barney, with real or counterfeit joy; 'cub id, sir; cub id."

"Here! you get on first," said Sikes, putting Oliver in front of him. "Quicker! or I shall tread upon your heels."

Muttering a curse upon his tardiness, Sikes pushed Oliver before him; and they entered a low dark room with a smoky fire, two or three broken chairs, a table, and a very old couch: on which, with his legs much higher than his head, a man was reposing at full length, smoking a long clay pipe. He was dressed in a smartly-cut snuff-coloured coat, with large brass buttons; an orange neckerchief; a coarse, staring, shawl-pattern waistcoat; and drab breeches. Mr. Crackit (for he it was) had no very great quantity of hair, either upon his head or face; but what he had, was of a reddish dye, and tortured into long corkscrew curls, through which he occasionally thrust some very dirty fingers, ornamented with large common rings. He was a trifle above the middle size, and apparently rather weak in the legs; but this circumstance by no means detracted from his own admiration of his top-boots, which he contemplated, in their elevated situation, with lively satisfaction.

"Bill, my boy!" said this figure, turning his head towards the door, "I'm glad to see you. I was almost afraid you'd given it up: in which case I should have made a personal wentur. Hallo!"

Uttering this exclamation in a tone of great surprise, as his eyes rested on Oliver, Mr. Toby Crackit brought himself into a sitting posture, and demanded who that was.

"The boy. Only the boy!" replied Sikes, drawing a chair towards the fire.

"Wud of Bister Fagid's lads," exclaimed Barney, with a grin.

"Fagin's, eh!" exclaimed Toby, looking at Oliver. "Wot an inwalable boy that'll make, for the old ladies' pockets in chapels! His mug is a fortin' to him."

"There—there's enough of that," interposed Sikes, impatiently; and stooping over his recumbant friend, he whispered a few words in his ear: at which Mr. Crackit laughed immensely, and honoured Oliver with a long stare of astonishment.

"Now," said Sikes, as he resumed his seat, "if you'll give us something to eat and drink while we're waiting, you'll put some heart in us; or in me, at all events. Sit down by the fire, younker, and rest yourself; for you'll have to go out with us again to-night, though not very far off."

Oliver looked at Sikes, in mute and timid wonder; and drawing a stool to the fire, sat with his aching head upon his hands, scarecely knowing where he was, or what was passing around him.

"Here," said Toby, as the young Jew placed some fragments of food, and a bottle upon the table, "Success to the crack!" He rose to honour the toast; and, carefully depositing his empty pipe in a corner, advanced to the table, filled a glass with spirits, and drank off its contents. Mr. Sikes did the same.

"A drain for the boy," said Toby, half-filling a wine-glass. "Down with it, innocence."

"Indeed," said Oliver, looking piteously up into the man's face; "indeed, I—"

"Down with it!" echoed Toby. "Do you think I don't know what's good for you? Tell him to drink it, Bill."

"He had better!" said Sikes clapping his hand upon his pocket. "Burn my body, if he isn't more trouble than a whole family of Dodgers. Drink it, you perwerse imp; drink it!"

Frightened by the menacing gestures of the two men, Oliver hastily swallowed the contents of the glass, and immediately fell into a violent fit of coughing: which delighted Toby Crackit and Barney, and even drew a smile from the surly Mr. Sikes.

This done, and Sikes having satisfied his appetite (Oliver could eat nothing but a small crust of bread which they made him swallow), the two men laid themselves down on chairs for a short nap. Oliver retained his stool by the fire; Barney wrapped in a blanket, stretched himself on the floor: close outside the fender.

They slept, or appeared to sleep, for some time; nobody stirring but Barney, who rose once or twice to throw coals on the fire. Oliver fell into a heavy doze: imagining himself straying along the gloomy lanes, or wandering about the dark churchyard, or retracing some one or other of the scenes of the past day: when he was roused by Toby Crackit jumping up and declaring it was half-past one.

In an instant, the other two were on their legs, and all were actively engaged in busy preparation. Sikes and his companion enveloped their necks and chins in large dark shawls, and drew on their great-coats; Barney, opening a cupboard, brought forth several articles, which he hastily crammed into the pockets.

"Barkers for me, Barney," said Toby Crackit.

"Here they are," replied Barney, producing a pair of pistols. "You loaded them yourself."

"All right!" replied Toby, stowing them away. "The persuaders?"

"I've got 'em," replied Sikes.

"Crape, keys, centre-bits, darkies—nothing forgotten?" inquired Toby: fastening a small crowbar to a loop inside the skirt of his coat.

"All right," rejoined his companion. "Bring them bits of timber, Barney. That's the time of day."

With these words, he took a thick stick from Barney's hands, who, having delivered another to Toby, busied himself in fastening on Oliver's cape.

"Now then!" said Sikes, holding out his hand.

Oliver: who was completely stupified by the unwonted exercise, and the air, and the drink which had been forced upon him: put his hand mechanically into that which Sikes extended for the purpose.

"Take his other hand, Toby," said Sikes. "Look out, Barney."

The man went to the door, and returned to announce that all was quiet. The two robbers issued forth with Oliver between them. Barney, having made all fast, rolled himself up as before, and was soon asleep again.

It was now intensely dark. The fog was much heavier than it had been in the early part of the night; and the atmosphere was so damp, that, although no rain fell, Oliver's hair and eyebrows, within a few minutes after leaving the house, had become stiff with the half-frozen moisture that was floating about. They crossed the bridge, and kept on towards the lights which he had seen before. They were at no great distance off; and, as they walked pretty briskly, they soon arrived at Chertsey.

"Slap through the town," whispered Sikes; "there'll be nobody in the way, to-night, to see us."

Toby acquiesced; and they hurried through the main street of the little town, which at that late hour was wholly deserted. A dim light shone at intervals from some bed-room window; and the hoarse barking of dogs occasionally broke the silence of the night. But there was nobody abroad. They had cleared the town, as the church-bell struck two.

Quickening their pace, they turned up a road upon the left hand. After walking about a quarter of a mile, they stopped before a detached house surrounded by a wall: to the top of which, Toby Crackit, scarcely pausing to take breath, climbed in a twinkling.

"The boy next," said Toby. "Hoist him up; I'll catch hold of him."

Before Oliver had time to look round, Sikes had caught him under the arms; and in three or four seconds he and Toby were lying on the grass on the other side. Sikes followed directly. And they stole cautiously towards the house.

And now, for the first time, Oliver, well-nigh mad with grief and terror, saw that housebreaking and robbery, if not murder, were the objects of the expedition. He clasped his hands together, and involuntarily uttered a subdued exclamation of horror. A mist came before his eyes; the cold sweat stood upon his ashy face; his limbs failed him; and he sank upon his knees.

"Get up!" murmured Sikes, trembling with rage, and drawing the pistol from his pocket; "Get up, or I'll strew your brains upon the grass."

"Oh! for God's sake let me go!" cried Oliver; "let me run away and die in the fields. I will never come near London; never, never! Oh! pray have mercy on me, and do not make me steal. For the love of all the bright Angels that rest in Heaven, have mercy upon me!"

The man to whom this appeal was made, swore a dreadful oath, and had cocked the pistol, when Toby, striking it from his grasp, placed his hand upon the boy's mouth, and dragged him to the house.

"Hush!" cried the man; "it won't answer here. Say another word, and I'll do your business myself with a crack on the head. That makes no noise, and is quite as certain, and more genteel. Here, Bill, wrench the shutter open. He's game enough now, I'll engage. I've seen older hands of his age took the same way, for a minute or two, on a cold night."

Sikes, invoking terrific imprecations upon Fagin's head for sending Oliver on such an errand, plied the crowbar vigorously, but with little noise. After some delay, and some assistance from Toby, the shutter to which he had referred, swung open on its hinges.

It was a little lattice window, about five feet and a half above the ground, at the back of the house: which belonged to a scullery, or small brewing-place, at the end of the passage. The aperture was so small, that the inmates had probably not thought it worth while to defend it more securely; but it was large enough to admit a boy of Oliver's size, nevertheless. A very brief exercise of Mr. Sike's art, sufficed to overcome the fastening of the lattice; and it soon stood wide open also.

"Now listen, you young limb," whispered Sikes, drawing a dark lantern from his pocket, and throwing the glare full on Oliver's face; "I'm a going to put you through there. Take this light; go softly up the steps straight afore you, and along the little hall, to the street door; unfasten it, and let us in."

"There's a bolt at the top, you won't be able to reach," interposed Toby. "Stand upon one of the hall chairs. There are three there, Bill, with a jolly large blue unicorn and gold pitchfork on 'em: which is the old lady's arms."

"Keep quiet, can't you?" replied Sikes, with a threatening look. "The room-door is open, is it?"

"Wide," replied Toby, after peeping in to satisfy himself. "The game of that is, that they always leave it open with a catch, so that the dog, who's got a bed in here, may walk up and down the passage when he feels wakeful. Ha! ha! Barney 'ticed him away to-night. So neat!"

Although Mr. Crackit spoke in a scarcely audible whisper, and laughed without noise, Sikes imperiously commanded him to be silent, and to get to work. Toby complied, by first producing his lantern, and placing it on the ground; then by planting himself firmly with his head against the wall beneath the window, and his hands upon his knees, so as to make a step of his back. This was no sooner done, than Sikes, mounting upon him, put Oliver gently through the window with his feet first; and, without leaving hold of his collar, planted him safely on the floor inside.

"Take this lantern," said Sikes, looking into the room. "You see the stairs afore you?"

Oliver, more dead than alive, gasped out, "Yes." Sikes, pointing to the street-door with the pistol-barrel, briefly advised him to take notice that he was within shot all the way; and that if he faltered, he would fall dead that instant.

"It's done in a minute," said Sikes, in the same low whisper. "Directly I leave go of you, do your work. Hark!"

"What's that?" whispered the other man.

They listened intently.

"Nothing," said Sikes, releasing his hold of Oliver. "Now!"

In the short time he had had to collect his senses, the boy had firmly resolved that, whether he died in the attempt or not, he would make one effort to dart upstairs from the hall, and alarm the family. Filled with this idea, he advanced at once, but stealthily.

"Come back!" suddenly cried Sikes aloud. "Back! back!"

Scared by the sudden breaking of the dead stillness of the place, and by a loud cry which followed it, Oliver let his lantern fall, and knew not whether to advance or fly.

The cry was repeated—a light appeared—a vision of two terrified half-dressed men at the top of the stairs swam before his eyes—a flash—a loud noise—a smoke—a crash somewhere, but where he knew not,—and he staggered back.

Sikes had disappeared for an instant; but he was up again, and had him by the collar before the smoke had cleared away. He fired his own pistol after the men, who were already retreating; and dragged the boy up.

"Clasp your arm tighter," said Sikes, as he drew him through the window. "Give me a shawl here. They've hit him. Quick! How the boy bleeds!"

Then came the loud ringing of a bell, mingled with the noise of fire-arms, and the shouts of men, and the sensation of being carried over uneven ground at a rapid pace. And then, the noises grew confused in the distance; and a cold deadly feeling crept over the boy's heart; and he saw or heard no more.

CHAPTER XXIII

Which Contains the Substance of a Pleasant Conversation Between
Mr. Bumble and a Lady; and Shows That Even a Beadle
May Be Susceptible on Some Points

The night was bitter cold. The snow lay on the ground, frozen into a hard thick crust, so that only the heaps that had drifted into byways and corners were affected by the sharp wind that howled abroad: which, as if expending increased fury on such prey as it found, caught it savagely up in clouds, and, whirling it into a thousand misty eddies, scattered it in air. Bleak, dark, and piercing cold, it was a night for the well-housed and fed to draw round the bright fire and thank God they were at home; and for the homeless, starving wretch to lay him down and die. Many hunger-worn outcasts close their eyes in our bare streets, at such times, who, let their crimes have been what they may, can hardly open them in a more bitter world.

Such was the aspect of out-of-doors affairs, when Mrs. Corney, the matron of the workhouse to which our readers have been already introduced as the birthplace of Oliver Twist, sat herself down before a cheerful fire in her own little room, and glanced, with no small degree of complacency, at a small round table: on which stood a tray of corresponding size, furnished with all necessary materials for the most grateful meal that matrons enjoy. In fact, Mrs. Corney was about to solace herself with a cup of tea. As she glanced from the table to the fireplace, where the smallest of all possible kettles was singing a small song in a small voice, her inward satisfaction evidently increased,—so much so, indeed, that Mrs. Corney smiled.

"Well!" said the matron, leaning her elbow on the table, and looking reflectively at the fire; "I'm sure we have all on us a great deal to be grateful for! A great deal, if we did but know it. Ah!"

Mrs. Corney shook her head mournfully, as if deploring the mental blindness of those paupers who did not know it; and thrusting a silver spoon (private property) into the inmost recesses of a two-ounce tin tea-caddy, proceeded to make the tea.

How slight a thing will disturb the equanimity of our frail minds! The black teapot, being very small and easily filled, ran over while Mrs. Corney was moralising; and the water slightly scalded Mrs. Corney's hand.

"Drat the pot!" said the worthy matron, setting it down very hastily on the hob; "a little stupid thing, that only holds a couple of cups! What use is it of, to anybody! Except," said Mrs. Corney, pausing, "except to a poor desolate creature like me. Oh dear!"

With these words, the matron dropped into her chair, and, once more resting her elbow on the table, thought of her solitary fate. The small teapot, and the single cup, had awakened in her mind sad recollections of Mr. Corney (who had not been dead more than five-and-twenty years); and she was overpowered.

"I shall never get another!" said Mrs. Corney, pettishly; "I shall never get another—like him."

Whether this remark bore reference to the husband, or the teapot, is uncertain. It might have been the latter; for Mrs. Corney looked at it as she spoke; and took it up afterwards. She had just tasted her first cup, when she was disturbed by a soft tap at the room-door.

"Oh, come in with you!" said Mrs. Corney, sharply. "Some of the old women dying, I suppose. They always die when I'm at meals. Don't stand there, letting the cold air in, don't. What's amiss now, eh?"

"Nothing, ma'am, nothing," replied a man's voice.

"Dear me!" exclaimed the matron, in a much sweeter tone, "is that Mr. Bumble?"

"At your service, ma'am," said Mr. Bumble, who had been stopping outside to rub his shoes clean, and to shake the snow off his coat; and who now made his appearance, bearing the cocked hat in one hand and a bundle in the other. "Shall I shut the door, ma'am?"

The lady modestly hesitated to reply, lest there should be any impropriety in holding an interview with Mr. Bumble, with closed doors. Mr. Bumble taking advantage of the hesitation, and being very cold himself, shut it without permission.

"Hard weather, Mr. Bumble," said the matron.

"Hard, indeed, ma'am," replied the beadle. "Anti-porochial weather this, ma'am. We have given away, Mrs. Corney, we have given away a matter of twenty quartern loaves and a cheese and a half, this very blessed afternoon; and yet them paupers are not contented."

"Of course not. When would they be, Mr. Bumble?" said the matron, sipping her tea.

"When, indeed, ma'am!" rejoined Mr. Bumble. "Why here's one man that, in consideration of his wife and large family, has a quartern loaf and a good pound of cheese, full weight. Is he grateful, ma'am? Is he grateful? Not a copper farthing's worth of it! What does he do, ma'am, but ask for a few coals; if it's only a pocket handkerchief full, he says! Coals! What would he do with coals? Toast his cheese with 'em and then come back for more. That's the way with these people, ma'am; give 'em a apron full of coals to-day, and they'll come back for another, the day after to-morrow, as brazen as alabaster."

The matron expressed her entire concurrence in this intelligible simile; and the beadle went on.

"I never," said Mr. Bumble, "see anything like the pitch it's got to. The day afore yesterday, a man—you have been a married woman, ma'am, and I may mention it to you—a man, with hardly a rag upon his back (here Mrs. Corney looked at the floor), goes to our overseer's door when he has got company coming to dinner; and says, he must be relieved, Mrs. Corney. As he wouldn't go away, and shocked the company very much, our overseer sent him out a pound of potatoes and half a pint of oatmeal. 'My heart!' says the ungrateful villain, 'what's the use of this to me? You might as well give me a pair of iron spectacles!' 'Very good,' says our overseer, taking 'em away again, 'you won't get anything else here.' 'Then I'll die in the streets!' says the vagrant. 'Oh no, you won't,' says our overseer."

"Ha! ha! That was very good! So like Mr. Grannett, wasn't it?" interposed the matron. "Well, Mr. Bumble?"

"Well, ma'am," rejoined the beadle, "he went away; and he did die in the streets. There's a obstinate pauper for you!"

"It beats anything I could have believed," observed the matron emphatically. "But don't you think out-of-door relief a very bad thing, any way, Mr. Bumble? You're a gentleman of experience, and ought to know. Come."

"Mrs. Corney," said the beadle, smiling as men smile who are conscious of superior information, "out-of-door relief, properly managed: properly managed, ma'am: is the porochial safeguard. The great principle of out-of-door relief is, to give the paupers exactly what they don't want; and then they get tired of coming."

"Dear me!" exclaimed Mrs. Corney. "Well, that is a good one, too!"

"Yes. Betwixt you and me, ma'am," returned Mr. Bumble, "that's the great principle; and that's the reason why, if you look at any cases that get into them owdacious newspapers, you'll always observe that sick families have been relieved with slices of cheese. That's the rule now, Mrs. Corney, all over the country. But, however," said the beadle, stopping to unpack his bundle, "these are official secrets, ma'am; not to be spoken of; except, as I may say, among the porochial officers, such as ourselves. This is the port wine, ma'am, that the board ordered for the infirmary; real, fresh, genuine port wine; only out of the cask this forenoon; clear as a bell, and no sediment!"

Having held the first bottle up to the light, and shaken it well to test its excellence, Mr. Bumble placed them both on top of a chest of drawers; folded the handkerchief in which they had been wrapped; put it carefully in his pocket; and took up his hat, as if to go.

"You'll have a very cold walk, Mr. Bumble," said the matron.

"It blows, ma'am," replied Mr. Bumble, turning up his coat-collar, "enough to cut one's ears off."

The matron looked, from the little kettle, to the beadle, who was moving towards the door; and as the beadle coughed, preparatory to bidding her good-night, bashfully inquired whether—whether he wouldn't take a cup of tea?

Mr. Bumble instantaneously turned back his collar again; laid his hat and stick upon a chair; and drew another chair up to the table. As he slowly seated himself, he looked at the lady. She fixed her eyes upon the little teapot. Mr. Bumble coughed again, and slightly smiled.

Mrs. Corney rose to get another cup and saucer from the closet. As she sat down, her eyes once again encountered those of the gallant beadle; she coloured, and applied herself to the task of making his tea. Again Mr. Bumble coughed—louder this time than he had coughed yet.

"Sweet? Mr. Bumble?" inquired the matron, taking up the sugar-basin.

"Very sweet, indeed, ma'am," replied Mr. Bumble. He fixed his eyes on Mrs. Corney as he said this; and if ever a beadle looked tender, Mr. Bumble was that beadle at that moment.

The tea was made, and handed in silence. Mr. Bumble, having spread a handkerchief over his knees to prevent the crumbs from sullying the splendour of his shorts, began to eat and drink; varying these amusements, occasionally, by fetching a deep sigh; which, however, had no injurious effect upon his appetite, but, on the contrary, rather seemed to facilitate his operations in the tea and toast department.

"You have a cat, ma'am, I see," said Mr. Bumble, glancing at one who, in the centre of her family, was basking before the fire; "and kittens too, I declare!"

"I am so fond of them, Mr. Bumble, you can't think," replied the matron. "They're so happy, so frolicsome, and so cheerful, that they are quite companions for me."

"Very nice animals, ma'am," replied Mr. Bumble, approvingly; "so very domestic."

"Oh, yes!" rejoined the matron with enthusiasm; "so fond of their home too, that it's quite a pleasure, I'm sure."

"Mrs. Corney, ma'am," said Mr. Bumble, slowly, and marking the time with his teaspoon, "I mean to say this, ma'am; that any cat, or kitten, that could live with you, ma'am, and not be fond of its home, must be a ass, ma'am."

"Oh, Mr. Bumble!" remonstrated Mrs. Corney.

"It's of no use disguising facts, ma'am," said Mr. Bumble, slowly flourishing the teaspoon with a kind of amorous dignity which made him doubly impressive; "I would drown it myself, with pleasure."

"Then you're a cruel man," said the matron vivaciously, as she held out her hand for the beadle's cup; "and a very hard-hearted man besides."

"Hard-hearted, ma'am?" said Mr. Bumble. "Hard?" Mr. Bumble resigned his cup without another word; squeezed Mrs. Corney's little finger as she took it; and inflicting two open-handed slaps upon his laced waistcoat, gave a mighty sigh, and hitched his chair a very little morsel farther from the fire.

It was a round table; and as Mrs. Corney and Mr. Bumble had been sitting opposite each other, with no great space between them, and fronting the fire, it will be seen that Mr. Bumble, in receding from the fire, and still keeping at the table, increased the distance between himself and Mrs. Corney; which proceeding, some prudent readers will doubtless be disposed to admire, and to consider an act of great heroism on Mr. Bumble's part: he being in some sort tempted by time, place, and opportunity, to give utterance to certain soft nothings, which however well they may become the lips of the light and thoughtless, do seem immeasurably beneath the dignity of judges of the land, members of parliament, ministers of state, lord mayors, and other great public functionaries, but more particularly beneath the stateliness and gravity of a beadle: who (as is well known) should be the sternest and most inflexible among them all.

Whatever were Mr. Bumble's intentions, however (and no doubt they were of the best): it unfortunately happened, as has been twice before remarked, that the table was a round one; consequently Mr. Bumble, moving his chair by little and little, soon began to diminish the distance between himself and the matron; and, continuing to travel round the outer edge of the circle, brought his chair, in time, close to that in which the matron was seated.

Indeed, the two chairs touched; and when they did so, Mr. Bumble stopped.

Now, if the matron had moved her chair to the right, she would have been scorched by the fire; and if to the left, she must have fallen into Mr. Bumble's arms; so (being a discreet matron, and no doubt foreseeing these consequences at a glance) she remained where she was, and handed Mr. Bumble another cup of tea.

"Hard-hearted, Mrs. Corney?" said Mr. Bumble, stirring his tea, and looking up into the matron's face; "are you hard-hearted, Mrs. Corney?"

"Dear me!" exclaimed the matron, "what a very curious question from a single man. What can you want to know for, Mr. Bumble?"

The beadle drank his tea to the last drop; finished a piece of toast; whisked the crumbs off his knees; wiped his lips; and deliberately kissed the matron.

"Mr. Bumble!" cried that discreet lady in a whisper; for the fright was so great, that she had quite lost her voice, "Mr. Bumble, I shall scream!" Mr. Bumble made no reply; but in a slow and dignified manner, put his arm round the matron's waist.

As the lady had stated her intention of screaming, of course she would have screamed at this additional boldness, but that the exertion was rendered unnecessary by a hasty knocking at the door: which was no sooner heard, than Mr. Bumble darted, with much agility, to the wine bottles, and began dusting them with great violence: while the matron sharply demanded who was there.

It is worthy of remark, as a curious physical instance of the efficacy of a sudden surprise in counteracting the effects of extreme fear, that her voice had quite recovered all its official asperity.

"If you please, mistress," said a withered old female pauper, hideously ugly: putting her head in at the door, "Old Sally is a-going fast."

"Well, what's that to me?" angrily demanded the matron. "I can't keep her alive, can I?"

"No, no, mistress," replied the old woman, "nobody can; she's far beyond the reach of help. I've seen a many people die; little babes and great strong men; and I know when death's a-coming, well enough. But she's troubled in her mind: and when the fits are not on her,—and that's not often, for she is dying very hard,—she says she has got something to tell, which you must hear. She'll never die quiet till you come, mistress."

At this intelligence, the worthy Mrs. Corney muttered a variety of invectives against old women who couldn't even die without purposely annoying their betters; and, muffling herself in a thick shawl which she hastily caught up, briefly requested Mr. Bumble to stay till she came back, lest anything particular should occur. Bidding the messenger walk fast, and not be all night hobbling up the stairs, she followed her from the room with a very ill grace, scolding all the way.

Mr. Bumble's conduct on being left to himself, was rather inexplicable. He opened the closet, counted the teaspoons, weighed the sugar-tongs, closely inspected a silver milk-pot to ascertain that it was of the genuine metal, and, having satisfied his curiosity on these points, put on his cocked hat corner-wise, and danced with much gravity four distinct times round the table.

Having gone through this very extraordinary performance, he took off the cocked hat again, and, spreading himself before the fire with his back towards it, seemed to be mentally engaged in taking an exact inventory of the furniture.

CHAPTER XXIV

*Treats on a Very Poor Subject. But Is a Short One, and May Be
Found of Importance in This History*

It was no unfit messenger of death, who had disturbed the quiet of the matron's
room. Her body was bent by age; her limbs trembled with palsy; her face, distorted
into a mumbling leer, resembled more the grotesque shaping of some wild pencil,
than the work of Nature's hand.

Alas! How few of Nature's faces are left alone to gladden us with their beauty!
The cares, and sorrows, and hungerings, of the world, change them as they change
hearts; and it is only when those passions sleep, and have lost their hold for ever, that
the troubled clouds pass off, and leave Heaven's surface clear. It is a common thing
for the countenances of the dead, even in that fixed and rigid state, to subside into the
long-forgotten expression of sleeping infancy, and settle into the very look of early
life; so calm, so peaceful, do they grow again, that those who knew them in their happy
childhood, kneel by the coffin's side in awe, and see the Angel even upon earth.

The old crone tottered along the passages, and up the stairs, muttering some
indistinct answers to the chidings of her companion; being at length compelled to
pause for breath, she gave the light into her hand, and remained behind to follow as
she might: while the more nimble superior made her way to the room where the sick
woman lay.

It was a bare garret-room, with a dim light burning at the farther end. There was
another old woman watching by the bed; the parish apothecary's apprentice was
standing by the fire, making a toothpick out of a quill.

"Cold night, Mrs. Corney," said this young gentleman, as the matron entered.

"Very cold, indeed, sir," replied the mistress, in her most civil tones, and dropping
a curtsey as she spoke.

"You should get better coals out of your contractors," said the apothecary's deputy,
breaking a lump on the top of the fire with the rusty poker; "these are not at all the
sort of thing for a cold night."

"They're the board's choosing, sir," returned the matron. "The least they could do,
would be to keep us pretty warm: for our places are hard enough."

The conversation was here interrupted by a moan from the sick woman.

"Oh!" said the young mag, turning his face towards the bed, as if he had previously
quite forgotten the patient, "it's all U.P. there, Mrs. Corney."

"It is, is it, sir?" asked the matron.

"If she lasts a couple of hours, I shall be surprised," said the apothecary's apprentice,
intent upon the toothpick's point. "It's a break-up of the system altogether. Is she
dozing, old lady?"

The attendant stooped over the bed, to ascertain; and nodded in the affirmative.

"Then perhaps she'll go off in that way, if you don't make a row," said the young
man. "Put the light on the floor. She won't see it there."

The attendant did as she was told: shaking her head meanwhile, to intimate that the woman would not die so easily; having done so, she resumed her seat by the side of the other nurse, who had by this time returned. The mistress, with an expression of impatience, wrapped herself in her shawl, and sat at the foot of the bed.

The apothecary's apprentice, having completed the manufacture of the toothpick, planted himself in front of the fire and made good use of it for ten minutes or so: when apparently growing rather dull, he wished Mrs. Corney joy of her job, and took himself off on tiptoe.

When they had sat in silence for some time, the two old women rose from the bed, and crouching over the fire, held out their withered hands to catch the heat. The flame threw a ghastly light on their shrivelled faces, and made their ugliness appear terrible, as, in this position, they began to converse in a low voice.

"Did she say any more, Anny dear, while I was gone?" inquired the messenger.

"Not a word," replied the other. "She plucked and tore at her arms for a little time; but I held her hands, and she soon dropped off. She hasn't much strength in her, so I easily kept her quiet. I ain't so weak for an old woman, although I am on parish allowance; no, no!"

"Did she drink the hot wine the doctor said she was to have?" demanded the first.

"I tried to get it down," rejoined the other. "But her teeth were tight set, and she clenched the mug so hard that it was as much as I could do to get it back again. So I drank it; and it did me good!"

Looking cautiously round, to ascertain that they were not overheard, the two hags cowered nearer to the fire, and chuckled heartily.

"I mind the time," said the first speaker, "when she would have done the same, and made rare fun of it afterwards."

"Ay, that she would," rejoined the other; "she had a merry heart. A many, many, beautiful corpses she laid out, as nice and neat as waxwork. My old eyes have seen them—ay, and those old hands touched them too; for I have helped her, scores of times."

Stretching forth her trembling fingers as she spoke, the old creature shook them exultingly before her face, and fumbling in her pocket, brought out an old time-discoloured tin snuff-box, from which she shook a few grains into the outstretched palm of her companion, and a few more into her own. While they were thus employed, the matron, who had been impatiently watching until the dying woman should awaken from her stupor, joined them by the fire, and sharply asked how long she was to wait?

"Not long, mistress," replied the second woman, looking up into her face. "We have none of us long to wait for Death. Patience, patience! He'll be here soon enough for us all."

"Hold your tongue, you doting idiot!" said the matron sternly. "You, Martha, tell me; has she been in this way before?"

"Often," answered the first woman.

"But will never be again," added the second one; "that is, she'll never wake again but once—and mind, mistress, that won't be for long!"

"Long or short," said the matron, snappishly, "she won't find me here when she does wake; take care, both of you, how you worry me again for nothing. It's no part of my duty to see all the old women in the house die, and I won't—that's more. Mind that, you impudent old harridans. If you make a fool of me again, I'll soon cure you, I warrant you!"

She was bouncing away, when a cry from the two women, who had turned towards the bed, caused her to look round. The patient had raised herself upright, and was stretching her arms towards them.

"Who's that?" she cried, in a hollow voice.

"Hush, hush!" said one of the women, stooping over her. "Lie down, lie down!"

"I'll never lie down again alive!" said the woman, struggling. "I will tell her! Come here! Nearer! Let me whisper in your ear."

She clutched the matron by the arm, and forcing her into a chair by the bedside, was about to speak, when looking round, she caught sight of the two old women bending forward in the attitude of eager listeners.

"Turn them away," said the woman, drowsily; "make haste! make haste!"

The two old crones, chiming in together, began pouring out many piteous lamentations that the poor dear was too far gone to know her best friends; and were uttering sundry protestations that they would never leave her, when the superior pushed them from the room, closed the door, and returned to the bedside. On being excluded, the old ladies changed their tone, and cried through the keyhole that old Sally was drunk; which, indeed, was not unlikely; since, in addition to a moderate dose of opium prescribed by the apothecary, she was labouring under the effects of a final taste of gin-and-water which had been privily administered, in the openness of their hearts, by the worthy old ladies themselves.

"Now listen to me," said the dying woman aloud, as if making a great effort to revive one latent spark of energy. "In this very room—in this very bed—I once nursed a pretty young creetur', that was brought into the house with her feet cut and bruised with walking, and all soiled with dust and blood. She gave birth to a boy, and died. Let me think—what was the year again!"

"Never mind the year," said the impatient auditor; "what about her?"

"Ay," murmured the sick woman, relapsing into her former drowsy state, "what about her?—what about—I know!" she cried, jumping fiercely up: her face flushed, and her eyes starting from her head—'I robbed her, so I did! She wasn't cold—I tell you she wasn't cold, when I stole it!"

"Stole what, for God's sake?" cried the matron, with a gesture as if she would call for help.

"It!" replied the woman, laying her hand over the other's mouth. "The only thing she had. She wanted clothes to keep her warm, and food to eat; but she had kept it safe, and had it in her bosom. It was gold, I tell you! Rich gold, that might have saved her life!"

"Gold!" echoed the matron, bending eagerly over the woman as she fell back. "Go on, go on—yes—what of it? Who was the mother? When was it?"

"She charge me to keep it safe," replied the woman with a groan, "and trusted me as the only woman about her. I stole it in my heart when she first showed it me hanging round her neck; and the child's death, perhaps, is on me besides! They would have treated him better, if they had known it all!"

"Known what?" asked the other. "Speak!"

"The boy grew so like his mother," said the woman, rambling on, and not heeding the question, "that I could never forget it when I saw his face. Poor girl! poor girl! She was so young, too! Such a gentle lamb! Wait; there's more to tell. I have not told you all, have I?"

"No, no," replied the matron, inclining her head to catch the words, as they came more faintly from the dying woman. "Be quick, or it may be too late!"

"The mother," said the woman, making a more violent effort than before; "the mother, when the pains of death first came upon her, whispered in my ear that if her baby was born alive, and thrived, the day might come when it would not feel so much disgraced to hear its poor young mother named. "And oh, kind Heaven!" she said, folding her thin hands together, "whether it be boy or girl, raise up some friends for it in this troubled world, and take pity upon a lonely desolate child, abandoned to its mercy!""

"The boy's name?" demanded the matron.

"They called him Oliver," replied the woman, feebly. "The gold I stole was—"

"Yes, yes—what?" cried the other.

She was bending eagerly over the woman to hear her reply; but drew back, instinctively, as she once again rose, slowly and stiffly, into a sitting posture; then, clutching the coverlid with both hands, muttered some indistinct sounds in her throat, and fell lifeless on the bed.

* * * * *

"Stone dead!" said one of the old women, hurrying in as soon as the door was opened.

"And nothing to tell, after all," rejoined the matron, walking carelessly away.

The two crones, to all appearance, too busily occupied in the preparations for their dreadful duties to make any reply, were left alone, hovering about the body.

CHAPTER XXV

Wherein This History Reverts to Mr. Fagin and Company

While these things were passing in the country workhouse, Mr. Fagin sat in the old den—the same from which Oliver had been removed by the girl— brooding over a dull, smoky fire. He held a pair of bellows upon his knee, with which he had apparently been endeavouring to rouse it into more cheerful action; but he had fallen into deep thought; and with his arms folded on them, and his chin resting on his thumbs, fixed his eyes, abstractedly, on the rusty bars.

At a table behind him sat the Artful Dodger, Master Charles Bates, and Mr. Chitling: all intent upon a game of whist; the Artful taking dummy against Master Bates and Mr. Chitling. The countenance of the first-named gentleman, peculiarly intelligent at all times, acquired great additional interest from his close observance of the game, and his attentive perusal of Mr. Chitling's hand; upon which, from time to time, as occasion served, he bestowed a variety of earnest glances: wisely regulating his own play by the result of his observations upon his neighbour's cards. It being a cold night, the Dodger wore his hat, as, indeed, was often his custom within doors. He also sustained a clay pipe between his teeth, which he only removed for a brief space when he deemed it necessary to apply for refreshment to a quart pot upon the table, which stood ready filled with gin-and-water for the accommodation of the company.

Master Bates was also attentive to the play; but being of a more excitable nature than his accomplished friend, it was observable that he more frequently applied himself to the gin-and-water, and moreover indulged in many jests and irrelevant remarks, all highly unbecoming a scientific rubber. Indeed, the Artful, presuming upon their close attachment, more than once took occasion to reason gravely with his companion upon these improprieties; all of which remonstrances, Master Bates received in extremely good part; merely requesting his friend to be "blowed," or to insert his head in a sack, or replying with some other neatly-turned witticism of a similar kind, the happy application of which, excited considerable admiration in the mind of Mr. Chitling. It was remarkable that the latter gentleman and his partner invariably lost; and that the circumstance, so far from angering Master Bates, appeared to afford him the highest amusement, inasmuch as he laughed most uproariously at the end of every deal, and protested that he had never seen such a jolly game in all his born days.

"That's two doubles and the rub," said Mr. Chitling, with a very long face, as he drew half-a-crown from his waistcoat-pocket. "I never see such a feller as you, Jack; you win everything. Even when we've good cards, Charley and I can't make nothing of 'em."

Either the master or the manner of this remark, which was made very ruefully, delighted Charley Bates so much, that his consequent shout of laughter roused the Jew from his reverie, and induced him to inquire what was the matter.

"Matter, Fagin!" cried Charley. "I wish you had watched the play. Tommy Chitling hasn't won a point; and I went partners with him against the Artfull and dumb."

"Ay, ay!" said the Jew, with a grin, which sufficiently demonstrated that he was at no loss to understand the reason. "Try 'em again, Tom; try 'em again."

"No more of it for me, thank 'ee, Fagin," replied Mr. Chitling; "I've had enough. That 'ere Dodger has such a run of luck that there's no standing again' him."

"Ha! ha! my dear," replied the Jew, "you must get up very early in the morning, to win against the Dodger."

"Morning!" said Charley Bates; "you must put your boots on over-night, and have a telescope at each eye, and a opera-glass between your shoulders, if you want to come over him."

Mr. Dawkins received these handsome compliments with much philosophy, and offered to cut any gentleman in company, for the first picture-card, at a shilling at a time. Nobody accepting the challenge, and his pipe being by this time smoked out, he proceeded to amuse himself by sketching a ground-plan of Newgate on the table with the piece of chalk which had served him in lieu of counters; whistling, meantime, with peculiar shrillness.

"How precious dull you are, Tommy!" said the Dodger, stopping short when there had been a long silence; and addressing Mr. Chitling. "What do you think he's thinking of, Fagin?"

"How should I know, my dear?" replied the Jew, looking round as he plied the bellows. "About his losses, maybe; or the little retirement in the country that he's just left, eh? Ha! ha! Is that it, my dear?"

"Not a bit of it," replied the Dodger, stopping the subject of discourse as Mr. Chitling was about to reply. "What do you say, Charley?"

"I should say," replied Master Bates, with a grin, "that he was uncommon sweet upon Betsy. See how he's a-blushing! Oh, my eye! here's a merry-go-rounder! Tommy Chitling's in love! Oh, Fagin, Fagin! what a spree!"

Thoroughly overpowered with the notion of Mr. Chitling being the victim of the tender passion, Master Bates threw himself back in his chair with such violence, that he lost his balance, and pitched over upon the floor; where (the accident abating nothing of his merriment) he lay at full length until his laugh was over, when he resumed his former position, and began another laugh.

"Never mind him, my dear," said the Jew, winking at Mr. Dawkins, and giving Master Bates a reproving tap with the nozzle of the bellows. "Betsy's a fine girl. Stick up to her, Tom. Stick up to her."

"What I mean to say, Fagin," replied Mr. Chitling, very red in the face, "is, that that isn't anything to anybody here."

"No more it is," replied the Jew; "Charley will talk. Don't mind him, my dear; don't mind him. Betsy's a fine girl. Do as she bids you, Tom, and you will make your fortune."

"So I do do as she bids me," replied Mr. Chitling; "I shouldn't have been milled, if it hadn't been for her advice. But it turned out a good job for you; didn't it, Fagin! And what's six weeks of it? It must come, some time or another, and why not in the winter time when you don't want to go out a-walking so much; eh, Fagin?"

"Ah, to be sure, my dear," replied the Jew.

"You wouldn't mind it again, Tom, would you," asked the Dodger, winking upon Charley and the Jew, "if Bet was all right?"

"I mean to say that I shouldn't," replied Tom, angrily. "There, now. Ah! Who'll say as much as that, I should like to know; eh, Fagin?"

"Nobody, my dear," replied the Jew; "not a soul, Tom. I don't know one of 'em that would do it besides you; not one of 'em, my dear."

"I might have got clear off, if I'd split upon her; mightn't I, Fagin?" angrily pursued the poor half-witted dupe. "A word from me would have done it; wouldn't it, Fagin?"

"To be sure it would, my dear," replied the Jew.

"But I didn't blab it; did I, Fagin?" demanded Tom, pouring question upon question with great volubility.

"No, no, to be sure," replied the Jew; "you were too stout-hearted for that. A deal too stout, my dear!"

"Perhaps I was," rejoined Tom, looking round; "and if I was, what's to laugh at, in that; eh, Fagin?"

The Jew, perceiving that Mr. Chitling was considerably roused, hastened to assure him that nobody was laughing; and to prove the gravity of the company, appealed to Master Bates, the principal offender. But, unfortunately, Charley, in opening his mouth to reply that he was never more serious in his life, was unable to prevent the escape of such a violent roar, that the abused Mr. Chitling, without any preliminary ceremonies, rushed across the room and aimed a blow at the offender; who, being skilful in evading pursuit, ducked to avoid it, and chose his time so well that it lighted on the chest of the merry old gentleman, and caused him to stagger to the wall, where he stood panting for breath, while Mr. Chitling looked on in intense dismay.

"Hark!" cried the Dodger at this moment, "I heard the tinkler.' Catching up the light, he crept softly upstairs.

The bell was rung again, with some impatience, while the party were in darkness. After a short pause, the Dodger reappeared, and whispered Fagin mysteriously.

"What!" cried the Jew, "alone?"

The Dodger nodded in the affirmative, and, shading the flame of the candle with his hand, gave Charley Bates a private intimation, in dumb show, that he had better not be funny just then. Having performed this friendly office, he fixed his eyes on the Jew's face, and awaited his directions.

The old man bit his yellow fingers, and meditated for some seconds; his face working with agitation the while, as if he dreaded something, and feared to know the worst. At length he raised his head.

"Where is he?" he asked.

The Dodger pointed to the floor above, and made a gesture, as if to leave the room.

"Yes," said the Jew, answering the mute inquiry; "bring him down. Hush! Quiet, Charley! Gently, Tom! Scarce, scarce!"

This brief direction to Charley Bates, and his recent antagonist, was softly and immediately obeyed. There was no sound of their whereabout, when the Dodger descended the stairs, bearing the light in his hand, and followed by a man in a coarse smock-frock; who, after casting a hurried glance round the room, pulled off a large wrapper which had concealed the lower portion of his face, and disclosed: all haggard, unwashed, and unshorn: the features of flash Toby Crackit.

"How are you, Faguey?" said this worthy, nodding to the Jew. "Pop that shawl away in my castor, Dodger, so that I may know where to find it when I cut; that's the time of day! You'll be a fine young cracksman afore the old file now."

With these words he pulled up the smock-frock; and, winding it round his middle, drew a chair to the fire, and placed his feet upon the hob.

"See there, Faguey," he said, pointing disconsolately to his top boots; "not a drop of Day and Martin since you know when; not a bubble of blacking, by Jove! But don't look at me in that way, man. All in good time. I can't talk about business till I've eat and drank; so produce the sustainance, and let's have a quiet fill-out for the first time these three days!"

The Jew motioned to the Dodger to place what eatables there were, upon the table; and, seating himself opposite the housebreaker, waited his leisure.

To judge from appearances, Toby was by no means in a hurry to open the conversation. At first, the Jew contented himself with patiently watching his countenance, as if to gain from its expression some clue to the intelligence he brought; but in vain.

He looked tired and worn, but there was the same complacent repose upon his features that they always wore: and through dirt, and beard, and whisker, there still shone, unimpaired, the self-satisfied smirk of flash Toby Crackit. Then the Jew, in an agony of impatience, watched every morsel he put into his mouth; pacing up and down the room, meanwhile, in irrepressible excitement. It was all of no use. Toby continued to eat with the utmost outward indifference, until he could eat no more; then, ordering the Dodger out, he closed the door, mixed a glass of spirits and water, and composed himself for talking.

"First and foremost, Faguey," said Toby.

"Yes, yes!" interposed the Jew, drawing up his chair.

Mr. Crackit stopped to take a draught of spirits and water, and to declare that the gin was excellent; then placing his feet against the low mantelpiece, so as to bring his boots to about the level of his eye, he quietly resumed.

"First and foremost, Faguey," said the housebreaker, "how's Bill?"

"What!" screamed the Jew, starting from his seat.

"Why, you don't mean to say——" began Toby, turning pale.

"Mean!" cried the Jew, stamping furiously on the ground. "Where are they? Sikes and the boy! Where are they? Where have they been? Where are they hiding? Why have they not been here?"

"The crack failed," said Toby faintly.

"I know it," replied the Jew, tearing a newspaper from his pocket and pointing to it. "What more?"

"They fired and hit the boy. We cut over the fields at the back, with him between us—straight as the crow flies—through hedge and ditch. They gave chase. Damme! the whole country was awake, and the dogs upon us."

"The boy!"

"Bill had him on his back, and scudded like the wind. We stopped to take him between us; his head hung down, and he was cold. They were close upon our heels; every man for himself, and each from the gallows! We parted company, and left the youngster lying in a ditch. Alive or dead, that's all I know about him."

The Jew stopped to hear no more; but uttering a loud yell, and twining his hands in his hair, rushed from the room, and from the house.

CHAPTER XXVI

In Which a Mysterious Character Appears Upon the Scene;
and Many Things, Inseparable From This History,
Are Done and Performed

The old man had gained the street corner, before he began to recover the effect of Toby Crackit's intelligence. He had relaxed nothing of his unusual speed; but was still pressing onward, in the same wild and disordered manner, when the sudden dashing past of a carriage: and a boisterous cry from the foot passengers, who saw his danger: drove him back upon the pavement. Avoiding, as much as was possible, all the main streets, and skulking only through the by-ways and alleys, he at length emerged on Snow Hill. Here he walked even faster than before; nor did he linger until he had again turned into a court; when, as if conscious that he was now in his proper element, he fell into his usual shuffling pace, and seemed to breathe more freely.

Near to the spot on which Snow Hill and Holborn Hill meet, opens, upon the right hand as you come out of the City, a narrow and dismal alley, leading to Saffron Hill. In its filthy shops are exposed for sale huge bunches of second-hand silk handkerchiefs, of all sizes and patterns; for here reside the traders who purchase them from pick-pockets. Hundreds of these handkerchiefs hang dangling from pegs outside the windows or flaunting from the door-posts; and the shelves, within, are piled with them. Confined as the limits of Field Lane are, it has its barber, its coffee-shop, its beer-shop, and its fried-fish warehouse. It is a commercial colony of itself: the emporium of petty larceny: visited at early morning, and setting-in of dusk, by silent merchants, who traffic in dark back-parlours, and who go as strangely as they come. Here, the clothesman, the shoe-vamper, and the rag-merchant, display their goods, as sign-boards to the petty thief; here, stores of old iron and bones, and heaps of mildewy fragments of woollen-stuff and linen, rust and rot in the grimy cellars.

It was into this place that the Jew turned. He was well known to the sallow denizens of the lane; for such of them as were on the look-out to buy or sell, nodded, familiarly, as he passed along. He replied to their salutations in the same way; but bestowed no closer recognition until he reached the further end of the alley; when he stopped, to address a salesman of small stature, who had squeezed as much of his person into a child's chair as the chair would hold, and was smoking a pipe at his warehouse door.

"Why, the sight of you, Mr. Fagin, would cure the hoptalmy!" said this respectable trader, in acknowledgment of the Jew's inquiry after his health.

"The neighbourhood was a little too hot, Lively," said Fagin, elevating his eyebrows, and crossing his hands upon his shoulders.

"Well, I've heerd that complaint of it, once or twice before," replied the trader; "but it soon cools down again; don't you find it so?"

Fagin nodded in the affirmative. Pointing in the direction of Saffron Hill, he inquired whether any one was up yonder to-night.

"At the Cripples?" inquired the man.

The Jew nodded.

"Let me see," pursued the merchant, reflecting.

"Yes, there's some half-dozen of 'em gone in, that I knows. I don't think your friend's there."

"Sikes is not, I suppose?" inquired the Jew, with a disappointed countenance.

"Non istwentus, as the lawyers say," replied the little man, shaking his head, and looking amazingly sly. "Have you got anything in my line to-night?"

"Nothing to-night," said the Jew, turning away.

"Are you going up to the Cripples, Fagin?" cried the little man, calling after him. "Stop! I don't mind if I have a drop there with you!"

But as the Jew, looking back, waved his hand to intimate that he preferred being alone; and, moreover, as the little man could not very easily disengage himself from the chair; the sign of the Cripples was, for a time, bereft of the advantage of Mr. Lively's presence. By the time he had got upon his legs, the Jew had disappeared; so Mr. Lively, after ineffectually standing on tiptoe, in the hope of catching sight of him, again forced himself into the little chair, and, exchanging a shake of the head with a lady in the opposite shop, in which doubt and mistrust were plainly mingled, resumed his pipe with a grave demeanour.

The Three Cripples, or rather the Cripples; which was the sign by which the establishment was familiarly known to its patrons: was the public-house in which Mr. Sikes and his dog have already figured. Merely making a sign to a man at the bar, Fagin walked straight upstairs, and opening the door of a room, and softly insinuating himself into the chamber, looked anxiously about: shading his eyes with his hand, as if in search of some particular person.

The room was illuminated by two gas-lights; the glare of which was prevented by the barred shutters, and closely-drawn curtains of faded red, from being visible outside. The ceiling was blackened, to prevent its colour from being injured by the flaring of the lamps; and the place was so full of dense tobacco smoke, that at first it was scarcely possible to discern anything more. By degrees, however, as some of it cleared away through the open door, an assemblage of heads, as confused as the noises that greeted the ear, might be made out; and as the eye grew more accustomed to the scene, the spectator gradually became aware of the presence of a numerous company, male and female, crowded round a long table: at the upper end of which, sat a chairman with a hammer of office in his hand; while a professional gentleman with a bluish nose, and his face tied up for the benefit of a toothache, presided at a jingling piano in a remote corner.

As Fagin stepped softly in, the professional gentleman, running over the keys by way of prelude, occasioned a general cry of order for a song; which having subsided, a young lady proceeded to entertain the company with a ballad in four verses, between each of which the accompanyist played the melody all through, as loud as he could.

When this was over, the chairman gave a sentiment, after which, the professional gentleman on the chairman's right and left volunteered a duet, and sang it, with great applause.

It was curious to observe some faces which stood out prominently from among the group. There was the chairman himself, (the landlord of the house,) a coarse, rough, heavy built fellow, who, while the songs were proceeding, rolled his eyes hither and thither, and, seeming to give himself up to joviality, had an eye for everything that was done, and an ear for everything that was said—and sharp ones, too. Near him were the singers: receiving, with professional indifference, the compliments of the company, and applying themselves, in turn, to a dozen proffered glasses of spirits and water, tendered by their more boisterous admirers; whose countenances, expressive of almost every vice in almost every grade, irresistibly attracted the attention, by their very repulsiveness. Cunning, ferocity, and drunkeness in all its stages, were there, in their strongest aspect; and women: some with the last lingering tinge of their early freshness almost fading as you looked: others with every mark and stamp of their sex utterly beaten out, and presenting but one loathsome blank of profligacy and crime; some mere girls, others but young women, and none past the prime of life; formed the darkest and saddest portion of this dreary picture.

Fagin, troubled by no grave emotions, looked eagerly from face to face while these proceedings were in progress; but apparently without meeting that of which he was in search. Succeeding, at length, in catching the eye of the man who occupied the chair, he beckoned to him slightly, and left the room, as quietly as he had entered it.

"What can I do for you, Mr. Fagin?" inquired the man, as he followed him out to the landing. "Won't you join us? They'll be delighted, every one of 'em."

The Jew shook his head impatiently, and said in a whisper, "Is he here?"

"No," replied the man.

"And no news of Barney?" inquired Fagin.

"None," replied the landlord of the Cripples; for it was he. "He won't stir till it's all safe. Depend on it, they're on the scent down there; and that if he moved, he'd blow upon the thing at once. He's all right enough, Barney is, else I should have heard of him. I'll pound it, that Barney's managing properly. Let him alone for that."

"Will he be here to-night?" asked the Jew, laying the same emphasis on the pronoun as before.

"Monks, do you mean?" inquired the landlord, hesitating.

"Hush!" said the Jew. "Yes."

"Certain," replied the man, drawing a gold watch from his fob; "I expected him here before now. If you'll wait ten minutes, he'll be——"

"No, no," said the Jew, hastily; as though, however desirous he might be to see the person in question, he was nevertheless relieved by his absence. "Tell him I came here to see him; and that he must come to me to-night. No, say to-morrow. As he is not here, to-morrow will be time enough."

"Good!" said the man. "Nothing more?"

"Not a word now," said the Jew, descending the stairs.

"I say," said the other, looking over the rails, and speaking in a hoarse whisper; "what a time this would be for a sell! I've got Phil Barker here: so drunk, that a boy might take him!"

"Ah! But it's not Phil Barker's time," said the Jew, looking up.

"Phil has something more to do, before we can afford to part with him; so go back to the company, my dear, and tell them to lead merry lives—while they last. Ha! ha! ha!"

The landlord reciprocated the old man's laugh; and returned to his guests. The Jew was no sooner alone, than his countenance resumed its former expression of anxiety and thought. After a brief reflection, he called a hack-cabriolet, and bade the man drive towards Bethnal Green. He dismissed him within some quarter of a mile of Mr. Sikes's residence, and performed the short remainder of the distance, on foot.

"Now," muttered the Jew, as he knocked at the door, "if there is any deep play here, I shall have it out of you, my girl, cunning as you are."

She was in her room, the woman said. Fagin crept softly upstairs, and entered it without any previous ceremony. The girl was alone; lying with her head upon the table, and her hair straggling over it.

"She has been drinking," thought the Jew, cooly, "or perhaps she is only miserable."

The old man turned to close the door, as he made this reflection; the noise thus occasioned, roused the girl. She eyed his crafty face narrowly, as she inquired to his recital of Toby Crackit's story. When it was concluded, she sank into her former attitude, but spoke not a word. She pushed the candle impatiently away; and once or twice as she feverishly changed her position, shuffled her feet upon the ground; but this was all.

During the silence, the Jew looked restlessly about the room, as if to assure himself that there were no appearances of Sikes having covertly returned. Apparently satisfied with his inspection, he coughed twice or thrice, and made as many efforts to open a conversation; but the girl heeded him no more than if he had been made of stone. At length he made another attempt; and rubbing his hands together, said, in his most conciliatory tone,

"And where should you think Bill was now, my dear?"

The girl moaned out some half intelligible reply, that she could not tell; and seemed, from the smothered noise that escaped her, to be crying.

"And the boy, too," said the Jew, straining his eyes to catch a glimpse of her face. "Poor leetle child! Left in a ditch, Nance; only think!"

"The child," said the girl, suddenly looking up, "is better where he is, than among us; and if no harm comes to Bill from it, I hope he lies dead in the ditch and that his young bones may rot there."

"What!" cried the Jew, in amazement.

"Ay, I do," returned the girl, meeting his gaze. "I shall be glad to have him away from my eyes, and to know that the worst is over. I can't bear to have him about me. The sight of him turns me against myself, and all of you."

"Pooh!" said the Jew, scornfully. "You're drunk."

"Am I?" cried the girl bitterly. "It's no fault of yours, if I am not! You'd never have me anything else, if you had your will, except now;—the humour doesn't suit you, doesn't it?"

"No!" rejoined the Jew, furiously. "It does not."

"Change it, then!" responded the girl, with a laugh.

"Change it!" exclaimed the Jew, exasperated beyond all bounds by his companion's unexpected obstinacy, and the vexation of the night, "I will change it! Listen to me, you drab. Listen to me, who with six words, can strangle Sikes as surely as if I had his bull's throat between my fingers now. If he comes back, and leaves the boy behind him; if he gets off free, and dead or alive, fails to restore him to me; murder him yourself if you would have him escape Jack Ketch. And do it the moment he sets foot in this room, or mind me, it will be too late!"

"What is all this?" cried the girl involuntarily.

"What is it?" pursued Fagin, mad with rage. "When the boy's worth hundreds of pounds to me, am I to lose what chance threw me in the way of getting safely, through the whims of a drunken gang that I could whistle away the lives of! And me bound, too, to a born devil that only wants the will, and has the power to, to—"

Panting for breath, the old man stammered for a word; and in that instant checked the torrent of his wrath, and changed his whole demeanour. A moment before, his clenched hands had grasped the air; his eyes had dilated; and his face grown livid with passion; but now, he shrunk into a chair, and, cowering together, trembled with the apprehension of having himself disclosed some hidden villainy. After a short silence, he ventured to look round at his companion. He appeared somewhat reassured, on beholding her in the same listless attitude from which he had first roused her.

"Nancy, dear!" croaked the Jew, in his usual voice. "Did you mind me, dear?"

"Don't worry me now, Fagin!" replied the girl, raising her head languidly. "If Bill has not done it this time, he will another. He has done many a good job for you, and will do many more when he can; and when he can't he won't; so no more about that."

"Regarding this boy, my dear?" said the Jew, rubbing the palms of his hands nervously together.

"The boy must take his chance with the rest," interrupted Nancy, hastily; "and I say again, I hope he is dead, and out of harm's way, and out of yours,—that is, if Bill comes to no harm. And if Toby got clear off, Bill's pretty sure to be safe; for Bill's worth two of Toby any time."

"And about what I was saying, my dear?" observed the Jew, keeping his glistening eye steadily upon her.

"Your must say it all over again, if it's anything you want me to do," rejoined Nancy; "and if it is, you had better wait till to-morrow. You put me up for a minute; but now I'm stupid again."

Fagin put several other questions: all with the same drift of ascertaining whether the girl had profited by his unguarded hints; but, she answered them so readily, and was withal so utterly unmoved by his searching looks, that his original impression of her being more than a trifle in liquor, was confirmed. Nancy, indeed, was not exempt from a failing which was very common among the Jew's female pupils; and in which, in their tenderer years, they were rather encouraged than checked. Her disordered appearance, and a wholesale perfume of Geneva which pervaded the apartment, afforded strong confirmatory evidence of the justice of the Jew's supposition; and when, after indulging in the temporary display of violence above described, she subsided, first into dullness, and afterwards into a compound of feelings: under the influence of which she shed tears one minute, and in the next gave utterance to various exclamations of "Never say die!" and divers calculations as to what might be the amount of the odds so long as a lady or gentleman was happy, Mr. Fagin, who had had considerable experience of such matters in his time, saw, with great satisfaction, that she was very far gone indeed.

Having eased his mind by this discovery; and having accomplished his twofold object of imparting to the girl what he had, that night, heard, and of ascertaining, with his own eyes, that Sikes had not returned, Mr. Fagin again turned his face homeward: leaving his young friend asleep, with her head upon the table.

It was within an hour of midnight. The weather being dark, and piercing cold, he had no great temptation to loiter. The sharp wind that scoured the streets, seemed to have cleared them of passengers, as of dust and mud, for few people were abroad, and they were to all appearance hastening fast home. It blew from the right quarter for the Jew, however, and straight before it he went: trembling, and shivering, as every fresh gust drove him rudely on his way.

He had reached the corner of his own street, and was already fumbling in his pocket for the door-key, when a dark figure emerged from a projecting entrance which lay in deep shadow, and, crossing the road, glided up to him unperceived.

"Fagin!" whispered a voice close to his ear.

"Ah!" said the Jew, turning quickly round, "is that—"

"Yes!" interrupted the stranger. "I have been lingering here these two hours. Where the devil have you been?"

"On your business, my dear," replied the Jew, glancing uneasily at his companion, and slackening his pace as he spoke. "On your business all night."

"Oh, of course!" said the stranger, with a sneer. "Well; and what's come of it?"

"Nothing good," said the Jew.

"Nothing bad, I hope?" said the stranger, stopping short, and turning a startled look on his companion.

The Jew shook his head, and was about to reply, when the stranger, interrupting him, motioned to the house, before which they had by this time arrived: remarking, that he had better say what he had got to say, under cover: for his blood was chilled with standing about so long, and the wind blew through him.

Fagin looked as if he could have willingly excused himself from taking home a visitor at that unseasonable hour; and, indeed, muttered something about having no fire; but his companion repeating his request in a peremptory manner, he unlocked the door, and requested him to close it softly, while he got a light.

"It's as dark as the grave," said the man, groping forward a few steps. "Make haste!"

"Shut the door," whispered Fagin from the end of the passage. As he spoke, it closed with a loud noise.

"That wasn't my doing," said the other man, feeling his way. "The wind blew it to, or it shut of its own accord: one or the other. Look sharp with the light, or I shall knock my brains out against something in this confounded hole."

Fagin stealthily descended the kitchen stairs. After a short absence, he returned with a lighted candle, and the intelligence that Toby Crackit was asleep in the back room below, and that the boys were in the front one. Beckoning the man to follow him, he led the way upstairs.

"We can say the few words we've got to say in here, my dear," said the Jew, throwing open a door on the first floor; "and as there are holes in the shutters, and we never show lights to our neighbours, we'll set the candle on the stairs. There!"

With those words, the Jew, stooping down, placed the candle on an upper flight of stairs, exactly opposite to the room door. This done, he led the way into the apartment; which was destitute of all movables save a broken arm-chair, and an old couch or sofa without covering, which stood behind the door. Upon this piece of furniture, the stranger sat himself with the air of a weary man; and the Jew, drawing up the arm-chair opposite, they sat face to face. It was not quite dark; the door was partially open; and the candle outside, threw a feeble reflection on the opposite wall.

They conversed for some time in whispers. Though nothing of the conversation was distinguishable beyond a few disjointed words here and there, a listener might easily have perceived that Fagin appeared to be defending himself against some remarks of the stranger; and that the latter was in a state of considerable irritation. They might have been talking, thus, for a quarter of an hour or more, when Monks—by which name the Jew had designated the strange man several times in the course of their colloquy—said, raising his voice a little,

"I tell you again, it was badly planned. Why not have kept him here among the rest, and made a sneaking, snivelling pickpocket of him at once?"

"Only hear him!" exclaimed the Jew, shrugging his shoulders.

"Why, do you mean to say you couldn't have done it, if you had chosen?" demanded Monks, sternly. "Haven't you done it, with other boys, scores of times? If you had had patience for a twelvemonth, at most, couldn't you have got him convicted, and sent safely out of the kingdom; perhaps for life?"

"Whose turn would that have served, my dear?" inquired the Jew humbly.

"Mine," replied Monks.

"But not mine," said the Jew, submissively. "He might have become of use to me. When there are two parties to a bargain, it is only reasonable that the interests of both should be consulted; is it, my good friend?"

"What then?" demanded Monks.

"I saw it was not easy to train him to the business," replied the Jew; "he was not like other boys in the same circumstances."

"Curse him, no!" muttered the man, "or he would have been a thief, long ago."

"I had no hold upon him to make him worse," pursued the Jew, anxiously watching the countenance of his companion. "His hand was not in. I had nothing to frighten him with; which we always must have in the beginning, or we labour in vain. What could I do? Send him out with the Dodger and Charley? We had enough of that, at first, my dear; I trembled for us all."

"That was not my doing," observed Monks.

"No, no, my dear!" renewed the Jew. "And I don't quarrel with it now; because, if it had never happened, you might never have clapped eyes on the boy to notice him, and so led to the discovery that it was him you were looking for. Well! I got him back for you by means of the girl; and then she begins to favour him."

"Throttle the girl!" said Monks, impatiently.

"Why, we can't afford to do that just now, my dear," replied the Jew, smiling; "and, besides, that sort of thing is not in our way; or, one of these days, I might be glad to have it done. I know what these girls are, Monks, well. As soon as the boy begins to harden, she'll care no more for him, than for a block of wood. You want him made a thief. If he is alive, I can make him one from this time; and, if—if—" said the Jew, drawing nearer to the other,—"it's not likely, mind,—but if the worst comes to the worst, and he is dead—"

"It's no fault of mine if he is!" interposed the other man, with a look of terror, and clasping the Jew's arm with trembling hands. "Mind that. Fagin! I had no hand in it. Anything but his death, I told you from the first. I won't shed blood; it's always found out, and haunts a man besides. If they shot him dead, I was not the cause; do you hear me? Fire this infernal den! What's that?"

"What!" cried the Jew, grasping the coward round the body, with both arms, as he sprung to his feet. "Where?"

"Yonder! replied the man, glaring at the opposite wall. "The shadow! I saw the shadow of a woman, in a cloak and bonnet, pass along the wainscot like a breath!"

The Jew released his hold, and they rushed tumultuously from the room. The candle, wasted by the draught, was standing where it had been placed. It showed them only the empty staircase, and their own white faces. They listened intently: a profound silence reigned throughout the house.

"It's your fancy," said the Jew, taking up the light and turning to his companion.

"I'll swear I saw it!" replied Monks, trembling. "It was bending forward when I saw it first; and when I spoke, it darted away."

The Jew glanced contemptuously at the pale face of his associate, and, telling him he could follow, if he pleased, ascended the stairs. They looked into all the rooms; they were cold, bare, and empty. They descended into the passage, and thence into the cellars below. The green damp hung upon the low walls; the tracks of the snail and slug glistened in the light of the candle; but all was still as death.

"What do you think now?" said the Jew, when they had regained the passage. "Besides ourselves, there's not a creature in the house except Toby and the boys; and they're safe enough. See here!"

As a proof of the fact, the Jew drew forth two keys from his pocket; and explained, that when he first went downstairs, he had locked them in, to prevent any intrusion on the conference.

This accumulated testimony effectually staggered Mr. Monks. His protestations had gradually become less and less vehement as they proceeded in their search without making any discovery; and, now, he gave vent to several very grim laughs, and confessed it could only have been his excited imagination. He declined any renewal of the conversation, however, for that night: suddenly remembering that it was past one o'clock. And so the amiable couple parted.

CHAPTER XXVII

Atones for the Unpoliteness of a Former Chapter;
Which Deserted a Lady, Most Unceremoniously

As it would be, by no means, seemly in a humble author to keep so mighty a personage as a beadle waiting, with his back to the fire, and the skirts of his coat gathered up under his arms, until such time as it might suit his pleasure to relieve him; and as it would still less become his station, or his gallantry to involve in the same neglect a lady on whom that beadle had looked with an eye of tenderness and affection, and in whose ear he had whispered sweet words, which, coming from such a quarter, might well thrill the bosom of maid or matron of whatsoever degree; the historian whose pen traces these words—trusting that he knows his place, and that he entertains a becoming reverence for those upon earth to whom high and important authority is delegated—hastens to pay them that respect which their position demands, and to treat them with all that duteous ceremony which their exalted rank, and (by consequence) great virtues, imperatively claim at his hands. Towards this end, indeed, he had purposed to introduce, in this place, a dissertation touching the divine right of beadles, and elucidative of the position, that a beadle can do no wrong: which could not fail to have been both pleasurable and profitable to the right-minded reader but which he is unfortunately compelled, by want of time and space, to postpone to some more convenient and fitting opportunity; on the arrival of which, he will be prepared to show, that a beadle properly constituted: that is to say, a parochial beadle, attached to a parochial workhouse, and attending in his official capacity the parochial church: is, in right and virtue of his office, possessed of all the excellences and best qualities of humanity; and that to none of those excellences, can mere companies' beadles, or court-of-law beadles, or even chapel-of-ease beadles (save the last, and they in a very lowly and inferior degree), lay the remotest sustainable claim.

Mr. Bumble had re-counted the teaspoons, re-weighed the sugar-tongs, made a closer inspection of the milk-pot, and ascertained to a nicety the exact condition of the furniture, down to the very horse-hair seats of the chairs; and had repeated each process full half a dozen times; before he began to think that it was time for Mrs. Corney to return. Thinking begets thinking; as there were no sounds of Mrs. Corney's approach, it occured to Mr. Bumble that it would be an innocent and virtuous way of spending the time, if he were further to allay his curiosity by a cursory glance at the interior of Mrs. Corney's chest of drawers.

Having listened at the keyhole, to assure himself that nobody was approaching the chamber, Mr. Bumble, beginning at the bottom, proceeded to make himself acquainted with the contents of the three long drawers: which, being filled with various garments of good fashion and texture, carefully preserved between two layers of old newspapers, speckled with dried lavender: seemed to yield him exceeding satisfaction. Arriving, in course of time, at the right-hand corner drawer (in which was the key), and beholding therein a small padlocked box, which, being shaken, gave forth a pleasant sound, as of the chinking of coin, Mr. Bumble returned with a stately walk to the fireplace; and, resuming his old attitude, said, with a grave and determined air, "I'll do it!" He followed up this remarkable declaration, by shaking his head in a waggish manner for ten minutes, as though he were remonstrating with himself for being such a pleasant dog; and then, he took a view of his legs in profile, with much seeming pleasure and interest.

He was still placidly engaged in this latter survey, when Mrs. Corney, hurrying into the room, threw herself, in a breathless state, on a chair by the fireside, and covering her eyes with one hand, placed the other over her heart, and gasped for breath.

"Mrs. Corney," said Mr. Bumble, stooping over the matron, "what is this, ma'am? Has anything happened, ma'am? Pray answer me: I'm on—on—" Mr. Bumble, in his alarm, could not immediately think of the word "tenterhooks," so he said "broken bottles."

"Oh, Mr. Bumble!" cried the lady, "I have been so dreadfully put out!"

"Put out, ma'am!" exclaimed Mr. Bumble; "who has dared to—? I know!" said Mr. Bumble, checking himself, with native majesty, "this is them wicious paupers!"

"It's dreadful to think of!" said the lady, shuddering.

"Then don't think of it, ma'am," rejoined Mr. Bumble.

"I can't help it," whimpered the lady.

"Then take something, ma'am," said Mr. Bumble soothingly. "A little of the wine?"

"Not for the world!" replied Mrs. Corney. "I couldn't,—oh! The top shelf in the right-hand corner—oh!" Uttering these words, the good lady pointed, distractedly, to the cupboard, and underwent a convulsion from internal spasms. Mr. Bumble rushed to the closet; and, snatching a pint green-glass bottle from the shelf thus incoherently indicated, filled a tea-cup with its contents, and held it to the lady's lips.

"I'm better now," said Mrs. Corney, falling back, after drinking half of it.

Mr. Bumble raised his eyes piously to the ceiling in thankfulness; and, bringing them down again to the brim of the cup, lifted it to his nose.

"Peppermint," exclaimed Mrs. Corney, in a faint voice, smiling gently on the beadle as she spoke. "Try it! There's a little—a little something else in it."

Mr. Bumble tasted the medicine with a doubtful look; smacked his lips; took another taste; and put the cup down empty.

"It's very comforting," said Mrs. Corney.

"Very much so indeed, ma'am," said the beadle. As he spoke, he drew a chair beside the matron, and tenderly inquired what had happened to distress her.

"Nothing," replied Mrs. Corney. "I am a foolish, excitable, weak creetur."

"Not weak, ma'am," retorted Mr. Bumble, drawing his chair a little closer. "Are you a weak creetur, Mrs. Corney?"

"We are all weak creeturs," said Mrs. Corney, laying down a general principle.

"So we are," said the beadle.

Nothing was said on either side, for a minute or two afterwards. By the expiration of that time, Mr. Bumble had illustrated the position by removing his left arm from the back of Mrs. Corney's chair, where it had previously rested, to Mrs. Corney's apron-string, round which it gradually became entwined.

"We are all weak creeturs," said Mr. Bumble.

Mrs. Corney sighed.

"Don't sigh, Mrs. Corney," said Mr. Bumble.

"I can't help it," said Mrs. Corney. And she sighed again.

"This is a very comfortable room, ma'am," said Mr. Bumble looking round. "Another room, and this, ma'am, would be a complete thing."

"It would be too much for one," murmured the lady.

"But not for two, ma'am," rejoined Mr. Bumble, in soft accents. "Eh, Mrs. Corney?"

Mrs. Corney drooped her head, when the beadle said this; the beadle drooped his, to get a view of Mrs. Corney's face. Mrs. Corney, with great propriety, turned her head away, and released her hand to get at her pocket-handkerchief; but insensibly replaced it in that of Mr. Bumble.

"The board allows you coals, don't they, Mrs. Corney?" inquired the beadle, affectionately pressing her hand.

"And candles," replied Mrs. Corney, slightly returning the pressure.

"Coals, candles, and house-rent free," said Mr. Bumble. "Oh, Mrs. Corney, what an Angel you are!"

The lady was not proof against this burst of feeling. She sank into Mr. Bumble's arms; and that gentleman in his agitation, imprinted a passionate kiss upon her chaste nose.

"Such porochial perfection!" exclaimed Mr. Bumble, rapturously. "You know that Mr. Slout is worse to-night, my fascinator?"

"Yes," replied Mrs. Corney, bashfully.

"He can't live a week, the doctor says," pursued Mr. Bumble. "He is the master of this establishment; his death will cause a wacancy; that wacancy must be filled up. Oh, Mrs. Corney, what a prospect this opens! What a opportunity for a jining of hearts and housekeepings!"

Mrs. Corney sobbed.

"The little word?" said Mr. Bumble, bending over the bashful beauty. "The one little, little, little word, my blessed Corney?"

"Ye—ye—yes!" sighed out the matron.

"One more," pursued the beadle; "compose your darling feelings for only one more. When is it to come off?"

Mrs. Corney twice essayed to speak: and twice failed. At length summoning up courage, she threw her arms around Mr. Bumble's neck, and said, it might be as soon as ever he pleased, and that he was "a irresistible duck."

Matters being thus amicably and satisfactorily arranged, the contract was solemnly ratified in another teacupful of the peppermint mixture; which was rendered the more necessary, by the flutter and agitation of the lady's spirits. While it was being disposed of, she acquainted Mr. Bumble with the old woman's decease.

"Very good," said that gentleman, sipping his peppermint; "I'll call at Sowerberry's as I go home, and tell him to send to-morrow morning. Was it that as frightened you, love?"

"It wasn't anything particular, dear," said the lady evasively.

"It must have been something, love," urged Mr. Bumble. "Won't you tell your own B.?"

"Not now," rejoined the lady; "one of these days. After we're married, dear."

"After we're married!" exclaimed Mr. Bumble. "It wasn't any impudence from any of them male paupers as—"

"No, no, love!" interposed the lady, hastily.

"If I thought it was," continued Mr. Bumble; "if I thought as any one of 'em had dared to lift his wulgar eyes to that lovely countenance—"

"They wouldn't have dared to do it, love," responded the lady.

"They had better not!" said Mr. Bumble, clenching his fist. "Let me see any man, porochial or extra-porochial, as would presume to do it; and I can tell him that he wouldn't do it a second time!"

Unembellished by any violence of gesticulation, this might have seemed no very high compliment to the lady's charms; but, as Mr. Bumble accompanied the threat with many warlike gestures, she was much touched with this proof of his devotion, and protested, with great admiration, that he was indeed a dove.

The dove then turned up his coat-collar, and put on his cocked hat; and, having exchanged a long and affectionate embrace with his future partner, once again braved the cold wind of the night: merely pausing, for a few minutes, in the male paupers' ward, to abuse them a little, with the view of satisfying himself that he could fill the office of workhouse-master with needful acerbity. Assured of his qualifications, Mr. Bumble left the building with a light heart, and bright visions of his future promotion: which served to occupy his mind until he reached the shop of the undertaker.

Now, Mr. and Mrs. Sowerberry having gone out to tea and supper: and Noah Claypole not being at any time disposed to take upon himself a greater amount of physical exertion than is necessary to a convenient performance of the two functions of eating and drinking, the shop was not closed, although it was past the usual hour of shutting-up. Mr. Bumble tapped with his cane on the counter several times; but, attracting no attention, and beholding a light shining through the glass-window of the little parlour at the back of the shop, he made bold to peep in and see what was going forward; and when he saw what was going forward, he was not a little surprised.

The cloth was laid for supper; the table was covered with bread and butter, plates and glasses; a porter-pot and a wine-bottle. At the upper end of the table, Mr. Noah Claypole lolled negligently in an easy-chair, with his legs thrown over one of the arms: an open clasp-knife in one hand, and a mass of buttered bread in the other. Close beside him stood Charlotte, opening oysters from a barrel: which Mr. Claypole condescended to swallow, with remarkable avidity. A more than ordinary redness in the region of the young gentleman's nose, and a kind of fixed wink in his right eye, denoted that he was in a slight degree intoxicated; these symptoms were confirmed by the intense relish with which he took his oysters, for which nothing but a strong appreciation of their cooling properties, in cases of internal fever, could have sufficiently accounted.

"Here's a delicious fat one, Noah, dear!" said Charlotte; "try him, do; only this one."

"What a delicious thing is a oyster!" remarked Mr. Claypole, after he had swallowed it. "What a pity it is, a number of 'em should ever make you feel uncomfortable; isn't it, Charlotte?"

"It's quite a cruelty," said Charlotte.

"So it is," acquiesced Mr. Claypole. "An't yer fond of oysters?"

"Not overmuch," replied Charlotte. "I like to see you eat 'em, Noah dear, better than eating 'em myself."

"Lor!" said Noah, reflectively; "how queer!"

"Have another," said Charlotte. "Here's one with such a beautiful, delicate beard!"

"I can't manage any more," said Noah. "I'm very sorry. Come here, Charlotte, and I'll kiss yer."

"What!" said Mr. Bumble, bursting into the room. "Say that again, sir."

Charlotte uttered a scream, and hid her face in her apron. Mr. Claypole, without making any further change in his position than suffering his legs to reach the ground, gazed at the beadle in drunken terror.

"Say it again, you wile, owdacious fellow!" said Mr. Bumble. "How dare you mention such a thing, sir? And how dare you encourage him, you insolent minx? Kiss her!" exclaimed Mr. Bumble, in strong indignation. "Faugh!"

"I didn't mean to do it!" said Noah, blubbering. "She's always a-kissing of me, whether I like it, or not."

"Oh, Noah," cried Charlotte, reproachfully.

"Yer are; yer know yer are!" retorted Noah. "She's always a-doin' of it, Mr. Bumble, sir; she chucks me under the chin, please, sir; and makes all manner of love!"

"Silence!" cried Mr. Bumble, sternly. "Take yourself downstairs, ma'am. Noah, you shut up the shop; say another word till your master comes home, at your peril; and, when he does come home, tell him that Mr. Bumble said he was to send a old woman's shell after breakfast to-morrow morning. Do you hear sir? Kissing!" cried Mr. Bumble, holding up his hands. "The sin and wickedness of the lower orders in this porochial district is frightful! If Parliament don't take their abominable courses under consideration, this country's ruined, and the character of the peasantry gone for ever!" With these words, the beadle strode, with a lofty and gloomy air, from the undertaker's premises.

And now that we have accompanied him so far on his road home, and have made all necessary preparations for the old woman's funeral, let us set on foot a few inquires after young Oliver Twist, and ascertain whether he be still lying in the ditch where Toby Crackit left him.

CHAPTER XXVIII

Looks After Oliver, and Proceeds With His Adventures

"Wolves tear your throats!" muttered Sikes, grinding his teeth. "I wish I was among some of you; you'd howl the hoarser for it."

As Sikes growled forth this imprecation, with the most desperate ferocity that his desperate nature was capable of, he rested the body of the wounded boy across his bended knee; and turned his head, for an instant, to look back at his pursuers.

There was little to be made out, in the mist and darkness; but the loud shouting of men vibrated through the air, and the barking of the neighbouring dogs, roused by the sound of the alarm bell, resounded in every direction.

"Stop, you white-livered hound!" cried the robber, shouting after Toby Crackit, who, making the best use of his long legs, was already ahead. "Stop!"

The repetition of the word, brought Toby to a dead stand-still. For he was not quite satisfied that he was beyond the range of pistol-shot; and Sikes was in no mood to be played with.

"Bear a hand with the boy," cried Sikes, beckoning furiously to his confederate. "Come back!"

Toby made a show of returning; but ventured, in a low voice, broken for want of breath, to intimate considerable reluctance as he came slowly along.

"Quicker!" cried Sikes, laying the boy in a dry ditch at his feet, and drawing a pistol from his pocket. "Don't play booty with me."

At this moment the noise grew louder. Sikes, again looking round, could discern that the men who had given chase were already climbing the gate of the field in which he stood; and that a couple of dogs were some paces in advance of them.

"It's all up, Bill!" cried Toby; "drop the kid, and show 'em your heels." With this parting advice, Mr. Crackit, preferring the chance of being shot by his friend, to the certainty of being taken by his enemies, fairly turned tail, and darted off at full speed. Sikes clenched his teeth; took one look around; threw over the prostrate form of Oliver, the cape in which he had been hurriedly muffled; ran along the front of the hedge, as if to distract the attention of those behind, from the spot where the boy lay; paused, for a second, before another hedge which met it at right angles; and whirling his pistol high into the air, cleared it at a bound, and was gone.

"Ho, ho, there!" cried a tremulous voice in the rear. "Pincher! Neptune! Come here, come here!"

The dogs, who, in common with their masters, seemed to have no particular relish for the sport in which they were engaged, readily answered to the command. Three men, who had by this time advanced some distance into the field, stopped to take counsel together.

"My advice, or, leastways, I should say, my orders, is," said the fattest man of the party, "that we 'mediately go home again."

"I am agreeable to anything which is agreeable to Mr. Giles," said a shorter man; who was by no means of a slim figure, and who was very pale in the face, and very polite: as frightened men frequently are.

"I shouldn't wish to appear ill-mannered, gentlemen," said the third, who had called the dogs back, "Mr. Giles ought to know."

"Certainly," replied the shorter man; "and whatever Mr. Giles says, it isn't our place to contradict him. No, no, I know my sitiwation! Thank my stars, I know my sitiwation." To tell the truth, the little man did seem to know his situation, and to know perfectly well that it was by no means a desirable one; for his teeth chattered in his head as he spoke.

"You are afraid, Brittles," said Mr. Giles.

"I an't," said Brittles.

"You are," said Giles.

"You're a falsehood, Mr. Giles," said Brittles.

"You're a lie, Brittles," said Mr. Giles.

Now, these four retorts arose from Mr. Giles's taunt; and Mr. Giles's taunt had arisen from his indignation at having the responsibility of going home again, imposed upon himself under cover of a compliment. The third man brought the dispute to a close, most philosophically.

"I'll tell you what it is, gentlemen," said he, "we're all afraid."

"Speak for yourself, sir," said Mr. Giles, who was the palest of the party.

"So I do," replied the man. "It's natural and proper to be afraid, under such circumstances. I am."

"So am I," said Brittles; "only there's no call to tell a man he is, so bounceably."

These frank admissions softened Mr. Giles, who at once owned that he was afraid; upon which, they all three faced about, and ran back again with the completest unanimity, until Mr. Giles (who had the shortest wind of the party, as was encumbered with a pitchfork) most handsomely insisted on stopping, to make an apology for his hastiness of speech.

"But it's wonderful," said Mr. Giles, when he had explained, "what a man will do, when his blood is up. I should have committed murder—I know I should—if we'd caught one of them rascals."

As the other two were impressed with a similar presentiment; and as their blood, like his, had all gone down again; some speculation ensued upon the cause of this sudden change in their temperament.

"I know what it was," said Mr. Giles; "it was the gate."

"I shouldn't wonder if it was," exclaimed Brittles, catching at the idea.

"You may depend upon it," said Giles, "that that gate stopped the flow of the excitement. I felt all mine suddenly going away, as I was climbing over it."

By a remarkable coincidence, the other two had been visited with the same unpleasant sensation at that precise moment. It was quite obvious, therefore, that it was the gate; especially as there was no doubt regarding the time at which the change had taken place, because all three remembered that they had come in sight of the robbers at the instant of its occurance.

This dialogue was held between the two men who had surprised the burglars, and a travelling tinker who had been sleeping in an outhouse, and who had been roused, together with his two mongrel curs, to join in the pursuit. Mr. Giles acted in the double capacity of butler and steward to the old lady of the mansion; Brittles was a lad of all-work: who, having entered her service a mere child, was treated as a promising young boy still, though he was something past thirty.

Encouraging each other with such converse as this; but, keeping very close together, notwithstanding, and looking apprehensively round, whenever a fresh gust rattled through the boughs; the three men hurried back to a tree, behind which they had left their lantern, lest its light should inform the thieves in what direction to fire. Catching up the light, they made the best of their way home, at a good round trot; and long after their dusky forms had ceased to be discernible, the light might have been seen twinkling and dancing in the distance, like some exhalation of the damp and gloomy atmosphere through which it was swiftly borne.

The air grew colder, as day came slowly on; and the mist rolled along the ground like a dense cloud of smoke. The grass was wet; the pathways, and low places, were all mire and water; the damp breath of an unwholesome wind went languidly by, with a hollow moaning. Still, Oliver lay motionless and insensible on the spot where Sikes had left him.

Morning drew on apace. The air become more sharp and piercing, as its first dull hue—the death of night, rather than the birth of day—glimmered faintly in the sky. The objects which had looked dim and terrible in the darkness, grew more and more defined, and gradually resolved into their familiar shapes. The rain came down, thick and fast, and pattered noisily among the leafless bushes. But, Oliver felt it not, as it beat against him; for he still lay stretched, helpless and unconscious, on his bed of clay.

At length, a low cry of pain broke the stillness that prevailed; and uttering it, the boy awoke. His left arm, rudely bandaged in a shawl, hung heavy and useless at his side; the bandage was saturated with blood. He was so weak, that he could scarcely raise himself into a sitting posture; when he had done so, he looked feebly round for help, and groaned with pain. Trembling in every joint, from cold and exhaustion, he made an effort to stand upright; but, shuddering from head to foot, fell prostrate on the ground.

After a short return of the stupor in which he had been so long plunged, Oliver: urged by a creeping sickness at his heart, which seemed to warn him that if he lay there, he must surely die: got upon his feet, and essayed to walk. His head was dizzy, and he staggered to and fro like a drunken man. But he kept up, nevertheless, and, with his head drooping languidly on his breast, went stumbling onward, he knew not whither.

And now, hosts of bewildering and confused ideas came crowding on his mind. He seemed to be still walking between Sikes and Crackit, who were angrily disputing—for the very words they said, sounded in his ears; and when he caught his own attention, as it were, by making some violent effort to save himself from falling, he found that he was talking to them. Then, he was alone with Sikes, plodding on as on the previous day; and as shadowy people passed them, he felt the robber's grasp upon his wrist.

Suddenly, he started back at the report of firearms; there rose into the air, loud cries and shouts; lights gleamed before his eyes; all was noise and tumult, as some unseen hand bore him hurriedly away. Through all these rapid visions, there ran an undefined, uneasy consciousness of pain, which wearied and tormented him incessantly.

Thus he staggered on, creeping, almost mechanically, between the bars of gates, or through hedge-gaps as they came in his way, until he reached a road. Here the rain began to fall so heavily, that it roused him.

He looked about, and saw that at no great distance there was a house, which perhaps he could reach. Pitying his condition, they might have compassion on him; and if they did not, it would be better, he thought, to die near human beings, than in the lonely open fields. He summoned up all his strength for one last trial, and bent his faltering steps towards it.

As he drew nearer to this house, a feeling come over him that he had seen it before. He remembered nothing of its details; but the shape and aspect of the building seemed familiar to him.

That garden wall! On the grass inside, he had fallen on his knees last night, and prayed the two men's mercy. It was the very house they had attempted to rob.

Oliver felt such fear come over him when he recognised the place, that, for the instant, he forgot the agony of his wound, and thought only of flight. Flight! He could scarcely stand: and if he were in full possession of all the best powers of his slight and youthful frame, whither could he fly? He pushed against the garden-gate; it was unlocked, and swung open on its hinges. He tottered across the lawn; climbed the steps; knocked faintly at the door; and, his whole strength failing him, sunk down against one of the pillars of the little portico.

It happened that about this time, Mr. Giles, Brittles, and the tinker, were recruiting themselves, after the fatigues and terrors of the night, with tea and sundries, in the kitchen. Not that it was Mr. Giles's habit to admit to too great familiarity the humbler servants: towards whom it was rather his wont to deport himself with a lofty affability, which, while it gratified, could not fail to remind them of his superior position in society. But, death, fires, and burglary, make all men equals; so Mr. Giles sat with his legs stretched out before the kitchen fender, leaning his left arm on the table, while, with his right, he illustrated a circumstantial and minute account of the robbery, to which his bearers (but especially the cook and housemaid, who were of the party) listened with breathless interest.

"It was about half-past two," said Mr. Giles, "or I wouldn't swear that it mightn't have been a little nearer three, when I woke up, and, turning round in my bed, as it might be so, (here Mr. Giles turned round in his chair, and pulled the corner of the table-cloth over him to imitate bed-clothes,) I fancied I heerd a noise."

At this point of the narrative the cook turned pale, and asked the housemaid to shut the door: who asked Brittles, who asked the tinker, who pretended not to hear.

"—Heerd a noise," continued Mr. Giles. "I says, at first, 'This is illusion'; and was composing myself off to sleep, when I heerd the noise again, distinct."

"What sort of a noise?" asked the cook.

"A kind of a busting noise," replied Mr. Giles, looking round him.

"More like the noise of powdering a iron bar on a nutmeg-grater," suggested Brittles.

"It was, when you heerd it, sir," rejoined Mr. Giles; "but, at this time, it had a busting sound. I turned down the clothes"; continued Giles, rolling back the table-cloth, "sat up in bed; and listened."

The cook and housemaid simultaneously ejaculated "Lor!" and drew their chairs closer together.

"I heerd it now, quite apparent," resumed Mr. Giles. "'Somebody,' I says, 'is forcing of a door, or window; what's to be done? I'll call up that poor lad, Brittles, and save him from being murdered in his bed; or his throat,' I says, 'may be cut from his right ear to his left, without his ever knowing it.'"

Here, all eyes were turned upon Brittles, who fixed his upon the speaker, and stared at him, with his mouth wide open, and his face expressive of the most unmitigated horror.

"I tossed off the clothes," said Giles, throwing away the table-cloth, and looking very hard at the cook and housemaid, "got softly out of bed; drew on a pair of—"

"Ladies present, Mr. Giles," murmured the tinker.

"—Of shoes, sir," said Giles, turning upon him, and laying great emphasis on the word; 'seized the loaded pistol that always goes upstairs with the plate-basket; and walked on tiptoes to his room. 'Brittles,' I says, when I had woke him, 'don't be frightened!'"

"So you did," observed Brittles, in a low voice.

"'We're dead men, I think, Brittles,' I says," continued Giles; "'but don't be frightened.'"

"Was he frightened?" asked the cook.

"Not a bit of it," replied Mr. Giles. "He was as firm—ah! pretty near as firm as I was."

"I should have died at once, I'm sure, if it had been me," observed the housemaid.

"You're a woman," retorted Brittles, plucking up a little.

"Brittles is right," said Mr. Giles, nodding his head, approvingly; "from a woman, nothing else was to be expected. We, being men, took a dark lantern that was standing on Brittle's hob, and groped our way downstairs in the pitch dark,—as it might be so."

Mr. Giles had risen from his seat, and taken two steps with his eyes shut, to accompany his description with appropriate action, when he started violently, in common with the rest of the company, and hurried back to his chair. The cook and housemaid screamed.

"It was a knock," said Mr. Giles, assuming perfect serenity. "Open the door, somebody."

Nobody moved.

"It seems a strange sort of a thing, a knock coming at such a time in the morning," said Mr. Giles, surveying the pale faces which surrounded him, and looking very blank himself; "but the door must be opened. Do you hear, somebody?"

Mr. Giles, as he spoke, looked at Brittles; but that young man, being naturally modest, probably considered himself nobody, and so held that the inquiry could not have any application to him; at all events, he tendered no reply. Mr. Giles directed an appealing glance at the tinker; but he had suddenly fallen asleep. The women were out of the question.

"If Brittles would rather open the door, in the presence of witnesses," said Mr. Giles, after a short silence, "I am ready to make one."

"So am I," said the tinker, waking up, as suddenly as he had fallen asleep.

Brittles capitulated on these terms; and the party being somewhat re-assured by the discovery (made on throwing open the shutters) that it was now broad day, took their way upstairs; with the dogs in front. The two women, who were afraid to stay below, brought up the rear. By the advice of Mr. Giles, they all talked very loud, to warn any evil-disposed person outside, that they were strong in numbers; and by a master-stoke of policy, originating in the brain of the same ingenious gentleman, the dogs' tails were well pinched, in the hall, to make them bark savagely.

These precautions having been taken, Mr. Giles held on fast by the tinker's arm (to prevent his running away, as he pleasantly said), and gave the word of command to open the door. Brittles obeyed; the group, peeping timorously over each other's shoulders, beheld no more formidable object than poor little Oliver Twist, speechless and exhausted, who raised his heavy eyes, and mutely solicited their compassion.

"A boy!" exclaimed Mr. Giles, valiantly, pushing the tinker into the background. "What's the matter with the—eh?—Why—Brittles—look here—don't you know?"

Brittles, who had got behind the door to open it, no sooner saw Oliver, than he uttered a loud cry. Mr. Giles, seizing the boy by one leg and one arm (fortunately not the broken limb) lugged him straight into the hall, and deposited him at full length on the floor thereof.

"Here he is!" bawled Giles, calling in a state of great excitement, up the staircase; "here's one of the thieves, ma'am! Here's a thief, miss! Wounded, miss! I shot him, miss; and Brittles held the light."

"—In a lantern, miss," cried Brittles, applying one hand to the side of his mouth, so that his voice might travel the better.

The two women-servants ran upstairs to carry the intelligence that Mr. Giles had captured a robber; and the tinker busied himself in endeavouring to restore Oliver, lest he should die before he could be hanged. In the midst of all this noise and commotion, there was heard a sweet female voice, which quelled it in an instant.

"Giles!" whispered the voice from the stair-head.

"I'm here, miss," replied Mr. Giles. "Don't be frightened, miss; I ain't much injured. He didn't make a very desperate resistance, miss! I was soon too many for him."

"Hush!" replied the young lady; "you frighten my aunt as much as the thieves did. Is the poor creature much hurt?"

"Wounded desperate, miss," replied Giles, with indescribable complacency.

"He looks as if he was a-going, miss," bawled Brittles, in the same manner as before. "Wouldn't you like to come and look at him, miss, in case he should?"

"Hush, pray; there's a good man!" rejoined the lady. "Wait quietly only one instant, while I speak to aunt."

With a footstep as soft and gentle as the voice, the speaker tripped away. She soon returned, with the direction that the wounded person was to be carried, carefully, upstairs to Mr. Giles's room; and that Brittles was to saddle the pony and betake himself instantly to Chertsey: from which place, he was to despatch, with all speed, a constable and doctor.

"But won't you take one look at him, first, miss?" asked Mr. Giles, with as much pride as if Oliver were some bird of rare plumage, that he had skilfully brought down. "Not one little peep, miss?"

"Not now, for the world," replied the young lady. "Poor fellow! Oh! treat him kindly, Giles for my sake!"

The old servant looked up at the speaker, as she turned away, with a glance as proud and admiring as if she had been his own child. Then, bending over Oliver, he helped to carry him upstairs, with the care and solicitude of a woman.

CHAPTER XXIX

Has an Introductory Account of the Inmates of the House, to Which Oliver Resorted

In a handsome room: though its furniture had rather the air of old-fashioned comfort, than of modern elegance: there sat two ladies at a well-spread breakfast-table. Mr. Giles, dressed with scrupulous care in a full suit of black, was in attendance upon them. He had taken his station some half-way between the side-board and the breakfast-table; and, with his body drawn up to its full height, his head thrown back, and inclined the merest trifle on one side, his left leg advanced, and his right hand thrust into his waist-coat, while his left hung down by his side, grasping a waiter, looked like one who laboured under a very agreeable sense of his own merits and importance.

Of the two ladies, one was well advanced in years; but the high-backed oaken chair in which she sat, was not more upright than she. Dressed with the utmost nicety and precision, in a quaint mixture of by-gone costume, with some slight concessions to the prevailing taste, which rather served to point the old style pleasantly than to impair its effect, she sat, in a stately manner, with her hands folded on the table before her. Her eyes (and age had dimmed but little of their brightness) were attentively upon her young companion.

The younger lady was in the lovely bloom and spring-time of womanhood; at that age, when, if ever angels be for God's good purposes enthroned in mortal forms, they may be, without impiety, supposed to abide in such as hers.

She was not past seventeen. Cast in so slight and exquisite a mould; so mild and gentle; so pure and beautiful; that earth seemed not her element, nor its rough creatures her fit companions. The very intelligence that shone in her deep blue eye, and was stamped upon her noble head, seemed scarcely of her age, or of the world; and yet the changing expression of sweetness and good humour, the thousand lights that played about the face, and left no shadow there; above all, the smile, the cheerful, happy smile, were made for Home, and fireside peace and happiness.

She was busily engaged in the little offices of the table. Chancing to raise her eyes as the elder lady was regarding her, she playfully put back her hair, which was simply braided on her forehead; and threw into her beaming look, such an expression of affection and artless loveliness, that blessed spirits might have smiled to look upon her.

"And Brittles has been gone upwards of an hour, has he?" asked the old lady, after a pause.

"An hour and twelve minutes, ma'am," replied Mr. Giles, referring to a silver watch, which he drew forth by a black ribbon.

"He is always slow," remarked the old lady.

"Brittles always was a slow boy, ma'am," replied the attendant. And seeing, by the bye, that Brittles had been a slow boy for upwards of thirty years, there appeared no great probability of his ever being a fast one.

"He gets worse instead of better, I think," said the elder lady.

"It is very inexcusable in him if he stops to play with any other boys," said the young lady, smiling.

Mr. Giles was apparently considering the propriety of indulging in a respectful smile himself, when a gig drove up to the garden-gate: out of which there jumped a fat gentleman, who ran straight up to the door: and who, getting quickly into the house by some mysterious process, burst into the room, and nearly overturned Mr. Giles and the breakfast-table together.

"I never heard of such a thing!" exclaimed the fat gentleman. "My dear Mrs. Maylie—bless my soul—in the silence of the night, too—I never heard of such a thing!"

With these expressions of condolence, the fat gentleman shook hands with both ladies, and drawing up a chair, inquired how they found themselves.

"You ought to be dead; positively dead with the fright," said the fat gentleman. "Why didn't you send? Bless me, my man should have come in a minute; and so would I; and my assistant would have been delighted; or anybody, I'm sure, under such circumstances. Dear, dear! So unexpected! In the silence of the night, too!"

The doctor seemed expecially troubled by the fact of the robbery having been unexpected, and attempted in the night-time; as if it were the established custom of gentlemen in the housebreaking way to transact business at noon, and to make an appointment, by post, a day or two previous.

"And you, Miss Rose," said the doctor, turning to the young lady, "I—"

"Oh! very much so, indeed," said Rose, interrupting him; "but there is a poor creature upstairs, whom aunt wishes you to see."

"Ah! to be sure," replied the doctor, "so there is. That was your handiwork, Giles, I understand."

Mr. Giles, who had been feverishly putting the tea-cups to rights, blushed very red, and said that he had had that honour.

"Honour, eh?" said the doctor; "well, I don't know; perhaps it's as honourable to hit a thief in a back kitchen, as to hit your man at twelve paces. Fancy that he fired in the air, and you've fought a duel, Giles."

Mr. Giles, who thought this light treatment of the matter an unjust attempt at diminishing his glory, answered respectfully, that it was not for the like of him to judge about that; but he rather thought it was no joke to the opposite party.

"Gad, that's true!" said the doctor. "Where is he? Show me the way. I'll look in again, as I come down, Mrs. Maylie. That's the little window that he got in at, eh? Well, I couldn't have believed it!"

Talking all the way, he followed Mr. Giles upstairs; and while he is going upstairs, the reader may be informed, that Mr. Losberne, a surgeon in the neighbourhood, known through a circuit of ten miles round as "the doctor," had grown fat, more from good-humour than from good living: and was as kind and hearty, and withal as eccentric an old bachelor, as will be found in five times that space, by any explorer alive.

The doctor was absent, much longer than either he or the ladies had anticipated. A large flat box was fetched out of the gig; and a bedroom bell was rung very often; and the servants ran up and down stairs perpetually; from which tokens it was justly concluded that something important was going on above. At length he returned; and in reply to an anxious inquiry after his patient; looked very mysterious, and closed the door, carefully.

"This is a very extraordinary thing, Mrs. Maylie," said the doctor, standing with his back to the door, as if to keep it shut.

"He is not in danger, I hope?" said the old lady.

"Why, that would not be an extraordinary thing, under the circumstances," replied the doctor; "though I don't think he is. Have you seen the thief?"

"No," rejoined the old lady.

"Nor heard anything about him?"

"No."

"I beg your pardon, ma'am, interposed Mr. Giles; "but I was going to tell you about him when Doctor Losberne came in."

The fact was, that Mr. Giles had not, at first, been able to bring his mind to the avowal, that he had only shot a boy. Such commendations had been bestowed upon his bravery, that he could not, for the life of him, help postponing the explanation for a few delicious minutes; during which he had flourished, in the very zenith of a brief reputation for undaunted courage.

"Rose wished to see the man," said Mrs. Maylie, "but I wouldn't hear of it."

"Humph!" rejoined the doctor. "There is nothing very alarming in his appearance. Have you any objection to see him in my presence?"

"If it be necessary," replied the old lady, "certainly not."

"Then I think it is necessary," said the doctor; "at all events, I am quite sure that you would deeply regret not having done so, if you postponed it. He is perfectly quiet and comfortable now. Allow me—Miss Rose, will you permit me? Not the slightest fear, I pledge you my honour!"

CHAPTER XXX

Relates What Oliver's New Visitors Thought of Him

With many loquacious assurances that they would be agreeably surprised in the aspect of the criminal, the doctor drew the young lady's arm through one of his; and offering his disengaged hand to Mrs. Maylie, led them, with much ceremony and stateliness, upstairs.

"Now," said the doctor, in a whisper, as he softly turned the handle of a bedroom-door, "let us hear what you think of him. He has not been shaved very recently, but he don't look at all ferocious notwithstanding. Stop, though! Let me first see that he is in visiting order."

Stepping before them, he looked into the room. Motioning them to advance, he closed the door when they had entered; and gently drew back the curtains of the bed. Upon it, in lieu of the dogged, black-visaged ruffian they had expected to behold, there lay a mere child: worn with pain and exhaustion, and sunk into a deep sleep. His wounded arm, bound and splintered up, was crossed upon his breast; his head reclined upon the other arm, which was half hidden by his long hair, as it streamed over the pillow.

The honest gentleman held the curtain in his hand, and looked on, for a minute or so, in silence. Whilst he was watching the patient thus, the younger lady glided softly past, and seating herself in a chair by the bedside, gathered Oliver's hair from his face. As she stooped over him, her tears fell upon his forehead.

The boy stirred, and smiled in his sleep, as though these marks of pity and compassion had awakened some pleasant dream of a love and affection he had never known. Thus, a strain of gentle music, or the rippling of water in a silent place, or the odour of a flower, or the mention of a familiar word, will sometimes call up sudden dim remembrances of scenes that never were, in this life; which vanish like a breath; which some brief memory of a happier existence, long gone by, would seem to have awakened; which no voluntary exertion of the mind can ever recall.

"What can this mean?" exclaimed the elder lady. "This poor child can never have been the pupil of robbers!"

"Vice," said the surgeon, replacing the curtain, "takes up her abode in many temples; and who can say that a fair outside shell not enshrine her?"

"But at so early an age!" urged Rose.

"My dear young lady," rejoined the surgeon, mournfully shaking his head; "crime, like death, is not confined to the old and withered alone. The youngest and fairest are too often its chosen victims."

"But, can you—oh! can you really believe that this delicate boy has been the voluntary associate of the worst outcasts of society?" said Rose.

The surgeon shook his head, in a manner which intimated that he feared it was very possible; and observing that they might disturb the patient, led the way into an adjoining apartment.

"But even if he has been wicked," pursued Rose, "think how young he is; think that he may never have known a mother's love, or the comfort of a home; that ill-usage and blows, or the want of bread, may have driven him to herd with men who have forced him to guilt. Aunt, dear aunt, for mercy's sake, think of this, before you let them drag this sick child to a prison, which in any case must be the grave of all his chances of amendment. Oh! as you love me, and know that I have never felt the want of parents in your goodness and affection, but that I might have done so, and might have been equally helpless and unprotected with this poor child, have pity upon him before it is too late!"

"My dear love," said the elder lady, as she folded the weeping girl to her bosom, "do you think I would harm a hair of his head?"

"Oh, no!" replied Rose, eagerly.

"No, surely," said the old lady; "my days are drawing to their close: and may mercy be shown to me as I show it to others! What can I do to save him, sir?"

"Let me think, ma'am," said the doctor; "let me think."

Mr. Losberne thrust his hands into his pockets, and took several turns up and down the room; often stopping, and balancing himself on his toes, and frowning frightfully. After various exclamations of "I've got it now" and "no, I haven't," and as many renewals of the walking and frowning, he at length made a dead halt, and spoke as follows:

"I think if you give me a full and unlimited commission to bully Giles, and that little boy, Brittles, I can manage it. Giles is a faithful fellow and an old servant, I know; but you can make it up to him in a thousand ways, and reward him for being such a good shot besides. You don't object to that?"

"Unless there is some other way of preserving the child," replied Mrs. Maylie.

"There is no other," said the doctor. "No other, take my word for it."

"Then my aunt invests you with full power," said Rose, smiling through her tears; "but pray don't be harder upon the poor fellows than is indispensably necessary."

"You seem to think," retorted the doctor, "that everybody is disposed to be hard-hearted to-day, except yourself, Miss Rose. I only hope, for the sake of the rising male sex generally, that you may be found in as vulnerable and soft-hearted a mood by the first eligible young fellow who appeals to your compassion; and I wish I were a young fellow, that I might avail myself, on the spot, of such a favourable opportunity for doing so, as the present."

"You are as great a boy as poor Brittles himself," returned Rose, blushing.

"Well," said the doctor, laughing heartily, "that is no very difficult matter. But to return to this boy. The great point of our agreement is yet to come. He will wake in an hour or so, I dare say; and although I have told that thick-headed constable-fellow downstairs that he musn't be moved or spoken to, on peril of his life, I think we may converse with him without danger. Now I make this stipulation—that I shall examine him in your presence, and that, if, from what he says, we judge, and I can show to the satisfaction of your cool reason, that he is a real and thorough bad one (which is more than possible), he shall be left to his fate, without any farther interference on my part, at all events."

"Oh no, aunt!" entreated Rose.

"Oh yes, aunt!" said the doctor. "Is is a bargain?"

"He cannot be hardened in vice," said Rose; "It is impossible."

"Very good," retorted the doctor; "then so much the more reason for acceding to my proposition."

Finally the treaty was entered into; and the parties thereunto sat down to wait, with some impatience, until Oliver should awake.

The patience of the two ladies was destined to undergo a longer trial than Mr. Losberne had led them to expect; for hour after hour passed on, and still Oliver slumbered heavily. It was evening, indeed, before the kind-hearted doctor brought them the intelligence, that he was at length sufficiently restored to be spoken to. The boy was very ill, he said, and weak from the loss of blood; but his mind was so troubled with anxiety to disclose something, that he deemed it better to give him the opportunity, than to insist upon his remaining quiet until next morning: which he should otherwise have done.

The conference was a long one. Oliver told them all his simple history, and was often compelled to stop, by pain and want of strength. It was a solemn thing, to hear, in the darkened room, the feeble voice of the sick child recounting a weary catalogue of evils and calamities which hard men had brought upon him. Oh! if when we oppress and grind our fellow-creatures, we bestowed but one thought on the dark evidences of human error, which, like dense and heavy clouds, are rising, slowly it is true, but not less surely, to Heaven, to pour their after-vengeance on our heads; if we heard but one instant, in imagination, the deep testimony of dead men's voices, which no power can stifle, and no pride shut out; where would be the injury and injustice, the suffering, misery, cruelty, and wrong, that each day's life brings with it!

Oliver's pillow was smoothed by gentle hands that night; and loveliness and virtue watched him as he slept. He felt calm and happy, and could have died without a murmur.

The momentous interview was no sooner concluded, and Oliver composed to rest again, than the doctor, after wiping his eyes, and condemning them for being weak all at once, betook himself downstairs to open upon Mr. Giles. And finding nobody about the parlours, it occurred to him, that he could perhaps originate the proceedings with better effect in the kitchen; so into the kitchen he went.

There were assembled, in that lower house of the domestic parliament, the women-servants, Mr. Brittles, Mr. Giles, the tinker (who had received a special invitation to regale himself for the remainder of the day, in consideration of his services), and the constable. The latter gentleman had a large staff, a large head, large features, and large half-boots; and he looked as if he had been taking a proportionate allowance of ale—as indeed he had.

The adventures of the previous night were still under discussion; for Mr. Giles was expatiating upon his presence of mind, when the doctor entered; Mr. Brittles, with a mug of ale in his hand, was corroborating everything, before his superior said it.

"Sit still!" said the doctor, waving his hand.

"Thank you, sir, said Mr. Giles. "Misses wished some ale to be given out, sir; and as I felt no ways inclined for my own little room, sir, and was disposed for company, I am taking mine among 'em here."

Brittles headed a low murmur, by which the ladies and gentlemen generally were understood to express the gratification they derived from Mr. Giles's condescension. Mr. Giles looked round with a patronising air, as much as to say that so long as they behaved properly, he would never desert them.

"How is the patient to-night, sir?" asked Giles.

"So-so'; returned the doctor. "I am afraid you have got yourself into a scrape there, Mr. Giles."

"I hope you don't mean to say, sir," said Mr. Giles, trembling, "that he's going to die. If I thought it, I should never be happy again. I wouldn't cut a boy off: no, not even Brittles here; not for all the plate in the county, sir."

"That's not the point," said the doctor, mysteriously. "Mr. Giles, are you a Protestant?"

"Yes, sir, I hope so," faltered Mr. Giles, who had turned very pale.

"And what are you, boy?" said the doctor, turning sharply upon Brittles.

"Lord bless me, sir!" replied Brittles, starting violently; "I'm the same as Mr. Giles, sir."

"Then tell me this," said the doctor, "both of you, both of you! Are you going to take upon yourselves to swear, that that boy upstairs is the boy that was put through the little window last night? Out with it! Come! We are prepared for you!"

The doctor, who was universally considered one of the best-tempered creatures on earth, made this demand in such a dreadful tone of anger, that Giles and Brittles, who were considerably muddled by ale and excitement, stared at each other in a state of stupefaction.

"Pay attention to the reply, constable, will you?" said the doctor, shaking his forefinger with great solemnity of manner, and tapping the bridge of his nose with it, to bespeak the exercise of that worthy's utmost acuteness. "Something may come of this before long."

The constable looked as wise as he could, and took up his staff of office: which had been reclining indolently in the chimney-corner.

"It's a simple question of identity, you will observe," said the doctor.

"That's what it is, sir," replied the constable, coughing with great violence; for he had finished his ale in a hurry, and some of it had gone the wrong way.

"Here's the house broken into," said the doctor, "and a couple of men catch one moment's glimpse of a boy, in the midst of gunpowder smoke, and in all the distraction of alarm and darkness. Here's a boy comes to that very same house, next morning, and because he happens to have his arm tied up, these men lay violent hands upon him—by doing which, they place his life in great danger—and swear he is the thief. Now, the question is, whether these men are justified by the fact; if not, in what situation do they place themselves?"

The constable nodded profoundly. He said, if that wasn't law, he would be glad to know what was.

"I ask you again," thundered the doctor, "are you, on your solemn oaths, able to identify that boy?"

Brittles looked doubtfully at Mr. Giles; Mr. Giles looked doubtfully at Brittles; the constable put his hand behind his ear, to catch the reply; the two women and the tinker leaned forward to listen; the doctor glanced keenly round; when a ring was heard at the gate, and at the same moment, the sound of wheels.

"It's the runners!" cried Brittles, to all appearance much relieved.

"The what?" exclaimed the doctor, aghast in his turn.

"The Bow Street officers, sir," replied Brittles, taking up a candle; "me and Mr. Giles sent for 'em this morning."

"What?" cried the doctor.

"Yes," replied Brittles; "I sent a message up by the coachman, and I only wonder they weren't here before, sir."

"You did, did you? Then confound your—slow coaches down here; that's all," said the doctor, walking away.

CHAPTER XXXI

Involves a Critical Position

"Who's that?" inquired Brittles, opening the door a little way, with the chain up, and peeping out, shading the candle with his hand.

"Open the door," replied a man outside; "it's the officers from Bow Street, as was sent to to-day."

Much comforted by this assurance, Brittles opened the door to its full width, and confronted a portly man in a great-coat; who walked in, without saying anything more, and wiped his shoes on the mat, as coolly as if he lived there.

"Just send somebody out to relieve my mate, will you, young man?" said the officer; "he's in the gig, a-minding the prad. Have you got a coach 'us here, that you could put it up in, for five or ten minutes?"

Brittles replying in the affirmative, and pointing out the building, the portly man stepped back to the garden-gate, and helped his companion to put up the gig: while Brittles lighted them, in a state of great admiration. This done, they returned to the house, and, being shown into a parlour, took off their great-coats and hats, and showed like what they were.

The man who had knocked at the door, was a stout personage of middle height, aged about fifty: with shiny black hair, cropped pretty close; half-whiskers, a round face, and sharp eyes. The other was a red-headed, bony man, in top-boots; with a rather ill-favoured countenance, and a turned-up sinister-looking nose.

"Tell your governor that Blathers and Duff is here, will you?" said the stouter man, smoothing down his hair, and laying a pair of handcuffs on the table. "Oh! Good-evening, master. Can I have a word or two with you in private, if you please?"

This was addressed to Mr. Losberne, who now made his appearance; that gentleman, motioning Brittles to retire, brought in the two ladies, and shut the door.

"This is the lady of the house," said Mr. Losberne, motioning towards Mrs. Maylie.

Mr. Blathers made a bow. Being desired to sit down, he put his hat on the floor, and taking a chair, motioned to Duff to do the same. The latter gentleman, who did not appear quite so much accustomed to good society, or quite so much at his ease in it—one of the two—seated himself, after undergoing several muscular affections of the limbs, and the head of his stick into his mouth, with some embarrassment.

"Now, with regard to this here robbery, master," said Blathers. "What are the circumstances?"

Mr. Losberne, who appeared desirous of gaining time, recounted them at great length, and with much circumlocution. Messrs. Blathers and Duff looked very knowing meanwhile, and occasionally exchanged a nod.

"I can't say, for certain, till I see the work, of course," said Blathers; "but my opinion at once is,—I don't mind committing myself to that extent,—that this wasn't done by a yokel; eh, Duff?"

"Certainly not," replied Duff.

"And, translating the word yokel for the benefit of the ladies, I apprehend your meaning to be, that this attempt was not made by a countryman?" said Mr. Losberne, with a smile.

"That's it, master," replied Blathers. "This is all about the robbery, is it?"

"All," replied the doctor.

"Now, what is this, about this here boy that the servants are a-talking on?" said Blathers.

"Nothing at all," replied the doctor. "One of the frightened servants chose to take it into his head, that he had something to do with this attempt to break into the house; but it's nonsense: sheer absurdity."

"Wery easy disposed of, if it is," remarked Duff.

"What he says is quite correct," observed Blathers, nodding his head in a confirmatory way, and playing carelessly with the handcuffs, as if they were a pair of castanets. "Who is the boy? What account does he give of himself? Where did he come from? He didn't drop out of the clouds, did he, master?"

"Of course not," replied the doctor, with a nervous glance at the two ladies. "I know his whole history: but we can talk about that presently. You would like, first, to see the place where the thieves made their attempt, I suppose?"

"Certainly," rejoined Mr. Blathers. "We had better inspect the premises first, and examine the servants afterwards. That's the usual way of doing business."

Lights were then procured; and Messrs. Blathers and Duff, attended by the native constable, Brittles, Giles, and everybody else in short, went into the little room at the end of the passage and looked out at the window; and afterwards went round by way of the lawn, and looked in at the window; and after that, had a candle handed out to inspect the shutter with; and after that, a lantern to trace the footsteps with; and after that, a pitchfork to poke the bushes with. This done, amidst the breathless interest of all beholders, they came in again; and Mr. Giles and Brittles were put through a melodramatic representation of their share in the previous night's adventures: which they performed some six times over: contradicting each other, in not more than one important respect, the first time, and in not more than a dozen the last. This consummation being arrived at, Blathers and Duff cleared the room, and held a long council together, compared with which, for secrecy and solemnity, a consultation of great doctors on the knottiest point in medicine, would be mere child's play.

Meanwhile, the doctor walked up and down the next room in a very uneasy state; and Mrs. Maylie and Rose looked on, with anxious faces.

"Upon my word," he said, making a halt, after a great number of very rapid turns, "I hardly know what to do."

"Surely," said Rose, "the poor child's story, faithfully repeated to these men, will be sufficient to exonerate him."

"I doubt it, my dear young lady," said the doctor, shaking his head. "I don't think it would exonerate him, either with them, or with legal functionaries of a higher grade. What is he, after all, they would say? A runaway. Judged by mere worldly considerations and probabilities, his story is a very doubtful one."

"You believe it, surely?" interrupted Rose.

"I believe it, strange as it is; and perhaps I may be an old fool for doing so," rejoined the doctor; "but I don't think it is exactly the tale for a practical police-officer, nevertheless."

"Why not?" demanded Rose.

"Because, my pretty cross-examiner," replied the doctor: "because, viewed with their eyes, there are many ugly points about it; he can only prove the parts that look ill, and none of those that look well. Confound the fellows, they will have the why and the wherefore, and will take nothing for granted. On his own showing, you see, he has been the companion of thieves for some time past; he has been carried to a police-officer, on a charge of picking a gentleman's pocket; he has been taken away, forcibly, from that gentleman's house, to a place which he cannot describe or point out, and of the situation of which he has not the remotest idea. He is brought down to Chertsey, by men who seem to have taken a violent fancy to him, whether he will or no; and is put through a window to rob a house; and then, just at the very moment when he is going to alarm the inmates, and so do the very thing that would set him all to rights, there rushes into the way, a blundering dog of a half-bred butler, and shoots him! As if on purpose to prevent his doing any good for himself! Don't you see all this?"

"I see it, of course," replied Rose, smiling at the doctor's impetuosity; "but still I do not see anything in it, to criminate the poor child."

"No," replied the doctor; "of course not! Bless the bright eyes of your sex! They never see, whether for good or bad, more than one side of any question; and that is, always, the one which first presents itself to them."

Having given vent to this result of experience, the doctor put his hands into his pockets, and walked up and down the room with even greater rapidity than before.

"The more I think of it," said the doctor, "the more I see that it will occasion endless trouble and difficulty if we put these men in possession of the boy's real story. I am certain it will not be believed; and even if they can do nothing to him in the end, still the dragging it forward, and giving publicity to all the doubts that will be cast upon it, must interfere, materially, with your benevolent plan of rescuing him from misery."

"Oh! what is to be done?" cried Rose. "Dear, dear! why did they send for these people?"

"Why, indeed!" exclaimed Mrs. Maylie. "I would not have had them here, for the world."

"All I know is," said Mr. Losberne, at last: sitting down with a kind of desperate calmness, "that we must try and carry it off with a bold face. The object is a good one, and that must be our excuse. The boy has strong symptoms of fever upon him, and is in no condition to be talked to any more; that's one comfort. We must make the best of it; and if bad be the best, it is no fault of ours. Come in!"

"Well, master," said Blathers, entering the room followed by his colleague, and making the door fast, before he said any more. "This warn't a put-up thing."

"And what the devil's a put-up thing?" demanded the doctor, impatiently.

"We call it a put-up robbery, ladies," said Blathers, turning to them, as if he pitied their ignorance, but had a contempt for the doctor's, "when the servants is in it."

"Nobody suspected them, in this case," said Mrs. Maylie.

"Wery likely not, ma'am," replied Blathers; "but they might have been in it, for all that."

"More likely on that wery account," said Duff.

"We find it was a town hand," said Blathers, continuing his report; "for the style of work is first-rate."

"Wery pretty indeed it is," remarked Duff, in an undertone.

"There was two of 'em in it," continued Blathers; "and they had a boy with 'em; that's plain from the size of the window. That's all to be said at present. We'll see this lad that you've got upstairs at once, if you please."

"Perhaps they will take something to drink first, Mrs. Maylie?" said the doctor: his face brightening, as if some new thought had occurred to him.

"Oh! to be sure!" exclaimed Rose, eagerly. "You shall have it immediately, if you will."

"Why, thank you, miss!" said Blathers, drawing his coat-sleeve across his mouth; "it's dry work, this sort of duty. Anythink that's handy, miss; don't put yourself out of the way, on our accounts."

"What shall it be?" asked the doctor, following the young lady to the sideboard.

"A little drop of spirits, master, if it's all the same," replied Blathers. "It's a cold ride from London, ma'am; and I always find that spirits comes home warmer to the feelings."

This interesting communication was addressed to Mrs. Maylie, who received it very graciously. While it was being conveyed to her, the doctor slipped out of the room.

"Ah!" said Mr. Blathers: not holding his wine-glass by the stem, but grasping the bottom between the thumb and forefinger of his left hand: and placing it in front of his chest; "I have seen a good many pieces of business like this, in my time, ladies."

"That crack down in the back lane at Edmonton, Blathers," said Mr. Duff, assisting his colleague's memory.

"That was something in this way, warn't it?" rejoined Mr. Blathers; "that was done by Conkey Chickweed, that was."

"You always gave that to him' replied Duff. "It was the Family Pet, I tell you. Conkey hadn't any more to do with it than I had."

"Get out!" retorted Mr. Blathers; "I know better. Do you mind that time when Conkey was robbed of his money, though? What a start that was! Better than any novel-book I ever see!"

"What was that?" inquired Rose: anxious to encourage any symptoms of good-humour in the unwelcome visitors.

"It was a robbery, miss, that hardly anybody would have been down upon," said Blathers. "This here Conkey Chickweed—"

"Conkey means Nosey, ma'am," interposed Duff.

"Of course the lady knows that, don't she?" demanded Mr. Blathers. "Always interrupting, you are, partner! This here Conkey Chickweed, miss, kept a public-house over Battlebridge way, and he had a cellar, where a good many young lords went to see cock-fighting, and badger-drawing, and that; and a wery intellectual manner the sports was conducted in, for I've seen 'em off 'en. He warn't one of the family, at that time; and one night he was robbed of three hundred and twenty-seven guineas in a canvas bag, that was stole out of his bedroom in the dead of night, by a tall man with a black patch over his eye, who had concealed himself under the bed, and after committing the robbery, jumped slap out of window: which was only a story high. He was wery quick about it. But Conkey was quick, too; for he fired a blunderbuss arter him, and roused the neighbourhood. They set up a hue-and-cry, directly, and when they came to look about 'em, found that Conkey had hit the robber; for there was traces of blood, all the way to some palings a good distance off; and there they lost 'em. However, he had made off with the blunt; and, consequently, the name of Mr. Chickweed, licensed witler, appeared in the Gazette among the other bankrupts; and all manner of benefits and subscriptions, and I don't know what all, was got up for the poor man, who was in a wery low state of mind about his loss, and went up and down the streets, for three or four days, a pulling his hair off in such a desperate manner that many people was afraid he might be going to make away with himself. One day he came up to the office, all in a hurry, and had a private interview with the magistrate, who, after a deal of talk, rings the bell, and orders Jem Spyers in (Jem was a active officer), and tells him to go and assist Mr. Chickweed in apprehending the man as robbed his house. 'I see him, Spyers,' said Chickweed, 'pass my house yesterday morning,' 'Why didn't you up, and collar him!' says Spyers. 'I was so struck all of a heap, that you might have fractured my skull with a toothpick,' says the poor man; 'but we're sure to have him; for between ten and eleven o'clock at night he passed again.' Spyers no sooner heard this, than he put some clean linen and a comb, in his pocket, in case he should have to stop a day or two; and away he goes, and sets himself down at one of the public-house windows behind the little red curtain, with his hat on, all ready to bolt out, at a moment's notice. He was smoking his pipe here, late at night, when all of a sudden Chickweed roars out, 'Here he is! Stop thief! Murder!' Jem Spyers dashes out; and there he sees Chickweed, a-tearing down the street full cry. Away goes Spyers; on goes Chickweed; round turns the people; everybody roars out, 'Thieves!' and Chickweed himself keeps on shouting, all the time, like mad. Spyers loses sight of him a minute as he turns a corner; shoots round; sees a little crowd; dives in; 'Which is the man?' 'D—me!' says Chickweed, 'I've lost him again!' It was a remarkable occurrence, but he warn't to be seen nowhere, so they went back to the public-house. Next morning, Spyers took his old place, and looked out, from behind the curtain, for a tall man with a black patch over his eye, till his own two eyes ached again. At last, he couldn't help shutting 'em, to ease 'em a minute; and the very moment he did so, he hears Chickweed a-roaring out, 'Here he is!' Off he starts once more, with Chickweed half-way down the street ahead of him; and after twice as long a run as the yesterday's one, the man's lost again! This was done, once or twice more, till one-half the neighbours gave out that Mr. Chickweed had been robbed by the devil, who was playing tricks with him arterwards; and the other half, that poor Mr. Chickweed had gone mad with grief."

"What did Jem Spyers say?" inquired the doctor; who had returned to the room shortly after the commencement of the story.

"Jem Spyers," resumed the officer, "for a long time said nothing at all, and listened to everything without seeming to, which showed he understood his business. But, one morning, he walked into the bar, and taking out his snuffbox, says 'Chickweed, I've found out who done this here robbery.' 'Have you?' said Chickweed. 'Oh, my dear Spyers, only let me have wengeance, and I shall die contented! Oh, my dear Spyers, where is the villain!' 'Come!' said Spyers, offering him a pinch of snuff, 'none of that gammon! You did it yourself.' So he had; and a good bit of money he had made by it, too; and nobody would never have found it out, if he hadn't been so precious anxious to keep up appearances!" said Mr. Blathers, putting down his wine-glass, and clinking the handcuffs together.

"Very curious, indeed," observed the doctor. "Now, if you please, you can walk upstairs."

"If you please, sir," returned Mr. Blathers. Closely following Mr. Losberne, the two officers ascended to Oliver's bedroom; Mr. Giles preceding the party, with a lighted candle.

Oliver had been dozing; but looked worse, and was more feverish than he had appeared yet. Being assisted by the doctor, he managed to sit up in bed for a minute or so; and looked at the strangers without at all understanding what was going forward—in fact, without seeming to recollect where he was, or what had been passing.

"This," said Mr. Losberne, speaking softly, but with great vehemence notwithstanding, 'this is the lad, who, being accidently wounded by a spring-gun in some boyish trespass on Mr. What-d' ye-call-him's grounds, at the back here, comes to the house for assistance this morning, and is immediately laid hold of and maltreated, by that ingenious gentleman with the candle in his hand: who has placed his life in considerable danger, as I can professionally certify."

Messrs. Blathers and Duff looked at Mr. Giles, as he was thus recommended to their notice. The bewildered butler gazed from them towards Oliver, and from Oliver towards Mr. Losberne, with a most ludicrous mixture of fear and perplexity.

"You don't mean to deny that, I suppose?" said the doctor, laying Oliver gently down again.

"It was all done for the—for the best, sir," answered Giles. "I am sure I thought it was the boy, or I wouldn't have meddled with him. I am not of an inhuman disposition, sir."

"Thought it was what boy?" inquired the senior officer.

"The housebreaker's boy, sir!" replied Giles. "They—they certainly had a boy."

"Well? Do you think so now?" inquired Blathers.

"Think what, now?" replied Giles, looking vacantly at his questioner.

"Think it's the same boy, Stupid-head?" rejoined Blathers, impatiently.

"I don't know; I really don't know," said Giles, with a rueful countenance. "I couldn't swear to him."

"What do you think?" asked Mr. Blathers.

"I don't know what to think," replied poor Giles. "I don't think it is the boy; indeed, I'm almost certain that it isn't. You know it can't be."

"Has this man been a-drinking, sir?" inquired Blathers, turning to the doctor.

"What a precious muddle-headed chap you are!" said Duff, addressing Mr. Giles, with supreme contempt.

Mr. Losberne had been feeling the patient's pulse during this short dialogue; but he now rose from the chair by the bedside, and remarked, that if the officers had any doubts upon the subject, they would perhaps like to step into the next room, and have Brittles before them.

Acting upon this suggestion, they adjourned to a neighbouring apartment, where Mr. Brittles, being called in, involved himself and his respected superior in such a wonderful maze of fresh contradictions and impossibilities, as tended to throw no particular light on anything, but the fact of his own strong mystification; except, indeed, his declarations that he shouldn't know the real boy, if he were put before him that instant; that he had only taken Oliver to be he, because Mr. Giles had said he was; and that Mr. Giles had, five minutes previously, admitted in the kitchen, that he began to be very much afraid he had been a little too hasty.

Among other ingenious surmises, the question was then raised, whether Mr. Giles had really hit anybody; and upon examination of the fellow pistol to that which he had fired, it turned out to have no more destructive loading than gunpowder and brown paper: a discovery which made a considerable impression on everybody but the doctor, who had drawn the ball about ten minutes before. Upon no one, however, did it make a greater impression than on Mr. Giles himself; who, after labouring, for some hours, under the fear of having mortally wounded a fellow-creature, eagerly caught at this new idea, and favoured it to the utmost. Finally, the officers, without troubling themselves very much about Oliver, left the Chertsey constable in the house, and took up their rest for that night in the town; promising to return the next morning.

With the next morning, there came a rumour, that two men and a boy were in the cage at Kingston, who had been apprehended over night under suspicious circumstances; and to Kingston Messrs. Blathers and Duff journeyed accordingly. The suspicious circumstances, however, resolving themselves, on investigation, into the one fact, that they had been discovered sleeping under a haystack; which, although a great crime, is only punishable by imprisonment, and is, in the merciful eye of the English law, and its comprehensive love of all the King's subjects, held to be no satisfactory proof, in the absence of all other evidence, that the sleeper, or sleepers, have committed burglary accompanied with violence, and have therefore rendered themselves liable to the punishment of death; Messrs. Blathers and Duff came back again, as wise as they went.

In short, after some more examination, and a great deal more conversation, a neighbouring magistrate was readily induced to take the joint bail of Mrs. Maylie and Mr. Losberne for Oliver's appearance if he should ever be called upon; and Blathers and Duff, being rewarded with a couple of guineas, returned to town with divided opinions on the subject of their expedition: the latter gentleman on a mature consideration of all the circumstances, inclining to the belief that the burglarious attempt had originated with the Family Pet; and the former being equally disposed to concede the full merit of it to the great Mr. Conkey Chickweed.

Meanwhile, Oliver gradually throve and prospered under the united care of Mrs. Maylie, Rose, and the kind-hearted Mr. Losberne. If fervent prayers, gushing from hearts overcharged with gratitude, be heard in heaven—and if they be not, what prayers are!—the blessings which the orphan child called down upon them, sunk into their souls, diffusing peace and happiness.

CHAPTER XXXII

Of the Happy Life Oliver Began to Lead With His Kind Friends

Oliver's ailings were neither slight nor few. In addition to the pain and delay attendant on a broken limb, his exposure to the wet and cold had brought on fever and ague: which hung about him for many weeks, and reduced him sadly. But, at length, he began, by slow degrees, to get better, and to be able to say sometimes, in a few tearful words, how deeply he felt the goodness of the two sweet ladies, and how ardently he hoped that when he grew strong and well again, he could do something to show his gratitude; only something, which would let them see the love and duty with which his breast was full; something, however slight, which would prove to them that their gentle kindness had not been cast away; but that the poor boy whom their charity had rescued from misery, or death, was eager to serve them with his whole heart and soul.

"Poor fellow!" said Rose, when Oliver had been one day feebly endeavouring to utter the words of thankfulness that rose to his pale lips; "you shall have many opportunities of serving us, if you will. We are going into the country, and my aunt intends that you shall accompany us. The quiet place, the pure air, and all the pleasure and beauties of spring, will restore you in a few days. We will employ you in a hundred ways, when you can bear the trouble."

"The trouble!" cried Oliver. "Oh! dear lady, if I could but work for you; if I could only give you pleasure by watering your flowers, or watching your birds, or running up and down the whole day long, to make you happy; what would I give to do it!"

"You shall give nothing at all," said Miss Maylie, smiling; "for, as I told you before, we shall employ you in a hundred ways; and if you only take half the trouble to please us, that you promise now, you will make me very happy indeed."

"Happy, ma'am!" cried Oliver; "how kind of you to say so!"

"You will make me happier than I can tell you," replied the young lady. "To think that my dear good aunt should have been the means of rescuing any one from such sad misery as you have described to us, would be an unspeakable pleasure to me; but to know that the object of her goodness and compassion was sincerely grateful and attached, in consequence, would delight me, more than you can well imagine. Do you understand me?" she inquired, watching Oliver's thoughtful face.

"Oh yes, ma'am, yes!" replied Oliver eagerly; "but I was thinking that I am ungrateful now."

"To whom?" inquired the young lady.

"To the kind gentleman, and the dear old nurse, who took so much care of me before," rejoined Oliver. "If they knew how happy I am, they would be pleased, I am sure."

"I am sure they would," rejoined Oliver's benefactress; "and Mr. Losberne has already been kind enough to promise that when you are well enough to bear the journey, he will carry you to see them."

"Has he, ma'am?" cried Oliver, his face brightening with pleasure. "I don't know what I shall do for joy when I see their kind faces once again!"

In a short time Oliver was sufficiently recovered to undergo the fatigue of this expedition. One morning he and Mr. Losberne set out, accordingly, in a little carriage which belonged to Mrs. Maylie. When they came to Chertsey Bridge, Oliver turned very pale, and uttered a loud exclamation.

"What's the matter with the boy?" cried the doctor, as usual, all in a bustle. "Do you see anything—hear anything—feel anything—eh?"

"That, sir," cried Oliver, pointing out of the carriage window. "That house!"

"Yes; well, what of it? Stop coachman. Pull up here," cried the doctor. "What of the house, my man; eh?"

"The thieves—the house they took me to!" whispered Oliver.

"The devil it is!" cried the doctor. "Hallo, there! let me out!"

But, before the coachman could dismount from his box, he had tumbled out of the coach, by some means or other; and, running down to the deserted tenement, began kicking at the door like a madman.

"Halloa?" said a little ugly hump-backed man: opening the door so suddenly, that the doctor, from the very impetus of his last kick, nearly fell forward into the passage. "What's the matter here?"

"Matter!" exclaimed the other, collaring him, without a moment's reflection. "A good deal. Robbery is the matter."

"There'll be Murder the matter, too," replied the hump-backed man, coolly, "if you don't take your hands off. Do you hear me?"

"I hear you," said the doctor, giving his captive a hearty shake.

"Where's—confound the fellow, what's his rascally name—Sikes; that's it. Where's Sikes, you thief?"

The hump-backed man stared, as if in excess of amazement and indignation; then, twisting himself, dexterously, from the doctor's grasp, growled forth a volley of horrid oaths, and retired into the house. Before he could shut the door, however, the doctor had passed into the parlour, without a word of parley.

He looked anxiously round; not an article of furniture; not a vestige of anything, animate or inanimate; not even the position of the cupboards; answered Oliver's description!

"Now!" said the hump-backed man, who had watched him keenly, "what do you mean by coming into my house, in this violent way? Do you want to rob me, or to murder me? Which is it?"

"Did you ever know a man come out to do either, in a chariot and pair, you ridiculous old vampire?" said the irritable doctor.

"What do you want, then?" demanded the hunchback. "Will you take yourself off, before I do you a mischief? Curse you!"

"As soon as I think proper," said Mr. Losberne, looking into the other parlour; which, like the first, bore no resemblance whatever to Oliver's account of it. "I shall find you out, some day, my friend."

"Will you?" sneered the ill-favoured cripple. "If you ever want me, I'm here. I haven't lived here mad and all alone, for five-and-twenty years, to be scared by you. You shall pay for this; you shall pay for this.' And so saying, the mis-shapen little demon set up a yell, and danced upon the ground, as if wild with rage.

"Stupid enough, this," muttered the doctor to himself; "the boy must have made a mistake. Here! Put that in your pocket, and shut yourself up again.' With these words he flung the hunchback a piece of money, and returned to the carriage.

The man followed to the chariot door, uttering the wildest imprecations and curses all the way; but as Mr. Losberne turned to speak to the driver, he looked into the carriage, and eyed Oliver for an instant with a glance so sharp and fierce and at the same time so furious and vindictive, that, waking or sleeping, he could not forget it for months afterwards. He continued to utter the most fearful imprecations, until the driver had resumed his seat; and when they were once more on their way, they could see him some distance behind: beating his feet upon the ground, and tearing his hair, in transports of real or pretended rage.

"I am an ass!" said the doctor, after a long silence. "Did you know that before, Oliver?"

"No, sir."

"Then don't forget it another time."

"An ass," said the doctor again, after a further silence of some minutes. "Even if it had been the right place, and the right fellows had been there, what could I have done, single-handed? And if I had had assistance, I see no good that I should have done, except leading to my own exposure, and an unavoidable statement of the manner in which I have hushed up this business. That would have served me right, though. I am always involving myself in some scrape or other, by acting on impulse. It might have done me good."

Now, the fact was that the excellent doctor had never acted upon anything but impulse all through his life, and it was no bad compliment to the nature of the impulses which governed him, that so far from being involved in any peculiar troubles or misfortunes, he had the warmest respect and esteem of all who knew him. If the truth must be told, he was a little out of temper, for a minute or two, at being disappointed in procuring corroborative evidence of Oliver's story on the very first occasion on which he had a chance of obtaining any. He soon came round again, however; and finding that Oliver's replies to his questions, were still as straightforward and consistent, and still delivered with as much apparent sincerity and truth, as they had ever been, he made up his mind to attach full credence to them, from that time forth.

As Oliver knew the name of the street in which Mr. Brownlow resided, they were enabled to drive straight thither. When the coach turned into it, his heart beat so violently, that he could scarcely draw his breath.

"Now, my boy, which house is it?" inquired Mr. Losberne.

"That! That!" replied Oliver, pointing eagerly out of the window. "The white house. Oh! make haste! Pray make haste! I feel as if I should die: it makes me tremble so."

"Come, come!" said the good doctor, patting him on the shoulder. "You will see them directly, and they will be overjoyed to find you safe and well."

"Oh! I hope so!" cried Oliver. "They were so good to me; so very, very good to me."

The coach rolled on. It stopped. No; that was the wrong house; the next door. It went on a few paces, and stopped again. Oliver looked up at the windows, with tears of happy expectation coursing down his face.

Alas! the white house was empty, and there was a bill in the window. "To Let."

"Knock at the next door," cried Mr. Losberne, taking Oliver's arm in his. "What has become of Mr. Brownlow, who used to live in the adjoining house, do you know?"

The servant did not know; but would go and inquire. She presently returned, and said, that Mr. Brownlow had sold off his goods, and gone to the West Indies, six weeks before. Oliver clasped his hands, and sank feebly backward.

"Has his housekeeper gone too?" inquired Mr. Losberne, after a moment's pause.

"Yes, sir'; replied the servant. "The old gentleman, the housekeeper, and a gentleman who was a friend of Mr. Brownlow's, all went together."

"Then turn towards home again," said Mr. Losberne to the driver; "and don't stop to bait the horses, till you get out of this confounded London!"

"The book-stall keeper, sir?" said Oliver. "I know the way there. See him, pray, sir! Do see him!"

"My poor boy, this is disappointment enough for one day," said the doctor. "Quite enough for both of us. If we go to the book-stall keeper's, we shall certainly find that he is dead, or has set his house on fire, or run away. No; home again straight!" And in obedience to the doctor's impulse, home they went.

This bitter disappointment caused Oliver much sorrow and grief, even in the midst of his happiness; for he had pleased himself, many times during his illness, with thinking of all that Mr. Brownlow and Mrs. Bedwin would say to him: and what delight it would be to tell them how many long days and nights he had passed in reflecting on what they had done for him, and in bewailing his cruel separation from them. The hope of eventually clearing himself with them, too, and explaining how he had been forced away, had buoyed him up, and sustained him, under many of his recent trials; and now, the idea that they should have gone so far, and carried with them the belief that he was an impostor and a robber—a belief which might remain uncontradicted to his dying day—was almost more than he could bear.

The circumstance occasioned no alteration, however, in the behaviour of his benefactors. After another fortnight, when the fine warm weather had fairly begun, and every tree and flower was putting forth its young leaves and rich blossoms, they made preparations for quitting the house at Chertsey, for some months.

Sending the plate, which had so excited Fagin's cupidity, to the banker's; and leaving Giles and another servant in care of the house, they departed to a cottage at some distance in the country, and took Oliver with them.

Who can describe the pleasure and delight, the peace of mind and soft tranquillity, the sickly boy felt in the balmy air, and among the green hills and rich woods, of an inland village! Who can tell how scenes of peace and quietude sink into the minds of pain-worn dwellers in close and noisy places, and carry their own freshness, deep into their jaded hearts! Men who have lived in crowded, pent-up streets, through lives of toil, and who have never wished for change; men, to whom custom has indeed been second nature, and who have come almost to love each brick and stone that formed the narrow boundaries of their daily walks; even they, with the hand of death upon them, have been known to yearn at last for one short glimpse of Nature's face; and, carried far from the scenes of their old pains and pleasures, have seemed to pass at once into a new state of being. Crawling forth, from day to day, to some green sunny spot, they have had such memories wakened up within them by the sight of the sky, and hill and plain, and glistening water, that a foretaste of heaven itself has soothed their quick decline, and they have sunk into their tombs, as peacefully as the sun whose setting they watched from their lonely chamber window but a few hours before, faded from their dim and feeble sight! The memories which peaceful country scenes call up, are not of this world, nor of its thoughts and hopes. Their gentle influence may teach us how to weave fresh garlands for the graves of those we loved: may purify our thoughts, and bear down before it old enmity and hatred; but beneath all this, there lingers, in the least reflective mind, a vague and half-formed consciousness of having held such feelings long before, in some remote and distant time, which calls up solemn thoughts of distant times to come, and bends down pride and worldliness beneath it.

It was a lovely spot to which they repaired. Oliver, whose days had been spent among squalid crowds, and in the midst of noise and brawling, seemed to enter on a new existence there. The rose and honeysuckle clung to the cottage walls; the ivy crept round the trunks of the trees; and the garden-flowers perfumed the air with delicious odours. Hard by, was a little churchyard; not crowded with tall unsightly gravestones, but full of humble mounds, covered with fresh turf and moss: beneath which, the old people of the village lay at rest. Oliver often wandered here; and, thinking of the wretched grave in which his mother lay, would sometimes sit him down and sob unseen; but, when he raised his eyes to the deep sky overhead, he would cease to think of her as lying in the ground, and would weep for her, sadly, but without pain.

It was a happy time. The days were peaceful and serene; the nights brought with them neither fear nor care; no languishing in a wretched prison, or associating with wretched men; nothing but pleasant and happy thoughts. Every morning he went to a white-headed old gentleman, who lived near the little church: who taught him to read better, and to write: and who spoke so kindly, and took such pains, that Oliver could never try enough to please him. Then, he would walk with Mrs. Maylie and Rose, and hear them talk of books; or perhaps sit near them, in some shady place, and listen whilst the young lady read: which he could have done, until it grew too dark to see the letters. Then, he had his own lesson for the next day to prepare; and at this, he would work hard, in a little room which looked into the garden, till evening came slowly on, when the ladies would walk out again, and he with them: listening with such pleasure to all they said: and so happy if they wanted a flower that he could climb to reach, or had forgotten anything he could run to fetch: that he could never be quick enough about it. When it became quite dark, and they returned home, the young lady would sit down to the piano, and play some pleasant air, or sing, in a low and gentle voice, some old song which it pleased her aunt to hear. There would be no candles lighted at such times as these; and Oliver would sit by one of the windows, listening to the sweet music, in a perfect rapture.

And when Sunday came, how differently the day was spent, from any way in which he had ever spent it yet! and how happily too; like all the other days in that most happy time! There was the little church, in the morning, with the green leaves fluttering at the windows: the birds singing without: and the sweet-smelling air stealing in at the low porch, and filling the homely building with its fragrance. The poor people were so neat and clean, and knelt so reverently in prayer, that it seemed a pleasure, not a tedious duty, their assembling there together; and though the singing might be rude, it was real, and sounded more musical (to Oliver's ears at least) than any he had ever heard in church before. Then, there were the walks as usual, and many calls at the clean houses of the labouring men; and at night, Oliver read a chapter or two from the Bible, which he had been studying all the week, and in the performance of which duty he felt more proud and pleased, than if he had been the clergyman himself.

In the morning, Oliver would be a-foot by six o'clock, roaming the fields, and plundering the hedges, far and wide, for nosegays of wild flowers, with which he would return laden, home; and which it took great care and consideration to arrange, to the best advantage, for the embellishment of the breakfast-table. There was fresh groundsel, too, for Miss Maylie's birds, with which Oliver, who had been studying the subject under the able tuition of the village clerk, would decorate the cages, in the most approved taste. When the birds were made all spruce and smart for the day, there was usually some little commission of charity to execute in the village; or, failing that, there was rare cricket-playing, sometimes, on the green; or, failing that, there was always something to do in the garden, or about the plants, to which Oliver (who had studied this science also, under the same master, who was a gardener by trade,) applied himself with hearty good-will, until Miss Rose made her appearance: when there were a thousand commendations to be bestowed on all he had done.

So three months glided away; three months which, in the life of the most blessed and favoured of mortals, might have been unmingled happiness, and which, in Oliver's were true felicity. With the purest and most amiable generosity on one side; and the truest, warmest, soul-felt gratitude on the other; it is no wonder that, by the end of that short time, Oliver Twist had become completely domesticated with the old lady and her niece, and that the fervent attachment of his young and sensitive heart, was repaid by their pride in, and attachment to, himself.

CHAPTER XXXIII

Wherein the Happiness of Oliver and His Friends, Experiences a Sudden Check

Spring flew swiftly by, and summer came. If the village had been beautiful at first it was now in the full glow and luxuriance of its richness. The great trees, which had looked shrunken and bare in the earlier months, had now burst into strong life and health; and stretching forth their green arms over the thirsty ground, converted open and naked spots into choice nooks, where was a deep and pleasant shade from which to look upon the wide prospect, steeped in sunshine, which lay stretched beyond. The earth had donned her mantle of brightest green; and shed her richest perfumes abroad. It was the prime and vigour of the year; all things were glad and flourishing.

Still, the same quiet life went on at the little cottage, and the same cheerful serenity prevailed among its inmates. Oliver had long since grown stout and healthy; but health or sickness made no difference in his warm feelings of a great many people. He was still the same gentle, attached, affectionate creature that he had been when pain and suffering had wasted his strength, and when he was dependent for every slight attention, and comfort on those who tended him.

One beautiful night, when they had taken a longer walk than was customary with them: for the day had been unusually warm, and there was a brilliant moon, and a light wind had sprung up, which was unusually refreshing. Rose had been in high spirits, too, and they had walked on, in merry conversation, until they had far exceeded their ordinary bounds. Mrs. Maylie being fatigued, they returned more slowly home. The young lady merely throwing off her simple bonnet, sat down to the piano as usual. After running abstractedly over the keys for a few minutes, she fell into a low and very solemn air; and as she played it, they heard a sound as if she were weeping.

"Rose, my dear!" said the elder lady.

Rose made no reply, but played a little quicker, as though the words had roused her from some painful thoughts.

"Rose, my love!" cried Mrs. Maylie, rising hastily, and bending over her. "What is this? In tears! My dear child, what distresses you?"

"Nothing, aunt; nothing," replied the young lady. "I don't know what it is; I can't describe it; but I feel—"

"Not ill, my love?" interposed Mrs. Maylie.

"No, no! Oh, not ill!" replied Rose: shuddering as though some deadly chillness were passing over her, while she spoke; "I shall be better presently. Close the window, pray!"

Oliver hastened to comply with her request. The young lady, making an effort to recover her cheerfulness, strove to play some livelier tune; but her fingers dropped powerless over the keys. Covering her face with her hands, she sank upon a sofa, and gave vent to the tears which she was now unable to repress.

"My child!" said the elderly lady, folding her arms about her, "I never saw you so before."

"I would not alarm you if I could avoid it," rejoined Rose; "but indeed I have tried very hard, and cannot help this. I fear I am ill, aunt."

She was, indeed; for, when candles were brought, they saw that in the very short time which had elapsed since their return home, the hue of her countenance had changed to a marble whiteness. Its expression had lost nothing of its beauty; but it was changed; and there was an anxious haggard look about the gentle face, which it had never worn before. Another minute, and it was suffused with a crimson flush: and a heavy wildness came over the soft blue eye. Again this disappeared, like the shadow thrown by a passing cloud; and she was once more deadly pale.

Oliver, who watched the old lady anxiously, observed that she was alarmed by these appearances; and so in truth, was he; but seeing that she affected to make light of them, he endeavoured to do the same, and they so far succeeded, that when Rose was persuaded by her aunt to retire for the night, she was in better spirits; and appeared even in better health: assuring them that she felt certain she should rise in the morning, quite well.

"I hope," said Oliver, when Mrs. Maylie returned, "that nothing is the matter? She don't look well to-night, but—"

The old lady motioned to him not to speak; and sitting herself down in a dark corner of the room, remained silent for some time. At length, she said, in a trembling voice:

"I hope not, Oliver. I have been very happy with her for some years: too happy, perhaps. It may be time that I should meet with some misfortune; but I hope it is not this."

"What?" inquired Oliver.

"The heavy blow," said the old lady, "of losing the dear girl who has so long been my comfort and happiness."

"Oh! God forbid!" exclaimed Oliver, hastily.

"Amen to that, my child!" said the old lady, wringing her hands.

"Surely there is no danger of anything so dreadful?" said Oliver. "Two hours ago, she was quite well."

"She is very ill now," rejoined Mrs. Maylies; "and will be worse, I am sure. My dear, dear Rose! Oh, what shall I do without her!"

She gave way to such great grief, that Oliver, suppressing his own emotion, ventured to remonstrate with her; and to beg, earnestly, that, for the sake of the dear young lady herself, she would be more calm.

"And consider, ma'am," said Oliver, as the tears forced themselves into his eyes, despite of his efforts to the contrary. "Oh! consider how young and good she is, and what pleasure and comfort she gives to all about her. I am sure—certain—quite certain—that, for your sake, who are so good yourself; and for her own; and for the sake of all she makes so happy; she will not die. Heaven will never let her die so young."

"Hush!" said Mrs. Maylie, laying her hand on Oliver's head. "You think like a child, poor boy. But you teach me my duty, notwithstanding. I had forgotten it for a moment, Oliver, but I hope I may be pardoned, for I am old, and have seen enough of illness and death to know the agony of separation from the objects of our love. I have seen enough, too, to know that it is not always the youngest and best who are spared to those that love them; but this should give us comfort in our sorrow; for Heaven is just; and such things teach us, impressively, that there is a brighter world than this; and that the passage to it is speedy. God's will be done! I love her; and He knows how well!"

Oliver was surprised to see that as Mrs. Maylie said these words, she checked her lamentations as though by one effort; and drawing herself up as she spoke, became composed and firm. He was still more astonished to find that this firmness lasted; and that, under all the care and watching which ensued, Mrs. Maylie was every ready and collected: performing all the duties which had devolved upon her, steadily, and, to all external appearances, even cheerfully. But he was young, and did not know what strong minds are capable of, under trying circumstances. How should he, when their possessors so seldom know themselves?

An anxious night ensued. When morning came, Mrs. Maylie's predictions were but too well verified. Rose was in the first stage of a high and dangerous fever.

"We must be active, Oliver, and not give way to useless grief," said Mrs. Maylie, laying her finger on her lip, as she looked steadily into his face; "this letter must be sent, with all possible expedition, to Mr. Losberne. It must be carried to the market-town: which is not more than four miles off, by the footpath across the field: and thence dispatched, by an express on horseback, straight to Chertsey. The people at the inn will undertake to do this: and I can trust to you to see it done, I know."

Oliver could make no reply, but looked his anxiety to be gone at once.

"Here is another letter," said Mrs. Maylie, pausing to reflect; "but whether to send it now, or wait until I see how Rose goes on, I scarcely know. I would not forward it, unless I feared the worst."

"Is it for Chertsey, too, ma'am?" inquired Oliver; impatient to execute his commission, and holding out his trembling hand for the letter.

"No," replied the old lady, giving it to him mechanically. Oliver glanced at it, and saw that it was directed to Harry Maylie, Esquire, at some great lord's house in the country; where, he could not make out.

"Shall it go, ma'am?" asked Oliver, looking up, impatiently.

"I think not," replied Mrs. Maylie, taking it back. "I will wait until to-morrow."

With these words, she gave Oliver her purse, and he started off, without more delay, at the greatest speed he could muster.

Swiftly he ran across the fields, and down the little lanes which sometimes divided them: now almost hidden by the high corn on either side, and now emerging on an open field, where the mowers and haymakers were busy at their work: nor did he stop once, save now and then, for a few seconds, to recover breath, until he came, in a great heat, and covered with dust, on the little market-place of the market-town.

Here he paused, and looked about for the inn. There were a white bank, and a red brewery, and a yellow town-hall; and in one corner there was a large house, with all the wood about it painted green: before which was the sign of "The George." To this he hastened, as soon as it caught his eye.

He spoke to a postboy who was dozing under the gateway; and who, after hearing what he wanted, referred him to the ostler; who after hearing all he had to say again, referred him to the landlord; who was a tall gentleman in a blue neckcloth, a white hat, drab breeches, and boots with tops to match, leaning against a pump by the stable-door, picking his teeth with a silver toothpick.

This gentleman walked with much deliberation into the bar to make out the bill: which took a long time making out: and after it was ready, and paid, a horse had to be saddled, and a man to be dressed, which took up ten good minutes more. Meanwhile Oliver was in such a desperate state of impatience and anxiety, that he felt as if he could have jumped upon the horse himself, and galloped away, full tear, to the next stage. At length, all was ready; and the little parcel having been handed up, with many injunctions and entreaties for its speedy delivery, the man set spurs to his horse, and rattling over the uneven paving of the market-place, was out of the town, and galloping along the turnpike-road, in a couple of minutes.

As it was something to feel certain that assistance was sent for, and that no time had been lost, Oliver hurried up the inn-yard, with a somewhat lighter heart. He was turning out of the gateway when he accidently stumbled against a tall man wrapped in a cloak, who was at that moment coming out of the inn door.

"Hah!" cried the man, fixing his eyes on Oliver, and suddenly recoiling. "What the devil's this?"

"I beg your pardon, sir," said Oliver; "I was in a great hurry to get home, and didn't see you were coming."

"Death!" muttered the man to himself, glaring at the boy with his large dark eyes. "Who would have thought it! Grind him to ashes! He'd start up from a stone coffin, to come in my way!"

"I am sorry," stammered Oliver, confused by the strange man's wild look. "I hope I have not hurt you!"

"Rot you!" murmured the man, in a horrible passion; between his clenched teeth; "if I had only had the courage to say the word, I might have been free of you in a night. Curses on your head, and black death on your heart, you imp! What are you doing here?"

The man shook his fist, as he uttered these words incoherently. He advanced towards Oliver, as if with the intention of aiming a blow at him, but fell violently on the ground: writhing and foaming, in a fit.

Oliver gazed, for a moment, at the struggles of the madman (for such he supposed him to be); and then darted into the house for help. Having seen him safely carried into the hotel, he turned his face homewards, running as fast as he could, to make up for lost time: and recalling with a great deal of astonishment and some fear, the extraordinary behaviour of the person from whom he had just parted.

The circumstance did not dwell in his recollection long, however: for when he reached the cottage, there was enough to occupy his mind, and to drive all considerations of self completely from his memory.

Rose Maylie had rapidly grown worse; before mid-night she was delirious. A medical practitioner, who resided on the spot, was in constant attendance upon her; and after first seeing the patient, he had taken Mrs. Maylie aside, and pronounced her disorder to be one of a most alarming nature. "In fact," he said, "it would be little short of a miracle, if she recovered."

How often did Oliver start from his bed that night, and stealing out, with noiseless footstep, to the staircase, listen for the slightest sound from the sick chamber! How often did a tremble shake his frame, and cold drops of terror start upon his brow, when a sudden trampling of feet caused him to fear that something too dreadful to think of, had even then occurred! And what had been the fervency of all the prayers he had ever muttered, compared with those he poured forth, now, in the agony and passion of his supplication for the life and health of the gentle creature, who was tottering on the deep grave's verge!

Oh! the suspense, the fearful, acute suspense, of standing idly by while the life of one we dearly love, is trembling in the balance! Oh! the racking thoughts that crowd upon the mind, and make the heart beat violently, and the breath come thick, by the force of the images they conjure up before it; the desperate anxiety to be doing something to relieve the pain, or lessen the danger, which we have no power to alleviate; the sinking of soul and spirit, which the sad remembrance of our helplessness produces; what tortures can equal these; what reflections or endeavours can, in the full tide and fever of the time, allay them!

Morning came; and the little cottage was lonely and still. People spoke in whispers; anxious faces appeared at the gate, from time to time; women and children went away in tears. All the livelong day, and for hours after it had grown dark, Oliver paced softly up and down the garden, raising his eyes every instant to the sick chamber, and shuddering to see the darkened window, looking as if death lay stretched inside. Late that night, Mr. Losberne arrived. "It is hard," said the good doctor, turning away as he spoke; "so young; so much beloved; but there is very little hope."

Another morning. The sun shone brightly; as brightly as if it looked upon no misery or care; and, with every leaf and flower in full bloom about her; with life, and health, and sounds and sights of joy, surrounding her on every side: the fair young creature lay, wasting fast. Oliver crept away to the old churchyard, and sitting down on one of the green mounds, wept and prayed for her, in silence.

There was such peace and beauty in the scene; so much of brightness and mirth in the sunny landscape; such blithesome music in the songs of the summer birds; such freedom in the rapid flight of the rook, careering overhead; so much of life and joyousness in all; that, when the boy raised his aching eyes, and looked about, the thought instinctively occurred to him, that this was not a time for death; that Rose could surely never die when humbler things were all so glad and gay; that graves were for cold and cheerless winter: not for sunlight and fragrance. He almost thought that shrouds were for the old and shrunken; and that they never wrapped the young and graceful form in their ghastly folds.

A knell from the church bell broke harshly on these youthful thoughts. Another! Again! It was tolling for the funeral service. A group of humble mourners entered the gate: wearing white favours; for the corpse was young. They stood uncovered by a grave; and there was a mother—a mother once—among the weeping train. But the sun shone brightly, and the birds sang on.

Oliver turned homeward, thinking on the many kindnesses he had received from the young lady, and wishing that the time could come again, that he might never cease showing her how grateful and attached he was. He had no cause for self-reproach on the score of neglect, or want of thought, for he had been devoted to her service; and yet a hundred little occasions rose up before him, on which he fancied he might have been more zealous, and more earnest, and wished he had been. We need be careful how we deal with those about us, when every death carries to some small circle of survivors, thoughts of so much omitted, and so little done—of so many things forgotten, and so many more which might have been repaired! There is no remorse so deep as that which is unavailing; if we would be spared its tortures, let us remember this, in time.

When he reached home Mrs. Maylie was sitting in the little parlour. Oliver's heart sank at sight of her; for she had never left the bedside of her niece; and he trembled to think what change could have driven her away. He learnt that she had fallen into a deep sleep, from which she would waken, either to recovery and life, or to bid them farewell, and die.

They sat, listening, and afraid to speak, for hours. The untasted meal was removed, with looks which showed that their thoughts were elsewhere, they watched the sun as he sank lower and lower, and, at length, cast over sky and earth those brilliant hues which herald his departure. Their quick ears caught the sound of an approaching footstep. They both involuntarily darted to the door, as Mr. Losberne entered.

"What of Rose?" cried the old lady. "Tell me at once! I can bear it; anything but suspense! Oh, tell me! in the name of Heaven!"

"You must compose yourself," said the doctor supporting her. "Be calm, my dear ma'am, pray."

"Let me go, in God's name! My dear child! She is dead! She is dying!"

"No!" cried the doctor, passionately. "As He is good and merciful, she will live to bless us all, for years to come."

The lady fell upon her knees, and tried to fold her hands together; but the energy which had supported her so long, fled up to Heaven with her first thanksgiving; and she sank into the friendly arms which were extended to receive her.

CHAPTER XXXIV

Contains Some Introductory Particulars Relative to a Young Gentleman Who Now Arrives Upon the Scene; and a New Adventure Which Happened to Oliver

It was almost too much happiness to bear. Oliver felt stunned and stupefied by the unexpected intelligence; he could not weep, or speak, or rest. He had scarcely the power of understanding anything that had passed, until, after a long ramble in the quiet evening air, a burst of tears came to his relief, and he seemed to awaken, all at once, to a full sense of the joyful change that had occurred, and the almost insupportable load of anguish which had been taken from his breast.

The night was fast closing in, when he returned homeward: laden with flowers which he had culled, with peculiar care, for the adornment of the sick chamber. As he walked briskly along the road, he heard behind him, the noise of some vehicle, approaching at a furious pace. Looking round, he saw that it was a post-chaise, driven at great speed; and as the horses were galloping, and the road was narrow, he stood leaning against a gate until it should have passed him.

As it dashed on, Oliver caught a glimpse of a man in a white nightcap, whose face seemed familiar to him, although his view was so brief that he could not identify the person. In another second or two, the nightcap was thrust out of the chaise-window, and a stentorian voice bellowed to the driver to stop: which he did, as soon as he could pull up his horses. Then, the nightcap once again appeared: and the same voice called Oliver by his name.

"Here!" cried the voice. "Oliver, what's the news? Miss Rose! Master O-li-ver!"

"Is is you, Giles?" cried Oliver, running up to the chaise-door.

Giles popped out his nightcap again, preparatory to making some reply, when he was suddenly pulled back by a young gentleman who occupied the other corner of the chaise, and who eagerly demanded what was the news.

"In a word!" cried the gentleman, "Better or worse?"

"Better—much better!" replied Oliver, hastily.

"Thank Heaven!" exclaimed the gentleman. "You are sure?"

"Quite, sir," replied Oliver. "The change took place only a few hours ago; and Mr. Losberne says, that all danger is at an end."

The gentleman said not another word, but, opening the chaise-door, leaped out, and taking Oliver hurriedly by the arm, led him aside.

"You are quite certain? There is no possibility of any mistake on your part, my boy, is there?" demanded the gentleman in a tremulous voice. "Do not deceive me, by awakening hopes that are not to be fulfilled."

"I would not for the world, sir," replied Oliver. "Indeed you may believe me. Mr. Losberne's words were, that she would live to bless us all for many years to come. I heard him say so."

The tears stood in Oliver's eyes as he recalled the scene which was the beginning of so much happiness; and the gentleman turned his face away, and remained silent, for some minutes. Oliver thought he heard him sob, more than once; but he feared to interrupt him by any fresh remark—for he could well guess what his feelings were—and so stood apart, feigning to be occupied with his nosegay.

All this time, Mr. Giles, with the white nightcap on, had been sitting on the steps of the chaise, supporting an elbow on each knee, and wiping his eyes with a blue cotton pocket-handkerchief dotted with white spots. That the honest fellow had not been feigning emotion, was abundantly demonstrated by the very red eyes with which he regarded the young gentleman, when he turned round and addressed him.

"I think you had better go on to my mother's in the chaise, Giles," said he. "I would rather walk slowly on, so as to gain a little time before I see her. You can say I am coming."

"I beg your pardon, Mr. Harry," said Giles: giving a final polish to his ruffled countenance with the handkerchief; "but if you would leave the postboy to say that, I should be very much obliged to you. It wouldn't be proper for the maids to see me in this state, sir; I should never have any more authority with them if they did."

"Well," rejoined Harry Maylie, smiling, "you can do as you like. Let him go on with the luggage, if you wish it, and do you follow with us. Only first exchange that nightcap for some more appropriate covering, or we shall be taken for madmen."

Mr. Giles, reminded of his unbecoming costume, snatched off and pocketed his nightcap; and substituted a hat, of grave and sober shape, which he took out of the chaise. This done, the postboy drove off; Giles, Mr. Maylie, and Oliver, followed at their leisure.

As they walked along, Oliver glanced from time to time with much interest and curiosity at the new comer. He seemed about five-and-twenty years of age, and was of the middle height; his countenance was frank and handsome; and his demeanor easy and prepossessing. Notwithstanding the difference between youth and age, he bore so strong a likeness to the old lady, that Oliver would have had no great difficulty in imagining their relationship, if he had not already spoken of her as his mother.

Mrs. Maylie was anxiously waiting to receive her son when he reached the cottage. The meeting did not take place without great emotion on both sides.

"Mother!" whispered the young man; "why did you not write before?"

"I did," replied Mrs. Maylie; "but, on reflection, I determined to keep back the letter until I had heard Mr. Losberne's opinion."

"But why," said the young man, "why run the chance of that occurring which so nearly happened? If Rose had—I cannot utter that word now—if this illness had terminated differently, how could you ever have forgiven yourself! How could I ever have know happiness again!"

"If that had been the case, Harry," said Mrs. Maylie, "I fear your happiness would have been effectually blighted, and that your arrival here, a day sooner or a day later, would have been of very, very little import."

"And who can wonder if it be so, mother?" rejoined the young man; "or why should I say, if?—It is—it is—you know it, mother—you must know it!"

"I know that she deserves the best and purest love the heart of man can offer," said Mrs. Maylie; "I know that the devotion and affection of her nature require no ordinary return, but one that shall be deep and lasting. If I did not feel this, and know, besides, that a changed behaviour in one she loved would break her heart, I should not feel my task so difficult of performance, or have to encounter so many struggles in my own bosom, when I take what seems to me to be the strict line of duty."

"This is unkind, mother," said Harry. "Do you still suppose that I am a boy ignorant of my own mind, and mistaking the impulses of my own soul?"

"I think, my dear son," returned Mrs. Maylie, laying her hand upon his shoulder, "that youth has many generous impulses which do not last; and that among them are some, which, being gratified, become only the more fleeting. Above all, I think" said the lady, fixing her eyes on her son's face, "that if an enthusiastic, ardent, and ambitious man marry a wife on whose name there is a stain, which, though it originate in no fault of hers, may be visited by cold and sordid people upon her, and upon his children also: and, in exact proportion to his success in the world, be cast in his teeth, and made the subject of sneers against him: he may, no matter how generous and good his nature, one day repent of the connection he formed in early life. And she may have the pain of knowing that he does so."

"Mother," said the young man, impatiently, "he would be a selfish brute, unworthy alike of the name of man and of the woman you describe, who acted thus."

"You think so now, Harry," replied his mother.

"And ever will!" said the young man. "The mental agony I have suffered, during the last two days, wrings from me the avowal to you of a passion which, as you well know, is not one of yesterday, nor one I have lightly formed. On Rose, sweet, gentle girl! my heart is set, as firmly as ever heart of man was set on woman. I have no thought, no view, no hope in life, beyond her; and if you oppose me in this great stake, you take my peace and happiness in your hands, and cast them to the wind. Mother, think better of this, and of me, and do not disregard the happiness of which you seem to think so little."

"Harry," said Mrs. Maylie, "it is because I think so much of warm and sensitive hearts, that I would spare them from being wounded. But we have said enough, and more than enough, on this matter, just now."

"Let it rest with Rose, then," interposed Harry. "You will not press these overstrained opinions of yours, so far, as to throw any obstacle in my way?"

"I will not," rejoined Mrs. Maylie; "but I would have you consider—"

"I have considered!" was the impatient reply; "Mother, I have considered, years and years. I have considered, ever since I have been capable of serious reflection. My feelings remain unchanged, as they ever will; and why should I suffer the pain of a delay in giving them vent, which can be productive of no earthly good? No! Before I leave this place, Rose shall hear me."

"She shall," said Mrs. Maylie.

"There is something in your manner, which would almost imply that she will hear me coldly, mother," said the young man.

"Not coldly," rejoined the old lady; "far from it."

"How then?" urged the young man. "She has formed no other attachment?"

"No, indeed," replied his mother; "you have, or I mistake, too strong a hold on her affections already. What I would say," resumed the old lady, stopping her son as he was about to speak, "is this. Before you stake your all on this chance; before you suffer yourself to be carried to the highest point of hope; reflect for a few moments, my dear child, on Rose's history, and consider what effect the knowledge of her doubtful birth may have on her decision: devoted as she is to us, with all the intensity of her noble mind, and with that perfect sacrifice of self which, in all matters, great or trifling, has always been her characteristic."

"What do you mean?"

"That I leave you to discover," replied Mrs. Maylie. "I must go back to her. God bless you!"

"I shall see you again to-night?" said the young man, eagerly.

"By and by," replied the lady; "when I leave Rose."

"You will tell her I am here?" said Harry.

"Of course," replied Mrs. Maylie.

"And say how anxious I have been, and how much I have suffered, and how I long to see her. You will not refuse to do this, mother?"

"No," said the old lady; "I will tell her all." And pressing her son's hand, affectionately, she hastened from the room.

Mr. Losberne and Oliver had remained at another end of the apartment while this hurried conversation was proceeding. The former now held out his hand to Harry Maylie; and hearty salutations were exchanged between them. The doctor then communicated, in reply to multifarious questions from his young friend, a precise account of his patient's situation; which was quite as consolatory and full of promise, as Oliver's statement had encouraged him to hope; and to the whole of which, Mr. Giles, who affected to be busy about the luggage, listened with greedy ears.

"Have you shot anything particular, lately, Giles?" inquired the doctor, when he had concluded.

"Nothing particular, sir," replied Mr. Giles, colouring up to the eyes.

"Nor catching any thieves, nor identifying any house-breakers?" said the doctor.

"None at all, sir," replied Mr. Giles, with much gravity.

"Well," said the doctor, "I am sorry to hear it, because you do that sort of thing admirably. Pray, how is Brittles?"

"The boy is very well, sir," said Mr. Giles, recovering his usual tone of patronage; "and sends his respectful duty, sir."

"That's well," said the doctor. "Seeing you here, reminds me, Mr. Giles, that on the day before that on which I was called away so hurriedly, I executed, at the request of your good mistress, a small commission in your favour. Just step into this corner a moment, will you?"

Mr. Giles walked into the corner with much importance, and some wonder, and was honoured with a short whispering conference with the doctor, on the termination of which, he made a great many bows, and retired with steps of unusual stateliness. The subject matter of this conference was not disclosed in the parlour, but the kitchen was speedily enlightened concerning it; for Mr. Giles walked straight thither, and having called for a mug of ale, announced, with an air of majesty, which was highly effective, that it had pleased his mistress, in consideration of his gallant behaviour on the occasion of that attempted robbery, to deposit, in the local savings-bank, the sum of five-and-twenty pounds, for his sole use and benefit. At this, the two women-servants lifted up their hands and eyes, and supposed that Mr. Giles, pulling out his shirt-frill, replied, "No, no"; and that if they observed that he was at all haughty to his inferiors, he would thank them to tell him so. And then he made a great many other remarks, no less illustrative of his humility, which were received with equal favour and applause, and were, withal, as original and as much to the purpose, as the remarks of great men commonly are.

Above stairs, the remainder of the evening passed cheerfully away; for the doctor was in high spirits; and however fatigued or thoughtful Harry Maylie might have been at first, he was not proof against the worthy gentleman's good humour, which displayed itself in a great variety of sallies and professional recollections, and an abundance of small jokes, which struck Oliver as being the drollest things he had ever heard, and caused him to laugh proportionately; to the evident satisfaction of the doctor, who laughed immoderately at himself, and made Harry laugh almost as heartily, by the very force of sympathy. So, they were as pleasant a party as, under the circumstances, they could well have been; and it was late before they retired, with light and thankful hearts, to take that rest of which, after the doubt and suspense they had recently undergone, they stood much in need.

Oliver rose next morning, in better heart, and went about his usual occupations, with more hope and pleasure than he had known for many days. The birds were once more hung out, to sing, in their old places; and the sweetest wild flowers that could be found, were once more gathered to gladden Rose with their beauty. The melancholy which had seemed to the sad eyes of the anxious boy to hang, for days past, over every object, beautiful as all were, was dispelled by magic. The dew seemed to sparkle more brightly on the green leaves; the air to rustle among them with a sweeter music; and the sky itself to look more blue and bright. Such is the influence which the condition of our own thoughts, exercise, even over the appearance of external objects. Men who look on nature, and their fellow-men, and cry that all is dark and gloomy, are in the right; but the sombre colours are reflections from their own jaundiced eyes and hearts. The real hues are delicate, and need a clearer vision.

It is worthy of remark, and Oliver did not fail to note it at the time, that his morning expeditions were no longer made alone. Harry Maylie, after the very first morning when he met Oliver coming laden home, was seized with such a passion for flowers, and displayed such a taste in their arrangement, as left his young companion far behind. If Oliver were behindhand in these respects, he knew where the best were to be found; and morning after morning they scoured the country together, and brought home the fairest that blossomed. The window of the young lady's chamber was opened now; for she loved to feel the rich summer air stream in, and revive her with its freshness; but there always stood in water, just inside the lattice, one particular little bunch, which was made up with great care, every morning. Oliver could not help noticing that the withered flowers were never thrown away, although the little vase was regularly replenished; nor, could he help observing, that whenever the doctor came into the garden, he invariably cast his eyes up to that particular corner, and nodded his head most expressively, as he set forth on his morning's walk. Pending these observations, the days were flying by; and Rose was rapidly recovering.

Nor did Oliver's time hang heavy on his hands, although the young lady had not yet left her chamber, and there were no evening walks, save now and then, for a short distance, with Mrs. Maylie. He applied himself, with redoubled assiduity, to the instructions of the white-headed old gentleman, and laboured so hard that his quick progress surprised even himself. It was while he was engaged in this pursuit, that he was greatly startled and distressed by a most unexpected occurrence.

The little room in which he was accustomed to sit, when busy at his books, was on the ground-floor, at the back of the house. It was quite a cottage-room, with a lattice-window: around which were clusters of jessamine and honeysuckle, that crept over the casement, and filled the place with their delicious perfume. It looked into a garden, whence a wicket-gate opened into a small paddock; all beyond, was fine meadow-land and wood. There was no other dwelling near, in that direction; and the prospect it commanded was very extensive.

One beautiful evening, when the first shades of twilight were beginning to settle upon the earth, Oliver sat at this window, intent upon his books. He had been poring over them for some time; and, as the day had been uncommonly sultry, and he had exerted himself a great deal, it is no disparagement to the authors, whoever they may have been, to say, that gradually and by slow degrees, he fell asleep.

There is a kind of sleep that steals upon us sometimes, which, while it holds the body prisoner, does not free the mind from a sense of things about it, and enable it to ramble at its pleasure. So far as an overpowering heaviness, a prostration of strength, and an utter inability to control our thoughts or power of motion, can be called sleep, this is it; and yet, we have a consciousness of all that is going on about us, and, if we dream at such a time, words which are really spoken, or sounds which really exist at the moment, accommodate themselves with surprising readiness to our visions, until reality and imagination become so strangely blended that it is afterwards almost matter of impossibility to separate the two. Nor is this, the most striking phenomenon incidental to such a state. It is an undoubted fact, that although our senses of touch and sight be for the time dead, yet our sleeping thoughts, and the visionary scenes that pass before us, will be influenced and materially influenced, by the mere silent presence of some external object; which may not have been near us when we closed our eyes: and of whose vicinity we have had no waking consciousness.

Oliver knew, perfectly well, that he was in his own little room; that his books were lying on the table before him; that the sweet air was stirring among the creeping plants outside. And yet he was asleep. Suddenly, the scene changed; the air became close and confined; and he thought, with a glow of terror, that he was in the Jew's house again. There sat the hideous old man, in his accustomed corner, pointing at him, and whispering to another man, with his face averted, who sat beside him.

"Hush, my dear!" he thought he heard the Jew say; "it is he, sure enough. Come away."

"He!" the other man seemed to answer; "could I mistake him, think you? If a crowd of ghosts were to put themselves into his exact shape, and he stood amongst them, there is something that would tell me how to point him out. If you buried him fifty feet deep, and took me across his grave, I fancy I should know, if there wasn't a mark above it, that he lay buried there?"

The man seemed to say this, with such dreadful hatred, that Oliver awoke with the fear, and started up.

Good Heaven! what was that, which sent the blood tingling to his heart, and deprived him of his voice, and of power to move! There—there—at the window—close before him—so close, that he could have almost touched him before he started back: with his eyes peering into the room, and meeting his: there stood the Jew! And beside him, white with rage or fear, or both, were the scowling features of the man who had accosted him in the inn-yard.

It was but an instant, a glance, a flash, before his eyes; and they were gone. But they had recognised him, and he them; and their look was as firmly impressed upon his memory, as if it had been deeply carved in stone, and set before him from his birth. He stood transfixed for a moment; then, leaping from the window into the garden, called loudly for help.

CHAPTER XXXV

*Containing the Unsatisfactory Result of Oliver's Adventure; and a
Conversation of Some Importance Between Harry Maylie and Rose*

When the inmates of the house, attracted by Oliver's cries, hurried to the spot from which they proceeded, they found him, pale and agitated, pointing in the direction of the meadows behind the house, and scarcely able to articulate the words, "The Jew! the Jew!"

Mr. Giles was at a loss to comprehend what this outcry meant; but Harry Maylie, whose perceptions were something quicker, and who had heard Oliver's history from his mother, understood it at once.

"What direction did he take?" he asked, catching up a heavy stick which was standing in a corner.

"That," replied Oliver, pointing out the course the man had taken; "I missed them in an instant."

"Then, they are in the ditch!" said Harry. "Follow! And keep as near me, as you can.' So saying, he sprang over the hedge, and darted off with a speed which rendered it matter of exceeding difficulty for the others to keep near him.

Giles followed as well as he could; and Oliver followed too; and in the course of a minute or two, Mr. Losberne, who had been out walking, and just then returned, tumbled over the hedge after them, and picking himself up with more agility than he could have been supposed to possess, struck into the same course at no contemptible speed, shouting all the while, most prodigiously, to know what was the matter.

On they all went; nor stopped they once to breathe, until the leader, striking off into an angle of the field indicated by Oliver, began to search, narrowly, the ditch and hedge adjoining; which afforded time for the remainder of the party to come up; and for Oliver to communicate to Mr. Losberne the circumstances that had led to so vigorous a pursuit.

The search was all in vain. There were not even the traces of recent footsteps, to be seen. They stood now, on the summit of a little hill, commanding the open fields in every direction for three or four miles. There was the village in the hollow on the left; but, in order to gain that, after pursuing the track Oliver had pointed out, the men must have made a circuit of open ground, which it was impossible they could have accomplished in so short a time. A thick wood skirted the meadow-land in another direction; but they could not have gained that covert for the same reason.

"It must have been a dream, Oliver," said Harry Maylie.

"Oh no, indeed, sir," replied Oliver, shuddering at the very recollection of the old wretch's countenance; "I saw him too plainly for that. I saw them both, as plainly as I see you now."

"Who was the other?" inquired Harry and Mr. Losberne, together.

"The very same man I told you of, who came so suddenly upon me at the inn," said Oliver. "We had our eyes fixed full upon each other; and I could swear to him."

"They took this way?" demanded Harry: "are you sure?"

"As I am that the men were at the window," replied Oliver, pointing down, as he spoke, to the hedge which divided the cottage-garden from the meadow. "The tall man leaped over, just there; and the Jew, running a few paces to the right, crept through that gap."

The two gentlemen watched Oliver's earnest face, as he spoke, and looking from him to each other, seemed to feel satisfied of the accuracy of what he said. Still, in no direction were there any appearances of the trampling of men in hurried flight. The grass was long; but it was trodden down nowhere, save where their own feet had crushed it. The sides and brinks of the ditches were of damp clay; but in no one place could they discern the print of men's shoes, or the slightest mark which would indicate that any feet had pressed the ground for hours before.

"This is strange!" said Harry.

"Strange?" echoed the doctor. "Blathers and Duff, themselves, could make nothing of it."

Notwithstanding the evidently useless nature of their search, they did not desist until the coming on of night rendered its further prosecution hopeless; and even then, they gave it up with reluctance. Giles was dispatched to the different ale-houses in the village, furnished with the best description Oliver could give of the appearance and dress of the strangers. Of these, the Jew was, at all events, sufficiently remarkable to be remembered, supposing he had been seen drinking, or loitering about; but Giles returned without any intelligence, calculated to dispel or lessen the mystery.

On the next day, fresh search was made, and the inquiries renewed; but with no better success. On the day following, Oliver and Mr. Maylie repaired to the market-town, in the hope of seeing or hearing something of the men there; but this effort was equally fruitless. After a few days, the affair began to be forgotten, as most affairs are, when wonder, having no fresh food to support it, dies away of itself.

Meanwhile, Rose was rapidly recovering. She had left her room: was able to go out; and mixing once more with the family, carried joy into the hearts of all.

But, although this happy change had a visible effect on the little circle; and although cheerful voices and merry laughter were once more heard in the cottage; there was at times, an unwonted restraint upon some there: even upon Rose herself: which Oliver could not fail to remark. Mrs. Maylie and her son were often closeted together for a long time; and more than once Rose appeared with traces of tears upon her face. After Mr. Losberne had fixed a day for his departure to Chertsey, these symptoms increased; and it became evident that something was in progress which affected the peace of the young lady, and of somebody else besides.

At length, one morning, when Rose was alone in the breakfast-parlour, Harry Maylie entered; and, with some hesitation, begged permission to speak with her for a few moments.

"A few—a very few—will suffice, Rose," said the young man, drawing his chair towards her. "What I shall have to say, has already presented itself to your mind; the most cherished hopes of my heart are not unknown to you, though from my lips you have not heard them stated."

Rose had been very pale from the moment of his entrance; but that might have been the effect of her recent illness. She merely bowed; and bending over some plants that stood near, waited in silence for him to proceed.

"I—I—ought to have left here, before," said Harry.

"You should, indeed," replied Rose. "Forgive me for saying so, but I wish you had."

"I was brought here, by the most dreadful and agonising of all apprehensions," said the young man; "the fear of losing the one dear being on whom my every wish and hope are fixed. You had been dying; trembling between earth and heaven. We know that when the young, the beautiful, and good, are visited with sickness, their pure spirits insensibly turn towards their bright home of lasting rest; we know, Heaven help us! that the best and fairest of our kind, too often fade in blooming."

There were tears in the eyes of the gentle girl, as these words were spoken; and when one fell upon the flower over which she bent, and glistened brightly in its cup, making it more beautiful, it seemed as though the outpouring of her fresh young heart, claimed kindred naturally, with the loveliest things in nature.

"A creature," continued the young man, passionately, "a creature as fair and innocent of guile as one of God's own angels, fluttered between life and death. Oh! who could hope, when the distant world to which she was akin, half opened to her view, that she would return to the sorrow and calamity of this! Rose, Rose, to know that you were passing away like some soft shadow, which a light from above, casts upon the earth; to have no hope that you would be spared to those who linger here; hardly to know a reason why you should be; to feel that you belonged to that bright sphere whither so many of the fairest and the best have winged their early flight; and yet to pray, amid all these consolations, that you might be restored to those who loved you—these were distractions almost too great to bear. They were mine, by day and night; and with them, came such a rushing torrent of fears, and apprehensions, and selfish regrets, lest you should die, and never know how devotedly I loved you, as almost bore down sense and reason in its course. You recovered. Day by day, and almost hour by hour, some drop of health came back, and mingling with the spent and feeble stream of life which circulated languidly within you, swelled it again to a high and rushing tide. I have watched you change almost from death, to life, with eyes that turned blind with their eagerness and deep affection. Do not tell me that you wish I had lost this; for it has softened my heart to all mankind."

"I did not mean that," said Rose, weeping; "I only wish you had left here, that you might have turned to high and noble pursuits again; to pursuits well worthy of you."

"There is no pursuit more worthy of me: more worthy of the highest nature that exists: than the struggle to win such a heart as yours," said the young man, taking her hand. "Rose, my own dear Rose! For years—for years—I have loved you; hoping to win my way to fame, and then come proudly home and tell you it had been pursued only for you to share; thinking, in my daydreams, how I would remind you, in that happy moment, of the many silent tokens I had given of a boy's attachment, and claim your hand, as in redemption of some old mute contract that had been sealed between us! That time has not arrived; but here, with not fame won, and no young vision realised, I offer you the heart so long your own, and stake my all upon the words with which you greet the offer."

"Your behaviour has ever been kind and noble." said Rose, mastering the emotions by which she was agitated. "As you believe that I am not insensible or ungrateful, so hear my answer."

"It is, that I may endeavour to deserve you; it is, dear Rose?"

"It is," replied Rose, "that you must endeavour to forget me; not as your old and dearly-attached companion, for that would wound me deeply; but, as the object of your love. Look into the world; think how many hearts you would be proud to gain, are there. Confide some other passion to me, if you will; I will be the truest, warmest, and most faithful friend you have."

There was a pause, during which, Rose, who had covered her face with one hand, gave free vent to her tears. Harry still retained the other.

"And your reasons, Rose," he said, at length, in a low voice; "your reasons for this decision?"

"You have a right to know them," rejoined Rose. "You can say nothing to alter my resolution. It is a duty that I must perform. I owe it, alike to others, and to myself."

"To yourself?"

"Yes, Harry. I owe it to myself, that I, a friendless, portionless, girl, with a blight upon my name, should not give your friends reason to suspect that I had sordidly yielded to your first passion, and fastened myself, a clog, on all your hopes and projects. I owe it to you and yours, to prevent you from opposing, in the warmth of your generous nature, this great obstacle to your progress in the world."

"If your inclinations chime with your sense of duty—' Harry began.

"They do not," replied Rose, colouring deeply.

"Then you return my love?" said Harry. "Say but that, dear Rose; say but that; and soften the bitterness of this hard disappointment!"

"If I could have done so, without doing heavy wrong to him I loved," rejoined Rose, "I could have—"

"Have received this declaration very differently?" said Harry. "Do not conceal that from me, at least, Rose."

"I could," said Rose. "Stay!" she added, disengaging her hand, "why should we prolong this painful interview? Most painful to me, and yet productive of lasting happiness, notwithstanding; for it will be happiness to know that I once held the high place in your regard which I now occupy, and every triumph you achieve in life will animate me with new fortitude and firmness. Farewell, Harry! As we have met to-day, we meet no more; but in other relations than those in which this conversation have placed us, we may be long and happily entwined; and may every blessing that the prayers of a true and earnest heart can call down from the source of all truth and sincerity, cheer and prosper you!"

"Another word, Rose," said Harry. "Your reason in your own words. From your own lips, let me hear it!"

"The prospect before you," answered Rose, firmly, "is a brilliant one. All the honours to which great talents and powerful connections can help men in public life, are in store for you. But those connections are proud; and I will neither mingle with such as may hold in scorn the mother who gave me life; nor bring disgrace or failure on the son of her who has so well supplied that mother's place. In a word," said the young lady, turning away, as her temporary firmness forsook her, "there is a stain upon my name, which the world visits on innocent heads. I will carry it into no blood but my own; and the reproach shall rest alone on me."

"One word more, Rose. Dearest Rose! one more!" cried Harry, throwing himself before her. "If I had been less—less fortunate, the world would call it—if some obscure and peaceful life had been my destiny—if I had been poor, sick, helpless—would you have turned from me then? Or has my probable advancement to riches and honour, given this scruple birth?"

"Do not press me to reply," answered Rose. "The question does not arise, and never will. It is unfair, almost unkind, to urge it."

"If your answer be what I almost dare to hope it is," retorted Harry, "it will shed a gleam of happiness upon my lonely way, and light the path before me. It is not an idle thing to do so much, by the utterance of a few brief words, for one who loves you beyond all else. Oh, Rose: in the name of my ardent and enduring attachment; in the name of all I have suffered for you, and all you doom me to undergo; answer me this one question!"

"Then, if your lot had been differently cast," rejoined Rose; "if you had been even a little, but not so far, above me; if I could have been a help and comfort to you in any humble scene of peace and retirement, and not a blot and drawback in ambitious and distinguished crowds; I should have been spared this trial. I have every reason to be happy, very happy, now; but then, Harry, I own I should have been happier."

Busy recollections of old hopes, cherished as a girl, long ago, crowded into the mind of Rose, while making this avowal; but they brought tears with them, as old hopes will when they come back withered; and they relieved her.

"I cannot help this weakness, and it makes my purpose stronger," said Rose, extending her hand. "I must leave you now, indeed."

"I ask one promise," said Harry. "Once, and only once more,—say within a year, but it may be much sooner,—I may speak to you again on this subject, for the last time."

"Not to press me to alter my right determination," replied Rose, with a melancholy smile; "it will be useless."

"No," said Harry; "to hear you repeat it, if you will—finally repeat it! I will lay at your feet, whatever of station of fortune I may possess; and if you still adhere to your present resolution, will not seek, by word or act, to change it."

"Then let it be so," rejoined Rose; "it is but one pang the more, and by that time I may be enabled to bear it better."

She extended her hand again. But the young man caught her to his bosom; and imprinting one kiss on her beautiful forehead, hurried from the room.

CHAPTER XXXVI

Is a Very Short One, and May Appear of No Great Importance In its Place,
But it Should Be Read Notwithstanding, as a Sequel to the Last,
and a Key to One That Will Follow When its Time Arrives

"And so you are resolved to be my travelling companion this morning; eh?"
said the doctor, as Harry Maylie joined him and Oliver at the breakfast-table.
"Why, you are not in the same mind or intention two half-hours together!"

"You will tell me a different tale one of these days," said Harry, colouring without
any perceptible reason.

"I hope I may have good cause to do so," replied Mr. Losberne; "though I confess
I don't think I shall. But yesterday morning you had made up your mind, in a great
hurry, to stay here, and to accompany your mother, like a dutiful son, to the sea-side.
Before noon, you announce that you are going to do me the honour of accompanying
me as far as I go, on your road to London. And at night, you urge me, with great
mystery, to start before the ladies are stirring; the consequence of which is, that young
Oliver here is pinned down to his breakfast when he ought to be ranging the meadows
after botanical phenomena of all kinds. Too bad, isn't it, Oliver?"

"I should have been very sorry not to have been at home when you and Mr. Maylie
went away, sir," rejoined Oliver.

"That's a fine fellow," said the doctor; "you shall come and see me when you return.
But, to speak seriously, Harry; has any communication from the great nobs produced
this sudden anxiety on your part to be gone?"

"The great nobs," replied Harry, 'under which designation, I presume, you include
my most stately uncle, have not communicated with me at all, since I have been here;
nor, at this time of the year, is it likely that anything would occur to render necessary
my immediate attendance among them."

"Well," said the doctor, "you are a queer fellow. But of course they will get you into
parliament at the election before Christmas, and these sudden shiftings and changes
are no bad preparation for political life. There's something in that. Good training is
always desirable, whether the race be for place, cup, or sweepstakes."

Harry Maylie looked as if he could have followed up this short dialogue by one
or two remarks that would have staggered the doctor not a little; but he contented
himself with saying, "We shall see," and pursued the subject no farther. The post-
chaise drove up to the door shortly afterwards; and Giles coming in for the luggage,
the good doctor bustled out, to see it packed.

"Oliver," said Harry Maylie, in a low voice, "let me speak a word with you."

Oliver walked into the window-recess to which Mr. Maylie beckoned him; much
surprised at the mixture of sadness and boisterous spirits, which his whole behaviour
displayed.

"You can write well now?" said Harry, laying his hand upon his arm.

"I hope so, sir," replied Oliver.

"I shall not be at home again, perhaps for some time; I wish you would write to me—say once a fort-night: every alternate Monday: to the General Post Office in London. Will you?"

"Oh! certainly, sir; I shall be proud to do it," exclaimed Oliver, greatly delighted with the commission.

"I should like to know how—how my mother and Miss Maylie are," said the young man; "and you can fill up a sheet by telling me what walks you take, and what you talk about, and whether she—they, I mean—seem happy and quite well. You understand me?"

"Oh! quite, sir, quite," replied Oliver.

"I would rather you did not mention it to them," said Harry, hurrying over his words; "because it might make my mother anxious to write to me oftener, and it is a trouble and worry to her. Let it be a secret between you and me; and mind you tell me everything! I depend upon you."

Oliver, quite elated and honoured by a sense of his importance, faithfully promised to be secret and explicit in his communications. Mr. Maylie took leave of him, with many assurances of his regard and protection.

The doctor was in the chaise; Giles (who, it had been arranged, should be left behind) held the door open in his hand; and the women-servants were in the garden, looking on. Harry cast one slight glance at the latticed window, and jumped into the carriage.

"Drive on!" he cried, "hard, fast, full gallop! Nothing short of flying will keep pace with me, to-day."

"Halloa!" cried the doctor, letting down the front glass in a great hurry, and shouting to the postillion; "something very short of flying will keep pace with me. Do you hear?"

Jingling and clattering, till distance rendered its noise inaudible, and its rapid progress only perceptible to the eye, the vehicle wound its way along the road, almost hidden in a cloud of dust: now wholly disappearing, and now becoming visible again, as intervening objects, or the intricacies of the way, permitted. It was not until even the dusty cloud was no longer to be seen, that the gazers dispersed.

And there was one looker-on, who remained with eyes fixed upon the spot where the carriage had disappeared, long after it was many miles away; for, behind the white curtain which had shrouded her from view when Harry raised his eyes towards the window, sat Rose herself.

"He seems in high spirits and happy," she said, at length. "I feared for a time he might be otherwise. I was mistaken. I am very, very glad."

Tears are signs of gladness as well as grief; but those which coursed down Rose's face, as she sat pensively at the window, still gazing in the same direction, seemed to tell more of sorrow than of joy.

CHAPTER XXXVII

In Which the Reader May Perceive a Contrast,
Not Uncommon in Matrimonial Cases

Mr. Bumble sat in the workhouse parlour, with his eyes moodily fixed on the cheerless grate, whence, as it was summer time, no brighter gleam proceeded, than the reflection of certain sickly rays of the sun, which were sent back from its cold and shining surface. A paper fly-cage dangled from the ceiling, to which he occasionally raised his eyes in gloomy thought; and, as the heedless insects hovered round the gaudy net-work, Mr. Bumble would heave a deep sigh, while a more gloomy shadow overspread his countenance. Mr. Bumble was meditating; it might be that the insects brought to mind, some painful passage in his own past life.

Nor was Mr. Bumble's gloom the only thing calculated to awaken a pleasing melancholy in the bosom of a spectator. There were not wanting other appearances, and those closely connected with his own person, which announced that a great change had taken place in the position of his affairs. The laced coat, and the cocked hat; where were they? He still wore knee-breeches, and dark cotton stockings on his nether limbs; but they were not the breeches. The coat was wide-skirted; and in that respect like the coat, but, oh how different! The mighty cocked hat was replaced by a modest round one. Mr. Bumble was no longer a beadle.

There are some promotions in life, which, independent of the more substantial rewards they offer, require peculiar value and dignity from the coats and waistcoats connected with them. A field-marshal has his uniform; a bishop his silk apron; a counsellor his silk gown; a beadle his cocked hat. Strip the bishop of his apron, or the beadle of his hat and lace; what are they? Men. Mere men. Dignity, and even holiness too, sometimes, are more questions of coat and waistcoat than some people imagine.

Mr. Bumble had married Mrs. Corney, and was master of the workhouse. Another beadle had come into power. On him the cocked hat, gold-laced coat, and staff, had all three descended.

"And to-morrow two months it was done!" said Mr. Bumble, with a sigh. "It seems a age."

Mr. Bumble might have meant that he had concentrated a whole existence of happiness into the short space of eight weeks; but the sigh—there was a vast deal of meaning in the sigh.

"I sold myself," said Mr. Bumble, pursuing the same train of relection, "for six teaspoons, a pair of sugar-tongs, and a milk-pot; with a small quantity of second-hand furniture, and twenty pound in money. I went very reasonable. Cheap, dirt cheap!"

"Cheap!" cried a shrill voice in Mr. Bumble's ear: "you would have been dear at any price; and dear enough I paid for you, Lord above knows that!"

Mr. Bumble turned, and encountered the face of his interesting consort, who, imperfectly comprehending the few words she had overheard of his complaint, had hazarded the foregoing remark at a venture.

"Mrs. Bumble, ma'am!" said Mr. Bumble, with a sentimental sternness.

"Well!" cried the lady.

"Have the goodness to look at me," said Mr. Bumble, fixing his eyes upon her. (If she stands such a eye as that," said Mr. Bumble to himself, "she can stand anything. It is a eye I never knew to fail with paupers. If it fails with her, my power is gone.')

Whether an exceedingly small expansion of eye be sufficient to quell paupers, who, being lightly fed, are in no very high condition; or whether the late Mrs. Corney was particularly proof against eagle glances; are matters of opinion. The matter of fact, is, that the matron was in no way overpowered by Mr. Bumble's scowl, but, on the contrary, treated it with great disdain, and even raised a laugh thereat, which sounded as though it were genuine.

On hearing this most unexpected sound, Mr. Bumble looked, first incredulous, and afterwards amazed. He then relapsed into his former state; nor did he rouse himself until his attention was again awakened by the voice of his partner.

"Are you going to sit snoring there, all day?" inquired Mrs. Bumble.

"I am going to sit here, as long as I think proper, ma'am," rejoined Mr. Bumble; "and although I was not snoring, I shall snore, gape, sneeze, laugh, or cry, as the humour strikes me; such being my prerogative."

"Your prerogative!" sneered Mrs. Bumble, with ineffable contempt.

"I said the word, ma'am," said Mr. Bumble. "The prerogative of a man is to command."

"And what's the prerogative of a woman, in the name of Goodness?" cried the relict of Mr. Corney deceased.

"To obey, ma'am," thundered Mr. Bumble. "Your late unfortunate husband should have taught it you; and then, perhaps, he might have been alive now. I wish he was, poor man!"

Mrs. Bumble, seeing at a glance, that the decisive moment had now arrived, and that a blow struck for the mastership on one side or other, must necessarily be final and conclusive, no sooner heard this allusion to the dead and gone, than she dropped into a chair, and with a loud scream that Mr. Bumble was a hard-hearted brute, fell into a paroxysm of tears.

But, tears were not the things to find their way to Mr. Bumble's soul; his heart was waterproof. Like washable beaver hats that improve with rain, his nerves were rendered stouter and more vigorous, by showers of tears, which, being tokens of weakness, and so far tacit admissions of his own power, pleased and exalted him. He eyed his good lady with looks of great satisfaction, and begged, in an encouraging manner, that she should cry her hardest: the exercise being looked upon, by the faculty, as strongly conducive to health.

"It opens the lungs, washes the countenance, exercises the eyes, and softens down the temper," said Mr. Bumble. "So cry away."

As he discharged himself of this pleasantry, Mr. Bumble took his hat from a peg, and putting it on, rather rakishly, on one side, as a man might, who felt he had asserted his superiority in a becoming manner, thrust his hands into his pockets, and sauntered towards the door, with much ease and waggishness depicted in his whole appearance.

Now, Mrs. Corney that was, had tried the tears, because they were less troublesome than a manual assault; but, she was quite prepared to make trial of the latter mode of proceeding, as Mr. Bumble was not long in discovering.

The first proof he experienced of the fact, was conveyed in a hollow sound, immediately succeeded by the sudden flying off of his hat to the opposite end of the room. This preliminary proceeding laying bare his head, the expert lady, clasping him tightly round the throat with one hand, inflicted a shower of blows (dealt with singular vigour and dexterity) upon it with the other. This done, she created a little variety by scratching his face, and tearing his hair; and, having, by this time, inflicted as much punishment as she deemed necessary for the offence, she pushed him over a chair, which was luckily well situated for the purpose: and defied him to talk about his prerogative again, if he dared.

"Get up!" said Mrs. Bumble, in a voice of command. "And take yourself away from here, unless you want me to do something desperate."

Mr. Bumble rose with a very rueful countenance: wondering much what something desperate might be. Picking up his hat, he looked towards the door.

"Are you going?" demanded Mrs. Bumble.

"Certainly, my dear, certainly," rejoined Mr. Bumble, making a quicker motion towards the door. "I didn't intend to—I'm going, my dear! You are so very violent, that really I—"

At this instant, Mrs. Bumble stepped hastily forward to replace the carpet, which had been kicked up in the scuffle. Mr. Bumble immediately darted out of the room, without bestowing another thought on his unfinished sentence: leaving the late Mrs. Corney in full possession of the field.

Mr. Bumble was fairly taken by surprise, and fairly beaten. He had a decided propensity for bullying: derived no inconsiderable pleasure from the exercise of petty cruelty; and, consequently, was (it is needless to say) a coward. This is by no means a disparagement to his character; for many official personages, who are held in high respect and admiration, are the victims of similar infirmities. The remark is made, indeed, rather in his favour than otherwise, and with a view of impressing the reader with a just sense of his qualifications for office.

But, the measure of his degradation was not yet full. After making a tour of the house, and thinking, for the first time, that the poor-laws really were too hard on people; and that men who ran away from their wives, leaving them chargeable to the parish, ought, in justice to be visited with no punishment at all, but rather rewarded as meritorious individuals who had suffered much; Mr. Bumble came to a room where some of the female paupers were usually employed in washing the parish linen: when the sound of voices in conversation, now proceeded.

"Hem!" said Mr. Bumble, summoning up all his native dignity. "These women at least shall continue to respect the prerogative. Hallo! hallo there! What do you mean by this noise, you hussies?"

With these words, Mr. Bumble opened the door, and walked in with a very fierce and angry manner: which was at once exchanged for a most humiliated and cowering air, as his eyes unexpectedly rested on the form of his lady wife.

"My dear," said Mr. Bumble, "I didn't know you were here."

"Didn't know I was here!" repeated Mrs. Bumble. "What do you do here?"

"I thought they were talking rather too much to be doing their work properly, my dear," replied Mr. Bumble: glancing distractedly at a couple of old women at the wash-tub, who were comparing notes of admiration at the workhouse-master's humility.

"You thought they were talking too much?" said Mrs. Bumble. "What business is it of yours?"

"Why, my dear—" urged Mr. Bumble submissively.

"What business is it of yours?" demanded Mrs. Bumble, again.

"It's very true, you're matron here, my dear," submitted Mr. Bumble; "but I thought you mightn't be in the way just then."

"I'll tell you what, Mr. Bumble," returned his lady. "We don't want any of your interference. You're a great deal too fond of poking your nose into things that don't concern you, making everybody in the house laugh, the moment your back is turned, and making yourself look like a fool every hour in the day. Be off; come!"

Mr. Bumble, seeing with excruciating feelings, the delight of the two old paupers, who were tittering together most rapturously, hesitated for an instant. Mrs. Bumble, whose patience brooked no delay, caught up a bowl of soap-suds, and motioning him towards the door, ordered him instantly to depart, on pain of receiving the contents upon his portly person.

What could Mr. Bumble do? He looked dejectedly round, and slunk away; and, as he reached the door, the titterings of the paupers broke into a shrill chuckle of irrepressible delight. It wanted but this. He was degraded in their eyes; he had lost caste and station before the very paupers; he had fallen from all the height and pomp of beadleship, to the lowest depth of the most snubbed hen-peckery.

"All in two months!" said Mr. Bumble, filled with dismal thoughts. "Two months! No more than two months ago, I was not only my own master, but everybody else's, so far as the porochial workhouse was concerned, and now!—"

It was too much. Mr. Bumble boxed the ears of the boy who opened the gate for him (for he had reached the portal in his reverie); and walked, distractedly, into the street.

He walked up one street, and down another, until exercise had abated the first passion of his grief; and then the revulsion of feeling made him thirsty. He passed a great many public-houses; but, at length paused before one in a by-way, whose parlour, as he gathered from a hasty peep over the blinds, was deserted, save by one solitary customer. It began to rain, heavily, at the moment. This determined him. Mr. Bumble stepped in; and ordering something to drink, as he passed the bar, entered the apartment into which he had looked from the street.

The man who was seated there, was tall and dark, and wore a large cloak. He had the air of a stranger; and seemed, by a certain haggardness in his look, as well as by the dusty soils on his dress, to have travelled some distance. He eyed Bumble askance, as he entered, but scarcely deigned to nod his head in acknowledgment of his salutation.

Mr. Bumble had quite dignity enough for two; supposing even that the stranger had been more familiar: so he drank his gin-and-water in silence, and read the paper with great show of pomp and circumstance.

It so happened, however: as it will happen very often, when men fall into company under such circumstances: that Mr. Bumble felt, every now and then, a powerful inducement, which he could not resist, to steal a look at the stranger: and that whenever he did so, he withdrew his eyes, in some confusion, to find that the stranger was at that moment stealing a look at him. Mr. Bumble's awkwardness was enhanced by the very remarkable expression of the stranger's eye, which was keen and bright, but shadowed by a scowl of distrust and suspicion, unlike anything he had ever observed before, and repulsive to behold.

When they had encountered each other's glance several times in this way, the stranger, in a harsh, deep voice, broke silence.

"Were you looking for me," he said, "when you peered in at the window?"

"Not that I am aware of, unless you're Mr.——" Here Mr. Bumble stopped short; for he was curious to know the stranger's name, and thought in his impatience, he might supply the blank.

"I see you were not," said the stranger; an expression of quiet sarcasm playing about his mouth; "or you have known my name. You don't know it. I would recommend you not to ask for it."

"I meant no harm, young man," observed Mr. Bumble, majestically.

"And have done none," said the stranger.

Another silence succeeded this short dialogue: which was again broken by the stranger.

"I have seen you before, I think?" said he. "You were differently dressed at that time, and I only passed you in the street, but I should know you again. You were beadle here, once; were you not?"

"I was," said Mr. Bumble, in some surprise; "porochial beadle."

"Just so," rejoined the other, nodding his head. "It was in that character I saw you. What are you now?"

"Master of the workhouse," rejoined Mr. Bumble, slowly and impressively, to check any undue familiarity the stranger might otherwise assume. "Master of the workhouse, young man!"

"You have the same eye to your own interest, that you always had, I doubt not?" resumed the stranger, looking keenly into Mr. Bumble's eyes, as he raised them in astonishment at the question.

"Don't scruple to answer freely, man. I know you pretty well, you see."

"I suppose, a married man," replied Mr. Bumble, shading his eyes with his hand, and surveying the stranger, from head to foot, in evident perplexity, "is not more averse to turning an honest penny when he can, than a single one. Porochial officers are not so well paid that they can afford to refuse any little extra fee, when it comes to them in a civil and proper manner."

The stranger smiled, and nodded his head again: as much to say, he had not mistaken his man; then rang the bell.

"Fill this glass again," he said, handing Mr. Bumble's empty tumbler to the landlord. "Let it be strong and hot. You like it so, I suppose?"

"Not too strong," replied Mr. Bumble, with a delicate cough.

"You understand what that means, landlord!" said the stranger, drily.

The host smiled, disappeared, and shortly afterwards returned with a steaming jorum: of which, the first gulp brought the water into Mr. Bumble's eyes.

"Now listen to me," said the stranger, after closing the door and window. "I came down to this place, to-day, to find you out; and, by one of those chances which the devil throws in the way of his friends sometimes, you walked into the very room I was sitting in, while you were uppermost in my mind. I want some information from you. I don't ask you to give it for nothing, slight as it is. Put up that, to begin with."

As he spoke, he pushed a couple of sovereigns across the table to his companion, carefully, as though unwilling that the chinking of money should be heard without. When Mr. Bumble had scrupulously examined the coins, to see that they were genuine, and had put them up, with much satisfaction, in his waistcoat-pocket, he went on:

"Carry your memory back—let me see—twelve years, last winter."

"It's a long time," said Mr. Bumble. "Very good. I've done it."

"The scene, the workhouse."

"Good!"

"And the time, night."

"Yes."

"And the place, the crazy hole, wherever it was, in which miserable drabs brought forth the life and health so often denied to themselves—gave birth to puling children for the parish to rear; and hid their shame, rot 'em in the grave!"

"The lying-in room, I suppose?" said Mr. Bumble, not quite following the stranger's excited description.

"Yes," said the stranger. "A boy was born there."

"A many boys," observed Mr. Bumble, shaking his head, despondingly.

"A murrain on the young devils!" cried the stranger; "I speak of one; a meek-looking, pale-faced boy, who was apprenticed down here, to a coffin-maker—I wish he had made his coffin, and screwed his body in it—and who afterwards ran away to London, as it was supposed."

"Why, you mean Oliver! Young Twist!" said Mr. Bumble; "I remember him, of course. There wasn't a obstinater young rascal—"

"It's not of him I want to hear; I've heard enough of him," said the stranger, stopping Mr. Bumble in the outset of a tirade on the subject of poor Oliver's vices. "It's of a woman; the hag that nursed his mother. Where is she?"

"Where is she?" said Mr. Bumble, whom the gin-and-water had rendered facetious. "It would be hard to tell. There's no midwifery there, whichever place she's gone to; so I suppose she's out of employment, anyway."

"What do you mean?" demanded the stranger, sternly.

"That she died last winter," rejoined Mr. Bumble.

The man looked fixedly at him when he had given this information, and although he did not withdraw his eyes for some time afterwards, his gaze gradually became vacant and abstracted, and he seemed lost in thought. For some time, he appeared doubtful whether he ought to be relieved or disappointed by the intelligence; but at length he breathed more freely; and withdrawing his eyes, observed that it was no great matter. With that he rose, as if to depart.

But Mr. Bumble was cunning enough; and he at once saw that an opportunity was opened, for the lucrative disposal of some secret in the possession of his better half. He well remembered the night of old Sally's death, which the occurrences of that day had given him good reason to recollect, as the occasion on which he had proposed to Mrs. Corney; and although that lady had never confided to him the disclosure of which she had been the solitary witness, he had heard enough to know that it related to something that had occurred in the old woman's attendance, as workhouse nurse, upon the young mother of Oliver Twist. Hastily calling this circumstance to mind, he informed the stranger, with an air of mystery, that one woman had been closeted with the old harridan shortly before she died; and that she could, as he had reason to believe, throw some light on the subject of his inquiry.

"How can I find her?" said the stranger, thrown off his guard; and plainly showing that all his fears (whatever they were) were aroused afresh by the intelligence.

"Only through me," rejoined Mr. Bumble.

"When?" cried the stranger, hastily.

"To-morrow," rejoined Bumble.

"At nine in the evening," said the stranger, producing a scrap of paper, and writing down upon it, an obscure address by the water-side, in characters that betrayed his agitation; "at nine in the evening, bring her to me there. I needn't tell you to be secret. It's your interest."

With these words, he led the way to the door, after stopping to pay for the liquor that had been drunk. Shortly remarking that their roads were different, he departed, without more ceremony than an emphatic repetition of the hour of appointment for the following night.

On glancing at the address, the parochial functionary observed that it contained no name. The stranger had not gone far, so he made after him to ask it.

"What do you want?" cried the man, turning quickly round, as Bumble touched him on the arm. "Following me?"

"Only to ask a question," said the other, pointing to the scrap of paper. "What name am I to ask for?"

"Monks!" rejoined the man; and strode hastily, away.

CHAPTER XXXVIII

*Containing an Account of What Passed Between Mr. and Mrs. Bumble,
and Mr. Monks, at Their Nocturnal Interview*

It was a dull, close, overcast summer evening. The clouds, which had been threatening all day, spread out in a dense and sluggish mass of vapour, already yielded large drops of rain, and seemed to presage a violent thunder-storm, when Mr. and Mrs. Bumble, turning out of the main street of the town, directed their course towards a scattered little colony of ruinous houses, distant from it some mile and a-half, or thereabouts, and erected on a low unwholesome swamp, bordering upon the river.

They were both wrapped in old and shabby outer garments, which might, perhaps, serve the double purpose of protecting their persons from the rain, and sheltering them from observation. The husband carried a lantern, from which, however, no light yet shone; and trudged on, a few paces in front, as though—the way being dirty—to give his wife the benefit of treading in his heavy footprints. They went on, in profound silence; every now and then, Mr. Bumble relaxed his pace, and turned his head as if to make sure that his helpmate was following; then, discovering that she was close at his heels, he mended his rate of walking, and proceeded, at a considerable increase of speed, towards their place of destination.

This was far from being a place of doubtful character; for it had long been known as the residence of none but low ruffians, who, under various pretences of living by their labour, subsisted chiefly on plunder and crime. It was a collection of mere hovels: some, hastily built with loose bricks: others, of old worm-eaten ship-timber: jumbled together without any attempt at order or arrangement, and planted, for the most part, within a few feet of the river's bank. A few leaky boats drawn up on the mud, and made fast to the dwarf wall which skirted it: and here and there an oar or coil of rope: appeared, at first, to indicate that the inhabitants of these miserable cottages pursued some avocation on the river; but a glance at the shattered and useless condition of the articles thus displayed, would have led a passer-by, without much difficulty, to the conjecture that they were disposed there, rather for the preservation of appearances, than with any view to their being actually employed.

In the heart of this cluster of huts; and skirting the river, which its upper stories overhung; stood a large building, formerly used as a manufactory of some kind. It had, in its day, probably furnished employment to the inhabitants of the surrounding tenements. But it had long since gone to ruin. The rat, the worm, and the action of the damp, had weakened and rotted the piles on which it stood; and a considerable portion of the building had already sunk down into the water; while the remainder, tottering and bending over the dark stream, seemed to wait a favourable opportunity of following its old companion, and involving itself in the same fate.

It was before this ruinous building that the worthy couple paused, as the first peal of distant thunder reverberated in the air, and the rain commenced pouring violently down.

"The place should be somewhere here," said Bumble, consulting a scrap of paper he held in his hand.

"Halloa there!" cried a voice from above.

Following the sound, Mr. Bumble raised his head and descried a man looking out of a door, breast-high, on the second story.

"Stand still, a minute," cried the voice; "I'll be with you directly." With which the head disappeared, and the door closed.

"Is that the man?" asked Mr. Bumble's good lady.

Mr. Bumble nodded in the affirmative.

"Then, mind what I told you," said the matron: "and be careful to say as little as you can, or you'll betray us at once."

Mr. Bumble, who had eyed the building with very rueful looks, was apparently about to express some doubts relative to the advisability of proceeding any further with the enterprise just then, when he was prevented by the appearance of Monks: who opened a small door, near which they stood, and beckoned them inwards.

"Come in!" he cried impatiently, stamping his foot upon the ground. "Don't keep me here!"

The woman, who had hesitated at first, walked boldly in, without any other invitation. Mr. Bumble, who was ashamed or afraid to lag behind, followed: obviously very ill at ease and with scarcely any of that remarkable dignity which was usually his chief characteristic.

"What the devil made you stand lingering there, in the wet?" said Monks, turning round, and addressing Bumble, after he had bolted the door behind them.

"We—we were only cooling ourselves," stammered Bumble, looking apprehensively about him.

"Cooling yourselves!" retorted Monks. "Not all the rain that ever fell, or ever will fall, will put as much of hell's fire out, as a man can carry about with him. You won't cool yourself so easily; don't think it!"

With this agreeable speech, Monks turned short upon the matron, and bent his gaze upon her, till even she, who was not easily cowed, was fain to withdraw her eyes, and turn them towards the ground.

"This is the woman, is it?" demanded Monks.

"Hem! That is the woman," replied Mr. Bumble, mindful of his wife's caution.

"You think women never can keep secrets, I suppose?" said the matron, interposing, and returning, as she spoke, the searching look of Monks.

"I know they will always keep one till it's found out," said Monks.

"And what may that be?" asked the matron.

"The loss of their own good name," replied Monks. "So, by the same rule, if a woman's a party to a secret that might hang or transport her, I'm not afraid of her telling it to anybody; not I! Do you understand, mistress?"

"No," rejoined the matron, slightly colouring as she spoke.

"Of course you don't!" said Monks. "How should you?"

Bestowing something half-way between a smile and a frown upon his two companions, and again beckoning them to follow him, the man hastened across the apartment, which was of considerable extent, but low in the roof. He was preparing to ascend a steep staircase, or rather ladder, leading to another floor of warehouses above: when a bright flash of lightning streamed down the aperture, and a peal of thunder followed, which shook the crazy building to its centre.

"Hear it!" he cried, shrinking back. "Hear it! Rolling and crashing on as if it echoed through a thousand caverns where the devils were hiding from it. I hate the sound!"

He remained silent for a few moments; and then, removing his hands suddenly from his face, showed, to the unspeakable discomposure of Mr. Bumble, that it was much distorted and discoloured.

"These fits come over me, now and then," said Monks, observing his alarm; "and thunder sometimes brings them on. Don't mind me now; it's all over for this once."

Thus speaking, he led the way up the ladder; and hastily closing the window-shutter of the room into which it led, lowered a lantern which hung at the end of a rope and pulley passed through one of the heavy beams in the ceiling: and which cast a dim light upon an old table and three chairs that were placed beneath it.

"Now," said Monks, when they had all three seated themselves, "the sooner we come to our business, the better for all. The woman know what it is, does she?"

The question was addressed to Bumble; but his wife anticipated the reply, by intimating that she was perfectly acquainted with it.

"He is right in saying that you were with this hag the night she died; and that she told you something——"

"About the mother of the boy you named," replied the matron interrupting him. "Yes."

"The first question is, of what nature was her communication?" said Monks.

"That's the second," observed the woman with much deliberation. "The first is, what may the communication be worth?"

"Who the devil can tell that, without knowing of what kind it is?" asked Monks.

"Nobody better than you, I am persuaded," answered Mrs. Bumble: who did not want for spirit, as her yoke-fellow could abundantly testify.

"Humph!" said Monks significantly, and with a look of eager inquiry; "there may be money's worth to get, eh?"

"Perhaps there may," was the composed reply.

"Something that was taken from her," said Monks. "Something that she wore. Something that——"

"You had better bid," interrupted Mrs. Bumble. "I have heard enough, already, to assure me that you are the man I ought to talk to."

Mr. Bumble, who had not yet been admitted by his better half into any greater share of the secret than he had originally possessed, listened to this dialogue with outstretched neck and distended eyes: which he directed towards his wife and Monks, by turns, in undisguised astonishment; increased, if possible, when the latter sternly demanded, what sum was required for the disclosure.

"What's it worth to you?" asked the woman, as collectedly as before.

"It may be nothing; it may be twenty pounds," replied Monks. "Speak out, and let me know which."

"Add five pounds to the sum you have named; give me five-and-twenty pounds in gold," said the woman; "and I'll tell you all I know. Not before."

"Five-and-twenty pounds!" exclaimed Monks, drawing back.

"I spoke as plainly as I could," replied Mrs. Bumble. "It's not a large sum, either."

"Not a large sum for a paltry secret, that may be nothing when it's told!" cried Monks impatiently; "and which has been lying dead for twelve years past or more!"

"Such matters keep well, and, like good wine, often double their value in course of time," answered the matron, still preserving the resolute indifference she had assumed. "As to lying dead, there are those who will lie dead for twelve thousand years to come, or twelve million, for anything you or I know, who will tell strange tales at last!"

"What if I pay it for nothing?" asked Monks, hesitating.

"You can easily take it away again," replied the matron. "I am but a woman; alone here; and unprotected."

"Not alone, my dear, nor unprotected, neither," submitted Mr. Bumble, in a voice tremulous with fear: "I am here, my dear. And besides," said Mr. Bumble, his teeth chattering as he spoke, "Mr. Monks is too much of a gentleman to attempt any violence on porochial persons. Mr. Monks is aware that I am not a young man, my dear, and also that I am a little run to seed, as I may say; bu he has heerd: I say I have no doubt Mr. Monks has heerd, my dear: that I am a very determined officer, with very uncommon strength, if I'm once roused. I only want a little rousing; that's all."

As Mr. Bumble spoke, he made a melancholy feint of grasping his lantern with fierce determination; and plainly showed, by the alarmed expression of every feature, that he did want a little rousing, and not a little, prior to making any very warlike demonstration: unless, indeed, against paupers, or other person or persons trained down for the purpose.

"You are a fool," said Mrs. Bumble, in reply; "and had better hold your tongue."

"He had better have cut it out, before he came, if he can't speak in a lower tone," said Monks, grimly. "So! He's your husband, eh?"

"He my husband!" tittered the matron, parrying the question.

"I thought as much, when you came in," rejoined Monks, marking the angry glance which the lady darted at her spouse as she spoke. "So much the better; I have less hesitation in dealing with two people, when I find that there's only one will between them. I'm in earnest. See here!"

He thrust his hand into a side-pocket; and producing a canvas bag, told out twenty-five sovereigns on the table, and pushed them over to the woman.

"Now," he said, "gather them up; and when this cursed peal of thunder, which I feel is coming up to break over the house-top, is gone, let's hear your story."

The thunder, which seemed in fact much nearer, and to shiver and break almost over their heads, having subsided, Monks, raising his face from the table, bent forward to listen to what the woman should say. The faces of the three nearly touched, as the two men leant over the small table in their eagerness to hear, and the woman also leant forward to render her whisper audible. The sickly rays of the suspended lantern falling directly upon them, aggravated the paleness and anxiety of their countenances: which, encircled by the deepest gloom and darkness, looked ghastly in the extreme.

"When this woman, that we called old Sally, died," the matron began, "she and I were alone."

"Was there no one by?" asked Monks, in the same hollow whisper; "No sick wretch or idiot in some other bed? No one who could hear, and might, by possibility, understand?"

"Not a soul," replied the woman; "we were alone. I stood alone beside the body when death came over it."

"Good," said Monks, regarding her attentively. "Go on."

"She spoke of a young creature," resumed the matron, "who had brought a child into the world some years before; not merely in the same room, but in the same bed, in which she then lay dying."

"Ay?" said Monks, with quivering lip, and glancing over his shoulder, "Blood! How things come about!"

"The child was the one you named to him last night," said the matron, nodding carelessly towards her husband; "the mother this nurse had robbed."

"In life?" asked Monks.

"In death," replied the woman, with something like a shudder. "She stole from the corpse, when it had hardly turned to one, that which the dead mother had prayed her, with her last breath, to keep for the infant's sake."

"She sold it," cried Monks, with desperate eagerness; "did she sell it? Where? When? To whom? How long before?"

"As she told me, with great difficulty, that she had done this," said the matron, "she fell back and died."

"Without saying more?" cried Monks, in a voice which, from its very suppression, seemed only the more furious. "It's a lie! I'll not be played with. She said more. I'll tear the life out of you both, but I'll know what it was."

"She didn't utter another word," said the woman, to all appearance unmoved (as Mr. Bumble was very far from being) by the strange man's violence; "but she clutched my gown, violently, with one hand, which was partly closed; and when I saw that she was dead, and so removed the hand by force, I found it clasped a scrap of dirty paper."

"Which contained—" interposed Monks, stretching forward.

"Nothing," replied the woman; "it was a pawnbroker's duplicate."

"For what?" demanded Monks.

"In good time I'll tell you.' said the woman. "I judge that she had kept the trinket, for some time, in the hope of turning it to better account; and then had pawned it; and had saved or scraped together money to pay the pawnbroker's interest year by year, and prevent its running out; so that if anything came of it, it could still be redeemed. Nothing had come of it; and, as I tell you, she died with the scrap of paper, all worn and tattered, in her hand. The time was out in two days; I thought something might one day come of it too; and so redeemed the pledge."

"Where is it now?" asked Monks quickly.

"There," replied the woman. And, as if glad to be relieved of it, she hastily threw upon the table a small kid bag scarcely large enough for a French watch, which Monks pouncing upon, tore open with trembling hands. It contained a little gold locket: in which were two locks of hair, and a plain gold wedding-ring.

"It has the word 'Agnes' engraved on the inside," said the woman.

"There is a blank left for the surname; and then follows the date; which is within a year before the child was born. I found out that."

"And this is all?" said Monks, after a close and eager scrutiny of the contents of the little packet.

"All," replied the woman.

Mr. Bumble drew a long breath, as if he were glad to find that the story was over, and no mention made of taking the five-and-twenty pounds back again; and now he took courage to wipe the perspiration which had been trickling over his nose, unchecked, during the whole of the previous dialogue.

"I know nothing of the story, beyond what I can guess at," said his wife addressing Monks, after a short silence; "and I want to know nothing; for it's safer not. But I may ask you two questions, may I?"

"You may ask," said Monks, with some show of surprise; "but whether I answer or not is another question."

"—Which makes three," observed Mr. Bumble, essaying a stroke of facetiousness.

"Is that what you expected to get from me?" demanded the matron.

"It is," replied Monks. "The other question?"

"What do you propose to do with it? Can it be used against me?"

"Never," rejoined Monks; "nor against me either. See here! But don't move a step forward, or your life is not worth a bulrush."

With these words, he suddenly wheeled the table aside, and pulling an iron ring in the boarding, threw back a large trap-door which opened close at Mr. Bumble's feet, and caused that gentleman to retire several paces backward, with great precipitation.

"Look down," said Monks, lowering the lantern into the gulf. "Don't fear me. I could have let you down, quietly enough, when you were seated over it, if that had been my game."

Thus encouraged, the matron drew near to the brink; and even Mr. Bumble himself, impelled by curiosity, ventured to do the same. The turbid water, swollen by the heavy rain, was rushing rapidly on below; and all other sounds were lost in the noise of its plashing and eddying against the green and slimy piles. There had once been a water-mill beneath; the tide foaming and chafing round the few rotten stakes, and fragments of machinery that yet remained, seemed to dart onward, with a new impulse, when freed from the obstacles which had unavailingly attempted to stem its headlong course.

"If you flung a man's body down there, where would it be to-morrow morning?" said Monks, swinging the lantern to and fro in the dark well.

"Twelve miles down the river, and cut to pieces besides," replied Bumble, recoiling at the thought.

Monks drew the little packet from his breast, where he had hurriedly thrust it; and tying it to a leaden weight, which had formed a part of some pulley, and was lying on the floor, dropped it into the stream. It fell straight, and true as a die; clove the water with a scarcely audible splash; and was gone.

The three looking into each other's faces, seemed to breathe more freely.

"There!" said Monks, closing the trap-door, which fell heavily back into its former position. "If the sea ever gives up its dead, as books say it will, it will keep its gold and silver to itself, and that trash among it. We have nothing more to say, and may break up our pleasant party."

"By all means," observed Mr. Bumble, with great alacrity.

"You'll keep a quiet tongue in your head, will you?" said Monks, with a threatening look. "I am not afraid of your wife."

"You may depend upon me, young man," answered Mr. Bumble, bowing himself gradually towards the ladder, with excessive politeness. "On everybody's account, young man; on my own, you know, Mr. Monks."

"I am glad, for your sake, to hear it," remarked Monks. "Light your lantern! And get away from here as fast as you can."

It was fortunate that the conversation terminated at this point, or Mr. Bumble, who had bowed himself to within six inches of the ladder, would infallibly have pitched headlong into the room below. He lighted his lantern from that which Monks had detached from the rope, and now carried in his hand; and making no effort to prolong the discourse, descended in silence, followed by his wife. Monks brought up the rear, after pausing on the steps to satisfy himself that there were no other sounds to be heard than the beating of the rain without, and the rushing of the water.

They traversed the lower room, slowly, and with caution; for Monks started at every shadow; and Mr. Bumble, holding his lantern a foot above the ground, walked not only with remarkable care, but with a marvellously light step for a gentleman of his figure: looking nervously about him for hidden trap-doors. The gate at which they had entered, was softly unfastened and opened by Monks; merely exchanging a nod with their mysterious acquaintance, the married couple emerged into the wet and darkness outside.

They were no sooner gone, than Monks, who appeared to entertain an invincible repugnance to being left alone, called to a boy who had been hidden somewhere below. Bidding him go first, and bear the light, he returned to the chamber he had just quitted.

CHAPTER XXXIX

*Introduces Some Respectable Characters With Whom the Reader
Is Already Acquainted, and Shows How Monks and the Jew
Laid Their Worthy Heads Together*

On the evening following that upon which the three worthies mentioned in the last chapter, disposed of their little matter of business as therein narrated, Mr. William Sikes, awakening from a nap, drowsily growled forth an inquiry what time of night it was.

The room in which Mr. Sikes propounded this question, was not one of those he had tenanted, previous to the Chertsey expedition, although it was in the same quarter of the town, and was situated at no great distance from his former lodgings. It was not, in appearance, so desirable a habitation as his old quarters: being a mean and badly-furnished apartment, of very limited size; lighted only by one small window in the shelving roof, and abutting on a close and dirty lane. Nor were there wanting other indications of the good gentleman's having gone down in the world of late: for a great scarcity of furniture, and total absence of comfort, together with the disappearance of all such small moveables as spare clothes and linen, bespoke a state of extreme poverty; while the meagre and attenuated condition of Mr. Sikes himself would have fully confirmed these symptoms, if they had stood in any need of corroboration.

The housebreaker was lying on the bed, wrapped in his white great-coat, by way of dressing-gown, and displaying a set of features in no degree improved by the cadaverous hue of illness, and the addition of a soiled nightcap, and a stiff, black beard of a week's growth. The dog sat at the bedside: now eyeing his master with a wistful look, and now pricking his ears, and uttering a low growl as some noise in the street, or in the lower part of the house, attracted his attention. Seated by the window, busily engaged in patching an old waistcoat which formed a portion of the robber's ordinary dress, was a female: so pale and reduced with watching and privation, that there would have been considerable difficulty in recognising her as the same Nancy who has already figured in this tale, but for the voice in which she replied to Mr. Sikes's question.

"Not long gone seven," said the girl. "How do you feel to-night, Bill?"

"As weak as water," replied Mr. Sikes, with an imprecation on his eyes and limbs. "Here; lend us a hand, and let me get off this thundering bed anyhow."

Illness had not improved Mr. Sikes's temper; for, as the girl raised him up and led him to a chair, he muttered various curses on her awkwardness, and struck her.

"Whining are you?" said Sikes. "Come! Don't stand snivelling there. If you can't do anything better than that, cut off altogether. D'ye hear me?"

"I hear you," replied the girl, turning her face aside, and forcing a laugh. "What fancy have you got in your head now?"

"Oh! you've thought better of it, have you?" growled Sikes, marking the tear which trembled in her eye. "All the better for you, you have."

"Why, you don't mean to say, you'd be hard upon me to-night, Bill," said the girl, laying her hand upon his shoulder.

"No!" cried Mr. Sikes. "Why not?"

"Such a number of nights," said the girl, with a touch of woman's tenderness, which communicated something like sweetness of tone, even to her voice: "such a number of nights as I've been patient with you, nursing and caring for you, as if you had been a child: and this the first that I've seen you like yourself; you wouldn't have served me as you did just now, if you'd thought of that, would you? Come, come; say you wouldn't."

"Well, then," rejoined Mr. Sikes, "I wouldn't. Why, damme, now, the girls's whining again!"

"It's nothing," said the girl, throwing herself into a chair. "Don't you seem to mind me. It'll soon be over."

"What'll be over?" demanded Mr. Sikes in a savage voice. "What foolery are you up to, now, again? Get up and bustle about, and don't come over me with your woman's nonsense."

At any other time, this remonstrance, and the tone in which it was delivered, would have had the desired effect; but the girl being really weak and exhausted, dropped her head over the back of the chair, and fainted, before Mr. Sikes could get out a few of the appropriate oaths with which, on similar occasions, he was accustomed to garnish his threats. Not knowing, very well, what to do, in this uncommon emergency; for Miss Nancy's hysterics were usually of that violent kind which the patient fights and struggles out of, without much assistance; Mr. Sikes tried a little blasphemy: and finding that mode of treatment wholly ineffectual, called for assistance.

"What's the matter here, my dear?" said Fagin, looking in.

"Lend a hand to the girl, can't you?" replied Sikes impatiently. "Don't stand chattering and grinning at me!"

With an exclamation of surprise, Fagin hastened to the girl's assistance, while Mr. John Dawkins (otherwise the Artful Dodger), who had followed his venerable friend into the room, hastily deposited on the floor a bundle with which he was laden; and snatching a bottle from the grasp of Master Charles Bates who came close at his heels, uncorked it in a twinkling with his teeth, and poured a portion of its contents down the patient's throat: previously taking a taste, himself, to prevent mistakes.

"Give her a whiff of fresh air with the bellows, Charley," said Mr. Dawkins; "and you slap her hands, Fagin, while Bill undoes the petticuts."

These united restoratives, administered with great energy: especially that department consigned to Master Bates, who appeared to consider his share in the proceedings, a piece of unexampled pleasantry: were not long in producing the desired effect. The girl gradually recovered her senses; and, staggering to a chair by the bedside, hid her face upon the pillow: leaving Mr. Sikes to confront the new comers, in some astonishment at their unlooked-for appearance.

"Why, what evil wind has blowed you here?" he asked Fagin.

"No evil wind at all, my dear, for evil winds blow nobody any good; and I've brought something good with me, that you'll be glad to see. Dodger, my dear, open the bundle; and give Bill the little trifles that we spent all our money on, this morning."

In compliance with Mr. Fagin's request, the Artful untied this bundle, which was of large size, and formed of an old table-cloth; and handed the articles it contained, one by one, to Charley Bates: who placed them on the table, with various encomiums on their rarity and excellence.

"Sitch a rabbit pie, Bill," exclaimed that young gentleman, disclosing to view a huge pasty; "sitch delicate creeturs, with sitch tender limbs, Bill, that the wery bones melt in your mouth, and there's no occasion to pick 'em; half a pound of seven and six-penny green, so precious strong that if you mix it with biling water, it'll go nigh to blow the lid of the tea-pot off; a pound and a half of moist sugar that the niggers didn't work at all at, afore they got it up to sitch a pitch of goodness,—oh no! Two half-quartern brans; pound of best fresh; piece of double Glo'ster; and, to wind up all, some of the richest sort you ever lushed!"

Uttering this last panegyric, Master Bates produced, from one of his extensive pockets, a full-sized wine-bottle, carefully corked; while Mr. Dawkins, at the same instant, poured out a wine-glassful of raw spirits from the bottle he carried: which the invalid tossed down his throat without a moment's hesitation.

"Ah!" said Fagin, rubbing his hands with great satisfaction. "You'll do, Bill; you'll do now."

"Do!" exclaimed Mr. Sikes; "I might have been done for, twenty times over, afore you'd have done anything to help me. What do you mean by leaving a man in this state, three weeks and more, you false-hearted wagabond?"

"Only hear him, boys!" said Fagin, shrugging his shoulders. "And us come to bring him all these beau-ti-ful things."

"The things is well enough in their way," observed Mr. Sikes: a little soothed as he glanced over the table; "but what have you got to say for yourself, why you should leave me here, down in the mouth, health, blunt, and everything else; and take no more notice of me, all this mortal time, than if I was that 'ere dog.—Drive him down, Charley!"

"I never see such a jolly dog as that," cried Master Bates, doing as he was desired. "Smelling the grub like a old lady a going to market! He'd make his fortun' on the stage that dog would, and rewive the drayma besides."

"Hold your din," cried Sikes, as the dog retreated under the bed: still growling angrily. "What have you got to say for yourself, you withered old fence, eh?"

"I was away from London, a week and more, my dear, on a plant," replied the Jew.

"And what about the other fortnight?" demanded Sikes. "What about the other fortnight that you've left me lying here, like a sick rat in his hole?"

"I couldn't help it, Bill. I can't go into a long explanation before company; but I couldn't help it, upon my honour."

"Upon your what?" growled Sikes, with excessive disgust. "Here! Cut me off a piece of that pie, one of you boys, to take the taste of that out of my mouth, or it'll choke me dead."

"Don't be out of temper, my dear," urged Fagin, submissively. "I have never forgot you, Bill; never once."

"No! I'll pound it that you han't," replied Sikes, with a bitter grin. "You've been scheming and plotting away, every hour that I have laid shivering and burning here; and Bill was to do this; and Bill was to do that; and Bill was to do it all, dirt cheap, as soon as he got well: and was quite poor enough for your work. If it hadn't been for the girl, I might have died."

"There now, Bill," remonstrated Fagin, eagerly catching at the word. "If it hadn't been for the girl! Who but poor ould Fagin was the means of your having such a handy girl about you?"

"He says true enough there!" said Nancy, coming hastily forward. "Let him be; let him be."

Nancy's appearance gave a new turn to the conversation; for the boys, receiving a sly wink from the wary old Jew, began to ply her with liquor: of which, however, she took very sparingly; while Fagin, assuming an unusual flow of spirits, gradually brought Mr. Sikes into a better temper, by affecting to regard his threats as a little pleasant banter; and, moreover, by laughing very heartily at one or two rough jokes, which, after repeated applications to the spirit-bottle, he condescended to make.

"It's all very well," said Mr. Sikes; "but I must have some blunt from you to-night."

"I haven't a piece of coin about me," replied the Jew.

"Then you've got lots at home," retorted Sikes; "and I must have some from there."

"Lots!" cried Fagin, holding up is hands. "I haven't so much as would—"

"I don't know how much you've got, and I dare say you hardly know yourself, as it would take a pretty long time to count it," said Sikes; "but I must have some to-night; and that's flat."

"Well, well," said Fagin, with a sigh, "I'll send the Artful round presently."

"You won't do nothing of the kind," rejoined Mr. Sikes. "The Artful's a deal too artful, and would forget to come, or lose his way, or get dodged by traps and so be perwented, or anything for an excuse, if you put him up to it. Nancy shall go to the ken and fetch it, to make all sure; and I'll lie down and have a snooze while she's gone."

After a great deal of haggling and squabbling, Fagin beat down the amount of the required advance from five pounds to three pounds four and sixpence: protesting with many solemn asseverations that that would only leave him eighteen-pence to keep house with; Mr. Sikes sullenly remarking that if he couldn't get any more he must accompany him home; with the Dodger and Master Bates put the eatables in the cupboard. The Jew then, taking leave of his affectionate friend, returned homeward, attended by Nancy and the boys: Mr. Sikes, meanwhile, flinging himself on the bed, and composing himself to sleep away the time until the young lady's return.

In due course, they arrived at Fagin's abode, where they found Toby Crackit and Mr. Chitling intent upon their fifteenth game at cribbage, which it is scarcely necessary to say the latter gentleman lost, and with it, his fifteenth and last sixpence: much to the amusement of his young friends. Mr. Crackit, apparently somewhat ashamed at being found relaxing himself with a gentleman so much his inferior in station and mental endowments, yawned, and inquiring after Sikes, took up his hat to go.

"Has nobody been, Toby?" asked Fagin.

"Not a living leg," answered Mr. Crackit, pulling up his collar; "it's been as dull as swipes. You ought to stand something handsome, Fagin, to recompense me for keeping house so long. Damme, I'm as flat as a juryman; and should have gone to sleep, as fast as Newgate, if I hadn't had the good natur' to amuse this youngster. Horrid dull, I'm blessed if I an't!"

With these and other ejaculations of the same kind, Mr. Toby Crackit swept up his winnings, and crammed them into his waistcoat pocket with a haughty air, as though such small pieces of silver were wholly beneath the consideration of a man of his figure; this done, he swaggered out of the room, with so much elegance and gentility, that Mr. Chitling, bestowing numerous admiring glances on his legs and boots till they were out of sight, assured the company that he considered his acquaintance cheap at fifteen sixpences an interview, and that he didn't value his losses the snap of his little finger.

"Wot a rum chap you are, Tom!" said Master Bates, highly amused by this declaration.

"Not a bit of it," replied Mr. Chitling. "Am I, Fagin?"

"A very clever fellow, my dear," said Fagin, patting him on the shoulder, and winking to his other pupils.

"And Mr. Crackit is a heavy swell; an't he, Fagin?" asked Tom.

"No doubt at all of that, my dear."

"And it is a creditable thing to have his acquaintance; an't it, Fagin?" pursued Tom.

"Very much so, indeed, my dear. They're only jealous, Tom, because he won't give it to them."

"Ah!" cried Tom, triumphantly, "that's where it is! He has cleaned me out. But I can go and earn some more, when I like; can't I, Fagin?"

"To be sure you can, and the sooner you go the better, Tom; so make up your loss at once, and don't lose any more time. Dodger! Charley! It's time you were on the lay. Come! It's near ten, and nothing done yet."

In obedience to this hint, the boys, nodding to Nancy, took up their hats, and left the room; the Dodger and his vivacious friend indulging, as they went, in many witticisms at the expense of Mr. Chitling; in whose conduct, it is but justice to say, there was nothing very conspicuous or peculiar: inasmuch as there are a great number of spirited young bloods upon town, who pay a much higher price than Mr. Chitling for being seen in good society: and a great number of fine gentlemen (composing the good society aforesaid) who established their reputation upon very much the same footing as flash Toby Crackit.

"Now," said Fagin, when they had left the room, "I'll go and get you that cash, Nancy. This is only the key of a little cupboard where I keep a few odd things the boys get, my dear. I never lock up my money, for I've got none to lock up, my dear—ha! ha! ha!—none to lock up. It's a poor trade, Nancy, and no thanks; but I'm fond of seeing the young people about me; and I bear it all, I bear it all. Hush!" he said, hastily concealing the key in his breast; "who's that? Listen!"

The girl, who was sitting at the table with her arms folded, appeared in no way interested in the arrival: or to care whether the person, whoever he was, came or went: until the murmur of a man's voice reached her ears. The instant she caught the sound, she tore off her bonnet and shawl, with the rapidity of lightning, and thrust them under the table. The Jew, turning round immediately afterwards, she muttered a complaint of the heat: in a tone of languor that contrasted, very remarkably, with the extreme haste and violence of this action: which, however, had been unobserved by Fagin, who had his back towards her at the time.

"Bah!" he whispered, as though nettled by the interruption; "it's the man I expected before; he's coming downstairs. Not a word about the money while he's here, Nance. He won't stop long. Not ten minutes, my dear."

Laying his skinny forefinger upon his lip, the Jew carried a candle to the door, as a man's step was heard upon the stairs without. He reached it, at the same moment as the visitor, who, coming hastily into the room, was close upon the girl before he observed her.

It was Monks.

"Only one of my young people," said Fagin, observing that Monks drew back, on beholding a stranger. "Don't move, Nancy."

The girl drew closer to the table, and glancing at Monks with an air of careless levity, withdrew her eyes; but as he turned towards Fagin, she stole another look;

so keen and searching, and full of purpose, that if there had been any bystander to observe the change, he could hardly have believed the two looks to have proceeded from the same person.

"Any news?" inquired Fagin.

"Great."

"And—and—good?" asked Fagin, hesitating as though he feared to vex the other man by being too sanguine.

"Not bad, any way," replied Monks with a smile. "I have been prompt enough this time. Let me have a word with you."

The girl drew closer to the table, and made no offer to leave the room, although she could see that Monks was pointing to her. The Jew: perhaps fearing she might say something aloud about the money, if he endeavoured to get rid of her: pointed upward, and took Monks out of the room.

"Not that infernal hole we were in before," she could hear the man say as they went upstairs. Fagin laughed; and making some reply which did not reach her, seemed, by the creaking of the boards, to lead his companion to the second story.

Before the sound of their footsteps had ceased to echo through the house, the girl had slipped off her shoes; and drawing her gown loosely over her head, and muffling her arms in it, stood at the door, listening with breathless interest. The moment the noise ceased, she glided from the room; ascended the stairs with incredible softness and silence; and was lost in the gloom above.

The room remained deserted for a quarter of an hour or more; the girl glided back with the same unearthly tread; and, immediately afterwards, the two men were heard descending. Monks went at once into the street; and the Jew crawled upstairs again for the money. When he returned, the girl was adjusting her shawl and bonnet, as if preparing to be gone.

"Why, Nance!" exclaimed the Jew, starting back as he put down the candle, "how pale you are!"

"Pale!" echoed the girl, shading her eyes with her hands, as if to look steadily at him.

"Quite horrible. What have you been doing to yourself?"

"Nothing that I know of, except sitting in this close place for I don't know how long and all," replied the girl carelessly. "Come! Let me get back; that's a dear."

With a sigh for every piece of money, Fagin told the amount into her hand. They parted without more conversation, merely interchanging a "good-night."

When the girl got into the open street, she sat down upon a doorstep; and seemed, for a few moments, wholly bewildered and unable to pursue her way. Suddenly she arose; and hurrying on, in a direction quite opposite to that in which Sikes was awaiting her returned, quickened her pace, until it gradually resolved into a violent run. After completely exhausting herself, she stopped to take breath: and, as if suddenly recollecting herself, and deploring her inability to do something she was bent upon, wrung her hands, and burst into tears.

It might be that her tears relieved her, or that she felt the full hopelessness of her condition; but she turned back; and hurrying with nearly as great rapidity in the contrary direction; partly to recover lost time, and partly to keep pace with the violent current of her own thoughts: soon reached the dwelling where she had left the housebreaker.

If she betrayed any agitation, when she presented herself to Mr. Sikes, he did not observe it; for merely inquiring if she had brought the money, and receiving a reply in the affirmative, he uttered a growl of satisfaction, and replacing his head upon the pillow, resumed the slumbers which her arrival had interrupted.

It was fortunate for her that the possession of money occasioned him so much employment next day in the way of eating and drinking; and withal had so beneficial an effect in smoothing down the asperities of his temper; that he had neither time nor inclination to be very critical upon her behaviour and deportment. That she had all the abstracted and nervous manner of one who is on the eve of some bold and hazardous step, which it has required no common struggle to resolve upon, would have been obvious to the lynx-eyed Fagin, who would most probably have taken the alarm at once; but Mr. Sikes lacking the niceties of discrimination, and being troubled with no more subtle misgivings than those which resolve themselves into a dogged roughness of behaviour towards everybody; and being, furthermore, in an unusually amiable condition, as has been already observed; saw nothing unusual in her demeanor, and indeed, troubled himself so little about her, that, had her agitation been far more perceptible than it was, it would have been very unlikely to have awakened his suspicions.

As that day closed in, the girl's excitement increased; and, when night came on, and she sat by, watching until the housebreaker should drink himself asleep, there was an unusual paleness in her cheek, and a fire in her eye, that even Sikes observed with astonishment.

Mr. Sikes being weak from the fever, was lying in bed, taking hot water with his gin to render it less inflammatory; and had pushed his glass towards Nancy to be replenished for the third or fourth time, when these symptoms first struck him.

"Why, burn my body!" said the man, raising himself on his hands as he stared the girl in the face. "You look like a corpse come to life again. What's the matter?"

"Matter!" replied the girl. "Nothing. What do you look at me so hard for?"

"What foolery is this?" demanded Sikes, grasping her by the arm, and shaking her roughly. "What is it? What do you mean? What are you thinking of?"

"Of many things, Bill," replied the girl, shivering, and as she did so, pressing her hands upon her eyes. "But, Lord! What odds in that?"

The tone of forced gaiety in which the last words were spoken, seemed to produce a deeper impression on Sikes than the wild and rigid look which had preceded them.

"I tell you wot it is," said Sikes; "if you haven't caught the fever, and got it comin' on, now, there's something more than usual in the wind, and something dangerous too. You're not a-going to——. No, damme! you wouldn't do that!"

"Do what?" asked the girl.

"There ain't," said Sikes, fixing his eyes upon her, and muttering the words to himself; "there ain't a stauncher-hearted gal going, or I'd have cut her throat three months ago. She's got the fever coming on; that's it."

Fortifying himself with this assurance, Sikes drained the glass to the bottom, and then, with many grumbling oaths, called for his physic. The girl jumped up, with great alacrity; poured it quickly out, but with her back towards him; and held the vessel to his lips, while he drank off the contents.

"Now," said the robber, "come and sit aside of me, and put on your own face; or I'll alter it so, that you won't know it agin when you do want it."

The girl obeyed. Sikes, locking her hand in his, fell back upon the pillow: turning his eyes upon her face. They closed; opened again; closed once more; again opened. He shifted his position restlessly; and, after dozing again, and again, for two or three minutes, and as often springing up with a look of terror, and gazing vacantly about him, was suddenly stricken, as it were, while in the very attitude of rising, into a deep and heavy sleep. The grasp of his hand relaxed; the upraised arm fell languidly by his side; and he lay like one in a profound trance.

"The laudanum has taken effect at last," murmured the girl, as she rose from the bedside. "I may be too late, even now."

She hastily dressed herself in her bonnet and shawl: looking fearfully round, from time to time, as if, despite the sleeping draught, she expected every moment to feel the pressure of Sikes's heavy hand upon her shoulder; then, stooping softly over the bed, she kissed the robber's lips; and then opening and closing the room-door with noiseless touch, hurried from the house.

A watchman was crying half-past nine, down a dark passage through which she had to pass, in gaining the main thoroughfare.

"Has it long gone the half-hour?" asked the girl.

"It'll strike the hour in another quarter," said the man: raising his lantern to her face.

"And I cannot get there in less than an hour or more," muttered Nancy: brushing swiftly past him, and gliding rapidly down the street.

Many of the shops were already closing in the back lanes and avenues through which she tracked her way, in making from Spitalfields towards the West-End of London. The clock struck ten, increasing her impatience. She tore along the narrow pavement: elbowing the passengers from side to side; and darting almost under the horses' heads, crossed crowded streets, where clusters of persons were eagerly watching their opportunity to do the like.

"The woman is mad!" said the people, turning to look after her as she rushed away.

When she reached the more wealthy quarter of the town, the streets were comparatively deserted; and here her headlong progress excited a still greater curiosity in the stragglers whom she hurried past. Some quickened their pace behind, as though to see whither she was hastening at such an unusual rate; and a few made head upon her, and looked back, surprised at her undiminished speed; but they fell off one by one; and when she neared her place of destination, she was alone.

It was a family hotel in a quiet but handsome street near Hyde Park. As the brilliant light of the lamp which burnt before its door, guided her to the spot, the clock struck eleven. She had loitered for a few paces as though irresolute, and making up her mind to advance; but the sound determined her, and she stepped into the hall. The porter's seat was vacant. She looked round with an air of incertitude, and advanced towards the stairs.

"Now, young woman!" said a smartly-dressed female, looking out from a door behind her, "who do you want here?"

"A lady who is stopping in this house," answered the girl.

"A lady!" was the reply, accompanied with a scornful look. "What lady?"

"Miss Maylie," said Nancy.

The young woman, who had by this time, noted her appearance, replied only by a look of virtuous disdain; and summoned a man to answer her. To him, Nancy repeated her request.

"What name am I to say?" asked the waiter.

"It's of no use saying any," replied Nancy.

"Nor business?" said the man.

"No, nor that neither," rejoined the girl. "I must see the lady."

"Come!" said the man, pushing her towards the door. "None of this. Take yourself off."

"I shall be carried out if I go!" said the girl violently; "and I can make that a job that two of you won't like to do. Isn't there anybody here," she said, looking round, "that will see a simple message carried for a poor wretch like me?"

This appeal produced an effect on a good-tempered-faced man-cook, who with some of the other servants was looking on, and who stepped forward to interfere.

"Take it up for her, Joe; can't you?" said this person.

"What's the good?" replied the man. "You don't suppose the young lady will see such as her; do you?"

This allusion to Nancy's doubtful character, raised a vast quantity of chaste wrath in the bosoms of four housemaids, who remarked, with great fervour, that the creature was a disgrace to her sex; and strongly advocated her being thrown, ruthlessly, into the kennel.

"Do what you like with me," said the girl, turning to the men again; "but do what I ask you first, and I ask you to give this message for God Almighty's sake."

The soft-hearted cook added his intercession, and the result was that the man who had first appeared undertook its delivery.

"What's it to be?" said the man, with one foot on the stairs.

"That a young woman earnestly asks to speak to Miss Maylie alone," said Nancy; "and that if the lady will only hear the first word she has to say, she will know whether to hear her business, or to have her turned out of doors as an impostor."

"I say," said the man, "you're coming it strong!"

"You give the message," said the girl firmly; "and let me hear the answer."

The man ran upstairs. Nancy remained, pale and almost breathless, listening with quivering lip to the very audible expressions of scorn, of which the chaste housemaids were very prolific; and of which they became still more so, when the man returned, and said the young woman was to walk upstairs.

"It's no good being proper in this world," said the first housemaid.

"Brass can do better than the gold what has stood the fire," said the second.

The third contented herself with wondering "what ladies was made of'; and the fourth took the first in a quartette of "Shameful!" with which the Dianas concluded.

Regardless of all this: for she had weightier matters at heart: Nancy followed the man, with trembling limbs, to a small ante-chamber, lighted by a lamp from the ceiling. Here he left her, and retired.

CHAPTER XL

A Strange Interview, Which Is a Sequel to the Last Chapter

The girl's life had been squandered in the streets, and among the most noisome of the stews and dens of London, but there was something of the woman's original nature left in her still; and when she heard a light step approaching the door opposite to that by which she had entered, and thought of the wide contrast which the small room would in another moment contain, she felt burdened with the sense of her own deep shame, and shrunk as though she could scarcely bear the presence of her with whom she had sought this interview.

But struggling with these better feelings was pride,—the vice of the lowest and most debased creatures no less than of the high and self-assured. The miserable companion of thieves and ruffians, the fallen outcast of low haunts, the associate of the scourings of the jails and hulks, living within the shadow of the gallows itself,—even this degraded being felt too proud to betray a feeble gleam of the womanly feeling which she thought a weakness, but which alone connected her with that humanity, of which her wasting life had obliterated so many, many traces when a very child.

She raised her eyes sufficiently to observe that the figure which presented itself was that of a slight and beautiful girl; then, bending them on the ground, she tossed her head with affected carelessness as she said:

"It's a hard matter to get to see you, lady. If I had taken offence, and gone away, as many would have done, you'd have been sorry for it one day, and not without reason either."

"I am very sorry if any one has behaved harshly to you," replied Rose. "Do not think of that. Tell me why you wished to see me. I am the person you inquired for."

The kind tone of this answer, the sweet voice, the gentle manner, the absence of any accent of haughtiness or displeasure, took the girl completely by surprise, and she burst into tears.

"Oh, lady, lady!" she said, clasping her hands passionately before her face, "if there was more like you, there would be fewer like me,—there would—there would!"

"Sit down," said Rose, earnestly. "If you are in poverty or affliction I shall be truly glad to relieve you if I can,—I shall indeed. Sit down."

"Let me stand, lady," said the girl, still weeping, "and do not speak to me so kindly till you know me better. It is growing late. Is—is—that door shut?"

"Yes," said Rose, recoiling a few steps, as if to be nearer assistance in case she should require it. "Why?"

"Because," said the girl, "I am about to put my life and the lives of others in your hands. I am the girl that dragged little Oliver back to old Fagin's on the night he went out from the house in Pentonville."

"You!" said Rose Maylie.

"I, lady!" replied the girl. "I am the infamous creature you have heard of, that lives among the thieves, and that never from the first moment I can recollect my eyes and senses opening on London streets have known any better life, or kinder words than they have given me, so help me God! Do not mind shrinking openly from me, lady. I am younger than you would think, to look at me, but I am well used to it. The poorest women fall back, as I make my way along the crowded pavement."

"What dreadful things are these!" said Rose, involuntarily falling from her strange companion.

"Thank Heaven upon your knees, dear lady," cried the girl, "that you had friends to care for and keep you in your childhood, and that you were never in the midst of cold and hunger, and riot and drunkenness, and—and—something worse than all—as I have been from my cradle. I may use the word, for the alley and the gutter were mine, as they will be my deathbed."

"I pity you!" said Rose, in a broken voice. "It wrings my heart to hear you!"

"Heaven bless you for your goodness!" rejoined the girl. "If you knew what I am sometimes, you would pity me, indeed. But I have stolen away from those who would surely murder me, if they knew I had been here, to tell you what I have overheard. Do you know a man named Monks?"

"No," said Rose.

"He knows you," replied the girl; "and knew you were here, for it was by hearing him tell the place that I found you out."

"I never heard the name," said Rose.

"Then he goes by some other amongst us," rejoined the girl, "which I more than thought before. Some time ago, and soon after Oliver was put into your house on the night of the robbery, I—suspecting this man—listened to a conversation held between him and Fagin in the dark. I found out, from what I heard, that Monks—the man I asked you about, you know—"

"Yes," said Rose, "I understand."

"—That Monks," pursued the girl, "had seen him accidently with two of our boys on the day we first lost him, and had known him directly to be the same child that he was watching for, though I couldn't make out why. A bargain was struck with Fagin, that if Oliver was got back he should have a certain sum; and he was to have more for making him a thief, which this Monks wanted for some purpose of his own."

"For what purpose?" asked Rose.

"He caught sight of my shadow on the wall as I listened, in the hope of finding out," said the girl; "and there are not many people besides me that could have got out of their way in time to escape discovery. But I did; and I saw him no more till last night."

"And what occurred then?"

"I'll tell you, lady. Last night he came again. Again they went upstairs, and I, wrapping myself up so that my shadow would not betray me, again listened at the door. The first words I heard Monks say were these: 'So the only proofs of the boy's identity lie at the bottom of the river, and the old hag that received them from the mother is rotting in her coffin.' They laughed, and talked of his success in doing this; and Monks, talking on about the boy, and getting very wild, said that though he

THE ADVENTURES OF OLIVER TWIST

had got the young devil's money safely now, he'd rather have had it the other way; for, what a game it would have been to have brought down the boast of the father's will, by driving him through every jail in town, and then hauling him up for some capital felony which Fagin could easily manage, after having made a good profit of him besides."

"What is all this!" said Rose.

"The truth, lady, though it comes from my lips," replied the girl. "Then, he said, with oaths common enough in my ears, but strange to yours, that if he could gratify his hatred by taking the boy's life without bringing his own neck in danger, he would; but, as he couldn't, he'd be upon the watch to meet him at every turn in life; and if he took advantage of his birth and history, he might harm him yet. "In short, Fagin,' he says, "Jew as you are, you never laid such snares as I'll contrive for my young brother, Oliver.'"

"His brother!" exclaimed Rose.

"Those were his words," said Nancy, glancing uneasily round, as she had scarcely ceased to do, since she began to speak, for a vision of Sikes haunted her perpetually. "And more. When he spoke of you and the other lady, and said it seemed contrived by Heaven, or the devil, against him, that Oliver should come into your hands, he laughed, and said there was some comfort in that too, for how many thousands and hundreds of thousands of pounds would you not give, if you had them, to know who your two-legged spaniel was."

"You do not mean," said Rose, turning very pale, "to tell me that this was said in earnest?"

"He spoke in hard and angry earnest, if a man ever did," replied the girl, shaking her head. "He is an earnest man when his hatred is up. I know many who do worse things; but I'd rather listen to them all a dozen times, than to that Monks once. It is growing late, and I have to reach home without suspicion of having been on such an errand as this. I must get back quickly."

"But what can I do?" said Rose. "To what use can I turn this communication without you? Back! Why do you wish to return to companions you paint in such terrible colors? If you repeat this information to a gentleman whom I can summon in an instant from the next room, you can be consigned to some place of safety without half an hour's delay."

"I wish to go back," said the girl. "I must go back, because—how can I tell such things to an innocent lady like you?—because among the men I have told you of, there is one: the most desperate among them all; that I can't leave: no, not even to be saved from the life I am leading now."

"Your having interfered in this dear boy's behalf before," said Rose; "your coming here, at so great a risk, to tell me what you have heard; your manner, which convinces me of the truth of what you say; your evident contrition, and sense of shame; all lead me to believe that you might yet be reclaimed. Oh!" said the earnest girl, folding her hands as the tears coursed down her face, "do not turn a deaf ear to the entreaties of one of your own sex; the first—the first, I do believe, who ever appealed to you in the voice of pity and compassion. Do hear my words, and let me save you yet, for better things."

"Lady," cried the girl, sinking on her knees, "dear, sweet, angel lady, you are the first that ever blessed me with such words as these, and if I had heard them years ago, they might have turned me from a life of sin and sorrow; but it is too late, it is too late!"

"It is never too late," said Rose, "for penitence and atonement."

"It is," cried the girl, writhing in agony of her mind; "I cannot leave him now! I could not be his death."

"Why should you be?" asked Rose.

"Nothing could save him," cried the girl. "If I told others what I have told you, and led to their being taken, he would be sure to die. He is the boldest, and has been so cruel!"

"Is it possible," cried Rose, "that for such a man as this, you can resign every future hope, and the certainty of immediate rescue? It is madness."

"I don't know what it is," answered the girl; "I only know that it is so, and not with me alone, but with hundreds of others as bad and wretched as myself. I must go back. Whether it is God's wrath for the wrong I have done, I do not know; but I am drawn back to him through every suffering and ill usage; and I should be, I believe, if I knew that I was to die by his hand at last."

"What am I to do?" said Rose. "I should not let you depart from me thus."

"You should, lady, and I know you will," rejoined the girl, rising. "You will not stop my going because I have trusted in your goodness, and forced no promise from you, as I might have done."

"Of what use, then, is the communication you have made?" said Rose. "This mystery must be investigated, or how will its disclosure to me, benefit Oliver, whom you are anxious to serve?"

"You must have some kind gentleman about you that will hear it as a secret, and advise you what to do," rejoined the girl.

"But where can I find you again when it is necessary?" asked Rose. "I do not seek to know where these dreadful people live, but where will you be walking or passing at any settled period from this time?"

"Will you promise me that you will have my secret strictly kept, and come alone, or with the only other person that knows it; and that I shall not be watched or followed?" asked the girl.

"I promise you solemnly," answered Rose.

"Every Sunday night, from eleven until the clock strikes twelve," said the girl without hesitation, "I will walk on London Bridge if I am alive."

"Stay another moment," interposed Rose, as the girl moved hurriedly towards the door. "Think once again on your own condition, and the opportunity you have of escaping from it. You have a claim on me: not only as the voluntary bearer of this intelligence, but as a woman lost almost beyond redemption. Will you return to this gang of robbers, and to this man, when a word can save you? What fascination is it that can take you back, and make you cling to wickedness and misery? Oh! is there no chord in your heart that I can touch! Is there nothing left, to which I can appeal against this terrible infatuation!"

"When ladies as young, and good, and beautiful as you are," replied the girl steadily, "give away your hearts, love will carry you all lengths—even such as you, who have home, friends, other admirers, everything, to fill them. When such as I, who have no certain roof but the coffinlid, and no friend in sickness or death but the hospital nurse, set our rotten hearts on any man, and let him fill the place that has been a blank through all our wretched lives, who can hope to cure us? Pity us, lady—pity us for having only one feeling of the woman left, and for having that turned, by a heavy judgment, from a comfort and a pride, into a new means of violence and suffering."

"You will," said Rose, after a pause, "take some money from me, which may enable you to live without dishonesty—at all events until we meet again?"

"Not a penny," replied the girl, waving her hand.

"Do not close your heart against all my efforts to help you," said Rose, stepping gently forward. "I wish to serve you indeed."

"You would serve me best, lady," replied the girl, wringing her hands, "if you could take my life at once; for I have felt more grief to think of what I am, to-night, than I ever did before, and it would be something not to die in the hell in which I have lived. God bless you, sweet lady, and send as much happiness on your head as I have brought shame on mine!"

Thus speaking, and sobbing aloud, the unhappy creature turned away; while Rose Maylie, overpowered by this extraordinary interview, which had more the semblance of a rapid dream than an actual occurrence, sank into a chair, and endeavoured to collect her wandering thoughts.

CHAPTER XLI

Containing Fresh Discoveries, and Showing that Surprises, Like Misfortunes, Seldom Come Alone

Her situation was, indeed, one of no common trial and difficulty. While she felt the most eager and burning desire to penetrate the mystery in which Oliver's history was enveloped, she could not but hold sacred the confidence which the miserable woman with whom she had just conversed, had reposed in her, as a young and guileless girl. Her words and manner had touched Rose Maylie's heart; and, mingled with her love for her young charge, and scarcely less intense in its truth and fervour, was her fond wish to win the outcast back to repentance and hope.

They purposed remaining in London only three days, prior to departing for some weeks to a distant part of the coast. It was now midnight of the first day. What course of action could she determine upon, which could be adopted in eight-and-forty hours? Or how could she postpone the journey without exciting suspicion?

Mr. Losberne was with them, and would be for the next two days; but Rose was too well acquainted with the excellent gentleman's impetuosity, and foresaw too clearly the wrath with which, in the first explosion of his indignation, he would regard the instrument of Oliver's recapture, to trust him with the secret, when her representations in the girl's behalf could be seconded by no experienced person. These were all reasons for the greatest caution and most circumspect behaviour in communicating it to Mrs. Maylie, whose first impulse would infallibly be to hold a conference with the worthy doctor on the subject. As to resorting to any legal adviser, even if she had known how to do so, it was scarcely to be thought of, for the same reason. Once the thought occurred to her of seeking assistance from Harry; but this awakened the recollection of their last parting, and it seemed unworthy of her to call him back, when—the tears rose to her eyes as she pursued this train of reflection—he might have by this time learnt to forget her, and to be happier away.

Disturbed by these different reflections; inclining now to one course and then to another, and again recoiling from all, as each successive consideration presented itself to her mind; Rose passed a sleepless and anxious night. After more communing with herself next day, she arrived at the desperate conclusion of consulting Harry.

"If it be painful to him," she thought, "to come back here, how painful it will be to me! But perhaps he will not come; he may write, or he may come himself, and studiously abstain from meeting me—he did when he went away. I hardly thought he would; but it was better for us both." And here Rose dropped the pen, and turned away, as though the very paper which was to be her messenger should not see her weep.

She had taken up the same pen, and laid it down again fifty times, and had considered and reconsidered the first line of her letter without writing the first word, when Oliver, who had been walking in the streets, with Mr. Giles for a body-guard, entered the room in such breathless haste and violent agitation, as seemed to betoken some new cause of alarm.

"What makes you look so flurried?" asked Rose, advancing to meet him.

"I hardly know how; I feel as if I should be choked," replied the boy. "Oh dear! To think that I should see him at last, and you should be able to know that I have told you the truth!"

"I never thought you had told us anything but the truth," said Rose, soothing him. "But what is this?—of whom do you speak?"

"I have seen the gentleman," replied Oliver, scarcely able to articulate, "the gentleman who was so good to me—Mr. Brownlow, that we have so often talked about."

"Where?" asked Rose.

"Getting out of a coach," replied Oliver, shedding tears of delight, "and going into a house. I didn't speak to him—I couldn't speak to him, for he didn't see me, and I trembled so, that I was not able to go up to him. But Giles asked, for me, whether he lived there, and they said he did. Look here," said Oliver, opening a scrap of paper, "here it is; here's where he lives—I'm going there directly! Oh, dear me, dear me! What shall I do when I come to see him and hear him speak again!"

With her attention not a little distracted by these and a great many other incoherent exclamations of joy, Rose read the address, which was Craven Street, in the Strand. She very soon determined upon turning the discovery to account.

"Quick!" she said. "Tell them to fetch a hackney-coach, and be ready to go with me. I will take you there directly, without a minute's loss of time. I will only tell my aunt that we are going out for an hour, and be ready as soon as you are."

Oliver needed no prompting to despatch, and in little more than five minutes they were on their way to Craven Street. When they arrived there, Rose left Oliver in the coach, under pretence of preparing the old gentleman to receive him; and sending up her card by the servant, requested to see Mr. Brownlow on very pressing business. The servant soon returned, to beg that she would walk upstairs; and following him into an upper room, Miss Maylie was presented to an elderly gentleman of benevolent appearance, in a bottle-green coat. At no great distance from whom, was seated another old gentleman, in nankeen breeches and gaiters; who did not look particularly benevolent, and who was sitting with his hands clasped on the top of a thick stick, and his chin propped thereupon.

"Dear me," said the gentleman, in the bottle-green coat, hastily rising with great politeness, "I beg your pardon, young lady—I imagined it was some importunate person who—I beg you will excuse me. Be seated, pray."

"Mr. Brownlow, I believe, sir?" said Rose, glancing from the other gentleman to the one who had spoken.

"That is my name," said the old gentleman. "This is my friend, Mr. Grimwig. Grimwig, will you leave us for a few minutes?"

"I believe," interposed Miss Maylie, "that at this period of our interview, I need not give that gentleman the trouble of going away. If I am correctly informed, he is cognizant of the business on which I wish to speak to you."

Mr. Brownlow inclined his head. Mr. Grimwig, who had made one very stiff bow, and risen from his chair, made another very stiff bow, and dropped into it again.

"I shall surprise you very much, I have no doubt," said Rose, naturally embarrassed; "but you once showed great benevolence and goodness to a very dear young friend of mine, and I am sure you will take an interest in hearing of him again."

"Indeed!" said Mr. Brownlow.

"Oliver Twist you knew him as," replied Rose.

The words no sooner escaped her lips, than Mr. Grimwig, who had been affecting to dip into a large book that lay on the table, upset it with a great crash, and falling back in his chair, discharged from his features every expression but one of unmitigated wonder, and indulged in a prolonged and vacant stare; then, as if ashamed of having betrayed so much emotion, he jerked himself, as it were, by a convulsion into his former attitude, and looking out straight before him emitted a long deep whistle, which seemed, at last, not to be discharged on empty air, but to die away in the innermost recesses of his stomach.

Mr. Browlow was no less surprised, although his astonishment was not expressed in the same eccentric manner. He drew his chair nearer to Miss Maylie's, and said,

"Do me the favour, my dear young lady, to leave entirely out of the question that goodness and benevolence of which you speak, and of which nobody else knows anything; and if you have it in your power to produce any evidence which will alter the unfavourable opinion I was once induced to entertain of that poor child, in Heaven's name put me in possession of it."

"A bad one! I'll eat my head if he is not a bad one," growled Mr. Grimwig, speaking by some ventriloquial power, without moving a muscle of his face.

"He is a child of a noble nature and a warm heart," said Rose, colouring; "and that Power which has thought fit to try him beyond his years, has planted in his breast affections and feelings which would do honour to many who have numbered his days six times over."

"I'm only sixty-one," said Mr. Grimwig, with the same rigid face. "And, as the devil's in it if this Oliver is not twelve years old at least, I don't see the application of that remark."

"Do not heed my friend, Miss Maylie," said Mr. Brownlow; "he does not mean what he says."

"Yes, he does," growled Mr. Grimwig.

"No, he does not," said Mr. Brownlow, obviously rising in wrath as he spoke.

"He'll eat his head, if he doesn't," growled Mr. Grimwig.

"He would deserve to have it knocked off, if he does," said Mr. Brownlow.

"And he'd uncommonly like to see any man offer to do it," responded Mr. Grimwig, knocking his stick upon the floor.

Having gone thus far, the two old gentlemen severally took snuff, and afterwards shook hands, according to their invariable custom.

"Now, Miss Maylie," said Mr. Brownlow, "to return to the subject in which your humanity is so much interested. Will you let me know what intelligence you have of this poor child: allowing me to promise that I exhausted every means in my power of discovering him, and that since I have been absent from this country, my first impression that he had imposed upon me, and had been persuaded by his former associates to rob me, has been considerably shaken."

Rose, who had had time to collect her thoughts, at once related, in a few natural words, all that had befallen Oliver since he left Mr. Brownlow's house; reserving Nancy's information for that gentleman's private ear, and concluding with the assurance that his only sorrow, for some months past, had been not being able to meet with his former benefactor and friend.

"Thank God!" said the old gentleman. "This is great happiness to me, great happiness. But you have not told me where he is now, Miss Maylie. You must pardon my finding fault with you,—but why not have brought him?"

"He is waiting in a coach at the door," replied Rose.

"At this door!" cried the old gentleman. With which he hurried out of the room, down the stairs, up the coachsteps, and into the coach, without another word.

When the room-door closed behind him, Mr. Grimwig lifted up his head, and converting one of the hind legs of his chair into a pivot, described three distinct circles with the assistance of his stick and the table; sitting in it all the time. After performing this evolution, he rose and limped as fast as he could up and down the room at least a dozen times, and then stopping suddenly before Rose, kissed her without the slightest preface.

"Hush!" he said, as the young lady rose in some alarm at this unusual proceeding. "Don't be afraid. I'm old enough to be your grandfather. You're a sweet girl. I like you. Here they are!"

In fact, as he threw himself at one dexterous dive into his former seat, Mr. Brownlow returned, accompanied by Oliver, whom Mr. Grimwig received very graciously; and if the gratification of that moment had been the only reward for all her anxiety and care in Oliver's behalf, Rose Maylie would have been well repaid.

"There is somebody else who should not be forgotten, by the bye," said Mr. Brownlow, ringing the bell. "Send Mrs. Bedwin here, if you please."

The old housekeeper answered the summons with all dispatch; and dropping a curtsey at the door, waited for orders.

"Why, you get blinder every day, Bedwin," said Mr. Brownlow, rather testily.

"Well, that I do, sir," replied the old lady. "People's eyes, at my time of life, don't improve with age, sir."

"I could have told you that," rejoined Mr. Brownlow; "but put on your glasses, and see if you can't find out what you were wanted for, will you?"

The old lady began to rummage in her pocket for her spectacles. But Oliver's patience was not proof against this new trial; and yielding to his first impulse, he sprang into her arms.

"God be good to me!" cried the old lady, embracing him; "it is my innocent boy!"

"My dear old nurse!" cried Oliver.

"He would come back—I knew he would," said the old lady, holding him in her arms. "How well he looks, and how like a gentleman's son he is dressed again! Where have you been, this long, long while? Ah! the same sweet face, but not so pale; the same soft eye, but not so sad. I have never forgotten them or his quiet smile, but have seen them every day, side by side with those of my own dear children, dead and gone since I was a lightsome young creature.' Running on thus, and now holding Oliver from her to mark how he had grown, now clasping him to her and passing her fingers fondly through his hair, the good soul laughed and wept upon his neck by turns.

Leaving her and Oliver to compare notes at leisure, Mr. Brownlow led the way into another room; and there, heard from Rose a full narration of her interview with Nancy, which occasioned him no little surprise and perplexity. Rose also explained her reasons for not confiding in her friend Mr. Losberne in the first instance. The old gentleman considered that she had acted prudently, and readily undertook to hold solemn conference with the worthy doctor himself. To afford him an early opportunity for the execution of this design, it was arranged that he should call at the hotel at eight o'clock that evening, and that in the meantime Mrs. Maylie should be cautiously informed of all that had occurred. These preliminaries adjusted, Rose and Oliver returned home.

Rose had by no means overrated the measure of the good doctor's wrath. Nancy's history was no sooner unfolded to him, than he poured forth a shower of mingled threats and execrations; threatened to make her the first victim of the combined ingenuity of Messrs. Blathers and Duff; and actually put on his hat preparatory to sallying forth to obtain the assistance of those worthies. And, doubtless, he would, in this first outbreak, have carried the intention into effect without a moment's consideration of the consequences, if he had not been restrained, in part, by corresponding violence on the side of Mr. Brownlow, who was himself of an irascible temperament, and party by such arguments and representations as seemed best calculated to dissuade him from his hotbrained purpose.

"Then what the devil is to be done?" said the impetuous doctor, when they had rejoined the two ladies. "Are we to pass a vote of thanks to all these vagabonds, male and female, and beg them to accept a hundred pounds, or so, apiece, as a trifling mark of our esteem, and some slight acknowledgment of their kindness to Oliver?"

"Not exactly that," rejoined Mr. Brownlow, laughing; "but we must proceed gently and with great care."

"Gentleness and care," exclaimed the doctor. "I'd send them one and all to——"

"Never mind where," interposed Mr. Brownlow. "But reflect whether sending them anywhere is likely to attain the object we have in view."

"What object?" asked the doctor.

"Simply, the discovery of Oliver's parentage, and regaining for him the inheritance of which, if this story be true, he has been fraudulently deprived."

"Ah!" said Mr. Losberne, cooling himself with his pocket-handkerchief; "I almost forgot that."

"You see," pursued Mr. Brownlow; "placing this poor girl entirely out of the question, and supposing it were possible to bring these scoundrels to justice without compromising her safety, what good should we bring about?"

"Hanging a few of them at least, in all probability," suggested the doctor, "and transporting the rest."

"Very good," replied Mr. Brownlow, smiling; "but no doubt they will bring that about for themselves in the fulness of time, and if we step in to forestall them, it seems to me that we shall be performing a very Quixotic act, in direct opposition to our own interest—or at least to Oliver's, which is the same thing."

"How?" inquired the doctor.

"Thus. It is quite clear that we shall have extreme difficulty in getting to the bottom of this mystery, unless we can bring this man, Monks, upon his knees. That can only be done by stratagem, and by catching him when he is not surrounded by these people. For, suppose he were apprehended, we have no proof against him. He is not even (so far as we know, or as the facts appear to us) concerned with the gang in any of their robberies. If he were not discharged, it is very unlikely that he could receive any further punishment than being committed to prison as a rogue and vagabond; and of course ever afterwards his mouth would be so obstinately closed that he might as well, for our purposes, be deaf, dumb, blind, and an idiot."

"Then," said the doctor impetuously, "I put it to you again, whether you think it reasonable that this promise to the girl should be considered binding; a promise made with the best and kindest intentions, but really——"

"Do not discuss the point, my dear young lady, pray," said Mr. Brownlow, interrupting Rose as she was about to speak. "The promise shall be kept. I don't think it will, in the slightest degree, interfere with our proceedings. But, before we can resolve upon any precise course of action, it will be necessary to see the girl; to ascertain from her whether she will point out this Monks, on the understanding that he is to be dealt with by us, and not by the law; or, if she will not, or cannot do that, to procure from her such an account of his haunts and description of his person, as will enable us to identify him. She cannot be seen until next Sunday night; this is

Tuesday. I would suggest that in the meantime, we remain perfectly quiet, and keep these matters secret even from Oliver himself."

Although Mr. Losberne received with many wry faces a proposal involving a delay of five whole days, he was fain to admit that no better course occurred to him just then; and as both Rose and Mrs. Maylie sided very strongly with Mr. Brownlow, that gentleman's proposition was carried unanimously.

"I should like," he said, "to call in the aid of my friend Grimwig. He is a strange creature, but a shrewd one, and might prove of material assistance to us; I should say that he was bred a lawyer, and quitted the Bar in disgust because he had only one brief and a motion of course, in twenty years, though whether that is recommendation or not, you must determine for yourselves."

"I have no objection to your calling in your friend if I may call in mine," said the doctor.

"We must put it to the vote," replied Mr. Brownlow, "who may he be?"

"That lady's son, and this young lady's—very old friend," said the doctor, motioning towards Mrs. Maylie, and concluding with an expressive glance at her niece.

Rose blushed deeply, but she did not make any audible objection to this motion (possibly she felt in a hopeless minority); and Harry Maylie and Mr. Grimwig were accordingly added to the committee.

"We stay in town, of course," said Mrs. Maylie, "while there remains the slightest prospect of prosecuting this inquiry with a chance of success. I will spare neither trouble nor expense in behalf of the object in which we are all so deeply interested, and I am content to remain here, if it be for twelve months, so long as you assure me that any hope remains."

"Good!" rejoined Mr. Brownlow. "And as I see on the faces about me, a disposition to inquire how it happened that I was not in the way to corroborate Oliver's tale, and had so suddenly left the kingdom, let me stipulate that I shall be asked no questions until such time as I may deem it expedient to forestall them by telling my own story. Believe me, I make this request with good reason, for I might otherwise excite hopes destined never to be realised, and only increase difficulties and disappointments already quite numerous enough. Come! Supper has been announced, and young Oliver, who is all alone in the next room, will have begun to think, by this time, that we have wearied of his company, and entered into some dark conspiracy to thrust him forth upon the world."

With these words, the old gentleman gave his hand to Mrs. Maylie, and escorted her into the supper-room. Mr. Losberne followed, leading Rose; and the council was, for the present, effectually broken up.

CHAPTER XLII

An Old Acquaintance of Oliver's, Exhibiting Decided Marks of Genius,
Becomes a Public Character in the Metropolis

Upon the night when Nancy, having lulled Mr. Sikes to sleep, hurried on her self-imposed mission to Rose Maylie, there advanced towards London, by the Great North Road, two persons, upon whom it is expedient that this history should bestow some attention.

They were a man and woman; or perhaps they would be better described as a male and female: for the former was one of those long-limbed, knock-kneed, shambling, bony people, to whom it is difficult to assign any precise age,—looking as they do, when they are yet boys, like undergrown men, and when they are almost men, like overgrown boys. The woman was young, but of a robust and hardy make, as she need have been to bear the weight of the heavy bundle which was strapped to her back. Her companion was not encumbered with much luggage, as there merely dangled from a stick which he carried over his shoulder, a small parcel wrapped in a common handkerchief, and apparently light enough. This circumstance, added to the length of his legs, which were of unusual extent, enabled him with much ease to keep some half-dozen paces in advance of his companion, to whom he occasionally turned with an impatient jerk of the head: as if reproaching her tardiness, and urging her to greater exertion.

Thus, they had toiled along the dusty road, taking little heed of any object within sight, save when they stepped aside to allow a wider passage for the mail-coaches which were whirling out of town, until they passed through Highgate archway; when the foremost traveller stopped and called impatiently to his companion,

"Come on, can't yer? What a lazybones yer are, Charlotte."

"It's a heavy load, I can tell you," said the female, coming up, almost breathless with fatigue.

"Heavy! What are yer talking about? What are yer made for?" rejoined the male traveller, changing his own little bundle as he spoke, to the other shoulder. "Oh, there yer are, resting again! Well, if yer ain't enough to tire anybody's patience out, I don't know what is!"

"Is it much farther?" asked the woman, resting herself against a bank, and looking up with the perspiration streaming from her face.

"Much farther! Yer as good as there," said the long-legged tramper, pointing out before him. "Look there! Those are the lights of London."

"They're a good two mile off, at least," said the woman despondingly.

"Never mind whether they're two mile off, or twenty," said Noah Claypole; for he it was; "but get up and come on, or I'll kick yer, and so I give yer notice."

As Noah's red nose grew redder with anger, and as he crossed the road while speaking, as if fully prepared to put his threat into execution, the woman rose without any further remark, and trudged onward by his side.

"Where do you mean to stop for the night, Noah?" she asked, after they had walked a few hundred yards.

"How should I know?" replied Noah, whose temper had been considerably impaired by walking.

"Near, I hope," said Charlotte.

"No, not near," replied Mr. Claypole. "There! Not near; so don't think it."

"Why not?"

"When I tell yer that I don't mean to do a thing, that's enough, without any why or because either," replied Mr. Claypole with dignity.

"Well, you needn't be so cross," said his companion.

"A pretty thing it would be, wouldn't it to go and stop at the very first public-house outside the town, so that Sowerberry, if he come up after us, might poke in his old nose, and have us taken back in a cart with handcuffs on," said Mr. Claypole in a jeering tone. "No! I shall go and lose myself among the narrowest streets I can find, and not stop till we come to the very out-of-the-wayest house I can set eyes on. "Cod, yer may thanks yer stars I've got a head; for if we hadn't gone, at first, the wrong road a purpose, and come back across country, yer'd have been locked up hard and fast a week ago, my lady. And serve yer right for being a fool."

"I know I ain't as cunning as you are," replied Charlotte; "but don't put all the blame on me, and say I should have been locked up. You would have been if I had been, any way."

"Yer took the money from the till, yer know yer did," said Mr. Claypole.

"I took it for you, Noah, dear," rejoined Charlotte.

"Did I keep it?" asked Mr. Claypole.

"No; you trusted in me, and let me carry it like a dear, and so you are," said the lady, chucking him under the chin, and drawing her arm through his.

This was indeed the case; but as it was not Mr. Claypole's habit to repose a blind and foolish confidence in anybody, it should be observed, in justice to that gentleman, that he had trusted Charlotte to this extent, in order that, if they were pursued, the money might be found on her: which would leave him an opportunity of asserting his innocence of any theft, and would greatly facilitate his chances of escape. Of course, he entered at this juncture, into no explanation of his motives, and they walked on very lovingly together.

In pursuance of this cautious plan, Mr. Claypole went on, without halting, until he arrived at the Angel at Islington, where he wisely judged, from the crowd of passengers and numbers of vehicles, that London began in earnest. Just pausing to observe which appeared the most crowded streets, and consequently the most to be avoided, he crossed into Saint John's Road, and was soon deep in the obscurity of the intricate and dirty ways, which, lying between Gray's Inn Lane and Smithfield, render that part of the town one of the lowest and worst that improvement has left in the midst of London.

Through these streets, Noah Claypole walked, dragging Charlotte after him; now stepping into the kennel to embrace at a glance the whole external character of some small public-house; now jogging on again, as some fancied appearance induced him to believe it too public for his purpose. At length, he stopped in front of one, more humble in appearance and more dirty than any he had yet seen; and, having crossed over and surveyed it from the opposite pavement, graciously announced his intention of putting up there, for the night.

"So give us the bundle," said Noah, unstrapping it from the woman's shoulders, and slinging it over his own; "and don't yer speak, except when yer spoke to. What's the name of the house—t-h-r—three what?"

"Cripples," said Charlotte.

"Three Cripples," repeated Noah, "and a very good sign too. Now, then! Keep close at my heels, and come along." With these injunctions, he pushed the rattling door with his shoulder, and entered the house, followed by his companion.

There was nobody in the bar but a young Jew, who, with his two elbows on the counter, was reading a dirty newspaper. He stared very hard at Noah, and Noah stared very hard at him.

If Noah had been attired in his charity-boy's dress, there might have been some reason for the Jew opening his eyes so wide; but as he had discarded the coat and badge, and wore a short smock-frock over his leathers, there seemed no particular reason for his appearance exciting so much attention in a public-house.

"Is this the Three Cripples?" asked Noah.

"That is the dabe of this 'ouse," replied the Jew.

"A gentleman we met on the road, coming up from the country, recommended us here," said Noah, nudging Charlotte, perhaps to call her attention to this most ingenious device for attracting respect, and perhaps to warn her to betray no surprise. "We want to sleep here to-night."

"I'b dot certaid you cad," said Barney, who was the attendant sprite; "but I'll idquire."

"Show us the tap, and give us a bit of cold meat and a drop of beer while yer inquiring, will yer?" said Noah.

Barney complied by ushering them into a small back-room, and setting the required viands before them; having done which, he informed the travellers that they could be lodged that night, and left the amiable couple to their refreshment.

Now, this back-room was immediately behind the bar, and some steps lower, so that any person connected with the house, undrawing a small curtain which concealed a single pane of glass fixed in the wall of the last-named apartment, about five feet from its flooring, could not only look down upon any guests in the back-room without any great hazard of being observed (the glass being in a dark angle of the wall, between which and a large upright beam the observer had to thrust himself), but could, by applying his ear to the partition, ascertain with tolerable distinctness, their subject of conversation. The landlord of the house had not withdrawn his eye from this place of espial for five minutes, and Barney had only just returned from making the communication above related, when Fagin, in the course of his evening's business, came into the bar to inquire after some of his young pupils.

"Hush!" said Barney: "stradegers id the next roob."

"Strangers!" repeated the old man in a whisper.

"Ah! Ad rub uds too," added Barney. "Frob the cuttry, but subthig in your way, or I'b bistaked."

Fagin appeared to receive this communication with great interest.

Mounting a stool, he cautiously applied his eye to the pane of glass, from which secret post he could see Mr. Claypole taking cold beef from the dish, and porter from the pot, and administering homeopathic doses of both to Charlotte, who sat patiently by, eating and drinking at his pleasure.

"Aha!" he whispered, looking round to Barney, "I like that fellow's looks. He'd be of use to us; he knows how to train the girl already. Don't make as much noise as a mouse, my dear, and let me hear 'em talk—let me hear 'em."

He again applied his eye to the glass, and turning his ear to the partition, listened attentively: with a subtle and eager look upon his face, that might have appertained to some old goblin.

"So I mean to be a gentleman," said Mr. Claypole, kicking out his legs, and continuing a conversation, the commencement of which Fagin had arrived too late to hear. "No more jolly old coffins, Charlotte, but a gentleman's life for me: and, if yer like, yer shall be a lady."

"I should like that well enough, dear," replied Charlotte; "but tills ain't to be emptied every day, and people to get clear off after it."

"Tills be blowed!" said Mr. Claypole; "there's more things besides tills to be emptied."

"What do you mean?" asked his companion.

"Pockets, women's ridicules, houses, mail-coaches, banks!" said Mr. Claypole, rising with the porter.

"But you can't do all that, dear," said Charlotte.

"I shall look out to get into company with them as can," replied Noah. "They'll be able to make us useful some way or another. Why, you yourself are worth fifty women; I never see such a precious sly and deceitful creetur as yer can be when I let yer."

"Lor, how nice it is to hear yer say so!" exclaimed Charlotte, imprinting a kiss upon his ugly face.

"There, that'll do: don't yer be too affectionate, in case I'm cross with yer," said Noah, disengaging himself with great gravity. "I should like to be the captain of some band, and have the whopping of 'em, and follering 'em about, unbeknown to themselves. That would suit me, if there was good profit; and if we could only get in with some gentleman of this sort, I say it would be cheap at that twenty-pound note you've got,—especially as we don't very well know how to get rid of it ourselves."

After expressing this opinion, Mr. Claypole looked into the porter-pot with an aspect of deep wisdom; and having well shaken its contents, nodded condescendingly to Charlotte, and took a draught, wherewith he appeared greatly refreshed. He was meditating another, when the sudden opening of the door, and the appearance of a stranger, interrupted him.

The stranger was Mr. Fagin. And very amiable he looked, and a very low bow he made, as he advanced, and setting himself down at the nearest table, ordered something to drink of the grinning Barney.

"A pleasant night, sir, but cool for the time of year," said Fagin, rubbing his hands. "From the country, I see, sir?"

"How do yer see that?" asked Noah Claypole.

"We have not so much dust as that in London," replied Fagin, pointing from Noah's shoes to those of his companion, and from them to the two bundles.

"Yer a sharp feller," said Noah. "Ha! ha! only hear that, Charlotte!"

"Why, one need be sharp in this town, my dear," replied the Jew, sinking his voice to a confidential whisper; "and that's the truth."

Fagin followed up this remark by striking the side of his nose with his right forefinger,—a gesture which Noah attempted to imitate, though not with complete success, in consequence of his own nose not being large enough for the purpose. However, Mr. Fagin seemed to interpret the endeavour as expressing a perfect coincidence with his opinion, and put about the liquor which Barney reappeared with, in a very friendly manner.

"Good stuff that," observed Mr. Claypole, smacking his lips.

"Dear!" said Fagin. "A man need be always emptying a till, or a pocket, or a woman's reticule, or a house, or a mail-coach, or a bank, if he drinks it regularly."

Mr. Claypole no sooner heard this extract from his own remarks than he fell back in his chair, and looked from the Jew to Charlotte with a countenance of ashy paleness and excessive terror.

"Don't mind me, my dear," said Fagin, drawing his chair closer. "Ha! ha! it was lucky it was only me that heard you by chance. It was very lucky it was only me."

"I didn't take it," stammered Noah, no longer stretching out his legs like an independent gentleman, but coiling them up as well as he could under his chair; "it was all her doing; yer've got it now, Charlotte, yer know yer have."

"No matter who's got it, or who did it, my dear," replied Fagin, glancing, nevertheless, with a hawk's eye at the girl and the two bundles. "I'm in that way myself, and I like you for it."

"In what way?" asked Mr. Claypole, a little recovering.

"In that way of business," rejoined Fagin; "and so are the people of the house. You've hit the right nail upon the head, and are as safe here as you could be. There is not a safer place in all this town than is the Cripples; that is, when I like to make it so. And I have taken a fancy to you and the young woman; so I've said the word, and you may make your minds easy."

Noah Claypole's mind might have been at ease after this assurance, but his body certainly was not; for he shuffled and writhed about, into various uncouth positions: eyeing his new friend meanwhile with mingled fear and suspicion.

"I'll tell you more," said Fagin, after he had reassured the girl, by dint of friendly nods and muttered encouragements. "I have got a friend that I think can gratify your darling wish, and put you in the right way, where you can take whatever department of the business you think will suit you best at first, and be taught all the others."

"Yer speak as if yer were in earnest," replied Noah.

"What advantage would it be to me to be anything else?" inquired Fagin, shrugging his shoulders. "Here! Let me have a word with you outside."

"There's no occasion to trouble ourselves to move," said Noah, getting his legs by gradual degrees abroad again. "She'll take the luggage upstairs the while. Charlotte, see to them bundles."

This mandate, which had been delivered with great majesty, was obeyed without the slightest demur; and Charlotte made the best of her way off with the packages while Noah held the door open and watched her out.

"She's kept tolerably well under, ain't she?" he asked as he resumed his seat: in the tone of a keeper who had tamed some wild animal.

"Quite perfect," rejoined Fagin, clapping him on the shoulder. "You're a genius, my dear."

"Why, I suppose if I wasn't, I shouldn't be here," replied Noah. "But, I say, she'll be back if yer lose time."

"Now, what do you think?" said Fagin. "If you was to like my friend, could you do better than join him?"

"Is he in a good way of business; that's where it is!" responded Noah, winking one of his little eyes.

"The top of the tree; employs a power of hands; has the very best society in the profession."

"Regular town-maders?" asked Mr. Claypole.

"Not a countryman among 'em; and I don't think he'd take you, even on my recommendation, if he didn't run rather short of assistants just now," replied Fagin.

"Should I have to hand over?" said Noah, slapping his breeches-pocket.

"It couldn't possibly be done without," replied Fagin, in a most decided manner.

"Twenty pound, though—it's a lot of money!"

"Not when it's in a note you can't get rid of," retorted Fagin. "Number and date taken, I suppose? Payment stopped at the Bank? Ah! It's not worth much to him. It'll have to go abroad, and he couldn't sell it for a great deal in the market."

"When could I see him?" asked Noah doubtfully.

"To-morrow morning."

"Where?"

"Here."

"Um!" said Noah. "What's the wages?"

"Live like a gentleman—board and lodging, pipes and spirits free—half of all you earn, and half of all the young woman earns," replied Mr. Fagin.

Whether Noah Claypole, whose rapacity was none of the least comprehensive, would have acceded even to these glowing terms, had he been a perfectly free agent, is very doubtful; but as he recollected that, in the event of his refusal, it was in the power of his new acquaintance to give him up to justice immediately (and more unlikely things had come to pass), he gradually relented, and said he thought that would suit him.

"But, yer see," observed Noah, "as she will be able to do a good deal, I should like to take something very light."

"A little fancy work?" suggested Fagin.

"Ah! something of that sort," replied Noah. "What do you think would suit me now? Something not too trying for the strength, and not very dangerous, you know. That's the sort of thing!"

"I heard you talk of something in the spy way upon the others, my dear," said Fagin. "My friend wants somebody who would do that well, very much."

"Why, I did mention that, and I shouldn't mind turning my hand to it sometimes," rejoined Mr. Claypole slowly; "but it wouldn't pay by itself, you know."

"That's true!" observed the Jew, ruminating or pretending to ruminate. "No, it might not."

"What do you think, then?" asked Noah, anxiously regarding him. "Something in the sneaking way, where it was pretty sure work, and not much more risk than being at home."

"What do you think of the old ladies?" asked Fagin. "There's a good deal of money made in snatching their bags and parcels, and running round the corner."

"Don't they holler out a good deal, and scratch sometimes?" asked Noah, shaking his head. "I don't think that would answer my purpose. Ain't there any other line open?"

"Stop!" said Fagin, laying his hand on Noah's knee. "The kinchin lay."

"What's that?" demanded Mr. Claypole.

"The kinchins, my dear," said Fagin, "is the young children that's sent on errands by their mothers, with sixpences and shillings; and the lay is just to take their money away—they've always got it ready in their hands,—then knock 'em into the kennel, and walk off very slow, as if there were nothing else the matter but a child fallen down and hurt itself. Ha! ha! ha!"

"Ha! ha!" roared Mr. Claypole, kicking up his legs in an ecstasy. "Lord, that's the very thing!"

"To be sure it is," replied Fagin; "and you can have a few good beats chalked out in Camden Town, and Battle Bridge, and neighborhoods like that, where they're always going errands; and you can upset as many kinchins as you want, any hour in the day. Ha! ha! ha!"

With this, Fagin poked Mr. Claypole in the side, and they joined in a burst of laughter both long and loud.

"Well, that's all right!" said Noah, when he had recovered himself, and Charlotte had returned. "What time to-morrow shall we say?"

"Will ten do?" asked Fagin, adding, as Mr. Claypole nodded assent, "What name shall I tell my good friend."

"Mr. Bolter," replied Noah, who had prepared himself for such emergency. "Mr. Morris Bolter. This is Mrs. Bolter."

"Mrs. Bolter's humble servant," said Fagin, bowing with grotesque politeness. "I hope I shall know her better very shortly."

"Do you hear the gentleman, Charlotte?" thundered Mr. Claypole.

"Yes, Noah, dear!" replied Mrs. Bolter, extending her hand.

"She calls me Noah, as a sort of fond way of talking," said Mr. Morris Bolter, late Claypole, turning to Fagin. "You understand?"

"Oh yes, I understand—perfectly," replied Fagin, telling the truth for once. "Good-night! Good-night!"

With many adieus and good wishes, Mr. Fagin went his way. Noah Claypole, bespeaking his good lady's attention, proceeded to enlighten her relative to the arrangement he had made, with all that haughtiness and air of superiority, becoming, not only a member of the sterner sex, but a gentleman who appreciated the dignity of a special appointment on the kinchin lay, in London and its vicinity.

CHAPTER XLIII

Wherein Is Shown How the Artful Dodger Got into Trouble

"And so it was you that was your own friend, was it?" asked Mr. Claypole, otherwise Bolter, when, by virtue of the compact entered into between them, he had removed next day to Fagin's house. "'Cod, I thought as much last night!"

"Every man's his own friend, my dear," replied Fagin, with his most insinuating grin. "He hasn't as good a one as himself anywhere."

"Except sometimes," replied Morris Bolter, assuming the air of a man of the world. "Some people are nobody's enemies but their own, yer know."

"Don't believe that," said Fagin. "When a man's his own enemy, it's only because he's too much his own friend; not because he's careful for everybody but himself. Pooh! pooh! There ain't such a thing in nature."

"There oughn't to be, if there is," replied Mr. Bolter.

"That stands to reason. Some conjurers say that number three is the magic number, and some say number seven. It's neither, my friend, neither. It's number one."

"Ha! ha!" cried Mr. Bolter. "Number one for ever."

"In a little community like ours, my dear," said Fagin, who felt it necessary to qualify this position, "we have a general number one, without considering me too as the same, and all the other young people."

"Oh, the devil!" exclaimed Mr. Bolter.

"You see," pursued Fagin, affecting to disregard this interruption, "we are so mixed up together, and identified in our interests, that it must be so. For instance, it's your object to take care of number one—meaning yourself."

"Certainly," replied Mr. Bolter. "Yer about right there."

"Well! You can't take care of yourself, number one, without taking care of me, number one."

"Number two, you mean," said Mr. Bolter, who was largely endowed with the quality of selfishness.

"No, I don't!" retorted Fagin. "I'm of the same importance to you, as you are to yourself."

"I say," interrupted Mr. Bolter, "yer a very nice man, and I'm very fond of yer; but we ain't quite so thick together, as all that comes to."

"Only think," said Fagin, shrugging his shoulders, and stretching out his hands; "only consider. You've done what's a very pretty thing, and what I love you for doing; but what at the same time would put the cravat round your throat, that's so very easily tied and so very difficult to unloose—in plain English, the halter!"

Mr. Bolter put his hand to his neckerchief, as if he felt it inconveniently tight; and murmured an assent, qualified in tone but not in substance.

"The gallows," continued Fagin, "the gallows, my dear, is an ugly finger-post, which points out a very short and sharp turning that has stopped many a bold fellow's career on the broad highway. To keep in the easy road, and keep it at a distance, is object number one with you."

"Of course it is," replied Mr. Bolter. "What do yer talk about such things for?"

"Only to show you my meaning clearly," said the Jew, raising his eyebrows. "To be able to do that, you depend upon me. To keep my little business all snug, I depend upon you. The first is your number one, the second my number one. The more you value your number one, the more careful you must be of mine; so we come at last to what I told you at first—that a regard for number one holds us all together, and must do so, unless we would all go to pieces in company."

"That's true," rejoined Mr. Bolter, thoughtfully. "Oh! yer a cunning old codger!"

Mr. Fagin saw, with delight, that this tribute to his powers was no mere compliment, but that he had really impressed his recruit with a sense of his wily genius, which it was most important that he should entertain in the outset of their acquaintance. To strengthen an impression so desirable and useful, he followed up the blow by acquainting him, in some detail, with the magnitude and extent of his operations; blending truth and fiction together, as best served his purpose; and bringing both to bear, with so much art, that Mr. Bolter's respect visibly increased, and became tempered, at the same time, with a degree of wholesome fear, which it was highly desirable to awaken.

"It's this mutual trust we have in each other that consoles me under heavy losses," said Fagin. "My best hand was taken from me, yesterday morning."

"You don't mean to say he died?" cried Mr. Bolter.

"No, no," replied Fagin, "not so bad as that. Not quite so bad."

"What, I suppose he was—"

"Wanted," interposed Fagin. "Yes, he was wanted."

"Very particular?" inquired Mr. Bolter.

"No," replied Fagin, "not very. He was charged with attempting to pick a pocket, and they found a silver snuff-box on him,—his own, my dear, his own, for he took snuff himself, and was very fond of it. They remanded him till to-day, for they thought they knew the owner. Ah! he was worth fifty boxes, and I'd give the price of as many to have him back. You should have known the Dodger, my dear; you should have known the Dodger."

"Well, but I shall know him, I hope; don't yer think so?" said Mr. Bolter.

"I'm doubtful about it," replied Fagin, with a sigh. "If they don't get any fresh evidence, it'll only be a summary conviction, and we shall have him back again after six weeks or so; but, if they do, it's a case of lagging. They know what a clever lad he is; he'll be a lifer. They'll make the Artful nothing less than a lifer."

"What do you mean by lagging and a lifer?" demanded Mr. Bolter. "What's the good of talking in that way to me; why don't yer speak so as I can understand yer?"

Fagin was about to translate these mysterious expressions into the vulgar tongue; and, being interpreted, Mr. Bolter would have been informed that they represented that combination of words, "transportation for life," when the dialogue was cut short by the entry of Master Bates, with his hands in his breeches-pockets, and his face twisted into a look of semi-comical woe.

"It's all up, Fagin," said Charley, when he and his new companion had been made known to each other.

"What do you mean?"

"They've found the gentleman as owns the box; two or three more's a coming to "dentify him; and the Artful's booked for a passage out," replied Master Bates. "I must have a full suit of mourning, Fagin, and a hatband, to wisit him in, afore he sets out upon his travels. To think of Jack Dawkins—lummy Jack—the Dodger—the Artful Dodger—going abroad for a common twopenny-halfpenny sneeze-box! I never thought he'd a done it under a gold watch, chain, and seals, at the lowest. Oh, why didn't he rob some rich old gentleman of all his walables, and go out as a gentleman, and not like a common prig, without no honour nor glory!"

With this expression of feeling for his unfortunate friend, Master Bates sat himself on the nearest chair with an aspect of chagrin and despondency.

"What do you talk about his having neither honour nor glory for!" exclaimed Fagin, darting an angry look at his pupil. "Wasn't he always the top-sawyer among you all! Is there one of you that could touch him or come near him on any scent! Eh?"

"Not one," replied Master Bates, in a voice rendered husky by regret; "not one."

"Then what do you talk of?" replied Fagin angrily; "what are you blubbering for?"

"'Cause it isn't on the rec-ord, is it?" said Charley, chafed into perfect defiance of his venerable friend by the current of his regrets; "'cause it can't come out in the 'dictment; 'cause nobody will never know half of what he was. How will he stand in the Newgate Calendar? P'raps not be there at all. Oh, my eye, my eye, wot a blow it is!"

"Ha! ha!" cried Fagin, extending his right hand, and turning to Mr. Bolter in a fit of chuckling which shook him as though he had the palsy; "see what a pride they take in their profession, my dear. Ain't it beautiful?"

Mr. Bolter nodded assent, and Fagin, after contemplating the grief of Charley Bates for some seconds with evident satisfaction, stepped up to that young gentleman and patted him on the shoulder.

"Never mind, Charley," said Fagin soothingly; "it'll come out, it'll be sure to come out. They'll all know what a clever fellow he was; he'll show it himself, and not disgrace his old pals and teachers. Think how young he is too! What a distinction, Charley, to be lagged at his time of life!"

"Well, it is a honour that is!" said Charley, a little consoled.

"He shall have all he wants," continued the Jew. "He shall be kept in the Stone Jug, Charley, like a gentleman. Like a gentleman! With his beer every day, and money in his pocket to pitch and toss with, if he can't spend it."

"No, shall he though?" cried Charley Bates.

"Ay, that he shall," replied Fagin, "and we'll have a big-wig, Charley: one that's got the greatest gift of the gab: to carry on his defence; and he shall make a speech for himself too, if he likes; and we'll read it all in the papers—'Artful Dodger—shrieks of laughter—here the court was convulsed'—eh, Charley, eh?"

"Ha! ha!" laughed Master Bates, "what a lark that would be, wouldn't it, Fagin? I say, how the Artful would bother 'em wouldn't he?"

"Would!" cried Fagin. "He shall—he will!"

"Ah, to be sure, so he will," repeated Charley, rubbing his hands.

"I think I see him now," cried the Jew, bending his eyes upon his pupil.

"So do I," cried Charley Bates. "Ha! ha! ha! so do I. I see it all afore me, upon my soul I do, Fagin. What a game! What a regular game! All the big-wigs trying to look solemn, and Jack Dawkins addressing of 'em as intimate and comfortable as if he was the judge's own son making a speech arter dinner—ha! ha! ha!"

In fact, Mr. Fagin had so well humoured his young friend's eccentric disposition, that Master Bates, who had at first been disposed to consider the imprisoned Dodger rather in the light of a victim, now looked upon him as the chief actor in a scene of most uncommon and exquisite humour, and felt quite impatient for the arrival of the time when his old companion should have so favourable an opportunity of displaying his abilities.

"We must know how he gets on to-day, by some handy means or other," said Fagin. "Let me think."

"Shall I go?" asked Charley.

"Not for the world," replied Fagin. "Are you mad, my dear, stark mad, that you'd walk into the very place where—No, Charley, no. One is enough to lose at a time."

"You don't mean to go yourself, I suppose?" said Charley with a humorous leer.

"That wouldn't quite fit," replied Fagin shaking his head.

"Then why don't you send this new cove?" asked Master Bates, laying his hand on Noah's arm. "Nobody knows him."

"Why, if he didn't mind—" observed Fagin.

"Mind!" interposed Charley. "What should he have to mind?"

"Really nothing, my dear," said Fagin, turning to Mr. Bolter, "really nothing."

"Oh, I dare say about that, yer know," observed Noah, backing towards the door, and shaking his head with a kind of sober alarm. "No, no—none of that. It's not in my department, that ain't."

"Wot department has he got, Fagin?" inquired Master Bates, surveying Noah's lank form with much disgust. "The cutting away when there's anything wrong, and the eating all the wittles when there's everything right; is that his branch?"

"Never mind," retorted Mr. Bolter; "and don't yer take liberties with yer superiors, little boy, or yer'll find yerself in the wrong shop."

Master Bates laughed so vehemently at this magnificent threat, that it was some time before Fagin could interpose, and represent to Mr. Bolter that he incurred no possible danger in visiting the police-office; that, inasmuch as no account of the little affair in which he had engaged, nor any description of his person, had yet been forwarded to the metropolis, it was very probable that he was not even suspected of having resorted to it for shelter; and that, if he were properly disguised, it would be as safe a spot for him to visit as any in London, inasmuch as it would be, of all places, the very last, to which he could be supposed likely to resort of his own free will.

Persuaded, in part, by these representations, but overborne in a much greater degree by his fear of Fagin, Mr. Bolter at length consented, with a very bad grace, to undertake the expedition. By Fagin's directions, he immediately substituted for his own attire, a waggoner's frock, velveteen breeches, and leather leggings: all of which articles the Jew had at hand. He was likewise furnished with a felt hat well garnished with turnpike tickets; and a carter's whip. Thus equipped, he was to saunter into the office, as some country fellow from Covent Garden market might be supposed to do for the gratification of his curiosity; and as he was as awkward, ungainly, and raw-boned a fellow as need be, Mr. Fagin had no fear but that he would look the part to perfection.

These arrangements completed, he was informed of the necessary signs and tokens by which to recognise the Artful Dodger, and was conveyed by Master Bates through dark and winding ways to within a very short distance of Bow Street. Having described the precise situation of the office, and accompanied it with copious directions how he was to walk straight up the passage, and when he got into the side, and pull off his hat as he went into the room, Charley Bates bade him hurry on alone, and promised to bide his return on the spot of their parting.

Noah Claypole, or Morris Bolter as the reader pleases, punctually followed the directions he had received, which—Master Bates being pretty well acquainted with the locality—were so exact that he was enabled to gain the magisterial presence without asking any question, or meeting with any interruption by the way.

He found himself jostled among a crowd of people, chiefly women, who were huddled together in a dirty frowsy room, at the upper end of which was a raised platform railed off from the rest, with a dock for the prisoners on the left hand against the wall, a box for the witnesses in the middle, and a desk for the magistrates on the right; the awful locality last named, being screened off by a partition which concealed the bench from the common gaze, and left the vulgar to imagine (if they could) the full majesty of justice.

There were only a couple of women in the dock, who were nodding to their admiring friends, while the clerk read some depositions to a couple of policemen and a man in plain clothes who leant over the table. A jailer stood reclining against the dock-rail, tapping his nose listlessly with a large key, except when he repressed an undue tendency to conversation among the idlers, by proclaiming silence; or looked sternly up to bid some woman "Take that baby out," when the gravity of justice was disturbed by feeble cries, half-smothered in the mother's shawl, from some meagre infant. The room smelt close and unwholesome; the walls were dirt-discoloured; and the ceiling blackened. There was an old smoky bust over the mantel-shelf, and a dusty clock above the dock—the only thing present, that seemed to go on as it ought; for depravity, or poverty, or an habitual acquaintance with both, had left a taint on all the animate matter, hardly less unpleasant than the thick greasy scum on every inanimate object that frowned upon it.

Noah looked eagerly about him for the Dodger; but although there were several women who would have done very well for that distinguished character's mother or sister, and more than one man who might be supposed to bear a strong resemblance to his father, nobody at all answering the description given him of Mr. Dawkins was to be seen. He waited in a state of much suspense and uncertainty until the women, being committed for trial, went flaunting out; and then was quickly relieved by the appearance of another prisoner who he felt at once could be no other than the object of his visit.

It was indeed Mr. Dawkins, who, shuffling into the office with the big coat sleeves tucked up as usual, his left hand in his pocket, and his hat in his right hand, preceded the jailer, with a rolling gait altogether indescribable, and, taking his place in the dock, requested in an audible voice to know what he was placed in that 'ere disgraceful sitivation for.

"Hold your tongue, will you?" said the jailer.

"I'm an Englishman, ain't I?" rejoined the Dodger. "Where are my priwileges?"

"You'll get your privileges soon enough," retorted the jailer, "and pepper with 'em."

"We'll see wot the Secretary of State for the Home Affairs has got to say to the beaks, if I don't," replied Mr. Dawkins. "Now then! Wot is this here business? I shall thank the madg'strates to dispose of this here little affair, and not to keep me while they read the paper, for I've got an appointment with a genelman in the City, and as I am a man of my word and wery punctual in business matters, he'll go away if I ain't there to my time, and then pr'aps ther won't be an action for damage against them as kep me away. Oh no, certainly not!"

At this point, the Dodger, with a show of being very particular with a view to proceedings to be had thereafter, desired the jailer to communicate "the names of them two files as was on the bench." Which so tickled the spectators, that they laughed almost as heartily as Master Bates could have done if he had heard the request.

"Silence there!" cried the jailer.

"What is this?" inquired one of the magistrates.

"A pick-pocketing case, your worship."

"Has the boy ever been here before?"

"He ought to have been, a many times," replied the jailer. "He has been pretty well everywhere else. I know him well, your worship."

"Oh! you know me, do you?" cried the Artful, making a note of the statement. "Wery good. That's a case of deformation of character, any way."

Here there was another laugh, and another cry of silence.

"Now then, where are the witnesses?" said the clerk.

"Ah! that's right," added the Dodger. "Where are they? I should like to see 'em."

This wish was immediately gratified, for a policeman stepped forward who had seen the prisoner attempt the pocket of an unknown gentleman in a crowd, and indeed take a handkerchief therefrom, which, being a very old one, he deliberately put back again, after trying it on his own countenance. For this reason, he took the Dodger into custody as soon as he could get near him, and the said Dodger, being searched, had upon his person a silver snuff-box, with the owner's name engraved upon the lid. This gentleman had been discovered on reference to the Court Guide, and being then and there present, swore that the snuff-box was his, and that he had missed it on the previous day, the moment he had disengaged himself from the crowd before referred to. He had also remarked a young gentleman in the throng, particularly active in making his way about, and that young gentleman was the prisoner before him.

"Have you anything to ask this witness, boy?" said the magistrate.

"I wouldn't abase myself by descending to hold no conversation with him," replied the Dodger.

"Have you anything to say at all?"

"Do you hear his worship ask if you've anything to say?" inquired the jailer, nudging the silent Dodger with his elbow.

"I beg your pardon," said the Dodger, looking up with an air of abstraction. "Did you redress yourself to me, my man?"

"I never see such an out-and-out young wagabond, your worship," observed the officer with a grin. "Do you mean to say anything, you young shaver?"

"No," replied the Dodger, "not here, for this ain't the shop for justice: besides which, my attorney is a-breakfasting this morning with the Wice President of the House of Commons; but I shall have something to say elsewhere, and so will he, and so will a wery numerous and 'spectable circle of acquaintance as'll make them beaks wish they'd never been born, or that they'd got their footmen to hang 'em up to their own hat-pegs, afore they let 'em come out this morning to try it on upon me. I'll—"

"There! He's fully committed!" interposed the clerk. "Take him away."

"Come on," said the jailer.

"Oh ah! I'll come on," replied the Dodger, brushing his hat with the palm of his hand. "Ah! (to the Bench) it's no use your looking frightened; I won't show you no mercy, not a ha'porth of it. You'll pay for this, my fine fellers. I wouldn't be you for something! I wouldn't go free, now, if you was to fall down on your knees and ask me. Here, carry me off to prison! Take me away!"

With these last words, the Dodger suffered himself to be led off by the collar; threatening, till he got into the yard, to make a parliamentary business of it; and then grinning in the officer's face, with great glee and self-approval.

Having seen him locked up by himself in a little cell, Noah made the best of his way back to where he had left Master Bates. After waiting here some time, he was joined by that young gentleman, who had prudently abstained from showing himself until he had looked carefully abroad from a snug retreat, and ascertained that his new friend had not been followed by any impertinent person.

The two hastened back together, to bear to Mr. Fagin the animating news that the Dodger was doing full justice to his bringing-up, and establishing for himself a glorious reputation.

CHAPTER XLIV

The Time Arrives for Nancy to Redeem Her Pledge to Rose Maylie. She Fails

Adept as she was, in all the arts of cunning and dissimulation, the girl Nancy could not wholly conceal the effect which the knowledge of the step she had taken, wrought upon her mind. She remembered that both the crafty Jew and the brutal Sikes had confided to her schemes, which had been hidden from all others: in the full confidence that she was trustworthy and beyond the reach of their suspicion. Vile as those schemes were, desperate as were their originators, and bitter as were her feelings towards Fagin, who had led her, step by step, deeper and deeper down into an abyss of crime and misery, whence was no escape; still, there were times when, even towards him, she felt some relenting, lest her disclosure should bring him within the iron grasp he had so long eluded, and he should fall at last—richly as he merited such a fate—by her hand.

But, these were the mere wanderings of a mind unable wholly to detach itself from old companions and associations, though enabled to fix itself steadily on one object, and resolved not to be turned aside by any consideration. Her fears for Sikes would have been more powerful inducements to recoil while there was yet time; but she had stipulated that her secret should be rigidly kept, she had dropped no clue which could lead to his discovery, she had refused, even for his sake, a refuge from all the guilt and wretchedness that encompasses her—and what more could she do! She was resolved.

Though all her mental struggles terminated in this conclusion, they forced themselves upon her, again and again, and left their traces too. She grew pale and thin, even within a few days. At times, she took no heed of what was passing before her, or no part in conversations where once, she would have been the loudest. At other times, she laughed without merriment, and was noisy without a moment afterwards—she sat silent and dejected, brooding with her head upon her hands, while the very effort by which she roused herself, told, more forcibly than even these indications, that she was ill at ease, and that her thoughts were occupied with matters very different and distant from those in the course of discussion by her companions.

It was Sunday night, and the bell of the nearest church struck the hour. Sikes and the Jew were talking, but they paused to listen. The girl looked up from the low seat on which she crouched, and listened too. Eleven.

"An hour this side of midnight," said Sikes, raising the blind to look out and returning to his seat. "Dark and heavy it is too. A good night for business this."

"Ah!" replied Fagin. "What a pity, Bill, my dear, that there's none quite ready to be done."

"You're right for once," replied Sikes gruffly. "It is a pity, for I'm in the humour too."

Fagin sighed, and shook his head despondingly.

"We must make up for lost time when we've got things into a good train. That's all I know," said Sikes.

"That's the way to talk, my dear," replied Fagin, venturing to pat him on the shoulder. "It does me good to hear you."

"Does you good, does it!" cried Sikes. "Well, so be it."

"Ha! ha! ha!" laughed Fagin, as if he were relieved by even this concession. "You're like yourself to-night, Bill. Quite like yourself."

"I don't feel like myself when you lay that withered old claw on my shoulder, so take it away," said Sikes, casting off the Jew's hand.

"It make you nervous, Bill,—reminds you of being nabbed, does it?" said Fagin, determined not to be offended.

"Reminds me of being nabbed by the devil," returned Sikes. "There never was another man with such a face as yours, unless it was your father, and I suppose he is singeing his grizzled red beard by this time, unless you came straight from the old 'un without any father at all betwixt you; which I shouldn't wonder at, a bit."

Fagin offered no reply to this compliment: but, pulling Sikes by the sleeve, pointed his finger towards Nancy, who had taken advantage of the foregoing conversation to put on her bonnet, and was now leaving the room.

"Hallo!" cried Sikes. "Nance. Where's the gal going to at this time of night?"

"Not far."

"What answer's that?" retorted Sikes. "Do you hear me?"

"I don't know where," replied the girl.

"Then I do," said Sikes, more in the spirit of obstinacy than because he had any real objection to the girl going where she listed. "Nowhere. Sit down."

"I'm not well. I told you that before," rejoined the girl. "I want a breath of air."

"Put your head out of the winder," replied Sikes.

"There's not enough there," said the girl. "I want it in the street."

"Then you won't have it," replied Sikes. With which assurance he rose, locked the door, took the key out, and pulling her bonnet from her head, flung it up to the top of an old press. "There," said the robber. "Now stop quietly where you are, will you?"

"It's not such a matter as a bonnet would keep me," said the girl turning very pale. "What do you mean, Bill? Do you know what you're doing?"

"Know what I'm—Oh!" cried Sikes, turning to Fagin, "she's out of her senses, you know, or she daren't talk to me in that way."

"You'll drive me on the something desperate," muttered the girl placing both hands upon her breast, as though to keep down by force some violent outbreak. "Let me go, will you,—this minute—this instant."

"No!" said Sikes.

"Tell him to let me go, Fagin. He had better. It'll be better for him. Do you hear me?" cried Nancy stamping her foot upon the ground.

"Hear you!" repeated Sikes turning round in his chair to confront her. "Aye! And if I hear you for half a minute longer, the dog shall have such a grip on your throat as'll tear some of that screaming voice out. Wot has come over you, you jade! Wot is it?"

"Let me go," said the girl with great earnestness; then sitting herself down on the floor, before the door, she said, "Bill, let me go; you don't know what you are doing. You don't, indeed. For only one hour—do—do!"

"Cut my limbs off one by one!" cried Sikes, seizing her roughly by the arm, "If I don't think the gal's stark raving mad. Get up."

"Not till you let me go—not till you let me go—Never—never!" screamed the girl. Sikes looked on, for a minute, watching his opportunity, and suddenly pinioning her hands dragged her, struggling and wrestling with him by the way, into a small room adjoining, where he sat himself on a bench, and thrusting her into a chair, held her down by force. She struggled and implored by turns until twelve o'clock had struck, and then, wearied and exhausted, ceased to contest the point any further. With a caution, backed by many oaths, to make no more efforts to go out that night, Sikes left her to recover at leisure and rejoined Fagin.

"Whew!" said the housebreaker wiping the perspiration from his face. "Wot a precious strange gal that is!"

"You may say that, Bill," replied Fagin thoughtfully. "You may say that."

"Wot did she take it into her head to go out to-night for, do you think?" asked Sikes. "Come; you should know her better than me. Wot does it mean?"

"Obstinacy; woman's obstinacy, I suppose, my dear."

"Well, I suppose it is," growled Sikes. "I thought I had tamed her, but she's as bad as ever."

"Worse," said Fagin thoughtfully. "I never knew her like this, for such a little cause."

"Nor I," said Sikes. "I think she's got a touch of that fever in her blood yet, and it won't come out—eh?"

"Like enough."

"I'll let her a little blood, without troubling the doctor, if she's took that way again," said Sikes.

Fagin nodded an expressive approval of this mode of treatment.

"She was hanging about me all day, and night too, when I was stretched on my back; and you, like a blackhearted wolf as you are, kept yourself aloof," said Sikes. "We was poor too, all the time, and I think, one way or other, it's worried and fretted her; and that being shut up here so long has made her restless—eh?"

"That's it, my dear," replied the Jew in a whisper. "Hush!"

As he uttered these words, the girl herself appeared and resumed her former seat. Her eyes were swollen and red; she rocked herself to and fro; tossed her head; and, after a little time, burst out laughing.

"Why, now she's on the other tack!" exclaimed Sikes, turning a look of excessive surprise on his companion.

Fagin nodded to him to take no further notice just then; and, in a few minutes, the girl subsided into her accustomed demeanour. Whispering Sikes that there was no fear of her relapsing, Fagin took up his hat and bade him good-night. He paused when he reached the room-door, and looking round, asked if somebody would light him down the dark stairs.

"Light him down," said Sikes, who was filling his pipe. "It's a pity he should break his neck himself, and disappoint the sight-seers. Show him a light."

Nancy followed the old man downstairs, with a candle. When they reached the passage, he laid his finger on his lip, and drawing close to the girl, said, in a whisper.

"What is it, Nancy, dear?"

"What do you mean?" replied the girl, in the same tone.

"The reason of all this," replied Fagin. "If he"—he pointed with his skinny fore-finger up the stairs—"is so hard with you (he's a brute, Nance, a brute-beast), why don't you—"

"Well?" said the girl, as Fagin paused, with his mouth almost touching her ear, and his eyes looking into hers.

"No matter just now. We'll talk of this again. You have a friend in me, Nance; a staunch friend. I have the means at hand, quiet and close. If you want revenge on those that treat you like a dog—like a dog! worse than his dog, for he humours him sometimes—come to me. I say, come to me. He is the mere hound of a day, but you know me of old, Nance."

"I know you well," replied the girl, without manifesting the least emotion. "Good-night."

She shrank back, as Fagin offered to lay his hand on hers, but said good-night again, in a steady voice, and, answering his parting look with a nod of intelligence, closed the door between them.

Fagin walked towards his home, intent upon the thoughts that were working within his brain. He had conceived the idea—not from what had just passed though that had tended to confirm him, but slowly and by degrees—that Nancy, wearied of the housebreaker's brutality, had conceived an attachment for some new friend. Her altered manner, her repeated absences from home alone, her comparative indifference to the interests of the gang for which she had once been so zealous, and, added to these, her desperate impatience to leave home that night at a particular hour, all favoured the supposition, and rendered it, to him at least, almost matter of certainty. The object of this new liking was not among his myrmidons. He would be a valuable acquisition with such an assistant as Nancy, and must (thus Fagin argued) be secured without delay.

There was another, and a darker object, to be gained. Sikes knew too much, and his ruffian taunts had not galled Fagin the less, because the wounds were hidden. The girl must know, well, that if she shook him off, she could never be safe from his fury, and that it would be surely wreaked—to the maiming of limbs, or perhaps the loss of life—on the object of her more recent fancy.

"With a little persuasion," thought Fagin, "what more likely than that she would consent to poison him? Women have done such things, and worse, to secure the same object before now. There would be the dangerous villain: the man I hate: gone; another secured in his place; and my influence over the girl, with a knowledge of this crime to back it, unlimited."

These things passed through the mind of Fagin, during the short time he sat alone, in the housebreaker's room; and with them uppermost in his thoughts, he had taken the opportunity afterwards afforded him, of sounding the girl in the broken hints he threw out at parting. There was no expression of surprise, no assumption of an inability to understand his meaning. The girl clearly comprehended it. Her glance at parting showed that.

But perhaps she would recoil from a plot to take the life of Sikes, and that was one of the chief ends to be attained. "How," thought Fagin, as he crept homeward, "can I increase my influence with her? What new power can I acquire?"

Such brains are fertile in expedients. If, without extracting a confession from herself, he laid a watch, discovered the object of her altered regard, and threatened to reveal the whole history to Sikes (of whom she stood in no common fear) unless she entered into his designs, could he not secure her compliance?

"I can," said Fagin, almost aloud. "She durst not refuse me then. Not for her life, not for her life! I have it all. The means are ready, and shall be set to work. I shall have you yet!"

He cast back a dark look, and a threatening motion of the hand, towards the spot where he had left the bolder villain; and went on his way: busying his bony hands in the folds of his tattered garment, which he wrenched tightly in his grasp, as though there were a hated enemy crushed with every motion of his fingers.

CHAPTER XLV

Noah Claypole Is Employed by Fagin on a Secret Mission

The old man was up, betimes, next morning, and waited impatiently for the appearance of his new associate, who after a delay that seemed interminable, at length presented himself, and commenced a voracious assault on the breakfast.

"Bolter," said Fagin, drawing up a chair and seating himself opposite Morris Bolter.

"Well, here I am," returned Noah. "What's the matter? Don't yer ask me to do anything till I have done eating. That's a great fault in this place. Yer never get time enough over yer meals."

"You can talk as you eat, can't you?" said Fagin, cursing his dear young friend's greediness from the very bottom of his heart.

"Oh yes, I can talk. I get on better when I talk," said Noah, cutting a monstrous slice of bread. "Where's Charlotte?"

"Out," said Fagin. "I sent her out this morning with the other young woman, because I wanted us to be alone."

"Oh!" said Noah. "I wish yer'd ordered her to make some buttered toast first. Well. Talk away. Yer won't interrupt me."

There seemed, indeed, no great fear of anything interrupting him, as he had evidently sat down with a determination to do a great deal of business.

"You did well yesterday, my dear," said Fagin. "Beautiful! Six shillings and ninepence halfpenny on the very first day! The kinchin lay will be a fortune to you."

"Don't you forget to add three pint-pots and a milk-can," said Mr. Bolter.

"No, no, my dear. The pint-pots were great strokes of genius: but the milk-can was a perfect masterpiece."

"Pretty well, I think, for a beginner," remarked Mr. Bolter complacently. "The pots I took off airy railings, and the milk-can was standing by itself outside a public-house. I thought it might get rusty with the rain, or catch cold, yer know. Eh? Ha! ha! ha!"

Fagin affected to laugh very heartily; and Mr. Bolter having had his laugh out, took a series of large bites, which finished his first hunk of bread and butter, and assisted himself to a second.

"I want you, Bolter," said Fagin, leaning over the table, "to do a piece of work for me, my dear, that needs great care and caution."

"I say," rejoined Bolter, "don't yer go shoving me into danger, or sending me any more o' yer police-offices. That don't suit me, that don't; and so I tell yer."

"That's not the smallest danger in it—not the very smallest," said the Jew; "it's only to dodge a woman."

"An old woman?" demanded Mr. Bolter.

"A young one," replied Fagin.

"I can do that pretty well, I know," said Bolter. "I was a regular cunning sneak when I was at school. What am I to dodge her for? Not to—"

"Not to do anything, but to tell me where she goes, who she sees, and, if possible, what she says; to remember the street, if it is a street, or the house, if it is a house; and to bring me back all the information you can."

"What'll yer give me?" asked Noah, setting down his cup, and looking his employer, eagerly, in the face.

"If you do it well, a pound, my dear. One pound," said Fagin, wishing to interest him in the scent as much as possible. "And that's what I never gave yet, for any job of work where there wasn't valuable consideration to be gained."

"Who is she?" inquired Noah.

"One of us."

"Oh Lor!" cried Noah, curling up his nose. "Yer doubtful of her, are yer?"

"She has found out some new friends, my dear, and I must know who they are," replied Fagin.

"I see," said Noah. "Just to have the pleasure of knowing them, if they're respectable people, eh? Ha! ha! ha! I'm your man."

"I knew you would be," cried Fagin, elated by the success of his proposal.

"Of course, of course," replied Noah. "Where is she? Where am I to wait for her? Where am I to go?"

"All that, my dear, you shall hear from me. I'll point her out at the proper time," said Fagin. "You keep ready, and leave the rest to me."

That night, and the next, and the next again, the spy sat booted and equipped in his carter's dress: ready to turn out at a word from Fagin. Six nights passed—six long weary nights—and on each, Fagin came home with a disappointed face, and briefly intimated that it was not yet time. On the seventh, he returned earlier, and with an exultation he could not conceal. It was Sunday.

"She goes abroad to-night," said Fagin, "and on the right errand, I'm sure; for she has been alone all day, and the man she is afraid of will not be back much before daybreak. Come with me. Quick!"

Noah started up without saying a word; for the Jew was in a state of such intense excitement that it infected him. They left the house stealthily, and hurrying through a labyrinth of streets, arrived at length before a public-house, which Noah recognised as the same in which he had slept, on the night of his arrival in London.

It was past eleven o'clock, and the door was closed. It opened softly on its hinges as Fagin gave a low whistle. They entered, without noise; and the door was closed behind them.

Scarcely venturing to whisper, but substituting dumb show for words, Fagin, and the young Jew who had admitted them, pointed out the pane of glass to Noah, and signed to him to climb up and observe the person in the adjoining room.

"Is that the woman?" he asked, scarcely above his breath.

Fagin nodded yes.

"I can't see her face well," whispered Noah. "She is looking down, and the candle is behind her."

"Stay there," whispered Fagin. He signed to Barney, who withdrew. In an instant, the lad entered the room adjoining, and, under pretence of snuffing the candle, moved it in the required position, and, speaking to the girl, caused her to raise her face.

"I see her now," cried the spy.

"Plainly?"

"I should know her among a thousand."

He hastily descended, as the room-door opened, and the girl came out. Fagin drew him behind a small partition which was curtained off, and they held their breaths as she passed within a few feet of their place of concealment, and emerged by the door at which they had entered.

"Hist!" cried the lad who held the door. "Dow."

Noah exchanged a look with Fagin, and darted out.

"To the left," whispered the lad; "take the left had, and keep od the other side."

He did so; and, by the light of the lamps, saw the girl's retreating figure, already at some distance before him. He advanced as near as he considered prudent, and kept on the opposite side of the street, the better to observe her motions. She looked nervously round, twice or thrice, and once stopped to let two men who were following close behind her, pass on. She seemed to gather courage as she advanced, and to walk with a steadier and firmer step. The spy preserved the same relative distance between them, and followed: with his eye upon her.

CHAPTER XLVI

The Appointment Kept

The church clocks chimed three quarters past eleven, as two figures emerged on London Bridge. One, which advanced with a swift and rapid step, was that of a woman who looked eagerly about her as though in quest of some expected object; the other figure was that of a man, who slunk along in the deepest shadow he could find, and, at some distance, accommodated his pace to hers: stopping when she stopped: and as she moved again, creeping stealthily on: but never allowing himself, in the ardour of his pursuit, to gain upon her footsteps. Thus, they crossed the bridge, from the Middlesex to the Surrey shore, when the woman, apparently disappointed in her anxious scrutiny of the foot-passengers, turned back. The movement was sudden; but he who watched her, was not thrown off his guard by it; for, shrinking into one of the recesses which surmount the piers of the bridge, and leaning over the parapet the better to conceal his figure, he suffered her to pass on the opposite pavement. When she was about the same distance in advance as she had been before, he slipped quietly down, and followed her again. At nearly the centre of the bridge, she stopped. The man stopped too.

It was a very dark night. The day had been unfavourable, and at that hour and place there were few people stirring. Such as there were, hurried quickly past: very possibly without seeing, but certainly without noticing, either the woman, or the man who kept her in view. Their appearance was not calculated to attract the importunate regards of such of London's destitute population, as chanced to take their way over the bridge that night in search of some cold arch or doorless hovel wherein to lay their heads; they stood there in silence: neither speaking nor spoken to, by any one who passed.

A mist hung over the river, deepening the red glare of the fires that burnt upon the small craft moored off the different wharfs, and rendering darker and more indistinct the murky buildings on the banks. The old smoke-stained storehouses on either side, rose heavy and dull from the dense mass of roofs and gables, and frowned sternly upon water too black to reflect even their lumbering shapes. The tower of old Saint Saviour's Church, and the spire of Saint Magnus, so long the giant-warders of the ancient bridge, were visible in the gloom; but the forest of shipping below bridge, and the thickly scattered spires of churches above, were nearly all hidden from sight.

The girl had taken a few restless turns to and fro—closely watched meanwhile by her hidden observer—when the heavy bell of St. Paul's tolled for the death of another day. Midnight had come upon the crowded city. The palace, the night-cellar, the jail, the madhouse: the chambers of birth and death, of health and sickness, the rigid face of the corpse and the calm sleep of the child: midnight was upon them all.

The hour had not struck two minutes, when a young lady, accompanied by a grey-haired gentleman, alighted from a hackney-carriage within a short distance of the bridge, and, having dismissed the vehicle, walked straight towards it. They had scarcely set foot upon its pavement, when the girl started, and immediately made towards them.

They walked onward, looking about them with the air of persons who entertained some very slight expectation which had little chance of being realised, when they were suddenly joined by this new associate. They halted with an exclamation of surprise, but suppressed it immediately; for a man in the garments of a countryman came close up—brushed against them, indeed—at that precise moment.

"Not here," said Nancy hurriedly, "I am afraid to speak to you here. Come away—out of the public road—down the steps yonder!"

As she uttered these words, and indicated, with her hand, the direction in which she wished them to proceed, the countryman looked round, and roughly asking what they took up the whole pavement for, passed on.

The steps to which the girl had pointed, were those which, on the Surrey bank, and on the same side of the bridge as Saint Saviour's Church, form a landing-stairs from the river. To this spot, the man bearing the appearance of a countryman, hastened unobserved; and after a moment's survey of the place, he began to descend.

These stairs are a part of the bridge; they consist of three flights. Just below the end of the second, going down, the stone wall on the left terminates in an ornamental pilaster facing towards the Thames. At this point the lower steps widen: so that a person turning that angle of the wall, is necessarily unseen by any others on the stairs who chance to be above him, if only a step. The countryman looked hastily round, when he reached this point; and as there seemed no better place of concealment, and, the tide being out, there was plenty of room, he slipped aside, with his back to the pilaster, and there waited: pretty certain that they would come no lower, and that even if he could not hear what was said, he could follow them again, with safety.

So tardily stole the time in this lonely place, and so eager was the spy to penetrate the motives of an interview so different from what he had been led to expect, that he more than once gave the matter up for lost, and persuaded himself, either that they had stopped far above, or had resorted to some entirely different spot to hold their mysterious conversation. He was on the point of emerging from his hiding-place, and regaining the road above, when he heard the sound of footsteps, and directly afterwards of voices almost close at his ear.

He drew himself straight upright against the wall, and, scarcely breathing, listened attentively.

"This is far enough," said a voice, which was evidently that of the gentleman. "I will not suffer the young lady to go any farther. Many people would have distrusted you too much to have come even so far, but you see I am willing to humour you."

"To humour me!" cried the voice of the girl whom he had followed. "You're considerate, indeed, sir. To humour me! Well, well, it's no matter."

"Why, for what," said the gentleman in a kinder tone, "for what purpose can you have brought us to this strange place? Why not have let me speak to you, above there, where it is light, and there is something stirring, instead of bringing us to this dark and dismal hole?"

"I told you before," replied Nancy, "that I was afraid to speak to you there. I don't know why it is," said the girl, shuddering, "but I have such a fear and dread upon me to-night that I can hardly stand."

"A fear of what?" asked the gentleman, who seemed to pity her.

"I scarcely know of what," replied the girl. "I wish I did. Horrible thoughts of death, and shrouds with blood upon them, and a fear that has made me burn as if I was on fire, have been upon me all day. I was reading a book to-night, to wile the time away, and the same things came into the print."

"Imagination," said the gentleman, soothing her.

"No imagination," replied the girl in a hoarse voice. "I'll swear I saw "coffin" written in every page of the book in large black letters,—aye, and they carried one close to me, in the streets to-night."

"There is nothing unusual in that," said the gentleman. "They have passed me often."

"Real ones," rejoined the girl. "This was not."

There was something so uncommon in her manner, that the flesh of the concealed listener crept as he heard the girl utter these words, and the blood chilled within him. He had never experienced a greater relief than in hearing the sweet voice of the young lady as she begged her to be calm, and not allow herself to become the prey of such fearful fancies.

"Speak to her kindly," said the young lady to her companion. "Poor creature! She seems to need it."

"Your haughty religious people would have held their heads up to see me as I am to-night, and preached of flames and vengeance," cried the girl. "Oh, dear lady, why ar'n't those who claim to be God's own folks as gentle and as kind to us poor wretches as you, who, having youth, and beauty, and all that they have lost, might be a little proud instead of so much humbler?"

"Ah!" said the gentleman. "A Turk turns his face, after washing it well, to the East, when he says his prayers; these good people, after giving their faces such a rub against the World as to take the smiles off, turn with no less regularity, to the darkest side of Heaven. Between the Mussulman and the Pharisee, commend me to the first!"

These words appeared to be addressed to the young lady, and were perhaps uttered with the view of affording Nancy time to recover herself. The gentleman, shortly afterwards, addressed himself to her.

"You were not here last Sunday night," he said.

"I couldn't come," replied Nancy; "I was kept by force."

"By whom?"

"Him that I told the young lady of before."

"You were not suspected of holding any communication with anybody on the subject which has brought us here to-night, I hope?" asked the old gentleman.

"No," replied the girl, shaking her head. "It's not very easy for me to leave him unless he knows why; I couldn't give him a drink of laudanum before I came away."

"Did he awake before you returned?" inquired the gentleman.

"No; and neither he nor any of them suspect me."

"Good," said the gentleman. "Now listen to me."

"I am ready," replied the girl, as he paused for a moment.

"This young lady," the gentleman began, "has communicated to me, and to some other friends who can be safely trusted, what you told her nearly a fortnight since. I confess to you that I had doubts, at first, whether you were to be implicitly relied upon, but now I firmly believe you are."

"I am," said the girl earnestly.

"I repeat that I firmly believe it. To prove to you that I am disposed to trust you, I tell you without reserve, that we propose to extort the secret, whatever it may be, from the fear of this man Monks. But if—if—" said the gentleman, "he cannot be secured, or, if secured, cannot be acted upon as we wish, you must deliver up the Jew."

"Fagin," cried the girl, recoiling.

"That man must be delivered up by you," said the gentleman.

"I will not do it! I will never do it!" replied the girl. "Devil that he is, and worse than devil as he has been to me, I will never do that."

"You will not?" said the gentleman, who seemed fully prepared for this answer.

"Never!" returned the girl.

"Tell me why?"

"For one reason," rejoined the girl firmly, "for one reason, that the lady knows and will stand by me in, I know she will, for I have her promise: and for this other reason, besides, that, bad life as he has led, I have led a bad life too; there are many of us who have kept the same courses together, and I'll not turn upon them, who might—any of them—have turned upon me, but didn't, bad as they are."

"Then," said the gentleman, quickly, as if this had been the point he had been aiming to attain; "put Monks into my hands, and leave him to me to deal with."

"What if he turns against the others?"

"I promise you that in that case, if the truth is forced from him, there the matter will rest; there must be circumstances in Oliver's little history which it would be painful to drag before the public eye, and if the truth is once elicited, they shall go scot free."

"And if it is not?" suggested the girl.

"Then," pursued the gentleman, "this Fagin shall not be brought to justice without your consent. In such a case I could show you reasons, I think, which would induce you to yield it."

"Have I the lady's promise for that?" asked the girl.

"You have," replied Rose. "My true and faithful pledge."

"Monks would never learn how you knew what you do?" said the girl, after a short pause.

"Never," replied the gentleman. "The intelligence should be brought to bear upon him, that he could never even guess."

"I have been a liar, and among liars from a little child," said the girl after another interval of silence, "but I will take your words."

After receiving an assurance from both, that she might safely do so, she proceeded in a voice so low that it was often difficult for the listener to discover even the purport of what she said, to describe, by name and situation, the public-house whence she had been followed that night. From the manner in which she occasionally paused, it appeared as if the gentleman were making some hasty notes of the information she communicated. When she had thoroughly explained the localities of the place, the best position from which to watch it without exciting observation, and the night and hour on which Monks was most in the habit of frequenting it, she seemed to consider for a few moments, for the purpose of recalling his features and appearances more forcibly to her recollection.

"He is tall," said the girl, "and a strongly made man, but not stout; he has a lurking walk; and as he walks, constantly looks over his shoulder, first on one side, and then on the other. Don't forget that, for his eyes are sunk in his head so much deeper than any other man's, that you might almost tell him by that alone. His face is dark, like his hair and eyes; and, although he can't be more than six or eight and twenty, withered and haggard. His lips are often discoloured and disfigured with the marks of teeth; for he has desperate fits, and sometimes even bites his hands and covers them with wounds—why did you start?" said the girl, stopping suddenly.

The gentleman replied, in a hurried manner, that he was not conscious of having done so, and begged her to proceed.

"Part of this," said the girl, "I have drawn out from other people at the house I tell you of, for I have only seen him twice, and both times he was covered up in a large cloak. I think that's all I can give you to know him by. Stay though," she added. "Upon his throat: so high that you can see a part of it below his neckerchief when he turns his face: there is—"

"A broad red mark, like a burn or scald?" cried the gentleman.

"How's this?" said the girl. "You know him!"

The young lady uttered a cry of surprise, and for a few moments they were so still that the listener could distinctly hear them breathe.

"I think I do," said the gentleman, breaking silence. "I should by your description. We shall see. Many people are singularly like each other. It may not be the same."

As he expressed himself to this effect, with assumed carelessness, he took a step or two nearer the concealed spy, as the latter could tell from the distinctness with which he heard him mutter, "It must be he!"

"Now," he said, returning: so it seemed by the sound: to the spot where he had stood before, "you have given us most valuable assistance, young woman, and I wish you to be the better for it. What can I do to serve you?"

"Nothing," replied Nancy.

"You will not persist in saying that," rejoined the gentleman, with a voice and emphasis of kindness that might have touched a much harder and more obdurate heart. "Think now. Tell me."

"Nothing, sir," rejoined the girl, weeping. "You can do nothing to help me. I am past all hope, indeed."

"You put yourself beyond its pale," said the gentleman. "The past has been a dreary waste with you, of youthful energies mis-spent, and such priceless treasures lavished, as the Creator bestows but once and never grants again, but, for the future, you may hope. I do not say that it is in our power to offer you peace of heart and mind, for that must come as you seek it; but a quiet asylum, either in England, or, if you fear to remain here, in some foreign country, it is not only within the compass of our ability but our most anxious wish to secure you. Before the dawn of morning, before this river wakes to the first glimpse of day-light, you shall be placed as entirely beyond the reach of your former associates, and leave as utter an absence of all trace behind you, as if you were to disappear from the earth this moment. Come! I would not have you go back to exchange one word with any old companion, or take one look at any old haunt, or breathe the very air which is pestilence and death to you. Quit them all, while there is time and opportunity!"

"She will be persuaded now," cried the young lady. "She hesitates, I am sure."

"I fear not, my dear," said the gentleman.

"No sir, I do not," replied the girl, after a short struggle. "I am chained to my old life. I loathe and hate it now, but I cannot leave it. I must have gone too far to turn back,—and yet I don't know, for if you had spoken to me so, some time ago, I should have laughed it off. But," she said, looking hastily round, "this fear comes over me again. I must go home."

"Home!" repeated the young lady, with great stress upon the word.

"Home, lady," rejoined the girl. "To such a home as I have raised for myself with the work of my whole life. Let us part. I shall be watched or seen. Go! Go! If I have done you any service all I ask is, that you leave me, and let me go my way alone."

"It is useless," said the gentleman, with a sigh. "We compromise her safety, perhaps, by staying here. We may have detained her longer than she expected already."

"Yes, yes," urged the girl. "You have."

"What," cried the young lady, "can be the end of this poor creature's life!"

"What!" repeated the girl. "Look before you, lady. Look at that dark water. How many times do you read of such as I who spring into the tide, and leave no living thing, to care for, or bewail them. It may be years hence, or it may be only months, but I shall come to that at last."

"Do not speak thus, pray," returned the young lady, sobbing.

"It will never reach your ears, dear lady, and God forbid such horrors should!" replied the girl. "Good-night, good-night!"

The gentleman turned away.

"This purse," cried the young lady. "Take it for my sake, that you may have some resource in an hour of need and trouble."

"No!" replied the girl. "I have not done this for money. Let me have that to think of. And yet—give me something that you have worn: I should like to have something— no, no, not a ring—your gloves or handkerchief—anything that I can keep, as having belonged to you, sweet lady. There. Bless you! God bless you. Good-night, good-night!"

The violent agitation of the girl, and the apprehension of some discovery which would subject her to ill-usage and violence, seemed to determine the gentleman to leave her, as she requested.

The sound of retreating footsteps were audible and the voices ceased.

The two figures of the young lady and her companion soon afterwards appeared upon the bridge. They stopped at the summit of the stairs.

"Hark!" cried the young lady, listening. "Did she call! I thought I heard her voice."

"No, my love," replied Mr. Brownlow, looking sadly back. "She has not moved, and will not till we are gone."

Rose Maylie lingered, but the old gentleman drew her arm through his, and led her, with gentle force, away. As they disappeared, the girl sunk down nearly at her full length upon one of the stone stairs, and vented the anguish of her heart in bitter tears.

After a time she arose, and with feeble and tottering steps ascended the street. The astonished listener remained motionless on his post for some minutes afterwards, and having ascertained, with many cautious glances round him, that he was again alone, crept slowly from his hiding-place, and returned, stealthily and in the shade of the wall, in the same manner as he had descended.

Peeping out, more than once, when he reached the top, to make sure that he was unobserved, Noah Claypole darted away at his utmost speed, and made for the Jew's house as fast as his legs would carry him.

CHAPTER XLVII

Fatal Consequences

It was nearly two hours before day-break; that time which in the autumn of the year, may be truly called the dead of night; when the streets are silent and deserted; when even sounds appear to slumber, and profligacy and riot have staggered home to dream; it was at this still and silent hour, that Fagin sat watching in his old lair, with face so distorted and pale, and eyes so red and blood-shot, that he looked less like a man, than like some hideous phantom, moist from the grave, and worried by an evil spirit.

He sat crouching over a cold hearth, wrapped in an old torn coverlet, with his face turned towards a wasting candle that stood upon a table by his side. His right hand was raised to his lips, and as, absorbed in thought, he bit his long black nails, he disclosed among his toothless gums a few such fangs as should have been a dog's or rat's.

Stretched upon a mattress on the floor, lay Noah Claypole, fast asleep. Towards him the old man sometimes directed his eyes for an instant, and then brought them back again to the candle; which with a long-burnt wick drooping almost double, and hot grease falling down in clots upon the table, plainly showed that his thoughts were busy elsewhere.

Indeed they were. Mortification at the overthrow of his notable scheme; hatred of the girl who had dared to palter with strangers; and utter distrust of the sincerity of her refusal to yield him up; bitter disappointment at the loss of his revenge on Sikes; the fear of detection, and ruin, and death; and a fierce and deadly rage kindled by all; these were the passionate considerations which, following close upon each other with rapid and ceaseless whirl, shot through the brain of Fagin, as every evil thought and blackest purpose lay working at his heart.

He sat without changing his attitude in the least, or appearing to take the smallest heed of time, until his quick ear seemed to be attracted by a footstep in the street.

"At last," he muttered, wiping his dry and fevered mouth. "At last!"

The bell rang gently as he spoke. He crept upstairs to the door, and presently returned accompanied by a man muffled to the chin, who carried a bundle under one arm. Sitting down and throwing back his outer coat, the man displayed the burly frame of Sikes.

"There!" he said, laying the bundle on the table. "Take care of that, and do the most you can with it. It's been trouble enough to get; I thought I should have been here, three hours ago."

Fagin laid his hand upon the bundle, and locking it in the cupboard, sat down again without speaking. But he did not take his eyes off the robber, for an instant, during this action; and now that they sat over against each other, face to face, he looked fixedly at him, with his lips quivering so violently, and his face so altered by the emotions which had mastered him, that the housebreaker involuntarily drew back his chair, and surveyed him with a look of real affright.

"Wot now?" cried Sikes. "Wot do you look at a man so for?"

Fagin raised his right hand, and shook his trembling forefinger in the air; but his passion was so great, that the power of speech was for the moment gone.

"Damme!" said Sikes, feeling in his breast with a look of alarm. "He's gone mad. I must look to myself here."

"No, no," rejoined Fagin, finding his voice. "It's not—you're not the person, Bill. I've no—no fault to find with you."

"Oh, you haven't, haven't you?" said Sikes, looking sternly at him, and ostentatiously passing a pistol into a more convenient pocket. "That's lucky—for one of us. Which one that is, don't matter."

"I've got that to tell you, Bill," said Fagin, drawing his chair nearer, "will make you worse than me."

"Aye?" returned the robber with an incredulous air. "Tell away! Look sharp, or Nance will think I'm lost."

"Lost!" cried Fagin. "She has pretty well settled that, in her own mind, already."

Sikes looked with an aspect of great perplexity into the Jew's face, and reading no satisfactory explanation of the riddle there, clenched his coat collar in his huge hand and shook him soundly.

"Speak, will you!" he said; "or if you don't, it shall be for want of breath. Open your mouth and say wot you've got to say in plain words. Out with it, you thundering old cur, out with it!"

"Suppose that lad that's laying there—" Fagin began.

Sikes turned round to where Noah was sleeping, as if he had not previously observed him. "Well!" he said, resuming his former position.

"Suppose that lad," pursued Fagin, "was to peach—to blow upon us all—first seeking out the right folks for the purpose, and then having a meeting with 'em in the street to paint our likenesses, describe every mark that they might know us by, and the crib where we might be most easily taken. Suppose he was to do all this, and besides to blow upon a plant we've all been in, more or less—of his own fancy; not grabbed, trapped, tried, earwigged by the parson and brought to it on bread and water,—but of his own fancy; to please his own taste; stealing out at nights to find those most interested against us, and peaching to them. Do you hear me?" cried the Jew, his eyes flashing with rage. "Suppose he did all this, what then?"

"What then!" replied Sikes; with a tremendous oath. "If he was left alive till I came, I'd grind his skull under the iron heel of my boot into as many grains as there are hairs upon his head."

"What if I did it!" cried Fagin almost in a yell. "I, that knows so much, and could hang so many besides myself!"

"I don't know," replied Sikes, clenching his teeth and turning white at the mere suggestion. "I'd do something in the jail that 'ud get me put in irons; and if I was tried along with you, I'd fall upon you with them in the open court, and beat your brains out afore the people. I should have such strength," muttered the robber, poising his brawny arm, "that I could smash your head as if a loaded waggon had gone over it."

"You would?"

"Would I!" said the housebreaker. "Try me."

"If it was Charley, or the Dodger, or Bet, or—"

"I don't care who," replied Sikes impatiently. "Whoever it was, I'd serve them the same."

Fagin looked hard at the robber; and, motioning him to be silent, stooped over the bed upon the floor, and shook the sleeper to rouse him. Sikes leant forward in his chair: looking on with his hands upon his knees, as if wondering much what all this questioning and preparation was to end in.

"Bolter, Bolter! Poor lad!" said Fagin, looking up with an expression of devilish anticipation, and speaking slowly and with marked emphasis. "He's tired—tired with watching for her so long,—watching for her, Bill."

"Wot d'ye mean?" asked Sikes, drawing back.

Fagin made no answer, but bending over the sleeper again, hauled him into a sitting posture. When his assumed name had been repeated several times, Noah rubbed his eyes, and, giving a heavy yawn, looked sleepily about him.

"Tell me that again—once again, just for him to hear," said the Jew, pointing to Sikes as he spoke.

"Tell yer what?" asked the sleepy Noah, shaking himself pettishly.

"That about— Nancy," said Fagin, clutching Sikes by the wrist, as if to prevent his leaving the house before he had heard enough. "You followed her?"

"Yes."

"To London Bridge?"

"Yes."

"Where she met two people."

"So she did."

"A gentleman and a lady that she had gone to of her own accord before, who asked her to give up all her pals, and Monks first, which she did—and to describe him, which she did—and to tell her what house it was that we meet at, and go to, which she did— and where it could be best watched from, which she did—and what time the people went there, which she did. She did all this. She told it all every word without a threat, without a murmur—she did—did she not?" cried Fagin, half mad with fury.

"All right," replied Noah, scratching his head. "That's just what it was!"

"What did they say, about last Sunday?"

"About last Sunday!" replied Noah, considering. "Why I told yer that before."

"Again. Tell it again!" cried Fagin, tightening his grasp on Sikes, and brandishing his other hand aloft, as the foam flew from his lips.

"They asked her," said Noah, who, as he grew more wakeful, seemed to have a dawning perception who Sikes was, "they asked her why she didn't come, last Sunday, as she promised. She said she couldn't."

"Why—why? Tell him that."

"Because she was forcibly kept at home by Bill, the man she had told them of before," replied Noah.

"What more of him?" cried Fagin. "What more of the man she had told them of before? Tell him that, tell him that."

"Why, that she couldn't very easily get out of doors unless he knew where she was going to," said Noah; "and so the first time she went to see the lady, she—ha! ha! ha! it made me laugh when she said it, that it did—she gave him a drink of laudanum."

"Hell's fire!" cried Sikes, breaking fiercely from the Jew. "Let me go!"

Flinging the old man from him, he rushed from the room, and darted, wildly and furiously, up the stairs.

"Bill, Bill!" cried Fagin, following him hastily. "A word. Only a word."

The word would not have been exchanged, but that the housebreaker was unable to open the door: on which he was expending fruitless oaths and violence, when the Jew came panting up.

"Let me out," said Sikes. "Don't speak to me; it's not safe. Let me out, I say!"

"Hear me speak a word," rejoined Fagin, laying his hand upon the lock. "You won't be—"

"Well," replied the other.

"You won't be—too—violent, Bill?"

The day was breaking, and there was light enough for the men to see each other's faces. They exchanged one brief glance; there was a fire in the eyes of both, which could not be mistaken.

"I mean," said Fagin, showing that he felt all disguise was now useless, "not too violent for safety. Be crafty, Bill, and not too bold."

Sikes made no reply; but, pulling open the door, of which Fagin had turned the lock, dashed into the silent streets.

Without one pause, or moment's consideration; without once turning his head to the right or left, or raising his eyes to the sky, or lowering them to the ground, but looking straight before him with savage resolution: his teeth so tightly compressed that the strained jaw seemed starting through his skin; the robber held on his headlong course, nor muttered a word, nor relaxed a muscle, until he reached his own door. He opened it, softly, with a key; strode lightly up the stairs; and entering his own room, double-locked the door, and lifting a heavy table against it, drew back the curtain of the bed.

The girl was lying, half-dressed, upon it. He had roused her from her sleep, for she raised herself with a hurried and startled look.

"Get up!" said the man.

"It is you, Bill!" said the girl, with an expression of pleasure at his return.

"It is," was the reply. "Get up."

There was a candle burning, but the man hastily drew it from the candlestick, and hurled it under the grate. Seeing the faint light of early day without, the girl rose to undraw the curtain.

"Let it be," said Sikes, thrusting his hand before her. "There's enough light for wot I've got to do."

"Bill," said the girl, in the low voice of alarm, "why do you look like that at me!"

The robber sat regarding her, for a few seconds, with dilated nostrils and heaving breast; and then, grasping her by the head and throat, dragged her into the middle of the room, and looking once towards the door, placed his heavy hand upon her mouth.

"Bill, Bill!" gasped the girl, wrestling with the strength of mortal fear, "I—I won't scream or cry—not once—hear me—speak to me—tell me what I have done!"

"You know, you she devil!" returned the robber, suppressing his breath. "You were watched to-night; every word you said was heard."

"Then spare my life for the love of Heaven, as I spared yours," rejoined the girl, clinging to him. "Bill, dear Bill, you cannot have the heart to kill me. Oh! think of all I have given up, only this one night, for you. You shall have time to think, and save yourself this crime; I will not loose my hold, you cannot throw me off. Bill, Bill, for dear God's sake, for your own, for mine, stop before you spill my blood! I have been true to you, upon my guilty soul I have!"

The man struggled violently, to release his arms; but those of the girl were clasped round his, and tear her as he would, he could not tear them away.

"Bill," cried the girl, striving to lay her head upon his breast, "the gentleman and that dear lady, told me to-night of a home in some foreign country where I could end my days in solitude and peace. Let me see them again, and beg them, on my knees, to show the same mercy and goodness to you; and let us both leave this dreadful place, and far apart lead better lives, and forget how we have lived, except in prayers, and never see each other more. It is never too late to repent. They told me so—I feel it now—but we must have time—a little, little time!"

The housebreaker freed one arm, and grasped his pistol. The certainty of immediate detection if he fired, flashed across his mind even in the midst of his fury; and he beat it twice with all the force he could summon, upon the upturned face that almost touched his own.

She staggered and fell: nearly blinded with the blood that rained down from a deep gash in her forehead; but raising herself, with difficulty, on her knees, drew from her bosom a white handkerchief—Rose Maylie's own—and holding it up, in her folded hands, as high towards Heaven as her feeble strength would allow, breathed one prayer for mercy to her Maker.

It was a ghastly figure to look upon. The murderer staggering backward to the wall, and shutting out the sight with his hand, seized a heavy club and struck her down.

CHAPTER XLVIII

The Flight of Sikes

Of all bad deeds that, under cover of the darkness, had been committed within wide London's bounds since night hung over it, that was the worst. Of all the horrors that rose with an ill scent upon the morning air, that was the foulest and most cruel.

The sun—the bright sun, that brings back, not light alone, but new life, and hope, and freshness to man—burst upon the crowded city in clear and radiant glory. Through costly-coloured glass and paper-mended window, through cathedral dome and rotten crevice, it shed its equal ray. It lighted up the room where the murdered woman lay. It did. He tried to shut it out, but it would stream in. If the sight had been a ghastly one in the dull morning, what was it, now, in all that brilliant light!

He had not moved; he had been afraid to stir. There had been a moan and motion of the hand; and, with terror added to rage, he had struck and struck again. Once he threw a rug over it; but it was worse to fancy the eyes, and imagine them moving towards him, than to see them glaring upward, as if watching the reflection of the pool of gore that quivered and danced in the sunlight on the ceiling. He had plucked it off again. And there was the body—mere flesh and blood, no more—but such flesh, and so much blood!

He struck a light, kindled a fire, and thrust the club into it. There was hair upon the end, which blazed and shrunk into a light cinder, and, caught by the air, whirled up the chimney. Even that frightened him, sturdy as he was; but he held the weapon till it broke, and then piled it on the coals to burn away, and smoulder into ashes. He washed himself, and rubbed his clothes; there were spots that would not be removed, but he cut the pieces out, and burnt them. How those stains were dispersed about the room! The very feet of the dog were bloody.

All this time he had, never once, turned his back upon the corpse; no, not for a moment. Such preparations completed, he moved, backward, towards the door: dragging the dog with him, lest he should soil his feet anew and carry out new evidence of the crime into the streets. He shut the door softly, locked it, took the key, and left the house.

He crossed over, and glanced up at the window, to be sure that nothing was visible from the outside. There was the curtain still drawn, which she would have opened to admit the light she never saw again. It lay nearly under there. He knew that. God, how the sun poured down upon the very spot!

The glance was instantaneous. It was a relief to have got free of the room. He whistled on the dog, and walked rapidly away.

He went through Islington; strode up the hill at Highgate on which stands the stone in honour of Whittington; turned down to Highgate Hill, unsteady of purpose, and uncertain where to go; struck off to the right again, almost as soon as he began to descend it; and taking the foot-path across the fields, skirted Caen Wood, and so came on Hampstead Heath. Traversing the hollow by the Vale of Heath, he mounted the opposite bank, and crossing the road which joins the villages of Hampstead and Highgate, made along the remaining portion of the heath to the fields at North End, in one of which he laid himself down under a hedge, and slept.

Soon he was up again, and away,—not far into the country, but back towards London by the high-road—then back again—then over another part of the same ground as he already traversed—then wandering up and down in fields, and lying on ditches' brinks to rest, and starting up to make for some other spot, and do the same, and ramble on again.

Where could he go, that was near and not too public, to get some meat and drink? Hendon. That was a good place, not far off, and out of most people's way. Thither he directed his steps,—running sometimes, and sometimes, with a strange perversity, loitering at a snail's pace, or stopping altogether and idly breaking the hedges with a stick. But when he got there, all the people he met—the very children at the doors—seemed to view him with suspicion. Back he turned again, without the courage to purchase bit or drop, though he had tasted no food for many hours; and once more he lingered on the Heath, uncertain where to go.

He wandered over miles and miles of ground, and still came back to the old place. Morning and noon had passed, and the day was on the wane, and still he rambled to and fro, and up and down, and round and round, and still lingered about the same spot. At last he got away, and shaped his course for Hatfield.

It was nine o'clock at night, when the man, quite tired out, and the dog, limping and lame from the unaccustomed exercise, turned down the hill by the church of the quiet village, and plodding along the little street, crept into a small public-house, whose scanty light had guided them to the spot. There was a fire in the tap-room, and some country-labourers were drinking before it.

They made room for the stranger, but he sat down in the furthest corner, and ate and drank alone, or rather with his dog: to whom he cast a morsel of food from time to time.

The conversation of the men assembled here, turned upon the neighbouring land, and farmers; and when those topics were exhausted, upon the age of some old man who had been buried on the previous Sunday; the young men present considering him very old, and the old men present declaring him to have been quite young—not older, one white-haired grandfather said, than he was—with ten or fifteen year of life in him at least—if he had taken care; if he had taken care.

There was nothing to attract attention, or excite alarm in this. The robber, after paying his reckoning, sat silent and unnoticed in his corner, and had almost dropped asleep, when he was half wakened by the noisy entrance of a new comer.

This was an antic fellow, half pedlar and half mountebank, who travelled about the country on foot to vend hones, strops, razors, washballs, harness-paste, medicine for dogs and horses, cheap perfumery, cosmetics, and such-like wares, which he carried in a case slung to his back. His entrance was the signal for various homely jokes with the countrymen, which slackened not until he had made his supper, and opened his box of treasures, when he ingeniously contrived to unite business with amusement.

"And what be that stoof? Good to eat, Harry?" asked a grinning countryman, pointing to some composition-cakes in one corner.

"This," said the fellow, producing one, "this is the infallible and invaluable composition for removing all sorts of stain, rust, dirt, mildew, spick, speck, spot, or spatter, from silk, satin, linen, cambric, cloth, crape, stuff, carpet, merino, muslin, bombazeen, or woollen stuff. Wine-stains, fruit-stains, beer-stains, water-stains, paint-stains, pitch-stains, any stains, all come out at one rub with the infallible and invaluable composition. If a lady stains her honour, she has only need to swallow one cake and she's cured at once—for it's poison. If a gentleman wants to prove this, he has only need to bolt one little square, and he has put it beyond question— for it's quite as satisfactory as a pistol-bullet, and a great deal nastier in the flavour, consequently the more credit in taking it. One penny a square. With all these virtues, one penny a square!"

There were two buyers directly, and more of the listeners plainly hesitated. The vendor observing this, increased in loquacity.

"It's all bought up as fast as it can be made," said the fellow. "There are fourteen water-mills, six steam-engines, and a galvanic battery, always a-working upon it, and they can't make it fast enough, though the men work so hard that they die off, and the widows is pensioned directly, with twenty pound a-year for each of the children, and a premium of fifty for twins. One penny a square! Two half-pence is all the same, and four farthings is received with joy. One penny a square! Wine-stains, fruit-stains, beer-stains, water-stains, paint-stains, pitch-stains, mud-stains, blood-stains! Here is a stain upon the hat of a gentleman in company, that I'll take clean out, before he can order me a pint of ale."

"Hah!" cried Sikes starting up. "Give that back."

"I'll take it clean out, sir," replied the man, winking to the company, "before you can come across the room to get it. Gentlemen all, observe the dark stain upon this gentleman's hat, no wider than a shilling, but thicker than a half-crown. Whether it is a wine-stain, fruit-stain, beer-stain, water-stain, paint-stain, pitch-stain, mud-stain, or blood-stain—"

The man got no further, for Sikes with a hideous imprecation overthrew the table, and tearing the hat from him, burst out of the house.

With the same perversity of feeling and irresolution that had fastened upon him, despite himself, all day, the murderer, finding that he was not followed, and that they most probably considered him some drunken sullen fellow, turned back up the town, and getting out of the glare of the lamps of a stage-coach that was standing in the street, was walking past, when he recognised the mail from London, and saw that it was standing at the little post-office. He almost knew what was to come; but he crossed over, and listened.

The guard was standing at the door, waiting for the letter-bag. A man, dressed like a game-keeper, came up at the moment, and he handed him a basket which lay ready on the pavement.

"That's for your people," said the guard. "Now, look alive in there, will you. Damn that 'ere bag, it warn't ready night afore last; this won't do, you know!"

"Anything new up in town, Ben?" asked the game-keeper, drawing back to the window-shutters, the better to admire the horses.

"No, nothing that I knows on," replied the man, pulling on his gloves. "Corn's up a little. I heerd talk of a murder, too, down Spitalfields way, but I don't reckon much upon it."

"Oh, that's quite true," said a gentleman inside, who was looking out of the window. "And a dreadful murder it was."

"Was it, sir?" rejoined the guard, touching his hat. "Man or woman, pray, sir?"

"A woman," replied the gentleman. "It is supposed—"

"Now, Ben," replied the coachman impatiently.

"Damn that 'ere bag," said the guard; "are you gone to sleep in there?"

"Coming!" cried the office keeper, running out.

"Coming," growled the guard. "Ah, and so's the young 'ooman of property that's going to take a fancy to me, but I don't know when. Here, give hold. All ri—ight!"

The horn sounded a few cheerful notes, and the coach was gone.

Sikes remained standing in the street, apparently unmoved by what he had just heard, and agitated by no stronger feeling than a doubt where to go. At length he went back again, and took the road which leads from Hatfield to St. Albans.

He went on doggedly; but as he left the town behind him, and plunged into the solitude and darkness of the road, he felt a dread and awe creeping upon him which shook him to the core. Every object before him, substance or shadow, still or moving, took the semblance of some fearful thing; but these fears were nothing compared to the sense that haunted him of that morning's ghastly figure following at his heels. He could trace its shadow in the gloom, supply the smallest item of the outline, and note how stiff and solemn it seemed to stalk along. He could hear its garments rustling in the leaves, and every breath of wind came laden with that last low cry. If he stopped it did the same. If he ran, it followed—not running too: that would have been a relief: but like a corpse endowed with the mere machinery of life, and borne on one slow melancholy wind that never rose or fell.

At times, he turned, with desperate determination, resolved to beat this phantom off, though it should look him dead; but the hair rose on his head, and his blood stood still, for it had turned with him and was behind him then. He had kept it before him that morning, but it was behind now—always. He leaned his back against a bank, and felt that it stood above him, visibly out against the cold night-sky. He threw himself upon the road—on his back upon the road. At his head it stood, silent, erect, and still—a living grave-stone, with its epitaph in blood.

Let no man talk of murderers escaping justice, and hint that Providence must sleep. There were twenty score of violent deaths in one long minute of that agony of fear.

There was a shed in a field he passed, that offered shelter for the night. Before the door, were three tall poplar trees, which made it very dark within; and the wind moaned through them with a dismal wail. He could not walk on, till daylight came again; and here he stretched himself close to the wall—to undergo new torture.

For now, a vision came before him, as constant and more terrible than that from which he had escaped. Those widely staring eyes, so lustreless and so glassy, that he had better borne to see them than think upon them, appeared in the midst of the darkness: light in themselves, but giving light to nothing. There were but two, but they were everywhere. If he shut out the sight, there came the room with every well-known object—some, indeed, that he would have forgotten, if he had gone over its contents from memory—each in its accustomed place. The body was in its place, and its eyes were as he saw them when he stole away. He got up, and rushed into the field without. The figure was behind him. He re-entered the shed, and shrunk down once more. The eyes were there, before he had laid himself along.

And here he remained in such terror as none but he can know, trembling in every limb, and the cold sweat starting from every pore, when suddenly there arose upon the night-wind the noise of distant shouting, and the roar of voices mingled in alarm and wonder. Any sound of men in that lonely place, even though it conveyed a real cause of alarm, was something to him. He regained his strength and energy at the prospect of personal danger; and springing to his feet, rushed into the open air.

The broad sky seemed on fire. Rising into the air with showers of sparks, and rolling one above the other, were sheets of flame, lighting the atmosphere for miles round, and driving clouds of smoke in the direction where he stood. The shouts grew louder as new voices swelled the roar, and he could hear the cry of Fire! mingled with the ringing of an alarm-bell, the fall of heavy bodies, and the crackling of flames as they twined round some new obstacle, and shot aloft as though refreshed by food. The noise increased as he looked. There were people there—men and women—light, bustle. It was like new life to him. He darted onward—straight, headlong—dashing through brier and brake, and leaping gate and fence as madly as his dog, who careered with loud and sounding bark before him.

He came upon the spot. There were half-dressed figures tearing to and fro, some endeavouring to drag the frightened horses from the stables, others driving the cattle from the yard and out-houses, and others coming laden from the burning pile, amidst a shower of falling sparks, and the tumbling down of red-hot beams. The apertures, where doors and windows stood an hour ago, disclosed a mass of raging fire; walls rocked and crumbled into the burning well; the molten lead and iron poured down, white hot, upon the ground. Women and children shrieked, and men encouraged each other with noisy shouts and cheers. The clanking of the engine-pumps, and the spirting and hissing of the water as it fell upon the blazing wood, added to the tremendous roar. He shouted, too, till he was hoarse; and flying from memory and himself, plunged into the thickest of the throng. Hither and thither he dived that night: now working at the pumps, and now hurrying through the smoke and flame, but never ceasing to engage himself wherever noise and men were thickest. Up and down the ladders, upon the roofs of buildings, over floors that quaked and trembled with his weight, under the lee of falling bricks and stones, in every part of that great fire was he; but he bore a charmed life, and had neither scratch nor bruise, nor weariness nor thought, till morning dawned again, and only smoke and blackened ruins remained.

This mad excitement over, there returned, with ten-fold force, the dreadful consciousness of his crime. He looked suspiciously about him, for the men were conversing in groups, and he feared to be the subject of their talk. The dog obeyed the significant beck of his finger, and they drew off, stealthily, together. He passed near an engine where some men were seated, and they called to him to share in their refreshment. He took some bread and meat; and as he drank a draught of beer, heard the firemen, who were from London, talking about the murder. "He has gone to

Birmingham, they say," said one: "but they'll have him yet, for the scouts are out, and by to-morrow night there'll be a cry all through the country."

He hurried off, and walked till he almost dropped upon the ground; then lay down in a lane, and had a long, but broken and uneasy sleep. He wandered on again, irresolute and undecided, and oppressed with the fear of another solitary night.

Suddenly, he took the desperate resolution to going back to London.

"There's somebody to speak to there, at all event," he thought. "A good hiding-place, too. They'll never expect to nab me there, after this country scent. Why can't I lie by for a week or so, and, forcing blunt from Fagin, get abroad to France? Damme, I'll risk it."

He acted upon this impulse without delay, and choosing the least frequented roads began his journey back, resolved to lie concealed within a short distance of the metropolis, and, entering it at dusk by a circuitous route, to proceed straight to that part of it which he had fixed on for his destination.

The dog, though. If any description of him were out, it would not be forgotten that the dog was missing, and had probably gone with him. This might lead to his apprehension as he passed along the streets. He resolved to drown him, and walked on, looking about for a pond: picking up a heavy stone and tying it to his handkerchief as he went.

The animal looked up into his master's face while these preparations were making; whether his instinct apprehended something of their purpose, or the robber's sidelong look at him was sterner than ordinary, he skulked a little farther in the rear than usual, and cowered as he came more slowly along. When his master halted at the brink of a pool, and looked round to call him, he stopped outright.

"Do you hear me call? Come here!" cried Sikes.

The animal came up from the very force of habit; but as Sikes stooped to attach the handkerchief to his throat, he uttered a low growl and started back.

"Come back!" said the robber.

The dog wagged his tail, but moved not. Sikes made a running noose and called him again.

The dog advanced, retreated, paused an instant, and scoured away at his hardest speed.

The man whistled again and again, and sat down and waited in the expectation that he would return. But no dog appeared, and at length he resumed his journey.

CHAPTER XLIX

*Monks and Mr. Brownlow at Length Meet. Their Conversation,
and the Intelligence That Interrupts It*

The twilight was beginning to close in, when Mr. Brownlow alighted from a hackney-coach at his own door, and knocked softly. The door being opened, a sturdy man got out of the coach and stationed himself on one side of the steps, while another man, who had been seated on the box, dismounted too, and stood upon the other side. At a sign from Mr. Brownlow, they helped out a third man, and taking him between them, hurried him into the house. This man was Monks.

They walked in the same manner up the stairs without speaking, and Mr. Brownlow, preceding them, led the way into a back-room. At the door of this apartment, Monks, who had ascended with evident reluctance, stopped. The two men looked at the old gentleman as if for instructions.

"He knows the alternative," said Mr. Browlow. "If he hesitates or moves a finger but as you bid him, drag him into the street, call for the aid of the police, and impeach him as a felon in my name."

"How dare you say this of me?" asked Monks.

"How dare you urge me to it, young man?" replied Mr. Brownlow, confronting him with a steady look. "Are you mad enough to leave this house? Unhand him. There, sir. You are free to go, and we to follow. But I warn you, by all I hold most solemn and most sacred, that instant will have you apprehended on a charge of fraud and robbery. I am resolute and immoveable. If you are determined to be the same, your blood be upon your own head!"

"By what authority am I kidnapped in the street, and brought here by these dogs?" asked Monks, looking from one to the other of the men who stood beside him.

"By mine," replied Mr. Brownlow. "Those persons are indemnified by me. If you complain of being deprived of your liberty—you had power and opportunity to retrieve it as you came along, but you deemed it advisable to remain quiet—I say again, throw yourself for protection on the law. I will appeal to the law too; but when you have gone too far to recede, do not sue to me for leniency, when the power will have passed into other hands; and do not say I plunged you down the gulf into which you rushed, yourself."

Monks was plainly disconcerted, and alarmed besides. He hesitated.

"You will decide quickly," said Mr. Brownlow, with perfect firmness and composure. "If you wish me to prefer my charges publicly, and consign you to a punishment the extent of which, although I can, with a shudder, foresee, I cannot control, once more, I say, for you know the way. If not, and you appeal to my forbearance, and the mercy of those you have deeply injured, seat yourself, without a word, in that chair. It has waited for you two whole days."

Monks muttered some unintelligible words, but wavered still.

"You will be prompt," said Mr. Brownlow. "A word from me, and the alternative has gone for ever."

Still the man hesitated.

"I have not the inclination to parley," said Mr. Brownlow, "and, as I advocate the dearest interests of others, I have not the right."

"Is there—" demanded Monks with a faltering tongue,—"is there—no middle course?"

"None."

Monks looked at the old gentleman, with an anxious eye; but, reading in his countenance nothing but severity and determination, walked into the room, and, shrugging his shoulders, sat down.

"Lock the door on the outside," said Mr. Brownlow to the attendants, "and come when I ring."

The men obeyed, and the two were left alone together.

"This is pretty treatment, sir," said Monks, throwing down his hat and cloak, "from my father's oldest friend."

"It is because I was your father's oldest friend, young man," returned Mr. Brownlow; "it is because the hopes and wishes of young and happy years were bound up with him, and that fair creature of his blood and kindred who rejoined her God in youth, and left me here a solitary, lonely man: it is because he knelt with me beside his only sisters' death-bed when he was yet a boy, on the morning that would—but Heaven willed otherwise—have made her my young wife; it is because my seared heart clung to him, from that time forth, through all his trials and errors, till he died; it is because old recollections and associations filled my heart, and even the sight of you brings with it old thoughts of him; it is because of all these things that I am moved to treat you gently now—yes, Edward Leeford, even now—and blush for your unworthiness who bear the name."

"What has the name to do with it?" asked the other, after contemplating, half in silence, and half in dogged wonder, the agitation of his companion. "What is the name to me?"

"Nothing," replied Mr. Brownlow, "nothing to you. But it was hers, and even at this distance of time brings back to me, an old man, the glow and thrill which I once felt, only to hear it repeated by a stranger. I am very glad you have changed it— very—very."

"This is all mighty fine," said Monks (to retain his assumed designation) after a long silence, during which he had jerked himself in sullen defiance to and fro, and Mr. Brownlow had sat, shading his face with his hand. "But what do you want with me?"

"You have a brother," said Mr. Brownlow, rousing himself: "a brother, the whisper of whose name in your ear when I came behind you in the street, was, in itself, almost enough to make you accompany me hither, in wonder and alarm."

"I have no brother," replied Monks. "You know I was an only child. Why do you talk to me of brothers? You know that, as well as I."

"Attend to what I do know, and you may not," said Mr. Brownlow. "I shall interest you by and by. I know that of the wretched marriage, into which family pride, and the most sordid and narrowest of all ambition, forced your unhappy father when a mere boy, you were the sole and most unnatural issue."

"I don't care for hard names," interrupted Monks with a jeering laugh. "You know the fact, and that's enough for me."

"But I also know," pursued the old gentleman, "the misery, the slow torture, the protracted anguish of that ill-assorted union. I know how listlessly and wearily each of that wretched pair dragged on their heavy chain through a world that was poisoned to them both. I know how cold formalities were succeeded by open taunts; how indifference gave place to dislike, dislike to hate, and hate to loathing, until at last they wrenched the clanking bond asunder, and retiring a wide space apart, carried each a galling fragment, of which nothing but death could break the rivets, to hide it in new society beneath the gayest looks they could assume. Your mother succeeded; she forgot it soon. But it rusted and cankered at your father's heart for years."

"Well, they were separated," said Monks, "and what of that?"

"When they had been separated for some time," returned Mr. Brownlow, "and your mother, wholly given up to continental frivolities, had utterly forgotten the young husband ten good years her junior, who, with prospects blighted, lingered on at home, he fell among new friends. This circumstance, at least, you know already."

"Not I," said Monks, turning away his eyes and beating his foot upon the ground, as a man who is determined to deny everything. "Not I."

"Your manner, no less than your actions, assures me that you have never forgotten it, or ceased to think of it with bitterness," returned Mr. Brownlow. "I speak of fifteen years ago, when you were not more than eleven years old, and your father but one-and-thirty—for he was, I repeat, a boy, when his father ordered him to marry. Must I go back to events which cast a shade upon the memory of your parent, or will you spare it, and disclose to me the truth?"

"I have nothing to disclose," rejoined Monks. "You must talk on if you will."

"These new friends, then," said Mr. Brownlow, "were a naval officer retired from active service, whose wife had died some half-a-year before, and left him with two children—there had been more, but, of all their family, happily but two survived. They were both daughters; one a beautiful creature of nineteen, and the other a mere child of two or three years old."

"What's this to me?" asked Monks.

"They resided," said Mr. Brownlow, without seeming to hear the interruption, "in a part of the country to which your father in his wandering had repaired, and where he had taken up his abode. Acquaintance, intimacy, friendship, fast followed on each other. Your father was gifted as few men are. He had his sister's soul and person. As the old officer knew him more and more, he grew to love him. I would that it had ended there. His daughter did the same."

The old gentleman paused; Monks was biting his lips, with his eyes fixed upon the floor; seeing this, he immediately resumed:

"The end of a year found him contracted, solemnly contracted, to that daughter; the object of the first, true, ardent, only passion of a guileless girl."

"Your tale is of the longest," observed Monks, moving restlessly in his chair.

"It is a true tale of grief and trial, and sorrow, young man," returned Mr. Brownlow, "and such tales usually are; if it were one of unmixed joy and happiness, it would be very brief. At length one of those rich relations to strengthen whose interest and importance your father had been sacrificed, as others are often—it is no uncommon case—died, and to repair the misery he had been instrumental in occasioning, left him his panacea for all griefs—Money. It was necessary that he should immediately repair to Rome, whither this man had sped for health, and where he had died, leaving his affairs in great confusion. He went; was seized with mortal illness there; was followed, the moment the intelligence reached Paris, by your mother who carried you with her; he died the day after her arrival, leaving no will—no will—so that the whole property fell to her and you."

At this part of the recital Monks held his breath, and listened with a face of intense eagerness, though his eyes were not directed towards the speaker. As Mr. Brownlow paused, he changed his position with the air of one who has experienced a sudden relief, and wiped his hot face and hands.

"Before he went abroad, and as he passed through London on his way," said Mr. Brownlow, slowly, and fixing his eyes upon the other's face, "he came to me."

"I never heard of that," interrupted Monks in a tone intended to appear incredulous, but savouring more of disagreeable surprise.

"He came to me, and left with me, among some other things, a picture—a portrait painted by himself—a likeness of this poor girl—which he did not wish to leave behind, and could not carry forward on his hasty journey. He was worn by anxiety and remorse almost to a shadow; talked in a wild, distracted way, of ruin and dishonour worked by himself; confided to me his intention to convert his whole property, at any loss, into money, and, having settled on his wife and you a portion of his recent acquisition, to fly the country—I guessed too well he would not fly alone—and never see it more. Even from me, his old and early friend, whose strong attachment had taken root in the earth that covered one most dear to both—even from me he withheld any more particular confession, promising to write and tell me all, and after that to see me once again, for the last time on earth. Alas! That was the last time. I had no letter, and I never saw him more."

"I went," said Mr. Brownlow, after a short pause, "I went, when all was over, to the scene of his—I will use the term the world would freely use, for worldly harshness or favour are now alike to him—of his guilty love, resolved that if my fears were realised that erring child should find one heart and home to shelter and compassionate her. The family had left that part a week before; they had called in such trifling debts as were outstanding, discharged them, and left the place by night. Why, or whither, none can tell."

Monks drew his breath yet more freely, and looked round with a smile of triumph.

"When your brother," said Mr. Brownlow, drawing nearer to the other's chair, "When your brother: a feeble, ragged, neglected child: was cast in my way by a stronger hand than chance, and rescued by me from a life of vice and infamy—"

"What?" cried Monks.

"By me," said Mr. Brownlow. "I told you I should interest you before long. I say by me—I see that your cunning associate suppressed my name, although for ought he knew, it would be quite strange to your ears. When he was rescued by me, then, and lay recovering from sickness in my house, his strong resemblance to this picture I have spoken of, struck me with astonishment. Even when I first saw him in all his dirt and misery, there was a lingering expression in his face that came upon me like a glimpse of some old friend flashing on one in a vivid dream. I need not tell you he was snared away before I knew his history—"

"Why not?" asked Monks hastily.

"Because you know it well."

"I!"

"Denial to me is vain," replied Mr. Brownlow. "I shall show you that I know more than that."

"You—you—can't prove anything against me," stammered Monks. "I defy you to do it!"

"We shall see," returned the old gentleman with a searching glance. "I lost the boy, and no efforts of mine could recover him. Your mother being dead, I knew that you alone could solve the mystery if anybody could, and as when I had last heard of you you were on your own estate in the West Indies—whither, as you well know, you retired upon your mother's death to escape the consequences of vicious courses here—I made the voyage. You had left it, months before, and were supposed to be in London, but no one could tell where. I returned. Your agents had no clue to your residence. You came and went, they said, as strangely as you had ever done: sometimes for days together and sometimes not for months: keeping to all appearance the same low haunts and mingling with the same infamous herd who had been your associates when a fierce ungovernable boy. I wearied them with new applications. I paced the streets by night and day, but until two hours ago, all my efforts were fruitless, and I never saw you for an instant."

"And now you do see me," said Monks, rising boldly, "what then? Fraud and robbery are high-sounding words—justified, you think, by a fancied resemblance in some young imp to an idle daub of a dead man's Brother! You don't even know that a child was born of this maudlin pair; you don't even know that."

"I did not," replied Mr. Brownlow, rising too; "but within the last fortnight I have learnt it all. You have a brother; you know it, and him. There was a will, which your mother destroyed, leaving the secret and the gain to you at her own death. It contained a reference to some child likely to be the result of this sad connection, which child was born, and accidentally encountered by you, when your suspicions were first awakened by his resemblance to your father. You repaired to the place of his birth. There existed proofs—proofs long suppressed—of his birth and parentage. Those proofs were destroyed by you, and now, in your own words to your accomplice the Jew, "the only proofs of the boy's identity lie at the bottom of the river, and the old hag that received them from the mother is rotting in her coffin." Unworthy son, coward, liar,—you, who hold your councils with thieves and murderers in dark rooms at night,—you, whose plots and wiles have brought a violent death upon the head of one worth millions such as you,—you, who from your cradle were gall and bitterness to your own father's heart, and in whom all evil passions, vice, and profligacy, festered, till they found a vent in a hideous disease which had made your face an index even to your mind—you, Edward Leeford, do you still brave me!"

"No, no, no!" returned the coward, overwhelmed by these accumulated charges.

"Every word!" cried the gentleman, "every word that has passed between you and this detested villain, is known to me. Shadows on the wall have caught your whispers, and brought them to my ear; the sight of the persecuted child has turned vice itself, and given it the courage and almost the attributes of virtue. Murder has been done, to which you were morally if not really a party."

"No, no," interposed Monks. "I—I knew nothing of that; I was going to inquire the truth of the story when you overtook me. I didn't know the cause. I thought it was a common quarrel."

"It was the partial disclosure of your secrets," replied Mr. Brownlow. "Will you disclose the whole?"

"Yes, I will."

"Set your hand to a statement of truth and facts, and repeat it before witnesses?"

"That I promise too."

"Remain quietly here, until such a document is drawn up, and proceed with me to such a place as I may deem most advisable, for the purpose of attesting it?"

"If you insist upon that, I'll do that also," replied Monks.

"You must do more than that," said Mr. Brownlow. "Make restitution to an innocent and unoffending child, for such he is, although the offspring of a guilty and most miserable love. You have not forgotten the provisions of the will. Carry them into execution so far as your brother is concerned, and then go where you please. In this world you need meet no more."

While Monks was pacing up and down, meditating with dark and evil looks on this proposal and the possibilities of evading it: torn by his fears on the one hand and his hatred on the other: the door was hurriedly unlocked, and a gentleman (Mr. Losberne) entered the room in violent agitation.

"The man will be taken," he cried. "He will be taken to-night!"

"The murderer?" asked Mr. Brownlow.

"Yes, yes," replied the other. "His dog has been seen lurking about some old haunt, and there seems little doubt that his master either is, or will be, there, under cover of the darkness. Spies are hovering about in every direction. I have spoken to the men who are charged with his capture, and they tell me he cannot escape. A reward of a hundred pounds is proclaimed by Government to-night."

"I will give fifty more," said Mr. Brownlow, "and proclaim it with my own lips upon the spot, if I can reach it. Where is Mr. Maylie?"

"Harry? As soon as he had seen your friend here, safe in a coach with you, he hurried off to where he heard this," replied the doctor, "and mounting his horse sallied forth to join the first party at some place in the outskirts agreed upon between them."

"Fagin," said Mr. Brownlow; "what of him?"

"When I last heard, he had not been taken, but he will be, or is, by this time. They're sure of him."

"Have you made up your mind?" asked Mr. Brownlow, in a low voice, of Monks.

"Yes," he replied. "You—you—will be secret with me?"

"I will. Remain here till I return. It is your only hope of safety."

They left the room, and the door was again locked.

"What have you done?" asked the doctor in a whisper.

"All that I could hope to do, and even more. Coupling the poor girl's intelligence with my previous knowledge, and the result of our good friend's inquiries on the spot, I left him no loophole of escape, and laid bare the whole villainy which by these lights became plain as day. Write and appoint the evening after to-morrow, at seven, for the meeting. We shall be down there, a few hours before, but shall require rest: especially the young lady, who may have greater need of firmness than either you or I can quite foresee just now. But my blood boils to avenge this poor murdered creature. Which way have they taken?"

"Drive straight to the office and you will be in time," replied Mr. Losberne. "I will remain here."

The two gentlemen hastily separated; each in a fever of excitement wholly uncontrollable.

CHAPTER L

The Pursuit and Escape

Near to that part of the Thames on which the church at Rotherhithe abuts, where the buildings on the banks are dirtiest and the vessels on the river blackest with the dust of colliers and the smoke of close-built low-roofed houses, there exists the filthiest, the strangest, the most extraordinary of the many localities that are hidden in London, wholly unknown, even by name, to the great mass of its inhabitants.

To reach this place, the visitor has to penetrate through a maze of close, narrow, and muddy streets, thronged by the roughest and poorest of waterside people, and devoted to the traffic they may be supposed to occasion. The cheapest and least delicate provisions are heaped in the shops; the coarsest and commonest articles of wearing apparel dangle at the salesman's door, and stream from the house-parapet and windows. Jostling with unemployed labourers of the lowest class, ballast-heavers, coal-whippers, brazen women, ragged children, and the raff and refuse of the river, he makes his way with difficulty along, assailed by offensive sights and smells from the narrow alleys which branch off on the right and left, and deafened by the clash of ponderous waggons that bear great piles of merchandise from the stacks of warehouses that rise from every corner. Arriving, at length, in streets remoter and less-frequented than those through which he has passed, he walks beneath tottering house-fronts projecting over the pavement, dismantled walls that seem to totter as he passes, chimneys half crushed half hesitating to fall, windows guarded by rusty iron bars that time and dirt have almost eaten away, every imaginable sign of desolation and neglect.

In such a neighborhood, beyond Dockhead in the Borough of Southwark, stands Jacob's Island, surrounded by a muddy ditch, six or eight feet deep and fifteen or twenty wide when the tide is in, once called Mill Pond, but known in the days of this story as Folly Ditch. It is a creek or inlet from the Thames, and can always be filled at high water by opening the sluices at the Lead Mills from which it took its old name. At such times, a stranger, looking from one of the wooden bridges thrown across it at Mill Lane, will see the inhabitants of the houses on either side lowering from their back doors and windows, buckets, pails, domestic utensils of all kinds, in which to haul the water up; and when his eye is turned from these operations to the houses themselves, his utmost astonishment will be excited by the scene before him. Crazy wooden galleries common to the backs of half a dozen houses, with holes from which to look upon the slime beneath; windows, broken and patched, with poles thrust out, on which to dry the linen that is never there; rooms so small, so filthy, so confined, that the air would seem too tainted even for the dirt and squalor which they shelter; wooden chambers thrusting themselves out above the mud, and threatening to fall into it—as some have done; dirt-besmeared walls and decaying foundations; every repulsive lineament of poverty, every loathsome indication of filth, rot, and garbage; all these ornament the banks of Folly Ditch.

In Jacob's Island, the warehouses are roofless and empty; the walls are crumbling down; the windows are windows no more; the doors are falling into the streets; the chimneys are blackened, but they yield no smoke. Thirty or forty years ago, before losses and chancery suits came upon it, it was a thriving place; but now it is a desolate island indeed. The houses have no owners; they are broken open, and entered upon by those who have the courage; and there they live, and there they die. They must have powerful motives for a secret residence, or be reduced to a destitute condition indeed, who seek a refuge in Jacob's Island.

In an upper room of one of these houses—a detached house of fair size, ruinous in other respects, but strongly defended at door and window: of which house the back commanded the ditch in manner already described—there were assembled three men, who, regarding each other every now and then with looks expressive of perplexity and expectation, sat for some time in profound and gloomy silence. One of these was Toby Crackit, another Mr. Chitling, and the third a robber of fifty years, whose nose had been almost beaten in, in some old scuffle, and whose face bore a frightful scar which might probably be traced to the same occasion. This man was a returned transport, and his name was Kags.

"I wish," said Toby turning to Mr. Chitling, "that you had picked out some other crib when the two old ones got too warm, and had not come here, my fine feller."

"Why didn't you, blunder-head!" said Kags.

"Well, I thought you'd have been a little more glad to see me than this," replied Mr. Chitling, with a melancholy air.

"Why, look'e, young gentleman," said Toby, "when a man keeps himself so very ex-clusive as I have done, and by that means has a snug house over his head with nobody a prying and smelling about it, it's rather a startling thing to have the honour of a wisit from a young gentleman (however respectable and pleasant a person he may be to play cards with at conweniency) circumstanced as you are."

"Especially, when the exclusive young man has got a friend stopping with him, that's arrived sooner than was expected from foreign parts, and is too modest to want to be presented to the Judges on his return," added Mr. Kags.

There was a short silence, after which Toby Crackit, seeming to abandon as hopeless any further effort to maintain his usual devil-may-care swagger, turned to Chitling and said,

"When was Fagin took then?"

"Just at dinner-time—two o'clock this afternoon. Charley and I made our lucky up the wash-us chimney, and Bolter got into the empty water-butt, head downwards; but his legs were so precious long that they stuck out at the top, and so they took him too."

"And Bet?"

"Poor Bet! She went to see the Body, to speak to who it was," replied Chitling, his countenance falling more and more, "and went off mad, screaming and raving, and beating her head against the boards; so they put a strait-weskut on her and took her to the hospital—and there she is."

"Wot's come of young Bates?" demanded Kags.

"He hung about, not to come over here afore dark, but he'll be here soon," replied Chitling. "There's nowhere else to go to now, for the people at the Cripples are all in custody, and the bar of the ken—I went up there and see it with my own eyes—is filled with traps."

"This is a smash," observed Toby, biting his lips. "There's more than one will go with this."

"The sessions are on," said Kags: "if they get the inquest over, and Bolter turns King's evidence: as of course he will, from what he's said already: they can prove Fagin an accessory before the fact, and get the trial on on Friday, and he'll swing in six days from this, by G——!"

"You should have heard the people groan," said Chitling; "the officers fought like devils, or they'd have torn him away. He was down once, but they made a ring round him, and fought their way along. You should have seen how he looked about him, all muddy and bleeding, and clung to them as if they were his dearest friends. I can see 'em now, not able to stand upright with the pressing of the mob, and draggin him along amongst 'em; I can see the people jumping up, one behind another, and snarling with their teeth and making at him; I can see the blood upon his hair and beard, and hear the cries with which the women worked themselves into the centre of the crowd at the street corner, and swore they'd tear his heart out!"

The horror-stricken witness of this scene pressed his hands upon his ears, and with his eyes closed got up and paced violently to and fro, like one distracted.

While he was thus engaged, and the two men sat by in silence with their eyes fixed upon the floor, a pattering noise was heard upon the stairs, and Sikes's dog bounded into the room. They ran to the window, downstairs, and into the street. The dog had jumped in at an open window; he made no attempt to follow them, nor was his master to be seen.

"What's the meaning of this?" said Toby when they had returned. "He can't be coming here. I——I—hope not."

"If he was coming here, he'd have come with the dog," said Kags, stooping down to examine the animal, who lay panting on the floor. "Here! Give us some water for him; he has run himself faint."

"He's drunk it all up, every drop," said Chitling after watching the dog some time in silence. "Covered with mud—lame—half blind—he must have come a long way."

"Where can he have come from!" exclaimed Toby. "He's been to the other kens of course, and finding them filled with strangers come on here, where he's been many a time and often. But where can he have come from first, and how comes he here alone without the other!"

"He"—(none of them called the murderer by his old name)—"He can't have made away with himself. What do you think?" said Chitling.

Toby shook his head.

"If he had," said Kags, "the dog 'ud want to lead us away to where he did it. No. I think he's got out of the country, and left the dog behind. He must have given him the slip somehow, or he wouldn't be so easy."

This solution, appearing the most probable one, was adopted as the right; the dog, creeping under a chair, coiled himself up to sleep, without more notice from anybody.

It being now dark, the shutter was closed, and a candle lighted and placed upon the table. The terrible events of the last two days had made a deep impression on all three, increased by the danger and uncertainty of their own position. They drew their chairs closer together, starting at every sound. They spoke little, and that in whispers, and were as silent and awe-stricken as if the remains of the murdered woman lay in the next room.

They had sat thus, some time, when suddenly was heard a hurried knocking at the door below.

"Young Bates," said Kags, looking angrily round, to check the fear he felt himself.

The knocking came again. No, it wasn't he. He never knocked like that.

Crackit went to the window, and shaking all over, drew in his head. There was no need to tell them who it was; his pale face was enough. The dog too was on the alert in an instant, and ran whining to the door.

"We must let him in," he said, taking up the candle.

"Isn't there any help for it?" asked the other man in a hoarse voice.

"None. He must come in."

"Don't leave us in the dark," said Kags, taking down a candle from the chimney-piece, and lighting it, with such a trembling hand that the knocking was twice repeated before he had finished.

Crackit went down to the door, and returned followed by a man with the lower part of his face buried in a handkerchief, and another tied over his head under his hat. He drew them slowly off. Blanched face, sunken eyes, hollow cheeks, beard of three days' growth, wasted flesh, short thick breath; it was the very ghost of Sikes.

He laid his hand upon a chair which stood in the middle of the room, but shuddering as he was about to drop into it, and seeming to glance over his shoulder, dragged it back close to the wall—as close as it would go—and ground it against it—and sat down.

Not a word had been exchanged. He looked from one to another in silence. If an eye were furtively raised and met his, it was instantly averted. When his hollow voice broke silence, they all three started. They seemed never to have heard its tones before.

"How came that dog here?" he asked.

"Alone. Three hours ago."

"To-night's paper says that Fagin's took. Is it true, or a lie?"

"True."

They were silent again.

"Damn you all!" said Sikes, passing his hand across his forehead.

"Have you nothing to say to me?"

There was an uneasy movement among them, but nobody spoke.

"You that keep this house," said Sikes, turning his face to Crackit, "do you mean to sell me, or to let me lie here till this hunt is over?"

"You may stop here, if you think it safe," returned the person addressed, after some hesitation.

Sikes carried his eyes slowly up the wall behind him: rather trying to turn his head than actually doing it: and said, "Is—it—the body—is it buried?"

They shook their heads.

"Why isn't it!" he retorted with the same glance behind him. "Wot do they keep such ugly things above the ground for?—Who's that knocking?"

Crackit intimated, by a motion of his hand as he left the room, that there was nothing to fear; and directly came back with Charley Bates behind him. Sikes sat opposite the door, so that the moment the boy entered the room he encountered his figure.

"Toby," said the boy falling back, as Sikes turned his eyes towards him, "why didn't you tell me this, downstairs?"

There had been something so tremendous in the shrinking off of the three, that the wretched man was willing to propitiate even this lad. Accordingly he nodded, and made as though he would shake hands with him.

"Let me go into some other room," said the boy, retreating still farther.

"Charley!" said Sikes, stepping forward. "Don't you—don't you know me?"

"Don't come nearer me," answered the boy, still retreating, and looking, with horror in his eyes, upon the murderer's face. "You monster!"

The man stopped half-way, and they looked at each other; but Sikes's eyes sunk gradually to the ground.

"Witness you three," cried the boy shaking his clenched fist, and becoming more and more excited as he spoke. "Witness you three—I'm not afraid of him—if they come here after him, I'll give him up; I will. I tell you out at once. He may kill me for it if he likes, or if he dares, but if I am here I'll give him up. I'd give him up if he was to be boiled alive. Murder! Help! If there's the pluck of a man among you three, you'll help me. Murder! Help! Down with him!"

Pouring out these cries, and accompanying them with violent gesticulation, the boy actually threw himself, single-handed, upon the strong man, and in the intensity of his energy and the suddenness of his surprise, brought him heavily to the ground.

The three spectators seemed quite stupefied. They offered no interference, and the boy and man rolled on the ground together; the former, heedless of the blows that showered upon him, wrenching his hands tighter and tighter in the garments about the murderer's breast, and never ceasing to call for help with all his might.

The contest, however, was too unequal to last long. Sikes had him down, and his knee was on his throat, when Crackit pulled him back with a look of alarm, and pointed to the window. There were lights gleaming below, voices in loud and earnest conversation, the tramp of hurried footsteps—endless they seemed in number—crossing the nearest wooden bridge. One man on horseback seemed to be among the crowd; for there was the noise of hoofs rattling on the uneven pavement. The gleam of lights increased; the footsteps came more thickly and noisily on. Then, came a loud knocking at the door, and then a hoarse murmur from such a multitude of angry voices as would have made the boldest quail.

"Help!" shrieked the boy in a voice that rent the air.

"He's here! Break down the door!"

"In the King's name," cried the voices without; and the hoarse cry arose again, but louder.

"Break down the door!" screamed the boy. "I tell you they'll never open it. Run straight to the room where the light is. Break down the door!"

Strokes, thick and heavy, rattled upon the door and lower window-shutters as he ceased to speak, and a loud huzzah burst from the crowd; giving the listener, for the first time, some adequate idea of its immense extent.

"Open the door of some place where I can lock this screeching Hell-babe," cried Sikes fiercely; running to and fro, and dragging the boy, now, as easily as if he were an empty sack. "That door. Quick!" He flung him in, bolted it, and turned the key. "Is the downstairs door fast?"

"Double-locked and chained," replied Crackit, who, with the other two men, still remained quite helpless and bewildered.

"The panels—are they strong?"

"Lined with sheet-iron."

"And the windows too?"

"Yes, and the windows."

"Damn you!" cried the desperate ruffian, throwing up the sash and menacing the crowd. "Do your worst! I'll cheat you yet!"

Of all the terrific yells that ever fell on mortal ears, none could exceed the cry of the infuriated throng. Some shouted to those who were nearest to set the house on fire; others roared to the officers to shoot him dead. Among them all, none showed such fury as the man on horseback, who, throwing himself out of the saddle, and bursting through the crowd as if he were parting water, cried, beneath the window, in a voice that rose above all others, "Twenty guineas to the man who brings a ladder!"

The nearest voices took up the cry, and hundreds echoed it. Some called for ladders, some for sledge-hammers; some ran with torches to and fro as if to seek them, and still came back and roared again; some spent their breath in impotent curses and execrations; some pressed forward with the ecstasy of madmen, and thus impeded the progress of those below; some among the boldest attempted to climb up by the water-spout and crevices in the wall; and all waved to and fro, in the darkness beneath, like a field of corn moved by an angry wind: and joined from time to time in one loud furious roar.

"The tide," cried the murderer, as he staggered back into the room, and shut the faces out, "the tide was in as I came up. Give me a rope, a long rope. They're all in front. I may drop into the Folly Ditch, and clear off that way. Give me a rope, or I shall do three more murders and kill myself."

The panic-stricken men pointed to where such articles were kept; the murderer, hastily selecting the longest and strongest cord, hurried up to the house-top.

All the window in the rear of the house had been long ago bricked up, except one small trap in the room where the boy was locked, and that was too small even for the passage of his body. But, from this aperture, he had never ceased to call on those without, to guard the back; and thus, when the murderer emerged at last on the house-top by the door in the roof, a loud shout proclaimed the fact to those in front, who immediately began to pour round, pressing upon each other in an unbroken stream.

He planted a board, which he had carried up with him for the purpose, so firmly against the door that it must be matter of great difficulty to open it from the inside; and creeping over the tiles, looked over the low parapet.

The water was out, and the ditch a bed of mud.

The crowd had been hushed during these few moments, watching his motions and doubtful of his purpose, but the instant they perceived it and knew it was defeated, they raised a cry of triumphant execration to which all their previous shouting had been whispers. Again and again it rose. Those who were at too great a distance to know its meaning, took up the sound; it echoed and re-echoed; it seemed as though the whole city had poured its population out to curse him.

On pressed the people from the front—on, on, on, in a strong struggling current of angry faces, with here and there a glaring torch to lighten them up, and show them out in all their wrath and passion. The houses on the opposite side of the ditch had been entered by the mob; sashes were thrown up, or torn bodily out; there were tiers and tiers of faces in every window; cluster upon cluster of people clinging to every house-top. Each little bridge (and there were three in sight) bent beneath the weight of the crowd upon it. Still the current poured on to find some nook or hole from which to vent their shouts, and only for an instant see the wretch.

"They have him now," cried a man on the nearest bridge. "Hurrah!"

The crowd grew light with uncovered heads; and again the shout uprose.

"I will give fifty pounds," cried an old gentleman from the same quarter, "to the man who takes him alive. I will remain here, till he come to ask me for it."

There was another roar. At this moment the word was passed among the crowd that the door was forced at last, and that he who had first called for the ladder had mounted into the room. The stream abruptly turned, as this intelligence ran from mouth to mouth; and the people at the windows, seeing those upon the bridges pouring back, quitted their stations, and running into the street, joined the concourse that now thronged pell-mell to the spot they had left: each man crushing and striving with his neighbor, and all panting with impatience to get near the door, and look upon the criminal as the officers brought him out. The cries and shrieks of those who were pressed almost to suffocation, or trampled down and trodden under foot in the confusion, were dreadful; the narrow ways were completely blocked up; and at this time, between the rush of some to regain the space in front of the house, and the unavailing struggles of others to extricate themselves from the mass, the immediate attention was distracted from the murderer, although the universal eagerness for his capture was, if possible, increased.

The man had shrunk down, thoroughly quelled by the ferocity of the crowd, and the impossibility of escape; but seeing this sudden change with no less rapidity than it had occurred, he sprang upon his feet, determined to make one last effort for his life by dropping into the ditch, and, at the risk of being stifled, endeavouring to creep away in the darkness and confusion.

Roused into new strength and energy, and stimulated by the noise within the house which announced that an entrance had really been effected, he set his foot against the stack of chimneys, fastened one end of the rope tightly and firmly round it, and with the other made a strong running noose by the aid of his hands and teeth almost in a second. He could let himself down by the cord to within a less distance of the ground than his own height, and had his knife ready in his hand to cut it then and drop.

At the very instant when he brought the loop over his head previous to slipping it beneath his arm-pits, and when the old gentleman before-mentioned (who had clung so tight to the railing of the bridge as to resist the force of the crowd, and retain his position) earnestly warned those about him that the man was about to lower himself down—at that very instant the murderer, looking behind him on the roof, threw his arms above his head, and uttered a yell of terror.

"The eyes again!" he cried in an unearthly screech.

Staggering as if struck by lightning, he lost his balance and tumbled over the parapet. The noose was on his neck. It ran up with his weight, tight as a bow-string, and swift as the arrow it speeds. He fell for five-and-thirty feet. There was a sudden jerk, a terrific convulsion of the limbs; and there he hung, with the open knife clenched in his stiffening hand.

The old chimney quivered with the shock, but stood it bravely. The murderer swung lifeless against the wall; and the boy, thrusting aside the dangling body which obscured his view, called to the people to come and take him out, for God's sake.

A dog, which had lain concealed till now, ran backwards and forwards on the parapet with a dismal howl, and collecting himself for a spring, jumped for the dead man's shoulders. Missing his aim, he fell into the ditch, turning completely over as he went; and striking his head against a stone, dashed out his brains.

CHAPTER LI

*Affording an Explanation of More Mysteries Than One, and Comprehending
a Proposal of Marriage With No Word of Settlement or Pin-Money*

The events narrated in the last chapter were yet but two days old, when Oliver
found himself, at three o'clock in the afternoon, in a travelling-carriage rolling
fast towards his native town. Mrs. Maylie, and Rose, and Mrs. Bedwin, and the good
doctor were with him: and Mr. Brownlow followed in a post-chaise, accompanied by
one other person whose name had not been mentioned.

They had not talked much upon the way; for Oliver was in a flutter of agitation
and uncertainty which deprived him of the power of collecting his thoughts, and
almost of speech, and appeared to have scarcely less effect on his companions, who
shared it, in at least an equal degree. He and the two ladies had been very carefully
made acquainted by Mr. Brownlow with the nature of the admissions which had been
forced from Monks; and although they knew that the object of their present journey
was to complete the work which had been so well begun, still the whole matter was
enveloped in enough of doubt and mystery to leave them in endurance of the most
intense suspense.

The same kind friend had, with Mr. Losberne's assistance, cautiously stopped all
channels of communication through which they could receive intelligence of the
dreadful occurrences that so recently taken place. "It was quite true," he said, "that
they must know them before long, but it might be at a better time than the present, and
it could not be at a worse.' So, they travelled on in silence: each busied with reflections
on the object which had brought them together: and no one disposed to give utterance
to the thoughts which crowded upon all.

But if Oliver, under these influences, had remained silent while they journeyed
towards his birth-place by a road he had never seen, how the whole current of his
recollections ran back to old times, and what a crowd of emotions were wakened
up in his breast, when they turned into that which he had traversed on foot: a poor
houseless, wandering boy, without a friend to help him, or a roof to shelter his head.

"See there, there!" cried Oliver, eagerly clasping the hand of Rose, and pointing
out at the carriage window; "that's the stile I came over; there are the hedges I crept
behind, for fear any one should overtake me and force me back! Yonder is the path
across the fields, leading to the old house where I was a little child! Oh Dick, Dick, my
dear old friend, if I could only see you now!"

"You will see him soon," replied Rose, gently taking his folded hands between her
own. "You shall tell him how happy you are, and how rich you have grown, and that
in all your happiness you have none so great as the coming back to make him happy
too."

"Yes, yes," said Oliver, "and we'll—we'll take him away from here, and have him
clothed and taught, and send him to some quiet country place where he may grow
strong and well,—shall we?"

Rose nodded "yes," for the boy was smiling through such happy tears that she could not speak.

"You will be kind and good to him, for you are to every one," said Oliver. "It will make you cry, I know, to hear what he can tell; but never mind, never mind, it will be all over, and you will smile again—I know that too—to think how changed he is; you did the same with me. He said "God bless you" to me when I ran away," cried the boy with a burst of affectionate emotion; "and I will say "God bless you" now, and show him how I love him for it!"

As they approached the town, and at length drove through its narrow streets, it became matter of no small difficulty to restrain the boy within reasonable bounds. There was Sowerberry's the undertaker's just as it used to be, only smaller and less imposing in appearance than he remembered it—there were all the well-known shops and houses, with almost every one of which he had some slight incident connected—there was Gamfield's cart, the very cart he used to have, standing at the old public-house door—there was the workhouse, the dreary prison of his youthful days, with its dismal windows frowning on the street—there was the same lean porter standing at the gate, at sight of whom Oliver involuntarily shrunk back, and then laughed at himself for being so foolish, then cried, then laughed again—there were scores of faces at the doors and windows that he knew quite well—there was nearly everything as if he had left it but yesterday, and all his recent life had been but a happy dream.

But it was pure, earnest, joyful reality. They drove straight to the door of the chief hotel (which Oliver used to stare up at, with awe, and think a mighty palace, but which had somehow fallen off in grandeur and size); and here was Mr. Grimwig all ready to receive them, kissing the young lady, and the old one too, when they got out of the coach, as if he were the grandfather of the whole party, all smiles and kindness, and not offering to eat his head—no, not once; not even when he contradicted a very old postboy about the nearest road to London, and maintained he knew it best, though he had only come that way once, and that time fast asleep. There was dinner prepared, and there were bedrooms ready, and everything was arranged as if by magic.

Notwithstanding all this, when the hurry of the first half-hour was over, the same silence and constraint prevailed that had marked their journey down. Mr. Brownlow did not join them at dinner, but remained in a separate room. The two other gentlemen hurried in and out with anxious faces, and, during the short intervals when they were present, conversed apart. Once, Mrs. Maylie was called away, and after being absent for nearly an hour, returned with eyes swollen with weeping. All these things made Rose and Oliver, who were not in any new secrets, nervous and uncomfortable. They sat wondering, in silence; or, if they exchanged a few words, spoke in whispers, as if they were afraid to hear the sound of their own voices.

At length, when nine o'clock had come, and they began to think they were to hear no more that night, Mr. Losberne and Mr. Grimwig entered the room, followed by Mr. Brownlow and a man whom Oliver almost shrieked with surprise to see; for they told him it was his brother, and it was the same man he had met at the market-town, and seen looking in with Fagin at the window of his little room. Monks cast a look of hate, which, even then, he could not dissemble, at the astonished boy, and sat down near the door. Mr. Brownlow, who had papers in his hand, walked to a table near which Rose and Oliver were seated.

"This is a painful task," said he, "but these declarations, which have been signed in London before many gentlemen, must be in substance repeated here. I would have spared you the degradation, but we must hear them from your own lips before we part, and you know why."

"Go on," said the person addressed, turning away his face. "Quick. I have almost done enough, I think. Don't keep me here."

"This child," said Mr. Brownlow, drawing Oliver to him, and laying his hand upon his head, "is your half-brother; the illegitimate son of your father, my dear friend Edwin Leeford, by poor young Agnes Fleming, who died in giving him birth."

"Yes," said Monks, scowling at the trembling boy: the beating of whose heart he might have heard. "That is the bastard child."

"The term you use," said Mr. Brownlow, sternly, "is a reproach to those long since passed beyond the feeble censure of the world. It reflects disgrace on no one living, except you who use it. Let that pass. He was born in this town."

"In the workhouse of this town," was the sullen reply. "You have the story there." He pointed impatiently to the papers as he spoke.

"I must have it here, too," said Mr. Brownlow, looking round upon the listeners.

"Listen then! You!" returned Monks. "His father being taken ill at Rome, was joined by his wife, my mother, from whom he had been long separated, who went from Paris and took me with her—to look after his property, for what I know, for she had no great affection for him, nor he for her. He knew nothing of us, for his senses were gone, and he slumbered on till next day, when he died. Among the papers in his desk, were two, dated on the night his illness first came on, directed to yourself'; he addressed himself to Mr. Brownlow; "and enclosed in a few short lines to you, with an intimation on the cover of the package that it was not to be forwarded till after he was dead. One of these papers was a letter to this girl Agnes; the other a will."

"What of the letter?" asked Mr. Brownlow.

"The letter?—A sheet of paper crossed and crossed again, with a penitent confession, and prayers to God to help her. He had palmed a tale on the girl that some secret mystery—to be explained one day—prevented his marrying her just then; and so she had gone on, trusting patiently to him, until she trusted too far, and lost what none could ever give her back. She was, at that time, within a few months of her confinement. He told her all he had meant to do, to hide her shame, if he had lived, and prayed her, if he died, not to curse his memory, or think the consequences of their sin would be visited on her or their young child; for all the guilt was his. He reminded her of the day he had given her the little locket and the ring with her christian name engraved upon it, and a blank left for that which he hoped one day to have bestowed upon her—prayed her yet to keep it, and wear it next her heart, as she had done before—and then ran on, wildly, in the same words, over and over again, as if he had gone distracted. I believe he had."

"The will," said Mr. Brownlow, as Oliver's tears fell fast.

Monks was silent.

"The will," said Mr. Brownlow, speaking for him, "was in the same spirit as the letter. He talked of miseries which his wife had brought upon him; of the rebellious disposition, vice, malice, and premature bad passions of you his only son, who had been trained to hate him; and left you, and your mother, each an annuity of eight hundred pounds. The bulk of his property he divided into two equal portions—one for Agnes Fleming, and the other for their child, if it should be born alive, and ever come of age. If it were a girl, it was to inherit the money unconditionally; but if a boy, only on the stipulation that in his minority he should never have stained his name with any public act of dishonour, meanness, cowardice, or wrong. He did this, he said, to mark his confidence in the other, and his conviction—only strengthened by approaching death—that the child would share her gentle heart, and noble nature. If he were disappointed in this expectation, then the money was to come to you: for then, and not till then, when both children were equal, would he recognise your prior claim upon his purse, who had none upon his heart, but had, from an infant, repulsed him with coldness and aversion."

"My mother," said Monks, in a louder tone, "did what a woman should have done. She burnt this will. The letter never reached its destination; but that, and other proofs, she kept, in case they ever tried to lie away the blot. The girl's father had the truth from her with every aggravation that her violent hate—I love her for it now—could add. Goaded by shame and dishonour he fled with his children into a remote corner of Wales, changing his very name that his friends might never know of his retreat; and here, no great while afterwards, he was found dead in his bed. The girl had left her home, in secret, some weeks before; he had searched for her, on foot, in every town and village near; it was on the night when he returned home, assured that she had destroyed herself, to hide her shame and his, that his old heart broke."

There was a short silence here, until Mr. Brownlow took up the thread of the narrative.

"Years after this," he said, "this man's—Edward Leeford's—mother came to me. He had left her, when only eighteen; robbed her of jewels and money; gambled, squandered, forged, and fled to London: where for two years he had associated with the lowest outcasts. She was sinking under a painful and incurable disease, and wished to recover him before she died. Inquiries were set on foot, and strict searches made. They were unavailing for a long time, but ultimately successful; and he went back with her to France."

"There she died," said Monks, "after a lingering illness; and, on her death-bed, she bequeathed these secrets to me, together with her unquenchable and deadly hatred of all whom they involved—though she need not have left me that, for I had inherited it long before. She would not believe that the girl had destroyed herself, and the child too, but was filled with the impression that a male child had been born, and was alive. I swore to her, if ever it crossed my path, to hunt it down; never to let it rest; to pursue it with the bitterest and most unrelenting animosity; to vent upon it the hatred that I deeply felt, and to spit upon the empty vaunt of that insulting will by draggin it, if I could, to the very gallows-foot. She was right. He came in my way at last. I began well; and, but for babbling drabs, I would have finished as I began!"

As the villain folded his arms tight together, and muttered curses on himself in the impotence of baffled malice, Mr. Brownlow turned to the terrified group beside him, and explained that the Jew, who had been his old accomplice and confidant, had a large reward for keeping Oliver ensnared: of which some part was to be given up, in the event of his being rescued: and that a dispute on this head had led to their visit to the country house for the purpose of identifying him.

"The locket and ring?" said Mr. Brownlow, turning to Monks.

"I bought them from the man and woman I told you of, who stole them from the nurse, who stole them from the corpse," answered Monks without raising his eyes. "You know what became of them."

Mr. Brownlow merely nodded to Mr. Grimwig, who disappearing with great alacrity, shortly returned, pushing in Mrs. Bumble, and dragging her unwilling consort after him.

"Do my hi's deceive me!" cried Mr. Bumble, with ill-feigned enthusiasm, "or is that little Oliver? Oh O-li-ver, if you know'd how I've been a-grieving for you——"

"Hold your tongue, fool," murmured Mrs. Bumble.

"Isn't natur, natur, Mrs. Bumble?" remonstrated the workhouse master. "Can't I be supposed to feel—I as brought him up porochially—when I see him a-setting here among ladies and gentlemen of the very affablest description! I always loved that boy as if he'd been my—my—my own grandfather," said Mr. Bumble, halting for an appropriate comparison. "Master Oliver, my dear, you remember the blessed gentleman in the white waistcoat? Ah! he went to heaven last week, in a oak coffin with plated handles, Oliver."

"Come, sir," said Mr. Grimwig, tartly; "suppress your feelings."

"I will do my endeavours, sir," replied Mr. Bumble. "How do you do, sir? I hope you are very well."

This salutation was addressed to Mr. Brownlow, who had stepped up to within a short distance of the respectable couple. He inquired, as he pointed to Monks,

"Do you know that person?"

"No," replied Mrs. Bumble flatly.

"Perhaps you don't?" said Mr. Brownlow, addressing her spouse.

"I never saw him in all my life," said Mr. Bumble.

"Nor sold him anything, perhaps?"

"No," replied Mrs. Bumble.

"You never had, perhaps, a certain gold locket and ring?" said Mr. Brownlow.

"Certainly not," replied the matron. "Why are we brought here to answer to such nonsense as this?"

Again Mr. Brownlow nodded to Mr. Grimwig; and again that gentleman limped away with extraordinary readiness. But not again did he return with a stout man and wife; for this time, he led in two palsied women, who shook and tottered as they walked.

"You shut the door the night old Sally died," said the foremost one, raising her shrivelled hand, "but you couldn't shut out the sound, nor stop the chinks."

"No, no," said the other, looking round her and wagging her toothless jaws. "No, no, no."

"We heard her try to tell you what she'd done, and saw you take a paper from her hand, and watched you too, next day, to the pawnbroker's shop," said the first.

"Yes," added the second, "and it was a 'locket and gold ring.' We found out that, and saw it given you. We were by. Oh! we were by."

"And we know more than that," resumed the first, "for she told us often, long ago, that the young mother had told her that, feeling she should never get over it, she was on her way, at the time that she was taken ill, to die near the grave of the father of the child."

"Would you like to see the pawnbroker himself?" asked Mr. Grimwig with a motion towards the door.

"No," replied the woman; "if he—she pointed to Monks—'has been coward enough to confess, as I see he has, and you have sounded all these hags till you have found the right ones, I have nothing more to say. I did sell them, and they're where you'll never get them. What then?"

"Nothing," replied Mr. Brownlow, "except that it remains for us to take care that neither of you is employed in a situation of trust again. You may leave the room."

"I hope," said Mr. Bumble, looking about him with great ruefulness, as Mr. Grimwig disappeared with the two old women: "I hope that this unfortunate little circumstance will not deprive me of my porochial office?"

"Indeed it will," replied Mr. Brownlow. "You may make up your mind to that, and think yourself well off besides."

"It was all Mrs. Bumble. She would do it," urged Mr. Bumble; first looking round to ascertain that his partner had left the room.

"That is no excuse," replied Mr. Brownlow. "You were present on the occasion of the destruction of these trinkets, and indeed are the more guilty of the two, in the eye of the law; for the law supposes that your wife acts under your direction."

"If the law supposes that," said Mr. Bumble, squeezing his hat emphatically in both hands, "the law is a ass—a idiot. If that's the eye of the law, the law is a bachelor; and the worst I wish the law is, that his eye may be opened by experience—by experience."

Laying great stress on the repetition of these two words, Mr. Bumble fixed his hat on very tight, and putting his hands in his pockets, followed his helpmate downstairs.

"Young lady," said Mr. Brownlow, turning to Rose, "give me your hand. Do not tremble. You need not fear to hear the few remaining words we have to say."

"If they have—I do not know how they can, but if they have—any reference to me," said Rose, "pray let me hear them at some other time. I have not strength or spirits now."

"Nay," returned the old gentleman, drawing her arm through his; "you have more fortitude than this, I am sure. Do you know this young lady, sir?"

"Yes," replied Monks.

"I never saw you before," said Rose faintly.

"I have seen you often," returned Monks.

"The father of the unhappy Agnes had two daughters," said Mr. Brownlow. "What was the fate of the other—the child?"

"The child," replied Monks, "when her father died in a strange place, in a strange name, without a letter, book, or scrap of paper that yielded the faintest clue by which his friends or relatives could be traced—the child was taken by some wretched cottagers, who reared it as their own."

"Go on," said Mr. Brownlow, signing to Mrs. Maylie to approach. "Go on!"

"You couldn't find the spot to which these people had repaired," said Monks, "but where friendship fails, hatred will often force a way. My mother found it, after a year of cunning search—ay, and found the child."

"She took it, did she?"

"No. The people were poor and began to sicken—at least the man did—of their fine humanity; so she left it with them, giving them a small present of money which would not last long, and promised more, which she never meant to send. She didn't quite rely, however, on their discontent and poverty for the child's unhappiness, but told the history of the sister's shame, with such alterations as suited her; bade them take good heed of the child, for she came of bad blood; and told them she was illegitimate, and sure to go wrong at one time or other. The circumstances countenanced all this; the people believed it; and there the child dragged on an existence, miserable enough even to satisfy us, until a widow lady, residing, then, at Chester, saw the girl by chance, pitied her, and took her home. There was some cursed spell, I think, against us; for in spite of all our efforts she remained there and was happy. I lost sight of her, two or three years ago, and saw her no more until a few months back."

"Do you see her now?"

"Yes. Leaning on your arm."

"But not the less my niece," cried Mrs. Maylie, folding the fainting girl in her arms; "not the less my dearest child. I would not lose her now, for all the treasures of the world. My sweet companion, my own dear girl!"

"The only friend I ever had," cried Rose, clinging to her. "The kindest, best of friends. My heart will burst. I cannot bear all this."

"You have borne more, and have been, through all, the best and gentlest creature that ever shed happiness on every one she knew," said Mrs. Maylie, embracing her tenderly. "Come, come, my love, remember who this is who waits to clasp you in his arms, poor child! See here—look, look, my dear!"

"Not aunt," cried Oliver, throwing his arms about her neck; "I'll never call her aunt—sister, my own dear sister, that something taught my heart to love so dearly from the first! Rose, dear, darling Rose!"

Let the tears which fell, and the broken words which were exchanged in the long close embrace between the orphans, be sacred. A father, sister, and mother, were gained, and lost, in that one moment. Joy and grief were mingled in the cup; but there were no bitter tears: for even grief itself arose so softened, and clothed in such sweet and tender recollections, that it became a solemn pleasure, and lost all character of pain.

They were a long, long time alone. A soft tap at the door, at length announced that some one was without. Oliver opened it, glided away, and gave place to Harry Maylie.

"I know it all," he said, taking a seat beside the lovely girl. "Dear Rose, I know it all."

"I am not here by accident," he added after a lengthened silence; "nor have I heard all this to-night, for I knew it yesterday—only yesterday. Do you guess that I have come to remind you of a promise?"

"Stay," said Rose. "You do know all."

"All. You gave me leave, at any time within a year, to renew the subject of our last discourse."

"I did."

"Not to press you to alter your determination," pursued the young man, "but to hear you repeat it, if you would. I was to lay whatever of station or fortune I might possess at your feet, and if you still adhered to your former determination, I pledged myself, by no word or act, to seek to change it."

"The same reasons which influenced me then, will influence me now," said Rose firmly. "If I ever owed a strict and rigid duty to her, whose goodness saved me from a life of indigence and suffering, when should I ever feel it, as I should to-night? It is a struggle," said Rose, "but one I am proud to make; it is a pang, but one my heart shall bear."

"The disclosure of to-night,"—Harry began.

"The disclosure of to-night," replied Rose softly, "leaves me in the same position, with reference to you, as that in which I stood before."

"You harden your heart against me, Rose," urged her lover.

"Oh Harry, Harry," said the young lady, bursting into tears; "I·wish I could, and spare myself this pain."

"Then why inflict it on yourself?" said Harry, taking her hand. "Think, dear Rose, think what you have heard to-night."

"And what have I heard! What have I heard!" cried Rose. "That a sense of his deep disgrace so worked upon my own father that he shunned all—there, we have said enough, Harry, we have said enough."

"Not yet, not yet," said the young man, detaining her as she rose. "My hopes, my wishes, prospects, feeling: every thought in life except my love for you: have undergone a change. I offer you, now, no distinction among a bustling crowd; no mingling with a world of malice and detraction, where the blood is called into honest cheeks by aught but real disgrace and shame; but a home—a heart and home—yes, dearest Rose, and those, and those alone, are all I have to offer."

"What do you mean!" she faltered.

"I mean but this—that when I left you last, I left you with a firm determination to level all fancied barriers between yourself and me; resolved that if my world could not be yours, I would make yours mine; that no pride of birth should curl the lip at you, for I would turn from it. This I have done. Those who have shrunk from me because of this, have shrunk from you, and proved you so far right. Such power and patronage: such relatives of influence and rank: as smiled upon me then, look coldly now; but there are smiling fields and waving trees in England's richest county; and by one village church—mine, Rose, my own!—there stands a rustic dwelling which you can make me prouder of, than all the hopes I have renounced, measured a thousandfold. This is my rank and station now, and here I lay it down!"

* * * * *

"It's a trying thing waiting supper for lovers," said Mr. Grimwig, waking up, and pulling his pocket-handkerchief from over his head.

Truth to tell, the supper had been waiting a most unreasonable time. Neither Mrs. Maylie, nor Harry, nor Rose (who all came in together), could offer a word in extenuation.

"I had serious thoughts of eating my head to-night," said Mr. Grimwig, "for I began to think I should get nothing else. I'll take the liberty, if you'll allow me, of saluting the bride that is to be."

Mr. Grimwig lost no time in carrying this notice into effect upon the blushing girl; and the example, being contagious, was followed both by the doctor and Mr. Brownlow: some people affirm that Harry Maylie had been observed to set it, originally, in a dark room adjoining; but the best authorities consider this downright scandal: he being young and a clergyman.

"Oliver, my child," said Mrs. Maylie, "where have you been, and why do you look so sad? There are tears stealing down your face at this moment. What is the matter?"

It is a world of disappointment: often to the hopes we most cherish, and hopes that do our nature the greatest honour.

Poor Dick was dead!

CHAPTER LII

Fagin's Last Night Alive

The court was paved, from floor to roof, with human faces. Inquisitive and eager eyes peered from every inch of space. From the rail before the dock, away into the sharpest angle of the smallest corner in the galleries, all looks were fixed upon one man—Fagin. Before him and behind: above, below, on the right and on the left: he seemed to stand surrounded by a firmament, all bright with gleaming eyes.

He stood there, in all this glare of living light, with one hand resting on the wooden slab before him, the other held to his ear, and his head thrust forward to enable him to catch with greater distinctness every word that fell from the presiding judge, who was delivering his charge to the jury. At times, he turned his eyes sharply upon them to observe the effect of the slightest featherweight in his favour; and when the points against him were stated with terrible distinctness, looked towards his counsel, in mute appeal that he would, even then, urge something in his behalf. Beyond these manifestations of anxiety, he stirred not hand or foot. He had scarcely moved since the trial began; and now that the judge ceased to speak, he still remained in the same strained attitude of close attention, with his gaze bent on him, as though he listened still.

A slight bustle in the court, recalled him to himself. Looking round, he saw that the juryman had turned together, to consider their verdict. As his eyes wandered to the gallery, he could see the people rising above each other to see his face: some hastily applying their glasses to their eyes: and others whispering their neighbours with looks expressive of abhorrence. A few there were, who seemed unmindful of him, and looked only to the jury, in impatient wonder how they could delay. But in no one face—not even among the women, of whom there were many there—could he read the faintest sympathy with himself, or any feeling but one of all-absorbing interest that he should be condemned.

As he saw all this in one bewildered glance, the deathlike stillness came again, and looking back he saw that the jurymen had turned towards the judge. Hush!

They only sought permission to retire.

He looked, wistfully, into their faces, one by one when they passed out, as though to see which way the greater number leant; but that was fruitless. The jailer touched him on the shoulder. He followed mechanically to the end of the dock, and sat down on a chair. The man pointed it out, or he would not have seen it.

He looked up into the gallery again. Some of the people were eating, and some fanning themselves with handkerchiefs; for the crowded place was very hot. There was one young man sketching his face in a little note-book. He wondered whether it was like, and looked on when the artist broke his pencil-point, and made another with his knife, as any idle spectator might have done.

In the same way, when he turned his eyes towards the judge, his mind began to busy itself with the fashion of his dress, and what it cost, and how he put it on. There was an old fat gentleman on the bench, too, who had gone out, some half an hour before, and now come back. He wondered within himself whether this man had been to get his dinner, what he had had, and where he had had it; and pursued this train of careless thought until some new object caught his eye and roused another.

Not that, all this time, his mind was, for an instant, free from one oppressive overwhelming sense of the grave that opened at his feet; it was ever present to him, but in a vague and general way, and he could not fix his thoughts upon it. Thus, even while he trembled, and turned burning hot at the idea of speedy death, he fell to counting the iron spikes before him, and wondering how the head of one had been broken off, and whether they would mend it, or leave it as it was. Then, he thought of all the horrors of the gallows and the scaffold—and stopped to watch a man sprinkling the floor to cool it—and then went on to think again.

At length there was a cry of silence, and a breathless look from all towards the door. The jury returned, and passed him close. He could glean nothing from their faces; they might as well have been of stone. Perfect stillness ensued—not a rustle—not a breath—Guilty.

The building rang with a tremendous shout, and another, and another, and then it echoed loud groans, that gathered strength as they swelled out, like angry thunder. It was a peal of joy from the populace outside, greeting the news that he would die on Monday.

The noise subsided, and he was asked if he had anything to say why sentence of death should not be passed upon him. He had resumed his listening attitude, and looked intently at his questioner while the demand was made; but it was twice repeated before he seemed to hear it, and then he only muttered that he was an old man—an old man—and so, dropping into a whisper, was silent again.

The judge assumed the black cap, and the prisoner still stood with the same air and gesture. A woman in the gallery, uttered some exclamation, called forth by this dread solemnity; he looked hastily up as if angry at the interruption, and bent forward yet more attentively. The address was solemn and impressive; the sentence fearful to hear. But he stood, like a marble figure, without the motion of a nerve. His haggard face was still thrust forward, his under-jaw hanging down, and his eyes staring out before him, when the jailer put his hand upon his arm, and beckoned him away. He gazed stupidly about him for an instant, and obeyed.

They led him through a paved room under the court, where some prisoners were waiting till their turns came, and others were talking to their friends, who crowded round a grate which looked into the open yard. There was nobody there to speak to him; but, as he passed, the prisoners fell back to render him more visible to the people who were clinging to the bars: and they assailed him with opprobrious names, and screeched and hissed. He shook his fist, and would have spat upon them; but his conductors hurried him on, through a gloomy passage lighted by a few dim lamps, into the interior of the prison.

Here, he was searched, that he might not have about him the means of anticipating the law; this ceremony performed, they led him to one of the condemned cells, and left him there—alone.

He sat down on a stone bench opposite the door, which served for seat and bedstead; and casting his blood-shot eyes upon the ground, tried to collect his thoughts. After awhile, he began to remember a few disjointed fragments of what the judge had said: though it had seemed to him, at the time, that he could not hear a word. These gradually fell into their proper places, and by degrees suggested more: so that in a little time he had the whole, almost as it was delivered. To be hanged by the neck, till he was dead—that was the end. To be hanged by the neck till he was dead.

As it came on very dark, he began to think of all the men he had known who had died upon the scaffold; some of them through his means. They rose up, in such quick succession, that he could hardly count them. He had seen some of them die,—and had joked too, because they died with prayers upon their lips. With what a rattling noise the drop went down; and how suddenly they changed, from strong and vigorous men to dangling heaps of clothes!

Some of them might have inhabited that very cell—sat upon that very spot. It was very dark; why didn't they bring a light? The cell had been built for many years. Scores of men must have passed their last hours there. It was like sitting in a vault strewn with dead bodies—the cap, the noose, the pinioned arms, the faces that he knew, even beneath that hideous veil.—Light, light!

At length, when his hands were raw with beating against the heavy door and walls, two men appeared: one bearing a candle, which he thrust into an iron candlestick fixed against the wall: the other dragging in a mattress on which to pass the night; for the prisoner was to be left alone no more.

Then came the night—dark, dismal, silent night. Other watchers are glad to hear this church-clock strike, for they tell of life and coming day. To him they brought

despair. The boom of every iron bell came laden with the one, deep, hollow sound—
Death. What availed the noise and bustle of cheerful morning, which penetrated even
there, to him? It was another form of knell, with mockery added to the warning.

The day passed off. Day? There was no day; it was gone as soon as come—and
night came on again; night so long, and yet so short; long in its dreadful silence, and
short in its fleeting hours. At one time he raved and blasphemed; and at another
howled and tore his hair. Venerable men of his own persuasion had come to pray
beside him, but he had driven them away with curses. They renewed their charitable
efforts, and he beat them off.

Saturday night. He had only one night more to live. And as he thought of this, the
day broke—Sunday.

It was not until the night of this last awful day, that a withering sense of his
helpless, desperate state came in its full intensity upon his blighted soul; not that he
had ever held any defined or positive hope of mercy, but that he had never been able
to consider more than the dim probability of dying so soon. He had spoken little to
either of the two men, who relieved each other in their attendance upon him; and
they, for their parts, made no effort to rouse his attention. He had sat there, awake,
but dreaming. Now, he started up, every minute, and with gasping mouth and burning
skin, hurried to and fro, in such a paroxysm of fear and wrath that even they—used
to such sights—recoiled from him with horror. He grew so terrible, at last, in all the
tortures of his evil conscience, that one man could not bear to sit there, eyeing him
alone; and so the two kept watch together.

He cowered down upon his stone bed, and thought of the past. He had been
wounded with some missiles from the crowd on the day of his capture, and his head
was bandaged with a linen cloth. His red hair hung down upon his bloodless face;
his beard was torn, and twisted into knots; his eyes shone with a terrible light; his
unwashed flesh crackled with the fever that burnt him up. Eight—nine—then. If it
was not a trick to frighten him, and those were the real hours treading on each other's
heels, where would he be, when they came round again! Eleven! Another struck,
before the voice of the previous hour had ceased to vibrate. At eight, he would be the
only mourner in his own funeral train; at eleven—

Those dreadful walls of Newgate, which have hidden so much misery and such
unspeakable anguish, not only from the eyes, but, too often, and too long, from the
thoughts, of men, never held so dread a spectacle as that. The few who lingered as
they passed, and wondered what the man was doing who was to be hanged to-morrow,
would have slept but ill that night, if they could have seen him.

From early in the evening until nearly midnight, little groups of two and three
presented themselves at the lodge-gate, and inquired, with anxious faces, whether any
reprieve had been received. These being answered in the negative, communicated the
welcome intelligence to clusters in the street, who pointed out to one another the door
from which he must come out, and showed where the scaffold would be built, and,
walking with unwilling steps away, turned back to conjure up the scene. By degrees
they fell off, one by one; and, for an hour, in the dead of night, the street was left to
solitude and darkness.

The space before the prison was cleared, and a few strong barriers, painted black, had been already thrown across the road to break the pressure of the expected crowd, when Mr. Brownlow and Oliver appeared at the wicket, and presented an order of admission to the prisoner, signed by one of the sheriffs. They were immediately admitted into the lodge.

"Is the young gentleman to come too, sir?" said the man whose duty it was to conduct them. "It's not a sight for children, sir."

"It is not indeed, my friend," rejoined Mr. Brownlow; "but my business with this man is intimately connected with him; and as this child has seen him in the full career of his success and villainy, I think it as well—even at the cost of some pain and fear—that he should see him now."

These few words had been said apart, so as to be inaudible to Oliver. The man touched his hat; and glancing at Oliver with some curiosity, opened another gate, opposite to that by which they had entered, and led them on, through dark and winding ways, towards the cells.

"This," said the man, stopping in a gloomy passage where a couple of workmen were making some preparations in profound silence "this is the place he passes through. If you step this way, you can see the door he goes out at."

He led them into a stone kitchen, fitted with coppers for dressing the prison food, and pointed to a door. There was an open grating above it, through which came the sound of men's voices, mingled with the noise of hammering, and the throwing down of boards. There were putting up the scaffold.

From this place, they passed through several strong gates, opened by other turnkeys from the inner side; and, having entered an open yard, ascended a flight of narrow steps, and came into a passage with a row of strong doors on the left hand. Motioning them to remain where they were, the turnkey knocked at one of these with his bunch of keys. The two attendants, after a little whispering, came out into the passage, stretching themselves as if glad of the temporary relief, and motioned the visitors to follow the jailer into the cell. They did so.

The condemned criminal was seated on his bed, rocking himself from side to side, with a countenance more like that of a snared beast than the face of a man. His mind was evidently wandering to his old life, for he continued to mutter, without appearing conscious of their presence otherwise than as a part of his vision.

"Good boy, Charley—well done—" he mumbled. "Oliver, too, ha! ha! ha! Oliver too—quite the gentleman now—quite the—take that boy away to bed!"

The jailer took the disengaged hand of Oliver; and, whispering him not to be alarmed, looked on without speaking.

"Take him away to bed!" cried Fagin. "Do you hear me, some of you? He has been the—the—somehow the cause of all this. It's worth the money to bring him up to it—Bolter's throat, Bill; never mind the girl—Bolter's throat as deep as you can cut. Saw his head off!"

"Fagin," said the jailer.

"That's me!" cried the Jew, falling instantly, into the attitude of listening he had assumed upon his trial. "An old man, my Lord; a very old, old man!"

"Here," said the turnkey, laying his hand upon his breast to keep him down. "Here's somebody wants to see you, to ask you some questions, I suppose. Fagin, Fagin! Are you a man?"

"I shan't be one long," he replied, looking up with a face retaining no human expression but rage and terror. "Strike them all dead! What right have they to butcher me?"

As he spoke he caught sight of Oliver and Mr. Brownlow. Shrinking to the furthest corner of the seat, he demanded to know what they wanted there.

"Steady," said the turnkey, still holding him down. "Now, sir, tell him what you want. Quick, if you please, for he grows worse as the time gets on."

"You have some papers," said Mr. Brownlow advancing, "which were placed in your hands, for better security, by a man called Monks."

"It's all a lie together," replied Fagin. "I haven't one—not one."

"For the love of God," said Mr. Brownlow solemnly, "do not say that now, upon the very verge of death; but tell me where they are. You know that Sikes is dead; that Monks has confessed; that there is no hope of any further gain. Where are those papers?"

"Oliver," cried Fagin, beckoning to him. "Here, here! Let me whisper to you."

"I am not afraid," said Oliver in a low voice, as he relinquished Mr. Brownlow's hand.

"The papers," said Fagin, drawing Oliver towards him, "are in a canvas bag, in a hole a little way up the chimney in the top front-room. I want to talk to you, my dear. I want to talk to you."

"Yes, yes," returned Oliver. "Let me say a prayer. Do! Let me say one prayer. Say only one, upon your knees, with me, and we will talk till morning."

"Outside, outside," replied Fagin, pushing the boy before him towards the door, and looking vacantly over his head. "Say I've gone to sleep—they'll believe you. You can get me out, if you take me so. Now then, now then!"

"Oh! God forgive this wretched man!" cried the boy with a burst of tears.

"That's right, that's right," said Fagin. "That'll help us on. This door first. If I shake and tremble, as we pass the gallows, don't you mind, but hurry on. Now, now, now!"

"Have you nothing else to ask him, sir?" inquired the turnkey.

"No other question," replied Mr. Brownlow. "If I hoped we could recall him to a sense of his position—"

"Nothing will do that, sir," replied the man, shaking his head. "You had better leave him."

The door of the cell opened, and the attendants returned.

"Press on, press on," cried Fagin. "Softly, but not so slow. Faster, faster!"

The men laid hands upon him, and disengaging Oliver from his grasp, held him back. He struggled with the power of desperation, for an instant; and then sent up cry upon cry that penetrated even those massive walls, and rang in their ears until they reached the open yard.

It was some time before they left the prison. Oliver nearly swooned after this frightful scene, and was so weak that for an hour or more, he had not the strength to walk.

Day was dawning when they again emerged. A great multitude had already assembled; the windows were filled with people, smoking and playing cards to beguile the time; the crowd were pushing, quarrelling, joking. Everything told of life and animation, but one dark cluster of objects in the centre of all—the black stage, the cross-beam, the rope, and all the hideous apparatus of death.

CHAPTER LIII

And Last

The fortunes of those who have figured in this tale are nearly closed. The little that remains to their historian to relate, is told in few and simple words.

Before three months had passed, Rose Fleming and Harry Maylie were married in the village church which was henceforth to be the scene of the young clergyman's labours; on the same day they entered into possession of their new and happy home.

Mrs. Maylie took up her abode with her son and daughter-in-law, to enjoy, during the tranquil remainder of her days, the greatest felicity that age and worth can know—the contemplation of the happiness of those on whom the warmest affections and tenderest cares of a well-spent life, have been unceasingly bestowed.

It appeared, on full and careful investigation, that if the wreck of property remaining in the custody of Monks (which had never prospered either in his hands or in those of his mother) were equally divided between himself and Oliver, it would yield, to each, little more than three thousand pounds. By the provisions of his father's will, Oliver would have been entitled to the whole; but Mr. Brownlow, unwilling to deprive the elder son of the opportunity of retrieving his former vices and pursuing an honest career, proposed this mode of distribution, to which his young charge joyfully acceded.

Monks, still bearing that assumed name, retired with his portion to a distant part of the New World; where, having quickly squandered it, he once more fell into his old courses, and, after undergoing a long confinement for some fresh act of fraud and knavery, at length sunk under an attack of his old disorder, and died in prison. As far from home, died the chief remaining members of his friend Fagin's gang.

Mr. Brownlow adopted Oliver as his son. Removing with him and the old housekeeper to within a mile of the parsonage-house, where his dear friends resided, he gratified the only remaining wish of Oliver's warm and earnest heart, and thus linked together a little society, whose condition approached as nearly to one of perfect happiness as can ever be known in this changing world.

Soon after the marriage of the young people, the worthy doctor returned to Chertsey, where, bereft of the presence of his old friends, he would have been discontented if his temperament had admitted of such a feeling; and would have turned quite peevish if he had known how. For two or three months, he contented himself with hinting that he feared the air began to disagree with him; then, finding that the place really no longer was, to him, what it had been, he settled his business on his assistant, took a bachelor's cottage outside the village of which his young friend was pastor, and instantaneously recovered. Here he took to gardening, planting, fishing, carpentering, and various other pursuits of a similar kind: all undertaken with his characteristic impetuosity. In each and all he has since become famous throughout the neighborhood, as a most profound authority.

Before his removal, he had managed to contract a strong friendship for Mr. Grimwig, which that eccentric gentleman cordially reciprocated. He is accordingly visited by Mr. Grimwig a great many times in the course of the year. On all such occasions, Mr. Grimwig plants, fishes, and carpenters, with great ardour; doing everything in a very singular and unprecedented manner, but always maintaining with his favourite asseveration, that his mode is the right one. On Sundays, he never fails to criticise the sermon to the young clergyman's face: always informing Mr. Losberne, in strict confidence afterwards, that he considers it an excellent performance, but deems it as well not to say so. It is a standing and very favourite joke, for Mr. Brownlow to rally him on his old prophecy concerning Oliver, and to remind him of the night on which they sat with the watch between them, waiting his return; but Mr. Grimwig contends that he was right in the main, and, in proof thereof, remarks that Oliver did not come back after all; which always calls forth a laugh on his side, and increases his good humour.

Mr. Noah Claypole: receiving a free pardon from the Crown in consequence of being admitted approver against Fagin: and considering his profession not altogether as safe a one as he could wish: was, for some little time, at a loss for the means of a livelihood, not burdened with too much work. After some consideration, he went into business as an Informer, in which calling he realises a genteel subsistence. His plan is, to walk out once a week during church time attended by Charlotte in respectable attire. The lady faints away at the doors of charitable publicans, and the gentleman being accommodated with three-penny worth of brandy to restore her, lays an information next day, and pockets half the penalty. Sometimes Mr. Claypole faints himself, but the result is the same.

Mr. and Mrs. Bumble, deprived of their situations, were gradually reduced to great indigence and misery, and finally became paupers in that very same workhouse in which they had once lorded it over others. Mr. Bumble has been heard to say, that in this reverse and degradation, he has not even spirits to be thankful for being separated from his wife.

As to Mr. Giles and Brittles, they still remain in their old posts, although the former is bald, and the last-named boy quite grey. They sleep at the parsonage, but divide their attentions so equally among its inmates, and Oliver and Mr. Brownlow, and Mr. Losberne, that to this day the villagers have never been able to discover to which establishment they properly belong.

Master Charles Bates, appalled by Sikes's crime, fell into a train of reflection whether an honest life was not, after all, the best. Arriving at the conclusion that it certainly was, he turned his back upon the scenes of the past, resolved to amend it in some new sphere of action. He struggled hard, and suffered much, for some time; but, having a contented disposition, and a good purpose, succeeded in the end; and, from being a farmer's drudge, and a carrier's lad, he is now the merriest young grazier in all Northamptonshire.

And now, the hand that traces these words, falters, as it approaches the conclusion of its task; and would weave, for a little longer space, the thread of these adventures.

I would fain linger yet with a few of those among whom I have so long moved, and share their happiness by endeavouring to depict it. I would show Rose Maylie in all the bloom and grace of early womanhood, shedding on her secluded path in life soft and gentle light, that fell on all who trod it with her, and shone into their hearts. I would paint her the life and joy of the fire-side circle and the lively summer group; I would follow her through the sultry fields at noon, and hear the low tones of her sweet voice in the moonlit evening walk; I would watch her in all her goodness and charity abroad, and the smiling untiring discharge of domestic duties at home; I would paint her and her dead sister's child happy in their love for one another, and passing whole hours together in picturing the friends whom they had so sadly lost; I would summon before me, once again, those joyous little faces that clustered round her knee, and listen to their merry prattle; I would recall the tones of that clear laugh, and conjure up the sympathising tear that glistened in the soft blue eye. These, and a thousand looks and smiles, and turns of thought and speech—I would fain recall them every one.

How Mr. Brownlow went on, from day to day, filling the mind of his adopted child with stores of knowledge, and becoming attached to him, more and more, as his nature developed itself, and showed the thriving seeds of all he wished him to become—how he traced in him new traits of his early friend, that awakened in his own bosom old remembrances, melancholy and yet sweet and soothing—how the two orphans, tried by adversity, remembered its lessons in mercy to others, and mutual love, and fervent thanks to Him who had protected and preserved them—these are all matters which need not to be told. I have said that they were truly happy; and without strong affection and humanity of heart, and gratitude to that Being whose code is Mercy, and whose great attribute is Benevolence to all things that breathe, happiness can never be attained.

Within the altar of the old village church there stands a white marble tablet, which bears as yet but one word: "AGNES." There is no coffin in that tomb; and may it be many, many years, before another name is placed above it! But, if the spirits of the Dead ever come back to earth, to visit spots hallowed by the love—the love beyond the grave—of those whom they knew in life, I believe that the shade of Agnes sometimes hovers round that solemn nook. I believe it none the less because that nook is in a Church, and she was weak and erring.

A Christmas Carol

IN PROSE BEING
A Ghost Story of Christmas

PREFACE

I have endeavoured in this Ghostly little book, to raise the Ghost of
an Idea, which shall not put my readers out of humour with themselves,
with each other, with the season, or with me. May it haunt their houses
pleasantly, and no one wish to lay it.

Their faithful Friend and Servant,

C. D.

December, 1843.

STAVE I: MARLEY'S GHOST

MARLEY was dead: to begin with. There is no doubt whatever about that. The
register of his burial was signed by the clergyman, the clerk, the undertaker, and
the chief mourner. Scrooge signed it: and Scrooge's name was good upon 'Change,
for anything he chose to put his hand to. Old Marley was as dead as a door-nail.

Mind! I don't mean to say that I know, of my own knowledge, what there is
particularly dead about a door-nail. I might have been inclined, myself, to regard
a coffin-nail as the deadest piece of ironmongery in the trade. But the wisdom of
our ancestors is in the simile; and my unhallowed hands shall not disturb it, or the
Country's done for. You will therefore permit me to repeat, emphatically, that Marley
was as dead as a door-nail.

Scrooge knew he was dead? Of course he did. How could it be otherwise? Scrooge
and he were partners for I don't know how many years. Scrooge was his sole executor,
his sole administrator, his sole assign, his sole residuary legatee, his sole friend, and
sole mourner. And even Scrooge was not so dreadfully cut up by the sad event, but that
he was an excellent man of business on the very day of the funeral, and solemnised it
with an undoubted bargain.

The mention of Marley's funeral brings me back to the point I started from. There
is no doubt that Marley was dead. This must be distinctly understood, or nothing
wonderful can come of the story I am going to relate. If we were not perfectly
convinced that Hamlet's Father died before the play began, there would be nothing
more remarkable in his taking a stroll at night, in an easterly wind, upon his own
ramparts, than there would be in any other middle-aged gentleman rashly turning out

after dark in a breezy spot—say Saint Paul's Churchyard for instance—literally to astonish his son's weak mind.

Scrooge never painted out Old Marley's name. There it stood, years afterwards, above the warehouse door: Scrooge and Marley. The firm was known as Scrooge and Marley. Sometimes people new to the business called Scrooge Scrooge, and sometimes Marley, but he answered to both names. It was all the same to him.

Oh! But he was a tight-fisted hand at the grind-stone, Scrooge! a squeezing, wrenching, grasping, scraping, clutching, covetous, old sinner! Hard and sharp as flint, from which no steel had ever struck out generous fire; secret, and self-contained, and solitary as an oyster. The cold within him froze his old features, nipped his pointed nose, shrivelled his cheek, stiffened his gait; made his eyes red, his thin lips blue; and spoke out shrewdly in his grating voice. A frosty rime was on his head, and on his eyebrows, and his wiry chin. He carried his own low temperature always about with him; he iced his office in the dog-days; and didn't thaw it one degree at Christmas.

External heat and cold had little influence on Scrooge. No warmth could warm, no wintry weather chill him. No wind that blew was bitterer than he, no falling snow was more intent upon its purpose, no pelting rain less open to entreaty. Foul weather didn't know where to have him. The heaviest rain, and snow, and hail, and sleet, could boast of the advantage over him in only one respect. They often "came down" handsomely, and Scrooge never did.

Nobody ever stopped him in the street to say, with gladsome looks, "My dear Scrooge, how are you? When will you come to see me?" No beggars implored him to bestow a trifle, no children asked him what it was o'clock, no man or woman ever once in all his life inquired the way to such and such a place, of Scrooge. Even the blind men's dogs appeared to know him; and when they saw him coming on, would tug their owners into doorways and up courts; and then would wag their tails as though they said, "No eye at all is better than an evil eye, dark master!"

But what did Scrooge care! It was the very thing he liked. To edge his way along the crowded paths of life, warning all human sympathy to keep its distance, was what the knowing ones call "nuts" to Scrooge.

Once upon a time—of all the good days in the year, on Christmas Eve—old Scrooge sat busy in his counting-house. It was cold, bleak, biting weather: foggy withal: and he could hear the people in the court outside, go wheezing up and down, beating their hands upon their breasts, and stamping their feet upon the pavement stones to warm them. The city clocks had only just gone three, but it was quite dark already—it had not been light all day—and candles were flaring in the windows of the neighbouring offices, like ruddy smears upon the palpable brown air. The fog came pouring in at every chink and keyhole, and was so dense without, that although the court was of the narrowest, the houses opposite were mere phantoms. To see the dingy cloud come drooping down, obscuring everything, one might have thought that Nature lived hard by, and was brewing on a large scale.

The door of Scrooge's counting-house was open that he might keep his eye upon his clerk, who in a dismal little cell beyond, a sort of tank, was copying letters. Scrooge had a very small fire, but the clerk's fire was so very much smaller that it looked like one coal. But he couldn't replenish it, for Scrooge kept the coal-box in his own room;

and so surely as the clerk came in with the shovel, the master predicted that it would be necessary for them to part. Wherefore the clerk put on his white comforter, and tried to warm himself at the candle; in which effort, not being a man of a strong imagination, he failed.

"A merry Christmas, uncle! God save you!" cried a cheerful voice. It was the voice of Scrooge's nephew, who came upon him so quickly that this was the first intimation he had of his approach.

"Bah!" said Scrooge, "Humbug!"

He had so heated himself with rapid walking in the fog and frost, this nephew of Scrooge's, that he was all in a glow; his face was ruddy and handsome; his eyes sparkled, and his breath smoked again.

"Christmas a humbug, uncle!" said Scrooge's nephew. "You don't mean that, I am sure?"

"I do," said Scrooge. "Merry Christmas! What right have you to be merry? What reason have you to be merry? You're poor enough."

"Come, then," returned the nephew gaily. "What right have you to be dismal? What reason have you to be morose? You're rich enough."

Scrooge having no better answer ready on the spur of the moment, said, "Bah!" again; and followed it up with "Humbug."

"Don't be cross, uncle!" said the nephew.

"What else can I be," returned the uncle, "when I live in such a world of fools as this? Merry Christmas! Out upon merry Christmas! What's Christmas time to you but a time for paying bills without money; a time for finding yourself a year older, but not an hour richer; a time for balancing your books and having every item in 'em through a round dozen of months presented dead against you? If I could work my will," said Scrooge indignantly, "every idiot who goes about with 'Merry Christmas' on his lips, should be boiled with his own pudding, and buried with a stake of holly through his heart. He should!"

"Uncle!" pleaded the nephew.

"Nephew!" returned the uncle sternly, "keep Christmas in your own way, and let me keep it in mine."

"Keep it!" repeated Scrooge's nephew. "But you don't keep it."

"Let me leave it alone, then," said Scrooge. "Much good may it do you! Much good it has ever done you!"

"There are many things from which I might have derived good, by which I have not profited, I dare say," returned the nephew. "Christmas among the rest. But I am sure I have always thought of Christmas time, when it has come round—apart from the veneration due to its sacred name and origin, if anything belonging to it can be apart from that—as a good time; a kind, forgiving, charitable, pleasant time; the only time I know of, in the long calendar of the year, when men and women seem by one consent to open their shut-up hearts freely, and to think of people below them as if they really were fellow-passengers to the grave, and not another race of creatures bound on other journeys. And therefore, uncle, though it has never put a scrap of gold or silver in my pocket, I believe that it has done me good, and will do me good; and I say, God bless it!"

The clerk in the Tank involuntarily applauded. Becoming immediately sensible of the impropriety, he poked the fire, and extinguished the last frail spark for ever.

"Let me hear another sound from you," said Scrooge, "and you'll keep your Christmas by losing your situation! You're quite a powerful speaker, sir," he added, turning to his nephew. "I wonder you don't go into Parliament."

"Don't be angry, uncle. Come! Dine with us to-morrow."

Scrooge said that he would see him—yes, indeed he did. He went the whole length of the expression, and said that he would see him in that extremity first.

"But why?" cried Scrooge's nephew. "Why?"

"Why did you get married?" said Scrooge.

"Because I fell in love."

"Because you fell in love!" growled Scrooge, as if that were the only one thing in the world more ridiculous than a merry Christmas. "Good afternoon!"

"Nay, uncle, but you never came to see me before that happened. Why give it as a reason for not coming now?"

"Good afternoon," said Scrooge.

"I want nothing from you; I ask nothing of you; why cannot we be friends?"

"Good afternoon," said Scrooge.

"I am sorry, with all my heart, to find you so resolute. We have never had any quarrel, to which I have been a party. But I have made the trial in homage to Christmas, and I'll keep my Christmas humour to the last. So A Merry Christmas, uncle!"

"Good afternoon!" said Scrooge.

"And A Happy New Year!"

"Good afternoon!" said Scrooge.

His nephew left the room without an angry word, notwithstanding. He stopped at the outer door to bestow the greetings of the season on the clerk, who, cold as he was, was warmer than Scrooge; for he returned them cordially.

"There's another fellow," muttered Scrooge; who overheard him: "my clerk, with fifteen shillings a week, and a wife and family, talking about a merry Christmas. I'll retire to Bedlam."

This lunatic, in letting Scrooge's nephew out, had let two other people in. They were portly gentlemen, pleasant to behold, and now stood, with their hats off, in Scrooge's office. They had books and papers in their hands, and bowed to him.

"Scrooge and Marley's, I believe," said one of the gentlemen, referring to his list. "Have I the pleasure of addressing Mr. Scrooge, or Mr. Marley?"

"Mr. Marley has been dead these seven years," Scrooge replied. "He died seven years ago, this very night."

"We have no doubt his liberality is well represented by his surviving partner," said the gentleman, presenting his credentials.

It certainly was; for they had been two kindred spirits. At the ominous word "liberality," Scrooge frowned, and shook his head, and handed the credentials back.

"At this festive season of the year, Mr. Scrooge," said the gentleman, taking up a pen, "it is more than usually desirable that we should make some slight provision for the Poor and destitute, who suffer greatly at the present time. Many thousands are in want of common necessaries; hundreds of thousands are in want of common comforts, sir."

"Are there no prisons?" asked Scrooge.

"Plenty of prisons," said the gentleman, laying down the pen again.

"And the Union workhouses?" demanded Scrooge. "Are they still in operation?"

"They are. Still," returned the gentleman, "I wish I could say they were not."

"The Treadmill and the Poor Law are in full vigour, then?" said Scrooge.

"Both very busy, sir."

"Oh! I was afraid, from what you said at first, that something had occurred to stop them in their useful course," said Scrooge. "I'm very glad to hear it."

"Under the impression that they scarcely furnish Christian cheer of mind or body to the multitude," returned the gentleman, "a few of us are endeavouring to raise a fund to buy the Poor some meat and drink, and means of warmth. We choose this time, because it is a time, of all others, when Want is keenly felt, and Abundance rejoices. What shall I put you down for?"

"Nothing!" Scrooge replied.

"You wish to be anonymous?"

"I wish to be left alone," said Scrooge. "Since you ask me what I wish, gentlemen, that is my answer. I don't make merry myself at Christmas and I can't afford to make idle people merry. I help to support the establishments I have mentioned—they cost enough; and those who are badly off must go there."

"Many can't go there; and many would rather die."

"If they would rather die," said Scrooge, "they had better do it, and decrease the surplus population. Besides—excuse me—I don't know that."

"But you might know it," observed the gentleman.

"It's not my business," Scrooge returned. "It's enough for a man to understand his own business, and not to interfere with other people's. Mine occupies me constantly. Good afternoon, gentlemen!"

Seeing clearly that it would be useless to pursue their point, the gentlemen withdrew. Scrooge resumed his labours with an improved opinion of himself, and in a more facetious temper than was usual with him.

Meanwhile the fog and darkness thickened so, that people ran about with flaring links, proffering their services to go before horses in carriages, and conduct them on their way. The ancient tower of a church, whose gruff old bell was always peeping slily down at Scrooge out of a Gothic window in the wall, became invisible, and struck the hours and quarters in the clouds, with tremulous vibrations afterwards as if its teeth were chattering in its frozen head up there. The cold became intense. In the main street, at the corner of the court, some labourers were repairing the gas-pipes, and had lighted a great fire in a brazier, round which a party of ragged men and boys were gathered: warming their hands and winking their eyes before the blaze in rapture. The water-plug being left in solitude, its overflowings sullenly congealed, and turned to misanthropic ice. The brightness of the shops where holly sprigs and berries crackled in the lamp heat of the windows, made pale faces ruddy as they passed. Poulterers' and grocers' trades became a splendid joke: a glorious pageant, with which it was next to impossible to believe that such dull principles as bargain and sale had anything to do. The Lord Mayor, in the stronghold of the mighty Mansion House, gave orders to his fifty cooks and butlers to keep Christmas as a Lord Mayor's household should; and even the little tailor, whom he had fined five shillings on the previous Monday for being drunk and bloodthirsty in the streets, stirred up to-morrow's pudding in his garret, while his lean wife and the baby sallied out to buy the beef.

Foggier yet, and colder. Piercing, searching, biting cold. If the good Saint Dunstan had but nipped the Evil Spirit's nose with a touch of such weather as that, instead of using his familiar weapons, then indeed he would have roared to lusty purpose. The owner of one scant young nose, gnawed and mumbled by the hungry cold as bones are gnawed by dogs, stooped down at Scrooge's keyhole to regale him with a Christmas carol: but at the first sound of

> "God bless you, merry gentleman!
> May nothing you dismay!"

Scrooge seized the ruler with such energy of action, that the singer fled in terror, leaving the keyhole to the fog and even more congenial frost.

At length the hour of shutting up the counting-house arrived. With an ill-will Scrooge dismounted from his stool, and tacitly admitted the fact to the expectant clerk in the Tank, who instantly snuffed his candle out, and put on his hat.

"You'll want all day to-morrow, I suppose?" said Scrooge.

"If quite convenient, sir."

"It's not convenient," said Scrooge, "and it's not fair. If I was to stop half-a-crown for it, you'd think yourself ill-used, I'll be bound?"

The clerk smiled faintly.

"And yet," said Scrooge, "you don't think me ill-used, when I pay a day's wages for no work."

The clerk observed that it was only once a year.

"A poor excuse for picking a man's pocket every twenty-fifth of December!" said Scrooge, buttoning his great-coat to the chin. "But I suppose you must have the whole day. Be here all the earlier next morning."

The clerk promised that he would; and Scrooge walked out with a growl. The office was closed in a twinkling, and the clerk, with the long ends of his white comforter dangling below his waist (for he boasted no great-coat), went down a slide on Cornhill, at the end of a lane of boys, twenty times, in honour of its being Christmas Eve, and then ran home to Camden Town as hard as he could pelt, to play at blindman's-buff.

Scrooge took his melancholy dinner in his usual melancholy tavern; and having read all the newspapers, and beguiled the rest of the evening with his banker's-book, went home to bed. He lived in chambers which had once belonged to his deceased partner. They were a gloomy suite of rooms, in a lowering pile of building up a yard, where it had so little business to be, that one could scarcely help fancying it must have run there when it was a young house, playing at hide-and-seek with other houses, and forgotten the way out again. It was old enough now, and dreary enough, for nobody lived in it but Scrooge, the other rooms being all let out as offices. The yard was so dark that even Scrooge, who knew its every stone, was fain to grope with his hands.

The fog and frost so hung about the black old gateway of the house, that it seemed as if the Genius of the Weather sat in mournful meditation on the threshold.

Now, it is a fact, that there was nothing at all particular about the knocker on the door, except that it was very large. It is also a fact, that Scrooge had seen it, night and morning, during his whole residence in that place; also that Scrooge had as little of what is called fancy about him as any man in the city of London, even including—which is a bold word—the corporation, aldermen, and livery. Let it also be borne in mind that Scrooge had not bestowed one thought on Marley, since his last mention of his seven years' dead partner that afternoon. And then let any man explain to me, if he can, how it happened that Scrooge, having his key in the lock of the door, saw in the knocker, without its undergoing any intermediate process of change—not a knocker, but Marley's face.

Marley's face. It was not in impenetrable shadow as the other objects in the yard were, but had a dismal light about it, like a bad lobster in a dark cellar. It was not angry or ferocious, but looked at Scrooge as Marley used to look: with ghostly spectacles turned up on its ghostly forehead. The hair was curiously stirred, as if by breath or hot air; and, though the eyes were wide open, they were perfectly motionless. That, and its livid colour, made it horrible; but its horror seemed to be in spite of the face and beyond its control, rather than a part of its own expression.

As Scrooge looked fixedly at this phenomenon, it was a knocker again.

To say that he was not startled, or that his blood was not conscious of a terrible sensation to which it had been a stranger from infancy, would be untrue. But he put his hand upon the key he had relinquished, turned it sturdily, walked in, and lighted his candle.

He did pause, with a moment's irresolution, before he shut the door; and he did look cautiously behind it first, as if he half expected to be terrified with the sight of Marley's pigtail sticking out into the hall. But there was nothing on the back of the door, except the screws and nuts that held the knocker on, so he said "Pooh, pooh!" and closed it with a bang.

The sound resounded through the house like thunder. Every room above, and every cask in the wine-merchant's cellars below, appeared to have a separate peal of echoes of its own. Scrooge was not a man to be frightened by echoes. He fastened the door, and walked across the hall, and up the stairs; slowly too: trimming his candle as he went.

You may talk vaguely about driving a coach-and-six up a good old flight of stairs, or through a bad young Act of Parliament; but I mean to say you might have got a hearse up that staircase, and taken it broadwise, with the splinter-bar towards the wall and the door towards the balustrades: and done it easy. There was plenty of width for that, and room to spare; which is perhaps the reason why Scrooge thought he saw a locomotive hearse going on before him in the gloom. Half-a-dozen gas-lamps out of the street wouldn't have lighted the entry too well, so you may suppose that it was pretty dark with Scrooge's dip.

Up Scrooge went, not caring a button for that. Darkness is cheap, and Scrooge liked it. But before he shut his heavy door, he walked through his rooms to see that all was right. He had just enough recollection of the face to desire to do that.

Sitting-room, bedroom, lumber-room. All as they should be. Nobody under the table, nobody under the sofa; a small fire in the grate; spoon and basin ready; and the little saucepan of gruel (Scrooge had a cold in his head) upon the hob. Nobody under the bed; nobody in the closet; nobody in his dressing-gown, which was hanging up in a suspicious attitude against the wall. Lumber-room as usual. Old fire-guard, old shoes, two fish-baskets, washing-stand on three legs, and a poker.

Quite satisfied, he closed his door, and locked himself in; double-locked himself in, which was not his custom. Thus secured against surprise, he took off his cravat; put on his dressing-gown and slippers, and his nightcap; and sat down before the fire to take his gruel.

It was a very low fire indeed; nothing on such a bitter night. He was obliged to sit close to it, and brood over it, before he could extract the least sensation of warmth from such a handful of fuel. The fireplace was an old one, built by some Dutch merchant long ago, and paved all round with quaint Dutch tiles, designed to illustrate the Scriptures. There were Cains and Abels, Pharaoh's daughters; Queens of Sheba, Angelic messengers descending through the air on clouds like feather-beds, Abrahams, Belshazzars, Apostles putting off to sea in butter-boats, hundreds of figures to attract his thoughts; and yet that face of Marley, seven years dead, came like the ancient Prophet's rod, and swallowed up the whole. If each smooth tile had been a blank at first, with power to shape some picture on its surface from the disjointed fragments of his thoughts, there would have been a copy of old Marley's head on every one.

"Humbug!" said Scrooge; and walked across the room.

After several turns, he sat down again. As he threw his head back in the chair, his glance happened to rest upon a bell, a disused bell, that hung in the room, and communicated for some purpose now forgotten with a chamber in the highest story of the building. It was with great astonishment, and with a strange, inexplicable dread, that as he looked, he saw this bell begin to swing. It swung so softly in the outset that it scarcely made a sound; but soon it rang out loudly, and so did every bell in the house.

This might have lasted half a minute, or a minute, but it seemed an hour. The bells ceased as they had begun, together. They were succeeded by a clanking noise, deep down below; as if some person were dragging a heavy chain over the casks in the wine-merchant's cellar. Scrooge then remembered to have heard that ghosts in haunted houses were described as dragging chains.

The cellar-door flew open with a booming sound, and then he heard the noise much louder, on the floors below; then coming up the stairs; then coming straight towards his door.

"It's humbug still!" said Scrooge. "I won't believe it."

His colour changed though, when, without a pause, it came on through the heavy door, and passed into the room before his eyes. Upon its coming in, the dying flame leaped up, as though it cried, "I know him; Marley's Ghost!" and fell again.

The same face: the very same. Marley in his pigtail, usual waistcoat, tights and boots; the tassels on the latter bristling, like his pigtail, and his coat-skirts, and the hair upon his head. The chain he drew was clasped about his middle. It was long, and wound about him like a tail; and it was made (for Scrooge observed it closely) of cash-boxes, keys, padlocks, ledgers, deeds, and heavy purses wrought in steel. His body was transparent; so that Scrooge, observing him, and looking through his waistcoat, could see the two buttons on his coat behind.

Scrooge had often heard it said that Marley had no bowels, but he had never believed it until now.

No, nor did he believe it even now. Though he looked the phantom through and through, and saw it standing before him; though he felt the chilling influence of its death-cold eyes; and marked the very texture of the folded kerchief bound about its head and chin, which wrapper he had not observed before; he was still incredulous, and fought against his senses.

"How now!" said Scrooge, caustic and cold as ever. "What do you want with me?"

"Much!"—Marley's voice, no doubt about it.

"Who are you?"

"Ask me who I was."

"Who were you then?" said Scrooge, raising his voice. "You're particular, for a shade." He was going to say "to a shade," but substituted this, as more appropriate.

"In life I was your partner, Jacob Marley."

"Can you—can you sit down?" asked Scrooge, looking doubtfully at him.

"I can."

"Do it, then."

Scrooge asked the question, because he didn't know whether a ghost so transparent might find himself in a condition to take a chair; and felt that in the event of its being impossible, it might involve the necessity of an embarrassing explanation. But the ghost sat down on the opposite side of the fireplace, as if he were quite used to it.

"You don't believe in me," observed the Ghost.

"I don't," said Scrooge.

"What evidence would you have of my reality beyond that of your senses?"

"I don't know," said Scrooge.

"Why do you doubt your senses?"

"Because," said Scrooge, "a little thing affects them. A slight disorder of the stomach makes them cheats. You may be an undigested bit of beef, a blot of mustard, a crumb of cheese, a fragment of an underdone potato. There's more of gravy than of grave about you, whatever you are!"

Scrooge was not much in the habit of cracking jokes, nor did he feel, in his heart, by any means waggish then. The truth is, that he tried to be smart, as a means of distracting his own attention, and keeping down his terror; for the spectre's voice disturbed the very marrow in his bones.

To sit, staring at those fixed glazed eyes, in silence for a moment, would play, Scrooge felt, the very deuce with him. There was something very awful, too, in the spectre's being provided with an infernal atmosphere of its own. Scrooge could not feel it himself, but this was clearly the case; for though the Ghost sat perfectly motionless, its hair, and skirts, and tassels, were still agitated as by the hot vapour from an oven.

"You see this toothpick?" said Scrooge, returning quickly to the charge, for the reason just assigned; and wishing, though it were only for a second, to divert the vision's stony gaze from himself.

"I do," replied the Ghost.

"You are not looking at it," said Scrooge.

"But I see it," said the Ghost, "notwithstanding."

"Well!" returned Scrooge, "I have but to swallow this, and be for the rest of my days persecuted by a legion of goblins, all of my own creation. Humbug, I tell you! humbug!"

At this the spirit raised a frightful cry, and shook its chain with such a dismal and appalling noise, that Scrooge held on tight to his chair, to save himself from falling in a swoon. But how much greater was his horror, when the phantom taking off the bandage round its head, as if it were too warm to wear indoors, its lower jaw dropped down upon its breast!

Scrooge fell upon his knees, and clasped his hands before his face.

"Mercy!" he said. "Dreadful apparition, why do you trouble me?"

"Man of the worldly mind!" replied the Ghost, "do you believe in me or not?"

"I do," said Scrooge. "I must. But why do spirits walk the earth, and why do they come to me?"

"It is required of every man," the Ghost returned, "that the spirit within him should walk abroad among his fellowmen, and travel far and wide; and if that spirit goes not forth in life, it is condemned to do so after death. It is doomed to wander through the world—oh, woe is me!—and witness what it cannot share, but might have shared on earth, and turned to happiness!"

Again the spectre raised a cry, and shook its chain and wrung its shadowy hands.

"You are fettered," said Scrooge, trembling. "Tell me why?"

"I wear the chain I forged in life," replied the Ghost. "I made it link by link, and yard by yard; I girded it on of my own free will, and of my own free will I wore it. Is its pattern strange to you?"

Scrooge trembled more and more.

"Or would you know," pursued the Ghost, "the weight and length of the strong coil you bear yourself? It was full as heavy and as long as this, seven Christmas Eves ago. You have laboured on it, since. It is a ponderous chain!"

Scrooge glanced about him on the floor, in the expectation of finding himself surrounded by some fifty or sixty fathoms of iron cable: but he could see nothing.

"Jacob," he said, imploringly. "Old Jacob Marley, tell me more. Speak comfort to me, Jacob!"

"I have none to give," the Ghost replied. "It comes from other regions, Ebenezer Scrooge, and is conveyed by other ministers, to other kinds of men. Nor can I tell you what I would. A very little more is all permitted to me. I cannot rest, I cannot stay, I cannot linger anywhere. My spirit never walked beyond our counting-house—mark me!—in life my spirit never roved beyond the narrow limits of our money-changing hole; and weary journeys lie before me!"

It was a habit with Scrooge, whenever he became thoughtful, to put his hands in his breeches pockets. Pondering on what the Ghost had said, he did so now, but without lifting up his eyes, or getting off his knees.

"You must have been very slow about it, Jacob," Scrooge observed, in a business-like manner, though with humility and deference.

"Slow!" the Ghost repeated.

"Seven years dead," mused Scrooge. "And travelling all the time!"

"The whole time," said the Ghost. "No rest, no peace. Incessant torture of remorse."

"You travel fast?" said Scrooge.

"On the wings of the wind," replied the Ghost.

"You might have got over a great quantity of ground in seven years," said Scrooge.

The Ghost, on hearing this, set up another cry, and clanked its chain so hideously in the dead silence of the night, that the Ward would have been justified in indicting it for a nuisance.

"Oh! captive, bound, and double-ironed," cried the phantom, "not to know, that ages of incessant labour by immortal creatures, for this earth must pass into eternity before the good of which it is susceptible is all developed. Not to know that any Christian spirit working kindly in its little sphere, whatever it may be, will find its mortal life too short for its vast means of usefulness. Not to know that no space of regret can make amends for one life's opportunity misused! Yet such was I! Oh! such was I!"

"But you were always a good man of business, Jacob," faltered Scrooge, who now began to apply this to himself.

"Business!" cried the Ghost, wringing its hands again. "Mankind was my business. The common welfare was my business; charity, mercy, forbearance, and benevolence, were, all, my business. The dealings of my trade were but a drop of water in the comprehensive ocean of my business!"

It held up its chain at arm's length, as if that were the cause of all its unavailing grief, and flung it heavily upon the ground again.

"At this time of the rolling year," the spectre said, "I suffer most. Why did I walk through crowds of fellow-beings with my eyes turned down, and never raise them to that blessed Star which led the Wise Men to a poor abode! Were there no poor homes to which its light would have conducted me!"

Scrooge was very much dismayed to hear the spectre going on at this rate, and began to quake exceedingly.

"Hear me!" cried the Ghost. "My time is nearly gone."

"I will," said Scrooge. "But don't be hard upon me! Don't be flowery, Jacob! Pray!"

"How it is that I appear before you in a shape that you can see, I may not tell. I have sat invisible beside you many and many a day."

It was not an agreeable idea. Scrooge shivered, and wiped the perspiration from his brow.

"That is no light part of my penance," pursued the Ghost. "I am here to-night to warn you, that you have yet a chance and hope of escaping my fate. A chance and hope of my procuring, Ebenezer."

"You were always a good friend to me," said Scrooge. "Thank'ee!"

"You will be haunted," resumed the Ghost, "by Three Spirits."

Scrooge's countenance fell almost as low as the Ghost's had done.

"Is that the chance and hope you mentioned, Jacob?" he demanded, in a faltering voice.

"It is."

"I—I think I'd rather not," said Scrooge.

"Without their visits," said the Ghost, "you cannot hope to shun the path I tread. Expect the first to-morrow, when the bell tolls One."

"Couldn't I take 'em all at once, and have it over, Jacob?" hinted Scrooge.

"Expect the second on the next night at the same hour. The third upon the next night when the last stroke of Twelve has ceased to vibrate. Look to see me no more; and look that, for your own sake, you remember what has passed between us!"

When it had said these words, the spectre took its wrapper from the table, and bound it round its head, as before. Scrooge knew this, by the smart sound its teeth made, when the jaws were brought together by the bandage. He ventured to raise his eyes again, and found his supernatural visitor confronting him in an erect attitude, with its chain wound over and about its arm.

The apparition walked backward from him; and at every step it took, the window raised itself a little, so that when the spectre reached it, it was wide open.

It beckoned Scrooge to approach, which he did. When they were within two paces of each other, Marley's Ghost held up its hand, warning him to come no nearer. Scrooge stopped.

Not so much in obedience, as in surprise and fear: for on the raising of the hand, he became sensible of confused noises in the air; incoherent sounds of lamentation and regret; wailings inexpressibly sorrowful and self-accusatory. The spectre, after listening for a moment, joined in the mournful dirge; and floated out upon the bleak, dark night.

Scrooge followed to the window: desperate in his curiosity. He looked out.

The air was filled with phantoms, wandering hither and thither in restless haste, and moaning as they went. Every one of them wore chains like Marley's Ghost; some few (they might be guilty governments) were linked together; none were free. Many had been personally known to Scrooge in their lives. He had been quite familiar with one old ghost, in a white waistcoat, with a monstrous iron safe attached to its ankle, who cried piteously at being unable to assist a wretched woman with an infant, whom it saw below, upon a door-step. The misery with them all was, clearly, that they sought to interfere, for good, in human matters, and had lost the power for ever.

Whether these creatures faded into mist, or mist enshrouded them, he could not tell. But they and their spirit voices faded together; and the night became as it had been when he walked home.

Scrooge closed the window, and examined the door by which the Ghost had entered. It was double-locked, as he had locked it with his own hands, and the bolts were undisturbed. He tried to say "Humbug!" but stopped at the first syllable. And being, from the emotion he had undergone, or the fatigues of the day, or his glimpse of the Invisible World, or the dull conversation of the Ghost, or the lateness of the hour, much in need of repose; went straight to bed, without undressing, and fell asleep upon the instant.

STAVE II: THE FIRST OF THE THREE SPIRITS

WHEN Scrooge awoke, it was so dark, that looking out of bed, he could scarcely distinguish the transparent window from the opaque walls of his chamber. He was endeavouring to pierce the darkness with his ferret eyes, when the chimes of a neighbouring church struck the four quarters. So he listened for the hour.

To his great astonishment the heavy bell went on from six to seven, and from seven to eight, and regularly up to twelve; then stopped. Twelve! It was past two when he went to bed. The clock was wrong. An icicle must have got into the works. Twelve!

He touched the spring of his repeater, to correct this most preposterous clock. Its rapid little pulse beat twelve: and stopped.

"Why, it isn't possible," said Scrooge, "that I can have slept through a whole day and far into another night. It isn't possible that anything has happened to the sun, and this is twelve at noon!"

The idea being an alarming one, he scrambled out of bed, and groped his way to the window. He was obliged to rub the frost off with the sleeve of his dressing-gown before he could see anything; and could see very little then. All he could make out was, that it was still very foggy and extremely cold, and that there was no noise of people running to and fro, and making a great stir, as there unquestionably would have been if night had beaten off bright day, and taken possession of the world. This was a great relief, because "three days after sight of this First of Exchange pay to Mr. Ebenezer Scrooge or his order," and so forth, would have become a mere United States' security if there were no days to count by.

Scrooge went to bed again, and thought, and thought, and thought it over and over and over, and could make nothing of it. The more he thought, the more perplexed he was; and the more he endeavoured not to think, the more he thought.

Marley's Ghost bothered him exceedingly. Every time he resolved within himself, after mature inquiry, that it was all a dream, his mind flew back again, like a strong spring released, to its first position, and presented the same problem to be worked all through, "Was it a dream or not?"

Scrooge lay in this state until the chime had gone three quarters more, when he remembered, on a sudden, that the Ghost had warned him of a visitation when the bell tolled one. He resolved to lie awake until the hour was passed; and, considering that he could no more go to sleep than go to Heaven, this was perhaps the wisest resolution in his power.

The quarter was so long, that he was more than once convinced he must have sunk into a doze unconsciously, and missed the clock. At length it broke upon his listening ear.

"Ding, dong!"

"A quarter past," said Scrooge, counting.

"Ding, dong!"

"Half-past!" said Scrooge.

"Ding, dong!"

"A quarter to it," said Scrooge.

"Ding, dong!"

"The hour itself," said Scrooge, triumphantly, "and nothing else!"

He spoke before the hour bell sounded, which it now did with a deep, dull, hollow, melancholy ONE. Light flashed up in the room upon the instant, and the curtains of his bed were drawn.

The curtains of his bed were drawn aside, I tell you, by a hand. Not the curtains at his feet, nor the curtains at his back, but those to which his face was addressed. The curtains of his bed were drawn aside; and Scrooge, starting up into a half-recumbent attitude, found himself face to face with the unearthly visitor who drew them: as close to it as I am now to you, and I am standing in the spirit at your elbow.

It was a strange figure—like a child: yet not so like a child as like an old man, viewed through some supernatural medium, which gave him the appearance of having receded from the view, and being diminished to a child's proportions. Its hair, which hung about its neck and down its back, was white as if with age; and yet the face had not a wrinkle in it, and the tenderest bloom was on the skin. The arms were very long and muscular; the hands the same, as if its hold were of uncommon strength. Its legs and feet, most delicately formed, were, like those upper members, bare. It wore a tunic of the purest white; and round its waist was bound a lustrous belt, the sheen of which was beautiful. It held a branch of fresh green holly in its hand; and, in singular contradiction of that wintry emblem, had its dress trimmed with summer flowers. But the strangest thing about it was, that from the crown of its head there sprung a bright clear jet of light, by which all this was visible; and which was doubtless the occasion of its using, in its duller moments, a great extinguisher for a cap, which it now held under its arm.

Even this, though, when Scrooge looked at it with increasing steadiness, was not its strangest quality. For as its belt sparkled and glittered now in one part and now in another, and what was light one instant, at another time was dark, so the figure itself fluctuated in its distinctness: being now a thing with one arm, now with one leg, now with twenty legs, now a pair of legs without a head, now a head without a body: of which dissolving parts, no outline would be visible in the dense gloom wherein they melted away. And in the very wonder of this, it would be itself again; distinct and clear as ever.

"Are you the Spirit, sir, whose coming was foretold to me?" asked Scrooge.

"I am!"

The voice was soft and gentle. Singularly low, as if instead of being so close beside him, it were at a distance.

"Who, and what are you?" Scrooge demanded.

"I am the Ghost of Christmas Past."

"Long Past?" inquired Scrooge: observant of its dwarfish stature.

"No. Your past."

Perhaps, Scrooge could not have told anybody why, if anybody could have asked him; but he had a special desire to see the Spirit in his cap; and begged him to be covered.

"What!" exclaimed the Ghost, "would you so soon put out, with worldly hands, the light I give? Is it not enough that you are one of those whose passions made this cap, and force me through whole trains of years to wear it low upon my brow!"

Scrooge reverently disclaimed all intention to offend or any knowledge of having wilfully "bonneted" the Spirit at any period of his life. He then made bold to inquire what business brought him there.

"Your welfare!" said the Ghost.

Scrooge expressed himself much obliged, but could not help thinking that a night of unbroken rest would have been more conducive to that end. The Spirit must have heard him thinking, for it said immediately:

"Your reclamation, then. Take heed!"

It put out its strong hand as it spoke, and clasped him gently by the arm.

"Rise! and walk with me!"

It would have been in vain for Scrooge to plead that the weather and the hour were not adapted to pedestrian purposes; that bed was warm, and the thermometer a long way below freezing; that he was clad but lightly in his slippers, dressing-gown, and nightcap; and that he had a cold upon him at that time. The grasp, though gentle as a woman's hand, was not to be resisted. He rose: but finding that the Spirit made towards the window, clasped his robe in supplication.

"I am a mortal," Scrooge remonstrated, "and liable to fall."

"Bear but a touch of my hand there," said the Spirit, laying it upon his heart, "and you shall be upheld in more than this!"

As the words were spoken, they passed through the wall, and stood upon an open country road, with fields on either hand. The city had entirely vanished. Not a vestige of it was to be seen. The darkness and the mist had vanished with it, for it was a clear, cold, winter day, with snow upon the ground.

"Good Heaven!" said Scrooge, clasping his hands together, as he looked about him. "I was bred in this place. I was a boy here!"

The Spirit gazed upon him mildly. Its gentle touch, though it had been light and instantaneous, appeared still present to the old man's sense of feeling. He was conscious of a thousand odours floating in the air, each one connected with a thousand thoughts, and hopes, and joys, and cares long, long, forgotten!

"Your lip is trembling," said the Ghost. "And what is that upon your cheek?"

Scrooge muttered, with an unusual catching in his voice, that it was a pimple; and begged the Ghost to lead him where he would.

"You recollect the way?" inquired the Spirit.

"Remember it!" cried Scrooge with fervour; "I could walk it blindfold."

"Strange to have forgotten it for so many years!" observed the Ghost. "Let us go on."

They walked along the road, Scrooge recognising every gate, and post, and tree; until a little market-town appeared in the distance, with its bridge, its church, and winding river. Some shaggy ponies now were seen trotting towards them with boys upon their backs, who called to other boys in country gigs and carts, driven by farmers. All these boys were in great spirits, and shouted to each other, until the broad fields were so full of merry music, that the crisp air laughed to hear it!

"These are but shadows of the things that have been," said the Ghost. "They have no consciousness of us."

The jocund travellers came on; and as they came, Scrooge knew and named them every one. Why was he rejoiced beyond all bounds to see them! Why did his cold eye glisten, and his heart leap up as they went past! Why was he filled with gladness when he heard them give each other Merry Christmas, as they parted at cross-roads and bye-ways, for their several homes! What was merry Christmas to Scrooge? Out upon merry Christmas! What good had it ever done to him?

"The school is not quite deserted," said the Ghost. "A solitary child, neglected by his friends, is left there still."

Scrooge said he knew it. And he sobbed.

They left the high-road, by a well-remembered lane, and soon approached a mansion of dull red brick, with a little weathercock-surmounted cupola, on the roof, and a bell hanging in it. It was a large house, but one of broken fortunes; for the spacious offices were little used, their walls were damp and mossy, their windows broken, and their gates decayed. Fowls clucked and strutted in the stables; and the coach-houses and sheds were over-run with grass. Nor was it more retentive of its ancient state, within; for entering the dreary hall, and glancing through the open doors of many rooms, they found them poorly furnished, cold, and vast. There was an earthy savour in the air, a chilly bareness in the place, which associated itself somehow with too much getting up by candle-light, and not too much to eat.

They went, the Ghost and Scrooge, across the hall, to a door at the back of the house. It opened before them, and disclosed a long, bare, melancholy room, made barer still by lines of plain deal forms and desks. At one of these a lonely boy was reading near a feeble fire; and Scrooge sat down upon a form, and wept to see his poor forgotten self as he used to be.

Not a latent echo in the house, not a squeak and scuffle from the mice behind the panelling, not a drip from the half-thawed water-spout in the dull yard behind, not a sigh among the leafless boughs of one despondent poplar, not the idle swinging of an empty store-house door, no, not a clicking in the fire, but fell upon the heart of Scrooge with a softening influence, and gave a freer passage to his tears.

The Spirit touched him on the arm, and pointed to his younger self, intent upon his reading. Suddenly a man, in foreign garments: wonderfully real and distinct to look at: stood outside the window, with an axe stuck in his belt, and leading by the bridle an ass laden with wood.

"Why, it's Ali Baba!" Scrooge exclaimed in ecstasy. "It's dear old honest Ali Baba! Yes, yes, I know! One Christmas time, when yonder solitary child was left here all alone, he did come, for the first time, just like that. Poor boy! And Valentine," said Scrooge, "and his wild brother, Orson; there they go! And what's his name, who was put down in his drawers, asleep, at the Gate of Damascus; don't you see him! And the Sultan's Groom turned upside down by the Genii; there he is upon his head! Serve him right. I'm glad of it. What business had he to be married to the Princess!"

To hear Scrooge expending all the earnestness of his nature on such subjects, in a most extraordinary voice between laughing and crying; and to see his heightened and excited face; would have been a surprise to his business friends in the city, indeed.

"There's the Parrot!" cried Scrooge. "Green body and yellow tail, with a thing like a lettuce growing out of the top of his head; there he is! Poor Robin Crusoe, he called him, when he came home again after sailing round the island. 'Poor Robin Crusoe, where have you been, Robin Crusoe?' The man thought he was dreaming, but he wasn't. It was the Parrot, you know. There goes Friday, running for his life to the little creek! Halloa! Hoop! Halloo!"

Then, with a rapidity of transition very foreign to his usual character, he said, in pity for his former self, "Poor boy!" and cried again.

"I wish," Scrooge muttered, putting his hand in his pocket, and looking about him, after drying his eyes with his cuff: "but it's too late now."

"What is the matter?" asked the Spirit.

"Nothing," said Scrooge. "Nothing. There was a boy singing a Christmas Carol at my door last night. I should like to have given him something: that's all."

The Ghost smiled thoughtfully, and waved its hand: saying as it did so, "Let us see another Christmas!"

Scrooge's former self grew larger at the words, and the room became a little darker and more dirty. The panels shrunk, the windows cracked; fragments of plaster fell out of the ceiling, and the naked laths were shown instead; but how all this was brought about, Scrooge knew no more than you do. He only knew that it was quite correct; that everything had happened so; that there he was, alone again, when all the other boys had gone home for the jolly holidays.

He was not reading now, but walking up and down despairingly. Scrooge looked at the Ghost, and with a mournful shaking of his head, glanced anxiously towards the door.

It opened; and a little girl, much younger than the boy, came darting in, and putting her arms about his neck, and often kissing him, addressed him as her "Dear, dear brother."

"I have come to bring you home, dear brother!" said the child, clapping her tiny hands, and bending down to laugh. "To bring you home, home, home!"

"Home, little Fan?" returned the boy.

"Yes!" said the child, brimful of glee. "Home, for good and all. Home, for ever and ever. Father is so much kinder than he used to be, that home's like Heaven! He spoke so gently to me one dear night when I was going to bed, that I was not afraid to ask him once more if you might come home; and he said Yes, you should; and sent me in a coach to bring you. And you're to be a man!" said the child, opening her eyes, "and are never to come back here; but first, we're to be together all the Christmas long, and have the merriest time in all the world."

"You are quite a woman, little Fan!" exclaimed the boy.

She clapped her hands and laughed, and tried to touch his head; but being too little, laughed again, and stood on tiptoe to embrace him. Then she began to drag him, in her childish eagerness, towards the door; and he, nothing loth to go, accompanied her.

A terrible voice in the hall cried, "Bring down Master Scrooge's box, there!" and in the hall appeared the schoolmaster himself, who glared on Master Scrooge with a ferocious condescension, and threw him into a dreadful state of mind by shaking hands with him. He then conveyed him and his sister into the veriest old well of a shivering best-parlour that ever was seen, where the maps upon the wall, and the celestial and terrestrial globes in the windows, were waxy with cold. Here he produced a decanter of curiously light wine, and a block of curiously heavy cake, and administered instalments of those dainties to the young people: at the same time, sending out a meagre servant to offer a glass of "something" to the postboy, who answered that he thanked the gentleman, but if it was the same tap as he had tasted before, he had rather not. Master Scrooge's trunk being by this time tied on to the top of the chaise, the children bade the schoolmaster good-bye right willingly; and getting into it, drove gaily down the garden-sweep: the quick wheels dashing the hoar-frost and snow from off the dark leaves of the evergreens like spray.

"Always a delicate creature, whom a breath might have withered," said the Ghost. "But she had a large heart!"

"So she had," cried Scrooge. "You're right. I will not gainsay it, Spirit. God forbid!"

"She died a woman," said the Ghost, "and had, as I think, children."

"One child," Scrooge returned.

"True," said the Ghost. "Your nephew!"

Scrooge seemed uneasy in his mind; and answered briefly, "Yes."

Although they had but that moment left the school behind them, they were now in the busy thoroughfares of a city, where shadowy passengers passed and repassed; where shadowy carts and coaches battled for the way, and all the strife and tumult of a real city were. It was made plain enough, by the dressing of the shops, that here too it was Christmas time again; but it was evening, and the streets were lighted up.

The Ghost stopped at a certain warehouse door, and asked Scrooge if he knew it.

"Know it!" said Scrooge. "Was I apprenticed here!"

They went in. At sight of an old gentleman in a Welsh wig, sitting behind such a high desk, that if he had been two inches taller he must have knocked his head against the ceiling, Scrooge cried in great excitement:

"Why, it's old Fezziwig! Bless his heart; it's Fezziwig alive again!"

Old Fezziwig laid down his pen, and looked up at the clock, which pointed to the hour of seven. He rubbed his hands; adjusted his capacious waistcoat; laughed all over himself, from his shoes to his organ of benevolence; and called out in a comfortable, oily, rich, fat, jovial voice:

"Yo ho, there! Ebenezer! Dick!"

Scrooge's former self, now grown a young man, came briskly in, accompanied by his fellow-'prentice.

"Dick Wilkins, to be sure!" said Scrooge to the Ghost. "Bless me, yes. There he is. He was very much attached to me, was Dick. Poor Dick! Dear, dear!"

"Yo ho, my boys!" said Fezziwig. "No more work to-night. Christmas Eve, Dick. Christmas, Ebenezer! Let's have the shutters up," cried old Fezziwig, with a sharp clap of his hands, "before a man can say Jack Robinson!"

You wouldn't believe how those two fellows went at it! They charged into the street with the shutters—one, two, three—had 'em up in their places—four, five, six—barred 'em and pinned 'em—seven, eight, nine—and came back before you could have got to twelve, panting like race-horses.

"Hilli-ho!" cried old Fezziwig, skipping down from the high desk, with wonderful agility. "Clear away, my lads, and let's have lots of room here! Hilli-ho, Dick! Chirrup, Ebenezer!"

Clear away! There was nothing they wouldn't have cleared away, or couldn't have cleared away, with old Fezziwig looking on. It was done in a minute. Every movable was packed off, as if it were dismissed from public life for evermore; the floor was swept and watered, the lamps were trimmed, fuel was heaped upon the fire; and the warehouse was as snug, and warm, and dry, and bright a ball-room, as you would desire to see upon a winter's night.

In came a fiddler with a music-book, and went up to the lofty desk, and made an orchestra of it, and tuned like fifty stomach-aches. In came Mrs. Fezziwig, one vast substantial smile. In came the three Miss Fezziwigs, beaming and lovable. In came the six young followers whose hearts they broke. In came all the young men and women employed in the business. In came the housemaid, with her cousin, the baker. In came the cook, with her brother's particular friend, the milkman. In came the boy from over the way, who was suspected of not having board enough from his master; trying to hide himself behind the girl from next door but one, who was proved to have had her ears pulled by her mistress. In they all came, one after another; some shyly, some boldly, some gracefully, some awkwardly, some pushing, some pulling; in they all came, anyhow and everyhow. Away they all went, twenty couple at once; hands half round and back again the other way; down the middle and up again; round and round in various stages of affectionate grouping; old top couple always turning up in the wrong place; new top couple starting off again, as soon as they got there; all top couples at last, and not a bottom one to help them! When this result was brought about, old Fezziwig, clapping his hands to stop the dance, cried out, "Well done!" and the fiddler plunged his hot face into a pot of porter, especially provided for that purpose. But scorning rest, upon his reappearance, he instantly began again, though there were no dancers yet, as if the other fiddler had been carried home, exhausted, on a shutter, and he were a bran-new man resolved to beat him out of sight, or perish.

There were more dances, and there were forfeits, and more dances, and there was cake, and there was negus, and there was a great piece of Cold Roast, and there was a great piece of Cold Boiled, and there were mince-pies, and plenty of beer. But the great effect of the evening came after the Roast and Boiled, when the fiddler (an artful dog, mind! The sort of man who knew his business better than you or I could have told it him!) struck up "Sir Roger de Coverley." Then old Fezziwig stood out to dance with Mrs. Fezziwig. Top couple, too; with a good stiff piece of work cut out for them;

three or four and twenty pair of partners; people who were not to be trifled with; people who would dance, and had no notion of walking.

But if they had been twice as many—ah, four times—old Fezziwig would have been a match for them, and so would Mrs. Fezziwig. As to her, she was worthy to be his partner in every sense of the term. If that's not high praise, tell me higher, and I'll use it. A positive light appeared to issue from Fezziwig's calves. They shone in every part of the dance like moons. You couldn't have predicted, at any given time, what would have become of them next. And when old Fezziwig and Mrs. Fezziwig had gone all through the dance; advance and retire, both hands to your partner, bow and curtsey, corkscrew, thread-the-needle, and back again to your place; Fezziwig "cut"—cut so deftly, that he appeared to wink with his legs, and came upon his feet again without a stagger.

When the clock struck eleven, this domestic ball broke up. Mr. and Mrs. Fezziwig took their stations, one on either side of the door, and shaking hands with every person individually as he or she went out, wished him or her a Merry Christmas. When everybody had retired but the two 'prentices, they did the same to them; and thus the cheerful voices died away, and the lads were left to their beds; which were under a counter in the back-shop.

During the whole of this time, Scrooge had acted like a man out of his wits. His heart and soul were in the scene, and with his former self. He corroborated everything, remembered everything, enjoyed everything, and underwent the strangest agitation. It was not until now, when the bright faces of his former self and Dick were turned from them, that he remembered the Ghost, and became conscious that it was looking full upon him, while the light upon its head burnt very clear.

"A small matter," said the Ghost, "to make these silly folks so full of gratitude."

"Small!" echoed Scrooge.

The Spirit signed to him to listen to the two apprentices, who were pouring out their hearts in praise of Fezziwig: and when he had done so, said,

"Why! Is it not? He has spent but a few pounds of your mortal money: three or four perhaps. Is that so much that he deserves this praise?"

"It isn't that," said Scrooge, heated by the remark, and speaking unconsciously like his former, not his latter, self. "It isn't that, Spirit. He has the power to render us happy or unhappy; to make our service light or burdensome; a pleasure or a toil. Say that his power lies in words and looks; in things so slight and insignificant that it is impossible to add and count 'em up: what then? The happiness he gives, is quite as great as if it cost a fortune."

He felt the Spirit's glance, and stopped.

"What is the matter?" asked the Ghost.

"Nothing particular," said Scrooge.

"Something, I think?" the Ghost insisted.

"No," said Scrooge, "No. I should like to be able to say a word or two to my clerk just now. That's all."

His former self turned down the lamps as he gave utterance to the wish; and Scrooge and the Ghost again stood side by side in the open air.

"My time grows short," observed the Spirit. "Quick!"

This was not addressed to Scrooge, or to any one whom he could see, but it produced an immediate effect. For again Scrooge saw himself. He was older now; a man in the prime of life. His face had not the harsh and rigid lines of later years; but it had begun to wear the signs of care and avarice. There was an eager, greedy, restless motion in the eye, which showed the passion that had taken root, and where the shadow of the growing tree would fall.

He was not alone, but sat by the side of a fair young girl in a mourning-dress: in whose eyes there were tears, which sparkled in the light that shone out of the Ghost of Christmas Past.

"It matters little," she said, softly. "To you, very little. Another idol has displaced me; and if it can cheer and comfort you in time to come, as I would have tried to do, I have no just cause to grieve."

"What Idol has displaced you?" he rejoined.

"A golden one."

"This is the even-handed dealing of the world!" he said. "There is nothing on which it is so hard as poverty; and there is nothing it professes to condemn with such severity as the pursuit of wealth!"

"You fear the world too much," she answered, gently. "All your other hopes have merged into the hope of being beyond the chance of its sordid reproach. I have seen your nobler aspirations fall off one by one, until the master-passion, Gain, engrosses you. Have I not?"

"What then?" he retorted. "Even if I have grown so much wiser, what then? I am not changed towards you."

She shook her head.

"Am I?"

"Our contract is an old one. It was made when we were both poor and content to be so, until, in good season, we could improve our worldly fortune by our patient industry. You are changed. When it was made, you were another man."

"I was a boy," he said impatiently.

"Your own feeling tells you that you were not what you are," she returned. "I am. That which promised happiness when we were one in heart, is fraught with misery now that we are two. How often and how keenly I have thought of this, I will not say. It is enough that I have thought of it, and can release you."

"Have I ever sought release?"

"In words. No. Never."

"In what, then?"

"In a changed nature; in an altered spirit; in another atmosphere of life; another Hope as its great end. In everything that made my love of any worth or value in your sight. If this had never been between us," said the girl, looking mildly, but with steadiness, upon him; "tell me, would you seek me out and try to win me now? Ah, no!"

He seemed to yield to the justice of this supposition, in spite of himself. But he said with a struggle, "You think not."

"I would gladly think otherwise if I could," she answered, "Heaven knows! When I have learned a Truth like this, I know how strong and irresistible it must be. But if you were free to-day, to-morrow, yesterday, can even I believe that you would choose a dowerless girl—you who, in your very confidence with her, weigh everything by Gain: or, choosing her, if for a moment you were false enough to your one guiding principle to do so, do I not know that your repentance and regret would surely follow? I do; and I release you. With a full heart, for the love of him you once were."

He was about to speak; but with her head turned from him, she resumed.

"You may—the memory of what is past half makes me hope you will—have pain in this. A very, very brief time, and you will dismiss the recollection of it, gladly, as an unprofitable dream, from which it happened well that you awoke. May you be happy in the life you have chosen!"

She left him, and they parted.

"Spirit!" said Scrooge, "show me no more! Conduct me home. Why do you delight to torture me?"

"One shadow more!" exclaimed the Ghost.

"No more!" cried Scrooge. "No more. I don't wish to see it. Show me no more!"

But the relentless Ghost pinioned him in both his arms, and forced him to observe what happened next.

They were in another scene and place; a room, not very large or handsome, but full of comfort. Near to the winter fire sat a beautiful young girl, so like that last that Scrooge believed it was the same, until he saw her, now a comely matron, sitting opposite her daughter. The noise in this room was perfectly tumultuous, for there were more children there, than Scrooge in his agitated state of mind could count; and, unlike the celebrated herd in the poem, they were not forty children conducting themselves like one, but every child was conducting itself like forty. The consequences were uproarious beyond belief; but no one seemed to care; on the contrary, the mother and daughter laughed heartily, and enjoyed it very much; and the latter, soon beginning to mingle in the sports, got pillaged by the young brigands most ruthlessly. What would I not have given to be one of them! Though I never could have been so rude, no, no! I wouldn't for the wealth of all the world have crushed that braided hair, and torn it down; and for the precious little shoe, I wouldn't have plucked it off, God bless my soul! to save my life. As to measuring her waist in sport, as they did, bold young brood, I couldn't have done it; I should have expected my arm to have grown round it for a punishment, and never come straight again. And yet I should have dearly liked, I own, to have touched her lips; to have questioned her, that she might have opened them; to have looked upon the lashes of her downcast eyes, and never raised a blush; to have let loose waves of hair, an inch of which would be a keepsake beyond price: in short, I should have liked, I do confess, to have had the lightest licence of a child, and yet to have been man enough to know its value.

But now a knocking at the door was heard, and such a rush immediately ensued that she with laughing face and plundered dress was borne towards it the centre of a flushed and boisterous group, just in time to greet the father, who came home attended by a man laden with Christmas toys and presents. Then the shouting and the struggling, and the onslaught that was made on the defenceless porter! The scaling him with chairs for ladders to dive into his pockets, despoil him of brown-paper parcels, hold on tight by his cravat, hug him round his neck, pommel his back, and kick his legs in irrepressible affection! The shouts of wonder and delight with which the development of every package was received! The terrible announcement that the baby had been taken in the act of putting a doll's frying-pan into his mouth, and was more than suspected of having swallowed a fictitious turkey, glued on a wooden platter! The immense relief of finding this a false alarm! The joy, and gratitude, and ecstasy! They are all indescribable alike. It is enough that by degrees the children and their emotions got out of the parlour, and by one stair at a time, up to the top of the house; where they went to bed, and so subsided.

And now Scrooge looked on more attentively than ever, when the master of the house, having his daughter leaning fondly on him, sat down with her and her mother at his own fireside; and when he thought that such another creature, quite as graceful and as full of promise, might have called him father, and been a spring-time in the haggard winter of his life, his sight grew very dim indeed.

"Belle," said the husband, turning to his wife with a smile, "I saw an old friend of yours this afternoon."

"Who was it?"

"Guess!"

"How can I? Tut, don't I know?" she added in the same breath, laughing as he laughed. "Mr. Scrooge."

"Mr. Scrooge it was. I passed his office window; and as it was not shut up, and he had a candle inside, I could scarcely help seeing him. His partner lies upon the point of death, I hear; and there he sat alone. Quite alone in the world, I do believe."

"Spirit!" said Scrooge in a broken voice, "remove me from this place."

"I told you these were shadows of the things that have been," said the Ghost. "That they are what they are, do not blame me!"

"Remove me!" Scrooge exclaimed, "I cannot bear it!"

He turned upon the Ghost, and seeing that it looked upon him with a face, in which in some strange way there were fragments of all the faces it had shown him, wrestled with it.

"Leave me! Take me back. Haunt me no longer!"

In the struggle, if that can be called a struggle in which the Ghost with no visible resistance on its own part was undisturbed by any effort of its adversary, Scrooge observed that its light was burning high and bright; and dimly connecting that with its influence over him, he seized the extinguisher-cap, and by a sudden action pressed it down upon its head.

The Spirit dropped beneath it, so that the extinguisher covered its whole form; but though Scrooge pressed it down with all his force, he could not hide the light: which streamed from under it, in an unbroken flood upon the ground.

He was conscious of being exhausted, and overcome by an irresistible drowsiness; and, further, of being in his own bedroom. He gave the cap a parting squeeze, in which his hand relaxed; and had barely time to reel to bed, before he sank into a heavy sleep.

STAVE III: THE SECOND OF THE THREE SPIRITS

AWAKING in the middle of a prodigiously tough snore, and sitting up in bed to get his thoughts together, Scrooge had no occasion to be told that the bell was again upon the stroke of One. He felt that he was restored to consciousness in the right nick of time, for the especial purpose of holding a conference with the second messenger despatched to him through Jacob Marley's intervention. But finding that he turned uncomfortably cold when he began to wonder which of his curtains this new spectre would draw back, he put them every one aside with his own hands; and lying down again, established a sharp look-out all round the bed. For he wished to challenge the Spirit on the moment of its appearance, and did not wish to be taken by surprise, and made nervous.

Gentlemen of the free-and-easy sort, who plume themselves on being acquainted with a move or two, and being usually equal to the time-of-day, express the wide range of their capacity for adventure by observing that they are good for anything from pitch-and-toss to manslaughter; between which opposite extremes, no doubt, there lies a tolerably wide and comprehensive range of subjects. Without venturing for Scrooge quite as hardily as this, I don't mind calling on you to believe that he was ready for a good broad field of strange appearances, and that nothing between a baby and rhinoceros would have astonished him very much.

Now, being prepared for almost anything, he was not by any means prepared for nothing; and, consequently, when the Bell struck One, and no shape appeared, he was taken with a violent fit of trembling. Five minutes, ten minutes, a quarter of an hour went by, yet nothing came. All this time, he lay upon his bed, the very core and centre of a blaze of ruddy light, which streamed upon it when the clock proclaimed the hour; and which, being only light, was more alarming than a dozen ghosts, as he was powerless to make out what it meant, or would be at; and was sometimes apprehensive that he might be at that very moment an interesting case of spontaneous combustion, without having the consolation of knowing it. At last, however, he began to think—as you or I would have thought at first; for it is always the person not in the predicament who knows what ought to have been done in it, and would unquestionably have done it too—at last, I say, he began to think that the source and secret of this ghostly light might be in the adjoining room, from whence, on further tracing it, it seemed to shine. This idea taking full possession of his mind, he got up softly and shuffled in his slippers to the door.

The moment Scrooge's hand was on the lock, a strange voice called him by his name, and bade him enter. He obeyed.

It was his own room. There was no doubt about that. But it had undergone a surprising transformation. The walls and ceiling were so hung with living green, that it looked a perfect grove; from every part of which, bright gleaming berries glistened. The crisp leaves of holly, mistletoe, and ivy reflected back the light, as if so many little mirrors had been scattered there; and such a mighty blaze went roaring up the chimney, as that dull petrification of a hearth had never known in Scrooge's time, or Marley's, or for many and many a winter season gone. Heaped up on the floor, to form a kind of throne, were turkeys, geese, game, poultry, brawn, great joints of meat, sucking-pigs, long wreaths of sausages, mince-pies, plum-puddings, barrels of oysters, red-hot chestnuts, cherry-cheeked apples, juicy oranges, luscious pears, immense twelfth-cakes, and seething bowls of punch, that made the chamber dim with their delicious steam. In easy state upon this couch, there sat a jolly Giant, glorious to see; who bore a glowing torch, in shape not unlike Plenty's horn, and held it up, high up, to shed its light on Scrooge, as he came peeping round the door.

"Come in!" exclaimed the Ghost. "Come in! and know me better, man!"

Scrooge entered timidly, and hung his head before this Spirit. He was not the dogged Scrooge he had been; and though the Spirit's eyes were clear and kind, he did not like to meet them.

"I am the Ghost of Christmas Present," said the Spirit. "Look upon me!"

Scrooge reverently did so. It was clothed in one simple green robe, or mantle, bordered with white fur. This garment hung so loosely on the figure, that its capacious breast was bare, as if disdaining to be warded or concealed by any artifice. Its feet, observable beneath the ample folds of the garment, were also bare; and on its head it wore no other covering than a holly wreath, set here and there with shining icicles. Its dark brown curls were long and free; free as its genial face, its sparkling eye, its open hand, its cheery voice, its unconstrained demeanour, and its joyful air. Girded round its middle was an antique scabbard; but no sword was in it, and the ancient sheath was eaten up with rust.

"You have never seen the like of me before!" exclaimed the Spirit.

"Never," Scrooge made answer to it.

"Have never walked forth with the younger members of my family; meaning (for I am very young) my elder brothers born in these later years?" pursued the Phantom.

"I don't think I have," said Scrooge. "I am afraid I have not. Have you had many brothers, Spirit?"

"More than eighteen hundred," said the Ghost.

"A tremendous family to provide for!" muttered Scrooge.

The Ghost of Christmas Present rose.

"Spirit," said Scrooge submissively, "conduct me where you will. I went forth last night on compulsion, and I learnt a lesson which is working now. To-night, if you have aught to teach me, let me profit by it."

"Touch my robe!"

Scrooge did as he was told, and held it fast.

Holly, mistletoe, red berries, ivy, turkeys, geese, game, poultry, brawn, meat, pigs, sausages, oysters, pies, puddings, fruit, and punch, all vanished instantly. So did the room, the fire, the ruddy glow, the hour of night, and they stood in the city streets on Christmas morning, where (for the weather was severe) the people made a rough, but brisk and not unpleasant kind of music, in scraping the snow from the pavement in front of their dwellings, and from the tops of their houses, whence it was mad delight to the boys to see it come plumping down into the road below, and splitting into artificial little snow-storms.

The house fronts looked black enough, and the windows blacker, contrasting with the smooth white sheet of snow upon the roofs, and with the dirtier snow upon the ground; which last deposit had been ploughed up in deep furrows by the heavy wheels of carts and waggons; furrows that crossed and re-crossed each other hundreds of times where the great streets branched off; and made intricate channels, hard to trace in the thick yellow mud and icy water. The sky was gloomy, and the shortest streets were choked up with a dingy mist, half thawed, half frozen, whose heavier particles descended in a shower of sooty atoms, as if all the chimneys in Great Britain had, by one consent, caught fire, and were blazing away to their dear hearts' content. There was nothing very cheerful in the climate or the town, and yet was there an air of cheerfulness abroad that the clearest summer air and brightest summer sun might have endeavoured to diffuse in vain.

For, the people who were shovelling away on the housetops were jovial and full of glee; calling out to one another from the parapets, and now and then exchanging a facetious snowball—better-natured missile far than many a wordy jest—laughing heartily if it went right and not less heartily if it went wrong. The poulterers' shops were still half open, and the fruiterers' were radiant in their glory. There were great, round, pot-bellied baskets of chestnuts, shaped like the waistcoats of jolly old gentlemen, lolling at the doors, and tumbling out into the street in their apoplectic opulence. There were ruddy, brown-faced, broad-girthed Spanish Onions, shining in the fatness of their growth like Spanish Friars, and winking from their shelves in wanton slyness at the girls as they went by, and glanced demurely at the hung-up mistletoe. There were pears and apples, clustered high in blooming pyramids; there were bunches of grapes, made, in the shopkeepers' benevolence to dangle from conspicuous hooks, that people's mouths might water gratis as they passed; there were piles of filberts, mossy and brown, recalling, in their fragrance, ancient walks among the woods, and pleasant shufflings ankle deep through withered leaves; there were Norfolk Biffins, squat and swarthy, setting off the yellow of the oranges and lemons, and, in the great compactness of their juicy persons, urgently entreating and beseeching to be carried home in paper bags and eaten after dinner. The very gold and silver fish, set forth among these choice fruits in a bowl, though members of a dull and stagnant-blooded race, appeared to know that there was something going on; and, to a fish, went gasping round and round their little world in slow and passionless excitement.

The Grocers'! oh, the Grocers'! nearly closed, with perhaps two shutters down, or one; but through those gaps such glimpses! It was not alone that the scales descending on the counter made a merry sound, or that the twine and roller parted company so briskly, or that the canisters were rattled up and down like juggling tricks, or even that the blended scents of tea and coffee were so grateful to the nose, or even that the raisins were so plentiful and rare, the almonds so extremely white, the sticks of cinnamon so long and straight, the other spices so delicious, the candied fruits so caked and spotted with molten sugar as to make the coldest lookers-on feel faint and subsequently bilious. Nor was it that the figs were moist and pulpy, or that the French plums blushed in modest tartness from their highly-decorated boxes, or that everything was good to eat and in its Christmas dress; but the customers were all so hurried and so eager in the hopeful promise of the day, that they tumbled up against each other at the door, crashing their wicker baskets wildly, and left their purchases upon the counter, and came running back to fetch them, and committed hundreds of the like mistakes, in the best humour possible; while the Grocer and his people were so frank and fresh that the polished hearts with which they fastened their aprons behind might have been their own, worn outside for general inspection, and for Christmas daws to peck at if they chose.

But soon the steeples called good people all, to church and chapel, and away they came, flocking through the streets in their best clothes, and with their gayest faces. And at the same time there emerged from scores of bye-streets, lanes, and nameless turnings, innumerable people, carrying their dinners to the bakers' shops. The sight of these poor revellers appeared to interest the Spirit very much, for he stood with Scrooge beside him in a baker's doorway, and taking off the covers as their bearers passed, sprinkled incense on their dinners from his torch. And it was a very uncommon kind of torch, for once or twice when there were angry words between some dinner-carriers who had jostled each other, he shed a few drops of water on them from it, and their good humour was restored directly. For they said, it was a shame to quarrel upon Christmas Day. And so it was! God love it, so it was!

In time the bells ceased, and the bakers were shut up; and yet there was a genial shadowing forth of all these dinners and the progress of their cooking, in the thawed blotch of wet above each baker's oven; where the pavement smoked as if its stones were cooking too.

"Is there a peculiar flavour in what you sprinkle from your torch?" asked Scrooge.

"There is. My own."

"Would it apply to any kind of dinner on this day?" asked Scrooge.

"To any kindly given. To a poor one most."

"Why to a poor one most?" asked Scrooge.

"Because it needs it most."

"Spirit," said Scrooge, after a moment's thought, "I wonder you, of all the beings in the many worlds about us, should desire to cramp these people's opportunities of innocent enjoyment."

"I!" cried the Spirit.

"You would deprive them of their means of dining every seventh day, often the only day on which they can be said to dine at all," said Scrooge. "Wouldn't you?"

"I!" cried the Spirit.

"You seek to close these places on the Seventh Day?" said Scrooge. "And it comes to the same thing."

"I seek!" exclaimed the Spirit.

"Forgive me if I am wrong. It has been done in your name, or at least in that of your family," said Scrooge.

"There are some upon this earth of yours," returned the Spirit, "who lay claim to know us, and who do their deeds of passion, pride, ill-will, hatred, envy, bigotry, and selfishness in our name, who are as strange to us and all our kith and kin, as if they had never lived. Remember that, and charge their doings on themselves, not us."

Scrooge promised that he would; and they went on, invisible, as they had been before, into the suburbs of the town. It was a remarkable quality of the Ghost (which Scrooge had observed at the baker's), that notwithstanding his gigantic size, he could accommodate himself to any place with ease; and that he stood beneath a low roof quite as gracefully and like a supernatural creature, as it was possible he could have done in any lofty hall.

And perhaps it was the pleasure the good Spirit had in showing off this power of his, or else it was his own kind, generous, hearty nature, and his sympathy with all poor men, that led him straight to Scrooge's clerk's; for there he went, and took Scrooge with him, holding to his robe; and on the threshold of the door the Spirit smiled, and stopped to bless Bob Cratchit's dwelling with the sprinkling of his torch. Think of that! Bob had but fifteen "Bob" a-week himself; he pocketed on Saturdays but fifteen copies of his Christian name; and yet the Ghost of Christmas Present blessed his four-roomed house!

Then up rose Mrs. Cratchit, Cratchit's wife, dressed out but poorly in a twice-turned gown, but brave in ribbons, which are cheap and make a goodly show for sixpence; and she laid the cloth, assisted by Belinda Cratchit, second of her daughters, also brave in ribbons; while Master Peter Cratchit plunged a fork into the saucepan of potatoes, and getting the corners of his monstrous shirt collar (Bob's private property, conferred upon his son and heir in honour of the day) into his mouth, rejoiced to find himself so gallantly attired, and yearned to show his linen in the fashionable Parks. And now two smaller Cratchits, boy and girl, came tearing in, screaming that outside the baker's they had smelt the goose, and known it for their own; and basking in luxurious thoughts of sage and onion, these young Cratchits danced about the table, and exalted Master Peter Cratchit to the skies, while he (not proud, although his collars nearly choked him) blew the fire, until the slow potatoes bubbling up, knocked loudly at the saucepan-lid to be let out and peeled.

"What has ever got your precious father then?" said Mrs. Cratchit. "And your brother, Tiny Tim! And Martha warn't as late last Christmas Day by half-an-hour?"

"Here's Martha, mother!" said a girl, appearing as she spoke.

"Here's Martha, mother!" cried the two young Cratchits. "Hurrah! There's such a goose, Martha!"

"Why, bless your heart alive, my dear, how late you are!" said Mrs. Cratchit, kissing her a dozen times, and taking off her shawl and bonnet for her with officious zeal.

"We'd a deal of work to finish up last night," replied the girl, "and had to clear away this morning, mother!"

"Well! Never mind so long as you are come," said Mrs. Cratchit. "Sit ye down before the fire, my dear, and have a warm, Lord bless ye!"

"No, no! There's father coming," cried the two young Cratchits, who were everywhere at once. "Hide, Martha, hide!"

So Martha hid herself, and in came little Bob, the father, with at least three feet of comforter exclusive of the fringe, hanging down before him; and his threadbare clothes darned up and brushed, to look seasonable; and Tiny Tim upon his shoulder. Alas for Tiny Tim, he bore a little crutch, and had his limbs supported by an iron frame!

"Why, where's our Martha?" cried Bob Cratchit, looking round.

"Not coming," said Mrs. Cratchit.

"Not coming!" said Bob, with a sudden declension in his high spirits; for he had been Tim's blood horse all the way from church, and had come home rampant. "Not coming upon Christmas Day!"

Martha didn't like to see him disappointed, if it were only in joke; so she came out prematurely from behind the closet door, and ran into his arms, while the two young Cratchits hustled Tiny Tim, and bore him off into the wash-house, that he might hear the pudding singing in the copper.

"And how did little Tim behave?" asked Mrs. Cratchit, when she had rallied Bob on his credulity, and Bob had hugged his daughter to his heart's content.

"As good as gold," said Bob, "and better. Somehow he gets thoughtful, sitting by himself so much, and thinks the strangest things you ever heard. He told me, coming home, that he hoped the people saw him in the church, because he was a cripple, and it might be pleasant to them to remember upon Christmas Day, who made lame beggars walk, and blind men see."

Bob's voice was tremulous when he told them this, and trembled more when he said that Tiny Tim was growing strong and hearty.

His active little crutch was heard upon the floor, and back came Tiny Tim before another word was spoken, escorted by his brother and sister to his stool before the fire; and while Bob, turning up his cuffs—as if, poor fellow, they were capable of being made more shabby—compounded some hot mixture in a jug with gin and lemons, and stirred it round and round and put it on the hob to simmer; Master Peter, and the two ubiquitous young Cratchits went to fetch the goose, with which they soon returned in high procession.

Such a bustle ensued that you might have thought a goose the rarest of all birds; a feathered phenomenon, to which a black swan was a matter of course—and in truth it was something very like it in that house. Mrs. Cratchit made the gravy (ready beforehand in a little saucepan) hissing hot; Master Peter mashed the potatoes with incredible vigour; Miss Belinda sweetened up the apple-sauce; Martha dusted the hot plates; Bob took Tiny Tim beside him in a tiny corner at the table; the two young Cratchits set chairs for everybody, not forgetting themselves, and mounting guard upon their posts, crammed spoons into their mouths, lest they should shriek for goose before their turn came to be helped. At last the dishes were set on, and grace was said. It was succeeded by a breathless pause, as Mrs. Cratchit, looking slowly all along the carving-knife, prepared to plunge it in the breast; but when she did, and when the long expected gush of stuffing issued forth, one murmur of delight arose all round the board, and even Tiny Tim, excited by the two young Cratchits, beat on the table with the handle of his knife, and feebly cried Hurrah!

There never was such a goose. Bob said he didn't believe there ever was such a goose cooked. Its tenderness and flavour, size and cheapness, were the themes of universal admiration. Eked out by apple-sauce and mashed potatoes, it was a sufficient dinner for the whole family; indeed, as Mrs. Cratchit said with great delight (surveying one small atom of a bone upon the dish), they hadn't ate it all at last! Yet every one had had enough, and the youngest Cratchits in particular, were steeped in sage and onion to the eyebrows! But now, the plates being changed by Miss Belinda, Mrs. Cratchit left the room alone—too nervous to bear witnesses—to take the pudding up and bring it in.

Suppose it should not be done enough! Suppose it should break in turning out! Suppose somebody should have got over the wall of the back-yard, and stolen it, while they were merry with the goose—a supposition at which the two young Cratchits became livid! All sorts of horrors were supposed.

Hallo! A great deal of steam! The pudding was out of the copper. A smell like a washing-day! That was the cloth. A smell like an eating-house and a pastrycook's next door to each other, with a laundress's next door to that! That was the pudding! In half a minute Mrs. Cratchit entered—flushed, but smiling proudly—with the pudding, like a speckled cannon-ball, so hard and firm, blazing in half of half-a-quartern of ignited brandy, and bedight with Christmas holly stuck into the top.

"Oh, a wonderful pudding!" Bob Cratchit said, and calmly too, that he regarded it as the greatest success achieved by Mrs. Cratchit since their marriage. Mrs. Cratchit said that now the weight was off her mind, she would confess she had had her doubts about the quantity of flour. Everybody had something to say about it, but nobody said or thought it was at all a small pudding for a large family. It would have been flat heresy to do so. Any Cratchit would have blushed to hint at such a thing.

At last the dinner was all done, the cloth was cleared, the hearth swept, and the fire made up. The compound in the jug being tasted, and considered perfect, apples and oranges were put upon the table, and a shovel-full of chestnuts on the fire. Then all the Cratchit family drew round the hearth, in what Bob Cratchit called a circle, meaning half a one; and at Bob Cratchit's elbow stood the family display of glass. Two tumblers, and a custard-cup without a handle.

These held the hot stuff from the jug, however, as well as golden goblets would have done; and Bob served it out with beaming looks, while the chestnuts on the fire sputtered and cracked noisily. Then Bob proposed:

"A Merry Christmas to us all, my dears. God bless us!"

Which all the family re-echoed.

"God bless us every one!" said Tiny Tim, the last of all.

He sat very close to his father's side upon his little stool. Bob held his withered little hand in his, as if he loved the child, and wished to keep him by his side, and dreaded that he might be taken from him.

"Spirit," said Scrooge, with an interest he had never felt before, "tell me if Tiny Tim will live."

"I see a vacant seat," replied the Ghost, "in the poor chimney-corner, and a crutch without an owner, carefully preserved. If these shadows remain unaltered by the Future, the child will die."

"No, no," said Scrooge. "Oh, no, kind Spirit! say he will be spared."

"If these shadows remain unaltered by the Future, none other of my race," returned the Ghost, "will find him here. What then? If he be like to die, he had better do it, and decrease the surplus population."

Scrooge hung his head to hear his own words quoted by the Spirit, and was overcome with penitence and grief.

"Man," said the Ghost, "if man you be in heart, not adamant, forbear that wicked cant until you have discovered What the surplus is, and Where it is. Will you decide what men shall live, what men shall die? It may be, that in the sight of Heaven, you are more worthless and less fit to live than millions like this poor man's child. Oh God! to hear the Insect on the leaf pronouncing on the too much life among his hungry brothers in the dust!"

Scrooge bent before the Ghost's rebuke, and trembling cast his eyes upon the ground. But he raised them speedily, on hearing his own name.

"Mr. Scrooge!" said Bob; "I'll give you Mr. Scrooge, the Founder of the Feast!"

"The Founder of the Feast indeed!" cried Mrs. Cratchit, reddening. "I wish I had him here. I'd give him a piece of my mind to feast upon, and I hope he'd have a good appetite for it."

"My dear," said Bob, "the children! Christmas Day."

"It should be Christmas Day, I am sure," said she, "on which one drinks the health of such an odious, stingy, hard, unfeeling man as Mr. Scrooge. You know he is, Robert! Nobody knows it better than you do, poor fellow!"

"My dear," was Bob's mild answer, "Christmas Day."

"I'll drink his health for your sake and the Day's," said Mrs. Cratchit, "not for his. Long life to him! A merry Christmas and a happy new year! He'll be very merry and very happy, I have no doubt!"

The children drank the toast after her. It was the first of their proceedings which had no heartiness. Tiny Tim drank it last of all, but he didn't care twopence for it. Scrooge was the Ogre of the family. The mention of his name cast a dark shadow on the party, which was not dispelled for full five minutes.

After it had passed away, they were ten times merrier than before, from the mere relief of Scrooge the Baleful being done with. Bob Cratchit told them how he had a situation in his eye for Master Peter, which would bring in, if obtained, full five-and-sixpence weekly. The two young Cratchits laughed tremendously at the idea of Peter's being a man of business; and Peter himself looked thoughtfully at the fire from between his collars, as if he were deliberating what particular investments he should favour when he came into the receipt of that bewildering income. Martha, who was a poor apprentice at a milliner's, then told them what kind of work she had to do, and how many hours she worked at a stretch, and how she meant to lie abed to-morrow morning for a good long rest; to-morrow being a holiday she passed at home. Also how she had seen a countess and a lord some days before, and how the lord "was much about as tall as Peter;" at which Peter pulled up his collars so high that you couldn't have seen his head if you had been there. All this time the chestnuts and the jug went round and round; and by-and-bye they had a song, about a lost child travelling in the snow, from Tiny Tim, who had a plaintive little voice, and sang it very well indeed.

There was nothing of high mark in this. They were not a handsome family; they were not well dressed; their shoes were far from being water-proof; their clothes were scanty; and Peter might have known, and very likely did, the inside of a pawnbroker's. But, they were happy, grateful, pleased with one another, and contented with the time; and when they faded, and looked happier yet in the bright sprinklings of the Spirit's torch at parting, Scrooge had his eye upon them, and especially on Tiny Tim, until the last.

By this time it was getting dark, and snowing pretty heavily; and as Scrooge and the Spirit went along the streets, the brightness of the roaring fires in kitchens, parlours, and all sorts of rooms, was wonderful. Here, the flickering of the blaze showed preparations for a cosy dinner, with hot plates baking through and through before the fire, and deep red curtains, ready to be drawn to shut out cold and darkness. There all the children of the house were running out into the snow to meet their married sisters, brothers, cousins, uncles, aunts, and be the first to greet them. Here, again, were shadows on the window-blind of guests assembling; and there a group of handsome girls, all hooded and fur-booted, and all chattering at once, tripped lightly off to some near neighbour's house; where, woe upon the single man who saw them enter—artful witches, well they knew it—in a glow!

But, if you had judged from the numbers of people on their way to friendly gatherings, you might have thought that no one was at home to give them welcome when they got there, instead of every house expecting company, and piling up its fires half-chimney high. Blessings on it, how the Ghost exulted! How it bared its breadth of breast, and opened its capacious palm, and floated on, outpouring, with a generous hand, its bright and harmless mirth on everything within its reach! The very lamplighter, who ran on before, dotting the dusky street with specks of light, and who was dressed to spend the evening somewhere, laughed out loudly as the Spirit passed, though little kenned the lamplighter that he had any company but Christmas!

And now, without a word of warning from the Ghost, they stood upon a bleak and desert moor, where monstrous masses of rude stone were cast about, as though it were the burial-place of giants; and water spread itself wheresoever it listed, or would have done so, but for the frost that held it prisoner; and nothing grew but moss and furze, and coarse rank grass. Down in the west the setting sun had left a streak of fiery red, which glared upon the desolation for an instant, like a sullen eye, and frowning lower, lower, lower yet, was lost in the thick gloom of darkest night.

"What place is this?" asked Scrooge.

"A place where Miners live, who labour in the bowels of the earth," returned the Spirit. "But they know me. See!"

A light shone from the window of a hut, and swiftly they advanced towards it. Passing through the wall of mud and stone, they found a cheerful company assembled round a glowing fire. An old, old man and woman, with their children and their children's children, and another generation beyond that, all decked out gaily in their holiday attire. The old man, in a voice that seldom rose above the howling of the wind upon the barren waste, was singing them a Christmas song—it had been a very old song when he was a boy—and from time to time they all joined in the chorus. So surely as they raised their voices, the old man got quite blithe and loud; and so surely as they stopped, his vigour sank again.

The Spirit did not tarry here, but bade Scrooge hold his robe, and passing on above the moor, sped—whither? Not to sea? To sea. To Scrooge's horror, looking back, he saw the last of the land, a frightful range of rocks, behind them; and his ears were deafened by the thundering of water, as it rolled and roared, and raged among the dreadful caverns it had worn, and fiercely tried to undermine the earth.

Built upon a dismal reef of sunken rocks, some league or so from shore, on which the waters chafed and dashed, the wild year through, there stood a solitary lighthouse. Great heaps of sea-weed clung to its base, and storm-birds—born of the wind one might suppose, as sea-weed of the water—rose and fell about it, like the waves they skimmed.

But even here, two men who watched the light had made a fire, that through the loophole in the thick stone wall shed out a ray of brightness on the awful sea. Joining their horny hands over the rough table at which they sat, they wished each other Merry Christmas in their can of grog; and one of them: the elder, too, with his face all damaged and scarred with hard weather, as the figure-head of an old ship might be: struck up a sturdy song that was like a Gale in itself.

Again the Ghost sped on, above the black and heaving sea—on, on—until, being far away, as he told Scrooge, from any shore, they lighted on a ship. They stood beside the helmsman at the wheel, the look-out in the bow, the officers who had the watch; dark, ghostly figures in their several stations; but every man among them hummed a Christmas tune, or had a Christmas thought, or spoke below his breath to his companion of some bygone Christmas Day, with homeward hopes belonging to it. And every man on board, waking or sleeping, good or bad, had had a kinder word for another on that day than on any day in the year; and had shared to some extent in its festivities; and had remembered those he cared for at a distance, and had known that they delighted to remember him.

It was a great surprise to Scrooge, while listening to the moaning of the wind, and thinking what a solemn thing it was to move on through the lonely darkness over an unknown abyss, whose depths were secrets as profound as Death: it was a great surprise to Scrooge, while thus engaged, to hear a hearty laugh. It was a much greater surprise to Scrooge to recognise it as his own nephew's and to find himself in a bright, dry, gleaming room, with the Spirit standing smiling by his side, and looking at that same nephew with approving affability!

"Ha, ha!" laughed Scrooge's nephew. "Ha, ha, ha!"

If you should happen, by any unlikely chance, to know a man more blest in a laugh than Scrooge's nephew, all I can say is, I should like to know him too. Introduce him to me, and I'll cultivate his acquaintance.

It is a fair, even-handed, noble adjustment of things, that while there is infection in disease and sorrow, there is nothing in the world so irresistibly contagious as laughter and good-humour. When Scrooge's nephew laughed in this way: holding his sides, rolling his head, and twisting his face into the most extravagant contortions: Scrooge's niece, by marriage, laughed as heartily as he. And their assembled friends being not a bit behindhand, roared out lustily.

"Ha, ha! Ha, ha, ha, ha!"

"He said that Christmas was a humbug, as I live!" cried Scrooge's nephew. "He believed it too!"

"More shame for him, Fred!" said Scrooge's niece, indignantly. Bless those women; they never do anything by halves. They are always in earnest.

She was very pretty: exceedingly pretty. With a dimpled, surprised-looking, capital face; a ripe little mouth, that seemed made to be kissed—as no doubt it was; all kinds of good little dots about her chin, that melted into one another when she laughed; and the sunniest pair of eyes you ever saw in any little creature's head. Altogether she was what you would have called provoking, you know; but satisfactory, too. Oh, perfectly satisfactory.

"He's a comical old fellow," said Scrooge's nephew, "that's the truth: and not so pleasant as he might be. However, his offences carry their own punishment, and I have nothing to say against him."

"I'm sure he is very rich, Fred," hinted Scrooge's niece. "At least you always tell me so."

"What of that, my dear!" said Scrooge's nephew. "His wealth is of no use to him. He don't do any good with it. He don't make himself comfortable with it. He hasn't the satisfaction of thinking—ha, ha, ha!—that he is ever going to benefit US with it."

"I have no patience with him," observed Scrooge's niece. Scrooge's niece's sisters, and all the other ladies, expressed the same opinion.

"Oh, I have!" said Scrooge's nephew. "I am sorry for him; I couldn't be angry with him if I tried. Who suffers by his ill whims! Himself, always. Here, he takes it into his head to dislike us, and he won't come and dine with us. What's the consequence? He don't lose much of a dinner."

"Indeed, I think he loses a very good dinner," interrupted Scrooge's niece. Everybody else said the same, and they must be allowed to have been competent judges, because they had just had dinner; and, with the dessert upon the table, were clustered round the fire, by lamplight.

"Well! I'm very glad to hear it," said Scrooge's nephew, "because I haven't great faith in these young housekeepers. What do you say, Topper?"

Topper had clearly got his eye upon one of Scrooge's niece's sisters, for he answered that a bachelor was a wretched outcast, who had no right to express an opinion on the subject. Whereat Scrooge's niece's sister—the plump one with the lace tucker: not the one with the roses—blushed.

"Do go on, Fred," said Scrooge's niece, clapping her hands. "He never finishes what he begins to say! He is such a ridiculous fellow!"

Scrooge's nephew revelled in another laugh, and as it was impossible to keep the infection off; though the plump sister tried hard to do it with aromatic vinegar; his example was unanimously followed.

"I was only going to say," said Scrooge's nephew, "that the consequence of his taking a dislike to us, and not making merry with us, is, as I think, that he loses some pleasant moments, which could do him no harm. I am sure he loses pleasanter companions than he can find in his own thoughts, either in his mouldy old office, or his dusty chambers. I mean to give him the same chance every year, whether he likes it or not, for I pity him. He may rail at Christmas till he dies, but he can't help thinking better of it—I defy him—if he finds me going there, in good temper, year after year, and saying Uncle Scrooge, how are you? If it only puts him in the vein to leave his poor clerk fifty pounds, that's something; and I think I shook him yesterday."

It was their turn to laugh now at the notion of his shaking Scrooge. But being thoroughly good-natured, and not much caring what they laughed at, so that they laughed at any rate, he encouraged them in their merriment, and passed the bottle joyously.

After tea, they had some music. For they were a musical family, and knew what they were about, when they sung a Glee or Catch, I can assure you: especially Topper, who could growl away in the bass like a good one, and never swell the large veins in his forehead, or get red in the face over it. Scrooge's niece played well upon the harp; and played among other tunes a simple little air (a mere nothing: you might learn to whistle it in two minutes), which had been familiar to the child who fetched Scrooge from the boarding-school, as he had been reminded by the Ghost of Christmas Past. When this strain of music sounded, all the things that Ghost had shown him, came upon his mind; he softened more and more; and thought that if he could have listened to it often, years ago, he might have cultivated the kindnesses of life for his own happiness with his own hands, without resorting to the sexton's spade that buried Jacob Marley.

But they didn't devote the whole evening to music. After a while they played at forfeits; for it is good to be children sometimes, and never better than at Christmas, when its mighty Founder was a child himself. Stop! There was first a game at blind-man's buff. Of course there was. And I no more believe Topper was really blind than I believe he had eyes in his boots. My opinion is, that it was a done thing between him and Scrooge's nephew; and that the Ghost of Christmas Present knew it. The way he went after that plump sister in the lace tucker, was an outrage on the credulity of human nature. Knocking down the fire-irons, tumbling over the chairs, bumping against the piano, smothering himself among the curtains, wherever she went, there went he! He always knew where the plump sister was. He wouldn't catch anybody else. If you had fallen up against him (as some of them did), on purpose, he would have made a feint of endeavouring to seize you, which would have been an affront to your understanding, and would instantly have sidled off in the direction of the plump sister. She often cried out that it wasn't fair; and it really was not. But when at last, he caught her; when, in spite of all her silken rustlings, and her rapid flutterings past him, he got her into a corner whence there was no escape; then his conduct was the most execrable. For his pretending not to know her; his pretending that it was necessary to touch her head-dress, and further to assure himself of her identity by pressing a certain ring upon her finger, and a certain chain about her neck; was vile, monstrous! No doubt she told him her opinion of it, when, another blind-man being in office, they were so very confidential together, behind the curtains.

Scrooge's niece was not one of the blind-man's buff party, but was made comfortable with a large chair and a footstool, in a snug corner, where the Ghost and Scrooge were close behind her. But she joined in the forfeits, and loved her love to admiration with all the letters of the alphabet. Likewise at the game of How, When, and Where, she was very great, and to the secret joy of Scrooge's nephew, beat her sisters hollow: though they were sharp girls too, as Topper could have told you. There might have been twenty people there, young and old, but they all played, and so did Scrooge; for wholly forgetting in the interest he had in what was going on, that his voice made no sound in their ears, he sometimes came out with his guess quite loud, and very often guessed quite right, too; for the sharpest needle, best Whitechapel, warranted not to cut in the eye, was not sharper than Scrooge; blunt as he took it in his head to be.

The Ghost was greatly pleased to find him in this mood, and looked upon him with such favour, that he begged like a boy to be allowed to stay until the guests departed. But this the Spirit said could not be done.

"Here is a new game," said Scrooge. "One half hour, Spirit, only one!"

It was a Game called Yes and No, where Scrooge's nephew had to think of something, and the rest must find out what; he only answering to their questions yes or no, as the case was. The brisk fire of questioning to which he was exposed, elicited from him that he was thinking of an animal, a live animal, rather a disagreeable animal, a savage animal, an animal that growled and grunted sometimes, and talked sometimes, and lived in London, and walked about the streets, and wasn't made a show of, and wasn't led by anybody, and didn't live in a menagerie, and was never killed in a market, and was not a horse, or an ass, or a cow, or a bull, or a tiger, or a dog, or a pig, or a cat, or a bear. At every fresh question that was put to him, this nephew burst into a fresh roar of laughter; and was so inexpressibly tickled, that he was obliged to get up off the sofa and stamp. At last the plump sister, falling into a similar state, cried out:

"I have found it out! I know what it is, Fred! I know what it is!"

"What is it?" cried Fred.

"It's your Uncle Scro-o-o-o-oge!"

Which it certainly was. Admiration was the universal sentiment, though some objected that the reply to "Is it a bear?" ought to have been "Yes;" inasmuch as an answer in the negative was sufficient to have diverted their thoughts from Mr. Scrooge, supposing they had ever had any tendency that way.

"He has given us plenty of merriment, I am sure," said Fred, "and it would be ungrateful not to drink his health. Here is a glass of mulled wine ready to our hand at the moment; and I say, 'Uncle Scrooge!'"

"Well! Uncle Scrooge!" they cried.

"A Merry Christmas and a Happy New Year to the old man, whatever he is!" said Scrooge's nephew. "He wouldn't take it from me, but may he have it, nevertheless. Uncle Scrooge!"

Uncle Scrooge had imperceptibly become so gay and light of heart, that he would have pledged the unconscious company in return, and thanked them in an inaudible speech, if the Ghost had given him time. But the whole scene passed off in the breath of the last word spoken by his nephew; and he and the Spirit were again upon their travels.

Much they saw, and far they went, and many homes they visited, but always with a happy end. The Spirit stood beside sick beds, and they were cheerful; on foreign lands, and they were close at home; by struggling men, and they were patient in their greater hope; by poverty, and it was rich. In almshouse, hospital, and jail, in misery's every refuge, where vain man in his little brief authority had not made fast the door, and barred the Spirit out, he left his blessing, and taught Scrooge his precepts.

It was a long night, if it were only a night; but Scrooge had his doubts of this, because the Christmas Holidays appeared to be condensed into the space of time they passed together. It was strange, too, that while Scrooge remained unaltered in his outward form, the Ghost grew older, clearly older. Scrooge had observed this change, but never spoke of it, until they left a children's Twelfth Night party, when, looking at the Spirit as they stood together in an open place, he noticed that its hair was grey.

"Are spirits' lives so short?" asked Scrooge.

"My life upon this globe, is very brief," replied the Ghost. "It ends to-night."

"To-night!" cried Scrooge.

"To-night at midnight. Hark! The time is drawing near."

The chimes were ringing the three quarters past eleven at that moment.

"Forgive me if I am not justified in what I ask," said Scrooge, looking intently at the Spirit's robe, "but I see something strange, and not belonging to yourself, protruding from your skirts. Is it a foot or a claw?"

"It might be a claw, for the flesh there is upon it," was the Spirit's sorrowful reply. "Look here."

From the foldings of its robe, it brought two children; wretched, abject, frightful, hideous, miserable. They knelt down at its feet, and clung upon the outside of its garment.

"Oh, Man! look here. Look, look, down here!" exclaimed the Ghost.

They were a boy and girl. Yellow, meagre, ragged, scowling, wolfish; but prostrate, too, in their humility. Where graceful youth should have filled their features out, and touched them with its freshest tints, a stale and shrivelled hand, like that of age, had pinched, and twisted them, and pulled them into shreds. Where angels might have sat enthroned, devils lurked, and glared out menacing. No change, no degradation, no perversion of humanity, in any grade, through all the mysteries of wonderful creation, has monsters half so horrible and dread.

Scrooge started back, appalled. Having them shown to him in this way, he tried to say they were fine children, but the words choked themselves, rather than be parties to a lie of such enormous magnitude.

"Spirit! are they yours?" Scrooge could say no more.

"They are Man's," said the Spirit, looking down upon them. "And they cling to me, appealing from their fathers. This boy is Ignorance. This girl is Want. Beware them both, and all of their degree, but most of all beware this boy, for on his brow I see that written which is Doom, unless the writing be erased. Deny it!" cried the Spirit, stretching out its hand towards the city. "Slander those who tell it ye! Admit it for your factious purposes, and make it worse. And bide the end!"

"Have they no refuge or resource?" cried Scrooge.

"Are there no prisons?" said the Spirit, turning on him for the last time with his own words. "Are there no workhouses?"

The bell struck twelve.

Scrooge looked about him for the Ghost, and saw it not. As the last stroke ceased to vibrate, he remembered the prediction of old Jacob Marley, and lifting up his eyes, beheld a solemn Phantom, draped and hooded, coming, like a mist along the ground, towards him.

STAVE IV: THE LAST OF THE SPIRITS

THE Phantom slowly, gravely, silently, approached. When it came near him, Scrooge bent down upon his knee; for in the very air through which this Spirit moved it seemed to scatter gloom and mystery.

It was shrouded in a deep black garment, which concealed its head, its face, its form, and left nothing of it visible save one outstretched hand. But for this it would have been difficult to detach its figure from the night, and separate it from the darkness by which it was surrounded.

He felt that it was tall and stately when it came beside him, and that its mysterious presence filled him with a solemn dread. He knew no more, for the Spirit neither spoke nor moved.

"I am in the presence of the Ghost of Christmas Yet To Come?" said Scrooge.

The Spirit answered not, but pointed onward with its hand.

"You are about to show me shadows of the things that have not happened, but will happen in the time before us," Scrooge pursued. "Is that so, Spirit?"

The upper portion of the garment was contracted for an instant in its folds, as if the Spirit had inclined its head. That was the only answer he received.

Although well used to ghostly company by this time, Scrooge feared the silent shape so much that his legs trembled beneath him, and he found that he could hardly stand when he prepared to follow it. The Spirit paused a moment, as observing his condition, and giving him time to recover.

But Scrooge was all the worse for this. It thrilled him with a vague uncertain horror, to know that behind the dusky shroud, there were ghostly eyes intently fixed upon him, while he, though he stretched his own to the utmost, could see nothing but a spectral hand and one great heap of black.

"Ghost of the Future!" he exclaimed, "I fear you more than any spectre I have seen. But as I know your purpose is to do me good, and as I hope to live to be another man from what I was, I am prepared to bear you company, and do it with a thankful heart. Will you not speak to me?"

It gave him no reply. The hand was pointed straight before them.

"Lead on!" said Scrooge. "Lead on! The night is waning fast, and it is precious time to me, I know. Lead on, Spirit!"

The Phantom moved away as it had come towards him. Scrooge followed in the shadow of its dress, which bore him up, he thought, and carried him along.

They scarcely seemed to enter the city; for the city rather seemed to spring up about them, and encompass them of its own act. But there they were, in the heart of it; on 'Change, amongst the merchants; who hurried up and down, and chinked the money in their pockets, and conversed in groups, and looked at their watches, and trifled thoughtfully with their great gold seals; and so forth, as Scrooge had seen them often.

The Spirit stopped beside one little knot of business men. Observing that the hand was pointed to them, Scrooge advanced to listen to their talk.

"No," said a great fat man with a monstrous chin, "I don't know much about it, either way. I only know he's dead."

"When did he die?" inquired another.

"Last night, I believe."

"Why, what was the matter with him?" asked a third, taking a vast quantity of snuff out of a very large snuff-box. "I thought he'd never die."

"God knows," said the first, with a yawn.

"What has he done with his money?" asked a red-faced gentleman with a pendulous excrescence on the end of his nose, that shook like the gills of a turkey-cock.

"I haven't heard," said the man with the large chin, yawning again. "Left it to his company, perhaps. He hasn't left it to me. That's all I know."

This pleasantry was received with a general laugh.

"It's likely to be a very cheap funeral," said the same speaker; "for upon my life I don't know of anybody to go to it. Suppose we make up a party and volunteer?"

"I don't mind going if a lunch is provided," observed the gentleman with the excrescence on his nose. "But I must be fed, if I make one."

Another laugh.

"Well, I am the most disinterested among you, after all," said the first speaker, "for I never wear black gloves, and I never eat lunch. But I'll offer to go, if anybody else will. When I come to think of it, I'm not at all sure that I wasn't his most particular friend; for we used to stop and speak whenever we met. Bye, bye!"

Speakers and listeners strolled away, and mixed with other groups. Scrooge knew the men, and looked towards the Spirit for an explanation.

The Phantom glided on into a street. Its finger pointed to two persons meeting. Scrooge listened again, thinking that the explanation might lie here.

He knew these men, also, perfectly. They were men of business: very wealthy, and of great importance. He had made a point always of standing well in their esteem: in a business point of view, that is; strictly in a business point of view.

"How are you?" said one.

"How are you?" returned the other.

"Well!" said the first. "Old Scratch has got his own at last, hey?"

"So I am told," returned the second. "Cold, isn't it?"

"Seasonable for Christmas time. You're not a skater, I suppose?"

"No. No. Something else to think of. Good morning!"

Not another word. That was their meeting, their conversation, and their parting.

Scrooge was at first inclined to be surprised that the Spirit should attach importance to conversations apparently so trivial; but feeling assured that they must have some hidden purpose, he set himself to consider what it was likely to be. They could scarcely be supposed to have any bearing on the death of Jacob, his old partner, for that was Past, and this Ghost's province was the Future. Nor could he think of any one immediately connected with himself, to whom he could apply them. But nothing doubting that to whomsoever they applied they had some latent moral for his own improvement, he resolved to treasure up every word he heard, and everything he saw; and especially to observe the shadow of himself when it appeared. For he had an expectation that the conduct of his future self would give him the clue he missed, and would render the solution of these riddles easy.

He looked about in that very place for his own image; but another man stood in his accustomed corner, and though the clock pointed to his usual time of day for being there, he saw no likeness of himself among the multitudes that poured in through the porch. It gave him little surprise, however; for he had been revolving in his mind a change of life, and thought and hoped he saw his new-born resolutions carried out in this.

Quiet and dark, beside him stood the Phantom, with its outstretched hand. When he roused himself from his thoughtful quest, he fancied from the turn of the hand, and its situation in reference to himself, that the Unseen Eyes were looking at him keenly. It made him shudder, and feel very cold.

They left the busy scene, and went into an obscure part of the town, where Scrooge had never penetrated before, although he recognised its situation, and its bad repute. The ways were foul and narrow; the shops and houses wretched; the people half-naked, drunken, slipshod, ugly. Alleys and archways, like so many cesspools, disgorged their offences of smell, and dirt, and life, upon the straggling streets; and the whole quarter reeked with crime, with filth, and misery.

Far in this den of infamous resort, there was a low-browed, beetling shop, below a pent-house roof, where iron, old rags, bottles, bones, and greasy offal, were bought. Upon the floor within, were piled up heaps of rusty keys, nails, chains, hinges, files, scales, weights, and refuse iron of all kinds. Secrets that few would like to scrutinise were bred and hidden in mountains of unseemly rags, masses of corrupted fat, and sepulchres of bones. Sitting in among the wares he dealt in, by a charcoal stove, made of old bricks, was a grey-haired rascal, nearly seventy years of age; who had screened himself from the cold air without, by a frousy curtaining of miscellaneous tatters, hung upon a line; and smoked his pipe in all the luxury of calm retirement.

Scrooge and the Phantom came into the presence of this man, just as a woman with a heavy bundle slunk into the shop. But she had scarcely entered, when another woman, similarly laden, came in too; and she was closely followed by a man in faded black, who was no less startled by the sight of them, than they had been upon the recognition of each other. After a short period of blank astonishment, in which the old man with the pipe had joined them, they all three burst into a laugh.

"Let the charwoman alone to be the first!" cried she who had entered first. "Let the laundress alone to be the second; and let the undertaker's man alone to be the third. Look here, old Joe, here's a chance! If we haven't all three met here without meaning it!"

"You couldn't have met in a better place," said old Joe, removing his pipe from his mouth. "Come into the parlour. You were made free of it long ago, you know; and the other two an't strangers. Stop till I shut the door of the shop. Ah! How it skreeks! There an't such a rusty bit of metal in the place as its own hinges, I believe; and I'm sure there's no such old bones here, as mine. Ha, ha! We're all suitable to our calling, we're well matched. Come into the parlour. Come into the parlour."

The parlour was the space behind the screen of rags. The old man raked the fire together with an old stair-rod, and having trimmed his smoky lamp (for it was night), with the stem of his pipe, put it in his mouth again.

While he did this, the woman who had already spoken threw her bundle on the floor, and sat down in a flaunting manner on a stool; crossing her elbows on her knees, and looking with a bold defiance at the other two.

"What odds then! What odds, Mrs. Dilber?" said the woman. "Every person has a right to take care of themselves. He always did."

"That's true, indeed!" said the laundress. "No man more so."

"Why then, don't stand staring as if you was afraid, woman; who's the wiser? We're not going to pick holes in each other's coats, I suppose?"

"No, indeed!" said Mrs. Dilber and the man together. "We should hope not."

"Very well, then!" cried the woman. "That's enough. Who's the worse for the loss of a few things like these? Not a dead man, I suppose."

"No, indeed," said Mrs. Dilber, laughing.

"If he wanted to keep 'em after he was dead, a wicked old screw," pursued the woman, "why wasn't he natural in his lifetime? If he had been, he'd have had somebody to look after him when he was struck with Death, instead of lying gasping out his last there, alone by himself."

"It's the truest word that ever was spoke," said Mrs. Dilber. "It's a judgment on him."

"I wish it was a little heavier judgment," replied the woman; "and it should have been, you may depend upon it, if I could have laid my hands on anything else. Open that bundle, old Joe, and let me know the value of it. Speak out plain. I'm not afraid to be the first, nor afraid for them to see it. We know pretty well that we were helping ourselves, before we met here, I believe. It's no sin. Open the bundle, Joe."

But the gallantry of her friends would not allow of this; and the man in faded black, mounting the breach first, produced his plunder. It was not extensive. A seal or two, a pencil-case, a pair of sleeve-buttons, and a brooch of no great value, were all. They were severally examined and appraised by old Joe, who chalked the sums he was disposed to give for each, upon the wall, and added them up into a total when he found there was nothing more to come.

"That's your account," said Joe, "and I wouldn't give another sixpence, if I was to be boiled for not doing it. Who's next?"

Mrs. Dilber was next. Sheets and towels, a little wearing apparel, two old-fashioned silver teaspoons, a pair of sugar-tongs, and a few boots. Her account was stated on the wall in the same manner.

"I always give too much to ladies. It's a weakness of mine, and that's the way I ruin myself," said old Joe. "That's your account. If you asked me for another penny, and made it an open question, I'd repent of being so liberal and knock off half-a-crown."

"And now undo my bundle, Joe," said the first woman.

Joe went down on his knees for the greater convenience of opening it, and having unfastened a great many knots, dragged out a large and heavy roll of some dark stuff.

"What do you call this?" said Joe. "Bed-curtains!"

"Ah!" returned the woman, laughing and leaning forward on her crossed arms. "Bed-curtains!"

"You don't mean to say you took 'em down, rings and all, with him lying there?" said Joe.

"Yes I do," replied the woman. "Why not?"

"You were born to make your fortune," said Joe, "and you'll certainly do it."

"I certainly shan't hold my hand, when I can get anything in it by reaching it out, for the sake of such a man as He was, I promise you, Joe," returned the woman coolly. "Don't drop that oil upon the blankets, now."

"His blankets?" asked Joe.

"Whose else's do you think?" replied the woman. "He isn't likely to take cold without 'em, I dare say."

"I hope he didn't die of anything catching? Eh?" said old Joe, stopping in his work, and looking up.

"Don't you be afraid of that," returned the woman. "I an't so fond of his company that I'd loiter about him for such things, if he did. Ah! you may look through that shirt till your eyes ache; but you won't find a hole in it, nor a threadbare place. It's the best he had, and a fine one too. They'd have wasted it, if it hadn't been for me."

"What do you call wasting of it?" asked old Joe.

"Putting it on him to be buried in, to be sure," replied the woman with a laugh. "Somebody was fool enough to do it, but I took it off again. If calico an't good enough for such a purpose, it isn't good enough for anything. It's quite as becoming to the body. He can't look uglier than he did in that one."

Scrooge listened to this dialogue in horror. As they sat grouped about their spoil, in the scanty light afforded by the old man's lamp, he viewed them with a detestation and disgust, which could hardly have been greater, though they had been obscene demons, marketing the corpse itself.

"Ha, ha!" laughed the same woman, when old Joe, producing a flannel bag with money in it, told out their several gains upon the ground. "This is the end of it, you see! He frightened every one away from him when he was alive, to profit us when he was dead! Ha, ha, ha!"

"Spirit!" said Scrooge, shuddering from head to foot. "I see, I see. The case of this unhappy man might be my own. My life tends that way, now. Merciful Heaven, what is this!"

He recoiled in terror, for the scene had changed, and now he almost touched a bed: a bare, uncurtained bed: on which, beneath a ragged sheet, there lay a something covered up, which, though it was dumb, announced itself in awful language.

The room was very dark, too dark to be observed with any accuracy, though Scrooge glanced round it in obedience to a secret impulse, anxious to know what kind of room it was. A pale light, rising in the outer air, fell straight upon the bed; and on it, plundered and bereft, unwatched, unwept, uncared for, was the body of this man.

Scrooge glanced towards the Phantom. Its steady hand was pointed to the head. The cover was so carelessly adjusted that the slightest raising of it, the motion of a finger upon Scrooge's part, would have disclosed the face. He thought of it, felt how easy it would be to do, and longed to do it; but had no more power to withdraw the veil than to dismiss the spectre at his side.

Oh cold, cold, rigid, dreadful Death, set up thine altar here, and dress it with such terrors as thou hast at thy command: for this is thy dominion! But of the loved, revered, and honoured head, thou canst not turn one hair to thy dread purposes, or make one feature odious. It is not that the hand is heavy and will fall down when released; it is not that the heart and pulse are still; but that the hand WAS open, generous, and true; the heart brave, warm, and tender; and the pulse a man's. Strike, Shadow, strike! And see his good deeds springing from the wound, to sow the world with life immortal!

No voice pronounced these words in Scrooge's ears, and yet he heard them when he looked upon the bed. He thought, if this man could be raised up now, what would be his foremost thoughts? Avarice, hard-dealing, griping cares? They have brought him to a rich end, truly!

He lay, in the dark empty house, with not a man, a woman, or a child, to say that he was kind to me in this or that, and for the memory of one kind word I will be kind to him. A cat was tearing at the door, and there was a sound of gnawing rats beneath the hearth-stone. What they wanted in the room of death, and why they were so restless and disturbed, Scrooge did not dare to think.

"Spirit!" he said, "this is a fearful place. In leaving it, I shall not leave its lesson, trust me. Let us go!"

Still the Ghost pointed with an unmoved finger to the head.

"I understand you," Scrooge returned, "and I would do it, if I could. But I have not the power, Spirit. I have not the power."

Again it seemed to look upon him.

"If there is any person in the town, who feels emotion caused by this man's death," said Scrooge quite agonised, "show that person to me, Spirit, I beseech you!"

The Phantom spread its dark robe before him for a moment, like a wing; and withdrawing it, revealed a room by daylight, where a mother and her children were.

She was expecting some one, and with anxious eagerness; for she walked up and down the room; started at every sound; looked out from the window; glanced at the clock; tried, but in vain, to work with her needle; and could hardly bear the voices of the children in their play.

At length the long-expected knock was heard. She hurried to the door, and met her husband; a man whose face was careworn and depressed, though he was young. There was a remarkable expression in it now; a kind of serious delight of which he felt ashamed, and which he struggled to repress.

He sat down to the dinner that had been hoarding for him by the fire; and when she asked him faintly what news (which was not until after a long silence), he appeared embarrassed how to answer.

"Is it good?" she said, "or bad?"—to help him.

"Bad," he answered.

"We are quite ruined?"

"No. There is hope yet, Caroline."

"If he relents," she said, amazed, "there is! Nothing is past hope, if such a miracle has happened."

"He is past relenting," said her husband. "He is dead."

She was a mild and patient creature if her face spoke truth; but she was thankful in her soul to hear it, and she said so, with clasped hands. She prayed forgiveness the next moment, and was sorry; but the first was the emotion of her heart.

"What the half-drunken woman whom I told you of last night, said to me, when I tried to see him and obtain a week's delay; and what I thought was a mere excuse to avoid me; turns out to have been quite true. He was not only very ill, but dying, then."

"To whom will our debt be transferred?"

"I don't know. But before that time we shall be ready with the money; and even though we were not, it would be a bad fortune indeed to find so merciless a creditor in his successor. We may sleep to-night with light hearts, Caroline!"

Yes. Soften it as they would, their hearts were lighter. The children's faces, hushed and clustered round to hear what they so little understood, were brighter; and it was a happier house for this man's death! The only emotion that the Ghost could show him, caused by the event, was one of pleasure.

"Let me see some tenderness connected with a death," said Scrooge; "or that dark chamber, Spirit, which we left just now, will be for ever present to me."

The Ghost conducted him through several streets familiar to his feet; and as they went along, Scrooge looked here and there to find himself, but nowhere was he to be seen. They entered poor Bob Cratchit's house; the dwelling he had visited before; and found the mother and the children seated round the fire.

Quiet. Very quiet. The noisy little Cratchits were as still as statues in one corner, and sat looking up at Peter, who had a book before him. The mother and her daughters were engaged in sewing. But surely they were very quiet!

"And He took a child, and set him in the midst of them."

Where had Scrooge heard those words? He had not dreamed them. The boy must have read them out, as he and the Spirit crossed the threshold. Why did he not go on?

The mother laid her work upon the table, and put her hand up to her face.

"The colour hurts my eyes," she said.

The colour? Ah, poor Tiny Tim!

"They're better now again," said Cratchit's wife. "It makes them weak by candle-light; and I wouldn't show weak eyes to your father when he comes home, for the world. It must be near his time."

"Past it rather," Peter answered, shutting up his book. "But I think he has walked a little slower than he used, these few last evenings, mother."

They were very quiet again. At last she said, and in a steady, cheerful voice, that only faltered once:

"I have known him walk with—I have known him walk with Tiny Tim upon his shoulder, very fast indeed."

"And so have I," cried Peter. "Often."

"And so have I," exclaimed another. So had all.

"But he was very light to carry," she resumed, intent upon her work, "and his father loved him so, that it was no trouble: no trouble. And there is your father at the door!"

She hurried out to meet him; and little Bob in his comforter—he had need of it, poor fellow—came in. His tea was ready for him on the hob, and they all tried who should help him to it most. Then the two young Cratchits got upon his knees and laid, each child a little cheek, against his face, as if they said, "Don't mind it, father. Don't be grieved!"

Bob was very cheerful with them, and spoke pleasantly to all the family. He looked at the work upon the table, and praised the industry and speed of Mrs. Cratchit and the girls. They would be done long before Sunday, he said.

"Sunday! You went to-day, then, Robert?" said his wife.

"Yes, my dear," returned Bob. "I wish you could have gone. It would have done you good to see how green a place it is. But you'll see it often. I promised him that I would walk there on a Sunday. My little, little child!" cried Bob. "My little child!"

He broke down all at once. He couldn't help it. If he could have helped it, he and his child would have been farther apart perhaps than they were.

He left the room, and went up-stairs into the room above, which was lighted cheerfully, and hung with Christmas. There was a chair set close beside the child, and there were signs of some one having been there, lately. Poor Bob sat down in it, and when he had thought a little and composed himself, he kissed the little face. He was reconciled to what had happened, and went down again quite happy.

They drew about the fire, and talked; the girls and mother working still. Bob told them of the extraordinary kindness of Mr. Scrooge's nephew, whom he had scarcely seen but once, and who, meeting him in the street that day, and seeing that he looked a little—"just a little down you know," said Bob, inquired what had happened to distress him. "On which," said Bob, "for he is the pleasantest-spoken gentleman you ever heard, I told him. 'I am heartily sorry for it, Mr. Cratchit,' he said, 'and heartily sorry for your good wife.' By the bye, how he ever knew that, I don't know."

"Knew what, my dear?"

"Why, that you were a good wife," replied Bob.

"Everybody knows that!" said Peter.

"Very well observed, my boy!" cried Bob. "I hope they do. 'Heartily sorry,' he said, 'for your good wife. If I can be of service to you in any way,' he said, giving me his card, 'that's where I live. Pray come to me.' Now, it wasn't," cried Bob, "for the sake of anything he might be able to do for us, so much as for his kind way, that this was quite delightful. It really seemed as if he had known our Tiny Tim, and felt with us."

"I'm sure he's a good soul!" said Mrs. Cratchit.

"You would be surer of it, my dear," returned Bob, "if you saw and spoke to him. I shouldn't be at all surprised—mark what I say!—if he got Peter a better situation."

"Only hear that, Peter," said Mrs. Cratchit.

"And then," cried one of the girls, "Peter will be keeping company with some one, and setting up for himself."

"Get along with you!" retorted Peter, grinning.

"It's just as likely as not," said Bob, "one of these days; though there's plenty of time for that, my dear. But however and whenever we part from one another, I am sure we shall none of us forget poor Tiny Tim—shall we—or this first parting that there was among us?"

"Never, father!" cried they all.

"And I know," said Bob, "I know, my dears, that when we recollect how patient and how mild he was; although he was a little, little child; we shall not quarrel easily among ourselves, and forget poor Tiny Tim in doing it."

"No, never, father!" they all cried again.

"I am very happy," said little Bob, "I am very happy!"

Mrs. Cratchit kissed him, his daughters kissed him, the two young Cratchits kissed him, and Peter and himself shook hands. Spirit of Tiny Tim, thy childish essence was from God!

"Spectre," said Scrooge, "something informs me that our parting moment is at hand. I know it, but I know not how. Tell me what man that was whom we saw lying dead?"

The Ghost of Christmas Yet To Come conveyed him, as before—though at a different time, he thought: indeed, there seemed no order in these latter visions, save that they were in the Future—into the resorts of business men, but showed him not himself. Indeed, the Spirit did not stay for anything, but went straight on, as to the end just now desired, until besought by Scrooge to tarry for a moment.

"This court," said Scrooge, "through which we hurry now, is where my place of occupation is, and has been for a length of time. I see the house. Let me behold what I shall be, in days to come!"

The Spirit stopped; the hand was pointed elsewhere.

"The house is yonder," Scrooge exclaimed. "Why do you point away?"

The inexorable finger underwent no change.

Scrooge hastened to the window of his office, and looked in. It was an office still, but not his. The furniture was not the same, and the figure in the chair was not himself. The Phantom pointed as before.

He joined it once again, and wondering why and whither he had gone, accompanied it until they reached an iron gate. He paused to look round before entering.

A churchyard. Here, then; the wretched man whose name he had now to learn, lay underneath the ground. It was a worthy place. Walled in by houses; overrun by grass and weeds, the growth of vegetation's death, not life; choked up with too much burying; fat with repleted appetite. A worthy place!

The Spirit stood among the graves, and pointed down to One. He advanced towards it trembling. The Phantom was exactly as it had been, but he dreaded that he saw new meaning in its solemn shape.

"Before I draw nearer to that stone to which you point," said Scrooge, "answer me one question. Are these the shadows of the things that Will be, or are they shadows of things that May be, only?"

Still the Ghost pointed downward to the grave by which it stood.

"Men's courses will foreshadow certain ends, to which, if persevered in, they must lead," said Scrooge. "But if the courses be departed from, the ends will change. Say it is thus with what you show me!"

The Spirit was immovable as ever.

Scrooge crept towards it, trembling as he went; and following the finger, read upon the stone of the neglected grave his own name, EBENEZER SCROOGE.

"Am I that man who lay upon the bed?" he cried, upon his knees.

The finger pointed from the grave to him, and back again.

"No, Spirit! Oh no, no!"

The finger still was there.

"Spirit!" he cried, tight clutching at its robe, "hear me! I am not the man I was. I will not be the man I must have been but for this intercourse. Why show me this, if I am past all hope!"

For the first time the hand appeared to shake.

"Good Spirit," he pursued, as down upon the ground he fell before it: "Your nature intercedes for me, and pities me. Assure me that I yet may change these shadows you have shown me, by an altered life!"

The kind hand trembled.

"I will honour Christmas in my heart, and try to keep it all the year. I will live in the Past, the Present, and the Future. The Spirits of all Three shall strive within me. I will not shut out the lessons that they teach. Oh, tell me I may sponge away the writing on this stone!"

In his agony, he caught the spectral hand. It sought to free itself, but he was strong in his entreaty, and detained it. The Spirit, stronger yet, repulsed him.

Holding up his hands in a last prayer to have his fate reversed, he saw an alteration in the Phantom's hood and dress. It shrunk, collapsed, and dwindled down into a bedpost.

STAVE V: THE END OF IT

YES! and the bedpost was his own. The bed was his own, the room was his own. Best and happiest of all, the Time before him was his own, to make amends in!

"I will live in the Past, the Present, and the Future!" Scrooge repeated, as he scrambled out of bed. "The Spirits of all Three shall strive within me. Oh Jacob Marley! Heaven, and the Christmas Time be praised for this! I say it on my knees, old Jacob; on my knees!"

He was so fluttered and so glowing with his good intentions, that his broken voice would scarcely answer to his call. He had been sobbing violently in his conflict with the Spirit, and his face was wet with tears.

"They are not torn down," cried Scrooge, folding one of his bed-curtains in his arms, "they are not torn down, rings and all. They are here—I am here—the shadows of the things that would have been, may be dispelled. They will be. I know they will!"

His hands were busy with his garments all this time; turning them inside out, putting them on upside down, tearing them, mislaying them, making them parties to every kind of extravagance.

"I don't know what to do!" cried Scrooge, laughing and crying in the same breath; and making a perfect Laocooen of himself with his stockings. "I am as light as a feather, I am as happy as an angel, I am as merry as a schoolboy. I am as giddy as a drunken man. A merry Christmas to everybody! A happy New Year to all the world. Hallo here! Whoop! Hallo!"

He had frisked into the sitting-room, and was now standing there: perfectly winded.

"There's the saucepan that the gruel was in!" cried Scrooge, starting off again, and going round the fireplace. "There's the door, by which the Ghost of Jacob Marley entered! There's the corner where the Ghost of Christmas Present, sat! There's the window where I saw the wandering Spirits! It's all right, it's all true, it all happened. Ha ha ha!"

Really, for a man who had been out of practice for so many years, it was a splendid laugh, a most illustrious laugh. The father of a long, long line of brilliant laughs!

"I don't know what day of the month it is!" said Scrooge. "I don't know how long I've been among the Spirits. I don't know anything. I'm quite a baby. Never mind. I don't care. I'd rather be a baby. Hallo! Whoop! Hallo here!"

He was checked in his transports by the churches ringing out the lustiest peals he had ever heard. Clash, clang, hammer; ding, dong, bell. Bell, dong, ding; hammer, clang, clash! Oh, glorious, glorious!

Running to the window, he opened it, and put out his head. No fog, no mist; clear, bright, jovial, stirring, cold; cold, piping for the blood to dance to; Golden sunlight; Heavenly sky; sweet fresh air; merry bells. Oh, glorious! Glorious!

"What's to-day!" cried Scrooge, calling downward to a boy in Sunday clothes, who perhaps had loitered in to look about him.

"EH?" returned the boy, with all his might of wonder.

"What's to-day, my fine fellow?" said Scrooge.

"To-day!" replied the boy. "Why, CHRISTMAS DAY."

"It's Christmas Day!" said Scrooge to himself. "I haven't missed it. The Spirits have done it all in one night. They can do anything they like. Of course they can. Of course they can. Hallo, my fine fellow!"

"Hallo!" returned the boy.

"Do you know the Poulterer's, in the next street but one, at the corner?" Scrooge inquired.

"I should hope I did," replied the lad.

"An intelligent boy!" said Scrooge. "A remarkable boy! Do you know whether they've sold the prize Turkey that was hanging up there?—Not the little prize Turkey: the big one?"

"What, the one as big as me?" returned the boy.

"What a delightful boy!" said Scrooge. "It's a pleasure to talk to him. Yes, my buck!"

"It's hanging there now," replied the boy.

"Is it?" said Scrooge. "Go and buy it."

"Walk-ER!" exclaimed the boy.

"No, no," said Scrooge, "I am in earnest. Go and buy it, and tell 'em to bring it here, that I may give them the direction where to take it. Come back with the man, and I'll give you a shilling. Come back with him in less than five minutes and I'll give you half-a-crown!"

The boy was off like a shot. He must have had a steady hand at a trigger who could have got a shot off half so fast.

"I'll send it to Bob Cratchit's!" whispered Scrooge, rubbing his hands, and splitting with a laugh. "He sha'n't know who sends it. It's twice the size of Tiny Tim. Joe Miller never made such a joke as sending it to Bob's will be!"

The hand in which he wrote the address was not a steady one, but write it he did, somehow, and went down-stairs to open the street door, ready for the coming of the poulterer's man. As he stood there, waiting his arrival, the knocker caught his eye.

"I shall love it, as long as I live!" cried Scrooge, patting it with his hand. "I scarcely ever looked at it before. What an honest expression it has in its face! It's a wonderful knocker!—Here's the Turkey! Hallo! Whoop! How are you! Merry Christmas!"

It was a Turkey! He never could have stood upon his legs, that bird. He would have snapped 'em short off in a minute, like sticks of sealing-wax.

"Why, it's impossible to carry that to Camden Town," said Scrooge. "You must have a cab."

The chuckle with which he said this, and the chuckle with which he paid for the Turkey, and the chuckle with which he paid for the cab, and the chuckle with which he recompensed the boy, were only to be exceeded by the chuckle with which he sat down breathless in his chair again, and chuckled till he cried.

Shaving was not an easy task, for his hand continued to shake very much; and shaving requires attention, even when you don't dance while you are at it. But if he had cut the end of his nose off, he would have put a piece of sticking-plaister over it, and been quite satisfied.

He dressed himself "all in his best," and at last got out into the streets. The people were by this time pouring forth, as he had seen them with the Ghost of Christmas Present; and walking with his hands behind him, Scrooge regarded every one with a delighted smile. He looked so irresistibly pleasant, in a word, that three or four good-humoured fellows said, "Good morning, sir! A merry Christmas to you!" And Scrooge said often afterwards, that of all the blithe sounds he had ever heard, those were the blithest in his ears.

He had not gone far, when coming on towards him he beheld the portly gentleman, who had walked into his counting-house the day before, and said, "Scrooge and Marley's, I believe?" It sent a pang across his heart to think how this old gentleman would look upon him when they met; but he knew what path lay straight before him, and he took it.

"My dear sir," said Scrooge, quickening his pace, and taking the old gentleman by both his hands. "How do you do? I hope you succeeded yesterday. It was very kind of you. A merry Christmas to you, sir!"

"Mr. Scrooge?"

"Yes," said Scrooge. "That is my name, and I fear it may not be pleasant to you. Allow me to ask your pardon. And will you have the goodness"—here Scrooge whispered in his ear.

"Lord bless me!" cried the gentleman, as if his breath were taken away. "My dear Mr. Scrooge, are you serious?"

"If you please," said Scrooge. "Not a farthing less. A great many back-payments are included in it, I assure you. Will you do me that favour?"

"My dear sir," said the other, shaking hands with him. "I don't know what to say to such munifi—"

"Don't say anything, please," retorted Scrooge. "Come and see me. Will you come and see me?"

"I will!" cried the old gentleman. And it was clear he meant to do it.

"Thank'ee," said Scrooge. "I am much obliged to you. I thank you fifty times. Bless you!"

He went to church, and walked about the streets, and watched the people hurrying to and fro, and patted children on the head, and questioned beggars, and looked down into the kitchens of houses, and up to the windows, and found that everything could yield him pleasure. He had never dreamed that any walk—that anything—could give him so much happiness. In the afternoon he turned his steps towards his nephew's house.

He passed the door a dozen times, before he had the courage to go up and knock. But he made a dash, and did it:

"Is your master at home, my dear?" said Scrooge to the girl. Nice girl! Very.

"Yes, sir."

"Where is he, my love?" said Scrooge.

"He's in the dining-room, sir, along with mistress. I'll show you up-stairs, if you please."

"Thank'ee. He knows me," said Scrooge, with his hand already on the dining-room lock. "I'll go in here, my dear."

He turned it gently, and sidled his face in, round the door. They were looking at the table (which was spread out in great array); for these young housekeepers are always nervous on such points, and like to see that everything is right.

"Fred!" said Scrooge.

Dear heart alive, how his niece by marriage started! Scrooge had forgotten, for the moment, about her sitting in the corner with the footstool, or he wouldn't have done it, on any account.

"Why bless my soul!" cried Fred, "who's that?"

"It's I. Your uncle Scrooge. I have come to dinner. Will you let me in, Fred?"

Let him in! It is a mercy he didn't shake his arm off. He was at home in five minutes. Nothing could be heartier. His niece looked just the same. So did Topper when he came. So did the plump sister when she came. So did every one when they came. Wonderful party, wonderful games, wonderful unanimity, won-der-ful happiness!

But he was early at the office next morning. Oh, he was early there. If he could only be there first, and catch Bob Cratchit coming late! That was the thing he had set his heart upon.

And he did it; yes, he did! The clock struck nine. No Bob. A quarter past. No Bob. He was full eighteen minutes and a half behind his time. Scrooge sat with his door wide open, that he might see him come into the Tank.

His hat was off, before he opened the door; his comforter too. He was on his stool in a jiffy; driving away with his pen, as if he were trying to overtake nine o'clock.

"Hallo!" growled Scrooge, in his accustomed voice, as near as he could feign it. "What do you mean by coming here at this time of day?"

"I am very sorry, sir," said Bob. "I am behind my time."

"You are?" repeated Scrooge. "Yes. I think you are. Step this way, sir, if you please."

"It's only once a year, sir," pleaded Bob, appearing from the Tank. "It shall not be repeated. I was making rather merry yesterday, sir."

"Now, I'll tell you what, my friend," said Scrooge, "I am not going to stand this sort of thing any longer. And therefore," he continued, leaping from his stool, and giving Bob such a dig in the waistcoat that he staggered back into the Tank again; "and therefore I am about to raise your salary!"

Bob trembled, and got a little nearer to the ruler. He had a momentary idea of knocking Scrooge down with it, holding him, and calling to the people in the court for help and a strait-waistcoat.

"A merry Christmas, Bob!" said Scrooge, with an earnestness that could not be mistaken, as he clapped him on the back. "A merrier Christmas, Bob, my good fellow, than I have given you, for many a year! I'll raise your salary, and endeavour to assist your struggling family, and we will discuss your affairs this very afternoon, over a Christmas bowl of smoking bishop, Bob! Make up the fires, and buy another coal-scuttle before you dot another i, Bob Cratchit!"

Scrooge was better than his word. He did it all, and infinitely more; and to Tiny Tim, who did NOT die, he was a second father. He became as good a friend, as good a master, and as good a man, as the good old city knew, or any other good old city, town, or borough, in the good old world. Some people laughed to see the alteration in him, but he let them laugh, and little heeded them; for he was wise enough to know that nothing ever happened on this globe, for good, at which some people did not have their fill of laughter in the outset; and knowing that such as these would be blind anyway, he thought it quite as well that they should wrinkle up their eyes in grins, as have the malady in less attractive forms. His own heart laughed: and that was quite enough for him.

He had no further intercourse with Spirits, but lived upon the Total Abstinence Principle, ever afterwards; and it was always said of him, that he knew how to keep Christmas well, if any man alive possessed the knowledge. May that be truly said of us, and all of us! And so, as Tiny Tim observed, God bless Us, Every One!

A Tale of Two Cities

A Story of The French Revolution

I. THE PERIOD

It was the best of times, it was the worst of times, it was the age of wisdom, it was the age of foolishness, it was the epoch of belief, it was the epoch of incredulity, it was the season of Light, it was the season of Darkness, it was the spring of hope, it was the winter of despair, we had everything before us, we had nothing before us, we were all going direct to Heaven, we were all going direct the other way—in short, the period was so far like the present period, that some of its noisiest authorities insisted on its being received, for good or for evil, in the superlative degree of comparison only.

There were a king with a large jaw and a queen with a plain face, on the throne of England; there were a king with a large jaw and a queen with a fair face, on the throne of France. In both countries it was clearer than crystal to the lords of the State preserves of loaves and fishes, that things in general were settled for ever.

It was the year of Our Lord one thousand seven hundred and seventy-five. Spiritual revelations were conceded to England at that favoured period, as at this. Mrs. Southcott had recently attained her five-and-twentieth blessed birthday, of whom a prophetic private in the Life Guards had heralded the sublime appearance by announcing that arrangements were made for the swallowing up of London and Westminster. Even the Cock-lane ghost had been laid only a round dozen of years, after rapping out its messages, as the spirits of this very year last past (supernaturally deficient in originality) rapped out theirs. Mere messages in the earthly order of events had lately come to the English Crown and People, from a congress of British subjects in America: which, strange to relate, have proved more important to the human race than any communications yet received through any of the chickens of the Cock-lane brood.

France, less favoured on the whole as to matters spiritual than her sister of the shield and trident, rolled with exceeding smoothness down hill, making paper money and spending it. Under the guidance of her Christian pastors, she entertained herself, besides, with such humane achievements as sentencing a youth to have his hands cut off, his tongue torn out with pincers, and his body burned alive, because he had not kneeled down in the rain to do honour to a dirty procession of monks which passed within his view, at a distance of some fifty or sixty yards. It is likely enough that, rooted in the woods of France and Norway, there were growing trees, when that sufferer was put to death, already marked by the Woodman, Fate, to come down and be sawn into boards, to make a certain movable framework with a sack and a knife in it, terrible in history. It is likely enough that in the rough outhouses of some tillers of the heavy lands adjacent to Paris, there were sheltered from the weather that very day, rude carts, bespattered with rustic mire, snuffed about by pigs, and roosted in by poultry, which the Farmer, Death, had already set apart to be his tumbrils of the Revolution. But that Woodman and that Farmer, though they work unceasingly, work silently, and no one heard them as they went about with muffled tread: the rather, forasmuch as to entertain any suspicion that they were awake, was to be atheistical and traitorous.

In England, there was scarcely an amount of order and protection to justify much national boasting. Daring burglaries by armed men, and highway robberies, took place in the capital itself every night; families were publicly cautioned not to go out of town without removing their furniture to upholsterers' warehouses for security; the highwayman in the dark was a City tradesman in the light, and, being recognised and challenged by his fellow- tradesman whom he stopped in his character of "the Captain," gallantly shot him through the head and rode away; the mail was waylaid by seven robbers, and the guard shot three dead, and then got shot dead himself by the other four, "in consequence of the failure of his ammunition:" after which the mail was robbed in peace; that magnificent potentate, the Lord Mayor of London, was made to stand and deliver on Turnham Green, by one highwayman, who despoiled the illustrious creature in sight of all his retinue; prisoners in London gaols fought battles with their turnkeys, and the majesty of the law fired blunderbusses in among them, loaded with rounds of shot and ball; thieves snipped off diamond crosses from the necks of noble lords at Court drawing-rooms; musketeers went into St. Giles's, to search for contraband goods, and the mob fired on the musketeers, and the musketeers fired on the mob, and nobody thought any of these occurrences much out of the common way. In the midst of them, the hangman, ever busy and ever worse than useless, was in constant requisition; now, stringing up long rows of miscellaneous criminals; now, hanging a housebreaker on Saturday who had been taken on Tuesday; now, burning people in the hand at Newgate by the dozen, and now burning pamphlets at the door of Westminster Hall; to-day, taking the life of an atrocious murderer, and to-morrow of a wretched pilferer who had robbed a farmer's boy of sixpence.

All these things, and a thousand like them, came to pass in and close upon the dear old year one thousand seven hundred and seventy-five. Environed by them, while the Woodman and the Farmer worked unheeded, those two of the large jaws, and those other two of the plain and the fair faces, trod with stir enough, and carried their divine rights with a high hand. Thus did the year one thousand seven hundred and seventy-five conduct their Greatnesses, and myriads of small creatures—the creatures of this chronicle among the rest—along the roads that lay before them.

II. THE MAIL

It was the Dover road that lay, on a Friday night late in November, before the first of the persons with whom this history has business. The Dover road lay, as to him, beyond the Dover mail, as it lumbered up Shooter's Hill. He walked up hill in the mire by the side of the mail, as the rest of the passengers did; not because they had the least relish for walking exercise, under the circumstances, but because the hill, and the harness, and the mud, and the mail, were all so heavy, that the horses had three times already come to a stop, besides once drawing the coach across the road, with the mutinous intent of taking it back to Blackheath. Reins and whip and coachman and guard, however, in combination, had read that article of war which forbade a purpose otherwise strongly in favour of the argument, that some brute animals are endued with Reason; and the team had capitulated and returned to their duty.

With drooping heads and tremulous tails, they mashed their way through the thick mud, floundering and stumbling between whiles, as if they were falling to pieces at the larger joints. As often as the driver rested them and brought them to a stand, with a wary "Wo-ho! so-ho-then!" the near leader violently shook his head and everything upon it—like an unusually emphatic horse, denying that the coach could be got up the hill. Whenever the leader made this rattle, the passenger started, as a nervous passenger might, and was disturbed in mind.

There was a steaming mist in all the hollows, and it had roamed in its forlornness up the hill, like an evil spirit, seeking rest and finding none. A clammy and intensely cold mist, it made its slow way through the air in ripples that visibly followed and overspread one another, as the waves of an unwholesome sea might do. It was dense enough to shut out everything from the light of the coach-lamps but these its own workings, and a few yards of road; and the reek of the labouring horses steamed into it, as if they had made it all.

Two other passengers, besides the one, were plodding up the hill by the side of the mail. All three were wrapped to the cheekbones and over the ears, and wore jack-boots. Not one of the three could have said, from anything he saw, what either of the other two was like; and each was hidden under almost as many wrappers from the eyes of the mind, as from the eyes of the body, of his two companions. In those days, travellers were very shy of being confidential on a short notice, for anybody on the road might be a robber or in league with robbers. As to the latter, when every posting-house and ale-house could produce somebody in "the Captain's" pay, ranging from the landlord to the lowest stable non-descript, it was the likeliest thing upon the cards. So the guard of the Dover mail thought to himself, that Friday night in November, one thousand seven hundred and seventy-five, lumbering up Shooter's Hill, as he stood on his own particular perch behind the mail, beating his feet, and keeping an eye and a hand on the arm-chest before him, where a loaded blunderbuss lay at the top of six or eight loaded horse-pistols, deposited on a substratum of cutlass.

The Dover mail was in its usual genial position that the guard suspected the passengers, the passengers suspected one another and the guard, they all suspected everybody else, and the coachman was sure of nothing but the horses; as to which cattle he could with a clear conscience have taken his oath on the two Testaments that they were not fit for the journey.

"Wo-ho!" said the coachman. "So, then! One more pull and you're at the top and be damned to you, for I have had trouble enough to get you to it!—Joe!"

"Halloa!" the guard replied.

"What o'clock do you make it, Joe?"

"Ten minutes, good, past eleven."

"My blood!" ejaculated the vexed coachman, "and not atop of Shooter's yet! Tst! Yah! Get on with you!"

The emphatic horse, cut short by the whip in a most decided negative, made a decided scramble for it, and the three other horses followed suit. Once more, the Dover mail struggled on, with the jack-boots of its passengers squashing along by its side. They had stopped when the coach stopped, and they kept close company with it. If any one of the three had had the hardihood to propose to another to walk on a little ahead into the mist and darkness, he would have put himself in a fair way of getting shot instantly as a highwayman.

The last burst carried the mail to the summit of the hill. The horses stopped to breathe again, and the guard got down to skid the wheel for the descent, and open the coach-door to let the passengers in.

"Tst! Joe!" cried the coachman in a warning voice, looking down from his box.

"What do you say, Tom?"

They both listened.

"I say a horse at a canter coming up, Joe."

"*I* say a horse at a gallop, Tom," returned the guard, leaving his hold of the door, and mounting nimbly to his place. "Gentlemen! In the king's name, all of you!"

With this hurried adjuration, he cocked his blunderbuss, and stood on the offensive.

The passenger booked by this history, was on the coach-step, getting in; the two other passengers were close behind him, and about to follow. He remained on the step, half in the coach and half out of; they remained in the road below him. They all looked from the coachman to the guard, and from the guard to the coachman, and listened. The coachman looked back and the guard looked back, and even the emphatic leader pricked up his ears and looked back, without contradicting.

The stillness consequent on the cessation of the rumbling and labouring of the coach, added to the stillness of the night, made it very quiet indeed. The panting of the horses communicated a tremulous motion to the coach, as if it were in a state of agitation. The hearts of the passengers beat loud enough perhaps to be heard; but at any rate, the quiet pause was audibly expressive of people out of breath, and holding the breath, and having the pulses quickened by expectation.

The sound of a horse at a gallop came fast and furiously up the hill.

"So-ho!" the guard sang out, as loud as he could roar. "Yo there! Stand! I shall fire!"

The pace was suddenly checked, and, with much splashing and floundering, a man's voice called from the mist, "Is that the Dover mail?"

"Never you mind what it is!" the guard retorted. "What are you?"

"*Is* that the Dover mail?"

"Why do you want to know?"

"I want a passenger, if it is."

"What passenger?"

"Mr. Jarvis Lorry."

Our booked passenger showed in a moment that it was his name. The guard, the coachman, and the two other passengers eyed him distrustfully.

"Keep where you are," the guard called to the voice in the mist, "because, if I should make a mistake, it could never be set right in your lifetime. Gentleman of the name of Lorry answer straight."

"What is the matter?" asked the passenger, then, with mildly quavering speech. "Who wants me? Is it Jerry?"

("I don't like Jerry's voice, if it is Jerry," growled the guard to himself. "He's hoarser than suits me, is Jerry.")

"Yes, Mr. Lorry."

"What is the matter?"

"A despatch sent after you from over yonder. T. and Co."

"I know this messenger, guard," said Mr. Lorry, getting down into the road—assisted from behind more swiftly than politely by the other two passengers, who immediately scrambled into the coach, shut the door, and pulled up the window. "He may come close; there's nothing wrong."

"I hope there ain't, but I can't make so 'Nation sure of that," said the guard, in gruff soliloquy. "Hallo you!"

"Well! And hallo you!" said Jerry, more hoarsely than before.

"Come on at a footpace! d'ye mind me? And if you've got holsters to that saddle o' yourn, don't let me see your hand go nigh 'em. For I'm a devil at a quick mistake, and when I make one it takes the form of Lead. So now let's look at you."

The figures of a horse and rider came slowly through the eddying mist, and came to the side of the mail, where the passenger stood. The rider stooped, and, casting up his eyes at the guard, handed the passenger a small folded paper. The rider's horse was blown, and both horse and rider were covered with mud, from the hoofs of the horse to the hat of the man.

"Guard!" said the passenger, in a tone of quiet business confidence.

The watchful guard, with his right hand at the stock of his raised blunderbuss, his left at the barrel, and his eye on the horseman, answered curtly, "Sir."

"There is nothing to apprehend. I belong to Tellson's Bank. You must know Tellson's Bank in London. I am going to Paris on business. A crown to drink. I may read this?"

"If so be as you're quick, sir."

He opened it in the light of the coach-lamp on that side, and read—first to himself and then aloud: "'Wait at Dover for Mam'selle.' It's not long, you see, guard. Jerry, say that my answer was, RECALLED TO LIFE."

Jerry started in his saddle. "That's a Blazing strange answer, too," said he, at his hoarsest.

"Take that message back, and they will know that I received this, as well as if I wrote. Make the best of your way. Good night."

With those words the passenger opened the coach-door and got in; not at all assisted by his fellow-passengers, who had expeditiously secreted their watches and purses in their boots, and were now making a general pretence of being asleep. With no more definite purpose than to escape the hazard of originating any other kind of action.

The coach lumbered on again, with heavier wreaths of mist closing round it as it began the descent. The guard soon replaced his blunderbuss in his arm-chest, and, having looked to the rest of its contents, and having looked to the supplementary pistols that he wore in his belt, looked to a smaller chest beneath his seat, in which there were a few smith's tools, a couple of torches, and a tinder-box. For he was furnished with that completeness that if the coach-lamps had been blown and stormed out, which did occasionally happen, he had only to shut himself up inside, keep the flint and steel sparks well off the straw, and get a light with tolerable safety and ease (if he were lucky) in five minutes.

"Tom!" softly over the coach roof.

"Hallo, Joe."

"Did you hear the message?"

"I did, Joe."

"What did you make of it, Tom?"

"Nothing at all, Joe."

"That's a coincidence, too," the guard mused, "for I made the same of it myself."

Jerry, left alone in the mist and darkness, dismounted meanwhile, not only to ease his spent horse, but to wipe the mud from his face, and shake the wet out of his hat-brim, which might be capable of holding about half a gallon. After standing with the bridle over his heavily-splashed arm, until the wheels of the mail were no longer within hearing and the night was quite still again, he turned to walk down the hill.

"After that there gallop from Temple Bar, old lady, I won't trust your fore-legs till I get you on the level," said this hoarse messenger, glancing at his mare. "'Recalled to life.' That's a Blazing strange message. Much of that wouldn't do for you, Jerry! I say, Jerry! You'd be in a Blazing bad way, if recalling to life was to come into fashion, Jerry!"

III. THE NIGHT SHADOWS

A wonderful fact to reflect upon, that every human creature is constituted to be that profound secret and mystery to every other. A solemn consideration, when I enter a great city by night, that every one of those darkly clustered houses encloses its own secret; that every room in every one of them encloses its own secret; that every beating heart in the hundreds of thousands of breasts there, is, in some of its imaginings, a secret to the heart nearest it! Something of the awfulness, even of Death itself, is referable to this. No more can I turn the leaves of this dear book that I loved, and vainly hope in time to read it all. No more can I look into the depths of this unfathomable water, wherein, as momentary lights glanced into it, I have had glimpses of buried treasure and other things submerged. It was appointed that the book should shut with a spring, for ever and for ever, when I had read but a page. It was appointed that the water should be locked in an eternal frost, when the light was playing on its surface, and I stood in ignorance on the shore. My friend is dead, my neighbour is dead, my love, the darling of my soul, is dead; it is the inexorable consolidation and perpetuation of the secret that was always in that individuality, and which I shall carry in mine to my life's end. In any of the burial-places of this city through which I pass, is there a sleeper more inscrutable than its busy inhabitants are, in their innermost personality, to me, or than I am to them?

As to this, his natural and not to be alienated inheritance, the messenger on horseback had exactly the same possessions as the King, the first Minister of State, or the richest merchant in London. So with the three passengers shut up in the narrow compass of one lumbering old mail coach; they were mysteries to one another, as complete as if each had been in his own coach and six, or his own coach and sixty, with the breadth of a county between him and the next.

The messenger rode back at an easy trot, stopping pretty often at ale-houses by the way to drink, but evincing a tendency to keep his own counsel, and to keep his hat cocked over his eyes. He had eyes that assorted very well with that decoration, being of a surface black, with no depth in the colour or form, and much too near together—as if they were afraid of being found out in something, singly, if they kept too far apart. They had a sinister expression, under an old cocked-hat like a three-cornered spittoon, and over a great muffler for the chin and throat, which descended nearly to the wearer's knees. When he stopped for drink, he moved this muffler with his left hand, only while he poured his liquor in with his right; as soon as that was done, he muffled again.

"No, Jerry, no!" said the messenger, harping on one theme as he rode. "It wouldn't do for you, Jerry. Jerry, you honest tradesman, it wouldn't suit *your* line of business! Recalled—! Bust me if I don't think he'd been a drinking!"

His message perplexed his mind to that degree that he was fain, several times, to take off his hat to scratch his head. Except on the crown, which was raggedly bald, he had stiff, black hair, standing jaggedly all over it, and growing down hill almost to his broad, blunt nose. It was so like Smith's work, so much more like the top of a strongly spiked wall than a head of hair, that the best of players at leap-frog might have declined him, as the most dangerous man in the world to go over.

While he trotted back with the message he was to deliver to the night watchman in his box at the door of Tellson's Bank, by Temple Bar, who was to deliver it to greater authorities within, the shadows of the night took such shapes to him as arose out of the message, and took such shapes to the mare as arose out of *her* private topics of uneasiness. They seemed to be numerous, for she shied at every shadow on the road.

What time, the mail-coach lumbered, jolted, rattled, and bumped upon its tedious way, with its three fellow-inscrutables inside. To whom, likewise, the shadows of the night revealed themselves, in the forms their dozing eyes and wandering thoughts suggested.

Tellson's Bank had a run upon it in the mail. As the bank passenger—with an arm drawn through the leathern strap, which did what lay in it to keep him from pounding against the next passenger, and driving him into his corner, whenever the coach got a special jolt—nodded in his place, with half-shut eyes, the little coach-windows, and the coach-lamp dimly gleaming through them, and the bulky bundle of opposite passenger, became the bank, and did a great stroke of business. The rattle of the harness was the chink of money, and more drafts were honoured in five minutes than even Tellson's, with all its foreign and home connection, ever paid in thrice the time. Then the strong-rooms underground, at Tellson's, with such of their valuable stores and secrets as were known to the passenger (and it was not a little that he knew about them), opened before him, and he went in among them with the great keys and the feebly-burning candle, and found them safe, and strong, and sound, and still, just as he had last seen them.

But, though the bank was almost always with him, and though the coach (in a confused way, like the presence of pain under an opiate) was always with him, there was another current of impression that never ceased to run, all through the night. He was on his way to dig some one out of a grave.

Now, which of the multitude of faces that showed themselves before him was the true face of the buried person, the shadows of the night did not indicate; but they were all the faces of a man of five-and- forty by years, and they differed principally in the passions they expressed, and in the ghastliness of their worn and wasted state. Pride, contempt, defiance, stubbornness, submission, lamentation, succeeded one another; so did varieties of sunken cheek, cadaverous colour, emaciated hands and figures. But the face was in the main one face, and every head was prematurely white. A hundred times the dozing passenger inquired of this spectre:

"Buried how long?"

The answer was always the same: "Almost eighteen years."

"You had abandoned all hope of being dug out?"

"Long ago."

"You know that you are recalled to life?"

"They tell me so."

"I hope you care to live?"

"I can't say."

"Shall I show her to you? Will you come and see her?"

The answers to this question were various and contradictory. Sometimes the broken reply was, "Wait! It would kill me if I saw her too soon." Sometimes, it was given in a tender rain of tears, and then it was, "Take me to her." Sometimes it was staring and bewildered, and then it was, "I don't know her. I don't understand."

After such imaginary discourse, the passenger in his fancy would dig, and dig, dig—now with a spade, now with a great key, now with his hands—to dig this wretched creature out. Got out at last, with earth hanging about his face and hair, he would suddenly fan away to dust. The passenger would then start to himself, and lower the window, to get the reality of mist and rain on his cheek.

Yet even when his eyes were opened on the mist and rain, on the moving patch of light from the lamps, and the hedge at the roadside retreating by jerks, the night shadows outside the coach would fall into the train of the night shadows within. The real Banking-house by Temple Bar, the real business of the past day, the real strong rooms, the real express sent after him, and the real message returned, would all be there. Out of the midst of them, the ghostly face would rise, and he would accost it again.

"Buried how long?"

"Almost eighteen years."

"I hope you care to live?"

"I can't say."

Dig—dig—dig—until an impatient movement from one of the two passengers would admonish him to pull up the window, draw his arm securely through the leathern strap, and speculate upon the two slumbering forms, until his mind lost its hold of them, and they again slid away into the bank and the grave.

"Buried how long?"

"Almost eighteen years."

"You had abandoned all hope of being dug out?"

"Long ago."

The words were still in his hearing as just spoken—distinctly in his hearing as ever spoken words had been in his life—when the weary passenger started to the consciousness of daylight, and found that the shadows of the night were gone.

He lowered the window, and looked out at the rising sun. There was a ridge of ploughed land, with a plough upon it where it had been left last night when the horses were unyoked; beyond, a quiet coppice-wood, in which many leaves of burning red and golden yellow still remained upon the trees. Though the earth was cold and wet, the sky was clear, and the sun rose bright, placid, and beautiful.

"Eighteen years!" said the passenger, looking at the sun. "Gracious Creator of day! To be buried alive for eighteen years!"

IV. THE PREPARATION

When the mail got successfully to Dover, in the course of the forenoon, the head drawer at the Royal George Hotel opened the coach-door as his custom was. He did it with some flourish of ceremony, for a mail journey from London in winter was an achievement to congratulate an adventurous traveller upon.

By that time, there was only one adventurous traveller left be congratulated: for the two others had been set down at their respective roadside destinations. The mildewy inside of the coach, with its damp and dirty straw, its disagreeable smell, and its obscurity, was rather like a larger dog-kennel. Mr. Lorry, the passenger, shaking himself out of it in chains of straw, a tangle of shaggy wrapper, flapping hat, and muddy legs, was rather like a larger sort of dog.

"There will be a packet to Calais, tomorrow, drawer?"

"Yes, sir, if the weather holds and the wind sets tolerable fair. The tide will serve pretty nicely at about two in the afternoon, sir. Bed, sir?"

"I shall not go to bed till night; but I want a bedroom, and a barber."

"And then breakfast, sir? Yes, sir. That way, sir, if you please. Show Concord! Gentleman's valise and hot water to Concord. Pull off gentleman's boots in Concord. (You will find a fine sea-coal fire, sir.) Fetch barber to Concord. Stir about there, now, for Concord!"

The Concord bed-chamber being always assigned to a passenger by the mail, and passengers by the mail being always heavily wrapped up from head to foot, the room had the odd interest for the establishment of the Royal George, that although but one kind of man was seen to go into it, all kinds and varieties of men came out of it. Consequently, another drawer, and two porters, and several maids and the landlady, were all loitering by accident at various points of the road between the Concord and the coffee-room, when a gentleman of sixty, formally dressed in a brown suit of clothes, pretty well worn, but very well kept, with large square cuffs and large flaps to the pockets, passed along on his way to his breakfast.

The coffee-room had no other occupant, that forenoon, than the gentleman in brown. His breakfast-table was drawn before the fire, and as he sat, with its light shining on him, waiting for the meal, he sat so still, that he might have been sitting for his portrait.

Very orderly and methodical he looked, with a hand on each knee, and a loud watch ticking a sonorous sermon under his flapped waist-coat, as though it pitted its gravity and longevity against the levity and evanescence of the brisk fire. He had a good leg, and was a little vain of it, for his brown stockings fitted sleek and close, and were of a fine texture; his shoes and buckles, too, though plain, were trim. He wore an odd little sleek crisp flaxen wig, setting very close to his head: which wig, it is to be presumed, was made of hair, but which looked far more as though it were spun from filaments of silk or glass. His linen, though not of a fineness in accordance with his stockings, was as white as the tops of the waves that broke upon the neighbouring beach, or the specks of sail that glinted in the sunlight far at sea. A face habitually suppressed and quieted, was still lighted up under the quaint wig by a pair of moist bright eyes that it must have cost their owner, in years gone by, some pains to drill to the composed and reserved expression of Tellson's Bank. He had a healthy colour in his cheeks, and his face, though lined, bore few traces of anxiety. But, perhaps the confidential bachelor clerks in Tellson's Bank were principally occupied with the cares of other people; and perhaps second-hand cares, like second-hand clothes, come easily off and on.

Completing his resemblance to a man who was sitting for his portrait, Mr. Lorry dropped off to sleep. The arrival of his breakfast roused him, and he said to the drawer, as he moved his chair to it:

"I wish accommodation prepared for a young lady who may come here at any time to-day. She may ask for Mr. Jarvis Lorry, or she may only ask for a gentleman from Tellson's Bank. Please to let me know."

"Yes, sir. Tellson's Bank in London, sir?"

"Yes."

"Yes, sir. We have oftentimes the honour to entertain your gentlemen in their travelling backwards and forwards betwixt London and Paris, sir. A vast deal of travelling, sir, in Tellson and Company's House."

"Yes. We are quite a French House, as well as an English one."

"Yes, sir. Not much in the habit of such travelling yourself, I think, sir?"

"Not of late years. It is fifteen years since we—since I—came last from France."

"Indeed, sir? That was before my time here, sir. Before our people's time here, sir. The George was in other hands at that time, sir."

"I believe so."

"But I would hold a pretty wager, sir, that a House like Tellson and Company was flourishing, a matter of fifty, not to speak of fifteen years ago?"

"You might treble that, and say a hundred and fifty, yet not be far from the truth."

"Indeed, sir!"

Rounding his mouth and both his eyes, as he stepped backward from the table, the waiter shifted his napkin from his right arm to his left, dropped into a comfortable attitude, and stood surveying the guest while he ate and drank, as from an observatory or watchtower. According to the immemorial usage of waiters in all ages.

When Mr. Lorry had finished his breakfast, he went out for a stroll on the beach. The little narrow, crooked town of Dover hid itself away from the beach, and ran its head into the chalk cliffs, like a marine ostrich. The beach was a desert of heaps of sea and stones tumbling wildly about, and the sea did what it liked, and what it liked was destruction. It thundered at the town, and thundered at the cliffs, and brought the coast down, madly. The air among the houses was of so strong a piscatory flavour that one might have supposed sick fish went up to be dipped in it, as sick people went down to be dipped in the sea. A little fishing was done in the port, and a quantity of strolling about by night, and looking seaward: particularly at those times when the tide made, and was near flood. Small tradesmen, who did no business whatever, sometimes unaccountably realised large fortunes, and it was remarkable that nobody in the neighbourhood could endure a lamplighter.

As the day declined into the afternoon, and the air, which had been at intervals clear enough to allow the French coast to be seen, became again charged with mist and vapour, Mr. Lorry's thoughts seemed to cloud too. When it was dark, and he sat before the coffee-room fire, awaiting his dinner as he had awaited his breakfast, his mind was busily digging, digging, digging, in the live red coals.

A bottle of good claret after dinner does a digger in the red coals no harm, otherwise than as it has a tendency to throw him out of work. Mr. Lorry had been idle a long time, and had just poured out his last glassful of wine with as complete an appearance of satisfaction as is ever to be found in an elderly gentleman of a fresh complexion who has got to the end of a bottle, when a rattling of wheels came up the narrow street, and rumbled into the inn-yard.

He set down his glass untouched. "This is Mam'selle!" said he.

In a very few minutes the waiter came in to announce that Miss Manette had arrived from London, and would be happy to see the gentleman from Tellson's.

"So soon?"

Miss Manette had taken some refreshment on the road, and required none then, and was extremely anxious to see the gentleman from Tellson's immediately, if it suited his pleasure and convenience.

The gentleman from Tellson's had nothing left for it but to empty his glass with an air of stolid desperation, settle his odd little flaxen wig at the ears, and follow the waiter to Miss Manette's apartment. It was a large, dark room, furnished in a funereal manner with black horsehair, and loaded with heavy dark tables. These had been oiled and oiled, until the two tall candles on the table in the middle of the room were gloomily reflected on every leaf; as if *they* were buried, in deep graves of black mahogany, and no light to speak of could be expected from them until they were dug out.

The obscurity was so difficult to penetrate that Mr. Lorry, picking his way over the well-worn Turkey carpet, supposed Miss Manette to be, for the moment, in some adjacent room, until, having got past the two tall candles, he saw standing to receive him by the table between them and the fire, a young lady of not more than seventeen, in a riding-cloak, and still holding her straw travelling- hat by its ribbon in her hand.

As his eyes rested on a short, slight, pretty figure, a quantity of golden hair, a pair of blue eyes that met his own with an inquiring look, and a forehead with a singular capacity (remembering how young and smooth it was), of rifting and knitting itself into an expression that was not quite one of perplexity, or wonder, or alarm, or merely of a bright fixed attention, though it included all the four expressions—as his eyes rested on these things, a sudden vivid likeness passed before him, of a child whom he had held in his arms on the passage across that very Channel, one cold time, when the hail drifted heavily and the sea ran high. The likeness passed away, like a breath along the surface of the gaunt pier-glass behind her, on the frame of which, a hospital procession of negro cupids, several headless and all cripples, were offering black baskets of Dead Sea fruit to black divinities of the feminine gender—and he made his formal bow to Miss Manette.

"Pray take a seat, sir." In a very clear and pleasant young voice; a little foreign in its accent, but a very little indeed.

"I kiss your hand, miss," said Mr. Lorry, with the manners of an earlier date, as he made his formal bow again, and took his seat.

"I received a letter from the Bank, sir, yesterday, informing me that some intelligence—or discovery—"

"The word is not material, miss; either word will do."

"—respecting the small property of my poor father, whom I never saw—so long dead—"

Mr. Lorry moved in his chair, and cast a troubled look towards the hospital procession of negro cupids. As if *they* had any help for anybody in their absurd baskets!

"—rendered it necessary that I should go to Paris, there to communicate with a gentleman of the Bank, so good as to be despatched to Paris for the purpose."

"Myself."

"As I was prepared to hear, sir."

She curtseyed to him (young ladies made curtseys in those days), with a pretty desire to convey to him that she felt how much older and wiser he was than she. He made her another bow.

"I replied to the Bank, sir, that as it was considered necessary, by those who know, and who are so kind as to advise me, that I should go to France, and that as I am an orphan and have no friend who could go with me, I should esteem it highly if I might be permitted to place myself, during the journey, under that worthy gentleman's protection. The gentleman had left London, but I think a messenger was sent after him to beg the favour of his waiting for me here."

"I was happy," said Mr. Lorry, "to be entrusted with the charge. I shall be more happy to execute it."

"Sir, I thank you indeed. I thank you very gratefully. It was told me by the Bank that the gentleman would explain to me the details of the business, and that I must prepare myself to find them of a surprising nature. I have done my best to prepare myself, and I naturally have a strong and eager interest to know what they are."

"Naturally," said Mr. Lorry. "Yes—I—"

After a pause, he added, again settling the crisp flaxen wig at the ears, "It is very difficult to begin."

He did not begin, but, in his indecision, met her glance. The young forehead lifted itself into that singular expression—but it was pretty and characteristic, besides being singular—and she raised her hand, as if with an involuntary action she caught at, or stayed some passing shadow.

"Are you quite a stranger to me, sir?"

"Am I not?" Mr. Lorry opened his hands, and extended them outwards with an argumentative smile.

Between the eyebrows and just over the little feminine nose, the line of which was as delicate and fine as it was possible to be, the expression deepened itself as she took her seat thoughtfully in the chair by which she had hitherto remained standing. He watched her as she mused, and the moment she raised her eyes again, went on:

"In your adopted country, I presume, I cannot do better than address you as a young English lady, Miss Manette?"

"If you please, sir."

"Miss Manette, I am a man of business. I have a business charge to acquit myself of. In your reception of it, don't heed me any more than if I was a speaking machine—truly, I am not much else. I will, with your leave, relate to you, miss, the story of one of our customers."

"Story!"

He seemed wilfully to mistake the word she had repeated, when he added, in a hurry, "Yes, customers; in the banking business we usually call our connection our customers. He was a French gentleman; a scientific gentleman; a man of great acquirements—a Doctor."

"Not of Beauvais?"

"Why, yes, of Beauvais. Like Monsieur Manette, your father, the gentleman was of Beauvais. Like Monsieur Manette, your father, the gentleman was of repute in Paris. I had the honour of knowing him there. Our relations were business relations, but confidential. I was at that time in our French House, and had been—oh! twenty years."

"At that time—I may ask, at what time, sir?"

"I speak, miss, of twenty years ago. He married—an English lady—and I was one of the trustees. His affairs, like the affairs of many other French gentlemen and French families, were entirely in Tellson's hands. In a similar way I am, or I have been, trustee of one kind or other for scores of our customers. These are mere business relations, miss; there is no friendship in them, no particular interest, nothing like sentiment. I have passed from one to another, in the course of my business life, just as I pass from one of our customers to another in the course of my business day; in short, I have no feelings; I am a mere machine. To go on—"

"But this is my father's story, sir; and I begin to think"—the curiously roughened forehead was very intent upon him—"that when I was left an orphan through my mother's surviving my father only two years, it was you who brought me to England. I am almost sure it was you."

Mr. Lorry took the hesitating little hand that confidingly advanced to take his, and he put it with some ceremony to his lips. He then conducted the young lady straightway to her chair again, and, holding the chair-back with his left hand, and using his right by turns to rub his chin, pull his wig at the ears, or point what he said, stood looking down into her face while she sat looking up into his.

"Miss Manette, it *was* I. And you will see how truly I spoke of myself just now, in saying I had no feelings, and that all the relations I hold with my fellow-creatures are mere business relations, when you reflect that I have never seen you since. No; you have been the ward of Tellson's House since, and I have been busy with the other business of Tellson's House since. Feelings! I have no time for them, no chance of them. I pass my whole life, miss, in turning an immense pecuniary Mangle."

After this odd description of his daily routine of employment, Mr. Lorry flattened his flaxen wig upon his head with both hands (which was most unnecessary, for nothing could be flatter than its shining surface was before), and resumed his former attitude.

"So far, miss (as you have remarked), this is the story of your regretted father. Now comes the difference. If your father had not died when he did—Don't be frightened! How you start!"

She did, indeed, start. And she caught his wrist with both her hands.

"Pray," said Mr. Lorry, in a soothing tone, bringing his left hand from the back of the chair to lay it on the supplicatory fingers that clasped him in so violent a tremble: "pray control your agitation—a matter of business. As I was saying—"

Her look so discomposed him that he stopped, wandered, and began anew:

"As I was saying; if Monsieur Manette had not died; if he had suddenly and silently disappeared; if he had been spirited away; if it had not been difficult to guess to what dreadful place, though no art could trace him; if he had an enemy in some compatriot who could exercise a privilege that I in my own time have known the boldest people afraid to speak of in a whisper, across the water there; for instance, the privilege of filling up blank forms for the consignment of any one to the oblivion of a prison for any length of time; if his wife had implored the king, the queen, the court, the clergy, for any tidings of him, and all quite in vain;—then the history of your father would have been the history of this unfortunate gentleman, the Doctor of Beauvais."

"I entreat you to tell me more, sir."

"I will. I am going to. You can bear it?"

"I can bear anything but the uncertainty you leave me in at this moment."

"You speak collectedly, and you—*are* collected. That's good!" (Though his manner was less satisfied than his words.) "A matter of business. Regard it as a matter of business—business that must be done. Now if this doctor's wife, though a lady of great courage and spirit, had suffered so intensely from this cause before her little child was born—"

"The little child was a daughter, sir."

"A daughter. A-a-matter of business—don't be distressed. Miss, if the poor lady had suffered so intensely before her little child was born, that she came to the determination of sparing the poor child the inheritance of any part of the agony she had known the pains of, by rearing her in the belief that her father was dead—No, don't kneel! In Heaven's name why should you kneel to me!"

"For the truth. O dear, good, compassionate sir, for the truth!"

"A—a matter of business. You confuse me, and how can I transact business if I am confused? Let us be clear-headed. If you could kindly mention now, for instance, what nine times ninepence are, or how many shillings in twenty guineas, it would be so encouraging. I should be so much more at my ease about your state of mind."

Without directly answering to this appeal, she sat so still when he had very gently raised her, and the hands that had not ceased to clasp his wrists were so much more steady than they had been, that she communicated some reassurance to Mr. Jarvis Lorry.

"That's right, that's right. Courage! Business! You have business before you; useful business. Miss Manette, your mother took this course with you. And when she died—I believe broken-hearted—having never slackened her unavailing search for your father, she left you, at two years old, to grow to be blooming, beautiful, and happy, without the dark cloud upon you of living in uncertainty whether your father soon wore his heart out in prison, or wasted there through many lingering years."

As he said the words he looked down, with an admiring pity, on the flowing golden hair; as if he pictured to himself that it might have been already tinged with grey.

"You know that your parents had no great possession, and that what they had was secured to your mother and to you. There has been no new discovery, of money, or of any other property; but—"

He felt his wrist held closer, and he stopped. The expression in the forehead, which had so particularly attracted his notice, and which was now immovable, had deepened into one of pain and horror.

"But he has been—been found. He is alive. Greatly changed, it is too probable; almost a wreck, it is possible; though we will hope the best. Still, alive. Your father has been taken to the house of an old servant in Paris, and we are going there: I, to identify him if I can: you, to restore him to life, love, duty, rest, comfort."

A shiver ran through her frame, and from it through his. She said, in a low, distinct, awe-stricken voice, as if she were saying it in a dream,

"I am going to see his Ghost! It will be his Ghost—not him!"

Mr. Lorry quietly chafed the hands that held his arm. "There, there, there! See now, see now! The best and the worst are known to you, now. You are well on your way to the poor wronged gentleman, and, with a fair sea voyage, and a fair land journey, you will be soon at his dear side."

She repeated in the same tone, sunk to a whisper, "I have been free, I have been happy, yet his Ghost has never haunted me!"

"Only one thing more," said Mr. Lorry, laying stress upon it as a wholesome means of enforcing her attention: "he has been found under another name; his own, long forgotten or long concealed. It would be worse than useless now to inquire which; worse than useless to seek to know whether he has been for years overlooked, or always designedly held prisoner. It would be worse than useless now to make any inquiries, because it would be dangerous. Better not to mention the subject, anywhere or in any way, and to remove him—for a while at all events—out of France. Even I, safe as an Englishman, and even Tellson's, important as they are to French credit, avoid all naming of the matter. I carry about me, not a scrap of writing openly referring to it. This is a secret service altogether. My credentials, entries, and memoranda, are all comprehended in the one line, 'Recalled to Life;' which may mean anything. But what is the matter! She doesn't notice a word! Miss Manette!"

Perfectly still and silent, and not even fallen back in her chair, she sat under his hand, utterly insensible; with her eyes open and fixed upon him, and with that last expression looking as if it were carved or branded into her forehead. So close was her hold upon his arm, that he feared to detach himself lest he should hurt her; therefore he called out loudly for assistance without moving.

A wild-looking woman, whom even in his agitation, Mr. Lorry observed to be all of a red colour, and to have red hair, and to be dressed in some extraordinary tight-fitting fashion, and to have on her head a most wonderful bonnet like a Grenadier wooden measure, and good measure too, or a great Stilton cheese, came running into the room in advance of the inn servants, and soon settled the question of his detachment from the poor young lady, by laying a brawny hand upon his chest, and sending him flying back against the nearest wall.

("I really think this must be a man!" was Mr. Lorry's breathless reflection, simultaneously with his coming against the wall.)

"Why, look at you all!" bawled this figure, addressing the inn servants. "Why don't you go and fetch things, instead of standing there staring at me? I am not so much to look at, am I? Why don't you go and fetch things? I'll let you know, if you don't bring smelling-salts, cold water, and vinegar, quick, I will."

There was an immediate dispersal for these restoratives, and she softly laid the patient on a sofa, and tended her with great skill and gentleness: calling her "my precious!" and "my bird!" and spreading her golden hair aside over her shoulders with great pride and care.

"And you in brown!" she said, indignantly turning to Mr. Lorry; "couldn't you tell her what you had to tell her, without frightening her to death? Look at her, with her pretty pale face and her cold hands. Do you call *that* being a Banker?"

Mr. Lorry was so exceedingly disconcerted by a question so hard to answer, that he could only look on, at a distance, with much feebler sympathy and humility, while the strong woman, having banished the inn servants under the mysterious penalty of "letting them know" something not mentioned if they stayed there, staring, recovered her charge by a regular series of gradations, and coaxed her to lay her drooping head upon her shoulder.

"I hope she will do well now," said Mr. Lorry.

"No thanks to you in brown, if she does. My darling pretty!"

"I hope," said Mr. Lorry, after another pause of feeble sympathy and humility, "that you accompany Miss Manette to France?"

"A likely thing, too!" replied the strong woman. "If it was ever intended that I should go across salt water, do you suppose Providence would have cast my lot in an island?"

This being another question hard to answer, Mr. Jarvis Lorry withdrew to consider it.

V. THE WINE-SHOP

A large cask of wine had been dropped and broken, in the street. The accident had happened in getting it out of a cart; the cask had tumbled out with a run, the hoops had burst, and it lay on the stones just outside the door of the wine-shop, shattered like a walnut-shell.

All the people within reach had suspended their business, or their idleness, to run to the spot and drink the wine. The rough, irregular stones of the street, pointing every way, and designed, one might have thought, expressly to lame all living creatures that approached them, had dammed it into little pools; these were surrounded, each by its own jostling group or crowd, according to its size. Some men kneeled down, made scoops of their two hands joined, and sipped, or tried to help women, who bent over their shoulders, to sip, before the wine had all run out between their fingers. Others, men and women, dipped in the puddles with little mugs of mutilated earthenware, or even with handkerchiefs from women's heads, which were squeezed dry into infants' mouths; others made small mud- embankments, to stem the wine as it ran; others, directed by lookers-on up at high windows, darted here and there, to cut off little streams of wine that started away in new directions; others devoted themselves to the sodden and lee-dyed pieces of the cask, licking, and even champing the moister wine-rotted fragments with eager relish. There was no drainage to carry off the wine, and not only did it all get taken up, but so much mud got taken up along with it, that there might have been a scavenger in the street, if anybody acquainted with it could have believed in such a miraculous presence.

A shrill sound of laughter and of amused voices—voices of men, women, and children—resounded in the street while this wine game lasted. There was little roughness in the sport, and much playfulness. There was a special companionship in it, an observable inclination on the part of every one to join some other one, which led, especially among the luckier or lighter-hearted, to frolicsome embraces, drinking of healths, shaking of hands, and even joining of hands and dancing, a dozen together. When the wine was gone, and the places where it had been most abundant were raked into a gridiron-pattern by fingers, these demonstrations ceased, as suddenly as they had broken out. The man who had left his saw sticking in the firewood he was cutting, set it in motion again; the women who had left on a door-step the little pot of hot ashes, at which she had been trying to soften the pain in her own starved fingers and toes, or in those of her child, returned to it; men with bare arms, matted locks, and cadaverous faces, who had emerged into the winter light from cellars, moved away, to descend again; and a gloom gathered on the scene that appeared more natural to it than sunshine.

The wine was red wine, and had stained the ground of the narrow street in the suburb of Saint Antoine, in Paris, where it was spilled. It had stained many hands, too, and many faces, and many naked feet, and many wooden shoes. The hands of the man who sawed the wood, left red marks on the billets; and the forehead of the woman who nursed her baby, was stained with the stain of the old rag she wound about her head again. Those who had been greedy with the staves of the cask, had acquired a tigerish smear about the mouth; and one tall joker so besmirched, his head more out of a long squalid bag of a nightcap than in it, scrawled upon a wall with his finger dipped in muddy wine-lees—BLOOD.

The time was to come, when that wine too would be spilled on the street-stones, and when the stain of it would be red upon many there.

And now that the cloud settled on Saint Antoine, which a momentary gleam had driven from his sacred countenance, the darkness of it was heavy—cold, dirt, sickness, ignorance, and want, were the lords in waiting on the saintly presence—nobles of great power all of them; but, most especially the last. Samples of a people that had undergone a terrible grinding and regrinding in the mill, and certainly not in the fabulous mill which ground old people young, shivered at every corner, passed in and out at every doorway, looked from every window, fluttered in every vestige of a garment that the wind shook. The mill which had worked them down, was the mill that grinds young people old; the children had ancient faces and grave voices; and upon them, and upon the grown faces, and ploughed into every furrow of age and coming up afresh, was the sigh, Hunger. It was prevalent everywhere. Hunger was pushed out of the tall houses, in the wretched clothing that hung upon poles and lines; Hunger was patched into them with straw and rag and wood and paper; Hunger was repeated in every fragment of the small modicum of firewood that the man sawed off; Hunger stared down from the smokeless chimneys, and started up from the filthy street that had no offal, among its refuse, of anything to eat. Hunger was the inscription on the baker's shelves, written in every small loaf of his scanty stock of bad bread; at the sausage-shop, in every dead-dog preparation that was offered for sale. Hunger rattled its dry bones among the roasting chestnuts in the turned cylinder; Hunger was shred into atomics in every farthing porringer of husky chips of potato, fried with some reluctant drops of oil.

Its abiding place was in all things fitted to it. A narrow winding street, full of offence and stench, with other narrow winding streets diverging, all peopled by rags and nightcaps, and all smelling of rags and nightcaps, and all visible things with a brooding look upon them that looked ill. In the hunted air of the people there was yet some wild-beast thought of the possibility of turning at bay. Depressed and slinking though they were, eyes of fire were not wanting among them; nor compressed lips, white with what they suppressed; nor foreheads knitted into the likeness of the gallows-rope they mused about enduring, or inflicting. The trade signs (and they were almost as many as the shops) were, all, grim illustrations of Want. The butcher and the porkman painted up, only the leanest scrags of meat; the baker, the coarsest of meagre loaves. The people rudely pictured as drinking in the wine-shops, croaked over their scanty measures of thin wine and beer, and were gloweringly confidential together. Nothing was represented in a flourishing condition, save tools and weapons; but, the cutler's knives and axes were sharp and bright, the smith's hammers were heavy, and the gunmaker's stock was murderous. The crippling stones of the pavement, with their many little reservoirs of mud and water, had no footways, but broke off abruptly at the doors. The kennel, to make amends, ran down the middle of the street—when it ran at all: which was only after heavy rains, and then it ran, by many eccentric fits, into the houses. Across the streets, at wide intervals, one clumsy lamp was slung by a rope and pulley; at night, when the lamplighter had let these down, and lighted, and hoisted them again, a feeble grove of dim wicks swung in a sickly manner overhead, as if they were at sea. Indeed they were at sea, and the ship and crew were in peril of tempest.

For, the time was to come, when the gaunt scarecrows of that region should have watched the lamplighter, in their idleness and hunger, so long, as to conceive the idea of improving on his method, and hauling up men by those ropes and pulleys, to flare upon the darkness of their condition. But, the time was not come yet; and every wind that blew over France shook the rags of the scarecrows in vain, for the birds, fine of song and feather, took no warning.

The wine-shop was a corner shop, better than most others in its appearance and degree, and the master of the wine-shop had stood outside it, in a yellow waistcoat and green breeches, looking on at the struggle for the lost wine. "It's not my affair," said he, with a final shrug of the shoulders. "The people from the market did it. Let them bring another."

There, his eyes happening to catch the tall joker writing up his joke, he called to him across the way:

"Say, then, my Gaspard, what do you do there?"

The fellow pointed to his joke with immense significance, as is often the way with his tribe. It missed its mark, and completely failed, as is often the way with his tribe too.

"What now? Are you a subject for the mad hospital?" said the wine-shop keeper, crossing the road, and obliterating the jest with a handful of mud, picked up for the purpose, and smeared over it. "Why do you write in the public streets? Is there—tell me thou—is there no other place to write such words in?"

In his expostulation he dropped his cleaner hand (perhaps accidentally, perhaps not) upon the joker's heart. The joker rapped it with his own, took a nimble spring upward, and came down in a fantastic dancing attitude, with one of his stained shoes jerked off his foot into his hand, and held out. A joker of an extremely, not to say wolfishly practical character, he looked, under those circumstances.

"Put it on, put it on," said the other. "Call wine, wine; and finish there." With that advice, he wiped his soiled hand upon the joker's dress, such as it was—quite deliberately, as having dirtied the hand on his account; and then recrossed the road and entered the wine-shop.

This wine-shop keeper was a bull-necked, martial-looking man of thirty, and he should have been of a hot temperament, for, although it was a bitter day, he wore no coat, but carried one slung over his shoulder. His shirt-sleeves were rolled up, too, and his brown arms were bare to the elbows. Neither did he wear anything more on his head than his own crisply-curling short dark hair. He was a dark man altogether, with good eyes and a good bold breadth between them. Good-humoured looking on the whole, but implacable-looking, too; evidently a man of a strong resolution and a set purpose; a man not desirable to be met, rushing down a narrow pass with a gulf on either side, for nothing would turn the man.

Madame Defarge, his wife, sat in the shop behind the counter as he came in. Madame Defarge was a stout woman of about his own age, with a watchful eye that seldom seemed to look at anything, a large hand heavily ringed, a steady face, strong features, and great composure of manner. There was a character about Madame Defarge, from which one might have predicated that she did not often make mistakes against herself in any of the reckonings over which she presided. Madame Defarge being sensitive to cold, was wrapped in fur, and had a quantity of bright shawl twined about her head, though not to the concealment of her large earrings. Her knitting was before her, but she had laid it down to pick her teeth with a toothpick. Thus engaged, with her right elbow supported by her left hand, Madame Defarge said nothing when her lord came in, but coughed just one grain of cough. This, in combination with the lifting of her darkly defined eyebrows over her toothpick by the breadth of a line, suggested to her husband that he would do well to look round the shop among the customers, for any new customer who had dropped in while he stepped over the way.

The wine-shop keeper accordingly rolled his eyes about, until they rested upon an elderly gentleman and a young lady, who were seated in a corner. Other company were there: two playing cards, two playing dominoes, three standing by the counter lengthening out a short supply of wine. As he passed behind the counter, he took notice that the elderly gentleman said in a look to the young lady, "This is our man."

"What the devil do *you* do in that galley there?" said Monsieur Defarge to himself; "I don't know you."

But, he feigned not to notice the two strangers, and fell into discourse with the triumvirate of customers who were drinking at the counter.

"How goes it, Jacques?" said one of these three to Monsieur Defarge. "Is all the spilt wine swallowed?"

"Every drop, Jacques," answered Monsieur Defarge.

When this interchange of Christian name was effected, Madame Defarge, picking her teeth with her toothpick, coughed another grain of cough, and raised her eyebrows by the breadth of another line.

"It is not often," said the second of the three, addressing Monsieur Defarge, "that many of these miserable beasts know the taste of wine, or of anything but black bread and death. Is it not so, Jacques?"

"It is so, Jacques," Monsieur Defarge returned.

At this second interchange of the Christian name, Madame Defarge, still using her toothpick with profound composure, coughed another grain of cough, and raised her eyebrows by the breadth of another line.

The last of the three now said his say, as he put down his empty drinking vessel and smacked his lips.

"Ah! So much the worse! A bitter taste it is that such poor cattle always have in their mouths, and hard lives they live, Jacques. Am I right, Jacques?"

"You are right, Jacques," was the response of Monsieur Defarge.

This third interchange of the Christian name was completed at the moment when Madame Defarge put her toothpick by, kept her eyebrows up, and slightly rustled in her seat.

"Hold then! True!" muttered her husband. "Gentlemen—my wife!"

The three customers pulled off their hats to Madame Defarge, with three flourishes. She acknowledged their homage by bending her head, and giving them a quick look.

Then she glanced in a casual manner round the wine-shop, took up her knitting with great apparent calmness and repose of spirit, and became absorbed in it.

"Gentlemen," said her husband, who had kept his bright eye observantly upon her, "good day. The chamber, furnished bachelor-fashion, that you wished to see, and were inquiring for when I stepped out, is on the fifth floor. The doorway of the staircase gives on the little courtyard close to the left here," pointing with his hand, "near to the window of my establishment. But, now that I remember, one of you has already been there, and can show the way. Gentlemen, adieu!"

They paid for their wine, and left the place. The eyes of Monsieur Defarge were studying his wife at her knitting when the elderly gentleman advanced from his corner, and begged the favour of a word.

"Willingly, sir," said Monsieur Defarge, and quietly stepped with him to the door.

Their conference was very short, but very decided. Almost at the first word, Monsieur Defarge started and became deeply attentive. It had not lasted a minute, when he nodded and went out. The gentleman then beckoned to the young lady, and they, too, went out. Madame Defarge knitted with nimble fingers and steady eyebrows, and saw nothing.

Mr. Jarvis Lorry and Miss Manette, emerging from the wine-shop thus, joined Monsieur Defarge in the doorway to which he had directed his own company just before. It opened from a stinking little black courtyard, and was the general public entrance to a great pile of houses, inhabited by a great number of people. In the gloomy tile-paved entry to the gloomy tile-paved staircase, Monsieur Defarge bent down on one knee to the child of his old master, and put her hand to his lips. It was a gentle action, but not at all gently done; a very remarkable transformation had come over him in a few seconds. He had no good-humour in his face, nor any openness of aspect left, but had become a secret, angry, dangerous man.

"It is very high; it is a little difficult. Better to begin slowly." Thus, Monsieur Defarge, in a stern voice, to Mr. Lorry, as they began ascending the stairs.

"Is he alone?" the latter whispered.

"Alone! God help him, who should be with him!" said the other, in the same low voice.

"Is he always alone, then?"

"Yes."

"Of his own desire?"

"Of his own necessity. As he was, when I first saw him after they found me and demanded to know if I would take him, and, at my peril be discreet—as he was then, so he is now."

"He is greatly changed?"

"Changed!"

The keeper of the wine-shop stopped to strike the wall with his hand, and mutter a tremendous curse. No direct answer could have been half so forcible. Mr. Lorry's spirits grew heavier and heavier, as he and his two companions ascended higher and higher.

Such a staircase, with its accessories, in the older and more crowded parts of Paris, would be bad enough now; but, at that time, it was vile indeed to unaccustomed and unhardened senses. Every little habitation within the great foul nest of one high building—that is to say, the room or rooms within every door that opened on the general staircase—left its own heap of refuse on its own landing, besides flinging other refuse from its own windows. The uncontrollable and hopeless mass of decomposition so engendered, would have polluted the air, even if poverty and deprivation had not loaded it with their intangible impurities; the two bad sources combined made it almost insupportable. Through such an atmosphere, by a steep dark shaft of dirt and poison, the way lay. Yielding to his own disturbance of mind, and to his young companion's agitation, which became greater every instant, Mr. Jarvis Lorry twice stopped to rest. Each of these stoppages was made at a doleful grating, by which any languishing good airs that were left uncorrupted, seemed to escape, and all spoilt and sickly vapours seemed to crawl in. Through the rusted bars, tastes, rather than glimpses, were caught of the jumbled neighbourhood; and nothing within range, nearer or lower than the summits of the two great towers of Notre-Dame, had any promise on it of healthy life or wholesome aspirations.

At last, the top of the staircase was gained, and they stopped for the third time. There was yet an upper staircase, of a steeper inclination and of contracted dimensions, to be ascended, before the garret story was reached. The keeper of the wine-shop, always going a little in advance, and always going on the side which Mr. Lorry took, as though he dreaded to be asked any question by the young lady, turned himself about here, and, carefully feeling in the pockets of the coat he carried over his shoulder, took out a key.

"The door is locked then, my friend?" said Mr. Lorry, surprised.

"Ay. Yes," was the grim reply of Monsieur Defarge.

"You think it necessary to keep the unfortunate gentleman so retired?"

"I think it necessary to turn the key." Monsieur Defarge whispered it closer in his ear, and frowned heavily.

"Why?"

"Why! Because he has lived so long, locked up, that he would be frightened—rave—tear himself to pieces—die—come to I know not what harm—if his door was left open."

"Is it possible!" exclaimed Mr. Lorry.

"Is it possible!" repeated Defarge, bitterly. "Yes. And a beautiful world we live in, when it *is* possible, and when many other such things are possible, and not only possible, but done—done, see you!—under that sky there, every day. Long live the Devil. Let us go on."

This dialogue had been held in so very low a whisper, that not a word of it had reached the young lady's ears. But, by this time she trembled under such strong emotion, and her face expressed such deep anxiety, and, above all, such dread and terror, that Mr. Lorry felt it incumbent on him to speak a word or two of reassurance.

"Courage, dear miss! Courage! Business! The worst will be over in a moment; it is but passing the room-door, and the worst is over. Then, all the good you bring to him, all the relief, all the happiness you bring to him, begin. Let our good friend here, assist you on that side. That's well, friend Defarge. Come, now. Business, business!"

They went up slowly and softly. The staircase was short, and they were soon at the top. There, as it had an abrupt turn in it, they came all at once in sight of three men, whose heads were bent down close together at the side of a door, and who were intently looking into the room to which the door belonged, through some chinks or holes in the wall. On hearing footsteps close at hand, these three turned, and rose, and showed themselves to be the three of one name who had been drinking in the wine-shop.

"I forgot them in the surprise of your visit," explained Monsieur Defarge. "Leave us, good boys; we have business here."

The three glided by, and went silently down.

There appearing to be no other door on that floor, and the keeper of the wine-shop going straight to this one when they were left alone, Mr. Lorry asked him in a whisper, with a little anger:

"Do you make a show of Monsieur Manette?"

"I show him, in the way you have seen, to a chosen few."

"Is that well?"

"*I* think it is well."

"Who are the few? How do you choose them?"

"I choose them as real men, of my name—Jacques is my name—to whom the sight is likely to do good. Enough; you are English; that is another thing. Stay there, if you please, a little moment."

With an admonitory gesture to keep them back, he stooped, and looked in through the crevice in the wall. Soon raising his head again, he struck twice or thrice upon the door—evidently with no other object than to make a noise there. With the same intention, he drew the key across it, three or four times, before he put it clumsily into the lock, and turned it as heavily as he could.

The door slowly opened inward under his hand, and he looked into the room and said something. A faint voice answered something. Little more than a single syllable could have been spoken on either side.

He looked back over his shoulder, and beckoned them to enter. Mr. Lorry got his arm securely round the daughter's waist, and held her; for he felt that she was sinking.

"A-a-a-business, business!" he urged, with a moisture that was not of business shining on his cheek. "Come in, come in!"

"I am afraid of it," she answered, shuddering.

"Of it? What?"

"I mean of him. Of my father."

Rendered in a manner desperate, by her state and by the beckoning of their conductor, he drew over his neck the arm that shook upon his shoulder, lifted her a little, and hurried her into the room. He sat her down just within the door, and held her, clinging to him.

Defarge drew out the key, closed the door, locked it on the inside, took out the key again, and held it in his hand. All this he did, methodically, and with as loud and harsh an accompaniment of noise as he could make. Finally, he walked across the room with a measured tread to where the window was. He stopped there, and faced round.

The garret, built to be a depository for firewood and the like, was dim and dark: for, the window of dormer shape, was in truth a door in the roof, with a little crane over it for the hoisting up of stores from the street: unglazed, and closing up the middle in two pieces, like any other door of French construction. To exclude the cold, one half of this door was fast closed, and the other was opened but a very little way. Such a scanty portion of light was admitted through these means, that it was difficult, on first coming in, to see anything; and long habit alone could have slowly formed in any one, the ability to do any work requiring nicety in such obscurity. Yet, work of that kind was being done in the garret; for, with his back towards the door, and his face towards the window where the keeper of the wine-shop stood looking at him, a white-haired man sat on a low bench, stooping forward and very busy, making shoes.

VI. THE SHOEMAKER

"Good day!" said Monsieur Defarge, looking down at the white head that bent low over the shoemaking.

It was raised for a moment, and a very faint voice responded to the salutation, as if it were at a distance:

"Good day!"

"You are still hard at work, I see?"

After a long silence, the head was lifted for another moment, and the voice replied, "Yes—I am working." This time, a pair of haggard eyes had looked at the questioner, before the face had dropped again.

The faintness of the voice was pitiable and dreadful. It was not the faintness of physical weakness, though confinement and hard fare no doubt had their part in it. Its deplorable peculiarity was, that it was the faintness of solitude and disuse. It was like the last feeble echo of a sound made long and long ago. So entirely had it lost the life and resonance of the human voice, that it affected the senses like a once beautiful colour faded away into a poor weak stain. So sunken and suppressed it was, that it was like a voice underground. So expressive it was, of a hopeless and lost creature, that a famished traveller, wearied out by lonely wandering in a wilderness, would have remembered home and friends in such a tone before lying down to die.

Some minutes of silent work had passed: and the haggard eyes had looked up again: not with any interest or curiosity, but with a dull mechanical perception, beforehand, that the spot where the only visitor they were aware of had stood, was not yet empty.

"I want," said Defarge, who had not removed his gaze from the shoemaker, "to let in a little more light here. You can bear a little more?"

The shoemaker stopped his work; looked with a vacant air of listening, at the floor on one side of him; then similarly, at the floor on the other side of him; then, upward at the speaker.

"What did you say?"

"You can bear a little more light?"

"I must bear it, if you let it in." (Laying the palest shadow of a stress upon the second word.)

The opened half-door was opened a little further, and secured at that angle for the time. A broad ray of light fell into the garret, and showed the workman with an unfinished shoe upon his lap, pausing in his labour. His few common tools and various scraps of leather were at his feet and on his bench. He had a white beard, raggedly cut, but not very long, a hollow face, and exceedingly bright eyes. The hollowness and thinness of his face would have caused them to look large, under his yet dark eyebrows and his confused white hair, though they had been really otherwise; but, they were naturally large, and looked unnaturally so. His yellow rags of shirt lay open at the throat, and showed his body to be withered and worn. He, and his old canvas frock, and his loose stockings, and all his poor tatters of clothes, had, in a long seclusion from direct light and air, faded down to such a dull uniformity of parchment-yellow, that it would have been hard to say which was which.

He had put up a hand between his eyes and the light, and the very bones of it seemed transparent. So he sat, with a steadfastly vacant gaze, pausing in his work. He never looked at the figure before him, without first looking down on this side of himself, then on that, as if he had lost the habit of associating place with sound; he never spoke, without first wandering in this manner, and forgetting to speak.

"Are you going to finish that pair of shoes to-day?" asked Defarge, motioning to Mr. Lorry to come forward.

"What did you say?"

"Do you mean to finish that pair of shoes to-day?"

"I can't say that I mean to. I suppose so. I don't know."

But, the question reminded him of his work, and he bent over it again.

Mr. Lorry came silently forward, leaving the daughter by the door. When he had stood, for a minute or two, by the side of Defarge, the shoemaker looked up. He showed no surprise at seeing another figure, but the unsteady fingers of one of his hands strayed to his lips as he looked at it (his lips and his nails were of the same pale lead- colour), and then the hand dropped to his work, and he once more bent over the shoe. The look and the action had occupied but an instant.

"You have a visitor, you see," said Monsieur Defarge.

"What did you say?"

"Here is a visitor."

The shoemaker looked up as before, but without removing a hand from his work.

"Come!" said Defarge. "Here is monsieur, who knows a well-made shoe when he sees one. Show him that shoe you are working at. Take it, monsieur."

Mr. Lorry took it in his hand.

"Tell monsieur what kind of shoe it is, and the maker's name."

There was a longer pause than usual, before the shoemaker replied:

"I forget what it was you asked me. What did you say?"

"I said, couldn't you describe the kind of shoe, for monsieur's information?"

"It is a lady's shoe. It is a young lady's walking-shoe. It is in the present mode. I never saw the mode. I have had a pattern in my hand." He glanced at the shoe with some little passing touch of pride.

"And the maker's name?" said Defarge.

Now that he had no work to hold, he laid the knuckles of the right hand in the hollow of the left, and then the knuckles of the left hand in the hollow of the right, and then passed a hand across his bearded chin, and so on in regular changes, without a moment's intermission. The task of recalling him from the vagrancy into which he always sank when he had spoken, was like recalling some very weak person from a swoon, or endeavouring, in the hope of some disclosure, to stay the spirit of a fast-dying man.

"Did you ask me for my name?"

"Assuredly I did."

"One Hundred and Five, North Tower."

"Is that all?"

"One Hundred and Five, North Tower."

With a weary sound that was not a sigh, nor a groan, he bent to work again, until the silence was again broken.

"You are not a shoemaker by trade?" said Mr. Lorry, looking steadfastly at him.

His haggard eyes turned to Defarge as if he would have transferred the question to him: but as no help came from that quarter, they turned back on the questioner when they had sought the ground.

"I am not a shoemaker by trade? No, I was not a shoemaker by trade. I-I learnt it here. I taught myself. I asked leave to——"

He lapsed away, even for minutes, ringing those measured changes on his hands the whole time. His eyes came slowly back, at last, to the face from which they had wandered; when they rested on it, he started, and resumed, in the manner of a sleeper that moment awake, reverting to a subject of last night.

"I asked leave to teach myself, and I got it with much difficulty after a long while, and I have made shoes ever since."

As he held out his hand for the shoe that had been taken from him, Mr. Lorry said, still looking steadfastly in his face:

"Monsieur Manette, do you remember nothing of me?"

The shoe dropped to the ground, and he sat looking fixedly at the questioner.

"Monsieur Manette"; Mr. Lorry laid his hand upon Defarge's arm; "do you remember nothing of this man? Look at him. Look at me. Is there no old banker, no old business, no old servant, no old time, rising in your mind, Monsieur Manette?"

As the captive of many years sat looking fixedly, by turns, at Mr. Lorry and at Defarge, some long obliterated marks of an actively intent intelligence in the middle of the forehead, gradually forced themselves through the black mist that had fallen on him. They were overclouded again, they were fainter, they were gone; but they had been there. And so exactly was the expression repeated on the fair young face of her who had crept along the wall to a point where she could see him, and where she now stood looking at him, with hands which at first had been only raised in frightened compassion, if not even to keep him off and shut out the sight of him, but which were now extending towards him, trembling with eagerness to lay the spectral face upon her warm young breast, and love it back to life and hope—so exactly was the expression repeated (though in stronger characters) on her fair young face, that it looked as though it had passed like a moving light, from him to her.

Darkness had fallen on him in its place. He looked at the two, less and less attentively, and his eyes in gloomy abstraction sought the ground and looked about him in the old way. Finally, with a deep long sigh, he took the shoe up, and resumed his work.

"Have you recognised him, monsieur?" asked Defarge in a whisper.

"Yes; for a moment. At first I thought it quite hopeless, but I have unquestionably seen, for a single moment, the face that I once knew so well. Hush! Let us draw further back. Hush!"

She had moved from the wall of the garret, very near to the bench on which he sat. There was something awful in his unconsciousness of the figure that could have put out its hand and touched him as he stooped over his labour.

Not a word was spoken, not a sound was made. She stood, like a spirit, beside him, and he bent over his work.

It happened, at length, that he had occasion to change the instrument in his hand, for his shoemaker's knife. It lay on that side of him which was not the side on which she stood. He had taken it up, and was stooping to work again, when his eyes caught the skirt of her dress. He raised them, and saw her face. The two spectators started forward, but she stayed them with a motion of her hand. She had no fear of his striking at her with the knife, though they had.

He stared at her with a fearful look, and after a while his lips began to form some words, though no sound proceeded from them. By degrees, in the pauses of his quick and laboured breathing, he was heard to say:

"What is this?"

With the tears streaming down her face, she put her two hands to her lips, and kissed them to him; then clasped them on her breast, as if she laid his ruined head there.

"You are not the gaoler's daughter?"

She sighed "No."

"Who are you?"

Not yet trusting the tones of her voice, she sat down on the bench beside him. He recoiled, but she laid her hand upon his arm. A strange thrill struck him when she did so, and visibly passed over his frame; he laid the knife down softly, as he sat staring at her.

Her golden hair, which she wore in long curls, had been hurriedly pushed aside, and fell down over her neck. Advancing his hand by little and little, he took it up and looked at it. In the midst of the action he went astray, and, with another deep sigh, fell to work at his shoemaking.

But not for long. Releasing his arm, she laid her hand upon his shoulder. After looking doubtfully at it, two or three times, as if to be sure that it was really there, he laid down his work, put his hand to his neck, and took off a blackened string with a scrap of folded rag attached to it. He opened this, carefully, on his knee, and it contained a very little quantity of hair: not more than one or two long golden hairs, which he had, in some old day, wound off upon his finger.

He took her hair into his hand again, and looked closely at it. "It is the same. How can it be! When was it! How was it!"

As the concentrated expression returned to his forehead, he seemed to become conscious that it was in hers too. He turned her full to the light, and looked at her.

"She had laid her head upon my shoulder, that night when I was summoned out—she had a fear of my going, though I had none—and when I was brought to the North Tower they found these upon my sleeve. 'You will leave me them? They can never help me to escape in the body, though they may in the spirit.' Those were the words I said. I remember them very well."

He formed this speech with his lips many times before he could utter it. But when he did find spoken words for it, they came to him coherently, though slowly.

"How was this?—*Was it you?*"

Once more, the two spectators started, as he turned upon her with a frightful suddenness. But she sat perfectly still in his grasp, and only said, in a low voice, "I entreat you, good gentlemen, do not come near us, do not speak, do not move!"

"Hark!" he exclaimed. "Whose voice was that?"

His hands released her as he uttered this cry, and went up to his white hair, which they tore in a frenzy. It died out, as everything but his shoemaking did die out of him, and he refolded his little packet and tried to secure it in his breast; but he still looked at her, and gloomily shook his head.

"No, no, no; you are too young, too blooming. It can't be. See what the prisoner is. These are not the hands she knew, this is not the face she knew, this is not a voice she ever heard. No, no. She was—and He was—before the slow years of the North Tower—ages ago. What is your name, my gentle angel?"

Hailing his softened tone and manner, his daughter fell upon her knees before him, with her appealing hands upon his breast.

"O, sir, at another time you shall know my name, and who my mother was, and who my father, and how I never knew their hard, hard history. But I cannot tell you at this time, and I cannot tell you here. All that I may tell you, here and now, is, that I pray to you to touch me and to bless me. Kiss me, kiss me! O my dear, my dear!"

His cold white head mingled with her radiant hair, which warmed and lighted it as though it were the light of Freedom shining on him.

"If you hear in my voice—I don't know that it is so, but I hope it is—if you hear in my voice any resemblance to a voice that once was sweet music in your ears, weep for it, weep for it! If you touch, in touching my hair, anything that recalls a beloved head that lay on your breast when you were young and free, weep for it, weep for it! If, when I hint to you of a Home that is before us, where I will be true to you with all my duty and with all my faithful service, I bring back the remembrance of a Home long desolate, while your poor heart pined away, weep for it, weep for it!"

She held him closer round the neck, and rocked him on her breast like a child.

"If, when I tell you, dearest dear, that your agony is over, and that I have come here to take you from it, and that we go to England to be at peace and at rest, I cause you to think of your useful life laid waste, and of our native France so wicked to you, weep for it, weep for it! And if, when I shall tell you of my name, and of my father who is living, and of my mother who is dead, you learn that I have to kneel to my honoured father, and implore his pardon for having never for his sake striven all day and lain awake and wept all night, because the love of my poor mother hid his torture from me, weep for it, weep for it! Weep for her, then, and for me! Good gentlemen, thank God! I feel his sacred tears upon my face, and his sobs strike against my heart. O, see! Thank God for us, thank God!"

He had sunk in her arms, and his face dropped on her breast: a sight so touching, yet so terrible in the tremendous wrong and suffering which had gone before it, that the two beholders covered their faces.

When the quiet of the garret had been long undisturbed, and his heaving breast and shaken form had long yielded to the calm that must follow all storms—emblem to humanity, of the rest and silence into which the storm called Life must hush at last—they came forward to raise the father and daughter from the ground. He had gradually dropped to the floor, and lay there in a lethargy, worn out. She had nestled down with him, that his head might lie upon her arm; and her hair drooping over him curtained him from the light.

"If, without disturbing him," she said, raising her hand to Mr. Lorry as he stooped over them, after repeated blowings of his nose, "all could be arranged for our leaving Paris at once, so that, from the very door, he could be taken away—"

"But, consider. Is he fit for the journey?" asked Mr. Lorry.

"More fit for that, I think, than to remain in this city, so dreadful to him."

"It is true," said Defarge, who was kneeling to look on and hear. "More than that; Monsieur Manette is, for all reasons, best out of France. Say, shall I hire a carriage and post-horses?"

"That's business," said Mr. Lorry, resuming on the shortest notice his methodical manners; "and if business is to be done, I had better do it."

"Then be so kind," urged Miss Manette, "as to leave us here. You see how composed he has become, and you cannot be afraid to leave him with me now. Why should you be? If you will lock the door to secure us from interruption, I do not doubt that you will find him, when you come back, as quiet as you leave him. In any case, I will take care of him until you return, and then we will remove him straight."

Both Mr. Lorry and Defarge were rather disinclined to this course, and in favour of one of them remaining. But, as there were not only carriage and horses to be seen to, but travelling papers; and as time pressed, for the day was drawing to an end, it came at last to their hastily dividing the business that was necessary to be done, and hurrying away to do it.

Then, as the darkness closed in, the daughter laid her head down on the hard ground close at the father's side, and watched him. The darkness deepened and deepened, and they both lay quiet, until a light gleamed through the chinks in the wall.

Mr. Lorry and Monsieur Defarge had made all ready for the journey, and had brought with them, besides travelling cloaks and wrappers, bread and meat, wine, and hot coffee. Monsieur Defarge put this provender, and the lamp he carried, on the shoemaker's bench (there was nothing else in the garret but a pallet bed), and he and Mr. Lorry roused the captive, and assisted him to his feet.

No human intelligence could have read the mysteries of his mind, in the scared blank wonder of his face. Whether he knew what had happened, whether he recollected what they had said to him, whether he knew that he was free, were questions which no sagacity could have solved. They tried speaking to him; but, he was so confused, and so very slow to answer, that they took fright at his bewilderment, and agreed for the time to tamper with him no more. He had a wild, lost manner of occasionally clasping his head in his hands, that had not been seen in him before; yet, he had some pleasure in the mere sound of his daughter's voice, and invariably turned to it when she spoke.

In the submissive way of one long accustomed to obey under coercion, he ate and drank what they gave him to eat and drink, and put on the cloak and other wrappings, that they gave him to wear. He readily responded to his daughter's drawing her arm through his, and took—and kept—her hand in both his own.

They began to descend; Monsieur Defarge going first with the lamp, Mr. Lorry closing the little procession. They had not traversed many steps of the long main staircase when he stopped, and stared at the roof and round at the wails.

"You remember the place, my father? You remember coming up here?"

"What did you say?"

But, before she could repeat the question, he murmured an answer as if she had repeated it.

"Remember? No, I don't remember. It was so very long ago."

That he had no recollection whatever of his having been brought from his prison to that house, was apparent to them. They heard him mutter, "One Hundred and Five, North Tower;" and when he looked about him, it evidently was for the strong fortress-walls which had long encompassed him. On their reaching the courtyard he instinctively altered his tread, as being in expectation of a drawbridge; and when there was no drawbridge, and he saw the carriage waiting in the open street, he dropped his daughter's hand and clasped his head again.

No crowd was about the door; no people were discernible at any of the many windows; not even a chance passerby was in the street. An unnatural silence and desertion reigned there. Only one soul was to be seen, and that was Madame Defarge—who leaned against the door-post, knitting, and saw nothing.

The prisoner had got into a coach, and his daughter had followed him, when Mr. Lorry's feet were arrested on the step by his asking, miserably, for his shoemaking tools and the unfinished shoes. Madame Defarge immediately called to her husband that she would get them, and went, knitting, out of the lamplight, through the courtyard. She quickly brought them down and handed them in;—and immediately afterwards leaned against the door-post, knitting, and saw nothing.

Defarge got upon the box, and gave the word "To the Barrier!" The postilion cracked his whip, and they clattered away under the feeble over-swinging lamps.

Under the over-swinging lamps—swinging ever brighter in the better streets, and ever dimmer in the worse—and by lighted shops, gay crowds, illuminated coffee-houses, and theatre-doors, to one of the city gates. Soldiers with lanterns, at the guard-house there. "Your papers, travellers!" "See here then, Monsieur the Officer," said Defarge, getting down, and taking him gravely apart, "these are the papers of monsieur inside, with the white head. They were consigned to me, with him, at the—" He dropped his voice, there was a flutter among the military lanterns, and one of them being handed into the coach by an arm in uniform, the eyes connected with the arm looked, not an every day or an every night look, at monsieur with the white head. "It is well. Forward!" from the uniform. "Adieu!" from Defarge. And so, under a short grove of feebler and feebler over-swinging lamps, out under the great grove of stars.

Beneath that arch of unmoved and eternal lights; some, so remote from this little earth that the learned tell us it is doubtful whether their rays have even yet discovered it, as a point in space where anything is suffered or done: the shadows of the night were broad and black. All through the cold and restless interval, until dawn, they once more whispered in the ears of Mr. Jarvis Lorry—sitting opposite the buried man who had been dug out, and wondering what subtle powers were for ever lost to him, and what were capable of restoration—the old inquiry:

"I hope you care to be recalled to life?"

And the old answer:

"I can't say."

Book The Second—The Golden Thread

I. FIVE YEARS LATER

Tellson's Bank by Temple Bar was an old-fashioned place, even in the year one thousand seven hundred and eighty. It was very small, very dark, very ugly, very incommodious. It was an old-fashioned place, moreover, in the moral attribute that the partners in the House were proud of its smallness, proud of its darkness, proud of its ugliness, proud of its incommodiousness. They were even boastful of its eminence in those particulars, and were fired by an express conviction that, if it were less objectionable, it would be less respectable. This was no passive belief, but an active weapon which they flashed at more convenient places of business. Tellson's (they said) wanted no elbow-room, Tellson's wanted no light, Tellson's wanted no embellishment. Noakes and Co.'s might, or Snooks Brothers' might; but Tellson's, thank Heaven!—

Any one of these partners would have disinherited his son on the question of rebuilding Tellson's. In this respect the House was much on a par with the Country; which did very often disinherit its sons for suggesting improvements in laws and customs that had long been highly objectionable, but were only the more respectable.

Thus it had come to pass, that Tellson's was the triumphant perfection of inconvenience. After bursting open a door of idiotic obstinacy with a weak rattle in its throat, you fell into Tellson's down two steps, and came to your senses in a miserable little shop, with two little counters, where the oldest of men made your cheque shake as if the wind rustled it, while they examined the signature by the dingiest of windows, which were always under a shower-bath of mud from Fleet-street, and which were made the dingier by their own iron bars proper, and the heavy shadow of Temple Bar. If your business necessitated your seeing "the House," you were put into a species of Condemned Hold at the back, where you meditated on a misspent life, until the House came with its hands in its pockets, and you could hardly blink at it in the dismal twilight. Your money came out of, or went into, wormy old wooden drawers, particles of which flew up your nose and down your throat when they were opened and shut. Your bank-notes had a musty odour, as if they were fast decomposing into rags again. Your plate was stowed away among the neighbouring cesspools, and evil communications corrupted its good polish in a day or two. Your deeds got into extemporised strong-rooms made of kitchens and sculleries, and fretted all the fat out of their parchments into the banking-house air. Your lighter boxes of family papers went up-stairs into a Barmecide room, that always had a great dining-table in it and never had a dinner, and where, even in the year one thousand seven hundred and eighty, the first letters written to you by your old love, or by your little children, were but newly released from the horror of being ogled through the windows, by the heads exposed on Temple Bar with an insensate brutality and ferocity worthy of Abyssinia or Ashantee.

But indeed, at that time, putting to death was a recipe much in vogue with all trades and professions, and not least of all with Tellson's. Death is Nature's remedy for all things, and why not Legislation's? Accordingly, the forger was put to Death; the utterer of a bad note was put to Death; the unlawful opener of a letter was put to Death; the purloiner of forty shillings and sixpence was put to Death; the holder of a horse at Tellson's door, who made off with it, was put to Death; the coiner of a bad shilling was put to Death; the sounders of three-fourths of the notes in the whole gamut of Crime, were put to Death. Not that it did the least good in the way of prevention—it might almost have been worth remarking that the fact was exactly the reverse—but, it cleared off (as to this world) the trouble of each particular case, and left nothing else connected with it to be looked after. Thus, Tellson's, in its day, like greater places of business, its contemporaries, had taken so many lives, that, if the heads laid low before it had been ranged on Temple Bar instead of being privately disposed of, they would probably have excluded what little light the ground floor had, in a rather significant manner.

Cramped in all kinds of dun cupboards and hutches at Tellson's, the oldest of men carried on the business gravely. When they took a young man into Tellson's London house, they hid him somewhere till he was old. They kept him in a dark place, like a cheese, until he had the full Tellson flavour and blue-mould upon him. Then only was he permitted to be seen, spectacularly poring over large books, and casting his breeches and gaiters into the general weight of the establishment.

Outside Tellson's—never by any means in it, unless called in—was an odd-job-man, an occasional porter and messenger, who served as the live sign of the house. He was never absent during business hours, unless upon an errand, and then he was represented by his son: a grisly urchin of twelve, who was his express image. People understood that Tellson's, in a stately way, tolerated the odd-job-man. The house had always tolerated some person in that capacity, and time and tide had drifted this person to the post. His surname was Cruncher, and on the youthful occasion of his renouncing by proxy the works of darkness, in the easterly parish church of Hounsditch, he had received the added appellation of Jerry.

The scene was Mr. Cruncher's private lodging in Hanging-sword-alley, Whitefriars: the time, half-past seven of the clock on a windy March morning, Anno Domini seventeen hundred and eighty. (Mr. Cruncher himself always spoke of the year of our Lord as Anna Dominoes: apparently under the impression that the Christian era dated from the invention of a popular game, by a lady who had bestowed her name upon it.)

Mr. Cruncher's apartments were not in a savoury neighbourhood, and were but two in number, even if a closet with a single pane of glass in it might be counted as one. But they were very decently kept. Early as it was, on the windy March morning, the room in which he lay abed was already scrubbed throughout; and between the cups and saucers arranged for breakfast, and the lumbering deal table, a very clean white cloth was spread.

Mr. Cruncher reposed under a patchwork counterpane, like a Harlequin at home. At first, he slept heavily, but, by degrees, began to roll and surge in bed, until he rose above the surface, with his spiky hair looking as if it must tear the sheets to ribbons. At which juncture, he exclaimed, in a voice of dire exasperation:

"Bust me, if she ain't at it agin!"

A woman of orderly and industrious appearance rose from her knees in a corner, with sufficient haste and trepidation to show that she was the person referred to.

"What!" said Mr. Cruncher, looking out of bed for a boot. "You're at it agin, are you?"

After hailing the mom with this second salutation, he threw a boot at the woman as a third. It was a very muddy boot, and may introduce the odd circumstance connected with Mr. Cruncher's domestic economy, that, whereas he often came home after banking hours with clean boots, he often got up next morning to find the same boots covered with clay.

"What," said Mr. Cruncher, varying his apostrophe after missing his mark—"what are you up to, Aggerawayter?"

"I was only saying my prayers."

"Saying your prayers! You're a nice woman! What do you mean by flopping yourself down and praying agin me?"

"I was not praying against you; I was praying for you."

"You weren't. And if you were, I won't be took the liberty with. Here! your mother's a nice woman, young Jerry, going a praying agin your father's prosperity. You've got a dutiful mother, you have, my son. You've got a religious mother, you have, my boy: going and flopping herself down, and praying that the bread-and-butter may be snatched out of the mouth of her only child."

Master Cruncher (who was in his shirt) took this very ill, and, turning to his mother, strongly deprecated any praying away of his personal board.

"And what do you suppose, you conceited female," said Mr. Cruncher, with unconscious inconsistency, "that the worth of *your* prayers may be? Name the price that you put *your* prayers at!"

"They only come from the heart, Jerry. They are worth no more than that."

"Worth no more than that," repeated Mr. Cruncher. "They ain't worth much, then. Whether or no, I won't be prayed agin, I tell you. I can't afford it. I'm not a going to be made unlucky by *your* sneaking. If you must go flopping yourself down, flop in favour of your husband and child, and not in opposition to 'em. If I had had any but a unnat'ral wife, and this poor boy had had any but a unnat'ral mother, I might have made some money last week instead of being counter-prayed and countermined and religiously circumwented into the worst of luck. B-u-u-ust me!" said Mr. Cruncher, who all this time had been putting on his clothes, "if I ain't, what with piety and one blowed thing and another, been choused this last week into as bad luck as ever a poor devil of a honest tradesman met with! Young Jerry, dress yourself, my boy, and while I clean my boots keep a eye upon your mother now and then, and if you see any signs of more flopping, give me a call. For, I tell you," here he addressed his wife once more, "I won't be gone agin, in this manner. I am as rickety as a hackney-coach, I'm as sleepy as laudanum, my lines is strained to that degree that I shouldn't know, if it wasn't for the pain in 'em, which was me and which somebody else, yet I'm none the better for it in pocket; and it's my suspicion that you've been at it from morning to night to prevent me from being the better for it in pocket, and I won't put up with it, Aggerawayter, and what do you say now!"

Growling, in addition, such phrases as "Ah! yes! You're religious, too. You wouldn't put yourself in opposition to the interests of your husband and child, would you? Not you!" and throwing off other sarcastic sparks from the whirling grindstone of his indignation, Mr. Cruncher betook himself to his boot-cleaning and his general preparation for business. In the meantime, his son, whose head was garnished with tenderer spikes, and whose young eyes stood close by one another, as his father's did, kept the required watch upon his mother. He greatly disturbed that poor woman at intervals, by darting out of his sleeping closet, where he made his toilet, with a suppressed cry of "You are going to flop, mother.—Halloa, father!" and, after raising this fictitious alarm, darting in again with an undutiful grin.

Mr. Cruncher's temper was not at all improved when he came to his breakfast. He resented Mrs. Cruncher's saying grace with particular animosity.

"Now, Aggerawayter! What are you up to? At it again?"

His wife explained that she had merely "asked a blessing."

"Don't do it!" said Mr. Crunches looking about, as if he rather expected to see the loaf disappear under the efficacy of his wife's petitions. "I ain't a going to be blest out of house and home. I won't have my wittles blest off my table. Keep still!"

Exceedingly red-eyed and grim, as if he had been up all night at a party which had taken anything but a convivial turn, Jerry Cruncher worried his breakfast rather than ate it, growling over it like any four-footed inmate of a menagerie. Towards nine o'clock he smoothed his ruffled aspect, and, presenting as respectable and business-like an exterior as he could overlay his natural self with, issued forth to the occupation of the day.

It could scarcely be called a trade, in spite of his favourite description of himself as "a honest tradesman." His stock consisted of a wooden stool, made out of a broken-backed chair cut down, which stool, young Jerry, walking at his father's side, carried every morning to beneath the banking-house window that was nearest Temple Bar: where, with the addition of the first handful of straw that could be gleaned from any passing vehicle to keep the cold and wet from the odd-job-man's feet, it formed the encampment for the day. On this post of his, Mr. Cruncher was as well known to Fleet-street and the Temple, as the Bar itself,—and was almost as in-looking.

Encamped at a quarter before nine, in good time to touch his three- cornered hat to the oldest of men as they passed in to Tellson's, Jerry took up his station on this windy

March morning, with young Jerry standing by him, when not engaged in making forays through the Bar, to inflict bodily and mental injuries of an acute description on passing boys who were small enough for his amiable purpose. Father and son, extremely like each other, looking silently on at the morning traffic in Fleet-street, with their two heads as near to one another as the two eyes of each were, bore a considerable resemblance to a pair of monkeys. The resemblance was not lessened by the accidental circumstance, that the mature Jerry bit and spat out straw, while the twinkling eyes of the youthful Jerry were as restlessly watchful of him as of everything else in Fleet-street.

The head of one of the regular indoor messengers attached to Tellson's establishment was put through the door, and the word was given:

"Porter wanted!"

"Hooray, father! Here's an early job to begin with!"

Having thus given his parent God speed, young Jerry seated himself on the stool, entered on his reversionary interest in the straw his father had been chewing, and cogitated.

"Al-ways rusty! His fingers is al-ways rusty!" muttered young Jerry. "Where does my father get all that iron rust from? He don't get no iron rust here!"

II. A SIGHT

"You know the Old Bailey, well, no doubt?" said one of the oldest of clerks to Jerry the messenger.

"Ye-es, sir," returned Jerry, in something of a dogged manner. "I *do* know the Bailey."

"Just so. And you know Mr. Lorry."

"I know Mr. Lorry, sir, much better than I know the Bailey. Much better," said Jerry, not unlike a reluctant witness at the establishment in question, "than I, as a honest tradesman, wish to know the Bailey."

"Very well. Find the door where the witnesses go in, and show the door-keeper this note for Mr. Lorry. He will then let you in."

"Into the court, sir?"

"Into the court."

Mr. Cruncher's eyes seemed to get a little closer to one another, and to interchange the inquiry, "What do you think of this?"

"Am I to wait in the court, sir?" he asked, as the result of that conference.

"I am going to tell you. The door-keeper will pass the note to Mr. Lorry, and do you make any gesture that will attract Mr. Lorry's attention, and show him where you stand. Then what you have to do, is, to remain there until he wants you."

"Is that all, sir?"

"That's all. He wishes to have a messenger at hand. This is to tell him you are there."

As the ancient clerk deliberately folded and superscribed the note, Mr. Cruncher, after surveying him in silence until he came to the blotting-paper stage, remarked:

"I suppose they'll be trying Forgeries this morning?"

"Treason!"

"That's quartering," said Jerry. "Barbarous!"

"It is the law," remarked the ancient clerk, turning his surprised spectacles upon him. "It is the law."

"It's hard in the law to spile a man, I think. Ifs hard enough to kill him, but it's wery hard to spile him, sir."

"Not at all," retained the ancient clerk. "Speak well of the law. Take care of your chest and voice, my good friend, and leave the law to take care of itself. I give you that advice."

"It's the damp, sir, what settles on my chest and voice," said Jerry. "I leave you to judge what a damp way of earning a living mine is."

"Well, well," said the old clerk; "we all have our various ways of gaining a livelihood. Some of us have damp ways, and some of us have dry ways. Here is the letter. Go along."

Jerry took the letter, and, remarking to himself with less internal deference than he made an outward show of, "You are a lean old one, too," made his bow, informed his son, in passing, of his destination, and went his way.

They hanged at Tyburn, in those days, so the street outside Newgate had not obtained one infamous notoriety that has since attached to it. But, the gaol was a vile place, in which most kinds of debauchery and villainy were practised, and where dire diseases were bred, that came into court with the prisoners, and sometimes rushed straight from the dock at my Lord Chief Justice himself, and pulled him off the bench. It had more than once happened, that the Judge in the black cap pronounced his own doom as certainly as the prisoner's, and even died before him. For the rest, the Old Bailey was famous as a kind of deadly inn-yard, from which pale travellers set out continually, in carts and coaches, on a violent passage into the other world: traversing some two miles and a half of public street and road, and shaming few good citizens, if any. So powerful is use, and so desirable to be good use in the beginning. It was famous, too, for the pillory, a wise old institution, that inflicted a punishment of which no one could foresee the extent; also, for the whipping-post, another dear old institution, very humanising and softening to behold in action; also, for extensive transactions in blood-money, another fragment of ancestral wisdom, systematically leading to the most frightful mercenary crimes that could be committed under Heaven. Altogether, the Old Bailey, at that date, was a choice illustration of the precept, that "Whatever is is right;" an aphorism that would be as final as it is lazy, did it not include the troublesome consequence, that nothing that ever was, was wrong.

Making his way through the tainted crowd, dispersed up and down this hideous scene of action, with the skill of a man accustomed to make his way quietly, the messenger found out the door he sought, and handed in his letter through a trap in it. For, people then paid to see the play at the Old Bailey, just as they paid to see the play in Bedlam—only the former entertainment was much the dearer. Therefore, all the Old Bailey doors were well guarded—except, indeed, the social doors by which the criminals got there, and those were always left wide open.

After some delay and demur, the door grudgingly turned on its hinges a very little way, and allowed Mr. Jerry Cruncher to squeeze himself into court.

"What's on?" he asked, in a whisper, of the man he found himself next to.

"Nothing yet."

"What's coming on?"

"The Treason case."

"The quartering one, eh?"

"Ah!" returned the man, with a relish; "he'll be drawn on a hurdle to be half hanged, and then he'll be taken down and sliced before his own face, and then his inside will be taken out and burnt while he looks on, and then his head will be chopped off, and he'll be cut into quarters. That's the sentence."

"If he's found Guilty, you mean to say?" Jerry added, by way of proviso.

"Oh! they'll find him guilty," said the other. "Don't you be afraid of that."

Mr. Cruncher's attention was here diverted to the door-keeper, whom he saw making his way to Mr. Lorry, with the note in his hand. Mr. Lorry sat at a table, among the gentlemen in wigs: not far from a wigged gentleman, the prisoner's counsel, who had a great bundle of papers before him: and nearly opposite another wigged gentleman with his hands in his pockets, whose whole attention, when Mr. Cruncher looked at him then or afterwards, seemed to be concentrated on the ceiling of the court. After some gruff coughing and rubbing of his chin and signing with his hand, Jerry attracted the notice of Mr. Lorry, who had stood up to look for him, and who quietly nodded and sat down again.

"What's *he* got to do with the case?" asked the man he had spoken with.

"Blest if I know," said Jerry.

"What have *you* got to do with it, then, if a person may inquire?"

"Blest if I know that either," said Jerry.

The entrance of the Judge, and a consequent great stir and settling down in the court, stopped the dialogue. Presently, the dock became the central point of interest. Two gaolers, who had been standing there, went out, and the prisoner was brought in, and put to the bar.

Everybody present, except the one wigged gentleman who looked at the ceiling, stared at him. All the human breath in the place, rolled at him, like a sea, or a wind, or a fire. Eager faces strained round pillars and corners, to get a sight of him; spectators in back rows stood up, not to miss a hair of him; people on the floor of the court, laid their hands on the shoulders of the people before them, to help themselves, at anybody's cost, to a view of him—stood a-tiptoe, got upon ledges, stood upon next to nothing, to see every inch of him. Conspicuous among these latter, like an animated bit of the spiked wall of Newgate, Jerry stood: aiming at the prisoner the beery breath of a whet he had taken as he came along, and discharging it to mingle with the waves of other beer, and gin, and tea, and coffee, and what not, that flowed at him, and already broke upon the great windows behind him in an impure mist and rain.

The object of all this staring and blaring, was a young man of about five-and-twenty, well-grown and well-looking, with a sunburnt cheek and a dark eye. His condition was that of a young gentleman. He was plainly dressed in black, or very dark grey, and his hair, which was long and dark, was gathered in a ribbon at the back of his neck; more to be out of his way than for ornament. As an emotion of the mind will express itself through any covering of the body, so the paleness which his situation engendered came through the brown upon his cheek, showing the soul to be stronger than the sun. He was otherwise quite self-possessed, bowed to the Judge, and stood quiet.

The sort of interest with which this man was stared and breathed at, was not a sort that elevated humanity. Had he stood in peril of a less horrible sentence—had there been a chance of any one of its savage details being spared—by just so much would he have lost in his fascination. The form that was to be doomed to be so shamefully mangled, was the sight; the immortal creature that was to be so butchered and torn asunder, yielded the sensation. Whatever gloss the various spectators put upon the interest, according to their several arts and powers of self-deceit, the interest was, at the root of it, Ogreish.

Silence in the court! Charles Darnay had yesterday pleaded Not Guilty to an indictment denouncing him (with infinite jingle and jangle) for that he was a false traitor to our serene, illustrious, excellent, and so forth, prince, our Lord the King, by reason of his having, on divers occasions, and by divers means and ways, assisted Lewis, the French King, in his wars against our said serene, illustrious, excellent, and so forth; that was to say, by coming and going, between the dominions of our said serene, illustrious, excellent, and so forth, and those of the said French Lewis, and wickedly, falsely, traitorously, and otherwise evil-adverbiously, revealing to the said French Lewis what forces our said serene, illustrious, excellent, and so forth, had in preparation to send to Canada and North America. This much, Jerry, with his head becoming more and more spiky as the law terms bristled it, made out with huge satisfaction, and so arrived circuitously at the understanding that the aforesaid, and over and over again aforesaid, Charles Darnay, stood there before him upon his trial; that the jury were swearing in; and that Mr. Attorney-General was making ready to speak.

The accused, who was (and who knew he was) being mentally hanged, beheaded, and quartered, by everybody there, neither flinched from the situation, nor assumed any theatrical air in it. He was quiet and attentive; watched the opening proceedings with a grave interest; and stood with his hands resting on the slab of wood before him, so composedly, that they had not displaced a leaf of the herbs with which it was strewn. The court was all bestrewn with herbs and sprinkled with vinegar, as a precaution against gaol air and gaol fever.

Over the prisoner's head there was a mirror, to throw the light down upon him. Crowds of the wicked and the wretched had been reflected in it, and had passed from its surface and this earth's together. Haunted in a most ghastly manner that abominable place would have been, if the glass could ever have rendered back its reflections, as the ocean is one day to give up its dead. Some passing thought of the infamy and disgrace for which it had been reserved, may have struck the prisoner's mind. Be that as it may, a change in his position making him conscious of a bar of light across his face, he looked up; and when he saw the glass his face flushed, and his right hand pushed the herbs away.

It happened, that the action turned his face to that side of the court which was on his left. About on a level with his eyes, there sat, in that corner of the Judge's bench, two persons upon whom his look immediately rested; so immediately, and so much to the changing of his aspect, that all the eyes that were turned upon him, turned to them.

The spectators saw in the two figures, a young lady of little more than twenty, and a gentleman who was evidently her father; a man of a very remarkable appearance in respect of the absolute whiteness of his hair, and a certain indescribable intensity of face: not of an active kind, but pondering and self-communing. When this expression was upon him, he looked as if he were old; but when it was stirred and broken up—as it was now, in a moment, on his speaking to his daughter—he became a handsome man, not past the prime of life.

His daughter had one of her hands drawn through his arm, as she sat by him, and the other pressed upon it. She had drawn close to him, in her dread of the scene, and in her pity for the prisoner. Her forehead had been strikingly expressive of an engrossing terror and compassion that saw nothing but the peril of the accused. This had been so very noticeable, so very powerfully and naturally shown, that starers who had had no pity for him were touched by her; and the whisper went about, "Who are they?"

Jerry, the messenger, who had made his own observations, in his own manner, and who had been sucking the rust off his fingers in his absorption, stretched his neck to hear who they were. The crowd about him had pressed and passed the inquiry on to the nearest attendant, and from him it had been more slowly pressed and passed back; at last it got to Jerry:

"Witnesses."

"For which side?"

"Against."

"Against what side?"

"The prisoner's."

The Judge, whose eyes had gone in the general direction, recalled them, leaned back in his seat, and looked steadily at the man whose life was in his hand, as Mr. Attorney-General rose to spin the rope, grind the axe, and hammer the nails into the scaffold.

III. A DISAPPOINTMENT

Mr. Attorney-General had to inform the jury, that the prisoner before them, though young in years, was old in the treasonable practices which claimed the forfeit of his life. That this correspondence with the public enemy was not a correspondence of to-day, or of yesterday, or even of last year, or of the year before. That, it was certain the prisoner had, for longer than that, been in the habit of passing and repassing between France and England, on secret business of which he could give no honest account. That, if it were in the nature of traitorous ways to thrive (which happily it never was), the real wickedness and guilt of his business might have remained undiscovered. That Providence, however, had put it into the heart of a person who was beyond fear and beyond reproach, to ferret out the nature of the prisoner's schemes, and, struck with horror, to disclose them to his Majesty's Chief Secretary of State and most honourable Privy Council. That, this patriot would be produced before them. That, his position and attitude were, on the whole, sublime. That, he had been the prisoner's friend, but, at once in an auspicious and an evil hour detecting his infamy, had resolved to immolate the traitor he could no longer cherish in his bosom, on the sacred altar of his country. That, if statues were decreed in Britain, as in ancient Greece and Rome, to public benefactors, this shining citizen would assuredly have had one. That, as they were not so decreed, he probably would not have one. That, Virtue, as had been observed by the poets (in many passages which he well knew the jury would have, word for word, at the tips of their tongues; whereat the jury's countenances displayed a guilty consciousness that they knew nothing about the passages), was in a manner contagious; more especially the bright virtue known as patriotism, or love of country. That, the lofty example of this immaculate and unimpeachable witness for the Crown, to refer to whom however unworthily was an honour, had communicated itself to the prisoner's servant, and had engendered in him a holy determination to examine his master's table-drawers and pockets, and secrete his papers. That, he (Mr. Attorney-General) was prepared to hear some disparagement attempted of this admirable servant; but that, in a general way, he preferred him to his (Mr. Attorney-General's) brothers and sisters, and honoured him more than his (Mr. Attorney-General's) father and mother. That, he called with confidence on the jury to come and do likewise. That, the evidence of these two witnesses, coupled with the documents of their discovering that would be produced, would show the prisoner to have been furnished with lists of his Majesty's forces, and of their disposition and preparation, both by sea and land, and would leave no doubt that he had habitually conveyed such information to a hostile power. That, these lists could not be proved to be in the prisoner's handwriting; but that it was all the same; that, indeed, it was rather the better for the prosecution, as showing the prisoner to be artful in his precautions. That, the proof would go back five years, and would show the prisoner already engaged in these pernicious missions, within a few weeks before the date of the very first action fought between the British troops and the Americans. That, for these reasons, the jury, being a loyal jury (as he knew they were), and being a responsible jury (as *they* knew they were), must positively find the prisoner Guilty, and make an end of him, whether they liked it or not. That, they never could lay their heads upon their pillows; that, they never could tolerate the idea of their wives laying their heads upon their pillows; that, they never could endure the notion of their children laying their heads upon their pillows; in short, that there never more could be, for them or theirs, any laying of heads upon pillows at all, unless the prisoner's head was taken off. That head Mr. Attorney-General concluded by demanding of them, in the name of everything he could think of with a round turn in it, and on the faith of his solemn asseveration that he already considered the prisoner as good as dead and gone.

When the Attorney-General ceased, a buzz arose in the court as if a cloud of great blue-flies were swarming about the prisoner, in anticipation of what he was soon to become. When toned down again, the unimpeachable patriot appeared in the witness-box.

Mr. Solicitor-General then, following his leader's lead, examined the patriot: John Barsad, gentleman, by name. The story of his pure soul was exactly what Mr.

Attorney-General had described it to be—perhaps, if it had a fault, a little too exactly. Having released his noble bosom of its burden, he would have modestly withdrawn himself, but that the wigged gentleman with the papers before him, sitting not far from Mr. Lorry, begged to ask him a few questions. The wigged gentleman sitting opposite, still looking at the ceiling of the court.

Had he ever been a spy himself? No, he scorned the base insinuation. What did he live upon? His property. Where was his property? He didn't precisely remember where it was. What was it? No business of anybody's. Had he inherited it? Yes, he had. From whom? Distant relation. Very distant? Rather. Ever been in prison? Certainly not. Never in a debtors' prison? Didn't see what that had to do with it. Never in a debtors' prison?—Come, once again. Never? Yes. How many times? Two or three times. Not five or six? Perhaps. Of what profession? Gentleman. Ever been kicked? Might have been. Frequently? No. Ever kicked downstairs? Decidedly not; once received a kick on the top of a staircase, and fell downstairs of his own accord. Kicked on that occasion for cheating at dice? Something to that effect was said by the intoxicated liar who committed the assault, but it was not true. Swear it was not true? Positively. Ever live by cheating at play? Never. Ever live by play? Not more than other gentlemen do. Ever borrow money of the prisoner? Yes. Ever pay him? No. Was not this intimacy with the prisoner, in reality a very slight one, forced upon the prisoner in coaches, inns, and packets? No. Sure he saw the prisoner with these lists? Certain. Knew no more about the lists? No. Had not procured them himself, for instance? No. Expect to get anything by this evidence? No. Not in regular government pay and employment, to lay traps? Oh dear no. Or to do anything? Oh dear no. Swear that? Over and over again. No motives but motives of sheer patriotism? None whatever.

The virtuous servant, Roger Cly, swore his way through the case at a great rate. He had taken service with the prisoner, in good faith and simplicity, four years ago. He had asked the prisoner, aboard the Calais packet, if he wanted a handy fellow, and the prisoner had engaged him. He had not asked the prisoner to take the handy fellow as an act of charity—never thought of such a thing. He began to have suspicions of the prisoner, and to keep an eye upon him, soon afterwards. In arranging his clothes, while travelling, he had seen similar lists to these in the prisoner's pockets, over and over again. He had taken these lists from the drawer of the prisoner's desk. He had not put them there first. He had seen the prisoner show these identical lists to French gentlemen at Calais, and similar lists to French gentlemen, both at Calais and Boulogne. He loved his country, and couldn't bear it, and had given information. He had never been suspected of stealing a silver tea-pot; he had been maligned respecting a mustard-pot, but it turned out to be only a plated one. He had known the last witness seven or eight years; that was merely a coincidence. He didn't call it a particularly curious coincidence; most coincidences were curious. Neither did he call it a curious coincidence that true patriotism was *his* only motive too. He was a true Briton, and hoped there were many like him.

The blue-flies buzzed again, and Mr. Attorney-General called Mr. Jarvis Lorry.

"Mr. Jarvis Lorry, are you a clerk in Tellson's bank?"

"I am."

"On a certain Friday night in November one thousand seven hundred and seventy-five, did business occasion you to travel between London and Dover by the mail?"

"It did."

"Were there any other passengers in the mail?"

"Two."

"Did they alight on the road in the course of the night?"

"They did."

"Mr. Lorry, look upon the prisoner. Was he one of those two passengers?"

"I cannot undertake to say that he was."

"Does he resemble either of these two passengers?"

"Both were so wrapped up, and the night was so dark, and we were all so reserved, that I cannot undertake to say even that."

"Mr. Lorry, look again upon the prisoner. Supposing him wrapped up as those two passengers were, is there anything in his bulk and stature to render it unlikely that he was one of them?"

"No."

"You will not swear, Mr. Lorry, that he was not one of them?"

"No."

"So at least you say he may have been one of them?"

"Yes. Except that I remember them both to have been—like myself—timorous of highwaymen, and the prisoner has not a timorous air."

"Did you ever see a counterfeit of timidity, Mr. Lorry?"

"I certainly have seen that."

"Mr. Lorry, look once more upon the prisoner. Have you seen him, to your certain knowledge, before?"

"I have."

"When?"

"I was returning from France a few days afterwards, and, at Calais, the prisoner came on board the packet-ship in which I returned, and made the voyage with me."

"At what hour did he come on board?"

"At a little after midnight."

"In the dead of the night. Was he the only passenger who came on board at that untimely hour?"

"He happened to be the only one."

"Never mind about 'happening,' Mr. Lorry. He was the only passenger who came on board in the dead of the night?"

"He was."

"Were you travelling alone, Mr. Lorry, or with any companion?"

"With two companions. A gentleman and lady. They are here."

"They are here. Had you any conversation with the prisoner?"

"Hardly any. The weather was stormy, and the passage long and rough, and I lay on a sofa, almost from shore to shore."

"Miss Manette!"

The young lady, to whom all eyes had been turned before, and were now turned again, stood up where she had sat. Her father rose with her, and kept her hand drawn through his arm.

"Miss Manette, look upon the prisoner."

To be confronted with such pity, and such earnest youth and beauty, was far more trying to the accused than to be confronted with all the crowd. Standing, as it were, apart with her on the edge of his grave, not all the staring curiosity that looked on, could, for the moment, nerve him to remain quite still. His hurried right hand parcelled out the herbs before him into imaginary beds of flowers in a garden; and his efforts to control and steady his breathing shook the lips from which the colour rushed to his heart. The buzz of the great flies was loud again.

"Miss Manette, have you seen the prisoner before?"

"Yes, sir."

"Where?"

"On board of the packet-ship just now referred to, sir, and on the same occasion."

"You are the young lady just now referred to?"

"O! most unhappily, I am!"

The plaintive tone of her compassion merged into the less musical voice of the Judge, as he said something fiercely: "Answer the questions put to you, and make no remark upon them."

"Miss Manette, had you any conversation with the prisoner on that passage across the Channel?"

"Yes, sir."

"Recall it."

In the midst of a profound stillness, she faintly began: "When the gentleman came on board—"

"Do you mean the prisoner?" inquired the Judge, knitting his brows.

"Yes, my Lord."

"Then say the prisoner."

"When the prisoner came on board, he noticed that my father," turning her eyes lovingly to him as he stood beside her, "was much fatigued and in a very weak state of health. My father was so reduced that I was afraid to take him out of the air, and I had made a bed for him on the deck near the cabin steps, and I sat on the deck at his side to take care of him. There were no other passengers that night, but we four. The prisoner was so good as to beg permission to advise me how I could shelter my father from the wind and weather, better than I had done. I had not known how to do it well, not understanding how the wind would set when we were out of the harbour. He did it for me. He expressed great gentleness and kindness for my father's state, and I am sure he felt it. That was the manner of our beginning to speak together."

"Let me interrupt you for a moment. Had he come on board alone?"

"No."

"How many were with him?"

"Two French gentlemen."

"Had they conferred together?"

"They had conferred together until the last moment, when it was necessary for the French gentlemen to be landed in their boat."

"Had any papers been handed about among them, similar to these lists?"

"Some papers had been handed about among them, but I don't know what papers."

"Like these in shape and size?"

"Possibly, but indeed I don't know, although they stood whispering very near to me: because they stood at the top of the cabin steps to have the light of the lamp that was hanging there; it was a dull lamp, and they spoke very low, and I did not hear what they said, and saw only that they looked at papers."

"Now, to the prisoner's conversation, Miss Manette."

"The prisoner was as open in his confidence with me—which arose out of my helpless situation—as he was kind, and good, and useful to my father. I hope," bursting into tears, "I may not repay him by doing him harm to-day."

Buzzing from the blue-flies.

"Miss Manette, if the prisoner does not perfectly understand that you give the evidence which it is your duty to give—which you must give—and which you cannot escape from giving—with great unwillingness, he is the only person present in that condition. Please to go on."

"He told me that he was travelling on business of a delicate and difficult nature, which might get people into trouble, and that he was therefore travelling under an assumed name. He said that this business had, within a few days, taken him to France, and might, at intervals, take him backwards and forwards between France and England for a long time to come."

"Did he say anything about America, Miss Manette? Be particular."

"He tried to explain to me how that quarrel had arisen, and he said that, so far as he could judge, it was a wrong and foolish one on England's part. He added, in a jesting way, that perhaps George Washington might gain almost as great a name in history as George the Third. But there was no harm in his way of saying this: it was said laughingly, and to beguile the time."

Any strongly marked expression of face on the part of a chief actor in a scene of great interest to whom many eyes are directed, will be unconsciously imitated by the spectators. Her forehead was painfully anxious and intent as she gave this evidence, and, in the pauses when she stopped for the Judge to write it down, watched its effect upon the counsel for and against. Among the lookers-on there was the same expression in all quarters of the court; insomuch, that a great majority of the foreheads there, might have been mirrors reflecting the witness, when the Judge looked up from his notes to glare at that tremendous heresy about George Washington.

Mr. Attorney-General now signified to my Lord, that he deemed it necessary, as a matter of precaution and form, to call the young lady's father, Doctor Manette. Who was called accordingly.

"Doctor Manette, look upon the prisoner. Have you ever seen him before?"

"Once. When he called at my lodgings in London. Some three years, or three years and a half ago."

"Can you identify him as your fellow-passenger on board the packet, or speak to his conversation with your daughter?"

"Sir, I can do neither."

"Is there any particular and special reason for your being unable to do either?"

He answered, in a low voice, "There is."

"Has it been your misfortune to undergo a long imprisonment, without trial, or even accusation, in your native country, Doctor Manette?"

He answered, in a tone that went to every heart, "A long imprisonment."

"Were you newly released on the occasion in question?"

"They tell me so."

"Have you no remembrance of the occasion?"

"None. My mind is a blank, from some time—I cannot even say what time—when I employed myself, in my captivity, in making shoes, to the time when I found myself living in London with my dear daughter here. She had become familiar to me, when a gracious God restored my faculties; but, I am quite unable even to say how she had become familiar. I have no remembrance of the process."

Mr. Attorney-General sat down, and the father and daughter sat down together.

A singular circumstance then arose in the case. The object in hand being to show that the prisoner went down, with some fellow-plotter untracked, in the Dover mail on that Friday night in November five years ago, and got out of the mail in the night, as a blind, at a place where he did not remain, but from which he travelled back some dozen miles or more, to a garrison and dockyard, and there collected information; a witness was called to identify him as having been at the precise time required, in the coffee-room of an hotel in that garrison-and-dockyard town, waiting for another person. The prisoner's counsel was cross-examining this witness with no result, except that he had never seen the prisoner on any other occasion, when the wigged gentleman who had all this time been looking at the ceiling of the court, wrote a word or two on a little piece of paper, screwed it up, and tossed it to him. Opening this piece of paper in the next pause, the counsel looked with great attention and curiosity at the prisoner.

"You say again you are quite sure that it was the prisoner?"

The witness was quite sure.

"Did you ever see anybody very like the prisoner?"

Not so like (the witness said) as that he could be mistaken.

"Look well upon that gentleman, my learned friend there," pointing to him who had tossed the paper over, "and then look well upon the prisoner. How say you? Are they very like each other?"

Allowing for my learned friend's appearance being careless and slovenly if not debauched, they were sufficiently like each other to surprise, not only the witness, but everybody present, when they were thus brought into comparison. My Lord being prayed to bid my learned friend lay aside his wig, and giving no very gracious consent, the likeness became much more remarkable. My Lord inquired of Mr. Stryver (the prisoner's counsel), whether they were next to try Mr. Carton (name of my learned friend) for treason? But, Mr. Stryver replied to my Lord, no; but he would ask the witness to tell him whether what happened once, might happen twice; whether he would have been so confident if he had seen this illustration of his rashness sooner, whether he would be so confident, having seen it; and more. The upshot of which, was, to smash this witness like a crockery vessel, and shiver his part of the case to useless lumber.

Mr. Cruncher had by this time taken quite a lunch of rust off his fingers in his following of the evidence. He had now to attend while Mr. Stryver fitted the prisoner's case on the jury, like a compact suit of clothes; showing them how the patriot, Barsad, was a hired spy and traitor, an unblushing trafficker in blood, and one of the greatest scoundrels upon earth since accursed Judas—which he certainly did look rather like. How the virtuous servant, Cly, was his friend and partner, and was worthy to be; how the watchful eyes of those forgers and false swearers had rested on the prisoner as a victim, because some family affairs in France, he being of French extraction, did require his making those passages across the Channel—though what those affairs were, a consideration for others who were near and dear to him, forbade him, even for his life, to disclose. How the evidence that had been warped and wrested from the young lady, whose anguish in giving it they had witnessed, came to nothing, involving the mere little innocent gallantries and politenesses likely to pass between any young gentleman and young lady so thrown together;—with the exception of that reference to George Washington, which was altogether too extravagant and impossible to be regarded in any other light than as a monstrous joke. How it would be a weakness in the government to break down in this attempt to practise for popularity on the lowest national antipathies and fears, and therefore Mr. Attorney-General had made the most of it; how, nevertheless, it rested upon nothing, save that vile and infamous character of evidence too often disfiguring such cases, and of which the State Trials of this country were full. But, there my Lord interposed (with as grave a face as if it had not been true), saying that he could not sit upon that Bench and suffer those allusions.

Mr. Stryver then called his few witnesses, and Mr. Cruncher had next to attend while Mr. Attorney-General turned the whole suit of clothes Mr. Stryver had fitted on the jury, inside out; showing how Barsad and Cly were even a hundred times better than he had thought them, and the prisoner a hundred times worse. Lastly, came my Lord himself, turning the suit of clothes, now inside out, now outside in, but on the whole decidedly trimming and shaping them into grave-clothes for the prisoner.

And now, the jury turned to consider, and the great flies swarmed again.

Mr. Carton, who had so long sat looking at the ceiling of the court, changed neither his place nor his attitude, even in this excitement. While his teamed friend, Mr. Stryver, massing his papers before him, whispered with those who sat near, and from time to time glanced anxiously at the jury; while all the spectators moved more or less, and grouped themselves anew; while even my Lord himself arose from his seat, and slowly paced up and down his platform, not unattended by a suspicion in the minds of the audience that his state was feverish; this one man sat leaning back, with his torn gown half off him, his untidy wig put on just as it had happened to fight on his head after its removal, his hands in his pockets, and his eyes on the ceiling as they had been all day. Something especially reckless in his demeanour, not only gave him a disreputable look, but so diminished the strong resemblance he undoubtedly bore to the prisoner (which his momentary earnestness, when they were compared together, had strengthened), that many of the lookers-on, taking note of him now, said to one another they would hardly have thought the two were so alike. Mr. Cruncher made the observation to his next neighbour, and added, "I'd hold half a guinea that *he* don't get no law-work to do. Don't look like the sort of one to get any, do he?"

Yet, this Mr. Carton took in more of the details of the scene than he appeared to take in; for now, when Miss Manette's head dropped upon her father's breast, he was the first to see it, and to say audibly: "Officer! look to that young lady. Help the gentleman to take her out. Don't you see she will fall!"

There was much commiseration for her as she was removed, and much sympathy with her father. It had evidently been a great distress to him, to have the days of his imprisonment recalled. He had shown strong internal agitation when he was questioned, and that pondering or brooding look which made him old, had been upon him, like a heavy cloud, ever since. As he passed out, the jury, who had turned back and paused a moment, spoke, through their foreman.

They were not agreed, and wished to retire. My Lord (perhaps with George Washington on his mind) showed some surprise that they were not agreed, but signified his pleasure that they should retire under watch and ward, and retired himself. The trial had lasted all day, and the lamps in the court were now being lighted. It began to be rumoured that the jury would be out a long while. The spectators dropped off to get refreshment, and the prisoner withdrew to the back of the dock, and sat down.

Mr. Lorry, who had gone out when the young lady and her father went out, now reappeared, and beckoned to Jerry: who, in the slackened interest, could easily get near him.

"Jerry, if you wish to take something to eat, you can. But, keep in the way. You will be sure to hear when the jury come in. Don't be a moment behind them, for I want you to take the verdict back to the bank. You are the quickest messenger I know, and will get to Temple Bar long before I can."

Jerry had just enough forehead to knuckle, and he knuckled it in acknowledgment of this communication and a shilling. Mr. Carton came up at the moment, and touched Mr. Lorry on the arm.

"How is the young lady?"

"She is greatly distressed; but her father is comforting her, and she feels the better for being out of court."

"I'll tell the prisoner so. It won't do for a respectable bank gentleman like you, to be seen speaking to him publicly, you know."

Mr. Lorry reddened as if he were conscious of having debated the point in his mind, and Mr. Carton made his way to the outside of the bar. The way out of court lay in that direction, and Jerry followed him, all eyes, ears, and spikes.

"Mr. Darnay!"

The prisoner came forward directly.

"You will naturally be anxious to hear of the witness, Miss Manette. She will do very well. You have seen the worst of her agitation."

"I am deeply sorry to have been the cause of it. Could you tell her so for me, with my fervent acknowledgments?"

"Yes, I could. I will, if you ask it."

Mr. Carton's manner was so careless as to be almost insolent. He stood, half turned from the prisoner, lounging with his elbow against the bar.

"I do ask it. Accept my cordial thanks."

"What," said Carton, still only half turned towards him, "do you expect, Mr. Darnay?"

"The worst."

"It's the wisest thing to expect, and the likeliest. But I think their withdrawing is in your favour."

Loitering on the way out of court not being allowed, Jerry heard no more: but left them—so like each other in feature, so unlike each other in manner—standing side by side, both reflected in the glass above them.

An hour and a half limped heavily away in the thief-and-rascal crowded passages below, even though assisted off with mutton pies and ale. The hoarse messenger, uncomfortably seated on a form after taking that refection, had dropped into a doze, when a loud murmur and a rapid tide of people setting up the stairs that led to the court, carried him along with them.

"Jerry! Jerry!" Mr. Lorry was already calling at the door when he got there.

"Here, sir! It's a fight to get back again. Here I am, sir!"

Mr. Lorry handed him a paper through the throng. "Quick! Have you got it?"

"Yes, sir."

Hastily written on the paper was the word "AQUITTED."

"If you had sent the message, 'Recalled to Life,' again," muttered Jerry, as he turned, "I should have known what you meant, this time."

He had no opportunity of saying, or so much as thinking, anything else, until he was clear of the Old Bailey; for, the crowd came pouring out with a vehemence that nearly took him off his legs, and a loud buzz swept into the street as if the baffled blue-flies were dispersing in search of other carrion.

IV. CONGRATULATORY

From the dimly-lighted passages of the court, the last sediment of the human stew that had been boiling there all day, was straining off, when Doctor Manette, Lucie Manette, his daughter, Mr. Lorry, the solicitor for the defence, and its counsel, Mr. Stryver, stood gathered round Mr. Charles Darnay—just released—congratulating him on his escape from death.

It would have been difficult by a far brighter light, to recognise in Doctor Manette, intellectual of face and upright of bearing, the shoemaker of the garret in Paris. Yet, no one could have looked at him twice, without looking again: even though the opportunity of observation had not extended to the mournful cadence of his low grave voice, and to the abstraction that overclouded him fitfully, without any apparent reason. While one external cause, and that a reference to his long lingering agony, would always—as on the trial—evoke this condition from the depths of his soul, it was also in its nature to arise of itself, and to draw a gloom over him, as incomprehensible to those unacquainted with his story as if they had seen the shadow of the actual Bastille thrown upon him by a summer sun, when the substance was three hundred miles away.

Only his daughter had the power of charming this black brooding from his mind. She was the golden thread that united him to a Past beyond his misery, and to a Present beyond his misery: and the sound of her voice, the light of her face, the touch of her hand, had a strong beneficial influence with him almost always. Not absolutely always, for she could recall some occasions on which her power had failed; but they were few and slight, and she believed them over.

Mr. Darnay had kissed her hand fervently and gratefully, and had turned to Mr. Stryver, whom he warmly thanked. Mr. Stryver, a man of little more than thirty, but looking twenty years older than he was, stout, loud, red, bluff, and free from any drawback of delicacy, had a pushing way of shouldering himself (morally and physically) into companies and conversations, that argued well for his shouldering his way up in life.

He still had his wig and gown on, and he said, squaring himself at his late client to that degree that he squeezed the innocent Mr. Lorry clean out of the group: "I am glad to have brought you off with honour, Mr. Darnay. It was an infamous prosecution, grossly infamous; but not the less likely to succeed on that account."

"You have laid me under an obligation to you for life—in two senses," said his late client, taking his hand.

"I have done my best for you, Mr. Darnay; and my best is as good as another man's, I believe."

It clearly being incumbent on some one to say, "Much better," Mr. Lorry said it; perhaps not quite disinterestedly, but with the interested object of squeezing himself back again.

"You think so?" said Mr. Stryver. "Well! you have been present all day, and you ought to know. You are a man of business, too."

"And as such," quoth Mr. Lorry, whom the counsel learned in the law had now shouldered back into the group, just as he had previously shouldered him out of it—"as such I will appeal to Doctor Manette, to break up this conference and order us all to our homes. Miss Lucie looks ill, Mr. Darnay has had a terrible day, we are worn out."

"Speak for yourself, Mr. Lorry," said Stryver; "I have a night's work to do yet. Speak for yourself."

"I speak for myself," answered Mr. Lorry, "and for Mr. Darnay, and for Miss Lucie, and—Miss Lucie, do you not think I may speak for us all?" He asked her the question pointedly, and with a glance at her father.

His face had become frozen, as it were, in a very curious look at Darnay: an intent look, deepening into a frown of dislike and distrust, not even unmixed with fear. With this strange expression on him his thoughts had wandered away.

"My father," said Lucie, softly laying her hand on his.

He slowly shook the shadow off, and turned to her.

"Shall we go home, my father?"

With a long breath, he answered "Yes."

The friends of the acquitted prisoner had dispersed, under the impression—which he himself had originated—that he would not be released that night. The lights were nearly all extinguished in the passages, the iron gates were being closed with a jar and a rattle, and the dismal place was deserted until to-morrow morning's interest of gallows, pillory, whipping-post, and branding-iron, should repeople it. Walking between her father and Mr. Darnay, Lucie Manette passed into the open air. A hackney-coach was called, and the father and daughter departed in it.

Mr. Stryver had left them in the passages, to shoulder his way back to the robing-room. Another person, who had not joined the group, or interchanged a word with any one of them, but who had been leaning against the wall where its shadow was darkest, had silently strolled out after the rest, and had looked on until the coach drove away. He now stepped up to where Mr. Lorry and Mr. Darnay stood upon the pavement.

"So, Mr. Lorry! Men of business may speak to Mr. Darnay now?"

Nobody had made any acknowledgment of Mr. Carton's part in the day's proceedings; nobody had known of it. He was unrobed, and was none the better for it in appearance.

"If you knew what a conflict goes on in the business mind, when the business mind is divided between good-natured impulse and business appearances, you would be amused, Mr. Darnay."

Mr. Lorry reddened, and said, warmly, "You have mentioned that before, sir. We men of business, who serve a House, are not our own masters. We have to think of the House more than ourselves."

"*I* know, *I* know," rejoined Mr. Carton, carelessly. "Don't be nettled, Mr. Lorry. You are as good as another, I have no doubt: better, I dare say."

"And indeed, sir," pursued Mr. Lorry, not minding him, "I really don't know what you have to do with the matter. If you'll excuse me, as very much your elder, for saying so, I really don't know that it is your business."

"Business! Bless you, *I* have no business," said Mr. Carton.

"It is a pity you have not, sir."

"I think so, too."

"If you had," pursued Mr. Lorry, "perhaps you would attend to it."

"Lord love you, no!—I shouldn't," said Mr. Carton.

"Well, sir!" cried Mr. Lorry, thoroughly heated by his indifference, "business is a very good thing, and a very respectable thing. And, sir, if business imposes its restraints and its silences and impediments, Mr. Darnay as a young gentleman of generosity knows how to make allowance for that circumstance. Mr. Darnay, good night, God bless you, sir! I hope you have been this day preserved for a prosperous and happy life.—Chair there!"

Perhaps a little angry with himself, as well as with the barrister, Mr. Lorry bustled into the chair, and was carried off to Tellson's. Carton, who smelt of port wine, and did not appear to be quite sober, laughed then, and turned to Darnay:

"This is a strange chance that throws you and me together. This must be a strange night to you, standing alone here with your counterpart on these street stones?"

"I hardly seem yet," returned Charles Darnay, "to belong to this world again."

"I don't wonder at it; it's not so long since you were pretty far advanced on your way to another. You speak faintly."

"I begin to think I *am* faint."

"Then why the devil don't you dine? I dined, myself, while those numskulls were deliberating which world you should belong to—this, or some other. Let me show you the nearest tavern to dine well at."

Drawing his arm through his own, he took him down Ludgate-hill to Fleet-street, and so, up a covered way, into a tavern. Here, they were shown into a little room, where Charles Darnay was soon recruiting his strength with a good plain dinner and good wine: while Carton sat opposite to him at the same table, with his separate bottle of port before him, and his fully half-insolent manner upon him.

"Do you feel, yet, that you belong to this terrestrial scheme again, Mr. Darnay?"

"I am frightfully confused regarding time and place; but I am so far mended as to feel that."

"It must be an immense satisfaction!"

He said it bitterly, and filled up his glass again: which was a large one.

"As to me, the greatest desire I have, is to forget that I belong to it. It has no good in it for me—except wine like this—nor I for it. So we are not much alike in that particular. Indeed, I begin to think we are not much alike in any particular, you and I."

Confused by the emotion of the day, and feeling his being there with this Double of coarse deportment, to be like a dream, Charles Darnay was at a loss how to answer; finally, answered not at all.

"Now your dinner is done," Carton presently said, "why don't you call a health, Mr. Darnay; why don't you give your toast?"

"What health? What toast?"

"Why, it's on the tip of your tongue. It ought to be, it must be, I'll swear it's there."

"Miss Manette, then!"

"Miss Manette, then!"

Looking his companion full in the face while he drank the toast, Carton flung his glass over his shoulder against the wall, where it shivered to pieces; then, rang the bell, and ordered in another.

"That's a fair young lady to hand to a coach in the dark, Mr. Darnay!" he said, ruing his new goblet.

A slight frown and a laconic "Yes," were the answer.

"That's a fair young lady to be pitied by and wept for by! How does it feel? Is it worth being tried for one's life, to be the object of such sympathy and compassion, Mr. Darnay?"

Again Darnay answered not a word.

"She was mightily pleased to have your message, when I gave it her. Not that she showed she was pleased, but I suppose she was."

The allusion served as a timely reminder to Darnay that this disagreeable companion had, of his own free will, assisted him in the strait of the day. He turned the dialogue to that point, and thanked him for it.

"I neither want any thanks, nor merit any," was the careless rejoinder. "It was nothing to do, in the first place; and I don't know why I did it, in the second. Mr. Darnay, let me ask you a question."

"Willingly, and a small return for your good offices."

"Do you think I particularly like you?"

"Really, Mr. Carton," returned the other, oddly disconcerted, "I have not asked myself the question."

"But ask yourself the question now."

"You have acted as if you do; but I don't think you do."

"*I* don't think I do," said Carton. "I begin to have a very good opinion of your understanding."

"Nevertheless," pursued Darnay, rising to ring the bell, "there is nothing in that, I hope, to prevent my calling the reckoning, and our parting without ill-blood on either side."

Carton rejoining, "Nothing in life!" Darnay rang. "Do you call the whole reckoning?" said Carton. On his answering in the affirmative, "Then bring me another pint of this same wine, drawer, and come and wake me at ten."

The bill being paid, Charles Darnay rose and wished him good night. Without returning the wish, Carton rose too, with something of a threat of defiance in his manner, and said, "A last word, Mr. Darnay: you think I am drunk?"

"I think you have been drinking, Mr. Carton."

"Think? You know I have been drinking."

"Since I must say so, I know it."

"Then you shall likewise know why. I am a disappointed drudge, sir. I care for no man on earth, and no man on earth cares for me."

"Much to be regretted. You might have used your talents better."

"May be so, Mr. Darnay; may be not. Don't let your sober face elate you, however; you don't know what it may come to. Good night!"

When he was left alone, this strange being took up a candle, went to a glass that hung against the wall, and surveyed himself minutely in it.

"Do you particularly like the man?" he muttered, at his own image; "why should you particularly like a man who resembles you? There is nothing in you to like; you know that. Ah, confound you! What a change you have made in yourself! A good reason for taking to a man, that he shows you what you have fallen away from, and what you might have been! Change places with him, and would you have been looked at by those blue eyes as he was, and commiserated by that agitated face as he was? Come on, and have it out in plain words! You hate the fellow."

He resorted to his pint of wine for consolation, drank it all in a few minutes, and fell asleep on his arms, with his hair straggling over the table, and a long winding-sheet in the candle dripping down upon him.

V. THE JACKAL

Those were drinking days, and most men drank hard. So very great is the improvement Time has brought about in such habits, that a moderate statement of the quantity of wine and punch which one man would swallow in the course of a night, without any detriment to his reputation as a perfect gentleman, would seem, in these days, a ridiculous exaggeration. The learned profession of the law was certainly not behind any other learned profession in its Bacchanalian propensities; neither was Mr. Stryver, already fast shouldering his way to a large and lucrative practice, behind his compeers in this particular, any more than in the drier parts of the legal race.

A favourite at the Old Bailey, and eke at the Sessions, Mr. Stryver had begun cautiously to hew away the lower staves of the ladder on which he mounted. Sessions and Old Bailey had now to summon their favourite, specially, to their longing arms; and shouldering itself towards the visage of the Lord Chief Justice in the Court of King's Bench, the florid countenance of Mr. Stryver might be daily seen, bursting out of the bed of wigs, like a great sunflower pushing its way at the sun from among a rank garden-full of flaring companions.

It had once been noted at the Bar, that while Mr. Stryver was a glib man, and an unscrupulous, and a ready, and a bold, he had not that faculty of extracting the essence from a heap of statements, which is among the most striking and necessary of the advocate's accomplishments. But, a remarkable improvement came upon him as to this. The more business he got, the greater his power seemed to grow of getting at its pith and marrow; and however late at night he sat carousing with Sydney Carton, he always had his points at his fingers' ends in the morning.

Sydney Carton, idlest and most unpromising of men, was Stryver's great ally. What the two drank together, between Hilary Term and Michaelmas, might have floated a king's ship. Stryver never had a case in hand, anywhere, but Carton was there, with his hands in his pockets, staring at the ceiling of the court; they went the same Circuit, and even there they prolonged their usual orgies late into the night, and Carton was rumoured to be seen at broad day, going home stealthily and unsteadily to his lodgings, like a dissipated cat. At last, it began to get about, among such as were interested in the matter, that although Sydney Carton would never be a lion, he was an amazingly good jackal, and that he rendered suit and service to Stryver in that humble capacity.

"Ten o'clock, sir," said the man at the tavern, whom he had charged to wake him— "ten o'clock, sir."

"*What's* the matter?"

"Ten o'clock, sir."

"What do you mean? Ten o'clock at night?"

"Yes, sir. Your honour told me to call you."

"Oh! I remember. Very well, very well."

After a few dull efforts to get to sleep again, which the man dexterously combated by stirring the fire continuously for five minutes, he got up, tossed his hat on, and walked out. He turned into the Temple, and, having revived himself by twice pacing the pavements of King's Bench-walk and Paper-buildings, turned into the Stryver chambers.

The Stryver clerk, who never assisted at these conferences, had gone home, and the Stryver principal opened the door. He had his slippers on, and a loose bed-gown, and his throat was bare for his greater ease. He had that rather wild, strained, seared marking about the eyes, which may be observed in all free livers of his class, from the portrait of Jeffries downward, and which can be traced, under various disguises of Art, through the portraits of every Drinking Age.

"You are a little late, Memory," said Stryver.

"About the usual time; it may be a quarter of an hour later."

They went into a dingy room lined with books and littered with papers, where there was a blazing fire. A kettle steamed upon the hob, and in the midst of the wreck of papers a table shone, with plenty of wine upon it, and brandy, and rum, and sugar, and lemons.

"You have had your bottle, I perceive, Sydney."

"Two to-night, I think. I have been dining with the day's client; or seeing him dine—it's all one!"

"That was a rare point, Sydney, that you brought to bear upon the identification. How did you come by it? When did it strike you?"

"I thought he was rather a handsome fellow, and I thought I should have been much the same sort of fellow, if I had had any luck."

Mr. Stryver laughed till he shook his precocious paunch.

"You and your luck, Sydney! Get to work, get to work."

Sullenly enough, the jackal loosened his dress, went into an adjoining room, and came back with a large jug of cold water, a basin, and a towel or two. Steeping the towels in the water, and partially wringing them out, he folded them on his head in a manner hideous to behold, sat down at the table, and said, "Now I am ready!"

"Not much boiling down to be done to-night, Memory," said Mr. Stryver, gaily, as he looked among his papers.

"How much?"

"Only two sets of them."

"Give me the worst first."

"There they are, Sydney. Fire away!"

The lion then composed himself on his back on a sofa on one side of the drinking-table, while the jackal sat at his own paper-bestrewn table proper, on the other side of it, with the bottles and glasses ready to his hand. Both resorted to the drinking-table without stint, but each in a different way; the lion for the most part reclining with his hands in his waistband, looking at the fire, or occasionally flirting with some lighter document; the jackal, with knitted brows and intent face, so deep in his task, that his eyes did not even follow the hand he stretched out for his glass—which often groped about, for a minute or more, before it found the glass for his lips. Two or three times, the matter in hand became so knotty, that the jackal found it imperative on him to get up, and steep his towels anew. From these pilgrimages to the jug and basin, he returned with such eccentricities of damp headgear as no words can describe; which were made the more ludicrous by his anxious gravity.

At length the jackal had got together a compact repast for the lion, and proceeded to offer it to him. The lion took it with care and caution, made his selections from it, and his remarks upon it, and the jackal assisted both. When the repast was fully discussed, the lion put his hands in his waistband again, and lay down to mediate. The jackal then invigorated himself with a bum for his throttle, and a fresh application to his head, and applied himself to the collection of a second meal; this was administered to the lion in the same manner, and was not disposed of until the clocks struck three in the morning.

"And now we have done, Sydney, fill a bumper of punch," said Mr. Stryver.

The jackal removed the towels from his head, which had been steaming again, shook himself, yawned, shivered, and complied.

"You were very sound, Sydney, in the matter of those crown witnesses to-day. Every question told."

"I always am sound; am I not?"

"I don't gainsay it. What has roughened your temper? Put some punch to it and smooth it again."

With a deprecatory grunt, the jackal again complied.

"The old Sydney Carton of old Shrewsbury School," said Stryver, nodding his head over him as he reviewed him in the present and the past, "the old seesaw Sydney. Up one minute and down the next; now in spirits and now in despondency!"

"Ah!" returned the other, sighing: "yes! The same Sydney, with the same luck. Even then, I did exercises for other boys, and seldom did my own."

"And why not?"

"God knows. It was my way, I suppose."

He sat, with his hands in his pockets and his legs stretched out before him, looking at the fire.

"Carton," said his friend, squaring himself at him with a bullying air, as if the fire-grate had been the furnace in which sustained endeavour was forged, and the one delicate thing to be done for the old Sydney Carton of old Shrewsbury School was to shoulder him into it, "your way is, and always was, a lame way. You summon no energy and purpose. Look at me."

"Oh, botheration!" returned Sydney, with a lighter and more good- humoured laugh, "don't *you* be moral!"

"How have I done what I have done?" said Stryver; "how do I do what I do?"

"Partly through paying me to help you, I suppose. But it's not worth your while to apostrophise me, or the air, about it; what you want to do, you do. You were always in the front rank, and I was always behind."

"I had to get into the front rank; I was not born there, was I?"

"I was not present at the ceremony; but my opinion is you were," said Carton. At this, he laughed again, and they both laughed.

"Before Shrewsbury, and at Shrewsbury, and ever since Shrewsbury," pursued Carton, "you have fallen into your rank, and I have fallen into mine. Even when we were fellow-students in the Student-Quarter of Paris, picking up French, and French law, and other French crumbs that we didn't get much good of, you were always somewhere, and I was always nowhere."

"And whose fault was that?"

"Upon my soul, I am not sure that it was not yours. You were always driving and riving and shouldering and passing, to that restless degree that I had no chance for my life but in rust and repose. It's a gloomy thing, however, to talk about one's own past, with the day breaking. Turn me in some other direction before I go."

"Well then! Pledge me to the pretty witness," said Stryver, holding up his glass. "Are you turned in a pleasant direction?"

Apparently not, for he became gloomy again.

"Pretty witness," he muttered, looking down into his glass. "I have had enough of witnesses to-day and to-night; who's your pretty witness?"

"The picturesque doctor's daughter, Miss Manette."

"*She* pretty?"

"Is she not?"

"No."

"Why, man alive, she was the admiration of the whole Court!"

"Rot the admiration of the whole Court! Who made the Old Bailey a judge of beauty? She was a golden-haired doll!"

"Do you know, Sydney," said Mr. Stryver, looking at him with sharp eyes, and slowly drawing a hand across his florid face: "do you know, I rather thought, at the time, that you sympathised with the golden-haired doll, and were quick to see what happened to the golden-haired doll?"

"Quick to see what happened! If a girl, doll or no doll, swoons within a yard or two of a man's nose, he can see it without a perspective-glass. I pledge you, but I deny the beauty. And now I'll have no more drink; I'll get to bed."

When his host followed him out on the staircase with a candle, to light him down the stairs, the day was coldly looking in through its grimy windows. When he got out of the house, the air was cold and sad, the dull sky overcast, the river dark and dim, the whole scene like a lifeless desert. And wreaths of dust were spinning round and round before the morning blast, as if the desert-sand had risen far away, and the first spray of it in its advance had begun to overwhelm the city.

Waste forces within him, and a desert all around, this man stood still on his way across a silent terrace, and saw for a moment, lying in the wilderness before him, a mirage of honourable ambition, self-denial, and perseverance. In the fair city of this vision, there were airy galleries from which the loves and graces looked upon him, gardens in which the fruits of life hung ripening, waters of Hope that sparkled in his sight. A moment, and it was gone. Climbing to a high chamber in a well of houses, he threw himself down in his clothes on a neglected bed, and its pillow was wet with wasted tears.

Sadly, sadly, the sun rose; it rose upon no sadder sight than the man of good abilities and good emotions, incapable of their directed exercise, incapable of his own help and his own happiness, sensible of the blight on him, and resigning himself to let it eat him away.

VI. HUNDREDS OF PEOPLE

The quiet lodgings of Doctor Manette were in a quiet street-corner not far from Soho-square. On the afternoon of a certain fine Sunday when the waves of four months had roiled over the trial for treason, and carried it, as to the public interest and memory, far out to sea, Mr. Jarvis Lorry walked along the sunny streets from Clerkenwell where he lived, on his way to dine with the Doctor. After several relapses into business-absorption, Mr. Lorry had become the Doctor's friend, and the quiet street-corner was the sunny part of his life.

On this certain fine Sunday, Mr. Lorry walked towards Soho, early in the afternoon, for three reasons of habit. Firstly, because, on fine Sundays, he often walked out, before dinner, with the Doctor and Lucie; secondly, because, on unfavourable Sundays, he was accustomed to be with them as the family friend, talking, reading, looking out of window, and generally getting through the day; thirdly, because he happened to have his own little shrewd doubts to solve, and knew how the ways of the Doctor's household pointed to that time as a likely time for solving them.

A quainter corner than the corner where the Doctor lived, was not to be found in London. There was no way through it, and the front windows of the Doctor's lodgings commanded a pleasant little vista of street that had a congenial air of retirement on it. There were few buildings then, north of the Oxford-road, and forest-trees flourished, and wild flowers grew, and the hawthorn blossomed, in the now vanished fields. As a consequence, country airs circulated in Soho with vigorous freedom, instead of languishing into the parish like stray paupers without a settlement; and there was many a good south wall, not far off, on which the peaches ripened in their season.

The summer light struck into the corner brilliantly in the earlier part of the day; but, when the streets grew hot, the corner was in shadow, though not in shadow so remote but that you could see beyond it into a glare of brightness. It was a cool spot, staid but cheerful, a wonderful place for echoes, and a very harbour from the raging streets.

There ought to have been a tranquil bark in such an anchorage, and there was. The Doctor occupied two floors of a large stiff house, where several callings purported to be pursued by day, but whereof little was audible any day, and which was shunned by all of them at night. In a building at the back, attainable by a courtyard where a plane-tree rustled its green leaves, church-organs claimed to be made, and silver to be chased, and likewise gold to be beaten by some mysterious giant who had a golden arm starting out of the wall of the front hall—as if he had beaten himself precious, and menaced a similar conversion of all visitors. Very little of these trades, or of a lonely lodger rumoured to live up-stairs, or of a dim coach-trimming maker asserted to have a counting-house below, was ever heard or seen. Occasionally, a stray workman putting his coat on, traversed the hall, or a stranger peered about there, or a distant clink was heard across the courtyard, or a thump from the golden giant. These, however, were only the exceptions required to prove the rule that the sparrows in the plane-tree behind the house, and the echoes in the corner before it, had their own way from Sunday morning unto Saturday night.

Doctor Manette received such patients here as his old reputation, and its revival in the floating whispers of his story, brought him. His scientific knowledge, and his vigilance and skill in conducting ingenious experiments, brought him otherwise into moderate request, and he earned as much as he wanted.

These things were within Mr. Jarvis Lorry's knowledge, thoughts, and notice, when he rang the door-bell of the tranquil house in the corner, on the fine Sunday afternoon.

"Doctor Manette at home?"

Expected home.

"Miss Lucie at home?"

Expected home.

"Miss Pross at home?"

Possibly at home, but of a certainty impossible for handmaid to anticipate intentions of Miss Pross, as to admission or denial of the fact.

"As I am at home myself," said Mr. Lorry, "I'll go upstairs."

Although the Doctor's daughter had known nothing of the country of her birth, she appeared to have innately derived from it that ability to make much of little means, which is one of its most useful and most agreeable characteristics. Simple as the furniture was, it was set off by so many little adornments, of no value but for their taste and fancy, that its effect was delightful. The disposition of everything in the rooms, from the largest object to the least; the arrangement of colours, the elegant variety and contrast obtained by thrift in trifles, by delicate hands, clear eyes, and good sense; were at once so pleasant in themselves, and so expressive of their originator, that, as Mr. Lorry stood looking about him, the very chairs and tables seemed to ask him, with something of that peculiar expression which he knew so well by this time, whether he approved?

There were three rooms on a floor, and, the doors by which they communicated being put open that the air might pass freely through them all, Mr. Lorry, smilingly observant of that fanciful resemblance which he detected all around him, walked from one to another. The first was the best room, and in it were Lucie's birds, and flowers, and books, and desk, and work-table, and box of water-colours; the second was the Doctor's consulting-room, used also as the dining-room; the third, changingly speckled by the rustle of the plane-tree in the yard, was the Doctor's bedroom, and there, in a corner, stood the disused shoemaker's bench and tray of tools, much as it had stood on the fifth floor of the dismal house by the wine-shop, in the suburb of Saint Antoine in Paris.

"I wonder," said Mr. Lorry, pausing in his looking about, "that he keeps that reminder of his sufferings about him!"

"And why wonder at that?" was the abrupt inquiry that made him start.

It proceeded from Miss Pross, the wild red woman, strong of hand, whose acquaintance he had first made at the Royal George Hotel at Dover, and had since improved.

"I should have thought—" Mr. Lorry began.

"Pooh! You'd have thought!" said Miss Pross; and Mr. Lorry left off.

"How do you do?" inquired that lady then—sharply, and yet as if to express that she bore him no malice.

"I am pretty well, I thank you," answered Mr. Lorry, with meekness; "how are you?"

"Nothing to boast of," said Miss Pross.

"Indeed?"

"Ah! indeed!" said Miss Pross. "I am very much put out about my Ladybird."

"Indeed?"

"For gracious sake say something else besides 'indeed,' or you'll fidget me to death," said Miss Pross: whose character (dissociated from stature) was shortness.

"Really, then?" said Mr. Lorry, as an amendment.

"Really, is bad enough," returned Miss Pross, "but better. Yes, I am very much put out."

"May I ask the cause?"

"I don't want dozens of people who are not at all worthy of Ladybird, to come here looking after her," said Miss Pross.

"*Do* dozens come for that purpose?"

"Hundreds," said Miss Pross.

It was characteristic of this lady (as of some other people before her time and since) that whenever her original proposition was questioned, she exaggerated it.

"Dear me!" said Mr. Lorry, as the safest remark he could think of.

"I have lived with the darling—or the darling has lived with me, and paid me for it; which she certainly should never have done, you may take your affidavit, if I could have afforded to keep either myself or her for nothing—since she was ten years old. And it's really very hard," said Miss Pross.

Not seeing with precision what was very hard, Mr. Lorry shook his head; using that important part of himself as a sort of fairy cloak that would fit anything.

"All sorts of people who are not in the least degree worthy of the pet, are always turning up," said Miss Pross. "When you began it—"

"*I* began it, Miss Pross?"

"Didn't you? Who brought her father to life?"

"Oh! If *that* was beginning it—" said Mr. Lorry.

"It wasn't ending it, I suppose? I say, when you began it, it was hard enough; not that I have any fault to find with Doctor Manette, except that he is not worthy of such a daughter, which is no imputation on him, for it was not to be expected that anybody should be, under any circumstances. But it really is doubly and trebly hard to have crowds and multitudes of people turning up after him (I could have forgiven him), to take Ladybird's affections away from me."

Mr. Lorry knew Miss Pross to be very jealous, but he also knew her by this time to be, beneath the service of her eccentricity, one of those unselfish creatures—found only among women—who will, for pure love and admiration, bind themselves willing slaves, to youth when they have lost it, to beauty that they never had, to accomplishments that they were never fortunate enough to gain, to bright hopes that never shone upon their own sombre lives. He knew enough of the world to know that there is nothing in it better than the faithful service of the heart; so rendered and so free from any mercenary taint, he had such an exalted respect for it, that in the retributive arrangements made by his own mind—we all make such arrangements, more or less—he stationed Miss Pross much nearer to the lower Angels than many ladies immeasurably better got up both by Nature and Art, who had balances at Tellson's.

"There never was, nor will be, but one man worthy of Ladybird," said Miss Pross; "and that was my brother Solomon, if he hadn't made a mistake in life."

Here again: Mr. Lorry's inquiries into Miss Pross's personal history had established the fact that her brother Solomon was a heartless scoundrel who had stripped her of everything she possessed, as a stake to speculate with, and had abandoned her in her poverty for evermore, with no touch of compunction. Miss Pross's fidelity of belief in Solomon (deducting a mere trifle for this slight mistake) was quite a serious matter with Mr. Lorry, and had its weight in his good opinion of her.

"As we happen to be alone for the moment, and are both people of business," he said, when they had got back to the drawing-room and had sat down there in friendly relations, "let me ask you—does the Doctor, in talking with Lucie, never refer to the shoemaking time, yet?"

"Never."

"And yet keeps that bench and those tools beside him?"

"Ah!" returned Miss Pross, shaking her head. "But I don't say he don't refer to it within himself."

"Do you believe that he thinks of it much?"

"I do," said Miss Pross.

"Do you imagine—" Mr. Lorry had begun, when Miss Pross took him up short with:

"Never imagine anything. Have no imagination at all."

"I stand corrected; do you suppose—you go so far as to suppose, sometimes?"

"Now and then," said Miss Pross.

"Do you suppose," Mr. Lorry went on, with a laughing twinkle in his bright eye, as it looked kindly at her, "that Doctor Manette has any theory of his own, preserved through all those years, relative to the cause of his being so oppressed; perhaps, even to the name of his oppressor?"

"I don't suppose anything about it but what Ladybird tells me."

"And that is—?"

"That she thinks he has."

"Now don't be angry at my asking all these questions; because I am a mere dull man of business, and you are a woman of business."

"Dull?" Miss Pross inquired, with placidity.

Rather wishing his modest adjective away, Mr. Lorry replied, "No, no, no. Surely not. To return to business:—Is it not remarkable that Doctor Manette, unquestionably innocent of any crime as we are all well assured he is, should never touch upon that question? I will not say with me, though he had business relations with me many years ago, and we are now intimate; I will say with the fair daughter to whom he is so devotedly attached, and who is so devotedly attached to him? Believe me, Miss Pross, I don't approach the topic with you, out of curiosity, but out of zealous interest."

"Well! To the best of my understanding, and bad's the best, you'll tell me," said Miss Pross, softened by the tone of the apology, "he is afraid of the whole subject."

"Afraid?"

"It's plain enough, I should think, why he may be. It's a dreadful remembrance. Besides that, his loss of himself grew out of it. Not knowing how he lost himself, or how he recovered himself, he may never feel certain of not losing himself again. That alone wouldn't make the subject pleasant, I should think."

It was a profounder remark than Mr. Lorry had looked for. "True," said he, "and fearful to reflect upon. Yet, a doubt lurks in my mind, Miss Pross, whether it is good for Doctor Manette to have that suppression always shut up within him. Indeed, it is this doubt and the uneasiness it sometimes causes me that has led me to our present confidence."

"Can't be helped," said Miss Pross, shaking her head. "Touch that string, and he instantly changes for the worse. Better leave it alone. In short, must leave it alone, like or no like. Sometimes, he gets up in the dead of the night, and will be heard, by us overhead there, walking up and down, walking up and down, in his room. Ladybird has learnt to know then that his mind is walking up and down, walking up and down, in his old prison. She hurries to him, and they go on together, walking up and down, walking up and down, until he is composed. But he never says a word of the true reason of his restlessness, to her, and she finds it best not to hint at it to him. In silence they go walking up and down together, walking up and down together, till her love and company have brought him to himself."

Notwithstanding Miss Pross's denial of her own imagination, there was a perception of the pain of being monotonously haunted by one sad idea, in her repetition of the phrase, walking up and down, which testified to her possessing such a thing.

The corner has been mentioned as a wonderful corner for echoes; it had begun to echo so resoundingly to the tread of coming feet, that it seemed as though the very mention of that weary pacing to and fro had set it going.

"Here they are!" said Miss Pross, rising to break up the conference; "and now we shall have hundreds of people pretty soon!"

It was such a curious corner in its acoustical properties, such a peculiar Ear of a place, that as Mr. Lorry stood at the open window, looking for the father and daughter whose steps he heard, he fancied they would never approach. Not only would the echoes die away, as though the steps had gone; but, echoes of other steps that never came would be heard in their stead, and would die away for good when they seemed close at hand. However, father and daughter did at last appear, and Miss Pross was ready at the street door to receive them.

Miss Pross was a pleasant sight, albeit wild, and red, and grim, taking off her darling's bonnet when she came up-stairs, and touching it up with the ends of her handkerchief, and blowing the dust off it, and folding her mantle ready for laying by, and smoothing her rich hair with as much pride as she could possibly have taken in her own hair if she had been the vainest and handsomest of women. Her darling was a pleasant sight too, embracing her and thanking her, and protesting against her taking so much trouble for her—which last she only dared to do playfully, or Miss Pross, sorely hurt, would have retired to her own chamber and cried. The Doctor was a pleasant sight too, looking on at them, and telling Miss Pross how she spoilt Lucie, in accents and with eyes that had as much spoiling in them as Miss Pross had, and would have had more if it were possible. Mr. Lorry was a pleasant sight too, beaming at all this in his little wig, and thanking his bachelor stars for having lighted him in his declining years to a Home. But, no Hundreds of people came to see the sights, and Mr. Lorry looked in vain for the fulfilment of Miss Pross's prediction.

Dinner-time, and still no Hundreds of people. In the arrangements of the little household, Miss Pross took charge of the lower regions, and always acquitted herself marvellously. Her dinners, of a very modest quality, were so well cooked and so well served, and so neat in their contrivances, half English and half French, that nothing could be better. Miss Pross's friendship being of the thoroughly practical kind, she had ravaged Soho and the adjacent provinces, in search of impoverished French, who, tempted by shillings and half-crowns, would impart culinary mysteries to her. From these decayed sons and daughters of Gaul, she had acquired such wonderful arts, that the woman and girl who formed the staff of domestics regarded her as quite a Sorceress, or Cinderella's Godmother: who would send out for a fowl, a rabbit, a vegetable or two from the garden, and change them into anything she pleased.

On Sundays, Miss Pross dined at the Doctor's table, but on other days persisted in taking her meals at unknown periods, either in the lower regions, or in her own room on the second floor—a blue chamber, to which no one but her Ladybird ever gained admittance. On this occasion, Miss Pross, responding to Ladybird's pleasant face and pleasant efforts to please her, unbent exceedingly; so the dinner was very pleasant, too.

It was an oppressive day, and, after dinner, Lucie proposed that the wine should be carried out under the plane-tree, and they should sit there in the air. As everything turned upon her, and revolved about her, they went out under the plane-tree, and she carried the wine down for the special benefit of Mr. Lorry. She had installed herself, some time before, as Mr. Lorry's cup-bearer; and while they sat under the plane-tree, talking, she kept his glass replenished. Mysterious backs and ends of houses peeped at them as they talked, and the plane-tree whispered to them in its own way above their heads.

Still, the Hundreds of people did not present themselves. Mr. Darnay presented himself while they were sitting under the plane-tree, but he was only One.

Doctor Manette received him kindly, and so did Lucie. But, Miss Pross suddenly became afflicted with a twitching in the head and body, and retired into the house. She was not unfrequently the victim of this disorder, and she called it, in familiar conversation, "a fit of the jerks."

The Doctor was in his best condition, and looked specially young. The resemblance between him and Lucie was very strong at such times, and as they sat side by side, she leaning on his shoulder, and he resting his arm on the back of her chair, it was very agreeable to trace the likeness.

He had been talking all day, on many subjects, and with unusual vivacity. "Pray, Doctor Manette," said Mr. Darnay, as they sat under the plane-tree—and he said it in the natural pursuit of the topic in hand, which happened to be the old buildings of London—"have you seen much of the Tower?"

"Lucie and I have been there; but only casually. We have seen enough of it, to know that it teems with interest; little more."

"*I* have been there, as you remember," said Darnay, with a smile, though reddening a little angrily, "in another character, and not in a character that gives facilities for seeing much of it. They told me a curious thing when I was there."

"What was that?" Lucie asked.

"In making some alterations, the workmen came upon an old dungeon, which had been, for many years, built up and forgotten. Every stone of its inner wall was covered by inscriptions which had been carved by prisoners—dates, names, complaints, and prayers. Upon a corner stone in an angle of the wall, one prisoner, who seemed to have gone to execution, had cut as his last work, three letters. They were done with some very poor instrument, and hurriedly, with an unsteady hand. At first, they were read as D. I. C.; but, on being more carefully examined, the last letter was found to be G. There was no record or legend of any prisoner with those initials, and many fruitless guesses were made what the name could have been. At length, it was suggested that the letters were not initials, but the complete word, DIG. The floor was examined very carefully under the inscription, and, in the earth beneath a stone, or tile, or some fragment of paving, were found the ashes of a paper, mingled with the ashes of a small leathern case or bag. What the unknown prisoner had written will never be read, but he had written something, and hidden it away to keep it from the gaoler."

"My father," exclaimed Lucie, "you are ill!"

He had suddenly started up, with his hand to his head. His manner and his look quite terrified them all.

"No, my dear, not ill. There are large drops of rain falling, and they made me start. We had better go in."

He recovered himself almost instantly. Rain was really falling in large drops, and he showed the back of his hand with rain-drops on it. But, he said not a single word in reference to the discovery that had been told of, and, as they went into the house, the business eye of Mr. Lorry either detected, or fancied it detected, on his face, as it turned towards Charles Darnay, the same singular look that had been upon it when it turned towards him in the passages of the Court House.

He recovered himself so quickly, however, that Mr. Lorry had doubts of his business eye. The arm of the golden giant in the hall was not more steady than he was, when he stopped under it to remark to them that he was not yet proof against slight surprises (if he ever would be), and that the rain had startled him.

Tea-time, and Miss Pross making tea, with another fit of the jerks upon her, and yet no Hundreds of people. Mr. Carton had lounged in, but he made only Two.

The night was so very sultry, that although they sat with doors and windows open, they were overpowered by heat. When the tea-table was done with, they all moved to one of the windows, and looked out into the heavy twilight. Lucie sat by her father; Darnay sat beside her; Carton leaned against a window. The curtains were long and white, and some of the thunder-gusts that whirled into the corner, caught them up to the ceiling, and waved them like spectral wings.

"The rain-drops are still falling, large, heavy, and few," said Doctor Manette. "It comes slowly."

"It comes surely," said Carton.

They spoke low, as people watching and waiting mostly do; as people in a dark room, watching and waiting for Lightning, always do.

There was a great hurry in the streets of people speeding away to get shelter before the storm broke; the wonderful corner for echoes resounded with the echoes of footsteps coming and going, yet not a footstep was there.

"A multitude of people, and yet a solitude!" said Darnay, when they had listened for a while.

"Is it not impressive, Mr. Darnay?" asked Lucie. "Sometimes, I have sat here of an evening, until I have fancied—but even the shade of a foolish fancy makes me shudder to-night, when all is so black and solemn—"

"Let us shudder too. We may know what it is."

"It will seem nothing to you. Such whims are only impressive as we originate them, I think; they are not to be communicated. I have sometimes sat alone here of an evening, listening, until I have made the echoes out to be the echoes of all the footsteps that are coming by-and-bye into our lives."

"There is a great crowd coming one day into our lives, if that be so," Sydney Carton struck in, in his moody way.

The footsteps were incessant, and the hurry of them became more and more rapid. The corner echoed and re-echoed with the tread of feet; some, as it seemed, under the windows; some, as it seemed, in the room; some coming, some going, some breaking off, some stopping altogether; all in the distant streets, and not one within sight.

"Are all these footsteps destined to come to all of us, Miss Manette, or are we to divide them among us?"

"I don't know, Mr. Darnay; I told you it was a foolish fancy, but you asked for it. When I have yielded myself to it, I have been alone, and then I have imagined them the footsteps of the people who are to come into my life, and my father's."

"I take them into mine!" said Carton. "*I* ask no questions and make no stipulations. There is a great crowd bearing down upon us, Miss Manette, and I see them—by the Lightning." He added the last words, after there had been a vivid flash which had shown him lounging in the window.

"And I hear them!" he added again, after a peal of thunder. "Here they come, fast, fierce, and furious!"

It was the rush and roar of rain that he typified, and it stopped him, for no voice could be heard in it. A memorable storm of thunder and lightning broke with that sweep of water, and there was not a moment's interval in crash, and fire, and rain, until after the moon rose at midnight.

The great bell of Saint Paul's was striking one in the cleared air, when Mr. Lorry, escorted by Jerry, high-booted and bearing a lantern, set forth on his return-passage to Clerkenwell. There were solitary patches of road on the way between Soho and Clerkenwell, and Mr. Lorry, mindful of foot-pads, always retained Jerry for this service: though it was usually performed a good two hours earlier.

"What a night it has been! Almost a night, Jerry," said Mr. Lorry, "to bring the dead out of their graves."

"I never see the night myself, master—nor yet I don't expect to—what would do that," answered Jerry.

"Good night, Mr. Carton," said the man of business. "Good night, Mr. Darnay. Shall we ever see such a night again, together!"

Perhaps. Perhaps, see the great crowd of people with its rush and roar, bearing down upon them, too.

VII. MONSEIGNEUR IN TOWN

Monseigneur, one of the great lords in power at the Court, held his fortnightly reception in his grand hotel in Paris. Monseigneur was in his inner room, his sanctuary of sanctuaries, the Holiest of Holiests to the crowd of worshippers in the suite of rooms without. Monseigneur was about to take his chocolate. Monseigneur could swallow a great many things with ease, and was by some few sullen minds supposed to be rather rapidly swallowing France; but, his morning's chocolate could not so much as get into the throat of Monseigneur, without the aid of four strong men besides the Cook.

Yes. It took four men, all four ablaze with gorgeous decoration, and the Chief of them unable to exist with fewer than two gold watches in his pocket, emulative of the noble and chaste fashion set by Monseigneur, to conduct the happy chocolate to Monseigneur's lips. One lacquey carried the chocolate-pot into the sacred presence; a second, milled and frothed the chocolate with the little instrument he bore for that function; a third, presented the favoured napkin; a fourth (he of the two gold watches), poured the chocolate out. It was impossible for Monseigneur to dispense with one of these attendants on the chocolate and hold his high place under the admiring Heavens. Deep would have been the blot upon his escutcheon if his chocolate had been ignobly waited on by only three men; he must have died of two.

Monseigneur had been out at a little supper last night, where the Comedy and the Grand Opera were charmingly represented. Monseigneur was out at a little supper most nights, with fascinating company. So polite and so impressible was Monseigneur, that the Comedy and the Grand Opera had far more influence with him in the tiresome articles of state affairs and state secrets, than the needs of all France. A happy circumstance for France, as the like always is for all countries similarly favoured!—always was for England (by way of example), in the regretted days of the merry Stuart who sold it.

Monseigneur had one truly noble idea of general public business, which was, to let everything go on in its own way; of particular public business, Monseigneur had the other truly noble idea that it must all go his way—tend to his own power and pocket. Of his pleasures, general and particular, Monseigneur had the other truly noble idea, that the world was made for them. The text of his order (altered from the original by only a pronoun, which is not much) ran: "The earth and the fulness thereof are mine, saith Monseigneur."

Yet, Monseigneur had slowly found that vulgar embarrassments crept into his affairs, both private and public; and he had, as to both classes of affairs, allied himself perforce with a Farmer-General. As to finances public, because Monseigneur could not make anything at all of them, and must consequently let them out to somebody who could; as to finances private, because Farmer-Generals were rich, and Monseigneur, after generations of great luxury and expense, was growing poor. Hence Monseigneur had taken his sister from a convent, while there was yet time to ward off the impending veil, the cheapest garment she could wear, and had bestowed her as a prize upon a very rich Farmer-General, poor in family. Which Farmer-General, carrying an appropriate cane with a golden apple on the top of it, was now among the company in the outer rooms, much prostrated before by mankind—always excepting superior mankind of the blood of Monseigneur, who, his own wife included, looked down upon him with the loftiest contempt.

A sumptuous man was the Farmer-General. Thirty horses stood in his stables, twenty-four male domestics sat in his halls, six body-women waited on his wife. As one who pretended to do nothing but plunder and forage where he could, the Farmer-General—howsoever his matrimonial relations conduced to social morality—was at least the greatest reality among the personages who attended at the hotel of Monseigneur that day.

For, the rooms, though a beautiful scene to look at, and adorned with every device of decoration that the taste and skill of the time could achieve, were, in truth, not a sound business; considered with any reference to the scarecrows in the rags and nightcaps elsewhere (and not so far off, either, but that the watching towers of Notre Dame, almost equidistant from the two extremes, could see them both), they would have been an exceedingly uncomfortable business—if that could have been anybody's business, at the house of Monseigneur. Military officers destitute of military knowledge; naval officers with no idea of a ship; civil officers without a notion of affairs; brazen ecclesiastics, of the worst world worldly, with sensual eyes, loose tongues, and looser lives; all totally unfit for their several callings, all lying horribly in pretending to belong to them, but all nearly or remotely of the order of Monseigneur, and therefore foisted on all public employments from which anything was to be got; these were to be told off by the score and the score. People not immediately connected with Monseigneur or the State, yet equally unconnected with anything that was real, or with lives passed in travelling by any straight road to any true earthly end, were no less abundant. Doctors who made great fortunes out of dainty remedies for imaginary disorders that never existed, smiled upon their courtly patients in the ante-chambers of Monseigneur. Projectors who had discovered every kind of remedy for the little evils with which the State was touched, except the remedy of setting to work in earnest to root out a single sin, poured their distracting babble into any ears they could lay hold of, at the reception of Monseigneur. Unbelieving Philosophers who were remodelling the world with words, and making card-towers of Babel to scale the skies with, talked with Unbelieving Chemists who had an eye on the transmutation of metals, at this wonderful gathering accumulated by Monseigneur. Exquisite gentlemen of the finest breeding, which was at that remarkable time—and has been since—to be known by its fruits of indifference to every natural subject of human interest, were in the most exemplary state of exhaustion, at the hotel of Monseigneur. Such homes had these various notabilities left behind them in the fine world of Paris, that the spies among the assembled devotees of Monseigneur—forming a goodly half of the polite company—would have found it hard to discover among the angels of that sphere one solitary wife, who, in her manners and appearance, owned to being a Mother. Indeed, except for the mere act of bringing a troublesome creature into this world—which does not go far towards the realisation of the name of mother—there was no such thing known to the fashion. Peasant women kept the unfashionable babies close, and brought them up, and charming grandmammas of sixty dressed and supped as at twenty.

The leprosy of unreality disfigured every human creature in attendance upon Monseigneur. In the outermost room were half a dozen exceptional people who had had, for a few years, some vague misgiving in them that things in general were going rather wrong. As a promising way of setting them right, half of the half-dozen had become members of a fantastic sect of Convulsionists, and were even then considering within themselves whether they should foam, rage, roar, and turn cataleptic on the spot—thereby setting up a highly intelligible finger-post to the Future, for Monseigneur's guidance. Besides these Dervishes, were other three who had rushed into another sect, which mended matters with a jargon about "the Centre of Truth:" holding that Man had got out of the Centre of Truth—which did not need much demonstration—but had not got out of the Circumference, and that he was to be kept from flying out of the Circumference, and was even to be shoved back into the Centre, by fasting and seeing of spirits. Among these, accordingly, much discoursing with spirits went on—and it did a world of good which never became manifest.

But, the comfort was, that all the company at the grand hotel of Monseigneur were perfectly dressed. If the Day of Judgment had only been ascertained to be a dress day, everybody there would have been eternally correct. Such frizzling and powdering and sticking up of hair, such delicate complexions artificially preserved and mended, such gallant swords to look at, and such delicate honour to the sense of smell, would surely keep anything going, for ever and ever. The exquisite gentlemen of the finest breeding wore little pendent trinkets that chinked as they languidly moved; these golden fetters rang like precious little bells; and what with that ringing, and with the rustle of silk and brocade and fine linen, there was a flutter in the air that fanned Saint Antoine and his devouring hunger far away.

Dress was the one unfailing talisman and charm used for keeping all things in their places. Everybody was dressed for a Fancy Ball that was never to leave off. From the Palace of the Tuileries, through Monseigneur and the whole Court, through the Chambers, the Tribunals of Justice, and all society (except the scarecrows), the Fancy Ball descended to the Common Executioner: who, in pursuance of the charm, was required to officiate "frizzled, powdered, in a gold-laced coat, pumps, and white silk stockings." At the gallows and the wheel—the axe was a rarity—Monsieur Paris, as it was the episcopal mode among his brother Professors of the provinces, Monsieur Orleans, and the rest, to call him, presided in this dainty dress. And who among the company at Monseigneur's reception in that seventeen hundred and eightieth year of our Lord, could possibly doubt, that a system rooted in a frizzled hangman, powdered, gold-laced, pumped, and white-silk stockinged, would see the very stars out!

Monseigneur having eased his four men of their burdens and taken his chocolate, caused the doors of the Holiest of Holiests to be thrown open, and issued forth. Then, what submission, what cringing and fawning, what servility, what abject humiliation! As to bowing down in body and spirit, nothing in that way was left for Heaven— which may have been one among other reasons why the worshippers of Monseigneur never troubled it.

Bestowing a word of promise here and a smile there, a whisper on one happy slave and a wave of the hand on another, Monseigneur affably passed through his rooms to the remote region of the Circumference of Truth. There, Monseigneur turned, and came back again, and so in due course of time got himself shut up in his sanctuary by the chocolate sprites, and was seen no more.

The show being over, the flutter in the air became quite a little storm, and the precious little bells went ringing downstairs. There was soon but one person left of all the crowd, and he, with his hat under his arm and his snuff-box in his hand, slowly passed among the mirrors on his way out.

"I devote you," said this person, stopping at the last door on his way, and turning in the direction of the sanctuary, "to the Devil!"

With that, he shook the snuff from his fingers as if he had shaken the dust from his feet, and quietly walked downstairs.

He was a man of about sixty, handsomely dressed, haughty in manner, and with a face like a fine mask. A face of a transparent paleness; every feature in it clearly defined; one set expression on it. The nose, beautifully formed otherwise, was very slightly pinched at the top of each nostril. In those two compressions, or dints, the only little change that the face ever showed, resided. They persisted in changing colour sometimes, and they would be occasionally dilated and contracted by something like a faint pulsation; then, they gave a look of treachery, and cruelty, to the whole countenance. Examined with attention, its capacity of helping such a look was to be found in the line of the mouth, and the lines of the orbits of the eyes, being much too horizontal and thin; still, in the effect of the face made, it was a handsome face, and a remarkable one.

Its owner went downstairs into the courtyard, got into his carriage, and drove away. Not many people had talked with him at the reception; he had stood in a little space apart, and Monseigneur might have been warmer in his manner. It appeared, under the circumstances, rather agreeable to him to see the common people dispersed before his horses, and often barely escaping from being run down. His man drove as if he were charging an enemy, and the furious recklessness of the man brought no check into the face, or to the lips, of the master. The complaint had sometimes made itself audible, even in that deaf city and dumb age, that, in the narrow streets without footways, the fierce patrician custom of hard driving endangered and maimed the mere vulgar in a barbarous manner. But, few cared enough for that to think of it a second time, and, in this matter, as in all others, the common wretches were left to get out of their difficulties as they could.

With a wild rattle and clatter, and an inhuman abandonment of consideration not easy to be understood in these days, the carriage dashed through streets and swept round corners, with women screaming before it, and men clutching each other and clutching children out of its way. At last, swooping at a street corner by a fountain, one of its wheels came to a sickening little jolt, and there was a loud cry from a number of voices, and the horses reared and plunged.

But for the latter inconvenience, the carriage probably would not have stopped; carriages were often known to drive on, and leave their wounded behind, and why not? But the frightened valet had got down in a hurry, and there were twenty hands at the horses' bridles.

"What has gone wrong?" said Monsieur, calmly looking out.

A tall man in a nightcap had caught up a bundle from among the feet of the horses, and had laid it on the basement of the fountain, and was down in the mud and wet, howling over it like a wild animal.

"Pardon, Monsieur the Marquis!" said a ragged and submissive man, "it is a child."

"Why does he make that abominable noise? Is it his child?"

"Excuse me, Monsieur the Marquis—it is a pity—yes."

The fountain was a little removed; for the street opened, where it was, into a space some ten or twelve yards square. As the tall man suddenly got up from the ground, and came running at the carriage, Monsieur the Marquis clapped his hand for an instant on his sword-hilt.

"Killed!" shrieked the man, in wild desperation, extending both arms at their length above his head, and staring at him. "Dead!"

The people closed round, and looked at Monsieur the Marquis. There was nothing revealed by the many eyes that looked at him but watchfulness and eagerness; there was no visible menacing or anger. Neither did the people say anything; after the first cry, they had been silent, and they remained so. The voice of the submissive man who had spoken, was flat and tame in its extreme submission. Monsieur the Marquis ran his eyes over them all, as if they had been mere rats come out of their holes.

He took out his purse.

"It is extraordinary to me," said he, "that you people cannot take care of yourselves and your children. One or the other of you is for ever in the way. How do I know what injury you have done my horses. See! Give him that."

He threw out a gold coin for the valet to pick up, and all the heads craned forward that all the eyes might look down at it as it fell. The tall man called out again with a most unearthly cry, "Dead!"

He was arrested by the quick arrival of another man, for whom the rest made way. On seeing him, the miserable creature fell upon his shoulder, sobbing and crying, and pointing to the fountain, where some women were stooping over the motionless bundle, and moving gently about it. They were as silent, however, as the men.

"I know all, I know all," said the last comer. "Be a brave man, my Gaspard! It is better for the poor little plaything to die so, than to live. It has died in a moment without pain. Could it have lived an hour as happily?"

"You are a philosopher, you there," said the Marquis, smiling. "How do they call you?"

"They call me Defarge."

"Of what trade?"

"Monsieur the Marquis, vendor of wine."

"Pick up that, philosopher and vendor of wine," said the Marquis, throwing him another gold coin, "and spend it as you will. The horses there; are they right?"

Without deigning to look at the assemblage a second time, Monsieur the Marquis leaned back in his seat, and was just being driven away with the air of a gentleman who had accidentally broke some common thing, and had paid for it, and could afford to pay for it; when his ease was suddenly disturbed by a coin flying into his carriage, and ringing on its floor.

"Hold!" said Monsieur the Marquis. "Hold the horses! Who threw that?"

He looked to the spot where Defarge the vendor of wine had stood, a moment before; but the wretched father was grovelling on his face on the pavement in that spot, and the figure that stood beside him was the figure of a dark stout woman, knitting.

"You dogs!" said the Marquis, but smoothly, and with an unchanged front, except as to the spots on his nose: "I would ride over any of you very willingly, and exterminate you from the earth. If I knew which rascal threw at the carriage, and if that brigand were sufficiently near it, he should be crushed under the wheels."

So cowed was their condition, and so long and hard their experience of what such a man could do to them, within the law and beyond it, that not a voice, or a hand, or even an eye was raised. Among the men, not one. But the woman who stood knitting looked up steadily, and looked the Marquis in the face. It was not for his dignity to notice it; his contemptuous eyes passed over her, and over all the other rats; and he leaned back in his seat again, and gave the word "Go on!"

He was driven on, and other carriages came whirling by in quick succession; the Minister, the State-Projector, the Farmer-General, the Doctor, the Lawyer, the Ecclesiastic, the Grand Opera, the Comedy, the whole Fancy Ball in a bright continuous flow, came whirling by. The rats had crept out of their holes to look on, and they remained looking on for hours; soldiers and police often passing between them and the spectacle, and making a barrier behind which they slunk, and through which they peeped. The father had long ago taken up his bundle and bidden himself away with it, when the women who had tended the bundle while it lay on the base of the fountain, sat there watching the running of the water and the rolling of the Fancy Ball—when the one woman who had stood conspicuous, knitting, still knitted on with the steadfastness of Fate. The water of the fountain ran, the swift river ran, the day ran into evening, so much life in the city ran into death according to rule, time and tide waited for no man, the rats were sleeping close together in their dark holes again, the Fancy Ball was lighted up at supper, all things ran their course.

VIII. MONSEIGNEUR IN THE COUNTRY

A beautiful landscape, with the corn bright in it, but not abundant. Patches of poor rye where corn should have been, patches of poor peas and beans, patches of most coarse vegetable substitutes for wheat. On inanimate nature, as on the men and women who cultivated it, a prevalent tendency towards an appearance of vegetating unwillingly—a dejected disposition to give up, and wither away.

Monsieur the Marquis in his travelling carriage (which might have been lighter), conducted by four post-horses and two postilions, fagged up a steep hill. A blush on the countenance of Monsieur the Marquis was no impeachment of his high breeding; it was not from within; it was occasioned by an external circumstance beyond his control—the setting sun.

The sunset struck so brilliantly into the travelling carriage when it gained the hill-top, that its occupant was steeped in crimson. "It will die out," said Monsieur the Marquis, glancing at his hands, "directly."

In effect, the sun was so low that it dipped at the moment. When the heavy drag had been adjusted to the wheel, and the carriage slid down hill, with a cinderous smell, in a cloud of dust, the red glow departed quickly; the sun and the Marquis going down together, there was no glow left when the drag was taken off.

But, there remained a broken country, bold and open, a little village at the bottom of the hill, a broad sweep and rise beyond it, a church- tower, a windmill, a forest for the chase, and a crag with a fortress on it used as a prison. Round upon all these darkening objects as the night drew on, the Marquis looked, with the air of one who was coming near home.

The village had its one poor street, with its poor brewery, poor tannery, poor tavern, poor stable-yard for relays of post-horses, poor fountain, all usual poor appointments. It had its poor people too. All its people were poor, and many of them were sitting at their doors, shredding spare onions and the like for supper, while many were at the fountain, washing leaves, and grasses, and any such small yieldings of the earth that could be eaten. Expressive sips of what made them poor, were not wanting; the tax for the state, the tax for the church, the tax for the lord, tax local and tax general, were to be paid here and to be paid there, according to solemn inscription in the little village, until the wonder was, that there was any village left unswallowed.

Few children were to be seen, and no dogs. As to the men and women, their choice on earth was stated in the prospect—Life on the lowest terms that could sustain it, down in the little village under the mill; or captivity and Death in the dominant prison on the crag.

Heralded by a courier in advance, and by the cracking of his postilions' whips, which twined snake-like about their heads in the evening air, as if he came attended by the Furies, Monsieur the Marquis drew up in his travelling carriage at the posting-house gate. It was hard by the fountain, and the peasants suspended their operations to look at him. He looked at them, and saw in them, without knowing it, the slow sure filing down of misery-worn face and figure, that was to make the meagreness of Frenchmen an English superstition which should survive the truth through the best part of a hundred years.

Monsieur the Marquis cast his eyes over the submissive faces that drooped before him, as the like of himself had drooped before Monseigneur of the Court—only the difference was, that these faces drooped merely to suffer and not to propitiate—when a grizzled mender of the roads joined the group.

"Bring me hither that fellow!" said the Marquis to the courier.

The fellow was brought, cap in hand, and the other fellows closed round to look and listen, in the manner of the people at the Paris fountain.

"I passed you on the road?"

"Monseigneur, it is true. I had the honour of being passed on the road."

"Coming up the hill, and at the top of the hill, both?"

"Monseigneur, it is true."

"What did you look at, so fixedly?"

"Monseigneur, I looked at the man."

He stooped a little, and with his tattered blue cap pointed under the carriage. All his fellows stooped to look under the carriage.

"What man, pig? And why look there?"

"Pardon, Monseigneur; he swung by the chain of the shoe—the drag."

"Who?" demanded the traveller.

"Monseigneur, the man."

"May the Devil carry away these idiots! How do you call the man? You know all the men of this part of the country. Who was he?"

"Your clemency, Monseigneur! He was not of this part of the country. Of all the days of my life, I never saw him."

"Swinging by the chain? To be suffocated?"

"With your gracious permission, that was the wonder of it, Monseigneur. His head hanging over—like this!"

He turned himself sideways to the carriage, and leaned back, with his face thrown up to the sky, and his head hanging down; then recovered himself, fumbled with his cap, and made a bow.

"What was he like?"

"Monseigneur, he was whiter than the miller. All covered with dust, white as a spectre, tall as a spectre!"

The picture produced an immense sensation in the little crowd; but all eyes, without comparing notes with other eyes, looked at Monsieur the Marquis. Perhaps, to observe whether he had any spectre on his conscience.

"Truly, you did well," said the Marquis, felicitously sensible that such vermin were not to ruffle him, "to see a thief accompanying my carriage, and not open that great mouth of yours. Bah! Put him aside, Monsieur Gabelle!"

Monsieur Gabelle was the Postmaster, and some other taxing functionary united; he had come out with great obsequiousness to assist at this examination, and had held the examined by the drapery of his arm in an official manner.

"Bah! Go aside!" said Monsieur Gabelle.

"Lay hands on this stranger if he seeks to lodge in your village to-night, and be sure that his business is honest, Gabelle."

"Monseigneur, I am flattered to devote myself to your orders."

"Did he run away, fellow?—where is that Accursed?"

The accursed was already under the carriage with some half-dozen particular friends, pointing out the chain with his blue cap. Some half-dozen other particular friends promptly hauled him out, and presented him breathless to Monsieur the Marquis.

"Did the man run away, Dolt, when we stopped for the drag?"

"Monseigneur, he precipitated himself over the hill-side, head first, as a person plunges into the river."

"See to it, Gabelle. Go on!"

The half-dozen who were peering at the chain were still among the wheels, like sheep; the wheels turned so suddenly that they were lucky to save their skins and bones; they had very little else to save, or they might not have been so fortunate.

The burst with which the carriage started out of the village and up the rise beyond, was soon checked by the steepness of the hill. Gradually, it subsided to a foot pace, swinging and lumbering upward among the many sweet scents of a summer night. The postilions, with a thousand gossamer gnats circling about them in lieu of the Furies, quietly mended the points to the lashes of their whips; the valet walked by the horses; the courier was audible, trotting on ahead into the dun distance.

At the steepest point of the hill there was a little burial-ground, with a Cross and a new large figure of Our Saviour on it; it was a poor figure in wood, done by some inexperienced rustic carver, but he had studied the figure from the life—his own life, maybe—for it was dreadfully spare and thin.

To this distressful emblem of a great distress that had long been growing worse, and was not at its worst, a woman was kneeling. She turned her head as the carriage came up to her, rose quickly, and presented herself at the carriage-door.

"It is you, Monseigneur! Monseigneur, a petition."

With an exclamation of impatience, but with his unchangeable face, Monseigneur looked out.

"How, then! What is it? Always petitions!"

"Monseigneur. For the love of the great God! My husband, the forester."

"What of your husband, the forester? Always the same with you people. He cannot pay something?"

"He has paid all, Monseigneur. He is dead."

"Well! He is quiet. Can I restore him to you?"

"Alas, no, Monseigneur! But he lies yonder, under a little heap of poor grass."

"Well?"

"Monseigneur, there are so many little heaps of poor grass?"

"Again, well?"

She looked an old woman, but was young. Her manner was one of passionate grief; by turns she clasped her veinous and knotted hands together with wild energy, and laid one of them on the carriage-door—tenderly, caressingly, as if it had been a human breast, and could be expected to feel the appealing touch.

"Monseigneur, hear me! Monseigneur, hear my petition! My husband died of want; so many die of want; so many more will die of want."

"Again, well? Can I feed them?"

"Monseigneur, the good God knows; but I don't ask it. My petition is, that a morsel of stone or wood, with my husband's name, may be placed over him to show where he lies. Otherwise, the place will be quickly forgotten, it will never be found when I am dead of the same malady, I shall be laid under some other heap of poor grass. Monseigneur, they are so many, they increase so fast, there is so much want. Monseigneur! Monseigneur!"

The valet had put her away from the door, the carriage had broken into a brisk trot, the postilions had quickened the pace, she was left far behind, and Monseigneur, again escorted by the Furies, was rapidly diminishing the league or two of distance that remained between him and his chateau.

The sweet scents of the summer night rose all around him, and rose, as the rain falls, impartially, on the dusty, ragged, and toil-worn group at the fountain not far away; to whom the mender of roads, with the aid of the blue cap without which he was nothing, still enlarged upon his man like a spectre, as long as they could bear it. By degrees, as they could bear no more, they dropped off one by one, and lights twinkled in little casements; which lights, as the casements darkened, and more stars came out, seemed to have shot up into the sky instead of having been extinguished.

The shadow of a large high-roofed house, and of many over-hanging trees, was upon Monsieur the Marquis by that time; and the shadow was exchanged for the light of a flambeau, as his carriage stopped, and the great door of his chateau was opened to him.

"Monsieur Charles, whom I expect; is he arrived from England?"

"Monseigneur, not yet."

IX. THE GORGON'S HEAD

It was a heavy mass of building, that chateau of Monsieur the Marquis, with a large stone courtyard before it, and two stone sweeps of staircase meeting in a stone terrace before the principal door. A stony business altogether, with heavy stone balustrades, and stone urns, and stone flowers, and stone faces of men, and stone heads of lions, in all directions. As if the Gorgon's head had surveyed it, when it was finished, two centuries ago.

Up the broad flight of shallow steps, Monsieur the Marquis, flambeau preceded, went from his carriage, sufficiently disturbing the darkness to elicit loud remonstrance from an owl in the roof of the great pile of stable building away among the trees. All else was so quiet, that the flambeau carried up the steps, and the other flambeau held at the great door, burnt as if they were in a close room of state, instead of being in the open night-air. Other sound than the owl's voice there was none, save the failing of a fountain into its stone basin; for, it was one of those dark nights that hold their breath by the hour together, and then heave a long low sigh, and hold their breath again.

The great door clanged behind him, and Monsieur the Marquis crossed a hall grim with certain old boar-spears, swords, and knives of the chase; grimmer with certain heavy riding-rods and riding-whips, of which many a peasant, gone to his benefactor Death, had felt the weight when his lord was angry.

Avoiding the larger rooms, which were dark and made fast for the night, Monsieur the Marquis, with his flambeau-bearer going on before, went up the staircase to a door in a corridor. This thrown open, admitted him to his own private apartment of three rooms: his bed-chamber and two others. High vaulted rooms with cool uncarpeted floors, great dogs upon the hearths for the burning of wood in winter time, and all luxuries befitting the state of a marquis in a luxurious age and country. The fashion of the last Louis but one, of the line that was never to break—the fourteenth Louis— was conspicuous in their rich furniture; but, it was diversified by many objects that were illustrations of old pages in the history of France.

A supper-table was laid for two, in the third of the rooms; a round room, in one of the chateau's four extinguisher-topped towers. A small lofty room, with its window wide open, and the wooden jalousie-blinds closed, so that the dark night only showed in slight horizontal lines of black, alternating with their broad lines of stone colour.

"My nephew," said the Marquis, glancing at the supper preparation; "they said he was not arrived."

Nor was he; but, he had been expected with Monseigneur.

"Ah! It is not probable he will arrive to-night; nevertheless, leave the table as it is. I shall be ready in a quarter of an hour."

In a quarter of an hour Monseigneur was ready, and sat down alone to his sumptuous and choice supper. His chair was opposite to the window, and he had taken his soup, and was raising his glass of Bordeaux to his lips, when he put it down.

"What is that?" he calmly asked, looking with attention at the horizontal lines of black and stone colour.

"Monseigneur? That?"

"Outside the blinds. Open the blinds."

It was done.

"Well?"

"Monseigneur, it is nothing. The trees and the night are all that are here."

The servant who spoke, had thrown the blinds wide, had looked out into the vacant darkness, and stood with that blank behind him, looking round for instructions.

"Good," said the imperturbable master. "Close them again."

That was done too, and the Marquis went on with his supper. He was half way through it, when he again stopped with his glass in his hand, hearing the sound of wheels. It came on briskly, and came up to the front of the chateau.

"Ask who is arrived."

It was the nephew of Monseigneur. He had been some few leagues behind Monseigneur, early in the afternoon. He had diminished the distance rapidly, but not so rapidly as to come up with Monseigneur on the road. He had heard of Monseigneur, at the posting-houses, as being before him.

He was to be told (said Monseigneur) that supper awaited him then and there, and that he was prayed to come to it. In a little while he came. He had been known in England as Charles Darnay.

Monseigneur received him in a courtly manner, but they did not shake hands.

"You left Paris yesterday, sir?" he said to Monseigneur, as he took his seat at table.

"Yesterday. And you?"

"I come direct."

"From London?"

"Yes."

"You have been a long time coming," said the Marquis, with a smile.

"On the contrary; I come direct."

"Pardon me! I mean, not a long time on the journey; a long time intending the journey."

"I have been detained by"—the nephew stopped a moment in his answer—"various business."

"Without doubt," said the polished uncle.

So long as a servant was present, no other words passed between them. When coffee had been served and they were alone together, the nephew, looking at the uncle and meeting the eyes of the face that was like a fine mask, opened a conversation.

"I have come back, sir, as you anticipate, pursuing the object that took me away. It carried me into great and unexpected peril; but it is a sacred object, and if it had carried me to death I hope it would have sustained me."

"Not to death," said the uncle; "it is not necessary to say, to death."

"I doubt, sir," returned the nephew, "whether, if it had carried me to the utmost brink of death, you would have cared to stop me there."

The deepened marks in the nose, and the lengthening of the fine straight lines in the cruel face, looked ominous as to that; the uncle made a graceful gesture of protest, which was so clearly a slight form of good breeding that it was not reassuring.

"Indeed, sir," pursued the nephew, "for anything I know, you may have expressly worked to give a more suspicious appearance to the suspicious circumstances that surrounded me."

"No, no, no," said the uncle, pleasantly.

"But, however that may be," resumed the nephew, glancing at him with deep distrust, "I know that your diplomacy would stop me by any means, and would know no scruple as to means."

"My friend, I told you so," said the uncle, with a fine pulsation in the two marks. "Do me the favour to recall that I told you so, long ago."

"I recall it."

"Thank you," said the Marquis—very sweetly indeed.

His tone lingered in the air, almost like the tone of a musical instrument.

"In effect, sir," pursued the nephew, "I believe it to be at once your bad fortune, and my good fortune, that has kept me out of a prison in France here."

"I do not quite understand," returned the uncle, sipping his coffee. "Dare I ask you to explain?"

"I believe that if you were not in disgrace with the Court, and had not been overshadowed by that cloud for years past, a letter de cachet would have sent me to some fortress indefinitely."

"It is possible," said the uncle, with great calmness. "For the honour of the family, I could even resolve to incommode you to that extent. Pray excuse me!"

"I perceive that, happily for me, the Reception of the day before yesterday was, as usual, a cold one," observed the nephew.

"I would not say happily, my friend," returned the uncle, with refined politeness; "I would not be sure of that. A good opportunity for consideration, surrounded by the advantages of solitude, might influence your destiny to far greater advantage than you influence it for yourself. But it is useless to discuss the question. I am, as you say, at a disadvantage. These little instruments of correction, these gentle aids to the power and honour of families, these slight favours that might so incommode you, are only to be obtained now by interest and importunity. They are sought by so many, and they are granted (comparatively) to so few! It used not to be so, but France in all such things is changed for the worse. Our not remote ancestors held the right of life and death over the surrounding vulgar. From this room, many such dogs have been taken out to be hanged; in the next room (my bedroom), one fellow, to our knowledge, was poniarded on the spot for professing some insolent delicacy respecting his daughter—*his* daughter? We have lost many privileges; a new philosophy has become the mode; and the assertion of our station, in these days, might (I do not go so far as to say would, but might) cause us real inconvenience. All very bad, very bad!"

The Marquis took a gentle little pinch of snuff, and shook his head; as elegantly despondent as he could becomingly be of a country still containing himself, that great means of regeneration.

"We have so asserted our station, both in the old time and in the modern time also," said the nephew, gloomily, "that I believe our name to be more detested than any name in France."

"Let us hope so," said the uncle. "Detestation of the high is the involuntary homage of the low."

"There is not," pursued the nephew, in his former tone, "a face I can look at, in all this country round about us, which looks at me with any deference on it but the dark deference of fear and slavery."

"A compliment," said the Marquis, "to the grandeur of the family, merited by the manner in which the family has sustained its grandeur. Hah!" And he took another gentle little pinch of snuff, and lightly crossed his legs.

But, when his nephew, leaning an elbow on the table, covered his eyes thoughtfully and dejectedly with his hand, the fine mask looked at him sideways with a stronger concentration of keenness, closeness, and dislike, than was comportable with its wearer's assumption of indifference.

"Repression is the only lasting philosophy. The dark deference of fear and slavery, my friend," observed the Marquis, "will keep the dogs obedient to the whip, as long as this roof," looking up to it, "shuts out the sky."

That might not be so long as the Marquis supposed. If a picture of the chateau as it was to be a very few years hence, and of fifty like it as they too were to be a very few years hence, could have been shown to him that night, he might have been at a loss to claim his own from the ghastly, fire-charred, plunder-wrecked rains. As for the roof he vaunted, he might have found *that* shutting out the sky in a new way—to wit, for ever, from the eyes of the bodies into which its lead was fired, out of the barrels of a hundred thousand muskets.

"Meanwhile," said the Marquis, "I will preserve the honour and repose of the family, if you will not. But you must be fatigued. Shall we terminate our conference for the night?"

"A moment more."

"An hour, if you please."

"Sir," said the nephew, "we have done wrong, and are reaping the fruits of wrong."

"*We* have done wrong?" repeated the Marquis, with an inquiring smile, and delicately pointing, first to his nephew, then to himself.

"Our family; our honourable family, whose honour is of so much account to both of us, in such different ways. Even in my father's time, we did a world of wrong, injuring every human creature who came between us and our pleasure, whatever it was. Why need I speak of my father's time, when it is equally yours? Can I separate my father's twin-brother, joint inheritor, and next successor, from himself?"

"Death has done that!" said the Marquis.

"And has left me," answered the nephew, "bound to a system that is frightful to me, responsible for it, but powerless in it; seeking to execute the last request of my dear mother's lips, and obey the last look of my dear mother's eyes, which implored me to have mercy and to redress; and tortured by seeking assistance and power in vain."

"Seeking them from me, my nephew," said the Marquis, touching him on the breast with his forefinger—they were now standing by the hearth—"you will for ever seek them in vain, be assured."

Every fine straight line in the clear whiteness of his face, was cruelly, craftily, and closely compressed, while he stood looking quietly at his nephew, with his snuff-box in his hand. Once again he touched him on the breast, as though his finger were the fine point of a small sword, with which, in delicate finesse, he ran him through the body, and said,

"My friend, I will die, perpetuating the system under which I have lived."

When he had said it, he took a culminating pinch of snuff, and put his box in his pocket.

"Better to be a rational creature," he added then, after ringing a small bell on the table, "and accept your natural destiny. But you are lost, Monsieur Charles, I see."

"This property and France are lost to me," said the nephew, sadly; "I renounce them."

"Are they both yours to renounce? France may be, but is the property? It is scarcely worth mentioning; but, is it yet?"

"I had no intention, in the words I used, to claim it yet. If it passed to me from you, to-morrow—"

"Which I have the vanity to hope is not probable."

"—or twenty years hence—"

"You do me too much honour," said the Marquis; "still, I prefer that supposition."

"—I would abandon it, and live otherwise and elsewhere. It is little to relinquish. What is it but a wilderness of misery and ruin!"

"Hah!" said the Marquis, glancing round the luxurious room.

"To the eye it is fair enough, here; but seen in its integrity, under the sky, and by the daylight, it is a crumbling tower of waste, mismanagement, extortion, debt, mortgage, oppression, hunger, nakedness, and suffering."

"Hah!" said the Marquis again, in a well-satisfied manner.

"If it ever becomes mine, it shall be put into some hands better qualified to free it slowly (if such a thing is possible) from the weight that drags it down, so that the miserable people who cannot leave it and who have been long wrung to the last point of endurance, may, in another generation, suffer less; but it is not for me. There is a curse on it, and on all this land."

"And you?" said the uncle. "Forgive my curiosity; do you, under your new philosophy, graciously intend to live?"

"I must do, to live, what others of my countrymen, even with nobility at their backs, may have to do some day-work."

"In England, for example?"

"Yes. The family honour, sir, is safe from me in this country. The family name can suffer from me in no other, for I bear it in no other."

The ringing of the bell had caused the adjoining bed-chamber to be lighted. It now shone brightly, through the door of communication. The Marquis looked that way, and listened for the retreating step of his valet.

"England is very attractive to you, seeing how indifferently you have prospered there," he observed then, turning his calm face to his nephew with a smile.

"I have already said, that for my prospering there, I am sensible I may be indebted to you, sir. For the rest, it is my Refuge."

"They say, those boastful English, that it is the Refuge of many. You know a compatriot who has found a Refuge there? A Doctor?"

"Yes."

"With a daughter?"

"Yes."

"Yes," said the Marquis. "You are fatigued. Good night!"

As he bent his head in his most courtly manner, there was a secrecy in his smiling face, and he conveyed an air of mystery to those words, which struck the eyes and ears of his nephew forcibly. At the same time, the thin straight lines of the setting of the eyes, and the thin straight lips, and the markings in the nose, curved with a sarcasm that looked handsomely diabolic.

"Yes," repeated the Marquis. "A Doctor with a daughter. Yes. So commences the new philosophy! You are fatigued. Good night!"

It would have been of as much avail to interrogate any stone face outside the chateau as to interrogate that face of his. The nephew looked at him, in vain, in passing on to the door.

"Good night!" said the uncle. "I look to the pleasure of seeing you again in the morning. Good repose! Light Monsieur my nephew to his chamber there!—And burn Monsieur my nephew in his bed, if you will," he added to himself, before he rang his little bell again, and summoned his valet to his own bedroom.

The valet come and gone, Monsieur the Marquis walked to and fro in his loose chamber-robe, to prepare himself gently for sleep, that hot still night. Rustling about the room, his softly-slippered feet making no noise on the floor, he moved like a refined tiger:—looked like some enchanted marquis of the impenitently wicked sort, in story, whose periodical change into tiger form was either just going off, or just coming on.

He moved from end to end of his voluptuous bedroom, looking again at the scraps of the day's journey that came unbidden into his mind; the slow toil up the hill at sunset, the setting sun, the descent, the mill, the prison on the crag, the little village in the hollow, the peasants at the fountain, and the mender of roads with his blue cap pointing out the chain under the carriage. That fountain suggested the Paris fountain, the little bundle lying on the step, the women bending over it, and the tall man with his arms up, crying, "Dead!"

"I am cool now," said Monsieur the Marquis, "and may go to bed."

So, leaving only one light burning on the large hearth, he let his thin gauze curtains fall around him, and heard the night break its silence with a long sigh as he composed himself to sleep.

The stone faces on the outer walls stared blindly at the black night for three heavy hours; for three heavy hours, the horses in the stables rattled at their racks, the dogs barked, and the owl made a noise with very little resemblance in it to the noise conventionally assigned to the owl by men-poets. But it is the obstinate custom of such creatures hardly ever to say what is set down for them.

For three heavy hours, the stone faces of the chateau, lion and human, stared blindly at the night. Dead darkness lay on all the landscape, dead darkness added its own hush to the hushing dust on all the roads. The burial-place had got to the pass that its little heaps of poor grass were undistinguishable from one another; the figure on the Cross might have come down, for anything that could be seen of it. In the village, taxers and taxed were fast asleep. Dreaming, perhaps, of banquets, as the starved usually do, and of ease and rest, as the driven slave and the yoked ox may, its lean inhabitants slept soundly, and were fed and freed.

The fountain in the village flowed unseen and unheard, and the fountain at the chateau dropped unseen and unheard—both melting away, like the minutes that were falling from the spring of Time—through three dark hours. Then, the grey water of both began to be ghostly in the light, and the eyes of the stone faces of the chateau were opened.

Lighter and lighter, until at last the sun touched the tops of the still trees, and poured its radiance over the hill. In the glow, the water of the chateau fountain seemed to turn to blood, and the stone faces crimsoned. The carol of the birds was loud and high, and, on the weather-beaten sill of the great window of the bed- chamber of Monsieur the Marquis, one little bird sang its sweetest song with all its might. At this, the nearest stone face seemed to stare amazed, and, with open mouth and dropped under-jaw, looked awe-stricken.

Now, the sun was full up, and movement began in the village. Casement windows opened, crazy doors were unbarred, and people came forth shivering—chilled, as yet, by the new sweet air. Then began the rarely lightened toil of the day among the village population. Some, to the fountain; some, to the fields; men and women here, to dig and delve; men and women there, to see to the poor live stock, and lead the bony cows out, to such pasture as could be found by the roadside. In the church and at the Cross, a kneeling figure or two; attendant on the latter prayers, the led cow, trying for a breakfast among the weeds at its foot.

The chateau awoke later, as became its quality, but awoke gradually and surely. First, the lonely boar-spears and knives of the chase had been reddened as of old; then, had gleamed trenchant in the morning sunshine; now, doors and windows were thrown open, horses in their stables looked round over their shoulders at the light and freshness pouring in at doorways, leaves sparkled and rustled at iron-grated windows, dogs pulled hard at their chains, and reared impatient to be loosed.

All these trivial incidents belonged to the routine of life, and the return of morning. Surely, not so the ringing of the great bell of the chateau, nor the running up and down the stairs; nor the hurried figures on the terrace; nor the booting and tramping here and there and everywhere, nor the quick saddling of horses and riding away?

What winds conveyed this hurry to the grizzled mender of roads, already at work on the hill-top beyond the village, with his day's dinner (not much to carry) lying in a bundle that it was worth no crow's while to peck at, on a heap of stones? Had the birds, carrying some grains of it to a distance, dropped one over him as they sow chance seeds? Whether or no, the mender of roads ran, on the sultry morning, as if for his life, down the hill, knee-high in dust, and never stopped till he got to the fountain.

All the people of the village were at the fountain, standing about in their depressed manner, and whispering low, but showing no other emotions than grim curiosity and surprise. The led cows, hastily brought in and tethered to anything that would hold them, were looking stupidly on, or lying down chewing the cud of nothing particularly repaying their trouble, which they had picked up in their interrupted saunter. Some of the people of the chateau, and some of those of the posting-house, and all the taxing authorities, were armed more or less, and were crowded on the other side of the little street in a purposeless way, that was highly fraught with nothing. Already, the mender of roads had penetrated into the midst of a group of fifty particular friends, and was smiting himself in the breast with his blue cap. What did all this portend, and what portended the swift hoisting-up of Monsieur Gabelle behind a servant on horseback, and the conveying away of the said Gabelle (double-laden though the horse was), at a gallop, like a new version of the German ballad of Leonora?

It portended that there was one stone face too many, up at the chateau.

The Gorgon had surveyed the building again in the night, and had added the one stone face wanting; the stone face for which it had waited through about two hundred years.

It lay back on the pillow of Monsieur the Marquis. It was like a fine mask, suddenly startled, made angry, and petrified. Driven home into the heart of the stone figure attached to it, was a knife. Round its hilt was a frill of paper, on which was scrawled:

"Drive him fast to his tomb. This, from Jacques."

X. TWO PROMISES

More months, to the number of twelve, had come and gone, and Mr. Charles Darnay was established in England as a higher teacher of the French language who was conversant with French literature. In this age, he would have been a Professor; in that age, he was a Tutor. He read with young men who could find any leisure and interest for the study of a living tongue spoken all over the world, and he cultivated a taste for its stores of knowledge and fancy. He could write of them, besides, in sound English, and render them into sound English. Such masters were not at that time easily found; Princes that had been, and Kings that were to be, were not yet of the Teacher class, and no ruined nobility had dropped out of Tellson's ledgers, to turn cooks and carpenters. As a tutor, whose attainments made the student's way unusually pleasant and profitable, and as an elegant translator who brought something to his work besides mere dictionary knowledge, young Mr. Darnay soon became known and encouraged. He was well acquainted, more-over, with the circumstances of his country, and those were of ever-growing interest. So, with great perseverance and untiring industry, he prospered.

In London, he had expected neither to walk on pavements of gold, nor to lie on beds of roses; if he had had any such exalted expectation, he would not have prospered. He had expected labour, and he found it, and did it and made the best of it. In this, his prosperity consisted.

A certain portion of his time was passed at Cambridge, where he read with undergraduates as a sort of tolerated smuggler who drove a contraband trade in European languages, instead of conveying Greek and Latin through the Custom-house. The rest of his time he passed in London.

Now, from the days when it was always summer in Eden, to these days when it is mostly winter in fallen latitudes, the world of a man has invariably gone one way— Charles Darnay's way—the way of the love of a woman.

He had loved Lucie Manette from the hour of his danger. He had never heard a sound so sweet and dear as the sound of her compassionate voice; he had never seen a face so tenderly beautiful, as hers when it was confronted with his own on the edge of the grave that had been dug for him. But, he had not yet spoken to her on the subject; the assassination at the deserted chateau far away beyond the heaving water and the long, long, dusty roads—the solid stone chateau which had itself become the mere mist of a dream—had been done a year, and he had never yet, by so much as a single spoken word, disclosed to her the state of his heart.

That he had his reasons for this, he knew full well. It was again a summer day when, lately arrived in London from his college occupation, he turned into the quiet corner in Soho, bent on seeking an opportunity of opening his mind to Doctor Manette. It was the close of the summer day, and he knew Lucie to be out with Miss Pross.

He found the Doctor reading in his arm-chair at a window. The energy which had at once supported him under his old sufferings and aggravated their sharpness, had been gradually restored to him. He was now a very energetic man indeed, with great firmness of purpose, strength of resolution, and vigour of action. In his recovered energy he was sometimes a little fitful and sudden, as he had at first been in the exercise of his other recovered faculties; but, this had never been frequently observable, and had grown more and more rare.

He studied much, slept little, sustained a great deal of fatigue with ease, and was equably cheerful. To him, now entered Charles Darnay, at sight of whom he laid aside his book and held out his hand.

"Charles Darnay! I rejoice to see you. We have been counting on your return these three or four days past. Mr. Stryver and Sydney Carton were both here yesterday, and both made you out to be more than due."

"I am obliged to them for their interest in the matter," he answered, a little coldly as to them, though very warmly as to the Doctor. "Miss Manette—"

"Is well," said the Doctor, as he stopped short, "and your return will delight us all. She has gone out on some household matters, but will soon be home."

"Doctor Manette, I knew she was from home. I took the opportunity of her being from home, to beg to speak to you."

There was a blank silence.

"Yes?" said the Doctor, with evident constraint. "Bring your chair here, and speak on."

He complied as to the chair, but appeared to find the speaking on less easy.

"I have had the happiness, Doctor Manette, of being so intimate here," so he at length began, "for some year and a half, that I hope the topic on which I am about to touch may not—"

He was stayed by the Doctor's putting out his hand to stop him. When he had kept it so a little while, he said, drawing it back:

"Is Lucie the topic?"

"She is."

"It is hard for me to speak of her at any time. It is very hard for me to hear her spoken of in that tone of yours, Charles Darnay."

"It is a tone of fervent admiration, true homage, and deep love, Doctor Manette!" he said deferentially.

There was another blank silence before her father rejoined:

"I believe it. I do you justice; I believe it."

His constraint was so manifest, and it was so manifest, too, that it originated in an unwillingness to approach the subject, that Charles Darnay hesitated.

"Shall I go on, sir?"

Another blank.

"Yes, go on."

"You anticipate what I would say, though you cannot know how earnestly I say it, how earnestly I feel it, without knowing my secret heart, and the hopes and fears and anxieties with which it has long been laden. Dear Doctor Manette, I love your daughter fondly, dearly, disinterestedly, devotedly. If ever there were love in the world, I love her. You have loved yourself; let your old love speak for me!"

The Doctor sat with his face turned away, and his eyes bent on the ground. At the last words, he stretched out his hand again, hurriedly, and cried:

"Not that, sir! Let that be! I adjure you, do not recall that!"

His cry was so like a cry of actual pain, that it rang in Charles Darnay's ears long after he had ceased. He motioned with the hand he had extended, and it seemed to be an appeal to Darnay to pause. The latter so received it, and remained silent.

"I ask your pardon," said the Doctor, in a subdued tone, after some moments. "I do not doubt your loving Lucie; you may be satisfied of it."

He turned towards him in his chair, but did not look at him, or raise his eyes. His chin dropped upon his hand, and his white hair overshadowed his face:

"Have you spoken to Lucie?"

"No."

"Nor written?"

"Never."

"It would be ungenerous to affect not to know that your self-denial is to be referred to your consideration for her father. Her father thanks you."

He offered his hand; but his eyes did not go with it.

"I know," said Darnay, respectfully, "how can I fail to know, Doctor Manette, I who have seen you together from day to day, that between you and Miss Manette there is an affection so unusual, so touching, so belonging to the circumstances in which it has been nurtured, that it can have few parallels, even in the tenderness between a father and child. I know, Doctor Manette—how can I fail to know—that, mingled with the affection and duty of a daughter who has become a woman, there is, in her heart, towards you, all the love and reliance of infancy itself. I know that, as in her childhood she had no parent, so she is now devoted to you with all the constancy and fervour of her present years and character, united to the trustfulness and attachment of the early days in which you were lost to her. I know perfectly well that if you had been restored to her from the world beyond this life, you could hardly be invested, in her sight, with a more sacred character than that in which you are always with her. I know that when she is clinging to you, the hands of baby, girl, and woman, all in one, are round your neck. I know that in loving you she sees and loves her mother at her own age, sees and loves you at my age, loves her mother broken-hearted, loves you through your dreadful trial and in your blessed restoration. I have known this, night and day, since I have known you in your home."

Her father sat silent, with his face bent down. His breathing was a little quickened; but he repressed all other signs of agitation.

"Dear Doctor Manette, always knowing this, always seeing her and you with this hallowed light about you, I have forborne, and forborne, as long as it was in the nature of man to do it. I have felt, and do even now feel, that to bring my love—even mine—between you, is to touch your history with something not quite so good as itself. But I love her. Heaven is my witness that I love her!"

"I believe it," answered her father, mournfully. "I have thought so before now. I believe it."

"But, do not believe," said Darnay, upon whose ear the mournful voice struck with a reproachful sound, "that if my fortune were so cast as that, being one day so happy as to make her my wife, I must at any time put any separation between her and you, I could or would breathe a word of what I now say. Besides that I should know it to be hopeless, I should know it to be a baseness. If I had any such possibility, even at a remote distance of years, harboured in my thoughts, and hidden in my heart—if it ever had been there—if it ever could be there—I could not now touch this honoured hand."

He laid his own upon it as he spoke.

"No, dear Doctor Manette. Like you, a voluntary exile from France; like you, driven from it by its distractions, oppressions, and miseries; like you, striving to live away from it by my own exertions, and trusting in a happier future; I look only to sharing your fortunes, sharing your life and home, and being faithful to you to the death. Not to divide with Lucie her privilege as your child, companion, and friend; but to come in aid of it, and bind her closer to you, if such a thing can be."

His touch still lingered on her father's hand. Answering the touch for a moment, but not coldly, her father rested his hands upon the arms of his chair, and looked up for the first time since the beginning of the conference. A struggle was evidently in his face; a struggle with that occasional look which had a tendency in it to dark doubt and dread.

"You speak so feelingly and so manfully, Charles Darnay, that I thank you with all my heart, and will open all my heart—or nearly so. Have you any reason to believe that Lucie loves you?"

"None. As yet, none."

"Is it the immediate object of this confidence, that you may at once ascertain that, with my knowledge?"

"Not even so. I might not have the hopefulness to do it for weeks; I might (mistaken or not mistaken) have that hopefulness to-morrow."

"Do you seek any guidance from me?"

"I ask none, sir. But I have thought it possible that you might have it in your power, if you should deem it right, to give me some."

"Do you seek any promise from me?"

"I do seek that."

"What is it?"

"I well understand that, without you, I could have no hope. I well understand that, even if Miss Manette held me at this moment in her innocent heart—do not think I have the presumption to assume so much—I could retain no place in it against her love for her father."

"If that be so, do you see what, on the other hand, is involved in it?"

"I understand equally well, that a word from her father in any suitor's favour, would outweigh herself and all the world. For which reason, Doctor Manette," said Darnay, modestly but firmly, "I would not ask that word, to save my life."

"I am sure of it. Charles Darnay, mysteries arise out of close love, as well as out of wide division; in the former case, they are subtle and delicate, and difficult to penetrate. My daughter Lucie is, in this one respect, such a mystery to me; I can make no guess at the state of her heart."

"May I ask, sir, if you think she is—" As he hesitated, her father supplied the rest.

"Is sought by any other suitor?"

"It is what I meant to say."

Her father considered a little before he answered:

"You have seen Mr. Carton here, yourself. Mr. Stryver is here too, occasionally. If it be at all, it can only be by one of these."

"Or both," said Darnay.

"I had not thought of both; I should not think either, likely. You want a promise from me. Tell me what it is."

"It is, that if Miss Manette should bring to you at any time, on her own part, such a confidence as I have ventured to lay before you, you will bear testimony to what I have said, and to your belief in it. I hope you may be able to think so well of me, as to urge no influence against me. I say nothing more of my stake in this; this is what I ask. The condition on which I ask it, and which you have an undoubted right to require, I will observe immediately."

"I give the promise," said the Doctor, "without any condition. I believe your object to be, purely and truthfully, as you have stated it. I believe your intention is to perpetuate, and not to weaken, the ties between me and my other and far dearer self. If she should ever tell me that you are essential to her perfect happiness, I will give her to you. If there were—Charles Darnay, if there were—"

The young man had taken his hand gratefully; their hands were joined as the Doctor spoke:

"—any fancies, any reasons, any apprehensions, anything whatsoever, new or old, against the man she really loved—the direct responsibility thereof not lying on his head—they should all be obliterated for her sake. She is everything to me; more to me than suffering, more to me than wrong, more to me—Well! This is idle talk."

So strange was the way in which he faded into silence, and so strange his fixed look when he had ceased to speak, that Darnay felt his own hand turn cold in the hand that slowly released and dropped it.

"You said something to me," said Doctor Manette, breaking into a smile. "What was it you said to me?"

He was at a loss how to answer, until he remembered having spoken of a condition. Relieved as his mind reverted to that, he answered:

"Your confidence in me ought to be returned with full confidence on my part. My present name, though but slightly changed from my mother's, is not, as you will remember, my own. I wish to tell you what that is, and why I am in England."

"Stop!" said the Doctor of Beauvais.

"I wish it, that I may the better deserve your confidence, and have no secret from you."

"Stop!"

For an instant, the Doctor even had his two hands at his ears; for another instant, even had his two hands laid on Darnay's lips.

"Tell me when I ask you, not now. If your suit should prosper, if Lucie should love you, you shall tell me on your marriage morning. Do you promise?"

"Willingly."

"Give me your hand. She will be home directly, and it is better she should not see us together to-night. Go! God bless you!"

It was dark when Charles Darnay left him, and it was an hour later and darker when Lucie came home; she hurried into the room alone—for Miss Pross had gone straight up-stairs—and was surprised to find his reading-chair empty.

"My father!" she called to him. "Father dear!"

Nothing was said in answer, but she heard a low hammering sound in his bedroom. Passing lightly across the intermediate room, she looked in at his door and came running back frightened, crying to herself, with her blood all chilled, "What shall I do! What shall I do!"

Her uncertainty lasted but a moment; she hurried back, and tapped at his door, and softly called to him. The noise ceased at the sound of her voice, and he presently came out to her, and they walked up and down together for a long time.

She came down from her bed, to look at him in his sleep that night. He slept heavily, and his tray of shoemaking tools, and his old unfinished work, were all as usual.

XI. A COMPANION PICTURE

"Sydney," said Mr. Stryver, on that self-same night, or morning, to his jackal; "mix another bowl of punch; I have something to say to you."

Sydney had been working double tides that night, and the night before, and the night before that, and a good many nights in succession, making a grand clearance among Mr. Stryver's papers before the setting in of the long vacation. The clearance was effected at last; the Stryver arrears were handsomely fetched up; everything was got rid of until November should come with its fogs atmospheric, and fogs legal, and bring grist to the mill again.

Sydney was none the livelier and none the soberer for so much application. It had taken a deal of extra wet-towelling to pull him through the night; a correspondingly extra quantity of wine had preceded the towelling; and he was in a very damaged condition, as he now pulled his turban off and threw it into the basin in which he had steeped it at intervals for the last six hours.

"Are you mixing that other bowl of punch?" said Stryver the portly, with his hands in his waistband, glancing round from the sofa where he lay on his back.

"I am."

"Now, look here! I am going to tell you something that will rather surprise you, and that perhaps will make you think me not quite as shrewd as you usually do think me. I intend to marry."

"*Do* you?"

"Yes. And not for money. What do you say now?"

"I don't feel disposed to say much. Who is she?"

"Guess."

"Do I know her?"

"Guess."

"I am not going to guess, at five o'clock in the morning, with my brains frying and sputtering in my head. If you want me to guess, you must ask me to dinner."

"Well then, I'll tell you," said Stryver, coming slowly into a sitting posture. "Sydney, I rather despair of making myself intelligible to you, because you are such an insensible dog."

"And you," returned Sydney, busy concocting the punch, "are such a sensitive and poetical spirit—"

"Come!" rejoined Stryver, laughing boastfully, "though I don't prefer any claim to being the soul of Romance (for I hope I know better), still I am a tenderer sort of fellow than *you*."

"You are a luckier, if you mean that."

"I don't mean that. I mean I am a man of more—more—"

"Say gallantry, while you are about it," suggested Carton.

"Well! I'll say gallantry. My meaning is that I am a man," said Stryver, inflating himself at his friend as he made the punch, "who cares more to be agreeable, who takes more pains to be agreeable, who knows better how to be agreeable, in a woman's society, than you do."

"Go on," said Sydney Carton.

"No; but before I go on," said Stryver, shaking his head in his bullying way, "I'll have this out with you. You've been at Doctor Manette's house as much as I have, or more than I have. Why, I have been ashamed of your moroseness there! Your manners have been of that silent and sullen and hangdog kind, that, upon my life and soul, I have been ashamed of you, Sydney!"

"It should be very beneficial to a man in your practice at the bar, to be ashamed of anything," returned Sydney; "you ought to be much obliged to me."

"You shall not get off in that way," rejoined Stryver, shouldering the rejoinder at him; "no, Sydney, it's my duty to tell you—and I tell you to your face to do you good—that you are a devilish ill-conditioned fellow in that sort of society. You are a disagreeable fellow."

Sydney drank a bumper of the punch he had made, and laughed.

"Look at me!" said Stryver, squaring himself; "I have less need to make myself agreeable than you have, being more independent in circumstances. Why do I do it?"

"I never saw you do it yet," muttered Carton.

"I do it because it's politic; I do it on principle. And look at me! I get on."

"You don't get on with your account of your matrimonial intentions," answered Carton, with a careless air; "I wish you would keep to that. As to me—will you never understand that I am incorrigible?"

He asked the question with some appearance of scorn.

"You have no business to be incorrigible," was his friend's answer, delivered in no very soothing tone.

"I have no business to be, at all, that I know of," said Sydney Carton. "Who is the lady?"

"Now, don't let my announcement of the name make you uncomfortable, Sydney," said Mr. Stryver, preparing him with ostentatious friendliness for the disclosure he was about to make, "because I know you don't mean half you say; and if you meant it all, it would be of no importance. I make this little preface, because you once mentioned the young lady to me in slighting terms."

"I did?"

"Certainly; and in these chambers."

Sydney Carton looked at his punch and looked at his complacent friend; drank his punch and looked at his complacent friend.

"You made mention of the young lady as a golden-haired doll. The young lady is Miss Manette. If you had been a fellow of any sensitiveness or delicacy of feeling in that kind of way, Sydney, I might have been a little resentful of your employing such a designation; but you are not. You want that sense altogether; therefore I am no more annoyed when I think of the expression, than I should be annoyed by a man's opinion of a picture of mine, who had no eye for pictures: or of a piece of music of mine, who had no ear for music."

Sydney Carton drank the punch at a great rate; drank it by bumpers, looking at his friend.

"Now you know all about it, Syd," said Mr. Stryver. "I don't care about fortune: she is a charming creature, and I have made up my mind to please myself: on the whole, I think I can afford to please myself. She will have in me a man already pretty well off, and a rapidly rising man, and a man of some distinction: it is a piece of good fortune for her, but she is worthy of good fortune. Are you astonished?"

Carton, still drinking the punch, rejoined, "Why should I be astonished?"

"You approve?"

Carton, still drinking the punch, rejoined, "Why should I not approve?"

"Well!" said his friend Stryver, "you take it more easily than I fancied you would, and are less mercenary on my behalf than I thought you would be; though, to be sure, you know well enough by this time that your ancient chum is a man of a pretty strong will. Yes, Sydney, I have had enough of this style of life, with no other as a change from it; I feel that it is a pleasant thing for a man to have a home when he feels inclined to go to it (when he doesn't, he can stay away), and I feel that Miss Manette will tell well in any station, and will always do me credit. So I have made up my mind. And now, Sydney, old boy, I want to say a word to *you* about *your* prospects. You are in a bad way, you know; you really are in a bad way. You don't know the value of money, you live hard, you'll knock up one of these days, and be ill and poor; you really ought to think about a nurse."

The prosperous patronage with which he said it, made him look twice as big as he was, and four times as offensive.

"Now, let me recommend you," pursued Stryver, "to look it in the face. I have looked it in the face, in my different way; look it in the face, you, in your different way. Marry. Provide somebody to take care of you. Never mind your having no enjoyment of women's society, nor understanding of it, nor tact for it. Find out somebody. Find out some respectable woman with a little property—somebody in the landlady way, or lodging-letting way—and marry her, against a rainy day. That's the kind of thing for *you*. Now think of it, Sydney."

"I'll think of it," said Sydney.

XII. THE FELLOW OF DELICACY

Mr. Stryver having made up his mind to that magnanimous bestowal of good fortune on the Doctor's daughter, resolved to make her happiness known to her before he left town for the Long Vacation. After some mental debating of the point, he came to the conclusion that it would be as well to get all the preliminaries done with, and they could then arrange at their leisure whether he should give her his hand a week or two before Michaelmas Term, or in the little Christmas vacation between it and Hilary.

As to the strength of his case, he had not a doubt about it, but clearly saw his way to the verdict. Argued with the jury on substantial worldly grounds—the only grounds ever worth taking into account—it was a plain case, and had not a weak spot in it. He called himself for the plaintiff, there was no getting over his evidence, the counsel for the defendant threw up his brief, and the jury did not even turn to consider. After trying it, Stryver, C. J., was satisfied that no plainer case could be.

Accordingly, Mr. Stryver inaugurated the Long Vacation with a formal proposal to take Miss Manette to Vauxhall Gardens; that failing, to Ranelagh; that unaccountably failing too, it behoved him to present himself in Soho, and there declare his noble mind.

Towards Soho, therefore, Mr. Stryver shouldered his way from the Temple, while the bloom of the Long Vacation's infancy was still upon it. Anybody who had seen him projecting himself into Soho while he was yet on Saint Dunstan's side of Temple Bar, bursting in his full-blown way along the pavement, to the jostlement of all weaker people, might have seen how safe and strong he was.

His way taking him past Tellson's, and he both banking at Tellson's and knowing Mr. Lorry as the intimate friend of the Manettes, it entered Mr. Stryver's mind to enter the bank, and reveal to Mr. Lorry the brightness of the Soho horizon. So, he pushed open the door with the weak rattle in its throat, stumbled down the two steps, got past the two ancient cashiers, and shouldered himself into the musty back closet where Mr. Lorry sat at great books ruled for figures, with perpendicular iron bars to his window as if that were ruled for figures too, and everything under the clouds were a sum.

"Halloa!" said Mr. Stryver. "How do you do? I hope you are well!"

It was Stryver's grand peculiarity that he always seemed too big for any place, or space. He was so much too big for Tellson's, that old clerks in distant corners looked up with looks of remonstrance, as though he squeezed them against the wall. The House itself, magnificently reading the paper quite in the far-off perspective, lowered displeased, as if the Stryver head had been butted into its responsible waistcoat.

The discreet Mr. Lorry said, in a sample tone of the voice he would recommend under the circumstances, "How do you do, Mr. Stryver? How do you do, sir?" and shook hands. There was a peculiarity in his manner of shaking hands, always to be seen in any clerk at Tellson's who shook hands with a customer when the House pervaded the air. He shook in a self-abnegating way, as one who shook for Tellson and Co.

"Can I do anything for you, Mr. Stryver?" asked Mr. Lorry, in his business character.

"Why, no, thank you; this is a private visit to yourself, Mr. Lorry; I have come for a private word."

"Oh indeed!" said Mr. Lorry, bending down his ear, while his eye strayed to the House afar off.

"I am going," said Mr. Stryver, leaning his arms confidentially on the desk: whereupon, although it was a large double one, there appeared to be not half desk enough for him: "I am going to make an offer of myself in marriage to your agreeable little friend, Miss Manette, Mr. Lorry."

"Oh dear me!" cried Mr. Lorry, rubbing his chin, and looking at his visitor dubiously.

"Oh dear me, sir?" repeated Stryver, drawing back. "Oh dear you, sir? What may your meaning be, Mr. Lorry?"

"My meaning," answered the man of business, "is, of course, friendly and appreciative, and that it does you the greatest credit, and—in short, my meaning is everything you could desire. But—really, you know, Mr. Stryver—" Mr. Lorry paused, and shook his head at him in the oddest manner, as if he were compelled against his will to add, internally, "you know there really is so much too much of you!"

"Well!" said Stryver, slapping the desk with his contentious hand, opening his eyes wider, and taking a long breath, "if I understand you, Mr. Lorry, I'll be hanged!"

Mr. Lorry adjusted his little wig at both ears as a means towards that end, and bit the feather of a pen.

"D—n it all, sir!" said Stryver, staring at him, "am I not eligible?"

"Oh dear yes! Yes. Oh yes, you're eligible!" said Mr. Lorry. "If you say eligible, you are eligible."

"Am I not prosperous?" asked Stryver.

"Oh! if you come to prosperous, you are prosperous," said Mr. Lorry.

"And advancing?"

"If you come to advancing you know," said Mr. Lorry, delighted to be able to make another admission, "nobody can doubt that."

"Then what on earth is your meaning, Mr. Lorry?" demanded Stryver, perceptibly crestfallen.

"Well! I—Were you going there now?" asked Mr. Lorry.

"Straight!" said Stryver, with a plump of his fist on the desk.

"Then I think I wouldn't, if I was you."

"Why?" said Stryver. "Now, I'll put you in a corner," forensically shaking a forefinger at him. "You are a man of business and bound to have a reason. State your reason. Why wouldn't you go?"

"Because," said Mr. Lorry, "I wouldn't go on such an object without having some cause to believe that I should succeed."

"D—n *me*!" cried Stryver, "but this beats everything."

Mr. Lorry glanced at the distant House, and glanced at the angry Stryver.

"Here's a man of business—a man of years—a man of experience—*in* a Bank," said Stryver; "and having summed up three leading reasons for complete success, he says there's no reason at all! Says it with his head on!" Mr. Stryver remarked upon the peculiarity as if it would have been infinitely less remarkable if he had said it with his head off.

"When I speak of success, I speak of success with the young lady; and when I speak of causes and reasons to make success probable, I speak of causes and reasons that will tell as such with the young lady. The young lady, my good sir," said Mr. Lorry, mildly tapping the Stryver arm, "the young lady. The young lady goes before all."

"Then you mean to tell me, Mr. Lorry," said Stryver, squaring his elbows, "that it is your deliberate opinion that the young lady at present in question is a mincing Fool?"

"Not exactly so. I mean to tell you, Mr. Stryver," said Mr. Lorry, reddening, "that I will hear no disrespectful word of that young lady from any lips; and that if I knew any man—which I hope I do not—whose taste was so coarse, and whose temper was so overbearing, that he could not restrain himself from speaking disrespectfully of that young lady at this desk, not even Tellson's should prevent my giving him a piece of my mind."

The necessity of being angry in a suppressed tone had put Mr. Stryver's blood-vessels into a dangerous state when it was his turn to be angry; Mr. Lorry's veins, methodical as their courses could usually be, were in no better state now it was his turn.

"That is what I mean to tell you, sir," said Mr. Lorry. "Pray let there be no mistake about it."

Mr. Stryver sucked the end of a ruler for a little while, and then stood hitting a tune out of his teeth with it, which probably gave him the toothache. He broke the awkward silence by saying:

"This is something new to me, Mr. Lorry. You deliberately advise me not to go up to Soho and offer myself—*my*self, Stryver of the King's Bench bar?"

"Do you ask me for my advice, Mr. Stryver?"

"Yes, I do."

"Very good. Then I give it, and you have repeated it correctly."

"And all I can say of it is," laughed Stryver with a vexed laugh, "that this—ha, ha!—beats everything past, present, and to come."

"Now understand me," pursued Mr. Lorry. "As a man of business, I am not justified in saying anything about this matter, for, as a man of business, I know nothing of it. But, as an old fellow, who has carried Miss Manette in his arms, who is the trusted friend of Miss Manette and of her father too, and who has a great affection for them both, I have spoken. The confidence is not of my seeking, recollect. Now, you think I may not be right?"

"Not I!" said Stryver, whistling. "I can't undertake to find third parties in common sense; I can only find it for myself. I suppose sense in certain quarters; you suppose mincing bread-and-butter nonsense. It's new to me, but you are right, I dare say."

"What I suppose, Mr. Stryver, I claim to characterise for myself—And understand me, sir," said Mr. Lorry, quickly flushing again, "I will not—not even at Tellson's—have it characterised for me by any gentleman breathing."

"There! I beg your pardon!" said Stryver.

"Granted. Thank you. Well, Mr. Stryver, I was about to say:—it might be painful to you to find yourself mistaken, it might be painful to Doctor Manette to have the task of being explicit with you, it might be very painful to Miss Manette to have the task of being explicit with you. You know the terms upon which I have the honour and happiness to stand with the family. If you please, committing you in no way, representing you in no way, I will undertake to correct my advice by the exercise of a little new observation and judgment expressly brought to bear upon it. If you should then be dissatisfied with it, you can but test its soundness for yourself; if, on the other hand, you should be satisfied with it, and it should be what it now is, it may spare all sides what is best spared. What do you say?"

"How long would you keep me in town?"

"Oh! It is only a question of a few hours. I could go to Soho in the evening, and come to your chambers afterwards."

"Then I say yes," said Stryver: "I won't go up there now, I am not so hot upon it as that comes to; I say yes, and I shall expect you to look in to-night. Good morning."

Then Mr. Stryver turned and burst out of the Bank, causing such a concussion of air on his passage through, that to stand up against it bowing behind the two counters, required the utmost remaining strength of the two ancient clerks. Those venerable and feeble persons were always seen by the public in the act of bowing, and were popularly believed, when they had bowed a customer out, still to keep on bowing in the empty office until they bowed another customer in.

The barrister was keen enough to divine that the banker would not have gone so far in his expression of opinion on any less solid ground than moral certainty. Unprepared as he was for the large pill he had to swallow, he got it down. "And now," said Mr. Stryver, shaking his forensic forefinger at the Temple in general, when it was down, "my way out of this, is, to put you all in the wrong."

It was a bit of the art of an Old Bailey tactician, in which he found great relief. "You shall not put me in the wrong, young lady," said Mr. Stryver; "I'll do that for you."

Accordingly, when Mr. Lorry called that night as late as ten o'clock, Mr. Stryver, among a quantity of books and papers littered out for the purpose, seemed to have nothing less on his mind than the subject of the morning. He even showed surprise when he saw Mr. Lorry, and was altogether in an absent and preoccupied state.

"Well!" said that good-natured emissary, after a full half-hour of bootless attempts to bring him round to the question. "I have been to Soho."

"To Soho?" repeated Mr. Stryver, coldly. "Oh, to be sure! What am I thinking of!"

"And I have no doubt," said Mr. Lorry, "that I was right in the conversation we had. My opinion is confirmed, and I reiterate my advice."

"I assure you," returned Mr. Stryver, in the friendliest way, "that I am sorry for it on your account, and sorry for it on the poor father's account. I know this must always be a sore subject with the family; let us say no more about it."

"I don't understand you," said Mr. Lorry.

"I dare say not," rejoined Stryver, nodding his head in a smoothing and final way; "no matter, no matter."

"But it does matter," Mr. Lorry urged.

"No it doesn't; I assure you it doesn't. Having supposed that there was sense where there is no sense, and a laudable ambition where there is not a laudable ambition, I am well out of my mistake, and no harm is done. Young women have committed similar follies often before, and have repented them in poverty and obscurity often before. In an unselfish aspect, I am sorry that the thing is dropped, because it would have been a bad thing for me in a worldly point of view; in a selfish aspect, I am glad that the thing has dropped, because it would have been a bad thing for me in a worldly point of view—it is hardly necessary to say I could have gained nothing by it. There is no harm at all done. I have not proposed to the young lady, and, between ourselves, I am by no means certain, on reflection, that I ever should have committed myself to that extent. Mr. Lorry, you cannot control the mincing vanities and giddinesses of empty-headed girls; you must not expect to do it, or you will always be disappointed. Now, pray say no more about it. I tell you, I regret it on account of others, but I am satisfied on my own account. And I am really very much obliged to you for allowing me to sound you, and for giving me your advice; you know the young lady better than I do; you were right, it never would have done."

Mr. Lorry was so taken aback, that he looked quite stupidly at Mr. Stryver shouldering him towards the door, with an appearance of showering generosity, forbearance, and goodwill, on his erring head. "Make the best of it, my dear sir," said Stryver; "say no more about it; thank you again for allowing me to sound you; good night!"

Mr. Lorry was out in the night, before he knew where he was. Mr. Stryver was lying back on his sofa, winking at his ceiling.

XIII. THE FELLOW OF NO DELICACY

If Sydney Carton ever shone anywhere, he certainly never shone in the house of Doctor Manette. He had been there often, during a whole year, and had always been the same moody and morose lounger there. When he cared to talk, he talked well; but, the cloud of caring for nothing, which overshadowed him with such a fatal darkness, was very rarely pierced by the light within him.

And yet he did care something for the streets that environed that house, and for the senseless stones that made their pavements. Many a night he vaguely and unhappily wandered there, when wine had brought no transitory gladness to him; many a dreary daybreak revealed his solitary figure lingering there, and still lingering there when the first beams of the sun brought into strong relief, removed beauties of architecture in spires of churches and lofty buildings, as perhaps the quiet time brought some sense of better things, else forgotten and unattainable, into his mind. Of late, the neglected bed in the Temple Court had known him more scantily than ever; and often when he had thrown himself upon it no longer than a few minutes, he had got up again, and haunted that neighbourhood.

On a day in August, when Mr. Stryver (after notifying to his jackal that "he had thought better of that marrying matter") had carried his delicacy into Devonshire, and when the sight and scent of flowers in the City streets had some waifs of goodness in them for the worst, of health for the sickliest, and of youth for the oldest, Sydney's feet still trod those stones. From being irresolute and purposeless, his feet became animated by an intention, and, in the working out of that intention, they took him to the Doctor's door.

He was shown up-stairs, and found Lucie at her work, alone. She had never been quite at her ease with him, and received him with some little embarrassment as he seated himself near her table. But, looking up at his face in the interchange of the first few common-places, she observed a change in it.

"I fear you are not well, Mr. Carton!"

"No. But the life I lead, Miss Manette, is not conducive to health. What is to be expected of, or by, such profligates?"

"Is it not—forgive me; I have begun the question on my lips—a pity to live no better life?"

"God knows it is a shame!"

"Then why not change it?"

Looking gently at him again, she was surprised and saddened to see that there were tears in his eyes. There were tears in his voice too, as he answered:

"It is too late for that. I shall never be better than I am. I shall sink lower, and be worse."

He leaned an elbow on her table, and covered his eyes with his hand. The table trembled in the silence that followed.

She had never seen him softened, and was much distressed. He knew her to be so, without looking at her, and said:

"Pray forgive me, Miss Manette. I break down before the knowledge of what I want to say to you. Will you hear me?"

"If it will do you any good, Mr. Carton, if it would make you happier, it would make me very glad!"

"God bless you for your sweet compassion!"

He unshaded his face after a little while, and spoke steadily.

"Don't be afraid to hear me. Don't shrink from anything I say. I am like one who died young. All my life might have been."

"No, Mr. Carton. I am sure that the best part of it might still be; I am sure that you might be much, much worthier of yourself."

"Say of you, Miss Manette, and although I know better—although in the mystery of my own wretched heart I know better—I shall never forget it!"

She was pale and trembling. He came to her relief with a fixed despair of himself which made the interview unlike any other that could have been holden.

"If it had been possible, Miss Manette, that you could have returned the love of the man you see before yourself—flung away, wasted, drunken, poor creature of misuse as you know him to be—he would have been conscious this day and hour, in spite of his happiness, that he would bring you to misery, bring you to sorrow and repentance, blight you, disgrace you, pull you down with him. I know very well that you can have no tenderness for me; I ask for none; I am even thankful that it cannot be."

"Without it, can I not save you, Mr. Carton? Can I not recall you—forgive me again!—to a better course? Can I in no way repay your confidence? I know this is a confidence," she modestly said, after a little hesitation, and in earnest tears, "I know you would say this to no one else. Can I turn it to no good account for yourself, Mr. Carton?"

He shook his head.

"To none. No, Miss Manette, to none. If you will hear me through a very little more, all you can ever do for me is done. I wish you to know that you have been the last dream of my soul. In my degradation I have not been so degraded but that the sight of you with your father, and of this home made such a home by you, has stirred old shadows that I thought had died out of me. Since I knew you, I have been troubled by a remorse that I thought would never reproach me again, and have heard whispers from old voices impelling me upward, that I thought were silent for ever. I have had unformed ideas of striving afresh, beginning anew, shaking off sloth and sensuality, and fighting out the abandoned fight. A dream, all a dream, that ends in nothing, and leaves the sleeper where he lay down, but I wish you to know that you inspired it."

"Will nothing of it remain? O Mr. Carton, think again! Try again!"

"No, Miss Manette; all through it, I have known myself to be quite undeserving. And yet I have had the weakness, and have still the weakness, to wish you to know with what a sudden mastery you kindled me, heap of ashes that I am, into fire—a fire, however, inseparable in its nature from myself, quickening nothing, lighting nothing, doing no service, idly burning away."

"Since it is my misfortune, Mr. Carton, to have made you more unhappy than you were before you knew me—"

"Don't say that, Miss Manette, for you would have reclaimed me, if anything could. You will not be the cause of my becoming worse."

"Since the state of your mind that you describe, is, at all events, attributable to some influence of mine—this is what I mean, if I can make it plain—can I use no influence to serve you? Have I no power for good, with you, at all?"

"The utmost good that I am capable of now, Miss Manette, I have come here to realise. Let me carry through the rest of my misdirected life, the remembrance that I opened my heart to you, last of all the world; and that there was something left in me at this time which you could deplore and pity."

"Which I entreated you to believe, again and again, most fervently, with all my heart, was capable of better things, Mr. Carton!"

"Entreat me to believe it no more, Miss Manette. I have proved myself, and I know better. I distress you; I draw fast to an end. Will you let me believe, when I recall this day, that the last confidence of my life was reposed in your pure and innocent breast, and that it lies there alone, and will be shared by no one?"

"If that will be a consolation to you, yes."

"Not even by the dearest one ever to be known to you?"

"Mr. Carton," she answered, after an agitated pause, "the secret is yours, not mine; and I promise to respect it."

"Thank you. And again, God bless you."

He put her hand to his lips, and moved towards the door.

"Be under no apprehension, Miss Manette, of my ever resuming this conversation by so much as a passing word. I will never refer to it again. If I were dead, that could not be surer than it is henceforth. In the hour of my death, I shall hold sacred the one good remembrance—and shall thank and bless you for it—that my last avowal of myself was made to you, and that my name, and faults, and miseries were gently carried in your heart. May it otherwise be light and happy!"

He was so unlike what he had ever shown himself to be, and it was so sad to think how much he had thrown away, and how much he every day kept down and perverted, that Lucie Manette wept mournfully for him as he stood looking back at her.

"Be comforted!" he said, "I am not worth such feeling, Miss Manette. An hour or two hence, and the low companions and low habits that I scorn but yield to, will render me less worth such tears as those, than any wretch who creeps along the streets. Be comforted! But, within myself, I shall always be, towards you, what I am now, though outwardly I shall be what you have heretofore seen me. The last supplication but one I make to you, is, that you will believe this of me."

"I will, Mr. Carton."

"My last supplication of all, is this; and with it, I will relieve you of a visitor with whom I well know you have nothing in unison, and between whom and you there is an impassable space. It is useless to say it, I know, but it rises out of my soul. For you, and for any dear to you, I would do anything. If my career were of that better kind that there was any opportunity or capacity of sacrifice in it, I would embrace any sacrifice for you and for those dear to you. Try to hold me in your mind, at some quiet times, as ardent and sincere in this one thing. The time will come, the time will not be long in coming, when new ties will be formed about you—ties that will bind you yet more tenderly and strongly to the home you so adorn—the dearest ties that will ever grace and gladden you. O Miss Manette, when the little picture of a happy father's face looks up in yours, when you see your own bright beauty springing up anew at your feet, think now and then that there is a man who would give his life, to keep a life you love beside you!"

He said, "Farewell!" said a last "God bless you!" and left her.

XIV. THE HONEST TRADESMAN

To the eyes of Mr. Jeremiah Cruncher, sitting on his stool in Fleet-street with his grisly urchin beside him, a vast number and variety of objects in movement were every day presented. Who could sit upon anything in Fleet-street during the busy hours of the day, and not be dazed and deafened by two immense processions, one ever tending westward with the sun, the other ever tending eastward from the sun, both ever tending to the plains beyond the range of red and purple where the sun goes down!

With his straw in his mouth, Mr. Cruncher sat watching the two streams, like the heathen rustic who has for several centuries been on duty watching one stream— saving that Jerry had no expectation of their ever running dry. Nor would it have been an expectation of a hopeful kind, since a small part of his income was derived from the pilotage of timid women (mostly of a full habit and past the middle term of life) from Tellson's side of the tides to the opposite shore. Brief as such companionship was in every separate instance, Mr. Cruncher never failed to become so interested in the lady as to express a strong desire to have the honour of drinking her very good health. And it was from the gifts bestowed upon him towards the execution of this benevolent purpose, that he recruited his finances, as just now observed.

Time was, when a poet sat upon a stool in a public place, and mused in the sight of men. Mr. Cruncher, sitting on a stool in a public place, but not being a poet, mused as little as possible, and looked about him.

It fell out that he was thus engaged in a season when crowds were few, and belated women few, and when his affairs in general were so unprosperous as to awaken a strong suspicion in his breast that Mrs. Cruncher must have been "flopping" in some pointed manner, when an unusual concourse pouring down Fleet-street westward, attracted his attention. Looking that way, Mr. Cruncher made out that some kind of funeral was coming along, and that there was popular objection to this funeral, which engendered uproar.

"Young Jerry," said Mr. Cruncher, turning to his offspring, "it's a buryin'."

"Hooroar, father!" cried Young Jerry.

The young gentleman uttered this exultant sound with mysterious significance. The elder gentleman took the cry so ill, that he watched his opportunity, and smote the young gentleman on the ear.

"What d'ye mean? What are you hooroaring at? What do you want to conwey to your own father, you young Rip? This boy is a getting too many for *me*!" said Mr. Cruncher, surveying him. "Him and his hooroars! Don't let me hear no more of you, or you shall feel some more of me. D'ye hear?"

"I warn't doing no harm," Young Jerry protested, rubbing his cheek.

"Drop it then," said Mr. Cruncher; "I won't have none of *your* no harms. Get a top of that there seat, and look at the crowd."

His son obeyed, and the crowd approached; they were bawling and hissing round a dingy hearse and dingy mourning coach, in which mourning coach there was only one mourner, dressed in the dingy trappings that were considered essential to the dignity of the position. The position appeared by no means to please him, however, with an increasing rabble surrounding the coach, deriding him, making grimaces at him, and incessantly groaning and calling out: "Yah! Spies! Tst! Yaha! Spies!" with many compliments too numerous and forcible to repeat.

Funerals had at all times a remarkable attraction for Mr. Cruncher; he always pricked up his senses, and became excited, when a funeral passed Tellson's. Naturally, therefore, a funeral with this uncommon attendance excited him greatly, and he asked of the first man who ran against him:

"What is it, brother? What's it about?"

"*I* don't know," said the man. "Spies! Yaha! Tst! Spies!"

He asked another man. "Who is it?"

"*I* don't know," returned the man, clapping his hands to his mouth nevertheless, and vociferating in a surprising heat and with the greatest ardour, "Spies! Yaha! Tst, tst! Spi—ies!"

At length, a person better informed on the merits of the case, tumbled against him, and from this person he learned that the funeral was the funeral of one Roger Cly.

"Was He a spy?" asked Mr. Cruncher.

"Old Bailey spy," returned his informant. "Yaha! Tst! Yah! Old Bailey Spi—i—ies!"

"Why, to be sure!" exclaimed Jerry, recalling the Trial at which he had assisted. "I've seen him. Dead, is he?"

"Dead as mutton," returned the other, "and can't be too dead. Have 'em out, there! Spies! Pull 'em out, there! Spies!"

The idea was so acceptable in the prevalent absence of any idea, that the crowd caught it up with eagerness, and loudly repeating the suggestion to have 'em out, and to pull 'em out, mobbed the two vehicles so closely that they came to a stop. On the crowd's opening the coach doors, the one mourner scuffled out of himself and was in their hands for a moment; but he was so alert, and made such good use of his time, that in another moment he was scouring away up a bye-street, after shedding his cloak, hat, long hatband, white pocket-handkerchief, and other symbolical tears.

These, the people tore to pieces and scattered far and wide with great enjoyment, while the tradesmen hurriedly shut up their shops; for a crowd in those times stopped at nothing, and was a monster much dreaded. They had already got the length of opening the hearse to take the coffin out, when some brighter genius proposed instead, its being escorted to its destination amidst general rejoicing. Practical suggestions being much needed, this suggestion, too, was received with acclamation, and the coach was immediately filled with eight inside and a dozen out, while as many people got on the roof of the hearse as could by any exercise of ingenuity stick upon it. Among the first of these volunteers was Jerry Cruncher himself, who modestly concealed his spiky head from the observation of Tellson's, in the further corner of the mourning coach.

The officiating undertakers made some protest against these changes in the ceremonies; but, the river being alarmingly near, and several voices remarking on the efficacy of cold immersion in bringing refractory members of the profession to reason, the protest was faint and brief. The remodelled procession started, with a chimney-sweep driving the hearse—advised by the regular driver, who was perched beside him, under close inspection, for the purpose—and with a pieman, also attended by his cabinet minister, driving the mourning coach. A bear-leader, a popular street character of the time, was impressed as an additional ornament, before the cavalcade had gone far down the Strand; and his bear, who was black and very mangy, gave quite an Undertaking air to that part of the procession in which he walked.

Thus, with beer-drinking, pipe-smoking, song-roaring, and infinite caricaturing of woe, the disorderly procession went its way, recruiting at every step, and all the shops shutting up before it. Its destination was the old church of Saint Pancras, far off in the fields. It got there in course of time; insisted on pouring into the burial-ground; finally, accomplished the interment of the deceased Roger Cly in its own way, and highly to its own satisfaction.

The dead man disposed of, and the crowd being under the necessity of providing some other entertainment for itself, another brighter genius (or perhaps the same) conceived the humour of impeaching casual passers-by, as Old Bailey spies, and wreaking vengeance on them. Chase was given to some scores of inoffensive persons who had never been near the Old Bailey in their lives, in the realisation of this fancy, and they were roughly hustled and maltreated. The transition to the sport of window-breaking, and thence to the plundering of public-houses, was easy and natural. At last, after several hours, when sundry summer-houses had been pulled down, and some area-railings had been torn up, to arm the more belligerent spirits, a rumour got about that the Guards were coming. Before this rumour, the crowd gradually melted away, and perhaps the Guards came, and perhaps they never came, and this was the usual progress of a mob.

Mr. Cruncher did not assist at the closing sports, but had remained behind in the churchyard, to confer and condole with the undertakers. The place had a soothing influence on him. He procured a pipe from a neighbouring public-house, and smoked it, looking in at the railings and maturely considering the spot.

"Jerry," said Mr. Cruncher, apostrophising himself in his usual way, "you see that there Cly that day, and you see with your own eyes that he was a young 'un and a straight made 'un."

Having smoked his pipe out, and ruminated a little longer, he turned himself about, that he might appear, before the hour of closing, on his station at Tellson's. Whether his meditations on mortality had touched his liver, or whether his general health had been previously at all amiss, or whether he desired to show a little attention to an eminent man, is not so much to the purpose, as that he made a short call upon his medical adviser—a distinguished surgeon—on his way back.

Young Jerry relieved his father with dutiful interest, and reported No job in his absence. The bank closed, the ancient clerks came out, the usual watch was set, and Mr. Cruncher and his son went home to tea.

"Now, I tell you where it is!" said Mr. Cruncher to his wife, on entering. "If, as a honest tradesman, my wenturs goes wrong to-night, I shall make sure that you've been praying again me, and I shall work you for it just the same as if I seen you do it."

The dejected Mrs. Cruncher shook her head.

"Why, you're at it afore my face!" said Mr. Cruncher, with signs of angry apprehension.

"I am saying nothing."

"Well, then; don't meditate nothing. You might as well flop as meditate. You may as well go again me one way as another. Drop it altogether."

"Yes, Jerry."

"Yes, Jerry," repeated Mr. Cruncher sitting down to tea. "Ah! It *is* yes, Jerry. That's about it. You may say yes, Jerry."

Mr. Cruncher had no particular meaning in these sulky corroborations, but made use of them, as people not unfrequently do, to express general ironical dissatisfaction.

"You and your yes, Jerry," said Mr. Cruncher, taking a bite out of his bread-and-butter, and seeming to help it down with a large invisible oyster out of his saucer. "Ah! I think so. I believe you."

"You are going out to-night?" asked his decent wife, when he took another bite.

"Yes, I am."

"May I go with you, father?" asked his son, briskly.

"No, you mayn't. I'm a going—as your mother knows—a fishing. That's where I'm going to. Going a fishing."

"Your fishing-rod gets rayther rusty; don't it, father?"

"Never you mind."

"Shall you bring any fish home, father?"

"If I don't, you'll have short commons, to-morrow," returned that gentleman, shaking his head; "that's questions enough for you; I ain't a going out, till you've been long abed."

He devoted himself during the remainder of the evening to keeping a most vigilant watch on Mrs. Cruncher, and sullenly holding her in conversation that she might be prevented from meditating any petitions to his disadvantage. With this view, he urged his son to hold her in conversation also, and led the unfortunate woman a hard life by dwelling on any causes of complaint he could bring against her, rather than he would leave her for a moment to her own reflections. The devoutest person could have rendered no greater homage to the efficacy of an honest prayer than he did in this distrust of his wife. It was as if a professed unbeliever in ghosts should be frightened by a ghost story.

"And mind you!" said Mr. Cruncher. "No games to-morrow! If I, as a honest tradesman, succeed in providing a jinte of meat or two, none of your not touching of it, and sticking to bread. If I, as a honest tradesman, am able to provide a little beer, none of your declaring on water. When you go to Rome, do as Rome does. Rome will be a ugly customer to you, if you don't. *I'm* your Rome, you know."

Then he began grumbling again:

"With your flying into the face of your own wittles and drink! I don't know how scarce you mayn't make the wittles and drink here, by your flopping tricks and your unfeeling conduct. Look at your boy: he *is* your'n, ain't he? He's as thin as a lath. Do you call yourself a mother, and not know that a mother's first duty is to blow her boy out?"

This touched Young Jerry on a tender place; who adjured his mother to perform her first duty, and, whatever else she did or neglected, above all things to lay especial stress on the discharge of that maternal function so affectingly and delicately indicated by his other parent.

Thus the evening wore away with the Cruncher family, until Young Jerry was ordered to bed, and his mother, laid under similar injunctions, obeyed them. Mr. Cruncher beguiled the earlier watches of the night with solitary pipes, and did not start upon his excursion until nearly one o'clock. Towards that small and ghostly hour, he rose up from his chair, took a key out of his pocket, opened a locked cupboard, and brought forth a sack, a crowbar of convenient size, a rope and chain, and other fishing tackle of that nature. Disposing these articles about him in skilful manner, he bestowed a parting defiance on Mrs. Cruncher, extinguished the light, and went out.

Young Jerry, who had only made a feint of undressing when he went to bed, was not long after his father. Under cover of the darkness he followed out of the room, followed down the stairs, followed down the court, followed out into the streets. He was in no uneasiness concerning his getting into the house again, for it was full of lodgers, and the door stood ajar all night.

Impelled by a laudable ambition to study the art and mystery of his father's honest calling, Young Jerry, keeping as close to house fronts, walls, and doorways, as his eyes were close to one another, held his honoured parent in view. The honoured parent steering Northward, had not gone far, when he was joined by another disciple of Izaak Walton, and the two trudged on together.

Within half an hour from the first starting, they were beyond the winking lamps, and the more than winking watchmen, and were out upon a lonely road. Another fisherman was picked up here—and that so silently, that if Young Jerry had been superstitious, he might have supposed the second follower of the gentle craft to have, all of a sudden, split himself into two.

The three went on, and Young Jerry went on, until the three stopped under a bank overhanging the road. Upon the top of the bank was a low brick wall, surmounted by an iron railing. In the shadow of bank and wall the three turned out of the road, and up a blind lane, of which the wall—there, risen to some eight or ten feet high—formed one side. Crouching down in a corner, peeping up the lane, the next object that Young Jerry saw, was the form of his honoured parent, pretty well defined against a watery and clouded moon, nimbly scaling an iron gate. He was soon over, and then the second fisherman got over, and then the third. They all dropped softly on the ground within the gate, and lay there a little—listening perhaps. Then, they moved away on their hands and knees.

It was now Young Jerry's turn to approach the gate: which he did, holding his breath. Crouching down again in a corner there, and looking in, he made out the three fishermen creeping through some rank grass! and all the gravestones in the churchyard—it was a large churchyard that they were in—looking on like ghosts in white, while the church tower itself looked on like the ghost of a monstrous giant. They did not creep far, before they stopped and stood upright. And then they began to fish.

They fished with a spade, at first. Presently the honoured parent appeared to be adjusting some instrument like a great corkscrew. Whatever tools they worked with, they worked hard, until the awful striking of the church clock so terrified Young Jerry, that he made off, with his hair as stiff as his father's.

But, his long-cherished desire to know more about these matters, not only stopped him in his running away, but lured him back again. They were still fishing perseveringly, when he peeped in at the gate for the second time; but, now they seemed to have got a bite. There was a screwing and complaining sound down below, and their bent figures were strained, as if by a weight. By slow degrees the weight broke away the earth upon it, and came to the surface. Young Jerry very well knew what it would be; but, when he saw it, and saw his honoured parent about to wrench it open, he was so frightened, being new to the sight, that he made off again, and never stopped until he had run a mile or more.

He would not have stopped then, for anything less necessary than breath, it being a spectral sort of race that he ran, and one highly desirable to get to the end of. He had a strong idea that the coffin he had seen was running after him; and, pictured as hopping on behind him, bolt upright, upon its narrow end, always on the point of overtaking him and hopping on at his side—perhaps taking his arm—it was a pursuer to shun. It was an inconsistent and ubiquitous fiend too, for, while it was making the whole night behind him dreadful, he darted out into the roadway to avoid dark alleys, fearful of its coming hopping out of them like a dropsical boy's-Kite without tail and wings. It hid in doorways too, rubbing its horrible shoulders against doors, and drawing them up to its ears, as if it were laughing. It got into shadows on the road, and lay cunningly on its back to trip him up. All this time it was incessantly hopping on behind and gaining on him, so that when the boy got to his own door he had reason for being half dead. And even then it would not leave him, but followed him upstairs with a bump on every stair, scrambled into bed with him, and bumped down, dead and heavy, on his breast when he fell asleep.

From his oppressed slumber, Young Jerry in his closet was awakened after daybreak and before sunrise, by the presence of his father in the family room. Something had gone wrong with him; at least, so Young Jerry inferred, from the circumstance of his holding Mrs. Cruncher by the ears, and knocking the back of her head against the head-board of the bed.

"I told you I would," said Mr. Cruncher, "and I did."

"Jerry, Jerry, Jerry!" his wife implored.

"You oppose yourself to the profit of the business," said Jerry, "and me and my partners suffer. You was to honour and obey; why the devil don't you?"

"I try to be a good wife, Jerry," the poor woman protested, with tears.

"Is it being a good wife to oppose your husband's business? Is it honouring your husband to dishonour his business? Is it obeying your husband to disobey him on the wital subject of his business?"

"You hadn't taken to the dreadful business then, Jerry."

"It's enough for you," retorted Mr. Cruncher, "to be the wife of a honest tradesman, and not to occupy your female mind with calculations when he took to his trade or when he didn't. A honouring and obeying wife would let his trade alone altogether. Call yourself a religious woman? If you're a religious woman, give me a irreligious one! You have no more nat'ral sense of duty than the bed of this here Thames river has of a pile, and similarly it must be knocked into you."

The altercation was conducted in a low tone of voice, and terminated in the honest tradesman's kicking off his clay-soiled boots, and lying down at his length on the floor. After taking a timid peep at him lying on his back, with his rusty hands under his head for a pillow, his son lay down too, and fell asleep again.

There was no fish for breakfast, and not much of anything else. Mr. Cruncher was out of spirits, and out of temper, and kept an iron pot-lid by him as a projectile for the correction of Mrs. Cruncher, in case he should observe any symptoms of her saying Grace. He was brushed and washed at the usual hour, and set off with his son to pursue his ostensible calling.

Young Jerry, walking with the stool under his arm at his father's side along sunny and crowded Fleet-street, was a very different Young Jerry from him of the previous night, running home through darkness and solitude from his grim pursuer. His cunning was fresh with the day, and his qualms were gone with the night—in which particulars it is not improbable that he had compeers in Fleet-street and the City of London, that fine morning.

"Father," said Young Jerry, as they walked along: taking care to keep at arm's length and to have the stool well between them: "what's a Resurrection-Man?"

Mr. Cruncher came to a stop on the pavement before he answered, "How should I know?"

"I thought you knowed everything, father," said the artless boy.

"Hem! Well," returned Mr. Cruncher, going on again, and lifting off his hat to give his spikes free play, "he's a tradesman."

"What's his goods, father?" asked the brisk Young Jerry.

"His goods," said Mr. Cruncher, after turning it over in his mind, "is a branch of Scientific goods."

"Persons' bodies, ain't it, father?" asked the lively boy.

"I believe it is something of that sort," said Mr. Cruncher.

"Oh, father, I should so like to be a Resurrection-Man when I'm quite growed up!"

Mr. Cruncher was soothed, but shook his head in a dubious and moral way. "It depends upon how you dewelop your talents. Be careful to dewelop your talents, and never to say no more than you can help to nobody, and there's no telling at the present time what you may not come to be fit for." As Young Jerry, thus encouraged, went on a few yards in advance, to plant the stool in the shadow of the Bar, Mr. Cruncher added to himself: "Jerry, you honest tradesman, there's hopes wot that boy will yet be a blessing to you, and a recompense to you for his mother!"

XV. KNITTING

There had been earlier drinking than usual in the wine-shop of Monsieur Defarge. As early as six o'clock in the morning, sallow faces peeping through its barred windows had descried other faces within, bending over measures of wine. Monsieur Defarge sold a very thin wine at the best of times, but it would seem to have been an unusually thin wine that he sold at this time. A sour wine, moreover, or a souring, for its influence on the mood of those who drank it was to make them gloomy. No vivacious Bacchanalian flame leaped out of the pressed grape of Monsieur Defarge: but, a smouldering fire that burnt in the dark, lay hidden in the dregs of it.

This had been the third morning in succession, on which there had been early drinking at the wine-shop of Monsieur Defarge. It had begun on Monday, and here was Wednesday come. There had been more of early brooding than drinking; for, many men had listened and whispered and slunk about there from the time of the opening of the door, who could not have laid a piece of money on the counter to save their souls. These were to the full as interested in the place, however, as if they could have commanded whole barrels of wine; and they glided from seat to seat, and from corner to corner, swallowing talk in lieu of drink, with greedy looks.

Notwithstanding an unusual flow of company, the master of the wine-shop was not visible. He was not missed; for, nobody who crossed the threshold looked for him, nobody asked for him, nobody wondered to see only Madame Defarge in her seat, presiding over the distribution of wine, with a bowl of battered small coins before her, as much defaced and beaten out of their original impress as the small coinage of humanity from whose ragged pockets they had come.

A suspended interest and a prevalent absence of mind, were perhaps observed by the spies who looked in at the wine-shop, as they looked in at every place, high and low, from the kings palace to the criminal's gaol. Games at cards languished, players at dominoes musingly built towers with them, drinkers drew figures on the tables with spilt drops of wine, Madame Defarge herself picked out the pattern on her sleeve with her toothpick, and saw and heard something inaudible and invisible a long way off.

Thus, Saint Antoine in this vinous feature of his, until midday. It was high noontide, when two dusty men passed through his streets and under his swinging lamps: of whom, one was Monsieur Defarge: the other a mender of roads in a blue cap. All adust and athirst, the two entered the wine-shop. Their arrival had lighted a kind of fire in the breast of Saint Antoine, fast spreading as they came along, which stirred and flickered in flames of faces at most doors and windows. Yet, no one had followed them, and no man spoke when they entered the wine-shop, though the eyes of every man there were turned upon them.

"Good day, gentlemen!" said Monsieur Defarge.

It may have been a signal for loosening the general tongue. It elicited an answering chorus of "Good day!"

"It is bad weather, gentlemen," said Defarge, shaking his head.

Upon which, every man looked at his neighbour, and then all cast down their eyes and sat silent. Except one man, who got up and went out.

"My wife," said Defarge aloud, addressing Madame Defarge: "I have travelled certain leagues with this good mender of roads, called Jacques. I met him—by accident—a day and half's journey out of Paris. He is a good child, this mender of roads, called Jacques. Give him to drink, my wife!"

A second man got up and went out. Madame Defarge set wine before the mender of roads called Jacques, who doffed his blue cap to the company, and drank. In the breast of his blouse he carried some coarse dark bread; he ate of this between whiles, and sat munching and drinking near Madame Defarge's counter. A third man got up and went out.

Defarge refreshed himself with a draught of wine—but, he took less than was given to the stranger, as being himself a man to whom it was no rarity—and stood waiting until the countryman had made his breakfast. He looked at no one present, and no one now looked at him; not even Madame Defarge, who had taken up her knitting, and was at work.

"Have you finished your repast, friend?" he asked, in due season.

"Yes, thank you."

"Come, then! You shall see the apartment that I told you you could occupy. It will suit you to a marvel."

Out of the wine-shop into the street, out of the street into a courtyard, out of the courtyard up a steep staircase, out of the staircase into a garret,—formerly the garret where a white-haired man sat on a low bench, stooping forward and very busy, making shoes.

No white-haired man was there now; but, the three men were there who had gone out of the wine-shop singly. And between them and the white-haired man afar off, was the one small link, that they had once looked in at him through the chinks in the wall.

Defarge closed the door carefully, and spoke in a subdued voice:

"Jacques One, Jacques Two, Jacques Three! This is the witness encountered by appointment, by me, Jacques Four. He will tell you all. Speak, Jacques Five!"

The mender of roads, blue cap in hand, wiped his swarthy forehead with it, and said, "Where shall I commence, monsieur?"

"Commence," was Monsieur Defarge's not unreasonable reply, "at the commencement."

"I saw him then, messieurs," began the mender of roads, "a year ago this running summer, underneath the carriage of the Marquis, hanging by the chain. Behold the manner of it. I leaving my work on the road, the sun going to bed, the carriage of the Marquis slowly ascending the hill, he hanging by the chain—like this."

Again the mender of roads went through the whole performance; in which he ought to have been perfect by that time, seeing that it had been the infallible resource and indispensable entertainment of his village during a whole year.

Jacques One struck in, and asked if he had ever seen the man before?

"Never," answered the mender of roads, recovering his perpendicular.

Jacques Three demanded how he afterwards recognised him then?

"By his tall figure," said the mender of roads, softly, and with his finger at his nose. "When Monsieur the Marquis demands that evening, 'Say, what is he like?' I make response, 'Tall as a spectre.'"

"You should have said, short as a dwarf," returned Jacques Two.

"But what did I know? The deed was not then accomplished, neither did he confide in me. Observe! Under those circumstances even, I do not offer my testimony. Monsieur the Marquis indicates me with his finger, standing near our little fountain, and says, 'To me! Bring that rascal!' My faith, messieurs, I offer nothing."

"He is right there, Jacques," murmured Defarge, to him who had interrupted. "Go on!"

"Good!" said the mender of roads, with an air of mystery. "The tall man is lost, and he is sought—how many months? Nine, ten, eleven?"

"No matter, the number," said Defarge. "He is well hidden, but at last he is unluckily found. Go on!"

"I am again at work upon the hill-side, and the sun is again about to go to bed. I am collecting my tools to descend to my cottage down in the village below, where it is already dark, when I raise my eyes, and see coming over the hill six soldiers. In the midst of them is a tall man with his arms bound—tied to his sides—like this!"

With the aid of his indispensable cap, he represented a man with his elbows bound fast at his hips, with cords that were knotted behind him.

"I stand aside, messieurs, by my heap of stones, to see the soldiers and their prisoner pass (for it is a solitary road, that, where any spectacle is well worth looking at), and at first, as they approach, I see no more than that they are six soldiers with a tall man bound, and that they are almost black to my sight—except on the side of the sun going to bed, where they have a red edge, messieurs. Also, I see that their long shadows are on the hollow ridge on the opposite side of the road, and are on the hill above it, and are like the shadows of giants. Also, I see that they are covered with dust, and that the dust moves with them as they come, tramp, tramp! But when they advance quite near to me, I recognise the tall man, and he recognises me. Ah, but he would be well content to precipitate himself over the hill-side once again, as on the evening when he and I first encountered, close to the same spot!"

He described it as if he were there, and it was evident that he saw it vividly; perhaps he had not seen much in his life.

"I do not show the soldiers that I recognise the tall man; he does not show the soldiers that he recognises me; we do it, and we know it, with our eyes. 'Come on!' says the chief of that company, pointing to the village, 'bring him fast to his tomb!' and they bring him faster. I follow. His arms are swelled because of being bound so tight, his wooden shoes are large and clumsy, and he is lame. Because he is lame, and consequently slow, they drive him with their guns—like this!"

He imitated the action of a man's being impelled forward by the butt-ends of muskets.

"As they descend the hill like madmen running a race, he falls. They laugh and pick him up again. His face is bleeding and covered with dust, but he cannot touch it; thereupon they laugh again. They bring him into the village; all the village runs to look; they take him past the mill, and up to the prison; all the village sees the prison gate open in the darkness of the night, and swallow him—like this!"

He opened his mouth as wide as he could, and shut it with a sounding snap of his teeth. Observant of his unwillingness to mar the effect by opening it again, Defarge said, "Go on, Jacques."

"All the village," pursued the mender of roads, on tiptoe and in a low voice, "withdraws; all the village whispers by the fountain; all the village sleeps; all the village dreams of that unhappy one, within the locks and bars of the prison on the crag, and never to come out of it, except to perish. In the morning, with my tools upon my shoulder, eating my morsel of black bread as I go, I make a circuit by the prison, on my way to my work. There I see him, high up, behind the bars of a lofty iron cage, bloody and dusty as last night, looking through. He has no hand free, to wave to me; I dare not call to him; he regards me like a dead man."

Defarge and the three glanced darkly at one another. The looks of all of them were dark, repressed, and revengeful, as they listened to the countryman's story; the manner of all of them, while it was secret, was authoritative too. They had the air of a rough tribunal; Jacques One and Two sitting on the old pallet-bed, each with his chin resting on his hand, and his eyes intent on the road-mender; Jacques Three, equally intent, on one knee behind them, with his agitated hand always gliding over the network of fine nerves about his mouth and nose; Defarge standing between them and the narrator, whom he had stationed in the light of the window, by turns looking from him to them, and from them to him.

"Go on, Jacques," said Defarge.

"He remains up there in his iron cage some days. The village looks at him by stealth, for it is afraid. But it always looks up, from a distance, at the prison on the crag; and in the evening, when the work of the day is achieved and it assembles to gossip at the fountain, all faces are turned towards the prison. Formerly, they were turned towards the posting-house; now, they are turned towards the prison. They whisper at the fountain, that although condemned to death he will not be executed; they say that petitions have been presented in Paris, showing that he was enraged and made mad by the death of his child; they say that a petition has been presented to the King himself. What do I know? It is possible. Perhaps yes, perhaps no."

"Listen then, Jacques," Number One of that name sternly interposed. "Know that a petition was presented to the King and Queen. All here, yourself excepted, saw the King take it, in his carriage in the street, sitting beside the Queen. It is Defarge whom you see here, who, at the hazard of his life, darted out before the horses, with the petition in his hand."

"And once again listen, Jacques!" said the kneeling Number Three: his fingers ever wandering over and over those fine nerves, with a strikingly greedy air, as if he hungered for something—that was neither food nor drink; "the guard, horse and foot, surrounded the petitioner, and struck him blows. You hear?"

"I hear, messieurs."

"Go on then," said Defarge.

"Again; on the other hand, they whisper at the fountain," resumed the countryman, "that he is brought down into our country to be executed on the spot, and that he will very certainly be executed. They even whisper that because he has slain Monseigneur, and because Monseigneur was the father of his tenants—serfs—what you will—he will be executed as a parricide. One old man says at the fountain, that his right hand, armed with the knife, will be burnt off before his face; that, into wounds which will be made in his arms, his breast, and his legs, there will be poured boiling oil, melted lead, hot resin, wax, and sulphur; finally, that he will be torn limb from limb by four strong horses. That old man says, all this was actually done to a prisoner who made an attempt on the life of the late King, Louis Fifteen. But how do I know if he lies? I am not a scholar."

"Listen once again then, Jacques!" said the man with the restless hand and the craving air. "The name of that prisoner was Damiens, and it was all done in open day, in the open streets of this city of Paris; and nothing was more noticed in the vast concourse that saw it done, than the crowd of ladies of quality and fashion, who were full of eager attention to the last—to the last, Jacques, prolonged until nightfall, when he had lost two legs and an arm, and still breathed! And it was done—why, how old are you?"

"Thirty-five," said the mender of roads, who looked sixty.

"It was done when you were more than ten years old; you might have seen it."

"Enough!" said Defarge, with grim impatience. "Long live the Devil! Go on."

"Well! Some whisper this, some whisper that; they speak of nothing else; even the fountain appears to fall to that tune. At length, on Sunday night when all the village is asleep, come soldiers, winding down from the prison, and their guns ring on the stones of the little street. Workmen dig, workmen hammer, soldiers laugh and sing; in the morning, by the fountain, there is raised a gallows forty feet high, poisoning the water."

The mender of roads looked *through* rather than *at* the low ceiling, and pointed as if he saw the gallows somewhere in the sky.

"All work is stopped, all assemble there, nobody leads the cows out, the cows are there with the rest. At midday, the roll of drums. Soldiers have marched into the prison in the night, and he is in the midst of many soldiers. He is bound as before, and in his mouth there is a gag—tied so, with a tight string, making him look almost as if he laughed." He suggested it, by creasing his face with his two thumbs, from the corners of his mouth to his ears. "On the top of the gallows is fixed the knife, blade upwards, with its point in the air. He is hanged there forty feet high—and is left hanging, poisoning the water."

They looked at one another, as he used his blue cap to wipe his face, on which the perspiration had started afresh while he recalled the spectacle.

"It is frightful, messieurs. How can the women and the children draw water! Who can gossip of an evening, under that shadow! Under it, have I said? When I left the village, Monday evening as the sun was going to bed, and looked back from the hill, the shadow struck across the church, across the mill, across the prison—seemed to strike across the earth, messieurs, to where the sky rests upon it!"

The hungry man gnawed one of his fingers as he looked at the other three, and his finger quivered with the craving that was on him.

"That's all, messieurs. I left at sunset (as I had been warned to do), and I walked on, that night and half next day, until I met (as I was warned I should) this comrade. With him, I came on, now riding and now walking, through the rest of yesterday and through last night. And here you see me!"

After a gloomy silence, the first Jacques said, "Good! You have acted and recounted faithfully. Will you wait for us a little, outside the door?"

"Very willingly," said the mender of roads. Whom Defarge escorted to the top of the stairs, and, leaving seated there, returned.

The three had risen, and their heads were together when he came back to the garret.

"How say you, Jacques?" demanded Number One. "To be registered?"

"To be registered, as doomed to destruction," returned Defarge.

"Magnificent!" croaked the man with the craving.

"The chateau, and all the race?" inquired the first.

"The chateau and all the race," returned Defarge. "Extermination."

The hungry man repeated, in a rapturous croak, "Magnificent!" and began gnawing another finger.

"Are you sure," asked Jacques Two, of Defarge, "that no embarrassment can arise from our manner of keeping the register? Without doubt it is safe, for no one beyond ourselves can decipher it; but shall we always be able to decipher it—or, I ought to say, will she?"

"Jacques," returned Defarge, drawing himself up, "if madame my wife undertook to keep the register in her memory alone, she would not lose a word of it—not a syllable of it. Knitted, in her own stitches and her own symbols, it will always be as plain to her as the sun. Confide in Madame Defarge. It would be easier for the weakest poltroon that lives, to erase himself from existence, than to erase one letter of his name or crimes from the knitted register of Madame Defarge."

There was a murmur of confidence and approval, and then the man who hungered, asked: "Is this rustic to be sent back soon? I hope so. He is very simple; is he not a little dangerous?"

"He knows nothing," said Defarge; "at least nothing more than would easily elevate himself to a gallows of the same height. I charge myself with him; let him remain with me; I will take care of him, and set him on his road. He wishes to see the fine world—the King, the Queen, and Court; let him see them on Sunday."

"What?" exclaimed the hungry man, staring. "Is it a good sign, that he wishes to see Royalty and Nobility?"

"Jacques," said Defarge; "judiciously show a cat milk, if you wish her to thirst for it. Judiciously show a dog his natural prey, if you wish him to bring it down one day."

Nothing more was said, and the mender of roads, being found already dozing on the topmost stair, was advised to lay himself down on the pallet-bed and take some rest. He needed no persuasion, and was soon asleep.

Worse quarters than Defarge's wine-shop, could easily have been found in Paris for a provincial slave of that degree. Saving for a mysterious dread of madame by which he was constantly haunted, his life was very new and agreeable. But, madame sat all day at her counter, so expressly unconscious of him, and so particularly determined not to perceive that his being there had any connection with anything below the surface, that he shook in his wooden shoes whenever his eye lighted on her. For, he contended with himself that it was impossible to foresee what that lady might pretend next; and he felt assured that if she should take it into her brightly ornamented head to pretend that she had seen him do a murder and afterwards flay the victim, she would infallibly go through with it until the play was played out.

Therefore, when Sunday came, the mender of roads was not enchanted (though he said he was) to find that madame was to accompany monsieur and himself to Versailles. It was additionally disconcerting to have madame knitting all the way there, in a public conveyance; it was additionally disconcerting yet, to have madame in the crowd in the afternoon, still with her knitting in her hands as the crowd waited to see the carriage of the King and Queen.

"You work hard, madame," said a man near her.

"Yes," answered Madame Defarge; "I have a good deal to do."

"What do you make, madame?"

"Many things."

"For instance—"

"For instance," returned Madame Defarge, composedly, "shrouds."

The man moved a little further away, as soon as he could, and the mender of roads fanned himself with his blue cap: feeling it mightily close and oppressive. If he needed a King and Queen to restore him, he was fortunate in having his remedy at hand; for, soon the large-faced King and the fair-faced Queen came in their golden coach, attended by the shining Bull's Eye of their Court, a glittering multitude of laughing ladies and fine lords; and in jewels and silks and powder and splendour and elegantly spurning figures and handsomely disdainful faces of both sexes, the mender of roads bathed himself, so much to his temporary intoxication, that he cried Long live the King, Long live the Queen, Long live everybody and everything! as if he had never heard of ubiquitous Jacques in his time. Then, there were gardens, courtyards, terraces, fountains, green banks, more King and Queen, more Bull's Eye, more lords and ladies, more Long live they all! until he absolutely wept with sentiment. During the whole of this scene, which lasted some three hours, he had plenty of shouting and weeping and sentimental company, and throughout Defarge held him by the collar, as if to restrain him from flying at the objects of his brief devotion and tearing them to pieces.

"Bravo!" said Defarge, clapping him on the back when it was over, like a patron; "you are a good boy!"

The mender of roads was now coming to himself, and was mistrustful of having made a mistake in his late demonstrations; but no.

"You are the fellow we want," said Defarge, in his ear; "you make these fools believe that it will last for ever. Then, they are the more insolent, and it is the nearer ended."

"Hey!" cried the mender of roads, reflectively; "that's true."

"These fools know nothing. While they despise your breath, and would stop it for ever and ever, in you or in a hundred like you rather than in one of their own horses or dogs, they only know what your breath tells them. Let it deceive them, then, a little longer; it cannot deceive them too much."

Madame Defarge looked superciliously at the client, and nodded in confirmation.

"As to you," said she, "you would shout and shed tears for anything, if it made a show and a noise. Say! Would you not?"

"Truly, madame, I think so. For the moment."

"If you were shown a great heap of dolls, and were set upon them to pluck them to pieces and despoil them for your own advantage, you would pick out the richest and gayest. Say! Would you not?"

"Truly yes, madame."

"Yes. And if you were shown a flock of birds, unable to fly, and were set upon them to strip them of their feathers for your own advantage, you would set upon the birds of the finest feathers; would you not?"

"It is true, madame."

"You have seen both dolls and birds to-day," said Madame Defarge, with a wave of her hand towards the place where they had last been apparent; "now, go home!"

XVI. STILL KNITTING

Madame Defarge and monsieur her husband returned amicably to the bosom of Saint Antoine, while a speck in a blue cap toiled through the darkness, and through the dust, and down the weary miles of avenue by the wayside, slowly tending towards that point of the compass where the chateau of Monsieur the Marquis, now in his grave, listened to the whispering trees. Such ample leisure had the stone faces, now, for listening to the trees and to the fountain, that the few village scarecrows who, in their quest for herbs to eat and fragments of dead stick to burn, strayed within sight of the great stone courtyard and terrace staircase, had it borne in upon their starved fancy that the expression of the faces was altered. A rumour just lived in the village— had a faint and bare existence there, as its people had—that when the knife struck home, the faces changed, from faces of pride to faces of anger and pain; also, that when that dangling figure was hauled up forty feet above the fountain, they changed again, and bore a cruel look of being avenged, which they would henceforth bear for ever. In the stone face over the great window of the bed-chamber where the murder was done, two fine dints were pointed out in the sculptured nose, which everybody recognised, and which nobody had seen of old; and on the scarce occasions when two or three ragged peasants emerged from the crowd to take a hurried peep at Monsieur the Marquis petrified, a skinny finger would not have pointed to it for a minute, before they all started away among the moss and leaves, like the more fortunate hares who could find a living there.

Chateau and hut, stone face and dangling figure, the red stain on the stone floor, and the pure water in the village well—thousands of acres of land—a whole province of France—all France itself—lay under the night sky, concentrated into a faint hair-breadth line. So does a whole world, with all its greatnesses and littlenesses, lie in a twinkling star. And as mere human knowledge can split a ray of light and analyse the manner of its composition, so, sublimer intelligences may read in the feeble shining of this earth of ours, every thought and act, every vice and virtue, of every responsible creature on it.

The Defarges, husband and wife, came lumbering under the starlight, in their public vehicle, to that gate of Paris whereunto their journey naturally tended. There was the usual stoppage at the barrier guardhouse, and the usual lanterns came glancing forth for the usual examination and inquiry. Monsieur Defarge alighted; knowing one or two of the soldiery there, and one of the police. The latter he was intimate with, and affectionately embraced.

When Saint Antoine had again enfolded the Defarges in his dusky wings, and they, having finally alighted near the Saint's boundaries, were picking their way on foot through the black mud and offal of his streets, Madame Defarge spoke to her husband:

"Say then, my friend; what did Jacques of the police tell thee?"

"Very little to-night, but all he knows. There is another spy commissioned for our quarter. There may be many more, for all that he can say, but he knows of one."

"Eh well!" said Madame Defarge, raising her eyebrows with a cool business air. "It is necessary to register him. How do they call that man?"

"He is English."

"So much the better. His name?"

"Barsad," said Defarge, making it French by pronunciation. But, he had been so careful to get it accurately, that he then spelt it with perfect correctness.

"Barsad," repeated madame. "Good. Christian name?"

"John."

"John Barsad," repeated madame, after murmuring it once to herself. "Good. His appearance; is it known?"

"Age, about forty years; height, about five feet nine; black hair; complexion dark; generally, rather handsome visage; eyes dark, face thin, long, and sallow; nose aquiline, but not straight, having a peculiar inclination towards the left cheek; expression, therefore, sinister."

"Eh my faith. It is a portrait!" said madame, laughing. "He shall be registered to-morrow."

They turned into the wine-shop, which was closed (for it was midnight), and where Madame Defarge immediately took her post at her desk, counted the small moneys that had been taken during her absence, examined the stock, went through the entries in the book, made other entries of her own, checked the serving man in every possible way, and finally dismissed him to bed. Then she turned out the contents of the bowl of money for the second time, and began knotting them up in her handkerchief, in a chain of separate knots, for safe keeping through the night. All this while, Defarge, with his pipe in his mouth, walked up and down, complacently admiring, but never interfering; in which condition, indeed, as to the business and his domestic affairs, he walked up and down through life.

The night was hot, and the shop, close shut and surrounded by so foul a neighbourhood, was ill-smelling. Monsieur Defarge's olfactory sense was by no means delicate, but the stock of wine smelt much stronger than it ever tasted, and so did the stock of rum and brandy and aniseed. He whiffed the compound of scents away, as he put down his smoked-out pipe.

"You are fatigued," said madame, raising her glance as she knotted the money. "There are only the usual odours."

"I am a little tired," her husband acknowledged.

"You are a little depressed, too," said madame, whose quick eyes had never been so intent on the accounts, but they had had a ray or two for him. "Oh, the men, the men!"

"But my dear!" began Defarge.

"But my dear!" repeated madame, nodding firmly; "but my dear! You are faint of heart to-night, my dear!"

"Well, then," said Defarge, as if a thought were wrung out of his breast, "it *is* a long time."

"It is a long time," repeated his wife; "and when is it not a long time? Vengeance and retribution require a long time; it is the rule."

"It does not take a long time to strike a man with Lightning," said Defarge.

"How long," demanded madame, composedly, "does it take to make and store the lightning? Tell me."

Defarge raised his head thoughtfully, as if there were something in that too.

"It does not take a long time," said madame, "for an earthquake to swallow a town. Eh well! Tell me how long it takes to prepare the earthquake?"

"A long time, I suppose," said Defarge.

"But when it is ready, it takes place, and grinds to pieces everything before it. In the meantime, it is always preparing, though it is not seen or heard. That is your consolation. Keep it."

She tied a knot with flashing eyes, as if it throttled a foe.

"I tell thee," said madame, extending her right hand, for emphasis, "that although it is a long time on the road, it is on the road and coming. I tell thee it never retreats, and never stops. I tell thee it is always advancing. Look around and consider the lives of all the world that we know, consider the faces of all the world that we know, consider the rage and discontent to which the Jacquerie addresses itself with more and more of certainty every hour. Can such things last? Bah! I mock you."

"My brave wife," returned Defarge, standing before her with his head a little bent, and his hands clasped at his back, like a docile and attentive pupil before his catechist, "I do not question all this. But it has lasted a long time, and it is possible—you know well, my wife, it is possible—that it may not come, during our lives."

"Eh well! How then?" demanded madame, tying another knot, as if there were another enemy strangled.

"Well!" said Defarge, with a half complaining and half apologetic shrug. "We shall not see the triumph."

"We shall have helped it," returned madame, with her extended hand in strong action. "Nothing that we do, is done in vain. I believe, with all my soul, that we shall see the triumph. But even if not, even if I knew certainly not, show me the neck of an aristocrat and tyrant, and still I would—"

Then madame, with her teeth set, tied a very terrible knot indeed.

"Hold!" cried Defarge, reddening a little as if he felt charged with cowardice; "I too, my dear, will stop at nothing."

"Yes! But it is your weakness that you sometimes need to see your victim and your opportunity, to sustain you. Sustain yourself without that. When the time comes, let loose a tiger and a devil; but wait for the time with the tiger and the devil chained—not shown—yet always ready."

Madame enforced the conclusion of this piece of advice by striking her little counter with her chain of money as if she knocked its brains out, and then gathering the heavy handkerchief under her arm in a serene manner, and observing that it was time to go to bed.

Next noontide saw the admirable woman in her usual place in the wine-shop, knitting away assiduously. A rose lay beside her, and if she now and then glanced at the flower, it was with no infraction of her usual preoccupied air. There were a few customers, drinking or not drinking, standing or seated, sprinkled about. The day was very hot, and heaps of flies, who were extending their inquisitive and adventurous perquisitions into all the glutinous little glasses near madame, fell dead at the bottom. Their decease made no impression on the other flies out promenading, who looked at them in the coolest manner (as if they themselves were elephants, or something as far removed), until they met the same fate. Curious to consider how heedless flies are!—perhaps they thought as much at Court that sunny summer day.

A figure entering at the door threw a shadow on Madame Defarge which she felt to be a new one. She laid down her knitting, and began to pin her rose in her head-dress, before she looked at the figure.

It was curious. The moment Madame Defarge took up the rose, the customers ceased talking, and began gradually to drop out of the wine-shop.

"Good day, madame," said the new-comer.

"Good day, monsieur."

She said it aloud, but added to herself, as she resumed her knitting: "Hah! Good day, age about forty, height about five feet nine, black hair, generally rather handsome visage, complexion dark, eyes dark, thin, long and sallow face, aquiline nose but not straight, having a peculiar inclination towards the left cheek which imparts a sinister expression! Good day, one and all!"

"Have the goodness to give me a little glass of old cognac, and a mouthful of cool fresh water, madame."

Madame complied with a polite air.

"Marvellous cognac this, madame!"

It was the first time it had ever been so complemented, and Madame Defarge knew enough of its antecedents to know better. She said, however, that the cognac was flattered, and took up her knitting. The visitor watched her fingers for a few moments, and took the opportunity of observing the place in general.

"You knit with great skill, madame."

"I am accustomed to it."

"A pretty pattern too!"

"_You_ think so?" said madame, looking at him with a smile.

"Decidedly. May one ask what it is for?"

"Pastime," said madame, still looking at him with a smile while her fingers moved nimbly.

"Not for use?"

"That depends. I may find a use for it one day. If I do—Well," said madame, drawing a breath and nodding her head with a stern kind of coquetry, "I'll use it!"

It was remarkable; but, the taste of Saint Antoine seemed to be decidedly opposed to a rose on the head-dress of Madame Defarge. Two men had entered separately, and had been about to order drink, when, catching sight of that novelty, they faltered, made a pretence of looking about as if for some friend who was not there, and went away. Nor, of those who had been there when this visitor entered, was there one left. They had all dropped off. The spy had kept his eyes open, but had been able to detect no sign. They had lounged away in a poverty-stricken, purposeless, accidental manner, quite natural and unimpeachable.

"*John*," thought madame, checking off her work as her fingers knitted, and her eyes looked at the stranger. "Stay long enough, and I shall knit 'BARSAD' before you go."

"You have a husband, madame?"

"I have."

"Children?"

"No children."

"Business seems bad?"

"Business is very bad; the people are so poor."

"Ah, the unfortunate, miserable people! So oppressed, too—as you say."

"As *you* say," madame retorted, correcting him, and deftly knitting an extra something into his name that boded him no good.

"Pardon me; certainly it was I who said so, but you naturally think so. Of course."

"*I* think?" returned madame, in a high voice. "I and my husband have enough to do to keep this wine-shop open, without thinking. All we think, here, is how to live. That is the subject *we* think of, and it gives us, from morning to night, enough to think about, without embarrassing our heads concerning others. *I* think for others? No, no."

The spy, who was there to pick up any crumbs he could find or make, did not allow his baffled state to express itself in his sinister face; but, stood with an air of gossiping gallantry, leaning his elbow on Madame Defarge's little counter, and occasionally sipping his cognac.

"A bad business this, madame, of Gaspard's execution. Ah! the poor Gaspard!" With a sigh of great compassion.

"My faith!" returned madame, coolly and lightly, "if people use knives for such purposes, they have to pay for it. He knew beforehand what the price of his luxury was; he has paid the price."

"I believe," said the spy, dropping his soft voice to a tone that invited confidence, and expressing an injured revolutionary susceptibility in every muscle of his wicked face: "I believe there is much compassion and anger in this neighbourhood, touching the poor fellow? Between ourselves."

"Is there?" asked madame, vacantly.

"Is there not?"

"—Here is my husband!" said Madame Defarge.

As the keeper of the wine-shop entered at the door, the spy saluted him by touching his hat, and saying, with an engaging smile, "Good day, Jacques!" Defarge stopped short, and stared at him.

"Good day, Jacques!" the spy repeated; with not quite so much confidence, or quite so easy a smile under the stare.

"You deceive yourself, monsieur," returned the keeper of the wine-shop. "You mistake me for another. That is not my name. I am Ernest Defarge."

"It is all the same," said the spy, airily, but discomfited too: "good day!"

"Good day!" answered Defarge, drily.

"I was saying to madame, with whom I had the pleasure of chatting when you entered, that they tell me there is—and no wonder!—much sympathy and anger in Saint Antoine, touching the unhappy fate of poor Gaspard."

"No one has told me so," said Defarge, shaking his head. "I know nothing of it."

Having said it, he passed behind the little counter, and stood with his hand on the back of his wife's chair, looking over that barrier at the person to whom they were both opposed, and whom either of them would have shot with the greatest satisfaction.

The spy, well used to his business, did not change his unconscious attitude, but drained his little glass of cognac, took a sip of fresh water, and asked for another glass of cognac. Madame Defarge poured it out for him, took to her knitting again, and hummed a little song over it.

"You seem to know this quarter well; that is to say, better than I do?" observed Defarge.

"Not at all, but I hope to know it better. I am so profoundly interested in its miserable inhabitants."

"Hah!" muttered Defarge.

"The pleasure of conversing with you, Monsieur Defarge, recalls to me," pursued the spy, "that I have the honour of cherishing some interesting associations with your name."

"Indeed!" said Defarge, with much indifference.

"Yes, indeed. When Doctor Manette was released, you, his old domestic, had the charge of him, I know. He was delivered to you. You see I am informed of the circumstances?"

"Such is the fact, certainly," said Defarge. He had had it conveyed to him, in an accidental touch of his wife's elbow as she knitted and warbled, that he would do best to answer, but always with brevity.

"It was to you," said the spy, "that his daughter came; and it was from your care that his daughter took him, accompanied by a neat brown monsieur; how is he called?—in a little wig—Lorry—of the bank of Tellson and Company—over to England."

"Such is the fact," repeated Defarge.

"Very interesting remembrances!" said the spy. "I have known Doctor Manette and his daughter, in England."

"Yes?" said Defarge.

"You don't hear much about them now?" said the spy.

"No," said Defarge.

"In effect," madame struck in, looking up from her work and her little song, "we never hear about them. We received the news of their safe arrival, and perhaps another letter, or perhaps two; but, since then, they have gradually taken their road in life—we, ours—and we have held no correspondence."

"Perfectly so, madame," replied the spy. "She is going to be married."

"Going?" echoed madame. "She was pretty enough to have been married long ago. You English are cold, it seems to me."

"Oh! You know I am English."

"I perceive your tongue is," returned madame; "and what the tongue is, I suppose the man is."

He did not take the identification as a compliment; but he made the best of it, and turned it off with a laugh. After sipping his cognac to the end, he added:

"Yes, Miss Manette is going to be married. But not to an Englishman; to one who, like herself, is French by birth. And speaking of Gaspard (ah, poor Gaspard! It was cruel, cruel!), it is a curious thing that she is going to marry the nephew of Monsieur the Marquis, for whom Gaspard was exalted to that height of so many feet; in other words, the present Marquis. But he lives unknown in England, he is no Marquis there; he is Mr. Charles Darnay. D'Aulnais is the name of his mother's family."

Madame Defarge knitted steadily, but the intelligence had a palpable effect upon her husband. Do what he would, behind the little counter, as to the striking of a light and the lighting of his pipe, he was troubled, and his hand was not trustworthy. The spy would have been no spy if he had failed to see it, or to record it in his mind.

Having made, at least, this one hit, whatever it might prove to be worth, and no customers coming in to help him to any other, Mr. Barsad paid for what he had drunk, and took his leave: taking occasion to say, in a genteel manner, before he departed, that he looked forward to the pleasure of seeing Monsieur and Madame Defarge again. For some minutes after he had emerged into the outer presence of Saint Antoine, the husband and wife remained exactly as he had left them, lest he should come back.

"Can it be true," said Defarge, in a low voice, looking down at his wife as he stood smoking with his hand on the back of her chair: "what he has said of Ma'amselle Manette?"

"As he has said it," returned madame, lifting her eyebrows a little, "it is probably false. But it may be true."

"If it is—" Defarge began, and stopped.

"If it is?" repeated his wife.

"—And if it does come, while we live to see it triumph—I hope, for her sake, Destiny will keep her husband out of France."

"Her husband's destiny," said Madame Defarge, with her usual composure, "will take him where he is to go, and will lead him to the end that is to end him. That is all I know."

"But it is very strange—now, at least, is it not very strange"—said Defarge, rather pleading with his wife to induce her to admit it, "that, after all our sympathy for Monsieur her father, and herself, her husband's name should be proscribed under your hand at this moment, by the side of that infernal dog's who has just left us?"

"Stranger things than that will happen when it does come," answered madame. "I have them both here, of a certainty; and they are both here for their merits; that is enough."

She rolled up her knitting when she had said those words, and presently took the rose out of the handkerchief that was wound about her head. Either Saint Antoine had an instinctive sense that the objectionable decoration was gone, or Saint Antoine was on the watch for its disappearance; howbeit, the Saint took courage to lounge in, very shortly afterwards, and the wine-shop recovered its habitual aspect.

In the evening, at which season of all others Saint Antoine turned himself inside out, and sat on door-steps and window-ledges, and came to the corners of vile streets and courts, for a breath of air, Madame Defarge with her work in her hand was accustomed to pass from place to place and from group to group: a Missionary—there were many like her—such as the world will do well never to breed again. All the women knitted. They knitted worthless things; but, the mechanical work was a mechanical substitute for eating and drinking; the hands moved for the jaws and the digestive apparatus: if the bony fingers had been still, the stomachs would have been more famine-pinched.

But, as the fingers went, the eyes went, and the thoughts. And as Madame Defarge moved on from group to group, all three went quicker and fiercer among every little knot of women that she had spoken with, and left behind.

Her husband smoked at his door, looking after her with admiration. "A great woman," said he, "a strong woman, a grand woman, a frightfully grand woman!"

Darkness closed around, and then came the ringing of church bells and the distant beating of the military drums in the Palace Courtyard, as the women sat knitting, knitting. Darkness encompassed them. Another darkness was closing in as surely, when the church bells, then ringing pleasantly in many an airy steeple over France, should be melted into thundering cannon; when the military drums should be beating to drown a wretched voice, that night all potent as the voice of Power and Plenty, Freedom and Life. So much was closing in about the women who sat knitting, knitting, that they their very selves were closing in around a structure yet unbuilt, where they were to sit knitting, knitting, counting dropping heads.

XVII. ONE NIGHT

Never did the sun go down with a brighter glory on the quiet corner in Soho, than one memorable evening when the Doctor and his daughter sat under the plane-tree together. Never did the moon rise with a milder radiance over great London, than on that night when it found them still seated under the tree, and shone upon their faces through its leaves.

Lucie was to be married to-morrow. She had reserved this last evening for her father, and they sat alone under the plane-tree.

"You are happy, my dear father?"

"Quite, my child."

They had said little, though they had been there a long time. When it was yet light enough to work and read, she had neither engaged herself in her usual work, nor had she read to him. She had employed herself in both ways, at his side under the tree, many and many a time; but, this time was not quite like any other, and nothing could make it so.

"And I am very happy to-night, dear father. I am deeply happy in the love that Heaven has so blessed—my love for Charles, and Charles's love for me. But, if my life were not to be still consecrated to you, or if my marriage were so arranged as that it would part us, even by the length of a few of these streets, I should be more unhappy and self-reproachful now than I can tell you. Even as it is—"

Even as it was, she could not command her voice.

In the sad moonlight, she clasped him by the neck, and laid her face upon his breast. In the moonlight which is always sad, as the light of the sun itself is—as the light called human life is—at its coming and its going.

"Dearest dear! Can you tell me, this last time, that you feel quite, quite sure, no new affections of mine, and no new duties of mine, will ever interpose between us? *I* know it well, but do you know it? In your own heart, do you feel quite certain?"

Her father answered, with a cheerful firmness of conviction he could scarcely have assumed, "Quite sure, my darling! More than that," he added, as he tenderly kissed her: "my future is far brighter, Lucie, seen through your marriage, than it could have been—nay, than it ever was—without it."

"If I could hope *that*, my father!—"

"Believe it, love! Indeed it is so. Consider how natural and how plain it is, my dear, that it should be so. You, devoted and young, cannot fully appreciate the anxiety I have felt that your life should not be wasted—"

She moved her hand towards his lips, but he took it in his, and repeated the word.

"—wasted, my child—should not be wasted, struck aside from the natural order of things—for my sake. Your unselfishness cannot entirely comprehend how much my mind has gone on this; but, only ask yourself, how could my happiness be perfect, while yours was incomplete?"

"If I had never seen Charles, my father, I should have been quite happy with you."

He smiled at her unconscious admission that she would have been unhappy without Charles, having seen him; and replied:

"My child, you did see him, and it is Charles. If it had not been Charles, it would have been another. Or, if it had been no other, I should have been the cause, and then the dark part of my life would have cast its shadow beyond myself, and would have fallen on you."

It was the first time, except at the trial, of her ever hearing him refer to the period of his suffering. It gave her a strange and new sensation while his words were in her ears; and she remembered it long afterwards.

"See!" said the Doctor of Beauvais, raising his hand towards the moon. "I have looked at her from my prison-window, when I could not bear her light. I have looked at her when it has been such torture to me to think of her shining upon what I had lost, that I have beaten my head against my prison-walls. I have looked at her, in a state so dun and lethargic, that I have thought of nothing but the number of horizontal lines I could draw across her at the full, and the number of perpendicular lines with which I could intersect them." He added in his inward and pondering manner, as he looked at the moon, "It was twenty either way, I remember, and the twentieth was difficult to squeeze in."

The strange thrill with which she heard him go back to that time, deepened as he dwelt upon it; but, there was nothing to shock her in the manner of his reference. He only seemed to contrast his present cheerfulness and felicity with the dire endurance that was over.

"I have looked at her, speculating thousands of times upon the unborn child from whom I had been rent. Whether it was alive. Whether it had been born alive, or the poor mother's shock had killed it. Whether it was a son who would some day avenge his father. (There was a time in my imprisonment, when my desire for vengeance was unbearable.) Whether it was a son who would never know his father's story; who might even live to weigh the possibility of his father's having disappeared of his own will and act. Whether it was a daughter who would grow to be a woman."

She drew closer to him, and kissed his cheek and his hand.

"I have pictured my daughter, to myself, as perfectly forgetful of me—rather, altogether ignorant of me, and unconscious of me. I have cast up the years of her age, year after year. I have seen her married to a man who knew nothing of my fate. I have altogether perished from the remembrance of the living, and in the next generation my place was a blank."

"My father! Even to hear that you had such thoughts of a daughter who never existed, strikes to my heart as if I had been that child."

"You, Lucie? It is out of the Consolation and restoration you have brought to me, that these remembrances arise, and pass between us and the moon on this last night.—What did I say just now?"

"She knew nothing of you. She cared nothing for you."

"So! But on other moonlight nights, when the sadness and the silence have touched me in a different way—have affected me with something as like a sorrowful sense of peace, as any emotion that had pain for its foundations could—I have imagined her as coming to me in my cell, and leading me out into the freedom beyond the fortress. I have seen her image in the moonlight often, as I now see you; except that I never held her in my arms; it stood between the little grated window and the door. But, you understand that that was not the child I am speaking of?"

"The figure was not; the—the—image; the fancy?"

"No. That was another thing. It stood before my disturbed sense of sight, but it never moved. The phantom that my mind pursued, was another and more real child. Of her outward appearance I know no more than that she was like her mother. The other had that likeness too—as you have—but was not the same. Can you follow me, Lucie? Hardly, I think? I doubt you must have been a solitary prisoner to understand these perplexed distinctions."

His collected and calm manner could not prevent her blood from running cold, as he thus tried to anatomise his old condition.

"In that more peaceful state, I have imagined her, in the moonlight, coming to me and taking me out to show me that the home of her married life was full of her loving remembrance of her lost father. My picture was in her room, and I was in her prayers. Her life was active, cheerful, useful; but my poor history pervaded it all."

"I was that child, my father, I was not half so good, but in my love that was I."

"And she showed me her children," said the Doctor of Beauvais, "and they had heard of me, and had been taught to pity me. When they passed a prison of the State, they kept far from its frowning walls, and looked up at its bars, and spoke in whispers. She could never deliver me; I imagined that she always brought me back after showing me such things. But then, blessed with the relief of tears, I fell upon my knees, and blessed her."

"I am that child, I hope, my father. O my dear, my dear, will you bless me as fervently to-morrow?"

"Lucie, I recall these old troubles in the reason that I have to-night for loving you better than words can tell, and thanking God for my great happiness. My thoughts, when they were wildest, never rose near the happiness that I have known with you, and that we have before us."

He embraced her, solemnly commended her to Heaven, and humbly thanked Heaven for having bestowed her on him. By-and-bye, they went into the house.

There was no one bidden to the marriage but Mr. Lorry; there was even to be no bridesmaid but the gaunt Miss Pross. The marriage was to make no change in their place of residence; they had been able to extend it, by taking to themselves the upper rooms formerly belonging to the apocryphal invisible lodger, and they desired nothing more.

Doctor Manette was very cheerful at the little supper. They were only three at table, and Miss Pross made the third. He regretted that Charles was not there; was more than half disposed to object to the loving little plot that kept him away; and drank to him affectionately.

So, the time came for him to bid Lucie good night, and they separated. But, in the stillness of the third hour of the morning, Lucie came downstairs again, and stole into his room; not free from unshaped fears, beforehand.

All things, however, were in their places; all was quiet; and he lay asleep, his white hair picturesque on the untroubled pillow, and his hands lying quiet on the coverlet. She put her needless candle in the shadow at a distance, crept up to his bed, and put her lips to his; then, leaned over him, and looked at him.

Into his handsome face, the bitter waters of captivity had worn; but, he covered up their tracks with a determination so strong, that he held the mastery of them even in his sleep. A more remarkable face in its quiet, resolute, and guarded struggle with an unseen assailant, was not to be beheld in all the wide dominions of sleep, that night.

She timidly laid her hand on his dear breast, and put up a prayer that she might ever be as true to him as her love aspired to be, and as his sorrows deserved. Then, she withdrew her hand, and kissed his lips once more, and went away. So, the sunrise came, and the shadows of the leaves of the plane-tree moved upon his face, as softly as her lips had moved in praying for him.

XVIII. NINE DAYS

The marriage-day was shining brightly, and they were ready outside the closed door of the Doctor's room, where he was speaking with Charles Darnay. They were ready to go to church; the beautiful bride, Mr. Lorry, and Miss Pross—to whom the event, through a gradual process of reconcilement to the inevitable, would have been one of absolute bliss, but for the yet lingering consideration that her brother Solomon should have been the bridegroom.

"And so," said Mr. Lorry, who could not sufficiently admire the bride, and who had been moving round her to take in every point of her quiet, pretty dress; "and so it was for this, my sweet Lucie, that I brought you across the Channel, such a baby! Lord bless me! How little I thought what I was doing! How lightly I valued the obligation I was conferring on my friend Mr. Charles!"

"You didn't mean it," remarked the matter-of-fact Miss Pross, "and therefore how could you know it? Nonsense!"

"Really? Well; but don't cry," said the gentle Mr. Lorry.

"I am not crying," said Miss Pross; "*you* are."

"I, my Pross?" (By this time, Mr. Lorry dared to be pleasant with her, on occasion.)

"You were, just now; I saw you do it, and I don't wonder at it. Such a present of plate as you have made 'em, is enough to bring tears into anybody's eyes. There's not a fork or a spoon in the collection," said Miss Pross, "that I didn't cry over, last night after the box came, till I couldn't see it."

"I am highly gratified," said Mr. Lorry, "though, upon my honour, I had no intention of rendering those trifling articles of remembrance invisible to any one. Dear me! This is an occasion that makes a man speculate on all he has lost. Dear, dear, dear! To think that there might have been a Mrs. Lorry, any time these fifty years almost!"

"Not at all!" From Miss Pross.

"You think there never might have been a Mrs. Lorry?" asked the gentleman of that name.

"Pooh!" rejoined Miss Pross; "you were a bachelor in your cradle."

"Well!" observed Mr. Lorry, beamingly adjusting his little wig, "that seems probable, too."

"And you were cut out for a bachelor," pursued Miss Pross, "before you were put in your cradle."

"Then, I think," said Mr. Lorry, "that I was very unhandsomely dealt with, and that I ought to have had a voice in the selection of my pattern. Enough! Now, my dear Lucie," drawing his arm soothingly round her waist, "I hear them moving in the next room, and Miss Pross and I, as two formal folks of business, are anxious not to lose the final opportunity of saying something to you that you wish to hear. You leave your good father, my dear, in hands as earnest and as loving as your own; he shall be taken every conceivable care of; during the next fortnight, while you are in Warwickshire and thereabouts, even Tellson's shall go to the wall (comparatively speaking) before him. And when, at the fortnight's end, he comes to join you and your beloved husband, on your other fortnight's trip in Wales, you shall say that we have sent him to you in the best health and in the happiest frame. Now, I hear Somebody's step coming to the door. Let me kiss my dear girl with an old-fashioned bachelor blessing, before Somebody comes to claim his own."

For a moment, he held the fair face from him to look at the well-remembered expression on the forehead, and then laid the bright golden hair against his little brown wig, with a genuine tenderness and delicacy which, if such things be old-fashioned, were as old as Adam.

The door of the Doctor's room opened, and he came out with Charles Darnay. He was so deadly pale—which had not been the case when they went in together—that no vestige of colour was to be seen in his face. But, in the composure of his manner he was unaltered, except that to the shrewd glance of Mr. Lorry it disclosed some shadowy indication that the old air of avoidance and dread had lately passed over him, like a cold wind.

He gave his arm to his daughter, and took her down-stairs to the chariot which Mr. Lorry had hired in honour of the day. The rest followed in another carriage, and soon, in a neighbouring church, where no strange eyes looked on, Charles Darnay and Lucie Manette were happily married.

Besides the glancing tears that shone among the smiles of the little group when it was done, some diamonds, very bright and sparkling, glanced on the bride's hand, which were newly released from the dark obscurity of one of Mr. Lorry's pockets. They returned home to breakfast, and all went well, and in due course the golden hair that had mingled with the poor shoemaker's white locks in the Paris garret, were mingled with them again in the morning sunlight, on the threshold of the door at parting.

It was a hard parting, though it was not for long. But her father cheered her, and said at last, gently disengaging himself from her enfolding arms, "Take her, Charles! She is yours!"

And her agitated hand waved to them from a chaise window, and she was gone.

The corner being out of the way of the idle and curious, and the preparations having been very simple and few, the Doctor, Mr. Lorry, and Miss Pross, were left quite alone. It was when they turned into the welcome shade of the cool old hall, that Mr. Lorry observed a great change to have come over the Doctor; as if the golden arm uplifted there, had struck him a poisoned blow.

He had naturally repressed much, and some revulsion might have been expected in him when the occasion for repression was gone. But, it was the old scared lost look that troubled Mr. Lorry; and through his absent manner of clasping his head and drearily wandering away into his own room when they got up-stairs, Mr. Lorry was reminded of Defarge the wine-shop keeper, and the starlight ride.

"I think," he whispered to Miss Pross, after anxious consideration, "I think we had best not speak to him just now, or at all disturb him. I must look in at Tellson's; so I will go there at once and come back presently. Then, we will take him a ride into the country, and dine there, and all will be well."

It was easier for Mr. Lorry to look in at Tellson's, than to look out of Tellson's. He was detained two hours. When he came back, he ascended the old staircase alone, having asked no question of the servant; going thus into the Doctor's rooms, he was stopped by a low sound of knocking.

"Good God!" he said, with a start. "What's that?"

Miss Pross, with a terrified face, was at his ear. "O me, O me! All is lost!" cried she, wringing her hands. "What is to be told to Ladybird? He doesn't know me, and is making shoes!"

Mr. Lorry said what he could to calm her, and went himself into the Doctor's room. The bench was turned towards the light, as it had been when he had seen the shoemaker at his work before, and his head was bent down, and he was very busy.

"Doctor Manette. My dear friend, Doctor Manette!"

The Doctor looked at him for a moment—half inquiringly, half as if he were angry at being spoken to—and bent over his work again.

He had laid aside his coat and waistcoat; his shirt was open at the throat, as it used to be when he did that work; and even the old haggard, faded surface of face had come back to him. He worked hard—impatiently—as if in some sense of having been interrupted.

Mr. Lorry glanced at the work in his hand, and observed that it was a shoe of the old size and shape. He took up another that was lying by him, and asked what it was.

"A young lady's walking shoe," he muttered, without looking up. "It ought to have been finished long ago. Let it be."

"But, Doctor Manette. Look at me!"

He obeyed, in the old mechanically submissive manner, without pausing in his work.

"You know me, my dear friend? Think again. This is not your proper occupation. Think, dear friend!"

Nothing would induce him to speak more. He looked up, for an instant at a time, when he was requested to do so; but, no persuasion would extract a word from him. He worked, and worked, and worked, in silence, and words fell on him as they would have fallen on an echoless wall, or on the air. The only ray of hope that Mr. Lorry could discover, was, that he sometimes furtively looked up without being asked. In that, there seemed a faint expression of curiosity or perplexity—as though he were trying to reconcile some doubts in his mind.

Two things at once impressed themselves on Mr. Lorry, as important above all others; the first, that this must be kept secret from Lucie; the second, that it must be kept secret from all who knew him. In conjunction with Miss Pross, he took immediate steps towards the latter precaution, by giving out that the Doctor was not well, and required a few days of complete rest. In aid of the kind deception to be practised on his daughter, Miss Pross was to write, describing his having been called away professionally, and referring to an imaginary letter of two or three hurried lines in his own hand, represented to have been addressed to her by the same post.

These measures, advisable to be taken in any case, Mr. Lorry took in the hope of his coming to himself. If that should happen soon, he kept another course in reserve; which was, to have a certain opinion that he thought the best, on the Doctor's case.

In the hope of his recovery, and of resort to this third course being thereby rendered practicable, Mr. Lorry resolved to watch him attentively, with as little appearance as possible of doing so. He therefore made arrangements to absent himself from Tellson's for the first time in his life, and took his post by the window in the same room.

He was not long in discovering that it was worse than useless to speak to him, since, on being pressed, he became worried. He abandoned that attempt on the first day, and resolved merely to keep himself always before him, as a silent protest against the delusion into which he had fallen, or was falling. He remained, therefore, in his seat near the window, reading and writing, and expressing in as many pleasant and natural ways as he could think of, that it was a free place.

Doctor Manette took what was given him to eat and drink, and worked on, that first day, until it was too dark to see—worked on, half an hour after Mr. Lorry could not have seen, for his life, to read or write. When he put his tools aside as useless, until morning, Mr. Lorry rose and said to him:

"Will you go out?"

He looked down at the floor on either side of him in the old manner, looked up in the old manner, and repeated in the old low voice:

"Out?"

"Yes; for a walk with me. Why not?"

He made no effort to say why not, and said not a word more. But, Mr. Lorry thought he saw, as he leaned forward on his bench in the dusk, with his elbows on his knees and his head in his hands, that he was in some misty way asking himself, "Why not?" The sagacity of the man of business perceived an advantage here, and determined to hold it.

Miss Pross and he divided the night into two watches, and observed him at intervals from the adjoining room. He paced up and down for a long time before he lay down; but, when he did finally lay himself down, he fell asleep. In the morning, he was up betimes, and went straight to his bench and to work.

On this second day, Mr. Lorry saluted him cheerfully by his name, and spoke to him on topics that had been of late familiar to them. He returned no reply, but it was evident that he heard what was said, and that he thought about it, however confusedly. This encouraged Mr. Lorry to have Miss Pross in with her work, several times during the day; at those times, they quietly spoke of Lucie, and of her father then present, precisely in the usual manner, and as if there were nothing amiss. This was done without any demonstrative accompaniment, not long enough, or often enough to harass him; and it lightened Mr. Lorry's friendly heart to believe that he looked up oftener, and that he appeared to be stirred by some perception of inconsistencies surrounding him.

When it fell dark again, Mr. Lorry asked him as before:

"Dear Doctor, will you go out?"

As before, he repeated, "Out?"

"Yes; for a walk with me. Why not?"

This time, Mr. Lorry feigned to go out when he could extract no answer from him, and, after remaining absent for an hour, returned. In the meanwhile, the Doctor had removed to the seat in the window, and had sat there looking down at the plane-tree; but, on Mr. Lorry's return, he slipped away to his bench.

The time went very slowly on, and Mr. Lorry's hope darkened, and his heart grew heavier again, and grew yet heavier and heavier every day. The third day came and went, the fourth, the fifth. Five days, six days, seven days, eight days, nine days.

With a hope ever darkening, and with a heart always growing heavier and heavier, Mr. Lorry passed through this anxious time. The secret was well kept, and Lucie was unconscious and happy; but he could not fail to observe that the shoemaker, whose hand had been a little out at first, was growing dreadfully skilful, and that he had never been so intent on his work, and that his hands had never been so nimble and expert, as in the dusk of the ninth evening.

XIX. AN OPINION

Worn out by anxious watching, Mr. Lorry fell asleep at his post. On the tenth morning of his suspense, he was startled by the shining of the sun into the room where a heavy slumber had overtaken him when it was dark night.

He rubbed his eyes and roused himself; but he doubted, when he had done so, whether he was not still asleep. For, going to the door of the Doctor's room and looking in, he perceived that the shoemaker's bench and tools were put aside again, and that the Doctor himself sat reading at the window. He was in his usual morning dress, and his face (which Mr. Lorry could distinctly see), though still very pale, was calmly studious and attentive.

Even when he had satisfied himself that he was awake, Mr. Lorry felt giddily uncertain for some few moments whether the late shoemaking might not be a disturbed dream of his own; for, did not his eyes show him his friend before him in his accustomed clothing and aspect, and employed as usual; and was there any sign within their range, that the change of which he had so strong an impression had actually happened?

It was but the inquiry of his first confusion and astonishment, the answer being obvious. If the impression were not produced by a real corresponding and sufficient cause, how came he, Jarvis Lorry, there? How came he to have fallen asleep, in his clothes, on the sofa in Doctor Manette's consulting-room, and to be debating these points outside the Doctor's bedroom door in the early morning?

Within a few minutes, Miss Pross stood whispering at his side. If he had had any particle of doubt left, her talk would of necessity have resolved it; but he was by that time clear-headed, and had none. He advised that they should let the time go by until the regular breakfast-hour, and should then meet the Doctor as if nothing unusual had occurred. If he appeared to be in his customary state of mind, Mr. Lorry would then cautiously proceed to seek direction and guidance from the opinion he had been, in his anxiety, so anxious to obtain.

Miss Pross, submitting herself to his judgment, the scheme was worked out with care. Having abundance of time for his usual methodical toilette, Mr. Lorry presented himself at the breakfast-hour in his usual white linen, and with his usual neat leg. The Doctor was summoned in the usual way, and came to breakfast.

So far as it was possible to comprehend him without overstepping those delicate and gradual approaches which Mr. Lorry felt to be the only safe advance, he at first supposed that his daughter's marriage had taken place yesterday. An incidental allusion, purposely thrown out, to the day of the week, and the day of the month, set him thinking and counting, and evidently made him uneasy. In all other respects, however, he was so composedly himself, that Mr. Lorry determined to have the aid he sought. And that aid was his own.

Therefore, when the breakfast was done and cleared away, and he and the Doctor were left together, Mr. Lorry said, feelingly:

"My dear Manette, I am anxious to have your opinion, in confidence, on a very curious case in which I am deeply interested; that is to say, it is very curious to me; perhaps, to your better information it may be less so."

Glancing at his hands, which were discoloured by his late work, the Doctor looked troubled, and listened attentively. He had already glanced at his hands more than once.

"Doctor Manette," said Mr. Lorry, touching him affectionately on the arm, "the case is the case of a particularly dear friend of mine. Pray give your mind to it, and advise me well for his sake—and above all, for his daughter's—his daughter's, my dear Manette."

"If I understand," said the Doctor, in a subdued tone, "some mental shock—?"

"Yes!"

"Be explicit," said the Doctor. "Spare no detail."

Mr. Lorry saw that they understood one another, and proceeded.

"My dear Manette, it is the case of an old and a prolonged shock, of great acuteness and severity to the affections, the feelings, the—the—as you express it—the mind. The mind. It is the case of a shock under which the sufferer was borne down, one cannot say for how long, because I believe he cannot calculate the time himself, and there are no other means of getting at it. It is the case of a shock from which the sufferer recovered, by a process that he cannot trace himself—as I once heard him publicly relate in a striking manner. It is the case of a shock from which he has recovered, so completely, as to be a highly intelligent man, capable of close application of mind, and great exertion of body, and of constantly making fresh additions to his stock of knowledge, which was already very large. But, unfortunately, there has been," he paused and took a deep breath—"a slight relapse."

The Doctor, in a low voice, asked, "Of how long duration?"

"Nine days and nights."

"How did it show itself? I infer," glancing at his hands again, "in the resumption of some old pursuit connected with the shock?"

"That is the fact."

"Now, did you ever see him," asked the Doctor, distinctly and collectedly, though in the same low voice, "engaged in that pursuit originally?"

"Once."

"And when the relapse fell on him, was he in most respects—or in all respects—as he was then?"

"I think in all respects."

"You spoke of his daughter. Does his daughter know of the relapse?"

"No. It has been kept from her, and I hope will always be kept from her. It is known only to myself, and to one other who may be trusted."

The Doctor grasped his hand, and murmured, "That was very kind. That was very thoughtful!" Mr. Lorry grasped his hand in return, and neither of the two spoke for a little while.

"Now, my dear Manette," said Mr. Lorry, at length, in his most considerate and most affectionate way, "I am a mere man of business, and unfit to cope with such intricate and difficult matters. I do not possess the kind of information necessary; I do not possess the kind of intelligence; I want guiding. There is no man in this world on whom I could so rely for right guidance, as on you. Tell me, how does this relapse come about? Is there danger of another? Could a repetition of it be prevented? How should a repetition of it be treated? How does it come about at all? What can I do for my friend? No man ever can have been more desirous in his heart to serve a friend, than I am to serve mine, if I knew how. But I don't know how to originate, in such a case. If your sagacity, knowledge, and experience, could put me on the right track, I might be able to do so much; unenlightened and undirected, I can do so little. Pray discuss it with me; pray enable me to see it a little more clearly, and teach me how to be a little more useful."

Doctor Manette sat meditating after these earnest words were spoken, and Mr. Lorry did not press him.

"I think it probable," said the Doctor, breaking silence with an effort, "that the relapse you have described, my dear friend, was not quite unforeseen by its subject."

"Was it dreaded by him?" Mr. Lorry ventured to ask.

"Very much." He said it with an involuntary shudder.

"You have no idea how such an apprehension weighs on the sufferer's mind, and how difficult—how almost impossible—it is, for him to force himself to utter a word upon the topic that oppresses him."

"Would he," asked Mr. Lorry, "be sensibly relieved if he could prevail upon himself to impart that secret brooding to any one, when it is on him?"

"I think so. But it is, as I have told you, next to impossible. I even believe it—in some cases—to be quite impossible."

"Now," said Mr. Lorry, gently laying his hand on the Doctor's arm again, after a short silence on both sides, "to what would you refer this attack?"

"I believe," returned Doctor Manette, "that there had been a strong and extraordinary revival of the train of thought and remembrance that was the first cause of the malady. Some intense associations of a most distressing nature were vividly recalled, I think. It is probable that there had long been a dread lurking in his mind, that those associations would be recalled—say, under certain circumstances— say, on a particular occasion. He tried to prepare himself in vain; perhaps the effort to prepare himself made him less able to bear it."

"Would he remember what took place in the relapse?" asked Mr. Lorry, with natural hesitation.

The Doctor looked desolately round the room, shook his head, and answered, in a low voice, "Not at all."

"Now, as to the future," hinted Mr. Lorry.

"As to the future," said the Doctor, recovering firmness, "I should have great hope. As it pleased Heaven in its mercy to restore him so soon, I should have great hope. He, yielding under the pressure of a complicated something, long dreaded and long vaguely foreseen and contended against, and recovering after the cloud had burst and passed, I should hope that the worst was over."

"Well, well! That's good comfort. I am thankful!" said Mr. Lorry.

"I am thankful!" repeated the Doctor, bending his head with reverence.

"There are two other points," said Mr. Lorry, "on which I am anxious to be instructed. I may go on?"

"You cannot do your friend a better service." The Doctor gave him his hand.

"To the first, then. He is of a studious habit, and unusually energetic; he applies himself with great ardour to the acquisition of professional knowledge, to the conducting of experiments, to many things. Now, does he do too much?"

"I think not. It may be the character of his mind, to be always in singular need of occupation. That may be, in part, natural to it; in part, the result of affliction. The less it was occupied with healthy things, the more it would be in danger of turning in the unhealthy direction. He may have observed himself, and made the discovery."

"You are sure that he is not under too great a strain?"

"I think I am quite sure of it."

"My dear Manette, if he were overworked now——"

"My dear Lorry, I doubt if that could easily be. There has been a violent stress in one direction, and it needs a counterweight."

"Excuse me, as a persistent man of business. Assuming for a moment, that he *was* overworked; it would show itself in some renewal of this disorder?"

"I do not think so. I do not think," said Doctor Manette with the firmness of self-conviction, "that anything but the one train of association would renew it. I think that, henceforth, nothing but some extraordinary jarring of that chord could renew it. After what has happened, and after his recovery, I find it difficult to imagine any such violent sounding of that string again. I trust, and I almost believe, that the circumstances likely to renew it are exhausted."

He spoke with the diffidence of a man who knew how slight a thing would overset the delicate organisation of the mind, and yet with the confidence of a man who had slowly won his assurance out of personal endurance and distress. It was not for his friend to abate that confidence. He professed himself more relieved and encouraged than he really was, and approached his second and last point. He felt it to be the most difficult of all; but, remembering his old Sunday morning conversation with Miss Pross, and remembering what he had seen in the last nine days, he knew that he must face it.

"The occupation resumed under the influence of this passing affliction so happily recovered from," said Mr. Lorry, clearing his throat, "we will call—Blacksmith's work, Blacksmith's work. We will say, to put a case and for the sake of illustration, that he had been used, in his bad time, to work at a little forge. We will say that he was unexpectedly found at his forge again. Is it not a pity that he should keep it by him?"

The Doctor shaded his forehead with his hand, and beat his foot nervously on the ground.

"He has always kept it by him," said Mr. Lorry, with an anxious look at his friend. "Now, would it not be better that he should let it go?"

Still, the Doctor, with shaded forehead, beat his foot nervously on the ground.

"You do not find it easy to advise me?" said Mr. Lorry. "I quite understand it to be a nice question. And yet I think——" And there he shook his head, and stopped.

"You see," said Doctor Manette, turning to him after an uneasy pause, "it is very hard to explain, consistently, the innermost workings of this poor man's mind. He once yearned so frightfully for that occupation, and it was so welcome when it came; no doubt it relieved his pain so much, by substituting the perplexity of the fingers for the perplexity of the brain, and by substituting, as he became more practised, the ingenuity of the hands, for the ingenuity of the mental torture; that he has never been able to bear the thought of putting it quite out of his reach. Even now, when I believe he is more hopeful of himself than he has ever been, and even speaks of himself with a kind of confidence, the idea that he might need that old employment, and not find it, gives him a sudden sense of terror, like that which one may fancy strikes to the heart of a lost child."

He looked like his illustration, as he raised his eyes to Mr. Lorry's face.

"But may not—mind! I ask for information, as a plodding man of business who only deals with such material objects as guineas, shillings, and bank-notes—may not the retention of the thing involve the retention of the idea? If the thing were gone, my dear Manette, might not the fear go with it? In short, is it not a concession to the misgiving, to keep the forge?"

There was another silence.

"You see, too," said the Doctor, tremulously, "it is such an old companion."

"I would not keep it," said Mr. Lorry, shaking his head; for he gained in firmness as he saw the Doctor disquieted. "I would recommend him to sacrifice it. I only want your authority. I am sure it does no good. Come! Give me your authority, like a dear good man. For his daughter's sake, my dear Manette!"

Very strange to see what a struggle there was within him!

"In her name, then, let it be done; I sanction it. But, I would not take it away while he was present. Let it be removed when he is not there; let him miss his old companion after an absence."

Mr. Lorry readily engaged for that, and the conference was ended. They passed the day in the country, and the Doctor was quite restored. On the three following days he remained perfectly well, and on the fourteenth day he went away to join Lucie and her husband. The precaution that had been taken to account for his silence, Mr. Lorry had previously explained to him, and he had written to Lucie in accordance with it, and she had no suspicions.

On the night of the day on which he left the house, Mr. Lorry went into his room with a chopper, saw, chisel, and hammer, attended by Miss Pross carrying a light. There, with closed doors, and in a mysterious and guilty manner, Mr. Lorry hacked the shoemaker's bench to pieces, while Miss Pross held the candle as if she were assisting at a murder—for which, indeed, in her grimness, she was no unsuitable figure. The burning of the body (previously reduced to pieces convenient for the purpose) was commenced without delay in the kitchen fire; and the tools, shoes, and leather, were buried in the garden. So wicked do destruction and secrecy appear to honest minds, that Mr. Lorry and Miss Pross, while engaged in the commission of their deed and in the removal of its traces, almost felt, and almost looked, like accomplices in a horrible crime.

XX. A PLEA

When the newly-married pair came home, the first person who appeared, to offer his congratulations, was Sydney Carton. They had not been at home many hours, when he presented himself. He was not improved in habits, or in looks, or in manner; but there was a certain rugged air of fidelity about him, which was new to the observation of Charles Darnay.

He watched his opportunity of taking Darnay aside into a window, and of speaking to him when no one overheard.

"Mr. Darnay," said Carton, "I wish we might be friends."

"We are already friends, I hope."

"You are good enough to say so, as a fashion of speech; but, I don't mean any fashion of speech. Indeed, when I say I wish we might be friends, I scarcely mean quite that, either."

Charles Darnay—as was natural—asked him, in all good-humour and good-fellowship, what he did mean?

"Upon my life," said Carton, smiling, "I find that easier to comprehend in my own mind, than to convey to yours. However, let me try. You remember a certain famous occasion when I was more drunk than—than usual?"

"I remember a certain famous occasion when you forced me to confess that you had been drinking."

"I remember it too. The curse of those occasions is heavy upon me, for I always remember them. I hope it may be taken into account one day, when all days are at an end for me! Don't be alarmed; I am not going to preach."

"I am not at all alarmed. Earnestness in you, is anything but alarming to me."

"Ah!" said Carton, with a careless wave of his hand, as if he waved that away. "On the drunken occasion in question (one of a large number, as you know), I was insufferable about liking you, and not liking you. I wish you would forget it."

"I forgot it long ago."

"Fashion of speech again! But, Mr. Darnay, oblivion is not so easy to me, as you represent it to be to you. I have by no means forgotten it, and a light answer does not help me to forget it."

"If it was a light answer," returned Darnay, "I beg your forgiveness for it. I had no other object than to turn a slight thing, which, to my surprise, seems to trouble you too much, aside. I declare to you, on the faith of a gentleman, that I have long dismissed it from my mind. Good Heaven, what was there to dismiss! Have I had nothing more important to remember, in the great service you rendered me that day?"

"As to the great service," said Carton, "I am bound to avow to you, when you speak of it in that way, that it was mere professional claptrap, I don't know that I cared what became of you, when I rendered it.—Mind! I say when I rendered it; I am speaking of the past."

"You make light of the obligation," returned Darnay, "but I will not quarrel with *your* light answer."

"Genuine truth, Mr. Darnay, trust me! I have gone aside from my purpose; I was speaking about our being friends. Now, you know me; you know I am incapable of all the higher and better flights of men. If you doubt it, ask Stryver, and he'll tell you so."

"I prefer to form my own opinion, without the aid of his."

"Well! At any rate you know me as a dissolute dog, who has never done any good, and never will."

"I don't know that you 'never will.'"

"But I do, and you must take my word for it. Well! If you could endure to have such a worthless fellow, and a fellow of such indifferent reputation, coming and going at odd times, I should ask that I might be permitted to come and go as a privileged person here; that I might be regarded as an useless (and I would add, if it were not for the resemblance I detected between you and me, an unornamental) piece of furniture, tolerated for its old service, and taken no notice of. I doubt if I should abuse the permission. It is a hundred to one if I should avail myself of it four times in a year. It would satisfy me, I dare say, to know that I had it."

"Will you try?"

"That is another way of saying that I am placed on the footing I have indicated. I thank you, Darnay. I may use that freedom with your name?"

"I think so, Carton, by this time."

They shook hands upon it, and Sydney turned away. Within a minute afterwards, he was, to all outward appearance, as unsubstantial as ever.

When he was gone, and in the course of an evening passed with Miss Pross, the Doctor, and Mr. Lorry, Charles Darnay made some mention of this conversation in general terms, and spoke of Sydney Carton as a problem of carelessness and recklessness. He spoke of him, in short, not bitterly or meaning to bear hard upon him, but as anybody might who saw him as he showed himself.

He had no idea that this could dwell in the thoughts of his fair young wife; but, when he afterwards joined her in their own rooms, he found her waiting for him with the old pretty lifting of the forehead strongly marked.

"We are thoughtful to-night!" said Darnay, drawing his arm about her.

"Yes, dearest Charles," with her hands on his breast, and the inquiring and attentive expression fixed upon him; "we are rather thoughtful to-night, for we have something on our mind to-night."

"What is it, my Lucie?"

"Will you promise not to press one question on me, if I beg you not to ask it?"

"Will I promise? What will I not promise to my Love?"

What, indeed, with his hand putting aside the golden hair from the cheek, and his other hand against the heart that beat for him!

"I think, Charles, poor Mr. Carton deserves more consideration and respect than you expressed for him to-night."

"Indeed, my own? Why so?"

"That is what you are not to ask me. But I think—I know—he does."

"If you know it, it is enough. What would you have me do, my Life?"

"I would ask you, dearest, to be very generous with him always, and very lenient on his faults when he is not by. I would ask you to believe that he has a heart he very, very seldom reveals, and that there are deep wounds in it. My dear, I have seen it bleeding."

"It is a painful reflection to me," said Charles Darnay, quite astounded, "that I should have done him any wrong. I never thought this of him."

"My husband, it is so. I fear he is not to be reclaimed; there is scarcely a hope that anything in his character or fortunes is reparable now. But, I am sure that he is capable of good things, gentle things, even magnanimous things."

She looked so beautiful in the purity of her faith in this lost man, that her husband could have looked at her as she was for hours.

"And, O my dearest Love!" she urged, clinging nearer to him, laying her head upon his breast, and raising her eyes to his, "remember how strong we are in our happiness, and how weak he is in his misery!"

The supplication touched him home. "I will always remember it, dear Heart! I will remember it as long as I live."

He bent over the golden head, and put the rosy lips to his, and folded her in his arms. If one forlorn wanderer then pacing the dark streets, could have heard her innocent disclosure, and could have seen the drops of pity kissed away by her husband from the soft blue eyes so loving of that husband, he might have cried to the night—and the words would not have parted from his lips for the first time—

"God bless her for her sweet compassion!"

XXI. ECHOING FOOTSTEPS

A wonderful corner for echoes, it has been remarked, that corner where the Doctor lived. Ever busily winding the golden thread which bound her husband, and her father, and herself, and her old directress and companion, in a life of quiet bliss, Lucie sat in the still house in the tranquilly resounding corner, listening to the echoing footsteps of years.

At first, there were times, though she was a perfectly happy young wife, when her work would slowly fall from her hands, and her eyes would be dimmed. For, there was something coming in the echoes, something light, afar off, and scarcely audible yet, that stirred her heart too much. Fluttering hopes and doubts—hopes, of a love as yet unknown to her: doubts, of her remaining upon earth, to enjoy that new delight— divided her breast. Among the echoes then, there would arise the sound of footsteps at her own early grave; and thoughts of the husband who would be left so desolate, and who would mourn for her so much, swelled to her eyes, and broke like waves.

That time passed, and her little Lucie lay on her bosom. Then, among the advancing echoes, there was the tread of her tiny feet and the sound of her prattling words.

Let greater echoes resound as they would, the young mother at the cradle side could always hear those coming. They came, and the shady house was sunny with a child's laugh, and the Divine friend of children, to whom in her trouble she had confided hers, seemed to take her child in his arms, as He took the child of old, and made it a sacred joy to her.

Ever busily winding the golden thread that bound them all together, weaving the service of her happy influence through the tissue of all their lives, and making it predominate nowhere, Lucie heard in the echoes of years none but friendly and soothing sounds. Her husband's step was strong and prosperous among them; her father's firm and equal. Lo, Miss Pross, in harness of string, awakening the echoes, as an unruly charger, whip-corrected, snorting and pawing the earth under the plane-tree in the garden!

Even when there were sounds of sorrow among the rest, they were not harsh nor cruel. Even when golden hair, like her own, lay in a halo on a pillow round the worn face of a little boy, and he said, with a radiant smile, "Dear papa and mamma, I am very sorry to leave you both, and to leave my pretty sister; but I am called, and I must go!" those were not tears all of agony that wetted his young mother's cheek, as the spirit departed from her embrace that had been entrusted to it. Suffer them and forbid them not. They see my Father's face. O Father, blessed words!

Thus, the rustling of an Angel's wings got blended with the other echoes, and they were not wholly of earth, but had in them that breath of Heaven. Sighs of the winds that blew over a little garden-tomb were mingled with them also, and both were audible to Lucie, in a hushed murmur—like the breathing of a summer sea asleep upon a sandy shore—as the little Lucie, comically studious at the task of the morning, or dressing a doll at her mother's footstool, chattered in the tongues of the Two Cities that were blended in her life.

The Echoes rarely answered to the actual tread of Sydney Carton. Some half-dozen times a year, at most, he claimed his privilege of coming in uninvited, and would sit among them through the evening, as he had once done often. He never came there heated with wine. And one other thing regarding him was whispered in the echoes, which has been whispered by all true echoes for ages and ages.

No man ever really loved a woman, lost her, and knew her with a blameless though an unchanged mind, when she was a wife and a mother, but her children had a strange sympathy with him—an instinctive delicacy of pity for him. What fine hidden sensibilities are touched in such a case, no echoes tell; but it is so, and it was so here. Carton was the first stranger to whom little Lucie held out her chubby arms, and he kept his place with her as she grew. The little boy had spoken of him, almost at the last. "Poor Carton! Kiss him for me!"

Mr. Stryver shouldered his way through the law, like some great engine forcing itself through turbid water, and dragged his useful friend in his wake, like a boat towed astern. As the boat so favoured is usually in a rough plight, and mostly under water, so, Sydney had a swamped life of it. But, easy and strong custom, unhappily so much easier and stronger in him than any stimulating sense of desert or disgrace, made it the life he was to lead; and he no more thought of emerging from his state of lion's jackal, than any real jackal may be supposed to think of rising to be a lion. Stryver was rich; had married a florid widow with property and three boys, who had nothing particularly shining about them but the straight hair of their dumpling heads.

These three young gentlemen, Mr. Stryver, exuding patronage of the most offensive quality from every pore, had walked before him like three sheep to the quiet corner in Soho, and had offered as pupils to Lucie's husband: delicately saying "Halloa! here are three lumps of bread-and- cheese towards your matrimonial picnic, Darnay!" The polite rejection of the three lumps of bread-and-cheese had quite bloated Mr. Stryver with indignation, which he afterwards turned to account in the training of the young gentlemen, by directing them to beware of the pride of Beggars, like that tutor-fellow. He was also in the habit of declaiming to Mrs. Stryver, over his full-bodied wine, on the arts Mrs. Darnay had once put in practice to "catch" him, and on the diamond-cut-diamond arts in himself, madam, which had rendered him "not to be caught." Some of his King's Bench familiars, who were occasionally parties to the full-bodied wine and the lie, excused him for the latter by saying that he had told it so often, that he believed it himself—which is surely such an incorrigible aggravation of an originally bad offence, as to justify any such offender's being carried off to some suitably retired spot, and there hanged out of the way.

These were among the echoes to which Lucie, sometimes pensive, sometimes amused and laughing, listened in the echoing corner, until her little daughter was six years old. How near to her heart the echoes of her child's tread came, and those of her own dear father's, always active and self-possessed, and those of her dear husband's, need not be told. Nor, how the lightest echo of their united home, directed by herself with such a wise and elegant thrift that it was more abundant than any waste, was music to her. Nor, how there were echoes all about her, sweet in her ears, of the many times her father had told her that he found her more devoted to him married (if that could be) than single, and of the many times her husband had said to her that no cares and duties seemed to divide her love for him or her help to him, and asked her "What is the magic secret, my darling, of your being everything to all of us, as if there were only one of us, yet never seeming to be hurried, or to have too much to do?"

But, there were other echoes, from a distance, that rumbled menacingly in the corner all through this space of time. And it was now, about little Lucie's sixth birthday, that they began to have an awful sound, as of a great storm in France with a dreadful sea rising.

On a night in mid-July, one thousand seven hundred and eighty-nine, Mr. Lorry came in late, from Tellson's, and sat himself down by Lucie and her husband in the dark window. It was a hot, wild night, and they were all three reminded of the old Sunday night when they had looked at the lightning from the same place.

"I began to think," said Mr. Lorry, pushing his brown wig back, "that I should have to pass the night at Tellson's. We have been so full of business all day, that we have not known what to do first, or which way to turn. There is such an uneasiness in Paris, that we have actually a run of confidence upon us! Our customers over there, seem not to be able to confide their property to us fast enough. There is positively a mania among some of them for sending it to England."

"That has a bad look," said Darnay—

"A bad look, you say, my dear Darnay? Yes, but we don't know what reason there is in it. People are so unreasonable! Some of us at Tellson's are getting old, and we really can't be troubled out of the ordinary course without due occasion."

"Still," said Darnay, "you know how gloomy and threatening the sky is."

"I know that, to be sure," assented Mr. Lorry, trying to persuade himself that his sweet temper was soured, and that he grumbled, "but I am determined to be peevish after my long day's botheration. Where is Manette?"

"Here he is," said the Doctor, entering the dark room at the moment.

"I am quite glad you are at home; for these hurries and forebodings by which I have been surrounded all day long, have made me nervous without reason. You are not going out, I hope?"

"No; I am going to play backgammon with you, if you like," said the Doctor.

"I don't think I do like, if I may speak my mind. I am not fit to be pitted against you to-night. Is the teaboard still there, Lucie? I can't see."

"Of course, it has been kept for you."

"Thank ye, my dear. The precious child is safe in bed?"

"And sleeping soundly."

"That's right; all safe and well! I don't know why anything should be otherwise than safe and well here, thank God; but I have been so put out all day, and I am not as young as I was! My tea, my dear! Thank ye. Now, come and take your place in the circle, and let us sit quiet, and hear the echoes about which you have your theory."

"Not a theory; it was a fancy."

"A fancy, then, my wise pet," said Mr. Lorry, patting her hand. "They are very numerous and very loud, though, are they not? Only hear them!"

Headlong, mad, and dangerous footsteps to force their way into anybody's life, footsteps not easily made clean again if once stained red, the footsteps raging in Saint Antoine afar off, as the little circle sat in the dark London window.

Saint Antoine had been, that morning, a vast dusky mass of scarecrows heaving to and fro, with frequent gleams of light above the billowy heads, where steel blades and bayonets shone in the sun. A tremendous roar arose from the throat of Saint Antoine, and a forest of naked arms struggled in the air like shrivelled branches of trees in a winter wind: all the fingers convulsively clutching at every weapon or semblance of a weapon that was thrown up from the depths below, no matter how far off.

Who gave them out, whence they last came, where they began, through what agency they crookedly quivered and jerked, scores at a time, over the heads of the crowd, like a kind of lightning, no eye in the throng could have told; but, muskets were being distributed—so were cartridges, powder, and ball, bars of iron and wood, knives, axes, pikes, every weapon that distracted ingenuity could discover or devise. People who could lay hold of nothing else, set themselves with bleeding hands to force stones and bricks out of their places in walls. Every pulse and heart in Saint Antoine was on high-fever strain and at high-fever heat. Every living creature there held life as of no account, and was demented with a passionate readiness to sacrifice it.

As a whirlpool of boiling waters has a centre point, so, all this raging circled round Defarge's wine-shop, and every human drop in the caldron had a tendency to be sucked towards the vortex where Defarge himself, already begrimed with gunpowder and sweat, issued orders, issued arms, thrust this man back, dragged this man forward, disarmed one to arm another, laboured and strove in the thickest of the uproar.

"Keep near to me, Jacques Three," cried Defarge; "and do you, Jacques One and Two, separate and put yourselves at the head of as many of these patriots as you can. Where is my wife?"

"Eh, well! Here you see me!" said madame, composed as ever, but not knitting to-day. Madame's resolute right hand was occupied with an axe, in place of the usual softer implements, and in her girdle were a pistol and a cruel knife.

"Where do you go, my wife?"

"I go," said madame, "with you at present. You shall see me at the head of women, by-and-bye."

"Come, then!" cried Defarge, in a resounding voice. "Patriots and friends, we are ready! The Bastille!"

With a roar that sounded as if all the breath in France had been shaped into the detested word, the living sea rose, wave on wave, depth on depth, and overflowed the city to that point. Alarm-bells ringing, drums beating, the sea raging and thundering on its new beach, the attack began.

Deep ditches, double drawbridge, massive stone walls, eight great towers, cannon, muskets, fire and smoke. Through the fire and through the smoke—in the fire and in the smoke, for the sea cast him up against a cannon, and on the instant he became a cannonier—Defarge of the wine-shop worked like a manful soldier, Two fierce hours.

Deep ditch, single drawbridge, massive stone walls, eight great towers, cannon, muskets, fire and smoke. One drawbridge down! "Work, comrades all, work! Work, Jacques One, Jacques Two, Jacques One Thousand, Jacques Two Thousand, Jacques Five-and-Twenty Thousand; in the name of all the Angels or the Devils—which you prefer—work!" Thus Defarge of the wine-shop, still at his gun, which had long grown hot.

"To me, women!" cried madame his wife. "What! We can kill as well as the men when the place is taken!" And to her, with a shrill thirsty cry, trooping women variously armed, but all armed alike in hunger and revenge.

Cannon, muskets, fire and smoke; but, still the deep ditch, the single drawbridge, the massive stone walls, and the eight great towers. Slight displacements of the raging sea, made by the falling wounded. Flashing weapons, blazing torches, smoking waggonloads of wet straw, hard work at neighbouring barricades in all directions, shrieks, volleys, execrations, bravery without stint, boom smash and rattle, and the furious sounding of the living sea; but, still the deep ditch, and the single drawbridge, and the massive stone walls, and the eight great towers, and still Defarge of the wine-shop at his gun, grown doubly hot by the service of Four fierce hours.

A white flag from within the fortress, and a parley—this dimly perceptible through the raging storm, nothing audible in it—suddenly the sea rose immeasurably wider and higher, and swept Defarge of the wine-shop over the lowered drawbridge, past the massive stone outer walls, in among the eight great towers surrendered!

So resistless was the force of the ocean bearing him on, that even to draw his breath or turn his head was as impracticable as if he had been struggling in the surf at the South Sea, until he was landed in the outer courtyard of the Bastille. There, against an angle of a wall, he made a struggle to look about him. Jacques Three was nearly at his side; Madame Defarge, still heading some of her women, was visible in the inner distance, and her knife was in her hand. Everywhere was tumult, exultation, deafening and maniacal bewilderment, astounding noise, yet furious dumb-show.

"The Prisoners!"

"The Records!"

"The secret cells!"

"The instruments of torture!"

"The Prisoners!"

Of all these cries, and ten thousand incoherences, "The Prisoners!" was the cry most taken up by the sea that rushed in, as if there were an eternity of people, as well as of time and space. When the foremost billows rolled past, bearing the prison officers with them, and threatening them all with instant death if any secret nook remained undisclosed, Defarge laid his strong hand on the breast of one of these men—a man with a grey head, who had a lighted torch in his hand—separated him from the rest, and got him between himself and the wall.

"Show me the North Tower!" said Defarge. "Quick!"

"I will faithfully," replied the man, "if you will come with me. But there is no one there."

"What is the meaning of One Hundred and Five, North Tower?" asked Defarge. "Quick!"

"The meaning, monsieur?"

"Does it mean a captive, or a place of captivity? Or do you mean that I shall strike you dead?"

"Kill him!" croaked Jacques Three, who had come close up.

"Monsieur, it is a cell."

"Show it me!"

"Pass this way, then."

Jacques Three, with his usual craving on him, and evidently disappointed by the dialogue taking a turn that did not seem to promise bloodshed, held by Defarge's arm as he held by the turnkey's. Their three heads had been close together during this brief discourse, and it had been as much as they could do to hear one another, even then: so tremendous was the noise of the living ocean, in its irruption into the Fortress, and its inundation of the courts and passages and staircases. All around outside, too, it beat the walls with a deep, hoarse roar, from which, occasionally, some partial shouts of tumult broke and leaped into the air like spray.

Through gloomy vaults where the light of day had never shone, past hideous doors of dark dens and cages, down cavernous flights of steps, and again up steep rugged ascents of stone and brick, more like dry waterfalls than staircases, Defarge, the turnkey, and Jacques Three, linked hand and arm, went with all the speed they could make. Here and there, especially at first, the inundation started on them and swept by; but when they had done descending, and were winding and climbing up a tower, they were alone. Hemmed in here by the massive thickness of walls and arches, the storm within the fortress and without was only audible to them in a dull, subdued way, as if the noise out of which they had come had almost destroyed their sense of hearing.

The turnkey stopped at a low door, put a key in a clashing lock, swung the door slowly open, and said, as they all bent their heads and passed in:

"One hundred and five, North Tower!"

There was a small, heavily-grated, unglazed window high in the wall, with a stone screen before it, so that the sky could be only seen by stooping low and looking up. There was a small chimney, heavily barred across, a few feet within. There was a heap of old feathery wood-ashes on the hearth. There was a stool, and table, and a straw bed. There were the four blackened walls, and a rusted iron ring in one of them.

"Pass that torch slowly along these walls, that I may see them," said Defarge to the turnkey.

The man obeyed, and Defarge followed the light closely with his eyes.

"Stop!—Look here, Jacques!"

"A. M.!" croaked Jacques Three, as he read greedily.

"Alexandre Manette," said Defarge in his ear, following the letters with his swart forefinger, deeply engrained with gunpowder. "And here he wrote 'a poor physician.' And it was he, without doubt, who scratched a calendar on this stone. What is that in your hand? A crowbar? Give it me!"

He had still the linstock of his gun in his own hand. He made a sudden exchange of the two instruments, and turning on the worm-eaten stool and table, beat them to pieces in a few blows.

"Hold the light higher!" he said, wrathfully, to the turnkey. "Look among those fragments with care, Jacques. And see! Here is my knife," throwing it to him; "rip open that bed, and search the straw. Hold the light higher, you!"

With a menacing look at the turnkey he crawled upon the hearth, and, peering up the chimney, struck and prised at its sides with the crowbar, and worked at the iron grating across it. In a few minutes, some mortar and dust came dropping down, which he averted his face to avoid; and in it, and in the old wood-ashes, and in a crevice in the chimney into which his weapon had slipped or wrought itself, he groped with a cautious touch.

"Nothing in the wood, and nothing in the straw, Jacques?"

"Nothing."

"Let us collect them together, in the middle of the cell. So! Light them, you!"

The turnkey fired the little pile, which blazed high and hot. Stooping again to come out at the low-arched door, they left it burning, and retraced their way to the courtyard; seeming to recover their sense of hearing as they came down, until they were in the raging flood once more.

They found it surging and tossing, in quest of Defarge himself. Saint Antoine was clamorous to have its wine-shop keeper foremost in the guard upon the governor who had defended the Bastille and shot the people. Otherwise, the governor would not be marched to the Hotel de Ville for judgment. Otherwise, the governor would escape, and the people's blood (suddenly of some value, after many years of worthlessness) be unavenged.

In the howling universe of passion and contention that seemed to encompass this grim old officer conspicuous in his grey coat and red decoration, there was but one quite steady figure, and that was a woman's. "See, there is my husband!" she cried, pointing him out. "See Defarge!" She stood immovable close to the grim old officer, and remained immovable close to him; remained immovable close to him through the streets, as Defarge and the rest bore him along; remained immovable close to him when he was got near his destination, and began to be struck at from behind; remained immovable close to him when the long-gathering rain of stabs and blows fell heavy; was so close to him when he dropped dead under it, that, suddenly animated, she put her foot upon his neck, and with her cruel knife—long ready—hewed off his head.

The hour was come, when Saint Antoine was to execute his horrible idea of hoisting up men for lamps to show what he could be and do. Saint Antoine's blood was up, and the blood of tyranny and domination by the iron hand was down—down on the steps of the Hotel de Ville where the governor's body lay—down on the sole of the shoe of Madame Defarge where she had trodden on the body to steady it for mutilation. "Lower the lamp yonder!" cried Saint Antoine, after glaring round for a new means of death; "here is one of his soldiers to be left on guard!" The swinging sentinel was posted, and the sea rushed on.

The sea of black and threatening waters, and of destructive upheaving of wave against wave, whose depths were yet unfathomed and whose forces were yet unknown. The remorseless sea of turbulently swaying shapes, voices of vengeance, and faces hardened in the furnaces of suffering until the touch of pity could make no mark on them.

But, in the ocean of faces where every fierce and furious expression was in vivid life, there were two groups of faces—each seven in number—so fixedly contrasting with the rest, that never did sea roll which bore more memorable wrecks with it. Seven faces of prisoners, suddenly released by the storm that had burst their tomb, were carried high overhead: all scared, all lost, all wondering and amazed, as if the Last Day were come, and those who rejoiced around them were lost spirits. Other seven faces there were, carried higher, seven dead faces, whose drooping eyelids and half-seen eyes awaited the Last Day. Impassive faces, yet with a suspended—not an abolished—expression on them; faces, rather, in a fearful pause, as having yet to raise the dropped lids of the eyes, and bear witness with the bloodless lips, "THOU DIDST IT!"

Seven prisoners released, seven gory heads on pikes, the keys of the accursed fortress of the eight strong towers, some discovered letters and other memorials of prisoners of old time, long dead of broken hearts,—such, and such—like, the loudly echoing footsteps of Saint Antoine escort through the Paris streets in mid-July, one thousand seven hundred and eighty-nine. Now, Heaven defeat the fancy of Lucie Darnay, and keep these feet far out of her life! For, they are headlong, mad, and dangerous; and in the years so long after the breaking of the cask at Defarge's wine-shop door, they are not easily purified when once stained red.

XXII. THE SEA STILL RISES

Haggard Saint Antoine had had only one exultant week, in which to soften his modicum of hard and bitter bread to such extent as he could, with the relish of fraternal embraces and congratulations, when Madame Defarge sat at her counter, as usual, presiding over the customers. Madame Defarge wore no rose in her head, for the great brotherhood of Spies had become, even in one short week, extremely chary of trusting themselves to the saint's mercies. The lamps across his streets had a portentously elastic swing with them.

Madame Defarge, with her arms folded, sat in the morning light and heat, contemplating the wine-shop and the street. In both, there were several knots of loungers, squalid and miserable, but now with a manifest sense of power enthroned on their distress. The raggedest nightcap, awry on the wretchedest head, had this crooked significance in it: "I know how hard it has grown for me, the wearer of this, to support life in myself; but do you know how easy it has grown for me, the wearer of this, to destroy life in you?" Every lean bare arm, that had been without work before, had this work always ready for it now, that it could strike. The fingers of the knitting women were vicious, with the experience that they could tear. There was a change in the appearance of Saint Antoine; the image had been hammering into this for hundreds of years, and the last finishing blows had told mightily on the expression.

Madame Defarge sat observing it, with such suppressed approval as was to be desired in the leader of the Saint Antoine women. One of her sisterhood knitted beside her. The short, rather plump wife of a starved grocer, and the mother of two children withal, this lieutenant had already earned the complimentary name of The Vengeance.

"Hark!" said The Vengeance. "Listen, then! Who comes?"

As if a train of powder laid from the outermost bound of Saint Antoine Quarter to the wine-shop door, had been suddenly fired, a fast-spreading murmur came rushing along.

"It is Defarge," said madame. "Silence, patriots!"

Defarge came in breathless, pulled off a red cap he wore, and looked around him! "Listen, everywhere!" said madame again. "Listen to him!" Defarge stood, panting, against a background of eager eyes and open mouths, formed outside the door; all those within the wine-shop had sprung to their feet.

"Say then, my husband. What is it?"

"News from the other world!"

"How, then?" cried madame, contemptuously. "The other world?"

"Does everybody here recall old Foulon, who told the famished people that they might eat grass, and who died, and went to Hell?"

"Everybody!" from all throats.

"The news is of him. He is among us!"

"Among us!" from the universal throat again. "And dead?"

"Not dead! He feared us so much—and with reason—that he caused himself to be represented as dead, and had a grand mock-funeral. But they have found him alive, hiding in the country, and have brought him in. I have seen him but now, on his way to the Hotel de Ville, a prisoner. I have said that he had reason to fear us. Say all! *Had* he reason?"

Wretched old sinner of more than threescore years and ten, if he had never known it yet, he would have known it in his heart of hearts if he could have heard the answering cry.

A moment of profound silence followed. Defarge and his wife looked steadfastly at one another. The Vengeance stooped, and the jar of a drum was heard as she moved it at her feet behind the counter.

"Patriots!" said Defarge, in a determined voice, "are we ready?"

Instantly Madame Defarge's knife was in her girdle; the drum was beating in the streets, as if it and a drummer had flown together by magic; and The Vengeance, uttering terrific shrieks, and flinging her arms about her head like all the forty Furies at once, was tearing from house to house, rousing the women.

The men were terrible, in the bloody-minded anger with which they looked from windows, caught up what arms they had, and came pouring down into the streets; but, the women were a sight to chill the boldest. From such household occupations as their bare poverty yielded, from their children, from their aged and their sick crouching on the bare ground famished and naked, they ran out with streaming hair, urging one another, and themselves, to madness with the wildest cries and actions. Villain Foulon taken, my sister! Old Foulon taken, my mother! Miscreant Foulon taken, my daughter! Then, a score of others ran into the midst of these, beating their breasts, tearing their hair, and screaming, Foulon alive! Foulon who told the starving people they might eat grass! Foulon who told my old father that he might eat grass, when I had no bread to give him! Foulon who told my baby it might suck grass, when these breasts where dry with want! O mother of God, this Foulon! O Heaven our suffering! Hear me, my dead baby and my withered father: I swear on my knees, on these stones, to avenge you on Foulon! Husbands, and brothers, and young men, Give us the blood of Foulon, Give us the head of Foulon, Give us the heart of Foulon, Give us the body and soul of Foulon, Rend Foulon to pieces, and dig him into the ground, that grass may grow from him! With these cries, numbers of the women, lashed into blind frenzy, whirled about, striking and tearing at their own friends until they dropped into a passionate swoon, and were only saved by the men belonging to them from being trampled under foot.

Nevertheless, not a moment was lost; not a moment! This Foulon was at the Hotel de Ville, and might be loosed. Never, if Saint Antoine knew his own sufferings, insults, and wrongs! Armed men and women flocked out of the Quarter so fast, and drew even these last dregs after them with such a force of suction, that within a quarter of an hour there was not a human creature in Saint Antoine's bosom but a few old crones and the wailing children.

No. They were all by that time choking the Hall of Examination where this old man, ugly and wicked, was, and overflowing into the adjacent open space and streets. The Defarges, husband and wife, The Vengeance, and Jacques Three, were in the first press, and at no great distance from him in the Hall.

"See!" cried madame, pointing with her knife. "See the old villain bound with ropes. That was well done to tie a bunch of grass upon his back. Ha, ha! That was well done. Let him eat it now!" Madame put her knife under her arm, and clapped her hands as at a play.

The people immediately behind Madame Defarge, explaining the cause of her satisfaction to those behind them, and those again explaining to others, and those to others, the neighbouring streets resounded with the clapping of hands. Similarly, during two or three hours of drawl, and the winnowing of many bushels of words, Madame Defarge's frequent expressions of impatience were taken up, with marvellous quickness, at a distance: the more readily, because certain men who had by some wonderful exercise of agility climbed up the external architecture to look in from the windows, knew Madame Defarge well, and acted as a telegraph between her and the crowd outside the building.

At length the sun rose so high that it struck a kindly ray as of hope or protection, directly down upon the old prisoner's head. The favour was too much to bear; in an instant the barrier of dust and chaff that had stood surprisingly long, went to the winds, and Saint Antoine had got him!

It was known directly, to the furthest confines of the crowd. Defarge had but sprung over a railing and a table, and folded the miserable wretch in a deadly embrace—Madame Defarge had but followed and turned her hand in one of the ropes with which he was tied—The Vengeance and Jacques Three were not yet up with them, and the men at the windows had not yet swooped into the Hall, like birds of prey from their high perches—when the cry seemed to go up, all over the city, "Bring him out! Bring him to the lamp!"

Down, and up, and head foremost on the steps of the building; now, on his knees; now, on his feet; now, on his back; dragged, and struck at, and stifled by the bunches of grass and straw that were thrust into his face by hundreds of hands; torn, bruised, panting, bleeding, yet always entreating and beseeching for mercy; now full of vehement agony of action, with a small clear space about him as the people drew one another back that they might see; now, a log of dead wood drawn through a forest of legs; he was hauled to the nearest street corner where one of the fatal lamps swung, and there Madame Defarge let him go—as a cat might have done to a mouse—and silently and composedly looked at him while they made ready, and while he besought her: the women passionately screeching at him all the time, and the men sternly calling out to have him killed with grass in his mouth. Once, he went aloft, and the rope broke, and they caught him shrieking; twice, he went aloft, and the rope broke, and they caught him shrieking; then, the rope was merciful, and held him, and his head was soon upon a pike, with grass enough in the mouth for all Saint Antoine to dance at the sight of.

Nor was this the end of the day's bad work, for Saint Antoine so shouted and danced his angry blood up, that it boiled again, on hearing when the day closed in that the son-in-law of the despatched, another of the people's enemies and insulters, was coming into Paris under a guard five hundred strong, in cavalry alone. Saint Antoine wrote his crimes on flaring sheets of paper, seized him—would have torn him out of the breast of an army to bear Foulon company—set his head and heart on pikes, and carried the three spoils of the day, in Wolf-procession through the streets.

Not before dark night did the men and women come back to the children, wailing and breadless. Then, the miserable bakers' shops were beset by long files of them, patiently waiting to buy bad bread; and while they waited with stomachs faint and empty, they beguiled the time by embracing one another on the triumphs of the day, and achieving them again in gossip. Gradually, these strings of ragged people shortened and frayed away; and then poor lights began to shine in high windows, and slender fires were made in the streets, at which neighbours cooked in common, afterwards supping at their doors.

Scanty and insufficient suppers those, and innocent of meat, as of most other sauce to wretched bread. Yet, human fellowship infused some nourishment into the flinty viands, and struck some sparks of cheerfulness out of them. Fathers and mothers who had had their full share in the worst of the day, played gently with their meagre children; and lovers, with such a world around them and before them, loved and hoped.

It was almost morning, when Defarge's wine-shop parted with its last knot of customers, and Monsieur Defarge said to madame his wife, in husky tones, while fastening the door:

"At last it is come, my dear!"

"Eh well!" returned madame. "Almost."

Saint Antoine slept, the Defarges slept: even The Vengeance slept with her starved grocer, and the drum was at rest. The drum's was the only voice in Saint Antoine that blood and hurry had not changed. The Vengeance, as custodian of the drum, could have wakened him up and had the same speech out of him as before the Bastille fell, or old Foulon was seized; not so with the hoarse tones of the men and women in Saint Antoine's bosom.

XXIII. FIRE RISES

There was a change on the village where the fountain fell, and where the mender of roads went forth daily to hammer out of the stones on the highway such morsels of bread as might serve for patches to hold his poor ignorant soul and his poor reduced body together. The prison on the crag was not so dominant as of yore; there were soldiers to guard it, but not many; there were officers to guard the soldiers, but not one of them knew what his men would do—beyond this: that it would probably not be what he was ordered.

Far and wide lay a ruined country, yielding nothing but desolation. Every green leaf, every blade of grass and blade of grain, was as shrivelled and poor as the miserable people. Everything was bowed down, dejected, oppressed, and broken. Habitations, fences, domesticated animals, men, women, children, and the soil that bore them—all worn out.

Monseigneur (often a most worthy individual gentleman) was a national blessing, gave a chivalrous tone to things, was a polite example of luxurious and shining fife, and a great deal more to equal purpose; nevertheless, Monseigneur as a class had, somehow or other, brought things to this. Strange that Creation, designed expressly for Monseigneur, should be so soon wrung dry and squeezed out! There must be something short-sighted in the eternal arrangements, surely! Thus it was, however; and the last drop of blood having been extracted from the flints, and the last screw of the rack having been turned so often that its purchase crumbled, and it now turned and turned with nothing to bite, Monseigneur began to run away from a phenomenon so low and unaccountable.

But, this was not the change on the village, and on many a village like it. For scores of years gone by, Monseigneur had squeezed it and wrung it, and had seldom graced it with his presence except for the pleasures of the chase—now, found in hunting the people; now, found in hunting the beasts, for whose preservation Monseigneur made edifying spaces of barbarous and barren wilderness. No. The change consisted in the appearance of strange faces of low caste, rather than in the disappearance of the high caste, chiselled, and otherwise beautified and beautifying features of Monseigneur.

For, in these times, as the mender of roads worked, solitary, in the dust, not often troubling himself to reflect that dust he was and to dust he must return, being for the most part too much occupied in thinking how little he had for supper and how much more he would eat if he had it—in these times, as he raised his eyes from his lonely labour, and viewed the prospect, he would see some rough figure approaching on foot, the like of which was once a rarity in those parts, but was now a frequent presence. As it advanced, the mender of roads would discern without surprise, that it was a shaggy-haired man, of almost barbarian aspect, tall, in wooden shoes that were clumsy even to the eyes of a mender of roads, grim, rough, swart, steeped in the mud and dust of many highways, dank with the marshy moisture of many low grounds, sprinkled with the thorns and leaves and moss of many byways through woods.

Such a man came upon him, like a ghost, at noon in the July weather, as he sat on his heap of stones under a bank, taking such shelter as he could get from a shower of hail.

The man looked at him, looked at the village in the hollow, at the mill, and at the prison on the crag. When he had identified these objects in what benighted mind he had, he said, in a dialect that was just intelligible:

"How goes it, Jacques?"

"All well, Jacques."

"Touch then!"

They joined hands, and the man sat down on the heap of stones.

"No dinner?"

"Nothing but supper now," said the mender of roads, with a hungry face.

"It is the fashion," growled the man. "I meet no dinner anywhere."

He took out a blackened pipe, filled it, lighted it with flint and steel, pulled at it until it was in a bright glow: then, suddenly held it from him and dropped something into it from between his finger and thumb, that blazed and went out in a puff of smoke.

"Touch then." It was the turn of the mender of roads to say it this time, after observing these operations. They again joined hands.

"To-night?" said the mender of roads.

"To-night," said the man, putting the pipe in his mouth.

"Where?"

"Here."

He and the mender of roads sat on the heap of stones looking silently at one another, with the hail driving in between them like a pigmy charge of bayonets, until the sky began to clear over the village.

"Show me!" said the traveller then, moving to the brow of the hill.

"See!" returned the mender of roads, with extended finger. "You go down here, and straight through the street, and past the fountain—"

"To the Devil with all that!" interrupted the other, rolling his eye over the landscape. "*I* go through no streets and past no fountains. Well?"

"Well! About two leagues beyond the summit of that hill above the village."

"Good. When do you cease to work?"

"At sunset."

"Will you wake me, before departing? I have walked two nights without resting. Let me finish my pipe, and I shall sleep like a child. Will you wake me?"

"Surely."

The wayfarer smoked his pipe out, put it in his breast, slipped off his great wooden shoes, and lay down on his back on the heap of stones. He was fast asleep directly.

As the road-mender plied his dusty labour, and the hail-clouds, rolling away, revealed bright bars and streaks of sky which were responded to by silver gleams upon the landscape, the little man (who wore a red cap now, in place of his blue one) seemed fascinated by the figure on the heap of stones. His eyes were so often turned towards it, that he used his tools mechanically, and, one would have said, to very poor account. The bronze face, the shaggy black hair and beard, the coarse woollen red cap, the rough medley dress of home-spun stuff and hairy skins of beasts, the powerful frame attenuated by spare living, and the sullen and desperate compression of the lips in sleep, inspired the mender of roads with awe. The traveller had travelled far, and his feet were footsore, and his ankles chafed and bleeding; his great shoes, stuffed with leaves and grass, had been heavy to drag over the many long leagues, and his clothes were chafed into holes, as he himself was into sores. Stooping down beside him, the road-mender tried to get a peep at secret weapons in his breast or where not; but, in vain, for he slept with his arms crossed upon him, and set as resolutely as his lips. Fortified towns with their stockades, guard-houses, gates, trenches, and drawbridges, seemed to the mender of roads, to be so much air as against this figure. And when he lifted his eyes from it to the horizon and looked around, he saw in his small fancy similar figures, stopped by no obstacle, tending to centres all over France.

The man slept on, indifferent to showers of hail and intervals of brightness, to sunshine on his face and shadow, to the paltering lumps of dull ice on his body and the diamonds into which the sun changed them, until the sun was low in the west, and the sky was glowing. Then, the mender of roads having got his tools together and all things ready to go down into the village, roused him.

"Good!" said the sleeper, rising on his elbow. "Two leagues beyond the summit of the hill?"

"About."

"About. Good!"

The mender of roads went home, with the dust going on before him according to the set of the wind, and was soon at the fountain, squeezing himself in among the lean kine brought there to drink, and appearing even to whisper to them in his whispering to all the village. When the village had taken its poor supper, it did not creep to bed, as it usually did, but came out of doors again, and remained there. A curious contagion of whispering was upon it, and also, when it gathered together at the fountain in the dark, another curious contagion of looking expectantly at the sky in one direction only. Monsieur Gabelle, chief functionary of the place, became uneasy; went out on his house-top alone, and looked in that direction too; glanced down from behind his chimneys at the darkening faces by the fountain below, and sent word to the sacristan who kept the keys of the church, that there might be need to ring the tocsin by-and-bye.

The night deepened. The trees environing the old chateau, keeping its solitary state apart, moved in a rising wind, as though they threatened the pile of building massive and dark in the gloom. Up the two terrace flights of steps the rain ran wildly, and beat at the great door, like a swift messenger rousing those within; uneasy rushes of wind went through the hall, among the old spears and knives, and passed lamenting up the stairs, and shook the curtains of the bed where the last Marquis had slept. East, West, North, and South, through the woods, four heavy-treading, unkempt figures crushed the high grass and cracked the branches, striding on cautiously to come together in the courtyard. Four lights broke out there, and moved away in different directions, and all was black again.

But, not for long. Presently, the chateau began to make itself strangely visible by some light of its own, as though it were growing luminous. Then, a flickering streak played behind the architecture of the front, picking out transparent places, and showing where balustrades, arches, and windows were. Then it soared higher, and grew broader and brighter. Soon, from a score of the great windows, flames burst forth, and the stone faces awakened, stared out of fire.

A faint murmur arose about the house from the few people who were left there, and there was a saddling of a horse and riding away. There was spurring and splashing through the darkness, and bridle was drawn in the space by the village fountain, and the horse in a foam stood at Monsieur Gabelle's door. "Help, Gabelle! Help, every one!" The tocsin rang impatiently, but other help (if that were any) there was none. The mender of roads, and two hundred and fifty particular friends, stood with folded arms at the fountain, looking at the pillar of fire in the sky. "It must be forty feet high," said they, grimly; and never moved.

The rider from the chateau, and the horse in a foam, clattered away through the village, and galloped up the stony steep, to the prison on the crag. At the gate, a group of officers were looking at the fire; removed from them, a group of soldiers. "Help, gentlemen—officers! The chateau is on fire; valuable objects may be saved from the flames by timely aid! Help, help!" The officers looked towards the soldiers who looked at the fire; gave no orders; and answered, with shrugs and biting of lips, "It must burn."

As the rider rattled down the hill again and through the street, the village was illuminating. The mender of roads, and the two hundred and fifty particular friends, inspired as one man and woman by the idea of lighting up, had darted into their houses, and were putting candles in every dull little pane of glass. The general scarcity of everything, occasioned candles to be borrowed in a rather peremptory manner of Monsieur Gabelle; and in a moment of reluctance and hesitation on that functionary's part, the mender of roads, once so submissive to authority, had remarked that carriages were good to make bonfires with, and that post-horses would roast.

The chateau was left to itself to flame and burn. In the roaring and raging of the conflagration, a red-hot wind, driving straight from the infernal regions, seemed to be blowing the edifice away. With the rising and falling of the blaze, the stone faces showed as if they were in torment. When great masses of stone and timber fell, the face with the two dints in the nose became obscured: anon struggled out of the smoke again, as if it were the face of the cruel Marquis, burning at the stake and contending with the fire.

The chateau burned; the nearest trees, laid hold of by the fire, scorched and shrivelled; trees at a distance, fired by the four fierce figures, begirt the blazing edifice with a new forest of smoke. Molten lead and iron boiled in the marble basin of the fountain; the water ran dry; the extinguisher tops of the towers vanished like ice before the heat, and trickled down into four rugged wells of flame. Great rents and splits branched out in the solid walls, like crystallisation; stupefied birds wheeled about and dropped into the furnace; four fierce figures trudged away, East, West, North, and South, along the night- enshrouded roads, guided by the beacon they had lighted, towards their next destination. The illuminated village had seized hold of the tocsin, and, abolishing the lawful ringer, rang for joy.

Not only that; but the village, light-headed with famine, fire, and bell-ringing, and bethinking itself that Monsieur Gabelle had to do with the collection of rent and taxes—though it was but a small instalment of taxes, and no rent at all, that Gabelle had got in those latter days—became impatient for an interview with him, and, surrounding his house, summoned him to come forth for personal conference. Whereupon, Monsieur Gabelle did heavily bar his door, and retire to hold counsel with himself. The result of that conference was, that Gabelle again withdrew himself to his housetop behind his stack of chimneys; this time resolved, if his door were broken in (he was a small Southern man of retaliative temperament), to pitch himself head foremost over the parapet, and crush a man or two below.

Probably, Monsieur Gabelle passed a long night up there, with the distant chateau for fire and candle, and the beating at his door, combined with the joy-ringing, for music; not to mention his having an ill-omened lamp slung across the road before his posting-house gate, which the village showed a lively inclination to displace in his favour. A trying suspense, to be passing a whole summer night on the brink of the black ocean, ready to take that plunge into it upon which Monsieur Gabelle had resolved! But, the friendly dawn appearing at last, and the rush-candles of the village guttering out, the people happily dispersed, and Monsieur Gabelle came down bringing his life with him for that while.

Within a hundred miles, and in the light of other fires, there were other functionaries less fortunate, that night and other nights, whom the rising sun found hanging across once-peaceful streets, where they had been born and bred; also, there were other villagers and townspeople less fortunate than the mender of roads and his fellows, upon whom the functionaries and soldiery turned with success, and whom they strung up in their turn. But, the fierce figures were steadily wending East, West, North, and South, be that as it would; and whosoever hung, fire burned. The altitude of the gallows that would turn to water and quench it, no functionary, by any stretch of mathematics, was able to calculate successfully.

XXIV. DRAWN TO THE LOADSTONE ROCK

In such risings of fire and risings of sea—the firm earth shaken by the rushes of an angry ocean which had now no ebb, but was always on the flow, higher and higher, to the terror and wonder of the beholders on the shore—three years of tempest were consumed. Three more birthdays of little Lucie had been woven by the golden thread into the peaceful tissue of the life of her home.

Many a night and many a day had its inmates listened to the echoes in the corner, with hearts that failed them when they heard the thronging feet. For, the footsteps had become to their minds as the footsteps of a people, tumultuous under a red flag and with their country declared in danger, changed into wild beasts, by terrible enchantment long persisted in.

Monseigneur, as a class, had dissociated himself from the phenomenon of his not being appreciated: of his being so little wanted in France, as to incur considerable danger of receiving his dismissal from it, and this life together. Like the fabled rustic who raised the Devil with infinite pains, and was so terrified at the sight of him that he could ask the Enemy no question, but immediately fled; so, Monseigneur, after boldly reading the Lord's Prayer backwards for a great number of years, and performing many other potent spells for compelling the Evil One, no sooner beheld him in his terrors than he took to his noble heels.

The shining Bull's Eye of the Court was gone, or it would have been the mark for a hurricane of national bullets. It had never been a good eye to see with—had long had the mote in it of Lucifer's pride, Sardanapalus's luxury, and a mole's blindness—but it had dropped out and was gone. The Court, from that exclusive inner circle to its outermost rotten ring of intrigue, corruption, and dissimulation, was all gone together. Royalty was gone; had been besieged in its Palace and "suspended," when the last tidings came over.

The August of the year one thousand seven hundred and ninety-two was come, and Monseigneur was by this time scattered far and wide.

As was natural, the head-quarters and great gathering-place of Monseigneur, in London, was Tellson's Bank. Spirits are supposed to haunt the places where their bodies most resorted, and Monseigneur without a guinea haunted the spot where his guineas used to be. Moreover, it was the spot to which such French intelligence as was most to be relied upon, came quickest. Again: Tellson's was a munificent house, and extended great liberality to old customers who had fallen from their high estate. Again: those nobles who had seen the coming storm in time, and anticipating plunder or confiscation, had made provident remittances to Tellson's, were always to be heard of there by their needy brethren. To which it must be added that every new-comer from France reported himself and his tidings at Tellson's, almost as a matter of course. For such variety of reasons, Tellson's was at that time, as to French intelligence, a kind of High Exchange; and this was so well known to the public, and the inquiries made there were in consequence so numerous, that Tellson's sometimes wrote the latest news out in a line or so and posted it in the Bank windows, for all who ran through Temple Bar to read.

On a steaming, misty afternoon, Mr. Lorry sat at his desk, and Charles Darnay stood leaning on it, talking with him in a low voice. The penitential den once set apart for interviews with the House, was now the news-Exchange, and was filled to overflowing. It was within half an hour or so of the time of closing.

"But, although you are the youngest man that ever lived," said Charles Darnay, rather hesitating, "I must still suggest to you——"

"I understand. That I am too old?" said Mr. Lorry.

"Unsettled weather, a long journey, uncertain means of travelling, a disorganised country, a city that may not be even safe for you."

"My dear Charles," said Mr. Lorry, with cheerful confidence, "you touch some of the reasons for my going: not for my staying away. It is safe enough for me; nobody will care to interfere with an old fellow of hard upon fourscore when there are so many people there much better worth interfering with. As to its being a disorganised city, if it were not a disorganised city there would be no occasion to send somebody from our House here to our House there, who knows the city and the business, of old, and is in Tellson's confidence. As to the uncertain travelling, the long journey, and the winter weather, if I were not prepared to submit myself to a few inconveniences for the sake of Tellson's, after all these years, who ought to be?"

"I wish I were going myself," said Charles Darnay, somewhat restlessly, and like one thinking aloud.

"Indeed! You are a pretty fellow to object and advise!" exclaimed Mr. Lorry. "You wish you were going yourself? And you a Frenchman born? You are a wise counsellor."

"My dear Mr. Lorry, it is because I am a Frenchman born, that the thought (which I did not mean to utter here, however) has passed through my mind often. One cannot help thinking, having had some sympathy for the miserable people, and having abandoned something to them," he spoke here in his former thoughtful manner, "that one might be listened to, and might have the power to persuade to some restraint. Only last night, after you had left us, when I was talking to Lucie——"

"When you were talking to Lucie," Mr. Lorry repeated. "Yes. I wonder you are not ashamed to mention the name of Lucie! Wishing you were going to France at this time of day!"

"However, I am not going," said Charles Darnay, with a smile. "It is more to the purpose that you say you are."

"And I am, in plain reality. The truth is, my dear Charles," Mr. Lorry glanced at the distant House, and lowered his voice, "you can have no conception of the difficulty with which our business is transacted, and of the peril in which our books and papers over yonder are involved. The Lord above knows what the compromising consequences would be to numbers of people, if some of our documents were seized or destroyed; and they might be, at any time, you know, for who can say that Paris is not set afire to-day, or sacked to-morrow! Now, a judicious selection from these with the least possible delay, and the burying of them, or otherwise getting of them out of harm's way, is within the power (without loss of precious time) of scarcely any one but myself, if any one. And shall I hang back, when Tellson's knows this and says this—Tellson's, whose bread I have eaten these sixty years—because I am a little stiff about the joints? Why, I am a boy, sir, to half a dozen old codgers here!"

"How I admire the gallantry of your youthful spirit, Mr. Lorry."

"Tut! Nonsense, sir!—And, my dear Charles," said Mr. Lorry, glancing at the House again, "you are to remember, that getting things out of Paris at this present time, no matter what things, is next to an impossibility. Papers and precious matters were this very day brought to us here (I speak in strict confidence; it is not business-like to whisper it, even to you), by the strangest bearers you can imagine, every one of whom had his head hanging on by a single hair as he passed the Barriers. At another time, our parcels would come and go, as easily as in business-like Old England; but now, everything is stopped."

"And do you really go to-night?"

"I really go to-night, for the case has become too pressing to admit of delay."

"And do you take no one with you?"

"All sorts of people have been proposed to me, but I will have nothing to say to any of them. I intend to take Jerry. Jerry has been my bodyguard on Sunday nights for a long time past and I am used to him. Nobody will suspect Jerry of being anything but an English bull-dog, or of having any design in his head but to fly at anybody who touches his master."

"I must say again that I heartily admire your gallantry and youthfulness."

"I must say again, nonsense, nonsense! When I have executed this little commission, I shall, perhaps, accept Tellson's proposal to retire and live at my ease. Time enough, then, to think about growing old."

This dialogue had taken place at Mr. Lorry's usual desk, with Monseigneur swarming within a yard or two of it, boastful of what he would do to avenge himself on the rascal-people before long. It was too much the way of Monseigneur under his reverses as a refugee, and it was much too much the way of native British orthodoxy, to talk of this terrible Revolution as if it were the only harvest ever known under the skies that had not been sown—as if nothing had ever been done, or omitted to be done, that had led to it—as if observers of the wretched millions in France, and of the misused and perverted resources that should have made them prosperous, had not seen it inevitably coming, years before, and had not in plain words recorded what they saw. Such vapouring, combined with the extravagant plots of Monseigneur for the restoration of a state of things that had utterly exhausted itself, and worn out Heaven and earth as well as itself, was hard to be endured without some remonstrance by any sane man who knew the truth. And it was such vapouring all about his ears, like a troublesome confusion of blood in his own head, added to a latent uneasiness in his mind, which had already made Charles Darnay restless, and which still kept him so.

Among the talkers, was Stryver, of the King's Bench Bar, far on his way to state promotion, and, therefore, loud on the theme: broaching to Monseigneur, his devices for blowing the people up and exterminating them from the face of the earth, and doing without them: and for accomplishing many similar objects akin in their nature to the abolition of eagles by sprinkling salt on the tails of the race. Him, Darnay heard with a particular feeling of objection; and Darnay stood divided between going away that he might hear no more, and remaining to interpose his word, when the thing that was to be, went on to shape itself out.

The House approached Mr. Lorry, and laying a soiled and unopened letter before him, asked if he had yet discovered any traces of the person to whom it was addressed? The House laid the letter down so close to Darnay that he saw the direction—the more quickly because it was his own right name. The address, turned into English, ran:

"Very pressing. To Monsieur heretofore the Marquis St. Evremonde, of France. Confided to the cares of Messrs. Tellson and Co., Bankers, London, England."

On the marriage morning, Doctor Manette had made it his one urgent and express request to Charles Darnay, that the secret of this name should be—unless he, the Doctor, dissolved the obligation—kept inviolate between them. Nobody else knew it to be his name; his own wife had no suspicion of the fact; Mr. Lorry could have none.

"No," said Mr. Lorry, in reply to the House; "I have referred it, I think, to everybody now here, and no one can tell me where this gentleman is to be found."

The hands of the clock verging upon the hour of closing the Bank, there was a general set of the current of talkers past Mr. Lorry's desk. He held the letter out inquiringly; and Monseigneur looked at it, in the person of this plotting and indignant refugee; and Monseigneur looked at it in the person of that plotting and indignant refugee; and This, That, and The Other, all had something disparaging to say, in French or in English, concerning the Marquis who was not to be found.

"Nephew, I believe—but in any case degenerate successor—of the polished Marquis who was murdered," said one. "Happy to say, I never knew him."

"A craven who abandoned his post," said another—this Monseigneur had been got out of Paris, legs uppermost and half suffocated, in a load of hay—"some years ago."

"Infected with the new doctrines," said a third, eyeing the direction through his glass in passing; "set himself in opposition to the last Marquis, abandoned the estates when he inherited them, and left them to the ruffian herd. They will recompense him now, I hope, as he deserves."

"Hey?" cried the blatant Stryver. "Did he though? Is that the sort of fellow? Let us look at his infamous name. D—n the fellow!"

Darnay, unable to restrain himself any longer, touched Mr. Stryver on the shoulder, and said:

"I know the fellow."

"Do you, by Jupiter?" said Stryver. "I am sorry for it."

"Why?"

"Why, Mr. Darnay? D'ye hear what he did? Don't ask, why, in these times."

"But I do ask why?"

"Then I tell you again, Mr. Darnay, I am sorry for it. I am sorry to hear you putting any such extraordinary questions. Here is a fellow, who, infected by the most pestilent and blasphemous code of devilry that ever was known, abandoned his property to the vilest scum of the earth that ever did murder by wholesale, and you ask me why I am sorry that a man who instructs youth knows him? Well, but I'll answer you. I am sorry because I believe there is contamination in such a scoundrel. That's why."

Mindful of the secret, Darnay with great difficulty checked himself, and said: "You may not understand the gentleman."

"I understand how to put *you* in a corner, Mr. Darnay," said Bully Stryver, "and I'll do it. If this fellow is a gentleman, I *don't* understand him. You may tell him so, with my compliments. You may also tell him, from me, that after abandoning his worldly goods and position to this butcherly mob, I wonder he is not at the head of them. But, no, gentlemen," said Stryver, looking all round, and snapping his fingers, "I know something of human nature, and I tell you that you'll never find a fellow like this fellow, trusting himself to the mercies of such precious *protégés*. No, gentlemen; he'll always show 'em a clean pair of heels very early in the scuffle, and sneak away."

With those words, and a final snap of his fingers, Mr. Stryver shouldered himself into Fleet-street, amidst the general approbation of his hearers. Mr. Lorry and Charles Darnay were left alone at the desk, in the general departure from the Bank.

"Will you take charge of the letter?" said Mr. Lorry. "You know where to deliver it?"

"I do."

"Will you undertake to explain, that we suppose it to have been addressed here, on the chance of our knowing where to forward it, and that it has been here some time?"

"I will do so. Do you start for Paris from here?"

"From here, at eight."

"I will come back, to see you off."

Very ill at ease with himself, and with Stryver and most other men, Darnay made the best of his way into the quiet of the Temple, opened the letter, and read it. These were its contents:

"Prison of the Abbaye, Paris. June 21, 1792.

"MONSIEUR HERETOFORE THE MARQUIS.

"After having long been in danger of my life at the hands of the village, I have been seized, with great violence and indignity, and brought a long journey on foot to Paris. On the road I have suffered a great deal. Nor is that all; my house has been destroyed—razed to the ground.

"The crime for which I am imprisoned, Monsieur heretofore the Marquis, and for which I shall be summoned before the tribunal, and shall lose my life (without your so generous help), is, they tell me, treason against the majesty of the people, in that I have acted against them for an emigrant. It is in vain I represent that I have acted for them, and not against, according to your commands. It is in vain I represent that, before the sequestration of emigrant property, I had remitted the imposts they had ceased to pay; that I had collected no rent; that I had had recourse to no process. The only response is, that I have acted for an emigrant, and where is that emigrant?

"Ah! most gracious Monsieur heretofore the Marquis, where is that emigrant? I cry in my sleep where is he? I demand of Heaven, will he not come to deliver me? No answer. Ah Monsieur heretofore the Marquis, I send my desolate cry across the sea, hoping it may perhaps reach your ears through the great bank of Tilson known at Paris!

"For the love of Heaven, of justice, of generosity, of the honour of your noble name, I supplicate you, Monsieur heretofore the Marquis, to succour and release me. My fault is, that I have been true to you. Oh Monsieur heretofore the Marquis, I pray you be you true to me!

"From this prison here of horror, whence I every hour tend nearer and nearer to destruction, I send you, Monsieur heretofore the Marquis, the assurance of my dolorous and unhappy service.

"Your afflicted—

"Gabelle."

The latent uneasiness in Darnay's mind was roused to vigourous life by this letter. The peril of an old servant and a good one, whose only crime was fidelity to himself and his family, stared him so reproachfully in the face, that, as he walked to and fro in the Temple considering what to do, he almost hid his face from the passersby.

He knew very well, that in his horror of the deed which had culminated the bad deeds and bad reputation of the old family house, in his resentful suspicions of his uncle, and in the aversion with which his conscience regarded the crumbling fabric that he was supposed to uphold, he had acted imperfectly. He knew very well, that in his love for Lucie, his renunciation of his social place, though by no means new to his own mind, had been hurried and incomplete. He knew that he ought to have systematically worked it out and supervised it, and that he had meant to do it, and that it had never been done.

The happiness of his own chosen English home, the necessity of being always actively employed, the swift changes and troubles of the time which had followed on one another so fast, that the events of this week annihilated the immature plans of last week, and the events of the week following made all new again; he knew very well, that to the force of these circumstances he had yielded:—not without disquiet, but still without continuous and accumulating resistance. That he had watched the times for a time of action, and that they had shifted and struggled until the time had gone by, and the nobility were trooping from France by every highway and byway, and their property was in course of confiscation and destruction, and their very names were blotting out, was as well known to himself as it could be to any new authority in France that might impeach him for it.

But, he had oppressed no man, he had imprisoned no man; he was so far from having harshly exacted payment of his dues, that he had relinquished them of his own will, thrown himself on a world with no favour in it, won his own private place there, and earned his own bread. Monsieur Gabelle had held the impoverished and involved estate on written instructions, to spare the people, to give them what little there was to give—such fuel as the heavy creditors would let them have in the winter, and such produce as could be saved from the same grip in the summer—and no doubt he had put the fact in plea and proof, for his own safety, so that it could not but appear now.

This favoured the desperate resolution Charles Darnay had begun to make, that he would go to Paris.

Yes. Like the mariner in the old story, the winds and streams had driven him within the influence of the Loadstone Rock, and it was drawing him to itself, and he must go. Everything that arose before his mind drifted him on, faster and faster, more and more steadily, to the terrible attraction. His latent uneasiness had been, that bad aims were being worked out in his own unhappy land by bad instruments, and that he who could not fail to know that he was better than they, was not there, trying to do something to stay bloodshed, and assert the claims of mercy and humanity. With this uneasiness half stifled, and half reproaching him, he had been brought to the pointed comparison of himself with the brave old gentleman in whom duty was so strong; upon that comparison (injurious to himself) had instantly followed the sneers of Monseigneur, which had stung him bitterly, and those of Stryver, which above all were coarse and galling, for old reasons. Upon those, had followed Gabelle's letter: the appeal of an innocent prisoner, in danger of death, to his justice, honour, and good name.

His resolution was made. He must go to Paris.

Yes. The Loadstone Rock was drawing him, and he must sail on, until he struck. He knew of no rock; he saw hardly any danger. The intention with which he had done what he had done, even although he had left it incomplete, presented it before him in an aspect that would be gratefully acknowledged in France on his presenting himself to assert it. Then, that glorious vision of doing good, which is so often the sanguine mirage of so many good minds, arose before him, and he even saw himself in the illusion with some influence to guide this raging Revolution that was running so fearfully wild.

As he walked to and fro with his resolution made, he considered that neither Lucie nor her father must know of it until he was gone. Lucie should be spared the pain of separation; and her father, always reluctant to turn his thoughts towards the dangerous ground of old, should come to the knowledge of the step, as a step taken, and not in the balance of suspense and doubt. How much of the incompleteness of his situation was referable to her father, through the painful anxiety to avoid reviving old associations of France in his mind, he did not discuss with himself. But, that circumstance too, had had its influence in his course.

He walked to and fro, with thoughts very busy, until it was time to return to Tellson's and take leave of Mr. Lorry. As soon as he arrived in Paris he would present himself to this old friend, but he must say nothing of his intention now.

A carriage with post-horses was ready at the Bank door, and Jerry was booted and equipped.

"I have delivered that letter," said Charles Darnay to Mr. Lorry. "I would not consent to your being charged with any written answer, but perhaps you will take a verbal one?"

"That I will, and readily," said Mr. Lorry, "if it is not dangerous."

"Not at all. Though it is to a prisoner in the Abbaye."

"What is his name?" said Mr. Lorry, with his open pocket-book in his hand.

"Gabelle."

"Gabelle. And what is the message to the unfortunate Gabelle in prison?"

"Simply, 'that he has received the letter, and will come.'"

"Any time mentioned?"

"He will start upon his journey to-morrow night."

"Any person mentioned?"

"No."

He helped Mr. Lorry to wrap himself in a number of coats and cloaks, and went out with him from the warm atmosphere of the old Bank, into the misty air of Fleet-street. "My love to Lucie, and to little Lucie," said Mr. Lorry at parting, "and take precious care of them till I come back." Charles Darnay shook his head and doubtfully smiled, as the carriage rolled away.

That night—it was the fourteenth of August—he sat up late, and wrote two fervent letters; one was to Lucie, explaining the strong obligation he was under to go to Paris, and showing her, at length, the reasons that he had, for feeling confident that he could become involved in no personal danger there; the other was to the Doctor, confiding Lucie and their dear child to his care, and dwelling on the same topics with the strongest assurances. To both, he wrote that he would despatch letters in proof of his safety, immediately after his arrival.

It was a hard day, that day of being among them, with the first reservation of their joint lives on his mind. It was a hard matter to preserve the innocent deceit of which they were profoundly unsuspicious. But, an affectionate glance at his wife, so happy and busy, made him resolute not to tell her what impended (he had been half moved to do it, so strange it was to him to act in anything without her quiet aid), and the day passed quickly. Early in the evening he embraced her, and her scarcely less dear namesake, pretending that he would return by-and-bye (an imaginary engagement took him out, and he had secreted a valise of clothes ready), and so he emerged into the heavy mist of the heavy streets, with a heavier heart.

The unseen force was drawing him fast to itself, now, and all the tides and winds were setting straight and strong towards it. He left his two letters with a trusty porter, to be delivered half an hour before midnight, and no sooner; took horse for Dover; and began his journey. "For the love of Heaven, of justice, of generosity, of the honour of your noble name!" was the poor prisoner's cry with which he strengthened his sinking heart, as he left all that was dear on earth behind him, and floated away for the Loadstone Rock.

Book the Third—the Track of a Storm

I. IN SECRET

The traveller fared slowly on his way, who fared towards Paris from England in the autumn of the year one thousand seven hundred and ninety-two. More than enough of bad roads, bad equipages, and bad horses, he would have encountered to delay him, though the fallen and unfortunate King of France had been upon his throne in all his glory; but, the changed times were fraught with other obstacles than these. Every town-gate and village taxing-house had its band of citizen- patriots, with their national muskets in a most explosive state of readiness, who stopped all comers and goers, cross-questioned them, inspected their papers, looked for their names in lists of their own, turned them back, or sent them on, or stopped them and laid them in hold, as their capricious judgment or fancy deemed best for the dawning Republic One and Indivisible, of Liberty, Equality, Fraternity, or Death.

A very few French leagues of his journey were accomplished, when Charles Darnay began to perceive that for him along these country roads there was no hope of return until he should have been declared a good citizen at Paris. Whatever might befall now, he must on to his journey's end. Not a mean village closed upon him, not a common barrier dropped across the road behind him, but he knew it to be another iron door in the series that was barred between him and England. The universal watchfulness so encompassed him, that if he had been taken in a net, or were being forwarded to his destination in a cage, he could not have felt his freedom more completely gone.

This universal watchfulness not only stopped him on the highway twenty times in a stage, but retarded his progress twenty times in a day, by riding after him and taking him back, riding before him and stopping him by anticipation, riding with him and keeping him in charge. He had been days upon his journey in France alone, when he went to bed tired out, in a little town on the high road, still a long way from Paris.

Nothing but the production of the afflicted Gabelle's letter from his prison of the Abbaye would have got him on so far. His difficulty at the guard-house in this small place had been such, that he felt his journey to have come to a crisis. And he was, therefore, as little surprised as a man could be, to find himself awakened at the small inn to which he had been remitted until morning, in the middle of the night.

Awakened by a timid local functionary and three armed patriots in rough red caps and with pipes in their mouths, who sat down on the bed.

"Emigrant," said the functionary, "I am going to send you on to Paris, under an escort."

"Citizen, I desire nothing more than to get to Paris, though I could dispense with the escort."

"Silence!" growled a red-cap, striking at the coverlet with the butt-end of his musket. "Peace, aristocrat!"

"It is as the good patriot says," observed the timid functionary. "You are an aristocrat, and must have an escort—and must pay for it."

"I have no choice," said Charles Darnay.

"Choice! Listen to him!" cried the same scowling red-cap. "As if it was not a favour to be protected from the lamp-iron!"

"It is always as the good patriot says," observed the functionary. "Rise and dress yourself, emigrant."

Darnay complied, and was taken back to the guard-house, where other patriots in rough red caps were smoking, drinking, and sleeping, by a watch-fire. Here he paid a heavy price for his escort, and hence he started with it on the wet, wet roads at three o'clock in the morning.

The escort were two mounted patriots in red caps and tri-coloured cockades, armed with national muskets and sabres, who rode one on either side of him.

The escorted governed his own horse, but a loose line was attached to his bridle, the end of which one of the patriots kept girded round his wrist. In this state they set forth with the sharp rain driving in their faces: clattering at a heavy dragoon trot over the uneven town pavement, and out upon the mire-deep roads. In this state they traversed without change, except of horses and pace, all the mire- deep leagues that lay between them and the capital.

They travelled in the night, halting an hour or two after daybreak, and lying by until the twilight fell. The escort were so wretchedly clothed, that they twisted straw round their bare legs, and thatched their ragged shoulders to keep the wet off. Apart from the personal discomfort of being so attended, and apart from such considerations of present danger as arose from one of the patriots being chronically drunk, and carrying his musket very recklessly, Charles Darnay did not allow the restraint that was laid upon him to awaken any serious fears in his breast; for, he reasoned with himself that it could have no reference to the merits of an individual case that was not yet stated, and of representations, confirmable by the prisoner in the Abbaye, that were not yet made.

But when they came to the town of Beauvais—which they did at eventide, when the streets were filled with people—he could not conceal from himself that the aspect of affairs was very alarming. An ominous crowd gathered to see him dismount of the posting-yard, and many voices called out loudly, "Down with the emigrant!"

He stopped in the act of swinging himself out of his saddle, and, resuming it as his safest place, said:

"Emigrant, my friends! Do you not see me here, in France, of my own will?"

"You are a cursed emigrant," cried a farrier, making at him in a furious manner through the press, hammer in hand; "and you are a cursed aristocrat!"

The postmaster interposed himself between this man and the rider's bridle (at which he was evidently making), and soothingly said, "Let him be; let him be! He will be judged at Paris."

"Judged!" repeated the farrier, swinging his hammer. "Ay! and condemned as a traitor." At this the crowd roared approval.

Checking the postmaster, who was for turning his horse's head to the yard (the drunken patriot sat composedly in his saddle looking on, with the line round his wrist), Darnay said, as soon as he could make his voice heard:

"Friends, you deceive yourselves, or you are deceived. I am not a traitor."

"He lies!" cried the smith. "He is a traitor since the decree. His life is forfeit to the people. His cursed life is not his own!"

At the instant when Darnay saw a rush in the eyes of the crowd, which another instant would have brought upon him, the postmaster turned his horse into the yard, the escort rode in close upon his horse's flanks, and the postmaster shut and barred the crazy double gates. The farrier struck a blow upon them with his hammer, and the crowd groaned; but, no more was done.

"What is this decree that the smith spoke of?" Darnay asked the postmaster, when he had thanked him, and stood beside him in the yard.

"Truly, a decree for selling the property of emigrants."

"When passed?"

"On the fourteenth."

"The day I left England!"

"Everybody says it is but one of several, and that there will be others—if there are not already—banishing all emigrants, and condemning all to death who return. That is what he meant when he said your life was not your own."

"But there are no such decrees yet?"

"What do I know!" said the postmaster, shrugging his shoulders; "there may be, or there will be. It is all the same. What would you have?"

They rested on some straw in a loft until the middle of the night, and then rode forward again when all the town was asleep. Among the many wild changes observable on familiar things which made this wild ride unreal, not the least was the seeming rarity of sleep. After long and lonely spurring over dreary roads, they would come to a cluster of poor cottages, not steeped in darkness, but all glittering with lights, and would find the people, in a ghostly manner in the dead of the night, circling hand in hand round a shrivelled tree of Liberty, or all drawn up together singing a Liberty song. Happily, however, there was sleep in Beauvais that night to help them out of it and they passed on once more into solitude and loneliness: jingling through the untimely cold and wet, among impoverished fields that had yielded no fruits of the earth that year, diversified by the blackened remains of burnt houses, and by the sudden emergence from ambuscade, and sharp reining up across their way, of patriot patrols on the watch on all the roads.

Daylight at last found them before the wall of Paris. The barrier was closed and strongly guarded when they rode up to it.

"Where are the papers of this prisoner?" demanded a resolute-looking man in authority, who was summoned out by the guard.

Naturally struck by the disagreeable word, Charles Darnay requested the speaker to take notice that he was a free traveller and French citizen, in charge of an escort which the disturbed state of the country had imposed upon him, and which he had paid for.

"Where," repeated the same personage, without taking any heed of him whatever, "are the papers of this prisoner?"

The drunken patriot had them in his cap, and produced them. Casting his eyes over Gabelle's letter, the same personage in authority showed some disorder and surprise, and looked at Darnay with a close attention.

He left escort and escorted without saying a word, however, and went into the guard-room; meanwhile, they sat upon their horses outside the gate. Looking about him while in this state of suspense, Charles Darnay observed that the gate was held by a mixed guard of soldiers and patriots, the latter far outnumbering the former; and that while ingress into the city for peasants' carts bringing in supplies, and for similar traffic and traffickers, was easy enough, egress, even for the homeliest people, was very difficult. A numerous medley of men and women, not to mention beasts and vehicles of various sorts, was waiting to issue forth; but, the previous identification was so strict, that they filtered through the barrier very slowly. Some of these people knew their turn for examination to be so far off, that they lay down on the ground to sleep or smoke, while others talked together, or loitered about. The red cap and tri-colour cockade were universal, both among men and women.

When he had sat in his saddle some half-hour, taking note of these things, Darnay found himself confronted by the same man in authority, who directed the guard to open the barrier. Then he delivered to the escort, drunk and sober, a receipt for the escorted, and requested him to dismount. He did so, and the two patriots, leading his tired horse, turned and rode away without entering the city.

He accompanied his conductor into a guard-room, smelling of common wine and tobacco, where certain soldiers and patriots, asleep and awake, drunk and sober, and in various neutral states between sleeping and waking, drunkenness and sobriety, were standing and lying about. The light in the guard-house, half derived from the waning oil-lamps of the night, and half from the overcast day, was in a correspondingly uncertain condition. Some registers were lying open on a desk, and an officer of a coarse, dark aspect, presided over these.

"Citizen Defarge," said he to Darnay's conductor, as he took a slip of paper to write on. "Is this the emigrant Evremonde?"

"This is the man."

"Your age, Evremonde?"

"Thirty-seven."

"Married, Evremonde?"

"Yes."

"Where married?"

"In England."

"Without doubt. Where is your wife, Evremonde?"

"In England."

"Without doubt. You are consigned, Evremonde, to the prison of La Force."

"Just Heaven!" exclaimed Darnay. "Under what law, and for what offence?"

The officer looked up from his slip of paper for a moment.

"We have new laws, Evremonde, and new offences, since you were here." He said it with a hard smile, and went on writing.

"I entreat you to observe that I have come here voluntarily, in response to that written appeal of a fellow-countryman which lies before you. I demand no more than the opportunity to do so without delay. Is not that my right?"

"Emigrants have no rights, Evremonde," was the stolid reply. The officer wrote until he had finished, read over to himself what he had written, sanded it, and handed it to Defarge, with the words "In secret."

Defarge motioned with the paper to the prisoner that he must accompany him. The prisoner obeyed, and a guard of two armed patriots attended them.

"Is it you," said Defarge, in a low voice, as they went down the guardhouse steps and turned into Paris, "who married the daughter of Doctor Manette, once a prisoner in the Bastille that is no more?"

"Yes," replied Darnay, looking at him with surprise.

"My name is Defarge, and I keep a wine-shop in the Quarter Saint Antoine. Possibly you have heard of me."

"My wife came to your house to reclaim her father? Yes!"

The word "wife" seemed to serve as a gloomy reminder to Defarge, to say with sudden impatience, "In the name of that sharp female newly-born, and called La Guillotine, why did you come to France?"

"You heard me say why, a minute ago. Do you not believe it is the truth?"

"A bad truth for you," said Defarge, speaking with knitted brows, and looking straight before him.

"Indeed I am lost here. All here is so unprecedented, so changed, so sudden and unfair, that I am absolutely lost. Will you render me a little help?"

"None." Defarge spoke, always looking straight before him.

"Will you answer me a single question?"

"Perhaps. According to its nature. You can say what it is."

"In this prison that I am going to so unjustly, shall I have some free communication with the world outside?"

"You will see."

"I am not to be buried there, prejudged, and without any means of presenting my case?"

"You will see. But, what then? Other people have been similarly buried in worse prisons, before now."

"But never by me, Citizen Defarge."

Defarge glanced darkly at him for answer, and walked on in a steady and set silence. The deeper he sank into this silence, the fainter hope there was—or so Darnay thought—of his softening in any slight degree. He, therefore, made haste to say:

"It is of the utmost importance to me (you know, Citizen, even better than I, of how much importance), that I should be able to communicate to Mr. Lorry of Tellson's Bank, an English gentleman who is now in Paris, the simple fact, without comment, that I have been thrown into the prison of La Force. Will you cause that to be done for me?"

"I will do," Defarge doggedly rejoined, "nothing for you. My duty is to my country and the People. I am the sworn servant of both, against you. I will do nothing for you."

Charles Darnay felt it hopeless to entreat him further, and his pride was touched besides. As they walked on in silence, he could not but see how used the people were to the spectacle of prisoners passing along the streets. The very children scarcely noticed him. A few passers turned their heads, and a few shook their fingers at him as an aristocrat; otherwise, that a man in good clothes should be going to prison, was no more remarkable than that a labourer in working clothes should be going to work. In one narrow, dark, and dirty street through which they passed, an excited orator, mounted on a stool, was addressing an excited audience on the crimes against the people, of the king and the royal family. The few words that he caught from this man's lips, first made it known to Charles Darnay that the king was in prison, and that the foreign ambassadors had one and all left Paris. On the road (except at Beauvais) he had heard absolutely nothing. The escort and the universal watchfulness had completely isolated him.

That he had fallen among far greater dangers than those which had developed themselves when he left England, he of course knew now. That perils had thickened about him fast, and might thicken faster and faster yet, he of course knew now. He could not but admit to himself that he might not have made this journey, if he could have foreseen the events of a few days. And yet his misgivings were not so dark as, imagined by the light of this later time, they would appear. Troubled as the future was, it was the unknown future, and in its obscurity there was ignorant hope. The horrible massacre, days and nights long, which, within a few rounds of the clock, was to set a great mark of blood upon the blessed garnering time of harvest, was as far out of his knowledge as if it had been a hundred thousand years away. The "sharp female newly-born, and called La Guillotine," was hardly known to him, or to the generality of people, by name. The frightful deeds that were to be soon done, were probably unimagined at that time in the brains of the doers. How could they have a place in the shadowy conceptions of a gentle mind?

Of unjust treatment in detention and hardship, and in cruel separation from his wife and child, he foreshadowed the likelihood, or the certainty; but, beyond this, he dreaded nothing distinctly. With this on his mind, which was enough to carry into a dreary prison courtyard, he arrived at the prison of La Force.

A man with a bloated face opened the strong wicket, to whom Defarge presented "The Emigrant Evremonde."

"What the Devil! How many more of them!" exclaimed the man with the bloated face.

Defarge took his receipt without noticing the exclamation, and withdrew, with his two fellow-patriots.

"What the Devil, I say again!" exclaimed the gaoler, left with his wife. "How many more!"

The gaoler's wife, being provided with no answer to the question, merely replied, "One must have patience, my dear!" Three turnkeys who entered responsive to a bell she rang, echoed the sentiment, and one added, "For the love of Liberty;" which sounded in that place like an inappropriate conclusion.

The prison of La Force was a gloomy prison, dark and filthy, and with a horrible smell of foul sleep in it. Extraordinary how soon the noisome flavour of imprisoned sleep, becomes manifest in all such places that are ill cared for!

"In secret, too," grumbled the gaoler, looking at the written paper. "As if I was not already full to bursting!"

He stuck the paper on a file, in an ill-humour, and Charles Darnay awaited his further pleasure for half an hour: sometimes, pacing to and fro in the strong arched room: sometimes, resting on a stone seat: in either case detained to be imprinted on the memory of the chief and his subordinates.

"Come!" said the chief, at length taking up his keys, "come with me, emigrant."

Through the dismal prison twilight, his new charge accompanied him by corridor and staircase, many doors clanging and locking behind them, until they came into a large, low, vaulted chamber, crowded with prisoners of both sexes. The women were seated at a long table, reading and writing, knitting, sewing, and embroidering; the men were for the most part standing behind their chairs, or lingering up and down the room.

In the instinctive association of prisoners with shameful crime and disgrace, the new-comer recoiled from this company. But the crowning unreality of his long unreal ride, was, their all at once rising to receive him, with every refinement of manner known to the time, and with all the engaging graces and courtesies of life.

So strangely clouded were these refinements by the prison manners and gloom, so spectral did they become in the inappropriate squalor and misery through which they were seen, that Charles Darnay seemed to stand in a company of the dead. Ghosts all! The ghost of beauty, the ghost of stateliness, the ghost of elegance, the ghost of pride, the ghost of frivolity, the ghost of wit, the ghost of youth, the ghost of age, all waiting their dismissal from the desolate shore, all turning on him eyes that were changed by the death they had died in coming there.

It struck him motionless. The gaoler standing at his side, and the other gaolers moving about, who would have been well enough as to appearance in the ordinary exercise of their functions, looked so extravagantly coarse contrasted with sorrowing mothers and blooming daughters who were there—with the apparitions of the coquette, the young beauty, and the mature woman delicately bred—that the inversion of all experience and likelihood which the scene of shadows presented, was heightened to its utmost. Surely, ghosts all. Surely, the long unreal ride some progress of disease that had brought him to these gloomy shades!

"In the name of the assembled companions in misfortune," said a gentleman of courtly appearance and address, coming forward, "I have the honour of giving you welcome to La Force, and of condoling with you on the calamity that has brought you among us. May it soon terminate happily! It would be an impertinence elsewhere, but it is not so here, to ask your name and condition?"

Charles Darnay roused himself, and gave the required information, in words as suitable as he could find.

"But I hope," said the gentleman, following the chief gaoler with his eyes, who moved across the room, "that you are not in secret?"

"I do not understand the meaning of the term, but I have heard them say so."

"Ah, what a pity! We so much regret it! But take courage; several members of our society have been in secret, at first, and it has lasted but a short time." Then he added, raising his voice, "I grieve to inform the society—in secret."

There was a murmur of commiseration as Charles Darnay crossed the room to a grated door where the gaoler awaited him, and many voices—among which, the soft and compassionate voices of women were conspicuous—gave him good wishes and encouragement. He turned at the grated door, to render the thanks of his heart; it closed under the gaoler's hand; and the apparitions vanished from his sight forever.

The wicket opened on a stone staircase, leading upward. When they had ascended forty steps (the prisoner of half an hour already counted them), the gaoler opened a low black door, and they passed into a solitary cell. It struck cold and damp, but was not dark.

"Yours," said the gaoler.

"Why am I confined alone?"

"How do I know!"

"I can buy pen, ink, and paper?"

"Such are not my orders. You will be visited, and can ask then. At present, you may buy your food, and nothing more."

There were in the cell, a chair, a table, and a straw mattress. As the gaoler made a general inspection of these objects, and of the four walls, before going out, a wandering fancy wandered through the mind of the prisoner leaning against the wall opposite to him, that this gaoler was so unwholesomely bloated, both in face and person, as to look like a man who had been drowned and filled with water. When the gaoler was gone, he thought in the same wandering way, "Now am I left, as if I were dead." Stopping then, to look down at the mattress, he turned from it with a sick feeling, and thought, "And here in these crawling creatures is the first condition of the body after death."

"Five paces by four and a half, five paces by four and a half, five paces by four and a half." The prisoner walked to and fro in his cell, counting its measurement, and the roar of the city arose like muffled drums with a wild swell of voices added to them. "He made shoes, he made shoes, he made shoes." The prisoner counted the measurement again, and paced faster, to draw his mind with him from that latter repetition. "The ghosts that vanished when the wicket closed. There was one among them, the appearance of a lady dressed in black, who was leaning in the embrasure of a window, and she had a light shining upon her golden hair, and she looked like * * * * Let us ride on again, for God's sake, through the illuminated villages with the people all awake! * * * * He made shoes, he made shoes, he made shoes. * * * * Five paces by four and a half." With such scraps tossing and rolling upward from the depths of his mind, the prisoner walked faster and faster, obstinately counting and counting; and the roar of the city changed to this extent—that it still rolled in like muffled drums, but with the wail of voices that he knew, in the swell that rose above them.

II. THE GRINDSTONE

Tellson's Bank, established in the Saint Germain Quarter of Paris, was in a wing of a large house, approached by a courtyard and shut off from the street by a high wall and a strong gate. The house belonged to a great nobleman who had lived in it until he made a flight from the troubles, in his own cook's dress, and got across the borders. A mere beast of the chase flying from hunters, he was still in his metempsychosis no other than the same Monseigneur, the preparation of whose chocolate for whose lips had once occupied three strong men besides the cook in question.

Monseigneur gone, and the three strong men absolving themselves from the sin of having drawn his high wages, by being more than ready and willing to cut his throat on the altar of the dawning Republic one and indivisible of Liberty, Equality, Fraternity, or Death, Monseigneur's house had been first sequestrated, and then confiscated. For, all things moved so fast, and decree followed decree with that fierce precipitation, that now upon the third night of the autumn month of September, patriot emissaries of the law were in possession of Monseigneur's house, and had marked it with the tri-colour, and were drinking brandy in its state apartments.

A place of business in London like Tellson's place of business in Paris, would soon have driven the House out of its mind and into the Gazette. For, what would staid British responsibility and respectability have said to orange-trees in boxes in a Bank courtyard, and even to a Cupid over the counter? Yet such things were. Tellson's had whitewashed the Cupid, but he was still to be seen on the ceiling, in the coolest linen, aiming (as he very often does) at money from morning to night. Bankruptcy must inevitably have come of this young Pagan, in Lombard-street, London, and also of a curtained alcove in the rear of the immortal boy, and also of a looking-glass let into the wall, and also of clerks not at all old, who danced in public on the slightest provocation. Yet, a French Tellson's could get on with these things exceedingly well, and, as long as the times held together, no man had taken fright at them, and drawn out his money.

What money would be drawn out of Tellson's henceforth, and what would lie there, lost and forgotten; what plate and jewels would tarnish in Tellson's hiding-places, while the depositors rusted in prisons, and when they should have violently perished; how many accounts with Tellson's never to be balanced in this world, must be carried over into the next; no man could have said, that night, any more than Mr. Jarvis Lorry could, though he thought heavily of these questions. He sat by a newly-lighted wood fire (the blighted and unfruitful year was prematurely cold), and on his honest and courageous face there was a deeper shade than the pendent lamp could throw, or any object in the room distortedly reflect—a shade of horror.

He occupied rooms in the Bank, in his fidelity to the House of which he had grown to be a part, like strong root-ivy. It chanced that they derived a kind of security from the patriotic occupation of the main building, but the true-hearted old gentleman never calculated about that. All such circumstances were indifferent to him, so that he did his duty. On the opposite side of the courtyard, under a colonnade, was extensive standing—for carriages—where, indeed, some carriages of Monseigneur yet stood. Against two of the pillars were fastened two great flaring flambeaux, and in the light of these, standing out in the open air, was a large grindstone: a roughly mounted thing which appeared to have hurriedly been brought there from some neighbouring smithy, or other workshop. Rising and looking out of window at these harmless objects, Mr. Lorry shivered, and retired to his seat by the fire. He had opened, not only the glass window, but the lattice blind outside it, and he had closed both again, and he shivered through his frame.

From the streets beyond the high wall and the strong gate, there came the usual night hum of the city, with now and then an indescribable ring in it, weird and unearthly, as if some unwonted sounds of a terrible nature were going up to Heaven.

"Thank God," said Mr. Lorry, clasping his hands, "that no one near and dear to me is in this dreadful town to-night. May He have mercy on all who are in danger!"

Soon afterwards, the bell at the great gate sounded, and he thought, "They have come back!" and sat listening. But, there was no loud irruption into the courtyard, as he had expected, and he heard the gate clash again, and all was quiet.

The nervousness and dread that were upon him inspired that vague uneasiness respecting the Bank, which a great change would naturally awaken, with such feelings roused. It was well guarded, and he got up to go among the trusty people who were watching it, when his door suddenly opened, and two figures rushed in, at sight of which he fell back in amazement.

Lucie and her father! Lucie with her arms stretched out to him, and with that old look of earnestness so concentrated and intensified, that it seemed as though it had been stamped upon her face expressly to give force and power to it in this one passage of her life.

"What is this?" cried Mr. Lorry, breathless and confused. "What is the matter? Lucie! Manette! What has happened? What has brought you here? What is it?"

With the look fixed upon him, in her paleness and wildness, she panted out in his arms, imploringly, "O my dear friend! My husband!"

"Your husband, Lucie?"

"Charles."

"What of Charles?"

"Here."

"Here, in Paris?"

"Has been here some days—three or four—I don't know how many—I can't collect my thoughts. An errand of generosity brought him here unknown to us; he was stopped at the barrier, and sent to prison."

The old man uttered an irrepressible cry. Almost at the same moment, the beg of the great gate rang again, and a loud noise of feet and voices came pouring into the courtyard.

"What is that noise?" said the Doctor, turning towards the window.

"Don't look!" cried Mr. Lorry. "Don't look out! Manette, for your life, don't touch the blind!"

The Doctor turned, with his hand upon the fastening of the window, and said, with a cool, bold smile:

"My dear friend, I have a charmed life in this city. I have been a Bastille prisoner. There is no patriot in Paris—in Paris? In France—who, knowing me to have been a prisoner in the Bastille, would touch me, except to overwhelm me with embraces, or carry me in triumph. My old pain has given me a power that has brought us through the barrier, and gained us news of Charles there, and brought us here. I knew it would be so; I knew I could help Charles out of all danger; I told Lucie so.—What is that noise?" His hand was again upon the window.

"Don't look!" cried Mr. Lorry, absolutely desperate. "No, Lucie, my dear, nor you!" He got his arm round her, and held her. "Don't be so terrified, my love. I solemnly swear to you that I know of no harm having happened to Charles; that I had no suspicion even of his being in this fatal place. What prison is he in?"

"La Force!"

"La Force! Lucie, my child, if ever you were brave and serviceable in your life— and you were always both—you will compose yourself now, to do exactly as I bid you; for more depends upon it than you can think, or I can say. There is no help for you in any action on your part to-night; you cannot possibly stir out. I say this, because what I must bid you to do for Charles's sake, is the hardest thing to do of all. You must instantly be obedient, still, and quiet. You must let me put you in a room at the back here. You must leave your father and me alone for two minutes, and as there are Life and Death in the world you must not delay."

"I will be submissive to you. I see in your face that you know I can do nothing else than this. I know you are true."

The old man kissed her, and hurried her into his room, and turned the key; then, came hurrying back to the Doctor, and opened the window and partly opened the blind, and put his hand upon the Doctor's arm, and looked out with him into the courtyard.

Looked out upon a throng of men and women: not enough in number, or near enough, to fill the courtyard: not more than forty or fifty in all. The people in possession of the house had let them in at the gate, and they had rushed in to work at the grindstone; it had evidently been set up there for their purpose, as in a convenient and retired spot.

But, such awful workers, and such awful work!

The grindstone had a double handle, and, turning at it madly were two men, whose faces, as their long hair flapped back when the whirlings of the grindstone brought their faces up, were more horrible and cruel than the visages of the wildest savages in their most barbarous disguise. False eyebrows and false moustaches were stuck upon them, and their hideous countenances were all bloody and sweaty, and all awry with howling, and all staring and glaring with beastly excitement and want of sleep. As these ruffians turned and turned, their matted locks now flung forward over their eyes, now flung backward over their necks, some women held wine to their mouths that they might drink; and what with dropping blood, and what with dropping wine, and what with the stream of sparks struck out of the stone, all their wicked atmosphere seemed gore and fire. The eye could not detect one creature in the group free from the smear of blood. Shouldering one another to get next at the sharpening-stone, were men stripped to the waist, with the stain all over their limbs and bodies; men in all sorts of rags, with the stain upon those rags; men devilishly set off with spoils of women's lace and silk and ribbon, with the stain dyeing those trifles through and through. Hatchets, knives, bayonets, swords, all brought to be sharpened, were all red with it. Some of the hacked swords were tied to the wrists of those who carried them, with strips of linen and fragments of dress: ligatures various in kind, but all deep of the one colour. And as the frantic wielders of these weapons snatched them from the stream of sparks and tore away into the streets, the same red hue was red in their frenzied eyes;—eyes which any unbrutalised beholder would have given twenty years of life, to petrify with a well-directed gun.

All this was seen in a moment, as the vision of a drowning man, or of any human creature at any very great pass, could see a world if it were there. They drew back from the window, and the Doctor looked for explanation in his friend's ashy face.

"They are," Mr. Lorry whispered the words, glancing fearfully round at the locked room, "murdering the prisoners. If you are sure of what you say; if you really have the power you think you have—as I believe you have—make yourself known to these devils, and get taken to La Force. It may be too late, I don't know, but let it not be a minute later!"

Doctor Manette pressed his hand, hastened bareheaded out of the room, and was in the courtyard when Mr. Lorry regained the blind.

His streaming white hair, his remarkable face, and the impetuous confidence of his manner, as he put the weapons aside like water, carried him in an instant to the heart of the concourse at the stone. For a few moments there was a pause, and a hurry, and a murmur, and the unintelligible sound of his voice; and then Mr. Lorry saw him, surrounded by all, and in the midst of a line of twenty men long, all linked shoulder to shoulder, and hand to shoulder, hurried out with cries of—"Live the Bastille prisoner! Help for the Bastille prisoner's kindred in La Force! Room for the Bastille prisoner in front there! Save the prisoner Evremonde at La Force!" and a thousand answering shouts.

He closed the lattice again with a fluttering heart, closed the window and the curtain, hastened to Lucie, and told her that her father was assisted by the people, and gone in search of her husband. He found her child and Miss Pross with her; but, it never occurred to him to be surprised by their appearance until a long time afterwards, when he sat watching them in such quiet as the night knew.

Lucie had, by that time, fallen into a stupor on the floor at his feet, clinging to his hand. Miss Pross had laid the child down on his own bed, and her head had gradually fallen on the pillow beside her pretty charge. O the long, long night, with the moans of the poor wife! And O the long, long night, with no return of her father and no tidings!

Twice more in the darkness the bell at the great gate sounded, and the irruption was repeated, and the grindstone whirled and spluttered. "What is it?" cried Lucie, affrighted. "Hush! The soldiers' swords are sharpened there," said Mr. Lorry. "The place is national property now, and used as a kind of armoury, my love."

Twice more in all; but, the last spell of work was feeble and fitful. Soon afterwards the day began to dawn, and he softly detached himself from the clasping hand, and cautiously looked out again. A man, so besmeared that he might have been a sorely wounded soldier creeping back to consciousness on a field of slain, was rising from the pavement by the side of the grindstone, and looking about him with a vacant air. Shortly, this worn-out murderer descried in the imperfect light one of the carriages of Monseigneur, and, staggering to that gorgeous vehicle, climbed in at the door, and shut himself up to take his rest on its dainty cushions.

The great grindstone, Earth, had turned when Mr. Lorry looked out again, and the sun was red on the courtyard. But, the lesser grindstone stood alone there in the calm morning air, with a red upon it that the sun had never given, and would never take away.

III. THE SHADOW

One of the first considerations which arose in the business mind of Mr. Lorry when business hours came round, was this:—that he had no right to imperil Tellson's by sheltering the wife of an emigrant prisoner under the Bank roof. His own possessions, safety, life, he would have hazarded for Lucie and her child, without a moment's demur; but the great trust he held was not his own, and as to that business charge he was a strict man of business.

At first, his mind reverted to Defarge, and he thought of finding out the wine-shop again and taking counsel with its master in reference to the safest dwelling-place in the distracted state of the city. But, the same consideration that suggested him, repudiated him; he lived in the most violent Quarter, and doubtless was influential there, and deep in its dangerous workings.

Noon coming, and the Doctor not returning, and every minute's delay tending to compromise Tellson's, Mr. Lorry advised with Lucie. She said that her father had spoken of hiring a lodging for a short term, in that Quarter, near the Banking-house. As there was no business objection to this, and as he foresaw that even if it were all well with Charles, and he were to be released, he could not hope to leave the city, Mr. Lorry went out in quest of such a lodging, and found a suitable one, high up in a removed by-street where the closed blinds in all the other windows of a high melancholy square of buildings marked deserted homes.

To this lodging he at once removed Lucie and her child, and Miss Pross: giving them what comfort he could, and much more than he had himself. He left Jerry with them, as a figure to fill a doorway that would bear considerable knocking on the head, and retained to his own occupations. A disturbed and doleful mind he brought to bear upon them, and slowly and heavily the day lagged on with him.

It wore itself out, and wore him out with it, until the Bank closed. He was again alone in his room of the previous night, considering what to do next, when he heard a foot upon the stair. In a few moments, a man stood in his presence, who, with a keenly observant look at him, addressed him by his name.

"Your servant," said Mr. Lorry. "Do you know me?"

He was a strongly made man with dark curling hair, from forty-five to fifty years of age. For answer he repeated, without any change of emphasis, the words:

"Do you know me?"

"I have seen you somewhere."

"Perhaps at my wine-shop?"

Much interested and agitated, Mr. Lorry said: "You come from Doctor Manette?"

"Yes. I come from Doctor Manette."

"And what says he? What does he send me?"

Defarge gave into his anxious hand, an open scrap of paper. It bore the words in the Doctor's writing:

"Charles is safe, but I cannot safely leave this place yet. I have obtained the favour that the bearer has a short note from Charles to his wife. Let the bearer see his wife."

It was dated from La Force, within an hour.

"Will you accompany me," said Mr. Lorry, joyfully relieved after reading this note aloud, "to where his wife resides?"

"Yes," returned Defarge.

Scarcely noticing as yet, in what a curiously reserved and mechanical way Defarge spoke, Mr. Lorry put on his hat and they went down into the courtyard. There, they found two women; one, knitting.

"Madame Defarge, surely!" said Mr. Lorry, who had left her in exactly the same attitude some seventeen years ago.

"It is she," observed her husband.

"Does Madame go with us?" inquired Mr. Lorry, seeing that she moved as they moved.

"Yes. That she may be able to recognise the faces and know the persons. It is for their safety."

Beginning to be struck by Defarge's manner, Mr. Lorry looked dubiously at him, and led the way. Both the women followed; the second woman being The Vengeance.

They passed through the intervening streets as quickly as they might, ascended the staircase of the new domicile, were admitted by Jerry, and found Lucie weeping, alone. She was thrown into a transport by the tidings Mr. Lorry gave her of her husband, and clasped the hand that delivered his note—little thinking what it had been doing near him in the night, and might, but for a chance, have done to him.

> "DEAREST,—Take courage. I am well, and your father has influence around me. You cannot answer this. Kiss our child for me."

That was all the writing. It was so much, however, to her who received it, that she turned from Defarge to his wife, and kissed one of the hands that knitted. It was a passionate, loving, thankful, womanly action, but the hand made no response—dropped cold and heavy, and took to its knitting again.

There was something in its touch that gave Lucie a check. She stopped in the act of putting the note in her bosom, and, with her hands yet at her neck, looked terrified at Madame Defarge. Madame Defarge met the lifted eyebrows and forehead with a cold, impassive stare.

"My dear," said Mr. Lorry, striking in to explain; "there are frequent risings in the streets; and, although it is not likely they will ever trouble you, Madame Defarge wishes to see those whom she has the power to protect at such times, to the end that she may know them—that she may identify them. I believe," said Mr. Lorry, rather halting in his reassuring words, as the stony manner of all the three impressed itself upon him more and more, "I state the case, Citizen Defarge?"

Defarge looked gloomily at his wife, and gave no other answer than a gruff sound of acquiescence.

"You had better, Lucie," said Mr. Lorry, doing all he could to propitiate, by tone and manner, "have the dear child here, and our good Pross. Our good Pross, Defarge, is an English lady, and knows no French."

The lady in question, whose rooted conviction that she was more than a match for any foreigner, was not to be shaken by distress and, danger, appeared with folded arms, and observed in English to The Vengeance, whom her eyes first encountered, "Well, I am sure, Boldface! I hope *you* are pretty well!" She also bestowed a British cough on Madame Defarge; but, neither of the two took much heed of her.

"Is that his child?" said Madame Defarge, stopping in her work for the first time, and pointing her knitting-needle at little Lucie as if it were the finger of Fate.

"Yes, madame," answered Mr. Lorry; "this is our poor prisoner's darling daughter, and only child."

The shadow attendant on Madame Defarge and her party seemed to fall so threatening and dark on the child, that her mother instinctively kneeled on the ground beside her, and held her to her breast. The shadow attendant on Madame Defarge and her party seemed then to fall, threatening and dark, on both the mother and the child.

"It is enough, my husband," said Madame Defarge. "I have seen them. We may go."

But, the suppressed manner had enough of menace in it—not visible and presented, but indistinct and withheld—to alarm Lucie into saying, as she laid her appealing hand on Madame Defarge's dress:

"You will be good to my poor husband. You will do him no harm. You will help me to see him if you can?"

"Your husband is not my business here," returned Madame Defarge, looking down at her with perfect composure. "It is the daughter of your father who is my business here."

"For my sake, then, be merciful to my husband. For my child's sake! She will put her hands together and pray you to be merciful. We are more afraid of you than of these others."

Madame Defarge received it as a compliment, and looked at her husband. Defarge, who had been uneasily biting his thumb-nail and looking at her, collected his face into a sterner expression.

"What is it that your husband says in that little letter?" asked Madame Defarge, with a lowering smile. "Influence; he says something touching influence?"

"That my father," said Lucie, hurriedly taking the paper from her breast, but with her alarmed eyes on her questioner and not on it, "has much influence around him."

"Surely it will release him!" said Madame Defarge. "Let it do so."

"As a wife and mother," cried Lucie, most earnestly, "I implore you to have pity on me and not to exercise any power that you possess, against my innocent husband, but to use it in his behalf. O sister-woman, think of me. As a wife and mother!"

Madame Defarge looked, coldly as ever, at the suppliant, and said, turning to her friend The Vengeance:

"The wives and mothers we have been used to see, since we were as little as this child, and much less, have not been greatly considered? We have known *their* husbands and fathers laid in prison and kept from them, often enough? All our lives, we have seen our sister-women suffer, in themselves and in their children, poverty, nakedness, hunger, thirst, sickness, misery, oppression and neglect of all kinds?"

"We have seen nothing else," returned The Vengeance.

"We have borne this a long time," said Madame Defarge, turning her eyes again upon Lucie. "Judge you! Is it likely that the trouble of one wife and mother would be much to us now?"

She resumed her knitting and went out. The Vengeance followed. Defarge went last, and closed the door.

"Courage, my dear Lucie," said Mr. Lorry, as he raised her. "Courage, courage! So far all goes well with us—much, much better than it has of late gone with many poor souls. Cheer up, and have a thankful heart."

"I am not thankless, I hope, but that dreadful woman seems to throw a shadow on me and on all my hopes."

"Tut, tut!" said Mr. Lorry; "what is this despondency in the brave little breast? A shadow indeed! No substance in it, Lucie."

But the shadow of the manner of these Defarges was dark upon himself, for all that, and in his secret mind it troubled him greatly.

IV. CALM IN STORM

Doctor Manette did not return until the morning of the fourth day of his absence. So much of what had happened in that dreadful time as could be kept from the knowledge of Lucie was so well concealed from her, that not until long afterwards, when France and she were far apart, did she know that eleven hundred defenceless prisoners of both sexes and all ages had been killed by the populace; that four days and nights had been darkened by this deed of horror; and that the air around her had been tainted by the slain. She only knew that there had been an attack upon the prisons, that all political prisoners had been in danger, and that some had been dragged out by the crowd and murdered.

To Mr. Lorry, the Doctor communicated under an injunction of secrecy on which he had no need to dwell, that the crowd had taken him through a scene of carnage to the prison of La Force. That, in the prison he had found a self-appointed Tribunal sitting, before which the prisoners were brought singly, and by which they were rapidly ordered to be put forth to be massacred, or to be released, or (in a few cases) to be sent back to their cells. That, presented by his conductors to this Tribunal, he had announced himself by name and profession as having been for eighteen years a secret and unaccused prisoner in the Bastille; that, one of the body so sitting in judgment had risen and identified him, and that this man was Defarge.

That, hereupon he had ascertained, through the registers on the table, that his son-in-law was among the living prisoners, and had pleaded hard to the Tribunal—of whom some members were asleep and some awake, some dirty with murder and some clean, some sober and some not—for his life and liberty. That, in the first frantic greetings lavished on himself as a notable sufferer under the overthrown system, it had been accorded to him to have Charles Darnay brought before the lawless Court, and examined. That, he seemed on the point of being at once released, when the tide in his favour met with some unexplained check (not intelligible to the Doctor), which led to a few words of secret conference. That, the man sitting as President had then informed Doctor Manette that the prisoner must remain in custody, but should, for his sake, be held inviolate in safe custody. That, immediately, on a signal, the prisoner was removed to the interior of the prison again; but, that he, the Doctor, had then so strongly pleaded for permission to remain and assure himself that his son-in-law was, through no malice or mischance, delivered to the concourse whose murderous yells outside the gate had often drowned the proceedings, that he had obtained the permission, and had remained in that Hall of Blood until the danger was over.

The sights he had seen there, with brief snatches of food and sleep by intervals, shall remain untold. The mad joy over the prisoners who were saved, had astounded him scarcely less than the mad ferocity against those who were cut to pieces. One prisoner there was, he said, who had been discharged into the street free, but at whom a mistaken savage had thrust a pike as he passed out. Being besought to go to him and dress the wound, the Doctor had passed out at the same gate, and had found him in the arms of a company of Samaritans, who were seated on the bodies of their victims. With an inconsistency as monstrous as anything in this awful nightmare, they had helped the healer, and tended the wounded man with the gentlest solicitude—had made a litter for him and escorted him carefully from the spot—had then caught up their weapons and plunged anew into a butchery so dreadful, that the Doctor had covered his eyes with his hands, and swooned away in the midst of it.

As Mr. Lorry received these confidences, and as he watched the face of his friend now sixty-two years of age, a misgiving arose within him that such dread experiences would revive the old danger.

But, he had never seen his friend in his present aspect: he had never at all known him in his present character. For the first time the Doctor felt, now, that his suffering was strength and power. For the first time he felt that in that sharp fire, he had slowly forged the iron which could break the prison door of his daughter's husband, and deliver him. "It all tended to a good end, my friend; it was not mere waste and ruin. As my beloved child was helpful in restoring me to myself, I will be helpful now in restoring the dearest part of herself to her; by the aid of Heaven I will do it!" Thus, Doctor Manette. And when Jarvis Lorry saw the kindled eyes, the resolute face, the calm strong look and bearing of the man whose life always seemed to him to have been stopped, like a clock, for so many years, and then set going again with an energy which had lain dormant during the cessation of its usefulness, he believed.

Greater things than the Doctor had at that time to contend with, would have yielded before his persevering purpose. While he kept himself in his place, as a physician, whose business was with all degrees of mankind, bond and free, rich and poor, bad and good, he used his personal influence so wisely, that he was soon the inspecting physician of three prisons, and among them of La Force. He could now assure Lucie that her husband was no longer confined alone, but was mixed with the general body of prisoners; he saw her husband weekly, and brought sweet messages to her, straight from his lips; sometimes her husband himself sent a letter to her (though never by the Doctor's hand), but she was not permitted to write to him: for, among the many wild suspicions of plots in the prisons, the wildest of all pointed at emigrants who were known to have made friends or permanent connections abroad.

This new life of the Doctor's was an anxious life, no doubt; still, the sagacious Mr. Lorry saw that there was a new sustaining pride in it. Nothing unbecoming tinged the pride; it was a natural and worthy one; but he observed it as a curiosity. The Doctor knew, that up to that time, his imprisonment had been associated in the minds of his daughter and his friend, with his personal affliction, deprivation, and weakness. Now that this was changed, and he knew himself to be invested through that old trial with forces to which they both looked for Charles's ultimate safety and deliverance, he became so far exalted by the change, that he took the lead and direction, and required them as the weak, to trust to him as the strong. The preceding relative positions of himself and Lucie were reversed, yet only as the liveliest gratitude and affection could reverse them, for he could have had no pride but in rendering some service to her who had rendered so much to him. "All curious to see," thought Mr. Lorry, in his amiably shrewd way, "but all natural and right; so, take the lead, my dear friend, and keep it; it couldn't be in better hands."

But, though the Doctor tried hard, and never ceased trying, to get Charles Darnay set at liberty, or at least to get him brought to trial, the public current of the time set too strong and fast for him. The new era began; the king was tried, doomed, and beheaded; the Republic of Liberty, Equality, Fraternity, or Death, declared for victory or death against the world in arms; the black flag waved night and day from the great towers of Notre Dame; three hundred thousand men, summoned to rise against the tyrants of the earth, rose from all the varying soils of France, as if the dragon's teeth had been sown broadcast, and had yielded fruit equally on hill and plain, on rock, in gravel, and alluvial mud, under the bright sky of the South and under the clouds of the North, in fell and forest, in the vineyards and the olive-grounds and among the cropped grass and the stubble of the corn, along the fruitful banks of the broad rivers, and in the sand of the sea-shore. What private solicitude could rear itself against the deluge of the Year One of Liberty—the deluge rising from below, not falling from above, and with the windows of Heaven shut, not opened!

There was no pause, no pity, no peace, no interval of relenting rest, no measurement of time. Though days and nights circled as regularly as when time was young, and the evening and morning were the first day, other count of time there was none. Hold of it was lost in the raging fever of a nation, as it is in the fever of one patient. Now, breaking the unnatural silence of a whole city, the executioner showed the people the head of the king—and now, it seemed almost in the same breath, the head of his fair wife which had had eight weary months of imprisoned widowhood and misery, to turn it grey.

And yet, observing the strange law of contradiction which obtains in all such cases, the time was long, while it flamed by so fast. A revolutionary tribunal in the capital, and forty or fifty thousand revolutionary committees all over the land; a law of the Suspected, which struck away all security for liberty or life, and delivered over any good and innocent person to any bad and guilty one; prisons gorged with people who had committed no offence, and could obtain no hearing; these things became the established order and nature of appointed things, and seemed to be ancient usage before they were many weeks old. Above all, one hideous figure grew as familiar as if it had been before the general gaze from the foundations of the world—the figure of the sharp female called La Guillotine.

It was the popular theme for jests; it was the best cure for headache, it infallibly prevented the hair from turning grey, it imparted a peculiar delicacy to the complexion, it was the National Razor which shaved close: who kissed La Guillotine, looked through the little window and sneezed into the sack. It was the sign of the regeneration of the human race. It superseded the Cross. Models of it were worn on breasts from which the Cross was discarded, and it was bowed down to and believed in where the Cross was denied.

It sheared off heads so many, that it, and the ground it most polluted, were a rotten red. It was taken to pieces, like a toy-puzzle for a young Devil, and was put together again when the occasion wanted it. It hushed the eloquent, struck down the powerful, abolished the beautiful and good. Twenty-two friends of high public mark, twenty-one living and one dead, it had lopped the heads off, in one morning, in as many minutes. The name of the strong man of Old Scripture had descended to the chief functionary who worked it; but, so armed, he was stronger than his namesake, and blinder, and tore away the gates of God's own Temple every day.

Among these terrors, and the brood belonging to them, the Doctor walked with a steady head: confident in his power, cautiously persistent in his end, never doubting that he would save Lucie's husband at last. Yet the current of the time swept by, so strong and deep, and carried the time away so fiercely, that Charles had lain in prison one year and three months when the Doctor was thus steady and confident. So much more wicked and distracted had the Revolution grown in that December month, that the rivers of the South were encumbered with the bodies of the violently drowned by night, and prisoners were shot in lines and squares under the southern wintry sun. Still, the Doctor walked among the terrors with a steady head. No man better known than he, in Paris at that day; no man in a stranger situation. Silent, humane, indispensable in hospital and prison, using his art equally among assassins and victims, he was a man apart. In the exercise of his skill, the appearance and the story of the Bastille Captive removed him from all other men. He was not suspected or brought in question, any more than if he had indeed been recalled to life some eighteen years before, or were a Spirit moving among mortals.

V. THE WOOD-SAWYER

One year and three months. During all that time Lucie was never sure, from hour to hour, but that the Guillotine would strike off her husband's head next day. Every day, through the stony streets, the tumbrils now jolted heavily, filled with Condemned. Lovely girls; bright women, brown-haired, black-haired, and grey; youths; stalwart men and old; gentle born and peasant born; all red wine for La Guillotine, all daily brought into light from the dark cellars of the loathsome prisons, and carried to her through the streets to slake her devouring thirst. Liberty, equality, fraternity, or death;—the last, much the easiest to bestow, O Guillotine!

If the suddenness of her calamity, and the whirling wheels of the time, had stunned the Doctor's daughter into awaiting the result in idle despair, it would but have been with her as it was with many. But, from the hour when she had taken the white head to her fresh young bosom in the garret of Saint Antoine, she had been true to her duties. She was truest to them in the season of trial, as all the quietly loyal and good will always be.

As soon as they were established in their new residence, and her father had entered on the routine of his avocations, she arranged the little household as exactly as if her husband had been there. Everything had its appointed place and its appointed time. Little Lucie she taught, as regularly, as if they had all been united in their English home. The slight devices with which she cheated herself into the show of a belief that they would soon be reunited—the little preparations for his speedy return, the setting aside of his chair and his books—these, and the solemn prayer at night for one dear prisoner especially, among the many unhappy souls in prison and the shadow of death—were almost the only outspoken reliefs of her heavy mind.

She did not greatly alter in appearance. The plain dark dresses, akin to mourning dresses, which she and her child wore, were as neat and as well attended to as the brighter clothes of happy days. She lost her colour, and the old and intent expression was a constant, not an occasional, thing; otherwise, she remained very pretty and comely. Sometimes, at night on kissing her father, she would burst into the grief she had repressed all day, and would say that her sole reliance, under Heaven, was on him. He always resolutely answered: "Nothing can happen to him without my knowledge, and I know that I can save him, Lucie."

They had not made the round of their changed life many weeks, when her father said to her, on coming home one evening:

"My dear, there is an upper window in the prison, to which Charles can sometimes gain access at three in the afternoon. When he can get to it—which depends on many uncertainties and incidents—he might see you in the street, he thinks, if you stood in a certain place that I can show you. But you will not be able to see him, my poor child, and even if you could, it would be unsafe for you to make a sign of recognition."

"O show me the place, my father, and I will go there every day."

From that time, in all weathers, she waited there two hours. As the clock struck two, she was there, and at four she turned resignedly away. When it was not too wet or inclement for her child to be with her, they went together; at other times she was alone; but, she never missed a single day.

It was the dark and dirty corner of a small winding street. The hovel of a cutter of wood into lengths for burning, was the only house at that end; all else was wall. On the third day of her being there, he noticed her.

"Good day, citizeness."

"Good day, citizen."

This mode of address was now prescribed by decree. It had been established voluntarily some time ago, among the more thorough patriots; but, was now law for everybody.

"Walking here again, citizeness?"

"You see me, citizen!"

The wood-sawyer, who was a little man with a redundancy of gesture (he had once been a mender of roads), cast a glance at the prison, pointed at the prison, and putting his ten fingers before his face to represent bars, peeped through them jocosely.

"But it's not my business," said he. And went on sawing his wood.

Next day he was looking out for her, and accosted her the moment she appeared.

"What? Walking here again, citizeness?"

"Yes, citizen."

"Ah! A child too! Your mother, is it not, my little citizeness?"

"Do I say yes, mamma?" whispered little Lucie, drawing close to her.

"Yes, dearest."

"Yes, citizen."

"Ah! But it's not my business. My work is my business. See my saw! I call it my Little Guillotine. La, la, la; La, la, la! And off his head comes!"

The billet fell as he spoke, and he threw it into a basket.

"I call myself the Samson of the firewood guillotine. See here again! Loo, loo, loo; Loo, loo, loo! And off *her* head comes! Now, a child. Tickle, tickle; Pickle, pickle! And off *its* head comes. All the family!"

Lucie shuddered as he threw two more billets into his basket, but it was impossible to be there while the wood-sawyer was at work, and not be in his sight. Thenceforth, to secure his good will, she always spoke to him first, and often gave him drink-money, which he readily received.

He was an inquisitive fellow, and sometimes when she had quite forgotten him in gazing at the prison roof and grates, and in lifting her heart up to her husband, she would come to herself to find him looking at her, with his knee on his bench and his saw stopped in its work. "But it's not my business!" he would generally say at those times, and would briskly fall to his sawing again.

In all weathers, in the snow and frost of winter, in the bitter winds of spring, in the hot sunshine of summer, in the rains of autumn, and again in the snow and frost of winter, Lucie passed two hours of every day at this place; and every day on leaving it, she kissed the prison wall. Her husband saw her (so she learned from her father) it might be once in five or six times: it might be twice or thrice running: it might be, not for a week or a fortnight together. It was enough that he could and did see her when the chances served, and on that possibility she would have waited out the day, seven days a week.

These occupations brought her round to the December month, wherein her father walked among the terrors with a steady head. On a lightly-snowing afternoon she arrived at the usual corner. It was a day of some wild rejoicing, and a festival. She had seen the houses, as she came along, decorated with little pikes, and with little red caps stuck upon them; also, with tricoloured ribbons; also, with the standard inscription (tricoloured letters were the favourite), Republic One and Indivisible. Liberty, Equality, Fraternity, or Death!

The miserable shop of the wood-sawyer was so small, that its whole surface furnished very indifferent space for this legend. He had got somebody to scrawl it up for him, however, who had squeezed Death in with most inappropriate difficulty. On his house-top, he displayed pike and cap, as a good citizen must, and in a window he had stationed his saw inscribed as his "Little Sainte Guillotine"—for the great sharp female was by that time popularly canonised. His shop was shut and he was not there, which was a relief to Lucie, and left her quite alone.

But, he was not far off, for presently she heard a troubled movement and a shouting coming along, which filled her with fear. A moment afterwards, and a throng of people came pouring round the corner by the prison wall, in the midst of whom was the wood-sawyer hand in hand with The Vengeance. There could not be fewer than five hundred people, and they were dancing like five thousand demons. There was no other music than their own singing. They danced to the popular Revolution song, keeping a ferocious time that was like a gnashing of teeth in unison. Men and women danced together, women danced together, men danced together, as hazard had brought them together. At first, they were a mere storm of coarse red caps and coarse woollen rags; but, as they filled the place, and stopped to dance about Lucie, some ghastly apparition of a dance-figure gone raving mad arose among them. They advanced, retreated, struck at one another's hands, clutched at one another's heads, spun round alone, caught one another and spun round in pairs, until many of them dropped. While those were down, the rest linked hand in hand, and all spun round together: then the ring broke, and in separate rings of two and four they turned and turned until they all stopped at once, began again, struck, clutched, and tore, and then reversed the spin, and all spun round another way. Suddenly they stopped again, paused, struck out the time afresh, formed into lines the width of the public way, and, with their heads low down and their hands high up, swooped screaming off. No fight could have been half so terrible as this dance. It was so emphatically a fallen sport—a something, once innocent, delivered over to all devilry—a healthy pastime changed into a means of angering the blood, bewildering the senses, and steeling the heart. Such grace as was visible in it, made it the uglier, showing how warped and perverted all things good by nature were become. The maidenly bosom bared to this, the pretty almost-child's head thus distracted, the delicate foot mincing in this slough of blood and dirt, were types of the disjointed time.

This was the Carmagnole. As it passed, leaving Lucie frightened and bewildered in the doorway of the wood-sawyer's house, the feathery snow fell as quietly and lay as white and soft, as if it had never been.

"O my father!" for he stood before her when she lifted up the eyes she had momentarily darkened with her hand; "such a cruel, bad sight."

"I know, my dear, I know. I have seen it many times. Don't be frightened! Not one of them would harm you."

"I am not frightened for myself, my father. But when I think of my husband, and the mercies of these people—"

"We will set him above their mercies very soon. I left him climbing to the window, and I came to tell you. There is no one here to see. You may kiss your hand towards that highest shelving roof."

"I do so, father, and I send him my Soul with it!"

"You cannot see him, my poor dear?"

"No, father," said Lucie, yearning and weeping as she kissed her hand, "no."

A footstep in the snow. Madame Defarge. "I salute you, citizeness," from the Doctor. "I salute you, citizen." This in passing. Nothing more. Madame Defarge gone, like a shadow over the white road.

"Give me your arm, my love. Pass from here with an air of cheerfulness and courage, for his sake. That was well done;" they had left the spot; "it shall not be in vain. Charles is summoned for to-morrow."

"For to-morrow!"

"There is no time to lose. I am well prepared, but there are precautions to be taken, that could not be taken until he was actually summoned before the Tribunal. He has not received the notice yet, but I know that he will presently be summoned for to-morrow, and removed to the Conciergerie; I have timely information. You are not afraid?"

She could scarcely answer, "I trust in you."

"Do so, implicitly. Your suspense is nearly ended, my darling; he shall be restored to you within a few hours; I have encompassed him with every protection. I must see Lorry."

He stopped. There was a heavy lumbering of wheels within hearing. They both knew too well what it meant. One. Two. Three. Three tumbrils faring away with their dread loads over the hushing snow.

"I must see Lorry," the Doctor repeated, turning her another way.

The staunch old gentleman was still in his trust; had never left it. He and his books were in frequent requisition as to property confiscated and made national. What he could save for the owners, he saved. No better man living to hold fast by what Tellson's had in keeping, and to hold his peace.

A murky red and yellow sky, and a rising mist from the Seine, denoted the approach of darkness. It was almost dark when they arrived at the Bank. The stately residence of Monseigneur was altogether blighted and deserted. Above a heap of dust and ashes in the court, ran the letters: National Property. Republic One and Indivisible. Liberty, Equality, Fraternity, or Death!

Who could that be with Mr. Lorry—the owner of the riding-coat upon the chair—who must not be seen? From whom newly arrived, did he come out, agitated and surprised, to take his favourite in his arms? To whom did he appear to repeat her faltering words, when, raising his voice and turning his head towards the door of the room from which he had issued, he said: "Removed to the Conciergerie, and summoned for to-morrow?"

VI. TRIUMPH

The dread tribunal of five Judges, Public Prosecutor, and determined Jury, sat every day. Their lists went forth every evening, and were read out by the gaolers of the various prisons to their prisoners. The standard gaoler-joke was, "Come out and listen to the Evening Paper, you inside there!"

"Charles Evremonde, called Darnay!"

So at last began the Evening Paper at La Force.

When a name was called, its owner stepped apart into a spot reserved for those who were announced as being thus fatally recorded. Charles Evremonde, called Darnay, had reason to know the usage; he had seen hundreds pass away so.

His bloated gaoler, who wore spectacles to read with, glanced over them to assure himself that he had taken his place, and went through the list, making a similar short pause at each name. There were twenty-three names, but only twenty were responded to; for one of the prisoners so summoned had died in gaol and been forgotten, and two had already been guillotined and forgotten. The list was read, in the vaulted chamber where Darnay had seen the associated prisoners on the night of his arrival. Every one of those had perished in the massacre; every human creature he had since cared for and parted with, had died on the scaffold.

There were hurried words of farewell and kindness, but the parting was soon over. It was the incident of every day, and the society of La Force were engaged in the preparation of some games of forfeits and a little concert, for that evening. They crowded to the grates and shed tears there; but, twenty places in the projected entertainments had to be refilled, and the time was, at best, short to the lock-up hour, when the common rooms and corridors would be delivered over to the great dogs who kept watch there through the night. The prisoners were far from insensible or unfeeling; their ways arose out of the condition of the time. Similarly, though with a subtle difference, a species of fervour or intoxication, known, without doubt, to have led some persons to brave the guillotine unnecessarily, and to die by it, was not mere boastfulness, but a wild infection of the wildly shaken public mind. In seasons of pestilence, some of us will have a secret attraction to the disease—a terrible passing inclination to die of it. And all of us have like wonders hidden in our breasts, only needing circumstances to evoke them.

The passage to the Conciergerie was short and dark; the night in its vermin-haunted cells was long and cold. Next day, fifteen prisoners were put to the bar before Charles Darnay's name was called. All the fifteen were condemned, and the trials of the whole occupied an hour and a half.

"Charles Evremonde, called Darnay," was at length arraigned.

His judges sat upon the Bench in feathered hats; but the rough red cap and tricoloured cockade was the head-dress otherwise prevailing. Looking at the Jury and the turbulent audience, he might have thought that the usual order of things was reversed, and that the felons were trying the honest men. The lowest, cruelest, and worst populace of a city, never without its quantity of low, cruel, and bad, were the directing spirits of the scene: noisily commenting, applauding, disapproving, anticipating, and precipitating the result, without a check. Of the men, the greater part were armed in various ways; of the women, some wore knives, some daggers, some ate and drank as they looked on, many knitted. Among these last, was one, with a spare piece of knitting under her arm as she worked. She was in a front row, by the side of a man whom he had never seen since his arrival at the Barrier, but whom he directly remembered as Defarge. He noticed that she once or twice whispered in his ear, and that she seemed to be his wife; but, what he most noticed in the two figures was, that although they were posted as close to himself as they could be, they never looked towards him. They seemed to be waiting for something with a dogged determination, and they looked at the Jury, but at nothing else. Under the President sat Doctor Manette, in his usual quiet dress. As well as the prisoner could see, he and Mr. Lorry were the only men there, unconnected with the Tribunal, who wore their usual clothes, and had not assumed the coarse garb of the Carmagnole.

Charles Evremonde, called Darnay, was accused by the public prosecutor as an emigrant, whose life was forfeit to the Republic, under the decree which banished all emigrants on pain of Death. It was nothing that the decree bore date since his return to France. There he was, and there was the decree; he had been taken in France, and his head was demanded.

"Take off his head!" cried the audience. "An enemy to the Republic!"

The President rang his bell to silence those cries, and asked the prisoner whether it was not true that he had lived many years in England?

Undoubtedly it was.

Was he not an emigrant then? What did he call himself?

Not an emigrant, he hoped, within the sense and spirit of the law.

Why not? the President desired to know.

Because he had voluntarily relinquished a title that was distasteful to him, and a station that was distasteful to him, and had left his country—he submitted before the word emigrant in the present acceptation by the Tribunal was in use—to live by his own industry in England, rather than on the industry of the overladen people of France.

What proof had he of this?

He handed in the names of two witnesses; Theophile Gabelle, and Alexandre Manette.

But he had married in England? the President reminded him.

True, but not an English woman.

A citizeness of France?

Yes. By birth.

Her name and family?

"Lucie Manette, only daughter of Doctor Manette, the good physician who sits there."

This answer had a happy effect upon the audience. Cries in exaltation of the well-known good physician rent the hall. So capriciously were the people moved, that tears immediately rolled down several ferocious countenances which had been glaring at the prisoner a moment before, as if with impatience to pluck him out into the streets and kill him.

On these few steps of his dangerous way, Charles Darnay had set his foot according to Doctor Manette's reiterated instructions. The same cautious counsel directed every step that lay before him, and had prepared every inch of his road.

The President asked, why had he returned to France when he did, and not sooner?

He had not returned sooner, he replied, simply because he had no means of living in France, save those he had resigned; whereas, in England, he lived by giving instruction in the French language and literature. He had returned when he did, on the pressing and written entreaty of a French citizen, who represented that his life was endangered by his absence. He had come back, to save a citizen's life, and to bear his testimony, at whatever personal hazard, to the truth. Was that criminal in the eyes of the Republic?

The populace cried enthusiastically, "No!" and the President rang his bell to quiet them. Which it did not, for they continued to cry "No!" until they left off, of their own will.

The President required the name of that citizen. The accused explained that the citizen was his first witness. He also referred with confidence to the citizen's letter, which had been taken from him at the Barrier, but which he did not doubt would be found among the papers then before the President.

The Doctor had taken care that it should be there—had assured him that it would be there—and at this stage of the proceedings it was produced and read. Citizen Gabelle was called to confirm it, and did so. Citizen Gabelle hinted, with infinite delicacy and politeness, that in the pressure of business imposed on the Tribunal by the multitude of enemies of the Republic with which it had to deal, he had been slightly overlooked in his prison of the Abbaye—in fact, had rather passed out of the Tribunal's patriotic remembrance—until three days ago; when he had been summoned before it, and had been set at liberty on the Jury's declaring themselves satisfied that the accusation against him was answered, as to himself, by the surrender of the citizen Evremonde, called Darnay.

Doctor Manette was next questioned. His high personal popularity, and the clearness of his answers, made a great impression; but, as he proceeded, as he showed that the Accused was his first friend on his release from his long imprisonment; that, the accused had remained in England, always faithful and devoted to his daughter and himself in their exile; that, so far from being in favour with the Aristocrat government there, he had actually been tried for his life by it, as the foe of England and friend of the United States—as he brought these circumstances into view, with the greatest discretion and with the straightforward force of truth and earnestness, the Jury and the populace became one. At last, when he appealed by name to Monsieur Lorry, an English gentleman then and there present, who, like himself, had been a witness on that English trial and could corroborate his account of it, the Jury declared that they had heard enough, and that they were ready with their votes if the President were content to receive them.

At every vote (the Jurymen voted aloud and individually), the populace set up a shout of applause. All the voices were in the prisoner's favour, and the President declared him free.

Then, began one of those extraordinary scenes with which the populace sometimes gratified their fickleness, or their better impulses towards generosity and mercy, or which they regarded as some set-off against their swollen account of cruel rage. No man can decide now to which of these motives such extraordinary scenes were referable; it is probable, to a blending of all the three, with the second predominating. No sooner was the acquittal pronounced, than tears were shed as freely as blood at another time, and such fraternal embraces were bestowed upon the prisoner by as many of both sexes as could rush at him, that after his long and unwholesome confinement he was in danger of fainting from exhaustion; none the less because he knew very well, that the very same people, carried by another current, would have rushed at him with the very same intensity, to rend him to pieces and strew him over the streets.

His removal, to make way for other accused persons who were to be tried, rescued him from these caresses for the moment. Five were to be tried together, next, as enemies of the Republic, forasmuch as they had not assisted it by word or deed. So quick was the Tribunal to compensate itself and the nation for a chance lost, that these five came down to him before he left the place, condemned to die within twenty-four hours. The first of them told him so, with the customary prison sign of Death—a raised finger—and they all added in words, "Long live the Republic!"

The five had had, it is true, no audience to lengthen their proceedings, for when he and Doctor Manette emerged from the gate, there was a great crowd about it, in which there seemed to be every face he had seen in Court—except two, for which he looked in vain. On his coming out, the concourse made at him anew, weeping, embracing, and shouting, all by turns and all together, until the very tide of the river on the bank of which the mad scene was acted, seemed to run mad, like the people on the shore.

They put him into a great chair they had among them, and which they had taken either out of the Court itself, or one of its rooms or passages. Over the chair they had thrown a red flag, and to the back of it they had bound a pike with a red cap on its top. In this car of triumph, not even the Doctor's entreaties could prevent his being carried to his home on men's shoulders, with a confused sea of red caps heaving about him, and casting up to sight from the stormy deep such wrecks of faces, that he more than once misdoubted his mind being in confusion, and that he was in the tumbril on his way to the Guillotine.

In wild dreamlike procession, embracing whom they met and pointing him out, they carried him on. Reddening the snowy streets with the prevailing Republican colour, in winding and tramping through them, as they had reddened them below the snow with a deeper dye, they carried him thus into the courtyard of the building where he lived. Her father had gone on before, to prepare her, and when her husband stood upon his feet, she dropped insensible in his arms.

As he held her to his heart and turned her beautiful head between his face and the brawling crowd, so that his tears and her lips might come together unseen, a few of the people fell to dancing. Instantly, all the rest fell to dancing, and the courtyard overflowed with the Carmagnole. Then, they elevated into the vacant chair a young woman from the crowd to be carried as the Goddess of Liberty, and then swelling and overflowing out into the adjacent streets, and along the river's bank, and over the bridge, the Carmagnole absorbed them every one and whirled them away.

After grasping the Doctor's hand, as he stood victorious and proud before him; after grasping the hand of Mr. Lorry, who came panting in breathless from his struggle against the waterspout of the Carmagnole; after kissing little Lucie, who was lifted up to clasp her arms round his neck; and after embracing the ever zealous and faithful Pross who lifted her; he took his wife in his arms, and carried her up to their rooms.

"Lucie! My own! I am safe."

"O dearest Charles, let me thank God for this on my knees as I have prayed to Him."

They all reverently bowed their heads and hearts. When she was again in his arms, he said to her:

"And now speak to your father, dearest. No other man in all this France could have done what he has done for me."

She laid her head upon her father's breast, as she had laid his poor head on her own breast, long, long ago. He was happy in the return he had made her, he was recompensed for his suffering, he was proud of his strength. "You must not be weak, my darling," he remonstrated; "don't tremble so. I have saved him."

VII. A KNOCK AT THE DOOR

"I have saved him." It was not another of the dreams in which he had often come back; he was really here. And yet his wife trembled, and a vague but heavy fear was upon her.

All the air round was so thick and dark, the people were so passionately revengeful and fitful, the innocent were so constantly put to death on vague suspicion and black malice, it was so impossible to forget that many as blameless as her husband and as dear to others as he was to her, every day shared the fate from which he had been clutched, that her heart could not be as lightened of its load as she felt it ought to be. The shadows of the wintry afternoon were beginning to fall, and even now the dreadful carts were rolling through the streets. Her mind pursued them, looking for him among the Condemned; and then she clung closer to his real presence and trembled more.

Her father, cheering her, showed a compassionate superiority to this woman's weakness, which was wonderful to see. No garret, no shoemaking, no One Hundred and Five, North Tower, now! He had accomplished the task he had set himself, his promise was redeemed, he had saved Charles. Let them all lean upon him.

Their housekeeping was of a very frugal kind: not only because that was the safest way of life, involving the least offence to the people, but because they were not rich, and Charles, throughout his imprisonment, had had to pay heavily for his bad food, and for his guard, and towards the living of the poorer prisoners. Partly on this account, and partly to avoid a domestic spy, they kept no servant; the citizen and citizeness who acted as porters at the courtyard gate, rendered them occasional service; and Jerry (almost wholly transferred to them by Mr. Lorry) had become their daily retainer, and had his bed there every night.

It was an ordinance of the Republic One and Indivisible of Liberty, Equality, Fraternity, or Death, that on the door or doorpost of every house, the name of every inmate must be legibly inscribed in letters of a certain size, at a certain convenient height from the ground. Mr. Jerry Cruncher's name, therefore, duly embellished the doorpost down below; and, as the afternoon shadows deepened, the owner of that name himself appeared, from overlooking a painter whom Doctor Manette had employed to add to the list the name of Charles Evremonde, called Darnay.

In the universal fear and distrust that darkened the time, all the usual harmless ways of life were changed. In the Doctor's little household, as in very many others, the articles of daily consumption that were wanted were purchased every evening, in small quantities and at various small shops. To avoid attracting notice, and to give as little occasion as possible for talk and envy, was the general desire.

For some months past, Miss Pross and Mr. Cruncher had discharged the office of purveyors; the former carrying the money; the latter, the basket. Every afternoon at about the time when the public lamps were lighted, they fared forth on this duty, and made and brought home such purchases as were needful. Although Miss Pross, through her long association with a French family, might have known as much of their language as of her own, if she had had a mind, she had no mind in that direction; consequently she knew no more of that "nonsense" (as she was pleased to call it) than Mr. Cruncher did. So her manner of marketing was to plump a noun-substantive at the head of a shopkeeper without any introduction in the nature of an article, and, if it happened not to be the name of the thing she wanted, to look round for that thing, lay hold of it, and hold on by it until the bargain was concluded. She always made a bargain for it, by holding up, as a statement of its just price, one finger less than the merchant held up, whatever his number might be.

"Now, Mr. Cruncher," said Miss Pross, whose eyes were red with felicity; "if you are ready, I am."

Jerry hoarsely professed himself at Miss Pross's service. He had worn all his rust off long ago, but nothing would file his spiky head down.

"There's all manner of things wanted," said Miss Pross, "and we shall have a precious time of it. We want wine, among the rest. Nice toasts these Redheads will be drinking, wherever we buy it."

"It will be much the same to your knowledge, miss, I should think," retorted Jerry, "whether they drink your health or the Old Un's."

"Who's he?" said Miss Pross.

Mr. Cruncher, with some diffidence, explained himself as meaning "Old Nick's."

"Ha!" said Miss Pross, "it doesn't need an interpreter to explain the meaning of these creatures. They have but one, and it's Midnight Murder, and Mischief."

"Hush, dear! Pray, pray, be cautious!" cried Lucie.

"Yes, yes, yes, I'll be cautious," said Miss Pross; "but I may say among ourselves, that I do hope there will be no oniony and tobaccoey smotherings in the form of embracings all round, going on in the streets. Now, Ladybird, never you stir from that fire till I come back! Take care of the dear husband you have recovered, and don't move your pretty head from his shoulder as you have it now, till you see me again! May I ask a question, Doctor Manette, before I go?"

"I think you may take that liberty," the Doctor answered, smiling.

"For gracious sake, don't talk about Liberty; we have quite enough of that," said Miss Pross.

"Hush, dear! Again?" Lucie remonstrated.

"Well, my sweet," said Miss Pross, nodding her head emphatically, "the short and the long of it is, that I am a subject of His Most Gracious Majesty King George the

Third;" Miss Pross curtseyed at the name; "and as such, my maxim is, Confound their politics, Frustrate their knavish tricks, On him our hopes we fix, God save the King!"

Mr. Cruncher, in an access of loyalty, growlingly repeated the words after Miss Pross, like somebody at church.

"I am glad you have so much of the Englishman in you, though I wish you had never taken that cold in your voice," said Miss Pross, approvingly. "But the question, Doctor Manette. Is there"—it was the good creature's way to affect to make light of anything that was a great anxiety with them all, and to come at it in this chance manner—"is there any prospect yet, of our getting out of this place?"

"I fear not yet. It would be dangerous for Charles yet."

"Heigh-ho-hum!" said Miss Pross, cheerfully repressing a sigh as she glanced at her darling's golden hair in the light of the fire, "then we must have patience and wait: that's all. We must hold up our heads and fight low, as my brother Solomon used to say. Now, Mr. Cruncher!—Don't you move, Ladybird!"

They went out, leaving Lucie, and her husband, her father, and the child, by a bright fire. Mr. Lorry was expected back presently from the Banking House. Miss Pross had lighted the lamp, but had put it aside in a corner, that they might enjoy the fire-light undisturbed. Little Lucie sat by her grandfather with her hands clasped through his arm: and he, in a tone not rising much above a whisper, began to tell her a story of a great and powerful Fairy who had opened a prison-wall and let out a captive who had once done the Fairy a service. All was subdued and quiet, and Lucie was more at ease than she had been.

"What is that?" she cried, all at once.

"My dear!" said her father, stopping in his story, and laying his hand on hers, "command yourself. What a disordered state you are in! The least thing—nothing—startles you! *You*, your father's daughter!"

"I thought, my father," said Lucie, excusing herself, with a pale face and in a faltering voice, "that I heard strange feet upon the stairs."

"My love, the staircase is as still as Death."

As he said the word, a blow was struck upon the door.

"Oh father, father. What can this be! Hide Charles. Save him!"

"My child," said the Doctor, rising, and laying his hand upon her shoulder, "I *have* saved him. What weakness is this, my dear! Let me go to the door."

He took the lamp in his hand, crossed the two intervening outer rooms, and opened it. A rude clattering of feet over the floor, and four rough men in red caps, armed with sabres and pistols, entered the room.

"The Citizen Evremonde, called Darnay," said the first.

"Who seeks him?" answered Darnay.

"I seek him. We seek him. I know you, Evremonde; I saw you before the Tribunal to-day. You are again the prisoner of the Republic."

The four surrounded him, where he stood with his wife and child clinging to him.

"Tell me how and why am I again a prisoner?"

"It is enough that you return straight to the Conciergerie, and will know to-morrow. You are summoned for to-morrow."

Doctor Manette, whom this visitation had so turned into stone, that he stood with the lamp in his hand, as if be woe a statue made to hold it, moved after these words were spoken, put the lamp down, and confronting the speaker, and taking him, not ungently, by the loose front of his red woollen shirt, said:

"You know him, you have said. Do you know me?"

"Yes, I know you, Citizen Doctor."

"We all know you, Citizen Doctor," said the other three.

He looked abstractedly from one to another, and said, in a lower voice, after a pause:

"Will you answer his question to me then? How does this happen?"

"Citizen Doctor," said the first, reluctantly, "he has been denounced to the Section of Saint Antoine. This citizen," pointing out the second who had entered, "is from Saint Antoine."

The citizen here indicated nodded his head, and added:

"He is accused by Saint Antoine."

"Of what?" asked the Doctor.

"Citizen Doctor," said the first, with his former reluctance, "ask no more. If the Republic demands sacrifices from you, without doubt you as a good patriot will be happy to make them. The Republic goes before all. The People is supreme. Evremonde, we are pressed."

"One word," the Doctor entreated. "Will you tell me who denounced him?"

"It is against rule," answered the first; "but you can ask Him of Saint Antoine here."

The Doctor turned his eyes upon that man. Who moved uneasily on his feet, rubbed his beard a little, and at length said:

"Well! Truly it is against rule. But he is denounced—and gravely—by the Citizen and Citizeness Defarge. And by one other."

"What other?"

"Do *you* ask, Citizen Doctor?"

"Yes."

"Then," said he of Saint Antoine, with a strange look, "you will be answered to-morrow. Now, I am dumb!"

VIII. A HAND AT CARDS

Happily unconscious of the new calamity at home, Miss Pross threaded her way along the narrow streets and crossed the river by the bridge of the Pont-Neuf, reckoning in her mind the number of indispensable purchases she had to make. Mr. Cruncher, with the basket, walked at her side. They both looked to the right and to the left into most of the shops they passed, had a wary eye for all gregarious assemblages of people, and turned out of their road to avoid any very excited group of talkers. It was a raw evening, and the misty river, blurred to the eye with blazing lights and to the ear with harsh noises, showed where the barges were stationed in which the smiths worked, making guns for the Army of the Republic. Woe to the man who played tricks with *that* Army, or got undeserved promotion in it! Better for him that his beard had never grown, for the National Razor shaved him close.

Having purchased a few small articles of grocery, and a measure of oil for the lamp, Miss Pross bethought herself of the wine they wanted. After peeping into several wine-shops, she stopped at the sign of the Good Republican Brutus of Antiquity, not far from the National Palace, once (and twice) the Tuileries, where the aspect of things rather took her fancy. It had a quieter look than any other place of the same description they had passed, and, though red with patriotic caps, was not so red as the rest. Sounding Mr. Cruncher, and finding him of her opinion, Miss Pross resorted to the Good Republican Brutus of Antiquity, attended by her cavalier.

Slightly observant of the smoky lights; of the people, pipe in mouth, playing with limp cards and yellow dominoes; of the one bare- breasted, bare-armed, soot-begrimed workman reading a journal aloud, and of the others listening to him; of the weapons worn, or laid aside to be resumed; of the two or three customers fallen forward asleep, who in the popular high-shouldered shaggy black spencer looked, in that attitude, like slumbering bears or dogs; the two outlandish customers approached the counter, and showed what they wanted.

As their wine was measuring out, a man parted from another man in a corner, and rose to depart. In going, he had to face Miss Pross. No sooner did he face her, than Miss Pross uttered a scream, and clapped her hands.

In a moment, the whole company were on their feet. That somebody was assassinated by somebody vindicating a difference of opinion was the likeliest occurrence. Everybody looked to see somebody fall, but only saw a man and a woman standing staring at each other; the man with all the outward aspect of a Frenchman and a thorough Republican; the woman, evidently English.

What was said in this disappointing anti-climax, by the disciples of the Good Republican Brutus of Antiquity, except that it was something very voluble and loud, would have been as so much Hebrew or Chaldean to Miss Pross and her protector, though they had been all ears. But, they had no ears for anything in their surprise. For, it must be recorded, that not only was Miss Pross lost in amazement and agitation, but, Mr. Cruncher—though it seemed on his own separate and individual account—was in a state of the greatest wonder.

"What is the matter?" said the man who had caused Miss Pross to scream; speaking in a vexed, abrupt voice (though in a low tone), and in English.

"Oh, Solomon, dear Solomon!" cried Miss Pross, clapping her hands again. "After not setting eyes upon you or hearing of you for so long a time, do I find you here!"

"Don't call me Solomon. Do you want to be the death of me?" asked the man, in a furtive, frightened way.

"Brother, brother!" cried Miss Pross, bursting into tears. "Have I ever been so hard with you that you ask me such a cruel question?"

"Then hold your meddlesome tongue," said Solomon, "and come out, if you want to speak to me. Pay for your wine, and come out. Who's this man?"

Miss Pross, shaking her loving and dejected head at her by no means affectionate brother, said through her tears, "Mr. Cruncher."

"Let him come out too," said Solomon. "Does he think me a ghost?"

Apparently, Mr. Cruncher did, to judge from his looks. He said not a word, however, and Miss Pross, exploring the depths of her reticule through her tears with great difficulty paid for her wine. As she did so, Solomon turned to the followers of the Good Republican Brutus of Antiquity, and offered a few words of explanation in the French language, which caused them all to relapse into their former places and pursuits.

"Now," said Solomon, stopping at the dark street corner, "what do you want?"

"How dreadfully unkind in a brother nothing has ever turned my love away from!" cried Miss Pross, "to give me such a greeting, and show me no affection."

"There. Confound it! There," said Solomon, making a dab at Miss Pross's lips with his own. "Now are you content?"

Miss Pross only shook her head and wept in silence.

"If you expect me to be surprised," said her brother Solomon, "I am not surprised; I knew you were here; I know of most people who are here. If you really don't want to endanger my existence—which I half believe you do—go your ways as soon as possible, and let me go mine. I am busy. I am an official."

"My English brother Solomon," mourned Miss Pross, casting up her tear-fraught eyes, "that had the makings in him of one of the best and greatest of men in his native country, an official among foreigners, and such foreigners! I would almost sooner have seen the dear boy lying in his—"

"I said so!" cried her brother, interrupting. "I knew it. You want to be the death of me. I shall be rendered Suspected, by my own sister. Just as I am getting on!"

"The gracious and merciful Heavens forbid!" cried Miss Pross. "Far rather would I never see you again, dear Solomon, though I have ever loved you truly, and ever shall. Say but one affectionate word to me, and tell me there is nothing angry or estranged between us, and I will detain you no longer."

Good Miss Pross! As if the estrangement between them had come of any culpability of hers. As if Mr. Lorry had not known it for a fact, years ago, in the quiet corner in Soho, that this precious brother had spent her money and left her!

He was saying the affectionate word, however, with a far more grudging condescension and patronage than he could have shown if their relative merits and positions had been reversed (which is invariably the case, all the world over), when Mr. Cruncher, touching him on the shoulder, hoarsely and unexpectedly interposed with the following singular question:

"I say! Might I ask the favour? As to whether your name is John Solomon, or Solomon John?"

The official turned towards him with sudden distrust. He had not previously uttered a word.

"Come!" said Mr. Cruncher. "Speak out, you know." (Which, by the way, was more than he could do himself.) "John Solomon, or Solomon John? She calls you Solomon, and she must know, being your sister. And *I* know you're John, you know. Which of the two goes first? And regarding that name of Pross, likewise. That warn't your name over the water."

"What do you mean?"

"Well, I don't know all I mean, for I can't call to mind what your name was, over the water."

"No?"

"No. But I'll swear it was a name of two syllables."

"Indeed?"

"Yes. T'other one's was one syllable. I know you. You was a spy—witness at the Bailey. What, in the name of the Father of Lies, own father to yourself, was you called at that time?"

"Barsad," said another voice, striking in.

"That's the name for a thousand pound!" cried Jerry.

The speaker who struck in, was Sydney Carton. He had his hands behind him under the skirts of his riding-coat, and he stood at Mr. Cruncher's elbow as negligently as he might have stood at the Old Bailey itself.

"Don't be alarmed, my dear Miss Pross. I arrived at Mr. Lorry's, to his surprise, yesterday evening; we agreed that I would not present myself elsewhere until all was well, or unless I could be useful; I present myself here, to beg a little talk with your brother. I wish you had a better employed brother than Mr. Barsad. I wish for your sake Mr. Barsad was not a Sheep of the Prisons."

Sheep was a cant word of the time for a spy, under the gaolers. The spy, who was pale, turned paler, and asked him how he dared—

"I'll tell you," said Sydney. "I lighted on you, Mr. Barsad, coming out of the prison of the Conciergerie while I was contemplating the walls, an hour or more ago. You have a face to be remembered, and I remember faces well. Made curious by seeing you in that connection, and having a reason, to which you are no stranger, for associating you with the misfortunes of a friend now very unfortunate, I walked in your direction. I walked into the wine-shop here, close after you, and sat near you. I had no difficulty in deducing from your unreserved conversation, and the rumour openly going about among your admirers, the nature of your calling. And gradually, what I had done at random, seemed to shape itself into a purpose, Mr. Barsad."

"What purpose?" the spy asked.

"It would be troublesome, and might be dangerous, to explain in the street. Could you favour me, in confidence, with some minutes of your company—at the office of Tellson's Bank, for instance?"

"Under a threat?"

"Oh! Did I say that?"

"Then, why should I go there?"

"Really, Mr. Barsad, I can't say, if you can't."

"Do you mean that you won't say, sir?" the spy irresolutely asked.

"You apprehend me very clearly, Mr. Barsad. I won't."

Carton's negligent recklessness of manner came powerfully in aid of his quickness and skill, in such a business as he had in his secret mind, and with such a man as he had to do with. His practised eye saw it, and made the most of it.

"Now, I told you so," said the spy, casting a reproachful look at his sister; "if any trouble comes of this, it's your doing."

"Come, come, Mr. Barsad!" exclaimed Sydney. "Don't be ungrateful. But for my great respect for your sister, I might not have led up so pleasantly to a little proposal that I wish to make for our mutual satisfaction. Do you go with me to the Bank?"

"I'll hear what you have got to say. Yes, I'll go with you."

"I propose that we first conduct your sister safely to the corner of her own street. Let me take your arm, Miss Pross. This is not a good city, at this time, for you to be out in, unprotected; and as your escort knows Mr. Barsad, I will invite him to Mr. Lorry's with us. Are we ready? Come then!"

Miss Pross recalled soon afterwards, and to the end of her life remembered, that as she pressed her hands on Sydney's arm and looked up in his face, imploring him to do no hurt to Solomon, there was a braced purpose in the arm and a kind of inspiration in the eyes, which not only contradicted his light manner, but changed and raised the man. She was too much occupied then with fears for the brother who so little deserved her affection, and with Sydney's friendly reassurances, adequately to heed what she observed.

They left her at the corner of the street, and Carton led the way to Mr. Lorry's, which was within a few minutes' walk. John Barsad, or Solomon Pross, walked at his side.

Mr. Lorry had just finished his dinner, and was sitting before a cheery little log or two of fire—perhaps looking into their blaze for the picture of that younger elderly gentleman from Tellson's, who had looked into the red coals at the Royal George at Dover, now a good many years ago. He turned his head as they entered, and showed the surprise with which he saw a stranger.

"Miss Pross's brother, sir," said Sydney. "Mr. Barsad."

"Barsad?" repeated the old gentleman, "Barsad? I have an association with the name—and with the face."

"I told you you had a remarkable face, Mr. Barsad," observed Carton, coolly. "Pray sit down."

As he took a chair himself, he supplied the link that Mr. Lorry wanted, by saying to him with a frown, "Witness at that trial." Mr. Lorry immediately remembered, and regarded his new visitor with an undisguised look of abhorrence.

"Mr. Barsad has been recognised by Miss Pross as the affectionate brother you have heard of," said Sydney, "and has acknowledged the relationship. I pass to worse news. Darnay has been arrested again."

Struck with consternation, the old gentleman exclaimed, "What do you tell me! I left him safe and free within these two hours, and am about to return to him!"

"Arrested for all that. When was it done, Mr. Barsad?"

"Just now, if at all."

"Mr. Barsad is the best authority possible, sir," said Sydney, "and I have it from Mr. Barsad's communication to a friend and brother Sheep over a bottle of wine, that the arrest has taken place. He left the messengers at the gate, and saw them admitted by the porter. There is no earthly doubt that he is retaken."

Mr. Lorry's business eye read in the speaker's face that it was loss of time to dwell upon the point. Confused, but sensible that something might depend on his presence of mind, he commanded himself, and was silently attentive.

"Now, I trust," said Sydney to him, "that the name and influence of Doctor Manette may stand him in as good stead to-morrow—you said he would be before the Tribunal again to-morrow, Mr. Barsad?—"

"Yes; I believe so."

"—In as good stead to-morrow as to-day. But it may not be so. I own to you, I am shaken, Mr. Lorry, by Doctor Manette's not having had the power to prevent this arrest."

"He may not have known of it beforehand," said Mr. Lorry.

"But that very circumstance would be alarming, when we remember how identified he is with his son-in-law."

"That's true," Mr. Lorry acknowledged, with his troubled hand at his chin, and his troubled eyes on Carton.

"In short," said Sydney, "this is a desperate time, when desperate games are played for desperate stakes. Let the Doctor play the winning game; I will play the losing one. No man's life here is worth purchase. Any one carried home by the people to-day, may be condemned tomorrow. Now, the stake I have resolved to play for, in case of the worst, is a friend in the Conciergerie. And the friend I purpose to myself to win, is Mr. Barsad."

"You need have good cards, sir," said the spy.

"I'll run them over. I'll see what I hold,—Mr. Lorry, you know what a brute I am; I wish you'd give me a little brandy."

It was put before him, and he drank off a glassful—drank off another glassful—pushed the bottle thoughtfully away.

"Mr. Barsad," he went on, in the tone of one who really was looking over a hand at cards: "Sheep of the prisons, emissary of Republican committees, now turnkey, now prisoner, always spy and secret informer, so much the more valuable here for being English that an Englishman is less open to suspicion of subornation in those characters than a Frenchman, represents himself to his employers under a false name. That's a very good card. Mr. Barsad, now in the employ of the republican French government, was formerly in the employ of the aristocratic English government, the enemy of France and freedom. That's an excellent card. Inference clear as day in this region of suspicion, that Mr. Barsad, still in the pay of the aristocratic English government, is the spy of Pitt, the treacherous foe of the Republic crouching in its bosom, the English traitor and agent of all mischief so much spoken of and so difficult to find. That's a card not to be beaten. Have you followed my hand, Mr. Barsad?"

"Not to understand your play," returned the spy, somewhat uneasily.

"I play my Ace, Denunciation of Mr. Barsad to the nearest Section Committee. Look over your hand, Mr. Barsad, and see what you have. Don't hurry."

He drew the bottle near, poured out another glassful of brandy, and drank it off. He saw that the spy was fearful of his drinking himself into a fit state for the immediate denunciation of him. Seeing it, he poured out and drank another glassful.

"Look over your hand carefully, Mr. Barsad. Take time."

It was a poorer hand than he suspected. Mr. Barsad saw losing cards in it that Sydney Carton knew nothing of. Thrown out of his honourable employment in England, through too much unsuccessful hard swearing there—not because he was not wanted there; our English reasons for vaunting our superiority to secrecy and spies are of very modern date—he knew that he had crossed the Channel, and accepted service in France: first, as a tempter and an eavesdropper among his own countrymen there: gradually, as a tempter and an eavesdropper among the natives. He knew that under the overthrown government he had been a spy upon Saint Antoine and Defarge's wine-shop; had received from the watchful police such heads of information concerning Doctor Manette's imprisonment, release, and history, as should serve him for an introduction to familiar conversation with the Defarges; and tried them on Madame Defarge, and had broken down with them signally. He always remembered with fear and trembling, that that terrible woman had knitted when he talked with her, and had looked ominously at him as her fingers moved. He had since seen her, in the Section of Saint Antoine, over and over again produce her knitted registers, and denounce people whose lives the guillotine then surely swallowed up. He knew, as every one employed as he was did, that he was never safe; that flight was impossible; that he was tied fast under the shadow of the axe; and that in spite of his utmost tergiversation and treachery in furtherance of the reigning terror, a word might bring it down upon him. Once denounced, and on such grave grounds as had just now been suggested to his mind, he foresaw that the dreadful woman of whose unrelenting character he had seen many proofs, would produce against him that fatal register, and would quash his last chance of life. Besides that all secret men are men soon terrified, here were surely cards enough of one black suit, to justify the holder in growing rather livid as he turned them over.

"You scarcely seem to like your hand," said Sydney, with the greatest composure. "Do you play?"

"I think, sir," said the spy, in the meanest manner, as he turned to Mr. Lorry, "I may appeal to a gentleman of your years and benevolence, to put it to this other gentleman, so much your junior, whether he can under any circumstances reconcile it to his station to play that Ace of which he has spoken. I admit that *I* am a spy, and that it is considered a discreditable station—though it must be filled by somebody; but this gentleman is no spy, and why should he so demean himself as to make himself one?"

"I play my Ace, Mr. Barsad," said Carton, taking the answer on himself, and looking at his watch, "without any scruple, in a very few minutes."

"I should have hoped, gentlemen both," said the spy, always striving to hook Mr. Lorry into the discussion, "that your respect for my sister—"

"I could not better testify my respect for your sister than by finally relieving her of her brother," said Sydney Carton.

"You think not, sir?"

"I have thoroughly made up my mind about it."

The smooth manner of the spy, curiously in dissonance with his ostentatiously rough dress, and probably with his usual demeanour, received such a check from the inscrutability of Carton,—who was a mystery to wiser and honester men than he,—that it faltered here and failed him. While he was at a loss, Carton said, resuming his former air of contemplating cards:

"And indeed, now I think again, I have a strong impression that I have another good card here, not yet enumerated. That friend and fellow-Sheep, who spoke of himself as pasturing in the country prisons; who was he?"

"French. You don't know him," said the spy, quickly.

"French, eh?" repeated Carton, musing, and not appearing to notice him at all, though he echoed his word. "Well; he may be."

"Is, I assure you," said the spy; "though it's not important."

"Though it's not important," repeated Carton, in the same mechanical way— "though it's not important—No, it's not important. No. Yet I know the face."

"I think not. I am sure not. It can't be," said the spy.

"It-can't-be," muttered Sydney Carton, retrospectively, and idling his glass (which fortunately was a small one) again. "Can't-be. Spoke good French. Yet like a foreigner, I thought?"

"Provincial," said the spy.

"No. Foreign!" cried Carton, striking his open hand on the table, as a light broke clearly on his mind. "Cly! Disguised, but the same man. We had that man before us at the Old Bailey."

"Now, there you are hasty, sir," said Barsad, with a smile that gave his aquiline nose an extra inclination to one side; "there you really give me an advantage over you. Cly (who I will unreservedly admit, at this distance of time, was a partner of mine) has been dead several years. I attended him in his last illness. He was buried in London, at the church of Saint Pancras-in-the-Fields. His unpopularity with the blackguard multitude at the moment prevented my following his remains, but I helped to lay him in his coffin."

Here, Mr. Lorry became aware, from where he sat, of a most remarkable goblin shadow on the wall. Tracing it to its source, he discovered it to be caused by a sudden extraordinary rising and stiffening of all the risen and stiff hair on Mr. Cruncher's head.

"Let us be reasonable," said the spy, "and let us be fair. To show you how mistaken you are, and what an unfounded assumption yours is, I will lay before you a certificate of Cly's burial, which I happened to have carried in my pocket-book," with a hurried hand he produced and opened it, "ever since. There it is. Oh, look at it, look at it! You may take it in your hand; it's no forgery."

Here, Mr. Lorry perceived the reflection on the wall to elongate, and Mr. Cruncher rose and stepped forward. His hair could not have been more violently on end, if it had been that moment dressed by the Cow with the crumpled horn in the house that Jack built.

Unseen by the spy, Mr. Cruncher stood at his side, and touched him on the shoulder like a ghostly bailiff.

"That there Roger Cly, master," said Mr. Cruncher, with a taciturn and iron-bound visage. "So *you* put him in his coffin?"

"I did."

"Who took him out of it?"

Barsad leaned back in his chair, and stammered, "What do you mean?"

"I mean," said Mr. Cruncher, "that he warn't never in it. No! Not he! I'll have my head took off, if he was ever in it."

The spy looked round at the two gentlemen; they both looked in unspeakable astonishment at Jerry.

"I tell you," said Jerry, "that you buried paving-stones and earth in that there coffin. Don't go and tell me that you buried Cly. It was a take in. Me and two more knows it."

"How do you know it?"

"What's that to you? Ecod!" growled Mr. Cruncher, "it's you I have got a old grudge again, is it, with your shameful impositions upon tradesmen! I'd catch hold of your throat and choke you for half a guinea."

Sydney Carton, who, with Mr. Lorry, had been lost in amazement at this turn of the business, here requested Mr. Cruncher to moderate and explain himself.

"At another time, sir," he returned, evasively, "the present time is ill-conwenient for explainin'. What I stand to, is, that he knows well wot that there Cly was never in that there coffin. Let him say he was, in so much as a word of one syllable, and I'll either catch hold of his throat and choke him for half a guinea;" Mr. Cruncher dwelt upon this as quite a liberal offer; "or I'll out and announce him."

"Humph! I see one thing," said Carton. "I hold another card, Mr. Barsad. Impossible, here in raging Paris, with Suspicion filling the air, for you to outlive denunciation, when you are in communication with another aristocratic spy of the same antecedents as yourself, who, moreover, has the mystery about him of having feigned death and come to life again! A plot in the prisons, of the foreigner against the Republic. A strong card—a certain Guillotine card! Do you play?"

"No!" returned the spy. "I throw up. I confess that we were so unpopular with the outrageous mob, that I only got away from England at the risk of being ducked to death, and that Cly was so ferreted up and down, that he never would have got away at all but for that sham. Though how this man knows it was a sham, is a wonder of wonders to me."

"Never you trouble your head about this man," retorted the contentious Mr. Cruncher; "you'll have trouble enough with giving your attention to that gentleman. And look here! Once more!"—Mr. Cruncher could not be restrained from making rather an ostentatious parade of his liberality—"I'd catch hold of your throat and choke you for half a guinea."

The Sheep of the prisons turned from him to Sydney Carton, and said, with more decision, "It has come to a point. I go on duty soon, and can't overstay my time. You told me you had a proposal; what is it? Now, it is of no use asking too much of me. Ask me to do anything in my office, putting my head in great extra danger, and I had better trust my life to the chances of a refusal than the chances of consent. In short, I should make that choice. You talk of desperation. We are all desperate here. Remember! I may denounce you if I think proper, and I can swear my way through stone walls, and so can others. Now, what do you want with me?"

"Not very much. You are a turnkey at the Conciergerie?"

"I tell you once for all, there is no such thing as an escape possible," said the spy, firmly.

"Why need you tell me what I have not asked? You are a turnkey at the Conciergerie?"

"I am sometimes."

"You can be when you choose?"

"I can pass in and out when I choose."

Sydney Carton filled another glass with brandy, poured it slowly out upon the hearth, and watched it as it dropped. It being all spent, he said, rising:

"So far, we have spoken before these two, because it was as well that the merits of the cards should not rest solely between you and me. Come into the dark room here, and let us have one final word alone."

IX. THE GAME MADE

W hile Sydney Carton and the Sheep of the prisons were in the adjoining dark room, speaking so low that not a sound was heard, Mr. Lorry looked at Jerry in considerable doubt and mistrust. That honest tradesman's manner of receiving the look, did not inspire confidence; he changed the leg on which he rested, as often as if he had fifty of those limbs, and were trying them all; he examined his finger-nails with a very questionable closeness of attention; and whenever Mr. Lorry's eye caught his, he was taken with that peculiar kind of short cough requiring the hollow of a hand before it, which is seldom, if ever, known to be an infirmity attendant on perfect openness of character.

"Jerry," said Mr. Lorry. "Come here."

Mr. Cruncher came forward sideways, with one of his shoulders in advance of him.

"What have you been, besides a messenger?"

After some cogitation, accompanied with an intent look at his patron, Mr. Cruncher conceived the luminous idea of replying, "Agicultooral character."

"My mind misgives me much," said Mr. Lorry, angrily shaking a forefinger at him, "that you have used the respectable and great house of Tellson's as a blind, and that you have had an unlawful occupation of an infamous description. If you have, don't expect me to befriend you when you get back to England. If you have, don't expect me to keep your secret. Tellson's shall not be imposed upon."

"I hope, sir," pleaded the abashed Mr. Cruncher, "that a gentleman like yourself wot I've had the honour of odd jobbing till I'm grey at it, would think twice about harming of me, even if it wos so—I don't say it is, but even if it wos. And which it is to be took into account that if it wos, it wouldn't, even then, be all o' one side. There'd be two sides to it. There might be medical doctors at the present hour, a picking up their guineas where a honest tradesman don't pick up his fardens—fardens! no, nor yet his half fardens—half fardens! no, nor yet his quarter—a banking away like smoke at Tellson's, and a cocking their medical eyes at that tradesman on the sly, a going in and going out to their own carriages—ah! equally like smoke, if not more so. Well, that 'ud be imposing, too, on Tellson's. For you cannot sarse the goose and not the gander. And here's Mrs. Cruncher, or leastways wos in the Old England times, and would be to-morrow, if cause given, a floppin' again the business to that degree as is ruinating—stark ruinating! Whereas them medical doctors' wives don't flop—catch 'em at it! Or, if they flop, their toppings goes in favour of more patients, and how can you rightly have one without t'other? Then, wot with undertakers, and wot with parish clerks, and wot with sextons, and wot with private watchmen (all awaricious and all in it), a man wouldn't get much by it, even if it wos so. And wot little a man did get, would never prosper with him, Mr. Lorry. He'd never have no good of it; he'd want all along to be out of the line, if he, could see his way out, being once in—even if it wos so."

"Ugh!" cried Mr. Lorry, rather relenting, nevertheless, "I am shocked at the sight of you."

"Now, what I would humbly offer to you, sir," pursued Mr. Cruncher, "even if it wos so, which I don't say it is—"

"Don't prevaricate," said Mr. Lorry.

"No, I will *not*, sir," returned Mr. Crunches as if nothing were further from his thoughts or practice—"which I don't say it is—wot I would humbly offer to you, sir, would be this. Upon that there stool, at that there Bar, sets that there boy of mine, brought up and growed up to be a man, wot will errand you, message you, general-light-job you, till your heels is where your head is, if such should be your wishes. If it wos so, which I still don't say it is (for I will not prewaricate to you, sir), let that there boy keep his father's place, and take care of his mother; don't blow upon that boy's father—do not do it, sir—and let that father go into the line of the reg'lar diggin', and make amends for what he would have undug—if it wos so—by diggin' of 'em in with a will, and with conwictions respectin' the futur' keepin' of 'em safe. That, Mr. Lorry," said Mr. Cruncher, wiping his forehead with his arm, as an announcement that he had arrived at the peroration of his discourse, "is wot I would respectfully offer to you, sir. A man don't see all this here a goin' on dreadful round him, in the way of Subjects without heads, dear me, plentiful enough fur to bring the price down to porterage and hardly that, without havin' his serious thoughts of things. And these here would be mine, if it wos so, entreatin' of you fur to bear in mind that wot I said just now, I up and said in the good cause when I might have kep' it back."

"That at least is true," said Mr. Lorry. "Say no more now. It may be that I shall yet stand your friend, if you deserve it, and repent in action—not in words. I want no more words."

Mr. Cruncher knuckled his forehead, as Sydney Carton and the spy returned from the dark room. "Adieu, Mr. Barsad," said the former; "our arrangement thus made, you have nothing to fear from me."

He sat down in a chair on the hearth, over against Mr. Lorry. When they were alone, Mr. Lorry asked him what he had done?

"Not much. If it should go ill with the prisoner, I have ensured access to him, once."

Mr. Lorry's countenance fell.

"It is all I could do," said Carton. "To propose too much, would be to put this man's head under the axe, and, as he himself said, nothing worse could happen to him if he were denounced. It was obviously the weakness of the position. There is no help for it."

"But access to him," said Mr. Lorry, "if it should go ill before the Tribunal, will not save him."

"I never said it would."

Mr. Lorry's eyes gradually sought the fire; his sympathy with his darling, and the heavy disappointment of his second arrest, gradually weakened them; he was an old man now, overborne with anxiety of late, and his tears fell.

"You are a good man and a true friend," said Carton, in an altered voice. "Forgive me if I notice that you are affected. I could not see my father weep, and sit by, careless. And I could not respect your sorrow more, if you were my father. You are free from that misfortune, however."

Though he said the last words, with a slip into his usual manner, there was a true feeling and respect both in his tone and in his touch, that Mr. Lorry, who had never seen the better side of him, was wholly unprepared for. He gave him his hand, and Carton gently pressed it.

"To return to poor Darnay," said Carton. "Don't tell Her of this interview, or this arrangement. It would not enable Her to go to see him. She might think it was contrived, in case of the worse, to convey to him the means of anticipating the sentence."

Mr. Lorry had not thought of that, and he looked quickly at Carton to see if it were in his mind. It seemed to be; he returned the look, and evidently understood it.

"She might think a thousand things," Carton said, "and any of them would only add to her trouble. Don't speak of me to her. As I said to you when I first came, I had better not see her. I can put my hand out, to do any little helpful work for her that my hand can find to do, without that. You are going to her, I hope? She must be very desolate to-night."

"I am going now, directly."

"I am glad of that. She has such a strong attachment to you and reliance on you. How does she look?"

"Anxious and unhappy, but very beautiful."

"Ah!"

It was a long, grieving sound, like a sigh—almost like a sob. It attracted Mr. Lorry's eyes to Carton's face, which was turned to the fire. A light, or a shade (the old gentleman could not have said which), passed from it as swiftly as a change will sweep over a hill-side on a wild bright day, and he lifted his foot to put back one of the little flaming logs, which was tumbling forward. He wore the white riding-coat and top-boots, then in vogue, and the light of the fire touching their light surfaces made him look very pale, with his long brown hair, all untrimmed, hanging loose about him. His indifference to fire was sufficiently remarkable to elicit a word of remonstrance from Mr. Lorry; his boot was still upon the hot embers of the flaming log, when it had broken under the weight of his foot.

"I forgot it," he said.

Mr. Lorry's eyes were again attracted to his face. Taking note of the wasted air which clouded the naturally handsome features, and having the expression of prisoners' faces fresh in his mind, he was strongly reminded of that expression.

"And your duties here have drawn to an end, sir?" said Carton, turning to him.

"Yes. As I was telling you last night when Lucie came in so unexpectedly, I have at length done all that I can do here. I hoped to have left them in perfect safety, and then to have quitted Paris. I have my Leave to Pass. I was ready to go."

They were both silent.

"Yours is a long life to look back upon, sir?" said Carton, wistfully.

"I am in my seventy-eighth year."

"You have been useful all your life; steadily and constantly occupied; trusted, respected, and looked up to?"

"I have been a man of business, ever since I have been a man. Indeed, I may say that I was a man of business when a boy."

"See what a place you fill at seventy-eight. How many people will miss you when you leave it empty!"

"A solitary old bachelor," answered Mr. Lorry, shaking his head. "There is nobody to weep for me."

"How can you say that? Wouldn't She weep for you? Wouldn't her child?"

"Yes, yes, thank God. I didn't quite mean what I said."

"It *is* a thing to thank God for; is it not?"

"Surely, surely."

"If you could say, with truth, to your own solitary heart, to-night, 'I have secured to myself the love and attachment, the gratitude or respect, of no human creature; I have won myself a tender place in no regard; I have done nothing good or serviceable to be remembered by!' your seventy-eight years would be seventy-eight heavy curses; would they not?"

"You say truly, Mr. Carton; I think they would be."

Sydney turned his eyes again upon the fire, and, after a silence of a few moments, said:

"I should like to ask you:—Does your childhood seem far off? Do the days when you sat at your mother's knee, seem days of very long ago?"

Responding to his softened manner, Mr. Lorry answered:

"Twenty years back, yes; at this time of my life, no. For, as I draw closer and closer to the end, I travel in the circle, nearer and nearer to the beginning. It seems to be one of the kind smoothings and preparings of the way. My heart is touched now, by many remembrances that had long fallen asleep, of my pretty young mother (and I so old!), and by many associations of the days when what we call the World was not so real with me, and my faults were not confirmed in me."

"I understand the feeling!" exclaimed Carton, with a bright flush. "And you are the better for it?"

"I hope so."

Carton terminated the conversation here, by rising to help him on with his outer coat; "But you," said Mr. Lorry, reverting to the theme, "you are young."

"Yes," said Carton. "I am not old, but my young way was never the way to age. Enough of me."

"And of me, I am sure," said Mr. Lorry. "Are you going out?"

"I'll walk with you to her gate. You know my vagabond and restless habits. If I should prowl about the streets a long time, don't be uneasy; I shall reappear in the morning. You go to the Court to-morrow?"

"Yes, unhappily."

"I shall be there, but only as one of the crowd. My Spy will find a place for me. Take my arm, sir."

Mr. Lorry did so, and they went down-stairs and out in the streets. A few minutes brought them to Mr. Lorry's destination. Carton left him there; but lingered at a little distance, and turned back to the gate again when it was shut, and touched it. He had heard of her going to the prison every day. "She came out here," he said, looking about him, "turned this way, must have trod on these stones often. Let me follow in her steps."

It was ten o'clock at night when he stood before the prison of La Force, where she had stood hundreds of times. A little wood-sawyer, having closed his shop, was smoking his pipe at his shop-door.

"Good night, citizen," said Sydney Carton, pausing in going by; for, the man eyed him inquisitively.

"Good night, citizen."

"How goes the Republic?"

"You mean the Guillotine. Not ill. Sixty-three to-day. We shall mount to a hundred soon. Samson and his men complain sometimes, of being exhausted. Ha, ha, ha! He is so droll, that Samson. Such a Barber!"

"Do you often go to see him—"

"Shave? Always. Every day. What a barber! You have seen him at work?"

"Never."

"Go and see him when he has a good batch. Figure this to yourself, citizen; he shaved the sixty-three to-day, in less than two pipes! Less than two pipes. Word of honour!"

As the grinning little man held out the pipe he was smoking, to explain how he timed the executioner, Carton was so sensible of a rising desire to strike the life out of him, that he turned away.

"But you are not English," said the wood-sawyer, "though you wear English dress?"

"Yes," said Carton, pausing again, and answering over his shoulder.

"You speak like a Frenchman."

"I am an old student here."

"Aha, a perfect Frenchman! Good night, Englishman."

"Good night, citizen."

"But go and see that droll dog," the little man persisted, calling after him. "And take a pipe with you!"

Sydney had not gone far out of sight, when he stopped in the middle of the street under a glimmering lamp, and wrote with his pencil on a scrap of paper. Then, traversing with the decided step of one who remembered the way well, several dark and dirty streets—much dirtier than usual, for the best public thoroughfares remained uncleansed in those times of terror—he stopped at a chemist's shop, which the owner was closing with his own hands. A small, dim, crooked shop, kept in a tortuous, up-hill thoroughfare, by a small, dim, crooked man.

Giving this citizen, too, good night, as he confronted him at his counter, he laid the scrap of paper before him. "Whew!" the chemist whistled softly, as he read it. "Hi! hi! hi!"

Sydney Carton took no heed, and the chemist said:

"For you, citizen?"

"For me."

"You will be careful to keep them separate, citizen? You know the consequences of mixing them?"

"Perfectly."

Certain small packets were made and given to him. He put them, one by one, in the breast of his inner coat, counted out the money for them, and deliberately left the shop. "There is nothing more to do," said he, glancing upward at the moon, "until to-morrow. I can't sleep."

It was not a reckless manner, the manner in which he said these words aloud under the fast-sailing clouds, nor was it more expressive of negligence than defiance. It was the settled manner of a tired man, who had wandered and struggled and got lost, but who at length struck into his road and saw its end.

Long ago, when he had been famous among his earliest competitors as a youth of great promise, he had followed his father to the grave. His mother had died, years before. These solemn words, which had been read at his father's grave, arose in his mind as he went down the dark streets, among the heavy shadows, with the moon and the clouds sailing on high above him. "I am the resurrection and the life, saith the Lord: he that believeth in me, though he were dead, yet shall he live: and whosoever liveth and believeth in me, shall never die."

In a city dominated by the axe, alone at night, with natural sorrow rising in him for the sixty-three who had been that day put to death, and for to-morrow's victims then awaiting their doom in the prisons, and still of to-morrow's and to-morrow's, the chain of association that brought the words home, like a rusty old ship's anchor from the deep, might have been easily found. He did not seek it, but repeated them and went on.

With a solemn interest in the lighted windows where the people were going to rest, forgetful through a few calm hours of the horrors surrounding them; in the towers of the churches, where no prayers were said, for the popular revulsion had even travelled that length of self-destruction from years of priestly impostors, plunderers, and profligates; in the distant burial-places, reserved, as they wrote upon the gates, for Eternal Sleep; in the abounding gaols; and in the streets along which the sixties rolled to a death which had become so common and material, that no sorrowful story of a haunting Spirit ever arose among the people out of all the working of the Guillotine; with a solemn interest in the whole life and death of the city settling down to its short nightly pause in fury; Sydney Carton crossed the Seine again for the lighter streets.

Few coaches were abroad, for riders in coaches were liable to be suspected, and gentility hid its head in red nightcaps, and put on heavy shoes, and trudged. But, the theatres were all well filled, and the people poured cheerfully out as he passed, and went chatting home. At one of the theatre doors, there was a little girl with a mother, looking for a way across the street through the mud. He carried the child over, and before the timid arm was loosed from his neck asked her for a kiss.

"I am the resurrection and the life, saith the Lord: he that believeth in me, though he were dead, yet shall he live: and whosoever liveth and believeth in me, shall never die."

Now, that the streets were quiet, and the night wore on, the words were in the echoes of his feet, and were in the air. Perfectly calm and steady, he sometimes repeated them to himself as he walked; but, he heard them always.

The night wore out, and, as he stood upon the bridge listening to the water as it splashed the river-walls of the Island of Paris, where the picturesque confusion of houses and cathedral shone bright in the light of the moon, the day came coldly, looking like a dead face out of the sky. Then, the night, with the moon and the stars, turned pale and died, and for a little while it seemed as if Creation were delivered over to Death's dominion.

But, the glorious sun, rising, seemed to strike those words, that burden of the night, straight and warm to his heart in its long bright rays. And looking along them, with reverently shaded eyes, a bridge of light appeared to span the air between him and the sun, while the river sparkled under it.

The strong tide, so swift, so deep, and certain, was like a congenial friend, in the morning stillness. He walked by the stream, far from the houses, and in the light and warmth of the sun fell asleep on the bank. When he awoke and was afoot again, he lingered there yet a little longer, watching an eddy that turned and turned purposeless, until the stream absorbed it, and carried it on to the sea.—"Like me."

A trading-boat, with a sail of the softened colour of a dead leaf, then glided into his view, floated by him, and died away. As its silent track in the water disappeared, the prayer that had broken up out of his heart for a merciful consideration of all his poor blindnesses and errors, ended in the words, "I am the resurrection and the life."

Mr. Lorry was already out when he got back, and it was easy to surmise where the good old man was gone. Sydney Carton drank nothing but a little coffee, ate some bread, and, having washed and changed to refresh himself, went out to the place of trial.

The court was all astir and a-buzz, when the black sheep—whom many fell away from in dread—pressed him into an obscure corner among the crowd. Mr. Lorry was there, and Doctor Manette was there. She was there, sitting beside her father.

When her husband was brought in, she turned a look upon him, so sustaining, so encouraging, so full of admiring love and pitying tenderness, yet so courageous for his sake, that it called the healthy blood into his face, brightened his glance, and animated his heart. If there had been any eyes to notice the influence of her look, on Sydney Carton, it would have been seen to be the same influence exactly.

Before that unjust Tribunal, there was little or no order of procedure, ensuring to any accused person any reasonable hearing. There could have been no such Revolution, if all laws, forms, and ceremonies, had not first been so monstrously abused, that the suicidal vengeance of the Revolution was to scatter them all to the winds.

Every eye was turned to the jury. The same determined patriots and good republicans as yesterday and the day before, and to-morrow and the day after. Eager and prominent among them, one man with a craving face, and his fingers perpetually hovering about his lips, whose appearance gave great satisfaction to the spectators. A life- thirsting, cannibal-looking, bloody-minded juryman, the Jacques Three of St. Antoine. The whole jury, as a jury of dogs empannelled to try the deer.

Every eye then turned to the five judges and the public prosecutor. No favourable leaning in that quarter to-day. A fell, uncompromising, murderous business-meaning there. Every eye then sought some other eye in the crowd, and gleamed at it approvingly; and heads nodded at one another, before bending forward with a strained attention.

Charles Evremonde, called Darnay. Released yesterday. Reaccused and retaken yesterday. Indictment delivered to him last night. Suspected and Denounced enemy of the Republic, Aristocrat, one of a family of tyrants, one of a race proscribed, for that they had used their abolished privileges to the infamous oppression of the people. Charles Evremonde, called Darnay, in right of such proscription, absolutely Dead in Law.

To this effect, in as few or fewer words, the Public Prosecutor.

The President asked, was the Accused openly denounced or secretly?

"Openly, President."

"By whom?"

"Three voices. Ernest Defarge, wine-vendor of St. Antoine."

"Good."

"Therese Defarge, his wife."

"Good."

"Alexandre Manette, physician."

A great uproar took place in the court, and in the midst of it, Doctor Manette was seen, pale and trembling, standing where he had been seated.

"President, I indignantly protest to you that this is a forgery and a fraud. You know the accused to be the husband of my daughter. My daughter, and those dear to her, are far dearer to me than my life. Who and where is the false conspirator who says that I denounce the husband of my child!"

"Citizen Manette, be tranquil. To fail in submission to the authority of the Tribunal would be to put yourself out of Law. As to what is dearer to you than life, nothing can be so dear to a good citizen as the Republic."

Loud acclamations hailed this rebuke. The President rang his bell, and with warmth resumed.

"If the Republic should demand of you the sacrifice of your child herself, you would have no duty but to sacrifice her. Listen to what is to follow. In the meanwhile, be silent!"

Frantic acclamations were again raised. Doctor Manette sat down, with his eyes looking around, and his lips trembling; his daughter drew closer to him. The craving man on the jury rubbed his hands together, and restored the usual hand to his mouth.

Defarge was produced, when the court was quiet enough to admit of his being heard, and rapidly expounded the story of the imprisonment, and of his having been a mere boy in the Doctor's service, and of the release, and of the state of the prisoner when released and delivered to him. This short examination followed, for the court was quick with its work.

"You did good service at the taking of the Bastille, citizen?"

"I believe so."

Here, an excited woman screeched from the crowd: "You were one of the best patriots there. Why not say so? You were a cannonier that day there, and you were among the first to enter the accursed fortress when it fell. Patriots, I speak the truth!"

It was The Vengeance who, amidst the warm commendations of the audience, thus assisted the proceedings. The President rang his bell; but, The Vengeance, warming with encouragement, shrieked, "I defy that bell!" wherein she was likewise much commended.

"Inform the Tribunal of what you did that day within the Bastille, citizen."

"I knew," said Defarge, looking down at his wife, who stood at the bottom of the steps on which he was raised, looking steadily up at him; "I knew that this prisoner, of whom I speak, had been confined in a cell known as One Hundred and Five, North Tower. I knew it from himself. He knew himself by no other name than One Hundred and Five, North Tower, when he made shoes under my care. As I serve my gun that day, I resolve, when the place shall fall, to examine that cell. It falls. I mount to the cell, with a fellow-citizen who is one of the Jury, directed by a gaoler. I examine it, very closely. In a hole in the chimney, where a stone has been worked out and replaced, I find a written paper. This is that written paper. I have made it my business to examine some specimens of the writing of Doctor Manette. This is the writing of Doctor Manette. I confide this paper, in the writing of Doctor Manette, to the hands of the President."

"Let it be read."

In a dead silence and stillness—the prisoner under trial looking lovingly at his wife, his wife only looking from him to look with solicitude at her father, Doctor Manette keeping his eyes fixed on the reader, Madame Defarge never taking hers from the prisoner, Defarge never taking his from his feasting wife, and all the other eyes there intent upon the Doctor, who saw none of them—the paper was read, as follows.

X. THE SUBSTANCE OF THE SHADOW

"I, Alexandre Manette, unfortunate physician, native of Beauvais, and afterwards resident in Paris, write this melancholy paper in my doleful cell in the Bastille, during the last month of the year, 1767. I write it at stolen intervals, under every difficulty. I design to secrete it in the wall of the chimney, where I have slowly and laboriously made a place of concealment for it. Some pitying hand may find it there, when I and my sorrows are dust.

"These words are formed by the rusty iron point with which I write with difficulty in scrapings of soot and charcoal from the chimney, mixed with blood, in the last month of the tenth year of my captivity. Hope has quite departed from my breast. I know from terrible warnings I have noted in myself that my reason will not long remain unimpaired, but I solemnly declare that I am at this time in the possession of my right mind—that my memory is exact and circumstantial—and that I write the truth as I shall answer for these my last recorded words, whether they be ever read by men or not, at the Eternal Judgment-seat.

"One cloudy moonlight night, in the third week of December (I think the twenty-second of the month) in the year 1757, I was walking on a retired part of the quay by the Seine for the refreshment of the frosty air, at an hour's distance from my place of residence in the Street of the School of Medicine, when a carriage came along behind me, driven very fast. As I stood aside to let that carriage pass, apprehensive that it might otherwise run me down, a head was put out at the window, and a voice called to the driver to stop.

"The carriage stopped as soon as the driver could rein in his horses, and the same voice called to me by my name. I answered. The carriage was then so far in advance of me that two gentlemen had time to open the door and alight before I came up with it.

"I observed that they were both wrapped in cloaks, and appeared to conceal themselves. As they stood side by side near the carriage door, I also observed that they both looked of about my own age, or rather younger, and that they were greatly alike, in stature, manner, voice, and (as far as I could see) face too.

"'You are Doctor Manette?' said one.

"'I am.'

"'Doctor Manette, formerly of Beauvais,' said the other; 'the young physician, originally an expert surgeon, who within the last year or two has made a rising reputation in Paris?'

"'Gentlemen,' I returned, 'I am that Doctor Manette of whom you speak so graciously.'

"'We have been to your residence,' said the first, 'and not being so fortunate as to find you there, and being informed that you were probably walking in this direction, we followed, in the hope of overtaking you. Will you please to enter the carriage?'

"The manner of both was imperious, and they both moved, as these words were spoken, so as to place me between themselves and the carriage door. They were armed. I was not.

"'Gentlemen,' said I, 'pardon me; but I usually inquire who does me the honour to seek my assistance, and what is the nature of the case to which I am summoned.'

"The reply to this was made by him who had spoken second. 'Doctor, your clients are people of condition. As to the nature of the case, our confidence in your skill assures us that you will ascertain it for yourself better than we can describe it. Enough. Will you please to enter the carriage?'

"I could do nothing but comply, and I entered it in silence. They both entered after me—the last springing in, after putting up the steps. The carriage turned about, and drove on at its former speed.

"I repeat this conversation exactly as it occurred. I have no doubt that it is, word for word, the same. I describe everything exactly as it took place, constraining my mind not to wander from the task. Where I make the broken marks that follow here, I leave off for the time, and put my paper in its hiding-place.

* * *

"The carriage left the streets behind, passed the North Barrier, and emerged upon the country road. At two-thirds of a league from the Barrier—I did not estimate the distance at that time, but afterwards when I traversed it—it struck out of the main avenue, and presently stopped at a solitary house, We all three alighted, and walked, by a damp soft footpath in a garden where a neglected fountain had overflowed, to the door of the house. It was not opened immediately, in answer to the ringing of the bell, and one of my two conductors struck the man who opened it, with his heavy riding glove, across the face.

"There was nothing in this action to attract my particular attention, for I had seen common people struck more commonly than dogs. But, the other of the two, being angry likewise, struck the man in like manner with his arm; the look and bearing of the brothers were then so exactly alike, that I then first perceived them to be twin brothers.

"From the time of our alighting at the outer gate (which we found locked, and which one of the brothers had opened to admit us, and had relocked), I had heard cries proceeding from an upper chamber. I was conducted to this chamber straight, the cries growing louder as we ascended the stairs, and I found a patient in a high fever of the brain, lying on a bed.

"The patient was a woman of great beauty, and young; assuredly not much past twenty. Her hair was torn and ragged, and her arms were bound to her sides with sashes and handkerchiefs. I noticed that these bonds were all portions of a gentleman's dress. On one of them, which was a fringed scarf for a dress of ceremony, I saw the armorial bearings of a Noble, and the letter E.

"I saw this, within the first minute of my contemplation of the patient; for, in her restless strivings she had turned over on her face on the edge of the bed, had drawn the end of the scarf into her mouth, and was in danger of suffocation. My first act was to put out my hand to relieve her breathing; and in moving the scarf aside, the embroidery in the corner caught my sight.

"I turned her gently over, placed my hands upon her breast to calm her and keep her down, and looked into her face. Her eyes were dilated and wild, and she constantly uttered piercing shrieks, and repeated the words, 'My husband, my father, and my brother!' and then counted up to twelve, and said, 'Hush!' For an instant, and no more, she would pause to listen, and then the piercing shrieks would begin again, and she would repeat the cry, 'My husband, my father, and my brother!' and would count up to twelve, and say, 'Hush!' There was no variation in the order, or the manner. There was no cessation, but the regular moment's pause, in the utterance of these sounds.

"'How long,' I asked, 'has this lasted?'

"To distinguish the brothers, I will call them the elder and the younger; by the elder, I mean him who exercised the most authority. It was the elder who replied, 'Since about this hour last night.'

"'She has a husband, a father, and a brother?'

"'A brother.'

"'I do not address her brother?'

"He answered with great contempt, 'No.'

"'She has some recent association with the number twelve?'

"The younger brother impatiently rejoined, 'With twelve o'clock?'

"'See, gentlemen,' said I, still keeping my hands upon her breast, 'how useless I am, as you have brought me! If I had known what I was coming to see, I could have come provided. As it is, time must be lost. There are no medicines to be obtained in this lonely place.'

"The elder brother looked to the younger, who said haughtily, 'There is a case of medicines here;' and brought it from a closet, and put it on the table.

*　*　*

"I opened some of the bottles, smelt them, and put the stoppers to my lips. If I had wanted to use anything save narcotic medicines that were poisons in themselves, I would not have administered any of those.

"'Do you doubt them?' asked the younger brother.

"'You see, monsieur, I am going to use them,' I replied, and said no more.

"I made the patient swallow, with great difficulty, and after many efforts, the dose that I desired to give. As I intended to repeat it after a while, and as it was necessary to watch its influence, I then sat down by the side of the bed. There was a timid and suppressed woman in attendance (wife of the man down-stairs), who had retreated into a corner. The house was damp and decayed, indifferently furnished—evidently, recently occupied and temporarily used. Some thick old hangings had been nailed up before the windows, to deaden the sound of the shrieks. They continued to be uttered in their regular succession, with the cry, 'My husband, my father, and my brother!' the counting up to twelve, and 'Hush!' The frenzy was so violent, that I had not unfastened the bandages restraining the arms; but, I had looked to them, to see that they were not painful. The only spark of encouragement in the case, was, that my hand upon the sufferer's breast had this much soothing influence, that for minutes at a time it tranquillised the figure. It had no effect upon the cries; no pendulum could be more regular.

"For the reason that my hand had this effect (I assume), I had sat by the side of the bed for half an hour, with the two brothers looking on, before the elder said:

"'There is another patient.'

"I was startled, and asked, 'Is it a pressing case?'

"'You had better see,' he carelessly answered; and took up a light.

*　*　*

"The other patient lay in a back room across a second staircase, which was a species of loft over a stable. There was a low plastered ceiling to a part of it; the rest was open, to the ridge of the tiled roof, and there were beams across. Hay and straw were stored in that portion of the place, fagots for firing, and a heap of apples in sand. I had to pass through that part, to get at the other. My memory is circumstantial and unshaken. I try it with these details, and I see them all, in this my cell in the Bastille, near the close of the tenth year of my captivity, as I saw them all that night.

"On some hay on the ground, with a cushion thrown under his head, lay a handsome peasant boy—a boy of not more than seventeen at the most. He lay on his back, with his teeth set, his right hand clenched on his breast, and his glaring eyes looking straight upward. I could not see where his wound was, as I kneeled on one knee over him; but, I could see that he was dying of a wound from a sharp point.

"'I am a doctor, my poor fellow,' said I. 'Let me examine it.'

"'I do not want it examined,' he answered; 'let it be.'

"It was under his hand, and I soothed him to let me move his hand away. The wound was a sword-thrust, received from twenty to twenty- four hours before, but no skill could have saved him if it had been looked to without delay. He was then dying fast. As I turned my eyes to the elder brother, I saw him looking down at this handsome boy whose life was ebbing out, as if he were a wounded bird, or hare, or rabbit; not at all as if he were a fellow-creature.

"'How has this been done, monsieur?' said I.

"'A crazed young common dog! A serf! Forced my brother to draw upon him, and has fallen by my brother's sword—like a gentleman.'

"There was no touch of pity, sorrow, or kindred humanity, in this answer. The speaker seemed to acknowledge that it was inconvenient to have that different order of creature dying there, and that it would have been better if he had died in the usual obscure routine of his vermin kind. He was quite incapable of any compassionate feeling about the boy, or about his fate.

"The boy's eyes had slowly moved to him as he had spoken, and they now slowly moved to me.

"'Doctor, they are very proud, these Nobles; but we common dogs are proud too, sometimes. They plunder us, outrage us, beat us, kill us; but we have a little pride left, sometimes. She—have you seen her, Doctor?'

"The shrieks and the cries were audible there, though subdued by the distance. He referred to them, as if she were lying in our presence.

"I said, 'I have seen her.'

"'She is my sister, Doctor. They have had their shameful rights, these Nobles, in the modesty and virtue of our sisters, many years, but we have had good girls among us. I know it, and have heard my father say so. She was a good girl. She was betrothed to a good young man, too: a tenant of his. We were all tenants of his—that man's who stands there. The other is his brother, the worst of a bad race.'

"It was with the greatest difficulty that the boy gathered bodily force to speak; but, his spirit spoke with a dreadful emphasis.

"'We were so robbed by that man who stands there, as all we common dogs are by those superior Beings—taxed by him without mercy, obliged to work for him without pay, obliged to grind our corn at his mill, obliged to feed scores of his tame birds on our wretched crops, and forbidden for our lives to keep a single tame bird of our own, pillaged and plundered to that degree that when we chanced to have a bit of meat, we ate it in fear, with the door barred and the shutters closed, that his people should not see it and take it from us—I say, we were so robbed, and hunted, and were made so poor, that our father told us it was a dreadful thing to bring a child into the world, and that what we should most pray for, was, that our women might be barren and our miserable race die out!'

"I had never before seen the sense of being oppressed, bursting forth like a fire. I had supposed that it must be latent in the people somewhere; but, I had never seen it break out, until I saw it in the dying boy.

"'Nevertheless, Doctor, my sister married. He was ailing at that time, poor fellow, and she married her lover, that she might tend and comfort him in our cottage—our dog-hut, as that man would call it. She had not been married many weeks, when that man's brother saw her and admired her, and asked that man to lend her to him—for what are husbands among us! He was willing enough, but my sister was good and virtuous, and hated his brother with a hatred as strong as mine. What did the two then, to persuade her husband to use his influence with her, to make her willing?'

"The boy's eyes, which had been fixed on mine, slowly turned to the looker-on, and I saw in the two faces that all he said was true. The two opposing kinds of pride confronting one another, I can see, even in this Bastille; the gentleman's, all negligent indifference; the peasant's, all trodden-down sentiment, and passionate revenge.

"'You know, Doctor, that it is among the Rights of these Nobles to harness us common dogs to carts, and drive us. They so harnessed him and drove him. You know that it is among their Rights to keep us in their grounds all night, quieting the frogs, in order that their noble sleep may not be disturbed. They kept him out in the unwholesome mists at night, and ordered him back into his harness in the day. But he was not persuaded. No! Taken out of harness one day at noon, to feed—if he could find food—he sobbed twelve times, once for every stroke of the bell, and died on her bosom.'

"Nothing human could have held life in the boy but his determination to tell all his wrong. He forced back the gathering shadows of death, as he forced his clenched right hand to remain clenched, and to cover his wound.

"'Then, with that man's permission and even with his aid, his brother took her away; in spite of what I know she must have told his brother—and what that is, will not be long unknown to you, Doctor, if it is now—his brother took her away—for his pleasure and diversion, for a little while. I saw her pass me on the road. When I took the tidings home, our father's heart burst; he never spoke one of the words that filled it. I took my young sister (for I have another) to a place beyond the reach of this man, and where, at least, she will never be *his* vassal. Then, I tracked the brother here, and last night climbed in—a common dog, but sword in hand.—Where is the loft window? It was somewhere here?'

"The room was darkening to his sight; the world was narrowing around him. I glanced about me, and saw that the hay and straw were trampled over the floor, as if there had been a struggle.

"'She heard me, and ran in. I told her not to come near us till he was dead. He came in and first tossed me some pieces of money; then struck at me with a whip. But I, though a common dog, so struck at him as to make him draw. Let him break into as many pieces as he will, the sword that he stained with my common blood; he drew to defend himself—thrust at me with all his skill for his life.'

"My glance had fallen, but a few moments before, on the fragments of a broken sword, lying among the hay. That weapon was a gentleman's. In another place, lay an old sword that seemed to have been a soldier's.

"'Now, lift me up, Doctor; lift me up. Where is he?'

"'He is not here,' I said, supporting the boy, and thinking that he referred to the brother.

"'He! Proud as these nobles are, he is afraid to see me. Where is the man who was here? Turn my face to him.'

"I did so, raising the boy's head against my knee. But, invested for the moment with extraordinary power, he raised himself completely: obliging me to rise too, or I could not have still supported him.

"'Marquis,' said the boy, turned to him with his eyes opened wide, and his right hand raised, 'in the days when all these things are to be answered for, I summon you and yours, to the last of your bad race, to answer for them. I mark this cross of blood upon you, as a sign that I do it. In the days when all these things are to be answered for, I summon your brother, the worst of the bad race, to answer for them separately. I mark this cross of blood upon him, as a sign that I do it.'

"Twice, he put his hand to the wound in his breast, and with his forefinger drew a cross in the air. He stood for an instant with the finger yet raised, and as it dropped, he dropped with it, and I laid him down dead.

* * *

"When I returned to the bedside of the young woman, I found her raving in precisely the same order of continuity. I knew that this might last for many hours, and that it would probably end in the silence of the grave.

"I repeated the medicines I had given her, and I sat at the side of the bed until the night was far advanced. She never abated the piercing quality of her shrieks, never stumbled in the distinctness or the order of her words. They were always 'My husband, my father, and my brother! One, two, three, four, five, six, seven, eight, nine, ten, eleven, twelve. Hush!'

"This lasted twenty-six hours from the time when I first saw her. I had come and gone twice, and was again sitting by her, when she began to falter. I did what little could be done to assist that opportunity, and by-and-bye she sank into a lethargy, and lay like the dead.

"It was as if the wind and rain had lulled at last, after a long and fearful storm. I released her arms, and called the woman to assist me to compose her figure and the dress she had torn. It was then that I knew her condition to be that of one in whom the first expectations of being a mother have arisen; and it was then that I lost the little hope I had had of her.

"'Is she dead?' asked the Marquis, whom I will still describe as the elder brother, coming booted into the room from his horse.

"'Not dead,' said I; 'but like to die.'

"'What strength there is in these common bodies!' he said, looking down at her with some curiosity.

"'There is prodigious strength,' I answered him, 'in sorrow and despair.'

"He first laughed at my words, and then frowned at them. He moved a chair with his foot near to mine, ordered the woman away, and said in a subdued voice,

"'Doctor, finding my brother in this difficulty with these hinds, I recommended that your aid should be invited. Your reputation is high, and, as a young man with your fortune to make, you are probably mindful of your interest. The things that you see here, are things to be seen, and not spoken of.'

"I listened to the patient's breathing, and avoided answering.

"'Do you honour me with your attention, Doctor?'

"'Monsieur,' said I, 'in my profession, the communications of patients are always received in confidence.' I was guarded in my answer, for I was troubled in my mind with what I had heard and seen.

"Her breathing was so difficult to trace, that I carefully tried the pulse and the heart. There was life, and no more. Looking round as I resumed my seat, I found both the brothers intent upon me.

* * *

"I write with so much difficulty, the cold is so severe, I am so fearful of being detected and consigned to an underground cell and total darkness, that I must abridge this narrative. There is no confusion or failure in my memory; it can recall, and could detail, every word that was ever spoken between me and those brothers.

"She lingered for a week. Towards the last, I could understand some few syllables that she said to me, by placing my ear close to her lips. She asked me where she was, and I told her; who I was, and I told her. It was in vain that I asked her for her family name. She faintly shook her head upon the pillow, and kept her secret, as the boy had done.

"I had no opportunity of asking her any question, until I had told the brothers she was sinking fast, and could not live another day. Until then, though no one was ever presented to her consciousness save the woman and myself, one or other of them had always jealously sat behind the curtain at the head of the bed when I was there. But when it came to that, they seemed careless what communication I might hold with her; as if—the thought passed through my mind—I were dying too.

"I always observed that their pride bitterly resented the younger brother's (as I call him) having crossed swords with a peasant, and that peasant a boy. The only consideration that appeared to affect the mind of either of them was the consideration that this was highly degrading to the family, and was ridiculous. As often as I caught the younger brother's eyes, their expression reminded me that he disliked me deeply, for knowing what I knew from the boy. He was smoother and more polite to me than the elder; but I saw this. I also saw that I was an incumbrance in the mind of the elder, too.

"My patient died, two hours before midnight—at a time, by my watch, answering almost to the minute when I had first seen her. I was alone with her, when her forlorn young head drooped gently on one side, and all her earthly wrongs and sorrows ended.

"The brothers were waiting in a room down-stairs, impatient to ride away. I had heard them, alone at the bedside, striking their boots with their riding-whips, and loitering up and down.

"'At last she is dead?' said the elder, when I went in.

"'She is dead,' said I.

"'I congratulate you, my brother,' were his words as he turned round.

"He had before offered me money, which I had postponed taking. He now gave me a rouleau of gold. I took it from his hand, but laid it on the table. I had considered the question, and had resolved to accept nothing.

"'Pray excuse me,' said I. 'Under the circumstances, no.'

"They exchanged looks, but bent their heads to me as I bent mine to them, and we parted without another word on either side.

* * *

"I am weary, weary, weary—worn down by misery. I cannot read what I have written with this gaunt hand.

"Early in the morning, the rouleau of gold was left at my door in a little box, with my name on the outside. From the first, I had anxiously considered what I ought to do. I decided, that day, to write privately to the Minister, stating the nature of the two cases to which I had been summoned, and the place to which I had gone: in effect, stating all the circumstances. I knew what Court influence was, and what the immunities of the Nobles were, and I expected that the matter would never be heard of; but, I wished to relieve my own mind. I had kept the matter a profound secret, even from my wife; and this, too, I resolved to state in my letter. I had no apprehension whatever of my real danger; but I was conscious that there might be danger for others, if others were compromised by possessing the knowledge that I possessed.

"I was much engaged that day, and could not complete my letter that night. I rose long before my usual time next morning to finish it. It was the last day of the year. The letter was lying before me just completed, when I was told that a lady waited, who wished to see me.

* * *

"I am growing more and more unequal to the task I have set myself. It is so cold, so dark, my senses are so benumbed, and the gloom upon me is so dreadful.

"The lady was young, engaging, and handsome, but not marked for long life. She was in great agitation. She presented herself to me as the wife of the Marquis St. Evremonde. I connected the title by which the boy had addressed the elder brother, with the initial letter embroidered on the scarf, and had no difficulty in arriving at the conclusion that I had seen that nobleman very lately.

"My memory is still accurate, but I cannot write the words of our conversation. I suspect that I am watched more closely than I was, and I know not at what times I may be watched. She had in part suspected, and in part discovered, the main facts of the cruel story, of her husband's share in it, and my being resorted to. She did not know that the girl was dead. Her hope had been, she said in great distress, to show her, in secret, a woman's sympathy. Her hope had been to avert the wrath of Heaven from a House that had long been hateful to the suffering many.

"She had reasons for believing that there was a young sister living, and her greatest desire was, to help that sister. I could tell her nothing but that there was such a sister; beyond that, I knew nothing. Her inducement to come to me, relying on my confidence, had been the hope that I could tell her the name and place of abode. Whereas, to this wretched hour I am ignorant of both.

*　*　*

"These scraps of paper fail me. One was taken from me, with a warning, yesterday. I must finish my record to-day.

"She was a good, compassionate lady, and not happy in her marriage. How could she be! The brother distrusted and disliked her, and his influence was all opposed to her; she stood in dread of him, and in dread of her husband too. When I handed her down to the door, there was a child, a pretty boy from two to three years old, in her carriage.

"'For his sake, Doctor,' she said, pointing to him in tears, 'I would do all I can to make what poor amends I can. He will never prosper in his inheritance otherwise. I have a presentiment that if no other innocent atonement is made for this, it will one day be required of him. What I have left to call my own—it is little beyond the worth of a few jewels—I will make it the first charge of his life to bestow, with the compassion and lamenting of his dead mother, on this injured family, if the sister can be discovered.'

"She kissed the boy, and said, caressing him, 'It is for thine own dear sake. Thou wilt be faithful, little Charles?' The child answered her bravely, 'Yes!' I kissed her hand, and she took him in her arms, and went away caressing him. I never saw her more.

"As she had mentioned her husband's name in the faith that I knew it, I added no mention of it to my letter. I sealed my letter, and, not trusting it out of my own hands, delivered it myself that day.

"That night, the last night of the year, towards nine o'clock, a man in a black dress rang at my gate, demanded to see me, and softly followed my servant, Ernest Defarge, a youth, up-stairs. When my servant came into the room where I sat with my wife—O my wife, beloved of my heart! My fair young English wife!—we saw the man, who was supposed to be at the gate, standing silent behind him.

"An urgent case in the Rue St. Honore, he said. It would not detain me, he had a coach in waiting.

"It brought me here, it brought me to my grave. When I was clear of the house, a black muffler was drawn tightly over my mouth from behind, and my arms were pinioned. The two brothers crossed the road from a dark corner, and identified me with a single gesture. The Marquis took from his pocket the letter I had written, showed it me, burnt it in the light of a lantern that was held, and extinguished the ashes with his foot. Not a word was spoken. I was brought here, I was brought to my living grave.

"If it had pleased *God* to put it in the hard heart of either of the brothers, in all these frightful years, to grant me any tidings of my dearest wife—so much as to let me know by a word whether alive or dead—I might have thought that He had not quite abandoned them. But, now I believe that the mark of the red cross is fatal to them, and that they have no part in His mercies. And them and their descendants, to the last of their race, I, Alexandre Manette, unhappy prisoner, do this last night of the year 1767, in my unbearable agony, denounce to the times when all these things shall be answered for. I denounce them to Heaven and to earth."

A terrible sound arose when the reading of this document was done. A sound of craving and eagerness that had nothing articulate in it but blood. The narrative called up the most revengeful passions of the time, and there was not a head in the nation but must have dropped before it.

Little need, in presence of that tribunal and that auditory, to show how the Defarges had not made the paper public, with the other captured Bastille memorials borne in procession, and had kept it, biding their time. Little need to show that this detested family name had long been anathematised by Saint Antoine, and was wrought into the fatal register. The man never trod ground whose virtues and services would have sustained him in that place that day, against such denunciation.

And all the worse for the doomed man, that the denouncer was a well-known citizen, his own attached friend, the father of his wife. One of the frenzied aspirations of the populace was, for imitations of the questionable public virtues of antiquity, and for sacrifices and self-immolations on the people's altar. Therefore when the President said (else had his own head quivered on his shoulders), that the good physician of the Republic would deserve better still of the Republic by rooting out an obnoxious family of Aristocrats, and would doubtless feel a sacred glow and joy in making his daughter a widow and her child an orphan, there was wild excitement, patriotic fervour, not a touch of human sympathy.

"Much influence around him, has that Doctor?" murmured Madame Defarge, smiling to The Vengeance. "Save him now, my Doctor, save him!"

At every juryman's vote, there was a roar. Another and another. Roar and roar.

Unanimously voted. At heart and by descent an Aristocrat, an enemy of the Republic, a notorious oppressor of the People. Back to the Conciergerie, and Death within four-and-twenty hours!

XI. DUSK

The wretched wife of the innocent man thus doomed to die, fell under the sentence, as if she had been mortally stricken. But, she uttered no sound; and so strong was the voice within her, representing that it was she of all the world who must uphold him in his misery and not augment it, that it quickly raised her, even from that shock.

The Judges having to take part in a public demonstration out of doors, the Tribunal adjourned. The quick noise and movement of the court's emptying itself by many passages had not ceased, when Lucie stood stretching out her arms towards her husband, with nothing in her face but love and consolation.

"If I might touch him! If I might embrace him once! O, good citizens, if you would have so much compassion for us!"

There was but a gaoler left, along with two of the four men who had taken him last night, and Barsad. The people had all poured out to the show in the streets. Barsad proposed to the rest, "Let her embrace him then; it is but a moment." It was silently acquiesced in, and they passed her over the seats in the hall to a raised place, where he, by leaning over the dock, could fold her in his arms.

"Farewell, dear darling of my soul. My parting blessing on my love. We shall meet again, where the weary are at rest!"

They were her husband's words, as he held her to his bosom.

"I can bear it, dear Charles. I am supported from above: don't suffer for me. A parting blessing for our child."

"I send it to her by you. I kiss her by you. I say farewell to her by you."

"My husband. No! A moment!" He was tearing himself apart from her. "We shall not be separated long. I feel that this will break my heart by-and-bye; but I will do my duty while I can, and when I leave her, God will raise up friends for her, as He did for me."

Her father had followed her, and would have fallen on his knees to both of them, but that Darnay put out a hand and seized him, crying:

"No, no! What have you done, what have you done, that you should kneel to us! We know now, what a struggle you made of old. We know, now what you underwent when you suspected my descent, and when you knew it. We know now, the natural antipathy you strove against, and conquered, for her dear sake. We thank you with all our hearts, and all our love and duty. Heaven be with you!"

Her father's only answer was to draw his hands through his white hair, and wring them with a shriek of anguish.

"It could not be otherwise," said the prisoner. "All things have worked together as they have fallen out. It was the always-vain endeavour to discharge my poor mother's trust that first brought my fatal presence near you. Good could never come of such evil, a happier end was not in nature to so unhappy a beginning. Be comforted, and forgive me. Heaven bless you!"

As he was drawn away, his wife released him, and stood looking after him with her hands touching one another in the attitude of prayer, and with a radiant look upon her face, in which there was even a comforting smile. As he went out at the prisoners' door, she turned, laid her head lovingly on her father's breast, tried to speak to him, and fell at his feet.

Then, issuing from the obscure corner from which he had never moved, Sydney Carton came and took her up. Only her father and Mr. Lorry were with her. His arm trembled as it raised her, and supported her head. Yet, there was an air about him that was not all of pity—that had a flush of pride in it.

"Shall I take her to a coach? I shall never feel her weight."

He carried her lightly to the door, and laid her tenderly down in a coach. Her father and their old friend got into it, and he took his seat beside the driver.

When they arrived at the gateway where he had paused in the dark not many hours before, to picture to himself on which of the rough stones of the street her feet had trodden, he lifted her again, and carried her up the staircase to their rooms. There, he laid her down on a couch, where her child and Miss Pross wept over her.

"Don't recall her to herself," he said, softly, to the latter, "she is better so. Don't revive her to consciousness, while she only faints."

"Oh, Carton, Carton, dear Carton!" cried little Lucie, springing up and throwing her arms passionately round him, in a burst of grief. "Now that you have come, I think you will do something to help mamma, something to save papa! O, look at her, dear Carton! Can you, of all the people who love her, bear to see her so?"

He bent over the child, and laid her blooming cheek against his face. He put her gently from him, and looked at her unconscious mother.

"Before I go," he said, and paused—"I may kiss her?"

It was remembered afterwards that when he bent down and touched her face with his lips, he murmured some words. The child, who was nearest to him, told them afterwards, and told her grandchildren when she was a handsome old lady, that she heard him say, "A life you love."

When he had gone out into the next room, he turned suddenly on Mr. Lorry and her father, who were following, and said to the latter:

"You had great influence but yesterday, Doctor Manette; let it at least be tried. These judges, and all the men in power, are very friendly to you, and very recognisant of your services; are they not?"

"Nothing connected with Charles was concealed from me. I had the strongest assurances that I should save him; and I did." He returned the answer in great trouble, and very slowly.

"Try them again. The hours between this and to-morrow afternoon are few and short, but try."

"I intend to try. I will not rest a moment."

"That's well. I have known such energy as yours do great things before now—though never," he added, with a smile and a sigh together, "such great things as this. But try! Of little worth as life is when we misuse it, it is worth that effort. It would cost nothing to lay down if it were not."

"I will go," said Doctor Manette, "to the Prosecutor and the President straight, and I will go to others whom it is better not to name. I will write too, and—But stay! There is a Celebration in the streets, and no one will be accessible until dark."

"That's true. Well! It is a forlorn hope at the best, and not much the forlorner for being delayed till dark. I should like to know how you speed; though, mind! I expect nothing! When are you likely to have seen these dread powers, Doctor Manette?"

"Immediately after dark, I should hope. Within an hour or two from this."

"It will be dark soon after four. Let us stretch the hour or two. If I go to Mr. Lorry's at nine, shall I hear what you have done, either from our friend or from yourself?"

"Yes."

"May you prosper!"

Mr. Lorry followed Sydney to the outer door, and, touching him on the shoulder as he was going away, caused him to turn.

"I have no hope," said Mr. Lorry, in a low and sorrowful whisper.

"Nor have I."

"If any one of these men, or all of these men, were disposed to spare him—which is a large supposition; for what is his life, or any man's to them!—I doubt if they durst spare him after the demonstration in the court."

"And so do I. I heard the fall of the axe in that sound."

Mr. Lorry leaned his arm upon the door-post, and bowed his face upon it.

"Don't despond," said Carton, very gently; "don't grieve. I encouraged Doctor Manette in this idea, because I felt that it might one day be consolatory to her. Otherwise, she might think 'his life was want only thrown away or wasted,' and that might trouble her."

"Yes, yes, yes," returned Mr. Lorry, drying his eyes, "you are right. But he will perish; there is no real hope."

"Yes. He will perish: there is no real hope," echoed Carton.

And walked with a settled step, down-stairs.

XII. DARKNESS

Sydney Carton paused in the street, not quite decided where to go. "At Tellson's banking-house at nine," he said, with a musing face. "Shall I do well, in the mean time, to show myself? I think so. It is best that these people should know there is such a man as I here; it is a sound precaution, and may be a necessary preparation. But care, care, care! Let me think it out!"

Checking his steps which had begun to tend towards an object, he took a turn or two in the already darkening street, and traced the thought in his mind to its possible consequences. His first impression was confirmed. "It is best," he said, finally resolved, "that these people should know there is such a man as I here." And he turned his face towards Saint Antoine.

Defarge had described himself, that day, as the keeper of a wine-shop in the Saint Antoine suburb. It was not difficult for one who knew the city well, to find his house without asking any question. Having ascertained its situation, Carton came out of those closer streets again, and dined at a place of refreshment and fell sound asleep after dinner. For the first time in many years, he had no strong drink. Since last night he had taken nothing but a little light thin wine, and last night he had dropped the brandy slowly down on Mr. Lorry's hearth like a man who had done with it.

It was as late as seven o'clock when he awoke refreshed, and went out into the streets again. As he passed along towards Saint Antoine, he stopped at a shop-window where there was a mirror, and slightly altered the disordered arrangement of his loose cravat, and his coat- collar, and his wild hair. This done, he went on direct to Defarge's, and went in.

There happened to be no customer in the shop but Jacques Three, of the restless fingers and the croaking voice. This man, whom he had seen upon the Jury, stood drinking at the little counter, in conversation with the Defarges, man and wife. The Vengeance assisted in the conversation, like a regular member of the establishment.

As Carton walked in, took his seat and asked (in very indifferent French) for a small measure of wine, Madame Defarge cast a careless glance at him, and then a keener, and then a keener, and then advanced to him herself, and asked him what it was he had ordered.

He repeated what he had already said.

"English?" asked Madame Defarge, inquisitively raising her dark eyebrows.

After looking at her, as if the sound of even a single French word were slow to express itself to him, he answered, in his former strong foreign accent. "Yes, madame, yes. I am English!"

Madame Defarge returned to her counter to get the wine, and, as he took up a Jacobin journal and feigned to pore over it puzzling out its meaning, he heard her say, "I swear to you, like Evremonde!"

Defarge brought him the wine, and gave him Good Evening.

"How?"

"Good evening."

"Oh! Good evening, citizen," filling his glass. "Ah! and good wine. I drink to the Republic."

Defarge went back to the counter, and said, "Certainly, a little like." Madame sternly retorted, "I tell you a good deal like." Jacques Three pacifically remarked, "He is so much in your mind, see you, madame." The amiable Vengeance added, with a laugh, "Yes, my faith! And you are looking forward with so much pleasure to seeing him once more to-morrow!"

Carton followed the lines and words of his paper, with a slow forefinger, and with a studious and absorbed face. They were all leaning their arms on the counter close together, speaking low. After a silence of a few moments, during which they all looked towards him without disturbing his outward attention from the Jacobin editor, they resumed their conversation.

"It is true what madame says," observed Jacques Three. "Why stop? There is great force in that. Why stop?"

"Well, well," reasoned Defarge, "but one must stop somewhere. After all, the question is still where?"

"At extermination," said madame.

"Magnificent!" croaked Jacques Three. The Vengeance, also, highly approved.

"Extermination is good doctrine, my wife," said Defarge, rather troubled; "in general, I say nothing against it. But this Doctor has suffered much; you have seen him to-day; you have observed his face when the paper was read."

"I have observed his face!" repeated madame, contemptuously and angrily. "Yes. I have observed his face. I have observed his face to be not the face of a true friend of the Republic. Let him take care of his face!"

"And you have observed, my wife," said Defarge, in a deprecatory manner, "the anguish of his daughter, which must be a dreadful anguish to him!"

"I have observed his daughter," repeated madame; "yes, I have observed his daughter, more times than one. I have observed her to-day, and I have observed her other days. I have observed her in the court, and I have observed her in the street by the prison. Let me but lift my finger—!" She seemed to raise it (the listener's eyes were always on his paper), and to let it fall with a rattle on the ledge before her, as if the axe had dropped.

"The citizeness is superb!" croaked the Juryman.

"She is an Angel!" said The Vengeance, and embraced her.

"As to thee," pursued madame, implacably, addressing her husband, "if it depended on thee—which, happily, it does not—thou wouldst rescue this man even now."

"No!" protested Defarge. "Not if to lift this glass would do it! But I would leave the matter there. I say, stop there."

"See you then, Jacques," said Madame Defarge, wrathfully; "and see you, too, my little Vengeance; see you both! Listen! For other crimes as tyrants and oppressors, I have this race a long time on my register, doomed to destruction and extermination. Ask my husband, is that so."

"It is so," assented Defarge, without being asked.

"In the beginning of the great days, when the Bastille falls, he finds this paper of to-day, and he brings it home, and in the middle of the night when this place is clear and shut, we read it, here on this spot, by the light of this lamp. Ask him, is that so."

"It is so," assented Defarge.

"That night, I tell him, when the paper is read through, and the lamp is burnt out, and the day is gleaming in above those shutters and between those iron bars, that I have now a secret to communicate. Ask him, is that so."

"It is so," assented Defarge again.

"I communicate to him that secret. I smite this bosom with these two hands as I smite it now, and I tell him, 'Defarge, I was brought up among the fishermen of the sea-shore, and that peasant family so injured by the two Evremonde brothers, as that Bastille paper describes, is my family. Defarge, that sister of the mortally wounded boy upon the ground was my sister, that husband was my sister's husband, that unborn child was their child, that brother was my brother, that father was my father, those dead are my dead, and that summons to answer for those things descends to me!' Ask him, is that so."

"It is so," assented Defarge once more.

"Then tell Wind and Fire where to stop," returned madame; "but don't tell me."

Both her hearers derived a horrible enjoyment from the deadly nature of her wrath—the listener could feel how white she was, without seeing her—and both highly commended it. Defarge, a weak minority, interposed a few words for the memory of the compassionate wife of the Marquis; but only elicited from his own wife a repetition of her last reply. "Tell the Wind and the Fire where to stop; not me!"

Customers entered, and the group was broken up. The English customer paid for what he had had, perplexedly counted his change, and asked, as a stranger, to be directed towards the National Palace. Madame Defarge took him to the door, and put her arm on his, in pointing out the road. The English customer was not without his reflections then, that it might be a good deed to seize that arm, lift it, and strike under it sharp and deep.

But, he went his way, and was soon swallowed up in the shadow of the prison wall. At the appointed hour, he emerged from it to present himself in Mr. Lorry's room again, where he found the old gentleman walking to and fro in restless anxiety. He said he had been with Lucie until just now, and had only left her for a few minutes, to come and keep his appointment. Her father had not been seen, since he quitted the banking-house towards four o'clock. She had some faint hopes that his mediation might save Charles, but they were very slight. He had been more than five hours gone: where could he be?

Mr. Lorry waited until ten; but, Doctor Manette not returning, and he being unwilling to leave Lucie any longer, it was arranged that he should go back to her, and come to the banking-house again at midnight. In the meanwhile, Carton would wait alone by the fire for the Doctor.

He waited and waited, and the clock struck twelve; but Doctor Manette did not come back. Mr. Lorry returned, and found no tidings of him, and brought none. Where could he be?

They were discussing this question, and were almost building up some weak structure of hope on his prolonged absence, when they heard him on the stairs. The instant he entered the room, it was plain that all was lost.

Whether he had really been to any one, or whether he had been all that time traversing the streets, was never known. As he stood staring at them, they asked him no question, for his face told them everything.

"I cannot find it," said he, "and I must have it. Where is it?"

His head and throat were bare, and, as he spoke with a helpless look straying all around, he took his coat off, and let it drop on the floor.

"Where is my bench? I have been looking everywhere for my bench, and I can't find it. What have they done with my work? Time presses: I must finish those shoes."

They looked at one another, and their hearts died within them.

"Come, come!" said he, in a whimpering miserable way; "let me get to work. Give me my work."

Receiving no answer, he tore his hair, and beat his feet upon the ground, like a distracted child.

"Don't torture a poor forlorn wretch," he implored them, with a dreadful cry; "but give me my work! What is to become of us, if those shoes are not done to-night?"

Lost, utterly lost!

It was so clearly beyond hope to reason with him, or try to restore him, that—as if by agreement—they each put a hand upon his shoulder, and soothed him to sit down before the fire, with a promise that he should have his work presently. He sank into the chair, and brooded over the embers, and shed tears. As if all that had happened since the garret time were a momentary fancy, or a dream, Mr. Lorry saw him shrink into the exact figure that Defarge had had in keeping.

Affected, and impressed with terror as they both were, by this spectacle of ruin, it was not a time to yield to such emotions. His lonely daughter, bereft of her final hope and reliance, appealed to them both too strongly. Again, as if by agreement, they looked at one another with one meaning in their faces. Carton was the first to speak:

"The last chance is gone: it was not much. Yes; he had better be taken to her. But, before you go, will you, for a moment, steadily attend to me? Don't ask me why I make the stipulations I am going to make, and exact the promise I am going to exact; I have a reason—a good one."

"I do not doubt it," answered Mr. Lorry. "Say on."

The figure in the chair between them, was all the time monotonously rocking itself to and fro, and moaning. They spoke in such a tone as they would have used if they had been watching by a sick-bed in the night.

Carton stooped to pick up the coat, which lay almost entangling his feet. As he did so, a small case in which the Doctor was accustomed to carry the lists of his day's duties, fell lightly on the floor. Carton took it up, and there was a folded paper in it. "We should look at this!" he said. Mr. Lorry nodded his consent. He opened it, and exclaimed, "Thank *God!*"

"What is it?" asked Mr. Lorry, eagerly.

"A moment! Let me speak of it in its place. First," he put his hand in his coat, and took another paper from it, "that is the certificate which enables me to pass out of this city. Look at it. You see—Sydney Carton, an Englishman?"

Mr. Lorry held it open in his hand, gazing in his earnest face.

"Keep it for me until to-morrow. I shall see him to-morrow, you remember, and I had better not take it into the prison."

"Why not?"

"I don't know; I prefer not to do so. Now, take this paper that Doctor Manette has carried about him. It is a similar certificate, enabling him and his daughter and her child, at any time, to pass the barrier and the frontier! You see?"

"Yes!"

"Perhaps he obtained it as his last and utmost precaution against evil, yesterday. When is it dated? But no matter; don't stay to look; put it up carefully with mine and your own. Now, observe! I never doubted until within this hour or two, that he had, or could have such a paper. It is good, until recalled. But it may be soon recalled, and, I have reason to think, will be."

"They are not in danger?"

"They are in great danger. They are in danger of denunciation by Madame Defarge. I know it from her own lips. I have overheard words of that woman's, to-night, which have presented their danger to me in strong colours. I have lost no time, and since then, I have seen the spy. He confirms me. He knows that a wood-sawyer, living by the prison wall, is under the control of the Defarges, and has been rehearsed by Madame Defarge as to his having seen Her"—he never mentioned Lucie's name—"making signs and signals to prisoners. It is easy to foresee that the pretence will be the common one, a prison plot, and that it will involve her life—and perhaps her child's—and perhaps her father's—for both have been seen with her at that place. Don't look so horrified. You will save them all."

"Heaven grant I may, Carton! But how?"

"I am going to tell you how. It will depend on you, and it could depend on no better man. This new denunciation will certainly not take place until after to-morrow; probably not until two or three days afterwards; more probably a week afterwards. You know it is a capital crime, to mourn for, or sympathise with, a victim of the Guillotine. She and her father would unquestionably be guilty of this crime, and this woman (the inveteracy of whose pursuit cannot be described) would wait to add that strength to her case, and make herself doubly sure. You follow me?"

"So attentively, and with so much confidence in what you say, that for the moment I lose sight," touching the back of the Doctor's chair, "even of this distress."

"You have money, and can buy the means of travelling to the seacoast as quickly as the journey can be made. Your preparations have been completed for some days, to return to England. Early to-morrow have your horses ready, so that they may be in starting trim at two o'clock in the afternoon."

"It shall be done!"

His manner was so fervent and inspiring, that Mr. Lorry caught the flame, and was as quick as youth.

"You are a noble heart. Did I say we could depend upon no better man? Tell her, to-night, what you know of her danger as involving her child and her father. Dwell upon that, for she would lay her own fair head beside her husband's cheerfully." He faltered for an instant; then went on as before. "For the sake of her child and her father, press upon her the necessity of leaving Paris, with them and you, at that hour. Tell her that it was her husband's last arrangement. Tell her that more depends upon it than she dare believe, or hope. You think that her father, even in this sad state, will submit himself to her; do you not?"

"I am sure of it."

"I thought so. Quietly and steadily have all these arrangements made in the courtyard here, even to the taking of your own seat in the carriage. The moment I come to you, take me in, and drive away."

"I understand that I wait for you under all circumstances?"

"You have my certificate in your hand with the rest, you know, and will reserve my place. Wait for nothing but to have my place occupied, and then for England!"

"Why, then," said Mr. Lorry, grasping his eager but so firm and steady hand, "it does not all depend on one old man, but I shall have a young and ardent man at my side."

"By the help of Heaven you shall! Promise me solemnly that nothing will influence you to alter the course on which we now stand pledged to one another."

"Nothing, Carton."

"Remember these words to-morrow: change the course, or delay in it—for any reason—and no life can possibly be saved, and many lives must inevitably be sacrificed."

"I will remember them. I hope to do my part faithfully."

"And I hope to do mine. Now, good bye!"

Though he said it with a grave smile of earnestness, and though he even put the old man's hand to his lips, he did not part from him then. He helped him so far to arouse the rocking figure before the dying embers, as to get a cloak and hat put upon it, and to tempt it forth to find where the bench and work were hidden that it still moaningly besought to have. He walked on the other side of it and protected it to the courtyard of the house where the afflicted heart—so happy in the memorable time when he had revealed his own desolate heart to it—outwatched the awful night. He entered the courtyard and remained there for a few moments alone, looking up at the light in the window of her room. Before he went away, he breathed a blessing towards it, and a Farewell.

XIII. FIFTY-TWO

In the black prison of the Conciergerie, the doomed of the day awaited their fate. They were in number as the weeks of the year. Fifty-two were to roll that afternoon on the life-tide of the city to the boundless everlasting sea. Before their cells were quit of them, new occupants were appointed; before their blood ran into the blood spilled yesterday, the blood that was to mingle with theirs to-morrow was already set apart.

Two score and twelve were told off. From the farmer-general of seventy, whose riches could not buy his life, to the seamstress of twenty, whose poverty and obscurity could not save her. Physical diseases, engendered in the vices and neglects of men, will seize on victims of all degrees; and the frightful moral disorder, born of unspeakable suffering, intolerable oppression, and heartless indifference, smote equally without distinction.

Charles Darnay, alone in a cell, had sustained himself with no flattering delusion since he came to it from the Tribunal. In every line of the narrative he had heard, he had heard his condemnation. He had fully comprehended that no personal influence could possibly save him, that he was virtually sentenced by the millions, and that units could avail him nothing.

Nevertheless, it was not easy, with the face of his beloved wife fresh before him, to compose his mind to what it must bear. His hold on life was strong, and it was very, very hard, to loosen; by gradual efforts and degrees unclosed a little here, it clenched the tighter there; and when he brought his strength to bear on that hand and it yielded, this was closed again. There was a hurry, too, in all his thoughts, a turbulent and heated working of his heart, that contended against resignation. If, for a moment, he did feel resigned, then his wife and child who had to live after him, seemed to protest and to make it a selfish thing.

But, all this was at first. Before long, the consideration that there was no disgrace in the fate he must meet, and that numbers went the same road wrongfully, and trod it firmly every day, sprang up to stimulate him. Next followed the thought that much of the future peace of mind enjoyable by the dear ones, depended on his quiet fortitude. So, by degrees he calmed into the better state, when he could raise his thoughts much higher, and draw comfort down.

Before it had set in dark on the night of his condemnation, he had travelled thus far on his last way. Being allowed to purchase the means of writing, and a light, he sat down to write until such time as the prison lamps should be extinguished.

He wrote a long letter to Lucie, showing her that he had known nothing of her father's imprisonment, until he had heard of it from herself, and that he had been as ignorant as she of his father's and uncle's responsibility for that misery, until the paper had been read. He had already explained to her that his concealment from herself of the name he had relinquished, was the one condition—fully intelligible now—that her father had attached to their betrothal, and was the one promise he had still exacted on the morning of their marriage. He entreated her, for her father's sake, never to seek to know whether her father had become oblivious of the existence of the paper, or had had it recalled to him (for the moment, or for good), by the story of the Tower, on that old Sunday under the dear old plane-tree in the garden. If he had preserved any definite remembrance of it, there could be no doubt that he had supposed it destroyed with the Bastille, when he had found no mention of it among the relics of prisoners which the populace had discovered there, and which had been described to all the world. He besought her—though he added that he knew it was needless—to console her father, by impressing him through every tender means she could think of, with the truth that he had done nothing for which he could justly reproach himself, but had uniformly forgotten himself for their joint sakes. Next to her preservation of his own last grateful love and blessing, and her overcoming of her sorrow, to devote herself to their dear child, he adjured her, as they would meet in Heaven, to comfort her father.

To her father himself, he wrote in the same strain; but, he told her father that he expressly confided his wife and child to his care. And he told him this, very strongly, with the hope of rousing him from any despondency or dangerous retrospect towards which he foresaw he might be tending.

To Mr. Lorry, he commended them all, and explained his worldly affairs. That done, with many added sentences of grateful friendship and warm attachment, all was done. He never thought of Carton. His mind was so full of the others, that he never once thought of him.

He had time to finish these letters before the lights were put out. When he lay down on his straw bed, he thought he had done with this world.

But, it beckoned him back in his sleep, and showed itself in shining forms. Free and happy, back in the old house in Soho (though it had nothing in it like the real house), unaccountably released and light of heart, he was with Lucie again, and she told him it was all a dream, and he had never gone away. A pause of forgetfulness, and then he had even suffered, and had come back to her, dead and at peace, and yet there was no difference in him. Another pause of oblivion, and he awoke in the sombre morning, unconscious where he was or what had happened, until it flashed upon his mind, "this is the day of my death!"

Thus, had he come through the hours, to the day when the fifty-two heads were to fall. And now, while he was composed, and hoped that he could meet the end with quiet heroism, a new action began in his waking thoughts, which was very difficult to master.

He had never seen the instrument that was to terminate his life. How high it was from the ground, how many steps it had, where he would be stood, how he would be touched, whether the touching hands would be dyed red, which way his face would be turned, whether he would be the first, or might be the last: these and many similar questions, in nowise directed by his will, obtruded themselves over and over again, countless times. Neither were they connected with fear: he was conscious of no fear. Rather, they originated in a strange besetting desire to know what to do when the time came; a desire gigantically disproportionate to the few swift moments to which it referred; a wondering that was more like the wondering of some other spirit within his, than his own.

The hours went on as he walked to and fro, and the clocks struck the numbers he would never hear again. Nine gone for ever, ten gone for ever, eleven gone for ever, twelve coming on to pass away. After a hard contest with that eccentric action of thought which had last perplexed him, he had got the better of it. He walked up and down, softly repeating their names to himself. The worst of the strife was over. He could walk up and down, free from distracting fancies, praying for himself and for them.

Twelve gone for ever.

He had been apprised that the final hour was Three, and he knew he would be summoned some time earlier, inasmuch as the tumbrils jolted heavily and slowly through the streets. Therefore, he resolved to keep Two before his mind, as the hour, and so to strengthen himself in the interval that he might be able, after that time, to strengthen others.

Walking regularly to and fro with his arms folded on his breast, a very different man from the prisoner, who had walked to and fro at La Force, he heard One struck away from him, without surprise. The hour had measured like most other hours. Devoutly thankful to Heaven for his recovered self-possession, he thought, "There is but another now," and turned to walk again.

Footsteps in the stone passage outside the door. He stopped.

The key was put in the lock, and turned. Before the door was opened, or as it opened, a man said in a low voice, in English: "He has never seen me here; I have kept out of his way. Go you in alone; I wait near. Lose no time!"

The door was quickly opened and closed, and there stood before him face to face, quiet, intent upon him, with the light of a smile on his features, and a cautionary finger on his lip, Sydney Carton.

There was something so bright and remarkable in his look, that, for the first moment, the prisoner misdoubted him to be an apparition of his own imagining. But, he spoke, and it was his voice; he took the prisoner's hand, and it was his real grasp.

"Of all the people upon earth, you least expected to see me?" he said.

"I could not believe it to be you. I can scarcely believe it now. You are not"—the apprehension came suddenly into his mind—"a prisoner?"

"No. I am accidentally possessed of a power over one of the keepers here, and in virtue of it I stand before you. I come from her—your wife, dear Darnay."

The prisoner wrung his hand.

"I bring you a request from her."

"What is it?"

"A most earnest, pressing, and emphatic entreaty, addressed to you in the most pathetic tones of the voice so dear to you, that you well remember."

The prisoner turned his face partly aside.

"You have no time to ask me why I bring it, or what it means; I have no time to tell you. You must comply with it—take off those boots you wear, and draw on these of mine."

There was a chair against the wall of the cell, behind the prisoner. Carton, pressing forward, had already, with the speed of lightning, got him down into it, and stood over him, barefoot.

"Draw on these boots of mine. Put your hands to them; put your will to them. Quick!"

"Carton, there is no escaping from this place; it never can be done. You will only die with me. It is madness."

"It would be madness if I asked you to escape; but do I? When I ask you to pass out at that door, tell me it is madness and remain here. Change that cravat for this of mine, that coat for this of mine. While you do it, let me take this ribbon from your hair, and shake out your hair like this of mine!"

With wonderful quickness, and with a strength both of will and action, that appeared quite supernatural, he forced all these changes upon him. The prisoner was like a young child in his hands.

"Carton! Dear Carton! It is madness. It cannot be accomplished, it never can be done, it has been attempted, and has always failed. I implore you not to add your death to the bitterness of mine."

"Do I ask you, my dear Darnay, to pass the door? When I ask that, refuse. There are pen and ink and paper on this table. Is your hand steady enough to write?"

"It was when you came in."

"Steady it again, and write what I shall dictate. Quick, friend, quick!"

Pressing his hand to his bewildered head, Darnay sat down at the table. Carton, with his right hand in his breast, stood close beside him.

"Write exactly as I speak."

"To whom do I address it?"

"To no one." Carton still had his hand in his breast.

"Do I date it?"

"No."

The prisoner looked up, at each question. Carton, standing over him with his hand in his breast, looked down.

"'If you remember,'" said Carton, dictating, "'the words that passed between us, long ago, you will readily comprehend this when you see it. You do remember them, I know. It is not in your nature to forget them.'"

He was drawing his hand from his breast; the prisoner chancing to look up in his hurried wonder as he wrote, the hand stopped, closing upon something.

"Have you written 'forget them'?" Carton asked.

"I have. Is that a weapon in your hand?"

"No; I am not armed."

"What is it in your hand?"

"You shall know directly. Write on; there are but a few words more." He dictated again. "'I am thankful that the time has come, when I can prove them. That I do so is no subject for regret or grief.'" As he said these words with his eyes fixed on the writer, his hand slowly and softly moved down close to the writer's face.

The pen dropped from Darnay's fingers on the table, and he looked about him vacantly.

"What vapour is that?" he asked.

"Vapour?"

"Something that crossed me?"

"I am conscious of nothing; there can be nothing here. Take up the pen and finish. Hurry, hurry!"

As if his memory were impaired, or his faculties disordered, the prisoner made an effort to rally his attention. As he looked at Carton with clouded eyes and with an altered manner of breathing, Carton—his hand again in his breast—looked steadily at him.

"Hurry, hurry!"

The prisoner bent over the paper, once more.

"'If it had been otherwise;'" Carton's hand was again watchfully and softly stealing down; "'I never should have used the longer opportunity. If it had been otherwise;'" the hand was at the prisoner's face; "'I should but have had so much the more to answer for. If it had been otherwise—'" Carton looked at the pen and saw it was trailing off into unintelligible signs.

Carton's hand moved back to his breast no more. The prisoner sprang up with a reproachful look, but Carton's hand was close and firm at his nostrils, and Carton's left arm caught him round the waist. For a few seconds he faintly struggled with the man who had come to lay down his life for him; but, within a minute or so, he was stretched insensible on the ground.

Quickly, but with hands as true to the purpose as his heart was, Carton dressed himself in the clothes the prisoner had laid aside, combed back his hair, and tied it with the ribbon the prisoner had worn. Then, he softly called, "Enter there! Come in!" and the Spy presented himself.

"You see?" said Carton, looking up, as he kneeled on one knee beside the insensible figure, putting the paper in the breast: "is your hazard very great?"

"Mr. Carton," the Spy answered, with a timid snap of his fingers, "my hazard is not *that*, in the thick of business here, if you are true to the whole of your bargain."

"Don't fear me. I will be true to the death."

"You must be, Mr. Carton, if the tale of fifty-two is to be right. Being made right by you in that dress, I shall have no fear."

"Have no fear! I shall soon be out of the way of harming you, and the rest will soon be far from here, please God! Now, get assistance and take me to the coach."

"You?" said the Spy nervously.

"Him, man, with whom I have exchanged. You go out at the gate by which you brought me in?"

"Of course."

"I was weak and faint when you brought me in, and I am fainter now you take me out. The parting interview has overpowered me. Such a thing has happened here, often, and too often. Your life is in your own hands. Quick! Call assistance!"

"You swear not to betray me?" said the trembling Spy, as he paused for a last moment.

"Man, man!" returned Carton, stamping his foot; "have I sworn by no solemn vow already, to go through with this, that you waste the precious moments now? Take him yourself to the courtyard you know of, place him yourself in the carriage, show him yourself to Mr. Lorry, tell him yourself to give him no restorative but air, and to remember my words of last night, and his promise of last night, and drive away!"

The Spy withdrew, and Carton seated himself at the table, resting his forehead on his hands. The Spy returned immediately, with two men.

"How, then?" said one of them, contemplating the fallen figure. "So afflicted to find that his friend has drawn a prize in the lottery of Sainte Guillotine?"

"A good patriot," said the other, "could hardly have been more afflicted if the Aristocrat had drawn a blank."

They raised the unconscious figure, placed it on a litter they had brought to the door, and bent to carry it away.

"The time is short, Evremonde," said the Spy, in a warning voice.

"I know it well," answered Carton. "Be careful of my friend, I entreat you, and leave me."

"Come, then, my children," said Barsad. "Lift him, and come away!"

The door closed, and Carton was left alone. Straining his powers of listening to the utmost, he listened for any sound that might denote suspicion or alarm. There was none. Keys turned, doors clashed, footsteps passed along distant passages: no cry was raised, or hurry made, that seemed unusual. Breathing more freely in a little while, he sat down at the table, and listened again until the clock struck Two.

Sounds that he was not afraid of, for he divined their meaning, then began to be audible. Several doors were opened in succession, and finally his own. A gaoler, with a list in his hand, looked in, merely saying, "Follow me, Evremonde!" and he followed into a large dark room, at a distance. It was a dark winter day, and what with the shadows within, and what with the shadows without, he could but dimly discern the others who were brought there to have their arms bound. Some were standing; some seated. Some were lamenting, and in restless motion; but, these were few. The great majority were silent and still, looking fixedly at the ground.

As he stood by the wall in a dim corner, while some of the fifty-two were brought in after him, one man stopped in passing, to embrace him, as having a knowledge of him. It thrilled him with a great dread of discovery; but the man went on. A very few moments after that, a young woman, with a slight girlish form, a sweet spare face in which there was no vestige of colour, and large widely opened patient eyes, rose from the seat where he had observed her sitting, and came to speak to him.

"Citizen Evremonde," she said, touching him with her cold hand. "I am a poor little seamstress, who was with you in La Force."

He murmured for answer: "True. I forget what you were accused of?"

"Plots. Though the just Heaven knows that I am innocent of any. Is it likely? Who would think of plotting with a poor little weak creature like me?"

The forlorn smile with which she said it, so touched him, that tears started from his eyes.

"I am not afraid to die, Citizen Evremonde, but I have done nothing. I am not unwilling to die, if the Republic which is to do so much good to us poor, will profit by my death; but I do not know how that can be, Citizen Evremonde. Such a poor weak little creature!"

As the last thing on earth that his heart was to warm and soften to, it warmed and softened to this pitiable girl.

"I heard you were released, Citizen Evremonde. I hoped it was true?"

"It was. But, I was again taken and condemned."

"If I may ride with you, Citizen Evremonde, will you let me hold your hand? I am not afraid, but I am little and weak, and it will give me more courage."

As the patient eyes were lifted to his face, he saw a sudden doubt in them, and then astonishment. He pressed the work-worn, hunger-worn young fingers, and touched his lips.

"Are you dying for him?" she whispered.

"And his wife and child. Hush! Yes."

"O you will let me hold your brave hand, stranger?"

"Hush! Yes, my poor sister; to the last."

* * *

The same shadows that are falling on the prison, are falling, in that same hour of the early afternoon, on the Barrier with the crowd about it, when a coach going out of Paris drives up to be examined.

"Who goes here? Whom have we within? Papers!"

The papers are handed out, and read.

"Alexandre Manette. Physician. French. Which is he?"

This is he; this helpless, inarticulately murmuring, wandering old man pointed out.

"Apparently the Citizen-Doctor is not in his right mind? The Revolution-fever will have been too much for him?"

Greatly too much for him.

"Hah! Many suffer with it. Lucie. His daughter. French. Which is she?"

This is she.

"Apparently it must be. Lucie, the wife of Evremonde; is it not?"

It is.

"Hah! Evremonde has an assignation elsewhere. Lucie, her child. English. This is she?"

She and no other.

"Kiss me, child of Evremonde. Now, thou hast kissed a good Republican; something new in thy family; remember it! Sydney Carton. Advocate. English. Which is he?"

He lies here, in this corner of the carriage. He, too, is pointed out.

"Apparently the English advocate is in a swoon?"

It is hoped he will recover in the fresher air. It is represented that he is not in strong health, and has separated sadly from a friend who is under the displeasure of the Republic.

"Is that all? It is not a great deal, that! Many are under the displeasure of the Republic, and must look out at the little window. Jarvis Lorry. Banker. English. Which is he?"

"I am he. Necessarily, being the last."

It is Jarvis Lorry who has replied to all the previous questions. It is Jarvis Lorry who has alighted and stands with his hand on the coach door, replying to a group of officials. They leisurely walk round the carriage and leisurely mount the box, to look at what little luggage it carries on the roof; the country-people hanging about, press nearer to the coach doors and greedily stare in; a little child, carried by its mother, has its short arm held out for it, that it may touch the wife of an aristocrat who has gone to the Guillotine.

"Behold your papers, Jarvis Lorry, countersigned."

"One can depart, citizen?"

"One can depart. Forward, my postilions! A good journey!"

"I salute you, citizens.—And the first danger passed!"

These are again the words of Jarvis Lorry, as he clasps his hands, and looks upward. There is terror in the carriage, there is weeping, there is the heavy breathing of the insensible traveller.

"Are we not going too slowly? Can they not be induced to go faster?" asks Lucie, clinging to the old man.

"It would seem like flight, my darling. I must not urge them too much; it would rouse suspicion."

"Look back, look back, and see if we are pursued!"

"The road is clear, my dearest. So far, we are not pursued."

Houses in twos and threes pass by us, solitary farms, ruinous buildings, dye-works, tanneries, and the like, open country, avenues of leafless trees. The hard uneven pavement is under us, the soft deep mud is on either side. Sometimes, we strike into the skirting mud, to avoid the stones that clatter us and shake us; sometimes, we stick in ruts and sloughs there. The agony of our impatience is then so great, that in our wild alarm and hurry we are for getting out and running—hiding—doing anything but stopping.

Out of the open country, in again among ruinous buildings, solitary farms, dye-works, tanneries, and the like, cottages in twos and threes, avenues of leafless trees. Have these men deceived us, and taken us back by another road? Is not this the same place twice over? Thank Heaven, no. A village. Look back, look back, and see if we are pursued! Hush! the posting-house.

Leisurely, our four horses are taken out; leisurely, the coach stands in the little street, bereft of horses, and with no likelihood upon it of ever moving again; leisurely, the new horses come into visible existence, one by one; leisurely, the new postilions follow, sucking and plaiting the lashes of their whips; leisurely, the old postilions count their money, make wrong additions, and arrive at dissatisfied results. All the time, our overfraught hearts are beating at a rate that would far outstrip the fastest gallop of the fastest horses ever foaled.

At length the new postilions are in their saddles, and the old are left behind. We are through the village, up the hill, and down the hill, and on the low watery grounds. Suddenly, the postilions exchange speech with animated gesticulation, and the horses are pulled up, almost on their haunches. We are pursued?

"Ho! Within the carriage there. Speak then!"

"What is it?" asks Mr. Lorry, looking out at window.

"How many did they say?"

"I do not understand you."

"—At the last post. How many to the Guillotine to-day?"

"Fifty-two."

"I said so! A brave number! My fellow-citizen here would have it forty-two; ten more heads are worth having. The Guillotine goes handsomely. I love it. Hi forward. Whoop!"

The night comes on dark. He moves more; he is beginning to revive, and to speak intelligibly; he thinks they are still together; he asks him, by his name, what he has in his hand. O pity us, kind Heaven, and help us! Look out, look out, and see if we are pursued.

The wind is rushing after us, and the clouds are flying after us, and the moon is plunging after us, and the whole wild night is in pursuit of us; but, so far, we are pursued by nothing else.

XIV. THE KNITTING DONE

In that same juncture of time when the Fifty-Two awaited their fate Madame Defarge held darkly ominous council with The Vengeance and Jacques Three of the Revolutionary Jury. Not in the wine-shop did Madame Defarge confer with these ministers, but in the shed of the wood-sawyer, erst a mender of roads. The sawyer himself did not participate in the conference, but abided at a little distance, like an outer satellite who was not to speak until required, or to offer an opinion until invited.

"But our Defarge," said Jacques Three, "is undoubtedly a good Republican? Eh?"

"There is no better," the voluble Vengeance protested in her shrill notes, "in France."

"Peace, little Vengeance," said Madame Defarge, laying her hand with a slight frown on her lieutenant's lips, "hear me speak. My husband, fellow-citizen, is a good Republican and a bold man; he has deserved well of the Republic, and possesses its confidence. But my husband has his weaknesses, and he is so weak as to relent towards this Doctor."

"It is a great pity," croaked Jacques Three, dubiously shaking his head, with his cruel fingers at his hungry mouth; "it is not quite like a good citizen; it is a thing to regret."

"See you," said madame, "I care nothing for this Doctor, I. He may wear his head or lose it, for any interest I have in him; it is all one to me. But, the Evremonde people are to be exterminated, and the wife and child must follow the husband and father."

"She has a fine head for it," croaked Jacques Three. "I have seen blue eyes and golden hair there, and they looked charming when Samson held them up." Ogre that he was, he spoke like an epicure.

Madame Defarge cast down her eyes, and reflected a little.

"The child also," observed Jacques Three, with a meditative enjoyment of his words, "has golden hair and blue eyes. And we seldom have a child there. It is a pretty sight!"

"In a word," said Madame Defarge, coming out of her short abstraction, "I cannot trust my husband in this matter. Not only do I feel, since last night, that I dare not confide to him the details of my projects; but also I feel that if I delay, there is danger of his giving warning, and then they might escape."

"That must never be," croaked Jacques Three; "no one must escape. We have not half enough as it is. We ought to have six score a day."

"In a word," Madame Defarge went on, "my husband has not my reason for pursuing this family to annihilation, and I have not his reason for regarding this Doctor with any sensibility. I must act for myself, therefore. Come hither, little citizen."

The wood-sawyer, who held her in the respect, and himself in the submission, of mortal fear, advanced with his hand to his red cap.

"Touching those signals, little citizen," said Madame Defarge, sternly, "that she made to the prisoners; you are ready to bear witness to them this very day?"

"Ay, ay, why not!" cried the sawyer. "Every day, in all weathers, from two to four, always signalling, sometimes with the little one, sometimes without. I know what I know. I have seen with my eyes."

He made all manner of gestures while he spoke, as if in incidental imitation of some few of the great diversity of signals that he had never seen.

"Clearly plots," said Jacques Three. "Transparently!"

"There is no doubt of the Jury?" inquired Madame Defarge, letting her eyes turn to him with a gloomy smile.

"Rely upon the patriotic Jury, dear citizeness. I answer for my fellow-Jurymen."

"Now, let me see," said Madame Defarge, pondering again. "Yet once more! Can I spare this Doctor to my husband? I have no feeling either way. Can I spare him?"

"He would count as one head," observed Jacques Three, in a low voice. "We really have not heads enough; it would be a pity, I think."

"He was signalling with her when I saw her," argued Madame Defarge; "I cannot speak of one without the other; and I must not be silent, and trust the case wholly to him, this little citizen here. For, I am not a bad witness."

The Vengeance and Jacques Three vied with each other in their fervent protestations that she was the most admirable and marvellous of witnesses. The little citizen, not to be outdone, declared her to be a celestial witness.

"He must take his chance," said Madame Defarge. "No, I cannot spare him! You are engaged at three o'clock; you are going to see the batch of to-day executed.—You?"

The question was addressed to the wood-sawyer, who hurriedly replied in the affirmative: seizing the occasion to add that he was the most ardent of Republicans, and that he would be in effect the most desolate of Republicans, if anything prevented him from enjoying the pleasure of smoking his afternoon pipe in the contemplation of the droll national barber. He was so very demonstrative herein, that he might have been suspected (perhaps was, by the dark eyes that looked contemptuously at him out of Madame Defarge's head) of having his small individual fears for his own personal safety, every hour in the day.

"I," said madame, "am equally engaged at the same place. After it is over—say at eight to-night—come you to me, in Saint Antoine, and we will give information against these people at my Section."

The wood-sawyer said he would be proud and flattered to attend the citizeness. The citizeness looking at him, he became embarrassed, evaded her glance as a small dog would have done, retreated among his wood, and hid his confusion over the handle of his saw.

Madame Defarge beckoned the Juryman and The Vengeance a little nearer to the door, and there expounded her further views to them thus:

"She will now be at home, awaiting the moment of his death. She will be mourning and grieving. She will be in a state of mind to impeach the justice of the Republic. She will be full of sympathy with its enemies. I will go to her."

"What an admirable woman; what an adorable woman!" exclaimed Jacques Three, rapturously. "Ah, my cherished!" cried The Vengeance; and embraced her.

"Take you my knitting," said Madame Defarge, placing it in her lieutenant's hands, "and have it ready for me in my usual seat. Keep me my usual chair. Go you there, straight, for there will probably be a greater concourse than usual, to-day."

"I willingly obey the orders of my Chief," said The Vengeance with alacrity, and kissing her cheek. "You will not be late?"

"I shall be there before the commencement."

"And before the tumbrils arrive. Be sure you are there, my soul," said The Vengeance, calling after her, for she had already turned into the street, "before the tumbrils arrive!"

Madame Defarge slightly waved her hand, to imply that she heard, and might be relied upon to arrive in good time, and so went through the mud, and round the corner of the prison wall. The Vengeance and the Juryman, looking after her as she walked away, were highly appreciative of her fine figure, and her superb moral endowments.

There were many women at that time, upon whom the time laid a dreadfully disfiguring hand; but, there was not one among them more to be dreaded than this ruthless woman, now taking her way along the streets. Of a strong and fearless character, of shrewd sense and readiness, of great determination, of that kind of beauty which not only seems to impart to its possessor firmness and animosity, but to strike into others an instinctive recognition of those qualities; the troubled time would have heaved her up, under any circumstances. But, imbued from her childhood with a brooding sense of wrong, and an inveterate hatred of a class, opportunity had developed her into a tigress. She was absolutely without pity. If she had ever had the virtue in her, it had quite gone out of her.

It was nothing to her, that an innocent man was to die for the sins of his forefathers; she saw, not him, but them. It was nothing to her, that his wife was to be made a widow and his daughter an orphan; that was insufficient punishment, because they were her natural enemies and her prey, and as such had no right to live. To appeal to her, was made hopeless by her having no sense of pity, even for herself. If she had been laid low in the streets, in any of the many encounters in which she had been engaged, she would not have pitied herself; nor, if she had been ordered to the axe to-morrow, would she have gone to it with any softer feeling than a fierce desire to change places with the man who sent here there.

Such a heart Madame Defarge carried under her rough robe. Carelessly worn, it was a becoming robe enough, in a certain weird way, and her dark hair looked rich under her coarse red cap. Lying hidden in her bosom, was a loaded pistol. Lying hidden at her waist, was a sharpened dagger. Thus accoutred, and walking with the confident tread of such a character, and with the supple freedom of a woman who had habitually walked in her girlhood, bare-foot and bare-legged, on the brown sea-sand, Madame Defarge took her way along the streets.

Now, when the journey of the travelling coach, at that very moment waiting for the completion of its load, had been planned out last night, the difficulty of taking Miss Pross in it had much engaged Mr. Lorry's attention. It was not merely desirable to avoid overloading the coach, but it was of the highest importance that the time occupied in examining it and its passengers, should be reduced to the utmost; since their escape might depend on the saving of only a few seconds here and there. Finally, he had proposed, after anxious consideration, that Miss Pross and Jerry, who were at liberty to leave the city, should leave it at three o'clock in the lightest- wheeled conveyance known to that period. Unencumbered with luggage, they would soon overtake the coach, and, passing it and preceding it on the road, would order its horses in advance, and greatly facilitate its progress during the precious hours of the night, when delay was the most to be dreaded.

Seeing in this arrangement the hope of rendering real service in that pressing emergency, Miss Pross hailed it with joy. She and Jerry had beheld the coach start, had known who it was that Solomon brought, had passed some ten minutes in tortures of suspense, and were now concluding their arrangements to follow the coach, even as Madame Defarge, taking her way through the streets, now drew nearer and nearer to the else-deserted lodging in which they held their consultation.

"Now what do you think, Mr. Cruncher," said Miss Pross, whose agitation was so great that she could hardly speak, or stand, or move, or live: "what do you think of our not starting from this courtyard? Another carriage having already gone from here to-day, it might awaken suspicion."

"My opinion, miss," returned Mr. Cruncher, "is as you're right. Likewise wot I'll stand by you, right or wrong."

"I am so distracted with fear and hope for our precious creatures," said Miss Pross, wildly crying, "that I am incapable of forming any plan. Are *you* capable of forming any plan, my dear good Mr. Cruncher?"

"Respectin' a future spear o' life, miss," returned Mr. Cruncher, "I hope so. Respectin' any present use o' this here blessed old head o' mine, I think not. Would you do me the favour, miss, to take notice o' two promises and wows wot it is my wishes fur to record in this here crisis?"

"Oh, for gracious sake!" cried Miss Pross, still wildly crying, "record them at once, and get them out of the way, like an excellent man."

"First," said Mr. Cruncher, who was all in a tremble, and who spoke with an ashy and solemn visage, "them poor things well out o' this, never no more will I do it, never no more!"

"I am quite sure, Mr. Cruncher," returned Miss Pross, "that you never will do it again, whatever it is, and I beg you not to think it necessary to mention more particularly what it is."

"No, miss," returned Jerry, "it shall not be named to you. Second: them poor things well out o' this, and never no more will I interfere with Mrs. Cruncher's flopping, never no more!"

"Whatever housekeeping arrangement that may be," said Miss Pross, striving to dry her eyes and compose herself, "I have no doubt it is best that Mrs. Cruncher should have it entirely under her own superintendence.—O my poor darlings!"

"I go so far as to say, miss, moreover," proceeded Mr. Cruncher, with a most alarming tendency to hold forth as from a pulpit—"and let my words be took down and took to Mrs. Cruncher through yourself—that wot my opinions respectin' flopping has undergone a change, and that wot I only hope with all my heart as Mrs. Cruncher may be a flopping at the present time."

"There, there, there! I hope she is, my dear man," cried the distracted Miss Pross, "and I hope she finds it answering her expectations."

"Forbid it," proceeded Mr. Cruncher, with additional solemnity, additional slowness, and additional tendency to hold forth and hold out, "as anything wot I have ever said or done should be wisited on my earnest wishes for them poor creeturs now! Forbid it as we shouldn't all flop (if it was anyways conwenient) to get 'em out o' this here dismal risk! Forbid it, miss! Wot I say, for-*bid* it!" This was Mr. Cruncher's conclusion after a protracted but vain endeavour to find a better one.

And still Madame Defarge, pursuing her way along the streets, came nearer and nearer.

"If we ever get back to our native land," said Miss Pross, "you may rely upon my telling Mrs. Cruncher as much as I may be able to remember and understand of what you have so impressively said; and at all events you may be sure that I shall bear witness to your being thoroughly in earnest at this dreadful time. Now, pray let us think! My esteemed Mr. Cruncher, let us think!"

Still, Madame Defarge, pursuing her way along the streets, came nearer and nearer.

"If you were to go before," said Miss Pross, "and stop the vehicle and horses from coming here, and were to wait somewhere for me; wouldn't that be best?"

Mr. Cruncher thought it might be best.

"Where could you wait for me?" asked Miss Pross.

Mr. Cruncher was so bewildered that he could think of no locality but Temple Bar. Alas! Temple Bar was hundreds of miles away, and Madame Defarge was drawing very near indeed.

"By the cathedral door," said Miss Pross. "Would it be much out of the way, to take me in, near the great cathedral door between the two towers?"

"No, miss," answered Mr. Cruncher.

"Then, like the best of men," said Miss Pross, "go to the posting- house straight, and make that change."

"I am doubtful," said Mr. Cruncher, hesitating and shaking his head, "about leaving of you, you see. We don't know what may happen."

"Heaven knows we don't," returned Miss Pross, "but have no fear for me. Take me in at the cathedral, at Three o'Clock, or as near it as you can, and I am sure it will be better than our going from here. I feel certain of it. There! Bless you, Mr. Cruncher! Think-not of me, but of the lives that may depend on both of us!"

This exordium, and Miss Pross's two hands in quite agonised entreaty clasping his, decided Mr. Cruncher. With an encouraging nod or two, he immediately went out to alter the arrangements, and left her by herself to follow as she had proposed.

The having originated a precaution which was already in course of execution, was a great relief to Miss Pross. The necessity of composing her appearance so that it should attract no special notice in the streets, was another relief. She looked at her watch, and it was twenty minutes past two. She had no time to lose, but must get ready at once.

Afraid, in her extreme perturbation, of the loneliness of the deserted rooms, and of half-imagined faces peeping from behind every open door in them, Miss Pross got a basin of cold water and began laving her eyes, which were swollen and red. Haunted by her feverish apprehensions, she could not bear to have her sight obscured for a minute at a time by the dripping water, but constantly paused and looked round to see that there was no one watching her. In one of those pauses she recoiled and cried out, for she saw a figure standing in the room.

The basin fell to the ground broken, and the water flowed to the feet of Madame Defarge. By strange stern ways, and through much staining blood, those feet had come to meet that water.

Madame Defarge looked coldly at her, and said, "The wife of Evremonde; where is she?"

It flashed upon Miss Pross's mind that the doors were all standing open, and would suggest the flight. Her first act was to shut them. There were four in the room, and she shut them all. She then placed herself before the door of the chamber which Lucie had occupied.

Madame Defarge's dark eyes followed her through this rapid movement, and rested on her when it was finished. Miss Pross had nothing beautiful about her; years had not tamed the wildness, or softened the grimness, of her appearance; but, she too was a determined woman in her different way, and she measured Madame Defarge with her eyes, every inch.

"You might, from your appearance, be the wife of Lucifer," said Miss Pross, in her breathing. "Nevertheless, you shall not get the better of me. I am an Englishwoman."

Madame Defarge looked at her scornfully, but still with something of Miss Pross's own perception that they two were at bay. She saw a tight, hard, wiry woman before her, as Mr. Lorry had seen in the same figure a woman with a strong hand, in the years gone by. She knew full well that Miss Pross was the family's devoted friend; Miss Pross knew full well that Madame Defarge was the family's malevolent enemy.

"On my way yonder," said Madame Defarge, with a slight movement of her hand towards the fatal spot, "where they reserve my chair and my knitting for me, I am come to make my compliments to her in passing. I wish to see her."

"I know that your intentions are evil," said Miss Pross, "and you may depend upon it, I'll hold my own against them."

Each spoke in her own language; neither understood the other's words; both were very watchful, and intent to deduce from look and manner, what the unintelligible words meant.

"It will do her no good to keep herself concealed from me at this moment," said Madame Defarge. "Good patriots will know what that means. Let me see her. Go tell her that I wish to see her. Do you hear?"

"If those eyes of yours were bed-winches," returned Miss Pross, "and I was an English four-poster, they shouldn't loose a splinter of me. No, you wicked foreign woman; I am your match."

Madame Defarge was not likely to follow these idiomatic remarks in detail; but, she so far understood them as to perceive that she was set at naught.

"Woman imbecile and pig-like!" said Madame Defarge, frowning. "I take no answer from you. I demand to see her. Either tell her that I demand to see her, or stand out of the way of the door and let me go to her!" This, with an angry explanatory wave of her right arm.

"I little thought," said Miss Pross, "that I should ever want to understand your nonsensical language; but I would give all I have, except the clothes I wear, to know whether you suspect the truth, or any part of it."

Neither of them for a single moment released the other's eyes. Madame Defarge had not moved from the spot where she stood when Miss Pross first became aware of her; but, she now advanced one step.

"I am a Briton," said Miss Pross, "I am desperate. I don't care an English Twopence for myself. I know that the longer I keep you here, the greater hope there is for my Ladybird. I'll not leave a handful of that dark hair upon your head, if you lay a finger on me!"

Thus Miss Pross, with a shake of her head and a flash of her eyes between every rapid sentence, and every rapid sentence a whole breath. Thus Miss Pross, who had never struck a blow in her life.

But, her courage was of that emotional nature that it brought the irrepressible tears into her eyes. This was a courage that Madame Defarge so little comprehended as to mistake for weakness. "Ha, ha!" she laughed, "you poor wretch! What are you worth! I address myself to that Doctor." Then she raised her voice and called out, "Citizen Doctor! Wife of Evremonde! Child of Evremonde! Any person but this miserable fool, answer the Citizeness Defarge!"

Perhaps the following silence, perhaps some latent disclosure in the expression of Miss Pross's face, perhaps a sudden misgiving apart from either suggestion, whispered to Madame Defarge that they were gone. Three of the doors she opened swiftly, and looked in.

"Those rooms are all in disorder, there has been hurried packing, there are odds and ends upon the ground. There is no one in that room behind you! Let me look."

"Never!" said Miss Pross, who understood the request as perfectly as Madame Defarge understood the answer.

"If they are not in that room, they are gone, and can be pursued and brought back," said Madame Defarge to herself.

"As long as you don't know whether they are in that room or not, you are uncertain what to do," said Miss Pross to herself; "and you shall not know that, if I can prevent your knowing it; and know that, or not know that, you shall not leave here while I can hold you."

"I have been in the streets from the first, nothing has stopped me, I will tear you to pieces, but I will have you from that door," said Madame Defarge.

"We are alone at the top of a high house in a solitary courtyard, we are not likely to be heard, and I pray for bodily strength to keep you here, while every minute you are here is worth a hundred thousand guineas to my darling," said Miss Pross.

Madame Defarge made at the door. Miss Pross, on the instinct of the moment, seized her round the waist in both her arms, and held her tight. It was in vain for Madame Defarge to struggle and to strike; Miss Pross, with the vigorous tenacity of love, always so much stronger than hate, clasped her tight, and even lifted her from the floor in the struggle that they had. The two hands of Madame Defarge buffeted and tore her face; but, Miss Pross, with her head down, held her round the waist, and clung to her with more than the hold of a drowning woman.

Soon, Madame Defarge's hands ceased to strike, and felt at her encircled waist. "It is under my arm," said Miss Pross, in smothered tones, "you shall not draw it. I am stronger than you, I bless Heaven for it. I hold you till one or other of us faints or dies!"

Madame Defarge's hands were at her bosom. Miss Pross looked up, saw what it was, struck at it, struck out a flash and a crash, and stood alone—blinded with smoke.

All this was in a second. As the smoke cleared, leaving an awful stillness, it passed out on the air, like the soul of the furious woman whose body lay lifeless on the ground.

In the first fright and horror of her situation, Miss Pross passed the body as far from it as she could, and ran down the stairs to call for fruitless help. Happily, she bethought herself of the consequences of what she did, in time to check herself and go back. It was dreadful to go in at the door again; but, she did go in, and even went near it, to get the bonnet and other things that she must wear. These she put on, out on the staircase, first shutting and locking the door and taking away the key. She then sat down on the stairs a few moments to breathe and to cry, and then got up and hurried away.

By good fortune she had a veil on her bonnet, or she could hardly have gone along the streets without being stopped. By good fortune, too, she was naturally so peculiar in appearance as not to show disfigurement like any other woman. She needed both advantages, for the marks of gripping fingers were deep in her face, and her hair was torn, and her dress (hastily composed with unsteady hands) was clutched and dragged a hundred ways.

In crossing the bridge, she dropped the door key in the river. Arriving at the cathedral some few minutes before her escort, and waiting there, she thought, what if the key were already taken in a net, what if it were identified, what if the door were opened and the remains discovered, what if she were stopped at the gate, sent to prison, and charged with murder! In the midst of these fluttering thoughts, the escort appeared, took her in, and took her away.

"Is there any noise in the streets?" she asked him.

"The usual noises," Mr. Cruncher replied; and looked surprised by the question and by her aspect.

"I don't hear you," said Miss Pross. "What do you say?"

It was in vain for Mr. Cruncher to repeat what he said; Miss Pross could not hear him. "So I'll nod my head," thought Mr. Cruncher, amazed, "at all events she'll see that." And she did.

"Is there any noise in the streets now?" asked Miss Pross again, presently.

Again Mr. Cruncher nodded his head.

"I don't hear it."

"Gone deaf in an hour?" said Mr. Cruncher, ruminating, with his mind much disturbed; "wot's come to her?"

"I feel," said Miss Pross, "as if there had been a flash and a crash, and that crash was the last thing I should ever hear in this life."

"Blest if she ain't in a queer condition!" said Mr. Cruncher, more and more disturbed. "Wot can she have been a takin', to keep her courage up? Hark! There's the roll of them dreadful carts! You can hear that, miss?"

"I can hear," said Miss Pross, seeing that he spoke to her, "nothing. O, my good man, there was first a great crash, and then a great stillness, and that stillness seems to be fixed and unchangeable, never to be broken any more as long as my life lasts."

"If she don't hear the roll of those dreadful carts, now very nigh their journey's end," said Mr. Cruncher, glancing over his shoulder, "it's my opinion that indeed she never will hear anything else in this world."

And indeed she never did.

XV. THE FOOTSTEPS DIE OUT FOR EVER

Along the Paris streets, the death-carts rumble, hollow and harsh. Six tumbrils carry the day's wine to La Guillotine. All the devouring and insatiate Monsters imagined since imagination could record itself, are fused in the one realisation, Guillotine. And yet there is not in France, with its rich variety of soil and climate, a blade, a leaf, a root, a sprig, a peppercorn, which will grow to maturity under conditions more certain than those that have produced this horror. Crush humanity out of shape once more, under similar hammers, and it will twist itself into the same tortured forms. Sow the same seed of rapacious license and oppression over again, and it will surely yield the same fruit according to its kind.

Six tumbrils roll along the streets. Change these back again to what they were, thou powerful enchanter, Time, and they shall be seen to be the carriages of absolute monarchs, the equipages of feudal nobles, the toilettes of flaring Jezebels, the churches that are not my father's house but dens of thieves, the huts of millions of starving peasants! No; the great magician who majestically works out the appointed order of the Creator, never reverses his transformations. "If thou be changed into this shape by the will of God," say the seers to the enchanted, in the wise Arabian stories, "then remain so! But, if thou wear this form through mere passing conjuration, then resume thy former aspect!" Changeless and hopeless, the tumbrils roll along.

As the sombre wheels of the six carts go round, they seem to plough up a long crooked furrow among the populace in the streets. Ridges of faces are thrown to this side and to that, and the ploughs go steadily onward. So used are the regular inhabitants of the houses to the spectacle, that in many windows there are no people, and in some the occupation of the hands is not so much as suspended, while the eyes survey the faces in the tumbrils. Here and there, the inmate has visitors to see the sight; then he points his finger, with something of the complacency of a curator or authorised exponent, to this cart and to this, and seems to tell who sat here yesterday, and who there the day before.

Of the riders in the tumbrils, some observe these things, and all things on their last roadside, with an impassive stare; others, with a lingering interest in the ways of life and men. Some, seated with drooping heads, are sunk in silent despair; again, there are some so heedful of their looks that they cast upon the multitude such glances as they have seen in theatres, and in pictures. Several close their eyes, and think, or try to get their straying thoughts together. Only one, and he a miserable creature, of a crazed aspect, is so shattered and made drunk by horror, that he sings, and tries to dance. Not one of the whole number appeals by look or gesture, to the pity of the people.

There is a guard of sundry horsemen riding abreast of the tumbrils, and faces are often turned up to some of them, and they are asked some question. It would seem to be always the same question, for, it is always followed by a press of people towards the third cart. The horsemen abreast of that cart, frequently point out one man in it with their swords. The leading curiosity is, to know which is he; he stands at the back of the tumbril with his head bent down, to converse with a mere girl who sits on the side of the cart, and holds his hand. He has no curiosity or care for the scene about him, and always speaks to the girl. Here and there in the long street of St. Honore, cries are raised against him. If they move him at all, it is only to a quiet smile, as he shakes his hair a little more loosely about his face. He cannot easily touch his face, his arms being bound.

On the steps of a church, awaiting the coming-up of the tumbrils, stands the Spy and prison-sheep. He looks into the first of them: not there. He looks into the second: not there. He already asks himself, "Has he sacrificed me?" when his face clears, as he looks into the third.

"Which is Evremonde?" says a man behind him.

"That. At the back there."

"With his hand in the girl's?"

"Yes."

The man cries, "Down, Evremonde! To the Guillotine all aristocrats! Down, Evremonde!"

"Hush, hush!" the Spy entreats him, timidly.

"And why not, citizen?"

"He is going to pay the forfeit: it will be paid in five minutes more. Let him be at peace."

But the man continuing to exclaim, "Down, Evremonde!" the face of Evremonde is for a moment turned towards him. Evremonde then sees the Spy, and looks attentively at him, and goes his way.

The clocks are on the stroke of three, and the furrow ploughed among the populace is turning round, to come on into the place of execution, and end. The ridges thrown to this side and to that, now crumble in and close behind the last plough as it passes on, for all are following to the Guillotine. In front of it, seated in chairs, as in a garden of public diversion, are a number of women, busily knitting. On one of the fore-most chairs, stands The Vengeance, looking about for her friend.

"Therese!" she cries, in her shrill tones. "Who has seen her? Therese Defarge!"

"She never missed before," says a knitting-woman of the sisterhood.

"No; nor will she miss now," cries The Vengeance, petulantly. "Therese."

"Louder," the woman recommends.

Ay! Louder, Vengeance, much louder, and still she will scarcely hear thee. Louder yet, Vengeance, with a little oath or so added, and yet it will hardly bring her. Send other women up and down to seek her, lingering somewhere; and yet, although the messengers have done dread deeds, it is questionable whether of their own wills they will go far enough to find her!

"Bad Fortune!" cries The Vengeance, stamping her foot in the chair, "and here are the tumbrils! And Evremonde will be despatched in a wink, and she not here! See her knitting in my hand, and her empty chair ready for her. I cry with vexation and disappointment!"

As The Vengeance descends from her elevation to do it, the tumbrils begin to discharge their loads. The ministers of Sainte Guillotine are robed and ready. Crash!—A head is held up, and the knitting- women who scarcely lifted their eyes to look at it a moment ago when it could think and speak, count One.

The second tumbril empties and moves on; the third comes up. Crash!—And the knitting-women, never faltering or pausing in their Work, count Two.

The supposed Evremonde descends, and the seamstress is lifted out next after him. He has not relinquished her patient hand in getting out, but still holds it as he promised. He gently places her with her back to the crashing engine that constantly whirrs up and falls, and she looks into his face and thanks him.

"But for you, dear stranger, I should not be so composed, for I am naturally a poor little thing, faint of heart; nor should I have been able to raise my thoughts to Him who was put to death, that we might have hope and comfort here to-day. I think you were sent to me by Heaven."

"Or you to me," says Sydney Carton. "Keep your eyes upon me, dear child, and mind no other object."

"I mind nothing while I hold your hand. I shall mind nothing when I let it go, if they are rapid."

"They will be rapid. Fear not!"

The two stand in the fast-thinning throng of victims, but they speak as if they were alone. Eye to eye, voice to voice, hand to hand, heart to heart, these two children of the Universal Mother, else so wide apart and differing, have come together on the dark highway, to repair home together, and to rest in her bosom.

"Brave and generous friend, will you let me ask you one last question? I am very ignorant, and it troubles me—just a little."

"Tell me what it is."

"I have a cousin, an only relative and an orphan, like myself, whom I love very dearly. She is five years younger than I, and she lives in a farmer's house in the south country. Poverty parted us, and she knows nothing of my fate—for I cannot write—and if I could, how should I tell her! It is better as it is."

"Yes, yes: better as it is."

"What I have been thinking as we came along, and what I am still thinking now, as I look into your kind strong face which gives me so much support, is this:—If the Republic really does good to the poor, and they come to be less hungry, and in all ways to suffer less, she may live a long time: she may even live to be old."

"What then, my gentle sister?"

"Do you think:" the uncomplaining eyes in which there is so much endurance, fill with tears, and the lips part a little more and tremble: "that it will seem long to me, while I wait for her in the better land where I trust both you and I will be mercifully sheltered?"

"It cannot be, my child; there is no Time there, and no trouble there."

"You comfort me so much! I am so ignorant. Am I to kiss you now? Is the moment come?"

"Yes."

She kisses his lips; he kisses hers; they solemnly bless each other. The spare hand does not tremble as he releases it; nothing worse than a sweet, bright constancy is in the patient face. She goes next before him—is gone; the knitting-women count Twenty-Two.

"I am the Resurrection and the Life, saith the Lord: he that believeth in me, though he were dead, yet shall he live: and whosoever liveth and believeth in me shall never die."

The murmuring of many voices, the upturning of many faces, the pressing on of many footsteps in the outskirts of the crowd, so that it swells forward in a mass, like one great heave of water, all flashes away. Twenty-Three.

* * *

They said of him, about the city that night, that it was the peacefullest man's face ever beheld there. Many added that he looked sublime and prophetic.

One of the most remarkable sufferers by the same axe—a woman—had asked at the foot of the same scaffold, not long before, to be allowed to write down the thoughts that were inspiring her. If he had given any utterance to his, and they were prophetic, they would have been these:

"I see Barsad, and Cly, Defarge, The Vengeance, the Juryman, the Judge, long ranks of the new oppressors who have risen on the destruction of the old, perishing by this retributive instrument, before it shall cease out of its present use. I see a beautiful city and a brilliant people rising from this abyss, and, in their struggles to be truly free, in their triumphs and defeats, through long years to come, I see the evil of this time and of the previous time of which this is the natural birth, gradually making expiation for itself and wearing out.

"I see the lives for which I lay down my life, peaceful, useful, prosperous and happy, in that England which I shall see no more. I see Her with a child upon her bosom, who bears my name. I see her father, aged and bent, but otherwise restored, and faithful to all men in his healing office, and at peace. I see the good old man, so long their friend, in ten years' time enriching them with all he has, and passing tranquilly to his reward.

"I see that I hold a sanctuary in their hearts, and in the hearts of their descendants, generations hence. I see her, an old woman, weeping for me on the anniversary of this day. I see her and her husband, their course done, lying side by side in their last earthly bed, and I know that each was not more honoured and held sacred in the other's soul, than I was in the souls of both.

"I see that child who lay upon her bosom and who bore my name, a man winning his way up in that path of life which once was mine. I see him winning it so well, that my name is made illustrious there by the light of his. I see the blots I threw upon it, faded away. I see him, fore-most of just judges and honoured men, bringing a boy of my name, with a forehead that I know and golden hair, to this place—then fair to look upon, with not a trace of this day's disfigurement—and I hear him tell the child my story, with a tender and a faltering voice.

"It is a far, far better thing that I do, than I have ever done; it is a far, far better rest that I go to than I have ever known."

Great Expectations

CHAPTER I

My father's family name being Pirrip, and my Christian name Philip, my infant tongue could make of both names nothing longer or more explicit than Pip. So, I called myself Pip, and came to be called Pip.

I give Pirrip as my father's family name, on the authority of his tombstone and my sister,—Mrs. Joe Gargery, who married the blacksmith. As I never saw my father or my mother, and never saw any likeness of either of them (for their days were long before the days of photographs), my first fancies regarding what they were like were unreasonably derived from their tombstones. The shape of the letters on my father's, gave me an odd idea that he was a square, stout, dark man, with curly black hair. From the character and turn of the inscription, "Also Georgiana Wife of the Above," I drew a childish conclusion that my mother was freckled and sickly. To five little stone lozenges, each about a foot and a half long, which were arranged in a neat row beside their grave, and were sacred to the memory of five little brothers of mine,—who gave up trying to get a living, exceedingly early in that universal struggle,—I am indebted for a belief I religiously entertained that they had all been born on their backs with their hands in their trousers-pockets, and had never taken them out in this state of existence.

Ours was the marsh country, down by the river, within, as the river wound, twenty miles of the sea. My first most vivid and broad impression of the identity of things seems to me to have been gained on a memorable raw afternoon towards evening. At such a time I found out for certain that this bleak place overgrown with nettles was the churchyard; and that Philip Pirrip, late of this parish, and also Georgiana wife of the above, were dead and buried; and that Alexander, Bartholomew, Abraham, Tobias, and Roger, infant children of the aforesaid, were also dead and buried; and that the dark flat wilderness beyond the churchyard, intersected with dikes and mounds and gates, with scattered cattle feeding on it, was the marshes; and that the low leaden line beyond was the river; and that the distant savage lair from which the wind was rushing was the sea; and that the small bundle of shivers growing afraid of it all and beginning to cry, was Pip.

"Hold your noise!" cried a terrible voice, as a man started up from among the graves at the side of the church porch. "Keep still, you little devil, or I'll cut your throat!"

A fearful man, all in coarse gray, with a great iron on his leg. A man with no hat, and with broken shoes, and with an old rag tied round his head. A man who had been soaked in water, and smothered in mud, and lamed by stones, and cut by flints, and stung by nettles, and torn by briars; who limped, and shivered, and glared, and growled; and whose teeth chattered in his head as he seized me by the chin.

"Oh! Don't cut my throat, sir," I pleaded in terror. "Pray don't do it, sir."

"Tell us your name!" said the man. "Quick!"

"Pip, sir."

"Once more," said the man, staring at me. "Give it mouth!"

"Pip. Pip, sir."

"Show us where you live," said the man. "Pint out the place!"

I pointed to where our village lay, on the flat in-shore among the alder-trees and pollards, a mile or more from the church.

The man, after looking at me for a moment, turned me upside down, and emptied my pockets. There was nothing in them but a piece of bread. When the church came to itself,—for he was so sudden and strong that he made it go head over heels before me, and I saw the steeple under my feet,—when the church came to itself, I say, I was seated on a high tombstone, trembling while he ate the bread ravenously.

"You young dog," said the man, licking his lips, "what fat cheeks you ha' got."

I believe they were fat, though I was at that time undersized for my years, and not strong.

"Darn me if I couldn't eat 'em," said the man, with a threatening shake of his head, "and if I han't half a mind to't!"

I earnestly expressed my hope that he wouldn't, and held tighter to the tombstone on which he had put me; partly, to keep myself upon it; partly, to keep myself from crying.

"Now lookee here!" said the man. "Where's your mother?"

"There, sir!" said I.

He started, made a short run, and stopped and looked over his shoulder.

"There, sir!" I timidly explained. "Also Georgiana. That's my mother."

"Oh!" said he, coming back. "And is that your father alonger your mother?"

"Yes, sir," said I; "him too; late of this parish."

"Ha!" he muttered then, considering. "Who d'ye live with,—supposin' you're kindly let to live, which I han't made up my mind about?"

"My sister, sir,—Mrs. Joe Gargery,—wife of Joe Gargery, the blacksmith, sir."

"Blacksmith, eh?" said he. And looked down at his leg.

After darkly looking at his leg and me several times, he came closer to my tombstone, took me by both arms, and tilted me back as far as he could hold me; so that his eyes looked most powerfully down into mine, and mine looked most helplessly up into his.

"Now lookee here," he said, "the question being whether you're to be let to live. You know what a file is?"

"Yes, sir."

"And you know what wittles is?"

"Yes, sir."

After each question he tilted me over a little more, so as to give me a greater sense of helplessness and danger.

"You get me a file." He tilted me again. "And you get me wittles." He tilted me again. "You bring 'em both to me." He tilted me again. "Or I'll have your heart and liver out." He tilted me again.

I was dreadfully frightened, and so giddy that I clung to him with both hands, and said, "If you would kindly please to let me keep upright, sir, perhaps I shouldn't be sick, and perhaps I could attend more."

He gave me a most tremendous dip and roll, so that the church jumped over its own weathercock. Then, he held me by the arms, in an upright position on the top of the stone, and went on in these fearful terms:—

"You bring me, to-morrow morning early, that file and them wittles. You bring the lot to me, at that old Battery over yonder. You do it, and you never dare to say a word or dare to make a sign concerning your having seen such a person as me, or any person sumever, and you shall be let to live. You fail, or you go from my words in any partickler, no matter how small it is, and your heart and your liver shall be tore out, roasted, and ate. Now, I ain't alone, as you may think I am. There's a young man hid with me, in comparison with which young man I am a Angel. That young man hears the words I speak. That young man has a secret way pecooliar to himself, of getting at a boy, and at his heart, and at his liver. It is in wain for a boy to attempt to hide himself from that young man. A boy may lock his door, may be warm in bed, may tuck himself up, may draw the clothes over his head, may think himself comfortable and safe, but that young man will softly creep and creep his way to him and tear him open. I am a keeping that young man from harming of you at the present moment, with great difficulty. I find it wery hard to hold that young man off of your inside. Now, what do you say?"

I said that I would get him the file, and I would get him what broken bits of food I could, and I would come to him at the Battery, early in the morning.

"Say Lord strike you dead if you don't!" said the man.

I said so, and he took me down.

"Now," he pursued, "you remember what you've undertook, and you remember that young man, and you get home!"

"Goo-good night, sir," I faltered.

"Much of that!" said he, glancing about him over the cold wet flat. "I wish I was a frog. Or a eel!"

At the same time, he hugged his shuddering body in both his arms,—clasping himself, as if to hold himself together,—and limped towards the low church wall. As I saw him go, picking his way among the nettles, and among the brambles that bound the green mounds, he looked in my young eyes as if he were eluding the hands of the dead people, stretching up cautiously out of their graves, to get a twist upon his ankle and pull him in.

When he came to the low church wall, he got over it, like a man whose legs were numbed and stiff, and then turned round to look for me. When I saw him turning, I set my face towards home, and made the best use of my legs. But presently I looked over my shoulder, and saw him going on again towards the river, still hugging himself in both arms, and picking his way with his sore feet among the great stones dropped into the marshes here and there, for stepping-places when the rains were heavy or the tide was in.

The marshes were just a long black horizontal line then, as I stopped to look after him; and the river was just another horizontal line, not nearly so broad nor yet so black;

and the sky was just a row of long angry red lines and dense black lines intermixed. On the edge of the river I could faintly make out the only two black things in all the prospect that seemed to be standing upright; one of these was the beacon by which the sailors steered,—like an unhooped cask upon a pole,—an ugly thing when you were near it; the other, a gibbet, with some chains hanging to it which had once held a pirate. The man was limping on towards this latter, as if he were the pirate come to life, and come down, and going back to hook himself up again. It gave me a terrible turn when I thought so; and as I saw the cattle lifting their heads to gaze after him, I wondered whether they thought so too. I looked all round for the horrible young man, and could see no signs of him. But now I was frightened again, and ran home without stopping.

CHAPTER II

My sister, Mrs. Joe Gargery, was more than twenty years older than I, and had established a great reputation with herself and the neighbors because she had brought me up "by hand." Having at that time to find out for myself what the expression meant, and knowing her to have a hard and heavy hand, and to be much in the habit of laying it upon her husband as well as upon me, I supposed that Joe Gargery and I were both brought up by hand.

She was not a good-looking woman, my sister; and I had a general impression that she must have made Joe Gargery marry her by hand. Joe was a fair man, with curls of flaxen hair on each side of his smooth face, and with eyes of such a very undecided blue that they seemed to have somehow got mixed with their own whites. He was a mild, good-natured, sweet-tempered, easy-going, foolish, dear fellow,—a sort of Hercules in strength, and also in weakness.

My sister, Mrs. Joe, with black hair and eyes, had such a prevailing redness of skin that I sometimes used to wonder whether it was possible she washed herself with a nutmeg-grater instead of soap. She was tall and bony, and almost always wore a coarse apron, fastened over her figure behind with two loops, and having a square impregnable bib in front, that was stuck full of pins and needles. She made it a powerful merit in herself, and a strong reproach against Joe, that she wore this apron so much. Though I really see no reason why she should have worn it at all; or why, if she did wear it at all, she should not have taken it off, every day of her life.

Joe's forge adjoined our house, which was a wooden house, as many of the dwellings in our country were,—most of them, at that time. When I ran home from the churchyard, the forge was shut up, and Joe was sitting alone in the kitchen. Joe and I being fellow-sufferers, and having confidences as such, Joe imparted a confidence to me, the moment I raised the latch of the door and peeped in at him opposite to it, sitting in the chimney corner.

"Mrs. Joe has been out a dozen times, looking for you, Pip. And she's out now, making it a baker's dozen."

"Is she?"

"Yes, Pip," said Joe; "and what's worse, she's got Tickler with her."

At this dismal intelligence, I twisted the only button on my waistcoat round and round, and looked in great depression at the fire. Tickler was a wax-ended piece of cane, worn smooth by collision with my tickled frame.

"She sot down," said Joe, "and she got up, and she made a grab at Tickler, and she Ram-paged out. That's what she did," said Joe, slowly clearing the fire between the lower bars with the poker, and looking at it; "she Ram-paged out, Pip."

"Has she been gone long, Joe?" I always treated him as a larger species of child, and as no more than my equal.

"Well," said Joe, glancing up at the Dutch clock, "she's been on the Ram-page, this last spell, about five minutes, Pip. She's a coming! Get behind the door, old chap, and have the jack-towel betwixt you."

I took the advice. My sister, Mrs. Joe, throwing the door wide open, and finding an obstruction behind it, immediately divined the cause, and applied Tickler to its further investigation. She concluded by throwing me—I often served as a connubial missile—at Joe, who, glad to get hold of me on any terms, passed me on into the chimney and quietly fenced me up there with his great leg.

"Where have you been, you young monkey?" said Mrs. Joe, stamping her foot. "Tell me directly what you've been doing to wear me away with fret and fright and worrit, or I'd have you out of that corner if you was fifty Pips, and he was five hundred Gargerys."

"I have only been to the churchyard," said I, from my stool, crying and rubbing myself.

"Churchyard!" repeated my sister. "If it warn't for me you'd have been to the churchyard long ago, and stayed there. Who brought you up by hand?"

"You did," said I.

"And why did I do it, I should like to know?" exclaimed my sister.

I whimpered, "I don't know."

"I don't!" said my sister. "I'd never do it again! I know that. I may truly say I've never had this apron of mine off since born you were. It's bad enough to be a blacksmith's wife (and him a Gargery) without being your mother."

My thoughts strayed from that question as I looked disconsolately at the fire. For the fugitive out on the marshes with the ironed leg, the mysterious young man, the file, the food, and the dreadful pledge I was under to commit a larceny on those sheltering premises, rose before me in the avenging coals.

"Hah!" said Mrs. Joe, restoring Tickler to his station. "Churchyard, indeed! You may well say churchyard, you two." One of us, by the by, had not said it at all. "You'll drive me to the churchyard betwixt you, one of these days, and O, a pr-r-recious pair you'd be without me!"

As she applied herself to set the tea-things, Joe peeped down at me over his leg, as if he were mentally casting me and himself up, and calculating what kind of pair we practically should make, under the grievous circumstances foreshadowed. After that, he sat feeling his right-side flaxen curls and whisker, and following Mrs. Joe about with his blue eyes, as his manner always was at squally times.

My sister had a trenchant way of cutting our bread and butter for us, that never varied. First, with her left hand she jammed the loaf hard and fast against her bib,—

where it sometimes got a pin into it, and sometimes a needle, which we afterwards got into our mouths. Then she took some butter (not too much) on a knife and spread it on the loaf, in an apothecary kind of way, as if she were making a plaster,—using both sides of the knife with a slapping dexterity, and trimming and moulding the butter off round the crust. Then, she gave the knife a final smart wipe on the edge of the plaster, and then sawed a very thick round off the loaf: which she finally, before separating from the loaf, hewed into two halves, of which Joe got one, and I the other.

On the present occasion, though I was hungry, I dared not eat my slice. I felt that I must have something in reserve for my dreadful acquaintance, and his ally the still more dreadful young man. I knew Mrs. Joe's housekeeping to be of the strictest kind, and that my larcenous researches might find nothing available in the safe. Therefore I resolved to put my hunk of bread and butter down the leg of my trousers.

The effort of resolution necessary to the achievement of this purpose I found to be quite awful. It was as if I had to make up my mind to leap from the top of a high house, or plunge into a great depth of water. And it was made the more difficult by the unconscious Joe. In our already-mentioned freemasonry as fellow-sufferers, and in his good-natured companionship with me, it was our evening habit to compare the way we bit through our slices, by silently holding them up to each other's admiration now and then,—which stimulated us to new exertions. To-night, Joe several times invited me, by the display of his fast diminishing slice, to enter upon our usual friendly competition; but he found me, each time, with my yellow mug of tea on one knee, and my untouched bread and butter on the other. At last, I desperately considered that the thing I contemplated must be done, and that it had best be done in the least improbable manner consistent with the circumstances. I took advantage of a moment when Joe had just looked at me, and got my bread and butter down my leg.

Joe was evidently made uncomfortable by what he supposed to be my loss of appetite, and took a thoughtful bite out of his slice, which he didn't seem to enjoy. He turned it about in his mouth much longer than usual, pondering over it a good deal, and after all gulped it down like a pill. He was about to take another bite, and had just got his head on one side for a good purchase on it, when his eye fell on me, and he saw that my bread and butter was gone.

The wonder and consternation with which Joe stopped on the threshold of his bite and stared at me, were too evident to escape my sister's observation.

"What's the matter now?" said she, smartly, as she put down her cup.

"I say, you know!" muttered Joe, shaking his head at me in very serious remonstrance. "Pip, old chap! You'll do yourself a mischief. It'll stick somewhere. You can't have chawed it, Pip."

"What's the matter now?" repeated my sister, more sharply than before.

"If you can cough any trifle on it up, Pip, I'd recommend you to do it," said Joe, all aghast. "Manners is manners, but still your elth's your elth."

By this time, my sister was quite desperate, so she pounced on Joe, and, taking him by the two whiskers, knocked his head for a little while against the wall behind him, while I sat in the corner, looking guiltily on.

"Now, perhaps you'll mention what's the matter," said my sister, out of breath, "you staring great stuck pig."

Joe looked at her in a helpless way, then took a helpless bite, and looked at me again.

"You know, Pip," said Joe, solemnly, with his last bite in his cheek, and speaking in a confidential voice, as if we two were quite alone, "you and me is always friends, and I'd be the last to tell upon you, any time. But such a——" he moved his chair and looked about the floor between us, and then again at me—"such a most uncommon Bolt as that!"

"Been bolting his food, has he?" cried my sister.

"You know, old chap," said Joe, looking at me, and not at Mrs. Joe, with his bite still in his cheek, "I Bolted, myself, when I was your age—frequent—and as a boy I've been among a many Bolters; but I never see your Bolting equal yet, Pip, and it's a mercy you ain't Bolted dead."

My sister made a dive at me, and fished me up by the hair, saying nothing more than the awful words, "You come along and be dosed."

Some medical beast had revived Tar-water in those days as a fine medicine, and Mrs. Joe always kept a supply of it in the cupboard; having a belief in its virtues correspondent to its nastiness. At the best of times, so much of this elixir was administered to me as a choice restorative, that I was conscious of going about, smelling like a new fence. On this particular evening the urgency of my case demanded a pint of this mixture, which was poured down my throat, for my greater comfort, while Mrs. Joe held my head under her arm, as a boot would be held in a bootjack. Joe got off with half a pint; but was made to swallow that (much to his disturbance, as he sat slowly munching and meditating before the fire), "because he had had a turn." Judging from myself, I should say he certainly had a turn afterwards, if he had had none before.

Conscience is a dreadful thing when it accuses man or boy; but when, in the case of a boy, that secret burden co-operates with another secret burden down the leg of his trousers, it is (as I can testify) a great punishment. The guilty knowledge that I was going to rob Mrs. Joe—I never thought I was going to rob Joe, for I never thought of any of the housekeeping property as his—united to the necessity of always keeping one hand on my bread and butter as I sat, or when I was ordered about the kitchen on any small errand, almost drove me out of my mind. Then, as the marsh winds made the fire glow and flare, I thought I heard the voice outside, of the man with the iron on his leg who had sworn me to secrecy, declaring that he couldn't and wouldn't starve until to-morrow, but must be fed now. At other times, I thought, What if the young man who was with so much difficulty restrained from imbruing his hands in me should yield to a constitutional impatience, or should mistake the time, and should think himself accredited to my heart and liver to-night, instead of to-morrow! If ever anybody's hair stood on end with terror, mine must have done so then. But, perhaps, nobody's ever did?

It was Christmas Eve, and I had to stir the pudding for next day, with a copper-stick, from seven to eight by the Dutch clock. I tried it with the load upon my leg (and that made me think afresh of the man with the load on his leg), and found the tendency of exercise to bring the bread and butter out at my ankle, quite unmanageable. Happily I slipped away, and deposited that part of my conscience in my garret bedroom.

"Hark!" said I, when I had done my stirring, and was taking a final warm in the chimney corner before being sent up to bed; "was that great guns, Joe?"

"Ah!" said Joe. "There's another conwict off."

"What does that mean, Joe?" said I.

Mrs. Joe, who always took explanations upon herself, said, snappishly, "Escaped. Escaped." Administering the definition like Tar-water.

While Mrs. Joe sat with her head bending over her needlework, I put my mouth into the forms of saying to Joe, "What's a convict?" Joe put his mouth into the forms of returning such a highly elaborate answer, that I could make out nothing of it but the single word "Pip."

"There was a conwict off last night," said Joe, aloud, "after sunset-gun. And they fired warning of him. And now it appears they're firing warning of another."

"Who's firing?" said I.

"Drat that boy," interposed my sister, frowning at me over her work, "what a questioner he is. Ask no questions, and you'll be told no lies."

It was not very polite to herself, I thought, to imply that I should be told lies by her even if I did ask questions. But she never was polite unless there was company.

At this point Joe greatly augmented my curiosity by taking the utmost pains to open his mouth very wide, and to put it into the form of a word that looked to me like "sulks." Therefore, I naturally pointed to Mrs. Joe, and put my mouth into the form of saying, "her?" But Joe wouldn't hear of that, at all, and again opened his mouth very wide, and shook the form of a most emphatic word out of it. But I could make nothing of the word.

"Mrs. Joe," said I, as a last resort, "I should like to know—if you wouldn't much mind—where the firing comes from?"

"Lord bless the boy!" exclaimed my sister, as if she didn't quite mean that but rather the contrary. "From the Hulks!"

"Oh-h!" said I, looking at Joe. "Hulks!"

Joe gave a reproachful cough, as much as to say, "Well, I told you so."

"And please, what's Hulks?" said I.

"That's the way with this boy!" exclaimed my sister, pointing me out with her needle and thread, and shaking her head at me. "Answer him one question, and he'll ask you a dozen directly. Hulks are prison-ships, right 'cross th' meshes." We always used that name for marshes, in our country.

"I wonder who's put into prison-ships, and why they're put there?" said I, in a general way, and with quiet desperation.

It was too much for Mrs. Joe, who immediately rose. "I tell you what, young fellow," said she, "I didn't bring you up by hand to badger people's lives out. It would be blame to me and not praise, if I had. People are put in the Hulks because they murder, and because they rob, and forge, and do all sorts of bad; and they always begin by asking questions. Now, you get along to bed!"

I was never allowed a candle to light me to bed, and, as I went up stairs in the dark, with my head tingling,—from Mrs. Joe's thimble having played the tambourine upon it, to accompany her last words,—I felt fearfully sensible of the great convenience that the hulks were handy for me. I was clearly on my way there. I had begun by asking questions, and I was going to rob Mrs. Joe.

Since that time, which is far enough away now, I have often thought that few people know what secrecy there is in the young under terror. No matter how unreasonable the terror, so that it be terror. I was in mortal terror of the young man who wanted my heart and liver; I was in mortal terror of my interlocutor with the iron leg; I was in mortal terror of myself, from whom an awful promise had been extracted; I had no hope of deliverance through my all-powerful sister, who repulsed me at every turn; I am afraid to think of what I might have done on requirement, in the secrecy of my terror.

If I slept at all that night, it was only to imagine myself drifting down the river on a strong spring-tide, to the Hulks; a ghostly pirate calling out to me through a speaking-trumpet, as I passed the gibbet-station, that I had better come ashore and be hanged there at once, and not put it off. I was afraid to sleep, even if I had been inclined, for I knew that at the first faint dawn of morning I must rob the pantry. There was no doing it in the night, for there was no getting a light by easy friction then; to have got one I must have struck it out of flint and steel, and have made a noise like the very pirate himself rattling his chains.

As soon as the great black velvet pall outside my little window was shot with gray, I got up and went down stairs; every board upon the way, and every crack in every board calling after me, "Stop thief!" and "Get up, Mrs. Joe!" In the pantry, which was far more abundantly supplied than usual, owing to the season, I was very much alarmed by a hare hanging up by the heels, whom I rather thought I caught when my back was half turned, winking. I had no time for verification, no time for selection, no time for anything, for I had no time to spare. I stole some bread, some rind of cheese, about half a jar of mincemeat (which I tied up in my pocket-handkerchief with my last night's slice), some brandy from a stone bottle (which I decanted into a glass bottle I had secretly used for making that intoxicating fluid, Spanish-liquorice-water, up in my room: diluting the stone bottle from a jug in the kitchen cupboard), a meat bone with very little on it, and a beautiful round compact pork pie. I was nearly going away without the pie, but I was tempted to mount upon a shelf, to look what it was that was put away so carefully in a covered earthen ware dish in a corner, and I found it was the pie, and I took it in the hope that it was not intended for early use, and would not be missed for some time.

There was a door in the kitchen, communicating with the forge; I unlocked and unbolted that door, and got a file from among Joe's tools. Then I put the fastenings as I had found them, opened the door at which I had entered when I ran home last night, shut it, and ran for the misty marshes.

CHAPTER III

It was a rimy morning, and very damp. I had seen the damp lying on the outside of my little window, as if some goblin had been crying there all night, and using the window for a pocket-handkerchief. Now, I saw the damp lying on the bare hedges and spare grass, like a coarser sort of spiders' webs; hanging itself from twig to twig and blade to blade. On every rail and gate, wet lay clammy, and the marsh mist was so thick, that the wooden finger on the post directing people to our village—a direction which they never accepted, for they never came there—was invisible to me until I was quite close under it. Then, as I looked up at it, while it dripped, it seemed to my oppressed conscience like a phantom devoting me to the Hulks.

The mist was heavier yet when I got out upon the marshes, so that instead of my running at everything, everything seemed to run at me. This was very disagreeable to a guilty mind. The gates and dikes and banks came bursting at me through the mist, as if they cried as plainly as could be, "A boy with Somebody's else's pork pie! Stop him!" The cattle came upon me with like suddenness, staring out of their eyes, and steaming out of their nostrils, "Halloa, young thief!" One black ox, with a white cravat on,—who even had to my awakened conscience something of a clerical air,—fixed me so obstinately with his eyes, and moved his blunt head round in such an accusatory manner as I moved round, that I blubbered out to him, "I couldn't help it, sir! It wasn't for myself I took it!" Upon which he put down his head, blew a cloud of smoke out of his nose, and vanished with a kick-up of his hind-legs and a flourish of his tail.

All this time, I was getting on towards the river; but however fast I went, I couldn't warm my feet, to which the damp cold seemed riveted, as the iron was riveted to the leg of the man I was running to meet. I knew my way to the Battery, pretty straight, for I had been down there on a Sunday with Joe, and Joe, sitting on an old gun, had told me that when I was 'prentice to him, regularly bound, we would have such Larks there! However, in the confusion of the mist, I found myself at last too far to the right, and consequently had to try back along the river-side, on the bank of loose stones above the mud and the stakes that staked the tide out. Making my way along here with all despatch, I had just crossed a ditch which I knew to be very near the Battery, and had just scrambled up the mound beyond the ditch, when I saw the man sitting before me. His back was towards me, and he had his arms folded, and was nodding forward, heavy with sleep.

I thought he would be more glad if I came upon him with his breakfast, in that unexpected manner, so I went forward softly and touched him on the shoulder. He instantly jumped up, and it was not the same man, but another man!

And yet this man was dressed in coarse gray, too, and had a great iron on his leg, and was lame, and hoarse, and cold, and was everything that the other man was; except that he had not the same face, and had a flat broad-brimmed low-crowned felt hat on. All this I saw in a moment, for I had only a moment to see it in: he swore an oath at me, made a hit at me,—it was a round weak blow that missed me and almost knocked himself down, for it made him stumble,—and then he ran into the mist, stumbling twice as he went, and I lost him.

"It's the young man!" I thought, feeling my heart shoot as I identified him. I dare say I should have felt a pain in my liver, too, if I had known where it was.

I was soon at the Battery after that, and there was the right Man,—hugging himself and limping to and fro, as if he had never all night left off hugging and limping,—waiting for me. He was awfully cold, to be sure. I half expected to see him drop down before my face and die of deadly cold. His eyes looked so awfully hungry too, that when I handed him the file and he laid it down on the grass, it occurred to me he would have tried to eat it, if he had not seen my bundle. He did not turn me upside down this time to get at what I had, but left me right side upwards while I opened the bundle and emptied my pockets.

"What's in the bottle, boy?" said he.

"Brandy," said I.

He was already handing mincemeat down his throat in the most curious manner,—more like a man who was putting it away somewhere in a violent hurry, than a man who was eating it,—but he left off to take some of the liquor. He shivered all the while so violently, that it was quite as much as he could do to keep the neck of the bottle between his teeth, without biting it off.

"I think you have got the ague," said I.

"I'm much of your opinion, boy," said he.

"It's bad about here," I told him. "You've been lying out on the meshes, and they're dreadful aguish. Rheumatic too."

"I'll eat my breakfast afore they're the death of me," said he. "I'd do that, if I was going to be strung up to that there gallows as there is over there, directly afterwards. I'll beat the shivers so far, I'll bet you."

He was gobbling mincemeat, meatbone, bread, cheese, and pork pie, all at once: staring distrustfully while he did so at the mist all round us, and often stopping—even stopping his jaws—to listen. Some real or fancied sound, some clink upon the river or breathing of beast upon the marsh, now gave him a start, and he said, suddenly,—

"You're not a deceiving imp? You brought no one with you?"

"No, sir! No!"

"Nor giv' no one the office to follow you?"

"No!"

"Well," said he, "I believe you. You'd be but a fierce young hound indeed, if at your time of life you could help to hunt a wretched warmint hunted as near death and dunghill as this poor wretched warmint is!"

Something clicked in his throat as if he had works in him like a clock, and was going to strike. And he smeared his ragged rough sleeve over his eyes.

Pitying his desolation, and watching him as he gradually settled down upon the pie, I made bold to say, "I am glad you enjoy it."

"Did you speak?"

"I said I was glad you enjoyed it."

"Thankee, my boy. I do."

I had often watched a large dog of ours eating his food; and I now noticed a decided similarity between the dog's way of eating, and the man's. The man took strong sharp sudden bites, just like the dog. He swallowed, or rather snapped up, every mouthful, too soon and too fast; and he looked sideways here and there while he ate, as if he thought there was danger in every direction of somebody's coming to take the pie away. He was altogether too unsettled in his mind over it, to appreciate it comfortably I thought, or to have anybody to dine with him, without making a chop with his jaws at the visitor. In all of which particulars he was very like the dog.

"I am afraid you won't leave any of it for him," said I, timidly; after a silence during which I had hesitated as to the politeness of making the remark. "There's no more to be got where that came from." It was the certainty of this fact that impelled me to offer the hint.

"Leave any for him? Who's him?" said my friend, stopping in his crunching of pie-crust.

"The young man. That you spoke of. That was hid with you."

"Oh ah!" he returned, with something like a gruff laugh. "Him? Yes, yes! He don't want no wittles."

"I thought he looked as if he did," said I.

The man stopped eating, and regarded me with the keenest scrutiny and the greatest surprise.

"Looked? When?"

"Just now."

"Where?"

"Yonder," said I, pointing; "over there, where I found him nodding asleep, and thought it was you."

He held me by the collar and stared at me so, that I began to think his first idea about cutting my throat had revived.

"Dressed like you, you know, only with a hat," I explained, trembling; "and— and"—I was very anxious to put this delicately—"and with—the same reason for wanting to borrow a file. Didn't you hear the cannon last night?"

"Then there was firing!" he said to himself.

"I wonder you shouldn't have been sure of that," I returned, "for we heard it up at home, and that's farther away, and we were shut in besides."

"Why, see now!" said he. "When a man's alone on these flats, with a light head and a light stomach, perishing of cold and want, he hears nothin' all night, but guns firing, and voices calling. Hears? He sees the soldiers, with their red coats lighted up by the torches carried afore, closing in round him. Hears his number called, hears himself challenged, hears the rattle of the muskets, hears the orders 'Make ready! Present! Cover him steady, men!' and is laid hands on—and there's nothin'! Why, if I see one pursuing party last night—coming up in order, Damn 'em, with their tramp, tramp—I see a hundred. And as to firing! Why, I see the mist shake with the cannon, arter it was broad day,—But this man"; he had said all the rest, as if he had forgotten my being there; "did you notice anything in him?"

"He had a badly bruised face," said I, recalling what I hardly knew I knew.

"Not here?" exclaimed the man, striking his left cheek mercilessly, with the flat of his hand.

"Yes, there!"

"Where is he?" He crammed what little food was left, into the breast of his gray jacket. "Show me the way he went. I'll pull him down, like a bloodhound. Curse this iron on my sore leg! Give us hold of the file, boy."

I indicated in what direction the mist had shrouded the other man, and he looked up at it for an instant. But he was down on the rank wet grass, filing at his iron like a madman, and not minding me or minding his own leg, which had an old chafe upon it and was bloody, but which he handled as roughly as if it had no more feeling in it than the file. I was very much afraid of him again, now that he had worked himself into this fierce hurry, and I was likewise very much afraid of keeping away from home any longer. I told him I must go, but he took no notice, so I thought the best thing I could do was to slip off. The last I saw of him, his head was bent over his knee and he was working hard at his fetter, muttering impatient imprecations at it and at his leg. The last I heard of him, I stopped in the mist to listen, and the file was still going.

CHAPTER IV

I fully expected to find a Constable in the kitchen, waiting to take me up. But not only was there no Constable there, but no discovery had yet been made of the robbery. Mrs. Joe was prodigiously busy in getting the house ready for the festivities of the day, and Joe had been put upon the kitchen doorstep to keep him out of the dust-pan,—an article into which his destiny always led him, sooner or later, when my sister was vigorously reaping the floors of her establishment.

"And where the deuce ha' you been?" was Mrs. Joe's Christmas salutation, when I and my conscience showed ourselves.

I said I had been down to hear the Carols. "Ah! well!" observed Mrs. Joe. "You might ha' done worse." Not a doubt of that I thought.

"Perhaps if I warn't a blacksmith's wife, and (what's the same thing) a slave with her apron never off, I should have been to hear the Carols," said Mrs. Joe. "I'm rather partial to Carols, myself, and that's the best of reasons for my never hearing any."

Joe, who had ventured into the kitchen after me as the dustpan had retired before us, drew the back of his hand across his nose with a conciliatory air, when Mrs. Joe darted a look at him, and, when her eyes were withdrawn, secretly crossed his two forefingers, and exhibited them to me, as our token that Mrs. Joe was in a cross temper. This was so much her normal state, that Joe and I would often, for weeks together, be, as to our fingers, like monumental Crusaders as to their legs.

We were to have a superb dinner, consisting of a leg of pickled pork and greens, and a pair of roast stuffed fowls. A handsome mince-pie had been made yesterday morning (which accounted for the mincemeat not being missed), and the pudding was already on the boil. These extensive arrangements occasioned us to be cut off unceremoniously in respect of breakfast; "for I ain't," said Mrs. Joe,—"I ain't a going to have no formal cramming and busting and washing up now, with what I've got before me, I promise you!"

So, we had our slices served out, as if we were two thousand troops on a forced march instead of a man and boy at home; and we took gulps of milk and water, with apologetic countenances, from a jug on the dresser. In the meantime, Mrs. Joe put clean white curtains up, and tacked a new flowered flounce across the wide chimney to replace the old one, and uncovered the little state parlor across the passage, which was never uncovered at any other time, but passed the rest of the year in a cool haze of silver paper, which even extended to the four little white crockery poodles on the mantel-shelf, each with a black nose and a basket of flowers in his mouth, and each the counterpart of the other. Mrs. Joe was a very clean housekeeper, but had an exquisite art of making her cleanliness more uncomfortable and unacceptable than dirt itself. Cleanliness is next to Godliness, and some people do the same by their religion.

My sister, having so much to do, was going to church vicariously, that is to say, Joe and I were going. In his working—clothes, Joe was a well-knit characteristic-looking blacksmith; in his holiday clothes, he was more like a scarecrow in good circumstances, than anything else. Nothing that he wore then fitted him or seemed to belong to him; and everything that he wore then grazed him. On the present festive occasion he emerged from his room, when the blithe bells were going, the picture of misery, in a full suit of Sunday penitentials. As to me, I think my sister must have had some general idea that I was a young offender whom an Accoucheur Policeman had taken up (on my birthday) and delivered over to her, to be dealt with according to the outraged majesty of the law. I was always treated as if I had insisted on being born in opposition to the dictates of reason, religion, and morality, and against the dissuading arguments of my best friends. Even when I was taken to have a new suit of clothes, the tailor had orders to make them like a kind of Reformatory, and on no account to let me have the free use of my limbs.

Joe and I going to church, therefore, must have been a moving spectacle for compassionate minds. Yet, what I suffered outside was nothing to what I underwent within. The terrors that had assailed me whenever Mrs. Joe had gone near the pantry, or out of the room, were only to be equalled by the remorse with which my mind dwelt on what my hands had done. Under the weight of my wicked secret, I pondered whether the Church would be powerful enough to shield me from the vengeance of the terrible young man, if I divulged to that establishment. I conceived the idea that the time when the banns were read and when the clergyman said, "Ye are now to declare it!" would be the time for me to rise and propose a private conference in the vestry. I am far from being sure that I might not have astonished our small congregation by resorting to this extreme measure, but for its being Christmas Day and no Sunday.

Mr. Wopsle, the clerk at church, was to dine with us; and Mr. Hubble the wheelwright and Mrs. Hubble; and Uncle Pumblechook (Joe's uncle, but Mrs. Joe appropriated him), who was a well-to-do cornchandler in the nearest town, and drove his own chaise-cart. The dinner hour was half-past one. When Joe and I got home, we found the table laid, and Mrs. Joe dressed, and the dinner dressing, and the front door unlocked (it never was at any other time) for the company to enter by, and everything most splendid. And still, not a word of the robbery.

The time came, without bringing with it any relief to my feelings, and the company came. Mr. Wopsle, united to a Roman nose and a large shining bald forehead, had a deep voice which he was uncommonly proud of; indeed it was understood among his acquaintance that if you could only give him his head, he would read the clergyman into fits; he himself confessed that if the Church was "thrown open," meaning to competition, he would not despair of making his mark in it. The Church not being "thrown open," he was, as I have said, our clerk. But he punished the Amens tremendously; and when he gave out the psalm,—always giving the whole verse,— he looked all round the congregation first, as much as to say, "You have heard my friend overhead; oblige me with your opinion of this style!"

I opened the door to the company,—making believe that it was a habit of ours to open that door,—and I opened it first to Mr. Wopsle, next to Mr. and Mrs. Hubble, and last of all to Uncle Pumblechook. N.B. I was not allowed to call him uncle, under the severest penalties.

"Mrs. Joe," said Uncle Pumblechook, a large hard-breathing middle-aged slow man, with a mouth like a fish, dull staring eyes, and sandy hair standing upright on his head, so that he looked as if he had just been all but choked, and had that moment come to, "I have brought you as the compliments of the season—I have brought you, Mum, a bottle of sherry wine—and I have brought you, Mum, a bottle of port wine."

Every Christmas Day he presented himself, as a profound novelty, with exactly the same words, and carrying the two bottles like dumb-bells. Every Christmas Day, Mrs. Joe replied, as she now replied, "O, Un—cle Pum-ble—chook! This is kind!" Every Christmas Day, he retorted, as he now retorted, "It's no more than your merits. And now are you all bobbish, and how's Sixpennorth of halfpence?" meaning me.

We dined on these occasions in the kitchen, and adjourned, for the nuts and oranges and apples to the parlor; which was a change very like Joe's change from his working-clothes to his Sunday dress. My sister was uncommonly lively on the present occasion, and indeed was generally more gracious in the society of Mrs. Hubble than in other company. I remember Mrs. Hubble as a little curly sharp-edged person in sky-blue, who held a conventionally juvenile position, because she had married Mr. Hubble,—I don't know at what remote period,—when she was much younger than he. I remember Mr Hubble as a tough, high-shouldered, stooping old man, of a sawdusty fragrance, with his legs extraordinarily wide apart: so that in my short days I always saw some miles of open country between them when I met him coming up the lane.

Among this good company I should have felt myself, even if I hadn't robbed the pantry, in a false position. Not because I was squeezed in at an acute angle of the tablecloth, with the table in my chest, and the Pumblechookian elbow in my eye, nor because I was not allowed to speak (I didn't want to speak), nor because I was regaled with the scaly tips of the drumsticks of the fowls, and with those obscure corners of pork of which the pig, when living, had had the least reason to be vain. No; I should not have minded that, if they would only have left me alone. But they wouldn't leave me alone. They seemed to think the opportunity lost, if they failed to point the conversation at me, every now and then, and stick the point into me. I might have been an unfortunate little bull in a Spanish arena, I got so smartingly touched up by these moral goads.

It began the moment we sat down to dinner. Mr. Wopsle said grace with theatrical declamation,—as it now appears to me, something like a religious cross of the Ghost in Hamlet with Richard the Third,—and ended with the very proper aspiration that we might be truly grateful. Upon which my sister fixed me with her eye, and said, in a low reproachful voice, "Do you hear that? Be grateful."

"Especially," said Mr. Pumblechook, "be grateful, boy, to them which brought you up by hand."

Mrs. Hubble shook her head, and contemplating me with a mournful presentiment that I should come to no good, asked, "Why is it that the young are never grateful?" This moral mystery seemed too much for the company until Mr. Hubble tersely solved it by saying, "Naterally wicious." Everybody then murmured "True!" and looked at me in a particularly unpleasant and personal manner.

Joe's station and influence were something feebler (if possible) when there was company than when there was none. But he always aided and comforted me when he could, in some way of his own, and he always did so at dinner-time by giving me gravy, if there were any. There being plenty of gravy to-day, Joe spooned into my plate, at this point, about half a pint.

A little later on in the dinner, Mr. Wopsle reviewed the sermon with some severity, and intimated—in the usual hypothetical case of the Church being "thrown open"— what kind of sermon he would have given them. After favoring them with some heads of that discourse, he remarked that he considered the subject of the day's homily, ill chosen; which was the less excusable, he added, when there were so many subjects "going about."

"True again," said Uncle Pumblechook. "You've hit it, sir! Plenty of subjects going about, for them that know how to put salt upon their tails. That's what's wanted. A man needn't go far to find a subject, if he's ready with his salt-box." Mr. Pumblechook added, after a short interval of reflection, "Look at Pork alone. There's a subject! If you want a subject, look at Pork!"

"True, sir. Many a moral for the young," returned Mr. Wopsle,—and I knew he was going to lug me in, before he said it; "might be deduced from that text."

("You listen to this," said my sister to me, in a severe parenthesis.)

Joe gave me some more gravy.

"Swine," pursued Mr. Wopsle, in his deepest voice, and pointing his fork at my blushes, as if he were mentioning my Christian name,—"swine were the companions of the prodigal. The gluttony of Swine is put before us, as an example to the young." (I thought this pretty well in him who had been praising up the pork for being so plump and juicy.) "What is detestable in a pig is more detestable in a boy."

"Or girl," suggested Mr. Hubble.

"Of course, or girl, Mr. Hubble," assented Mr. Wopsle, rather irritably, "but there is no girl present."

"Besides," said Mr. Pumblechook, turning sharp on me, "think what you've got to be grateful for. If you'd been born a Squeaker—"

"He was, if ever a child was," said my sister, most emphatically.

Joe gave me some more gravy.

"Well, but I mean a four-footed Squeaker," said Mr. Pumblechook. "If you had been born such, would you have been here now? Not you—"

"Unless in that form," said Mr. Wopsle, nodding towards the dish.

"But I don't mean in that form, sir," returned Mr. Pumblechook, who had an objection to being interrupted; "I mean, enjoying himself with his elders and betters, and improving himself with their conversation, and rolling in the lap of luxury. Would he have been doing that? No, he wouldn't. And what would have been your destination?" turning on me again. "You would have been disposed of for so many shillings according to the market price of the article, and Dunstable the butcher would have come up to you as you lay in your straw, and he would have whipped you under his left arm, and with his right he would have tucked up his frock to get a penknife from out of his waistcoat-pocket, and he would have shed your blood and had your life. No bringing up by hand then. Not a bit of it!"

Joe offered me more gravy, which I was afraid to take.

"He was a world of trouble to you, ma'am," said Mrs. Hubble, commiserating my sister.

"Trouble?" echoed my sister; "trouble?" and then entered on a fearful catalogue of all the illnesses I had been guilty of, and all the acts of sleeplessness I had committed, and all the high places I had tumbled from, and all the low places I had tumbled into, and all the injuries I had done myself, and all the times she had wished me in my grave, and I had contumaciously refused to go there.

I think the Romans must have aggravated one another very much, with their noses. Perhaps, they became the restless people they were, in consequence. Anyhow, Mr. Wopsle's Roman nose so aggravated me, during the recital of my misdemeanours, that I should have liked to pull it until he howled. But, all I had endured up to this time was nothing in comparison with the awful feelings that took possession of me when the pause was broken which ensued upon my sister's recital, and in which pause everybody had looked at me (as I felt painfully conscious) with indignation and abhorrence.

"Yet," said Mr. Pumblechook, leading the company gently back to the theme from which they had strayed, "Pork—regarded as biled—is rich, too; ain't it?"

"Have a little brandy, uncle," said my sister.

O Heavens, it had come at last! He would find it was weak, he would say it was weak, and I was lost! I held tight to the leg of the table under the cloth, with both hands, and awaited my fate.

My sister went for the stone bottle, came back with the stone bottle, and poured his brandy out: no one else taking any. The wretched man trifled with his glass,—took it up, looked at it through the light, put it down,—prolonged my misery. All this time Mrs. Joe and Joe were briskly clearing the table for the pie and pudding.

I couldn't keep my eyes off him. Always holding tight by the leg of the table with my hands and feet, I saw the miserable creature finger his glass playfully, take it up, smile, throw his head back, and drink the brandy off. Instantly afterwards, the company were seized with unspeakable consternation, owing to his springing to his feet, turning round several times in an appalling spasmodic whooping-cough dance, and rushing out at the door; he then became visible through the window, violently plunging and expectorating, making the most hideous faces, and apparently out of his mind.

I held on tight, while Mrs. Joe and Joe ran to him. I didn't know how I had done it, but I had no doubt I had murdered him somehow. In my dreadful situation, it was a relief when he was brought back, and surveying the company all round as if they had disagreed with him, sank down into his chair with the one significant gasp, "Tar!"

I had filled up the bottle from the tar-water jug. I knew he would be worse by and by. I moved the table, like a Medium of the present day, by the vigor of my unseen hold upon it.

"Tar!" cried my sister, in amazement. "Why, how ever could Tar come there?"

But, Uncle Pumblechook, who was omnipotent in that kitchen, wouldn't hear the word, wouldn't hear of the subject, imperiously waved it all away with his hand, and asked for hot gin and water. My sister, who had begun to be alarmingly meditative, had to employ herself actively in getting the gin the hot water, the sugar, and the lemon-peel, and mixing them. For the time being at least, I was saved. I still held on to the leg of the table, but clutched it now with the fervor of gratitude.

By degrees, I became calm enough to release my grasp and partake of pudding. Mr. Pumblechook partook of pudding. All partook of pudding. The course terminated, and Mr. Pumblechook had begun to beam under the genial influence of gin and water. I began to think I should get over the day, when my sister said to Joe, "Clean plates,—cold."

I clutched the leg of the table again immediately, and pressed it to my bosom as if it had been the companion of my youth and friend of my soul. I foresaw what was coming, and I felt that this time I really was gone.

"You must taste," said my sister, addressing the guests with her best grace—"you must taste, to finish with, such a delightful and delicious present of Uncle Pumblechook's!"

Must they! Let them not hope to taste it!

"You must know," said my sister, rising, "it's a pie; a savory pork pie."

The company murmured their compliments. Uncle Pumblechook, sensible of having deserved well of his fellow-creatures, said,—quite vivaciously, all things considered,—"Well, Mrs. Joe, we'll do our best endeavors; let us have a cut at this same pie."

My sister went out to get it. I heard her steps proceed to the pantry. I saw Mr. Pumblechook balance his knife. I saw reawakening appetite in the Roman nostrils of Mr. Wopsle. I heard Mr. Hubble remark that "a bit of savory pork pie would lay atop of anything you could mention, and do no harm," and I heard Joe say, "You shall have some, Pip." I have never been absolutely certain whether I uttered a shrill yell of terror, merely in spirit, or in the bodily hearing of the company. I felt that I could bear no more, and that I must run away. I released the leg of the table, and ran for my life.

But I ran no farther than the house door, for there I ran head-foremost into a party of soldiers with their muskets, one of whom held out a pair of handcuffs to me, saying, "Here you are, look sharp, come on!"

CHAPTER V

The apparition of a file of soldiers ringing down the but-ends of their loaded muskets on our door-step, caused the dinner-party to rise from table in confusion, and caused Mrs. Joe re-entering the kitchen empty-handed, to stop short and stare, in her wondering lament of "Gracious goodness gracious me, what's gone—with the—pie!"

The sergeant and I were in the kitchen when Mrs. Joe stood staring; at which crisis I partially recovered the use of my senses. It was the sergeant who had spoken to me, and he was now looking round at the company, with his handcuffs invitingly extended towards them in his right hand, and his left on my shoulder.

"Excuse me, ladies and gentleman," said the sergeant, "but as I have mentioned at the door to this smart young shaver," (which he hadn't), "I am on a chase in the name of the king, and I want the blacksmith."

"And pray what might you want with him?" retorted my sister, quick to resent his being wanted at all.

"Missis," returned the gallant sergeant, "speaking for myself, I should reply, the honor and pleasure of his fine wife's acquaintance; speaking for the king, I answer, a little job done."

This was received as rather neat in the sergeant; insomuch that Mr. Pumblechook cried audibly, "Good again!"

"You see, blacksmith," said the sergeant, who had by this time picked out Joe with his eye, "we have had an accident with these, and I find the lock of one of 'em goes wrong, and the coupling don't act pretty. As they are wanted for immediate service, will you throw your eye over them?"

Joe threw his eye over them, and pronounced that the job would necessitate the lighting of his forge fire, and would take nearer two hours than one, "Will it? Then will you set about it at once, blacksmith?" said the off-hand sergeant, "as it's on his Majesty's service. And if my men can bear a hand anywhere, they'll make themselves useful." With that, he called to his men, who came trooping into the kitchen one after another, and piled their arms in a corner. And then they stood about, as soldiers do; now, with their hands loosely clasped before them; now, resting a knee or a shoulder; now, easing a belt or a pouch; now, opening the door to spit stiffly over their high stocks, out into the yard.

All these things I saw without then knowing that I saw them, for I was in an agony of apprehension. But beginning to perceive that the handcuffs were not for me, and that the military had so far got the better of the pie as to put it in the background, I collected a little more of my scattered wits.

"Would you give me the time?" said the sergeant, addressing himself to Mr. Pumblechook, as to a man whose appreciative powers justified the inference that he was equal to the time.

"It's just gone half past two."

"That's not so bad," said the sergeant, reflecting; "even if I was forced to halt here nigh two hours, that'll do. How far might you call yourselves from the marshes, hereabouts? Not above a mile, I reckon?"

"Just a mile," said Mrs. Joe.

"That'll do. We begin to close in upon 'em about dusk. A little before dusk, my orders are. That'll do."

"Convicts, sergeant?" asked Mr. Wopsle, in a matter-of-course way.

"Ay!" returned the sergeant, "two. They're pretty well known to be out on the marshes still, and they won't try to get clear of 'em before dusk. Anybody here seen anything of any such game?"

Everybody, myself excepted, said no, with confidence. Nobody thought of me.

"Well!" said the sergeant, "they'll find themselves trapped in a circle, I expect, sooner than they count on. Now, blacksmith! If you're ready, his Majesty the King is."

Joe had got his coat and waistcoat and cravat off, and his leather apron on, and passed into the forge. One of the soldiers opened its wooden windows, another lighted the fire, another turned to at the bellows, the rest stood round the blaze, which was soon roaring. Then Joe began to hammer and clink, hammer and clink, and we all looked on.

The interest of the impending pursuit not only absorbed the general attention, but even made my sister liberal. She drew a pitcher of beer from the cask for the soldiers, and invited the sergeant to take a glass of brandy. But Mr. Pumblechook said, sharply, "Give him wine, Mum. I'll engage there's no Tar in that:" so, the sergeant thanked him and said that as he preferred his drink without tar, he would take wine, if it was equally convenient. When it was given him, he drank his Majesty's health and compliments of the season, and took it all at a mouthful and smacked his lips.

"Good stuff, eh, sergeant?" said Mr. Pumblechook.

"I'll tell you something," returned the sergeant; "I suspect that stuff's of your providing."

Mr. Pumblechook, with a fat sort of laugh, said, "Ay, ay? Why?"

"Because," returned the sergeant, clapping him on the shoulder, "you're a man that knows what's what."

"D'ye think so?" said Mr. Pumblechook, with his former laugh. "Have another glass!"

"With you. Hob and nob," returned the sergeant. "The top of mine to the foot of yours,—the foot of yours to the top of mine,—Ring once, ring twice,—the best tune on the Musical Glasses! Your health. May you live a thousand years, and never be a worse judge of the right sort than you are at the present moment of your life!"

The sergeant tossed off his glass again and seemed quite ready for another glass. I noticed that Mr. Pumblechook in his hospitality appeared to forget that he had made a present of the wine, but took the bottle from Mrs. Joe and had all the credit of handing it about in a gush of joviality. Even I got some. And he was so very free of the wine that he even called for the other bottle, and handed that about with the same liberality, when the first was gone.

As I watched them while they all stood clustering about the forge, enjoying themselves so much, I thought what terrible good sauce for a dinner my fugitive friend on the marshes was. They had not enjoyed themselves a quarter so much, before the entertainment was brightened with the excitement he furnished. And now, when they were all in lively anticipation of "the two villains" being taken, and when the bellows seemed to roar for the fugitives, the fire to flare for them, the smoke to hurry away in pursuit of them, Joe to hammer and clink for them, and all the murky shadows on the wall to shake at them in menace as the blaze rose and sank, and the red-hot sparks dropped and died, the pale afternoon outside almost seemed in my pitying young fancy to have turned pale on their account, poor wretches.

At last, Joe's job was done, and the ringing and roaring stopped. As Joe got on his coat, he mustered courage to propose that some of us should go down with the soldiers and see what came of the hunt. Mr. Pumblechook and Mr. Hubble declined, on the plea of a pipe and ladies' society; but Mr. Wopsle said he would go, if Joe would. Joe said he was agreeable, and would take me, if Mrs. Joe approved. We never should have got leave to go, I am sure, but for Mrs. Joe's curiosity to know all about it and how it ended. As it was, she merely stipulated, "If you bring the boy back with his head blown to bits by a musket, don't look to me to put it together again."

The sergeant took a polite leave of the ladies, and parted from Mr. Pumblechook as from a comrade; though I doubt if he were quite as fully sensible of that gentleman's merits under arid conditions, as when something moist was going. His men resumed their muskets and fell in. Mr. Wopsle, Joe, and I, received strict charge to keep in the rear, and to speak no word after we reached the marshes. When we were all out in the raw air and were steadily moving towards our business, I treasonably whispered to Joe, "I hope, Joe, we shan't find them." and Joe whispered to me, "I'd give a shilling if they had cut and run, Pip."

We were joined by no stragglers from the village, for the weather was cold and threatening, the way dreary, the footing bad, darkness coming on, and the people had good fires in-doors and were keeping the day. A few faces hurried to glowing windows and looked after us, but none came out. We passed the finger-post, and held straight on to the churchyard. There we were stopped a few minutes by a signal from the sergeant's hand, while two or three of his men dispersed themselves among the graves, and also examined the porch. They came in again without finding anything, and then we struck out on the open marshes, through the gate at the side of the churchyard. A bitter sleet came rattling against us here on the east wind, and Joe took me on his back.

Now that we were out upon the dismal wilderness where they little thought I had been within eight or nine hours and had seen both men hiding, I considered for the first time, with great dread, if we should come upon them, would my particular convict suppose that it was I who had brought the soldiers there? He had asked me if I was a deceiving imp, and he had said I should be a fierce young hound if I joined the hunt against him. Would he believe that I was both imp and hound in treacherous earnest, and had betrayed him?

It was of no use asking myself this question now. There I was, on Joe's back, and there was Joe beneath me, charging at the ditches like a hunter, and stimulating Mr.

Wopsle not to tumble on his Roman nose, and to keep up with us. The soldiers were in front of us, extending into a pretty wide line with an interval between man and man. We were taking the course I had begun with, and from which I had diverged in the mist. Either the mist was not out again yet, or the wind had dispelled it. Under the low red glare of sunset, the beacon, and the gibbet, and the mound of the Battery, and the opposite shore of the river, were plain, though all of a watery lead color.

With my heart thumping like a blacksmith at Joe's broad shoulder, I looked all about for any sign of the convicts. I could see none, I could hear none. Mr. Wopsle had greatly alarmed me more than once, by his blowing and hard breathing; but I knew the sounds by this time, and could dissociate them from the object of pursuit. I got a dreadful start, when I thought I heard the file still going; but it was only a sheep-bell. The sheep stopped in their eating and looked timidly at us; and the cattle, their heads turned from the wind and sleet, stared angrily as if they held us responsible for both annoyances; but, except these things, and the shudder of the dying day in every blade of grass, there was no break in the bleak stillness of the marshes.

The soldiers were moving on in the direction of the old Battery, and we were moving on a little way behind them, when, all of a sudden, we all stopped. For there had reached us on the wings of the wind and rain, a long shout. It was repeated. It was at a distance towards the east, but it was long and loud. Nay, there seemed to be two or more shouts raised together,—if one might judge from a confusion in the sound.

To this effect the sergeant and the nearest men were speaking under their breath, when Joe and I came up. After another moment's listening, Joe (who was a good judge) agreed, and Mr. Wopsle (who was a bad judge) agreed. The sergeant, a decisive man, ordered that the sound should not be answered, but that the course should be changed, and that his men should make towards it "at the double." So we slanted to the right (where the East was), and Joe pounded away so wonderfully, that I had to hold on tight to keep my seat.

It was a run indeed now, and what Joe called, in the only two words he spoke all the time, "a Winder." Down banks and up banks, and over gates, and splashing into dikes, and breaking among coarse rushes: no man cared where he went. As we came nearer to the shouting, it became more and more apparent that it was made by more than one voice. Sometimes, it seemed to stop altogether, and then the soldiers stopped. When it broke out again, the soldiers made for it at a greater rate than ever, and we after them. After a while, we had so run it down, that we could hear one voice calling "Murder!" and another voice, "Convicts! Runaways! Guard! This way for the runaway convicts!" Then both voices would seem to be stifled in a struggle, and then would break out again. And when it had come to this, the soldiers ran like deer, and Joe too.

The sergeant ran in first, when we had run the noise quite down, and two of his men ran in close upon him. Their pieces were cocked and levelled when we all ran in.

"Here are both men!" panted the sergeant, struggling at the bottom of a ditch. "Surrender, you two! and confound you for two wild beasts! Come asunder!"

Water was splashing, and mud was flying, and oaths were being sworn, and blows were being struck, when some more men went down into the ditch to help the sergeant, and dragged out, separately, my convict and the other one. Both were bleeding and panting and execrating and struggling; but of course I knew them both directly.

"Mind!" said my convict, wiping blood from his face with his ragged sleeves, and shaking torn hair from his fingers: "I took him! I give him up to you! Mind that!"

"It's not much to be particular about," said the sergeant; "it'll do you small good, my man, being in the same plight yourself. Handcuffs there!"

"I don't expect it to do me any good. I don't want it to do me more good than it does now," said my convict, with a greedy laugh. "I took him. He knows it. That's enough for me."

The other convict was livid to look at, and, in addition to the old bruised left side of his face, seemed to be bruised and torn all over. He could not so much as get his breath to speak, until they were both separately handcuffed, but leaned upon a soldier to keep himself from falling.

"Take notice, guard,—he tried to murder me," were his first words.

"Tried to murder him?" said my convict, disdainfully. "Try, and not do it? I took him, and giv' him up; that's what I done. I not only prevented him getting off the marshes, but I dragged him here,—dragged him this far on his way back. He's a gentleman, if you please, this villain. Now, the Hulks has got its gentleman again, through me. Murder him? Worth my while, too, to murder him, when I could do worse and drag him back!"

The other one still gasped, "He tried—he tried to—murder me. Bear—bear witness."

"Lookee here!" said my convict to the sergeant. "Single-handed I got clear of the prison-ship; I made a dash and I done it. I could ha' got clear of these death-cold flats likewise—look at my leg: you won't find much iron on it—if I hadn't made the discovery that he was here. Let him go free? Let him profit by the means as I found out? Let him make a tool of me afresh and again? Once more? No, no, no. If I had died at the bottom there," and he made an emphatic swing at the ditch with his manacled hands, "I'd have held to him with that grip, that you should have been safe to find him in my hold."

The other fugitive, who was evidently in extreme horror of his companion, repeated, "He tried to murder me. I should have been a dead man if you had not come up."

"He lies!" said my convict, with fierce energy. "He's a liar born, and he'll die a liar. Look at his face; ain't it written there? Let him turn those eyes of his on me. I defy him to do it."

The other, with an effort at a scornful smile, which could not, however, collect the nervous working of his mouth into any set expression, looked at the soldiers, and looked about at the marshes and at the sky, but certainly did not look at the speaker.

"Do you see him?" pursued my convict. "Do you see what a villain he is? Do you see those grovelling and wandering eyes? That's how he looked when we were tried together. He never looked at me."

The other, always working and working his dry lips and turning his eyes restlessly about him far and near, did at last turn them for a moment on the speaker, with the words, "You are not much to look at," and with a half-taunting glance at the bound hands. At that point, my convict became so frantically exasperated, that he would have rushed upon him but for the interposition of the soldiers. "Didn't I tell you," said the other convict then, "that he would murder me, if he could?" And any one could see that he shook with fear, and that there broke out upon his lips curious white flakes, like thin snow.

"Enough of this parley," said the sergeant. "Light those torches."

As one of the soldiers, who carried a basket in lieu of a gun, went down on his knee to open it, my convict looked round him for the first time, and saw me. I had alighted from Joe's back on the brink of the ditch when we came up, and had not moved since. I looked at him eagerly when he looked at me, and slightly moved my hands and shook my head. I had been waiting for him to see me that I might try to assure him of my innocence. It was not at all expressed to me that he even comprehended my intention, for he gave me a look that I did not understand, and it all passed in a moment. But if he had looked at me for an hour or for a day, I could not have remembered his face ever afterwards, as having been more attentive.

The soldier with the basket soon got a light, and lighted three or four torches, and took one himself and distributed the others. It had been almost dark before, but now it seemed quite dark, and soon afterwards very dark. Before we departed from that spot, four soldiers standing in a ring, fired twice into the air. Presently we saw other torches kindled at some distance behind us, and others on the marshes on the opposite bank of the river. "All right," said the sergeant. "March."

We had not gone far when three cannon were fired ahead of us with a sound that seemed to burst something inside my ear. "You are expected on board," said the sergeant to my convict; "they know you are coming. Don't straggle, my man. Close up here."

The two were kept apart, and each walked surrounded by a separate guard. I had hold of Joe's hand now, and Joe carried one of the torches. Mr. Wopsle had been for going back, but Joe was resolved to see it out, so we went on with the party. There was a reasonably good path now, mostly on the edge of the river, with a divergence here and there where a dike came, with a miniature windmill on it and a muddy sluice-gate. When I looked round, I could see the other lights coming in after us. The torches we carried dropped great blotches of fire upon the track, and I could see those, too, lying smoking and flaring. I could see nothing else but black darkness. Our lights warmed the air about us with their pitchy blaze, and the two prisoners seemed rather to like that, as they limped along in the midst of the muskets. We could not go fast, because of their lameness; and they were so spent, that two or three times we had to halt while they rested.

After an hour or so of this travelling, we came to a rough wooden hut and a landing-place. There was a guard in the hut, and they challenged, and the sergeant answered. Then, we went into the hut, where there was a smell of tobacco and whitewash, and a bright fire, and a lamp, and a stand of muskets, and a drum, and a low wooden bedstead, like an overgrown mangle without the machinery, capable of holding about a dozen soldiers all at once. Three or four soldiers who lay upon it in their great-coats were not much interested in us, but just lifted their heads and took a sleepy stare, and then lay down again. The sergeant made some kind of report, and some entry in a book, and then the convict whom I call the other convict was drafted off with his guard, to go on board first.

My convict never looked at me, except that once. While we stood in the hut, he stood before the fire looking thoughtfully at it, or putting up his feet by turns upon the hob, and looking thoughtfully at them as if he pitied them for their recent adventures. Suddenly, he turned to the sergeant, and remarked,—

"I wish to say something respecting this escape. It may prevent some persons laying under suspicion alonger me."

"You can say what you like," returned the sergeant, standing coolly looking at him with his arms folded, "but you have no call to say it here. You'll have opportunity enough to say about it, and hear about it, before it's done with, you know."

"I know, but this is another pint, a separate matter. A man can't starve; at least I can't. I took some wittles, up at the willage over yonder,—where the church stands a'most out on the marshes."

"You mean stole," said the sergeant.

"And I'll tell you where from. From the blacksmith's."

"Halloa!" said the sergeant, staring at Joe.

"Halloa, Pip!" said Joe, staring at me.

"It was some broken wittles—that's what it was—and a dram of liquor, and a pie."

"Have you happened to miss such an article as a pie, blacksmith?" asked the sergeant, confidentially.

"My wife did, at the very moment when you came in. Don't you know, Pip?"

"So," said my convict, turning his eyes on Joe in a moody manner, and without the least glance at me,—"so you're the blacksmith, are you? Than I'm sorry to say, I've eat your pie."

"God knows you're welcome to it,—so far as it was ever mine," returned Joe, with a saving remembrance of Mrs. Joe. "We don't know what you have done, but we wouldn't have you starved to death for it, poor miserable fellow-creatur.—Would us, Pip?"

The something that I had noticed before, clicked in the man's throat again, and he turned his back. The boat had returned, and his guard were ready, so we followed him to the landing-place made of rough stakes and stones, and saw him put into the boat, which was rowed by a crew of convicts like himself. No one seemed surprised to see him, or interested in seeing him, or glad to see him, or sorry to see him, or spoke a word, except that somebody in the boat growled as if to dogs, "Give way, you!" which was the signal for the dip of the oars. By the light of the torches, we saw the black Hulk lying out a little way from the mud of the shore, like a wicked Noah's ark. Cribbed and barred and moored by massive rusty chains, the prison-ship seemed in my young eyes to be ironed like the prisoners. We saw the boat go alongside, and we saw him taken up the side and disappear. Then, the ends of the torches were flung hissing into the water, and went out, as if it were all over with him.

CHAPTER VI

M y state of mind regarding the pilfering from which I had been so unexpectedly exonerated did not impel me to frank disclosure; but I hope it had some dregs of good at the bottom of it.

I do not recall that I felt any tenderness of conscience in reference to Mrs. Joe, when the fear of being found out was lifted off me. But I loved Joe,—perhaps for no better reason in those early days than because the dear fellow let me love him,—and, as to him, my inner self was not so easily composed. It was much upon my mind (particularly when I first saw him looking about for his file) that I ought to tell Joe the whole truth. Yet I did not, and for the reason that I mistrusted that if I did, he would think me worse than I was. The fear of losing Joe's confidence, and of thenceforth sitting in the chimney corner at night staring drearily at my forever lost companion and friend, tied up my tongue. I morbidly represented to myself that if Joe knew it, I never afterwards could see him at the fireside feeling his fair whisker, without thinking that he was meditating on it. That, if Joe knew it, I never afterwards could see him glance, however casually, at yesterday's meat or pudding when it came on to-day's table, without thinking that he was debating whether I had been in the pantry. That, if Joe knew it, and at any subsequent period of our joint domestic life remarked that his beer was flat or thick, the conviction that he suspected Tar in it, would bring a rush of blood to my face. In a word, I was too cowardly to do what I knew to be right, as I had been too cowardly to avoid doing what I knew to be wrong. I had had no intercourse with the world at that time, and I imitated none of its many inhabitants who act in this manner. Quite an untaught genius, I made the discovery of the line of action for myself.

As I was sleepy before we were far away from the prison-ship, Joe took me on his back again and carried me home. He must have had a tiresome journey of it, for Mr. Wopsle, being knocked up, was in such a very bad temper that if the Church had been thrown open, he would probably have excommunicated the whole expedition, beginning with Joe and myself. In his lay capacity, he persisted in sitting down in the damp to such an insane extent, that when his coat was taken off to be dried at the kitchen fire, the circumstantial evidence on his trousers would have hanged him, if it had been a capital offence.

By that time, I was staggering on the kitchen floor like a little drunkard, through having been newly set upon my feet, and through having been fast asleep, and through waking in the heat and lights and noise of tongues. As I came to myself (with the aid of a heavy thump between the shoulders, and the restorative exclamation "Yah! Was there ever such a boy as this!" from my sister,) I found Joe telling them about the convict's confession, and all the visitors suggesting different ways by which he had got into the pantry. Mr. Pumblechook made out, after carefully surveying the premises, that he had first got upon the roof of the forge, and had then got upon the roof of the house, and had then let himself down the kitchen chimney by a rope made of his bedding cut into strips; and as Mr. Pumblechook was very positive and drove his own chaise-cart—over Everybody—it was agreed that it must be so. Mr. Wopsle, indeed, wildly cried out, "No!" with the feeble malice of a tired man; but, as he had no theory, and no coat on, he was unanimously set at naught,—not to mention his smoking hard behind, as he stood with his back to the kitchen fire to draw the damp out: which was not calculated to inspire confidence.

This was all I heard that night before my sister clutched me, as a slumberous offence to the company's eyesight, and assisted me up to bed with such a strong hand that I seemed to have fifty boots on, and to be dangling them all against the edges of the stairs. My state of mind, as I have described it, began before I was up in the morning, and lasted long after the subject had died out, and had ceased to be mentioned saving on exceptional occasions.

CHAPTER VII

At the time when I stood in the churchyard reading the family tombstones, I had just enough learning to be able to spell them out. My construction even of their simple meaning was not very correct, for I read "wife of the Above" as a complimentary reference to my father's exaltation to a better world; and if any one of my deceased relations had been referred to as "Below," I have no doubt I should have formed the worst opinions of that member of the family. Neither were my notions of the theological positions to which my Catechism bound me, at all accurate; for, I have a lively remembrance that I supposed my declaration that I was to "walk in the same all the days of my life," laid me under an obligation always to go through the village from our house in one particular direction, and never to vary it by turning down by the wheelwright's or up by the mill.

When I was old enough, I was to be apprenticed to Joe, and until I could assume that dignity I was not to be what Mrs. Joe called "Pompeyed," or (as I render it) pampered. Therefore, I was not only odd-boy about the forge, but if any neighbor happened to want an extra boy to frighten birds, or pick up stones, or do any such job, I was favored with the employment. In order, however, that our superior position might not be compromised thereby, a money-box was kept on the kitchen mantel-shelf, in to which it was publicly made known that all my earnings were dropped. I have an impression that they were to be contributed eventually towards the liquidation of the National Debt, but I know I had no hope of any personal participation in the treasure.

Mr. Wopsle's great-aunt kept an evening school in the village; that is to say, she was a ridiculous old woman of limited means and unlimited infirmity, who used to go to sleep from six to seven every evening, in the society of youth who paid two pence per week each, for the improving opportunity of seeing her do it. She rented a small cottage, and Mr. Wopsle had the room up stairs, where we students used to overhear him reading aloud in a most dignified and terrific manner, and occasionally bumping on the ceiling. There was a fiction that Mr. Wopsle "examined" the scholars once a quarter. What he did on those occasions was to turn up his cuffs, stick up his hair, and give us Mark Antony's oration over the body of Caesar. This was always followed by Collins's Ode on the Passions, wherein I particularly venerated Mr. Wopsle as Revenge throwing his blood-stained sword in thunder down, and taking the War-denouncing trumpet with a withering look. It was not with me then, as it was in later life, when I fell into the society of the Passions, and compared them with Collins and Wopsle, rather to the disadvantage of both gentlemen.

Mr. Wopsle's great-aunt, besides keeping this Educational Institution, kept in the same room—a little general shop. She had no idea what stock she had, or what the price of anything in it was; but there was a little greasy memorandum-book kept in a drawer, which served as a Catalogue of Prices, and by this oracle Biddy arranged all the shop transaction. Biddy was Mr. Wopsle's great-aunt's granddaughter; I confess myself quiet unequal to the working out of the problem, what relation she was to Mr. Wopsle. She was an orphan like myself; like me, too, had been brought up by hand. She was most noticeable, I thought, in respect of her extremities; for, her hair always wanted brushing, her hands always wanted washing, and her shoes always wanted mending and pulling up at heel. This description must be received with a week-day limitation. On Sundays, she went to church elaborated.

Much of my unassisted self, and more by the help of Biddy than of Mr. Wopsle's great-aunt, I struggled through the alphabet as if it had been a bramble-bush; getting considerably worried and scratched by every letter. After that I fell among those thieves, the nine figures, who seemed every evening to do something new to disguise themselves and baffle recognition. But, at last I began, in a purblind groping way, to read, write, and cipher, on the very smallest scale.

One night I was sitting in the chimney corner with my slate, expending great efforts on the production of a letter to Joe. I think it must have been a full year after our hunt upon the marshes, for it was a long time after, and it was winter and a hard frost. With an alphabet on the hearth at my feet for reference, I contrived in an hour or two to print and smear this epistle:—

"MI DEER JO i OPE U R KR WITE WELL i OPE i SHAL SON B HABELL 4 2 TEEDGE U JO AN THEN WE SHORL B SO GLODD AN WEN i M PRENGTD 2 U JO WOT LARX AN BLEVE ME INF XN PIP."

There was no indispensable necessity for my communicating with Joe by letter, inasmuch as he sat beside me and we were alone. But I delivered this written communication (slate and all) with my own hand, and Joe received it as a miracle of erudition.

"I say, Pip, old chap!" cried Joe, opening his blue eyes wide, "what a scholar you are! An't you?"

"I should like to be," said I, glancing at the slate as he held it; with a misgiving that the writing was rather hilly.

"Why, here's a J," said Joe, "and a O equal to anythink! Here's a J and a O, Pip, and a J-O, Joe."

I had never heard Joe read aloud to any greater extent than this monosyllable, and I had observed at church last Sunday, when I accidentally held our Prayer-Book upside down, that it seemed to suit his convenience quite as well as if it had been all right. Wishing to embrace the present occasion of finding out whether in teaching Joe, I should have to begin quite at the beginning, I said, "Ah! But read the rest, Jo."

"The rest, eh, Pip?" said Joe, looking at it with a slow, searching eye, "One, two, three. Why, here's three Js, and three Os, and three J-O, Joes in it, Pip!"

I leaned over Joe, and, with the aid of my forefinger read him the whole letter.

"Astonishing!" said Joe, when I had finished. "You ARE a scholar."

"How do you spell Gargery, Joe?" I asked him, with a modest patronage.

"I don't spell it at all," said Joe.

"But supposing you did?"

"It can't be supposed," said Joe. "Tho' I'm uncommon fond of reading, too."

"Are you, Joe?"

"On-common. Give me," said Joe, "a good book, or a good newspaper, and sit me down afore a good fire, and I ask no better. Lord!" he continued, after rubbing his knees a little, "when you do come to a J and a O, and says you, "Here, at last, is a J-O, Joe, how interesting reading is!"

I derived from this, that Joe's education, like Steam, was yet in its infancy, Pursuing the subject, I inquired,—

"Didn't you ever go to school, Joe, when you were as little as me?"

"No, Pip."

"Why didn't you ever go to school, Joe, when you were as little as me?"

"Well, Pip," said Joe, taking up the poker, and settling himself to his usual occupation when he was thoughtful, of slowly raking the fire between the lower bars; "I'll tell you. My father, Pip, he were given to drink, and when he were overtook with drink, he hammered away at my mother, most onmerciful. It were a'most the only hammering he did, indeed, 'xcepting at myself. And he hammered at me with a wigor only to be equalled by the wigor with which he didn't hammer at his anwil.—You're a listening and understanding, Pip?"

"Yes, Joe."

"'Consequence, my mother and me we ran away from my father several times; and then my mother she'd go out to work, and she'd say, "Joe," she'd say, "now, please God, you shall have some schooling, child," and she'd put me to school. But my father were that good in his hart that he couldn't abear to be without us. So, he'd come with a most tremenjous crowd and make such a row at the doors of the houses where we was, that they used to be obligated to have no more to do with us and to give us up to him. And then he took us home and hammered us. Which, you see, Pip," said Joe, pausing in his meditative raking of the fire, and looking at me, "were a drawback on my learning."

"Certainly, poor Joe!"

"Though mind you, Pip," said Joe, with a judicial touch or two of the poker on the top bar, "rendering unto all their doo, and maintaining equal justice betwixt man and man, my father were that good in his hart, don't you see?"

I didn't see; but I didn't say so.

"Well!" Joe pursued, "somebody must keep the pot a biling, Pip, or the pot won't bile, don't you know?"

I saw that, and said so.

"'Consequence, my father didn't make objections to my going to work; so I went to work to work at my present calling, which were his too, if he would have followed it, and I worked tolerable hard, I assure you, Pip. In time I were able to keep him, and I kep him till he went off in a purple leptic fit. And it were my intentions to have had put upon his tombstone that, Whatsume'er the failings on his part, Remember reader he were that good in his heart."

Joe recited this couplet with such manifest pride and careful perspicuity, that I asked him if he had made it himself.

"I made it," said Joe, "my own self. I made it in a moment. It was like striking out a horseshoe complete, in a single blow. I never was so much surprised in all my life,—couldn't credit my own ed,—to tell you the truth, hardly believed it were my own ed. As I was saying, Pip, it were my intentions to have had it cut over him; but poetry costs money, cut it how you will, small or large, and it were not done. Not to mention bearers, all the money that could be spared were wanted for my mother. She were in poor elth, and quite broke. She weren't long of following, poor soul, and her share of peace come round at last."

Joe's blue eyes turned a little watery; he rubbed first one of them, and then the other, in a most uncongenial and uncomfortable manner, with the round knob on the top of the poker.

"It were but lonesome then," said Joe, "living here alone, and I got acquainted with your sister. Now, Pip,"—Joe looked firmly at me as if he knew I was not going to agree with him;—"your sister is a fine figure of a woman."

I could not help looking at the fire, in an obvious state of doubt.

"Whatever family opinions, or whatever the world's opinions, on that subject may be, Pip, your sister is," Joe tapped the top bar with the poker after every word following, "a-fine-figure—of—a—woman!"

I could think of nothing better to say than "I am glad you think so, Joe."

"So am I," returned Joe, catching me up. "I am glad I think so, Pip. A little redness or a little matter of Bone, here or there, what does it signify to Me?"

I sagaciously observed, if it didn't signify to him, to whom did it signify?

"Certainly!" assented Joe. "That's it. You're right, old chap! When I got acquainted with your sister, it were the talk how she was bringing you up by hand. Very kind of her too, all the folks said, and I said, along with all the folks. As to you," Joe pursued with a countenance expressive of seeing something very nasty indeed, "if you could have been aware how small and flabby and mean you was, dear me, you'd have formed the most contemptible opinion of yourself!"

Not exactly relishing this, I said, "Never mind me, Joe."

"But I did mind you, Pip," he returned with tender simplicity. "When I offered to your sister to keep company, and to be asked in church at such times as she was willing and ready to come to the forge, I said to her, 'And bring the poor little child. God bless the poor little child,' I said to your sister, 'there's room for him at the forge!'"

I broke out crying and begging pardon, and hugged Joe round the neck: who dropped the poker to hug me, and to say, "Ever the best of friends; an't us, Pip? Don't cry, old chap!"

When this little interruption was over, Joe resumed:—

"Well, you see, Pip, and here we are! That's about where it lights; here we are! Now, when you take me in hand in my learning, Pip (and I tell you beforehand I am awful dull, most awful dull), Mrs. Joe mustn't see too much of what we're up to. It must be done, as I may say, on the sly. And why on the sly? I'll tell you why, Pip."

He had taken up the poker again; without which, I doubt if he could have proceeded in his demonstration.

"Your sister is given to government."

"Given to government, Joe?" I was startled, for I had some shadowy idea (and I am afraid I must add, hope) that Joe had divorced her in a favor of the Lords of the Admiralty, or Treasury.

"Given to government," said Joe. "Which I meantersay the government of you and myself."

"Oh!"

"And she an't over partial to having scholars on the premises," Joe continued, "and in partickler would not be over partial to my being a scholar, for fear as I might rise. Like a sort or rebel, don't you see?"

I was going to retort with an inquiry, and had got as far as "Why——" when Joe stopped me.

"Stay a bit. I know what you're a going to say, Pip; stay a bit! I don't deny that your sister comes the Mo-gul over us, now and again. I don't deny that she do throw us back-falls, and that she do drop down upon us heavy. At such times as when your sister is on the Ram-page, Pip," Joe sank his voice to a whisper and glanced at the door, "candor compels fur to admit that she is a Buster."

Joe pronounced this word, as if it began with at least twelve capital Bs.

"Why don't I rise? That were your observation when I broke it off, Pip?"

"Yes, Joe."

"Well," said Joe, passing the poker into his left hand, that he might feel his whisker; and I had no hope of him whenever he took to that placid occupation; "your sister's a master-mind. A master-mind."

"What's that?" I asked, in some hope of bringing him to a stand. But Joe was readier with his definition than I had expected, and completely stopped me by arguing circularly, and answering with a fixed look, "Her."

"And I ain't a master-mind," Joe resumed, when he had unfixed his look, and got back to his whisker. "And last of all, Pip,—and this I want to say very serious to you, old chap,—I see so much in my poor mother, of a woman drudging and slaving and breaking her honest hart and never getting no peace in her mortal days, that I'm dead afeerd of going wrong in the way of not doing what's right by a woman, and I'd fur rather of the two go wrong the t'other way, and be a little ill-conwenienced myself. I wish it was only me that got put out, Pip; I wish there warn't no Tickler for you, old chap; I wish I could take it all on myself; but this is the up-and-down-and-straight on it, Pip, and I hope you'll overlook shortcomings."

Young as I was, I believe that I dated a new admiration of Joe from that night. We were equals afterwards, as we had been before; but, afterwards at quiet times when I sat looking at Joe and thinking about him, I had a new sensation of feeling conscious that I was looking up to Joe in my heart.

"However," said Joe, rising to replenish the fire; "here's the Dutch-clock a working himself up to being equal to strike Eight of 'em, and she's not come home yet! I hope

Uncle Pumblechook's mare mayn't have set a forefoot on a piece o' ice, and gone down."

Mrs. Joe made occasional trips with Uncle Pumblechook on market-days, to assist him in buying such household stuffs and goods as required a woman's judgment; Uncle Pumblechook being a bachelor and reposing no confidences in his domestic servant. This was market-day, and Mrs. Joe was out on one of these expeditions.

Joe made the fire and swept the hearth, and then we went to the door to listen for the chaise-cart. It was a dry cold night, and the wind blew keenly, and the frost was white and hard. A man would die to-night of lying out on the marshes, I thought. And then I looked at the stars, and considered how awful if would be for a man to turn his face up to them as he froze to death, and see no help or pity in all the glittering multitude.

"Here comes the mare," said Joe, "ringing like a peal of bells!"

The sound of her iron shoes upon the hard road was quite musical, as she came along at a much brisker trot than usual. We got a chair out, ready for Mrs. Joe's alighting, and stirred up the fire that they might see a bright window, and took a final survey of the kitchen that nothing might be out of its place. When we had completed these preparations, they drove up, wrapped to the eyes. Mrs. Joe was soon landed, and Uncle Pumblechook was soon down too, covering the mare with a cloth, and we were soon all in the kitchen, carrying so much cold air in with us that it seemed to drive all the heat out of the fire.

"Now," said Mrs. Joe, unwrapping herself with haste and excitement, and throwing her bonnet back on her shoulders where it hung by the strings, "if this boy ain't grateful this night, he never will be!"

I looked as grateful as any boy possibly could, who was wholly uninformed why he ought to assume that expression.

"It's only to be hoped," said my sister, "that he won't be Pompeyed. But I have my fears."

"She ain't in that line, Mum," said Mr. Pumblechook. "She knows better."

She? I looked at Joe, making the motion with my lips and eyebrows, "She?" Joe looked at me, making the motion with his lips and eyebrows, "She?" My sister catching him in the act, he drew the back of his hand across his nose with his usual conciliatory air on such occasions, and looked at her.

"Well?" said my sister, in her snappish way. "What are you staring at? Is the house afire?"

"—Which some individual," Joe politely hinted, "mentioned—she."

"And she is a she, I suppose?" said my sister. "Unless you call Miss Havisham a he. And I doubt if even you'll go so far as that."

"Miss Havisham, up town?" said Joe.

"Is there any Miss Havisham down town?" returned my sister.

"She wants this boy to go and play there. And of course he's going. And he had better play there," said my sister, shaking her head at me as an encouragement to be extremely light and sportive, "or I'll work him."

I had heard of Miss Havisham up town,—everybody for miles round had heard of Miss Havisham up town,—as an immensely rich and grim lady who lived in a large and dismal house barricaded against robbers, and who led a life of seclusion.

"Well to be sure!" said Joe, astounded. "I wonder how she come to know Pip!"

"Noodle!" cried my sister. "Who said she knew him?"

"—Which some individual," Joe again politely hinted, "mentioned that she wanted him to go and play there."

"And couldn't she ask Uncle Pumblechook if he knew of a boy to go and play there? Isn't it just barely possible that Uncle Pumblechook may be a tenant of hers, and that he may sometimes—we won't say quarterly or half-yearly, for that would be requiring too much of you—but sometimes—go there to pay his rent? And couldn't she then ask Uncle Pumblechook if he knew of a boy to go and play there? And couldn't Uncle Pumblechook, being always considerate and thoughtful for us—though you may not think it, Joseph," in a tone of the deepest reproach, as if he were the most callous of nephews, "then mention this boy, standing Prancing here"—which I solemnly declare I was not doing—"that I have for ever been a willing slave to?"

"Good again!" cried Uncle Pumblechook. "Well put! Prettily pointed! Good indeed! Now Joseph, you know the case."

"No, Joseph," said my sister, still in a reproachful manner, while Joe apologetically drew the back of his hand across and across his nose, "you do not yet—though you may not think it—know the case. You may consider that you do, but you do not, Joseph. For you do not know that Uncle Pumblechook, being sensible that for anything we can tell, this boy's fortune may be made by his going to Miss Havisham's, has offered to take him into town to-night in his own chaise-cart, and to keep him to-night, and to take him with his own hands to Miss Havisham's to-morrow morning. And Lor-a-mussy me!" cried my sister, casting off her bonnet in sudden desperation, "here I stand talking to mere Mooncalfs, with Uncle Pumblechook waiting, and the mare catching cold at the door, and the boy grimed with crock and dirt from the hair of his head to the sole of his foot!"

With that, she pounced upon me, like an eagle on a lamb, and my face was squeezed into wooden bowls in sinks, and my head was put under taps of water-butts, and I was soaped, and kneaded, and towelled, and thumped, and harrowed, and rasped, until I really was quite beside myself. (I may here remark that I suppose myself to be better acquainted than any living authority, with the ridgy effect of a wedding-ring, passing unsympathetically over the human countenance.)

When my ablutions were completed, I was put into clean linen of the stiffest character, like a young penitent into sackcloth, and was trussed up in my tightest and fearfullest suit. I was then delivered over to Mr. Pumblechook, who formally received me as if he were the Sheriff, and who let off upon me the speech that I knew he had been dying to make all along: "Boy, be forever grateful to all friends, but especially unto them which brought you up by hand!"

"Good-bye, Joe!"

"God bless you, Pip, old chap!"

I had never parted from him before, and what with my feelings and what with soapsuds, I could at first see no stars from the chaise-cart. But they twinkled out one by one, without throwing any light on the questions why on earth I was going to play at Miss Havisham's, and what on earth I was expected to play at.

CHAPTER VIII

Mr. Pumblechook's premises in the High Street of the market town, were of a peppercorny and farinaceous character, as the premises of a cornchandler and seedsman should be. It appeared to me that he must be a very happy man indeed, to have so many little drawers in his shop; and I wondered when I peeped into one or two on the lower tiers, and saw the tied-up brown paper packets inside, whether the flower-seeds and bulbs ever wanted of a fine day to break out of those jails, and bloom.

It was in the early morning after my arrival that I entertained this speculation. On the previous night, I had been sent straight to bed in an attic with a sloping roof, which was so low in the corner where the bedstead was, that I calculated the tiles as being within a foot of my eyebrows. In the same early morning, I discovered a singular affinity between seeds and corduroys. Mr. Pumblechook wore corduroys, and so did his shopman; and somehow, there was a general air and flavor about the corduroys, so much in the nature of seeds, and a general air and flavor about the seeds, so much in the nature of corduroys, that I hardly knew which was which. The same opportunity served me for noticing that Mr. Pumblechook appeared to conduct his business by looking across the street at the saddler, who appeared to transact his business by keeping his eye on the coachmaker, who appeared to get on in life by putting his hands in his pockets and contemplating the baker, who in his turn folded his arms and stared at the grocer, who stood at his door and yawned at the chemist. The watchmaker, always poring over a little desk with a magnifying-glass at his eye, and always inspected by a group of smock-frocks poring over him through the glass of his shop-window, seemed to be about the only person in the High Street whose trade engaged his attention.

Mr. Pumblechook and I breakfasted at eight o'clock in the parlor behind the shop, while the shopman took his mug of tea and hunch of bread and butter on a sack of peas in the front premises. I considered Mr. Pumblechook wretched company. Besides being possessed by my sister's idea that a mortifying and penitential character ought to be imparted to my diet,—besides giving me as much crumb as possible in combination with as little butter, and putting such a quantity of warm water into my milk that it would have been more candid to have left the milk out altogether,—his conversation consisted of nothing but arithmetic. On my politely bidding him Good morning, he said, pompously, "Seven times nine, boy?" And how should I be able to answer, dodged in that way, in a strange place, on an empty stomach! I was hungry, but before I had swallowed a morsel, he began a running sum that lasted all through the breakfast. "Seven?" "And four?" "And eight?" "And six?" "And two?" "And ten?" And so on. And after each figure was disposed of, it was as much as I could do to get a bite or a sup, before the next came; while he sat at his ease guessing nothing, and eating bacon and hot roll, in (if I may be allowed the expression) a gorging and gormandizing manner.

For such reasons, I was very glad when ten o'clock came and we started for Miss Havisham's; though I was not at all at my ease regarding the manner in which I should acquit myself under that lady's roof. Within a quarter of an hour we came to Miss Havisham's house, which was of old brick, and dismal, and had a great many iron bars to it. Some of the windows had been walled up; of those that remained, all the lower were rustily barred. There was a courtyard in front, and that was barred; so we had to wait, after ringing the bell, until some one should come to open it. While we waited at the gate, I peeped in (even then Mr. Pumblechook said, "And fourteen?" but I pretended not to hear him), and saw that at the side of the house there was a large brewery. No brewing was going on in it, and none seemed to have gone on for a long long time.

A window was raised, and a clear voice demanded "What name?" To which my conductor replied, "Pumblechook." The voice returned, "Quite right," and the window was shut again, and a young lady came across the court-yard, with keys in her hand.

"This," said Mr. Pumblechook, "is Pip."

"This is Pip, is it?" returned the young lady, who was very pretty and seemed very proud; "come in, Pip."

Mr. Pumblechook was coming in also, when she stopped him with the gate.

"Oh!" she said. "Did you wish to see Miss Havisham?"

"If Miss Havisham wished to see me," returned Mr. Pumblechook, discomfited.

"Ah!" said the girl; "but you see she don't."

She said it so finally, and in such an undiscussible way, that Mr. Pumblechook, though in a condition of ruffled dignity, could not protest. But he eyed me severely,— as if I had done anything to him!—and departed with the words reproachfully delivered: "Boy! Let your behavior here be a credit unto them which brought you up by hand!" I was not free from apprehension that he would come back to propound through the gate, "And sixteen?" But he didn't.

My young conductress locked the gate, and we went across the courtyard. It was paved and clean, but grass was growing in every crevice. The brewery buildings had a little lane of communication with it, and the wooden gates of that lane stood open, and all the brewery beyond stood open, away to the high enclosing wall; and all was empty and disused. The cold wind seemed to blow colder there than outside the gate; and it made a shrill noise in howling in and out at the open sides of the brewery, like the noise of wind in the rigging of a ship at sea.

She saw me looking at it, and she said, "You could drink without hurt all the strong beer that's brewed there now, boy."

"I should think I could, miss," said I, in a shy way.

"Better not try to brew beer there now, or it would turn out sour, boy; don't you think so?"

"It looks like it, miss."

"Not that anybody means to try," she added, "for that's all done with, and the place will stand as idle as it is till it falls. As to strong beer, there's enough of it in the cellars already, to drown the Manor House."

"Is that the name of this house, miss?"

"One of its names, boy."

"It has more than one, then, miss?"

"One more. Its other name was Satis; which is Greek, or Latin, or Hebrew, or all three—or all one to me—for enough."

"Enough House," said I; "that's a curious name, miss."

"Yes," she replied; "but it meant more than it said. It meant, when it was given, that whoever had this house could want nothing else. They must have been easily satisfied in those days, I should think. But don't loiter, boy."

Though she called me "boy" so often, and with a carelessness that was far from complimentary, she was of about my own age. She seemed much older than I, of course, being a girl, and beautiful and self-possessed; and she was as scornful of me as if she had been one-and-twenty, and a queen.

We went into the house by a side door, the great front entrance had two chains across it outside,—and the first thing I noticed was, that the passages were all dark, and that she had left a candle burning there. She took it up, and we went through more passages and up a staircase, and still it was all dark, and only the candle lighted us.

At last we came to the door of a room, and she said, "Go in."

I answered, more in shyness than politeness, "After you, miss."

To this she returned: "Don't be ridiculous, boy; I am not going in." And scornfully walked away, and—what was worse—took the candle with her.

This was very uncomfortable, and I was half afraid. However, the only thing to be done being to knock at the door, I knocked, and was told from within to enter. I entered, therefore, and found myself in a pretty large room, well lighted with wax candles. No glimpse of daylight was to be seen in it. It was a dressing-room, as I supposed from the furniture, though much of it was of forms and uses then quite unknown to me. But prominent in it was a draped table with a gilded looking-glass, and that I made out at first sight to be a fine lady's dressing-table.

Whether I should have made out this object so soon if there had been no fine lady sitting at it, I cannot say. In an arm-chair, with an elbow resting on the table and her head leaning on that hand, sat the strangest lady I have ever seen, or shall ever see.

She was dressed in rich materials,—satins, and lace, and silks,—all of white. Her shoes were white. And she had a long white veil dependent from her hair, and she had bridal flowers in her hair, but her hair was white. Some bright jewels sparkled on her neck and on her hands, and some other jewels lay sparkling on the table. Dresses, less splendid than the dress she wore, and half-packed trunks, were scattered about. She had not quite finished dressing, for she had but one shoe on,—the other was on the table near her hand,—her veil was but half arranged, her watch and chain were not put on, and some lace for her bosom lay with those trinkets, and with her handkerchief, and gloves, and some flowers, and a Prayer-Book all confusedly heaped about the looking-glass.

It was not in the first few moments that I saw all these things, though I saw more of them in the first moments than might be supposed. But I saw that everything within my view which ought to be white, had been white long ago, and had lost its lustre and was faded and yellow. I saw that the bride within the bridal dress had withered like the dress, and like the flowers, and had no brightness left but the brightness of her sunken eyes. I saw that the dress had been put upon the rounded figure of a young woman, and that the figure upon which it now hung loose had shrunk to skin and bone. Once, I had been taken to see some ghastly waxwork at the Fair, representing I know not what impossible personage lying in state. Once, I had been taken to one of our old marsh churches to see a skeleton in the ashes of a rich dress that had been dug out of a vault under the church pavement. Now, waxwork and skeleton seemed to have dark eyes that moved and looked at me. I should have cried out, if I could.

"Who is it?" said the lady at the table.

"Pip, ma'am."

"Pip?"

"Mr. Pumblechook's boy, ma'am. Come—to play."

"Come nearer; let me look at you. Come close."

It was when I stood before her, avoiding her eyes, that I took note of the surrounding objects in detail, and saw that her watch had stopped at twenty minutes to nine, and that a clock in the room had stopped at twenty minutes to nine.

"Look at me," said Miss Havisham. "You are not afraid of a woman who has never seen the sun since you were born?"

I regret to state that I was not afraid of telling the enormous lie comprehended in the answer "No."

"Do you know what I touch here?" she said, laying her hands, one upon the other, on her left side.

"Yes, ma'am." (It made me think of the young man.)

"What do I touch?"

"Your heart."

"Broken!"

She uttered the word with an eager look, and with strong emphasis, and with a weird smile that had a kind of boast in it. Afterwards she kept her hands there for a little while, and slowly took them away as if they were heavy.

"I am tired," said Miss Havisham. "I want diversion, and I have done with men and women. Play."

I think it will be conceded by my most disputatious reader, that she could hardly have directed an unfortunate boy to do anything in the wide world more difficult to be done under the circumstances.

"I sometimes have sick fancies," she went on, "and I have a sick fancy that I want to see some play. There, there!" with an impatient movement of the fingers of her right hand; "play, play, play!"

For a moment, with the fear of my sister's working me before my eyes, I had a desperate idea of starting round the room in the assumed character of Mr. Pumblechook's chaise-cart. But I felt myself so unequal to the performance that I gave it up, and stood looking at Miss Havisham in what I suppose she took for a dogged manner, inasmuch as she said, when we had taken a good look at each other,—

"Are you sullen and obstinate?"

"No, ma'am, I am very sorry for you, and very sorry I can't play just now. If you complain of me I shall get into trouble with my sister, so I would do it if I could; but it's so new here, and so strange, and so fine,—and melancholy—." I stopped, fearing I might say too much, or had already said it, and we took another look at each other.

Before she spoke again, she turned her eyes from me, and looked at the dress she wore, and at the dressing-table, and finally at herself in the looking-glass.

"So new to him," she muttered, "so old to me; so strange to him, so familiar to me; so melancholy to both of us! Call Estella."

As she was still looking at the reflection of herself, I thought she was still talking to herself, and kept quiet.

"Call Estella," she repeated, flashing a look at me. "You can do that. Call Estella. At the door."

To stand in the dark in a mysterious passage of an unknown house, bawling Estella to a scornful young lady neither visible nor responsive, and feeling it a dreadful liberty so to roar out her name, was almost as bad as playing to order. But she answered at last, and her light came along the dark passage like a star.

Miss Havisham beckoned her to come close, and took up a jewel from the table, and tried its effect upon her fair young bosom and against her pretty brown hair. "Your own, one day, my dear, and you will use it well. Let me see you play cards with this boy."

"With this boy? Why, he is a common laboring boy!"

I thought I overheard Miss Havisham answer,—only it seemed so Unlikely,— "Well? You can break his heart."

"What do you play, boy?" asked Estella of myself, with the greatest disdain.

"Nothing but beggar my neighbor, miss."

"Beggar him," said Miss Havisham to Estella. So we sat down to cards.

It was then I began to understand that everything in the room had stopped, like the watch and the clock, a long time ago. I noticed that Miss Havisham put down the jewel exactly on the spot from which she had taken it up. As Estella dealt the cards, I glanced at the dressing-table again, and saw that the shoe upon it, once white, now yellow, had never been worn. I glanced down at the foot from which the shoe was absent, and saw that the silk stocking on it, once white, now yellow, had been trodden ragged. Without this arrest of everything, this standing still of all the pale decayed objects, not even the withered bridal dress on the collapsed form could have looked so like grave-clothes, or the long veil so like a shroud.

So she sat, corpse-like, as we played at cards; the frillings and trimmings on her bridal dress, looking like earthy paper. I knew nothing then of the discoveries that are occasionally made of bodies buried in ancient times, which fall to powder in the moment of being distinctly seen; but, I have often thought since, that she must have looked as if the admission of the natural light of day would have struck her to dust.

"He calls the knaves Jacks, this boy!" said Estella with disdain, before our first game was out. "And what coarse hands he has! And what thick boots!"

I had never thought of being ashamed of my hands before; but I began to consider them a very indifferent pair. Her contempt for me was so strong, that it became infectious, and I caught it.

She won the game, and I dealt. I misdealt, as was only natural, when I knew she was lying in wait for me to do wrong; and she denounced me for a stupid, clumsy laboring-boy.

"You say nothing of her," remarked Miss Havisham to me, as she looked on. "She says many hard things of you, but you say nothing of her. What do you think of her?"

"I don't like to say," I stammered.

"Tell me in my ear," said Miss Havisham, bending down.

"I think she is very proud," I replied, in a whisper.

"Anything else?"

"I think she is very pretty."

"Anything else?"

"I think she is very insulting." (She was looking at me then with a look of supreme aversion.)

"Anything else?"

"I think I should like to go home."

"And never see her again, though she is so pretty?"

"I am not sure that I shouldn't like to see her again, but I should like to go home now."

"You shall go soon," said Miss Havisham, aloud. "Play the game out."

Saving for the one weird smile at first, I should have felt almost sure that Miss Havisham's face could not smile. It had dropped into a watchful and brooding expression,—most likely when all the things about her had become transfixed,—and it looked as if nothing could ever lift it up again. Her chest had dropped, so that she stooped; and her voice had dropped, so that she spoke low, and with a dead lull upon her; altogether, she had the appearance of having dropped body and soul, within and without, under the weight of a crushing blow.

I played the game to an end with Estella, and she beggared me. She threw the cards down on the table when she had won them all, as if she despised them for having been won of me.

"When shall I have you here again?" said Miss Havisham. "Let me think."

I was beginning to remind her that to-day was Wednesday, when she checked me with her former impatient movement of the fingers of her right hand.

"There, there! I know nothing of days of the week; I know nothing of weeks of the year. Come again after six days. You hear?"

"Yes, ma'am."

"Estella, take him down. Let him have something to eat, and let him roam and look about him while he eats. Go, Pip."

I followed the candle down, as I had followed the candle up, and she stood it in the place where we had found it. Until she opened the side entrance, I had fancied, without thinking about it, that it must necessarily be night-time. The rush of the daylight quite confounded me, and made me feel as if I had been in the candlelight of the strange room many hours.

"You are to wait here, you boy," said Estella; and disappeared and closed the door.

I took the opportunity of being alone in the courtyard to look at my coarse hands and my common boots. My opinion of those accessories was not favorable. They had never troubled me before, but they troubled me now, as vulgar appendages. I determined to ask Joe why he had ever taught me to call those picture-cards Jacks, which ought to be called knaves. I wished Joe had been rather more genteelly brought up, and then I should have been so too.

She came back, with some bread and meat and a little mug of beer. She put the mug down on the stones of the yard, and gave me the bread and meat without looking at me, as insolently as if I were a dog in disgrace. I was so humiliated, hurt, spurned, offended, angry, sorry,—I cannot hit upon the right name for the smart—God knows what its name was,—that tears started to my eyes. The moment they sprang there, the girl looked at me with a quick delight in having been the cause of them. This gave me power to keep them back and to look at her: so, she gave a contemptuous toss—but with a sense, I thought, of having made too sure that I was so wounded—and left me.

But when she was gone, I looked about me for a place to hide my face in, and got behind one of the gates in the brewery-lane, and leaned my sleeve against the wall there, and leaned my forehead on it and cried. As I cried, I kicked the wall, and took a hard twist at my hair; so bitter were my feelings, and so sharp was the smart without a name, that needed counteraction.

My sister's bringing up had made me sensitive. In the little world in which children have their existence whosoever brings them up, there is nothing so finely perceived and so finely felt as injustice. It may be only small injustice that the child can be exposed to; but the child is small, and its world is small, and its rocking-horse stands as many hands high, according to scale, as a big-boned Irish hunter. Within myself, I had sustained, from my babyhood, a perpetual conflict with injustice. I had known, from the time when I could speak, that my sister, in her capricious and violent coercion, was unjust to me. I had cherished a profound conviction that her bringing me up by hand gave her no right to bring me up by jerks. Through all my punishments, disgraces, fasts, and vigils, and other penitential performances, I had nursed this assurance; and to my communing so much with it, in a solitary and unprotected way, I in great part refer the fact that I was morally timid and very sensitive.

I got rid of my injured feelings for the time by kicking them into the brewery wall, and twisting them out of my hair, and then I smoothed my face with my sleeve, and came from behind the gate. The bread and meat were acceptable, and the beer was warming and tingling, and I was soon in spirits to look about me.

To be sure, it was a deserted place, down to the pigeon-house in the brewery-yard, which had been blown crooked on its pole by some high wind, and would have made the pigeons think themselves at sea, if there had been any pigeons there to be rocked by it. But there were no pigeons in the dove-cot, no horses in the stable, no pigs in the sty, no malt in the storehouse, no smells of grains and beer in the copper or the vat. All the uses and scents of the brewery might have evaporated with its last reek of smoke. In a by-yard, there was a wilderness of empty casks, which had a certain sour remembrance of better days lingering about them; but it was too sour to be accepted as a sample of the beer that was gone,—and in this respect I remember those recluses as being like most others.

Behind the furthest end of the brewery, was a rank garden with an old wall; not so high but that I could struggle up and hold on long enough to look over it, and see that the rank garden was the garden of the house, and that it was overgrown with tangled weeds, but that there was a track upon the green and yellow paths, as if some one sometimes walked there, and that Estella was walking away from me even then. But she seemed to be everywhere. For when I yielded to the temptation presented by the casks, and began to walk on them, I saw her walking on them at the end of the yard of casks. She had her back towards me, and held her pretty brown hair spread out in her two hands, and never looked round, and passed out of my view directly. So, in the brewery itself,—by which I mean the large paved lofty place in which they used to make the beer, and where the brewing utensils still were. When I first went into it, and, rather oppressed by its gloom, stood near the door looking about me, I saw her pass among the extinguished fires, and ascend some light iron stairs, and go out by a gallery high overhead, as if she were going out into the sky.

It was in this place, and at this moment, that a strange thing happened to my fancy. I thought it a strange thing then, and I thought it a stranger thing long afterwards. I turned my eyes—a little dimmed by looking up at the frosty light—towards a great wooden beam in a low nook of the building near me on my right hand, and I saw a figure hanging there by the neck. A figure all in yellow white, with but one shoe to the feet; and it hung so, that I could see that the faded trimmings of the dress were like earthy paper, and that the face was Miss Havisham's, with a movement going over the whole countenance as if she were trying to call to me. In the terror of seeing the figure, and in the terror of being certain that it had not been there a moment before, I at first ran from it, and then ran towards it. And my terror was greatest of all when I found no figure there.

Nothing less than the frosty light of the cheerful sky, the sight of people passing beyond the bars of the court-yard gate, and the reviving influence of the rest of the bread and meat and beer, would have brought me round. Even with those aids, I might not have come to myself as soon as I did, but that I saw Estella approaching with the keys, to let me out. She would have some fair reason for looking down upon me, I thought, if she saw me frightened; and she would have no fair reason.

She gave me a triumphant glance in passing me, as if she rejoiced that my hands were so coarse and my boots were so thick, and she opened the gate, and stood holding it. I was passing out without looking at her, when she touched me with a taunting hand.

"Why don't you cry?"

"Because I don't want to."

"You do," said she. "You have been crying till you are half blind, and you are near crying again now."

She laughed contemptuously, pushed me out, and locked the gate upon me. I went straight to Mr. Pumblechook's, and was immensely relieved to find him not at home.

So, leaving word with the shopman on what day I was wanted at Miss Havisham's again, I set off on the four-mile walk to our forge; pondering, as I went along, on all I had seen, and deeply revolving that I was a common laboring-boy; that my hands were coarse; that my boots were thick; that I had fallen into a despicable habit of calling knaves Jacks; that I was much more ignorant than I had considered myself last night, and generally that I was in a low-lived bad way.

CHAPTER IX

When I reached home, my sister was very curious to know all about Miss Havisham's, and asked a number of questions. And I soon found myself getting heavily bumped from behind in the nape of the neck and the small of the back, and having my face ignominiously shoved against the kitchen wall, because I did not answer those questions at sufficient length.

If a dread of not being understood be hidden in the breasts of other young people to anything like the extent to which it used to be hidden in mine,—which I consider probable, as I have no particular reason to suspect myself of having been a monstrosity,—it is the key to many reservations. I felt convinced that if I described Miss Havisham's as my eyes had seen it, I should not be understood. Not only that, but I felt convinced that Miss Havisham too would not be understood; and although she was perfectly incomprehensible to me, I entertained an impression that there would be something coarse and treacherous in my dragging her as she really was (to say nothing of Miss Estella) before the contemplation of Mrs. Joe. Consequently, I said as little as I could, and had my face shoved against the kitchen wall.

The worst of it was that that bullying old Pumblechook, preyed upon by a devouring curiosity to be informed of all I had seen and heard, came gaping over in his chaise-cart at tea-time, to have the details divulged to him. And the mere sight of the torment, with his fishy eyes and mouth open, his sandy hair inquisitively on end, and his waistcoat heaving with windy arithmetic, made me vicious in my reticence.

"Well, boy," Uncle Pumblechook began, as soon as he was seated in the chair of honor by the fire. "How did you get on up town?"

I answered, "Pretty well, sir," and my sister shook her fist at me.

"Pretty well?" Mr. Pumblechook repeated. "Pretty well is no answer. Tell us what you mean by pretty well, boy?"

Whitewash on the forehead hardens the brain into a state of obstinacy perhaps. Anyhow, with whitewash from the wall on my forehead, my obstinacy was adamantine. I reflected for some time, and then answered as if I had discovered a new idea, "I mean pretty well."

My sister with an exclamation of impatience was going to fly at me,—I had no shadow of defence, for Joe was busy in the forge,—when Mr. Pumblechook interposed with "No! Don't lose your temper. Leave this lad to me, ma'am; leave this lad to me." Mr. Pumblechook then turned me towards him, as if he were going to cut my hair, and said,—

"First (to get our thoughts in order): Forty-three pence?"

I calculated the consequences of replying "Four Hundred Pound," and finding them against me, went as near the answer as I could—which was somewhere about eightpence off. Mr. Pumblechook then put me through my pence-table from "twelve pence make one shilling," up to "forty pence make three and fourpence," and then triumphantly demanded, as if he had done for me, "Now! How much is forty-three pence?" To which I replied, after a long interval of reflection, "I don't know." And I was so aggravated that I almost doubt if I did know.

Mr. Pumblechook worked his head like a screw to screw it out of me, and said, "Is forty-three pence seven and sixpence three fardens, for instance?"

"Yes!" said I. And although my sister instantly boxed my ears, it was highly gratifying to me to see that the answer spoilt his joke, and brought him to a dead stop.

"Boy! What like is Miss Havisham?" Mr. Pumblechook began again when he had recovered; folding his arms tight on his chest and applying the screw.

"Very tall and dark," I told him.

"Is she, uncle?" asked my sister.

Mr. Pumblechook winked assent; from which I at once inferred that he had never seen Miss Havisham, for she was nothing of the kind.

"Good!" said Mr. Pumblechook conceitedly. ("This is the way to have him! We are beginning to hold our own, I think, Mum?")

"I am sure, uncle," returned Mrs. Joe, "I wish you had him always; you know so well how to deal with him."

"Now, boy! What was she a doing of, when you went in today?" asked Mr. Pumblechook.

"She was sitting," I answered, "in a black velvet coach."

Mr. Pumblechook and Mrs. Joe stared at one another—as they well Might—and both repeated, "In a black velvet coach?"

"Yes," said I. "And Miss Estella—that's her niece, I think—handed her in cake and wine at the coach-window, on a gold plate. And we all had cake and wine on gold plates. And I got up behind the coach to eat mine, because she told me to."

"Was anybody else there?" asked Mr. Pumblechook.

"Four dogs," said I.

"Large or small?"

"Immense," said I. "And they fought for veal-cutlets out of a silver basket."

Mr. Pumblechook and Mrs. Joe stared at one another again, in utter amazement. I was perfectly frantic,—a reckless witness under the torture,—and would have told them anything.

"Where was this coach, in the name of gracious?" asked my sister.

"In Miss Havisham's room." They stared again. "But there weren't any horses to it." I added this saving clause, in the moment of rejecting four richly caparisoned coursers which I had had wild thoughts of harnessing.

"Can this be possible, uncle?" asked Mrs. Joe. "What can the boy mean?"

"I'll tell you, Mum," said Mr. Pumblechook. "My opinion is, it's a sedan-chair. She's flighty, you know,—very flighty,—quite flighty enough to pass her days in a sedan-chair."

"Did you ever see her in it, uncle?" asked Mrs. Joe.

"How could I," he returned, forced to the admission, "when I never see her in my life? Never clapped eyes upon her!"

"Goodness, uncle! And yet you have spoken to her?"

"Why, don't you know," said Mr. Pumblechook, testily, "that when I have been there, I have been took up to the outside of her door, and the door has stood ajar, and she has spoke to me that way. Don't say you don't know that, Mum. Howsever, the boy went there to play. What did you play at, boy?"

"We played with flags," I said. (I beg to observe that I think of myself with amazement, when I recall the lies I told on this occasion.)

"Flags!" echoed my sister.

"Yes," said I. "Estella waved a blue flag, and I waved a red one, and Miss Havisham waved one sprinkled all over with little gold stars, out at the coach-window. And then we all waved our swords and hurrahed."

"Swords!" repeated my sister. "Where did you get swords from?"

"Out of a cupboard," said I. "And I saw pistols in it,—and jam,—and pills. And there was no daylight in the room, but it was all lighted up with candles."

"That's true, Mum," said Mr. Pumblechook, with a grave nod. "That's the state of the case, for that much I've seen myself." And then they both stared at me, and I, with an obtrusive show of artlessness on my countenance, stared at them, and plaited the right leg of my trousers with my right hand.

If they had asked me any more questions, I should undoubtedly have betrayed myself, for I was even then on the point of mentioning that there was a balloon in the yard, and should have hazarded the statement but for my invention being divided between that phenomenon and a bear in the brewery. They were so much occupied, however, in discussing the marvels I had already presented for their consideration, that I escaped. The subject still held them when Joe came in from his work to have a cup of tea. To whom my sister, more for the relief of her own mind than for the gratification of his, related my pretended experiences.

Now, when I saw Joe open his blue eyes and roll them all round the kitchen in helpless amazement, I was overtaken by penitence; but only as regarded him,—not in the least as regarded the other two. Towards Joe, and Joe only, I considered myself a young monster, while they sat debating what results would come to me from Miss Havisham's acquaintance and favor. They had no doubt that Miss Havisham would "do something" for me; their doubts related to the form that something would take. My sister stood out for "property." Mr. Pumblechook was in favor of a handsome premium for binding me apprentice to some genteel trade,—say, the corn and seed trade, for instance. Joe fell into the deepest disgrace with both, for offering the bright suggestion that I might only be presented with one of the dogs who had fought for the veal-cutlets. "If a fool's head can't express better opinions than that," said my sister, "and you have got any work to do, you had better go and do it." So he went.

After Mr. Pumblechook had driven off, and when my sister was washing up, I stole into the forge to Joe, and remained by him until he had done for the night. Then I said, "Before the fire goes out, Joe, I should like to tell you something."

"Should you, Pip?" said Joe, drawing his shoeing-stool near the forge. "Then tell us. What is it, Pip?"

"Joe," said I, taking hold of his rolled-up shirt sleeve, and twisting it between my finger and thumb, "you remember all that about Miss Havisham's?"

"Remember?" said Joe. "I believe you! Wonderful!"

"It's a terrible thing, Joe; it ain't true."

"What are you telling of, Pip?" cried Joe, falling back in the greatest amazement. "You don't mean to say it's—"

"Yes I do; it's lies, Joe."

"But not all of it? Why sure you don't mean to say, Pip, that there was no black welwet co—ch?" For, I stood shaking my head. "But at least there was dogs, Pip? Come, Pip," said Joe, persuasively, "if there warn't no weal-cutlets, at least there was dogs?"

"No, Joe."

"A dog?" said Joe. "A puppy? Come?"

"No, Joe, there was nothing at all of the kind."

As I fixed my eyes hopelessly on Joe, Joe contemplated me in dismay. "Pip, old chap! This won't do, old fellow! I say! Where do you expect to go to?"

"It's terrible, Joe; ain't it?"

"Terrible?" cried Joe. "Awful! What possessed you?"

"I don't know what possessed me, Joe," I replied, letting his shirt sleeve go, and sitting down in the ashes at his feet, hanging my head; "but I wish you hadn't taught me to call Knaves at cards Jacks; and I wish my boots weren't so thick nor my hands so coarse."

And then I told Joe that I felt very miserable, and that I hadn't been able to explain myself to Mrs. Joe and Pumblechook, who were so rude to me, and that there had been a beautiful young lady at Miss Havisham's who was dreadfully proud, and that she had said I was common, and that I knew I was common, and that I wished I was not common, and that the lies had come of it somehow, though I didn't know how.

This was a case of metaphysics, at least as difficult for Joe to deal with as for me. But Joe took the case altogether out of the region of metaphysics, and by that means vanquished it.

"There's one thing you may be sure of, Pip," said Joe, after some rumination, "namely, that lies is lies. Howsever they come, they didn't ought to come, and they come from the father of lies, and work round to the same. Don't you tell no more of 'em, Pip. That ain't the way to get out of being common, old chap. And as to being common, I don't make it out at all clear. You are oncommon in some things. You're oncommon small. Likewise you're a oncommon scholar."

"No, I am ignorant and backward, Joe."

"Why, see what a letter you wrote last night! Wrote in print even! I've seen letters—Ah! and from gentlefolks!—that I'll swear weren't wrote in print," said Joe.

"I have learnt next to nothing, Joe. You think much of me. It's only that."

"Well, Pip," said Joe, "be it so or be it son't, you must be a common scholar afore you can be a oncommon one, I should hope! The king upon his throne, with his crown upon his ed, can't sit and write his acts of Parliament in print, without having begun, when he were a unpromoted Prince, with the alphabet.—Ah!" added Joe, with a shake of the head that was full of meaning, "and begun at A. too, and worked his way to Z. And I know what that is to do, though I can't say I've exactly done it."

There was some hope in this piece of wisdom, and it rather encouraged me.

"Whether common ones as to callings and earnings," pursued Joe, reflectively, "mightn't be the better of continuing for to keep company with common ones, instead of going out to play with oncommon ones,—which reminds me to hope that there were a flag, perhaps?"

"No, Joe."

"(I'm sorry there weren't a flag, Pip). Whether that might be or mightn't be, is a thing as can't be looked into now, without putting your sister on the Rampage; and that's a thing not to be thought of as being done intentional. Lookee here, Pip, at what is said to you by a true friend. Which this to you the true friend say. If you can't get to be oncommon through going straight, you'll never get to do it through going crooked. So don't tell no more on 'em, Pip, and live well and die happy."

"You are not angry with me, Joe?"

"No, old chap. But bearing in mind that them were which I meantersay of a stunning and outdacious sort,—alluding to them which bordered on weal-cutlets and dog-fighting,—a sincere well-wisher would adwise, Pip, their being dropped into your meditations, when you go up stairs to bed. That's all, old chap, and don't never do it no more."

When I got up to my little room and said my prayers, I did not forget Joe's recommendation, and yet my young mind was in that disturbed and unthankful state, that I thought long after I laid me down, how common Estella would consider Joe, a mere blacksmith; how thick his boots, and how coarse his hands. I thought how Joe and my sister were then sitting in the kitchen, and how I had come up to bed from the kitchen, and how Miss Havisham and Estella never sat in a kitchen, but were far above the level of such common doings. I fell asleep recalling what I "used to do" when I was at Miss Havisham's; as though I had been there weeks or months, instead of hours; and as though it were quite an old subject of remembrance, instead of one that had arisen only that day.

That was a memorable day to me, for it made great changes in me. But it is the same with any life. Imagine one selected day struck out of it, and think how different its course would have been. Pause you who read this, and think for a moment of the long chain of iron or gold, of thorns or flowers, that would never have bound you, but for the formation of the first link on one memorable day.

CHAPTER X

The felicitous idea occurred to me a morning or two later when I woke, that the best step I could take towards making myself uncommon was to get out of Biddy everything she knew. In pursuance of this luminous conception I mentioned to Biddy when I went to Mr. Wopsle's great-aunt's at night, that I had a particular reason for wishing to get on in life, and that I should feel very much obliged to her if she would impart all her learning to me. Biddy, who was the most obliging of girls, immediately said she would, and indeed began to carry out her promise within five minutes.

The Educational scheme or Course established by Mr. Wopsle's great-aunt may be resolved into the following synopsis. The pupils ate apples and put straws down one another's backs, until Mr. Wopsle's great-aunt collected her energies, and made an indiscriminate totter at them with a birch-rod. After receiving the charge with every mark of derision, the pupils formed in line and buzzingly passed a ragged book from hand to hand. The book had an alphabet in it, some figures and tables, and a little spelling,—that is to say, it had had once. As soon as this volume began to circulate, Mr. Wopsle's great-aunt fell into a state of coma, arising either from sleep or a rheumatic paroxysm. The pupils then entered among themselves upon a competitive examination on the subject of Boots, with the view of ascertaining who could tread the hardest upon whose toes. This mental exercise lasted until Biddy made a rush at them and distributed three defaced Bibles (shaped as if they had been unskilfully cut off the chump end of something), more illegibly printed at the best than any curiosities of literature I have since met with, speckled all over with ironmould, and having various specimens of the insect world smashed between their leaves. This part of the Course was usually lightened by several single combats between Biddy and refractory students. When the fights were over, Biddy gave out the number of a page, and then we all read aloud what we could,—or what we couldn't—in a frightful chorus; Biddy leading with a high, shrill, monotonous voice, and none of us having the least notion of, or reverence for, what we were reading about. When this horrible din had lasted a certain time, it mechanically awoke Mr. Wopsle's great-aunt, who staggered at a boy fortuitously, and pulled his ears. This was understood to terminate the Course for the evening, and we emerged into the air with shrieks of intellectual victory. It is fair to remark that there was no prohibition against any pupil's entertaining himself with a slate or even with the ink (when there was any), but that it was not easy to pursue that branch of study in the winter season, on account of the little general shop in which the classes were holden—and which was also Mr. Wopsle's great-aunt's sitting-room and bedchamber—being but faintly illuminated through the agency of one low-spirited dip-candle and no snuffers.

It appeared to me that it would take time to become uncommon, under these circumstances: nevertheless, I resolved to try it, and that very evening Biddy entered on our special agreement, by imparting some information from her little catalogue of Prices, under the head of moist sugar, and lending me, to copy at home, a large old English D which she had imitated from the heading of some newspaper, and which I supposed, until she told me what it was, to be a design for a buckle.

Of course there was a public-house in the village, and of course Joe liked sometimes to smoke his pipe there. I had received strict orders from my sister to call for him at the Three Jolly Bargemen, that evening, on my way from school, and bring him home at my peril. To the Three Jolly Bargemen, therefore, I directed my steps.

There was a bar at the Jolly Bargemen, with some alarmingly long chalk scores in it on the wall at the side of the door, which seemed to me to be never paid off. They had been there ever since I could remember, and had grown more than I had. But there was a quantity of chalk about our country, and perhaps the people neglected no opportunity of turning it to account.

It being Saturday night, I found the landlord looking rather grimly at these records; but as my business was with Joe and not with him, I merely wished him good evening, and passed into the common room at the end of the passage, where there was a bright large kitchen fire, and where Joe was smoking his pipe in company with Mr. Wopsle and a stranger. Joe greeted me as usual with "Halloa, Pip, old chap!" and the moment he said that, the stranger turned his head and looked at me.

He was a secret-looking man whom I had never seen before. His head was all on one side, and one of his eyes was half shut up, as if he were taking aim at something with an invisible gun. He had a pipe in his mouth, and he took it out, and, after slowly blowing all his smoke away and looking hard at me all the time, nodded. So, I nodded, and then he nodded again, and made room on the settle beside him that I might sit down there.

But as I was used to sit beside Joe whenever I entered that place of resort, I said "No, thank you, sir," and fell into the space Joe made for me on the opposite settle. The strange man, after glancing at Joe, and seeing that his attention was otherwise engaged, nodded to me again when I had taken my seat, and then rubbed his leg—in a very odd way, as it struck me.

"You was saying," said the strange man, turning to Joe, "that you was a blacksmith."

"Yes. I said it, you know," said Joe.

"What'll you drink, Mr.—? You didn't mention your name, by the bye."

Joe mentioned it now, and the strange man called him by it. "What'll you drink, Mr. Gargery? At my expense? To top up with?"

"Well," said Joe, "to tell you the truth, I ain't much in the habit of drinking at anybody's expense but my own."

"Habit? No," returned the stranger, "but once and away, and on a Saturday night too. Come! Put a name to it, Mr. Gargery."

"I wouldn't wish to be stiff company," said Joe. "Rum."

"Rum," repeated the stranger. "And will the other gentleman originate a sentiment."

"Rum," said Mr. Wopsle.

"Three Rums!" cried the stranger, calling to the landlord. "Glasses round!"

"This other gentleman," observed Joe, by way of introducing Mr. Wopsle, "is a gentleman that you would like to hear give it out. Our clerk at church."

"Aha!" said the stranger, quickly, and cocking his eye at me. "The lonely church, right out on the marshes, with graves round it!"

"That's it," said Joe.

The stranger, with a comfortable kind of grunt over his pipe, put his legs up on the settle that he had to himself. He wore a flapping broad-brimmed traveller's hat, and under it a handkerchief tied over his head in the manner of a cap: so that he showed no hair. As he looked at the fire, I thought I saw a cunning expression, followed by a half-laugh, come into his face.

"I am not acquainted with this country, gentlemen, but it seems a solitary country towards the river."

"Most marshes is solitary," said Joe.

"No doubt, no doubt. Do you find any gypsies, now, or tramps, or vagrants of any sort, out there?"

"No," said Joe; "none but a runaway convict now and then. And we don't find them, easy. Eh, Mr. Wopsle?"

Mr. Wopsle, with a majestic remembrance of old discomfiture, assented; but not warmly.

"Seems you have been out after such?" asked the stranger.

"Once," returned Joe. "Not that we wanted to take them, you understand; we went out as lookers on; me, and Mr. Wopsle, and Pip. Didn't us, Pip?"

"Yes, Joe."

The stranger looked at me again,—still cocking his eye, as if he were expressly taking aim at me with his invisible gun,—and said, "He's a likely young parcel of bones that. What is it you call him?"

"Pip," said Joe.

"Christened Pip?"

"No, not christened Pip."

"Surname Pip?"

"No," said Joe, "it's a kind of family name what he gave himself when a infant, and is called by."

"Son of yours?"

"Well," said Joe, meditatively, not, of course, that it could be in anywise necessary to consider about it, but because it was the way at the Jolly Bargemen to seem to consider deeply about everything that was discussed over pipes,—"well—no. No, he ain't."

"Nevvy?" said the strange man.

"Well," said Joe, with the same appearance of profound cogitation, "he is not—no, not to deceive you, he is not—my nevvy."

"What the Blue Blazes is he?" asked the stranger. Which appeared to me to be an inquiry of unnecessary strength.

Mr. Wopsle struck in upon that; as one who knew all about relationships, having professional occasion to bear in mind what female relations a man might not marry; and expounded the ties between me and Joe. Having his hand in, Mr. Wopsle finished off with a most terrifically snarling passage from Richard the Third, and seemed to think he had done quite enough to account for it when he added, "—as the poet says."

And here I may remark that when Mr. Wopsle referred to me, he considered it a necessary part of such reference to rumple my hair and poke it into my eyes. I cannot conceive why everybody of his standing who visited at our house should always have put me through the same inflammatory process under similar circumstances. Yet I do not call to mind that I was ever in my earlier youth the subject of remark in our social family circle, but some large-handed person took some such ophthalmic steps to patronize me.

All this while, the strange man looked at nobody but me, and looked at me as if he were determined to have a shot at me at last, and bring me down. But he said nothing after offering his Blue Blazes observation, until the glasses of rum and water were brought; and then he made his shot, and a most extraordinary shot it was.

It was not a verbal remark, but a proceeding in dumb-show, and was pointedly addressed to me. He stirred his rum and water pointedly at me, and he tasted his rum and water pointedly at me. And he stirred it and he tasted it; not with a spoon that was brought to him, but with a file.

He did this so that nobody but I saw the file; and when he had done it he wiped the file and put it in a breast-pocket. I knew it to be Joe's file, and I knew that he knew my convict, the moment I saw the instrument. I sat gazing at him, spell-bound. But he now reclined on his settle, taking very little notice of me, and talking principally about turnips.

There was a delicious sense of cleaning-up and making a quiet pause before going on in life afresh, in our village on Saturday nights, which stimulated Joe to dare to stay out half an hour longer on Saturdays than at other times. The half-hour and the rum and water running out together, Joe got up to go, and took me by the hand.

"Stop half a moment, Mr. Gargery," said the strange man. "I think I've got a bright new shilling somewhere in my pocket, and if I have, the boy shall have it."

He looked it out from a handful of small change, folded it in some crumpled paper, and gave it to me. "Yours!" said he. "Mind! Your own."

I thanked him, staring at him far beyond the bounds of good manners, and holding tight to Joe. He gave Joe good-night, and he gave Mr. Wopsle good-night (who went out with us), and he gave me only a look with his aiming eye,—no, not a look, for he shut it up, but wonders may be done with an eye by hiding it.

On the way home, if I had been in a humor for talking, the talk must have been all on my side, for Mr. Wopsle parted from us at the door of the Jolly Bargemen, and Joe went all the way home with his mouth wide open, to rinse the rum out with as much air as possible. But I was in a manner stupefied by this turning up of my old misdeed and old acquaintance, and could think of nothing else.

My sister was not in a very bad temper when we presented ourselves in the kitchen, and Joe was encouraged by that unusual circumstance to tell her about the bright shilling. "A bad un, I'll be bound," said Mrs. Joe triumphantly, "or he wouldn't have given it to the boy! Let's look at it."

I took it out of the paper, and it proved to be a good one. "But what's this?" said Mrs. Joe, throwing down the shilling and catching up the paper. "Two One-Pound notes?"

Nothing less than two fat sweltering one-pound notes that seemed to have been on terms of the warmest intimacy with all the cattle-markets in the county. Joe caught up his hat again, and ran with them to the Jolly Bargemen to restore them to their owner. While he was gone, I sat down on my usual stool and looked vacantly at my sister, feeling pretty sure that the man would not be there.

Presently, Joe came back, saying that the man was gone, but that he, Joe, had left word at the Three Jolly Bargemen concerning the notes. Then my sister sealed them up in a piece of paper, and put them under some dried rose-leaves in an ornamental teapot on the top of a press in the state parlor. There they remained, a nightmare to me, many and many a night and day.

I had sadly broken sleep when I got to bed, through thinking of the strange man taking aim at me with his invisible gun, and of the guiltily coarse and common thing it was, to be on secret terms of conspiracy with convicts,—a feature in my low career that I had previously forgotten. I was haunted by the file too. A dread possessed me that when I least expected it, the file would reappear. I coaxed myself to sleep by thinking of Miss Havisham's, next Wednesday; and in my sleep I saw the file coming at me out of a door, without seeing who held it, and I screamed myself awake.

CHAPTER XI

At the appointed time I returned to Miss Havisham's, and my hesitating ring at the gate brought out Estella. She locked it after admitting me, as she had done before, and again preceded me into the dark passage where her candle stood. She took no notice of me until she had the candle in her hand, when she looked over her shoulder, superciliously saying, "You are to come this way to-day," and took me to quite another part of the house.

The passage was a long one, and seemed to pervade the whole square basement of the Manor House. We traversed but one side of the square, however, and at the end of it she stopped, and put her candle down and opened a door. Here, the daylight reappeared, and I found myself in a small paved courtyard, the opposite side of which was formed by a detached dwelling-house, that looked as if it had once belonged to the manager or head clerk of the extinct brewery. There was a clock in the outer wall of this house. Like the clock in Miss Havisham's room, and like Miss Havisham's watch, it had stopped at twenty minutes to nine.

We went in at the door, which stood open, and into a gloomy room with a low ceiling, on the ground-floor at the back. There was some company in the room, and Estella said to me as she joined it, "You are to go and stand there boy, till you are wanted." "There", being the window, I crossed to it, and stood "there," in a very uncomfortable state of mind, looking out.

It opened to the ground, and looked into a most miserable corner of the neglected garden, upon a rank ruin of cabbage-stalks, and one box-tree that had been clipped round long ago, like a pudding, and had a new growth at the top of it, out of shape and of a different color, as if that part of the pudding had stuck to the saucepan and got burnt. This was my homely thought, as I contemplated the box-tree. There had been some light snow, overnight, and it lay nowhere else to my knowledge; but, it had not quite melted from the cold shadow of this bit of garden, and the wind caught it up in little eddies and threw it at the window, as if it pelted me for coming there.

I divined that my coming had stopped conversation in the room, and that its other occupants were looking at me. I could see nothing of the room except the shining of the fire in the window-glass, but I stiffened in all my joints with the consciousness that I was under close inspection.

There were three ladies in the room and one gentleman. Before I had been standing at the window five minutes, they somehow conveyed to me that they were all toadies and humbugs, but that each of them pretended not to know that the others were toadies and humbugs: because the admission that he or she did know it, would have made him or her out to be a toady and humbug.

They all had a listless and dreary air of waiting somebody's pleasure, and the most talkative of the ladies had to speak quite rigidly to repress a yawn. This lady, whose name was Camilla, very much reminded me of my sister, with the difference that she was older, and (as I found when I caught sight of her) of a blunter cast of features. Indeed, when I knew her better I began to think it was a Mercy she had any features at all, so very blank and high was the dead wall of her face.

"Poor dear soul!" said this lady, with an abruptness of manner quite my sister's. "Nobody's enemy but his own!"

"It would be much more commendable to be somebody else's enemy," said the gentleman; "far more natural."

"Cousin Raymond," observed another lady, "we are to love our neighbor."

"Sarah Pocket," returned Cousin Raymond, "if a man is not his own neighbor, who is?"

Miss Pocket laughed, and Camilla laughed and said (checking a yawn), "The idea!" But I thought they seemed to think it rather a good idea too. The other lady, who had not spoken yet, said gravely and emphatically, "Very true!"

"Poor soul!" Camilla presently went on (I knew they had all been looking at me in the mean time), "he is so very strange! Would anyone believe that when Tom's wife died, he actually could not be induced to see the importance of the children's having the deepest of trimmings to their mourning? 'Good Lord!' says he, 'Camilla, what can it signify so long as the poor bereaved little things are in black?' So like Matthew! The idea!"

"Good points in him, good points in him," said Cousin Raymond; "Heaven forbid I should deny good points in him; but he never had, and he never will have, any sense of the proprieties."

"You know I was obliged," said Camilla,—"I was obliged to be firm. I said, 'It WILL NOT DO, for the credit of the family.' I told him that, without deep trimmings, the family was disgraced. I cried about it from breakfast till dinner. I injured my digestion. And at last he flung out in his violent way, and said, with a D, 'Then do as you like.' Thank Goodness it will always be a consolation to me to know that I instantly went out in a pouring rain and bought the things."

"He paid for them, did he not?" asked Estella.

"It's not the question, my dear child, who paid for them," returned Camilla. "I bought them. And I shall often think of that with peace, when I wake up in the night."

The ringing of a distant bell, combined with the echoing of some cry or call along the passage by which I had come, interrupted the conversation and caused Estella to say to me, "Now, boy!" On my turning round, they all looked at me with the utmost contempt, and, as I went out, I heard Sarah Pocket say, "Well I am sure! What next!" and Camilla add, with indignation, "Was there ever such a fancy! The i-de-a!"

As we were going with our candle along the dark passage, Estella stopped all of a sudden, and, facing round, said in her taunting manner, with her face quite close to mine,—

"Well?"

"Well, miss?" I answered, almost falling over her and checking myself.

She stood looking at me, and, of course, I stood looking at her.

"Am I pretty?"

"Yes; I think you are very pretty."

"Am I insulting?"

"Not so much so as you were last time," said I.

"Not so much so?"

"No."

She fired when she asked the last question, and she slapped my face with such force as she had, when I answered it.

"Now?" said she. "You little coarse monster, what do you think of me now?"

"I shall not tell you."

"Because you are going to tell up stairs. Is that it?"

"No," said I, "that's not it."

"Why don't you cry again, you little wretch?"

"Because I'll never cry for you again," said I. Which was, I suppose, as false a declaration as ever was made; for I was inwardly crying for her then, and I know what I know of the pain she cost me afterwards.

We went on our way up stairs after this episode; and, as we were going up, we met a gentleman groping his way down.

"Whom have we here?" asked the gentleman, stopping and looking at me.

"A boy," said Estella.

He was a burly man of an exceedingly dark complexion, with an exceedingly large head, and a corresponding large hand. He took my chin in his large hand and turned up my face to have a look at me by the light of the candle. He was prematurely bald on the top of his head, and had bushy black eyebrows that wouldn't lie down but stood up bristling. His eyes were set very deep in his head, and were disagreeably sharp and suspicious. He had a large watch-chain, and strong black dots where his beard and whiskers would have been if he had let them. He was nothing to me, and I could have had no foresight then, that he ever would be anything to me, but it happened that I had this opportunity of observing him well.

"Boy of the neighborhood? Hey?" said he.

"Yes, sir," said I.

"How do you come here?"

"Miss Havisham sent for me, sir," I explained.

"Well! Behave yourself. I have a pretty large experience of boys, and you're a bad set of fellows. Now mind!" said he, biting the side of his great forefinger as he frowned at me, "you behave yourself!"

With those words, he released me—which I was glad of, for his hand smelt of scented soap—and went his way down stairs. I wondered whether he could be a doctor; but no, I thought; he couldn't be a doctor, or he would have a quieter and more persuasive manner. There was not much time to consider the subject, for we were soon in Miss Havisham's room, where she and everything else were just as I had left them. Estella left me standing near the door, and I stood there until Miss Havisham cast her eyes upon me from the dressing-table.

"So!" she said, without being startled or surprised: "the days have worn away, have they?"

"Yes, ma'am. To-day is—"

"There, there, there!" with the impatient movement of her fingers. "I don't want to know. Are you ready to play?"

I was obliged to answer in some confusion, "I don't think I am, ma'am."

"Not at cards again?" she demanded, with a searching look.

"Yes, ma'am; I could do that, if I was wanted."

"Since this house strikes you old and grave, boy," said Miss Havisham, impatiently, "and you are unwilling to play, are you willing to work?"

I could answer this inquiry with a better heart than I had been able to find for the other question, and I said I was quite willing.

"Then go into that opposite room," said she, pointing at the door behind me with her withered hand, "and wait there till I come."

I crossed the staircase landing, and entered the room she indicated. From that room, too, the daylight was completely excluded, and it had an airless smell that was oppressive. A fire had been lately kindled in the damp old-fashioned grate, and it was more disposed to go out than to burn up, and the reluctant smoke which hung in the room seemed colder than the clearer air,—like our own marsh mist. Certain wintry branches of candles on the high chimney-piece faintly lighted the chamber; or it would be more expressive to say, faintly troubled its darkness. It was spacious, and I dare say had once been handsome, but every discernible thing in it was covered with dust and mould, and dropping to pieces. The most prominent object was a long table with a tablecloth spread on it, as if a feast had been in preparation when the house and the clocks all stopped together. An epergne or centre-piece of some kind was in the middle of this cloth; it was so heavily overhung with cobwebs that its form was quite undistinguishable; and, as I looked along the yellow expanse out of which I remember its seeming to grow, like a black fungus, I saw speckle-legged spiders with blotchy bodies running home to it, and running out from it, as if some circumstances of the greatest public importance had just transpired in the spider community.

I heard the mice too, rattling behind the panels, as if the same occurrence were important to their interests. But the black beetles took no notice of the agitation, and groped about the hearth in a ponderous elderly way, as if they were short-sighted and hard of hearing, and not on terms with one another.

These crawling things had fascinated my attention, and I was watching them from a distance, when Miss Havisham laid a hand upon my shoulder. In her other hand she had a crutch-headed stick on which she leaned, and she looked like the Witch of the place.

"This," said she, pointing to the long table with her stick, "is where I will be laid when I am dead. They shall come and look at me here."

With some vague misgiving that she might get upon the table then and there and die at once, the complete realization of the ghastly waxwork at the Fair, I shrank under her touch.

"What do you think that is?" she asked me, again pointing with her stick; "that, where those cobwebs are?"

"I can't guess what it is, ma'am."

"It's a great cake. A bride-cake. Mine!"

She looked all round the room in a glaring manner, and then said, leaning on me while her hand twitched my shoulder, "Come, come, come! Walk me, walk me!"

I made out from this, that the work I had to do, was to walk Miss Havisham round and round the room. Accordingly, I started at once, and she leaned upon my shoulder, and we went away at a pace that might have been an imitation (founded on my first impulse under that roof) of Mr. Pumblechook's chaise-cart.

She was not physically strong, and after a little time said, "Slower!" Still, we went at an impatient fitful speed, and as we went, she twitched the hand upon my shoulder, and worked her mouth, and led me to believe that we were going fast because her thoughts went fast. After a while she said, "Call Estella!" so I went out on the landing and roared that name as I had done on the previous occasion. When her light appeared, I returned to Miss Havisham, and we started away again round and round the room.

If only Estella had come to be a spectator of our proceedings, I should have felt sufficiently discontented; but as she brought with her the three ladies and the gentleman whom I had seen below, I didn't know what to do. In my politeness, I would have stopped; but Miss Havisham twitched my shoulder, and we posted on,—with a shame-faced consciousness on my part that they would think it was all my doing.

"Dear Miss Havisham," said Miss Sarah Pocket. "How well you look!"

"I do not," returned Miss Havisham. "I am yellow skin and bone."

Camilla brightened when Miss Pocket met with this rebuff; and she murmured, as she plaintively contemplated Miss Havisham, "Poor dear soul! Certainly not to be expected to look well, poor thing. The idea!"

"And how are you?" said Miss Havisham to Camilla. As we were close to Camilla then, I would have stopped as a matter of course, only Miss Havisham wouldn't stop. We swept on, and I felt that I was highly obnoxious to Camilla.

"Thank you, Miss Havisham," she returned, "I am as well as can be expected."

"Why, what's the matter with you?" asked Miss Havisham, with exceeding sharpness.

"Nothing worth mentioning," replied Camilla. "I don't wish to make a display of my feelings, but I have habitually thought of you more in the night than I am quite equal to."

"Then don't think of me," retorted Miss Havisham.

"Very easily said!" remarked Camilla, amiably repressing a sob, while a hitch came into her upper lip, and her tears overflowed. "Raymond is a witness what ginger and sal volatile I am obliged to take in the night. Raymond is a witness what nervous jerkings I have in my legs. Chokings and nervous jerkings, however, are nothing new to me when I think with anxiety of those I love. If I could be less affectionate and sensitive, I should have a better digestion and an iron set of nerves. I am sure I wish it could be so. But as to not thinking of you in the night—The idea!" Here, a burst of tears.

The Raymond referred to, I understood to be the gentleman present, and him I understood to be Mr. Camilla. He came to the rescue at this point, and said in a consolatory and complimentary voice, "Camilla, my dear, it is well known that your family feelings are gradually undermining you to the extent of making one of your legs shorter than the other."

"I am not aware," observed the grave lady whose voice I had heard but once, "that to think of any person is to make a great claim upon that person, my dear."

Miss Sarah Pocket, whom I now saw to be a little dry, brown, corrugated old woman, with a small face that might have been made of walnut-shells, and a large mouth like a cat's without the whiskers, supported this position by saying, "No, indeed, my dear. Hem!"

"Thinking is easy enough," said the grave lady.

"What is easier, you know?" assented Miss Sarah Pocket.

"Oh, yes, yes!" cried Camilla, whose fermenting feelings appeared to rise from her legs to her bosom. "It's all very true! It's a weakness to be so affectionate, but I can't help it. No doubt my health would be much better if it was otherwise, still I wouldn't change my disposition if I could. It's the cause of much suffering, but it's a consolation to know I posses it, when I wake up in the night." Here another burst of feeling.

Miss Havisham and I had never stopped all this time, but kept going round and round the room; now brushing against the skirts of the visitors, now giving them the whole length of the dismal chamber.

"There's Matthew!" said Camilla. "Never mixing with any natural ties, never coming here to see how Miss Havisham is! I have taken to the sofa with my staylace cut, and have lain there hours insensible, with my head over the side, and my hair all down, and my feet I don't know where—"

("Much higher than your head, my love," said Mr. Camilla.)

"I have gone off into that state, hours and hours, on account of Matthew's strange and inexplicable conduct, and nobody has thanked me."

"Really I must say I should think not!" interposed the grave lady.

"You see, my dear," added Miss Sarah Pocket (a blandly vicious personage), "the question to put to yourself is, who did you expect to thank you, my love?"

"Without expecting any thanks, or anything of the sort," resumed Camilla, "I have remained in that state, hours and hours, and Raymond is a witness of the extent to which I have choked, and what the total inefficacy of ginger has been, and I have been heard at the piano-forte tuner's across the street, where the poor mistaken children have even supposed it to be pigeons cooing at a distance,—and now to be told—" Here Camilla put her hand to her throat, and began to be quite chemical as to the formation of new combinations there.

When this same Matthew was mentioned, Miss Havisham stopped me and herself, and stood looking at the speaker. This change had a great influence in bringing Camilla's chemistry to a sudden end.

"Matthew will come and see me at last," said Miss Havisham, sternly, "when I am laid on that table. That will be his place,—there," striking the table with her stick, "at my head! And yours will be there! And your husband's there! And Sarah Pocket's there! And Georgiana's there! Now you all know where to take your stations when you come to feast upon me. And now go!"

At the mention of each name, she had struck the table with her stick in a new place. She now said, "Walk me, walk me!" and we went on again.

"I suppose there's nothing to be done," exclaimed Camilla, "but comply and depart. It's something to have seen the object of one's love and duty for even so short a time. I shall think of it with a melancholy satisfaction when I wake up in the night. I wish Matthew could have that comfort, but he sets it at defiance. I am determined not to make a display of my feelings, but it's very hard to be told one wants to feast on one's relations,—as if one was a Giant,—and to be told to go. The bare idea!"

Mr. Camilla interposing, as Mrs. Camilla laid her hand upon her heaving bosom, that lady assumed an unnatural fortitude of manner which I supposed to be expressive of an intention to drop and choke when out of view, and kissing her hand to Miss Havisham, was escorted forth. Sarah Pocket and Georgiana contended who should remain last; but Sarah was too knowing to be outdone, and ambled round Georgiana with that artful slipperiness that the latter was obliged to take precedence. Sarah Pocket then made her separate effect of departing with, "Bless you, Miss Havisham dear!" and with a smile of forgiving pity on her walnut-shell countenance for the weaknesses of the rest.

While Estella was away lighting them down, Miss Havisham still walked with her hand on my shoulder, but more and more slowly. At last she stopped before the fire, and said, after muttering and looking at it some seconds,—

"This is my birthday, Pip."

I was going to wish her many happy returns, when she lifted her stick.

"I don't suffer it to be spoken of. I don't suffer those who were here just now, or any one to speak of it. They come here on the day, but they dare not refer to it."

Of course I made no further effort to refer to it.

"On this day of the year, long before you were born, this heap of decay," stabbing with her crutched stick at the pile of cobwebs on the table, but not touching it, "was brought here. It and I have worn away together. The mice have gnawed at it, and sharper teeth than teeth of mice have gnawed at me."

She held the head of her stick against her heart as she stood looking at the table; she in her once white dress, all yellow and withered; the once white cloth all yellow and withered; everything around in a state to crumble under a touch.

"When the ruin is complete," said she, with a ghastly look, "and when they lay me dead, in my bride's dress on the bride's table,—which shall be done, and which will be the finished curse upon him,—so much the better if it is done on this day!"

She stood looking at the table as if she stood looking at her own figure lying there. I remained quiet. Estella returned, and she too remained quiet. It seemed to me that we continued thus for a long time. In the heavy air of the room, and the heavy darkness that brooded in its remoter corners, I even had an alarming fancy that Estella and I might presently begin to decay.

At length, not coming out of her distraught state by degrees, but in an instant, Miss Havisham said, "Let me see you two play cards; why have you not begun?" With that, we returned to her room, and sat down as before; I was beggared, as before; and again, as before, Miss Havisham watched us all the time, directed my attention to Estella's beauty, and made me notice it the more by trying her jewels on Estella's breast and hair.

Estella, for her part, likewise treated me as before, except that she did not condescend to speak. When we had played some half-dozen games, a day was appointed for my return, and I was taken down into the yard to be fed in the former dog-like manner. There, too, I was again left to wander about as I liked.

It is not much to the purpose whether a gate in that garden wall which I had scrambled up to peep over on the last occasion was, on that last occasion, open or shut. Enough that I saw no gate then, and that I saw one now. As it stood open, and as I knew that Estella had let the visitors out,—for she had returned with the keys in her hand,—I strolled into the garden, and strolled all over it. It was quite a wilderness, and there were old melon-frames and cucumber-frames in it, which seemed in their decline to have produced a spontaneous growth of weak attempts at pieces of old hats and boots, with now and then a weedy offshoot into the likeness of a battered saucepan.

When I had exhausted the garden and a greenhouse with nothing in it but a fallen-down grape-vine and some bottles, I found myself in the dismal corner upon which I had looked out of the window. Never questioning for a moment that the house was now empty, I looked in at another window, and found myself, to my great surprise, exchanging a broad stare with a pale young gentleman with red eyelids and light hair.

This pale young gentleman quickly disappeared, and reappeared beside me. He had been at his books when I had found myself staring at him, and I now saw that he was inky.

"Halloa!" said he, "young fellow!"

Halloa being a general observation which I had usually observed to be best answered by itself, I said, "Halloa!" politely omitting young fellow.

"Who let you in?" said he.

"Miss Estella."

"Who gave you leave to prowl about?"

"Miss Estella."

"Come and fight," said the pale young gentleman.

What could I do but follow him? I have often asked myself the question since; but what else could I do? His manner was so final, and I was so astonished, that I followed where he led, as if I had been under a spell.

"Stop a minute, though," he said, wheeling round before we had gone many paces. "I ought to give you a reason for fighting, too. There it is!" In a most irritating manner he instantly slapped his hands against one another, daintily flung one of his legs up behind him, pulled my hair, slapped his hands again, dipped his head, and butted it into my stomach.

The bull-like proceeding last mentioned, besides that it was unquestionably to be regarded in the light of a liberty, was particularly disagreeable just after bread and meat. I therefore hit out at him and was going to hit out again, when he said, "Aha! Would you?" and began dancing backwards and forwards in a manner quite unparalleled within my limited experience.

"Laws of the game!" said he. Here, he skipped from his left leg on to his right. "Regular rules!" Here, he skipped from his right leg on to his left. "Come to the ground, and go through the preliminaries!" Here, he dodged backwards and forwards, and did all sorts of things while I looked helplessly at him.

I was secretly afraid of him when I saw him so dexterous; but I felt morally and physically convinced that his light head of hair could have had no business in the pit of my stomach, and that I had a right to consider it irrelevant when so obtruded on my attention. Therefore, I followed him without a word, to a retired nook of the garden, formed by the junction of two walls and screened by some rubbish. On his asking me if I was satisfied with the ground, and on my replying Yes, he begged my leave to absent himself for a moment, and quickly returned with a bottle of water and a sponge dipped in vinegar. "Available for both," he said, placing these against the wall. And then fell to pulling off, not only his jacket and waistcoat, but his shirt too, in a manner at once light-hearted, business-like, and bloodthirsty.

Although he did not look very healthy,—having pimples on his face, and a breaking out at his mouth,—these dreadful preparations quite appalled me. I judged him to be about my own age, but he was much taller, and he had a way of spinning himself about that was full of appearance. For the rest, he was a young gentleman in a gray suit (when not denuded for battle), with his elbows, knees, wrists, and heels considerably in advance of the rest of him as to development.

My heart failed me when I saw him squaring at me with every demonstration of mechanical nicety, and eyeing my anatomy as if he were minutely choosing his bone. I never have been so surprised in my life, as I was when I let out the first blow, and saw him lying on his back, looking up at me with a bloody nose and his face exceedingly fore-shortened.

But, he was on his feet directly, and after sponging himself with a great show of dexterity began squaring again. The second greatest surprise I have ever had in my life was seeing him on his back again, looking up at me out of a black eye.

His spirit inspired me with great respect. He seemed to have no strength, and he never once hit me hard, and he was always knocked down; but he would be up again in a moment, sponging himself or drinking out of the water-bottle, with the greatest satisfaction in seconding himself according to form, and then came at me with an air and a show that made me believe he really was going to do for me at last. He got heavily bruised, for I am sorry to record that the more I hit him, the harder I hit him; but he came up again and again and again, until at last he got a bad fall with the back of his head against the wall. Even after that crisis in our affairs, he got up and turned round and round confusedly a few times, not knowing where I was; but finally went on his knees to his sponge and threw it up: at the same time panting out, "That means you have won."

He seemed so brave and innocent, that although I had not proposed the contest, I felt but a gloomy satisfaction in my victory. Indeed, I go so far as to hope that I regarded myself while dressing as a species of savage young wolf or other wild beast. However, I got dressed, darkly wiping my sanguinary face at intervals, and I said, "Can I help you?" and he said "No thankee," and I said "Good afternoon," and he said "Same to you."

When I got into the courtyard, I found Estella waiting with the keys. But she neither asked me where I had been, nor why I had kept her waiting; and there was a bright flush upon her face, as though something had happened to delight her. Instead of going straight to the gate, too, she stepped back into the passage, and beckoned me.

"Come here! You may kiss me, if you like."

I kissed her cheek as she turned it to me. I think I would have gone through a great deal to kiss her cheek. But I felt that the kiss was given to the coarse common boy as a piece of money might have been, and that it was worth nothing.

What with the birthday visitors, and what with the cards, and what with the fight, my stay had lasted so long, that when I neared home the light on the spit of sand off the point on the marshes was gleaming against a black night-sky, and Joe's furnace was flinging a path of fire across the road.

CHAPTER XII

My mind grew very uneasy on the subject of the pale young gentleman. The more I thought of the fight, and recalled the pale young gentleman on his back in various stages of puffy and incrimsoned countenance, the more certain it appeared that something would be done to me. I felt that the pale young gentleman's blood was on my head, and that the Law would avenge it. Without having any definite idea of the penalties I had incurred, it was clear to me that village boys could not go stalking about the country, ravaging the houses of gentlefolks and pitching into the studious youth of England, without laying themselves open to severe punishment. For some days, I even kept close at home, and looked out at the kitchen door with the greatest caution and trepidation before going on an errand, lest the officers of the County Jail should pounce upon me. The pale young gentleman's nose had stained my trousers, and I tried to wash out that evidence of my guilt in the dead of night. I had cut my knuckles against the pale young gentleman's teeth, and I twisted my imagination into a thousand tangles, as I devised incredible ways of accounting for that damnatory circumstance when I should be haled before the Judges.

When the day came round for my return to the scene of the deed of violence, my terrors reached their height. Whether myrmidons of Justice, specially sent down from London, would be lying in ambush behind the gate;—whether Miss Havisham, preferring to take personal vengeance for an outrage done to her house, might rise in those grave-clothes of hers, draw a pistol, and shoot me dead:—whether suborned boys—a numerous band of mercenaries—might be engaged to fall upon me in the brewery, and cuff me until I was no more;—it was high testimony to my confidence in the spirit of the pale young gentleman, that I never imagined him accessory to these retaliations; they always came into my mind as the acts of injudicious relatives of his, goaded on by the state of his visage and an indignant sympathy with the family features.

However, go to Miss Havisham's I must, and go I did. And behold! nothing came of the late struggle. It was not alluded to in any way, and no pale young gentleman was to be discovered on the premises. I found the same gate open, and I explored the garden, and even looked in at the windows of the detached house; but my view was suddenly stopped by the closed shutters within, and all was lifeless. Only in the corner where the combat had taken place could I detect any evidence of the young gentleman's existence. There were traces of his gore in that spot, and I covered them with garden-mould from the eye of man.

On the broad landing between Miss Havisham's own room and that other room in which the long table was laid out, I saw a garden-chair,—a light chair on wheels, that you pushed from behind. It had been placed there since my last visit, and I entered, that same day, on a regular occupation of pushing Miss Havisham in this chair (when she was tired of walking with her hand upon my shoulder) round her own room, and across the landing, and round the other room. Over and over and over again, we would make these journeys, and sometimes they would last as long as three hours at a stretch. I insensibly fall into a general mention of these journeys as numerous, because it was at once settled that I should return every alternate day at noon for these purposes, and because I am now going to sum up a period of at least eight or ten months.

As we began to be more used to one another, Miss Havisham talked more to me, and asked me such questions as what had I learnt and what was I going to be? I told her I was going to be apprenticed to Joe, I believed; and I enlarged upon my knowing nothing and wanting to know everything, in the hope that she might offer some help towards that desirable end. But she did not; on the contrary, she seemed to prefer my being ignorant. Neither did she ever give me any money,—or anything but my daily dinner,—nor ever stipulate that I should be paid for my services.

Estella was always about, and always let me in and out, but never told me I might kiss her again. Sometimes, she would coldly tolerate me; sometimes, she would condescend to me; sometimes, she would be quite familiar with me; sometimes, she would tell me energetically that she hated me. Miss Havisham would often ask me in a whisper, or when we were alone, "Does she grow prettier and prettier, Pip?" And when I said yes (for indeed she did), would seem to enjoy it greedily. Also, when we played at cards Miss Havisham would look on, with a miserly relish of Estella's moods, whatever they were. And sometimes, when her moods were so many and so contradictory of one another that I was puzzled what to say or do, Miss Havisham would embrace her with lavish fondness, murmuring something in her ear that sounded like "Break their hearts my pride and hope, break their hearts and have no mercy!"

There was a song Joe used to hum fragments of at the forge, of which the burden was Old Clem. This was not a very ceremonious way of rendering homage to a patron saint, but I believe Old Clem stood in that relation towards smiths. It was a song that imitated the measure of beating upon iron, and was a mere lyrical excuse for the introduction of Old Clem's respected name. Thus, you were to hammer boys round—Old Clem! With a thump and a sound—Old Clem! Beat it out, beat it out—Old Clem! With a clink for the stout—Old Clem! Blow the fire, blow the fire—Old Clem! Roaring dryer, soaring higher—Old Clem! One day soon after the appearance of the chair, Miss Havisham suddenly saying to me, with the impatient movement of her fingers, "There, there, there! Sing!" I was surprised into crooning this ditty as I pushed her over the floor. It happened so to catch her fancy that she took it up in a low brooding voice as if she were singing in her sleep. After that, it became customary with us to have it as we moved about, and Estella would often join in; though the whole strain was so subdued, even when there were three of us, that it made less noise in the grim old house than the lightest breath of wind.

What could I become with these surroundings? How could my character fail to be influenced by them? Is it to be wondered at if my thoughts were dazed, as my eyes were, when I came out into the natural light from the misty yellow rooms?

Perhaps I might have told Joe about the pale young gentleman, if I had not previously been betrayed into those enormous inventions to which I had confessed. Under the circumstances, I felt that Joe could hardly fail to discern in the pale young gentleman, an appropriate passenger to be put into the black velvet coach; therefore, I said nothing of him. Besides, that shrinking from having Miss Havisham and Estella discussed, which had come upon me in the beginning, grew much more potent as time went on. I reposed complete confidence in no one but Biddy; but I told poor Biddy everything. Why it came natural to me to do so, and why Biddy had a deep concern in everything I told her, I did not know then, though I think I know now.

Meanwhile, councils went on in the kitchen at home, fraught with almost insupportable aggravation to my exasperated spirit. That ass, Pumblechook, used often to come over of a night for the purpose of discussing my prospects with my sister; and I really do believe (to this hour with less penitence than I ought to feel), that if these hands could have taken a linchpin out of his chaise-cart, they would have done it. The miserable man was a man of that confined stolidity of mind, that he could not discuss my prospects without having me before him,—as it were, to operate upon,—and he would drag me up from my stool (usually by the collar) where I was quiet in a corner, and, putting me before the fire as if I were going to be cooked, would begin by saying, "Now, Mum, here is this boy! Here is this boy which you brought up by hand. Hold up your head, boy, and be forever grateful unto them which so did do. Now, Mum, with respections to this boy!" And then he would rumple my hair the wrong way,—which from my earliest remembrance, as already hinted, I have in my soul denied the right of any fellow-creature to do,—and would hold me before him by the sleeve,—a spectacle of imbecility only to be equalled by himself.

Then, he and my sister would pair off in such nonsensical speculations about Miss Havisham, and about what she would do with me and for me, that I used to want—quite painfully—to burst into spiteful tears, fly at Pumblechook, and pummel him all over. In these dialogues, my sister spoke to me as if she were morally wrenching one of my teeth out at every reference; while Pumblechook himself, self-constituted my patron, would sit supervising me with a depreciatory eye, like the architect of my fortunes who thought himself engaged on a very unremunerative job.

In these discussions, Joe bore no part. But he was often talked at, while they were in progress, by reason of Mrs. Joe's perceiving that he was not favorable to my being taken from the forge. I was fully old enough now to be apprenticed to Joe; and when Joe sat with the poker on his knees thoughtfully raking out the ashes between the lower bars, my sister would so distinctly construe that innocent action into opposition on his part, that she would dive at him, take the poker out of his hands, shake him, and put it away. There was a most irritating end to every one of these debates. All in a moment, with nothing to lead up to it, my sister would stop herself in a yawn, and catching sight of me as it were incidentally, would swoop upon me with, "Come! there's enough of you! You get along to bed; you've given trouble enough for one night, I hope!" As if I had besought them as a favor to bother my life out.

We went on in this way for a long time, and it seemed likely that we should continue to go on in this way for a long time, when one day Miss Havisham stopped short as she and I were walking, she leaning on my shoulder; and said with some displeasure,—

"You are growing tall, Pip!"

I thought it best to hint, through the medium of a meditative look, that this might be occasioned by circumstances over which I had no control.

She said no more at the time; but she presently stopped and looked at me again; and presently again; and after that, looked frowning and moody. On the next day of my attendance, when our usual exercise was over, and I had landed her at her dressing-table, she stayed me with a movement of her impatient fingers:—

"Tell me the name again of that blacksmith of yours."

"Joe Gargery, ma'am."

"Meaning the master you were to be apprenticed to?"

"Yes, Miss Havisham."

"You had better be apprenticed at once. Would Gargery come here with you, and bring your indentures, do you think?"

I signified that I had no doubt he would take it as an honor to be asked.

"Then let him come."

"At any particular time, Miss Havisham?"

"There, there! I know nothing about times. Let him come soon, and come along with you."

When I got home at night, and delivered this message for Joe, my sister "went on the Rampage," in a more alarming degree than at any previous period. She asked me and Joe whether we supposed she was door-mats under our feet, and how we dared to use her so, and what company we graciously thought she was fit for? When she had exhausted a torrent of such inquiries, she threw a candlestick at Joe, burst into a loud sobbing, got out the dustpan,—which was always a very bad sign,—put on her coarse apron, and began cleaning up to a terrible extent. Not satisfied with a dry cleaning, she took to a pail and scrubbing-brush, and cleaned us out of house and home, so that we stood shivering in the back-yard. It was ten o'clock at night before we ventured to creep in again, and then she asked Joe why he hadn't married a Negress Slave at once? Joe offered no answer, poor fellow, but stood feeling his whisker and looking dejectedly at me, as if he thought it really might have been a better speculation.

CHAPTER XIII

It was a trial to my feelings, on the next day but one, to see Joe arraying himself in his Sunday clothes to accompany me to Miss Havisham's. However, as he thought his court-suit necessary to the occasion, it was not for me tell him that he looked far better in his working-dress; the rather, because I knew he made himself so dreadfully uncomfortable, entirely on my account, and that it was for me he pulled up his shirt-collar so very high behind, that it made the hair on the crown of his head stand up like a tuft of feathers.

At breakfast-time my sister declared her intention of going to town with us, and being left at Uncle Pumblechook's and called for "when we had done with our fine ladies"—a way of putting the case, from which Joe appeared inclined to augur the worst. The forge was shut up for the day, and Joe inscribed in chalk upon the door (as it was his custom to do on the very rare occasions when he was not at work) the monosyllable HOUT, accompanied by a sketch of an arrow supposed to be flying in the direction he had taken.

We walked to town, my sister leading the way in a very large beaver bonnet, and carrying a basket like the Great Seal of England in plaited Straw, a pair of pattens, a spare shawl, and an umbrella, though it was a fine bright day. I am not quite clear whether these articles were carried penitentially or ostentatiously; but I rather think they were displayed as articles of property,—much as Cleopatra or any other sovereign lady on the Rampage might exhibit her wealth in a pageant or procession.

When we came to Pumblechook's, my sister bounced in and left us. As it was almost noon, Joe and I held straight on to Miss Havisham's house. Estella opened the gate as usual, and, the moment she appeared, Joe took his hat off and stood weighing it by the brim in both his hands; as if he had some urgent reason in his mind for being particular to half a quarter of an ounce.

Estella took no notice of either of us, but led us the way that I knew so well. I followed next to her, and Joe came last. When I looked back at Joe in the long passage, he was still weighing his hat with the greatest care, and was coming after us in long strides on the tips of his toes.

Estella told me we were both to go in, so I took Joe by the coat-cuff and conducted him into Miss Havisham's presence. She was seated at her dressing-table, and looked round at us immediately.

"Oh!" said she to Joe. "You are the husband of the sister of this boy?"

I could hardly have imagined dear old Joe looking so unlike himself or so like some extraordinary bird; standing as he did speechless, with his tuft of feathers ruffled, and his mouth open as if he wanted a worm.

"You are the husband," repeated Miss Havisham, "of the sister of this boy?"

It was very aggravating; but, throughout the interview, Joe persisted in addressing Me instead of Miss Havisham.

"Which I meantersay, Pip," Joe now observed in a manner that was at once expressive of forcible argumentation, strict confidence, and great politeness, "as I hup and married your sister, and I were at the time what you might call (if you was anyways inclined) a single man."

"Well!" said Miss Havisham. "And you have reared the boy, with the intention of taking him for your apprentice; is that so, Mr. Gargery?"

"You know, Pip," replied Joe, "as you and me were ever friends, and it were looked for'ard to betwixt us, as being calc'lated to lead to larks. Not but what, Pip, if you had ever made objections to the business,—such as its being open to black and sut, or such-like,—not but what they would have been attended to, don't you see?"

"Has the boy," said Miss Havisham, "ever made any objection? Does he like the trade?"

"Which it is well beknown to yourself, Pip," returned Joe, strengthening his former mixture of argumentation, confidence, and politeness, "that it were the wish of your own hart." (I saw the idea suddenly break upon him that he would adapt his epitaph to the occasion, before he went on to say) "And there weren't no objection on your part, and Pip it were the great wish of your hart!"

It was quite in vain for me to endeavor to make him sensible that he ought to speak to Miss Havisham. The more I made faces and gestures to him to do it, the more confidential, argumentative, and polite, he persisted in being to Me.

"Have you brought his indentures with you?" asked Miss Havisham.

"Well, Pip, you know," replied Joe, as if that were a little unreasonable, "you yourself see me put 'em in my 'at, and therefore you know as they are here." With which he took them out, and gave them, not to Miss Havisham, but to me. I am afraid I was ashamed of the dear good fellow,—I know I was ashamed of him,—when I saw that Estella stood at the back of Miss Havisham's chair, and that her eyes laughed mischievously. I took the indentures out of his hand and gave them to Miss Havisham.

"You expected," said Miss Havisham, as she looked them over, "no premium with the boy?"

"Joe!" I remonstrated, for he made no reply at all. "Why don't you answer—"

"Pip," returned Joe, cutting me short as if he were hurt, "which I meantersay that were not a question requiring a answer betwixt yourself and me, and which you know the answer to be full well No. You know it to be No, Pip, and wherefore should I say it?"

Miss Havisham glanced at him as if she understood what he really was better than I had thought possible, seeing what he was there; and took up a little bag from the table beside her.

"Pip has earned a premium here," she said, "and here it is. There are five-and-twenty guineas in this bag. Give it to your master, Pip."

As if he were absolutely out of his mind with the wonder awakened in him by her strange figure and the strange room, Joe, even at this pass, persisted in addressing me.

"This is wery liberal on your part, Pip," said Joe, "and it is as such received and grateful welcome, though never looked for, far nor near, nor nowheres. And now, old chap," said Joe, conveying to me a sensation, first of burning and then of freezing, for I felt as if that familiar expression were applied to Miss Havisham,—"and now, old chap, may we do our duty! May you and me do our duty, both on us, by one and another, and by them which your liberal present—have-conweyed—to be—for the satisfaction of mind-of—them as never—" here Joe showed that he felt he had fallen into frightful difficulties, until he triumphantly rescued himself with the words, "and from myself far be it!" These words had such a round and convincing sound for him that he said them twice.

"Good by, Pip!" said Miss Havisham. "Let them out, Estella."

"Am I to come again, Miss Havisham?" I asked.

"No. Gargery is your master now. Gargery! One word!"

Thus calling him back as I went out of the door, I heard her say to Joe in a distinct emphatic voice, "The boy has been a good boy here, and that is his reward. Of course, as an honest man, you will expect no other and no more."

How Joe got out of the room, I have never been able to determine; but I know that when he did get out he was steadily proceeding up stairs instead of coming down, and was deaf to all remonstrances until I went after him and laid hold of him. In another minute we were outside the gate, and it was locked, and Estella was gone. When we stood in the daylight alone again, Joe backed up against a wall, and said to me, "Astonishing!" And there he remained so long saying, "Astonishing" at intervals, so often, that I began to think his senses were never coming back. At length he prolonged his remark into "Pip, I do assure you this is as-TON-ishing!" and so, by degrees, became conversational and able to walk away.

I have reason to think that Joe's intellects were brightened by the encounter they had passed through, and that on our way to Pumblechook's he invented a subtle and deep design. My reason is to be found in what took place in Mr. Pumblechook's parlor: where, on our presenting ourselves, my sister sat in conference with that detested seedsman.

"Well?" cried my sister, addressing us both at once. "And what's happened to you? I wonder you condescend to come back to such poor society as this, I am sure I do!"

"Miss Havisham," said Joe, with a fixed look at me, like an effort of remembrance, "made it wery partick'ler that we should give her—were it compliments or respects, Pip?"

"Compliments," I said.

"Which that were my own belief," answered Joe; "her compliments to Mrs. J. Gargery—"

"Much good they'll do me!" observed my sister; but rather gratified too.

"And wishing," pursued Joe, with another fixed look at me, like another effort of remembrance, "that the state of Miss Havisham's elth were sitch as would have—allowed, were it, Pip?"

"Of her having the pleasure," I added.

"Of ladies' company," said Joe. And drew a long breath.

"Well!" cried my sister, with a mollified glance at Mr. Pumblechook. "She might have had the politeness to send that message at first, but it's better late than never. And what did she give young Rantipole here?"

"She giv' him," said Joe, "nothing."

Mrs. Joe was going to break out, but Joe went on.

"What she giv'," said Joe, "she giv' to his friends. 'And by his friends,' were her explanation, 'I mean into the hands of his sister Mrs. J. Gargery.' Them were her words; 'Mrs. J. Gargery.' She mayn't have know'd," added Joe, with an appearance of reflection, "whether it were Joe, or Jorge."

My sister looked at Pumblechook: who smoothed the elbows of his wooden arm-chair, and nodded at her and at the fire, as if he had known all about it beforehand.

"And how much have you got?" asked my sister, laughing. Positively laughing!

"What would present company say to ten pound?" demanded Joe.

"They'd say," returned my sister, curtly, "pretty well. Not too much, but pretty well."

"It's more than that, then," said Joe.

That fearful Impostor, Pumblechook, immediately nodded, and said, as he rubbed the arms of his chair, "It's more than that, Mum."

"Why, you don't mean to say—" began my sister.

"Yes I do, Mum," said Pumblechook; "but wait a bit. Go on, Joseph. Good in you! Go on!"

"What would present company say," proceeded Joe, "to twenty pound?"

"Handsome would be the word," returned my sister.

"Well, then," said Joe, "It's more than twenty pound."

That abject hypocrite, Pumblechook, nodded again, and said, with a patronizing laugh, "It's more than that, Mum. Good again! Follow her up, Joseph!"

"Then to make an end of it," said Joe, delightedly handing the bag to my sister; "it's five-and-twenty pound."

"It's five-and-twenty pound, Mum," echoed that basest of swindlers, Pumblechook, rising to shake hands with her; "and it's no more than your merits (as I said when my opinion was asked), and I wish you joy of the money!"

If the villain had stopped here, his case would have been sufficiently awful, but he blackened his guilt by proceeding to take me into custody, with a right of patronage that left all his former criminality far behind.

"Now you see, Joseph and wife," said Pumblechook, as he took me by the arm above the elbow, "I am one of them that always go right through with what they've begun. This boy must be bound, out of hand. That's my way. Bound out of hand."

"Goodness knows, Uncle Pumblechook," said my sister (grasping the money), "we're deeply beholden to you."

"Never mind me, Mum," returned that diabolical cornchandler. "A pleasure's a pleasure all the world over. But this boy, you know; we must have him bound. I said I'd see to it—to tell you the truth."

The Justices were sitting in the Town Hall near at hand, and we at once went over to have me bound apprentice to Joe in the Magisterial presence. I say we went over, but I was pushed over by Pumblechook, exactly as if I had that moment picked a pocket or fired a rick; indeed, it was the general impression in Court that I had been taken red-handed; for, as Pumblechook shoved me before him through the crowd, I heard some people say, "What's he done?" and others, "He's a young 'un, too, but looks bad, don't he?" One person of mild and benevolent aspect even gave me a tract ornamented with a woodcut of a malevolent young man fitted up with a perfect sausage-shop of fetters, and entitled TO BE READ IN MY CELL.

The Hall was a queer place, I thought, with higher pews in it than a church,—and with people hanging over the pews looking on,—and with mighty Justices (one with a powdered head) leaning back in chairs, with folded arms, or taking snuff, or going to sleep, or writing, or reading the newspapers,—and with some shining black portraits on the walls, which my unartistic eye regarded as a composition of hardbake and sticking-plaster. Here, in a corner my indentures were duly signed and attested, and I was "bound"; Mr. Pumblechook holding me all the while as if we had looked in on our way to the scaffold, to have those little preliminaries disposed of.

When we had come out again, and had got rid of the boys who had been put into great spirits by the expectation of seeing me publicly tortured, and who were much disappointed to find that my friends were merely rallying round me, we went back to Pumblechook's. And there my sister became so excited by the twenty-five guineas, that nothing would serve her but we must have a dinner out of that windfall at the Blue Boar, and that Pumblechook must go over in his chaise-cart, and bring the Hubbles and Mr. Wopsle.

It was agreed to be done; and a most melancholy day I passed. For, it inscrutably appeared to stand to reason, in the minds of the whole company, that I was an excrescence on the entertainment. And to make it worse, they all asked me from time to time,—in short, whenever they had nothing else to do,—why I didn't enjoy myself? And what could I possibly do then, but say I was enjoying myself,—when I wasn't!

However, they were grown up and had their own way, and they made the most of it. That swindling Pumblechook, exalted into the beneficent contriver of the whole occasion, actually took the top of the table; and, when he addressed them on the subject of my being bound, and had fiendishly congratulated them on my being liable to imprisonment if I played at cards, drank strong liquors, kept late hours or bad company, or indulged in other vagaries which the form of my indentures appeared to contemplate as next to inevitable, he placed me standing on a chair beside him to illustrate his remarks.

My only other remembrances of the great festival are, That they wouldn't let me go to sleep, but whenever they saw me dropping off, woke me up and told me to enjoy myself. That, rather late in the evening Mr. Wopsle gave us Collins's ode, and threw his bloodstained sword in thunder down, with such effect, that a waiter came in and said, "The Commercials underneath sent up their compliments, and it wasn't the Tumblers' Arms." That, they were all in excellent spirits on the road home, and sang, O Lady Fair! Mr. Wopsle taking the bass, and asserting with a tremendously strong voice (in reply to the inquisitive bore who leads that piece of music in a most impertinent manner, by wanting to know all about everybody's private affairs) that he was the man with his white locks flowing, and that he was upon the whole the weakest pilgrim going.

Finally, I remember that when I got into my little bedroom, I was truly wretched, and had a strong conviction on me that I should never like Joe's trade. I had liked it once, but once was not now.

CHAPTER XIV

It is a most miserable thing to feel ashamed of home. There may be black ingratitude in the thing, and the punishment may be retributive and well deserved; but that it is a miserable thing, I can testify.

Home had never been a very pleasant place to me, because of my sister's temper. But, Joe had sanctified it, and I had believed in it. I had believed in the best parlor as a most elegant saloon; I had believed in the front door, as a mysterious portal of the Temple of State whose solemn opening was attended with a sacrifice of roast fowls; I had believed in the kitchen as a chaste though not magnificent apartment; I had believed in the forge as the glowing road to manhood and independence. Within a single year all this was changed. Now it was all coarse and common, and I would not have had Miss Havisham and Estella see it on any account.

How much of my ungracious condition of mind may have been my own fault, how much Miss Havisham's, how much my sister's, is now of no moment to me or to any one. The change was made in me; the thing was done. Well or ill done, excusably or inexcusably, it was done.

Once, it had seemed to me that when I should at last roll up my shirt-sleeves and go into the forge, Joe's 'prentice, I should be distinguished and happy. Now the reality was in my hold, I only felt that I was dusty with the dust of small-coal, and that I had a weight upon my daily remembrance to which the anvil was a feather. There have been occasions in my later life (I suppose as in most lives) when I have felt for a time as if a thick curtain had fallen on all its interest and romance, to shut me out from anything save dull endurance any more. Never has that curtain dropped so heavy and blank, as when my way in life lay stretched out straight before me through the newly entered road of apprenticeship to Joe.

I remember that at a later period of my "time," I used to stand about the churchyard on Sunday evenings when night was falling, comparing my own perspective with the windy marsh view, and making out some likeness between them by thinking how flat and low both were, and how on both there came an unknown way and a dark mist and then the sea. I was quite as dejected on the first working-day of my apprenticeship as in that after-time; but I am glad to know that I never breathed a murmur to Joe while my indentures lasted. It is about the only thing I am glad to know of myself in that connection.

For, though it includes what I proceed to add, all the merit of what I proceed to add was Joe's. It was not because I was faithful, but because Joe was faithful, that I never ran away and went for a soldier or a sailor. It was not because I had a strong sense of the virtue of industry, but because Joe had a strong sense of the virtue of industry, that I worked with tolerable zeal against the grain. It is not possible to know how far the influence of any amiable honest-hearted duty-doing man flies out into the world; but it is very possible to know how it has touched one's self in going by, and I know right well that any good that intermixed itself with my apprenticeship came of plain contented Joe, and not of restlessly aspiring discontented me.

What I wanted, who can say? How can I say, when I never knew? What I dreaded was, that in some unlucky hour I, being at my grimiest and commonest, should lift up my eyes and see Estella looking in at one of the wooden windows of the forge. I was haunted by the fear that she would, sooner or later, find me out, with a black face and hands, doing the coarsest part of my work, and would exult over me and despise me. Often after dark, when I was pulling the bellows for Joe, and we were singing Old Clem, and when the thought how we used to sing it at Miss Havisham's would seem to show me Estella's face in the fire, with her pretty hair fluttering in the wind and her eyes scorning me,—often at such a time I would look towards those panels of black night in the wall which the wooden windows then were, and would fancy that I saw her just drawing her face away, and would believe that she had come at last.

After that, when we went in to supper, the place and the meal would have a more homely look than ever, and I would feel more ashamed of home than ever, in my own ungracious breast.

CHAPTER XV

As I was getting too big for Mr. Wopsle's great-aunt's room, my education under that preposterous female terminated. Not, however, until Biddy had imparted to me everything she knew, from the little catalogue of prices, to a comic song she had once bought for a half-penny. Although the only coherent part of the latter piece of literature were the opening lines,

When I went to Lunnon town sirs, Too rul loo rul Too rul loo rul Wasn't I done very brown sirs? Too rul loo rul Too rul loo rul—still, in my desire to be wiser, I got this composition by heart with the utmost gravity; nor do I recollect that I questioned its merit, except that I thought (as I still do) the amount of Too rul somewhat in excess of the poetry. In my hunger for information, I made proposals to Mr. Wopsle to bestow some intellectual crumbs upon me, with which he kindly complied. As it turned out, however, that he only wanted me for a dramatic lay-figure, to be contradicted and embraced and wept over and bullied and clutched and stabbed and knocked about in a variety of ways, I soon declined that course of instruction; though not until Mr. Wopsle in his poetic fury had severely mauled me.

Whatever I acquired, I tried to impart to Joe. This statement sounds so well, that I cannot in my conscience let it pass unexplained. I wanted to make Joe less ignorant and common, that he might be worthier of my society and less open to Estella's reproach.

The old Battery out on the marshes was our place of study, and a broken slate and a short piece of slate-pencil were our educational implements: to which Joe always added a pipe of tobacco. I never knew Joe to remember anything from one Sunday to another, or to acquire, under my tuition, any piece of information whatever. Yet he would smoke his pipe at the Battery with a far more sagacious air than anywhere else,—even with a learned air,—as if he considered himself to be advancing immensely. Dear fellow, I hope he did.

It was pleasant and quiet, out there with the sails on the river passing beyond the earthwork, and sometimes, when the tide was low, looking as if they belonged to sunken ships that were still sailing on at the bottom of the water. Whenever I watched the vessels standing out to sea with their white sails spread, I somehow thought of Miss Havisham and Estella; and whenever the light struck aslant, afar off, upon a cloud or sail or green hillside or water-line, it was just the same.—Miss Havisham and Estella and the strange house and the strange life appeared to have something to do with everything that was picturesque.

One Sunday when Joe, greatly enjoying his pipe, had so plumed himself on being "most awful dull," that I had given him up for the day, I lay on the earthwork for some time with my chin on my hand, descrying traces of Miss Havisham and Estella all over the prospect, in the sky and in the water, until at last I resolved to mention a thought concerning them that had been much in my head.

"Joe," said I; "don't you think I ought to make Miss Havisham a visit?"

"Well, Pip," returned Joe, slowly considering. "What for?"

"What for, Joe? What is any visit made for?"

"There is some wisits p'r'aps," said Joe, "as for ever remains open to the question, Pip. But in regard to wisiting Miss Havisham. She might think you wanted something,—expected something of her."

"Don't you think I might say that I did not, Joe?"

"You might, old chap," said Joe. "And she might credit it. Similarly she mightn't."

Joe felt, as I did, that he had made a point there, and he pulled hard at his pipe to keep himself from weakening it by repetition.

"You see, Pip," Joe pursued, as soon as he was past that danger, "Miss Havisham done the handsome thing by you. When Miss Havisham done the handsome thing by you, she called me back to say to me as that were all."

"Yes, Joe. I heard her."

"ALL," Joe repeated, very emphatically.

"Yes, Joe. I tell you, I heard her."

"Which I meantersay, Pip, it might be that her meaning were,—Make a end on it!—As you was!—Me to the North, and you to the South!—Keep in sunders!"

I had thought of that too, and it was very far from comforting to me to find that he had thought of it; for it seemed to render it more probable.

"But, Joe."

"Yes, old chap."

"Here am I, getting on in the first year of my time, and, since the day of my being bound, I have never thanked Miss Havisham, or asked after her, or shown that I remember her."

"That's true, Pip; and unless you was to turn her out a set of shoes all four round,—and which I meantersay as even a set of shoes all four round might not be acceptable as a present, in a total wacancy of hoofs—"

"I don't mean that sort of remembrance, Joe; I don't mean a present."

But Joe had got the idea of a present in his head and must harp upon it. "Or even," said he, "if you was helped to knocking her up a new chain for the front door,—or say a gross or two of shark-headed screws for general use,—or some light fancy article, such as a toasting-fork when she took her muffins,—or a gridiron when she took a sprat or such like—"

"I don't mean any present at all, Joe," I interposed.

"Well," said Joe, still harping on it as though I had particularly pressed it, "if I was yourself, Pip, I wouldn't. No, I would not. For what's a door-chain when she's got one always up? And shark-headers is open to misrepresentations. And if it was a toasting-fork, you'd go into brass and do yourself no credit. And the oncommonest workman can't show himself oncommon in a gridiron,—for a gridiron IS a gridiron," said Joe, steadfastly impressing it upon me, as if he were endeavouring to rouse me from a fixed delusion, "and you may haim at what you like, but a gridiron it will come out, either by your leave or again your leave, and you can't help yourself—"

"My dear Joe," I cried, in desperation, taking hold of his coat, "don't go on in that way. I never thought of making Miss Havisham any present."

"No, Pip," Joe assented, as if he had been contending for that, all along; "and what I say to you is, you are right, Pip."

"Yes, Joe; but what I wanted to say, was, that as we are rather slack just now, if you would give me a half-holiday to-morrow, I think I would go up-town and make a call on Miss Est—Havisham."

"Which her name," said Joe, gravely, "ain't Estavisham, Pip, unless she have been rechris'ened."

"I know, Joe, I know. It was a slip of mine. What do you think of it, Joe?"

In brief, Joe thought that if I thought well of it, he thought well of it. But, he was particular in stipulating that if I were not received with cordiality, or if I were not encouraged to repeat my visit as a visit which had no ulterior object but was simply one of gratitude for a favor received, then this experimental trip should have no successor. By these conditions I promised to abide.

Now, Joe kept a journeyman at weekly wages whose name was Orlick. He pretended that his Christian name was Dolge,—a clear Impossibility,—but he was a fellow of that obstinate disposition that I believe him to have been the prey of no delusion in this particular, but wilfully to have imposed that name upon the village as an affront to its understanding. He was a broadshouldered loose-limbed swarthy fellow of great strength, never in a hurry, and always slouching. He never even seemed to come to his work on purpose, but would slouch in as if by mere accident; and when he went to the Jolly Bargemen to eat his dinner, or went away at night, he would slouch out, like Cain or the Wandering Jew, as if he had no idea where he was going and no intention of ever coming back. He lodged at a sluice-keeper's out on the marshes, and on working-days would come slouching from his hermitage, with his hands in his pockets and his dinner loosely tied in a bundle round his neck and dangling on his back. On Sundays he mostly lay all day on the sluice-gates, or stood against ricks and barns. He always slouched, locomotively, with his eyes on the ground; and, when accosted or otherwise required to raise them, he looked up in a half-resentful, half-puzzled way, as though the only thought he ever had was, that it was rather an odd and injurious fact that he should never be thinking.

This morose journeyman had no liking for me. When I was very small and timid, he gave me to understand that the Devil lived in a black corner of the forge, and that he knew the fiend very well: also that it was necessary to make up the fire, once in seven years, with a live boy, and that I might consider myself fuel. When I became Joe's 'prentice, Orlick was perhaps confirmed in some suspicion that I should displace him; howbeit, he liked me still less. Not that he ever said anything, or did anything, openly importing hostility; I only noticed that he always beat his sparks in my direction, and that whenever I sang Old Clem, he came in out of time.

Dolge Orlick was at work and present, next day, when I reminded Joe of my half-holiday. He said nothing at the moment, for he and Joe had just got a piece of hot iron between them, and I was at the bellows; but by and by he said, leaning on his hammer,—

"Now, master! Sure you're not a going to favor only one of us. If Young Pip has a half-holiday, do as much for Old Orlick." I suppose he was about five-and-twenty, but he usually spoke of himself as an ancient person.

"Why, what'll you do with a half-holiday, if you get it?" said Joe.

"What'll I do with it! What'll he do with it? I'll do as much with it as him," said Orlick.

"As to Pip, he's going up town," said Joe.

"Well then, as to Old Orlick, he's a going up town," retorted that worthy. "Two can go up town. Tain't only one wot can go up town.

"Don't lose your temper," said Joe.

"Shall if I like," growled Orlick. "Some and their up-towning! Now, master! Come. No favoring in this shop. Be a man!"

The master refusing to entertain the subject until the journeyman was in a better temper, Orlick plunged at the furnace, drew out a red-hot bar, made at me with it as if he were going to run it through my body, whisked it round my head, laid it on the anvil, hammered it out,—as if it were I, I thought, and the sparks were my spirting blood,—and finally said, when he had hammered himself hot and the iron cold, and he again leaned on his hammer,—

"Now, master!"

"Are you all right now?" demanded Joe.

"Ah! I am all right," said gruff Old Orlick.

"Then, as in general you stick to your work as well as most men," said Joe, "let it be a half-holiday for all."

My sister had been standing silent in the yard, within hearing,—she was a most unscrupulous spy and listener,—and she instantly looked in at one of the windows.

"Like you, you fool!" said she to Joe, "giving holidays to great idle hulkers like that. You are a rich man, upon my life, to waste wages in that way. I wish I was his master!"

"You'd be everybody's master, if you durst," retorted Orlick, with an ill-favored grin.

("Let her alone," said Joe.)

"I'd be a match for all noodles and all rogues," returned my sister, beginning to work herself into a mighty rage. "And I couldn't be a match for the noodles, without being a match for your master, who's the dunder-headed king of the noodles. And I couldn't be a match for the rogues, without being a match for you, who are the blackest-looking and the worst rogue between this and France. Now!"

"You're a foul shrew, Mother Gargery," growled the journeyman. "If that makes a judge of rogues, you ought to be a good'un."

("Let her alone, will you?" said Joe.)

"What did you say?" cried my sister, beginning to scream. "What did you say? What did that fellow Orlick say to me, Pip? What did he call me, with my husband standing by? Oh! oh! oh!" Each of these exclamations was a shriek; and I must remark of my sister, what is equally true of all the violent women I have ever seen, that passion was no excuse for her, because it is undeniable that instead of lapsing into passion, she consciously and deliberately took extraordinary pains to force herself into it, and became blindly furious by regular stages; "what was the name he gave me before the base man who swore to defend me? Oh! Hold me! Oh!"

"Ah-h-h!" growled the journeyman, between his teeth, "I'd hold you, if you was my wife. I'd hold you under the pump, and choke it out of you."

("I tell you, let her alone," said Joe.)

"Oh! To hear him!" cried my sister, with a clap of her hands and a scream together,—which was her next stage. "To hear the names he's giving me! That Orlick! In my own house! Me, a married woman! With my husband standing by! Oh! Oh!" Here my sister, after a fit of clappings and screamings, beat her hands upon her bosom and upon her knees, and threw her cap off, and pulled her hair down,—which were the last stages on her road to frenzy. Being by this time a perfect Fury and a complete success, she made a dash at the door which I had fortunately locked.

What could the wretched Joe do now, after his disregarded parenthetical interruptions, but stand up to his journeyman, and ask him what he meant by interfering betwixt himself and Mrs. Joe; and further whether he was man enough to come on? Old Orlick felt that the situation admitted of nothing less than coming on, and was on his defence straightway; so, without so much as pulling off their singed and burnt aprons, they went at one another, like two giants. But, if any man in that neighborhood could stand uplong against Joe, I never saw the man. Orlick, as if he had been of no more account than the pale young gentleman, was very soon among the coal-dust, and in no hurry to come out of it. Then Joe unlocked the door and picked up my sister, who had dropped insensible at the window (but who had seen the fight first, I think), and who was carried into the house and laid down, and who was recommended to revive, and would do nothing but struggle and clench her hands in Joe's hair. Then, came that singular calm and silence which succeed all uproars; and then, with the vague sensation which I have always connected with such a lull,—namely, that it was Sunday, and somebody was dead,—I went up stairs to dress myself.

When I came down again, I found Joe and Orlick sweeping up, without any other traces of discomposure than a slit in one of Orlick's nostrils, which was neither expressive nor ornamental. A pot of beer had appeared from the Jolly Bargemen, and they were sharing it by turns in a peaceable manner. The lull had a sedative and philosophical influence on Joe, who followed me out into the road to say, as a parting observation that might do me good, "On the Rampage, Pip, and off the Rampage, Pip:—such is Life!"

With what absurd emotions (for we think the feelings that are very serious in a man quite comical in a boy) I found myself again going to Miss Havisham's, matters little here. Nor, how I passed and repassed the gate many times before I could make up my mind to ring. Nor, how I debated whether I should go away without ringing; nor, how I should undoubtedly have gone, if my time had been my own, to come back.

Miss Sarah Pocket came to the gate. No Estella.

"How, then? You here again?" said Miss Pocket. "What do you want?"

When I said that I only came to see how Miss Havisham was, Sarah evidently deliberated whether or no she should send me about my business. But unwilling to hazard the responsibility, she let me in, and presently brought the sharp message that I was to "come up."

Everything was unchanged, and Miss Havisham was alone.

"Well?" said she, fixing her eyes upon me. "I hope you want nothing? You'll get nothing."

"No indeed, Miss Havisham. I only wanted you to know that I am doing very well in my apprenticeship, and am always much obliged to you."

"There, there!" with the old restless fingers. "Come now and then; come on your birthday.—Ay!" she cried suddenly, turning herself and her chair towards me, "You are looking round for Estella? Hey?"

I had been looking round,—in fact, for Estella,—and I stammered that I hoped she was well.

"Abroad," said Miss Havisham; "educating for a lady; far out of reach; prettier than ever; admired by all who see her. Do you feel that you have lost her?"

There was such a malignant enjoyment in her utterance of the last words, and she broke into such a disagreeable laugh, that I was at a loss what to say. She spared me the trouble of considering, by dismissing me. When the gate was closed upon me by Sarah of the walnut-shell countenance, I felt more than ever dissatisfied with my home and with my trade and with everything; and that was all I took by that motion.

As I was loitering along the High Street, looking in disconsolately at the shop windows, and thinking what I would buy if I were a gentleman, who should come out of the bookshop but Mr. Wopsle. Mr. Wopsle had in his hand the affecting tragedy of George Barnwell, in which he had that moment invested sixpence, with the view of heaping every word of it on the head of Pumblechook, with whom he was going to drink tea. No sooner did he see me, than he appeared to consider that a special Providence had put a 'prentice in his way to be read at; and he laid hold of me, and insisted on my accompanying him to the Pumblechookian parlor. As I knew it would be miserable at home, and as the nights were dark and the way was dreary, and almost any companionship on the road was better than none, I made no great resistance;

consequently, we turned into Pumblechook's just as the street and the shops were lighting up.

As I never assisted at any other representation of George Barnwell, I don't know how long it may usually take; but I know very well that it took until half-past nine o' clock that night, and that when Mr. Wopsle got into Newgate, I thought he never would go to the scaffold, he became so much slower than at any former period of his disgraceful career. I thought it a little too much that he should complain of being cut short in his flower after all, as if he had not been running to seed, leaf after leaf, ever since his course began. This, however, was a mere question of length and wearisomeness. What stung me, was the identification of the whole affair with my unoffending self. When Barnwell began to go wrong, I declare that I felt positively apologetic, Pumblechook's indignant stare so taxed me with it. Wopsle, too, took pains to present me in the worst light. At once ferocious and maudlin, I was made to murder my uncle with no extenuating circumstances whatever; Millwood put me down in argument, on every occasion; it became sheer monomania in my master's daughter to care a button for me; and all I can say for my gasping and procrastinating conduct on the fatal morning, is, that it was worthy of the general feebleness of my character. Even after I was happily hanged and Wopsle had closed the book, Pumblechook sat staring at me, and shaking his head, and saying, "Take warning, boy, take warning!" as if it were a well-known fact that I contemplated murdering a near relation, provided I could only induce one to have the weakness to become my benefactor.

It was a very dark night when it was all over, and when I set out with Mr. Wopsle on the walk home. Beyond town, we found a heavy mist out, and it fell wet and thick. The turnpike lamp was a blur, quite out of the lamp's usual place apparently, and its rays looked solid substance on the fog. We were noticing this, and saying how that the mist rose with a change of wind from a certain quarter of our marshes, when we came upon a man, slouching under the lee of the turnpike house.

"Halloa!" we said, stopping. "Orlick there?"

"Ah!" he answered, slouching out. "I was standing by a minute, on the chance of company."

"You are late," I remarked.

Orlick not unnaturally answered, "Well? And you're late."

"We have been," said Mr. Wopsle, exalted with his late performance,—"we have been indulging, Mr. Orlick, in an intellectual evening."

Old Orlick growled, as if he had nothing to say about that, and we all went on together. I asked him presently whether he had been spending his half-holiday up and down town?

"Yes," said he, "all of it. I come in behind yourself. I didn't see you, but I must have been pretty close behind you. By the by, the guns is going again."

"At the Hulks?" said I.

"Ay! There's some of the birds flown from the cages. The guns have been going since dark, about. You'll hear one presently."

In effect, we had not walked many yards further, when the well-remembered boom came towards us, deadened by the mist, and heavily rolled away along the low grounds by the river, as if it were pursuing and threatening the fugitives.

"A good night for cutting off in," said Orlick. "We'd be puzzled how to bring down a jail-bird on the wing, to-night."

The subject was a suggestive one to me, and I thought about it in silence. Mr. Wopsle, as the ill-requited uncle of the evening's tragedy, fell to meditating aloud in his garden at Camberwell. Orlick, with his hands in his pockets, slouched heavily at my side. It was very dark, very wet, very muddy, and so we splashed along. Now and then, the sound of the signal cannon broke upon us again, and again rolled sulkily along the course of the river. I kept myself to myself and my thoughts. Mr. Wopsle died amiably at Camberwell, and exceedingly game on Bosworth Field, and in the greatest agonies at Glastonbury. Orlick sometimes growled, "Beat it out, beat it out,—Old Clem! With a clink for the stout,—Old Clem!" I thought he had been drinking, but he was not drunk.

Thus, we came to the village. The way by which we approached it took us past the Three Jolly Bargemen, which we were surprised to find—it being eleven o'clock—in a state of commotion, with the door wide open, and unwonted lights that had been hastily caught up and put down scattered about. Mr. Wopsle dropped in to ask what was the matter (surmising that a convict had been taken), but came running out in a great hurry.

"There's something wrong," said he, without stopping, "up at your place, Pip. Run all!"

"What is it?" I asked, keeping up with him. So did Orlick, at my side.

"I can't quite understand. The house seems to have been violently entered when Joe Gargery was out. Supposed by convicts. Somebody has been attacked and hurt."

We were running too fast to admit of more being said, and we made no stop until we got into our kitchen. It was full of people; the whole village was there, or in the yard; and there was a surgeon, and there was Joe, and there were a group of women, all on the floor in the midst of the kitchen. The unemployed bystanders drew back when they saw me, and so I became aware of my sister,—lying without sense or movement on the bare boards where she had been knocked down by a tremendous blow on the back of the head, dealt by some unknown hand when her face was turned towards the fire,—destined never to be on the Rampage again, while she was the wife of Joe.

CHAPTER XVI

With my head full of George Barnwell, I was at first disposed to believe that I must have had some hand in the attack upon my sister, or at all events that as her near relation, popularly known to be under obligations to her, I was a more legitimate object of suspicion than any one else. But when, in the clearer light of next morning, I began to reconsider the matter and to hear it discussed around me on all sides, I took another view of the case, which was more reasonable.

Joe had been at the Three Jolly Bargemen, smoking his pipe, from a quarter after eight o'clock to a quarter before ten. While he was there, my sister had been seen standing at the kitchen door, and had exchanged Good Night with a farm-laborer going home. The man could not be more particular as to the time at which he saw her (he got into dense confusion when he tried to be), than that it must have been before nine. When Joe went home at five minutes before ten, he found her struck down on the floor, and promptly called in assistance. The fire had not then burnt unusually low, nor was the snuff of the candle very long; the candle, however, had been blown out.

Nothing had been taken away from any part of the house. Neither, beyond the blowing out of the candle,—which stood on a table between the door and my sister, and was behind her when she stood facing the fire and was struck,—was there any disarrangement of the kitchen, excepting such as she herself had made, in falling and bleeding. But, there was one remarkable piece of evidence on the spot. She had been struck with something blunt and heavy, on the head and spine; after the blows were dealt, something heavy had been thrown down at her with considerable violence, as she lay on her face. And on the ground beside her, when Joe picked her up, was a convict's leg-iron which had been filed asunder.

Now, Joe, examining this iron with a smith's eye, declared it to have been filed asunder some time ago. The hue and cry going off to the Hulks, and people coming thence to examine the iron, Joe's opinion was corroborated. They did not undertake to say when it had left the prison-ships to which it undoubtedly had once belonged; but they claimed to know for certain that that particular manacle had not been worn by either of the two convicts who had escaped last night. Further, one of those two was already retaken, and had not freed himself of his iron.

Knowing what I knew, I set up an inference of my own here. I believed the iron to be my convict's iron,—the iron I had seen and heard him filing at, on the marshes,—but my mind did not accuse him of having put it to its latest use. For I believed one of two other persons to have become possessed of it, and to have turned it to this cruel account. Either Orlick, or the strange man who had shown me the file.

Now, as to Orlick; he had gone to town exactly as he told us when we picked him up at the turnpike, he had been seen about town all the evening, he had been in divers companies in several public-houses, and he had come back with myself and Mr. Wopsle. There was nothing against him, save the quarrel; and my sister had quarrelled with him, and with everybody else about her, ten thousand times. As to the strange man; if he had come back for his two bank-notes there could have been no dispute about them, because my sister was fully prepared to restore them. Besides, there had been no altercation; the assailant had come in so silently and suddenly, that she had been felled before she could look round.

It was horrible to think that I had provided the weapon, however undesignedly, but I could hardly think otherwise. I suffered unspeakable trouble while I considered and reconsidered whether I should at last dissolve that spell of my childhood and tell Joe all the story. For months afterwards, I every day settled the question finally in the negative, and reopened and reargued it next morning. The contention came, after all, to this;—the secret was such an old one now, had so grown into me and become a part of myself, that I could not tear it away. In addition to the dread that, having led up to so much mischief, it would be now more likely than ever to alienate Joe from me if he believed it, I had a further restraining dread that he would not believe it, but would assort it with the fabulous dogs and veal-cutlets as a monstrous invention. However, I temporized with myself, of course—for, was I not wavering between right and wrong, when the thing is always done?—and resolved to make a full disclosure if I should see any such new occasion as a new chance of helping in the discovery of the assailant.

The Constables and the Bow Street men from London—for, this happened in the days of the extinct red-waistcoated police—were about the house for a week or two, and did pretty much what I have heard and read of like authorities doing in other such cases. They took up several obviously wrong people, and they ran their heads very hard against wrong ideas, and persisted in trying to fit the circumstances to the ideas, instead of trying to extract ideas from the circumstances. Also, they stood about the door of the Jolly Bargemen, with knowing and reserved looks that filled the whole neighborhood with admiration; and they had a mysterious manner of taking their drink, that was almost as good as taking the culprit. But not quite, for they never did it.

Long after these constitutional powers had dispersed, my sister lay very ill in bed. Her sight was disturbed, so that she saw objects multiplied, and grasped at visionary teacups and wineglasses instead of the realities; her hearing was greatly impaired; her memory also; and her speech was unintelligible. When, at last, she came round so far as to be helped down stairs, it was still necessary to keep my slate always by her, that she might indicate in writing what she could not indicate in speech. As she was (very bad handwriting apart) a more than indifferent speller, and as Joe was a more than indifferent reader, extraordinary complications arose between them which I was always called in to solve. The administration of mutton instead of medicine, the substitution of Tea for Joe, and the baker for bacon, were among the mildest of my own mistakes.

However, her temper was greatly improved, and she was patient. A tremulous uncertainty of the action of all her limbs soon became a part of her regular state, and afterwards, at intervals of two or three months, she would often put her hands to her head, and would then remain for about a week at a time in some gloomy aberration of mind. We were at a loss to find a suitable attendant for her, until a circumstance happened conveniently to relieve us. Mr. Wopsle's great-aunt conquered a confirmed habit of living into which she had fallen, and Biddy became a part of our establishment.

It may have been about a month after my sister's reappearance in the kitchen, when Biddy came to us with a small speckled box containing the whole of her worldly effects, and became a blessing to the household. Above all, she was a blessing to Joe, for the dear old fellow was sadly cut up by the constant contemplation of the wreck of his wife, and had been accustomed, while attending on her of an evening, to turn to me every now and then and say, with his blue eyes moistened, "Such a fine figure of a woman as she once were, Pip!" Biddy instantly taking the cleverest charge of her as though she had studied her from infancy; Joe became able in some sort to appreciate the greater quiet of his life, and to get down to the Jolly Bargemen now and then for a change that did him good. It was characteristic of the police people that they had all more or less suspected poor Joe (though he never knew it), and that they had to a man concurred in regarding him as one of the deepest spirits they had ever encountered.

Biddy's first triumph in her new office, was to solve a difficulty that had completely vanquished me. I had tried hard at it, but had made nothing of it. Thus it was:—

Again and again and again, my sister had traced upon the slate, a character that looked like a curious T, and then with the utmost eagerness had called our attention to it as something she particularly wanted. I had in vain tried everything producible that began with a T, from tar to toast and tub. At length it had come into my head that the sign looked like a hammer, and on my lustily calling that word in my sister's ear, she had begun to hammer on the table and had expressed a qualified assent. Thereupon, I had brought in all our hammers, one after another, but without avail. Then I bethought me of a crutch, the shape being much the same, and I borrowed one in the village, and displayed it to my sister with considerable confidence. But she shook her head to that extent when she was shown it, that we were terrified lest in her weak and shattered state she should dislocate her neck.

When my sister found that Biddy was very quick to understand her, this mysterious sign reappeared on the slate. Biddy looked thoughtfully at it, heard my explanation, looked thoughtfully at my sister, looked thoughtfully at Joe (who was always represented on the slate by his initial letter), and ran into the forge, followed by Joe and me.

"Why, of course!" cried Biddy, with an exultant face. "Don't you see? It's him!"

Orlick, without a doubt! She had lost his name, and could only signify him by his hammer. We told him why we wanted him to come into the kitchen, and he slowly laid down his hammer, wiped his brow with his arm, took another wipe at it with his apron, and came slouching out, with a curious loose vagabond bend in the knees that strongly distinguished him.

I confess that I expected to see my sister denounce him, and that I was disappointed by the different result. She manifested the greatest anxiety to be on good terms with him, was evidently much pleased by his being at length produced, and motioned that she would have him given something to drink. She watched his countenance as if she were particularly wishful to be assured that he took kindly to his reception, she showed every possible desire to conciliate him, and there was an air of humble propitiation in all she did, such as I have seen pervade the bearing of a child towards a hard master. After that day, a day rarely passed without her drawing the hammer on her slate, and without Orlick's slouching in and standing doggedly before her, as if he knew no more than I did what to make of it.

CHAPTER XVII

I now fell into a regular routine of apprenticeship life, which was varied beyond the limits of the village and the marshes, by no more remarkable circumstance than the arrival of my birthday and my paying another visit to Miss Havisham. I found Miss Sarah Pocket still on duty at the gate; I found Miss Havisham just as I had left her, and she spoke of Estella in the very same way, if not in the very same words. The interview lasted but a few minutes, and she gave me a guinea when I was going, and told me to come again on my next birthday. I may mention at once that this became an annual custom. I tried to decline taking the guinea on the first occasion, but with no better effect than causing her to ask me very angrily, if I expected more? Then, and after that, I took it.

So unchanging was the dull old house, the yellow light in the darkened room, the faded spectre in the chair by the dressing-table glass, that I felt as if the stopping of the clocks had stopped Time in that mysterious place, and, while I and everything else outside it grew older, it stood still. Daylight never entered the house as to my thoughts and remembrances of it, any more than as to the actual fact. It bewildered me, and under its influence I continued at heart to hate my trade and to be ashamed of home.

Imperceptibly I became conscious of a change in Biddy, however. Her shoes came up at the heel, her hair grew bright and neat, her hands were always clean. She was not beautiful,—she was common, and could not be like Estella,—but she was pleasant and wholesome and sweet-tempered. She had not been with us more than a year (I remember her being newly out of mourning at the time it struck me), when I observed to myself one evening that she had curiously thoughtful and attentive eyes; eyes that were very pretty and very good.

It came of my lifting up my own eyes from a task I was poring at—writing some passages from a book, to improve myself in two ways at once by a sort of stratagem—and seeing Biddy observant of what I was about. I laid down my pen, and Biddy stopped in her needlework without laying it down.

"Biddy," said I, "how do you manage it? Either I am very stupid, or you are very clever."

"What is it that I manage? I don't know," returned Biddy, smiling.

She managed our whole domestic life, and wonderfully too; but I did not mean that, though that made what I did mean more surprising.

"How do you manage, Biddy," said I, "to learn everything that I learn, and always to keep up with me?" I was beginning to be rather vain of my knowledge, for I spent my birthday guineas on it, and set aside the greater part of my pocket-money for similar investment; though I have no doubt, now, that the little I knew was extremely dear at the price.

"I might as well ask you," said Biddy, "how you manage?"

"No; because when I come in from the forge of a night, any one can see me turning to at it. But you never turn to at it, Biddy."

"I suppose I must catch it like a cough," said Biddy, quietly; and went on with her sewing.

Pursuing my idea as I leaned back in my wooden chair, and looked at Biddy sewing away with her head on one side, I began to think her rather an extraordinary girl. For I called to mind now, that she was equally accomplished in the terms of our trade, and the names of our different sorts of work, and our various tools. In short, whatever I knew, Biddy knew. Theoretically, she was already as good a blacksmith as I, or better.

"You are one of those, Biddy," said I, "who make the most of every chance. You never had a chance before you came here, and see how improved you are!"

Biddy looked at me for an instant, and went on with her sewing. "I was your first teacher though; wasn't I?" said she, as she sewed.

"Biddy!" I exclaimed, in amazement. "Why, you are crying!"

"No I am not," said Biddy, looking up and laughing. "What put that in your head?"

What could have put it in my head but the glistening of a tear as it dropped on her work? I sat silent, recalling what a drudge she had been until Mr. Wopsle's great-aunt successfully overcame that bad habit of living, so highly desirable to be got rid of by some people. I recalled the hopeless circumstances by which she had been surrounded in the miserable little shop and the miserable little noisy evening school, with that miserable old bundle of incompetence always to be dragged and shouldered. I reflected that even in those untoward times there must have been latent in Biddy what was now developing, for, in my first uneasiness and discontent I had turned to her for help, as a matter of course. Biddy sat quietly sewing, shedding no more tears, and while I looked at her and thought about it all, it occurred to me that perhaps I had not been sufficiently grateful to Biddy. I might have been too reserved, and should have patronized her more (though I did not use that precise word in my meditations) with my confidence.

"Yes, Biddy," I observed, when I had done turning it over, "you were my first teacher, and that at a time when we little thought of ever being together like this, in this kitchen."

"Ah, poor thing!" replied Biddy. It was like her self-forgetfulness to transfer the remark to my sister, and to get up and be busy about her, making her more comfortable; "that's sadly true!"

"Well!" said I, "we must talk together a little more, as we used to do. And I must consult you a little more, as I used to do. Let us have a quiet walk on the marshes next Sunday, Biddy, and a long chat."

My sister was never left alone now; but Joe more than readily undertook the care of her on that Sunday afternoon, and Biddy and I went out together. It was summertime, and lovely weather. When we had passed the village and the church and the churchyard, and were out on the marshes and began to see the sails of the ships as they sailed on, I began to combine Miss Havisham and Estella with the prospect, in my usual way. When we came to the river-side and sat down on the bank, with the water rippling at our feet, making it all more quiet than it would have been without that sound, I resolved that it was a good time and place for the admission of Biddy into my inner confidence.

"Biddy," said I, after binding her to secrecy, "I want to be a gentleman."

"O, I wouldn't, if I was you!" she returned. "I don't think it would answer."

"Biddy," said I, with some severity, "I have particular reasons for wanting to be a gentleman."

"You know best, Pip; but don't you think you are happier as you are?"

"Biddy," I exclaimed, impatiently, "I am not at all happy as I am. I am disgusted with my calling and with my life. I have never taken to either, since I was bound. Don't be absurd."

"Was I absurd?" said Biddy, quietly raising her eyebrows; "I am sorry for that; I didn't mean to be. I only want you to do well, and to be comfortable."

"Well, then, understand once for all that I never shall or can be comfortable—or anything but miserable—there, Biddy!—unless I can lead a very different sort of life from the life I lead now."

"That's a pity!" said Biddy, shaking her head with a sorrowful air.

Now, I too had so often thought it a pity, that, in the singular kind of quarrel with myself which I was always carrying on, I was half inclined to shed tears of vexation and distress when Biddy gave utterance to her sentiment and my own. I told her she was right, and I knew it was much to be regretted, but still it was not to be helped.

"If I could have settled down," I said to Biddy, plucking up the short grass within reach, much as I had once upon a time pulled my feelings out of my hair and kicked them into the brewery wall,—"if I could have settled down and been but half as fond of the forge as I was when I was little, I know it would have been much better for me. You and I and Joe would have wanted nothing then, and Joe and I would perhaps have gone partners when I was out of my time, and I might even have grown up to keep company with you, and we might have sat on this very bank on a fine Sunday, quite different people. I should have been good enough for you; shouldn't I, Biddy?"

Biddy sighed as she looked at the ships sailing on, and returned for answer, "Yes; I am not over-particular." It scarcely sounded flattering, but I knew she meant well.

"Instead of that," said I, plucking up more grass and chewing a blade or two, "see how I am going on. Dissatisfied, and uncomfortable, and—what would it signify to me, being coarse and common, if nobody had told me so!"

Biddy turned her face suddenly towards mine, and looked far more attentively at me than she had looked at the sailing ships.

"It was neither a very true nor a very polite thing to say," she remarked, directing her eyes to the ships again. "Who said it?"

I was disconcerted, for I had broken away without quite seeing where I was going to. It was not to be shuffled off now, however, and I answered, "The beautiful young lady at Miss Havisham's, and she's more beautiful than anybody ever was, and I admire her dreadfully, and I want to be a gentleman on her account." Having made this lunatic confession, I began to throw my torn-up grass into the river, as if I had some thoughts of following it.

"Do you want to be a gentleman, to spite her or to gain her over?" Biddy quietly asked me, after a pause.

"I don't know," I moodily answered.

"Because, if it is to spite her," Biddy pursued, "I should think—but you know best—that might be better and more independently done by caring nothing for her words. And if it is to gain her over, I should think—but you know best—she was not worth gaining over."

Exactly what I myself had thought, many times. Exactly what was perfectly manifest to me at the moment. But how could I, a poor dazed village lad, avoid that wonderful inconsistency into which the best and wisest of men fall every day?

"It may be all quite true," said I to Biddy, "but I admire her dreadfully."

In short, I turned over on my face when I came to that, and got a good grasp on the hair on each side of my head, and wrenched it well. All the while knowing the madness of my heart to be so very mad and misplaced, that I was quite conscious it would have served my face right, if I had lifted it up by my hair, and knocked it against the pebbles as a punishment for belonging to such an idiot.

Biddy was the wisest of girls, and she tried to reason no more with me. She put her hand, which was a comfortable hand though roughened by work, upon my hands, one after another, and gently took them out of my hair. Then she softly patted my shoulder in a soothing way, while with my face upon my sleeve I cried a little,—exactly as I had done in the brewery yard,—and felt vaguely convinced that I was very much ill-used by somebody, or by everybody; I can't say which.

"I am glad of one thing," said Biddy, "and that is, that you have felt you could give me your confidence, Pip. And I am glad of another thing, and that is, that of course you know you may depend upon my keeping it and always so far deserving it. If your first teacher (dear! such a poor one, and so much in need of being taught herself!) had been your teacher at the present time, she thinks she knows what lesson she would set. But it would be a hard one to learn, and you have got beyond her, and it's of no use now." So, with a quiet sigh for me, Biddy rose from the bank, and said, with a fresh and pleasant change of voice, "Shall we walk a little farther, or go home?"

"Biddy," I cried, getting up, putting my arm round her neck, and giving her a kiss, "I shall always tell you everything."

"Till you're a gentleman," said Biddy.

"You know I never shall be, so that's always. Not that I have any occasion to tell you anything, for you know everything I know,—as I told you at home the other night."

"Ah!" said Biddy, quite in a whisper, as she looked away at the ships. And then repeated, with her former pleasant change, "shall we walk a little farther, or go home?"

I said to Biddy we would walk a little farther, and we did so, and the summer afternoon toned down into the summer evening, and it was very beautiful. I began to consider whether I was not more naturally and wholesomely situated, after all, in these circumstances, than playing beggar my neighbor by candle-light in the room with the stopped clocks, and being despised by Estella. I thought it would be very good for me if I could get her out of my head, with all the rest of those remembrances and fancies, and could go to work determined to relish what I had to do, and stick to it, and make the best of it. I asked myself the question whether I did not surely know that if Estella were beside me at that moment instead of Biddy, she would make me miserable? I was obliged to admit that I did know it for a certainty, and I said to myself, "Pip, what a fool you are!"

We talked a good deal as we walked, and all that Biddy said seemed right. Biddy was never insulting, or capricious, or Biddy to-day and somebody else to-morrow; she would have derived only pain, and no pleasure, from giving me pain; she would far rather have wounded her own breast than mine. How could it be, then, that I did not like her much the better of the two?

"Biddy," said I, when we were walking homeward, "I wish you could put me right."

"I wish I could!" said Biddy.

"If I could only get myself to fall in love with you,—you don't mind my speaking so openly to such an old acquaintance?"

"Oh dear, not at all!" said Biddy. "Don't mind me."

"If I could only get myself to do it, that would be the thing for me."

"But you never will, you see," said Biddy.

It did not appear quite so unlikely to me that evening, as it would have done if we had discussed it a few hours before. I therefore observed I was not quite sure of that. But Biddy said she was, and she said it decisively. In my heart I believed her to be right; and yet I took it rather ill, too, that she should be so positive on the point.

When we came near the churchyard, we had to cross an embankment, and get over a stile near a sluice-gate. There started up, from the gate, or from the rushes, or from the ooze (which was quite in his stagnant way), Old Orlick.

"Halloa!" he growled, "where are you two going?"

"Where should we be going, but home?"

"Well, then," said he, "I'm jiggered if I don't see you home!"

This penalty of being jiggered was a favorite supposititious case of his. He attached no definite meaning to the word that I am aware of, but used it, like his own pretended Christian name, to affront mankind, and convey an idea of something savagely damaging. When I was younger, I had had a general belief that if he had jiggered me personally, he would have done it with a sharp and twisted hook.

Biddy was much against his going with us, and said to me in a whisper, "Don't let him come; I don't like him." As I did not like him either, I took the liberty of saying that we thanked him, but we didn't want seeing home. He received that piece of information with a yell of laughter, and dropped back, but came slouching after us at a little distance.

Curious to know whether Biddy suspected him of having had a hand in that murderous attack of which my sister had never been able to give any account, I asked her why she did not like him.

"Oh!" she replied, glancing over her shoulder as he slouched after us, "because I—I am afraid he likes me."

"Did he ever tell you he liked you?" I asked indignantly.

"No," said Biddy, glancing over her shoulder again, "he never told me so; but he dances at me, whenever he can catch my eye."

However novel and peculiar this testimony of attachment, I did not doubt the accuracy of the interpretation. I was very hot indeed upon Old Orlick's daring to admire her; as hot as if it were an outrage on myself.

"But it makes no difference to you, you know," said Biddy, calmly.

"No, Biddy, it makes no difference to me; only I don't like it; I don't approve of it."

"Nor I neither," said Biddy. "Though that makes no difference to you."

"Exactly," said I; "but I must tell you I should have no opinion of you, Biddy, if he danced at you with your own consent."

I kept an eye on Orlick after that night, and, whenever circumstances were favorable to his dancing at Biddy, got before him to obscure that demonstration. He had struck root in Joe's establishment, by reason of my sister's sudden fancy for him, or I should have tried to get him dismissed. He quite understood and reciprocated my good intentions, as I had reason to know thereafter.

And now, because my mind was not confused enough before, I complicated its confusion fifty thousand-fold, by having states and seasons when I was clear that Biddy was immeasurably better than Estella, and that the plain honest working life to which I was born had nothing in it to be ashamed of, but offered me sufficient means of self-respect and happiness. At those times, I would decide conclusively that my disaffection to dear old Joe and the forge was gone, and that I was growing up in a fair way to be partners with Joe and to keep company with Biddy,—when all in a moment some confounding remembrance of the Havisham days would fall upon me like a destructive missile, and scatter my wits again. Scattered wits take a long time picking up; and often before I had got them well together, they would be dispersed in all directions by one stray thought, that perhaps after all Miss Havisham was going to make my fortune when my time was out.

If my time had run out, it would have left me still at the height of my perplexities, I dare say. It never did run out, however, but was brought to a premature end, as I proceed to relate.

CHAPTER XVIII

It was in the fourth year of my apprenticeship to Joe, and it was a Saturday night. There was a group assembled round the fire at the Three Jolly Bargemen, attentive to Mr. Wopsle as he read the newspaper aloud. Of that group I was one.

A highly popular murder had been committed, and Mr. Wopsle was imbrued in blood to the eyebrows. He gloated over every abhorrent adjective in the description, and identified himself with every witness at the Inquest. He faintly moaned, "I am done for," as the victim, and he barbarously bellowed, "I'll serve you out," as the murderer. He gave the medical testimony, in pointed imitation of our local practitioner; and he piped and shook, as the aged turnpike-keeper who had heard blows, to an extent so very paralytic as to suggest a doubt regarding the mental competency of that witness. The coroner, in Mr. Wopsle's hands, became Timon of Athens; the beadle, Coriolanus. He enjoyed himself thoroughly, and we all enjoyed ourselves, and were delightfully comfortable. In this cosey state of mind we came to the verdict Wilful Murder.

Then, and not sooner, I became aware of a strange gentleman leaning over the back of the settle opposite me, looking on. There was an expression of contempt on his face, and he bit the side of a great forefinger as he watched the group of faces.

"Well!" said the stranger to Mr. Wopsle, when the reading was done, "you have settled it all to your own satisfaction, I have no doubt?"

Everybody started and looked up, as if it were the murderer. He looked at everybody coldly and sarcastically.

"Guilty, of course?" said he. "Out with it. Come!"

"Sir," returned Mr. Wopsle, "without having the honor of your acquaintance, I do say Guilty." Upon this we all took courage to unite in a confirmatory murmur.

"I know you do," said the stranger; "I knew you would. I told you so. But now I'll ask you a question. Do you know, or do you not know, that the law of England supposes every man to be innocent, until he is proved—proved—to be guilty?"

"Sir," Mr. Wopsle began to reply, "as an Englishman myself, I—"

"Come!" said the stranger, biting his forefinger at him. "Don't evade the question. Either you know it, or you don't know it. Which is it to be?"

He stood with his head on one side and himself on one side, in a Bullying, interrogative manner, and he threw his forefinger at Mr. Wopsle,—as it were to mark him out—before biting it again.

"Now!" said he. "Do you know it, or don't you know it?"

"Certainly I know it," replied Mr. Wopsle.

"Certainly you know it. Then why didn't you say so at first? Now, I'll ask you another question,"—taking possession of Mr. Wopsle, as if he had a right to him,— "do you know that none of these witnesses have yet been cross-examined?"

Mr. Wopsle was beginning, "I can only say—" when the stranger stopped him.

"What? You won't answer the question, yes or no? Now, I'll try you again." Throwing his finger at him again. "Attend to me. Are you aware, or are you not aware, that none of these witnesses have yet been cross-examined? Come, I only want one word from you. Yes, or no?"

Mr. Wopsle hesitated, and we all began to conceive rather a poor opinion of him.

"Come!" said the stranger, "I'll help you. You don't deserve help, but I'll help you. Look at that paper you hold in your hand. What is it?"

"What is it?" repeated Mr. Wopsle, eyeing it, much at a loss.

"Is it," pursued the stranger in his most sarcastic and suspicious manner, "the printed paper you have just been reading from?"

"Undoubtedly."

"Undoubtedly. Now, turn to that paper, and tell me whether it distinctly states that the prisoner expressly said that his legal advisers instructed him altogether to reserve his defence?"

"I read that just now," Mr. Wopsle pleaded.

"Never mind what you read just now, sir; I don't ask you what you read just now. You may read the Lord's Prayer backwards, if you like,—and, perhaps, have done it before to-day. Turn to the paper. No, no, no my friend; not to the top of the column; you know better than that; to the bottom, to the bottom." (We all began to think Mr. Wopsle full of subterfuge.) "Well? Have you found it?"

"Here it is," said Mr. Wopsle.

"Now, follow that passage with your eye, and tell me whether it distinctly states that the prisoner expressly said that he was instructed by his legal advisers wholly to reserve his defence? Come! Do you make that of it?"

Mr. Wopsle answered, "Those are not the exact words."

"Not the exact words!" repeated the gentleman bitterly. "Is that the exact substance?"

"Yes," said Mr. Wopsle.

"Yes," repeated the stranger, looking round at the rest of the company with his right hand extended towards the witness, Wopsle. "And now I ask you what you say to the conscience of that man who, with that passage before his eyes, can lay his head upon his pillow after having pronounced a fellow-creature guilty, unheard?"

We all began to suspect that Mr. Wopsle was not the man we had thought him, and that he was beginning to be found out.

"And that same man, remember," pursued the gentleman, throwing his finger at Mr. Wopsle heavily,—"that same man might be summoned as a juryman upon this very trial, and, having thus deeply committed himself, might return to the bosom of his family and lay his head upon his pillow, after deliberately swearing that he would well and truly try the issue joined between Our Sovereign Lord the King and the prisoner at the bar, and would a true verdict give according to the evidence, so help him God!"

We were all deeply persuaded that the unfortunate Wopsle had gone too far, and had better stop in his reckless career while there was yet time.

The strange gentleman, with an air of authority not to be disputed, and with a manner expressive of knowing something secret about every one of us that would effectually do for each individual if he chose to disclose it, left the back of the settle, and came into the space between the two settles, in front of the fire, where he remained standing, his left hand in his pocket, and he biting the forefinger of his right.

"From information I have received," said he, looking round at us as we all quailed before him, "I have reason to believe there is a blacksmith among you, by name Joseph—or Joe—Gargery. Which is the man?"

"Here is the man," said Joe.

The strange gentleman beckoned him out of his place, and Joe went.

"You have an apprentice," pursued the stranger, "commonly known as Pip? Is he here?"

"I am here!" I cried.

The stranger did not recognize me, but I recognised him as the gentleman I had met on the stairs, on the occasion of my second visit to Miss Havisham. I had known him the moment I saw him looking over the settle, and now that I stood confronting him with his hand upon my shoulder, I checked off again in detail his large head, his dark complexion, his deep-set eyes, his bushy black eyebrows, his large watch-chain, his strong black dots of beard and whisker, and even the smell of scented soap on his great hand.

"I wish to have a private conference with you two," said he, when he had surveyed me at his leisure. "It will take a little time. Perhaps we had better go to your place of residence. I prefer not to anticipate my communication here; you will impart as much or as little of it as you please to your friends afterwards; I have nothing to do with that."

Amidst a wondering silence, we three walked out of the Jolly Bargemen, and in a wondering silence walked home. While going along, the strange gentleman occasionally looked at me, and occasionally bit the side of his finger. As we neared home, Joe vaguely acknowledging the occasion as an impressive and ceremonious one, went on ahead to open the front door. Our conference was held in the state parlor, which was feebly lighted by one candle.

It began with the strange gentleman's sitting down at the table, drawing the candle to him, and looking over some entries in his pocket-book. He then put up the pocket-book and set the candle a little aside, after peering round it into the darkness at Joe and me, to ascertain which was which.

"My name," he said, "is Jaggers, and I am a lawyer in London. I am pretty well known. I have unusual business to transact with you, and I commence by explaining that it is not of my originating. If my advice had been asked, I should not have been here. It was not asked, and you see me here. What I have to do as the confidential agent of another, I do. No less, no more."

Finding that he could not see us very well from where he sat, he got up, and threw one leg over the back of a chair and leaned upon it; thus having one foot on the seat of the chair, and one foot on the ground.

"Now, Joseph Gargery, I am the bearer of an offer to relieve you of this young fellow your apprentice. You would not object to cancel his indentures at his request and for his good? You would want nothing for so doing?"

"Lord forbid that I should want anything for not standing in Pip's way," said Joe, staring.

"Lord forbidding is pious, but not to the purpose," returned Mr. Jaggers. "The question is, Would you want anything? Do you want anything?"

"The answer is," returned Joe, sternly, "No."

I thought Mr. Jaggers glanced at Joe, as if he considered him a fool for his disinterestedness. But I was too much bewildered between breathless curiosity and surprise, to be sure of it.

"Very well," said Mr. Jaggers. "Recollect the admission you have made, and don't try to go from it presently."

"Who's a going to try?" retorted Joe.

"I don't say anybody is. Do you keep a dog?"

"Yes, I do keep a dog."

"Bear in mind then, that Brag is a good dog, but Holdfast is a better. Bear that in mind, will you?" repeated Mr. Jaggers, shutting his eyes and nodding his head at Joe, as if he were forgiving him something. "Now, I return to this young fellow. And the communication I have got to make is, that he has Great Expectations."

Joe and I gasped, and looked at one another.

"I am instructed to communicate to him," said Mr. Jaggers, throwing his finger at me sideways, "that he will come into a handsome property. Further, that it is the desire of the present possessor of that property, that he be immediately removed from his present sphere of life and from this place, and be brought up as a gentleman,—in a word, as a young fellow of great expectations."

My dream was out; my wild fancy was surpassed by sober reality; Miss Havisham was going to make my fortune on a grand scale.

"Now, Mr. Pip," pursued the lawyer, "I address the rest of what I have to say, to you. You are to understand, first, that it is the request of the person from whom I take my instructions that you always bear the name of Pip. You will have no objection, I dare say, to your great expectations being encumbered with that easy condition. But if you have any objection, this is the time to mention it."

My heart was beating so fast, and there was such a singing in my ears, that I could scarcely stammer I had no objection.

"I should think not! Now you are to understand, secondly, Mr. Pip, that the name of the person who is your liberal benefactor remains a profound secret, until the person chooses to reveal it. I am empowered to mention that it is the intention of the person to reveal it at first hand by word of mouth to yourself. When or where that intention may be carried out, I cannot say; no one can say. It may be years hence. Now, you are distinctly to understand that you are most positively prohibited from making any inquiry on this head, or any allusion or reference, however distant, to any individual whomsoever as the individual, in all the communications you may have with me. If you have a suspicion in your own breast, keep that suspicion in your own breast. It is not the least to the purpose what the reasons of this prohibition are; they may be the strongest and gravest reasons, or they may be mere whim. This is not for you to inquire into. The condition is laid down. Your acceptance of it, and your observance of it as binding, is the only remaining condition that I am charged with, by the person from whom I take my instructions, and for whom I am not otherwise responsible. That person is the person from whom you derive your expectations, and the secret is solely held by that person and by me. Again, not a very difficult condition with which to encumber such a rise in fortune; but if you have any objection to it, this is the time to mention it. Speak out."

Once more, I stammered with difficulty that I had no objection.

"I should think not! Now, Mr. Pip, I have done with stipulations." Though he called me Mr. Pip, and began rather to make up to me, he still could not get rid of a certain air of bullying suspicion; and even now he occasionally shut his eyes and threw his finger at me while he spoke, as much as to express that he knew all kinds of things to my disparagement, if he only chose to mention them. "We come next, to mere details of arrangement. You must know that, although I have used the term 'expectations' more than once, you are not endowed with expectations only. There is already lodged in my hands a sum of money amply sufficient for your suitable education and maintenance. You will please consider me your guardian. Oh!" for I was going to thank him, "I tell you at once, I am paid for my services, or I shouldn't render them. It is considered that you must be better educated, in accordance with your altered position, and that you will be alive to the importance and necessity of at once entering on that advantage."

I said I had always longed for it.

"Never mind what you have always longed for, Mr. Pip," he retorted; "keep to the record. If you long for it now, that's enough. Am I answered that you are ready to be placed at once under some proper tutor? Is that it?"

I stammered yes, that was it.

"Good. Now, your inclinations are to be consulted. I don't think that wise, mind, but it's my trust. Have you ever heard of any tutor whom you would prefer to another?"

I had never heard of any tutor but Biddy and Mr. Wopsle's great-aunt; so, I replied in the negative.

"There is a certain tutor, of whom I have some knowledge, who I think might suit the purpose," said Mr. Jaggers. "I don't recommend him, observe; because I never recommend anybody. The gentleman I speak of is one Mr. Matthew Pocket."

Ah! I caught at the name directly. Miss Havisham's relation. The Matthew whom Mr. and Mrs. Camilla had spoken of. The Matthew whose place was to be at Miss Havisham's head, when she lay dead, in her bride's dress on the bride's table.

"You know the name?" said Mr. Jaggers, looking shrewdly at me, and then shutting up his eyes while he waited for my answer.

My answer was, that I had heard of the name.

"Oh!" said he. "You have heard of the name. But the question is, what do you say of it?"

I said, or tried to say, that I was much obliged to him for his recommendation—

"No, my young friend!" he interrupted, shaking his great head very slowly. "Recollect yourself!"

Not recollecting myself, I began again that I was much obliged to him for his recommendation—

"No, my young friend," he interrupted, shaking his head and frowning and smiling both at once,—"no, no, no; it's very well done, but it won't do; you are too young to fix me with it. Recommendation is not the word, Mr. Pip. Try another."

Correcting myself, I said that I was much obliged to him for his mention of Mr. Matthew Pocket—

"That's more like it!" cried Mr. Jaggers.—And (I added), I would gladly try that gentleman.

"Good. You had better try him in his own house. The way shall be prepared for you, and you can see his son first, who is in London. When will you come to London?"

I said (glancing at Joe, who stood looking on, motionless), that I supposed I could come directly.

"First," said Mr. Jaggers, "you should have some new clothes to come in, and they should not be working-clothes. Say this day week. You'll want some money. Shall I leave you twenty guineas?"

He produced a long purse, with the greatest coolness, and counted them out on the table and pushed them over to me. This was the first time he had taken his leg from the chair. He sat astride of the chair when he had pushed the money over, and sat swinging his purse and eyeing Joe.

"Well, Joseph Gargery? You look dumbfoundered?"

"I am!" said Joe, in a very decided manner.

"It was understood that you wanted nothing for yourself, remember?"

"It were understood," said Joe. "And it are understood. And it ever will be similar according."

"But what," said Mr. Jaggers, swinging his purse,—"what if it was in my instructions to make you a present, as compensation?"

"As compensation what for?" Joe demanded.

"For the loss of his services."

Joe laid his hand upon my shoulder with the touch of a woman. I have often thought him since, like the steam-hammer that can crush a man or pat an egg-shell, in his combination of strength with gentleness. "Pip is that hearty welcome," said Joe, "to go free with his services, to honor and fortun', as no words can tell him. But if you think as Money can make compensation to me for the loss of the little child—what come to the forge—and ever the best of friends!—"

O dear good Joe, whom I was so ready to leave and so unthankful to, I see you again, with your muscular blacksmith's arm before your eyes, and your broad chest heaving, and your voice dying away. O dear good faithful tender Joe, I feel the loving tremble of your hand upon my arm, as solemnly this day as if it had been the rustle of an angel's wing!

But I encouraged Joe at the time. I was lost in the mazes of my future fortunes, and could not retrace the by-paths we had trodden together. I begged Joe to be comforted, for (as he said) we had ever been the best of friends, and (as I said) we ever would be so. Joe scooped his eyes with his disengaged wrist, as if he were bent on gouging himself, but said not another word.

Mr. Jaggers had looked on at this, as one who recognised in Joe the village idiot, and in me his keeper. When it was over, he said, weighing in his hand the purse he had ceased to swing:—

"Now, Joseph Gargery, I warn you this is your last chance. No half measures with me. If you mean to take a present that I have it in charge to make you, speak out, and you shall have it. If on the contrary you mean to say—" Here, to his great amazement, he was stopped by Joe's suddenly working round him with every demonstration of a fell pugilistic purpose.

"Which I meantersay," cried Joe, "that if you come into my place bull-baiting and badgering me, come out! Which I meantersay as sech if you're a man, come on! Which I meantersay that what I say, I meantersay and stand or fall by!"

I drew Joe away, and he immediately became placable; merely stating to me, in an obliging manner and as a polite expostulatory notice to any one whom it might happen to concern, that he were not a going to be bull-baited and badgered in his own place. Mr. Jaggers had risen when Joe demonstrated, and had backed near the door. Without evincing any inclination to come in again, he there delivered his valedictory remarks. They were these.

"Well, Mr. Pip, I think the sooner you leave here—as you are to be a gentleman— the better. Let it stand for this day week, and you shall receive my printed address in the meantime. You can take a hackney-coach at the stage-coach office in London, and come straight to me. Understand, that I express no opinion, one way or other, on the trust I undertake. I am paid for undertaking it, and I do so. Now, understand that, finally. Understand that!"

He was throwing his finger at both of us, and I think would have gone on, but for his seeming to think Joe dangerous, and going off.

Something came into my head which induced me to run after him, as he was going down to the Jolly Bargemen, where he had left a hired carriage.

"I beg your pardon, Mr. Jaggers."

"Halloa!" said he, facing round, "what's the matter?"

"I wish to be quite right, Mr. Jaggers, and to keep to your directions; so I thought I had better ask. Would there be any objection to my taking leave of any one I know, about here, before I go away?"

"No," said he, looking as if he hardly understood me.

"I don't mean in the village only, but up town?"

"No," said he. "No objection."

I thanked him and ran home again, and there I found that Joe had already locked the front door and vacated the state parlor, and was seated by the kitchen fire with a hand on each knee, gazing intently at the burning coals. I too sat down before the fire and gazed at the coals, and nothing was said for a long time.

My sister was in her cushioned chair in her corner, and Biddy sat at her needle-work before the fire, and Joe sat next Biddy, and I sat next Joe in the corner opposite my sister. The more I looked into the glowing coals, the more incapable I became of looking at Joe; the longer the silence lasted, the more unable I felt to speak.

At length I got out, "Joe, have you told Biddy?"

"No, Pip," returned Joe, still looking at the fire, and holding his knees tight, as if he had private information that they intended to make off somewhere, "which I left it to yourself, Pip."

"I would rather you told, Joe."

"Pip's a gentleman of fortun' then," said Joe, "and God bless him in it!"

Biddy dropped her work, and looked at me. Joe held his knees and looked at me. I looked at both of them. After a pause, they both heartily congratulated me; but there was a certain touch of sadness in their congratulations that I rather resented.

I took it upon myself to impress Biddy (and through Biddy, Joe) with the grave obligation I considered my friends under, to know nothing and say nothing about the maker of my fortune. It would all come out in good time, I observed, and in the meanwhile nothing was to be said, save that I had come into great expectations from a mysterious patron. Biddy nodded her head thoughtfully at the fire as she took up her work again, and said she would be very particular; and Joe, still detaining his knees, said, "Ay, ay, I'll be ekervally partickler, Pip;" and then they congratulated me again, and went on to express so much wonder at the notion of my being a gentleman that I didn't half like it.

Infinite pains were then taken by Biddy to convey to my sister some idea of what had happened. To the best of my belief, those efforts entirely failed. She laughed and nodded her head a great many times, and even repeated after Biddy, the words "Pip" and "Property." But I doubt if they had more meaning in them than an election cry, and I cannot suggest a darker picture of her state of mind.

I never could have believed it without experience, but as Joe and Biddy became more at their cheerful ease again, I became quite gloomy. Dissatisfied with my fortune, of course I could not be; but it is possible that I may have been, without quite knowing it, dissatisfied with myself.

Any how, I sat with my elbow on my knee and my face upon my hand, looking into the fire, as those two talked about my going away, and about what they should do without me, and all that. And whenever I caught one of them looking at me, though never so pleasantly (and they often looked at me,—particularly Biddy), I felt offended: as if they were expressing some mistrust of me. Though Heaven knows they never did by word or sign.

At those times I would get up and look out at the door; for our kitchen door opened at once upon the night, and stood open on summer evenings to air the room. The very stars to which I then raised my eyes, I am afraid I took to be but poor and humble stars for glittering on the rustic objects among which I had passed my life.

"Saturday night," said I, when we sat at our supper of bread and cheese and beer. "Five more days, and then the day before the day! They'll soon go."

"Yes, Pip," observed Joe, whose voice sounded hollow in his beer-mug. "They'll soon go."

"Soon, soon go," said Biddy.

"I have been thinking, Joe, that when I go down town on Monday, and order my new clothes, I shall tell the tailor that I'll come and put them on there, or that I'll have them sent to Mr. Pumblechook's. It would be very disagreeable to be stared at by all the people here."

"Mr. and Mrs. Hubble might like to see you in your new gen-teel figure too, Pip," said Joe, industriously cutting his bread, with his cheese on it, in the palm of his left hand, and glancing at my untasted supper as if he thought of the time when we used to compare slices. "So might Wopsle. And the Jolly Bargemen might take it as a compliment."

"That's just what I don't want, Joe. They would make such a business of it,—such a coarse and common business,—that I couldn't bear myself."

"Ah, that indeed, Pip!" said Joe. "If you couldn't abear yourself—"

Biddy asked me here, as she sat holding my sister's plate, "Have you thought about when you'll show yourself to Mr. Gargery, and your sister and me? You will show yourself to us; won't you?"

"Biddy," I returned with some resentment, "you are so exceedingly quick that it's difficult to keep up with you."

("She always were quick," observed Joe.)

"If you had waited another moment, Biddy, you would have heard me say that I shall bring my clothes here in a bundle one evening,—most likely on the evening before I go away."

Biddy said no more. Handsomely forgiving her, I soon exchanged an affectionate good night with her and Joe, and went up to bed. When I got into my little room, I sat down and took a long look at it, as a mean little room that I should soon be parted from and raised above, for ever. It was furnished with fresh young remembrances too, and even at the same moment I fell into much the same confused division of mind between it and the better rooms to which I was going, as I had been in so often between the forge and Miss Havisham's, and Biddy and Estella.

The sun had been shining brightly all day on the roof of my attic, and the room was warm. As I put the window open and stood looking out, I saw Joe come slowly forth at the dark door, below, and take a turn or two in the air; and then I saw Biddy come, and bring him a pipe and light it for him. He never smoked so late, and it seemed to hint to me that he wanted comforting, for some reason or other.

He presently stood at the door immediately beneath me, smoking his pipe, and Biddy stood there too, quietly talking to him, and I knew that they talked of me, for I heard my name mentioned in an endearing tone by both of them more than once. I would not have listened for more, if I could have heard more; so I drew away from the window, and sat down in my one chair by the bedside, feeling it very sorrowful and strange that this first night of my bright fortunes should be the loneliest I had ever known.

Looking towards the open window, I saw light wreaths from Joe's pipe floating there, and I fancied it was like a blessing from Joe,—not obtruded on me or paraded before me, but pervading the air we shared together. I put my light out, and crept into bed; and it was an uneasy bed now, and I never slept the old sound sleep in it any more.

CHAPTER XIX

Morning made a considerable difference in my general prospect of Life, and brightened it so much that it scarcely seemed the same. What lay heaviest on my mind was, the consideration that six days intervened between me and the day of departure; for I could not divest myself of a misgiving that something might happen to London in the meanwhile, and that, when I got there, it would be either greatly deteriorated or clean gone.

Joe and Biddy were very sympathetic and pleasant when I spoke of our approaching separation; but they only referred to it when I did. After breakfast, Joe brought out my indentures from the press in the best parlor, and we put them in the fire, and I felt that I was free. With all the novelty of my emancipation on me, I went to church with Joe, and thought perhaps the clergyman wouldn't have read that about the rich man and the kingdom of Heaven, if he had known all.

After our early dinner, I strolled out alone, purposing to finish off the marshes at once, and get them done with. As I passed the church, I felt (as I had felt during service in the morning) a sublime compassion for the poor creatures who were destined to go there, Sunday after Sunday, all their lives through, and to lie obscurely at last among the low green mounds. I promised myself that I would do something for them one of these days, and formed a plan in outline for bestowing a dinner of roast-beef and plum-pudding, a pint of ale, and a gallon of condescension, upon everybody in the village.

If I had often thought before, with something allied to shame, of my companionship with the fugitive whom I had once seen limping among those graves, what were my thoughts on this Sunday, when the place recalled the wretch, ragged and shivering, with his felon iron and badge! My comfort was, that it happened a long time ago, and that he had doubtless been transported a long way off, and that he was dead to me, and might be veritably dead into the bargain.

No more low, wet grounds, no more dikes and sluices, no more of these grazing cattle,—though they seemed, in their dull manner, to wear a more respectful air now, and to face round, in order that they might stare as long as possible at the possessor of such great expectations,—farewell, monotonous acquaintances of my childhood, henceforth I was for London and greatness; not for smith's work in general, and for you! I made my exultant way to the old Battery, and, lying down there to consider the question whether Miss Havisham intended me for Estella, fell asleep.

When I awoke, I was much surprised to find Joe sitting beside me, smoking his pipe. He greeted me with a cheerful smile on my opening my eyes, and said,—

"As being the last time, Pip, I thought I'd foller."

"And Joe, I am very glad you did so."

"Thankee, Pip."

"You may be sure, dear Joe," I went on, after we had shaken hands, "that I shall never forget you."

"No, no, Pip!" said Joe, in a comfortable tone, "I'm sure of that. Ay, ay, old chap! Bless you, it were only necessary to get it well round in a man's mind, to be certain on it. But it took a bit of time to get it well round, the change come so oncommon plump; didn't it?"

Somehow, I was not best pleased with Joe's being so mightily secure of me. I should have liked him to have betrayed emotion, or to have said, "It does you credit, Pip," or something of that sort. Therefore, I made no remark on Joe's first head; merely saying as to his second, that the tidings had indeed come suddenly, but that I had always wanted to be a gentleman, and had often and often speculated on what I would do, if I were one.

"Have you though?" said Joe. "Astonishing!"

"It's a pity now, Joe," said I, "that you did not get on a little more, when we had our lessons here; isn't it?"

"Well, I don't know," returned Joe. "I'm so awful dull. I'm only master of my own trade. It were always a pity as I was so awful dull; but it's no more of a pity now, than it was—this day twelvemonth—don't you see?"

What I had meant was, that when I came into my property and was able to do something for Joe, it would have been much more agreeable if he had been better qualified for a rise in station. He was so perfectly innocent of my meaning, however, that I thought I would mention it to Biddy in preference.

So, when we had walked home and had had tea, I took Biddy into our little garden by the side of the lane, and, after throwing out in a general way for the elevation of her spirits, that I should never forget her, said I had a favor to ask of her.

"And it is, Biddy," said I, "that you will not omit any opportunity of helping Joe on, a little."

"How helping him on?" asked Biddy, with a steady sort of glance.

"Well! Joe is a dear good fellow,—in fact, I think he is the dearest fellow that ever lived,—but he is rather backward in some things. For instance, Biddy, in his learning and his manners."

Although I was looking at Biddy as I spoke, and although she opened her eyes very wide when I had spoken, she did not look at me.

"O, his manners! won't his manners do then?" asked Biddy, plucking a black-currant leaf.

"My dear Biddy, they do very well here—"

"O! they do very well here?" interrupted Biddy, looking closely at the leaf in her hand.

"Hear me out,—but if I were to remove Joe into a higher sphere, as I shall hope to remove him when I fully come into my property, they would hardly do him justice."

"And don't you think he knows that?" asked Biddy.

It was such a very provoking question (for it had never in the most distant manner occurred to me), that I said, snappishly,—

"Biddy, what do you mean?"

Biddy, having rubbed the leaf to pieces between her hands,—and the smell of a black-currant bush has ever since recalled to me that evening in the little garden by the side of the lane,—said, "Have you never considered that he may be proud?"

"Proud?" I repeated, with disdainful emphasis.

"O! there are many kinds of pride," said Biddy, looking full at me and shaking her head; "pride is not all of one kind—"

"Well? What are you stopping for?" said I.

"Not all of one kind," resumed Biddy. "He may be too proud to let any one take him out of a place that he is competent to fill, and fills well and with respect. To tell you the truth, I think he is; though it sounds bold in me to say so, for you must know him far better than I do."

"Now, Biddy," said I, "I am very sorry to see this in you. I did not expect to see this in you. You are envious, Biddy, and grudging. You are dissatisfied on account of my rise in fortune, and you can't help showing it."

"If you have the heart to think so," returned Biddy, "say so. Say so over and over again, if you have the heart to think so."

"If you have the heart to be so, you mean, Biddy," said I, in a virtuous and superior tone; "don't put it off upon me. I am very sorry to see it, and it's a—it's a bad side of human nature. I did intend to ask you to use any little opportunities you might have after I was gone, of improving dear Joe. But after this I ask you nothing. I am extremely sorry to see this in you, Biddy," I repeated. "It's a—it's a bad side of human nature."

"Whether you scold me or approve of me," returned poor Biddy, "you may equally depend upon my trying to do all that lies in my power, here, at all times. And whatever opinion you take away of me, shall make no difference in my remembrance of you. Yet a gentleman should not be unjust neither," said Biddy, turning away her head.

I again warmly repeated that it was a bad side of human nature (in which sentiment, waiving its application, I have since seen reason to think I was right), and I walked down the little path away from Biddy, and Biddy went into the house, and I went out at the garden gate and took a dejected stroll until supper-time; again feeling it very sorrowful and strange that this, the second night of my bright fortunes, should be as lonely and unsatisfactory as the first.

But, morning once more brightened my view, and I extended my clemency to Biddy, and we dropped the subject. Putting on the best clothes I had, I went into town as early as I could hope to find the shops open, and presented myself before Mr. Trabb, the tailor, who was having his breakfast in the parlor behind his shop, and who did not think it worth his while to come out to me, but called me in to him.

"Well!" said Mr. Trabb, in a hail-fellow-well-met kind of way. "How are you, and what can I do for you?"

Mr. Trabb had sliced his hot roll into three feather-beds, and was slipping butter in between the blankets, and covering it up. He was a prosperous old bachelor, and his open window looked into a prosperous little garden and orchard, and there was a prosperous iron safe let into the wall at the side of his fireplace, and I did not doubt that heaps of his prosperity were put away in it in bags.

"Mr. Trabb," said I, "it's an unpleasant thing to have to mention, because it looks like boasting; but I have come into a handsome property."

A change passed over Mr. Trabb. He forgot the butter in bed, got up from the bedside, and wiped his fingers on the tablecloth, exclaiming, "Lord bless my soul!"

"I am going up to my guardian in London," said I, casually drawing some guineas out of my pocket and looking at them; "and I want a fashionable suit of clothes to go in. I wish to pay for them," I added—otherwise I thought he might only pretend to make them, "with ready money."

"My dear sir," said Mr. Trabb, as he respectfully bent his body, opened his arms, and took the liberty of touching me on the outside of each elbow, "don't hurt me by mentioning that. May I venture to congratulate you? Would you do me the favor of stepping into the shop?"

Mr. Trabb's boy was the most audacious boy in all that country-side. When I had entered he was sweeping the shop, and he had sweetened his labors by sweeping over me. He was still sweeping when I came out into the shop with Mr. Trabb, and he knocked the broom against all possible corners and obstacles, to express (as I understood it) equality with any blacksmith, alive or dead.

"Hold that noise," said Mr. Trabb, with the greatest sternness, "or I'll knock your head off!—Do me the favor to be seated, sir. Now, this," said Mr. Trabb, taking down a roll of cloth, and tiding it out in a flowing manner over the counter, preparatory to getting his hand under it to show the gloss, "is a very sweet article. I can recommend it for your purpose, sir, because it really is extra super. But you shall see some others. Give me Number Four, you!" (To the boy, and with a dreadfully severe stare; foreseeing the danger of that miscreant's brushing me with it, or making some other sign of familiarity.)

Mr. Trabb never removed his stern eye from the boy until he had deposited number four on the counter and was at a safe distance again. Then he commanded him to bring number five, and number eight. "And let me have none of your tricks here," said Mr. Trabb, "or you shall repent it, you young scoundrel, the longest day you have to live."

Mr. Trabb then bent over number four, and in a sort of deferential confidence recommended it to me as a light article for summer wear, an article much in vogue among the nobility and gentry, an article that it would ever be an honor to him to reflect upon a distinguished fellow-townsman's (if he might claim me for a fellow-townsman) having worn. "Are you bringing numbers five and eight, you vagabond," said Mr. Trabb to the boy after that, "or shall I kick you out of the shop and bring them myself?"

I selected the materials for a suit, with the assistance of Mr. Trabb's judgment, and re-entered the parlor to be measured. For although Mr. Trabb had my measure already, and had previously been quite contented with it, he said apologetically that it "wouldn't do under existing circumstances, sir,—wouldn't do at all." So, Mr. Trabb measured and calculated me in the parlor, as if I were an estate and he the finest species of surveyor, and gave himself such a world of trouble that I felt that no suit of clothes could possibly remunerate him for his pains. When he had at last done and had appointed to send the articles to Mr. Pumblechook's on the Thursday evening, he said, with his hand upon the parlor lock, "I know, sir, that London gentlemen cannot be expected to patronize local work, as a rule; but if you would give me a turn now and then in the quality of a townsman, I should greatly esteem it. Good morning, sir, much obliged.—Door!"

The last word was flung at the boy, who had not the least notion what it meant. But I saw him collapse as his master rubbed me out with his hands, and my first decided experience of the stupendous power of money was, that it had morally laid upon his back Trabb's boy.

After this memorable event, I went to the hatter's, and the bootmaker's, and the hosier's, and felt rather like Mother Hubbard's dog whose outfit required the services of so many trades. I also went to the coach-office and took my place for seven o'clock on Saturday morning. It was not necessary to explain everywhere that I had come into a handsome property; but whenever I said anything to that effect, it followed that the officiating tradesman ceased to have his attention diverted through the window by the High Street, and concentrated his mind upon me. When I had ordered everything I wanted, I directed my steps towards Pumblechook's, and, as I approached that gentleman's place of business, I saw him standing at his door.

He was waiting for me with great impatience. He had been out early with the chaise-cart, and had called at the forge and heard the news. He had prepared a collation for me in the Barnwell parlor, and he too ordered his shopman to "come out of the gangway" as my sacred person passed.

"My dear friend," said Mr. Pumblechook, taking me by both hands, when he and I and the collation were alone, "I give you joy of your good fortune. Well deserved, well deserved!"

This was coming to the point, and I thought it a sensible way of expressing himself.

"To think," said Mr. Pumblechook, after snorting admiration at me for some moments, "that I should have been the humble instrument of leading up to this, is a proud reward."

I begged Mr. Pumblechook to remember that nothing was to be ever said or hinted, on that point.

"My dear young friend," said Mr. Pumblechook; "if you will allow me to call you so—"

I murmured "Certainly," and Mr. Pumblechook took me by both hands again, and communicated a movement to his waistcoat, which had an emotional appearance, though it was rather low down, "My dear young friend, rely upon my doing my little all in your absence, by keeping the fact before the mind of Joseph.—Joseph!" said Mr. Pumblechook, in the way of a compassionate adjuration. "Joseph!! Joseph!!!" Thereupon he shook his head and tapped it, expressing his sense of deficiency in Joseph.

"But my dear young friend," said Mr. Pumblechook, "you must be hungry, you must be exhausted. Be seated. Here is a chicken had round from the Boar, here is a tongue had round from the Boar, here's one or two little things had round from the Boar, that I hope you may not despise. But do I," said Mr. Pumblechook, getting up again the moment after he had sat down, "see afore me, him as I ever sported with in his times of happy infancy? And may I—may I—?"

This May I, meant might he shake hands? I consented, and he was fervent, and then sat down again.

"Here is wine," said Mr. Pumblechook. "Let us drink, Thanks to Fortune, and may she ever pick out her favorites with equal judgment! And yet I cannot," said Mr. Pumblechook, getting up again, "see afore me One—and likewise drink to One—without again expressing—May I—may I—?"

I said he might, and he shook hands with me again, and emptied his glass and turned it upside down. I did the same; and if I had turned myself upside down before drinking, the wine could not have gone more direct to my head.

Mr. Pumblechook helped me to the liver wing, and to the best slice of tongue (none of those out-of-the-way No Thoroughfares of Pork now), and took, comparatively speaking, no care of himself at all. "Ah! poultry, poultry! You little thought," said Mr. Pumblechook, apostrophizing the fowl in the dish, "when you was a young fledgling, what was in store for you. You little thought you was to be refreshment beneath this humble roof for one as—Call it a weakness, if you will," said Mr. Pumblechook, getting up again, "but may I? may I—?"

It began to be unnecessary to repeat the form of saying he might, so he did it at once. How he ever did it so often without wounding himself with my knife, I don't know.

"And your sister," he resumed, after a little steady eating, "which had the honor of bringing you up by hand! It's a sad picter, to reflect that she's no longer equal to fully understanding the honor. May—"

I saw he was about to come at me again, and I stopped him.

"We'll drink her health," said I.

"Ah!" cried Mr. Pumblechook, leaning back in his chair, quite flaccid with admiration, "that's the way you know 'em, sir!" (I don't know who Sir was, but he certainly was not I, and there was no third person present); "that's the way you know the noble-minded, sir! Ever forgiving and ever affable. It might," said the servile Pumblechook, putting down his untasted glass in a hurry and getting up again, "to a common person, have the appearance of repeating—but may I—?"

When he had done it, he resumed his seat and drank to my sister. "Let us never be blind," said Mr. Pumblechook, "to her faults of temper, but it is to be hoped she meant well."

At about this time, I began to observe that he was getting flushed in the face; as to myself, I felt all face, steeped in wine and smarting.

I mentioned to Mr. Pumblechook that I wished to have my new clothes sent to his house, and he was ecstatic on my so distinguishing him. I mentioned my reason for desiring to avoid observation in the village, and he lauded it to the skies. There was nobody but himself, he intimated, worthy of my confidence, and—in short, might he? Then he asked me tenderly if I remembered our boyish games at sums, and how we had gone together to have me bound apprentice, and, in effect, how he had ever been my favorite fancy and my chosen friend? If I had taken ten times as many glasses of wine as I had, I should have known that he never had stood in that relation towards me, and should in my heart of hearts have repudiated the idea. Yet for all that, I remember feeling convinced that I had been much mistaken in him, and that he was a sensible, practical, good-hearted prime fellow.

By degrees he fell to reposing such great confidence in me, as to ask my advice in reference to his own affairs. He mentioned that there was an opportunity for a great amalgamation and monopoly of the corn and seed trade on those premises, if enlarged, such as had never occurred before in that or any other neighborhood. What alone was wanting to the realization of a vast fortune, he considered to be More Capital. Those were the two little words, more capital. Now it appeared to him (Pumblechook) that if that capital were got into the business, through a sleeping partner, sir,—which sleeping partner would have nothing to do but walk in, by self or deputy, whenever he pleased, and examine the books,—and walk in twice a year and take his profits away in his pocket, to the tune of fifty per cent,—it appeared to him that that might be an opening for a young gentleman of spirit combined with property, which would be worthy of his attention. But what did I think? He had great confidence in my opinion, and what did I think? I gave it as my opinion. "Wait a bit!" The united vastness and distinctness of this view so struck him, that he no longer asked if he might shake hands with me, but said he really must,—and did.

We drank all the wine, and Mr. Pumblechook pledged himself over and over again to keep Joseph up to the mark (I don't know what mark), and to render me efficient and constant service (I don't know what service). He also made known to me for the first time in my life, and certainly after having kept his secret wonderfully well, that he had always said of me, "That boy is no common boy, and mark me, his fortun' will be no common fortun'." He said with a tearful smile that it was a singular thing to think of now, and I said so too. Finally, I went out into the air, with a dim perception that there was something unwonted in the conduct of the sunshine, and found that I had slumberously got to the turnpike without having taken any account of the road.

There, I was roused by Mr. Pumblechook's hailing me. He was a long way down the sunny street, and was making expressive gestures for me to stop. I stopped, and he came up breathless.

"No, my dear friend," said he, when he had recovered wind for speech. "Not if I can help it. This occasion shall not entirely pass without that affability on your part.—May I, as an old friend and well-wisher? May I?"

We shook hands for the hundredth time at least, and he ordered a young carter out of my way with the greatest indignation. Then, he blessed me and stood waving his hand to me until I had passed the crook in the road; and then I turned into a field and had a long nap under a hedge before I pursued my way home.

I had scant luggage to take with me to London, for little of the little I possessed was adapted to my new station. But I began packing that same afternoon, and wildly packed up things that I knew I should want next morning, in a fiction that there was not a moment to be lost.

So, Tuesday, Wednesday, and Thursday, passed; and on Friday morning I went to Mr. Pumblechook's, to put on my new clothes and pay my visit to Miss Havisham. Mr. Pumblechook's own room was given up to me to dress in, and was decorated with clean towels expressly for the event. My clothes were rather a disappointment, of course. Probably every new and eagerly expected garment ever put on since clothes came in, fell a trifle short of the wearer's expectation. But after I had had my new suit on some half an hour, and had gone through an immensity of posturing with

Mr. Pumblechook's very limited dressing-glass, in the futile endeavor to see my legs, it seemed to fit me better. It being market morning at a neighboring town some ten miles off, Mr. Pumblechook was not at home. I had not told him exactly when I meant to leave, and was not likely to shake hands with him again before departing. This was all as it should be, and I went out in my new array, fearfully ashamed of having to pass the shopman, and suspicious after all that I was at a personal disadvantage, something like Joe's in his Sunday suit.

I went circuitously to Miss Havisham's by all the back ways, and rang at the bell constrainedly, on account of the stiff long fingers of my gloves. Sarah Pocket came to the gate, and positively reeled back when she saw me so changed; her walnut-shell countenance likewise turned from brown to green and yellow.

"You?" said she. "You? Good gracious! What do you want?"

"I am going to London, Miss Pocket," said I, "and want to say good by to Miss Havisham."

I was not expected, for she left me locked in the yard, while she went to ask if I were to be admitted. After a very short delay, she returned and took me up, staring at me all the way.

Miss Havisham was taking exercise in the room with the long spread table, leaning on her crutch stick. The room was lighted as of yore, and at the sound of our entrance, she stopped and turned. She was then just abreast of the rotted bride-cake.

"Don't go, Sarah," she said. "Well, Pip?"

"I start for London, Miss Havisham, to-morrow," I was exceedingly careful what I said, "and I thought you would kindly not mind my taking leave of you."

"This is a gay figure, Pip," said she, making her crutch stick play round me, as if she, the fairy godmother who had changed me, were bestowing the finishing gift.

"I have come into such good fortune since I saw you last, Miss Havisham," I murmured. "And I am so grateful for it, Miss Havisham!"

"Ay, ay!" said she, looking at the discomfited and envious Sarah, with delight. "I have seen Mr. Jaggers. I have heard about it, Pip. So you go to-morrow?"

"Yes, Miss Havisham."

"And you are adopted by a rich person?"

"Yes, Miss Havisham."

"Not named?"

"No, Miss Havisham."

"And Mr. Jaggers is made your guardian?"

"Yes, Miss Havisham."

She quite gloated on these questions and answers, so keen was her enjoyment of Sarah Pocket's jealous dismay. "Well!" she went on; "you have a promising career before you. Be good—deserve it—and abide by Mr. Jaggers's instructions." She looked at me, and looked at Sarah, and Sarah's countenance wrung out of her watchful face a cruel smile. "Good by, Pip!—you will always keep the name of Pip, you know."

"Yes, Miss Havisham."

"Good by, Pip!"

She stretched out her hand, and I went down on my knee and put it to my lips. I had not considered how I should take leave of her; it came naturally to me at the moment to do this. She looked at Sarah Pocket with triumph in her weird eyes, and so I left my fairy godmother, with both her hands on her crutch stick, standing in the midst of the dimly lighted room beside the rotten bride-cake that was hidden in cobwebs.

Sarah Pocket conducted me down, as if I were a ghost who must be seen out. She could not get over my appearance, and was in the last degree confounded. I said "Good by, Miss Pocket;" but she merely stared, and did not seem collected enough to know that I had spoken. Clear of the house, I made the best of my way back to Pumblechook's, took off my new clothes, made them into a bundle, and went back home in my older dress, carrying it—to speak the truth—much more at my ease too, though I had the bundle to carry.

And now, those six days which were to have run out so slowly, had run out fast and were gone, and to-morrow looked me in the face more steadily than I could look at it. As the six evenings had dwindled away, to five, to four, to three, to two, I had become more and more appreciative of the society of Joe and Biddy. On this last evening, I dressed my self out in my new clothes for their delight, and sat in my splendor until bedtime. We had a hot supper on the occasion, graced by the inevitable roast fowl, and we had some flip to finish with. We were all very low, and none the higher for pretending to be in spirits.

I was to leave our village at five in the morning, carrying my little hand-portmanteau, and I had told Joe that I wished to walk away all alone. I am afraid—sore afraid—that this purpose originated in my sense of the contrast there would be between me and Joe, if we went to the coach together. I had pretended with myself that there was nothing of this taint in the arrangement; but when I went up to my little room on this last night, I felt compelled to admit that it might be so, and had an impulse upon me to go down again and entreat Joe to walk with me in the morning. I did not.

All night there were coaches in my broken sleep, going to wrong places instead of to London, and having in the traces, now dogs, now cats, now pigs, now men,—never horses. Fantastic failures of journeys occupied me until the day dawned and the birds were singing. Then, I got up and partly dressed, and sat at the window to take a last look out, and in taking it fell asleep.

Biddy was astir so early to get my breakfast, that, although I did not sleep at the window an hour, I smelt the smoke of the kitchen fire when I started up with a terrible idea that it must be late in the afternoon. But long after that, and long after I had heard the clinking of the teacups and was quite ready, I wanted the resolution to go down stairs. After all, I remained up there, repeatedly unlocking and unstrapping my small portmanteau and locking and strapping it up again, until Biddy called to me that I was late.

It was a hurried breakfast with no taste in it. I got up from the meal, saying with a sort of briskness, as if it had only just occurred to me, "Well! I suppose I must be off!" and then I kissed my sister who was laughing and nodding and shaking in her usual chair, and kissed Biddy, and threw my arms around Joe's neck. Then I took up my little portmanteau and walked out. The last I saw of them was, when I presently heard a scuffle behind me, and looking back, saw Joe throwing an old shoe after me and Biddy throwing another old shoe. I stopped then, to wave my hat, and dear old Joe waved his strong right arm above his head, crying huskily "Hooroar!" and Biddy put her apron to her face.

I walked away at a good pace, thinking it was easier to go than I had supposed it would be, and reflecting that it would never have done to have had an old shoe thrown after the coach, in sight of all the High Street. I whistled and made nothing of going. But the village was very peaceful and quiet, and the light mists were solemnly rising, as if to show me the world, and I had been so innocent and little there, and all beyond was so unknown and great, that in a moment with a strong heave and sob I broke into tears. It was by the finger-post at the end of the village, and I laid my hand upon it, and said, "Good by, O my dear, dear friend!"

Heaven knows we need never be ashamed of our tears, for they are rain upon the blinding dust of earth, overlying our hard hearts. I was better after I had cried than before,—more sorry, more aware of my own ingratitude, more gentle. If I had cried before, I should have had Joe with me then.

So subdued I was by those tears, and by their breaking out again in the course of the quiet walk, that when I was on the coach, and it was clear of the town, I deliberated with an aching heart whether I would not get down when we changed horses and walk back, and have another evening at home, and a better parting. We changed, and I had not made up my mind, and still reflected for my comfort that it would be quite practicable to get down and walk back, when we changed again. And while I was occupied with these deliberations, I would fancy an exact resemblance to Joe in some man coming along the road towards us, and my heart would beat high.—As if he could possibly be there!

We changed again, and yet again, and it was now too late and too far to go back, and I went on. And the mists had all solemnly risen now, and the world lay spread before me.

THIS IS THE END OF THE FIRST STAGE OF PIP'S EXPECTATIONS.

CHAPTER XX

The journey from our town to the metropolis was a journey of about five hours. It was a little past midday when the four-horse stage-coach by which I was a passenger, got into the ravel of traffic frayed out about the Cross Keys, Wood Street, Cheapside, London.

We Britons had at that time particularly settled that it was treasonable to doubt our having and our being the best of everything: otherwise, while I was scared by the immensity of London, I think I might have had some faint doubts whether it was not rather ugly, crooked, narrow, and dirty.

Mr. Jaggers had duly sent me his address; it was, Little Britain, and he had written after it on his card, "just out of Smithfield, and close by the coach-office." Nevertheless, a hackney-coachman, who seemed to have as many capes to his greasy great-coat as he was years old, packed me up in his coach and hemmed me in with a folding and jingling barrier of steps, as if he were going to take me fifty miles. His getting on his box, which I remember to have been decorated with an old weather-stained pea-green hammercloth moth-eaten into rags, was quite a work of time. It was a wonderful equipage, with six great coronets outside, and ragged things behind for I don't know how many footmen to hold on by, and a harrow below them, to prevent amateur footmen from yielding to the temptation.

I had scarcely had time to enjoy the coach and to think how like a straw-yard it was, and yet how like a rag-shop, and to wonder why the horses' nose-bags were kept inside, when I observed the coachman beginning to get down, as if we were going to stop presently. And stop we presently did, in a gloomy street, at certain offices with an open door, whereon was painted MR. JAGGERS.

"How much?" I asked the coachman.

The coachman answered, "A shilling—unless you wish to make it more."

I naturally said I had no wish to make it more.

"Then it must be a shilling," observed the coachman. "I don't want to get into trouble. I know him!" He darkly closed an eye at Mr. Jaggers's name, and shook his head.

When he had got his shilling, and had in course of time completed the ascent to his box, and had got away (which appeared to relieve his mind), I went into the front office with my little portmanteau in my hand and asked, Was Mr. Jaggers at home?

"He is not," returned the clerk. "He is in Court at present. Am I addressing Mr. Pip?"

I signified that he was addressing Mr. Pip.

"Mr. Jaggers left word, would you wait in his room. He couldn't say how long he might be, having a case on. But it stands to reason, his time being valuable, that he won't be longer than he can help."

With those words, the clerk opened a door, and ushered me into an inner chamber at the back. Here, we found a gentleman with one eye, in a velveteen suit and knee-breeches, who wiped his nose with his sleeve on being interrupted in the perusal of the newspaper.

"Go and wait outside, Mike," said the clerk.

I began to say that I hoped I was not interrupting, when the clerk shoved this gentleman out with as little ceremony as I ever saw used, and tossing his fur cap out after him, left me alone.

Mr. Jaggers's room was lighted by a skylight only, and was a most dismal place; the skylight, eccentrically pitched like a broken head, and the distorted adjoining houses looking as if they had twisted themselves to peep down at me through it. There were not so many papers about, as I should have expected to see; and there were some odd objects about, that I should not have expected to see,—such as an old rusty pistol, a sword in a scabbard, several strange-looking boxes and packages, and two dreadful casts on a shelf, of faces peculiarly swollen, and twitchy about the nose. Mr. Jaggers's own high-backed chair was of deadly black horsehair, with rows of brass nails round it, like a coffin; and I fancied I could see how he leaned back in it, and bit his forefinger at the clients. The room was but small, and the clients seemed to have had a habit of backing up against the wall; the wall, especially opposite to Mr. Jaggers's chair, being greasy with shoulders. I recalled, too, that the one-eyed gentleman had shuffled forth against the wall when I was the innocent cause of his being turned out.

I sat down in the cliental chair placed over against Mr. Jaggers's chair, and became fascinated by the dismal atmosphere of the place. I called to mind that the clerk had the same air of knowing something to everybody else's disadvantage, as his master had. I wondered how many other clerks there were up-stairs, and whether they all claimed to have the same detrimental mastery of their fellow-creatures. I wondered what was the history of all the odd litter about the room, and how it came there. I wondered whether the two swollen faces were of Mr. Jaggers's family, and, if he were so unfortunate as to have had a pair of such ill-looking relations, why he stuck them on that dusty perch for the blacks and flies to settle on, instead of giving them a place at home. Of course I had no experience of a London summer day, and my spirits may have been oppressed by the hot exhausted air, and by the dust and grit that lay thick on everything. But I sat wondering and waiting in Mr. Jaggers's close room, until I really could not bear the two casts on the shelf above Mr. Jaggers's chair, and got up and went out.

When I told the clerk that I would take a turn in the air while I waited, he advised me to go round the corner and I should come into Smithfield. So I came into Smithfield; and the shameful place, being all asmear with filth and fat and blood and foam, seemed to stick to me. So, I rubbed it off with all possible speed by turning into a street where I saw the great black dome of Saint Paul's bulging at me from behind a grim stone building which a bystander said was Newgate Prison. Following the wall of the jail, I found the roadway covered with straw to deaden the noise of passing vehicles; and from this, and from the quantity of people standing about smelling strongly of spirits and beer, I inferred that the trials were on.

While I looked about me here, an exceedingly dirty and partially drunk minister of justice asked me if I would like to step in and hear a trial or so: informing me that he could give me a front place for half a crown, whence I should command a full view of the Lord Chief Justice in his wig and robes,—mentioning that awful personage like waxwork, and presently offering him at the reduced price of eighteen-pence. As I declined the proposal on the plea of an appointment, he was so good as to take me into a yard and show me where the gallows was kept, and also where people were publicly whipped, and then he showed me the Debtors' Door, out of which culprits came to be hanged; heightening the interest of that dreadful portal by giving me to understand that "four on 'em" would come out at that door the day after to-morrow at eight in the morning, to be killed in a row. This was horrible, and gave me a sickening idea of London; the more so as the Lord Chief Justice's proprietor wore (from his hat down to his boots and up again to his pocket-handkerchief inclusive) mildewed clothes which had evidently not belonged to him originally, and which I took it into my head he had bought cheap of the executioner. Under these circumstances I thought myself well rid of him for a shilling.

I dropped into the office to ask if Mr. Jaggers had come in yet, and I found he had not, and I strolled out again. This time, I made the tour of Little Britain, and turned into Bartholomew Close; and now I became aware that other people were waiting about for Mr. Jaggers, as well as I. There were two men of secret appearance lounging in Bartholomew Close, and thoughtfully fitting their feet into the cracks of the pavement as they talked together, one of whom said to the other when they first passed me, that "Jaggers would do it if it was to be done." There was a knot of three men and two women standing at a corner, and one of the women was crying on her dirty shawl, and the other comforted her by saying, as she pulled her own shawl over her shoulders, "Jaggers is for him, 'Melia, and what more could you have?" There was a red-eyed little Jew who came into the Close while I was loitering there, in company with a second little Jew whom he sent upon an errand; and while the messenger was gone, I remarked this Jew, who was of a highly excitable temperament, performing a jig of anxiety under a lamp-post and accompanying himself, in a kind of frenzy, with the words, "O Jaggerth, Jaggerth, Jaggerth! all otherth ith Cag-Maggerth, give me Jaggerth!" These testimonies to the popularity of my guardian made a deep impression on me, and I admired and wondered more than ever.

At length, as I was looking out at the iron gate of Bartholomew Close into Little Britain, I saw Mr. Jaggers coming across the road towards me. All the others who were waiting saw him at the same time, and there was quite a rush at him. Mr. Jaggers, putting a hand on my shoulder and walking me on at his side without saying anything to me, addressed himself to his followers.

First, he took the two secret men.

"Now, I have nothing to say to you," said Mr. Jaggers, throwing his finger at them. "I want to know no more than I know. As to the result, it's a toss-up. I told you from the first it was a toss-up. Have you paid Wemmick?"

"We made the money up this morning, sir," said one of the men, submissively, while the other perused Mr. Jaggers's face.

"I don't ask you when you made it up, or where, or whether you made it up at all. Has Wemmick got it?"

"Yes, sir," said both the men together.

"Very well; then you may go. Now, I won't have it!" said Mr Jaggers, waving his hand at them to put them behind him. "If you say a word to me, I'll throw up the case."

"We thought, Mr. Jaggers——" one of the men began, pulling off his hat.

"That's what I told you not to do," said Mr. Jaggers. "You thought! I think for you; that's enough for you. If I want you, I know where to find you; I don't want you to find me. Now I won't have it. I won't hear a word."

The two men looked at one another as Mr. Jaggers waved them behind again, and humbly fell back and were heard no more.

"And now you!" said Mr. Jaggers, suddenly stopping, and turning on the two women with the shawls, from whom the three men had meekly separated,—"Oh! Amelia, is it?"

"Yes, Mr. Jaggers."

"And do you remember," retorted Mr. Jaggers, "that but for me you wouldn't be here and couldn't be here?"

"O yes, sir!" exclaimed both women together. "Lord bless you, sir, well we knows that!"

"Then why," said Mr. Jaggers, "do you come here?"

"My Bill, sir!" the crying woman pleaded.

"Now, I tell you what!" said Mr. Jaggers. "Once for all. If you don't know that your Bill's in good hands, I know it. And if you come here bothering about your Bill, I'll make an example of both your Bill and you, and let him slip through my fingers. Have you paid Wemmick?"

"O yes, sir! Every farden."

"Very well. Then you have done all you have got to do. Say another word—one single word—and Wemmick shall give you your money back."

This terrible threat caused the two women to fall off immediately. No one remained now but the excitable Jew, who had already raised the skirts of Mr. Jaggers's coat to his lips several times.

"I don't know this man!" said Mr. Jaggers, in the same devastating strain: "What does this fellow want?"

"Ma thear Mithter Jaggerth. Hown brother to Habraham Latharuth?"

"Who's he?" said Mr. Jaggers. "Let go of my coat."

The suitor, kissing the hem of the garment again before relinquishing it, replied, "Habraham Latharuth, on thuthpithion of plate."

"You're too late," said Mr. Jaggers. "I am over the way."

"Holy father, Mithter Jaggerth!" cried my excitable acquaintance, turning white, "don't thay you're again Habraham Latharuth!"

"I am," said Mr. Jaggers, "and there's an end of it. Get out of the way."

"Mithter Jaggerth! Half a moment! My hown cuthen'th gone to Mithter Wemmick at thith prethent minute, to hoffer him hany termth. Mithter Jaggerth! Half a quarter of a moment! If you'd have the condethenthun to be bought off from the t'other thide—at hany thuperior prithe!—money no object!—Mithter Jaggerth—Mithter—!"

My guardian threw his supplicant off with supreme indifference, and left him dancing on the pavement as if it were red hot. Without further interruption, we reached the front office, where we found the clerk and the man in velveteen with the fur cap.

"Here's Mike," said the clerk, getting down from his stool, and approaching Mr. Jaggers confidentially.

"Oh!" said Mr. Jaggers, turning to the man, who was pulling a lock of hair in the middle of his forehead, like the Bull in Cock Robin pulling at the bell-rope; "your man comes on this afternoon. Well?"

"Well, Mas'r Jaggers," returned Mike, in the voice of a sufferer from a constitutional cold; "arter a deal o' trouble, I've found one, sir, as might do."

"What is he prepared to swear?"

"Well, Mas'r Jaggers," said Mike, wiping his nose on his fur cap this time; "in a general way, anythink."

Mr. Jaggers suddenly became most irate. "Now, I warned you before," said he, throwing his forefinger at the terrified client, "that if you ever presumed to talk in that way here, I'd make an example of you. You infernal scoundrel, how dare you tell ME that?"

The client looked scared, but bewildered too, as if he were unconscious what he had done.

"Spooney!" said the clerk, in a low voice, giving him a stir with his elbow. "Soft Head! Need you say it face to face?"

"Now, I ask you, you blundering booby," said my guardian, very sternly, "once more and for the last time, what the man you have brought here is prepared to swear?"

Mike looked hard at my guardian, as if he were trying to learn a lesson from his face, and slowly replied, "Ayther to character, or to having been in his company and never left him all the night in question."

"Now, be careful. In what station of life is this man?"

Mike looked at his cap, and looked at the floor, and looked at the ceiling, and looked at the clerk, and even looked at me, before beginning to reply in a nervous manner, "We've dressed him up like—" when my guardian blustered out,—

"What? You WILL, will you?"

("Spooney!" added the clerk again, with another stir.)

After some helpless casting about, Mike brightened and began again:—

"He is dressed like a 'spectable pieman. A sort of a pastry-cook."

"Is he here?" asked my guardian.

"I left him," said Mike, "a setting on some doorsteps round the corner."

"Take him past that window, and let me see him."

The window indicated was the office window. We all three went to it, behind the wire blind, and presently saw the client go by in an accidental manner, with a murderous-looking tall individual, in a short suit of white linen and a paper cap. This guileless confectioner was not by any means sober, and had a black eye in the green stage of recovery, which was painted over.

"Tell him to take his witness away directly," said my guardian to the clerk, in extreme disgust, "and ask him what he means by bringing such a fellow as that."

My guardian then took me into his own room, and while he lunched, standing, from a sandwich-box and a pocket-flask of sherry (he seemed to bully his very sandwich as he ate it), informed me what arrangements he had made for me. I was to go to "Barnard's Inn," to young Mr. Pocket's rooms, where a bed had been sent in for my accommodation; I was to remain with young Mr. Pocket until Monday; on Monday I was to go with him to his father's house on a visit, that I might try how I liked it. Also, I was told what my allowance was to be,—it was a very liberal one,—and had handed to me from one of my guardian's drawers, the cards of certain tradesmen with whom I was to deal for all kinds of clothes, and such other things as I could in reason want. "You will find your credit good, Mr. Pip," said my guardian, whose flask of sherry smelt like a whole caskful, as he hastily refreshed himself, "but I shall by this means be able to check your bills, and to pull you up if I find you outrunning the constable. Of course you'll go wrong somehow, but that's no fault of mine."

After I had pondered a little over this encouraging sentiment, I asked Mr. Jaggers if I could send for a coach? He said it was not worth while, I was so near my destination; Wemmick should walk round with me, if I pleased.

I then found that Wemmick was the clerk in the next room. Another clerk was rung down from up stairs to take his place while he was out, and I accompanied him into the street, after shaking hands with my guardian. We found a new set of people lingering outside, but Wemmick made a way among them by saying coolly yet decisively, "I tell you it's no use; he won't have a word to say to one of you;" and we soon got clear of them, and went on side by side.

CHAPTER XXI

Casting my eyes on Mr. Wemmick as we went along, to see what he was like in the light of day, I found him to be a dry man, rather short in stature, with a square wooden face, whose expression seemed to have been imperfectly chipped out with a dull-edged chisel. There were some marks in it that might have been dimples, if the material had been softer and the instrument finer, but which, as it was, were only dints. The chisel had made three or four of these attempts at embellishment over his nose, but had given them up without an effort to smooth them off. I judged him to be a bachelor from the frayed condition of his linen, and he appeared to have sustained a good many bereavements; for he wore at least four mourning rings, besides a brooch representing a lady and a weeping willow at a tomb with an urn on it. I noticed, too, that several rings and seals hung at his watch-chain, as if he were quite laden with remembrances of departed friends. He had glittering eyes,—small, keen, and black,—and thin wide mottled lips. He had had them, to the best of my belief, from forty to fifty years.

"So you were never in London before?" said Mr. Wemmick to me.

"No," said I.

"I was new here once," said Mr. Wemmick. "Rum to think of now!"

"You are well acquainted with it now?"

"Why, yes," said Mr. Wemmick. "I know the moves of it."

"Is it a very wicked place?" I asked, more for the sake of saying something than for information.

"You may get cheated, robbed, and murdered in London. But there are plenty of people anywhere, who'll do that for you."

"If there is bad blood between you and them," said I, to soften it off a little.

"O! I don't know about bad blood," returned Mr. Wemmick; "there's not much bad blood about. They'll do it, if there's anything to be got by it."

"That makes it worse."

"You think so?" returned Mr. Wemmick. "Much about the same, I should say."

He wore his hat on the back of his head, and looked straight before him: walking in a self-contained way as if there were nothing in the streets to claim his attention. His mouth was such a post-office of a mouth that he had a mechanical appearance of smiling. We had got to the top of Holborn Hill before I knew that it was merely a mechanical appearance, and that he was not smiling at all.

"Do you know where Mr. Matthew Pocket lives?" I asked Mr. Wemmick.

"Yes," said he, nodding in the direction. "At Hammersmith, west of London."

"Is that far?"

"Well! Say five miles."

"Do you know him?"

"Why, you're a regular cross-examiner!" said Mr. Wemmick, looking at me with an approving air. "Yes, I know him. I know him!"

There was an air of toleration or depreciation about his utterance of these words that rather depressed me; and I was still looking sideways at his block of a face in search of any encouraging note to the text, when he said here we were at Barnard's Inn. My depression was not alleviated by the announcement, for, I had supposed that establishment to be an hotel kept by Mr. Barnard, to which the Blue Boar in our town was a mere public-house. Whereas I now found Barnard to be a disembodied spirit, or a fiction, and his inn the dingiest collection of shabby buildings ever squeezed together in a rank corner as a club for Tom-cats.

We entered this haven through a wicket-gate, and were disgorged by an introductory passage into a melancholy little square that looked to me like a flat burying-ground. I thought it had the most dismal trees in it, and the most dismal sparrows, and the most dismal cats, and the most dismal houses (in number half a dozen or so), that I had ever seen. I thought the windows of the sets of chambers into which those houses were divided were in every stage of dilapidated blind and curtain, crippled flower-pot, cracked glass, dusty decay, and miserable makeshift; while To Let, To Let, To Let, glared at me from empty rooms, as if no new wretches ever came there, and the vengeance of the soul of Barnard were being slowly appeased by the gradual suicide of the present occupants and their unholy interment under the gravel. A frowzy mourning of soot and smoke attired this forlorn creation of Barnard, and it had strewn ashes on its head, and was undergoing penance and humiliation as a mere dust-hole. Thus far my sense of sight; while dry rot and wet rot and all the silent rots that rot in neglected roof and cellar,—rot of rat and mouse and bug and coaching-stables near at hand besides—addressed themselves faintly to my sense of smell, and moaned, "Try Barnard's Mixture."

So imperfect was this realisation of the first of my great expectations, that I looked in dismay at Mr. Wemmick. "Ah!" said he, mistaking me; "the retirement reminds you of the country. So it does me."

He led me into a corner and conducted me up a flight of stairs,—which appeared to me to be slowly collapsing into sawdust, so that one of those days the upper lodgers would look out at their doors and find themselves without the means of coming down,—to a set of chambers on the top floor. MR. POCKET, JUN., was painted on the door, and there was a label on the letter-box, "Return shortly."

"He hardly thought you'd come so soon," Mr. Wemmick explained. "You don't want me any more?"

"No, thank you," said I.

"As I keep the cash," Mr. Wemmick observed, "we shall most likely meet pretty often. Good day."

"Good day."

I put out my hand, and Mr. Wemmick at first looked at it as if he thought I wanted something. Then he looked at me, and said, correcting himself,—

"To be sure! Yes. You're in the habit of shaking hands?"

I was rather confused, thinking it must be out of the London fashion, but said yes.

"I have got so out of it!" said Mr. Wemmick,—"except at last. Very glad, I'm sure, to make your acquaintance. Good day!"

When we had shaken hands and he was gone, I opened the staircase window and had nearly beheaded myself, for, the lines had rotted away, and it came down like the guillotine. Happily it was so quick that I had not put my head out. After this escape, I was content to take a foggy view of the Inn through the window's encrusting dirt, and to stand dolefully looking out, saying to myself that London was decidedly overrated.

Mr. Pocket, Junior's, idea of Shortly was not mine, for I had nearly maddened myself with looking out for half an hour, and had written my name with my finger several times in the dirt of every pane in the window, before I heard footsteps on the stairs. Gradually there arose before me the hat, head, neckcloth, waistcoat, trousers, boots, of a member of society of about my own standing. He had a paper-bag under each arm and a pottle of strawberries in one hand, and was out of breath.

"Mr. Pip?" said he.

"Mr. Pocket?" said I.

"Dear me!" he exclaimed. "I am extremely sorry; but I knew there was a coach from your part of the country at midday, and I thought you would come by that one. The fact is, I have been out on your account,—not that that is any excuse,—for I thought, coming from the country, you might like a little fruit after dinner, and I went to Covent Garden Market to get it good."

For a reason that I had, I felt as if my eyes would start out of my head. I acknowledged his attention incoherently, and began to think this was a dream.

"Dear me!" said Mr. Pocket, Junior. "This door sticks so!"

As he was fast making jam of his fruit by wrestling with the door while the paper-bags were under his arms, I begged him to allow me to hold them. He relinquished them with an agreeable smile, and combated with the door as if it were a wild beast. It yielded so suddenly at last, that he staggered back upon me, and I staggered back upon the opposite door, and we both laughed. But still I felt as if my eyes must start out of my head, and as if this must be a dream.

"Pray come in," said Mr. Pocket, Junior. "Allow me to lead the way. I am rather bare here, but I hope you'll be able to make out tolerably well till Monday. My father thought you would get on more agreeably through to-morrow with me than with him, and might like to take a walk about London. I am sure I shall be very happy to show London to you. As to our table, you won't find that bad, I hope, for it will be supplied from our coffee-house here, and (it is only right I should add) at your expense, such being Mr. Jaggers's directions. As to our lodging, it's not by any means splendid, because I have my own bread to earn, and my father hasn't anything to give me, and I shouldn't be willing to take it, if he had. This is our sitting-room,—just such chairs and tables and carpet and so forth, you see, as they could spare from home. You mustn't give me credit for the tablecloth and spoons and castors, because they come for you from the coffee-house. This is my little bedroom; rather musty, but Barnard's is musty. This is your bedroom; the furniture's hired for the occasion, but I trust it will answer the purpose; if you should want anything, I'll go and fetch it. The chambers are retired, and we shall be alone together, but we shan't fight, I dare say. But dear me, I beg your pardon, you're holding the fruit all this time. Pray let me take these bags from you. I am quite ashamed."

As I stood opposite to Mr. Pocket, Junior, delivering him the bags, One, Two, I saw the starting appearance come into his own eyes that I knew to be in mine, and he said, falling back,—

"Lord bless me, you're the prowling boy!"

"And you," said I, "are the pale young gentleman!"

CHAPTER XXII

The pale young gentleman and I stood contemplating one another in Barnard's Inn, until we both burst out laughing. "The idea of its being you!" said he. "The idea of its being you!" said I. And then we contemplated one another afresh, and laughed again. "Well!" said the pale young gentleman, reaching out his hand good-humoredly, "it's all over now, I hope, and it will be magnanimous in you if you'll forgive me for having knocked you about so."

I derived from this speech that Mr. Herbert Pocket (for Herbert was the pale young gentleman's name) still rather confounded his intention with his execution. But I made a modest reply, and we shook hands warmly.

"You hadn't come into your good fortune at that time?" said Herbert Pocket.

"No," said I.

"No," he acquiesced: "I heard it had happened very lately. I was rather on the lookout for good fortune then."

"Indeed?"

"Yes. Miss Havisham had sent for me, to see if she could take a fancy to me. But she couldn't,—at all events, she didn't."

I thought it polite to remark that I was surprised to hear that.

"Bad taste," said Herbert, laughing, "but a fact. Yes, she had sent for me on a trial visit, and if I had come out of it successfully, I suppose I should have been provided for; perhaps I should have been what-you-may-called it to Estella."

"What's that?" I asked, with sudden gravity.

He was arranging his fruit in plates while we talked, which divided his attention, and was the cause of his having made this lapse of a word. "Affianced," he explained, still busy with the fruit. "Betrothed. Engaged. What's-his-named. Any word of that sort."

"How did you bear your disappointment?" I asked.

"Pooh!" said he, "I didn't care much for it. She's a Tartar."

"Miss Havisham?"

"I don't say no to that, but I meant Estella. That girl's hard and haughty and capricious to the last degree, and has been brought up by Miss Havisham to wreak revenge on all the male sex."

"What relation is she to Miss Havisham?"

"None," said he. "Only adopted."

"Why should she wreak revenge on all the male sex? What revenge?"

"Lord, Mr. Pip!" said he. "Don't you know?"

"No," said I.

"Dear me! It's quite a story, and shall be saved till dinner-time. And now let me take the liberty of asking you a question. How did you come there, that day?"

I told him, and he was attentive until I had finished, and then burst out laughing again, and asked me if I was sore afterwards? I didn't ask him if he was, for my conviction on that point was perfectly established.

"Mr. Jaggers is your guardian, I understand?" he went on.

"Yes."

"You know he is Miss Havisham's man of business and solicitor, and has her confidence when nobody else has?"

This was bringing me (I felt) towards dangerous ground. I answered with a constraint I made no attempt to disguise, that I had seen Mr. Jaggers in Miss Havisham's house on the very day of our combat, but never at any other time, and that I believed he had no recollection of having ever seen me there.

"He was so obliging as to suggest my father for your tutor, and he called on my father to propose it. Of course he knew about my father from his connection with Miss Havisham. My father is Miss Havisham's cousin; not that that implies familiar intercourse between them, for he is a bad courtier and will not propitiate her."

Herbert Pocket had a frank and easy way with him that was very taking. I had never seen any one then, and I have never seen any one since, who more strongly expressed to me, in every look and tone, a natural incapacity to do anything secret and mean. There was something wonderfully hopeful about his general air, and something that at the same time whispered to me he would never be very successful or rich. I don't know how this was. I became imbued with the notion on that first occasion before we sat down to dinner, but I cannot define by what means.

He was still a pale young gentleman, and had a certain conquered languor about him in the midst of his spirits and briskness, that did not seem indicative of natural strength. He had not a handsome face, but it was better than handsome: being extremely amiable and cheerful. His figure was a little ungainly, as in the days when my knuckles had taken such liberties with it, but it looked as if it would always be light and young. Whether Mr. Trabb's local work would have sat more gracefully on him than on me, may be a question; but I am conscious that he carried off his rather old clothes much better than I carried off my new suit.

As he was so communicative, I felt that reserve on my part would be a bad return unsuited to our years. I therefore told him my small story, and laid stress on my being forbidden to inquire who my benefactor was. I further mentioned that as I had been brought up a blacksmith in a country place, and knew very little of the ways of politeness, I would take it as a great kindness in him if he would give me a hint whenever he saw me at a loss or going wrong.

"With pleasure," said he, "though I venture to prophesy that you'll want very few hints. I dare say we shall be often together, and I should like to banish any needless restraint between us. Will you do me the favour to begin at once to call me by my Christian name, Herbert?"

I thanked him and said I would. I informed him in exchange that my Christian name was Philip.

"I don't take to Philip," said he, smiling, "for it sounds like a moral boy out of the spelling-book, who was so lazy that he fell into a pond, or so fat that he couldn't see out of his eyes, or so avaricious that he locked up his cake till the mice ate it, or so determined to go a bird's-nesting that he got himself eaten by bears who lived handy in the neighborhood. I tell you what I should like. We are so harmonious, and you have been a blacksmith,—would you mind it?"

"I shouldn't mind anything that you propose," I answered, "but I don't understand you."

"Would you mind Handel for a familiar name? There's a charming piece of music by Handel, called the Harmonious Blacksmith."

"I should like it very much."

"Then, my dear Handel," said he, turning round as the door opened, "here is the dinner, and I must beg of you to take the top of the table, because the dinner is of your providing."

This I would not hear of, so he took the top, and I faced him. It was a nice little dinner,—seemed to me then a very Lord Mayor's Feast,—and it acquired additional relish from being eaten under those independent circumstances, with no old people by, and with London all around us. This again was heightened by a certain gypsy character that set the banquet off; for while the table was, as Mr. Pumblechook might have said, the lap of luxury,—being entirely furnished forth from the coffee-house,—the circumjacent region of sitting-room was of a comparatively pastureless and shifty character; imposing on the waiter the wandering habits of putting the covers on the floor (where he fell over them), the melted butter in the arm-chair, the bread on the bookshelves, the cheese in the coal-scuttle, and the boiled fowl into my bed in the next room,—where I found much of its parsley and butter in a state of congelation when I retired for the night. All this made the feast delightful, and when the waiter was not there to watch me, my pleasure was without alloy.

We had made some progress in the dinner, when I reminded Herbert of his promise to tell me about Miss Havisham.

"True," he replied. "I'll redeem it at once. Let me introduce the topic, Handel, by mentioning that in London it is not the custom to put the knife in the mouth,—for fear of accidents,—and that while the fork is reserved for that use, it is not put further in than necessary. It is scarcely worth mentioning, only it's as well to do as other people do. Also, the spoon is not generally used over-hand, but under. This has two advantages. You get at your mouth better (which after all is the object), and you save a good deal of the attitude of opening oysters, on the part of the right elbow."

He offered these friendly suggestions in such a lively way, that we both laughed and I scarcely blushed.

"Now," he pursued, "concerning Miss Havisham. Miss Havisham, you must know, was a spoilt child. Her mother died when she was a baby, and her father denied her nothing. Her father was a country gentleman down in your part of the world, and was a brewer. I don't know why it should be a crack thing to be a brewer; but it is indisputable that while you cannot possibly be genteel and bake, you may be as genteel as never was and brew. You see it every day."

"Yet a gentleman may not keep a public-house; may he?" said I.

"Not on any account," returned Herbert; "but a public-house may keep a gentleman. Well! Mr. Havisham was very rich and very proud. So was his daughter."

"Miss Havisham was an only child?" I hazarded.

"Stop a moment, I am coming to that. No, she was not an only child; she had a half-brother. Her father privately married again—his cook, I rather think."

"I thought he was proud," said I.

"My good Handel, so he was. He married his second wife privately, because he was proud, and in course of time she died. When she was dead, I apprehend he first told his daughter what he had done, and then the son became a part of the family, residing in the house you are acquainted with. As the son grew a young man, he turned out riotous, extravagant, undutiful,—altogether bad. At last his father disinherited him; but he softened when he was dying, and left him well off, though not nearly so well off as Miss Havisham.—Take another glass of wine, and excuse my mentioning that society as a body does not expect one to be so strictly conscientious in emptying one's glass, as to turn it bottom upwards with the rim on one's nose."

I had been doing this, in an excess of attention to his recital. I thanked him, and apologised. He said, "Not at all," and resumed.

"Miss Havisham was now an heiress, and you may suppose was looked after as a great match. Her half-brother had now ample means again, but what with debts and what with new madness wasted them most fearfully again. There were stronger differences between him and her than there had been between him and his father, and it is suspected that he cherished a deep and mortal grudge against her as having influenced the father's anger. Now, I come to the cruel part of the story,—merely breaking off, my dear Handel, to remark that a dinner-napkin will not go into a tumbler."

Why I was trying to pack mine into my tumbler, I am wholly unable to say. I only know that I found myself, with a perseverance worthy of a much better cause, making the most strenuous exertions to compress it within those limits. Again I thanked him and apologized, and again he said in the cheerfullest manner, "Not at all, I am sure!" and resumed.

"There appeared upon the scene—say at the races, or the public balls, or anywhere else you like—a certain man, who made love to Miss Havisham. I never saw him (for this happened five-and-twenty years ago, before you and I were, Handel), but I have heard my father mention that he was a showy man, and the kind of man for the purpose. But that he was not to be, without ignorance or prejudice, mistaken for a gentleman, my father most strongly asseverates; because it is a principle of his that no man who was not a true gentleman at heart ever was, since the world began, a true gentleman in manner. He says, no varnish can hide the grain of the wood; and that the more varnish you put on, the more the grain will express itself. Well! This man pursued Miss Havisham closely, and professed to be devoted to her. I believe she had not shown much susceptibility up to that time; but all the susceptibility she possessed certainly came out then, and she passionately loved him. There is no doubt that she perfectly idolised him. He practised on her affection in that systematic way, that he got great sums of money from her, and he induced her to buy her brother out of a share in the brewery (which had been weakly left him by his father) at an immense price, on the plea that when he was her husband he must hold and manage it all. Your guardian was not at that time in Miss Havisham's counsels, and she was too haughty and too much in love to be advised by any one. Her relations were poor and scheming, with the exception of my father; he was poor enough, but not time-serving or jealous. The only independent one among them, he warned her that she was doing too much for this man, and was placing herself too unreservedly in his power. She took the first opportunity of angrily ordering my father out of the house, in his presence, and my father has never seen her since."

I thought of her having said, "Matthew will come and see me at last when I am laid dead upon that table;" and I asked Herbert whether his father was so inveterate against her?

"It's not that," said he, "but she charged him, in the presence of her intended husband, with being disappointed in the hope of fawning upon her for his own advancement, and, if he were to go to her now, it would look true—even to him— and even to her. To return to the man and make an end of him. The marriage day was fixed, the wedding dresses were bought, the wedding tour was planned out, the wedding guests were invited. The day came, but not the bridegroom. He wrote her a letter—"

"Which she received," I struck in, "when she was dressing for her marriage? At twenty minutes to nine?"

"At the hour and minute," said Herbert, nodding, "at which she afterwards stopped all the clocks. What was in it, further than that it most heartlessly broke the marriage off, I can't tell you, because I don't know. When she recovered from a bad illness that she had, she laid the whole place waste, as you have seen it, and she has never since looked upon the light of day."

"Is that all the story?" I asked, after considering it.

"All I know of it; and indeed I only know so much, through piecing it out for myself; for my father always avoids it, and, even when Miss Havisham invited me to go there, told me no more of it than it was absolutely requisite I should understand. But I have forgotten one thing. It has been supposed that the man to whom she gave her misplaced confidence acted throughout in concert with her half-brother; that it was a conspiracy between them; and that they shared the profits."

"I wonder he didn't marry her and get all the property," said I.

"He may have been married already, and her cruel mortification may have been a part of her half-brother's scheme," said Herbert. "Mind! I don't know that."

"What became of the two men?" I asked, after again considering the subject.

"They fell into deeper shame and degradation—if there can be deeper—and ruin."

"Are they alive now?"

"I don't know."

"You said just now that Estella was not related to Miss Havisham, but adopted. When adopted?"

Herbert shrugged his shoulders. "There has always been an Estella, since I have heard of a Miss Havisham. I know no more. And now, Handel," said he, finally throwing off the story as it were, "there is a perfectly open understanding between us. All that I know about Miss Havisham, you know."

"And all that I know," I retorted, "you know."

"I fully believe it. So there can be no competition or perplexity between you and me. And as to the condition on which you hold your advancement in life,—namely, that you are not to inquire or discuss to whom you owe it,—you may be very sure that it will never be encroached upon, or even approached, by me, or by any one belonging to me."

In truth, he said this with so much delicacy, that I felt the subject done with, even though I should be under his father's roof for years and years to come. Yet he said it with so much meaning, too, that I felt he as perfectly understood Miss Havisham to be my benefactress, as I understood the fact myself.

It had not occurred to me before, that he had led up to the theme for the purpose of clearing it out of our way; but we were so much the lighter and easier for having broached it, that I now perceived this to be the case. We were very gay and sociable, and I asked him, in the course of conversation, what he was? He replied, "A capitalist,—an Insurer of Ships." I suppose he saw me glancing about the room in search of some tokens of Shipping, or capital, for he added, "In the City."

I had grand ideas of the wealth and importance of Insurers of Ships in the City, and I began to think with awe of having laid a young Insurer on his back, blackened his enterprising eye, and cut his responsible head open. But again there came upon me, for my relief, that odd impression that Herbert Pocket would never be very successful or rich.

"I shall not rest satisfied with merely employing my capital in insuring ships. I shall buy up some good Life Assurance shares, and cut into the Direction. I shall also do a little in the mining way. None of these things will interfere with my chartering a few thousand tons on my own account. I think I shall trade," said he, leaning back in his chair, "to the East Indies, for silks, shawls, spices, dyes, drugs, and precious woods. It's an interesting trade."

"And the profits are large?" said I.

"Tremendous!" said he.

I wavered again, and began to think here were greater expectations than my own.

"I think I shall trade, also," said he, putting his thumbs in his waist-coat pockets, "to the West Indies, for sugar, tobacco, and rum. Also to Ceylon, specially for elephants' tusks."

"You will want a good many ships," said I.

"A perfect fleet," said he.

Quite overpowered by the magnificence of these transactions, I asked him where the ships he insured mostly traded to at present?

"I haven't begun insuring yet," he replied. "I am looking about me."

Somehow, that pursuit seemed more in keeping with Barnard's Inn. I said (in a tone of conviction), "Ah-h!"

"Yes. I am in a counting-house, and looking about me."

"Is a counting-house profitable?" I asked.

"To—do you mean to the young fellow who's in it?" he asked, in reply.

"Yes; to you."

"Why, n-no; not to me." He said this with the air of one carefully reckoning up and striking a balance. "Not directly profitable. That is, it doesn't pay me anything, and I have to—keep myself."

This certainly had not a profitable appearance, and I shook my head as if I would imply that it would be difficult to lay by much accumulative capital from such a source of income.

"But the thing is," said Herbert Pocket, "that you look about you. That's the grand thing. You are in a counting-house, you know, and you look about you."

It struck me as a singular implication that you couldn't be out of a counting-house, you know, and look about you; but I silently deferred to his experience.

"Then the time comes," said Herbert, "when you see your opening. And you go in, and you swoop upon it and you make your capital, and then there you are! When you have once made your capital, you have nothing to do but employ it."

This was very like his way of conducting that encounter in the garden; very like. His manner of bearing his poverty, too, exactly corresponded to his manner of bearing that defeat. It seemed to me that he took all blows and buffets now with just the same air as he had taken mine then. It was evident that he had nothing around him but the simplest necessaries, for everything that I remarked upon turned out to have been sent in on my account from the coffee-house or somewhere else.

Yet, having already made his fortune in his own mind, he was so unassuming with it that I felt quite grateful to him for not being puffed up. It was a pleasant addition to his naturally pleasant ways, and we got on famously. In the evening we went out for a walk in the streets, and went half-price to the Theatre; and next day we went to church at Westminster Abbey, and in the afternoon we walked in the Parks; and I wondered who shod all the horses there, and wished Joe did.

On a moderate computation, it was many months, that Sunday, since I had left Joe and Biddy. The space interposed between myself and them partook of that expansion, and our marshes were any distance off. That I could have been at our old church in my old church-going clothes, on the very last Sunday that ever was, seemed a combination of impossibilities, geographical and social, solar and lunar. Yet in the London streets so crowded with people and so brilliantly lighted in the dusk of evening, there were depressing hints of reproaches for that I had put the poor old kitchen at home so far away; and in the dead of night, the footsteps of some incapable impostor of a porter mooning about Barnard's Inn, under pretence of watching it, fell hollow on my heart.

On the Monday morning at a quarter before nine, Herbert went to the counting-house to report himself,—to look about him, too, I suppose,—and I bore him company. He was to come away in an hour or two to attend me to Hammersmith, and I was to wait about for him. It appeared to me that the eggs from which young Insurers were hatched were incubated in dust and heat, like the eggs of ostriches, judging from the places to which those incipient giants repaired on a Monday morning. Nor did the counting-house where Herbert assisted, show in my eyes as at all a good Observatory; being a back second floor up a yard, of a grimy presence in all particulars, and with a look into another back second floor, rather than a look out.

I waited about until it was noon, and I went upon 'Change, and I saw fluey men sitting there under the bills about shipping, whom I took to be great merchants, though I couldn't understand why they should all be out of spirits. When Herbert came, we went and had lunch at a celebrated house which I then quite venerated, but now believe to have been the most abject superstition in Europe, and where I could not help noticing, even then, that there was much more gravy on the tablecloths and knives and waiters' clothes, than in the steaks. This collation disposed of at a moderate price (considering the grease, which was not charged for), we went back to Barnard's Inn and got my little portmanteau, and then took coach for Hammersmith. We arrived there at two or three o'clock in the afternoon, and had very little way to walk to Mr. Pocket's house. Lifting the latch of a gate, we passed direct into a little garden overlooking the river, where Mr. Pocket's children were playing about. And unless I deceive myself on a point where my interests or prepossessions are certainly not concerned, I saw that Mr. and Mrs. Pocket's children were not growing up or being brought up, but were tumbling up.

Mrs. Pocket was sitting on a garden chair under a tree, reading, with her legs upon another garden chair; and Mrs. Pocket's two nurse-maids were looking about them while the children played. "Mamma," said Herbert, "this is young Mr. Pip." Upon which Mrs. Pocket received me with an appearance of amiable dignity.

"Master Alick and Miss Jane," cried one of the nurses to two of the children, "if you go a bouncing up against them bushes you'll fall over into the river and be drownded, and what'll your pa say then?"

At the same time this nurse picked up Mrs. Pocket's handkerchief, and said, "If that don't make six times you've dropped it, Mum!" Upon which Mrs. Pocket laughed and said, "Thank you, Flopson," and settling herself in one chair only, resumed her book. Her countenance immediately assumed a knitted and intent expression as if she had been reading for a week, but before she could have read half a dozen lines, she fixed her eyes upon me, and said, "I hope your mamma is quite well?" This unexpected inquiry put me into such a difficulty that I began saying in the absurdest way that if there had been any such person I had no doubt she would have been quite well and would have been very much obliged and would have sent her compliments, when the nurse came to my rescue.

"Well!" she cried, picking up the pocket-handkerchief, "if that don't make seven times! What ARE you a doing of this afternoon, Mum!" Mrs. Pocket received her property, at first with a look of unutterable surprise as if she had never seen it before, and then with a laugh of recognition, and said, "Thank you, Flopson," and forgot me, and went on reading.

I found, now I had leisure to count them, that there were no fewer than six little Pockets present, in various stages of tumbling up. I had scarcely arrived at the total when a seventh was heard, as in the region of air, wailing dolefully.

"If there ain't Baby!" said Flopson, appearing to think it most surprising. "Make haste up, Millers."

Millers, who was the other nurse, retired into the house, and by degrees the child's wailing was hushed and stopped, as if it were a young ventriloquist with something in its mouth. Mrs. Pocket read all the time, and I was curious to know what the book could be.

We were waiting, I supposed, for Mr. Pocket to come out to us; at any rate we waited there, and so I had an opportunity of observing the remarkable family phenomenon that whenever any of the children strayed near Mrs. Pocket in their play, they always tripped themselves up and tumbled over her,—always very much to her momentary astonishment, and their own more enduring lamentation. I was at a loss to account for this surprising circumstance, and could not help giving my mind to speculations about it, until by and by Millers came down with the baby, which baby was handed to Flopson, which Flopson was handing it to Mrs. Pocket, when she too went fairly head foremost over Mrs. Pocket, baby and all, and was caught by Herbert and myself.

"Gracious me, Flopson!" said Mrs. Pocket, looking off her book for a moment, "everybody's tumbling!"

"Gracious you, indeed, Mum!" returned Flopson, very red in the face; "what have you got there?"

"I got here, Flopson?" asked Mrs. Pocket.

"Why, if it ain't your footstool!" cried Flopson. "And if you keep it under your skirts like that, who's to help tumbling? Here! Take the baby, Mum, and give me your book."

Mrs. Pocket acted on the advice, and inexpertly danced the infant a little in her lap, while the other children played about it. This had lasted but a very short time, when Mrs. Pocket issued summary orders that they were all to be taken into the house for a nap. Thus I made the second discovery on that first occasion, that the nurture of the little Pockets consisted of alternately tumbling up and lying down.

Under these circumstances, when Flopson and Millers had got the children into the house, like a little flock of sheep, and Mr. Pocket came out of it to make my acquaintance, I was not much surprised to find that Mr. Pocket was a gentleman with a rather perplexed expression of face, and with his very gray hair disordered on his head, as if he didn't quite see his way to putting anything straight.

CHAPTER XXIII

M r. Pocket said he was glad to see me, and he hoped I was not sorry to see him. "For, I really am not," he added, with his son's smile, "an alarming personage." He was a young-looking man, in spite of his perplexities and his very gray hair, and his manner seemed quite natural. I use the word natural, in the sense of its being unaffected; there was something comic in his distraught way, as though it would have been downright ludicrous but for his own perception that it was very near being so. When he had talked with me a little, he said to Mrs. Pocket, with a rather anxious contraction of his eyebrows, which were black and handsome, "Belinda, I hope you have welcomed Mr. Pip?" And she looked up from her book, and said, "Yes." She then smiled upon me in an absent state of mind, and asked me if I liked the taste of orange-flower water? As the question had no bearing, near or remote, on any foregone or subsequent transaction, I consider it to have been thrown out, like her previous approaches, in general conversational condescension.

I found out within a few hours, and may mention at once, that Mrs. Pocket was the only daughter of a certain quite accidental deceased Knight, who had invented for himself a conviction that his deceased father would have been made a Baronet but for somebody's determined opposition arising out of entirely personal motives,—I forget whose, if I ever knew,—the Sovereign's, the Prime Minister's, the Lord Chancellor's, the Archbishop of Canterbury's, anybody's,—and had tacked himself on to the nobles of the earth in right of this quite supposititious fact. I believe he had been knighted himself for storming the English grammar at the point of the pen, in a desperate address engrossed on vellum, on the occasion of the laying of the first stone of some building or other, and for handing some Royal Personage either the trowel or the mortar. Be that as it may, he had directed Mrs. Pocket to be brought up from her cradle as one who in the nature of things must marry a title, and who was to be guarded from the acquisition of plebeian domestic knowledge.

So successful a watch and ward had been established over the young lady by this judicious parent, that she had grown up highly ornamental, but perfectly helpless and useless. With her character thus happily formed, in the first bloom of her youth she had encountered Mr. Pocket: who was also in the first bloom of youth, and not quite decided whether to mount to the Woolsack, or to roof himself in with a mitre. As his doing the one or the other was a mere question of time, he and Mrs. Pocket had taken Time by the forelock (when, to judge from its length, it would seem to have wanted cutting), and had married without the knowledge of the judicious parent. The judicious parent, having nothing to bestow or withhold but his blessing, had handsomely settled that dower upon them after a short struggle, and had informed Mr. Pocket that his wife was "a treasure for a Prince." Mr. Pocket had invested the Prince's treasure in the ways of the world ever since, and it was supposed to have brought him in but indifferent interest. Still, Mrs. Pocket was in general the object of a queer sort of respectful pity, because she had not married a title; while Mr. Pocket was the object of a queer sort of forgiving reproach, because he had never got one.

Mr. Pocket took me into the house and showed me my room: which was a pleasant one, and so furnished as that I could use it with comfort for my own private sitting-room. He then knocked at the doors of two other similar rooms, and introduced me to their occupants, by name Drummle and Startop. Drummle, an old-looking young man of a heavy order of architecture, was whistling. Startop, younger in years and appearance, was reading and holding his head, as if he thought himself in danger of exploding it with too strong a charge of knowledge.

Both Mr. and Mrs. Pocket had such a noticeable air of being in somebody else's hands, that I wondered who really was in possession of the house and let them live there, until I found this unknown power to be the servants. It was a smooth way of going on, perhaps, in respect of saving trouble; but it had the appearance of being expensive, for the servants felt it a duty they owed to themselves to be nice in their eating and drinking, and to keep a deal of company down stairs. They allowed a very liberal table to Mr. and Mrs. Pocket, yet it always appeared to me that by far the best part of the house to have boarded in would have been the kitchen,—always supposing the boarder capable of self-defence, for, before I had been there a week, a neighboring lady with whom the family were personally unacquainted, wrote in to say that she had seen Millers slapping the baby. This greatly distressed Mrs. Pocket, who burst into tears on receiving the note, and said that it was an extraordinary thing that the neighbors couldn't mind their own business.

By degrees I learnt, and chiefly from Herbert, that Mr. Pocket had been educated at Harrow and at Cambridge, where he had distinguished himself; but that when he had had the happiness of marrying Mrs. Pocket very early in life, he had impaired his prospects and taken up the calling of a Grinder. After grinding a number of dull blades,—of whom it was remarkable that their fathers, when influential, were always going to help him to preferment, but always forgot to do it when the blades had left the Grindstone,—he had wearied of that poor work and had come to London. Here, after gradually failing in loftier hopes, he had "read" with divers who had lacked opportunities or neglected them, and had refurbished divers others for special occasions, and had turned his acquirements to the account of literary compilation and correction, and on such means, added to some very moderate private resources, still maintained the house I saw.

Mr. and Mrs. Pocket had a toady neighbor; a widow lady of that highly sympathetic nature that she agreed with everybody, blessed everybody, and shed smiles and tears on everybody, according to circumstances. This lady's name was Mrs. Coiler, and I had the honor of taking her down to dinner on the day of my installation. She gave me to understand on the stairs, that it was a blow to dear Mrs. Pocket that dear Mr. Pocket should be under the necessity of receiving gentlemen to read with him. That did not extend to me, she told me in a gush of love and confidence (at that time, I had known her something less than five minutes); if they were all like Me, it would be quite another thing.

"But dear Mrs. Pocket," said Mrs. Coiler, "after her early disappointment (not that dear Mr. Pocket was to blame in that), requires so much luxury and elegance—"

"Yes, ma'am," I said, to stop her, for I was afraid she was going to cry.

"And she is of so aristocratic a disposition—"

"Yes, ma'am," I said again, with the same object as before.

"—That it is hard," said Mrs. Coiler, "to have dear Mr. Pocket's time and attention diverted from dear Mrs. Pocket."

I could not help thinking that it might be harder if the butcher's time and attention were diverted from dear Mrs. Pocket; but I said nothing, and indeed had enough to do in keeping a bashful watch upon my company manners.

It came to my knowledge, through what passed between Mrs. Pocket and Drummle while I was attentive to my knife and fork, spoon, glasses, and other instruments of self-destruction, that Drummle, whose Christian name was Bentley, was actually the next heir but one to a baronetcy. It further appeared that the book I had seen Mrs. Pocket reading in the garden was all about titles, and that she knew the exact date at which her grandpapa would have come into the book, if he ever had come at all. Drummle didn't say much, but in his limited way (he struck me as a sulky kind of fellow) he spoke as one of the elect, and recognised Mrs. Pocket as a woman and a sister. No one but themselves and Mrs. Coiler the toady neighbour showed any interest in this part of the conversation, and it appeared to me that it was painful to Herbert; but it promised to last a long time, when the page came in with the announcement of a domestic affliction. It was, in effect, that the cook had mislaid the beef. To my unutterable amazement, I now, for the first time, saw Mr. Pocket relieve his mind by going through a performance that struck me as very extraordinary, but which made no impression on anybody else, and with which I soon became as familiar as the rest. He laid down the carving-knife and fork,—being engaged in carving, at the moment,—put his two hands into his disturbed hair, and appeared to make an extraordinary effort to lift himself up by it. When he had done this, and had not lifted himself up at all, he quietly went on with what he was about.

Mrs. Coiler then changed the subject and began to flatter me. I liked it for a few moments, but she flattered me so very grossly that the pleasure was soon over. She had a serpentine way of coming close at me when she pretended to be vitally interested in the friends and localities I had left, which was altogether snaky and fork-tongued; and when she made an occasional bounce upon Startop (who said very little to her), or upon Drummle (who said less), I rather envied them for being on the opposite side of the table.

After dinner the children were introduced, and Mrs. Coiler made admiring comments on their eyes, noses, and legs,—a sagacious way of improving their minds. There were four little girls, and two little boys, besides the baby who might have been either, and the baby's next successor who was as yet neither. They were brought in by Flopson and Millers, much as though those two non-commissioned officers had been recruiting somewhere for children and had enlisted these, while Mrs. Pocket looked at the young Nobles that ought to have been as if she rather thought she had had the pleasure of inspecting them before, but didn't quite know what to make of them.

"Here! Give me your fork, Mum, and take the baby," said Flopson. "Don't take it that way, or you'll get its head under the table."

Thus advised, Mrs. Pocket took it the other way, and got its head upon the table; which was announced to all present by a prodigious concussion.

"Dear, dear! Give it me back, Mum," said Flopson; "and Miss Jane, come and dance to baby, do!"

One of the little girls, a mere mite who seemed to have prematurely taken upon herself some charge of the others, stepped out of her place by me, and danced to and from the baby until it left off crying, and laughed. Then, all the children laughed, and Mr. Pocket (who in the meantime had twice endeavoured to lift himself up by the hair) laughed, and we all laughed and were glad.

Flopson, by dint of doubling the baby at the joints like a Dutch doll, then got it safely into Mrs. Pocket's lap, and gave it the nut-crackers to play with; at the same time recommending Mrs. Pocket to take notice that the handles of that instrument were not likely to agree with its eyes, and sharply charging Miss Jane to look after the same. Then, the two nurses left the room, and had a lively scuffle on the staircase with a dissipated page who had waited at dinner, and who had clearly lost half his buttons at the gaming-table.

I was made very uneasy in my mind by Mrs. Pocket's falling into a discussion with Drummle respecting two baronetcies, while she ate a sliced orange steeped in sugar and wine, and, forgetting all about the baby on her lap, who did most appalling things with the nut-crackers. At length little Jane, perceiving its young brains to be imperilled, softly left her place, and with many small artifices coaxed the dangerous weapon away. Mrs. Pocket finishing her orange at about the same time, and not approving of this, said to Jane,—

"You naughty child, how dare you? Go and sit down this instant!"

"Mamma dear," lisped the little girl, "baby ood have put hith eyeth out."

"How dare you tell me so?" retorted Mrs. Pocket. "Go and sit down in your chair this moment!"

Mrs. Pocket's dignity was so crushing, that I felt quite abashed, as if I myself had done something to rouse it.

"Belinda," remonstrated Mr. Pocket, from the other end of the table, "how can you be so unreasonable? Jane only interfered for the protection of baby."

"I will not allow anybody to interfere," said Mrs. Pocket. "I am surprised, Matthew, that you should expose me to the affront of interference."

"Good God!" cried Mr. Pocket, in an outbreak of desolate desperation. "Are infants to be nut-crackered into their tombs, and is nobody to save them?"

"I will not be interfered with by Jane," said Mrs. Pocket, with a majestic glance at that innocent little offender. "I hope I know my poor grandpapa's position. Jane, indeed!"

Mr. Pocket got his hands in his hair again, and this time really did lift himself some inches out of his chair. "Hear this!" he helplessly exclaimed to the elements. "Babies are to be nut-crackered dead, for people's poor grandpapa's positions!" Then he let himself down again, and became silent.

We all looked awkwardly at the tablecloth while this was going on. A pause succeeded, during which the honest and irrepressible baby made a series of leaps and crows at little Jane, who appeared to me to be the only member of the family (irrespective of servants) with whom it had any decided acquaintance.

"Mr. Drummle," said Mrs. Pocket, "will you ring for Flopson? Jane, you undutiful little thing, go and lie down. Now, baby darling, come with ma!"

The baby was the soul of honor, and protested with all its might. It doubled itself up the wrong way over Mrs. Pocket's arm, exhibited a pair of knitted shoes and dimpled ankles to the company in lieu of its soft face, and was carried out in the highest state of mutiny. And it gained its point after all, for I saw it through the window within a few minutes, being nursed by little Jane.

It happened that the other five children were left behind at the dinner-table, through Flopson's having some private engagement, and their not being anybody else's business. I thus became aware of the mutual relations between them and Mr. Pocket, which were exemplified in the following manner. Mr. Pocket, with the normal perplexity of his face heightened and his hair rumpled, looked at them for some minutes, as if he couldn't make out how they came to be boarding and lodging in that establishment, and why they hadn't been billeted by Nature on somebody else. Then, in a distant Missionary way he asked them certain questions,—as why little Joe had that hole in his frill, who said, Pa, Flopson was going to mend it when she had time,—and how little Fanny came by that whitlow, who said, Pa, Millers was going to poultice it when she didn't forget. Then, he melted into parental tenderness, and gave them a shilling apiece and told them to go and play; and then as they went out, with one very strong effort to lift himself up by the hair he dismissed the hopeless subject.

In the evening there was rowing on the river. As Drummle and Startop had each a boat, I resolved to set up mine, and to cut them both out. I was pretty good at most exercises in which country boys are adepts, but as I was conscious of wanting elegance of style for the Thames,—not to say for other waters,—I at once engaged to place myself under the tuition of the winner of a prize-wherry who plied at our stairs, and to whom I was introduced by my new allies. This practical authority confused me very much by saying I had the arm of a blacksmith. If he could have known how nearly the compliment lost him his pupil, I doubt if he would have paid it.

There was a supper-tray after we got home at night, and I think we should all have enjoyed ourselves, but for a rather disagreeable domestic occurrence. Mr. Pocket was in good spirits, when a housemaid came in, and said, "If you please, sir, I should wish to speak to you."

"Speak to your master?" said Mrs. Pocket, whose dignity was roused again. "How can you think of such a thing? Go and speak to Flopson. Or speak to me—at some other time."

"Begging your pardon, ma'am," returned the housemaid, "I should wish to speak at once, and to speak to master."

Hereupon, Mr. Pocket went out of the room, and we made the best of ourselves until he came back.

"This is a pretty thing, Belinda!" said Mr. Pocket, returning with a countenance expressive of grief and despair. "Here's the cook lying insensibly drunk on the kitchen floor, with a large bundle of fresh butter made up in the cupboard ready to sell for grease!"

Mrs. Pocket instantly showed much amiable emotion, and said, "This is that odious Sophia's doing!"

"What do you mean, Belinda?" demanded Mr. Pocket.

"Sophia has told you," said Mrs. Pocket. "Did I not see her with my own eyes and hear her with my own ears, come into the room just now and ask to speak to you?"

"But has she not taken me down stairs, Belinda," returned Mr. Pocket, "and shown me the woman, and the bundle too?"

"And do you defend her, Matthew," said Mrs. Pocket, "for making mischief?"

Mr. Pocket uttered a dismal groan.

"Am I, grandpapa's granddaughter, to be nothing in the house?" said Mrs. Pocket. "Besides, the cook has always been a very nice respectful woman, and said in the most natural manner when she came to look after the situation, that she felt I was born to be a Duchess."

There was a sofa where Mr. Pocket stood, and he dropped upon it in the attitude of the Dying Gladiator. Still in that attitude he said, with a hollow voice, "Good night, Mr. Pip," when I deemed it advisable to go to bed and leave him.

CHAPTER XXIV

After two or three days, when I had established myself in my room and had gone backwards and forwards to London several times, and had ordered all I wanted of my tradesmen, Mr. Pocket and I had a long talk together. He knew more of my intended career than I knew myself, for he referred to his having been told by Mr. Jaggers that I was not designed for any profession, and that I should be well enough educated for my destiny if I could "hold my own" with the average of young men in prosperous circumstances. I acquiesced, of course, knowing nothing to the contrary.

He advised my attending certain places in London, for the acquisition of such mere rudiments as I wanted, and my investing him with the functions of explainer and director of all my studies. He hoped that with intelligent assistance I should meet with little to discourage me, and should soon be able to dispense with any aid but his. Through his way of saying this, and much more to similar purpose, he placed himself on confidential terms with me in an admirable manner; and I may state at once that he was always so zealous and honourable in fulfilling his compact with me, that he made me zealous and honourable in fulfilling mine with him. If he had shown indifference as a master, I have no doubt I should have returned the compliment as a pupil; he gave me no such excuse, and each of us did the other justice. Nor did I ever regard him as having anything ludicrous about him—or anything but what was serious, honest, and good—in his tutor communication with me.

When these points were settled, and so far carried out as that I had begun to work in earnest, it occurred to me that if I could retain my bedroom in Barnard's Inn, my life would be agreeably varied, while my manners would be none the worse for Herbert's society. Mr. Pocket did not object to this arrangement, but urged that before any step could possibly be taken in it, it must be submitted to my guardian. I felt that this delicacy arose out of the consideration that the plan would save Herbert some expense, so I went off to Little Britain and imparted my wish to Mr. Jaggers.

"If I could buy the furniture now hired for me," said I, "and one or two other little things, I should be quite at home there."

"Go it!" said Mr. Jaggers, with a short laugh. "I told you you'd get on. Well! How much do you want?"

I said I didn't know how much.

"Come!" retorted Mr. Jaggers. "How much? Fifty pounds?"

"O, not nearly so much."

"Five pounds?" said Mr. Jaggers.

This was such a great fall, that I said in discomfiture, "O, more than that."

"More than that, eh!" retorted Mr. Jaggers, lying in wait for me, with his hands in his pockets, his head on one side, and his eyes on the wall behind me; "how much more?"

"It is so difficult to fix a sum," said I, hesitating.

"Come!" said Mr. Jaggers. "Let's get at it. Twice five; will that do? Three times five; will that do? Four times five; will that do?"

I said I thought that would do handsomely.

"Four times five will do handsomely, will it?" said Mr. Jaggers, knitting his brows. "Now, what do you make of four times five?"

"What do I make of it?"

"Ah!" said Mr. Jaggers; "how much?"

"I suppose you make it twenty pounds," said I, smiling.

"Never mind what I make it, my friend," observed Mr. Jaggers, with a knowing and contradictory toss of his head. "I want to know what you make it."

"Twenty pounds, of course."

"Wemmick!" said Mr. Jaggers, opening his office door. "Take Mr. Pip's written order, and pay him twenty pounds."

This strongly marked way of doing business made a strongly marked impression on me, and that not of an agreeable kind. Mr. Jaggers never laughed; but he wore great bright creaking boots, and, in poising himself on these boots, with his large head bent down and his eyebrows joined together, awaiting an answer, he sometimes caused the boots to creak, as if they laughed in a dry and suspicious way. As he happened to go out now, and as Wemmick was brisk and talkative, I said to Wemmick that I hardly knew what to make of Mr. Jaggers's manner.

"Tell him that, and he'll take it as a compliment," answered Wemmick; "he don't mean that you should know what to make of it.—Oh!" for I looked surprised, "it's not personal; it's professional: only professional."

Wemmick was at his desk, lunching—and crunching—on a dry hard biscuit; pieces of which he threw from time to time into his slit of a mouth, as if he were posting them.

"Always seems to me," said Wemmick, "as if he had set a man-trap and was watching it. Suddenly-click—you're caught!"

Without remarking that man-traps were not among the amenities of life, I said I supposed he was very skilful?

"Deep," said Wemmick, "as Australia." Pointing with his pen at the office floor, to express that Australia was understood, for the purposes of the figure, to be symmetrically on the opposite spot of the globe. "If there was anything deeper," added Wemmick, bringing his pen to paper, "he'd be it."

Then, I said I supposed he had a fine business, and Wemmick said, "Ca-pi-tal!" Then I asked if there were many clerks? to which he replied,—

"We don't run much into clerks, because there's only one Jaggers, and people won't have him at second hand. There are only four of us. Would you like to see 'em? You are one of us, as I may say."

I accepted the offer. When Mr. Wemmick had put all the biscuit into the post, and had paid me my money from a cash-box in a safe, the key of which safe he kept somewhere down his back and produced from his coat-collar like an iron-pigtail, we went up stairs. The house was dark and shabby, and the greasy shoulders that had left their mark in Mr. Jaggers's room seemed to have been shuffling up and down the staircase for years. In the front first floor, a clerk who looked something between a publican and a rat-catcher—a large pale, puffed, swollen man—was attentively engaged with three or four people of shabby appearance, whom he treated as unceremoniously as everybody seemed to be treated who contributed to Mr. Jaggers's coffers. "Getting evidence together," said Mr. Wemmick, as we came out, "for the Bailey." In the room over that, a little flabby terrier of a clerk with dangling hair (his cropping seemed to have been forgotten when he was a puppy) was similarly engaged with a man with weak eyes, whom Mr. Wemmick presented to me as a smelter who kept his pot always boiling, and who would melt me anything I pleased,—and who was in an excessive white-perspiration, as if he had been trying his art on himself. In a back room, a high-shouldered man with a face-ache tied up in dirty flannel, who was dressed in old black clothes that bore the appearance of having been waxed, was stooping over his work of making fair copies of the notes of the other two gentlemen, for Mr. Jaggers's own use.

This was all the establishment. When we went down stairs again, Wemmick led me into my guardian's room, and said, "This you've seen already."

"Pray," said I, as the two odious casts with the twitchy leer upon them caught my sight again, "whose likenesses are those?"

"These?" said Wemmick, getting upon a chair, and blowing the dust off the horrible heads before bringing them down. "These are two celebrated ones. Famous clients of ours that got us a world of credit. This chap (why you must have come down in the night and been peeping into the inkstand, to get this blot upon your eyebrow, you old rascal!) murdered his master, and, considering that he wasn't brought up to evidence, didn't plan it badly."

"Is it like him?" I asked, recoiling from the brute, as Wemmick spat upon his eyebrow and gave it a rub with his sleeve.

"Like him? It's himself, you know. The cast was made in Newgate, directly after he was taken down. You had a particular fancy for me, hadn't you, Old Artful?" said Wemmick. He then explained this affectionate apostrophe, by touching his brooch representing the lady and the weeping willow at the tomb with the urn upon it, and saying, "Had it made for me, express!"

"Is the lady anybody?" said I.

"No," returned Wemmick. "Only his game. (You liked your bit of game, didn't you?) No; deuce a bit of a lady in the case, Mr. Pip, except one,—and she wasn't of this slender lady-like sort, and you wouldn't have caught her looking after this urn, unless there was something to drink in it." Wemmick's attention being thus directed to his brooch, he put down the cast, and polished the brooch with his pocket-handkerchief.

"Did that other creature come to the same end?" I asked. "He has the same look."

"You're right," said Wemmick; "it's the genuine look. Much as if one nostril was caught up with a horse-hair and a little fish-hook. Yes, he came to the same end; quite the natural end here, I assure you. He forged wills, this blade did, if he didn't also put the supposed testators to sleep too. You were a gentlemanly Cove, though" (Mr. Wemmick was again apostrophising), "and you said you could write Greek. Yah, Bounceable! What a liar you were! I never met such a liar as you!" Before putting his late friend on his shelf again, Wemmick touched the largest of his mourning rings and said, "Sent out to buy it for me, only the day before."

While he was putting up the other cast and coming down from the chair, the thought crossed my mind that all his personal jewelry was derived from like sources.

As he had shown no diffidence on the subject, I ventured on the liberty of asking him the question, when he stood before me, dusting his hands.

"O yes," he returned, "these are all gifts of that kind. One brings another, you see; that's the way of it. I always take 'em. They're curiosities. And they're property. They may not be worth much, but, after all, they're property and portable. It don't signify to you with your brilliant lookout, but as to myself, my guiding-star always is, 'Get hold of portable property'."

When I had rendered homage to this light, he went on to say, in a friendly manner:—

"If at any odd time when you have nothing better to do, you wouldn't mind coming over to see me at Walworth, I could offer you a bed, and I should consider it an honour. I have not much to show you; but such two or three curiosities as I have got you might like to look over; and I am fond of a bit of garden and a summer-house."

I said I should be delighted to accept his hospitality.

"Thankee," said he; "then we'll consider that it's to come off, when convenient to you. Have you dined with Mr. Jaggers yet?"

"Not yet."

"Well," said Wemmick, "he'll give you wine, and good wine. I'll give you punch, and not bad punch. And now I'll tell you something. When you go to dine with Mr. Jaggers, look at his housekeeper."

"Shall I see something very uncommon?"

"Well," said Wemmick, "you'll see a wild beast tamed. Not so very uncommon, you'll tell me. I reply, that depends on the original wildness of the beast, and the amount of taming. It won't lower your opinion of Mr. Jaggers's powers. Keep your eye on it."

I told him I would do so, with all the interest and curiosity that his preparation awakened. As I was taking my departure, he asked me if I would like to devote five minutes to seeing Mr. Jaggers "at it?"

For several reasons, and not least because I didn't clearly know what Mr. Jaggers would be found to be "at," I replied in the affirmative. We dived into the City, and came up in a crowded police-court, where a blood-relation (in the murderous sense) of the deceased, with the fanciful taste in brooches, was standing at the bar, uncomfortably chewing something; while my guardian had a woman under examination or cross-examination,—I don't know which,—and was striking her, and the bench, and everybody present, with awe. If anybody, of whatsoever degree, said a word that he didn't approve of, he instantly required to have it "taken down." If anybody wouldn't make an admission, he said, "I'll have it out of you!" and if anybody made an admission, he said, "Now I have got you!" The magistrates shivered under a single bite of his finger. Thieves and thief-takers hung in dread rapture on his words, and shrank when a hair of his eyebrows turned in their direction. Which side he was on I couldn't make out, for he seemed to me to be grinding the whole place in a mill; I only know that when I stole out on tiptoe, he was not on the side of the bench; for, he was making the legs of the old gentleman who presided, quite convulsive under the table, by his denunciations of his conduct as the representative of British law and justice in that chair that day.

CHAPTER XXV

Bentley Drummle, who was so sulky a fellow that he even took up a book as if its writer had done him an injury, did not take up an acquaintance in a more agreeable spirit. Heavy in figure, movement, and comprehension,—in the sluggish complexion of his face, and in the large, awkward tongue that seemed to loll about in his mouth as he himself lolled about in a room,—he was idle, proud, niggardly, reserved, and suspicious. He came of rich people down in Somersetshire, who had nursed this combination of qualities until they made the discovery that it was just of age and a blockhead. Thus, Bentley Drummle had come to Mr. Pocket when he was a head taller than that gentleman, and half a dozen heads thicker than most gentlemen.

Startop had been spoilt by a weak mother and kept at home when he ought to have been at school, but he was devotedly attached to her, and admired her beyond measure. He had a woman's delicacy of feature, and was—"as you may see, though you never saw her," said Herbert to me—"exactly like his mother." It was but natural that I should take to him much more kindly than to Drummle, and that, even in the earliest evenings of our boating, he and I should pull homeward abreast of one another, conversing from boat to boat, while Bentley Drummle came up in our wake alone, under the overhanging banks and among the rushes. He would always creep in-shore like some uncomfortable amphibious creature, even when the tide would have sent him fast upon his way; and I always think of him as coming after us in the dark or by the back-water, when our own two boats were breaking the sunset or the moonlight in mid-stream.

Herbert was my intimate companion and friend. I presented him with a half-share in my boat, which was the occasion of his often coming down to Hammersmith; and my possession of a half-share in his chambers often took me up to London. We used to walk between the two places at all hours. I have an affection for the road yet (though it is not so pleasant a road as it was then), formed in the impressibility of untried youth and hope.

When I had been in Mr. Pocket's family a month or two, Mr. and Mrs. Camilla turned up. Camilla was Mr. Pocket's sister. Georgiana, whom I had seen at Miss Havisham's on the same occasion, also turned up. She was a cousin,—an indigestive single woman, who called her rigidity religion, and her liver love. These people hated me with the hatred of cupidity and disappointment. As a matter of course, they fawned upon me in my prosperity with the basest meanness. Towards Mr. Pocket, as a grown-up infant with no notion of his own interests, they showed the complacent forbearance I had heard them express. Mrs. Pocket they held in contempt; but they allowed the poor soul to have been heavily disappointed in life, because that shed a feeble reflected light upon themselves.

These were the surroundings among which I settled down, and applied myself to my education. I soon contracted expensive habits, and began to spend an amount of money that within a few short months I should have thought almost fabulous; but through good and evil I stuck to my books. There was no other merit in this, than my having sense enough to feel my deficiencies. Between Mr. Pocket and Herbert I got on fast; and, with one or the other always at my elbow to give me the start I wanted, and clear obstructions out of my road, I must have been as great a dolt as Drummle if I had done less.

I had not seen Mr. Wemmick for some weeks, when I thought I would write him a note and propose to go home with him on a certain evening. He replied that it would give him much pleasure, and that he would expect me at the office at six o'clock. Thither I went, and there I found him, putting the key of his safe down his back as the clock struck.

"Did you think of walking down to Walworth?" said he.

"Certainly," said I, "if you approve."

"Very much," was Wemmick's reply, "for I have had my legs under the desk all day, and shall be glad to stretch them. Now, I'll tell you what I have got for supper, Mr. Pip. I have got a stewed steak,—which is of home preparation,—and a cold roast fowl,—which is from the cook's-shop. I think it's tender, because the master of the shop was a Juryman in some cases of ours the other day, and we let him down easy. I reminded him of it when I bought the fowl, and I said, 'Pick us out a good one, old Briton, because if we had chosen to keep you in the box another day or two, we could easily have done it.' He said to that, 'Let me make you a present of the best fowl in the shop.' I let him, of course. As far as it goes, it's property and portable. You don't object to an aged parent, I hope?"

I really thought he was still speaking of the fowl, until he added, "Because I have got an aged parent at my place." I then said what politeness required.

"So, you haven't dined with Mr. Jaggers yet?" he pursued, as we walked along.

"Not yet."

"He told me so this afternoon when he heard you were coming. I expect you'll have an invitation to-morrow. He's going to ask your pals, too. Three of 'em; ain't there?"

Although I was not in the habit of counting Drummle as one of my intimate associates, I answered, "Yes."

"Well, he's going to ask the whole gang,"—I hardly felt complimented by the word,—"and whatever he gives you, he'll give you good. Don't look forward to variety, but you'll have excellence. And there'sa nother rum thing in his house," proceeded Wemmick, after a moment's pause, as if the remark followed on the housekeeper understood; "he never lets a door or window be fastened at night."

"Is he never robbed?"

"That's it!" returned Wemmick. "He says, and gives it out publicly, 'I want to see the man who'll rob me.' Lord bless you, I have heard him, a hundred times, if I have heard him once, say to regular cracksmen in our front office, 'You know where I live; now, no bolt is ever drawn there; why don't you do a stroke of business with me? Come; can't I tempt you?' Not a man of them, sir, would be bold enough to try it on, for love or money."

"They dread him so much?" said I.

"Dread him," said Wemmick. "I believe you they dread him. Not but what he's artful, even in his defiance of them. No silver, sir. Britannia metal, every spoon."

"So they wouldn't have much," I observed, "even if they—"

"Ah! But he would have much," said Wemmick, cutting me short, "and they know it. He'd have their lives, and the lives of scores of 'em. He'd have all he could get. And it's impossible to say what he couldn't get, if he gave his mind to it."

I was falling into meditation on my guardian's greatness, when Wemmick remarked:—

"As to the absence of plate, that's only his natural depth, you know. A river's its natural depth, and he's his natural depth. Look at his watch-chain. That's real enough."

"It's very massive," said I.

"Massive?" repeated Wemmick. "I think so. And his watch is a gold repeater, and worth a hundred pound if it's worth a penny. Mr. Pip, there are about seven hundred thieves in this town who know all about that watch; there's not a man, a woman, or a child, among them, who wouldn't identify the smallest link in that chain, and drop it as if it was red hot, if inveigled into touching it."

At first with such discourse, and afterwards with conversation of a more general nature, did Mr. Wemmick and I beguile the time and the road, until he gave me to understand that we had arrived in the district of Walworth.

It appeared to be a collection of back lanes, ditches, and little gardens, and to present the aspect of a rather dull retirement. Wemmick's house was a little wooden cottage in the midst of plots of garden, and the top of it was cut out and painted like a battery mounted with guns.

"My own doing," said Wemmick. "Looks pretty; don't it?"

I highly commended it, I think it was the smallest house I ever saw; with the queerest gothic windows (by far the greater part of them sham), and a gothic door almost too small to get in at.

"That's a real flagstaff, you see," said Wemmick, "and on Sundays I run up a real flag. Then look here. After I have crossed this bridge, I hoist it up-so—and cut off the communication."

The bridge was a plank, and it crossed a chasm about four feet wide and two deep. But it was very pleasant to see the pride with which he hoisted it up and made it fast; smiling as he did so, with a relish and not merely mechanically.

"At nine o'clock every night, Greenwich time," said Wemmick, "the gun fires. There he is, you see! And when you hear him go, I think you'll say he's a Stinger."

The piece of ordnance referred to, was mounted in a separate fortress, constructed of lattice-work. It was protected from the weather by an ingenious little tarpaulin contrivance in the nature of an umbrella.

"Then, at the back," said Wemmick, "out of sight, so as not to impede the idea of fortifications,—for it's a principle with me, if you have an idea, carry it out and keep it up,—I don't know whether that's your opinion—"

I said, decidedly.

"—At the back, there's a pig, and there are fowls and rabbits; then, I knock together my own little frame, you see, and grow cucumbers; and you'll judge at supper what sort of a salad I can raise. So, sir," said Wemmick, smiling again, but seriously too, as he shook his head, "if you can suppose the little place besieged, it would hold out a devil of a time in point of provisions."

Then, he conducted me to a bower about a dozen yards off, but which was approached by such ingenious twists of path that it took quite a long time to get at; and in this retreat our glasses were already set forth. Our punch was cooling in an ornamental lake, on whose margin the bower was raised. This piece of water (with an island in the middle which might have been the salad for supper) was of a circular form, and he had constructed a fountain in it, which, when you set a little mill going and took a cork out of a pipe, played to that powerful extent that it made the back of your hand quite wet.

"I am my own engineer, and my own carpenter, and my own plumber, and my own gardener, and my own Jack of all Trades," said Wemmick, in acknowledging my compliments. "Well; it's a good thing, you know. It brushes the Newgate cobwebs away, and pleases the Aged. You wouldn't mind being at once introduced to the Aged, would you? It wouldn't put you out?"

I expressed the readiness I felt, and we went into the castle. There we found, sitting by a fire, a very old man in a flannel coat: clean, cheerful, comfortable, and well cared for, but intensely deaf.

"Well aged parent," said Wemmick, shaking hands with him in a cordial and jocose way, "how am you?"

"All right, John; all right!" replied the old man.

"Here's Mr. Pip, aged parent," said Wemmick, "and I wish you could hear his name. Nod away at him, Mr. Pip; that's what he likes. Nod away at him, if you please, like winking!"

"This is a fine place of my son's, sir," cried the old man, while I nodded as hard as I possibly could. "This is a pretty pleasure-ground, sir. This spot and these beautiful works upon it ought to be kept together by the Nation, after my son's time, for the people's enjoyment."

"You're as proud of it as Punch; ain't you, Aged?" said Wemmick, contemplating the old man, with his hard face really softened; "there's a nod for you;" giving him a tremendous one; "there's another for you;" giving him a still more tremendous one; "you like that, don't you? If you're not tired, Mr. Pip—though I know it's tiring to strangers—will you tip him one more? You can't think how it pleases him."

I tipped him several more, and he was in great spirits. We left him bestirring himself to feed the fowls, and we sat down to our punch in the arbor; where Wemmick told me, as he smoked a pipe, that it had taken him a good many years to bring the property up to its present pitch of perfection.

"Is it your own, Mr. Wemmick?"

"O yes," said Wemmick, "I have got hold of it, a bit at a time. It's a freehold, by George!"

"Is it indeed? I hope Mr. Jaggers admires it?"

"Never seen it," said Wemmick. "Never heard of it. Never seen the Aged. Never heard of him. No; the office is one thing, and private life is another. When I go into the office, I leave the Castle behind me, and when I come into the Castle, I leave the office behind me. If it's not in any way disagreeable to you, you'll oblige me by doing the same. I don't wish it professionally spoken about."

Of course I felt my good faith involved in the observance of his request. The punch being very nice, we sat there drinking it and talking, until it was almost nine o'clock. "Getting near gun-fire," said Wemmick then, as he laid down his pipe; "it's the Aged's treat."

Proceeding into the Castle again, we found the Aged heating the poker, with expectant eyes, as a preliminary to the performance of this great nightly ceremony. Wemmick stood with his watch in his hand until the moment was come for him to take the red-hot poker from the Aged, and repair to the battery. He took it, and went out, and presently the Stinger went off with a Bang that shook the crazy little box of a cottage as if it must fall to pieces, and made every glass and teacup in it ring. Upon this, the Aged—who I believe would have been blown out of his arm-chair but for holding on by the elbows—cried out exultingly, "He's fired! I heerd him!" and I nodded at the old gentleman until it is no figure of speech to declare that I absolutely could not see him.

The interval between that time and supper Wemmick devoted to showing me his collection of curiosities. They were mostly of a felonious character; comprising the pen with which a celebrated forgery had been committed, a distinguished razor or two, some locks of hair, and several manuscript confessions written under condemnation,— upon which Mr. Wemmick set particular value as being, to use his own words, "every one of 'em Lies, sir." These were agreeably dispersed among small specimens of china and glass, various neat trifles made by the proprietor of the museum, and some tobacco-stoppers carved by the Aged. They were all displayed in that chamber of the Castle into which I had been first inducted, and which served, not only as the general sitting-room but as the kitchen too, if I might judge from a saucepan on the hob, and a brazen bijou over the fireplace designed for the suspension of a roasting-jack.

There was a neat little girl in attendance, who looked after the Aged in the day. When she had laid the supper-cloth, the bridge was lowered to give her means of egress, and she withdrew for the night. The supper was excellent; and though the Castle was rather subject to dry-rot insomuch that it tasted like a bad nut, and though the pig might have been farther off, I was heartily pleased with my whole entertainment. Nor was there any drawback on my little turret bedroom, beyond there being such a very thin ceiling between me and the flagstaff, that when I lay down on my back in bed, it seemed as if I had to balance that pole on my forehead all night.

Wemmick was up early in the morning, and I am afraid I heard him cleaning my boots. After that, he fell to gardening, and I saw him from my gothic window pretending to employ the Aged, and nodding at him in a most devoted manner. Our breakfast was as good as the supper, and at half-past eight precisely we started for Little Britain. By degrees, Wemmick got dryer and harder as we went along, and his mouth tightened into a post-office again. At last, when we got to his place of business and he pulled out his key from his coat-collar, he looked as unconscious of his Walworth property as if the Castle and the drawbridge and the arbor and the lake and the fountain and the Aged, had all been blown into space together by the last discharge of the Stinger.

CHAPTER XXVI

It fell out as Wemmick had told me it would, that I had an early opportunity of comparing my guardian's establishment with that of his cashier and clerk. My guardian was in his room, washing his hands with his scented soap, when I went into the office from Walworth; and he called me to him, and gave me the invitation for myself and friends which Wemmick had prepared me to receive. "No ceremony," he stipulated, "and no dinner dress, and say to-morrow." I asked him where we should come to (for I had no idea where he lived), and I believe it was in his general objection to make anything like an admission, that he replied, "Come here, and I'll take you home with me." I embrace this opportunity of remarking that he washed his clients off, as if he were a surgeon or a dentist. He had a closet in his room, fitted up for the purpose, which smelt of the scented soap like a perfumer's shop. It had an unusually large jack-towel on a roller inside the door, and he would wash his hands, and wipe them and dry them all over this towel, whenever he came in from a police court or dismissed a client from his room. When I and my friends repaired to him at six o'clock next day, he seemed to have been engaged on a case of a darker complexion than usual, for we found him with his head butted into this closet, not only washing his hands, but laving his face and gargling his throat. And even when he had done all that, and had gone all round the jack-towel, he took out his penknife and scraped the case out of his nails before he put his coat on.

There were some people slinking about as usual when we passed out into the street, who were evidently anxious to speak with him; but there was something so conclusive in the halo of scented soap which encircled his presence, that they gave it up for that day. As we walked along westward, he was recognised ever and again by some face in the crowd of the streets, and whenever that happened he talked louder to me; but he never otherwise recognised anybody, or took notice that anybody recognised him.

He conducted us to Gerrard Street, Soho, to a house on the south side of that street. Rather a stately house of its kind, but dolefully in want of painting, and with dirty windows. He took out his key and opened the door, and we all went into a stone hall, bare, gloomy, and little used. So, up a dark brown staircase into a series of three dark brown rooms on the first floor. There were carved garlands on the panelled walls, and as he stood among them giving us welcome, I know what kind of loops I thought they looked like.

Dinner was laid in the best of these rooms; the second was his dressing-room; the third, his bedroom. He told us that he held the whole house, but rarely used more of it than we saw. The table was comfortably laid—no silver in the service, of course—and at the side of his chair was a capacious dumb-waiter, with a variety of bottles and decanters on it, and four dishes of fruit for dessert. I noticed throughout, that he kept everything under his own hand, and distributed everything himself.

There was a bookcase in the room; I saw from the backs of the books, that they were about evidence, criminal law, criminal biography, trials, acts of Parliament, and such things. The furniture was all very solid and good, like his watch-chain. It had an official look, however, and there was nothing merely ornamental to be seen. In a corner was a little table of papers with a shaded lamp: so that he seemed to bring the office home with him in that respect too, and to wheel it out of an evening and fall to work.

As he had scarcely seen my three companions until now,—for he and I had walked together,—he stood on the hearth-rug, after ringing the bell, and took a searching look at them. To my surprise, he seemed at once to be principally if not solely interested in Drummle.

"Pip," said he, putting his large hand on my shoulder and moving me to the window, "I don't know one from the other. Who's the Spider?"

"The spider?" said I.

"The blotchy, sprawly, sulky fellow."

"That's Bentley Drummle," I replied; "the one with the delicate face is Startop."

Not making the least account of "the one with the delicate face," he returned, "Bentley Drummle is his name, is it? I like the look of that fellow."

He immediately began to talk to Drummle: not at all deterred by his replying in his heavy reticent way, but apparently led on by it to screw discourse out of him. I was looking at the two, when there came between me and them the housekeeper, with the first dish for the table.

She was a woman of about forty, I supposed,—but I may have thought her younger than she was. Rather tall, of a lithe nimble figure, extremely pale, with large faded eyes, and a quantity of streaming hair. I cannot say whether any diseased affection of the heart caused her lips to be parted as if she were panting, and her face to bear a curious expression of suddenness and flutter; but I know that I had been to see Macbeth at the theatre, a night or two before, and that her face looked to me as if it were all disturbed by fiery air, like the faces I had seen rise out of the Witches' caldron.

She set the dish on, touched my guardian quietly on the arm with a finger to notify that dinner was ready, and vanished. We took our seats at the round table, and my guardian kept Drummle on one side of him, while Startop sat on the other. It was a noble dish of fish that the housekeeper had put on table, and we had a joint of equally choice mutton afterwards, and then an equally choice bird. Sauces, wines, all the accessories we wanted, and all of the best, were given out by our host from his dumb-waiter; and when they had made the circuit of the table, he always put them back again. Similarly, he dealt us clean plates and knives and forks, for each course, and dropped those just disused into two baskets on the ground by his chair. No other attendant than the housekeeper appeared. She set on every dish; and I always saw in her face, a face rising out of the caldron. Years afterwards, I made a dreadful likeness of that woman, by causing a face that had no other natural resemblance to it than it derived from flowing hair to pass behind a bowl of flaming spirits in a dark room.

Induced to take particular notice of the housekeeper, both by her own striking appearance and by Wemmick's preparation, I observed that whenever she was in the room she kept her eyes attentively on my guardian, and that she would remove her hands from any dish she put before him, hesitatingly, as if she dreaded his calling her back, and wanted him to speak when she was nigh, if he had anything to say. I fancied that I could detect in his manner a consciousness of this, and a purpose of always holding her in suspense.

Dinner went off gayly, and although my guardian seemed to follow rather than originate subjects, I knew that he wrenched the weakest part of our dispositions out of us. For myself, I found that I was expressing my tendency to lavish expenditure, and to patronize Herbert, and to boast of my great prospects, before I quite knew that I had opened my lips. It was so with all of us, but with no one more than Drummle: the development of whose inclination to gird in a grudging and suspicious way at the rest, was screwed out of him before the fish was taken off.

It was not then, but when we had got to the cheese, that our conversation turned upon our rowing feats, and that Drummle was rallied for coming up behind of a night in that slow amphibious way of his. Drummle upon this, informed our host that he much preferred our room to our company, and that as to skill he was more than our master, and that as to strength he could scatter us like chaff. By some invisible agency, my guardian wound him up to a pitch little short of ferocity about this trifle; and he fell to baring and spanning his arm to show how muscular it was, and we all fell to baring and spanning our arms in a ridiculous manner.

Now the housekeeper was at that time clearing the table; my guardian, taking no heed of her, but with the side of his face turned from her, was leaning back in his chair biting the side of his forefinger and showing an interest in Drummle, that, to me, was quite inexplicable. Suddenly, he clapped his large hand on the housekeeper's, like a trap, as she stretched it across the table. So suddenly and smartly did he do this, that we all stopped in our foolish contention.

"If you talk of strength," said Mr. Jaggers, "I'll show you a wrist. Molly, let them see your wrist."

Her entrapped hand was on the table, but she had already put her other hand behind her waist. "Master," she said, in a low voice, with her eyes attentively and entreatingly fixed upon him. "Don't."

"I'll show you a wrist," repeated Mr. Jaggers, with an immovable determination to show it. "Molly, let them see your wrist."

"Master," she again murmured. "Please!"

"Molly," said Mr. Jaggers, not looking at her, but obstinately looking at the opposite side of the room, "let them see both your wrists. Show them. Come!"

He took his hand from hers, and turned that wrist up on the table. She brought her other hand from behind her, and held the two out side by side. The last wrist was much disfigured,—deeply scarred and scarred across and across. When she held her hands out she took her eyes from Mr. Jaggers, and turned them watchfully on every one of the rest of us in succession.

"There's power here," said Mr. Jaggers, coolly tracing out the sinews with his forefinger. "Very few men have the power of wrist that this woman has. It's remarkable what mere force of grip there is in these hands. I have had occasion to notice many hands; but I never saw stronger in that respect, man's or woman's, than these."

While he said these words in a leisurely, critical style, she continued to look at every one of us in regular succession as we sat. The moment he ceased, she looked at him again. "That'll do, Molly," said Mr. Jaggers, giving her a slight nod; "you have been admired, and can go." She withdrew her hands and went out of the room, and

Mr. Jaggers, putting the decanters on from his dumb-waiter, filled his glass and passed round the wine.

"At half-past nine, gentlemen," said he, "we must break up. Pray make the best use of your time. I am glad to see you all. Mr. Drummle, I drink to you."

If his object in singling out Drummle were to bring him out still more, it perfectly succeeded. In a sulky triumph, Drummle showed his morose depreciation of the rest of us, in a more and more offensive degree, until he became downright intolerable. Through all his stages, Mr. Jaggers followed him with the same strange interest. He actually seemed to serve as a zest to Mr. Jaggers's wine.

In our boyish want of discretion I dare say we took too much to drink, and I know we talked too much. We became particularly hot upon some boorish sneer of Drummle's, to the effect that we were too free with our money. It led to my remarking, with more zeal than discretion, that it came with a bad grace from him, to whom Startop had lent money in my presence but a week or so before.

"Well," retorted Drummle; "he'll be paid."

"I don't mean to imply that he won't," said I, "but it might make you hold your tongue about us and our money, I should think."

"You should think!" retorted Drummle. "Oh Lord!"

"I dare say," I went on, meaning to be very severe, "that you wouldn't lend money to any of us if we wanted it."

"You are right," said Drummle. "I wouldn't lend one of you a sixpence. I wouldn't lend anybody a sixpence."

"Rather mean to borrow under those circumstances, I should say."

"You should say," repeated Drummle. "Oh Lord!"

This was so very aggravating—the more especially as I found myself making no way against his surly obtuseness—that I said, disregarding Herbert's efforts to check me,—

"Come, Mr. Drummle, since we are on the subject, I'll tell you what passed between Herbert here and me, when you borrowed that money."

"I don't want to know what passed between Herbert there and you," growled Drummle. And I think he added in a lower growl, that we might both go to the devil and shake ourselves.

"I'll tell you, however," said I, "whether you want to know or not. We said that as you put it in your pocket very glad to get it, you seemed to be immensely amused at his being so weak as to lend it."

Drummle laughed outright, and sat laughing in our faces, with his hands in his pockets and his round shoulders raised; plainly signifying that it was quite true, and that he despised us as asses all.

Hereupon Startop took him in hand, though with a much better grace than I had shown, and exhorted him to be a little more agreeable. Startop, being a lively, bright young fellow, and Drummle being the exact opposite, the latter was always disposed to resent him as a direct personal affront. He now retorted in a coarse, lumpish way, and Startop tried to turn the discussion aside with some small pleasantry that made us all laugh. Resenting this little success more than anything, Drummle, without any threat or warning, pulled his hands out of his pockets, dropped his round shoulders, swore, took up a large glass, and would have flung it at his adversary's head, but for our entertainer's dexterously seizing it at the instant when it was raised for that purpose.

"Gentlemen," said Mr. Jaggers, deliberately putting down the glass, and hauling out his gold repeater by its massive chain, "I am exceedingly sorry to announce that it's half past nine."

On this hint we all rose to depart. Before we got to the street door, Startop was cheerily calling Drummle "old boy," as if nothing had happened. But the old boy was so far from responding, that he would not even walk to Hammersmith on the same side of the way; so Herbert and I, who remained in town, saw them going down the street on opposite sides; Startop leading, and Drummle lagging behind in the shadow of the houses, much as he was wont to follow in his boat.

As the door was not yet shut, I thought I would leave Herbert there for a moment, and run up stairs again to say a word to my guardian. I found him in his dressing-room surrounded by his stock of boots, already hard at it, washing his hands of us.

I told him I had come up again to say how sorry I was that anything disagreeable should have occurred, and that I hoped he would not blame me much.

"Pooh!" said he, sluicing his face, and speaking through the water-drops; "it's nothing, Pip. I like that Spider though."

He had turned towards me now, and was shaking his head, and blowing, and towelling himself.

"I am glad you like him, sir," said I—"but I don't."

"No, no," my guardian assented; "don't have too much to do with him. Keep as clear of him as you can. But I like the fellow, Pip; he is one of the true sort. Why, if I was a fortune-teller—"

Looking out of the towel, he caught my eye.

"But I am not a fortune-teller," he said, letting his head drop into a festoon of towel, and towelling away at his two ears. "You know what I am, don't you? Good night, Pip."

"Good night, sir."

In about a month after that, the Spider's time with Mr. Pocket was up for good, and, to the great relief of all the house but Mrs. Pocket, he went home to the family hole.

CHAPTER XXVII

"MY DEAR MR PIP:—

"I write this by request of Mr. Gargery, for to let you know that he is going to London in company with Mr. Wopsle and would be glad if agreeable to be allowed to see you. He would call at Barnard's Hotel Tuesday morning at nine o'clock, when if not agreeable please leave word. Your poor sister is much the same as when you left. We talk of you in the kitchen every night, and wonder what you are saying and doing. If now considered in the light of a liberty, excuse it for the love of poor old days. No more, dear Mr. Pip, from your ever obliged, and affectionate servant,

"BIDDY."

"P.S. He wishes me most particular to write what larks. He says you will understand. I hope and do not doubt it will be agreeable to see him, even though a gentleman, for you had ever a good heart, and he is a worthy, worthy man. I have read him all, excepting only the last little sentence, and he wishes me most particular to write again what larks."

I received this letter by the post on Monday morning, and therefore its appointment was for next day. Let me confess exactly with what feelings I looked forward to Joe's coming.

Not with pleasure, though I was bound to him by so many ties; no; with considerable disturbance, some mortification, and a keen sense of incongruity. If I could have kept him away by paying money, I certainly would have paid money. My greatest reassurance was that he was coming to Barnard's Inn, not to Hammersmith, and consequently would not fall in Bentley Drummle's way. I had little objection to his being seen by Herbert or his father, for both of whom I had a respect; but I had the sharpest sensitiveness as to his being seen by Drummle, whom I held in contempt. So, throughout life, our worst weaknesses and meannesses are usually committed for the sake of the people whom we most despise.

I had begun to be always decorating the chambers in some quite unnecessary and inappropriate way or other, and very expensive those wrestles with Barnard proved to be. By this time, the rooms were vastly different from what I had found them, and I enjoyed the honour of occupying a few prominent pages in the books of a neighboring upholsterer. I had got on so fast of late, that I had even started a boy in boots,—top boots,—in bondage and slavery to whom I might have been said to pass my days. For, after I had made the monster (out of the refuse of my washerwoman's family), and had clothed him with a blue coat, canary waistcoat, white cravat, creamy breeches, and the boots already mentioned, I had to find him a little to do and a great deal to eat; and with both of those horrible requirements he haunted my existence.

This avenging phantom was ordered to be on duty at eight on Tuesday morning in the hall, (it was two feet square, as charged for floorcloth,) and Herbert suggested certain things for breakfast that he thought Joe would like. While I felt sincerely obliged to him for being so interested and considerate, I had an odd half-provoked sense of suspicion upon me, that if Joe had been coming to see him, he wouldn't have been quite so brisk about it.

However, I came into town on the Monday night to be ready for Joe, and I got up early in the morning, and caused the sitting-room and breakfast-table to assume their most splendid appearance. Unfortunately the morning was drizzly, and an angel could not have concealed the fact that Barnard was shedding sooty tears outside the window, like some weak giant of a Sweep.

As the time approached I should have liked to run away, but the Avenger pursuant to orders was in the hall, and presently I heard Joe on the staircase. I knew it was Joe, by his clumsy manner of coming up stairs,—his state boots being always too big for him,—and by the time it took him to read the names on the other floors in the course of his ascent. When at last he stopped outside our door, I could hear his finger tracing over the painted letters of my name, and I afterwards distinctly heard him breathing in at the keyhole. Finally he gave a faint single rap, and Pepper—such was the compromising name of the avenging boy—announced "Mr. Gargery!" I thought he never would have done wiping his feet, and that I must have gone out to lift him off the mat, but at last he came in.

"Joe, how are you, Joe?"

"Pip, how AIR you, Pip?"

With his good honest face all glowing and shining, and his hat put down on the floor between us, he caught both my hands and worked them straight up and down, as if I had been the last-patented Pump.

"I am glad to see you, Joe. Give me your hat."

But Joe, taking it up carefully with both hands, like a bird's-nest with eggs in it, wouldn't hear of parting with that piece of property, and persisted in standing talking over it in a most uncomfortable way.

"Which you have that growed," said Joe, "and that swelled, and that gentle-folked;" Joe considered a little before he discovered this word; "as to be sure you are a honor to your king and country."

"And you, Joe, look wonderfully well."

"Thank God," said Joe, "I'm ekerval to most. And your sister, she's no worse than she were. And Biddy, she's ever right and ready. And all friends is no backerder, if not no forarder. 'Ceptin Wopsle; he's had a drop."

All this time (still with both hands taking great care of the bird's-nest), Joe was rolling his eyes round and round the room, and round and round the flowered pattern of my dressing-gown.

"Had a drop, Joe?"

"Why yes," said Joe, lowering his voice, "he's left the Church and went into the playacting. Which the playacting have likeways brought him to London along with me. And his wish were," said Joe, getting the bird's-nest under his left arm for the moment, and groping in it for an egg with his right; "if no offence, as I would 'and you that."

I took what Joe gave me, and found it to be the crumpled play-bill of a small metropolitan theatre, announcing the first appearance, in that very week, of "the celebrated Provincial Amateur of Roscian renown, whose unique performance in the highest tragic walk of our National Bard has lately occasioned so great a sensation in local dramatic circles."

"Were you at his performance, Joe?" I inquired.

"I were," said Joe, with emphasis and solemnity.

"Was there a great sensation?"

"Why," said Joe, "yes, there certainly were a peck of orange-peel. Partickler when he see the ghost. Though I put it to yourself, sir, whether it were calc'lated to keep a man up to his work with a good hart, to be continiwally cutting in betwixt him and the Ghost with 'Amen!' A man may have had a misfortun' and been in the Church," said Joe, lowering his voice to an argumentative and feeling tone, "but that is no reason why you should put him out at such a time. Which I meantersay, if the ghost of a man's own father cannot be allowed to claim his attention, what can, Sir? Still more, when his mourning 'at is unfortunately made so small as that the weight of the black feathers brings it off, try to keep it on how you may."

A ghost-seeing effect in Joe's own countenance informed me that Herbert had entered the room. So, I presented Joe to Herbert, who held out his hand; but Joe backed from it, and held on by the bird's-nest.

"Your servant, Sir," said Joe, "which I hope as you and Pip"—here his eye fell on the Avenger, who was putting some toast on table, and so plainly denoted an intention to make that young gentleman one of the family, that I frowned it down and confused him more—"I meantersay, you two gentlemen,—which I hope as you get your elths in this close spot? For the present may be a werry good inn, according to London opinions," said Joe, confidentially, "and I believe its character do stand but I wouldn't keep a pig in it myself,—not in the case that I wished him to fatten wholesome and to eat with a meller flavor on him."

Having borne this flattering testimony to the merits of our dwelling-place, and having incidentally shown this tendency to call me "sir," Joe, being invited to sit down to table, looked all round the room for a suitable spot on which to deposit his hat,—as if it were only on some very few rare substances in nature that it could find a resting place,—and ultimately stood it on an extreme corner of the chimney-piece, from which it ever afterwards fell off at intervals.

"Do you take tea, or coffee, Mr. Gargery?" asked Herbert, who always presided of a morning.

"Thankee, Sir," said Joe, stiff from head to foot, "I'll take whichever is most agreeable to yourself."

"What do you say to coffee?"

"Thankee, Sir," returned Joe, evidently dispirited by the proposal, "since you are so kind as make chice of coffee, I will not run contrairy to your own opinions. But don't you never find it a little 'eating?"

"Say tea then," said Herbert, pouring it out.

Here Joe's hat tumbled off the mantel-piece, and he started out of his chair and picked it up, and fitted it to the same exact spot. As if it were an absolute point of good breeding that it should tumble off again soon.

"When did you come to town, Mr. Gargery?"

"Were it yesterday afternoon?" said Joe, after coughing behind his hand, as if he had had time to catch the whooping-cough since he came. "No it were not. Yes it were. Yes. It were yesterday afternoon" (with an appearance of mingled wisdom, relief, and strict impartiality).

"Have you seen anything of London yet?"

"Why, yes, Sir," said Joe, "me and Wopsle went off straight to look at the Blacking Ware'us. But we didn't find that it come up to its likeness in the red bills at the shop doors; which I meantersay," added Joe, in an explanatory manner, "as it is there drawd too architectooralooral."

I really believe Joe would have prolonged this word (mightily expressive to my mind of some architecture that I know) into a perfect Chorus, but for his attention being providentially attracted by his hat, which was toppling. Indeed, it demanded from him a constant attention, and a quickness of eye and hand, very like that exacted by wicket-keeping. He made extraordinary play with it, and showed the greatest skill; now, rushing at it and catching it neatly as it dropped; now, merely stopping it midway, beating it up, and humoring it in various parts of the room and against a good deal of the pattern of the paper on the wall, before he felt it safe to close with it; finally splashing it into the slop-basin, where I took the liberty of laying hands upon it.

As to his shirt-collar, and his coat-collar, they were perplexing to reflect upon,— insoluble mysteries both. Why should a man scrape himself to that extent, before he could consider himself full dressed? Why should he suppose it necessary to be purified by suffering for his holiday clothes? Then he fell into such unaccountable fits of meditation, with his fork midway between his plate and his mouth; had his eyes attracted in such strange directions; was afflicted with such remarkable coughs; sat so far from the table, and dropped so much more than he ate, and pretended that he hadn't dropped it; that I was heartily glad when Herbert left us for the City.

I had neither the good sense nor the good feeling to know that this was all my fault, and that if I had been easier with Joe, Joe would have been easier with me. I felt impatient of him and out of temper with him; in which condition he heaped coals of fire on my head.

"Us two being now alone, sir,"—began Joe.

"Joe," I interrupted, pettishly, "how can you call me, sir?"

Joe looked at me for a single instant with something faintly like reproach. Utterly preposterous as his cravat was, and as his collars were, I was conscious of a sort of dignity in the look.

"Us two being now alone," resumed Joe, "and me having the intentions and abilities to stay not many minutes more, I will now conclude—leastways begin—to mention what have led to my having had the present honour. For was it not," said Joe, with his old air of lucid exposition, "that my only wish were to be useful to you, I should not have had the honor of breaking wittles in the company and abode of gentlemen."

I was so unwilling to see the look again, that I made no remonstrance against this tone.

"Well, sir," pursued Joe, "this is how it were. I were at the Bargemen t'other night, Pip;"—whenever he subsided into affection, he called me Pip, and whenever he relapsed into politeness he called me sir; "when there come up in his shay-cart,

Pumblechook. Which that same identical," said Joe, going down a new track, "do comb my 'air the wrong way sometimes, awful, by giving out up and down town as it were him which ever had your infant companionation and were looked upon as a playfellow by yourself."

"Nonsense. It was you, Joe."

"Which I fully believed it were, Pip," said Joe, slightly tossing his head, "though it signify little now, sir. Well, Pip; this same identical, which his manners is given to blusterous, come to me at the Bargemen (wot a pipe and a pint of beer do give refreshment to the workingman, sir, and do not over stimilate), and his word were, 'Joseph, Miss Havisham she wish to speak to you.'"

"Miss Havisham, Joe?"

"'She wish,' were Pumblechook's word, 'to speak to you.'" Joe sat and rolled his eyes at the ceiling.

"Yes, Joe? Go on, please."

"Next day, sir," said Joe, looking at me as if I were a long way off, "having cleaned myself, I go and I see Miss A."

"Miss A., Joe? Miss Havisham?"

"Which I say, sir," replied Joe, with an air of legal formality, as if he were making his will, "Miss A., or otherways Havisham. Her expression air then as follering: 'Mr. Gargery. You air in correspondence with Mr. Pip?' Having had a letter from you, I were able to say 'I am.' (When I married your sister, sir, I said 'I will;' and when I answered your friend, Pip, I said 'I am.') 'Would you tell him, then,' said she, 'that which Estella has come home and would be glad to see him.'"

I felt my face fire up as I looked at Joe. I hope one remote cause of its firing may have been my consciousness that if I had known his errand, I should have given him more encouragement.

"Biddy," pursued Joe, "when I got home and asked her fur to write the message to you, a little hung back. Biddy says, 'I know he will be very glad to have it by word of mouth, it is holiday time, you want to see him, go!' I have now concluded, sir," said Joe, rising from his chair, "and, Pip, I wish you ever well and ever prospering to a greater and a greater height."

"But you are not going now, Joe?"

"Yes I am," said Joe.

"But you are coming back to dinner, Joe?"

"No I am not," said Joe.

Our eyes met, and all the "ir" melted out of that manly heart as he gave me his hand.

"Pip, dear old chap, life is made of ever so many partings welded together, as I may say, and one man's a blacksmith, and one's a whitesmith, and one's a goldsmith, and one's a coppersmith. Diwisions among such must come, and must be met as they come. If there's been any fault at all to-day, it's mine. You and me is not two figures to be together in London; nor yet anywheres else but what is private, and beknown, and understood among friends. It ain't that I am proud, but that I want to be right, as you shall never see me no more in these clothes. I'm wrong in these clothes. I'm wrong out of the forge, the kitchen, or off th' meshes. You won't find half so much fault in me if you think of me in my forge dress, with my hammer in my hand, or even my pipe. You won't find half so much fault in me if, supposing as you should ever wish to see me, you come and put your head in at the forge window and see Joe the blacksmith, there, at the old anvil, in the old burnt apron, sticking to the old work. I'm awful dull, but I hope I've beat out something nigh the rights of this at last. And so GOD bless you, dear old Pip, old chap, GOD bless you!"

I had not been mistaken in my fancy that there was a simple dignity in him. The fashion of his dress could no more come in its way when he spoke these words than it could come in its way in Heaven. He touched me gently on the forehead, and went out. As soon as I could recover myself sufficiently, I hurried out after him and looked for him in the neighboring streets; but he was gone.

CHAPTER XXVIII

It was clear that I must repair to our town next day, and in the first flow of my repentance, it was equally clear that I must stay at Joe's. But, when I had secured my box-place by to-morrow's coach, and had been down to Mr. Pocket's and back, I was not by any means convinced on the last point, and began to invent reasons and make excuses for putting up at the Blue Boar. I should be an inconvenience at Joe's; I was not expected, and my bed would not be ready; I should be too far from Miss Havisham's, and she was exacting and mightn't like it. All other swindlers upon earth are nothing to the self-swindlers, and with such pretences did I cheat myself. Surely a curious thing. That I should innocently take a bad half-crown of somebody else's manufacture is reasonable enough; but that I should knowingly reckon the spurious coin of my own make as good money! An obliging stranger, under pretence of compactly folding up my bank-notes for security's sake, abstracts the notes and gives me nutshells; but what is his sleight of hand to mine, when I fold up my own nutshells and pass them on myself as notes!

Having settled that I must go to the Blue Boar, my mind was much disturbed by indecision whether or not to take the Avenger. It was tempting to think of that expensive Mercenary publicly airing his boots in the archway of the Blue Boar's posting-yard; it was almost solemn to imagine him casually produced in the tailor's shop, and confounding the disrespectful senses of Trabb's boy. On the other hand, Trabb's boy might worm himself into his intimacy and tell him things; or, reckless and desperate wretch as I knew he could be, might hoot him in the High Street, My patroness, too, might hear of him, and not approve. On the whole, I resolved to leave the Avenger behind.

It was the afternoon coach by which I had taken my place, and, as winter had now come round, I should not arrive at my destination until two or three hours after dark. Our time of starting from the Cross Keys was two o'clock. I arrived on the ground with a quarter of an hour to spare, attended by the Avenger,—if I may connect that expression with one who never attended on me if he could possibly help it.

At that time it was customary to carry Convicts down to the dock-yards by stage-coach. As I had often heard of them in the capacity of outside passengers, and had more than once seen them on the high road dangling their ironed legs over the coach roof, I had no cause to be surprised when Herbert, meeting me in the yard, came up and told me there were two convicts going down with me. But I had a reason that was an old reason now for constitutionally faltering whenever I heard the word "convict."

"You don't mind them, Handel?" said Herbert.

"O no!"

"I thought you seemed as if you didn't like them?"

"I can't pretend that I do like them, and I suppose you don't particularly. But I don't mind them."

"See! There they are," said Herbert, "coming out of the Tap. What a degraded and vile sight it is!"

They had been treating their guard, I suppose, for they had a gaoler with them, and all three came out wiping their mouths on their hands. The two convicts were handcuffed together, and had irons on their legs,—irons of a pattern that I knew well. They wore the dress that I likewise knew well. Their keeper had a brace of pistols, and carried a thick-knobbed bludgeon under his arm; but he was on terms of good understanding with them, and stood with them beside him, looking on at the putting-to of the horses, rather with an air as if the convicts were an interesting Exhibition not formally open at the moment, and he the Curator. One was a taller and stouter man than the other, and appeared as a matter of course, according to the mysterious ways of the world, both convict and free, to have had allotted to him the smaller suit of clothes. His arms and legs were like great pincushions of those shapes, and his attire disguised him absurdly; but I knew his half-closed eye at one glance. There stood the man whom I had seen on the settle at the Three Jolly Bargemen on a Saturday night, and who had brought me down with his invisible gun!

It was easy to make sure that as yet he knew me no more than if he had never seen me in his life. He looked across at me, and his eye appraised my watch-chain, and then he incidentally spat and said something to the other convict, and they laughed and slued themselves round with a clink of their coupling manacle, and looked at something else. The great numbers on their backs, as if they were street doors; their coarse mangy ungainly outer surface, as if they were lower animals; their ironed legs, apologetically garlanded with pocket-handkerchiefs; and the way in which all present looked at them and kept from them; made them (as Herbert had said) a most disagreeable and degraded spectacle.

But this was not the worst of it. It came out that the whole of the back of the coach had been taken by a family removing from London, and that there were no places for the two prisoners but on the seat in front behind the coachman. Hereupon, a choleric gentleman, who had taken the fourth place on that seat, flew into a most violent passion, and said that it was a breach of contract to mix him up with such villainous company, and that it was poisonous, and pernicious, and infamous, and shameful, and I don't know what else. At this time the coach was ready and the coachman impatient, and we were all preparing to get up, and the prisoners had come over with their keeper,—bringing with them that curious flavor of bread-poultice, baize, rope-yarn, and hearthstone, which attends the convict presence.

"Don't take it so much amiss, sir," pleaded the keeper to the angry passenger; "I'll sit next you myself. I'll put 'em on the outside of the row. They won't interfere with you, sir. You needn't know they're there."

"And don't blame me," growled the convict I had recognised. "I don't want to go. I am quite ready to stay behind. As fur as I am concerned any one's welcome to my place."

"Or mine," said the other, gruffly. "I wouldn't have incommoded none of you, if I'd had my way." Then they both laughed, and began cracking nuts, and spitting the shells about.—As I really think I should have liked to do myself, if I had been in their place and so despised.

At length, it was voted that there was no help for the angry gentleman, and that he must either go in his chance company or remain behind. So he got into his place, still making complaints, and the keeper got into the place next him, and the convicts hauled themselves up as well as they could, and the convict I had recognised sat behind me with his breath on the hair of my head.

"Good by, Handel!" Herbert called out as we started. I thought what a blessed fortune it was, that he had found another name for me than Pip.

It is impossible to express with what acuteness I felt the convict's breathing, not only on the back of my head, but all along my spine. The sensation was like being touched in the marrow with some pungent and searching acid, it set my very teeth on edge. He seemed to have more breathing business to do than another man, and to make more noise in doing it; and I was conscious of growing high-shouldered on one side, in my shrinking endeavors to fend him off.

The weather was miserably raw, and the two cursed the cold. It made us all lethargic before we had gone far, and when we had left the Half-way House behind, we habitually dozed and shivered and were silent. I dozed off, myself, in considering the question whether I ought to restore a couple of pounds sterling to this creature before losing sight of him, and how it could best be done. In the act of dipping forward as if I were going to bathe among the horses, I woke in a fright and took the question up again.

But I must have lost it longer than I had thought, since, although I could recognize nothing in the darkness and the fitful lights and shadows of our lamps, I traced marsh country in the cold damp wind that blew at us. Cowering forward for warmth and to make me a screen against the wind, the convicts were closer to me than before. The very first words I heard them interchange as I became conscious, were the words of my own thought, "Two One Pound notes."

"How did he get 'em?" said the convict I had never seen.

"How should I know?" returned the other. "He had 'em stowed away somehows. Giv him by friends, I expect."

"I wish," said the other, with a bitter curse upon the cold, "that I had 'em here."

"Two one pound notes, or friends?"

"Two one pound notes. I'd sell all the friends I ever had for one, and think it a blessed good bargain. Well? So he says—?"

"So he says," resumed the convict I had recognised,—"it was all said and done in half a minute, behind a pile of timber in the Dock-yard,—'You're a going to be discharged?' Yes, I was. Would I find out that boy that had fed him and kep his secret, and give him them two one pound notes? Yes, I would. And I did."

"More fool you," growled the other. "I'd have spent 'em on a Man, in wittles and drink. He must have been a green one. Mean to say he knowed nothing of you?"

"Not a ha'porth. Different gangs and different ships. He was tried again for prison breaking, and got made a Lifer."

"And was that—Honor!—the only time you worked out, in this part of the country?"

"The only time."

"What might have been your opinion of the place?"

"A most beastly place. Mudbank, mist, swamp, and work; work, swamp, mist, and mudbank."

They both execrated the place in very strong language, and gradually growled themselves out, and had nothing left to say.

After overhearing this dialogue, I should assuredly have got down and been left in the solitude and darkness of the highway, but for feeling certain that the man had no suspicion of my identity. Indeed, I was not only so changed in the course of nature, but so differently dressed and so differently circumstanced, that it was not at all likely he could have known me without accidental help. Still, the coincidence of our being together on the coach, was sufficiently strange to fill me with a dread that some other coincidence might at any moment connect me, in his hearing, with my name. For this reason, I resolved to alight as soon as we touched the town, and put myself out of his hearing. This device I executed successfully. My little portmanteau was in the boot under my feet; I had but to turn a hinge to get it out; I threw it down before me, got down after it, and was left at the first lamp on the first stones of the town pavement. As to the convicts, they went their way with the coach, and I knew at what point they would be spirited off to the river. In my fancy, I saw the boat with its convict crew waiting for them at the slime-washed stairs,—again heard the gruff "Give way, you!" like and order to dogs,—again saw the wicked Noah's Ark lying out on the black water.

I could not have said what I was afraid of, for my fear was altogether undefined and vague, but there was great fear upon me. As I walked on to the hotel, I felt that a dread, much exceeding the mere apprehension of a painful or disagreeable recognition, made me tremble. I am confident that it took no distinctness of shape, and that it was the revival for a few minutes of the terror of childhood.

The coffee-room at the Blue Boar was empty, and I had not only ordered my dinner there, but had sat down to it, before the waiter knew me. As soon as he had apologized for the remissness of his memory, he asked me if he should send Boots for Mr. Pumblechook?

"No," said I, "certainly not."

The waiter (it was he who had brought up the Great Remonstrance from the Commercials, on the day when I was bound) appeared surprised, and took the earliest opportunity of putting a dirty old copy of a local newspaper so directly in my way, that I took it up and read this paragraph:—

Our readers will learn, not altogether without interest, in reference to the recent romantic rise in fortune of a young artificer in iron of this neighbourhood (what a theme, by the way, for the magic pen of our as yet not universally acknowledged townsman TOOBY, the poet of our columns!) that the youth's earliest patron, companion, and friend, was a highly respected individual not entirely unconnected with the corn and seed trade, and whose eminently convenient and commodious business premises are situate within a hundred miles of the High Street. It is not wholly irrespective of our personal feelings that we record HIM as the Mentor of our young Telemachus, for it is good to know that our town produced the founder of the latter's fortunes. Does the thought-contracted brow of the local Sage or the lustrous eye of local Beauty inquire whose fortunes? We believe that Quintin Matsys was the BLACKSMITH of Antwerp. VERB. SAP.

I entertain a conviction, based upon large experience, that if in the days of my prosperity I had gone to the North Pole, I should have met somebody there, wandering Esquimaux or civilized man, who would have told me that Pumblechook was my earliest patron and the founder of my fortunes.

CHAPTER XXIX

Betimes in the morning I was up and out. It was too early yet to go to Miss Havisham's, so I loitered into the country on Miss Havisham's side of town,—which was not Joe's side; I could go there to-morrow,—thinking about my patroness, and painting brilliant pictures of her plans for me.

She had adopted Estella, she had as good as adopted me, and it could not fail to be her intention to bring us together. She reserved it for me to restore the desolate house, admit the sunshine into the dark rooms, set the clocks a-going and the cold hearths a-blazing, tear down the cobwebs, destroy the vermin,—in short, do all the shining deeds of the young Knight of romance, and marry the Princess. I had stopped to look at the house as I passed; and its seared red brick walls, blocked windows, and strong green ivy clasping even the stacks of chimneys with its twigs and tendons, as if with sinewy old arms, had made up a rich attractive mystery, of which I was the hero. Estella was the inspiration of it, and the heart of it, of course. But, though she had taken such strong possession of me, though my fancy and my hope were so set upon her, though her influence on my boyish life and character had been all-powerful, I did not, even that romantic morning, invest her with any attributes save those she possessed. I mention this in this place, of a fixed purpose, because it is the clew by which I am to be followed into my poor labyrinth. According to my experience, the conventional notion of a lover cannot be always true. The unqualified truth is, that when I loved Estella with the love of a man, I loved her simply because I found her irresistible. Once for all; I knew to my sorrow, often and often, if not always, that I loved her against reason, against promise, against peace, against hope, against happiness, against all discouragement that could be. Once for all; I loved her none the less because I knew it, and it had no more influence in restraining me than if I had devoutly believed her to be human perfection.

I so shaped out my walk as to arrive at the gate at my old time. When I had rung at the bell with an unsteady hand, I turned my back upon the gate, while I tried to get my breath and keep the beating of my heart moderately quiet. I heard the side-door open, and steps come across the courtyard; but I pretended not to hear, even when the gate swung on its rusty hinges.

Being at last touched on the shoulder, I started and turned. I started much more naturally then, to find myself confronted by a man in a sober gray dress. The last man I should have expected to see in that place of porter at Miss Havisham's door.

"Orlick!"

"Ah, young master, there's more changes than yours. But come in, come in. It's opposed to my orders to hold the gate open."

I entered and he swung it, and locked it, and took the key out. "Yes!" said he, facing round, after doggedly preceding me a few steps towards the house. "Here I am!"

"How did you come here?"

"I come here," he retorted, "on my legs. I had my box brought alongside me in a barrow."

"Are you here for good?"

"I ain't here for harm, young master, I suppose."

I was not so sure of that. I had leisure to entertain the retort in my mind, while he slowly lifted his heavy glance from the pavement, up my legs and arms, to my face.

"Then you have left the forge?" I said.

"Do this look like a forge?" replied Orlick, sending his glance all round him with an air of injury. "Now, do it look like it?"

I asked him how long he had left Gargery's forge?

"One day is so like another here," he replied, "that I don't know without casting it up. However, I come here some time since you left."

"I could have told you that, Orlick."

"Ah!" said he, dryly. "But then you've got to be a scholar."

By this time we had come to the house, where I found his room to be one just within the side-door, with a little window in it looking on the courtyard. In its small proportions, it was not unlike the kind of place usually assigned to a gate-porter in Paris. Certain keys were hanging on the wall, to which he now added the gate key; and his patchwork-covered bed was in a little inner division or recess. The whole had a slovenly, confined, and sleepy look, like a cage for a human dormouse; while he, looming dark and heavy in the shadow of a corner by the window, looked like the human dormouse for whom it was fitted up,—as indeed he was.

"I never saw this room before," I remarked; "but there used to be no Porter here."

"No," said he; "not till it got about that there was no protection on the premises, and it come to be considered dangerous, with convicts and Tag and Rag and Bobtail going up and down. And then I was recommended to the place as a man who could give another man as good as he brought, and I took it. It's easier than bellowsing and hammering.—That's loaded, that is."

My eye had been caught by a gun with a brass-bound stock over the chimney-piece, and his eye had followed mine.

"Well," said I, not desirous of more conversation, "shall I go up to Miss Havisham?"

"Burn me, if I know!" he retorted, first stretching himself and then shaking himself; "my orders ends here, young master. I give this here bell a rap with this here hammer, and you go on along the passage till you meet somebody."

"I am expected, I believe?"

"Burn me twice over, if I can say!" said he.

Upon that, I turned down the long passage which I had first trodden in my thick boots, and he made his bell sound. At the end of the passage, while the bell was still reverberating, I found Sarah Pocket, who appeared to have now become constitutionally green and yellow by reason of me.

"Oh!" said she. "You, is it, Mr. Pip?"

"It is, Miss Pocket. I am glad to tell you that Mr. Pocket and family are all well."

"Are they any wiser?" said Sarah, with a dismal shake of the head; "they had better be wiser, than well. Ah, Matthew, Matthew! You know your way, sir?"

Tolerably, for I had gone up the staircase in the dark, many a time. I ascended it now, in lighter boots than of yore, and tapped in my old way at the door of Miss Havisham's room. "Pip's rap," I heard her say, immediately; "come in, Pip."

She was in her chair near the old table, in the old dress, with her two hands crossed on her stick, her chin resting on them, and her eyes on the fire. Sitting near her, with the white shoe, that had never been worn, in her hand, and her head bent as she looked at it, was an elegant lady whom I had never seen.

"Come in, Pip," Miss Havisham continued to mutter, without looking round or up; "come in, Pip, how do you do, Pip? so you kiss my hand as if I were a queen, eh?—Well?"

She looked up at me suddenly, only moving her eyes, and repeated in a grimly playful manner,—

"Well?"

"I heard, Miss Havisham," said I, rather at a loss, "that you were so kind as to wish me to come and see you, and I came directly."

"Well?"

The lady whom I had never seen before, lifted up her eyes and looked archly at me, and then I saw that the eyes were Estella's eyes. But she was so much changed, was so much more beautiful, so much more womanly, in all things winning admiration, had made such wonderful advance, that I seemed to have made none. I fancied, as I looked at her, that I slipped hopelessly back into the coarse and common boy again. O the sense of distance and disparity that came upon me, and the inaccessibility that came about her!

She gave me her hand. I stammered something about the pleasure I felt in seeing her again, and about my having looked forward to it, for a long, long time.

"Do you find her much changed, Pip?" asked Miss Havisham, with her greedy look, and striking her stick upon a chair that stood between them, as a sign to me to sit down there.

"When I came in, Miss Havisham, I thought there was nothing of Estella in the face or figure; but now it all settles down so curiously into the old—"

"What? You are not going to say into the old Estella?" Miss Havisham interrupted. "She was proud and insulting, and you wanted to go away from her. Don't you remember?"

I said confusedly that that was long ago, and that I knew no better then, and the like. Estella smiled with perfect composure, and said she had no doubt of my having been quite right, and of her having been very disagreeable.

"Is he changed?" Miss Havisham asked her.

"Very much," said Estella, looking at me.

"Less coarse and common?" said Miss Havisham, playing with Estella's hair.

Estella laughed, and looked at the shoe in her hand, and laughed again, and looked at me, and put the shoe down. She treated me as a boy still, but she lured me on.

We sat in the dreamy room among the old strange influences which had so wrought upon me, and I learnt that she had but just come home from France, and that she was going to London. Proud and wilful as of old, she had brought those qualities into such subjection to her beauty that it was impossible and out of nature—or I thought so—to separate them from her beauty. Truly it was impossible to dissociate her presence from all those wretched hankerings after money and gentility that had disturbed my boyhood,—from all those ill-regulated aspirations that had first made me ashamed of home and Joe,—from all those visions that had raised her face in the glowing fire, struck it out of the iron on the anvil, extracted it from the darkness of night to look in at the wooden window of the forge, and flit away. In a word, it was impossible for me to separate her, in the past or in the present, from the innermost life of my life.

It was settled that I should stay there all the rest of the day, and return to the hotel at night, and to London to-morrow. When we had conversed for a while, Miss Havisham sent us two out to walk in the neglected garden: on our coming in by and by, she said, I should wheel her about a little, as in times of yore.

So, Estella and I went out into the garden by the gate through which I had strayed to my encounter with the pale young gentleman, now Herbert; I, trembling in spirit and worshipping the very hem of her dress; she, quite composed and most decidedly not worshipping the hem of mine. As we drew near to the place of encounter, she stopped and said,—

"I must have been a singular little creature to hide and see that fight that day; but I did, and I enjoyed it very much."

"You rewarded me very much."

"Did I?" she replied, in an incidental and forgetful way. "I remember I entertained a great objection to your adversary, because I took it ill that he should be brought here to pester me with his company."

"He and I are great friends now."

"Are you? I think I recollect though, that you read with his father?"

"Yes."

I made the admission with reluctance, for it seemed to have a boyish look, and she already treated me more than enough like a boy.

"Since your change of fortune and prospects, you have changed your companions," said Estella.

"Naturally," said I.

"And necessarily," she added, in a haughty tone; "what was fit company for you once, would be quite unfit company for you now."

In my conscience, I doubt very much whether I had any lingering intention left of going to see Joe; but if I had, this observation put it to flight.

"You had no idea of your impending good fortune, in those times?" said Estella, with a slight wave of her hand, signifying in the fighting times.

"Not the least."

The air of completeness and superiourity with which she walked at my side, and the air of youthfulness and submission with which I walked at hers, made a contrast that I strongly felt. It would have rankled in me more than it did, if I had not regarded myself as eliciting it by being so set apart for her and assigned to her.

The garden was too overgrown and rank for walking in with ease, and after we had made the round of it twice or thrice, we came out again into the brewery yard. I showed her to a nicety where I had seen her walking on the casks, that first old day, and she said, with a cold and careless look in that direction, "Did I?" I reminded her where she had come out of the house and given me my meat and drink, and she said, "I don't remember." "Not remember that you made me cry?" said I. "No," said she, and shook her head and looked about her. I verily believe that her not remembering and not minding in the least, made me cry again, inwardly,—and that is the sharpest crying of all.

"You must know," said Estella, condescending to me as a brilliant and beautiful woman might, "that I have no heart,—if that has anything to do with my memory."

I got through some jargon to the effect that I took the liberty of doubting that. That I knew better. That there could be no such beauty without it.

"Oh! I have a heart to be stabbed in or shot in, I have no doubt," said Estella, "and of course if it ceased to beat I should cease to be. But you know what I mean. I have no softness there, no—sympathy—sentiment—nonsense."

What was it that was borne in upon my mind when she stood still and looked attentively at me? Anything that I had seen in Miss Havisham? No. In some of her looks and gestures there was that tinge of resemblance to Miss Havisham which may often be noticed to have been acquired by children, from grown person with whom they have been much associated and secluded, and which, when childhood is passed, will produce a remarkable occasional likeness of expression between faces that are otherwise quite different. And yet I could not trace this to Miss Havisham. I looked again, and though she was still looking at me, the suggestion was gone.

What was it?

"I am serious," said Estella, not so much with a frown (for her brow was smooth) as with a darkening of her face; "if we are to be thrown much together, you had better believe it at once. No!" imperiously stopping me as I opened my lips. "I have not bestowed my tenderness anywhere. I have never had any such thing."

In another moment we were in the brewery, so long disused, and she pointed to the high gallery where I had seen her going out on that same first day, and told me she remembered to have been up there, and to have seen me standing scared below. As my eyes followed her white hand, again the same dim suggestion that I could not possibly grasp crossed me. My involuntary start occasioned her to lay her hand upon my arm. Instantly the ghost passed once more and was gone.

What was it?

"What is the matter?" asked Estella. "Are you scared again?"

"I should be, if I believed what you said just now," I replied, to turn it off.

"Then you don't? Very well. It is said, at any rate. Miss Havisham will soon be expecting you at your old post, though I think that might be laid aside now, with other old belongings. Let us make one more round of the garden, and then go in. Come! You shall not shed tears for my cruelty to-day; you shall be my Page, and give me your shoulder."

Her handsome dress had trailed upon the ground. She held it in one hand now, and with the other lightly touched my shoulder as we walked. We walked round the ruined garden twice or thrice more, and it was all in bloom for me. If the green and yellow growth of weed in the chinks of the old wall had been the most precious flowers that ever blew, it could not have been more cherished in my remembrance.

There was no discrepancy of years between us to remove her far from me; we were of nearly the same age, though of course the age told for more in her case than in mine; but the air of inaccessibility which her beauty and her manner gave her, tormented me in the midst of my delight, and at the height of the assurance I felt that our patroness had chosen us for one another. Wretched boy!

At last we went back into the house, and there I heard, with surprise, that my guardian had come down to see Miss Havisham on business, and would come back to dinner. The old wintry branches of chandeliers in the room where the mouldering table was spread had been lighted while we were out, and Miss Havisham was in her chair and waiting for me.

It was like pushing the chair itself back into the past, when we began the old slow circuit round about the ashes of the bridal feast. But, in the funereal room, with that figure of the grave fallen back in the chair fixing its eyes upon her, Estella looked more bright and beautiful than before, and I was under stronger enchantment.

The time so melted away, that our early dinner-hour drew close at hand, and Estella left us to prepare herself. We had stopped near the centre of the long table, and Miss Havisham, with one of her withered arms stretched out of the chair, rested that clenched hand upon the yellow cloth. As Estella looked back over her shoulder before going out at the door, Miss Havisham kissed that hand to her, with a ravenous intensity that was of its kind quite dreadful.

Then, Estella being gone and we two left alone, she turned to me, and said in a whisper,—

"Is she beautiful, graceful, well-grown? Do you admire her?"

"Everybody must who sees her, Miss Havisham."

She drew an arm round my neck, and drew my head close down to hers as she sat in the chair. "Love her, love her, love her! How does she use you?"

Before I could answer (if I could have answered so difficult a question at all) she repeated, "Love her, love her, love her! If she favours you, love her. If she wounds you, love her. If she tears your heart to pieces,—and as it gets older and stronger it will tear deeper,—love her, love her, love her!"

Never had I seen such passionate eagerness as was joined to her utterance of these words. I could feel the muscles of the thin arm round my neck swell with the vehemence that possessed her.

"Hear me, Pip! I adopted her, to be loved. I bred her and educated her, to be loved. I developed her into what she is, that she might be loved. Love her!"

She said the word often enough, and there could be no doubt that she meant to say it; but if the often repeated word had been hate instead of love—despair—revenge— dire death—it could not have sounded from her lips more like a curse.

"I'll tell you," said she, in the same hurried passionate whisper, "what real love is. It is blind devotion, unquestioning self-humiliation, utter submission, trust and belief against yourself and against the whole world, giving up your whole heart and soul to the smiter—as I did!"

When she came to that, and to a wild cry that followed that, I caught her round the waist. For she rose up in the chair, in her shroud of a dress, and struck at the air as if she would as soon have struck herself against the wall and fallen dead.

All this passed in a few seconds. As I drew her down into her chair, I was conscious of a scent that I knew, and turning, saw my guardian in the room.

He always carried (I have not yet mentioned it, I think) a pocket-handkerchief of rich silk and of imposing proportions, which was of great value to him in his profession. I have seen him so terrify a client or a witness by ceremoniously unfolding this pocket-handkerchief as if he were immediately going to blow his nose, and then pausing, as if he knew he should not have time to do it before such client or witness committed himself, that the self-committal has followed directly, quite as a matter of course. When I saw him in the room he had this expressive pocket-handkerchief in both hands, and was looking at us. On meeting my eye, he said plainly, by a momentary and silent pause in that attitude, "Indeed? Singular!" and then put the handkerchief to its right use with wonderful effect.

Miss Havisham had seen him as soon as I, and was (like everybody else) afraid of him. She made a strong attempt to compose herself, and stammered that he was as punctual as ever.

"As punctual as ever," he repeated, coming up to us. "(How do you do, Pip? Shall I give you a ride, Miss Havisham? Once round?) And so you are here, Pip?"

I told him when I had arrived, and how Miss Havisham had wished me to come and see Estella. To which he replied, "Ah! Very fine young lady!" Then he pushed Miss Havisham in her chair before him, with one of his large hands, and put the other in his trousers-pocket as if the pocket were full of secrets.

"Well, Pip! How often have you seen Miss Estella before?" said he, when he came to a stop.

"How often?"

"Ah! How many times? Ten thousand times?"

"Oh! Certainly not so many."

"Twice?"

"Jaggers," interposed Miss Havisham, much to my relief, "leave my Pip alone, and go with him to your dinner."

He complied, and we groped our way down the dark stairs together. While we were still on our way to those detached apartments across the paved yard at the back, he asked me how often I had seen Miss Havisham eat and drink; offering me a breadth of choice, as usual, between a hundred times and once.

I considered, and said, "Never."

"And never will, Pip," he retorted, with a frowning smile. "She has never allowed herself to be seen doing either, since she lived this present life of hers. She wanders about in the night, and then lays hands on such food as she takes."

"Pray, sir," said I, "may I ask you a question?"

"You may," said he, "and I may decline to answer it. Put your question."

"Estella's name. Is it Havisham or—?" I had nothing to add.

"Or what?" said he.

"Is it Havisham?"

"It is Havisham."

This brought us to the dinner-table, where she and Sarah Pocket awaited us. Mr. Jaggers presided, Estella sat opposite to him, I faced my green and yellow friend. We dined very well, and were waited on by a maid-servant whom I had never seen in all my comings and goings, but who, for anything I know, had been in that mysterious house the whole time. After dinner a bottle of choice old port was placed before my guardian (he was evidently well acquainted with the vintage), and the two ladies left us.

Anything to equal the determined reticence of Mr. Jaggers under that roof I never saw elsewhere, even in him. He kept his very looks to himself, and scarcely directed his eyes to Estella's face once during dinner. When she spoke to him, he listened, and in due course answered, but never looked at her, that I could see. On the other hand, she often looked at him, with interest and curiosity, if not distrust, but his face never, showed the least consciousness. Throughout dinner he took a dry delight in making Sarah Pocket greener and yellower, by often referring in conversation with me to my expectations; but here, again, he showed no consciousness, and even made it appear that he extorted—and even did extort, though I don't know how—those references out of my innocent self.

And when he and I were left alone together, he sat with an air upon him of general lying by in consequence of information he possessed, that really was too much for me. He cross-examined his very wine when he had nothing else in hand. He held it between himself and the candle, tasted the port, rolled it in his mouth, swallowed it, looked at his glass again, smelt the port, tried it, drank it, filled again, and cross-examined the glass again, until I was as nervous as if I had known the wine to be telling him something to my disadvantage. Three or four times I feebly thought I would start conversation; but whenever he saw me going to ask him anything, he looked at me with his glass in his hand, and rolling his wine about in his mouth, as if requesting me to take notice that it was of no use, for he couldn't answer.

I think Miss Pocket was conscious that the sight of me involved her in the danger of being goaded to madness, and perhaps tearing off her cap,—which was a very hideous one, in the nature of a muslin mop,—and strewing the ground with her hair,—which assuredly had never grown on her head. She did not appear when we afterwards went up to Miss Havisham's room, and we four played at whist. In the interval, Miss Havisham, in a fantastic way, had put some of the most beautiful jewels from her dressing-table into Estella's hair, and about her bosom and arms; and I saw even my guardian look at her from under his thick eyebrows, and raise them a little, when her loveliness was before him, with those rich flushes of glitter and color in it.

Of the manner and extent to which he took our trumps into custody, and came out with mean little cards at the ends of hands, before which the glory of our Kings and Queens was utterly abased, I say nothing; nor, of the feeling that I had, respecting his looking upon us personally in the light of three very obvious and poor riddles that he had found out long ago. What I suffered from, was the incompatibility between his cold presence and my feelings towards Estella. It was not that I knew I could never bear to speak to him about her, that I knew I could never bear to hear him creak his boots at her, that I knew I could never bear to see him wash his hands of her; it was, that my admiration should be within a foot or two of him,—it was, that my feelings should be in the same place with him,—that, was the agonizing circumstance.

We played until nine o'clock, and then it was arranged that when Estella came to London I should be forewarned of her coming and should meet her at the coach; and then I took leave of her, and touched her and left her.

My guardian lay at the Boar in the next room to mine. Far into the night, Miss Havisham's words, "Love her, love her, love her!" sounded in my ears. I adapted them for my own repetition, and said to my pillow, "I love her, I love her, I love her!" hundreds of times. Then, a burst of gratitude came upon me, that she should be destined for me, once the blacksmith's boy. Then I thought if she were, as I feared, by no means rapturously grateful for that destiny yet, when would she begin to be interested in me? When should I awaken the heart within her that was mute and sleeping now?

Ah me! I thought those were high and great emotions. But I never thought there was anything low and small in my keeping away from Joe, because I knew she would be contemptuous of him. It was but a day gone, and Joe had brought the tears into my eyes; they had soon dried, God forgive me! soon dried.

CHAPTER XXX

After well considering the matter while I was dressing at the Blue Boar in the morning, I resolved to tell my guardian that I doubted Orlick's being the right sort of man to fill a post of trust at Miss Havisham's. "Why of course he is not the right sort of man, Pip," said my guardian, comfortably satisfied beforehand on the general head, "because the man who fills the post of trust never is the right sort of man." It seemed quite to put him into spirits to find that this particular post was not exceptionally held by the right sort of man, and he listened in a satisfied manner while I told him what knowledge I had of Orlick. "Very good, Pip," he observed, when I had concluded, "I'll go round presently, and pay our friend off." Rather alarmed by this summary action, I was for a little delay, and even hinted that our friend himself might be difficult to deal with. "Oh no he won't," said my guardian, making his pocket-handkerchief-point, with perfect confidence; "I should like to see him argue the question with me."

As we were going back together to London by the midday coach, and as I breakfasted under such terrors of Pumblechook that I could scarcely hold my cup, this gave me an opportunity of saying that I wanted a walk, and that I would go on along the London road while Mr. Jaggers was occupied, if he would let the coachman know that I would get into my place when overtaken. I was thus enabled to fly from the Blue Boar immediately after breakfast. By then making a loop of about a couple of miles into the open country at the back of Pumblechook's premises, I got round into the High Street again, a little beyond that pitfall, and felt myself in comparative security.

It was interesting to be in the quiet old town once more, and it was not disagreeable to be here and there suddenly recognised and stared after. One or two of the tradespeople even darted out of their shops and went a little way down the street before me, that they might turn, as if they had forgotten something, and pass me face to face,—on which occasions I don't know whether they or I made the worse pretence; they of not doing it, or I of not seeing it. Still my position was a distinguished one, and I was not at all dissatisfied with it, until Fate threw me in the way of that unlimited miscreant, Trabb's boy.

Casting my eyes along the street at a certain point of my progress, I beheld Trabb's boy approaching, lashing himself with an empty blue bag. Deeming that a serene and unconscious contemplation of him would best beseem me, and would be most likely to quell his evil mind, I advanced with that expression of countenance, and was rather congratulating myself on my success, when suddenly the knees of Trabb's boy smote together, his hair uprose, his cap fell off, he trembled violently in every limb, staggered out into the road, and crying to the populace, "Hold me! I'm so frightened!" feigned to be in a paroxysm of terror and contrition, occasioned by the dignity of my appearance. As I passed him, his teeth loudly chattered in his head, and with every mark of extreme humiliation, he prostrated himself in the dust.

This was a hard thing to bear, but this was nothing. I had not advanced another two hundred yards when, to my inexpressible terror, amazement, and indignation, I again beheld Trabb's boy approaching. He was coming round a narrow corner. His blue bag was slung over his shoulder, honest industry beamed in his eyes, a determination to proceed to Trabb's with cheerful briskness was indicated in his gait. With a shock he became aware of me, and was severely visited as before; but this time his motion was rotatory, and he staggered round and round me with knees more afflicted, and with uplifted hands as if beseeching for mercy. His sufferings were hailed with the greatest joy by a knot of spectators, and I felt utterly confounded.

I had not got as much further down the street as the post-office, when I again beheld Trabb's boy shooting round by a back way. This time, he was entirely changed. He wore the blue bag in the manner of my great-coat, and was strutting along the pavement towards me on the opposite side of the street, attended by a company of delighted young friends to whom he from time to time exclaimed, with a wave of his hand, "Don't know yah!" Words cannot state the amount of aggravation and injury wreaked upon me by Trabb's boy, when passing abreast of me, he pulled up his shirt-collar, twined his side-hair, stuck an arm akimbo, and smirked extravagantly by, wriggling his elbows and body, and drawling to his attendants, "Don't know yah, don't know yah, 'pon my soul don't know yah!" The disgrace attendant on his immediately afterwards taking to crowing and pursuing me across the bridge with crows, as from an exceedingly dejected fowl who had known me when I was a blacksmith, culminated the disgrace with which I left the town, and was, so to speak, ejected by it into the open country.

But unless I had taken the life of Trabb's boy on that occasion, I really do not even now see what I could have done save endure. To have struggled with him in the street, or to have exacted any lower recompense from him than his heart's best blood, would have been futile and degrading. Moreover, he was a boy whom no man could hurt; an invulnerable and dodging serpent who, when chased into a corner, flew out again between his captor's legs, scornfully yelping. I wrote, however, to Mr. Trabb by next day's post, to say that Mr. Pip must decline to deal further with one who could so far forget what he owed to the best interests of society, as to employ a boy who excited Loathing in every respectable mind.

The coach, with Mr. Jaggers inside, came up in due time, and I took my box-seat again, and arrived in London safe,—but not sound, for my heart was gone. As soon as I arrived, I sent a penitential codfish and barrel of oysters to Joe (as reparation for not having gone myself), and then went on to Barnard's Inn.

I found Herbert dining on cold meat, and delighted to welcome me back. Having despatched The Avenger to the coffee-house for an addition to the dinner, I felt that I must open my breast that very evening to my friend and chum. As confidence was out of the question with The Avenger in the hall, which could merely be regarded in the light of an antechamber to the keyhole, I sent him to the Play. A better proof of the severity of my bondage to that taskmaster could scarcely be afforded, than the degrading shifts to which I was constantly driven to find him employment. So mean is extremity, that I sometimes sent him to Hyde Park corner to see what o'clock it was.

Dinner done and we sitting with our feet upon the fender, I said to Herbert, "My dear Herbert, I have something very particular to tell you."

"My dear Handel," he returned, "I shall esteem and respect your confidence."

"It concerns myself, Herbert," said I, "and one other person."

Herbert crossed his feet, looked at the fire with his head on one side, and having looked at it in vain for some time, looked at me because I didn't go on.

"Herbert," said I, laying my hand upon his knee, "I love—I adore—Estella."

Instead of being transfixed, Herbert replied in an easy matter-of-course way, "Exactly. Well?"

"Well, Herbert? Is that all you say? Well?"

"What next, I mean?" said Herbert. "Of course I know that."

"How do you know it?" said I.

"How do I know it, Handel? Why, from you."

"I never told you."

"Told me! You have never told me when you have got your hair cut, but I have had senses to perceive it. You have always adored her, ever since I have known you. You brought your adoration and your portmanteau here together. Told me! Why, you have always told me all day long. When you told me your own story, you told me plainly that you began adoring her the first time you saw her, when you were very young indeed."

"Very well, then," said I, to whom this was a new and not unwelcome light, "I have never left off adoring her. And she has come back, a most beautiful and most elegant creature. And I saw her yesterday. And if I adored her before, I now doubly adore her."

"Lucky for you then, Handel," said Herbert, "that you are picked out for her and allotted to her. Without encroaching on forbidden ground, we may venture to say that there can be no doubt between ourselves of that fact. Have you any idea yet, of Estella's views on the adoration question?"

I shook my head gloomily. "Oh! She is thousands of miles away, from me," said I.

"Patience, my dear Handel: time enough, time enough. But you have something more to say?"

"I am ashamed to say it," I returned, "and yet it's no worse to say it than to think it. You call me a lucky fellow. Of course, I am. I was a blacksmith's boy but yesterday; I am—what shall I say I am—to-day?"

"Say a good fellow, if you want a phrase," returned Herbert, smiling, and clapping his hand on the back of mine—"a good fellow, with impetuosity and hesitation, boldness and diffidence, action and dreaming, curiously mixed in him."

I stopped for a moment to consider whether there really was this mixture in my character. On the whole, I by no means recognised the analysis, but thought it not worth disputing.

"When I ask what I am to call myself to-day, Herbert," I went on, "I suggest what I have in my thoughts. You say I am lucky. I know I have done nothing to raise myself in life, and that Fortune alone has raised me; that is being very lucky. And yet, when I think of Estella—"

("And when don't you, you know?" Herbert threw in, with his eyes on the fire; which I thought kind and sympathetic of him.)

"—Then, my dear Herbert, I cannot tell you how dependent and uncertain I feel, and how exposed to hundreds of chances. Avoiding forbidden ground, as you did just now, I may still say that on the constancy of one person (naming no person) all my expectations depend. And at the best, how indefinite and unsatisfactory, only to know so vaguely what they are!" In saying this, I relieved my mind of what had always been there, more or less, though no doubt most since yesterday.

"Now, Handel," Herbert replied, in his gay, hopeful way, "it seems to me that in the despondency of the tender passion, we are looking into our gift-horse's mouth with a magnifying-glass. Likewise, it seems to me that, concentrating our attention on the examination, we altogether overlook one of the best points of the animal. Didn't you tell me that your guardian, Mr. Jaggers, told you in the beginning, that you were not endowed with expectations only? And even if he had not told you so,—though that is a very large If, I grant,—could you believe that of all men in London, Mr. Jaggers is the man to hold his present relations towards you unless he were sure of his ground?"

I said I could not deny that this was a strong point. I said it (people often do so, in such cases) like a rather reluctant concession to truth and justice;—as if I wanted to deny it!

"I should think it was a strong point," said Herbert, "and I should think you would be puzzled to imagine a stronger; as to the rest, you must bide your guardian's time, and he must bide his client's time. You'll be one-and-twenty before you know where you are, and then perhaps you'll get some further enlightenment. At all events, you'll be nearer getting it, for it must come at last."

"What a hopeful disposition you have!" said I, gratefully admiring his cheery ways.

"I ought to have," said Herbert, "for I have not much else. I must acknowledge, by the by, that the good sense of what I have just said is not my own, but my father's. The only remark I ever heard him make on your story, was the final one, "The thing is settled and done, or Mr. Jaggers would not be in it." And now before I say anything more about my father, or my father's son, and repay confidence with confidence, I want to make myself seriously disagreeable to you for a moment,—positively repulsive."

"You won't succeed," said I.

"O yes I shall!" said he. "One, two, three, and now I am in for it. Handel, my good fellow;"—though he spoke in this light tone, he was very much in earnest,—"I have been thinking since we have been talking with our feet on this fender, that Estella surely cannot be a condition of your inheritance, if she was never referred to by your guardian. Am I right in so understanding what you have told me, as that he never referred to her, directly or indirectly, in any way? Never even hinted, for instance, that your patron might have views as to your marriage ultimately?"

"Never."

"Now, Handel, I am quite free from the flavor of sour grapes, upon my soul and honor! Not being bound to her, can you not detach yourself from her?—I told you I should be disagreeable."

I turned my head aside, for, with a rush and a sweep, like the old marsh winds coming up from the sea, a feeling like that which had subdued me on the morning when I left the forge, when the mists were solemnly rising, and when I laid my hand upon the village finger-post, smote upon my heart again. There was silence between us for a little while.

"Yes; but my dear Handel," Herbert went on, as if we had been talking, instead of silent, "its having been so strongly rooted in the breast of a boy whom nature and circumstances made so romantic, renders it very serious. Think of her bringing-up, and think of Miss Havisham. Think of what she is herself (now I am repulsive and you abominate me). This may lead to miserable things."

"I know it, Herbert," said I, with my head still turned away, "but I can't help it."

"You can't detach yourself?"

"No. Impossible!"

"You can't try, Handel?"

"No. Impossible!"

"Well!" said Herbert, getting up with a lively shake as if he had been asleep, and stirring the fire, "now I'll endeavor to make myself agreeable again!"

So he went round the room and shook the curtains out, put the chairs in their places, tidied the books and so forth that were lying about, looked into the hall, peeped into the letter-box, shut the door, and came back to his chair by the fire: where he sat down, nursing his left leg in both arms.

"I was going to say a word or two, Handel, concerning my father and my father's son. I am afraid it is scarcely necessary for my father's son to remark that my father's establishment is not particularly brilliant in its housekeeping."

"There is always plenty, Herbert," said I, to say something encouraging.

"O yes! and so the dustman says, I believe, with the strongest approval, and so does the marine-store shop in the back street. Gravely, Handel, for the subject is grave enough, you know how it is as well as I do. I suppose there was a time once when my father had not given matters up; but if ever there was, the time is gone. May I ask you if you have ever had an opportunity of remarking, down in your part of the country, that the children of not exactly suitable marriages are always most particularly anxious to be married?"

This was such a singular question, that I asked him in return, "Is it so?"

"I don't know," said Herbert, "that's what I want to know. Because it is decidedly the case with us. My poor sister Charlotte, who was next me and died before she was fourteen, was a striking example. Little Jane is the same. In her desire to be matrimonially established, you might suppose her to have passed her short existence in the perpetual contemplation of domestic bliss. Little Alick in a frock has already made arrangements for his union with a suitable young person at Kew. And indeed, I think we are all engaged, except the baby."

"Then you are?" said I.

"I am," said Herbert; "but it's a secret."

I assured him of my keeping the secret, and begged to be favored with further particulars. He had spoken so sensibly and feelingly of my weakness that I wanted to know something about his strength.

"May I ask the name?" I said.

"Name of Clara," said Herbert.

"Live in London?"

"Yes, perhaps I ought to mention," said Herbert, who had become curiously crestfallen and meek, since we entered on the interesting theme, "that she is rather below my mother's nonsensical family notions. Her father had to do with the victualling of passenger-ships. I think he was a species of purser."

"What is he now?" said I.

"He's an invalid now," replied Herbert.

"Living on—?"

"On the first floor," said Herbert. Which was not at all what I meant, for I had intended my question to apply to his means. "I have never seen him, for he has always kept his room overhead, since I have known Clara. But I have heard him constantly. He makes tremendous rows,—roars, and pegs at the floor with some frightful instrument." In looking at me and then laughing heartily, Herbert for the time recovered his usual lively manner.

"Don't you expect to see him?" said I.

"O yes, I constantly expect to see him," returned Herbert, "because I never hear him, without expecting him to come tumbling through the ceiling. But I don't know how long the rafters may hold."

When he had once more laughed heartily, he became meek again, and told me that the moment he began to realize Capital, it was his intention to marry this young lady. He added as a self-evident proposition, engendering low spirits, "But you can't marry, you know, while you're looking about you."

As we contemplated the fire, and as I thought what a difficult vision to realize this same Capital sometimes was, I put my hands in my pockets. A folded piece of paper in one of them attracting my attention, I opened it and found it to be the play-bill I had received from Joe, relative to the celebrated provincial amateur of Roscian renown. "And bless my heart," I involuntarily added aloud, "it's to-night!"

This changed the subject in an instant, and made us hurriedly resolve to go to the play. So, when I had pledged myself to comfort and abet Herbert in the affair of his heart by all practicable and impracticable means, and when Herbert had told me that his affianced already knew me by reputation and that I should be presented to her, and when we had warmly shaken hands upon our mutual confidence, we blew out our candles, made up our fire, locked our door, and issued forth in quest of Mr. Wopsle and Denmark.

CHAPTER XXXI

On our arrival in Denmark, we found the king and queen of that country elevated in two arm-chairs on a kitchen-table, holding a Court. The whole of the Danish nobility were in attendance; consisting of a noble boy in the wash-leather boots of a gigantic ancestor, a venerable Peer with a dirty face who seemed to have risen from the people late in life, and the Danish chivalry with a comb in its hair and a pair of white silk legs, and presenting on the whole a feminine appearance. My gifted townsman stood gloomily apart, with folded arms, and I could have wished that his curls and forehead had been more probable.

Several curious little circumstances transpired as the action proceeded. The late king of the country not only appeared to have been troubled with a cough at the time of his decease, but to have taken it with him to the tomb, and to have brought it back. The royal phantom also carried a ghostly manuscript round its truncheon, to which it had the appearance of occasionally referring, and that too, with an air of anxiety and a tendency to lose the place of reference which were suggestive of a state of mortality. It was this, I conceive, which led to the Shade's being advised by the gallery to "turn over!"—a recommendation which it took extremely ill. It was likewise to be noted of this majestic spirit, that whereas it always appeared with an air of having been out a long time and walked an immense distance, it perceptibly came from a closely contiguous wall. This occasioned its terrors to be received derisively. The Queen of Denmark, a very buxom lady, though no doubt historically brazen, was considered by the public to have too much brass about her; her chin being attached to her diadem by a broad band of that metal (as if she had a gorgeous toothache), her waist being encircled by another, and each of her arms by another, so that she was openly mentioned as "the kettle-drum." The noble boy in the ancestral boots was inconsistent, representing himself, as it were in one breath, as an able seaman, a strolling actor, a grave-digger, a clergyman, and a person of the utmost importance at a Court fencing-match, on the authority of whose practised eye and nice discrimination the finest strokes were judged. This gradually led to a want of toleration for him, and even—on his being detected in holy orders, and declining to perform the funeral service—to the general indignation taking the form of nuts. Lastly, Ophelia was a prey to such slow musical madness, that when, in course of time, she had taken off her white muslin scarf, folded it up, and buried it, a sulky man who had been long cooling his impatient nose against an iron bar in the front row of the gallery, growled, "Now the baby's put to bed let's have supper!" Which, to say the least of it, was out of keeping.

Upon my unfortunate townsman all these incidents accumulated with playful effect. Whenever that undecided Prince had to ask a question or state a doubt, the public helped him out with it. As for example; on the question whether 'twas nobler in the mind to suffer, some roared yes, and some no, and some inclining to both opinions said "Toss up for it;" and quite a Debating Society arose. When he asked what should such fellows as he do crawling between earth and heaven, he was encouraged with loud cries of "Hear, hear!" When he appeared with his stocking disordered (its disorder expressed, according to usage, by one very neat fold in the top, which I suppose to be always got up with a flat iron), a conversation took place in the gallery respecting the paleness of his leg, and whether it was occasioned by the turn the ghost had given him. On his taking the recorders,—very like a little black flute that had just been played in the orchestra and handed out at the door,—he was called upon unanimously for Rule Britannia. When he recommended the player not to saw the air thus, the sulky man said, "And don't you do it, neither; you're a deal worse than him!" And I grieve to add that peals of laughter greeted Mr. Wopsle on every one of these occasions.

But his greatest trials were in the churchyard, which had the appearance of a primeval forest, with a kind of small ecclesiastical wash-house on one side, and a turnpike gate on the other. Mr. Wopsle in a comprehensive black cloak, being descried entering at the turnpike, the gravedigger was admonished in a friendly way, "Look out! Here's the undertaker a coming, to see how you're a getting on with your work!" I believe it is well known in a constitutional country that Mr. Wopsle could not possibly have returned the skull, after moralizing over it, without dusting his fingers on a white napkin taken from his breast; but even that innocent and indispensable action did not pass without the comment, "Wai-ter!" The arrival of the body for interment (in an empty black box with the lid tumbling open), was the signal for a general joy, which was much enhanced by the discovery, among the bearers, of an individual obnoxious to identification. The joy attended Mr. Wopsle through his struggle with Laertes on the brink of the orchestra and the grave, and slackened no more until he had tumbled the king off the kitchen-table, and had died by inches from the ankles upward.

We had made some pale efforts in the beginning to applaud Mr. Wopsle; but they were too hopeless to be persisted in. Therefore we had sat, feeling keenly for him, but laughing, nevertheless, from ear to ear. I laughed in spite of myself all the time, the whole thing was so droll; and yet I had a latent impression that there was something decidedly fine in Mr. Wopsle's elocution,—not for old associations' sake, I am afraid, but because it was very slow, very dreary, very up-hill and down-hill, and very unlike any way in which any man in any natural circumstances of life or death ever expressed himself about anything. When the tragedy was over, and he had been called for and hooted, I said to Herbert, "Let us go at once, or perhaps we shall meet him."

We made all the haste we could down stairs, but we were not quick enough either. Standing at the door was a Jewish man with an unnatural heavy smear of eyebrow, who caught my eyes as we advanced, and said, when we came up with him,—

"Mr. Pip and friend?"

Identity of Mr. Pip and friend confessed.

"Mr. Waldengarver," said the man, "would be glad to have the honour."

"Waldengarver?" I repeated—when Herbert murmured in my ear, "Probably Wopsle."

"Oh!" said I. "Yes. Shall we follow you?"

"A few steps, please." When we were in a side alley, he turned and asked, "How did you think he looked?—I dressed him."

I don't know what he had looked like, except a funeral; with the addition of a large Danish sun or star hanging round his neck by a blue ribbon, that had given him the appearance of being insured in some extraordinary Fire Office. But I said he had looked very nice.

"When he come to the grave," said our conductor, "he showed his cloak beautiful. But, judging from the wing, it looked to me that when he see the ghost in the queen's apartment, he might have made more of his stockings."

I modestly assented, and we all fell through a little dirty swing door, into a sort of hot packing-case immediately behind it. Here Mr. Wopsle was divesting himself of his Danish garments, and here there was just room for us to look at him over one another's shoulders, by keeping the packing-case door, or lid, wide open.

"Gentlemen," said Mr. Wopsle, "I am proud to see you. I hope, Mr. Pip, you will excuse my sending round. I had the happiness to know you in former times, and the Drama has ever had a claim which has ever been acknowledged, on the noble and the affluent."

Meanwhile, Mr. Waldengarver, in a frightful perspiration, was trying to get himself out of his princely sables.

"Skin the stockings off Mr. Waldengarver," said the owner of that property, "or you'll bust 'em. Bust 'em, and you'll bust five-and-thirty shillings. Shakspeare never was complimented with a finer pair. Keep quiet in your chair now, and leave 'em to me."

With that, he went upon his knees, and began to flay his victim; who, on the first stocking coming off, would certainly have fallen over backward with his chair, but for there being no room to fall anyhow.

I had been afraid until then to say a word about the play. But then, Mr. Waldengarver looked up at us complacently, and said,—

"Gentlemen, how did it seem to you, to go, in front?"

Herbert said from behind (at the same time poking me), "Capitally." So I said "Capitally."

"How did you like my reading of the character, gentlemen?" said Mr. Waldengarver, almost, if not quite, with patronage.

Herbert said from behind (again poking me), "Massive and concrete." So I said boldly, as if I had originated it, and must beg to insist upon it, "Massive and concrete."

"I am glad to have your approbation, gentlemen," said Mr. Waldengarver, with an air of dignity, in spite of his being ground against the wall at the time, and holding on by the seat of the chair.

"But I'll tell you one thing, Mr. Waldengarver," said the man who was on his knees, "in which you're out in your reading. Now mind! I don't care who says contrairy; I tell you so. You're out in your reading of Hamlet when you get your legs in profile. The last Hamlet as I dressed, made the same mistakes in his reading at rehearsal, till I got him to put a large red wafer on each of his shins, and then at that rehearsal (which was the last) I went in front, sir, to the back of the pit, and whenever his reading brought him into profile, I called out 'I don't see no wafers!' And at night his reading was lovely."

Mr. Waldengarver smiled at me, as much as to say "a faithful Dependent—I overlook his folly;" and then said aloud, "My view is a little classic and thoughtful for them here; but they will improve, they will improve."

Herbert and I said together, O, no doubt they would improve.

"Did you observe, gentlemen," said Mr. Waldengarver, "that there was a man in the gallery who endeavored to cast derision on the service,—I mean, the representation?"

We basely replied that we rather thought we had noticed such a man. I added, "He was drunk, no doubt."

"O dear no, sir," said Mr. Wopsle, "not drunk. His employer would see to that, sir. His employer would not allow him to be drunk."

"You know his employer?" said I.

Mr. Wopsle shut his eyes, and opened them again; performing both ceremonies very slowly. "You must have observed, gentlemen," said he, "an ignorant and a blatant ass, with a rasping throat and a countenance expressive of low malignity, who went through—I will not say sustained—the role (if I may use a French expression) of Claudius, King of Denmark. That is his employer, gentlemen. Such is the profession!"

Without distinctly knowing whether I should have been more sorry for Mr. Wopsle if he had been in despair, I was so sorry for him as it was, that I took the opportunity of his turning round to have his braces put on,—which jostled us out at the doorway,—to ask Herbert what he thought of having him home to supper? Herbert said he thought it would be kind to do so; therefore I invited him, and he went to Barnard's with us, wrapped up to the eyes, and we did our best for him, and he sat until two o'clock in the morning, reviewing his success and developing his plans. I forget in detail what they were, but I have a general recollection that he was to begin with reviving the Drama, and to end with crushing it; inasmuch as his decease would leave it utterly bereft and without a chance or hope.

Miserably I went to bed after all, and miserably thought of Estella, and miserably dreamed that my expectations were all cancelled, and that I had to give my hand in marriage to Herbert's Clara, or play Hamlet to Miss Havisham's Ghost, before twenty thousand people, without knowing twenty words of it.

CHAPTER XXXII

One day when I was busy with my books and Mr. Pocket, I received a note by the post, the mere outside of which threw me into a great flutter; for, though I had never seen the handwriting in which it was addressed, I divined whose hand it was. It had no set beginning, as Dear Mr. Pip, or Dear Pip, or Dear Sir, or Dear Anything, but ran thus:—

> "I am to come to London the day after to-morrow by the midday coach.
> I believe it was settled you should meet me? At all events Miss Havisham
> has that impression, and I write in obedience to it. She sends you her
> regard.

> "Yours, ESTELLA."

If there had been time, I should probably have ordered several suits of clothes for this occasion; but as there was not, I was fain to be content with those I had. My appetite vanished instantly, and I knew no peace or rest until the day arrived. Not that its arrival brought me either; for, then I was worse than ever, and began haunting the coach-office in Wood Street, Cheapside, before the coach had left the Blue Boar in our town. For all that I knew this perfectly well, I still felt as if it were not safe to let the coach-office be out of my sight longer than five minutes at a time; and in this condition of unreason I had performed the first half-hour of a watch of four or five hours, when Wemmick ran against me.

"Halloa, Mr. Pip," said he; "how do you do? I should hardly have thought this was your beat."

I explained that I was waiting to meet somebody who was coming up by coach, and I inquired after the Castle and the Aged.

"Both flourishing thankye," said Wemmick, "and particularly the Aged. He's in wonderful feather. He'll be eighty-two next birthday. I have a notion of firing eighty-two times, if the neighborhood shouldn't complain, and that cannon of mine should prove equal to the pressure. However, this is not London talk. Where do you think I am going to?"

"To the office?" said I, for he was tending in that direction.

"Next thing to it," returned Wemmick, "I am going to Newgate. We are in a banker's-parcel case just at present, and I have been down the road taking a squint at the scene of action, and thereupon must have a word or two with our client."

"Did your client commit the robbery?" I asked.

"Bless your soul and body, no," answered Wemmick, very drily. "But he is accused of it. So might you or I be. Either of us might be accused of it, you know."

"Only neither of us is," I remarked.

"Yah!" said Wemmick, touching me on the breast with his forefinger; "you're a deep one, Mr. Pip! Would you like to have a look at Newgate? Have you time to spare?"

I had so much time to spare, that the proposal came as a relief, notwithstanding its irreconcilability with my latent desire to keep my eye on the coach-office. Muttering that I would make the inquiry whether I had time to walk with him, I went into the office, and ascertained from the clerk with the nicest precision and much to the trying of his temper, the earliest moment at which the coach could be expected,—which I knew beforehand, quite as well as he. I then rejoined Mr. Wemmick, and affecting to consult my watch, and to be surprised by the information I had received, accepted his offer.

We were at Newgate in a few minutes, and we passed through the lodge where some fetters were hanging up on the bare walls among the prison rules, into the interior of the jail. At that time jails were much neglected, and the period of exaggerated reaction consequent on all public wrongdoing—and which is always its heaviest and longest punishment—was still far off. So felons were not lodged and fed better than soldiers, (to say nothing of paupers,) and seldom set fire to their prisons with the excusable object of improving the flavor of their soup. It was visiting time when Wemmick took me in, and a potman was going his rounds with beer; and the prisoners, behind bars in yards, were buying beer, and talking to friends; and a frowzy, ugly, disorderly, depressing scene it was.

It struck me that Wemmick walked among the prisoners much as a gardener might walk among his plants. This was first put into my head by his seeing a shoot that had come up in the night, and saying, "What, Captain Tom? Are you there? Ah, indeed!" and also, "Is that Black Bill behind the cistern? Why I didn't look for you these two months; how do you find yourself?" Equally in his stopping at the bars and attending to anxious whisperers,—always singly,—Wemmick with his post-office in an immovable state, looked at them while in conference, as if he were taking particular notice of the advance they had made, since last observed, towards coming out in full blow at their trial.

He was highly popular, and I found that he took the familiar department of Mr. Jaggers's business; though something of the state of Mr. Jaggers hung about him too, forbidding approach beyond certain limits. His personal recognition of each successive client was comprised in a nod, and in his settling his hat a little easier on his head with both hands, and then tightening the post-office, and putting his hands in his pockets. In one or two instances there was a difficulty respecting the raising of fees, and then Mr. Wemmick, backing as far as possible from the insufficient money produced, said, "it's no use, my boy. I'm only a subordinate. I can't take it. Don't go on in that way with a subordinate. If you are unable to make up your quantum, my boy, you had better address yourself to a principal; there are plenty of principals in the profession, you know, and what is not worth the while of one, may be worth the while of another; that's my recommendation to you, speaking as a subordinate. Don't try on useless measures. Why should you? Now, who's next?"

Thus, we walked through Wemmick's greenhouse, until he turned to me and said, "Notice the man I shall shake hands with." I should have done so, without the preparation, as he had shaken hands with no one yet.

Almost as soon as he had spoken, a portly upright man (whom I can see now, as I write) in a well-worn olive-colored frock-coat, with a peculiar pallor overspreading the red in his complexion, and eyes that went wandering about when he tried to fix them, came up to a corner of the bars, and put his hand to his hat—which had a greasy and fatty surface like cold broth—with a half-serious and half-jocose military salute.

"Colonel, to you!" said Wemmick; "how are you, Colonel?"

"All right, Mr. Wemmick."

"Everything was done that could be done, but the evidence was too strong for us, Colonel."

"Yes, it was too strong, sir,—but I don't care."

"No, no," said Wemmick, coolly, "you don't care." Then, turning to me, "Served His Majesty this man. Was a soldier in the line and bought his discharge."

I said, "Indeed?" and the man's eyes looked at me, and then looked over my head, and then looked all round me, and then he drew his hand across his lips and laughed.

"I think I shall be out of this on Monday, sir," he said to Wemmick.

"Perhaps," returned my friend, "but there's no knowing."

"I am glad to have the chance of bidding you good by, Mr. Wemmick," said the man, stretching out his hand between two bars.

"Thankye," said Wemmick, shaking hands with him. "Same to you, Colonel."

"If what I had upon me when taken had been real, Mr. Wemmick," said the man, unwilling to let his hand go, "I should have asked the favor of your wearing another ring—in acknowledgment of your attentions."

"I'll accept the will for the deed," said Wemmick. "By the by; you were quite a pigeon-fancier." The man looked up at the sky. "I am told you had a remarkable breed of tumblers. Could you commission any friend of yours to bring me a pair, of you've no further use for 'em?"

"It shall be done, sir?"

"All right," said Wemmick, "they shall be taken care of. Good afternoon, Colonel. Good by!" They shook hands again, and as we walked away Wemmick said to me, "A Coiner, a very good workman. The Recorder's report is made to-day, and he is sure to be executed on Monday. Still you see, as far as it goes, a pair of pigeons are portable property all the same." With that, he looked back, and nodded at this dead plant, and then cast his eyes about him in walking out of the yard, as if he were considering what other pot would go best in its place.

As we came out of the prison through the lodge, I found that the great importance of my guardian was appreciated by the turnkeys, no less than by those whom they held in charge. "Well, Mr. Wemmick," said the turnkey, who kept us between the two studded and spiked lodge gates, and who carefully locked one before he unlocked the other, "what's Mr. Jaggers going to do with that water-side murder? Is he going to make it manslaughter, or what's he going to make of it?"

"Why don't you ask him?" returned Wemmick.

"O yes, I dare say!" said the turnkey.

"Now, that's the way with them here, Mr. Pip," remarked Wemmick, turning to me with his post-office elongated. "They don't mind what they ask of me, the subordinate; but you'll never catch 'em asking any questions of my principal."

"Is this young gentleman one of the 'prentices or articled ones of your office?" asked the turnkey, with a grin at Mr. Wemmick's humor.

"There he goes again, you see!" cried Wemmick, "I told you so! Asks another question of the subordinate before his first is dry! Well, supposing Mr. Pip is one of them?"

"Why then," said the turnkey, grinning again, "he knows what Mr. Jaggers is."

"Yah!" cried Wemmick, suddenly hitting out at the turnkey in a facetious way, "you're dumb as one of your own keys when you have to do with my principal, you know you are. Let us out, you old fox, or I'll get him to bring an action against you for false imprisonment."

The turnkey laughed, and gave us good day, and stood laughing at us over the spikes of the wicket when we descended the steps into the street.

"Mind you, Mr. Pip," said Wemmick, gravely in my ear, as he took my arm to be more confidential; "I don't know that Mr. Jaggers does a better thing than the way in which he keeps himself so high. He's always so high. His constant height is of a piece with his immense abilities. That Colonel durst no more take leave of him, than that turnkey durst ask him his intentions respecting a case. Then, between his height and them, he slips in his subordinate,—don't you see?—and so he has 'em, soul and body."

I was very much impressed, and not for the first time, by my guardian's subtlety. To confess the truth, I very heartily wished, and not for the first time, that I had had some other guardian of minor abilities.

Mr. Wemmick and I parted at the office in Little Britain, where suppliants for Mr. Jaggers's notice were lingering about as usual, and I returned to my watch in the street of the coach-office, with some three hours on hand. I consumed the whole time in thinking how strange it was that I should be encompassed by all this taint of prison and crime; that, in my childhood out on our lonely marshes on a winter evening, I should have first encountered it; that, it should have reappeared on two occasions, starting out like a stain that was faded but not gone; that, it should in this new way pervade my fortune and advancement. While my mind was thus engaged, I thought of the beautiful young Estella, proud and refined, coming towards me, and I thought with absolute abhorrence of the contrast between the jail and her. I wished that Wemmick had not met me, or that I had not yielded to him and gone with him, so that, of all days in the year on this day, I might not have had Newgate in my breath and on my clothes. I beat the prison dust off my feet as I sauntered to and fro, and I shook it out of my dress, and I exhaled its air from my lungs. So contaminated did I feel, remembering who was coming, that the coach came quickly after all, and I was not yet free from the soiling consciousness of Mr. Wemmick's conservatory, when I saw her face at the coach window and her hand waving to me.

What was the nameless shadow which again in that one instant had passed?

CHAPTER XXXIII

In her furred travelling-dress, Estella seemed more delicately beautiful than she had ever seemed yet, even in my eyes. Her manner was more winning than she had cared to let it be to me before, and I thought I saw Miss Havisham's influence in the change.

We stood in the Inn Yard while she pointed out her luggage to me, and when it was all collected I remembered—having forgotten everything but herself in the meanwhile—that I knew nothing of her destination.

"I am going to Richmond," she told me. "Our lesson is, that there are two Richmonds, one in Surrey and one in Yorkshire, and that mine is the Surrey Richmond. The distance is ten miles. I am to have a carriage, and you are to take me. This is my purse, and you are to pay my charges out of it. O, you must take the purse! We have no choice, you and I, but to obey our instructions. We are not free to follow our own devices, you and I."

As she looked at me in giving me the purse, I hoped there was an inner meaning in her words. She said them slightingly, but not with displeasure.

"A carriage will have to be sent for, Estella. Will you rest here a little?"

"Yes, I am to rest here a little, and I am to drink some tea, and you are to take care of me the while."

She drew her arm through mine, as if it must be done, and I requested a waiter who had been staring at the coach like a man who had never seen such a thing in his life, to show us a private sitting-room. Upon that, he pulled out a napkin, as if it were a magic clew without which he couldn't find the way up stairs, and led us to the black hole of the establishment, fitted up with a diminishing mirror (quite a superfluous article, considering the hole's proportions), an anchovy sauce-cruet, and somebody's pattens. On my objecting to this retreat, he took us into another room with a dinner-table for thirty, and in the grate a scorched leaf of a copy-book under a bushel of coal-dust. Having looked at this extinct conflagration and shaken his head, he took my order; which, proving to be merely, "Some tea for the lady," sent him out of the room in a very low state of mind.

I was, and I am, sensible that the air of this chamber, in its strong combination of stable with soup-stock, might have led one to infer that the coaching department was not doing well, and that the enterprising proprietor was boiling down the horses for the refreshment department. Yet the room was all in all to me, Estella being in it. I thought that with her I could have been happy there for life. (I was not at all happy there at the time, observe, and I knew it well.)

"Where are you going to, at Richmond?" I asked Estella.

"I am going to live," said she, "at a great expense, with a lady there, who has the power—or says she has—of taking me about, and introducing me, and showing people to me and showing me to people."

"I suppose you will be glad of variety and admiration?"

"Yes, I suppose so."

She answered so carelessly, that I said, "You speak of yourself as if you were some one else."

"Where did you learn how I speak of others? Come, come," said Estella, smiling delightfully, "you must not expect me to go to school to you; I must talk in my own way. How do you thrive with Mr. Pocket?"

"I live quite pleasantly there; at least—" It appeared to me that I was losing a chance.

"At least?" repeated Estella.

"As pleasantly as I could anywhere, away from you."

"You silly boy," said Estella, quite composedly, "how can you talk such nonsense? Your friend Mr. Matthew, I believe, is superior to the rest of his family?"

"Very superior indeed. He is nobody's enemy—"—"Don't add but his own," interposed Estella, "for I hate that class of man. But he really is disinterested, and above small jealousy and spite, I have heard?"

"I am sure I have every reason to say so."

"You have not every reason to say so of the rest of his people," said Estella, nodding at me with an expression of face that was at once grave and rallying, "for they beset Miss Havisham with reports and insinuations to your disadvantage. They watch you, misrepresent you, write letters about you (anonymous sometimes), and you are the torment and the occupation of their lives. You can scarcely realize to yourself the hatred those people feel for you."

"They do me no harm, I hope?"

Instead of answering, Estella burst out laughing. This was very singular to me, and I looked at her in considerable perplexity. When she left off—and she had not laughed languidly, but with real enjoyment—I said, in my diffident way with her,—

"I hope I may suppose that you would not be amused if they did me any harm."

"No, no you may be sure of that," said Estella. "You may be certain that I laugh because they fail. O, those people with Miss Havisham, and the tortures they undergo!" She laughed again, and even now when she had told me why, her laughter was very singular to me, for I could not doubt its being genuine, and yet it seemed too much for the occasion. I thought there must really be something more here than I knew; she saw the thought in my mind, and answered it.

"It is not easy for even you." said Estella, "to know what satisfaction it gives me to see those people thwarted, or what an enjoyable sense of the ridiculous I have when they are made ridiculous. For you were not brought up in that strange house from a mere baby. I was. You had not your little wits sharpened by their intriguing against you, suppressed and defenceless, under the mask of sympathy and pity and what not that is soft and soothing. I had. You did not gradually open your round childish eyes wider and wider to the discovery of that impostor of a woman who calculates her stores of peace of mind for when she wakes up in the night. I did."

It was no laughing matter with Estella now, nor was she summoning these remembrances from any shallow place. I would not have been the cause of that look of hers for all my expectations in a heap.

"Two things I can tell you," said Estella. "First, notwithstanding the proverb that constant dropping will wear away a stone, you may set your mind at rest that these people never will—never would, in hundred years—impair your ground with Miss Havisham, in any particular, great or small. Second, I am beholden to you as the cause of their being so busy and so mean in vain, and there is my hand upon it."

As she gave it to me playfully,—for her darker mood had been but Momentary,—I held it and put it to my lips. "You ridiculous boy," said Estella, "will you never take warning? Or do you kiss my hand in the same spirit in which I once let you kiss my cheek?"

"What spirit was that?" said I.

"I must think a moment. A spirit of contempt for the fawners and plotters."

"If I say yes, may I kiss the cheek again?"

"You should have asked before you touched the hand. But, yes, if you like."

I leaned down, and her calm face was like a statue's. "Now," said Estella, gliding away the instant I touched her cheek, "you are to take care that I have some tea, and you are to take me to Richmond."

Her reverting to this tone as if our association were forced upon us, and we were mere puppets, gave me pain; but everything in our intercourse did give me pain. Whatever her tone with me happened to be, I could put no trust in it, and build no hope on it; and yet I went on against trust and against hope. Why repeat it a thousand times? So it always was.

I rang for the tea, and the waiter, reappearing with his magic clew, brought in by degrees some fifty adjuncts to that refreshment, but of tea not a glimpse. A teaboard, cups and saucers, plates, knives and forks (including carvers), spoons (various), saltcellars, a meek little muffin confined with the utmost precaution under a strong iron cover, Moses in the bulrushes typified by a soft bit of butter in a quantity of parsley, a pale loaf with a powdered head, two proof impressions of the bars of the kitchen fireplace on triangular bits of bread, and ultimately a fat family urn; which the waiter staggered in with, expressing in his countenance burden and suffering. After a prolonged absence at this stage of the entertainment, he at length came back with a casket of precious appearance containing twigs. These I steeped in hot water, and so from the whole of these appliances extracted one cup of I don't know what for Estella.

The bill paid, and the waiter remembered, and the ostler not forgotten, and the chambermaid taken into consideration,—in a word, the whole house bribed into a state of contempt and animosity, and Estella's purse much lightened,—we got into our post-coach and drove away. Turning into Cheapside and rattling up Newgate Street, we were soon under the walls of which I was so ashamed.

"What place is that?" Estella asked me.

I made a foolish pretence of not at first recognizing it, and then told her. As she looked at it, and drew in her head again, murmuring, "Wretches!" I would not have confessed to my visit for any consideration.

"Mr. Jaggers," said I, by way of putting it neatly on somebody else, "has the reputation of being more in the secrets of that dismal place than any man in London."

"He is more in the secrets of every place, I think," said Estella, in a low voice.

"You have been accustomed to see him often, I suppose?"

"I have been accustomed to see him at uncertain intervals, ever since I can remember. But I know him no better now, than I did before I could speak plainly. What is your own experience of him? Do you advance with him?"

"Once habituated to his distrustful manner," said I, "I have done very well."

"Are you intimate?"

"I have dined with him at his private house."

"I fancy," said Estella, shrinking "that must be a curious place."

"It is a curious place."

I should have been chary of discussing my guardian too freely even with her; but I should have gone on with the subject so far as to describe the dinner in Gerrard Street, if we had not then come into a sudden glare of gas. It seemed, while it lasted, to be all alight and alive with that inexplicable feeling I had had before; and when we were out of it, I was as much dazed for a few moments as if I had been in lightning.

So we fell into other talk, and it was principally about the way by which we were travelling, and about what parts of London lay on this side of it, and what on that. The great city was almost new to her, she told me, for she had never left Miss Havisham's neighborhood until she had gone to France, and she had merely passed through London then in going and returning. I asked her if my guardian had any charge of her while she remained here? To that she emphatically said "God forbid!" and no more.

It was impossible for me to avoid seeing that she cared to attract me; that she made herself winning, and would have won me even if the task had needed pains. Yet this made me none the happier, for even if she had not taken that tone of our being disposed of by others, I should have felt that she held my heart in her hand because she wilfully chose to do it, and not because it would have wrung any tenderness in her to crush it and throw it away.

When we passed through Hammersmith, I showed her where Mr. Matthew Pocket lived, and said it was no great way from Richmond, and that I hoped I should see her sometimes.

"O yes, you are to see me; you are to come when you think proper; you are to be mentioned to the family; indeed you are already mentioned."

I inquired was it a large household she was going to be a member of?

"No; there are only two; mother and daughter. The mother is a lady of some station, though not averse to increasing her income."

"I wonder Miss Havisham could part with you again so soon."

"It is a part of Miss Havisham's plans for me, Pip," said Estella, with a sigh, as if she were tired; "I am to write to her constantly and see her regularly and report how I go on,—I and the jewels,—for they are nearly all mine now."

It was the first time she had ever called me by my name. Of course she did so purposely, and knew that I should treasure it up.

We came to Richmond all too soon, and our destination there was a house by the green,—a staid old house, where hoops and powder and patches, embroidered coats, rolled stockings, ruffles and swords, had had their court days many a time. Some ancient trees before the house were still cut into fashions as formal and unnatural as the hoops and wigs and stiff skirts; but their own allotted places in the great procession of the dead were not far off, and they would soon drop into them and go the silent way of the rest.

A bell with an old voice—which I dare say in its time had often said to the house, Here is the green farthingale, Here is the diamond-hilted sword, Here are the shoes with red heels and the blue solitaire—sounded gravely in the moonlight, and two cherry-colored maids came fluttering out to receive Estella. The doorway soon absorbed her boxes, and she gave me her hand and a smile, and said good night, and was absorbed likewise. And still I stood looking at the house, thinking how happy I should be if I lived there with her, and knowing that I never was happy with her, but always miserable.

I got into the carriage to be taken back to Hammersmith, and I got in with a bad heart-ache, and I got out with a worse heart-ache. At our own door, I found little Jane Pocket coming home from a little party escorted by her little lover; and I envied her little lover, in spite of his being subject to Flopson.

Mr. Pocket was out lecturing; for, he was a most delightful lecturer on domestic economy, and his treatises on the management of children and servants were considered the very best text-books on those themes. But Mrs. Pocket was at home, and was in a little difficulty, on account of the baby's having been accommodated with a needle-case to keep him quiet during the unaccountable absence (with a relative in the Foot Guards) of Millers. And more needles were missing than it could be regarded as quite wholesome for a patient of such tender years either to apply externally or to take as a tonic.

Mr. Pocket being justly celebrated for giving most excellent practical advice, and for having a clear and sound perception of things and a highly judicious mind, I had some notion in my heart-ache of begging him to accept my confidence. But happening to look up at Mrs. Pocket as she sat reading her book of dignities after prescribing Bed as a sovereign remedy for baby, I thought—Well—No, I wouldn't.

CHAPTER XXXIV

As I had grown accustomed to my expectations, I had insensibly begun to notice their effect upon myself and those around me. Their influence on my own character I disguised from my recognition as much as possible, but I knew very well that it was not all good. I lived in a state of chronic uneasiness respecting my behavior to Joe. My conscience was not by any means comfortable about Biddy. When I woke up in the night,—like Camilla,—I used to think, with a weariness on my spirits, that I should have been happier and better if I had never seen Miss Havisham's face, and had risen to manhood content to be partners with Joe in the honest old forge. Many a time of an evening, when I sat alone looking at the fire, I thought, after all there was no fire like the forge fire and the kitchen fire at home.

Yet Estella was so inseparable from all my restlessness and disquiet of mind, that I really fell into confusion as to the limits of my own part in its production. That is to say, supposing I had had no expectations, and yet had had Estella to think of, I could not make out to my satisfaction that I should have done much better. Now, concerning the influence of my position on others, I was in no such difficulty, and so

I perceived—though dimly enough perhaps—that it was not beneficial to anybody, and, above all, that it was not beneficial to Herbert. My lavish habits led his easy nature into expenses that he could not afford, corrupted the simplicity of his life, and disturbed his peace with anxieties and regrets. I was not at all remorseful for having unwittingly set those other branches of the Pocket family to the poor arts they practised; because such littlenesses were their natural bent, and would have been evoked by anybody else, if I had left them slumbering. But Herbert's was a very different case, and it often caused me a twinge to think that I had done him evil service in crowding his sparely furnished chambers with incongruous upholstery work, and placing the Canary-breasted Avenger at his disposal.

So now, as an infallible way of making little ease great ease, I began to contract a quantity of debt. I could hardly begin but Herbert must begin too, so he soon followed. At Startop's suggestion, we put ourselves down for election into a club called The Finches of the Grove: the object of which institution I have never divined, if it were not that the members should dine expensively once a fortnight, to quarrel among themselves as much as possible after dinner, and to cause six waiters to get drunk on the stairs. I know that these gratifying social ends were so invariably accomplished, that Herbert and I understood nothing else to be referred to in the first standing toast of the society: which ran "Gentlemen, may the present promotion of good feeling ever reign predominant among the Finches of the Grove."

The Finches spent their money foolishly (the Hotel we dined at was in Covent Garden), and the first Finch I saw when I had the honour of joining the Grove was Bentley Drummle, at that time floundering about town in a cab of his own, and doing a great deal of damage to the posts at the street corners. Occasionally, he shot himself out of his equipage headforemost over the apron; and I saw him on one occasion deliver himself at the door of the Grove in this unintentional way—like coals. But here I anticipate a little, for I was not a Finch, and could not be, according to the sacred laws of the society, until I came of age.

In my confidence in my own resources, I would willingly have taken Herbert's expenses on myself; but Herbert was proud, and I could make no such proposal to him. So he got into difficulties in every direction, and continued to look about him. When we gradually fell into keeping late hours and late company, I noticed that he looked about him with a desponding eye at breakfast-time; that he began to look about him more hopefully about mid-day; that he drooped when he came into dinner; that he seemed to descry Capital in the distance, rather clearly, after dinner; that he all but realized Capital towards midnight; and that at about two o'clock in the morning, he became so deeply despondent again as to talk of buying a rifle and going to America, with a general purpose of compelling buffaloes to make his fortune.

I was usually at Hammersmith about half the week, and when I was at Hammersmith I haunted Richmond, whereof separately by and by. Herbert would often come to Hammersmith when I was there, and I think at those seasons his father would occasionally have some passing perception that the opening he was looking for, had not appeared yet. But in the general tumbling up of the family, his tumbling out in life somewhere, was a thing to transact itself somehow. In the meantime Mr. Pocket grew grayer, and tried oftener to lift himself out of his perplexities by the hair. While

Mrs. Pocket tripped up the family with her footstool, read her book of dignities, lost her pocket-handkerchief, told us about her grandpapa, and taught the young idea how to shoot, by shooting it into bed whenever it attracted her notice.

As I am now generalizing a period of my life with the object of clearing my way before me, I can scarcely do so better than by at once completing the description of our usual manners and customs at Barnard's Inn.

We spent as much money as we could, and got as little for it as people could make up their minds to give us. We were always more or less miserable, and most of our acquaintance were in the same condition. There was a gay fiction among us that we were constantly enjoying ourselves, and a skeleton truth that we never did. To the best of my belief, our case was in the last aspect a rather common one.

Every morning, with an air ever new, Herbert went into the City to look about him. I often paid him a visit in the dark back-room in which he consorted with an ink-jar, a hat-peg, a coal-box, a string-box, an almanac, a desk and stool, and a ruler; and I do not remember that I ever saw him do anything else but look about him. If we all did what we undertake to do, as faithfully as Herbert did, we might live in a Republic of the Virtues. He had nothing else to do, poor fellow, except at a certain hour of every afternoon to "go to Lloyd's"—in observance of a ceremony of seeing his principal, I think. He never did anything else in connection with Lloyd's that I could find out, except come back again. When he felt his case unusually serious, and that he positively must find an opening, he would go on 'Change at a busy time, and walk in and out, in a kind of gloomy country dance figure, among the assembled magnates. "For," says Herbert to me, coming home to dinner on one of those special occasions, "I find the truth to be, Handel, that an opening won't come to one, but one must go to it,—so I have been."

If we had been less attached to one another, I think we must have hated one another regularly every morning. I detested the chambers beyond expression at that period of repentance, and could not endure the sight of the Avenger's livery; which had a more expensive and a less remunerative appearance then than at any other time in the four-and-twenty hours. As we got more and more into debt, breakfast became a hollower and hollower form, and, being on one occasion at breakfast-time threatened (by letter) with legal proceedings, "not unwholly unconnected," as my local paper might put it, "with jewelery," I went so far as to seize the Avenger by his blue collar and shake him off his feet,—so that he was actually in the air, like a booted Cupid,—for presuming to suppose that we wanted a roll.

At certain times—meaning at uncertain times, for they depended on our humor—I would say to Herbert, as if it were a remarkable discovery,—

"My dear Herbert, we are getting on badly."

"My dear Handel," Herbert would say to me, in all sincerity, if you will believe me, those very words were on my lips, by a strange coincidence."

"Then, Herbert," I would respond, "let us look into out affairs."

We always derived profound satisfaction from making an appointment for this purpose. I always thought this was business, this was the way to confront the thing, this was the way to take the foe by the throat. And I know Herbert thought so too.

We ordered something rather special for dinner, with a bottle of something similarly out of the common way, in order that our minds might be fortified for the occasion, and we might come well up to the mark. Dinner over, we produced a bundle of pens, a copious supply of ink, and a goodly show of writing and blotting paper. For there was something very comfortable in having plenty of stationery.

I would then take a sheet of paper, and write across the top of it, in a neat hand, the heading, "Memorandum of Pip's debts"; with Barnard's Inn and the date very carefully added. Herbert would also take a sheet of paper, and write across it with similar formalities, "Memorandum of Herbert's debts."

Each of us would then refer to a confused heap of papers at his side, which had been thrown into drawers, worn into holes in pockets, half burnt in lighting candles, stuck for weeks into the looking-glass, and otherwise damaged. The sound of our pens going refreshed us exceedingly, insomuch that I sometimes found it difficult to distinguish between this edifying business proceeding and actually paying the money. In point of meritorious character, the two things seemed about equal.

When we had written a little while, I would ask Herbert how he got on? Herbert probably would have been scratching his head in a most rueful manner at the sight of his accumulating figures.

"They are mounting up, Handel," Herbert would say; "upon my life, they are mounting up."

"Be firm, Herbert," I would retort, plying my own pen with great assiduity. "Look the thing in the face. Look into your affairs. Stare them out of countenance."

"So I would, Handel, only they are staring me out of countenance."

However, my determined manner would have its effect, and Herbert would fall to work again. After a time he would give up once more, on the plea that he had not got Cobbs's bill, or Lobbs's, or Nobbs's, as the case might be.

"Then, Herbert, estimate; estimate it in round numbers, and put it down."

"What a fellow of resource you are!" my friend would reply, with admiration. "Really your business powers are very remarkable."

I thought so too. I established with myself, on these occasions, the reputation of a first-rate man of business,—prompt, decisive, energetic, clear, cool-headed. When I had got all my responsibilities down upon my list, I compared each with the bill, and ticked it off. My self-approval when I ticked an entry was quite a luxurious sensation. When I had no more ticks to make, I folded all my bills up uniformly, docketed each on the back, and tied the whole into a symmetrical bundle. Then I did the same for Herbert (who modestly said he had not my administrative genius), and felt that I had brought his affairs into a focus for him.

My business habits had one other bright feature, which I called "leaving a Margin." For example; supposing Herbert's debts to be one hundred and sixty-four pounds four-and-twopence, I would say, "Leave a margin, and put them down at two hundred." Or, supposing my own to be four times as much, I would leave a margin, and put them down at seven hundred. I had the highest opinion of the wisdom of this same Margin, but I am bound to acknowledge that on looking back, I deem it to have been an expensive device. For, we always ran into new debt immediately, to the full extent of the margin, and sometimes, in the sense of freedom and solvency it imparted, got pretty far on into another margin.

But there was a calm, a rest, a virtuous hush, consequent on these examinations of our affairs that gave me, for the time, an admirable opinion of myself. Soothed by my exertions, my method, and Herbert's compliments, I would sit with his symmetrical bundle and my own on the table before me among the stationary, and feel like a Bank of some sort, rather than a private individual.

We shut our outer door on these solemn occasions, in order that we might not be interrupted. I had fallen into my serene state one evening, when we heard a letter dropped through the slit in the said door, and fall on the ground. "It's for you, Handel," said Herbert, going out and coming back with it, "and I hope there is nothing the matter." This was in allusion to its heavy black seal and border.

The letter was signed Trabb & Co., and its contents were simply, that I was an honored sir, and that they begged to inform me that Mrs. J. Gargery had departed this life on Monday last at twenty minutes past six in the evening, and that my attendance was requested at the interment on Monday next at three o'clock in the afternoon.

CHAPTER XXXV

It was the first time that a grave had opened in my road of life, and the gap it made in the smooth ground was wonderful. The figure of my sister in her chair by the kitchen fire, haunted me night and day. That the place could possibly be, without her, was something my mind seemed unable to compass; and whereas she had seldom or never been in my thoughts of late, I had now the strangest ideas that she was coming towards me in the street, or that she would presently knock at the door. In my rooms too, with which she had never been at all associated, there was at once the blankness of death and a perpetual suggestion of the sound of her voice or the turn of her face or figure, as if she were still alive and had been often there.

Whatever my fortunes might have been, I could scarcely have recalled my sister with much tenderness. But I suppose there is a shock of regret which may exist without much tenderness. Under its influence (and perhaps to make up for the want of the softer feeling) I was seized with a violent indignation against the assailant from whom she had suffered so much; and I felt that on sufficient proof I could have revengefully pursued Orlick, or any one else, to the last extremity.

Having written to Joe, to offer him consolation, and to assure him that I would come to the funeral, I passed the intermediate days in the curious state of mind I have glanced at. I went down early in the morning, and alighted at the Blue Boar in good time to walk over to the forge.

It was fine summer weather again, and, as I walked along, the times when I was a little helpless creature, and my sister did not spare me, vividly returned. But they returned with a gentle tone upon them that softened even the edge of Tickler. For now, the very breath of the beans and clover whispered to my heart that the day must come when it would be well for my memory that others walking in the sunshine should be softened as they thought of me.

At last I came within sight of the house, and saw that Trabb and Co. had put in a funereal execution and taken possession. Two dismally absurd persons, each ostentatiously exhibiting a crutch done up in a black bandage,—as if that instrument could possibly communicate any comfort to anybody,—were posted at the front door; and in one of them I recognised a postboy discharged from the Boar for turning a young couple into a sawpit on their bridal morning, in consequence of intoxication rendering it necessary for him to ride his horse clasped round the neck with both arms. All the children of the village, and most of the women, were admiring these sable warders and the closed windows of the house and forge; and as I came up, one of the two warders (the postboy) knocked at the door,—implying that I was far too much exhausted by grief to have strength remaining to knock for myself.

Another sable warder (a carpenter, who had once eaten two geese for a wager) opened the door, and showed me into the best parlor. Here, Mr. Trabb had taken unto himself the best table, and had got all the leaves up, and was holding a kind of black Bazaar, with the aid of a quantity of black pins. At the moment of my arrival, he had just finished putting somebody's hat into black long-clothes, like an African baby; so he held out his hand for mine. But I, misled by the action, and confused by the occasion, shook hands with him with every testimony of warm affection.

Poor dear Joe, entangled in a little black cloak tied in a large bow under his chin, was seated apart at the upper end of the room; where, as chief mourner, he had evidently been stationed by Trabb. When I bent down and said to him, "Dear Joe, how are you?" he said, "Pip, old chap, you knowed her when she were a fine figure of a—" and clasped my hand and said no more.

Biddy, looking very neat and modest in her black dress, went quietly here and there, and was very helpful. When I had spoken to Biddy, as I thought it not a time for talking I went and sat down near Joe, and there began to wonder in what part of the house it—she—my sister—was. The air of the parlor being faint with the smell of sweet-cake, I looked about for the table of refreshments; it was scarcely visible until one had got accustomed to the gloom, but there was a cut-up plum cake upon it, and there were cut-up oranges, and sandwiches, and biscuits, and two decanters that I knew very well as ornaments, but had never seen used in all my life; one full of port, and one of sherry. Standing at this table, I became conscious of the servile Pumblechook in a black cloak and several yards of hatband, who was alternately stuffing himself, and making obsequious movements to catch my attention. The moment he succeeded, he came over to me (breathing sherry and crumbs), and said in a subdued voice, "May I, dear sir?" and did. I then descried Mr. and Mrs. Hubble; the last-named in a decent speechless paroxysm in a corner. We were all going to "follow," and were all in course of being tied up separately (by Trabb) into ridiculous bundles.

"Which I meantersay, Pip," Joe whispered me, as we were being what Mr. Trabb called "formed" in the parlor, two and two,—and it was dreadfully like a preparation for some grim kind of dance; "which I meantersay, sir, as I would in preference have carried her to the church myself, along with three or four friendly ones wot come to it with willing harts and arms, but it were considered wot the neighbors would look down on such and would be of opinions as it were wanting in respect."

"Pocket-handkerchiefs out, all!" cried Mr. Trabb at this point, in a depressed business-like voice. "Pocket-handkerchiefs out! We are ready!"

So we all put our pocket-handkerchiefs to our faces, as if our noses were bleeding, and filed out two and two; Joe and I; Biddy and Pumblechook; Mr. and Mrs. Hubble. The remains of my poor sister had been brought round by the kitchen door, and, it being a point of Undertaking ceremony that the six bearers must be stifled and blinded under a horrible black velvet housing with a white border, the whole looked like a blind monster with twelve human legs, shuffling and blundering along, under the guidance of two keepers,—the postboy and his comrade.

The neighborhood, however, highly approved of these arrangements, and we were much admired as we went through the village; the more youthful and vigorous part of the community making dashes now and then to cut us off, and lying in wait to intercept us at points of vantage. At such times the more exuberant among them called out in an excited manner on our emergence round some corner of expectancy, "Here they come!" "Here they are!" and we were all but cheered. In this progress I was much annoyed by the abject Pumblechook, who, being behind me, persisted all the way as a delicate attention in arranging my streaming hatband, and smoothing my cloak. My thoughts were further distracted by the excessive pride of Mr. and Mrs. Hubble, who were surpassingly conceited and vainglorious in being members of so distinguished a procession.

And now the range of marshes lay clear before us, with the sails of the ships on the river growing out of it; and we went into the churchyard, close to the graves of my unknown parents, Philip Pirrip, late of this parish, and Also Georgiana, Wife of the Above. And there, my sister was laid quietly in the earth, while the larks sang high above it, and the light wind strewed it with beautiful shadows of clouds and trees.

Of the conduct of the worldly minded Pumblechook while this was doing, I desire to say no more than it was all addressed to me; and that even when those noble passages were read which remind humanity how it brought nothing into the world and can take nothing out, and how it fleeth like a shadow and never continueth long in one stay, I heard him cough a reservation of the case of a young gentleman who came unexpectedly into large property. When we got back, he had the hardihood to tell me that he wished my sister could have known I had done her so much honor, and to hint that she would have considered it reasonably purchased at the price of her death. After that, he drank all the rest of the sherry, and Mr. Hubble drank the port, and the two talked (which I have since observed to be customary in such cases) as if they were of quite another race from the deceased, and were notoriously immortal. Finally, he went away with Mr. and Mrs. Hubble,—to make an evening of it, I felt sure, and to tell the Jolly Bargemen that he was the founder of my fortunes and my earliest benefactor.

When they were all gone, and when Trabb and his men—but not his Boy; I looked for him—had crammed their mummery into bags, and were gone too, the house felt wholesomer. Soon afterwards, Biddy, Joe, and I, had a cold dinner together; but we dined in the best parlor, not in the old kitchen, and Joe was so exceedingly particular what he did with his knife and fork and the saltcellar and what not, that there was great restraint upon us. But after dinner, when I made him take his pipe, and when I had loitered with him about the forge, and when we sat down together on the great block of stone outside it, we got on better. I noticed that after the funeral Joe changed his clothes so far, as to make a compromise between his Sunday dress and working dress; in which the dear fellow looked natural, and like the Man he was.

He was very much pleased by my asking if I might sleep in my own little room, and I was pleased too; for I felt that I had done rather a great thing in making the request. When the shadows of evening were closing in, I took an opportunity of getting into the garden with Biddy for a little talk.

"Biddy," said I, "I think you might have written to me about these sad matters."

"Do you, Mr. Pip?" said Biddy. "I should have written if I had thought that."

"Don't suppose that I mean to be unkind, Biddy, when I say I consider that you ought to have thought that."

"Do you, Mr. Pip?"

She was so quiet, and had such an orderly, good, and pretty way with her, that I did not like the thought of making her cry again. After looking a little at her downcast eyes as she walked beside me, I gave up that point.

"I suppose it will be difficult for you to remain here now, Biddy dear?"

"Oh! I can't do so, Mr. Pip," said Biddy, in a tone of regret but still of quiet conviction. "I have been speaking to Mrs. Hubble, and I am going to her to-morrow. I hope we shall be able to take some care of Mr. Gargery, together, until he settles down."

"How are you going to live, Biddy? If you want any mo—"

"How am I going to live?" repeated Biddy, striking in, with a momentary flush upon her face. "I'll tell you, Mr. Pip. I am going to try to get the place of mistress in the new school nearly finished here. I can be well recommended by all the neighbors, and I hope I can be industrious and patient, and teach myself while I teach others. You know, Mr. Pip," pursued Biddy, with a smile, as she raised her eyes to my face, "the new schools are not like the old, but I learnt a good deal from you after that time, and have had time since then to improve."

"I think you would always improve, Biddy, under any circumstances."

"Ah! Except in my bad side of human nature," murmured Biddy.

It was not so much a reproach as an irresistible thinking aloud. Well! I thought I would give up that point too. So, I walked a little further with Biddy, looking silently at her downcast eyes.

"I have not heard the particulars of my sister's death, Biddy."

"They are very slight, poor thing. She had been in one of her bad states—though they had got better of late, rather than worse—for four days, when she came out of it in the evening, just at tea-time, and said quite plainly, 'Joe.' As she had never said any word for a long while, I ran and fetched in Mr. Gargery from the forge. She made signs to me that she wanted him to sit down close to her, and wanted me to put her arms round his neck. So I put them round his neck, and she laid her head down on his shoulder quite content and satisfied. And so she presently said 'Joe' again, and once 'Pardon,' and once 'Pip.' And so she never lifted her head up any more, and it was just an hour later when we laid it down on her own bed, because we found she was gone."

Biddy cried; the darkening garden, and the lane, and the stars that were coming out, were blurred in my own sight.

"Nothing was ever discovered, Biddy?"

"Nothing."

"Do you know what is become of Orlick?"

"I should think from the color of his clothes that he is working in the quarries."

"Of course you have seen him then?—Why are you looking at that dark tree in the lane?"

"I saw him there, on the night she died."

"That was not the last time either, Biddy?"

"No; I have seen him there, since we have been walking here.—It is of no use," said Biddy, laying her hand upon my arm, as I was for running out, "you know I would not deceive you; he was not there a minute, and he is gone."

It revived my utmost indignation to find that she was still pursued by this fellow, and I felt inveterate against him. I told her so, and told her that I would spend any money or take any pains to drive him out of that country. By degrees she led me into more temperate talk, and she told me how Joe loved me, and how Joe never complained of anything,—she didn't say, of me; she had no need; I knew what she meant,—but ever did his duty in his way of life, with a strong hand, a quiet tongue, and a gentle heart.

"Indeed, it would be hard to say too much for him," said I; "and Biddy, we must often speak of these things, for of course I shall be often down here now. I am not going to leave poor Joe alone."

Biddy said never a single word.

"Biddy, don't you hear me?"

"Yes, Mr. Pip."

"Not to mention your calling me Mr. Pip,—which appears to me to be in bad taste, Biddy,—what do you mean?"

"What do I mean?" asked Biddy, timidly.

"Biddy," said I, in a virtuously self-asserting manner, "I must request to know what you mean by this?"

"By this?" said Biddy.

"Now, don't echo," I retorted. "You used not to echo, Biddy."

"Used not!" said Biddy. "O Mr. Pip! Used!"

Well! I rather thought I would give up that point too. After another silent turn in the garden, I fell back on the main position.

"Biddy," said I, "I made a remark respecting my coming down here often, to see Joe, which you received with a marked silence. Have the goodness, Biddy, to tell me why."

"Are you quite sure, then, that you WILL come to see him often?" asked Biddy, stopping in the narrow garden walk, and looking at me under the stars with a clear and honest eye.

"O dear me!" said I, as if I found myself compelled to give up Biddy in despair. "This really is a very bad side of human nature! Don't say any more, if you please, Biddy. This shocks me very much."

For which cogent reason I kept Biddy at a distance during supper, and when I went up to my own old little room, took as stately a leave of her as I could, in my murmuring soul, deem reconcilable with the churchyard and the event of the day. As often as I was restless in the night, and that was every quarter of an hour, I reflected what an unkindness, what an injury, what an injustice, Biddy had done me.

Early in the morning I was to go. Early in the morning I was out, and looking in, unseen, at one of the wooden windows of the forge. There I stood, for minutes, looking at Joe, already at work with a glow of health and strength upon his face that made it show as if the bright sun of the life in store for him were shining on it.

"Good by, dear Joe!—No, don't wipe it off—for God's sake, give me your blackened hand!—I shall be down soon and often."

"Never too soon, sir," said Joe, "and never too often, Pip!"

Biddy was waiting for me at the kitchen door, with a mug of new milk and a crust of bread. "Biddy," said I, when I gave her my hand at parting, "I am not angry, but I am hurt."

"No, don't be hurt," she pleaded quite pathetically; "let only me be hurt, if I have been ungenerous."

Once more, the mists were rising as I walked away. If they disclosed to me, as I suspect they did, that I should not come back, and that Biddy was quite right, all I can say is,—they were quite right too.

CHAPTER XXXVI

Herbert and I went on from bad to worse, in the way of increasing our debts, looking into our affairs, leaving Margins, and the like exemplary transactions; and Time went on, whether or no, as he has a way of doing; and I came of age,—in fulfilment of Herbert's prediction, that I should do so before I knew where I was.

Herbert himself had come of age eight months before me. As he had nothing else than his majority to come into, the event did not make a profound sensation in Barnard's Inn. But we had looked forward to my one-and-twentieth birthday, with a crowd of speculations and anticipations, for we had both considered that my guardian could hardly help saying something definite on that occasion.

I had taken care to have it well understood in Little Britain when my birthday was. On the day before it, I received an official note from Wemmick, informing me that Mr. Jaggers would be glad if I would call upon him at five in the afternoon of the auspicious day. This convinced us that something great was to happen, and threw me into an unusual flutter when I repaired to my guardian's office, a model of punctuality.

In the outer office Wemmick offered me his congratulations, and incidentally rubbed the side of his nose with a folded piece of tissue-paper that I liked the look of. But he said nothing respecting it, and motioned me with a nod into my guardian's room. It was November, and my guardian was standing before his fire leaning his back against the chimney-piece, with his hands under his coattails.

"Well, Pip," said he, "I must call you Mr. Pip to-day. Congratulations, Mr. Pip."

We shook hands,—he was always a remarkably short shaker,—and I thanked him.

"Take a chair, Mr. Pip," said my guardian.

As I sat down, and he preserved his attitude and bent his brows at his boots, I felt at a disadvantage, which reminded me of that old time when I had been put upon a tombstone. The two ghastly casts on the shelf were not far from him, and their expression was as if they were making a stupid apoplectic attempt to attend to the conversation.

"Now my young friend," my guardian began, as if I were a witness in the box, "I am going to have a word or two with you."

"If you please, sir."

"What do you suppose," said Mr. Jaggers, bending forward to look at the ground, and then throwing his head back to look at the ceiling,—"what do you suppose you are living at the rate of?"

"At the rate of, sir?"

"At," repeated Mr. Jaggers, still looking at the ceiling, "the—rate—of?" And then looked all round the room, and paused with his pocket-handkerchief in his hand, half-way to his nose.

I had looked into my affairs so often, that I had thoroughly destroyed any slight notion I might ever have had of their bearings. Reluctantly, I confessed myself quite unable to answer the question. This reply seemed agreeable to Mr. Jaggers, who said, "I thought so!" and blew his nose with an air of satisfaction.

"Now, I have asked you a question, my friend," said Mr. Jaggers. "Have you anything to ask me?"

"Of course it would be a great relief to me to ask you several questions, sir; but I remember your prohibition."

"Ask one," said Mr. Jaggers.

"Is my benefactor to be made known to me to-day?"

"No. Ask another."

"Is that confidence to be imparted to me soon?"

"Waive that, a moment," said Mr. Jaggers, "and ask another."

I looked about me, but there appeared to be now no possible escape from the inquiry, "Have-I—anything to receive, sir?" On that, Mr. Jaggers said, triumphantly, "I thought we should come to it!" and called to Wemmick to give him that piece of paper. Wemmick appeared, handed it in, and disappeared.

"Now, Mr. Pip," said Mr. Jaggers, "attend, if you please. You have been drawing pretty freely here; your name occurs pretty often in Wemmick's cash-book; but you are in debt, of course?"

"I am afraid I must say yes, sir."

"You know you must say yes; don't you?" said Mr. Jaggers.

"Yes, sir."

"I don't ask you what you owe, because you don't know; and if you did know, you wouldn't tell me; you would say less. Yes, yes, my friend," cried Mr. Jaggers, waving his forefinger to stop me as I made a show of protesting: "it's likely enough that you think you wouldn't, but you would. You'll excuse me, but I know better than you. Now, take this piece of paper in your hand. You have got it? Very good. Now, unfold it and tell me what it is."

"This is a bank-note," said I, "for five hundred pounds."

"That is a bank-note," repeated Mr. Jaggers, "for five hundred pounds. And a very handsome sum of money too, I think. You consider it so?"

"How could I do otherwise!"

"Ah! But answer the question," said Mr. Jaggers.

"Undoubtedly."

"You consider it, undoubtedly, a handsome sum of money. Now, that handsome sum of money, Pip, is your own. It is a present to you on this day, in earnest of your expectations. And at the rate of that handsome sum of money per annum, and at no higher rate, you are to live until the donor of the whole appears. That is to say, you will now take your money affairs entirely into your own hands, and you will draw from Wemmick one hundred and twenty-five pounds per quarter, until you are in communication with the fountain-head, and no longer with the mere agent. As I have told you before, I am the mere agent. I execute my instructions, and I am paid for doing so. I think them injudicious, but I am not paid for giving any opinion on their merits."

I was beginning to express my gratitude to my benefactor for the great liberality with which I was treated, when Mr. Jaggers stopped me. "I am not paid, Pip," said he, coolly, "to carry your words to any one;" and then gathered up his coat-tails, as he had gathered up the subject, and stood frowning at his boots as if he suspected them of designs against him.

After a pause, I hinted,—

"There was a question just now, Mr. Jaggers, which you desired me to waive for a moment. I hope I am doing nothing wrong in asking it again?"

"What is it?" said he.

I might have known that he would never help me out; but it took me aback to have to shape the question afresh, as if it were quite new. "Is it likely," I said, after hesitating, "that my patron, the fountain-head you have spoken of, Mr. Jaggers, will soon—" there I delicately stopped.

"Will soon what?" asked Mr. Jaggers. "That's no question as it stands, you know."

"Will soon come to London," said I, after casting about for a precise form of words, "or summon me anywhere else?"

"Now, here," replied Mr. Jaggers, fixing me for the first time with his dark deep-set eyes, "we must revert to the evening when we first encountered one another in your village. What did I tell you then, Pip?"

"You told me, Mr. Jaggers, that it might be years hence when that person appeared."

"Just so," said Mr. Jaggers, "that's my answer."

As we looked full at one another, I felt my breath come quicker in my strong desire to get something out of him. And as I felt that it came quicker, and as I felt that he saw that it came quicker, I felt that I had less chance than ever of getting anything out of him.

"Do you suppose it will still be years hence, Mr. Jaggers?"

Mr. Jaggers shook his head,—not in negativing the question, but in altogether negativing the notion that he could anyhow be got to answer it,—and the two horrible casts of the twitched faces looked, when my eyes strayed up to them, as if they had come to a crisis in their suspended attention, and were going to sneeze.

"Come!" said Mr. Jaggers, warming the backs of his legs with the backs of his warmed hands, "I'll be plain with you, my friend Pip. That's a question I must not be asked. You'll understand that better, when I tell you it's a question that might compromise me. Come! I'll go a little further with you; I'll say something more."

He bent down so low to frown at his boots, that he was able to rub the calves of his legs in the pause he made.

"When that person discloses," said Mr. Jaggers, straightening himself, "you and that person will settle your own affairs. When that person discloses, my part in this business will cease and determine. When that person discloses, it will not be necessary for me to know anything about it. And that's all I have got to say."

We looked at one another until I withdrew my eyes, and looked thoughtfully at the floor. From this last speech I derived the notion that Miss Havisham, for some reason or no reason, had not taken him into her confidence as to her designing me for Estella; that he resented this, and felt a jealousy about it; or that he really did object to that scheme, and would have nothing to do with it. When I raised my eyes again, I found that he had been shrewdly looking at me all the time, and was doing so still.

"If that is all you have to say, sir," I remarked, "there can be nothing left for me to say."

He nodded assent, and pulled out his thief-dreaded watch, and asked me where I was going to dine? I replied at my own chambers, with Herbert. As a necessary sequence, I asked him if he would favor us with his company, and he promptly accepted the invitation. But he insisted on walking home with me, in order that I might make no extra preparation for him, and first he had a letter or two to write, and (of course) had his hands to wash. So I said I would go into the outer office and talk to Wemmick.

The fact was, that when the five hundred pounds had come into my pocket, a thought had come into my head which had been often there before; and it appeared to me that Wemmick was a good person to advise with concerning such thought.

He had already locked up his safe, and made preparations for going home. He had left his desk, brought out his two greasy office candlesticks and stood them in line with the snuffers on a slab near the door, ready to be extinguished; he had raked his fire low, put his hat and great-coat ready, and was beating himself all over the chest with his safe-key, as an athletic exercise after business.

"Mr. Wemmick," said I, "I want to ask your opinion. I am very desirous to serve a friend."

Wemmick tightened his post-office and shook his head, as if his opinion were dead against any fatal weakness of that sort.

"This friend," I pursued, "is trying to get on in commercial life, but has no money, and finds it difficult and disheartening to make a beginning. Now I want somehow to help him to a beginning."

"With money down?" said Wemmick, in a tone drier than any sawdust.

"With some money down," I replied, for an uneasy remembrance shot across me of that symmetrical bundle of papers at home—"with some money down, and perhaps some anticipation of my expectations."

"Mr. Pip," said Wemmick, "I should like just to run over with you on my fingers, if you please, the names of the various bridges up as high as Chelsea Reach. Let's see; there's London, one; Southwark, two; Blackfriars, three; Waterloo, four; Westminster, five; Vauxhall, six." He had checked off each bridge in its turn, with the handle of his safe-key on the palm of his hand. "There's as many as six, you see, to choose from."

"I don't understand you," said I.

"Choose your bridge, Mr. Pip," returned Wemmick, "and take a walk upon your bridge, and pitch your money into the Thames over the centre arch of your bridge, and you know the end of it. Serve a friend with it, and you may know the end of it too,—but it's a less pleasant and profitable end."

I could have posted a newspaper in his mouth, he made it so wide after saying this.

"This is very discouraging," said I.

"Meant to be so," said Wemmick.

"Then is it your opinion," I inquired, with some little indignation, "that a man should never—"

"—Invest portable property in a friend?" said Wemmick. "Certainly he should not. Unless he wants to get rid of the friend,—and then it becomes a question how much portable property it may be worth to get rid of him."

"And that," said I, "is your deliberate opinion, Mr. Wemmick?"

"That," he returned, "is my deliberate opinion in this office."

"Ah!" said I, pressing him, for I thought I saw him near a loophole here; "but would that be your opinion at Walworth?"

"Mr. Pip," he replied, with gravity, "Walworth is one place, and this office is another. Much as the Aged is one person, and Mr. Jaggers is another. They must not be confounded together. My Walworth sentiments must be taken at Walworth; none but my official sentiments can be taken in this office."

"Very well," said I, much relieved, "then I shall look you up at Walworth, you may depend upon it."

"Mr. Pip," he returned, "you will be welcome there, in a private and personal capacity."

We had held this conversation in a low voice, well knowing my guardian's ears to be the sharpest of the sharp. As he now appeared in his doorway, towelling his hands, Wemmick got on his great-coat and stood by to snuff out the candles. We all three went into the street together, and from the door-step Wemmick turned his way, and Mr. Jaggers and I turned ours.

I could not help wishing more than once that evening, that Mr. Jaggers had had an Aged in Gerrard Street, or a Stinger, or a Something, or a Somebody, to unbend his brows a little. It was an uncomfortable consideration on a twenty-first birthday, that coming of age at all seemed hardly worth while in such a guarded and suspicious world as he made of it. He was a thousand times better informed and cleverer than Wemmick, and yet I would a thousand times rather have had Wemmick to dinner.

And Mr. Jaggers made not me alone intensely melancholy, because, after he was gone, Herbert said of himself, with his eyes fixed on the fire, that he thought he must have committed a felony and forgotten the details of it, he felt so dejected and guilty.

CHAPTER XXXVII

Deeming Sunday the best day for taking Mr. Wemmick's Walworth sentiments, I devoted the next ensuing Sunday afternoon to a pilgrimage to the Castle. On arriving before the battlements, I found the Union Jack flying and the drawbridge up; but undeterred by this show of defiance and resistance, I rang at the gate, and was admitted in a most pacific manner by the Aged.

"My son, sir," said the old man, after securing the drawbridge, "rather had it in his mind that you might happen to drop in, and he left word that he would soon be home from his afternoon's walk. He is very regular in his walks, is my son. Very regular in everything, is my son."

I nodded at the old gentleman as Wemmick himself might have nodded, and we went in and sat down by the fireside.

"You made acquaintance with my son, sir," said the old man, in his chirping way, while he warmed his hands at the blaze, "at his office, I expect?" I nodded. "Hah! I have heerd that my son is a wonderful hand at his business, sir?" I nodded hard. "Yes; so they tell me. His business is the Law?" I nodded harder. "Which makes it more surprising in my son," said the old man, "for he was not brought up to the Law, but to the Wine-Coopering."

Curious to know how the old gentleman stood informed concerning the reputation of Mr. Jaggers, I roared that name at him. He threw me into the greatest confusion by laughing heartily and replying in a very sprightly manner, "No, to be sure; you're right." And to this hour I have not the faintest notion what he meant, or what joke he thought I had made.

As I could not sit there nodding at him perpetually, without making some other attempt to interest him, I shouted at inquiry whether his own calling in life had been "the Wine-Coopering." By dint of straining that term out of myself several times and tapping the old gentleman on the chest to associate it with him, I at last succeeded in making my meaning understood.

"No," said the old gentleman; "the warehousing, the warehousing. First, over yonder;" he appeared to mean up the chimney, but I believe he intended to refer me to Liverpool; "and then in the City of London here. However, having an infirmity—for I am hard of hearing, sir—"

I expressed in pantomime the greatest astonishment.

"—Yes, hard of hearing; having that infirmity coming upon me, my son he went into the Law, and he took charge of me, and he by little and little made out this elegant and beautiful property. But returning to what you said, you know," pursued the old man, again laughing heartily, "what I say is, No to be sure; you're right."

I was modestly wondering whether my utmost ingenuity would have enabled me to say anything that would have amused him half as much as this imaginary pleasantry, when I was startled by a sudden click in the wall on one side of the chimney, and the ghostly tumbling open of a little wooden flap with "JOHN" upon it. The old man, following my eyes, cried with great triumph, "My son's come home!" and we both went out to the drawbridge.

It was worth any money to see Wemmick waving a salute to me from the other side of the moat, when we might have shaken hands across it with the greatest ease. The Aged was so delighted to work the drawbridge, that I made no offer to assist him, but stood quiet until Wemmick had come across, and had presented me to Miss Skiffins; a lady by whom he was accompanied.

Miss Skiffins was of a wooden appearance, and was, like her escort, in the post-office branch of the service. She might have been some two or three years younger than Wemmick, and I judged her to stand possessed of portable property. The cut of her dress from the waist upward, both before and behind, made her figure very like a boy's kite; and I might have pronounced her gown a little too decidedly orange, and her gloves a little too intensely green. But she seemed to be a good sort of fellow, and showed a high regard for the Aged. I was not long in discovering that she was a frequent visitor at the Castle; for, on our going in, and my complimenting Wemmick on his ingenious contrivance for announcing himself to the Aged, he begged me to give my attention for a moment to the other side of the chimney, and disappeared. Presently another click came, and another little door tumbled open with "Miss Skiffins" on it; then Miss Skiffins shut up and John tumbled open; then Miss Skiffins and John both tumbled open together, and finally shut up together. On Wemmick's return from working these mechanical appliances, I expressed the great admiration with which I regarded them, and he said, "Well, you know, they're both pleasant and useful to the Aged. And by George, sir, it's a thing worth mentioning, that of all the people who come to this gate, the secret of those pulls is only known to the Aged, Miss Skiffins, and me!"

"And Mr. Wemmick made them," added Miss Skiffins, "with his own hands out of his own head."

While Miss Skiffins was taking off her bonnet (she retained her green gloves during the evening as an outward and visible sign that there was company), Wemmick invited me to take a walk with him round the property, and see how the island looked in wintertime. Thinking that he did this to give me an opportunity of taking his Walworth sentiments, I seized the opportunity as soon as we were out of the Castle.

Having thought of the matter with care, I approached my subject as if I had never hinted at it before. I informed Wemmick that I was anxious in behalf of Herbert Pocket, and I told him how we had first met, and how we had fought. I glanced at Herbert's home, and at his character, and at his having no means but such as he was dependent on his father for; those, uncertain and unpunctual. I alluded to the advantages I had derived in my first rawness and ignorance from his society, and I confessed that I feared I had but ill repaid them, and that he might have done better without me and my expectations. Keeping Miss Havisham in the background at a great distance, I still hinted at the possibility of my having competed with him in his prospects, and at the certainty of his possessing a generous soul, and being far above any mean distrusts, retaliations, or designs. For all these reasons (I told Wemmick), and because he was my young companion and friend, and I had a great affection for him, I wished my own good fortune to reflect some rays upon him, and therefore I sought advice from Wemmick's experience and knowledge of men and affairs, how I could best try with my resources to help Herbert to some present income,—say of a hundred a year, to keep him in good hope and heart,—and gradually to buy him on to some small partnership. I begged Wemmick, in conclusion, to understand that my help must always be rendered without Herbert's knowledge or suspicion, and that there was no one else in the world with whom I could advise. I wound up by laying my hand upon his shoulder, and saying, "I can't help confiding in you, though I know it must be troublesome to you; but that is your fault, in having ever brought me here."

Wemmick was silent for a little while, and then said with a kind of start, "Well you know, Mr. Pip, I must tell you one thing. This is devilish good of you."

"Say you'll help me to be good then," said I.

"Ecod," replied Wemmick, shaking his head, "that's not my trade."

"Nor is this your trading-place," said I.

"You are right," he returned. "You hit the nail on the head. Mr. Pip, I'll put on my considering-cap, and I think all you want to do may be done by degrees. Skiffins (that's her brother) is an accountant and agent. I'll look him up and go to work for you."

"I thank you ten thousand times."

"On the contrary," said he, "I thank you, for though we are strictly in our private and personal capacity, still it may be mentioned that there are Newgate cobwebs about, and it brushes them away."

After a little further conversation to the same effect, we returned into the Castle where we found Miss Skiffins preparing tea. The responsible duty of making the toast was delegated to the Aged, and that excellent old gentleman was so intent upon it that he seemed to me in some danger of melting his eyes. It was no nominal meal that we were going to make, but a vigorous reality. The Aged prepared such a hay-stack of buttered toast, that I could scarcely see him over it as it simmered on an iron stand hooked on to the top-bar; while Miss Skiffins brewed such a jorum of tea, that the pig in the back premises became strongly excited, and repeatedly expressed his desire to participate in the entertainment.

The flag had been struck, and the gun had been fired, at the right moment of time, and I felt as snugly cut off from the rest of Walworth as if the moat were thirty feet wide by as many deep. Nothing disturbed the tranquillity of the Castle, but the occasional tumbling open of John and Miss Skiffins: which little doors were a prey to some spasmodic infirmity that made me sympathetically uncomfortable until I got used to it. I inferred from the methodical nature of Miss Skiffins's arrangements that she made tea there every Sunday night; and I rather suspected that a classic brooch she wore, representing the profile of an undesirable female with a very straight nose and a very new moon, was a piece of portable property that had been given her by Wemmick.

We ate the whole of the toast, and drank tea in proportion, and it was delightful to see how warm and greasy we all got after it. The Aged especially, might have passed for some clean old chief of a savage tribe, just oiled. After a short pause of repose, Miss Skiffins—in the absence of the little servant who, it seemed, retired to the bosom of her family on Sunday afternoons—washed up the tea-things, in a trifling lady-like amateur manner that compromised none of us. Then, she put on her gloves again, and we drew round the fire, and Wemmick said, "Now, Aged Parent, tip us the paper."

Wemmick explained to me while the Aged got his spectacles out, that this was according to custom, and that it gave the old gentleman infinite satisfaction to read the news aloud. "I won't offer an apology," said Wemmick, "for he isn't capable of many pleasures—are you, Aged P.?"

"All right, John, all right," returned the old man, seeing himself spoken to.

"Only tip him a nod every now and then when he looks off his paper," said Wemmick, "and he'll be as happy as a king. We are all attention, Aged One."

"All right, John, all right!" returned the cheerful old man, so busy and so pleased, that it really was quite charming.

The Aged's reading reminded me of the classes at Mr. Wopsle's great-aunt's, with the pleasanter peculiarity that it seemed to come through a keyhole. As he wanted the candles close to him, and as he was always on the verge of putting either his head or the newspaper into them, he required as much watching as a powder-mill. But Wemmick was equally untiring and gentle in his vigilance, and the Aged read on, quite unconscious of his many rescues. Whenever he looked at us, we all expressed the greatest interest and amazement, and nodded until he resumed again.

As Wemmick and Miss Skiffins sat side by side, and as I sat in a shadowy corner, I observed a slow and gradual elongation of Mr. Wemmick's mouth, powerfully suggestive of his slowly and gradually stealing his arm round Miss Skiffins's waist. In course of time I saw his hand appear on the other side of Miss Skiffins; but at that moment Miss Skiffins neatly stopped him with the green glove, unwound his arm again as if it were an article of dress, and with the greatest deliberation laid it on the table before her. Miss Skiffins's composure while she did this was one of the most remarkable sights I have ever seen, and if I could have thought the act consistent with abstraction of mind, I should have deemed that Miss Skiffins performed it mechanically.

By and by, I noticed Wemmick's arm beginning to disappear again, and gradually fading out of view. Shortly afterwards, his mouth began to widen again. After an interval of suspense on my part that was quite enthralling and almost painful, I saw his hand appear on the other side of Miss Skiffins. Instantly, Miss Skiffins stopped it with the neatness of a placid boxer, took off that girdle or cestus as before, and laid it on the table. Taking the table to represent the path of virtue, I am justified in stating that during the whole time of the Aged's reading, Wemmick's arm was straying from the path of virtue and being recalled to it by Miss Skiffins.

At last, the Aged read himself into a light slumber. This was the time for Wemmick to produce a little kettle, a tray of glasses, and a black bottle with a porcelain-topped cork, representing some clerical dignitary of a rubicund and social aspect. With the aid of these appliances we all had something warm to drink, including the Aged, who was soon awake again. Miss Skiffins mixed, and I observed that she and Wemmick drank out of one glass. Of course I knew better than to offer to see Miss Skiffins home, and under the circumstances I thought I had best go first; which I did, taking a cordial leave of the Aged, and having passed a pleasant evening.

Before a week was out, I received a note from Wemmick, dated Walworth, stating that he hoped he had made some advance in that matter appertaining to our private and personal capacities, and that he would be glad if I could come and see him again upon it. So, I went out to Walworth again, and yet again, and yet again, and I saw him by appointment in the City several times, but never held any communication with him on the subject in or near Little Britain. The upshot was, that we found a worthy young merchant or shipping-broker, not long established in business, who wanted intelligent help, and who wanted capital, and who in due course of time and receipt would want a partner. Between him and me, secret articles were signed of which Herbert was the subject, and I paid him half of my five hundred pounds down, and engaged for sundry other payments: some, to fall due at certain dates out of my income: some, contingent on my coming into my property. Miss Skiffins's brother conducted the negotiation. Wemmick pervaded it throughout, but never appeared in it.

The whole business was so cleverly managed, that Herbert had not the least suspicion of my hand being in it. I never shall forget the radiant face with which he came home one afternoon, and told me, as a mighty piece of news, of his having fallen in with one Clarriker (the young merchant's name), and of Clarriker's having shown an extraordinary inclination towards him, and of his belief that the opening had come at last. Day by day as his hopes grew stronger and his face brighter, he must have thought me a more and more affectionate friend, for I had the greatest difficulty in restraining my tears of triumph when I saw him so happy. At length, the thing being done, and he having that day entered Clarriker's House, and he having talked to me for a whole evening in a flush of pleasure and success, I did really cry in good earnest when I went to bed, to think that my expectations had done some good to somebody.

A great event in my life, the turning point of my life, now opens on my view. But, before I proceed to narrate it, and before I pass on to all the changes it involved, I must give one chapter to Estella. It is not much to give to the theme that so long filled my heart.

CHAPTER XXXVIII

If that staid old house near the Green at Richmond should ever come to be haunted when I am dead, it will be haunted, surely, by my ghost. O the many, many nights and days through which the unquiet spirit within me haunted that house when Estella lived there! Let my body be where it would, my spirit was always wandering, wandering, wandering, about that house.

The lady with whom Estella was placed, Mrs. Brandley by name, was a widow, with one daughter several years older than Estella. The mother looked young, and the daughter looked old; the mother's complexion was pink, and the daughter's was yellow; the mother set up for frivolity, and the daughter for theology. They were in what is called a good position, and visited, and were visited by, numbers of people. Little, if any, community of feeling subsisted between them and Estella, but the understanding was established that they were necessary to her, and that she was necessary to them. Mrs. Brandley had been a friend of Miss Havisham's before the time of her seclusion.

In Mrs. Brandley's house and out of Mrs. Brandley's house, I suffered every kind and degree of torture that Estella could cause me. The nature of my relations with her, which placed me on terms of familiarity without placing me on terms of favor, conduced to my distraction. She made use of me to tease other admirers, and she turned the very familiarity between herself and me to the account of putting a constant slight on my devotion to her. If I had been her secretary, steward, half-brother, poor relation,—if I had been a younger brother of her appointed husband,—I could not have seemed to myself further from my hopes when I was nearest to her. The privilege of calling her by her name and hearing her call me by mine became, under the circumstances an aggravation of my trials; and while I think it likely that it almost maddened her other lovers, I know too certainly that it almost maddened me.

She had admirers without end. No doubt my jealousy made an admirer of every one who went near her; but there were more than enough of them without that.

I saw her often at Richmond, I heard of her often in town, and I used often to take her and the Brandleys on the water; there were picnics, fête days, plays, operas, concerts, parties, all sorts of pleasures, through which I pursued her,—and they were all miseries to me. I never had one hour's happiness in her society, and yet my mind all round the four-and-twenty hours was harping on the happiness of having her with me unto death.

Throughout this part of our intercourse,—and it lasted, as will presently be seen, for what I then thought a long time,—she habitually reverted to that tone which expressed that our association was forced upon us. There were other times when she would come to a sudden check in this tone and in all her many tones, and would seem to pity me.

"Pip, Pip," she said one evening, coming to such a check, when we sat apart at a darkening window of the house in Richmond; "will you never take warning?"

"Of what?"

"Of me."

"Warning not to be attracted by you, do you mean, Estella?"

"Do I mean! If you don't know what I mean, you are blind."

I should have replied that Love was commonly reputed blind, but for the reason that I always was restrained—and this was not the least of my miseries—by a feeling that it was ungenerous to press myself upon her, when she knew that she could not choose but obey Miss Havisham. My dread always was, that this knowledge on her part laid me under a heavy disadvantage with her pride, and made me the subject of a rebellious struggle in her bosom.

"At any rate," said I, "I have no warning given me just now, for you wrote to me to come to you, this time."

"That's true," said Estella, with a cold careless smile that always chilled me.

After looking at the twilight without, for a little while, she went on to say:—

"The time has come round when Miss Havisham wishes to have me for a day at Satis. You are to take me there, and bring me back, if you will. She would rather I did not travel alone, and objects to receiving my maid, for she has a sensitive horror of being talked of by such people. Can you take me?"

"Can I take you, Estella!"

"You can then? The day after to-morrow, if you please. You are to pay all charges out of my purse, You hear the condition of your going?"

"And must obey," said I.

This was all the preparation I received for that visit, or for others like it; Miss Havisham never wrote to me, nor had I ever so much as seen her handwriting. We went down on the next day but one, and we found her in the room where I had first beheld her, and it is needless to add that there was no change in Satis House.

She was even more dreadfully fond of Estella than she had been when I last saw them together; I repeat the word advisedly, for there was something positively dreadful in the energy of her looks and embraces. She hung upon Estella's beauty, hung upon her words, hung upon her gestures, and sat mumbling her own trembling fingers while she looked at her, as though she were devouring the beautiful creature she had reared.

From Estella she looked at me, with a searching glance that seemed to pry into my heart and probe its wounds. "How does she use you, Pip; how does she use you?" she asked me again, with her witch-like eagerness, even in Estella's hearing. But, when we sat by her flickering fire at night, she was most weird; for then, keeping Estella's hand drawn through her arm and clutched in her own hand, she extorted from her, by dint of referring back to what Estella had told her in her regular letters, the names and conditions of the men whom she had fascinated; and as Miss Havisham dwelt upon this roll, with the intensity of a mind mortally hurt and diseased, she sat with her other hand on her crutch stick, and her chin on that, and her wan bright eyes glaring at me, a very spectre.

I saw in this, wretched though it made me, and bitter the sense of dependence and even of degradation that it awakened,—I saw in this that Estella was set to wreak Miss Havisham's revenge on men, and that she was not to be given to me until she had gratified it for a term. I saw in this, a reason for her being beforehand assigned to me. Sending her out to attract and torment and do mischief, Miss Havisham sent her with the malicious assurance that she was beyond the reach of all admirers, and that all who staked upon that cast were secured to lose. I saw in this that I, too, was tormented by a perversion of ingenuity, even while the prize was reserved for me. I saw in this the reason for my being staved off so long and the reason for my late guardian's declining to commit himself to the formal knowledge of such a scheme. In a word, I saw in this Miss Havisham as I had her then and there before my eyes, and always had had her before my eyes; and I saw in this, the distinct shadow of the darkened and unhealthy house in which her life was hidden from the sun.

The candles that lighted that room of hers were placed in sconces on the wall. They were high from the ground, and they burnt with the steady dulness of artificial light in air that is seldom renewed. As I looked round at them, and at the pale gloom they made, and at the stopped clock, and at the withered articles of bridal dress upon the table and the ground, and at her own awful figure with its ghostly reflection thrown large by the fire upon the ceiling and the wall, I saw in everything the construction that my mind had come to, repeated and thrown back to me. My thoughts passed into the great room across the landing where the table was spread, and I saw it written, as it were, in the falls of the cobwebs from the centre-piece, in the crawlings of the spiders on the cloth, in the tracks of the mice as they betook their little quickened hearts behind the panels, and in the gropings and pausings of the beetles on the floor.

It happened on the occasion of this visit that some sharp words arose between Estella and Miss Havisham. It was the first time I had ever seen them opposed.

We were seated by the fire, as just now described, and Miss Havisham still had Estella's arm drawn through her own, and still clutched Estella's hand in hers, when Estella gradually began to detach herself. She had shown a proud impatience more than once before, and had rather endured that fierce affection than accepted or returned it.

"What!" said Miss Havisham, flashing her eyes upon her, "are you tired of me?"

"Only a little tired of myself," replied Estella, disengaging her arm, and moving to the great chimney-piece, where she stood looking down at the fire.

"Speak the truth, you ingrate!" cried Miss Havisham, passionately striking her stick upon the floor; "you are tired of me."

Estella looked at her with perfect composure, and again looked down at the fire. Her graceful figure and her beautiful face expressed a self-possessed indifference to the wild heat of the other, that was almost cruel.

"You stock and stone!" exclaimed Miss Havisham. "You cold, cold heart!"

"What?" said Estella, preserving her attitude of indifference as she leaned against the great chimney-piece and only moving her eyes; "do you reproach me for being cold? You?"

"Are you not?" was the fierce retort.

"You should know," said Estella. "I am what you have made me. Take all the praise, take all the blame; take all the success, take all the failure; in short, take me."

"O, look at her, look at her!" cried Miss Havisham, bitterly; "Look at her so hard and thankless, on the hearth where she was reared! Where I took her into this wretched breast when it was first bleeding from its stabs, and where I have lavished years of tenderness upon her!"

"At least I was no party to the compact," said Estella, "for if I could walk and speak, when it was made, it was as much as I could do. But what would you have? You have been very good to me, and I owe everything to you. What would you have?"

"Love," replied the other.

"You have it."

"I have not," said Miss Havisham.

"Mother by adoption," retorted Estella, never departing from the easy grace of her attitude, never raising her voice as the other did, never yielding either to anger or tenderness,—"mother by adoption, I have said that I owe everything to you. All I possess is freely yours. All that you have given me, is at your command to have again. Beyond that, I have nothing. And if you ask me to give you, what you never gave me, my gratitude and duty cannot do impossibilities."

"Did I never give her love!" cried Miss Havisham, turning wildly to me. "Did I never give her a burning love, inseparable from jealousy at all times, and from sharp pain, while she speaks thus to me! Let her call me mad, let her call me mad!"

"Why should I call you mad," returned Estella, "I, of all people? Does any one live, who knows what set purposes you have, half as well as I do? Does any one live, who knows what a steady memory you have, half as well as I do? I who have sat on this same hearth on the little stool that is even now beside you there, learning your lessons and looking up into your face, when your face was strange and frightened me!"

"Soon forgotten!" moaned Miss Havisham. "Times soon forgotten!"

"No, not forgotten," retorted Estella,—"not forgotten, but treasured up in my memory. When have you found me false to your teaching? When have you found me unmindful of your lessons? When have you found me giving admission here," she touched her bosom with her hand, "to anything that you excluded? Be just to me."

"So proud, so proud!" moaned Miss Havisham, pushing away her gray hair with both her hands.

"Who taught me to be proud?" returned Estella. "Who praised me when I learnt my lesson?"

"So hard, so hard!" moaned Miss Havisham, with her former action.

"Who taught me to be hard?" returned Estella. "Who praised me when I learnt my lesson?"

"But to be proud and hard to me!" Miss Havisham quite shrieked, as she stretched out her arms. "Estella, Estella, Estella, to be proud and hard to me!"

Estella looked at her for a moment with a kind of calm wonder, but was not otherwise disturbed; when the moment was past, she looked down at the fire again.

"I cannot think," said Estella, raising her eyes after a silence "why you should be so unreasonable when I come to see you after a separation. I have never forgotten your wrongs and their causes. I have never been unfaithful to you or your schooling. I have never shown any weakness that I can charge myself with."

"Would it be weakness to return my love?" exclaimed Miss Havisham. "But yes, yes, she would call it so!"

"I begin to think," said Estella, in a musing way, after another moment of calm wonder, "that I almost understand how this comes about. If you had brought up your adopted daughter wholly in the dark confinement of these rooms, and had never let her know that there was such a thing as the daylight by which she had never once seen your face,—if you had done that, and then, for a purpose had wanted her to understand the daylight and know all about it, you would have been disappointed and angry?"

Miss Havisham, with her head in her hands, sat making a low moaning, and swaying herself on her chair, but gave no answer.

"Or," said Estella,—"which is a nearer case,—if you had taught her, from the dawn of her intelligence, with your utmost energy and might, that there was such a thing as daylight, but that it was made to be her enemy and destroyer, and she must always turn against it, for it had blighted you and would else blight her;—if you had done this, and then, for a purpose, had wanted her to take naturally to the daylight and she could not do it, you would have been disappointed and angry?"

Miss Havisham sat listening (or it seemed so, for I could not see her face), but still made no answer.

"So," said Estella, "I must be taken as I have been made. The success is not mine, the failure is not mine, but the two together make me."

Miss Havisham had settled down, I hardly knew how, upon the floor, among the faded bridal relics with which it was strewn. I took advantage of the moment—I had sought one from the first—to leave the room, after beseeching Estella's attention to her, with a movement of my hand. When I left, Estella was yet standing by the great chimney-piece, just as she had stood throughout. Miss Havisham's gray hair was all adrift upon the ground, among the other bridal wrecks, and was a miserable sight to see.

It was with a depressed heart that I walked in the starlight for an hour and more, about the courtyard, and about the brewery, and about the ruined garden. When I at last took courage to return to the room, I found Estella sitting at Miss Havisham's knee, taking up some stitches in one of those old articles of dress that were dropping to pieces, and of which I have often been reminded since by the faded tatters of old banners that I have seen hanging up in cathedrals. Afterwards, Estella and I played at cards, as of yore,—only we were skilful now, and played French games,—and so the evening wore away, and I went to bed.

I lay in that separate building across the courtyard. It was the first time I had ever lain down to rest in Satis House, and sleep refused to come near me. A thousand Miss Havishams haunted me. She was on this side of my pillow, on that, at the head of the bed, at the foot, behind the half-opened door of the dressing-room, in the dressing-room, in the room overhead, in the room beneath,—everywhere. At last, when the night was slow to creep on towards two o'clock, I felt that I absolutely could no longer bear the place as a place to lie down in, and that I must get up. I therefore got up and put on my clothes, and went out across the yard into the long stone passage, designing to gain the outer courtyard and walk there for the relief of my mind. But I was no sooner in the passage than I extinguished my candle; for I saw Miss Havisham going along it in a ghostly manner, making a low cry. I followed her at a distance, and saw her go up the staircase. She carried a bare candle in her hand, which she had probably taken from one of the sconces in her own room, and was a most unearthly object by its light. Standing at the bottom of the staircase, I felt the mildewed air of the feast-chamber, without seeing her open the door, and I heard her walking there, and so across into her own room, and so across again into that, never ceasing the low cry. After a time, I tried in the dark both to get out, and to go back, but I could do neither until some streaks of day strayed in and showed me where to lay my hands. During the whole interval, whenever I went to the bottom of the staircase, I heard her footstep, saw her light pass above, and heard her ceaseless low cry.

Before we left next day, there was no revival of the difference between her and Estella, nor was it ever revived on any similar occasion; and there were four similar occasions, to the best of my remembrance. Nor, did Miss Havisham's manner towards Estella in anywise change, except that I believed it to have something like fear infused among its former characteristics.

It is impossible to turn this leaf of my life, without putting Bentley Drummle's name upon it; or I would, very gladly.

On a certain occasion when the Finches were assembled in force, and when good feeling was being promoted in the usual manner by nobody's agreeing with anybody else, the presiding Finch called the Grove to order, forasmuch as Mr. Drummle had not yet toasted a lady; which, according to the solemn constitution of the society, it was the brute's turn to do that day. I thought I saw him leer in an ugly way at me while the decanters were going round, but as there was no love lost between us, that might easily be. What was my indignant surprise when he called upon the company to pledge him to "Estella!"

"Estella who?" said I.

"Never you mind," retorted Drummle.

"Estella of where?" said I. "You are bound to say of where." Which he was, as a Finch.

"Of Richmond, gentlemen," said Drummle, putting me out of the question, "and a peerless beauty."

Much he knew about peerless beauties, a mean, miserable idiot! I whispered Herbert.

"I know that lady," said Herbert, across the table, when the toast had been honored.

"Do you?" said Drummle.

"And so do I," I added, with a scarlet face.

"Do you?" said Drummle. "O, Lord!"

This was the only retort—except glass or crockery—that the heavy creature was capable of making; but, I became as highly incensed by it as if it had been barbed with wit, and I immediately rose in my place and said that I could not but regard it as being like the honorable Finch's impudence to come down to that Grove,—we always talked about coming down to that Grove, as a neat Parliamentary turn of expression,—down to that Grove, proposing a lady of whom he knew nothing. Mr. Drummle, upon this, starting up, demanded what I meant by that? Whereupon I made him the extreme reply that I believed he knew where I was to be found.

Whether it was possible in a Christian country to get on without blood, after this, was a question on which the Finches were divided. The debate upon it grew so lively, indeed, that at least six more honorable members told six more, during the discussion, that they believed they knew where they were to be found. However, it was decided at last (the Grove being a Court of Honor) that if Mr. Drummle would bring never so slight a certificate from the lady, importing that he had the honor of her acquaintance, Mr. Pip must express his regret, as a gentleman and a Finch, for "having been betrayed into a warmth which." Next day was appointed for the production (lest our honor should take cold from delay), and next day Drummle appeared with a polite little avowal in Estella's hand, that she had had the honor of dancing with him several times. This left me no course but to regret that I had been "betrayed into a warmth which," and on the whole to repudiate, as untenable, the idea that I was to be found anywhere. Drummle and I then sat snorting at one another for an hour, while the Grove engaged in indiscriminate contradiction, and finally the promotion of good feeling was declared to have gone ahead at an amazing rate.

I tell this lightly, but it was no light thing to me. For, I cannot adequately express what pain it gave me to think that Estella should show any favor to a contemptible, clumsy, sulky booby, so very far below the average. To the present moment, I believe it to have been referable to some pure fire of generosity and disinterestedness in my love for her, that I could not endure the thought of her stooping to that hound. No doubt I should have been miserable whomsoever she had favored; but a worthier object would have caused me a different kind and degree of distress.

It was easy for me to find out, and I did soon find out, that Drummle had begun to follow her closely, and that she allowed him to do it. A little while, and he was always in pursuit of her, and he and I crossed one another every day. He held on, in a dull persistent way, and Estella held him on; now with encouragement, now with discouragement, now almost flattering him, now openly despising him, now knowing him very well, now scarcely remembering who he was.

The Spider, as Mr. Jaggers had called him, was used to lying in wait, however, and had the patience of his tribe. Added to that, he had a blockhead confidence in his money and in his family greatness, which sometimes did him good service,—almost taking the place of concentration and determined purpose. So, the Spider, doggedly watching Estella, outwatched many brighter insects, and would often uncoil himself and drop at the right nick of time.

At a certain Assembly Ball at Richmond (there used to be Assembly Balls at most places then), where Estella had outshone all other beauties, this blundering Drummle so hung about her, and with so much toleration on her part, that I resolved to speak to her concerning him. I took the next opportunity; which was when she was waiting for Mrs. Blandley to take her home, and was sitting apart among some flowers, ready to go. I was with her, for I almost always accompanied them to and from such places.

"Are you tired, Estella?"

"Rather, Pip."

"You should be."

"Say rather, I should not be; for I have my letter to Satis House to write, before I go to sleep."

"Recounting to-night's triumph?" said I. "Surely a very poor one, Estella."

"What do you mean? I didn't know there had been any."

"Estella," said I, "do look at that fellow in the corner yonder, who is looking over here at us."

"Why should I look at him?" returned Estella, with her eyes on me instead. "What is there in that fellow in the corner yonder,—to use your words,—that I need look at?"

"Indeed, that is the very question I want to ask you," said I. "For he has been hovering about you all night."

"Moths, and all sorts of ugly creatures," replied Estella, with a glance towards him, "hover about a lighted candle. Can the candle help it?"

"No," I returned; "but cannot the Estella help it?"

"Well!" said she, laughing, after a moment, "perhaps. Yes. Anything you like."

"But, Estella, do hear me speak. It makes me wretched that you should encourage a man so generally despised as Drummle. You know he is despised."

"Well?" said she.

"You know he is as ungainly within as without. A deficient, ill-tempered, lowering, stupid fellow."

"Well?" said she.

"You know he has nothing to recommend him but money and a ridiculous roll of addle-headed predecessors; now, don't you?"

"Well?" said she again; and each time she said it, she opened her lovely eyes the wider.

To overcome the difficulty of getting past that monosyllable, I took it from her, and said, repeating it with emphasis, "Well! Then, that is why it makes me wretched."

Now, if I could have believed that she favored Drummle with any idea of making me-me—wretched, I should have been in better heart about it; but in that habitual way of hers, she put me so entirely out of the question, that I could believe nothing of the kind.

"Pip," said Estella, casting her glance over the room, "don't be foolish about its effect on you. It may have its effect on others, and may be meant to have. It's not worth discussing."

"Yes it is," said I, "because I cannot bear that people should say, 'she throws away her graces and attractions on a mere boor, the lowest in the crowd.'"

"I can bear it," said Estella.

"Oh! don't be so proud, Estella, and so inflexible."

"Calls me proud and inflexible in this breath!" said Estella, opening her hands. "And in his last breath reproached me for stooping to a boor!"

"There is no doubt you do," said I, something hurriedly, "for I have seen you give him looks and smiles this very night, such as you never give to—me."

"Do you want me then," said Estella, turning suddenly with a fixed and serious, if not angry, look, "to deceive and entrap you?"

"Do you deceive and entrap him, Estella?"

"Yes, and many others,—all of them but you. Here is Mrs. Brandley. I'll say no more."

And now that I have given the one chapter to the theme that so filled my heart, and so often made it ache and ache again, I pass on unhindered, to the event that had impended over me longer yet; the event that had begun to be prepared for, before I knew that the world held Estella, and in the days when her baby intelligence was receiving its first distortions from Miss Havisham's wasting hands.

In the Eastern story, the heavy slab that was to fall on the bed of state in the flush of conquest was slowly wrought out of the quarry, the tunnel for the rope to hold it in its place was slowly carried through the leagues of rock, the slab was slowly raised and fitted in the roof, the rope was rove to it and slowly taken through the miles of hollow to the great iron ring. All being made ready with much labour, and the hour come, the sultan was aroused in the dead of the night, and the sharpened axe that was to sever the rope from the great iron ring was put into his hand, and he struck with it, and the rope parted and rushed away, and the ceiling fell. So, in my case; all the work, near and afar, that tended to the end, had been accomplished; and in an instant the blow was struck, and the roof of my stronghold dropped upon me.

CHAPTER XXXIX

I was three-and-twenty years of age. Not another word had I heard to enlighten me on the subject of my expectations, and my twenty-third birthday was a week gone. We had left Barnard's Inn more than a year, and lived in the Temple. Our chambers were in Garden-court, down by the river.

Mr. Pocket and I had for some time parted company as to our original relations, though we continued on the best terms. Notwithstanding my inability to settle to anything,—which I hope arose out of the restless and incomplete tenure on which I held my means,—I had a taste for reading, and read regularly so many hours a day. That matter of Herbert's was still progressing, and everything with me was as I have brought it down to the close of the last preceding chapter.

Business had taken Herbert on a journey to Marseilles. I was alone, and had a dull sense of being alone. Dispirited and anxious, long hoping that to-morrow or next week would clear my way, and long disappointed, I sadly missed the cheerful face and ready response of my friend.

It was wretched weather; stormy and wet, stormy and wet; and mud, mud, mud, deep in all the streets. Day after day, a vast heavy veil had been driving over London from the East, and it drove still, as if in the East there were an Eternity of cloud and wind. So furious had been the gusts, that high buildings in town had had the lead stripped off their roofs; and in the country, trees had been torn up, and sails of windmills carried away; and gloomy accounts had come in from the coast, of shipwreck and death. Violent blasts of rain had accompanied these rages of wind, and the day just closed as I sat down to read had been the worst of all.

Alterations have been made in that part of the Temple since that time, and it has not now so lonely a character as it had then, nor is it so exposed to the river. We lived at the top of the last house, and the wind rushing up the river shook the house that night, like discharges of cannon, or breakings of a sea. When the rain came with it and dashed against the windows, I thought, raising my eyes to them as they rocked, that I might have fancied myself in a storm-beaten lighthouse. Occasionally, the smoke came rolling down the chimney as though it could not bear to go out into such a night; and when I set the doors open and looked down the staircase, the staircase lamps were blown out; and when I shaded my face with my hands and looked through the black windows (opening them ever so little was out of the question in the teeth of such wind and rain), I saw that the lamps in the court were blown out, and that the lamps on the bridges and the shore were shuddering, and that the coal-fires in barges on the river were being carried away before the wind like red-hot splashes in the rain.

I read with my watch upon the table, purposing to close my book at eleven o'clock. As I shut it, Saint Paul's, and all the many church-clocks in the City—some leading, some accompanying, some following—struck that hour. The sound was curiously flawed by the wind; and I was listening, and thinking how the wind assailed and tore it, when I heard a footstep on the stair.

What nervous folly made me start, and awfully connect it with the footstep of my dead sister, matters not. It was past in a moment, and I listened again, and heard the footstep stumble in coming on. Remembering then, that the staircase-lights were blown out, I took up my reading-lamp and went out to the stair-head. Whoever was below had stopped on seeing my lamp, for all was quiet.

"There is some one down there, is there not?" I called out, looking down.

"Yes," said a voice from the darkness beneath.

"What floor do you want?"

"The top. Mr. Pip."

"That is my name.—There is nothing the matter?"

"Nothing the matter," returned the voice. And the man came on.

I stood with my lamp held out over the stair-rail, and he came slowly within its light. It was a shaded lamp, to shine upon a book, and its circle of light was very contracted; so that he was in it for a mere instant, and then out of it. In the instant, I had seen a face that was strange to me, looking up with an incomprehensible air of being touched and pleased by the sight of me.

Moving the lamp as the man moved, I made out that he was substantially dressed, but roughly, like a voyager by sea. That he had long iron-gray hair. That his age was about sixty. That he was a muscular man, strong on his legs, and that he was browned and hardened by exposure to weather. As he ascended the last stair or two, and the light of my lamp included us both, I saw, with a stupid kind of amazement, that he was holding out both his hands to me.

"Pray what is your business?" I asked him.

"My business?" he repeated, pausing. "Ah! Yes. I will explain my business, by your leave."

"Do you wish to come in?"

"Yes," he replied; "I wish to come in, master."

I had asked him the question inhospitably enough, for I resented the sort of bright and gratified recognition that still shone in his face. I resented it, because it seemed to imply that he expected me to respond to it. But I took him into the room I had just left, and, having set the lamp on the table, asked him as civilly as I could to explain himself.

He looked about him with the strangest air,—an air of wondering pleasure, as if he had some part in the things he admired,—and he pulled off a rough outer coat, and his hat. Then, I saw that his head was furrowed and bald, and that the long iron-gray hair grew only on its sides. But, I saw nothing that in the least explained him. On the contrary, I saw him next moment, once more holding out both his hands to me.

"What do you mean?" said I, half suspecting him to be mad.

He stopped in his looking at me, and slowly rubbed his right hand over his head. "It's disapinting to a man," he said, in a coarse broken voice, "arter having looked for'ard so distant, and come so fur; but you're not to blame for that,—neither on us is to blame for that. I'll speak in half a minute. Give me half a minute, please."

He sat down on a chair that stood before the fire, and covered his forehead with his large brown veinous hands. I looked at him attentively then, and recoiled a little from him; but I did not know him.

"There's no one nigh," said he, looking over his shoulder; "is there?"

"Why do you, a stranger coming into my rooms at this time of the night, ask that question?" said I.

"You're a game one," he returned, shaking his head at me with a deliberate affection, at once most unintelligible and most exasperating; "I'm glad you've grow'd up, a game one! But don't catch hold of me. You'd be sorry arterwards to have done it."

I relinquished the intention he had detected, for I knew him! Even yet I could not recall a single feature, but I knew him! If the wind and the rain had driven away the intervening years, had scattered all the intervening objects, had swept us to the churchyard where we first stood face to face on such different levels, I could not have known my convict more distinctly than I knew him now as he sat in the chair before the fire. No need to take a file from his pocket and show it to me; no need to take the handkerchief from his neck and twist it round his head; no need to hug himself with both his arms, and take a shivering turn across the room, looking back at me for recognition. I knew him before he gave me one of those aids, though, a moment before, I had not been conscious of remotely suspecting his identity.

He came back to where I stood, and again held out both his hands. Not knowing what to do,—for, in my astonishment I had lost my self-possession,—I reluctantly gave him my hands. He grasped them heartily, raised them to his lips, kissed them, and still held them.

"You acted noble, my boy," said he. "Noble, Pip! And I have never forgot it!"

At a change in his manner as if he were even going to embrace me, I laid a hand upon his breast and put him away.

"Stay!" said I. "Keep off! If you are grateful to me for what I did when I was a little child, I hope you have shown your gratitude by mending your way of life. If you have come here to thank me, it was not necessary. Still, however you have found me out, there must be something good in the feeling that has brought you here, and I will not repulse you; but surely you must understand that—I—"

My attention was so attracted by the singularity of his fixed look at me, that the words died away on my tongue.

"You was a saying," he observed, when we had confronted one another in silence, "that surely I must understand. What, surely must I understand?"

"That I cannot wish to renew that chance intercourse with you of long ago, under these different circumstances. I am glad to believe you have repented and recovered yourself. I am glad to tell you so. I am glad that, thinking I deserve to be thanked, you have come to thank me. But our ways are different ways, none the less. You are wet, and you look weary. Will you drink something before you go?"

He had replaced his neckerchief loosely, and had stood, keenly observant of me, biting a long end of it. "I think," he answered, still with the end at his mouth and still observant of me, "that I will drink (I thank you) afore I go."

There was a tray ready on a side-table. I brought it to the table near the fire, and asked him what he would have? He touched one of the bottles without looking at it or speaking, and I made him some hot rum and water. I tried to keep my hand steady while I did so, but his look at me as he leaned back in his chair with the long draggled end of his neckerchief between his teeth—evidently forgotten—made my hand very difficult to master. When at last I put the glass to him, I saw with amazement that his eyes were full of tears.

Up to this time I had remained standing, not to disguise that I wished him gone. But I was softened by the softened aspect of the man, and felt a touch of reproach. "I hope," said I, hurriedly putting something into a glass for myself, and drawing a chair to the table, "that you will not think I spoke harshly to you just now. I had no intention of doing it, and I am sorry for it if I did. I wish you well and happy!"

As I put my glass to my lips, he glanced with surprise at the end of his neckerchief, dropping from his mouth when he opened it, and stretched out his hand. I gave him mine, and then he drank, and drew his sleeve across his eyes and forehead.

"How are you living?" I asked him.

"I've been a sheep-farmer, stock-breeder, other trades besides, away in the new world," said he; "many a thousand mile of stormy water off from this."

"I hope you have done well?"

"I've done wonderfully well. There's others went out alonger me as has done well too, but no man has done nigh as well as me. I'm famous for it."

"I am glad to hear it."

"I hope to hear you say so, my dear boy."

Without stopping to try to understand those words or the tone in which they were spoken, I turned off to a point that had just come into my mind.

"Have you ever seen a messenger you once sent to me," I inquired, "since he undertook that trust?"

"Never set eyes upon him. I warn't likely to it."

"He came faithfully, and he brought me the two one-pound notes. I was a poor boy then, as you know, and to a poor boy they were a little fortune. But, like you, I have done well since, and you must let me pay them back. You can put them to some other poor boy's use." I took out my purse.

He watched me as I laid my purse upon the table and opened it, and he watched me as I separated two one-pound notes from its contents. They were clean and new, and I spread them out and handed them over to him. Still watching me, he laid them one upon the other, folded them long-wise, gave them a twist, set fire to them at the lamp, and dropped the ashes into the tray.

"May I make so bold," he said then, with a smile that was like a frown, and with a frown that was like a smile, "as ask you how you have done well, since you and me was out on them lone shivering marshes?"

"How?"

"Ah!"

He emptied his glass, got up, and stood at the side of the fire, with his heavy brown hand on the mantel-shelf. He put a foot up to the bars, to dry and warm it, and the wet boot began to steam; but, he neither looked at it, nor at the fire, but steadily looked at me. It was only now that I began to tremble.

When my lips had parted, and had shaped some words that were without sound, I forced myself to tell him (though I could not do it distinctly), that I had been chosen to succeed to some property.

"Might a mere warmint ask what property?" said he.

I faltered, "I don't know."

"Might a mere warmint ask whose property?" said he.

I faltered again, "I don't know."

"Could I make a guess, I wonder," said the Convict, "at your income since you come of age! As to the first figure now. Five?"

With my heart beating like a heavy hammer of disordered action, I rose out of my chair, and stood with my hand upon the back of it, looking wildly at him.

"Concerning a guardian," he went on. "There ought to have been some guardian, or such-like, whiles you was a minor. Some lawyer, maybe. As to the first letter of that lawyer's name now. Would it be J?"

All the truth of my position came flashing on me; and its disappointments, dangers, disgraces, consequences of all kinds, rushed in in such a multitude that I was borne down by them and had to struggle for every breath I drew.

"Put it," he resumed, "as the employer of that lawyer whose name begun with a J, and might be Jaggers,—put it as he had come over sea to Portsmouth, and had landed there, and had wanted to come on to you. 'However, you have found me out,' you says just now. Well! However, did I find you out? Why, I wrote from Portsmouth to a person in London, for particulars of your address. That person's name? Why, Wemmick."

I could not have spoken one word, though it had been to save my life. I stood, with a hand on the chair-back and a hand on my breast, where I seemed to be suffocating,—I stood so, looking wildly at him, until I grasped at the chair, when the room began to surge and turn. He caught me, drew me to the sofa, put me up against the cushions, and bent on one knee before me, bringing the face that I now well remembered, and that I shuddered at, very near to mine.

"Yes, Pip, dear boy, I've made a gentleman on you! It's me wot has done it! I swore that time, sure as ever I earned a guinea, that guinea should go to you. I swore arterwards, sure as ever I spec'lated and got rich, you should get rich. I lived rough, that you should live smooth; I worked hard, that you should be above work. What odds, dear boy? Do I tell it, fur you to feel a obligation? Not a bit. I tell it, fur you to know as that there hunted dunghill dog wot you kep life in, got his head so high that he could make a gentleman,—and, Pip, you're him!"

The abhorrence in which I held the man, the dread I had of him, the repugnance with which I shrank from him, could not have been exceeded if he had been some terrible beast.

"Look'ee here, Pip. I'm your second father. You're my son,—more to me nor any son. I've put away money, only for you to spend. When I was a hired-out shepherd in a solitary hut, not seeing no faces but faces of sheep till I half forgot wot men's and women's faces wos like, I see yourn. I drops my knife many a time in that hut when I was a-eating my dinner or my supper, and I says, 'Here's the boy again, a looking at me whiles I eats and drinks!' I see you there a many times, as plain as ever I see you on them misty marshes. 'Lord strike me dead!' I says each time,—and I goes out in the air to say it under the open heavens,—'but wot, if I gets liberty and money, I'll make that boy a gentleman!' And I done it. Why, look at you, dear boy! Look at these here lodgings o'yourn, fit for a lord! A lord? Ah! You shall show money with lords for wagers, and beat 'em!"

In his heat and triumph, and in his knowledge that I had been nearly fainting, he did not remark on my reception of all this. It was the one grain of relief I had.

"Look'ee here!" he went on, taking my watch out of my pocket, and turning towards him a ring on my finger, while I recoiled from his touch as if he had been a snake, "a gold 'un and a beauty: that's a gentleman's, I hope! A diamond all set round with rubies; that's a gentleman's, I hope! Look at your linen; fine and beautiful! Look at your clothes; better ain't to be got! And your books too," turning his eyes round the room, "mounting up, on their shelves, by hundreds! And you read 'em; don't you? I see you'd been a reading of 'em when I come in. Ha, ha, ha! You shall read 'em to me, dear boy! And if they're in foreign languages wot I don't understand, I shall be just as proud as if I did."

Again he took both my hands and put them to his lips, while my blood ran cold within me.

"Don't you mind talking, Pip," said he, after again drawing his sleeve over his eyes and forehead, as the click came in his throat which I well remembered,—and he was all the more horrible to me that he was so much in earnest; "you can't do better nor keep quiet, dear boy. You ain't looked slowly forward to this as I have; you wosn't prepared for this as I wos. But didn't you never think it might be me?"

"O no, no, no," I returned, "Never, never!"

"Well, you see it wos me, and single-handed. Never a soul in it but my own self and Mr. Jaggers."

"Was there no one else?" I asked.

"No," said he, with a glance of surprise: "who else should there be? And, dear boy, how good looking you have growed! There's bright eyes somewheres—eh? Isn't there bright eyes somewheres, wot you love the thoughts on?"

O Estella, Estella!

"They shall be yourn, dear boy, if money can buy 'em. Not that a gentleman like you, so well set up as you, can't win 'em off of his own game; but money shall back you! Let me finish wot I was a telling you, dear boy. From that there hut and that there hiring-out, I got money left me by my master (which died, and had been the same as me), and got my liberty and went for myself. In every single thing I went for, I went for you. 'Lord strike a blight upon it,' I says, wotever it was I went for, 'if it ain't for him!' It all prospered wonderful. As I giv' you to understand just now, I'm famous for it. It was the money left me, and the gains of the first few year wot I sent home to Mr. Jaggers—all for you—when he first come arter you, agreeable to my letter."

O that he had never come! That he had left me at the forge,—far from contented, yet, by comparison happy!

"And then, dear boy, it was a recompense to me, look'ee here, to know in secret that I was making a gentleman. The blood horses of them colonists might fling up the dust over me as I was walking; what do I say? I says to myself, 'I'm making a better gentleman nor ever you'll be!' When one of 'em says to another, 'He was a convict, a few year ago, and is a ignorant common fellow now, for all he's lucky,' what do I say? I says to myself, 'If I ain't a gentleman, nor yet ain't got no learning, I'm the owner of such. All on you owns stock and land; which on you owns a brought-up London gentleman?' This way I kep myself a going. And this way I held steady afore my mind that I would for certain come one day and see my boy, and make myself known to him, on his own ground."

He laid his hand on my shoulder. I shuddered at the thought that for anything I knew, his hand might be stained with blood.

"It warn't easy, Pip, for me to leave them parts, nor yet it warn't safe. But I held to it, and the harder it was, the stronger I held, for I was determined, and my mind firm made up. At last I done it. Dear boy, I done it!"

I tried to collect my thoughts, but I was stunned. Throughout, I had seemed to myself to attend more to the wind and the rain than to him; even now, I could not separate his voice from those voices, though those were loud and his was silent.

"Where will you put me?" he asked, presently. "I must be put somewheres, dear boy."

"To sleep?" said I.

"Yes. And to sleep long and sound," he answered; "for I've been sea-tossed and sea-washed, months and months."

"My friend and companion," said I, rising from the sofa, "is absent; you must have his room."

"He won't come back to-morrow; will he?"

"No," said I, answering almost mechanically, in spite of my utmost efforts; "not to-morrow."

"Because, look'ee here, dear boy," he said, dropping his voice, and laying a long finger on my breast in an impressive manner, "caution is necessary."

"How do you mean? Caution?"

"By G———, it's Death!"

"What's death?"

"I was sent for life. It's death to come back. There's been overmuch coming back of late years, and I should of a certainty be hanged if took."

Nothing was needed but this; the wretched man, after loading wretched me with his gold and silver chains for years, had risked his life to come to me, and I held it there in my keeping! If I had loved him instead of abhorring him; if I had been attracted to him by the strongest admiration and affection, instead of shrinking from him with the strongest repugnance; it could have been no worse. On the contrary, it would have been better, for his preservation would then have naturally and tenderly addressed my heart.

My first care was to close the shutters, so that no light might be seen from without, and then to close and make fast the doors. While I did so, he stood at the table drinking rum and eating biscuit; and when I saw him thus engaged, I saw my convict on the marshes at his meal again. It almost seemed to me as if he must stoop down presently, to file at his leg.

When I had gone into Herbert's room, and had shut off any other communication between it and the staircase than through the room in which our conversation had been held, I asked him if he would go to bed? He said yes, but asked me for some of my "gentleman's linen" to put on in the morning. I brought it out, and laid it ready for him, and my blood again ran cold when he again took me by both hands to give me good night.

I got away from him, without knowing how I did it, and mended the fire in the room where we had been together, and sat down by it, afraid to go to bed. For an hour or more, I remained too stunned to think; and it was not until I began to think, that I began fully to know how wrecked I was, and how the ship in which I had sailed was gone to pieces.

Miss Havisham's intentions towards me, all a mere dream; Estella not designed for me; I only suffered in Satis House as a convenience, a sting for the greedy relations, a model with a mechanical heart to practise on when no other practice was at hand; those were the first smarts I had. But, sharpest and deepest pain of all,—it was for the convict, guilty of I knew not what crimes, and liable to be taken out of those rooms where I sat thinking, and hanged at the Old Bailey door, that I had deserted Joe.

I would not have gone back to Joe now, I would not have gone back to Biddy now, for any consideration; simply, I suppose, because my sense of my own worthless conduct to them was greater than every consideration. No wisdom on earth could have given me the comfort that I should have derived from their simplicity and fidelity; but I could never, never, undo what I had done.

In every rage of wind and rush of rain, I heard pursuers. Twice, I could have sworn there was a knocking and whispering at the outer door. With these fears upon me, I began either to imagine or recall that I had had mysterious warnings of this man's approach. That, for weeks gone by, I had passed faces in the streets which I had thought like his. That these likenesses had grown more numerous, as he, coming over the sea, had drawn nearer. That his wicked spirit had somehow sent these messengers to mine, and that now on this stormy night he was as good as his word, and with me.

Crowding up with these reflections came the reflection that I had seen him with my childish eyes to be a desperately violent man; that I had heard that other convict reiterate that he had tried to murder him; that I had seen him down in the ditch tearing and fighting like a wild beast. Out of such remembrances I brought into the light of the fire a half-formed terror that it might not be safe to be shut up there with him in the dead of the wild solitary night. This dilated until it filled the room, and impelled me to take a candle and go in and look at my dreadful burden.

He had rolled a handkerchief round his head, and his face was set and lowering in his sleep. But he was asleep, and quietly too, though he had a pistol lying on the pillow. Assured of this, I softly removed the key to the outside of his door, and turned it on him before I again sat down by the fire. Gradually I slipped from the chair and lay on the floor. When I awoke without having parted in my sleep with the perception of my wretchedness, the clocks of the Eastward churches were striking five, the candles were wasted out, the fire was dead, and the wind and rain intensified the thick black darkness.

THIS IS THE END OF THE SECOND STAGE OF PIP'S EXPECTATIONS.

CHAPTER XL

It was fortunate for me that I had to take precautions to ensure (so far as I could) the safety of my dreaded visitor; for, this thought pressing on me when I awoke, held other thoughts in a confused concourse at a distance.

The impossibility of keeping him concealed in the chambers was self-evident. It could not be done, and the attempt to do it would inevitably engender suspicion. True, I had no Avenger in my service now, but I was looked after by an inflammatory old female, assisted by an animated rag-bag whom she called her niece, and to keep a room secret from them would be to invite curiosity and exaggeration. They both had weak eyes, which I had long attributed to their chronically looking in at keyholes, and they were always at hand when not wanted; indeed that was their only reliable quality besides larceny. Not to get up a mystery with these people, I resolved to announce in the morning that my uncle had unexpectedly come from the country.

This course I decided on while I was yet groping about in the darkness for the means of getting a light. Not stumbling on the means after all, I was fain to go out to the adjacent Lodge and get the watchman there to come with his lantern. Now, in groping my way down the black staircase I fell over something, and that something was a man crouching in a corner.

As the man made no answer when I asked him what he did there, but eluded my touch in silence, I ran to the Lodge and urged the watchman to come quickly; telling him of the incident on the way back. The wind being as fierce as ever, we did not care to endanger the light in the lantern by rekindling the extinguished lamps on the staircase, but we examined the staircase from the bottom to the top and found no one there. It then occurred to me as possible that the man might have slipped into my rooms; so, lighting my candle at the watchman's, and leaving him standing at the door, I examined them carefully, including the room in which my dreaded guest lay asleep. All was quiet, and assuredly no other man was in those chambers.

It troubled me that there should have been a lurker on the stairs, on that night of all nights in the year, and I asked the watchman, on the chance of eliciting some hopeful explanation as I handed him a dram at the door, whether he had admitted at his gate any gentleman who had perceptibly been dining out? Yes, he said; at different times of the night, three. One lived in Fountain Court, and the other two lived in the Lane, and he had seen them all go home. Again, the only other man who dwelt in the house of which my chambers formed a part had been in the country for some weeks, and he certainly had not returned in the night, because we had seen his door with his seal on it as we came up-stairs.

"The night being so bad, sir," said the watchman, as he gave me back my glass, "uncommon few have come in at my gate. Besides them three gentlemen that I have named, I don't call to mind another since about eleven o'clock, when a stranger asked for you."

"My uncle," I muttered. "Yes."

"You saw him, sir?"

"Yes. Oh yes."

"Likewise the person with him?"

"Person with him!" I repeated.

"I judged the person to be with him," returned the watchman. "The person stopped, when he stopped to make inquiry of me, and the person took this way when he took this way."

"What sort of person?"

The watchman had not particularly noticed; he should say a working person; to the best of his belief, he had a dust-colored kind of clothes on, under a dark coat. The watchman made more light of the matter than I did, and naturally; not having my reason for attaching weight to it.

When I had got rid of him, which I thought it well to do without prolonging explanations, my mind was much troubled by these two circumstances taken together. Whereas they were easy of innocent solution apart,—as, for instance, some diner out or diner at home, who had not gone near this watchman's gate, might have strayed to my staircase and dropped asleep there,—and my nameless visitor might have brought some one with him to show him the way,—still, joined, they had an ugly look to one as prone to distrust and fear as the changes of a few hours had made me.

I lighted my fire, which burnt with a raw pale flare at that time of the morning, and fell into a doze before it. I seemed to have been dozing a whole night when the clocks struck six. As there was full an hour and a half between me and daylight, I dozed again; now, waking up uneasily, with prolix conversations about nothing, in my ears; now, making thunder of the wind in the chimney; at length, falling off into a profound sleep from which the daylight woke me with a start.

All this time I had never been able to consider my own situation, nor could I do so yet. I had not the power to attend to it. I was greatly dejected and distressed, but in an incoherent wholesale sort of way. As to forming any plan for the future, I could as soon have formed an elephant. When I opened the shutters and looked out at the wet wild morning, all of a leaden hue; when I walked from room to room; when I sat down again shivering, before the fire, waiting for my laundress to appear; I thought how miserable I was, but hardly knew why, or how long I had been so, or on what day of the week I made the reflection, or even who I was that made it.

At last, the old woman and the niece came in,—the latter with a head not easily distinguishable from her dusty broom,—and testified surprise at sight of me and the fire. To whom I imparted how my uncle had come in the night and was then asleep, and how the breakfast preparations were to be modified accordingly. Then I washed and dressed while they knocked the furniture about and made a dust; and so, in a sort of dream or sleep-waking, I found myself sitting by the fire again, waiting for him—to come to breakfast.

By and by, his door opened and he came out. I could not bring myself to bear the sight of him, and I thought he had a worse look by daylight.

"I do not even know," said I, speaking low as he took his seat at the table, "by what name to call you. I have given out that you are my uncle."

"That's it, dear boy! Call me uncle."

"You assumed some name, I suppose, on board ship?"

"Yes, dear boy. I took the name of Provis."

"Do you mean to keep that name?"

"Why, yes, dear boy, it's as good as another,—unless you'd like another."

"What is your real name?" I asked him in a whisper.

"Magwitch," he answered, in the same tone; "chrisen'd Abel."

"What were you brought up to be?"

"A warmint, dear boy."

He answered quite seriously, and used the word as if it denoted some profession.

"When you came into the Temple last night—" said I, pausing to wonder whether that could really have been last night, which seemed so long ago.

"Yes, dear boy?"

"When you came in at the gate and asked the watchman the way here, had you any one with you?"

"With me? No, dear boy."

"But there was some one there?"

"I didn't take particular notice," he said, dubiously, "not knowing the ways of the place. But I think there was a person, too, come in alonger me."

"Are you known in London?"

"I hope not!" said he, giving his neck a jerk with his forefinger that made me turn hot and sick.

"Were you known in London, once?"

"Not over and above, dear boy. I was in the provinces mostly."

"Were you-tried—in London?"

"Which time?" said he, with a sharp look.

"The last time."

He nodded. "First knowed Mr. Jaggers that way. Jaggers was for me."

It was on my lips to ask him what he was tried for, but he took up a knife, gave it a flourish, and with the words, "And what I done is worked out and paid for!" fell to at his breakfast.

He ate in a ravenous way that was very disagreeable, and all his actions were uncouth, noisy, and greedy. Some of his teeth had failed him since I saw him eat on the marshes, and as he turned his food in his mouth, and turned his head sideways to bring his strongest fangs to bear upon it, he looked terribly like a hungry old dog. If I had begun with any appetite, he would have taken it away, and I should have sat much as I did,—repelled from him by an insurmountable aversion, and gloomily looking at the cloth.

"I'm a heavy grubber, dear boy," he said, as a polite kind of apology when he made an end of his meal, "but I always was. If it had been in my constitution to be a lighter grubber, I might ha' got into lighter trouble. Similarly, I must have my smoke. When I was first hired out as shepherd t'other side the world, it's my belief I should ha' turned into a molloncolly-mad sheep myself, if I hadn't a had my smoke."

As he said so, he got up from table, and putting his hand into the breast of the pea-coat he wore, brought out a short black pipe, and a handful of loose tobacco of the kind that is called Negro-head. Having filled his pipe, he put the surplus tobacco back again, as if his pocket were a drawer. Then, he took a live coal from the fire with the tongs, and lighted his pipe at it, and then turned round on the hearth-rug with his back to the fire, and went through his favorite action of holding out both his hands for mine.

"And this," said he, dandling my hands up and down in his, as he puffed at his pipe,—"and this is the gentleman what I made! The real genuine One! It does me good fur to look at you, Pip. All I stip'late, is, to stand by and look at you, dear boy!"

I released my hands as soon as I could, and found that I was beginning slowly to settle down to the contemplation of my condition. What I was chained to, and how heavily, became intelligible to me, as I heard his hoarse voice, and sat looking up at his furrowed bald head with its iron gray hair at the sides.

"I mustn't see my gentleman a footing it in the mire of the streets; there mustn't be no mud on his boots. My gentleman must have horses, Pip! Horses to ride, and horses to drive, and horses for his servant to ride and drive as well. Shall colonists have their horses (and blood 'uns, if you please, good Lord!) and not my London gentleman? No, no. We'll show 'em another pair of shoes than that, Pip; won't us?"

He took out of his pocket a great thick pocket-book, bursting with papers, and tossed it on the table.

"There's something worth spending in that there book, dear boy. It's yourn. All I've got ain't mine; it's yourn. Don't you be afeerd on it. There's more where that come from. I've come to the old country fur to see my gentleman spend his money like a gentleman. That'll be my pleasure. My pleasure 'ull be fur to see him do it. And blast you all!" he wound up, looking round the room and snapping his fingers once with a loud snap, "blast every one, from the judge in his wig, to the colonist a stirring up the dust, I'll show a better gentleman than the whole kit on you put together!"

"Stop!" said I, almost in a frenzy of fear and dislike, "I want to speak to you. I want to know what is to be done. I want to know how you are to be kept out of danger, how long you are going to stay, what projects you have."

"Look'ee here, Pip," said he, laying his hand on my arm in a suddenly altered and subdued manner; "first of all, look'ee here. I forgot myself half a minute ago. What I said was low; that's what it was; low. Look'ee here, Pip. Look over it. I ain't a going to be low."

"First," I resumed, half groaning, "what precautions can be taken against your being recognised and seized?"

"No, dear boy," he said, in the same tone as before, "that don't go first. Lowness goes first. I ain't took so many year to make a gentleman, not without knowing what's due to him. Look'ee here, Pip. I was low; that's what I was; low. Look over it, dear boy."

Some sense of the grimly-ludicrous moved me to a fretful laugh, as I replied, "I have looked over it. In Heaven's name, don't harp upon it!"

"Yes, but look'ee here," he persisted. "Dear boy, I ain't come so fur, not fur to be low. Now, go on, dear boy. You was a saying—"

"How are you to be guarded from the danger you have incurred?"

"Well, dear boy, the danger ain't so great. Without I was informed agen, the danger ain't so much to signify. There's Jaggers, and there's Wemmick, and there's you. Who else is there to inform?"

"Is there no chance person who might identify you in the street?" said I.

"Well," he returned, "there ain't many. Nor yet I don't intend to advertise myself in the newspapers by the name of A.M. come back from Botany Bay; and years have rolled away, and who's to gain by it? Still, look'ee here, Pip. If the danger had been fifty times as great, I should ha' come to see you, mind you, just the same."

"And how long do you remain?"

"How long?" said he, taking his black pipe from his mouth, and dropping his jaw as he stared at me. "I'm not a going back. I've come for good."

"Where are you to live?" said I. "What is to be done with you? Where will you be safe?"

"Dear boy," he returned, "there's disguising wigs can be bought for money, and there's hair powder, and spectacles, and black clothes,—shorts and what not. Others has done it safe afore, and what others has done afore, others can do agen. As to the where and how of living, dear boy, give me your own opinions on it."

"You take it smoothly now," said I, "but you were very serious last night, when you swore it was Death."

"And so I swear it is Death," said he, putting his pipe back in his mouth, "and Death by the rope, in the open street not fur from this, and it's serious that you should fully understand it to be so. What then, when that's once done? Here I am. To go back now 'ud be as bad as to stand ground—worse. Besides, Pip, I'm here, because I've meant it by you, years and years. As to what I dare, I'm a old bird now, as has dared all manner of traps since first he was fledged, and I'm not afeerd to perch upon a scarecrow. If there's Death hid inside of it, there is, and let him come out, and I'll face him, and then I'll believe in him and not afore. And now let me have a look at my gentleman agen."

Once more, he took me by both hands and surveyed me with an air of admiring proprietorship: smoking with great complacency all the while.

It appeared to me that I could do no better than secure him some quiet lodging hard by, of which he might take possession when Herbert returned: whom I expected in two or three days. That the secret must be confided to Herbert as a matter of unavoidable necessity, even if I could have put the immense relief I should derive from sharing it with him out of the question, was plain to me. But it was by no means so plain to Mr. Provis (I resolved to call him by that name), who reserved his consent to Herbert's participation until he should have seen him and formed a favorable judgment of his physiognomy. "And even then, dear boy," said he, pulling a greasy little clasped black Testament out of his pocket, "we'll have him on his oath."

To state that my terrible patron carried this little black book about the world solely to swear people on in cases of emergency, would be to state what I never quite established; but this I can say, that I never knew him put it to any other use. The book itself had the appearance of having been stolen from some court of justice, and perhaps his knowledge of its antecedents, combined with his own experience in that wise, gave him a reliance on its powers as a sort of legal spell or charm. On this first occasion of his producing it, I recalled how he had made me swear fidelity in the churchyard long ago, and how he had described himself last night as always swearing to his resolutions in his solitude.

As he was at present dressed in a seafaring slop suit, in which he looked as if he had some parrots and cigars to dispose of, I next discussed with him what dress he should wear. He cherished an extraordinary belief in the virtues of "shorts" as a disguise, and had in his own mind sketched a dress for himself that would have made him something between a dean and a dentist. It was with considerable difficulty that I won him over to the assumption of a dress more like a prosperous farmer's; and we arranged that he should cut his hair close, and wear a little powder. Lastly, as he had not yet been seen by the laundress or her niece, he was to keep himself out of their view until his change of dress was made.

It would seem a simple matter to decide on these precautions; but in my dazed, not to say distracted, state, it took so long, that I did not get out to further them until two or three in the afternoon. He was to remain shut up in the chambers while I was gone, and was on no account to open the door.

There being to my knowledge a respectable lodging-house in Essex Street, the back of which looked into the Temple, and was almost within hail of my windows, I first of all repaired to that house, and was so fortunate as to secure the second floor for my uncle, Mr. Provis. I then went from shop to shop, making such purchases as were necessary to the change in his appearance. This business transacted, I turned my face, on my own account, to Little Britain. Mr. Jaggers was at his desk, but, seeing me enter, got up immediately and stood before his fire.

"Now, Pip," said he, "be careful."

"I will, sir," I returned. For, coming along I had thought well of what I was going to say.

"Don't commit yourself," said Mr. Jaggers, "and don't commit any one. You understand—any one. Don't tell me anything: I don't want to know anything; I am not curious."

Of course I saw that he knew the man was come.

"I merely want, Mr. Jaggers," said I, "to assure myself that what I have been told is true. I have no hope of its being untrue, but at least I may verify it."

Mr. Jaggers nodded. "But did you say 'told' or 'informed'?" he asked me, with his head on one side, and not looking at me, but looking in a listening way at the floor. "Told would seem to imply verbal communication. You can't have verbal communication with a man in New South Wales, you know."

"I will say, informed, Mr. Jaggers."

"Good."

"I have been informed by a person named Abel Magwitch, that he is the benefactor so long unknown to me."

"That is the man," said Mr. Jaggers, "in New South Wales."

"And only he?" said I.

"And only he," said Mr. Jaggers.

"I am not so unreasonable, sir, as to think you at all responsible for my mistakes and wrong conclusions; but I always supposed it was Miss Havisham."

"As you say, Pip," returned Mr. Jaggers, turning his eyes upon me coolly, and taking a bite at his forefinger, "I am not at all responsible for that."

"And yet it looked so like it, sir," I pleaded with a downcast heart.

"Not a particle of evidence, Pip," said Mr. Jaggers, shaking his head and gathering up his skirts. "Take nothing on its looks; take everything on evidence. There's no better rule."

"I have no more to say," said I, with a sigh, after standing silent for a little while. "I have verified my information, and there's an end."

"And Magwitch—in New South Wales—having at last disclosed himself," said Mr. Jaggers, "you will comprehend, Pip, how rigidly throughout my communication with you, I have always adhered to the strict line of fact. There has never been the least departure from the strict line of fact. You are quite aware of that?"

"Quite, sir."

"I communicated to Magwitch—in New South Wales—when he first wrote to me—from New South Wales—the caution that he must not expect me ever to deviate from the strict line of fact. I also communicated to him another caution. He appeared to me to have obscurely hinted in his letter at some distant idea he had of seeing you in England here. I cautioned him that I must hear no more of that; that he was not at all likely to obtain a pardon; that he was expatriated for the term of his natural life; and that his presenting himself in this country would be an act of felony, rendering him liable to the extreme penalty of the law. I gave Magwitch that caution," said Mr. Jaggers, looking hard at me; "I wrote it to New South Wales. He guided himself by it, no doubt."

"No doubt," said I.

"I have been informed by Wemmick," pursued Mr. Jaggers, still looking hard at me, "that he has received a letter, under date Portsmouth, from a colonist of the name of Purvis, or—"

"Or Provis," I suggested.

"Or Provis—thank you, Pip. Perhaps it is Provis? Perhaps you know it's Provis?"

"Yes," said I.

"You know it's Provis. A letter, under date Portsmouth, from a colonist of the name of Provis, asking for the particulars of your address, on behalf of Magwitch. Wemmick sent him the particulars, I understand, by return of post. Probably it is through Provis that you have received the explanation of Magwitch—in New South Wales?"

"It came through Provis," I replied.

"Good day, Pip," said Mr. Jaggers, offering his hand; "glad to have seen you. In writing by post to Magwitch—in New South Wales—or in communicating with him through Provis, have the goodness to mention that the particulars and vouchers of our long account shall be sent to you, together with the balance; for there is still a balance remaining. Good day, Pip!"

We shook hands, and he looked hard at me as long as he could see me. I turned at the door, and he was still looking hard at me, while the two vile casts on the shelf seemed to be trying to get their eyelids open, and to force out of their swollen throats, "O, what a man he is!"

Wemmick was out, and though he had been at his desk he could have done nothing for me. I went straight back to the Temple, where I found the terrible Provis drinking rum and water and smoking negro-head, in safety.

Next day the clothes I had ordered all came home, and he put them on. Whatever he put on, became him less (it dismally seemed to me) than what he had worn before. To my thinking, there was something in him that made it hopeless to attempt to disguise him. The more I dressed him and the better I dressed him, the more he looked like the slouching fugitive on the marshes. This effect on my anxious fancy was partly referable, no doubt, to his old face and manner growing more familiar to me; but I believe too that he dragged one of his legs as if there were still a weight of iron on it, and that from head to foot there was Convict in the very grain of the man.

The influences of his solitary hut-life were upon him besides, and gave him a savage air that no dress could tame; added to these were the influences of his subsequent branded life among men, and, crowning all, his consciousness that he was dodging and hiding now. In all his ways of sitting and standing, and eating and drinking,—of brooding about in a high-shouldered reluctant style,—of taking out his great horn-handled jackknife and wiping it on his legs and cutting his food,—of lifting light glasses and cups to his lips, as if they were clumsy pannikins,—of chopping a wedge off his bread, and soaking up with it the last fragments of gravy round and round his plate, as if to make the most of an allowance, and then drying his finger-ends on it, and then swallowing it,—in these ways and a thousand other small nameless instances arising every minute in the day, there was Prisoner, Felon, Bondsman, plain as plain could be.

It had been his own idea to wear that touch of powder, and I had conceded the powder after overcoming the shorts. But I can compare the effect of it, when on, to nothing but the probable effect of rouge upon the dead; so awful was the manner in which everything in him that it was most desirable to repress, started through that thin layer of pretence, and seemed to come blazing out at the crown of his head. It was abandoned as soon as tried, and he wore his grizzled hair cut short.

Words cannot tell what a sense I had, at the same time, of the dreadful mystery that he was to me. When he fell asleep of an evening, with his knotted hands clenching the sides of the easy-chair, and his bald head tattooed with deep wrinkles falling forward on his breast, I would sit and look at him, wondering what he had done, and loading him with all the crimes in the Calendar, until the impulse was powerful on me to start up and fly from him. Every hour so increased my abhorrence of him, that I even think I might have yielded to this impulse in the first agonies of being so haunted, notwithstanding all he had done for me and the risk he ran, but for the knowledge that Herbert must soon come back. Once, I actually did start out of bed in the night, and begin to dress myself in my worst clothes, hurriedly intending to leave him there with everything else I possessed, and enlist for India as a private soldier.

I doubt if a ghost could have been more terrible to me, up in those lonely rooms in the long evenings and long nights, with the wind and the rain always rushing by. A ghost could not have been taken and hanged on my account, and the consideration that he could be, and the dread that he would be, were no small addition to my horrors. When he was not asleep, or playing a complicated kind of Patience with a ragged pack of cards of his own,—a game that I never saw before or since, and in which he recorded his winnings by sticking his jackknife into the table,—when he was not engaged in either of these pursuits, he would ask me to read to him,—"Foreign language, dear boy!" While I complied, he, not comprehending a single word, would stand before the fire surveying me with the air of an Exhibitor, and I would see him, between the fingers of the hand with which I shaded my face, appealing in dumb show to the furniture to take notice of my proficiency. The imaginary student pursued by the misshapen creature he had impiously made, was not more wretched than I, pursued by the creature who had made me, and recoiling from him with a stronger repulsion, the more he admired me and the fonder he was of me.

This is written of, I am sensible, as if it had lasted a year. It lasted about five days. Expecting Herbert all the time, I dared not go out, except when I took Provis for an airing after dark. At length, one evening when dinner was over and I had dropped into a slumber quite worn out,—for my nights had been agitated and my rest broken by fearful dreams,—I was roused by the welcome footstep on the staircase. Provis, who had been asleep too, staggered up at the noise I made, and in an instant I saw his jackknife shining in his hand.

"Quiet! It's Herbert!" I said; and Herbert came bursting in, with the airy freshness of six hundred miles of France upon him.

"Handel, my dear fellow, how are you, and again how are you, and again how are you? I seem to have been gone a twelvemonth! Why, so I must have been, for you have grown quite thin and pale! Handel, my—Halloa! I beg your pardon."

He was stopped in his running on and in his shaking hands with me, by seeing Provis. Provis, regarding him with a fixed attention, was slowly putting up his jackknife, and groping in another pocket for something else.

"Herbert, my dear friend," said I, shutting the double doors, while Herbert stood staring and wondering, "something very strange has happened. This is—a visitor of mine."

"It's all right, dear boy!" said Provis coming forward, with his little clasped black book, and then addressing himself to Herbert. "Take it in your right hand. Lord strike you dead on the spot, if ever you split in any way sumever! Kiss it!"

"Do so, as he wishes it," I said to Herbert. So, Herbert, looking at me with a friendly uneasiness and amazement, complied, and Provis immediately shaking hands with him, said, "Now you're on your oath, you know. And never believe me on mine, if Pip shan't make a gentleman on you!"

CHAPTER XLI

In vain should I attempt to describe the astonishment and disquiet of Herbert, when he and I and Provis sat down before the fire, and I recounted the whole of the secret. Enough, that I saw my own feelings reflected in Herbert's face, and not least among them, my repugnance towards the man who had done so much for me.

What would alone have set a division between that man and us, if there had been no other dividing circumstance, was his triumph in my story. Saving his troublesome sense of having been "low" on one occasion since his return,—on which point he began to hold forth to Herbert, the moment my revelation was finished,—he had no perception of the possibility of my finding any fault with my good fortune. His boast that he had made me a gentleman, and that he had come to see me support the character on his ample resources, was made for me quite as much as for himself. And that it was a highly agreeable boast to both of us, and that we must both be very proud of it, was a conclusion quite established in his own mind.

"Though, look'ee here, Pip's comrade," he said to Herbert, after having discoursed for some time, "I know very well that once since I come back—for half a minute— I've been low. I said to Pip, I knowed as I had been low. But don't you fret yourself on that score. I ain't made Pip a gentleman, and Pip ain't a going to make you a gentleman, not fur me not to know what's due to ye both. Dear boy, and Pip's comrade, you two may count upon me always having a gen-teel muzzle on. Muzzled I have been since that half a minute when I was betrayed into lowness, muzzled I am at the present time, muzzled I ever will be."

Herbert said, "Certainly," but looked as if there were no specific consolation in this, and remained perplexed and dismayed. We were anxious for the time when he would go to his lodging and leave us together, but he was evidently jealous of leaving us together, and sat late. It was midnight before I took him round to Essex Street, and saw him safely in at his own dark door. When it closed upon him, I experienced the first moment of relief I had known since the night of his arrival.

Never quite free from an uneasy remembrance of the man on the stairs, I had always looked about me in taking my guest out after dark, and in bringing him back; and I looked about me now. Difficult as it is in a large city to avoid the suspicion of being watched, when the mind is conscious of danger in that regard, I could not persuade myself that any of the people within sight cared about my movements. The few who were passing passed on their several ways, and the street was empty when I turned back into the Temple. Nobody had come out at the gate with us, nobody went in at the gate with me. As I crossed by the fountain, I saw his lighted back windows looking bright and quiet, and, when I stood for a few moments in the doorway of the building where I lived, before going up the stairs, Garden Court was as still and lifeless as the staircase was when I ascended it.

Herbert received me with open arms, and I had never felt before so blessedly what it is to have a friend. When he had spoken some sound words of sympathy and encouragement, we sat down to consider the question, What was to be done?

The chair that Provis had occupied still remaining where it had Stood,—for he had a barrack way with him of hanging about one spot, in one unsettled manner, and going through one round of observances with his pipe and his negro-head and his jackknife and his pack of cards, and what not, as if it were all put down for him on a slate,—I say his chair remaining where it had stood, Herbert unconsciously took it, but next moment started out of it, pushed it away, and took another. He had no occasion to say after that that he had conceived an aversion for my patron, neither had I occasion to confess my own. We interchanged that confidence without shaping a syllable.

"What," said I to Herbert, when he was safe in another chair,—"what is to be done?"

"My poor dear Handel," he replied, holding his head, "I am too stunned to think."

"So was I, Herbert, when the blow first fell. Still, something must be done. He is intent upon various new expenses,—horses, and carriages, and lavish appearances of all kinds. He must be stopped somehow."

"You mean that you can't accept—"

"How can I?" I interposed, as Herbert paused. "Think of him! Look at him!"

An involuntary shudder passed over both of us.

"Yet I am afraid the dreadful truth is, Herbert, that he is attached to me, strongly attached to me. Was there ever such a fate!"

"My poor dear Handel," Herbert repeated.

"Then," said I, "after all, stopping short here, never taking another penny from him, think what I owe him already! Then again: I am heavily in debt,—very heavily for me, who have now no expectations,—and I have been bred to no calling, and I am fit for nothing."

"Well, well, well!" Herbert remonstrated. "Don't say fit for nothing."

"What am I fit for? I know only one thing that I am fit for, and that is, to go for a soldier. And I might have gone, my dear Herbert, but for the prospect of taking counsel with your friendship and affection."

Of course I broke down there: and of course Herbert, beyond seizing a warm grip of my hand, pretended not to know it.

"Anyhow, my dear Handel," said he presently, "soldiering won't do. If you were to renounce this patronage and these favors, I suppose you would do so with some faint hope of one day repaying what you have already had. Not very strong, that hope, if you went soldiering! Besides, it's absurd. You would be infinitely better in Clarriker's house, small as it is. I am working up towards a partnership, you know."

Poor fellow! He little suspected with whose money.

"But there is another question," said Herbert. "This is an ignorant, determined man, who has long had one fixed idea. More than that, he seems to me (I may misjudge him) to be a man of a desperate and fierce character."

"I know he is," I returned. "Let me tell you what evidence I have seen of it." And I told him what I had not mentioned in my narrative, of that encounter with the other convict.

"See, then," said Herbert; "think of this! He comes here at the peril of his life, for the realization of his fixed idea. In the moment of realization, after all his toil and waiting, you cut the ground from under his feet, destroy his idea, and make his gains worthless to him. Do you see nothing that he might do, under the disappointment?"

"I have seen it, Herbert, and dreamed of it, ever since the fatal night of his arrival. Nothing has been in my thoughts so distinctly as his putting himself in the way of being taken."

"Then you may rely upon it," said Herbert, "that there would be great danger of his doing it. That is his power over you as long as he remains in England, and that would be his reckless course if you forsook him."

I was so struck by the horror of this idea, which had weighed upon me from the first, and the working out of which would make me regard myself, in some sort, as his murderer, that I could not rest in my chair, but began pacing to and fro. I said to Herbert, meanwhile, that even if Provis were recognised and taken, in spite of himself, I should be wretched as the cause, however innocently. Yes; even though I was so wretched in having him at large and near me, and even though I would far rather have worked at the forge all the days of my life than I would ever have come to this!

But there was no staving off the question, What was to be done?

"The first and the main thing to be done," said Herbert, "is to get him out of England. You will have to go with him, and then he may be induced to go."

"But get him where I will, could I prevent his coming back?"

"My good Handel, is it not obvious that with Newgate in the next street, there must be far greater hazard in your breaking your mind to him and making him reckless, here, than elsewhere. If a pretext to get him away could be made out of that other convict, or out of anything else in his life, now."

"There, again!" said I, stopping before Herbert, with my open hands held out, as if they contained the desperation of the case. "I know nothing of his life. It has almost made me mad to sit here of a night and see him before me, so bound up with my fortunes and misfortunes, and yet so unknown to me, except as the miserable wretch who terrified me two days in my childhood!"

Herbert got up, and linked his arm in mine, and we slowly walked to and fro together, studying the carpet.

"Handel," said Herbert, stopping, "you feel convinced that you can take no further benefits from him; do you?"

"Fully. Surely you would, too, if you were in my place?"

"And you feel convinced that you must break with him?"

"Herbert, can you ask me?"

"And you have, and are bound to have, that tenderness for the life he has risked on your account, that you must save him, if possible, from throwing it away. Then you must get him out of England before you stir a finger to extricate yourself. That done, extricate yourself, in Heaven's name, and we'll see it out together, dear old boy."

It was a comfort to shake hands upon it, and walk up and down again, with only that done.

"Now, Herbert," said I, "with reference to gaining some knowledge of his history. There is but one way that I know of. I must ask him point blank."

"Yes. Ask him," said Herbert, "when we sit at breakfast in the morning." For he had said, on taking leave of Herbert, that he would come to breakfast with us.

With this project formed, we went to bed. I had the wildest dreams concerning him, and woke unrefreshed; I woke, too, to recover the fear which I had lost in the night, of his being found out as a returned transport. Waking, I never lost that fear.

He came round at the appointed time, took out his jackknife, and sat down to his meal. He was full of plans "for his gentleman's coming out strong, and like a gentleman," and urged me to begin speedily upon the pocket-book which he had left in my possession. He considered the chambers and his own lodging as temporary residences, and advised me to look out at once for a "fashionable crib" near Hyde Park, in which he could have "a shake-down." When he had made an end of his breakfast, and was wiping his knife on his leg, I said to him, without a word of preface,—

"After you were gone last night, I told my friend of the struggle that the soldiers found you engaged in on the marshes, when we came up. You remember?"

"Remember!" said he. "I think so!"

"We want to know something about that man—and about you. It is strange to know no more about either, and particularly you, than I was able to tell last night. Is not this as good a time as another for our knowing more?"

"Well!" he said, after consideration. "You're on your oath, you know, Pip's comrade?"

"Assuredly," replied Herbert.

"As to anything I say, you know," he insisted. "The oath applies to all."

"I understand it to do so."

"And look'ee here! Wotever I done is worked out and paid for," he insisted again. "So be it."

He took out his black pipe and was going to fill it with negro-head, when, looking at the tangle of tobacco in his hand, he seemed to think it might perplex the thread of his narrative. He put it back again, stuck his pipe in a button-hole of his coat, spread a hand on each knee, and after turning an angry eye on the fire for a few silent moments, looked round at us and said what follows.

CHAPTER XLII

"Dear boy and Pip's comrade. I am not a going fur to tell you my life like a song, or a story-book. But to give it you short and handy, I'll put it at once into a mouthful of English. In jail and out of jail, in jail and out of jail, in jail and out of jail. There, you've got it. That's my life pretty much, down to such times as I got shipped off, arter Pip stood my friend.

"I've been done everything to, pretty well—except hanged. I've been locked up as much as a silver tea-kittle. I've been carted here and carted there, and put out of this town, and put out of that town, and stuck in the stocks, and whipped and worried and drove. I've no more notion where I was born than you have—if so much. I first become aware of myself down in Essex, a thieving turnips for my living. Summun had run away from me—a man—a tinker—and he'd took the fire with him, and left me wery cold.

"I know'd my name to be Magwitch, chrisen'd Abel. How did I know it? Much as I know'd the birds' names in the hedges to be chaffinch, sparrer, thrush. I might have thought it was all lies together, only as the birds' names come out true, I supposed mine did.

"So fur as I could find, there warn't a soul that see young Abel Magwitch, with us little on him as in him, but wot caught fright at him, and either drove him off, or took him up. I was took up, took up, took up, to that extent that I reg'larly grow'd up took up.

"This is the way it was, that when I was a ragged little creetur as much to be pitied as ever I see (not that I looked in the glass, for there warn't many insides of furnished houses known to me), I got the name of being hardened. "This is a terrible hardened one," they says to prison wisitors, picking out me. "May be said to live in jails, this boy. "Then they looked at me, and I looked at them, and they measured my head, some on 'em,—they had better a measured my stomach,—and others on 'em giv me tracts what I couldn't read, and made me speeches what I couldn't understand. They always went on agen me about the Devil. But what the Devil was I to do? I must put something into my stomach, mustn't I?—Howsomever, I'm a getting low, and I know what's due. Dear boy and Pip's comrade, don't you be afeerd of me being low.

"Tramping, begging, thieving, working sometimes when I could,—though that warn't as often as you may think, till you put the question whether you would ha' been over-ready to give me work yourselves,—a bit of a poacher, a bit of a laborer, a bit of a wagoner, a bit of a haymaker, a bit of a hawker, a bit of most things that don't pay and lead to trouble, I got to be a man. A deserting soldier in a Traveller's Rest, what lay hid up to the chin under a lot of taturs, learnt me to read; and a travelling Giant what signed his name at a penny a time learnt me to write. I warn't locked up as often now as formerly, but I wore out my good share of key-metal still.

"At Epsom races, a matter of over twenty years ago, I got acquainted wi' a man whose skull I'd crack wi' this poker, like the claw of a lobster, if I'd got it on this hob. His right name was Compeyson; and that's the man, dear boy, what you see me a pounding in the ditch, according to what you truly told your comrade arter I was gone last night.

"He set up fur a gentleman, this Compeyson, and he'd been to a public boarding-school and had learning. He was a smooth one to talk, and was a dab at the ways of gentlefolks. He was good-looking too. It was the night afore the great race, when I found him on the heath, in a booth that I know'd on. Him and some more was a sitting among the tables when I went in, and the landlord (which had a knowledge of me, and was a sporting one) called him out, and said, 'I think this is a man that might suit you,'—meaning I was.

"Compeyson, he looks at me very noticing, and I look at him. He has a watch and a chain and a ring and a breast-pin and a handsome suit of clothes.

"'To judge from appearances, you're out of luck,' says Compeyson to me.

"'Yes, master, and I've never been in it much.' (I had come out of Kingston Jail last on a vagrancy committal. Not but what it might have been for something else; but it warn't.)

"'Luck changes,' says Compeyson; 'perhaps yours is going to change.'

"I says, 'I hope it may be so. There's room.'

"'What can you do?' says Compeyson.

"'Eat and drink,' I says; 'if you'll find the materials.'

"Compeyson laughed, looked at me again very noticing, giv me five shillings, and appointed me for next night. Same place.

"I went to Compeyson next night, same place, and Compeyson took me on to be his man and pardner. And what was Compeyson's business in which we was to go pardners? Compeyson's business was the swindling, handwriting forging, stolen bank-note passing, and such-like. All sorts of traps as Compeyson could set with his head, and keep his own legs out of and get the profits from and let another man in for, was Compeyson's business. He'd no more heart than a iron file, he was as cold as death, and he had the head of the Devil afore mentioned.

"There was another in with Compeyson, as was called Arthur,—not as being so chrisen'd, but as a surname. He was in a Decline, and was a shadow to look at. Him and Compeyson had been in a bad thing with a rich lady some years afore, and they'd made a pot of money by it; but Compeyson betted and gamed, and he'd have run through the king's taxes. So, Arthur was a dying, and a dying poor and with the horrors on him, and Compeyson's wife (which Compeyson kicked mostly) was a having pity on him when she could, and Compeyson was a having pity on nothing and nobody.

"I might a took warning by Arthur, but I didn't; and I won't pretend I was partick'ler—for where 'ud be the good on it, dear boy and comrade? So I begun wi' Compeyson, and a poor tool I was in his hands. Arthur lived at the top of Compeyson's house (over nigh Brentford it was), and Compeyson kept a careful account agen him for board and lodging, in case he should ever get better to work it out. But Arthur soon settled the account. The second or third time as ever I see him, he come a tearing down into Compeyson's parlor late at night, in only a flannel gown, with his hair all in a sweat, and he says to Compeyson's wife, 'Sally, she really is upstairs alonger me, now, and I can't get rid of her. She's all in white,' he says, 'wi' white flowers in her hair, and she's awful mad, and she's got a shroud hanging over her arm, and she says she'll put it on me at five in the morning.'

"Says Compeyson: 'Why, you fool, don't you know she's got a living body? And how should she be up there, without coming through the door, or in at the window, and up the stairs?'

"'I don't know how she's there,' says Arthur, shivering dreadful with the horrors, 'but she's standing in the corner at the foot of the bed, awful mad. And over where her heart's broke—you broke it!—there's drops of blood.'

"Compeyson spoke hardy, but he was always a coward. 'Go up alonger this drivelling sick man,' he says to his wife, 'and Magwitch, lend her a hand, will you?' But he never come nigh himself.

"Compeyson's wife and me took him up to bed agen, and he raved most dreadful. 'Why look at her!' he cries out. 'She's a shaking the shroud at me! Don't you see her? Look at her eyes! Ain't it awful to see her so mad?' Next he cries, 'She'll put it on me, and then I'm done for! Take it away from her, take it away!' And then he catched hold of us, and kep on a talking to her, and answering of her, till I half believed I see her myself.

"Compeyson's wife, being used to him, giv him some liquor to get the horrors off, and by and by he quieted. 'O, she's gone! Has her keeper been for her?' he says. 'Yes,' says Compeyson's wife. 'Did you tell him to lock her and bar her in?' 'Yes.' 'And to take that ugly thing away from her?' 'Yes, yes, all right.' 'You're a good creetur,' he says, 'don't leave me, whatever you do, and thank you!'

"He rested pretty quiet till it might want a few minutes of five, and then he starts up with a scream, and screams out, 'Here she is! She's got the shroud again. She's unfolding it. She's coming out of the corner. She's coming to the bed. Hold me, both on you—one of each side—don't let her touch me with it. Hah! she missed me that time. Don't let her throw it over my shoulders. Don't let her lift me up to get it round me. She's lifting me up. Keep me down!' Then he lifted himself up hard, and was dead.

"Compeyson took it easy as a good riddance for both sides. Him and me was soon busy, and first he swore me (being ever artful) on my own book,—this here little black book, dear boy, what I swore your comrade on.

"Not to go into the things that Compeyson planned, and I done—which 'ud take a week—I'll simply say to you, dear boy, and Pip's comrade, that that man got me into such nets as made me his black slave. I was always in debt to him, always under his thumb, always a working, always a getting into danger. He was younger than me, but he'd got craft, and he'd got learning, and he overmatched me five hundred times told and no mercy. My Missis as I had the hard time wi'—Stop though! I ain't brought her in—"

He looked about him in a confused way, as if he had lost his place in the book of his remembrance; and he turned his face to the fire, and spread his hands broader on his knees, and lifted them off and put them on again.

"There ain't no need to go into it," he said, looking round once more. "The time wi' Compeyson was a'most as hard a time as ever I had; that said, all's said. Did I tell you as I was tried, alone, for misdemeanor, while with Compeyson?"

I answered, No.

"Well!" he said, "I was, and got convicted. As to took up on suspicion, that was twice or three times in the four or five year that it lasted; but evidence was wanting. At last, me and Compeyson was both committed for felony,—on a charge of putting stolen notes in circulation,—and there was other charges behind. Compeyson says to me, 'Separate defences, no communication,' and that was all. And I was so miserable poor, that I sold all the clothes I had, except what hung on my back, afore I could get Jaggers.

"When we was put in the dock, I noticed first of all what a gentleman Compeyson looked, wi' his curly hair and his black clothes and his white pocket-handkercher, and what a common sort of a wretch I looked. When the prosecution opened and the evidence was put short, aforehand, I noticed how heavy it all bore on me, and how light on him. When the evidence was giv in the box, I noticed how it was always me that had come for'ard, and could be swore to, how it was always me that the money had been paid to, how it was always me that had seemed to work the thing and get the profit. But when the defence come on, then I see the plan plainer; for, says the counsellor for Compeyson, 'My lord and gentlemen, here you has afore you, side by side, two persons as your eyes can separate wide; one, the younger, well brought up, who will be spoke to as such; one, the elder, ill brought up, who will be spoke to as such; one, the younger, seldom if ever seen in these here transactions, and only suspected; t'other, the elder, always seen in 'em and always wi'his guilt brought home. Can you doubt, if there is but one in it, which is the one, and, if there is two in it, which is much the worst one?' And such-like. And when it come to character, warn't it Compeyson as had been to the school, and warn't it his schoolfellows as was in this position and in that, and warn't it him as had been know'd by witnesses in such clubs and societies, and nowt to his disadvantage? And warn't it me as had been tried afore, and as had been know'd up hill and down dale in Bridewells and Lock-Ups! And when it come to speech-making, warn't it Compeyson as could speak to 'em wi' his face dropping every now and then into his white pocket-handkercher,—ah! and wi' verses in his speech, too,—and warn't it me as could only say, 'Gentlemen, this man at my side is a most precious rascal'? And when the verdict come, warn't it Compeyson as was recommended to mercy on account of good character and bad company, and giving up all the information he could agen me, and warn't it me as got never a word but Guilty? And when I says to Compeyson, 'Once out of this court, I'll smash that face of yourn!' ain't it Compeyson as prays the Judge to be protected, and gets two turnkeys stood betwixt us? And when we're sentenced, ain't it him as gets seven year, and me fourteen, and ain't it him as the Judge is sorry for, because he might a done so well, and ain't it me as the Judge perceives to be a old offender of wiolent passion, likely to come to worse?"

He had worked himself into a state of great excitement, but he checked it, took two or three short breaths, swallowed as often, and stretching out his hand towards me said, in a reassuring manner, "I ain't a going to be low, dear boy!"

He had so heated himself that he took out his handkerchief and wiped his face and head and neck and hands, before he could go on.

"I had said to Compeyson that I'd smash that face of his, and I swore Lord smash mine! to do it. We was in the same prison-ship, but I couldn't get at him for long, though I tried. At last I come behind him and hit him on the cheek to turn him round and get a smashing one at him, when I was seen and seized. The black-hole of that ship warn't a strong one, to a judge of black-holes that could swim and dive. I escaped to the shore, and I was a hiding among the graves there, envying them as was in 'em and all over, when I first see my boy!"

He regarded me with a look of affection that made him almost abhorrent to me again, though I had felt great pity for him.

"By my boy, I was giv to understand as Compeyson was out on them marshes too. Upon my soul, I half believe he escaped in his terror, to get quit of me, not knowing it was me as had got ashore. I hunted him down. I smashed his face. 'And now,' says I 'as the worst thing I can do, caring nothing for myself, I'll drag you back.' And I'd have swum off, towing him by the hair, if it had come to that, and I'd a got him aboard without the soldiers.

"Of course he'd much the best of it to the last,—his character was so good. He had escaped when he was made half wild by me and my murderous intentions; and his punishment was light. I was put in irons, brought to trial again, and sent for life. I didn't stop for life, dear boy and Pip's comrade, being here."

"He wiped himself again, as he had done before, and then slowly took his tangle of tobacco from his pocket, and plucked his pipe from his button-hole, and slowly filled it, and began to smoke.

"Is he dead?" I asked, after a silence.

"Is who dead, dear boy?"

"Compeyson."

"He hopes I am, if he's alive, you may be sure," with a fierce look. "I never heerd no more of him."

Herbert had been writing with his pencil in the cover of a book. He softly pushed the book over to me, as Provis stood smoking with his eyes on the fire, and I read in it:—

"Young Havisham's name was Arthur. Compeyson is the man who professed to be Miss Havisham's lover."

I shut the book and nodded slightly to Herbert, and put the book by; but we neither of us said anything, and both looked at Provis as he stood smoking by the fire.

CHAPTER XLIII

Why should I pause to ask how much of my shrinking from Provis might be traced to Estella? Why should I loiter on my road, to compare the state of mind in which I had tried to rid myself of the stain of the prison before meeting her at the coach-office, with the state of mind in which I now reflected on the abyss between Estella in her pride and beauty, and the returned transport whom I harbored? The road would be none the smoother for it, the end would be none the better for it, he would not be helped, nor I extenuated.

A new fear had been engendered in my mind by his narrative; or rather, his narrative had given form and purpose to the fear that was already there. If Compeyson were alive and should discover his return, I could hardly doubt the consequence. That, Compeyson stood in mortal fear of him, neither of the two could know much better than I; and that any such man as that man had been described to be would hesitate to release himself for good from a dreaded enemy by the safe means of becoming an informer was scarcely to be imagined.

Never had I breathed, and never would I breathe—or so I resolved—a word of Estella to Provis. But, I said to Herbert that, before I could go abroad, I must see both Estella and Miss Havisham. This was when we were left alone on the night of the day when Provis told us his story. I resolved to go out to Richmond next day, and I went.

On my presenting myself at Mrs. Brandley's, Estella's maid was called to tell that Estella had gone into the country. Where? To Satis House, as usual. Not as usual, I said, for she had never yet gone there without me; when was she coming back? There was an air of reservation in the answer which increased my perplexity, and the answer was, that her maid believed she was only coming back at all for a little while. I could make nothing of this, except that it was meant that I should make nothing of it, and I went home again in complete discomfiture.

Another night consultation with Herbert after Provis was gone home (I always took him home, and always looked well about me), led us to the conclusion that nothing should be said about going abroad until I came back from Miss Havisham's. In the mean time, Herbert and I were to consider separately what it would be best to say; whether we should devise any pretence of being afraid that he was under suspicious observation; or whether I, who had never yet been abroad, should propose an expedition. We both knew that I had but to propose anything, and he would consent. We agreed that his remaining many days in his present hazard was not to be thought of.

Next day I had the meanness to feign that I was under a binding promise to go down to Joe; but I was capable of almost any meanness towards Joe or his name. Provis was to be strictly careful while I was gone, and Herbert was to take the charge of him that I had taken. I was to be absent only one night, and, on my return, the gratification of his impatience for my starting as a gentleman on a greater scale was to be begun. It occurred to me then, and as I afterwards found to Herbert also, that he might be best got away across the water, on that pretence,—as, to make purchases, or the like.

Having thus cleared the way for my expedition to Miss Havisham's, I set off by the early morning coach before it was yet light, and was out on the open country road when the day came creeping on, halting and whimpering and shivering, and wrapped in patches of cloud and rags of mist, like a beggar. When we drove up to the Blue Boar after a drizzly ride, whom should I see come out under the gateway, toothpick in hand, to look at the coach, but Bentley Drummle!

As he pretended not to see me, I pretended not to see him. It was a very lame pretence on both sides; the lamer, because we both went into the coffee-room, where he had just finished his breakfast, and where I ordered mine. It was poisonous to me to see him in the town, for I very well knew why he had come there.

Pretending to read a smeary newspaper long out of date, which had nothing half so legible in its local news, as the foreign matter of coffee, pickles, fish sauces, gravy, melted butter, and wine with which it was sprinkled all over, as if it had taken the measles in a highly irregular form, I sat at my table while he stood before the fire. By degrees it became an enormous injury to me that he stood before the fire. And I got up, determined to have my share of it. I had to put my hand behind his legs for the poker when I went up to the fireplace to stir the fire, but still pretended not to know him.

"Is this a cut?" said Mr. Drummle.

"Oh!" said I, poker in hand; "it's you, is it? How do you do? I was wondering who it was, who kept the fire off."

With that, I poked tremendously, and having done so, planted myself side by side with Mr. Drummle, my shoulders squared and my back to the fire.

"You have just come down?" said Mr. Drummle, edging me a little away with his shoulder.

"Yes," said I, edging him a little away with my shoulder.

"Beastly place," said Drummle. "Your part of the country, I think?"

"Yes," I assented. "I am told it's very like your Shropshire."

"Not in the least like it," said Drummle.

Here Mr. Drummle looked at his boots and I looked at mine, and then Mr. Drummle looked at my boots, and I looked at his.

"Have you been here long?" I asked, determined not to yield an inch of the fire.

"Long enough to be tired of it," returned Drummle, pretending to yawn, but equally determined.

"Do you stay here long?"

"Can't say," answered Mr. Drummle. "Do you?"

"Can't say," said I.

I felt here, through a tingling in my blood, that if Mr. Drummle's shoulder had claimed another hair's breadth of room, I should have jerked him into the window; equally, that if my own shoulder had urged a similar claim, Mr. Drummle would have jerked me into the nearest box. He whistled a little. So did I.

"Large tract of marshes about here, I believe?" said Drummle.

"Yes. What of that?" said I.

Mr. Drummle looked at me, and then at my boots, and then said, "Oh!" and laughed.

"Are you amused, Mr. Drummle?"

"No," said he, "not particularly. I am going out for a ride in the saddle. I mean to explore those marshes for amusement. Out-of-the-way villages there, they tell me. Curious little public-houses—and smithies—and that. Waiter!"

"Yes, sir."

"Is that horse of mine ready?"

"Brought round to the door, sir."

"I say. Look here, you sir. The lady won't ride to-day; the weather won't do."

"Very good, sir."

"And I don't dine, because I'm going to dine at the lady's."

"Very good, sir."

Then, Drummle glanced at me, with an insolent triumph on his great-jowled face that cut me to the heart, dull as he was, and so exasperated me, that I felt inclined to take him in my arms (as the robber in the story-book is said to have taken the old lady) and seat him on the fire.

One thing was manifest to both of us, and that was, that until relief came, neither of us could relinquish the fire. There we stood, well squared up before it, shoulder to shoulder and foot to foot, with our hands behind us, not budging an inch. The horse was visible outside in the drizzle at the door, my breakfast was put on the table, Drummle's was cleared away, the waiter invited me to begin, I nodded, we both stood our ground.

"Have you been to the Grove since?" said Drummle.

"No," said I, "I had quite enough of the Finches the last time I was there."

"Was that when we had a difference of opinion?"

"Yes," I replied, very shortly.

"Come, come! They let you off easily enough," sneered Drummle. "You shouldn't have lost your temper."

"Mr. Drummle," said I, "you are not competent to give advice on that subject. When I lose my temper (not that I admit having done so on that occasion), I don't throw glasses."

"I do," said Drummle.

After glancing at him once or twice, in an increased state of smouldering ferocity, I said,—

"Mr. Drummle, I did not seek this conversation, and I don't think it an agreeable one."

"I am sure it's not," said he, superciliously over his shoulder; "I don't think anything about it."

"And therefore," I went on, "with your leave, I will suggest that we hold no kind of communication in future."

"Quite my opinion," said Drummle, "and what I should have suggested myself, or done—more likely—without suggesting. But don't lose your temper. Haven't you lost enough without that?"

"What do you mean, sir?"

"Waiter!" said Drummle, by way of answering me.

The waiter reappeared.

"Look here, you sir. You quite understand that the young lady don't ride to-day, and that I dine at the young lady's?"

"Quite so, sir!"

When the waiter had felt my fast-cooling teapot with the palm of his hand, and had looked imploringly at me, and had gone out, Drummle, careful not to move the shoulder next me, took a cigar from his pocket and bit the end off, but showed no sign of stirring. Choking and boiling as I was, I felt that we could not go a word further, without introducing Estella's name, which I could not endure to hear him utter; and therefore I looked stonily at the opposite wall, as if there were no one present, and forced myself to silence. How long we might have remained in this ridiculous position it is impossible to say, but for the incursion of three thriving farmers—laid on by the waiter, I think—who came into the coffee-room unbuttoning their great-coats and rubbing their hands, and before whom, as they charged at the fire, we were obliged to give way.

I saw him through the window, seizing his horse's mane, and mounting in his blundering brutal manner, and sidling and backing away. I thought he was gone, when he came back, calling for a light for the cigar in his mouth, which he had forgotten. A man in a dust-colored dress appeared with what was wanted,—I could not have said from where: whether from the inn yard, or the street, or where not,—and as Drummle leaned down from the saddle and lighted his cigar and laughed, with a jerk of his head towards the coffee-room windows, the slouching shoulders and ragged hair of this man whose back was towards me reminded me of Orlick.

Too heavily out of sorts to care much at the time whether it were he or no, or after all to touch the breakfast, I washed the weather and the journey from my face and hands, and went out to the memorable old house that it would have been so much the better for me never to have entered, never to have seen.

CHAPTER XLIV

In the room where the dressing-table stood, and where the wax-candles burnt on the wall, I found Miss Havisham and Estella; Miss Havisham seated on a settee near the fire, and Estella on a cushion at her feet. Estella was knitting, and Miss Havisham was looking on. They both raised their eyes as I went in, and both saw an alteration in me. I derived that, from the look they interchanged.

"And what wind," said Miss Havisham, "blows you here, Pip?"

Though she looked steadily at me, I saw that she was rather confused. Estella, pausing a moment in her knitting with her eyes upon me, and then going on, I fancied that I read in the action of her fingers, as plainly as if she had told me in the dumb alphabet, that she perceived I had discovered my real benefactor.

"Miss Havisham," said I, "I went to Richmond yesterday, to speak to Estella; and finding that some wind had blown her here, I followed."

Miss Havisham motioning to me for the third or fourth time to sit down, I took the chair by the dressing-table, which I had often seen her occupy. With all that ruin at my feet and about me, it seemed a natural place for me, that day.

"What I had to say to Estella, Miss Havisham, I will say before you, presently—in a few moments. It will not surprise you, it will not displease you. I am as unhappy as you can ever have meant me to be."

Miss Havisham continued to look steadily at me. I could see in the action of Estella's fingers as they worked that she attended to what I said; but she did not look up.

"I have found out who my patron is. It is not a fortunate discovery, and is not likely ever to enrich me in reputation, station, fortune, anything. There are reasons why I must say no more of that. It is not my secret, but another's."

As I was silent for a while, looking at Estella and considering how to go on, Miss Havisham repeated, "It is not your secret, but another's. Well?"

"When you first caused me to be brought here, Miss Havisham, when I belonged to the village over yonder, that I wish I had never left, I suppose I did really come here, as any other chance boy might have come,—as a kind of servant, to gratify a want or a whim, and to be paid for it?"

"Ay, Pip," replied Miss Havisham, steadily nodding her head; "you did."

"And that Mr. Jaggers—"

"Mr. Jaggers," said Miss Havisham, taking me up in a firm tone, "had nothing to do with it, and knew nothing of it. His being my lawyer, and his being the lawyer of your patron is a coincidence. He holds the same relation towards numbers of people, and it might easily arise. Be that as it may, it did arise, and was not brought about by any one."

Any one might have seen in her haggard face that there was no suppression or evasion so far.

"But when I fell into the mistake I have so long remained in, at least you led me on?" said I.

"Yes," she returned, again nodding steadily, "I let you go on."

"Was that kind?"

"Who am I," cried Miss Havisham, striking her stick upon the floor and flashing into wrath so suddenly that Estella glanced up at her in surprise,—"who am I, for God's sake, that I should be kind?"

It was a weak complaint to have made, and I had not meant to make it. I told her so, as she sat brooding after this outburst.

"Well, well, well!" she said. "What else?"

"I was liberally paid for my old attendance here," I said, to soothe her, "in being apprenticed, and I have asked these questions only for my own information. What follows has another (and I hope more disinterested) purpose. In humoring my mistake, Miss Havisham, you punished—practised on—perhaps you will supply whatever term expresses your intention, without offence—your self-seeking relations?"

"I did. Why, they would have it so! So would you. What has been my history, that I should be at the pains of entreating either them or you not to have it so! You made your own snares. I never made them."

Waiting until she was quiet again,—for this, too, flashed out of her in a wild and sudden way,—I went on.

"I have been thrown among one family of your relations, Miss Havisham, and have been constantly among them since I went to London. I know them to have been as honestly under my delusion as I myself. And I should be false and base if I did not tell you, whether it is acceptable to you or no, and whether you are inclined to give credence to it or no, that you deeply wrong both Mr. Matthew Pocket and his son Herbert, if you suppose them to be otherwise than generous, upright, open, and incapable of anything designing or mean."

"They are your friends," said Miss Havisham.

"They made themselves my friends," said I, "when they supposed me to have superseded them; and when Sarah Pocket, Miss Georgiana, and Mistress Camilla were not my friends, I think."

This contrasting of them with the rest seemed, I was glad to see, to do them good with her. She looked at me keenly for a little while, and then said quietly,—

"What do you want for them?"

"Only," said I, "that you would not confound them with the others. They may be of the same blood, but, believe me, they are not of the same nature."

Still looking at me keenly, Miss Havisham repeated,—

"What do you want for them?"

"I am not so cunning, you see," I said, in answer, conscious that I reddened a little, "as that I could hide from you, even if I desired, that I do want something. Miss Havisham, if you would spare the money to do my friend Herbert a lasting service in life, but which from the nature of the case must be done without his knowledge, I could show you how."

"Why must it be done without his knowledge?" she asked, settling her hands upon her stick, that she might regard me the more attentively.

"Because," said I, "I began the service myself, more than two years ago, without his knowledge, and I don't want to be betrayed. Why I fail in my ability to finish it, I cannot explain. It is a part of the secret which is another person's and not mine."

She gradually withdrew her eyes from me, and turned them on the fire. After watching it for what appeared in the silence and by the light of the slowly wasting candles to be a long time, she was roused by the collapse of some of the red coals, and looked towards me again—at first, vacantly—then, with a gradually concentrating attention. All this time Estella knitted on. When Miss Havisham had fixed her attention on me, she said, speaking as if there had been no lapse in our dialogue,—

"What else?"

"Estella," said I, turning to her now, and trying to command my trembling voice, "you know I love you. You know that I have loved you long and dearly."

She raised her eyes to my face, on being thus addressed, and her fingers plied their work, and she looked at me with an unmoved countenance. I saw that Miss Havisham glanced from me to her, and from her to me.

"I should have said this sooner, but for my long mistake. It induced me to hope that Miss Havisham meant us for one another. While I thought you could not help yourself, as it were, I refrained from saying it. But I must say it now."

Preserving her unmoved countenance, and with her fingers still going, Estella shook her head.

"I know," said I, in answer to that action,—"I know. I have no hope that I shall ever call you mine, Estella. I am ignorant what may become of me very soon, how poor I may be, or where I may go. Still, I love you. I have loved you ever since I first saw you in this house."

Looking at me perfectly unmoved and with her fingers busy, she shook her head again.

"It would have been cruel in Miss Havisham, horribly cruel, to practise on the susceptibility of a poor boy, and to torture me through all these years with a vain hope and an idle pursuit, if she had reflected on the gravity of what she did. But I think she did not. I think that, in the endurance of her own trial, she forgot mine, Estella."

I saw Miss Havisham put her hand to her heart and hold it there, as she sat looking by turns at Estella and at me.

"It seems," said Estella, very calmly, "that there are sentiments, fancies,—I don't know how to call them,—which I am not able to comprehend. When you say you love me, I know what you mean, as a form of words; but nothing more. You address nothing in my breast, you touch nothing there. I don't care for what you say at all. I have tried to warn you of this; now, have I not?"

I said in a miserable manner, "Yes."

"Yes. But you would not be warned, for you thought I did not mean it. Now, did you not think so?"

"I thought and hoped you could not mean it. You, so young, untried, and beautiful, Estella! Surely it is not in Nature."

"It is in my nature," she returned. And then she added, with a stress upon the words, "It is in the nature formed within me. I make a great difference between you and all other people when I say so much. I can do no more."

"Is it not true," said I, "that Bentley Drummle is in town here, and pursuing you?"

"It is quite true," she replied, referring to him with the indifference of utter contempt.

"That you encourage him, and ride out with him, and that he dines with you this very day?"

She seemed a little surprised that I should know it, but again replied, "Quite true."

"You cannot love him, Estella!"

Her fingers stopped for the first time, as she retorted rather angrily, "What have I told you? Do you still think, in spite of it, that I do not mean what I say?"

"You would never marry him, Estella?"

She looked towards Miss Havisham, and considered for a moment with her work in her hands. Then she said, "Why not tell you the truth? I am going to be married to him."

I dropped my face into my hands, but was able to control myself better than I could have expected, considering what agony it gave me to hear her say those words. When I raised my face again, there was such a ghastly look upon Miss Havisham's, that it impressed me, even in my passionate hurry and grief.

"Estella, dearest Estella, do not let Miss Havisham lead you into this fatal step. Put me aside for ever,—you have done so, I well know,—but bestow yourself on some worthier person than Drummle. Miss Havisham gives you to him, as the greatest slight and injury that could be done to the many far better men who admire you, and to the few who truly love you. Among those few there may be one who loves you even as dearly, though he has not loved you as long, as I. Take him, and I can bear it better, for your sake!"

My earnestness awoke a wonder in her that seemed as if it would have been touched with compassion, if she could have rendered me at all intelligible to her own mind.

"I am going," she said again, in a gentler voice, "to be married to him. The preparations for my marriage are making, and I shall be married soon. Why do you injuriously introduce the name of my mother by adoption? It is my own act."

"Your own act, Estella, to fling yourself away upon a brute?"

"On whom should I fling myself away?" she retorted, with a smile. "Should I fling myself away upon the man who would the soonest feel (if people do feel such things) that I took nothing to him? There! It is done. I shall do well enough, and so will my husband. As to leading me into what you call this fatal step, Miss Havisham would have had me wait, and not marry yet; but I am tired of the life I have led, which has very few charms for me, and I am willing enough to change it. Say no more. We shall never understand each other."

"Such a mean brute, such a stupid brute!" I urged, in despair.

"Don't be afraid of my being a blessing to him," said Estella; "I shall not be that. Come! Here is my hand. Do we part on this, you visionary boy—or man?"

"O Estella!" I answered, as my bitter tears fell fast on her hand, do what I would to restrain them; "even if I remained in England and could hold my head up with the rest, how could I see you Drummle's wife?"

"Nonsense," she returned,—"nonsense. This will pass in no time."

"Never, Estella!"

"You will get me out of your thoughts in a week."

"Out of my thoughts! You are part of my existence, part of myself. You have been in every line I have ever read since I first came here, the rough common boy whose poor heart you wounded even then. You have been in every prospect I have ever seen since,—on the river, on the sails of the ships, on the marshes, in the clouds, in the light, in the darkness, in the wind, in the woods, in the sea, in the streets. You have been the embodiment of every graceful fancy that my mind has ever become acquainted with. The stones of which the strongest London buildings are made are not more real, or more impossible to be displaced by your hands, than your presence and influence have been to me, there and everywhere, and will be. Estella, to the last hour of my life, you cannot choose but remain part of my character, part of the little good in me, part of the evil. But, in this separation, I associate you only with the good; and I will faithfully hold you to that always, for you must have done me far more good than harm, let me feel now what sharp distress I may. O God bless you, God forgive you!"

In what ecstasy of unhappiness I got these broken words out of myself, I don't know. The rhapsody welled up within me, like blood from an inward wound, and gushed out. I held her hand to my lips some lingering moments, and so I left her. But ever afterwards, I remembered,—and soon afterwards with stronger reason,—that while Estella looked at me merely with incredulous wonder, the spectral figure of Miss Havisham, her hand still covering her heart, seemed all resolved into a ghastly stare of pity and remorse.

All done, all gone! So much was done and gone, that when I went out at the gate, the light of the day seemed of a darker color than when I went in. For a while, I hid myself among some lanes and by-paths, and then struck off to walk all the way to London. For, I had by that time come to myself so far as to consider that I could not go back to the inn and see Drummle there; that I could not bear to sit upon the coach and be spoken to; that I could do nothing half so good for myself as tire myself out.

It was past midnight when I crossed London Bridge. Pursuing the narrow intricacies of the streets which at that time tended westward near the Middlesex shore of the river, my readiest access to the Temple was close by the river-side, through Whitefriars. I was not expected till to-morrow; but I had my keys, and, if Herbert were gone to bed, could get to bed myself without disturbing him.

As it seldom happened that I came in at that Whitefriars gate after the Temple was closed, and as I was very muddy and weary, I did not take it ill that the night-porter examined me with much attention as he held the gate a little way open for me to pass in. To help his memory I mentioned my name.

"I was not quite sure, sir, but I thought so. Here's a note, sir. The messenger that brought it, said would you be so good as read it by my lantern?"

Much surprised by the request, I took the note. It was directed to Philip Pip, Esquire, and on the top of the superscription were the words, "PLEASE READ THIS, HERE." I opened it, the watchman holding up his light, and read inside, in Wemmick's writing,—

"DON'T GO HOME."

CHAPTER XLV

Turning from the Temple gate as soon as I had read the warning, I made the best of my way to Fleet Street, and there got a late hackney chariot and drove to the Hummums in Covent Garden. In those times a bed was always to be got there at any hour of the night, and the chamberlain, letting me in at his ready wicket, lighted the candle next in order on his shelf, and showed me straight into the bedroom next in order on his list. It was a sort of vault on the ground floor at the back, with a despotic monster of a four-post bedstead in it, straddling over the whole place, putting one of his arbitrary legs into the fireplace and another into the doorway, and squeezing the wretched little washing-stand in quite a Divinely Righteous manner.

As I had asked for a night-light, the chamberlain had brought me in, before he left me, the good old constitutional rushlight of those virtuous days.—an object like the ghost of a walking-cane, which instantly broke its back if it were touched, which nothing could ever be lighted at, and which was placed in solitary confinement at the bottom of a high tin tower, perforated with round holes that made a staringly wide-awake pattern on the walls. When I had got into bed, and lay there footsore, weary, and wretched, I found that I could no more close my own eyes than I could close the eyes of this foolish Argus. And thus, in the gloom and death of the night, we stared at one another.

What a doleful night! How anxious, how dismal, how long! There was an inhospitable smell in the room, of cold soot and hot dust; and, as I looked up into the corners of the tester over my head, I thought what a number of blue-bottle flies from the butchers', and earwigs from the market, and grubs from the country, must be holding on up there, lying by for next summer. This led me to speculate whether any of them ever tumbled down, and then I fancied that I felt light falls on my face,—a disagreeable turn of thought, suggesting other and more objectionable approaches up my back. When I had lain awake a little while, those extraordinary voices with which silence teems began to make themselves audible. The closet whispered, the fireplace sighed, the little washing-stand ticked, and one guitar-string played occasionally in the chest of drawers. At about the same time, the eyes on the wall acquired a new expression, and in every one of those staring rounds I saw written, DON'T GO HOME.

Whatever night-fancies and night-noises crowded on me, they never warded off this DON'T GO HOME. It plaited itself into whatever I thought of, as a bodily pain would have done. Not long before, I had read in the newspapers, how a gentleman unknown had come to the Hummums in the night, and had gone to bed, and had destroyed himself, and had been found in the morning weltering in blood. It came into my head that he must have occupied this very vault of mine, and I got out of bed to assure myself that there were no red marks about; then opened the door to look out into the passages, and cheer myself with the companionship of a distant light, near which I knew the chamberlain to be dozing. But all this time, why I was not to go home, and what had happened at home, and when I should go home, and whether Provis was safe at home, were questions occupying my mind so busily, that one might have supposed there could be no more room in it for any other theme. Even when I thought of Estella, and how we had parted that day forever, and when I recalled all the circumstances of our parting, and all her looks and tones, and the action of her fingers while she knitted,—even then I was pursuing, here and there and everywhere, the caution, Don't go home. When at last I dozed, in sheer exhaustion of mind and body, it became a vast shadowy verb which I had to conjugate. Imperative mood, present tense: Do not thou go home, let him not go home, let us not go home, do not ye or you go home, let not them go home. Then potentially: I may not and I cannot go home; and I might not, could not, would not, and should not go home; until I felt that I was going distracted, and rolled over on the pillow, and looked at the staring rounds upon the wall again.

I had left directions that I was to be called at seven; for it was plain that I must see Wemmick before seeing any one else, and equally plain that this was a case in which his Walworth sentiments only could be taken. It was a relief to get out of the room where the night had been so miserable, and I needed no second knocking at the door to startle me from my uneasy bed.

The Castle battlements arose upon my view at eight o'clock. The little servant happening to be entering the fortress with two hot rolls, I passed through the postern and crossed the drawbridge in her company, and so came without announcement into the presence of Wemmick as he was making tea for himself and the Aged. An open door afforded a perspective view of the Aged in bed.

"Halloa, Mr. Pip!" said Wemmick. "You did come home, then?"

"Yes," I returned; "but I didn't go home."

"That's all right," said he, rubbing his hands. "I left a note for you at each of the Temple gates, on the chance. Which gate did you come to?"

I told him.

"I'll go round to the others in the course of the day and destroy the notes," said Wemmick; "it's a good rule never to leave documentary evidence if you can help it, because you don't know when it may be put in. I'm going to take a liberty with you. Would you mind toasting this sausage for the Aged P.?"

I said I should be delighted to do it.

"Then you can go about your work, Mary Anne," said Wemmick to the little servant; "which leaves us to ourselves, don't you see, Mr. Pip?" he added, winking, as she disappeared.

I thanked him for his friendship and caution, and our discourse proceeded in a low tone, while I toasted the Aged's sausage and he buttered the crumb of the Aged's roll.

"Now, Mr. Pip, you know," said Wemmick, "you and I understand one another. We are in our private and personal capacities, and we have been engaged in a confidential transaction before to-day. Official sentiments are one thing. We are extra official."

I cordially assented. I was so very nervous, that I had already lighted the Aged's sausage like a torch, and been obliged to blow it out.

"I accidentally heard, yesterday morning," said Wemmick, "being in a certain place where I once took you,—even between you and me, it's as well not to mention names when avoidable—"

"Much better not," said I. "I understand you."

"I heard there by chance, yesterday morning," said Wemmick, "that a certain person not altogether of uncolonial pursuits, and not unpossessed of portable property,—I don't know who it may really be,—we won't name this person—"

"Not necessary," said I.

"—Had made some little stir in a certain part of the world where a good many people go, not always in gratification of their own inclinations, and not quite irrespective of the government expense—"

In watching his face, I made quite a firework of the Aged's sausage, and greatly discomposed both my own attention and Wemmick's; for which I apologized.

"—By disappearing from such place, and being no more heard of thereabouts. From which," said Wemmick, "conjectures had been raised and theories formed. I also heard that you at your chambers in Garden Court, Temple, had been watched, and might be watched again."

"By whom?" said I.

"I wouldn't go into that," said Wemmick, evasively, "it might clash with official responsibilities. I heard it, as I have in my time heard other curious things in the same place. I don't tell it you on information received. I heard it."

He took the toasting-fork and sausage from me as he spoke, and set forth the Aged's breakfast neatly on a little tray. Previous to placing it before him, he went into the Aged's room with a clean white cloth, and tied the same under the old gentleman's chin, and propped him up, and put his nightcap on one side, and gave him quite a rakish air. Then he placed his breakfast before him with great care, and said, "All right, ain't you, Aged P.?" To which the cheerful Aged replied, "All right, John, my boy, all right!" As there seemed to be a tacit understanding that the Aged was not in a presentable state, and was therefore to be considered invisible, I made a pretence of being in complete ignorance of these proceedings.

"This watching of me at my chambers (which I have once had reason to suspect)," I said to Wemmick when he came back, "is inseparable from the person to whom you have adverted; is it?"

Wemmick looked very serious. "I couldn't undertake to say that, of my own knowledge. I mean, I couldn't undertake to say it was at first. But it either is, or it will be, or it's in great danger of being."

As I saw that he was restrained by fealty to Little Britain from saying as much as he could, and as I knew with thankfulness to him how far out of his way he went to say what he did, I could not press him. But I told him, after a little meditation over the fire, that I would like to ask him a question, subject to his answering or not answering, as he deemed right, and sure that his course would be right. He paused in his breakfast, and crossing his arms, and pinching his shirt-sleeves (his notion of in-door comfort was to sit without any coat), he nodded to me once, to put my question.

"You have heard of a man of bad character, whose true name is Compeyson?"

He answered with one other nod.

"Is he living?"

One other nod.

"Is he in London?"

He gave me one other nod, compressed the post-office exceedingly, gave me one last nod, and went on with his breakfast.

"Now," said Wemmick, "questioning being over," which he emphasized and repeated for my guidance, "I come to what I did, after hearing what I heard. I went to Garden Court to find you; not finding you, I went to Clarriker's to find Mr. Herbert."

"And him you found?" said I, with great anxiety.

"And him I found. Without mentioning any names or going into any details, I gave him to understand that if he was aware of anybody—Tom, Jack, or Richard—being about the chambers, or about the immediate neighborhood, he had better get Tom, Jack, or Richard out of the way while you were out of the way."

"He would be greatly puzzled what to do?"

"He was puzzled what to do; not the less, because I gave him my opinion that it was not safe to try to get Tom, Jack, or Richard too far out of the way at present. Mr. Pip, I'll tell you something. Under existing circumstances, there is no place like a great city when you are once in it. Don't break cover too soon. Lie close. Wait till things slacken, before you try the open, even for foreign air."

I thanked him for his valuable advice, and asked him what Herbert had done?

"Mr. Herbert," said Wemmick, "after being all of a heap for half an hour, struck out a plan. He mentioned to me as a secret, that he is courting a young lady who has, as no doubt you are aware, a bedridden Pa. Which Pa, having been in the Purser line of life, lies a-bed in a bow-window where he can see the ships sail up and down the river. You are acquainted with the young lady, most probably?"

"Not personally," said I.

The truth was, that she had objected to me as an expensive companion who did Herbert no good, and that, when Herbert had first proposed to present me to her, she had received the proposal with such very moderate warmth, that Herbert had felt himself obliged to confide the state of the case to me, with a view to the lapse of a little time before I made her acquaintance. When I had begun to advance Herbert's prospects by stealth, I had been able to bear this with cheerful philosophy: he and his affianced, for their part, had naturally not been very anxious to introduce a third person into their interviews; and thus, although I was assured that I had risen in Clara's esteem, and although the young lady and I had long regularly interchanged messages and remembrances by Herbert, I had never seen her. However, I did not trouble Wemmick with these particulars.

"The house with the bow-window," said Wemmick, "being by the river-side, down the Pool there between Limehouse and Greenwich, and being kept, it seems, by a very respectable widow who has a furnished upper floor to let, Mr. Herbert put it to me, what did I think of that as a temporary tenement for Tom, Jack, or Richard? Now, I thought very well of it, for three reasons I'll give you. That is to say: Firstly. It's altogether out of all your beats, and is well away from the usual heap of streets great and small. Secondly. Without going near it yourself, you could always hear of the safety of Tom, Jack, or Richard, through Mr. Herbert. Thirdly. After a while and when it might be prudent, if you should want to slip Tom, Jack, or Richard on board a foreign packet-boat, there he is—ready."

Much comforted by these considerations, I thanked Wemmick again and again, and begged him to proceed.

"Well, sir! Mr. Herbert threw himself into the business with a will, and by nine o'clock last night he housed Tom, Jack, or Richard,—whichever it may be,—you and I don't want to know,—quite successfully. At the old lodgings it was understood that he was summoned to Dover, and, in fact, he was taken down the Dover road and cornered out of it. Now, another great advantage of all this is, that it was done without you, and when, if any one was concerning himself about your movements, you must be known to be ever so many miles off and quite otherwise engaged. This diverts suspicion and confuses it; and for the same reason I recommended that, even if you came back last night, you should not go home. It brings in more confusion, and you want confusion."

Wemmick, having finished his breakfast, here looked at his watch, and began to get his coat on.

"And now, Mr. Pip," said he, with his hands still in the sleeves, "I have probably done the most I can do; but if I can ever do more,—from a Walworth point of view, and in a strictly private and personal capacity,—I shall be glad to do it. Here's the address. There can be no harm in your going here to-night, and seeing for yourself that all is well with Tom, Jack, or Richard, before you go home,—which is another reason for your not going home last night. But, after you have gone home, don't go back here. You are very welcome, I am sure, Mr. Pip"; his hands were now out of his sleeves, and I was shaking them; "and let me finally impress one important point upon you." He laid his hands upon my shoulders, and added in a solemn whisper: "Avail yourself of this evening to lay hold of his portable property. You don't know what may happen to him. Don't let anything happen to the portable property."

Quite despairing of making my mind clear to Wemmick on this point, I forbore to try.

"Time's up," said Wemmick, "and I must be off. If you had nothing more pressing to do than to keep here till dark, that's what I should advise. You look very much worried, and it would do you good to have a perfectly quiet day with the Aged,—he'll be up presently,—and a little bit of—you remember the pig?"

"Of course," said I.

"Well; and a little bit of him. That sausage you toasted was his, and he was in all respects a first-rater. Do try him, if it is only for old acquaintance sake. Good by, Aged Parent!" in a cheery shout.

"All right, John; all right, my boy!" piped the old man from within.

I soon fell asleep before Wemmick's fire, and the Aged and I enjoyed one another's society by falling asleep before it more or less all day. We had loin of pork for dinner, and greens grown on the estate; and I nodded at the Aged with a good intention whenever I failed to do it drowsily. When it was quite dark, I left the Aged preparing the fire for toast; and I inferred from the number of teacups, as well as from his glances at the two little doors in the wall, that Miss Skiffins was expected.

CHAPTER XLVI

Eight o'clock had struck before I got into the air, that was scented, not disagreeably, by the chips and shavings of the long-shore boat-builders, and mast, oar, and block makers. All that water-side region of the upper and lower Pool below Bridge was unknown ground to me; and when I struck down by the river, I found that the spot I wanted was not where I had supposed it to be, and was anything but easy to find. It was called Mill Pond Bank, Chinks's Basin; and I had no other guide to Chinks's Basin than the Old Green Copper Rope-walk.

It matters not what stranded ships repairing in dry docks I lost myself among, what old hulls of ships in course of being knocked to pieces, what ooze and slime and other dregs of tide, what yards of ship-builders and ship-breakers, what rusty anchors blindly biting into the ground, though for years off duty, what mountainous country of accumulated casks and timber, how many ropewalks that were not the Old Green Copper. After several times falling short of my destination and as often overshooting it, I came unexpectedly round a corner, upon Mill Pond Bank. It was a fresh kind of place, all circumstances considered, where the wind from the river had room to turn itself round; and there were two or three trees in it, and there was the stump of a ruined windmill, and there was the Old Green Copper Ropewalk,—whose long and narrow vista I could trace in the moonlight, along a series of wooden frames set in the ground, that looked like superannuated haymaking-rakes which had grown old and lost most of their teeth.

Selecting from the few queer houses upon Mill Pond Bank a house with a wooden front and three stories of bow-window (not bay-window, which is another thing), I looked at the plate upon the door, and read there, Mrs. Whimple. That being the name I wanted, I knocked, and an elderly woman of a pleasant and thriving appearance responded. She was immediately deposed, however, by Herbert, who silently led me into the parlor and shut the door. It was an odd sensation to see his very familiar face established quite at home in that very unfamiliar room and region; and I found myself looking at him, much as I looked at the corner-cupboard with the glass and china, the shells upon the chimney-piece, and the colored engravings on the wall, representing the death of Captain Cook, a ship-launch, and his Majesty King George the Third in a state coachman's wig, leather-breeches, and top-boots, on the terrace at Windsor.

"All is well, Handel," said Herbert, "and he is quite satisfied, though eager to see you. My dear girl is with her father; and if you'll wait till she comes down, I'll make you known to her, and then we'll go up stairs. That's her father."

I had become aware of an alarming growling overhead, and had probably expressed the fact in my countenance.

"I am afraid he is a sad old rascal," said Herbert, smiling, "but I have never seen him. Don't you smell rum? He is always at it."

"At rum?" said I.

"Yes," returned Herbert, "and you may suppose how mild it makes his gout. He persists, too, in keeping all the provisions up stairs in his room, and serving them out.

He keeps them on shelves over his head, and will weigh them all. His room must be like a chandler's shop."

While he thus spoke, the growling noise became a prolonged roar, and then died away.

"What else can be the consequence," said Herbert, in explanation, "if he will cut the cheese? A man with the gout in his right hand—and everywhere else—can't expect to get through a Double Gloucester without hurting himself."

He seemed to have hurt himself very much, for he gave another furious roar.

"To have Provis for an upper lodger is quite a godsend to Mrs. Whimple," said Herbert, "for of course people in general won't stand that noise. A curious place, Handel; isn't it?"

It was a curious place, indeed; but remarkably well kept and clean.

"Mrs. Whimple," said Herbert, when I told him so, "is the best of housewives, and I really do not know what my Clara would do without her motherly help. For, Clara has no mother of her own, Handel, and no relation in the world but old Gruffandgrim."

"Surely that's not his name, Herbert?"

"No, no," said Herbert, "that's my name for him. His name is Mr. Barley. But what a blessing it is for the son of my father and mother to love a girl who has no relations, and who can never bother herself or anybody else about her family!"

Herbert had told me on former occasions, and now reminded me, that he first knew Miss Clara Barley when she was completing her education at an establishment at Hammersmith, and that on her being recalled home to nurse her father, he and she had confided their affection to the motherly Mrs. Whimple, by whom it had been fostered and regulated with equal kindness and discretion, ever since. It was understood that nothing of a tender nature could possibly be confided to old Barley, by reason of his being totally unequal to the consideration of any subject more psychological than Gout, Rum, and Purser's stores.

As we were thus conversing in a low tone while Old Barley's sustained growl vibrated in the beam that crossed the ceiling, the room door opened, and a very pretty, slight, dark-eyed girl of twenty or so came in with a basket in her hand: whom Herbert tenderly relieved of the basket, and presented, blushing, as "Clara." She really was a most charming girl, and might have passed for a captive fairy, whom that truculent Ogre, Old Barley, had pressed into his service.

"Look here," said Herbert, showing me the basket, with a compassionate and tender smile, after we had talked a little; "here's poor Clara's supper, served out every night. Here's her allowance of bread, and here's her slice of cheese, and here's her rum,—which I drink. This is Mr. Barley's breakfast for to-morrow, served out to be cooked. Two mutton-chops, three potatoes, some split peas, a little flour, two ounces of butter, a pinch of salt, and all this black pepper. It's stewed up together, and taken hot, and it's a nice thing for the gout, I should think!"

There was something so natural and winning in Clara's resigned way of looking at these stores in detail, as Herbert pointed them out; and something so confiding, loving, and innocent in her modest manner of yielding herself to Herbert's embracing arm; and something so gentle in her, so much needing protection on Mill Pond Bank, by Chinks's Basin, and the Old Green Copper Ropewalk, with Old Barley growling in the beam,—that I would not have undone the engagement between her and Herbert for all the money in the pocket-book I had never opened.

I was looking at her with pleasure and admiration, when suddenly the growl swelled into a roar again, and a frightful bumping noise was heard above, as if a giant with a wooden leg were trying to bore it through the ceiling to come at us. Upon this Clara said to Herbert, "Papa wants me, darling!" and ran away.

"There is an unconscionable old shark for you!" said Herbert. "What do you suppose he wants now, Handel?"

"I don't know," said I. "Something to drink?"

"That's it!" cried Herbert, as if I had made a guess of extraordinary merit. "He keeps his grog ready mixed in a little tub on the table. Wait a moment, and you'll hear Clara lift him up to take some. There he goes!" Another roar, with a prolonged shake at the end. "Now," said Herbert, as it was succeeded by silence, "he's drinking. Now," said Herbert, as the growl resounded in the beam once more, "he's down again on his back!"

Clara returned soon afterwards, and Herbert accompanied me up stairs to see our charge. As we passed Mr. Barley's door, he was heard hoarsely muttering within, in a strain that rose and fell like wind, the following Refrain, in which I substitute good wishes for something quite the reverse:—

"Ahoy! Bless your eyes, here's old Bill Barley. Here's old Bill Barley, bless your eyes. Here's old Bill Barley on the flat of his back, by the Lord. Lying on the flat of his back like a drifting old dead flounder, here's your old Bill Barley, bless your eyes. Ahoy! Bless you."

In this strain of consolation, Herbert informed me the invisible Barley would commune with himself by the day and night together; Often, while it was light, having, at the same time, one eye at a telescope which was fitted on his bed for the convenience of sweeping the river.

In his two cabin rooms at the top of the house, which were fresh and airy, and in which Mr. Barley was less audible than below, I found Provis comfortably settled. He expressed no alarm, and seemed to feel none that was worth mentioning; but it struck me that he was softened,—indefinably, for I could not have said how, and could never afterwards recall how when I tried, but certainly.

The opportunity that the day's rest had given me for reflection had resulted in my fully determining to say nothing to him respecting Compeyson. For anything I knew, his animosity towards the man might otherwise lead to his seeking him out and rushing on his own destruction. Therefore, when Herbert and I sat down with him by his fire, I asked him first of all whether he relied on Wemmick's judgment and sources of information?

"Ay, ay, dear boy!" he answered, with a grave nod, "Jaggers knows."

"Then, I have talked with Wemmick," said I, "and have come to tell you what caution he gave me and what advice."

This I did accurately, with the reservation just mentioned; and I told him how Wemmick had heard, in Newgate prison (whether from officers or prisoners I could not say), that he was under some suspicion, and that my chambers had been watched; how Wemmick had recommended his keeping close for a time, and my keeping away from him; and what Wemmick had said about getting him abroad. I added, that of course, when the time came, I should go with him, or should follow close upon him, as might be safest in Wemmick's judgment. What was to follow that I did not touch upon; neither, indeed, was I at all clear or comfortable about it in my own mind, now that I saw him in that softer condition, and in declared peril for my sake. As to altering my way of living by enlarging my expenses, I put it to him whether in our present unsettled and difficult circumstances, it would not be simply ridiculous, if it were no worse?

He could not deny this, and indeed was very reasonable throughout. His coming back was a venture, he said, and he had always known it to be a venture. He would do nothing to make it a desperate venture, and he had very little fear of his safety with such good help.

Herbert, who had been looking at the fire and pondering, here said that something had come into his thoughts arising out of Wemmick's suggestion, which it might be worth while to pursue. "We are both good watermen, Handel, and could take him down the river ourselves when the right time comes. No boat would then be hired for the purpose, and no boatmen; that would save at least a chance of suspicion, and any chance is worth saving. Never mind the season; don't you think it might be a good thing if you began at once to keep a boat at the Temple stairs, and were in the habit of rowing up and down the river? You fall into that habit, and then who notices or minds? Do it twenty or fifty times, and there is nothing special in your doing it the twenty-first or fifty-first."

I liked this scheme, and Provis was quite elated by it. We agreed that it should be carried into execution, and that Provis should never recognize us if we came below Bridge, and rowed past Mill Pond Bank. But we further agreed that he should pull down the blind in that part of his window which gave upon the east, whenever he saw us and all was right.

Our conference being now ended, and everything arranged, I rose to go; remarking to Herbert that he and I had better not go home together, and that I would take half an hour's start of him. "I don't like to leave you here," I said to Provis, "though I cannot doubt your being safer here than near me. Good by!"

"Dear boy," he answered, clasping my hands, "I don't know when we may meet again, and I don't like good by. Say good night!"

"Good night! Herbert will go regularly between us, and when the time comes you may be certain I shall be ready. Good night, good night!"

We thought it best that he should stay in his own rooms; and we left him on the landing outside his door, holding a light over the stair-rail to light us down stairs. Looking back at him, I thought of the first night of his return, when our positions were reversed, and when I little supposed my heart could ever be as heavy and anxious at parting from him as it was now.

Old Barley was growling and swearing when we repassed his door, with no appearance of having ceased or of meaning to cease. When we got to the foot of the stairs, I asked Herbert whether he had preserved the name of Provis. He replied, certainly not, and that the lodger was Mr. Campbell. He also explained that the utmost known of Mr. Campbell there was, that he (Herbert) had Mr. Campbell consigned to him, and felt a strong personal interest in his being well cared for, and living a secluded life. So, when we went into the parlor where Mrs. Whimple and Clara were seated at work, I said nothing of my own interest in Mr. Campbell, but kept it to myself.

When I had taken leave of the pretty, gentle, dark-eyed girl, and of the motherly woman who had not outlived her honest sympathy with a little affair of true love, I felt as if the Old Green Copper Ropewalk had grown quite a different place. Old Barley might be as old as the hills, and might swear like a whole field of troopers, but there were redeeming youth and trust and hope enough in Chinks's Basin to fill it to overflowing. And then I thought of Estella, and of our parting, and went home very sadly.

All things were as quiet in the Temple as ever I had seen them. The windows of the rooms on that side, lately occupied by Provis, were dark and still, and there was no lounger in Garden Court. I walked past the fountain twice or thrice before I descended the steps that were between me and my rooms, but I was quite alone. Herbert, coming to my bedside when he came in,—for I went straight to bed, dispirited and fatigued,— made the same report. Opening one of the windows after that, he looked out into the moonlight, and told me that the pavement was a solemnly empty as the pavement of any cathedral at that same hour.

Next day I set myself to get the boat. It was soon done, and the boat was brought round to the Temple stairs, and lay where I could reach her within a minute or two. Then, I began to go out as for training and practice: sometimes alone, sometimes with Herbert. I was often out in cold, rain, and sleet, but nobody took much note of me after I had been out a few times. At first, I kept above Blackfriars Bridge; but as the hours of the tide changed, I took towards London Bridge. It was Old London Bridge in those days, and at certain states of the tide there was a race and fall of water there which gave it a bad reputation. But I knew well enough how to 'shoot' the bridge after seeing it done, and so began to row about among the shipping in the Pool, and down to Erith. The first time I passed Mill Pond Bank, Herbert and I were pulling a pair of oars; and, both in going and returning, we saw the blind towards the east come down. Herbert was rarely there less frequently than three times in a week, and he never brought me a single word of intelligence that was at all alarming. Still, I knew that there was cause for alarm, and I could not get rid of the notion of being watched. Once received, it is a haunting idea; how many undesigning persons I suspected of watching me, it would be hard to calculate.

In short, I was always full of fears for the rash man who was in hiding. Herbert had sometimes said to me that he found it pleasant to stand at one of our windows after dark, when the tide was running down, and to think that it was flowing, with everything it bore, towards Clara. But I thought with dread that it was flowing towards Magwitch, and that any black mark on its surface might be his pursuers, going swiftly, silently, and surely, to take him.

CHAPTER XLVII

Some weeks passed without bringing any change. We waited for Wemmick, and he made no sign. If I had never known him out of Little Britain, and had never enjoyed the privilege of being on a familiar footing at the Castle, I might have doubted him; not so for a moment, knowing him as I did.

My worldly affairs began to wear a gloomy appearance, and I was pressed for money by more than one creditor. Even I myself began to know the want of money (I mean of ready money in my own pocket), and to relieve it by converting some easily spared articles of jewelery into cash. But I had quite determined that it would be a heartless fraud to take more money from my patron in the existing state of my uncertain thoughts and plans. Therefore, I had sent him the unopened pocket-book by Herbert, to hold in his own keeping, and I felt a kind of satisfaction—whether it was a false kind or a true, I hardly know—in not having profited by his generosity since his revelation of himself.

As the time wore on, an impression settled heavily upon me that Estella was married. Fearful of having it confirmed, though it was all but a conviction, I avoided the newspapers, and begged Herbert (to whom I had confided the circumstances of our last interview) never to speak of her to me. Why I hoarded up this last wretched little rag of the robe of hope that was rent and given to the winds, how do I know? Why did you who read this, commit that not dissimilar inconsistency of your own last year, last month, last week?

It was an unhappy life that I lived; and its one dominant anxiety, towering over all its other anxieties, like a high mountain above a range of mountains, never disappeared from my view. Still, no new cause for fear arose. Let me start from my bed as I would, with the terror fresh upon me that he was discovered; let me sit listening, as I would with dread, for Herbert's returning step at night, lest it should be fleeter than ordinary, and winged with evil news,—for all that, and much more to like purpose, the round of things went on. Condemned to inaction and a state of constant restlessness and suspense, I rowed about in my boat, and waited, waited, waited, as I best could.

There were states of the tide when, having been down the river, I could not get back through the eddy-chafed arches and starlings of old London Bridge; then, I left my boat at a wharf near the Custom House, to be brought up afterwards to the Temple stairs. I was not averse to doing this, as it served to make me and my boat a commoner incident among the water-side people there. From this slight occasion sprang two meetings that I have now to tell of.

One afternoon, late in the month of February, I came ashore at the wharf at dusk. I had pulled down as far as Greenwich with the ebb tide, and had turned with the tide. It had been a fine bright day, but had become foggy as the sun dropped, and I had had to feel my way back among the shipping, pretty carefully. Both in going and returning, I had seen the signal in his window, All well.

As it was a raw evening, and I was cold, I thought I would comfort myself with dinner at once; and as I had hours of dejection and solitude before me if I went home to the Temple, I thought I would afterwards go to the play. The theatre where Mr. Wopsle had achieved his questionable triumph was in that water-side neighborhood (it is nowhere now), and to that theatre I resolved to go. I was aware that Mr. Wopsle had not succeeded in reviving the Drama, but, on the contrary, had rather partaken of its decline. He had been ominously heard of, through the play-bills, as a faithful Black, in connection with a little girl of noble birth, and a monkey. And Herbert had seen him as a predatory Tartar of comic propensities, with a face like a red brick, and an outrageous hat all over bells.

I dined at what Herbert and I used to call a geographical chop-house, where there were maps of the world in porter-pot rims on every half-yard of the tablecloths, and charts of gravy on every one of the knives,—to this day there is scarcely a single chop-house within the Lord Mayor's dominions which is not geographical,—and wore out the time in dozing over crumbs, staring at gas, and baking in a hot blast of dinners. By and by, I roused myself, and went to the play.

There, I found a virtuous boatswain in His Majesty's service,—a most excellent man, though I could have wished his trousers not quite so tight in some places, and not quite so loose in others,—who knocked all the little men's hats over their eyes, though he was very generous and brave, and who wouldn't hear of anybody's paying taxes, though he was very patriotic. He had a bag of money in his pocket, like a pudding in the cloth, and on that property married a young person in bed-furniture, with great rejoicings; the whole population of Portsmouth (nine in number at the last census) turning out on the beach to rub their own hands and shake everybody else's, and sing "Fill, fill!" A certain dark-complexioned Swab, however, who wouldn't fill, or do anything else that was proposed to him, and whose heart was openly stated (by the boatswain) to be as black as his figure-head, proposed to two other Swabs to get all mankind into difficulties; which was so effectually done (the Swab family having considerable political influence) that it took half the evening to set things right, and then it was only brought about through an honest little grocer with a white hat, black gaiters, and red nose, getting into a clock, with a gridiron, and listening, and coming out, and knocking everybody down from behind with the gridiron whom he couldn't confute with what he had overheard. This led to Mr. Wopsle's (who had never been heard of before) coming in with a star and garter on, as a plenipotentiary of great power direct from the Admiralty, to say that the Swabs were all to go to prison on the spot, and that he had brought the boatswain down the Union Jack, as a slight acknowledgment of his public services. The boatswain, unmanned for the first time, respectfully dried his eyes on the Jack, and then cheering up, and addressing Mr. Wopsle as Your Honour, solicited permission to take him by the fin. Mr. Wopsle, conceding his fin with a gracious dignity, was immediately shoved into a dusty corner, while everybody danced a hornpipe; and from that corner, surveying the public with a discontented eye, became aware of me.

The second piece was the last new grand comic Christmas pantomime, in the first scene of which, it pained me to suspect that I detected Mr. Wopsle with red worsted legs under a highly magnified phosphoric countenance and a shock of red curtain-fringe for his hair, engaged in the manufacture of thunderbolts in a mine, and displaying great cowardice when his gigantic master came home (very hoarse) to dinner. But he presently presented himself under worthier circumstances; for, the Genius of Youthful Love being in want of assistance,—on account of the parental brutality of an ignorant farmer who opposed the choice of his daughter's heart, by purposely falling upon the object, in a flour-sack, out of the first-floor window,—summoned a sententious Enchanter; and he, coming up from the antipodes rather unsteadily, after an apparently violent journey, proved to be Mr. Wopsle in a high-crowned hat, with a necromantic work in one volume under his arm. The business of this enchanter on earth being principally to be talked at, sung at, butted at, danced at, and flashed at with fires of various colors, he had a good deal of time on his hands. And I observed, with great surprise, that he devoted it to staring in my direction as if he were lost in amazement.

There was something so remarkable in the increasing glare of Mr. Wopsle's eye, and he seemed to be turning so many things over in his mind and to grow so confused, that I could not make it out. I sat thinking of it long after he had ascended to the clouds in a large watch-case, and still I could not make it out. I was still thinking of it when I came out of the theatre an hour afterwards, and found him waiting for me near the door.

"How do you do?" said I, shaking hands with him as we turned down the street together. "I saw that you saw me."

"Saw you, Mr. Pip!" he returned. "Yes, of course I saw you. But who else was there?"

"Who else?"

"It is the strangest thing," said Mr. Wopsle, drifting into his lost look again; "and yet I could swear to him."

Becoming alarmed, I entreated Mr. Wopsle to explain his meaning.

"Whether I should have noticed him at first but for your being there," said Mr. Wopsle, going on in the same lost way, "I can't be positive; yet I think I should."

Involuntarily I looked round me, as I was accustomed to look round me when I went home; for these mysterious words gave me a chill.

"Oh! He can't be in sight," said Mr. Wopsle. "He went out before I went off. I saw him go."

Having the reason that I had for being suspicious, I even suspected this poor actor. I mistrusted a design to entrap me into some admission. Therefore I glanced at him as we walked on together, but said nothing.

"I had a ridiculous fancy that he must be with you, Mr. Pip, till I saw that you were quite unconscious of him, sitting behind you there like a ghost."

My former chill crept over me again, but I was resolved not to speak yet, for it was quite consistent with his words that he might be set on to induce me to connect these references with Provis. Of course, I was perfectly sure and safe that Provis had not been there.

"I dare say you wonder at me, Mr. Pip; indeed, I see you do. But it is so very strange! You'll hardly believe what I am going to tell you. I could hardly believe it myself, if you told me."

"Indeed?" said I.

"No, indeed. Mr. Pip, you remember in old times a certain Christmas Day, when you were quite a child, and I dined at Gargery's, and some soldiers came to the door to get a pair of handcuffs mended?"

"I remember it very well."

"And you remember that there was a chase after two convicts, and that we joined in it, and that Gargery took you on his back, and that I took the lead, and you kept up with me as well as you could?"

"I remember it all very well." Better than he thought,—except the last clause.

"And you remember that we came up with the two in a ditch, and that there was a scuffle between them, and that one of them had been severely handled and much mauled about the face by the other?"

"I see it all before me."

"And that the soldiers lighted torches, and put the two in the centre, and that we went on to see the last of them, over the black marshes, with the torchlight shining on their faces,—I am particular about that,—with the torchlight shining on their faces, when there was an outer ring of dark night all about us?"

"Yes," said I. "I remember all that."

"Then, Mr. Pip, one of those two prisoners sat behind you tonight. I saw him over your shoulder."

"Steady!" I thought. I asked him then, "Which of the two do you suppose you saw?"

"The one who had been mauled," he answered readily, "and I'll swear I saw him! The more I think of him, the more certain I am of him."

"This is very curious!" said I, with the best assumption I could put on of its being nothing more to me. "Very curious indeed!"

I cannot exaggerate the enhanced disquiet into which this conversation threw me, or the special and peculiar terror I felt at Compeyson's having been behind me "like a ghost." For if he had ever been out of my thoughts for a few moments together since the hiding had begun, it was in those very moments when he was closest to me; and to think that I should be so unconscious and off my guard after all my care was as if I had shut an avenue of a hundred doors to keep him out, and then had found him at my elbow. I could not doubt, either, that he was there, because I was there, and that, however slight an appearance of danger there might be about us, danger was always near and active.

I put such questions to Mr. Wopsle as, When did the man come in? He could not tell me that; he saw me, and over my shoulder he saw the man. It was not until he had seen him for some time that he began to identify him; but he had from the first vaguely associated him with me, and known him as somehow belonging to me in the old village time. How was he dressed? Prosperously, but not noticeably otherwise; he thought, in black. Was his face at all disfigured? No, he believed not. I believed not too, for, although in my brooding state I had taken no especial notice of the people behind me, I thought it likely that a face at all disfigured would have attracted my attention.

When Mr. Wopsle had imparted to me all that he could recall or I extract, and when I had treated him to a little appropriate refreshment, after the fatigues of the evening, we parted. It was between twelve and one o'clock when I reached the Temple, and the gates were shut. No one was near me when I went in and went home.

Herbert had come in, and we held a very serious council by the fire. But there was nothing to be done, saving to communicate to Wemmick what I had that night found out, and to remind him that we waited for his hint. As I thought that I might compromise him if I went too often to the Castle, I made this communication by letter. I wrote it before I went to bed, and went out and posted it; and again no one was near me. Herbert and I agreed that we could do nothing else but be very cautious. And we were very cautious indeed,—more cautious than before, if that were possible,—and I for my part never went near Chinks's Basin, except when I rowed by, and then I only looked at Mill Pond Bank as I looked at anything else.

CHAPTER XLVIII

The second of the two meetings referred to in the last chapter occurred about a week after the first. I had again left my boat at the wharf below Bridge; the time was an hour earlier in the afternoon; and, undecided where to dine, I had strolled up into Cheapside, and was strolling along it, surely the most unsettled person in all the busy concourse, when a large hand was laid upon my shoulder by some one overtaking me. It was Mr. Jaggers's hand, and he passed it through my arm.

"As we are going in the same direction, Pip, we may walk together. Where are you bound for?"

"For the Temple, I think," said I.

"Don't you know?" said Mr. Jaggers.

"Well," I returned, glad for once to get the better of him in cross-examination, "I do not know, for I have not made up my mind."

"You are going to dine?" said Mr. Jaggers. "You don't mind admitting that, I suppose?"

"No," I returned, "I don't mind admitting that."

"And are not engaged?"

"I don't mind admitting also that I am not engaged."

"Then," said Mr. Jaggers, "come and dine with me."

I was going to excuse myself, when he added, "Wemmick's coming." So I changed my excuse into an acceptance,—the few words I had uttered, serving for the beginning of either,—and we went along Cheapside and slanted off to Little Britain, while the lights were springing up brilliantly in the shop windows, and the street lamp-lighters, scarcely finding ground enough to plant their ladders on in the midst of the afternoon's bustle, were skipping up and down and running in and out, opening more red eyes in the gathering fog than my rushlight tower at the Hummums had opened white eyes in the ghostly wall.

At the office in Little Britain there was the usual letter-writing, hand-washing, candle-snuffing, and safe-locking, that closed the business of the day. As I stood idle by Mr. Jaggers's fire, its rising and falling flame made the two casts on the shelf look as if they were playing a diabolical game at bo-peep with me; while the pair of coarse, fat office candles that dimly lighted Mr. Jaggers as he wrote in a corner were decorated with dirty winding-sheets, as if in remembrance of a host of hanged clients.

We went to Gerrard Street, all three together, in a hackney-coach: And, as soon as we got there, dinner was served. Although I should not have thought of making, in that place, the most distant reference by so much as a look to Wemmick's Walworth sentiments, yet I should have had no objection to catching his eye now and then in a friendly way. But it was not to be done. He turned his eyes on Mr. Jaggers whenever he raised them from the table, and was as dry and distant to me as if there were twin Wemmicks, and this was the wrong one.

"Did you send that note of Miss Havisham's to Mr. Pip, Wemmick?" Mr. Jaggers asked, soon after we began dinner.

"No, sir," returned Wemmick; "it was going by post, when you brought Mr. Pip into the office. Here it is." He handed it to his principal instead of to me.

"It's a note of two lines, Pip," said Mr. Jaggers, handing it on, "sent up to me by Miss Havisham on account of her not being sure of your address. She tells me that she wants to see you on a little matter of business you mentioned to her. You'll go down?"

"Yes," said I, casting my eyes over the note, which was exactly in those terms.

"When do you think of going down?"

"I have an impending engagement," said I, glancing at Wemmick, who was putting fish into the post-office, "that renders me rather uncertain of my time. At once, I think."

"If Mr. Pip has the intention of going at once," said Wemmick to Mr. Jaggers, "he needn't write an answer, you know."

Receiving this as an intimation that it was best not to delay, I settled that I would go to-morrow, and said so. Wemmick drank a glass of wine, and looked with a grimly satisfied air at Mr. Jaggers, but not at me.

"So, Pip! Our friend the Spider," said Mr. Jaggers, "has played his cards. He has won the pool."

It was as much as I could do to assent.

"Hah! He is a promising fellow—in his way—but he may not have it all his own way. The stronger will win in the end, but the stronger has to be found out first. If he should turn to, and beat her—"

"Surely," I interrupted, with a burning face and heart, "you do not seriously think that he is scoundrel enough for that, Mr. Jaggers?"

"I didn't say so, Pip. I am putting a case. If he should turn to and beat her, he may possibly get the strength on his side; if it should be a question of intellect, he certainly will not. It would be chance work to give an opinion how a fellow of that sort will turn out in such circumstances, because it's a toss-up between two results."

"May I ask what they are?"

"A fellow like our friend the Spider," answered Mr. Jaggers, "either beats or cringes. He may cringe and growl, or cringe and not growl; but he either beats or cringes. Ask Wemmick his opinion."

"Either beats or cringes," said Wemmick, not at all addressing himself to me.

"So here's to Mrs. Bentley Drummle," said Mr. Jaggers, taking a decanter of choicer wine from his dumb-waiter, and filling for each of us and for himself, "and may the question of supremacy be settled to the lady's satisfaction! To the satisfaction of the lady and the gentleman, it never will be. Now, Molly, Molly, Molly, Molly, how slow you are to-day!"

She was at his elbow when he addressed her, putting a dish upon the table. As she withdrew her hands from it, she fell back a step or two, nervously muttering some excuse. And a certain action of her fingers, as she spoke, arrested my attention.

"What's the matter?" said Mr. Jaggers.

"Nothing. Only the subject we were speaking of," said I, "was rather painful to me."

The action of her fingers was like the action of knitting. She stood looking at her master, not understanding whether she was free to go, or whether he had more to say to her and would call her back if she did go. Her look was very intent. Surely, I had seen exactly such eyes and such hands on a memorable occasion very lately!

He dismissed her, and she glided out of the room. But she remained before me as plainly as if she were still there. I looked at those hands, I looked at those eyes, I looked at that flowing hair; and I compared them with other hands, other eyes, other hair, that I knew of, and with what those might be after twenty years of a brutal husband and a stormy life. I looked again at those hands and eyes of the housekeeper, and thought of the inexplicable feeling that had come over me when I last walked—not alone—in the ruined garden, and through the deserted brewery. I thought how the same feeling had come back when I saw a face looking at me, and a hand waving to me from a stage-coach window; and how it had come back again and had flashed about me like lightning, when I had passed in a carriage—not alone—through a sudden glare of light in a dark street. I thought how one link of association had helped that identification in the theatre, and how such a link, wanting before, had been riveted for me now, when I had passed by a chance swift from Estella's name to the fingers with their knitting action, and the attentive eyes. And I felt absolutely certain that this woman was Estella's mother.

Mr. Jaggers had seen me with Estella, and was not likely to have missed the sentiments I had been at no pains to conceal. He nodded when I said the subject was painful to me, clapped me on the back, put round the wine again, and went on with his dinner.

Only twice more did the housekeeper reappear, and then her stay in the room was very short, and Mr. Jaggers was sharp with her. But her hands were Estella's hands, and her eyes were Estella's eyes, and if she had reappeared a hundred times I could have been neither more sure nor less sure that my conviction was the truth.

It was a dull evening, for Wemmick drew his wine, when it came round, quite as a matter of business,—just as he might have drawn his salary when that came round,—and with his eyes on his chief, sat in a state of perpetual readiness for cross-examination. As to the quantity of wine, his post-office was as indifferent and ready as any other post-office for its quantity of letters. From my point of view, he was the wrong twin all the time, and only externally like the Wemmick of Walworth.

We took our leave early, and left together. Even when we were groping among Mr. Jaggers's stock of boots for our hats, I felt that the right twin was on his way back; and we had not gone half a dozen yards down Gerrard Street in the Walworth direction, before I found that I was walking arm in arm with the right twin, and that the wrong twin had evaporated into the evening air.

"Well!" said Wemmick, "that's over! He's a wonderful man, without his living likeness; but I feel that I have to screw myself up when I dine with him,—and I dine more comfortably unscrewed."

I felt that this was a good statement of the case, and told him so.

"Wouldn't say it to anybody but yourself," he answered. "I know that what is said between you and me goes no further."

I asked him if he had ever seen Miss Havisham's adopted daughter, Mrs. Bentley Drummle. He said no. To avoid being too abrupt, I then spoke of the Aged and of Miss Skiffins. He looked rather sly when I mentioned Miss Skiffins, and stopped in the street to blow his nose, with a roll of the head, and a flourish not quite free from latent boastfulness.

"Wemmick," said I, "do you remember telling me, before I first went to Mr. Jaggers's private house, to notice that housekeeper?"

"Did I?" he replied. "Ah, I dare say I did. Deuce take me," he added, suddenly, "I know I did. I find I am not quite unscrewed yet."

"A wild beast tamed, you called her."

"And what do you call her?"

"The same. How did Mr. Jaggers tame her, Wemmick?"

"That's his secret. She has been with him many a long year."

"I wish you would tell me her story. I feel a particular interest in being acquainted with it. You know that what is said between you and me goes no further."

"Well!" Wemmick replied, "I don't know her story,—that is, I don't know all of it. But what I do know I'll tell you. We are in our private and personal capacities, of course."

"Of course."

"A score or so of years ago, that woman was tried at the Old Bailey for murder, and was acquitted. She was a very handsome young woman, and I believe had some gypsy blood in her. Anyhow, it was hot enough when it was up, as you may suppose."

"But she was acquitted."

"Mr. Jaggers was for her," pursued Wemmick, with a look full of meaning, "and worked the case in a way quite astonishing. It was a desperate case, and it was comparatively early days with him then, and he worked it to general admiration; in fact, it may almost be said to have made him. He worked it himself at the police-office, day after day for many days, contending against even a committal; and at the trial where he couldn't work it himself, sat under counsel, and—every one knew—put in all the salt and pepper. The murdered person was a woman,—a woman a good ten years older, very much larger, and very much stronger. It was a case of jealousy. They both led tramping lives, and this woman in Gerrard Street here had been married very young, over the broomstick (as we say), to a tramping man, and was a perfect fury in point of jealousy. The murdered woman,—more a match for the man, certainly, in point of years—was found dead in a barn near Hounslow Heath. There had been a violent struggle, perhaps a fight. She was bruised and scratched and torn, and had been held by the throat, at last, and choked. Now, there was no reasonable evidence to implicate any person but this woman, and on the improbabilities of her having been able to do it Mr. Jaggers principally rested his case. You may be sure," said Wemmick, touching me on the sleeve, "that he never dwelt upon the strength of her hands then, though he sometimes does now."

I had told Wemmick of his showing us her wrists, that day of the dinner party.

"Well, sir!" Wemmick went on; "it happened—happened, don't you see?—that this woman was so very artfully dressed from the time of her apprehension, that she looked much slighter than she really was; in particular, her sleeves are always remembered to have been so skilfully contrived that her arms had quite a delicate look. She had only a bruise or two about her,—nothing for a tramp,—but the backs of her hands were lacerated, and the question was, Was it with finger-nails? Now, Mr. Jaggers showed that she had struggled through a great lot of brambles which were not as high as her face; but which she could not have got through and kept her hands out of; and bits of those brambles were actually found in her skin and put in evidence, as well as the fact that the brambles in question were found on examination to have been broken through, and to have little shreds of her dress and little spots of blood upon them here and there. But the boldest point he made was this: it was attempted to be set up, in proof of her jealousy, that she was under strong suspicion of having, at about the time of the murder, frantically destroyed her child by this man—some three years old—to revenge herself upon him. Mr. Jaggers worked that in this way: 'We say these are not marks of finger-nails, but marks of brambles, and we show you the brambles. You say they are marks of finger-nails, and you set up the hypothesis that she destroyed her child. You must accept all consequences of that hypothesis. For anything we know, she may have destroyed her child, and the child in clinging to her may have scratched her hands. What then? You are not trying her for the murder of her child; why don't you? As to this case, if you will have scratches, we say that, for anything we know, you may have accounted for them, assuming for the sake of argument that you have not invented them?' To sum up, sir," said Wemmick, "Mr. Jaggers was altogether too many for the jury, and they gave in."

"Has she been in his service ever since?"

"Yes; but not only that," said Wemmick, "she went into his service immediately after her acquittal, tamed as she is now. She has since been taught one thing and another in the way of her duties, but she was tamed from the beginning."

"Do you remember the sex of the child?"

"Said to have been a girl."

"You have nothing more to say to me to-night?"

"Nothing. I got your letter and destroyed it. Nothing."

We exchanged a cordial good-night, and I went home, with new matter for my thoughts, though with no relief from the old.

CHAPTER XLIX

Putting Miss Havisham's note in my pocket, that it might serve as my credentials for so soon reappearing at Satis House, in case her waywardness should lead her to express any surprise at seeing me, I went down again by the coach next day. But I alighted at the Halfway House, and breakfasted there, and walked the rest of the distance; for I sought to get into the town quietly by the unfrequented ways, and to leave it in the same manner.

The best light of the day was gone when I passed along the quiet echoing courts behind the High Street. The nooks of ruin where the old monks had once had their refectories and gardens, and where the strong walls were now pressed into the service of humble sheds and stables, were almost as silent as the old monks in their graves. The cathedral chimes had at once a sadder and a more remote sound to me, as I hurried on avoiding observation, than they had ever had before; so, the swell of the old organ was borne to my ears like funeral music; and the rooks, as they hovered about the gray tower and swung in the bare high trees of the priory garden, seemed to call to me that the place was changed, and that Estella was gone out of it for ever.

An elderly woman, whom I had seen before as one of the servants who lived in the supplementary house across the back courtyard, opened the gate. The lighted candle stood in the dark passage within, as of old, and I took it up and ascended the staircase alone. Miss Havisham was not in her own room, but was in the larger room across the landing. Looking in at the door, after knocking in vain, I saw her sitting on the hearth in a ragged chair, close before, and lost in the contemplation of, the ashy fire.

Doing as I had often done, I went in, and stood touching the old chimney-piece, where she could see me when she raised her eyes. There was an air or utter loneliness upon her, that would have moved me to pity though she had wilfully done me a deeper injury than I could charge her with. As I stood compassionating her, and thinking how, in the progress of time, I too had come to be a part of the wrecked fortunes of that house, her eyes rested on me. She stared, and said in a low voice, "Is it real?"

"It is I, Pip. Mr. Jaggers gave me your note yesterday, and I have lost no time."

"Thank you. Thank you."

As I brought another of the ragged chairs to the hearth and sat down, I remarked a new expression on her face, as if she were afraid of me.

"I want," she said, "to pursue that subject you mentioned to me when you were last here, and to show you that I am not all stone. But perhaps you can never believe, now, that there is anything human in my heart?"

When I said some reassuring words, she stretched out her tremulous right hand, as though she was going to touch me; but she recalled it again before I understood the action, or knew how to receive it.

"You said, speaking for your friend, that you could tell me how to do something useful and good. Something that you would like done, is it not?"

"Something that I would like done very much."

"What is it?"

I began explaining to her that secret history of the partnership. I had not got far into it, when I judged from her looks that she was thinking in a discursive way of me, rather than of what I said. It seemed to be so; for, when I stopped speaking, many moments passed before she showed that she was conscious of the fact.

"Do you break off," she asked then, with her former air of being afraid of me, "because you hate me too much to bear to speak to me?"

"No, no," I answered, "how can you think so, Miss Havisham! I stopped because I thought you were not following what I said."

"Perhaps I was not," she answered, putting a hand to her head. "Begin again, and let me look at something else. Stay! Now tell me."

She set her hand upon her stick in the resolute way that sometimes was habitual to her, and looked at the fire with a strong expression of forcing herself to attend. I went on with my explanation, and told her how I had hoped to complete the transaction out of my means, but how in this I was disappointed. That part of the subject (I reminded her) involved matters which could form no part of my explanation, for they were the weighty secrets of another.

"So!" said she, assenting with her head, but not looking at me. "And how much money is wanting to complete the purchase?"

I was rather afraid of stating it, for it sounded a large sum. "Nine hundred pounds."

"If I give you the money for this purpose, will you keep my secret as you have kept your own?"

"Quite as faithfully."

"And your mind will be more at rest?"

"Much more at rest."

"Are you very unhappy now?"

She asked this question, still without looking at me, but in an unwonted tone of sympathy. I could not reply at the moment, for my voice failed me. She put her left arm across the head of her stick, and softly laid her forehead on it.

"I am far from happy, Miss Havisham; but I have other causes of disquiet than any you know of. They are the secrets I have mentioned."

After a little while, she raised her head, and looked at the fire Again.

"It is noble in you to tell me that you have other causes of unhappiness, Is it true?"

"Too true."

"Can I only serve you, Pip, by serving your friend? Regarding that as done, is there nothing I can do for you yourself?"

"Nothing. I thank you for the question. I thank you even more for the tone of the question. But there is nothing."

She presently rose from her seat, and looked about the blighted room for the means of writing. There were none there, and she took from her pocket a yellow set of ivory tablets, mounted in tarnished gold, and wrote upon them with a pencil in a case of tarnished gold that hung from her neck.

"You are still on friendly terms with Mr. Jaggers?"

"Quite. I dined with him yesterday."

"This is an authority to him to pay you that money, to lay out at your irresponsible discretion for your friend. I keep no money here; but if you would rather Mr. Jaggers knew nothing of the matter, I will send it to you."

"Thank you, Miss Havisham; I have not the least objection to receiving it from him."

She read me what she had written; and it was direct and clear, and evidently intended to absolve me from any suspicion of profiting by the receipt of the money. I took the tablets from her hand, and it trembled again, and it trembled more as she took off the chain to which the pencil was attached, and put it in mine. All this she did without looking at me.

"My name is on the first leaf. If you can ever write under my name, 'I forgive her,' though ever so long after my broken heart is dust pray do it!"

"O Miss Havisham," said I, "I can do it now. There have been sore mistakes; and my life has been a blind and thankless one; and I want forgiveness and direction far too much, to be bitter with you."

She turned her face to me for the first time since she had averted it, and, to my amazement, I may even add to my terror, dropped on her knees at my feet; with her folded hands raised to me in the manner in which, when her poor heart was young and fresh and whole, they must often have been raised to heaven from her mother's side.

To see her with her white hair and her worn face kneeling at my feet gave me a shock through all my frame. I entreated her to rise, and got my arms about her to help her up; but she only pressed that hand of mine which was nearest to her grasp, and hung her head over it and wept. I had never seen her shed a tear before, and, in the hope that the relief might do her good, I bent over her without speaking. She was not kneeling now, but was down upon the ground.

"O!" she cried, despairingly. "What have I done! What have I done!"

"If you mean, Miss Havisham, what have you done to injure me, let me answer. Very little. I should have loved her under any circumstances. Is she married?"

"Yes."

It was a needless question, for a new desolation in the desolate house had told me so.

"What have I done! What have I done!" She wrung her hands, and crushed her white hair, and returned to this cry over and over again. "What have I done!"

I knew not how to answer, or how to comfort her. That she had done a grievous thing in taking an impressionable child to mould into the form that her wild resentment, spurned affection, and wounded pride found vengeance in, I knew full well. But that, in shutting out the light of day, she had shut out infinitely more; that, in seclusion, she had secluded herself from a thousand natural and healing influences; that, her mind, brooding solitary, had grown diseased, as all minds do and must and will that reverse the appointed order of their Maker, I knew equally well. And could I look upon her without compassion, seeing her punishment in the ruin she was, in her profound unfitness for this earth on which she was placed, in the vanity of sorrow which had become a master mania, like the vanity of penitence, the vanity of remorse, the vanity of unworthiness, and other monstrous vanities that have been curses in this world?

"Until you spoke to her the other day, and until I saw in you a looking-glass that showed me what I once felt myself, I did not know what I had done. What have I done! What have I done!" And so again, twenty, fifty times over, What had she done!

"Miss Havisham," I said, when her cry had died away, "you may dismiss me from your mind and conscience. But Estella is a different case, and if you can ever undo any scrap of what you have done amiss in keeping a part of her right nature away from her, it will be better to do that than to bemoan the past through a hundred years."

"Yes, yes, I know it. But, Pip—my dear!" There was an earnest womanly compassion for me in her new affection. "My dear! Believe this: when she first came to me, I meant to save her from misery like my own. At first, I meant no more."

"Well, well!" said I. "I hope so."

"But as she grew, and promised to be very beautiful, I gradually did worse, and with my praises, and with my jewels, and with my teachings, and with this figure of myself always before her, a warning to back and point my lessons, I stole her heart away, and put ice in its place."

"Better," I could not help saying, "to have left her a natural heart, even to be bruised or broken."

With that, Miss Havisham looked distractedly at me for a while, and then burst out again, What had she done!

"If you knew all my story," she pleaded, "you would have some compassion for me and a better understanding of me."

"Miss Havisham," I answered, as delicately as I could, "I believe I may say that I do know your story, and have known it ever since I first left this neighborhood. It has inspired me with great commiseration, and I hope I understand it and its influences. Does what has passed between us give me any excuse for asking you a question relative to Estella? Not as she is, but as she was when she first came here?"

She was seated on the ground, with her arms on the ragged chair, and her head leaning on them. She looked full at me when I said this, and replied, "Go on."

"Whose child was Estella?"

She shook her head.

"You don't know?"

She shook her head again.

"But Mr. Jaggers brought her here, or sent her here?"

"Brought her here."

"Will you tell me how that came about?"

She answered in a low whisper and with caution: "I had been shut up in these rooms a long time (I don't know how long; you know what time the clocks keep here), when I told him that I wanted a little girl to rear and love, and save from my fate. I had first seen him when I sent for him to lay this place waste for me; having read of him in the newspapers, before I and the world parted. He told me that he would look about him for such an orphan child. One night he brought her here asleep, and I called her Estella."

"Might I ask her age then?"

"Two or three. She herself knows nothing, but that she was left an orphan and I adopted her."

So convinced I was of that woman's being her mother, that I wanted no evidence to establish the fact in my own mind. But, to any mind, I thought, the connection here was clear and straight.

What more could I hope to do by prolonging the interview? I had succeeded on behalf of Herbert, Miss Havisham had told me all she knew of Estella, I had said and done what I could to ease her mind. No matter with what other words we parted; we parted.

Twilight was closing in when I went down stairs into the natural air. I called to the woman who had opened the gate when I entered, that I would not trouble her just yet, but would walk round the place before leaving. For I had a presentiment that I should never be there again, and I felt that the dying light was suited to my last view of it.

By the wilderness of casks that I had walked on long ago, and on which the rain of years had fallen since, rotting them in many places, and leaving miniature swamps and pools of water upon those that stood on end, I made my way to the ruined garden. I went all round it; round by the corner where Herbert and I had fought our battle; round by the paths where Estella and I had walked. So cold, so lonely, so dreary all!

Taking the brewery on my way back, I raised the rusty latch of a little door at the garden end of it, and walked through. I was going out at the opposite door,—not easy to open now, for the damp wood had started and swelled, and the hinges were yielding, and the threshold was encumbered with a growth of fungus,—when I turned my head to look back. A childish association revived with wonderful force in the moment of the slight action, and I fancied that I saw Miss Havisham hanging to the beam. So strong was the impression, that I stood under the beam shuddering from head to foot before I knew it was a fancy,—though to be sure I was there in an instant.

The mournfulness of the place and time, and the great terror of this illusion, though it was but momentary, caused me to feel an indescribable awe as I came out between the open wooden gates where I had once wrung my hair after Estella had wrung my heart. Passing on into the front courtyard, I hesitated whether to call the woman to let me out at the locked gate of which she had the key, or first to go up stairs and assure myself that Miss Havisham was as safe and well as I had left her. I took the latter course and went up.

I looked into the room where I had left her, and I saw her seated in the ragged chair upon the hearth close to the fire, with her back towards me. In the moment when I was withdrawing my head to go quietly away, I saw a great flaming light spring up. In the same moment I saw her running at me, shrieking, with a whirl of fire blazing all about her, and soaring at least as many feet above her head as she was high.

I had a double-caped great-coat on, and over my arm another thick coat. That I got them off, closed with her, threw her down, and got them over her; that I dragged the great cloth from the table for the same purpose, and with it dragged down the heap of rottenness in the midst, and all the ugly things that sheltered there; that we were on the ground struggling like desperate enemies, and that the closer I covered her, the more wildly she shrieked and tried to free herself,—that this occurred I knew through the result, but not through anything I felt, or thought, or knew I did. I knew nothing until I knew that we were on the floor by the great table, and that patches of tinder yet alight were floating in the smoky air, which, a moment ago, had been her faded bridal dress.

Then, I looked round and saw the disturbed beetles and spiders running away over the floor, and the servants coming in with breathless cries at the door. I still held her forcibly down with all my strength, like a prisoner who might escape; and I doubt if I even knew who she was, or why we had struggled, or that she had been in flames, or that the flames were out, until I saw the patches of tinder that had been her garments no longer alight but falling in a black shower around us.

She was insensible, and I was afraid to have her moved, or even touched. Assistance was sent for, and I held her until it came, as if I unreasonably fancied (I think I did) that, if I let her go, the fire would break out again and consume her. When I got up, on the surgeon's coming to her with other aid, I was astonished to see that both my hands were burnt; for, I had no knowledge of it through the sense of feeling.

On examination it was pronounced that she had received serious hurts, but that they of themselves were far from hopeless; the danger lay mainly in the nervous shock. By the surgeon's directions, her bed was carried into that room and laid upon the great table, which happened to be well suited to the dressing of her injuries. When I saw her again, an hour afterwards, she lay, indeed, where I had seen her strike her stick, and had heard her say that she would lie one day.

Though every vestige of her dress was burnt, as they told me, she still had something of her old ghastly bridal appearance; for, they had covered her to the throat with white cotton-wool, and as she lay with a white sheet loosely overlying that, the phantom air of something that had been and was changed was still upon her.

I found, on questioning the servants, that Estella was in Paris, and I got a promise from the surgeon that he would write to her by the next post. Miss Havisham's family I took upon myself; intending to communicate with Mr. Matthew Pocket only, and leave him to do as he liked about informing the rest. This I did next day, through Herbert, as soon as I returned to town.

There was a stage, that evening, when she spoke collectedly of what had happened, though with a certain terrible vivacity. Towards midnight she began to wander in her speech; and after that it gradually set in that she said innumerable times in a low solemn voice, "What have I done!" And then, "When she first came, I meant to save her from misery like mine." And then, "Take the pencil and write under my name, 'I forgive her!'" She never changed the order of these three sentences, but she sometimes left out a word in one or other of them; never putting in another word, but always leaving a blank and going on to the next word.

As I could do no service there, and as I had, nearer home, that pressing reason for anxiety and fear which even her wanderings could not drive out of my mind, I decided, in the course of the night that I would return by the early morning coach, walking on a mile or so, and being taken up clear of the town. At about six o'clock of the morning, therefore, I leaned over her and touched her lips with mine, just as they said, not stopping for being touched, "Take the pencil and write under my name, 'I forgive her.'"

CHAPTER L

My hands had been dressed twice or thrice in the night, and again in the morning. My left arm was a good deal burned to the elbow, and, less severely, as high as the shoulder; it was very painful, but the flames had set in that direction, and I felt thankful it was no worse. My right hand was not so badly burnt but that I could move the fingers. It was bandaged, of course, but much less inconveniently than my left hand and arm; those I carried in a sling; and I could only wear my coat like a cloak, loose over my shoulders and fastened at the neck. My hair had been caught by the fire, but not my head or face.

When Herbert had been down to Hammersmith and seen his father, he came back to me at our chambers, and devoted the day to attending on me. He was the kindest of nurses, and at stated times took off the bandages, and steeped them in the cooling liquid that was kept ready, and put them on again, with a patient tenderness that I was deeply grateful for.

At first, as I lay quiet on the sofa, I found it painfully difficult, I might say impossible, to get rid of the impression of the glare of the flames, their hurry and noise, and the fierce burning smell. If I dozed for a minute, I was awakened by Miss Havisham's cries, and by her running at me with all that height of fire above her head. This pain of the mind was much harder to strive against than any bodily pain I suffered; and Herbert, seeing that, did his utmost to hold my attention engaged.

Neither of us spoke of the boat, but we both thought of it. That was made apparent by our avoidance of the subject, and by our agreeing—without agreement—to make my recovery of the use of my hands a question of so many hours, not of so many weeks.

My first question when I saw Herbert had been of course, whether all was well down the river? As he replied in the affirmative, with perfect confidence and cheerfulness, we did not resume the subject until the day was wearing away. But then, as Herbert changed the bandages, more by the light of the fire than by the outer light, he went back to it spontaneously.

"I sat with Provis last night, Handel, two good hours."

"Where was Clara?"

"Dear little thing!" said Herbert. "She was up and down with Gruffandgrim all the evening. He was perpetually pegging at the floor the moment she left his sight. I doubt if he can hold out long, though. What with rum and pepper,—and pepper and rum,—I should think his pegging must be nearly over."

"And then you will be married, Herbert?"

"How can I take care of the dear child otherwise?—Lay your arm out upon the back of the sofa, my dear boy, and I'll sit down here, and get the bandage off so gradually that you shall not know when it comes. I was speaking of Provis. Do you know, Handel, he improves?"

"I said to you I thought he was softened when I last saw him."

"So you did. And so he is. He was very communicative last night, and told me more of his life. You remember his breaking off here about some woman that he had had great trouble with.—Did I hurt you?"

I had started, but not under his touch. His words had given me a start.

"I had forgotten that, Herbert, but I remember it now you speak of it."

"Well! He went into that part of his life, and a dark wild part it is. Shall I tell you? Or would it worry you just now?"

"Tell me by all means. Every word."

Herbert bent forward to look at me more nearly, as if my reply had been rather more hurried or more eager than he could quite account for. "Your head is cool?" he said, touching it.

"Quite," said I. "Tell me what Provis said, my dear Herbert."

"It seems," said Herbert, "—there's a bandage off most charmingly, and now comes the cool one,—makes you shrink at first, my poor dear fellow, don't it? but it will be comfortable presently,—it seems that the woman was a young woman, and a jealous woman, and a revengeful woman; revengeful, Handel, to the last degree."

"To what last degree?"

"Murder.—Does it strike too cold on that sensitive place?"

"I don't feel it. How did she murder? Whom did she murder?" "Why, the deed may not have merited quite so terrible a name," said Herbert, "but, she was tried for it, and Mr. Jaggers defended her, and the reputation of that defence first made his name known to Provis. It was another and a stronger woman who was the victim, and there had been a struggle—in a barn. Who began it, or how fair it was, or how unfair, may be doubtful; but how it ended is certainly not doubtful, for the victim was found throttled."

"Was the woman brought in guilty?"

"No; she was acquitted.—My poor Handel, I hurt you!"

"It is impossible to be gentler, Herbert. Yes? What else?"

"This acquitted young woman and Provis had a little child; a little child of whom Provis was exceedingly fond. On the evening of the very night when the object of her jealousy was strangled as I tell you, the young woman presented herself before Provis for one moment, and swore that she would destroy the child (which was in her possession), and he should never see it again; then she vanished.—There's the worst arm comfortably in the sling once more, and now there remains but the right hand, which is a far easier job. I can do it better by this light than by a stronger, for my hand is steadiest when I don't see the poor blistered patches too distinctly.—You don't think your breathing is affected, my dear boy? You seem to breathe quickly."

"Perhaps I do, Herbert. Did the woman keep her oath?"

"There comes the darkest part of Provis's life. She did."

"That is, he says she did."

"Why, of course, my dear boy," returned Herbert, in a tone of surprise, and again bending forward to get a nearer look at me. "He says it all. I have no other information."

"No, to be sure."

"Now, whether," pursued Herbert, "he had used the child's mother ill, or whether he had used the child's mother well, Provis doesn't say; but she had shared some four or five years of the wretched life he described to us at this fireside, and he seems to have felt pity for her, and forbearance towards her. Therefore, fearing he should be called upon to depose about this destroyed child, and so be the cause of her death, he hid himself (much as he grieved for the child), kept himself dark, as he says, out of the way and out of the trial, and was only vaguely talked of as a certain man called Abel, out of whom the jealousy arose. After the acquittal she disappeared, and thus he lost the child and the child's mother."

"I want to ask—"

"A moment, my dear boy, and I have done. That evil genius, Compeyson, the worst of scoundrels among many scoundrels, knowing of his keeping out of the way at that time and of his reasons for doing so, of course afterwards held the knowledge over his head as a means of keeping him poorer and working him harder. It was clear last night that this barbed the point of Provis's animosity."

"I want to know," said I, "and particularly, Herbert, whether he told you when this happened?"

"Particularly? Let me remember, then, what he said as to that. His expression was, 'a round score o' year ago, and a'most directly after I took up wi' Compeyson.' How old were you when you came upon him in the little churchyard?"

"I think in my seventh year."

"Ay. It had happened some three or four years then, he said, and you brought into his mind the little girl so tragically lost, who would have been about your age."

"Herbert," said I, after a short silence, in a hurried way, "can you see me best by the light of the window, or the light of the fire?"

"By the firelight," answered Herbert, coming close again.

"Look at me."

"I do look at you, my dear boy."

"Touch me."

"I do touch you, my dear boy."

"You are not afraid that I am in any fever, or that my head is much disordered by the accident of last night?"

"N-no, my dear boy," said Herbert, after taking time to examine me. "You are rather excited, but you are quite yourself."

"I know I am quite myself. And the man we have in hiding down the river, is Estella's Father."

CHAPTER LI

What purpose I had in view when I was hot on tracing out and proving Estella's parentage, I cannot say. It will presently be seen that the question was not before me in a distinct shape until it was put before me by a wiser head than my own.

But when Herbert and I had held our momentous conversation, I was seized with a feverish conviction that I ought to hunt the matter down,—that I ought not to let it rest, but that I ought to see Mr. Jaggers, and come at the bare truth. I really do not know whether I felt that I did this for Estella's sake, or whether I was glad to transfer to the man in whose preservation I was so much concerned some rays of the romantic interest that had so long surrounded me. Perhaps the latter possibility may be the nearer to the truth.

Any way, I could scarcely be withheld from going out to Gerrard Street that night. Herbert's representations that, if I did, I should probably be laid up and stricken useless, when our fugitive's safety would depend upon me, alone restrained my impatience. On the understanding, again and again reiterated, that, come what would, I was to go to Mr. Jaggers to-morrow, I at length submitted to keep quiet, and to have my hurts looked after, and to stay at home. Early next morning we went out together, and at the corner of Giltspur Street by Smithfield, I left Herbert to go his way into the City, and took my way to Little Britain.

There were periodical occasions when Mr. Jaggers and Wemmick went over the office accounts, and checked off the vouchers, and put all things straight. On these occasions, Wemmick took his books and papers into Mr. Jaggers's room, and one of the up-stairs clerks came down into the outer office. Finding such clerk on Wemmick's post that morning, I knew what was going on; but I was not sorry to have Mr. Jaggers and Wemmick together, as Wemmick would then hear for himself that I said nothing to compromise him.

My appearance, with my arm bandaged and my coat loose over my shoulders, favored my object. Although I had sent Mr. Jaggers a brief account of the accident as soon as I had arrived in town, yet I had to give him all the details now; and the speciality of the occasion caused our talk to be less dry and hard, and less strictly regulated by the rules of evidence, than it had been before. While I described the disaster, Mr. Jaggers stood, according to his wont, before the fire. Wemmick leaned back in his chair, staring at me, with his hands in the pockets of his trousers, and his pen put horizontally into the post. The two brutal casts, always inseparable in my mind from the official proceedings, seemed to be congestively considering whether they didn't smell fire at the present moment.

My narrative finished, and their questions exhausted, I then produced Miss Havisham's authority to receive the nine hundred pounds for Herbert. Mr. Jaggers's eyes retired a little deeper into his head when I handed him the tablets, but he presently handed them over to Wemmick, with instructions to draw the check for his signature. While that was in course of being done, I looked on at Wemmick as he wrote, and Mr. Jaggers, poising and swaying himself on his well-polished boots, looked on at me. "I am sorry, Pip," said he, as I put the check in my pocket, when he had signed it, "that we do nothing for you."

"Miss Havisham was good enough to ask me," I returned, "whether she could do nothing for me, and I told her No."

"Everybody should know his own business," said Mr. Jaggers. And I saw Wemmick's lips form the words "portable property."

"I should not have told her No, if I had been you," said Mr Jaggers; "but every man ought to know his own business best."

"Every man's business," said Wemmick, rather reproachfully towards me, "is portable property."

As I thought the time was now come for pursuing the theme I had at heart, I said, turning on Mr. Jaggers:—

"I did ask something of Miss Havisham, however, sir. I asked her to give me some information relative to her adopted daughter, and she gave me all she possessed."

"Did she?" said Mr. Jaggers, bending forward to look at his boots and then straightening himself. "Hah! I don't think I should have done so, if I had been Miss Havisham. But she ought to know her own business best."

"I know more of the history of Miss Havisham's adopted child than Miss Havisham herself does, sir. I know her mother."

Mr. Jaggers looked at me inquiringly, and repeated "Mother?"

"I have seen her mother within these three days."

"Yes?" said Mr. Jaggers.

"And so have you, sir. And you have seen her still more recently."

"Yes?" said Mr. Jaggers.

"Perhaps I know more of Estella's history than even you do," said I. "I know her father too."

A certain stop that Mr. Jaggers came to in his manner—he was too self-possessed to change his manner, but he could not help its being brought to an indefinably attentive stop—assured me that he did not know who her father was. This I had strongly suspected from Provis's account (as Herbert had repeated it) of his having kept himself dark; which I pieced on to the fact that he himself was not Mr. Jaggers's client until some four years later, and when he could have no reason for claiming his identity. But, I could not be sure of this unconsciousness on Mr. Jaggers's part before, though I was quite sure of it now.

"So! You know the young lady's father, Pip?" said Mr. Jaggers.

"Yes," I replied, "and his name is Provis—from New South Wales."

Even Mr. Jaggers started when I said those words. It was the slightest start that could escape a man, the most carefully repressed and the sooner checked, but he did start, though he made it a part of the action of taking out his pocket-handkerchief. How Wemmick received the announcement I am unable to say; for I was afraid to look at him just then, lest Mr. Jaggers's sharpness should detect that there had been some communication unknown to him between us.

"And on what evidence, Pip," asked Mr. Jaggers, very coolly, as he paused with his handkerchief half way to his nose, "does Provis make this claim?"

"He does not make it," said I, "and has never made it, and has no knowledge or belief that his daughter is in existence."

For once, the powerful pocket-handkerchief failed. My reply was so Unexpected, that Mr. Jaggers put the handkerchief back into his pocket without completing the usual performance, folded his arms, and looked with stern attention at me, though with an immovable face.

Then I told him all I knew, and how I knew it; with the one reservation that I left him to infer that I knew from Miss Havisham what I in fact knew from Wemmick. I was very careful indeed as to that. Nor did I look towards Wemmick until I had finished all I had to tell, and had been for some time silently meeting Mr. Jaggers's look. When I did at last turn my eyes in Wemmick's direction, I found that he had unposted his pen, and was intent upon the table before him.

"Hah!" said Mr. Jaggers at last, as he moved towards the papers on the table. "What item was it you were at, Wemmick, when Mr. Pip came in?"

But I could not submit to be thrown off in that way, and I made a passionate, almost an indignant appeal, to him to be more frank and manly with me. I reminded him of the false hopes into which I had lapsed, the length of time they had lasted, and the discovery I had made: and I hinted at the danger that weighed upon my spirits. I represented myself as being surely worthy of some little confidence from him, in return for the confidence I had just now imparted. I said that I did not blame him, or suspect him, or mistrust him, but I wanted assurance of the truth from him. And if he asked me why I wanted it, and why I thought I had any right to it, I would tell him, little as he cared for such poor dreams, that I had loved Estella dearly and long, and that although I had lost her, and must live a bereaved life, whatever concerned her was still nearer and dearer to me than anything else in the world. And seeing that Mr. Jaggers stood quite still and silent, and apparently quite obdurate, under this appeal, I turned to Wemmick, and said, "Wemmick, I know you to be a man with a gentle heart. I have seen your pleasant home, and your old father, and all the innocent, cheerful playful ways with which you refresh your business life. And I entreat you to say a word for me to Mr. Jaggers, and to represent to him that, all circumstances considered, he ought to be more open with me!"

I have never seen two men look more oddly at one another than Mr. Jaggers and Wemmick did after this apostrophe. At first, a misgiving crossed me that Wemmick would be instantly dismissed from his employment; but it melted as I saw Mr. Jaggers relax into something like a smile, and Wemmick become bolder.

"What's all this?" said Mr. Jaggers. "You with an old father, and you with pleasant and playful ways?"

"Well!" returned Wemmick. "If I don't bring 'em here, what does it matter?"

"Pip," said Mr. Jaggers, laying his hand upon my arm, and smiling openly, "this man must be the most cunning impostor in all London."

"Not a bit of it," returned Wemmick, growing bolder and bolder. "I think you're another."

Again they exchanged their former odd looks, each apparently still distrustful that the other was taking him in.

"You with a pleasant home?" said Mr. Jaggers.

"Since it don't interfere with business," returned Wemmick, "let it be so. Now, I look at you, sir, I shouldn't wonder if you might be planning and contriving to have a pleasant home of your own one of these days, when you're tired of all this work."

Mr. Jaggers nodded his head retrospectively two or three times, and actually drew a sigh. "Pip," said he, "we won't talk about 'poor dreams;' you know more about such things than I, having much fresher experience of that kind. But now about this other matter. I'll put a case to you. Mind! I admit nothing."

He waited for me to declare that I quite understood that he expressly said that he admitted nothing.

"Now, Pip," said Mr. Jaggers, "put this case. Put the case that a woman, under such circumstances as you have mentioned, held her child concealed, and was obliged to communicate the fact to her legal adviser, on his representing to her that he must know, with an eye to the latitude of his defence, how the fact stood about that child. Put the case that, at the same time he held a trust to find a child for an eccentric rich lady to adopt and bring up."

"I follow you, sir."

"Put the case that he lived in an atmosphere of evil, and that all he saw of children was their being generated in great numbers for certain destruction. Put the case that he often saw children solemnly tried at a criminal bar, where they were held up to be seen; put the case that he habitually knew of their being imprisoned, whipped, transported, neglected, cast out, qualified in all ways for the hangman, and growing up to be hanged. Put the case that pretty nigh all the children he saw in his daily business life he had reason to look upon as so much spawn, to develop into the fish that were to come to his net,—to be prosecuted, defended, forsworn, made orphans, bedevilled somehow."

"I follow you, sir."

"Put the case, Pip, that here was one pretty little child out of the heap who could be saved; whom the father believed dead, and dared make no stir about; as to whom, over the mother, the legal adviser had this power: 'I know what you did, and how you did it. You came so and so, you did such and such things to divert suspicion. I have tracked you through it all, and I tell it you all. Part with the child, unless it should be necessary to produce it to clear you, and then it shall be produced. Give the child into my hands, and I will do my best to bring you off. If you are saved, your child is saved too; if you are lost, your child is still saved.' Put the case that this was done, and that the woman was cleared."

"I understand you perfectly."

"But that I make no admissions?"

"That you make no admissions." And Wemmick repeated, "No admissions."

"Put the case, Pip, that passion and the terror of death had a little shaken the woman's intellects, and that when she was set at liberty, she was scared out of the ways of the world, and went to him to be sheltered. Put the case that he took her in, and that he kept down the old, wild, violent nature whenever he saw an inkling of its breaking out, by asserting his power over her in the old way. Do you comprehend the imaginary case?"

"Quite."

"Put the case that the child grew up, and was married for money. That the mother was still living. That the father was still living. That the mother and father, unknown to one another, were dwelling within so many miles, furlongs, yards if you like, of one another. That the secret was still a secret, except that you had got wind of it. Put that last case to yourself very carefully."

"I do."

"I ask Wemmick to put it to himself very carefully."

And Wemmick said, "I do."

"For whose sake would you reveal the secret? For the father's? I think he would not be much the better for the mother. For the mother's? I think if she had done such a deed she would be safer where she was. For the daughter's? I think it would hardly serve her to establish her parentage for the information of her husband, and to drag her back to disgrace, after an escape of twenty years, pretty secure to last for life. But add the case that you had loved her, Pip, and had made her the subject of those 'poor dreams' which have, at one time or another, been in the heads of more men than you think likely, then I tell you that you had better—and would much sooner when you had thought well of it—chop off that bandaged left hand of yours with your bandaged right hand, and then pass the chopper on to Wemmick there, to cut that off too."

I looked at Wemmick, whose face was very grave. He gravely touched his lips with his forefinger. I did the same. Mr. Jaggers did the same. "Now, Wemmick," said the latter then, resuming his usual manner, "what item was it you were at when Mr. Pip came in?"

Standing by for a little, while they were at work, I observed that the odd looks they had cast at one another were repeated several times: with this difference now, that each of them seemed suspicious, not to say conscious, of having shown himself in a weak and unprofessional light to the other. For this reason, I suppose, they were now inflexible with one another; Mr. Jaggers being highly dictatorial, and Wemmick obstinately justifying himself whenever there was the smallest point in abeyance for a moment. I had never seen them on such ill terms; for generally they got on very well indeed together.

But they were both happily relieved by the opportune appearance of Mike, the client with the fur cap and the habit of wiping his nose on his sleeve, whom I had seen on the very first day of my appearance within those walls. This individual, who, either in his own person or in that of some member of his family, seemed to be always in trouble (which in that place meant Newgate), called to announce that his eldest daughter was taken up on suspicion of shoplifting. As he imparted this melancholy circumstance to Wemmick, Mr. Jaggers standing magisterially before the fire and taking no share in the proceedings, Mike's eye happened to twinkle with a tear.

"What are you about?" demanded Wemmick, with the utmost indignation. "What do you come snivelling here for?"

"I didn't go to do it, Mr. Wemmick."

"You did," said Wemmick. "How dare you? You're not in a fit state to come here, if you can't come here without spluttering like a bad pen. What do you mean by it?"

"A man can't help his feelings, Mr. Wemmick," pleaded Mike.

"His what?" demanded Wemmick, quite savagely. "Say that again!"

"Now look here my man," said Mr. Jaggers, advancing a step, and pointing to the door. "Get out of this office. I'll have no feelings here. Get out."

"It serves you right," said Wemmick, "Get out."

So, the unfortunate Mike very humbly withdrew, and Mr. Jaggers and Wemmick appeared to have re-established their good understanding, and went to work again with an air of refreshment upon them as if they had just had lunch.

CHAPTER LII

From Little Britain I went, with my check in my pocket, to Miss Skiffins's brother, the accountant; and Miss Skiffins's brother, the accountant, going straight to Clarriker's and bringing Clarriker to me, I had the great satisfaction of concluding that arrangement. It was the only good thing I had done, and the only completed thing I had done, since I was first apprised of my great expectations.

Clarriker informing me on that occasion that the affairs of the House were steadily progressing, that he would now be able to establish a small branch-house in the East which was much wanted for the extension of the business, and that Herbert in his new partnership capacity would go out and take charge of it, I found that I must have prepared for a separation from my friend, even though my own affairs had been more settled. And now, indeed, I felt as if my last anchor were loosening its hold, and I should soon be driving with the winds and waves.

But there was recompense in the joy with which Herbert would come home of a night and tell me of these changes, little imagining that he told me no news, and would sketch airy pictures of himself conducting Clara Barley to the land of the Arabian Nights, and of me going out to join them (with a caravan of camels, I believe), and of our all going up the Nile and seeing wonders. Without being sanguine as to my own part in those bright plans, I felt that Herbert's way was clearing fast, and that old Bill Barley had but to stick to his pepper and rum, and his daughter would soon be happily provided for.

We had now got into the month of March. My left arm, though it presented no bad symptoms, took, in the natural course, so long to heal that I was still unable to get a coat on. My right arm was tolerably restored; disfigured, but fairly serviceable.

On a Monday morning, when Herbert and I were at breakfast, I received the following letter from Wemmick by the post.

"Walworth. Burn this as soon as read. Early in the week, or say Wednesday, you might do what you know of, if you felt disposed to try it. Now burn."

When I had shown this to Herbert and had put it in the fire—but not before we had both got it by heart—we considered what to do. For, of course my being disabled could now be no longer kept out of view.

"I have thought it over again and again," said Herbert, "and I think I know a better course than taking a Thames waterman. Take Startop. A good fellow, a skilled hand, fond of us, and enthusiastic and honorable."

I had thought of him more than once.

"But how much would you tell him, Herbert?"

"It is necessary to tell him very little. Let him suppose it a mere freak, but a secret one, until the morning comes: then let him know that there is urgent reason for your getting Provis aboard and away. You go with him?"

"No doubt."

"Where?"

It had seemed to me, in the many anxious considerations I had given the point, almost indifferent what port we made for,—Hamburg, Rotterdam, Antwerp,—the place signified little, so that he was out of England. Any foreign steamer that fell in our way and would take us up would do. I had always proposed to myself to get him well down the river in the boat; certainly well beyond Gravesend, which was a critical place for search or inquiry if suspicion were afoot. As foreign steamers would leave London at about the time of high-water, our plan would be to get down the river by a previous ebb-tide, and lie by in some quiet spot until we could pull off to one. The time when one would be due where we lay, wherever that might be, could be calculated pretty nearly, if we made inquiries beforehand.

Herbert assented to all this, and we went out immediately after breakfast to pursue our investigations. We found that a steamer for Hamburg was likely to suit our purpose best, and we directed our thoughts chiefly to that vessel. But we noted down what other foreign steamers would leave London with the same tide, and we satisfied ourselves that we knew the build and color of each. We then separated for a few hours: I, to get at once such passports as were necessary; Herbert, to see Startop at his lodgings. We both did what we had to do without any hindrance, and when we met again at one o'clock reported it done. I, for my part, was prepared with passports; Herbert had seen Startop, and he was more than ready to join.

Those two should pull a pair of oars, we settled, and I would steer; our charge would be sitter, and keep quiet; as speed was not our object, we should make way enough. We arranged that Herbert should not come home to dinner before going to Mill Pond Bank that evening; that he should not go there at all to-morrow evening, Tuesday; that he should prepare Provis to come down to some stairs hard by the house, on Wednesday, when he saw us approach, and not sooner; that all the arrangements with him should be concluded that Monday night; and that he should be communicated with no more in any way, until we took him on board.

These precautions well understood by both of us, I went home.

On opening the outer door of our chambers with my key, I found a letter in the box, directed to me; a very dirty letter, though not ill-written. It had been delivered by hand (of course, since I left home), and its contents were these:—

"If you are not afraid to come to the old marshes to-night or tomorrow night at nine, and to come to the little sluice-house by the limekiln, you had better come. If you want information regarding your uncle Provis, you had much better come and tell no one, and lose no time. You must come alone. Bring this with you."

I had had load enough upon my mind before the receipt of this strange letter. What to do now, I could not tell. And the worst was, that I must decide quickly, or I should miss the afternoon coach, which would take me down in time for to-night. To-morrow night I could not think of going, for it would be too close upon the time of the flight. And again, for anything I knew, the proffered information might have some important bearing on the flight itself.

If I had had ample time for consideration, I believe I should still have gone. Having hardly any time for consideration,—my watch showing me that the coach started within half an hour,—I resolved to go. I should certainly not have gone, but for the reference to my Uncle Provis. That, coming on Wemmick's letter and the morning's busy preparation, turned the scale.

It is so difficult to become clearly possessed of the contents of almost any letter, in a violent hurry, that I had to read this mysterious epistle again twice, before its injunction to me to be secret got mechanically into my mind. Yielding to it in the same mechanical kind of way, I left a note in pencil for Herbert, telling him that as I should be so soon going away, I knew not for how long, I had decided to hurry down and back, to ascertain for myself how Miss Havisham was faring. I had then barely time to get my great-coat, lock up the chambers, and make for the coach-office by the short by-ways. If I had taken a hackney-chariot and gone by the streets, I should have missed my aim; going as I did, I caught the coach just as it came out of the yard. I was the only inside passenger, jolting away knee-deep in straw, when I came to myself.

For I really had not been myself since the receipt of the letter; it had so bewildered me, ensuing on the hurry of the morning. The morning hurry and flutter had been great; for, long and anxiously as I had waited for Wemmick, his hint had come like a surprise at last. And now I began to wonder at myself for being in the coach, and to doubt whether I had sufficient reason for being there, and to consider whether I should get out presently and go back, and to argue against ever heeding an anonymous communication, and, in short, to pass through all those phases of contradiction and indecision to which I suppose very few hurried people are strangers. Still, the reference to Provis by name mastered everything. I reasoned as I had reasoned already without knowing it,—if that be reasoning,—in case any harm should befall him through my not going, how could I ever forgive myself!

It was dark before we got down, and the journey seemed long and dreary to me, who could see little of it inside, and who could not go outside in my disabled state. Avoiding the Blue Boar, I put up at an inn of minor reputation down the town, and ordered some dinner. While it was preparing, I went to Satis House and inquired for Miss Havisham; she was still very ill, though considered something better.

My inn had once been a part of an ancient ecclesiastical house, and I dined in a little octagonal common-room, like a font. As I was not able to cut my dinner, the old landlord with a shining bald head did it for me. This bringing us into conversation, he was so good as to entertain me with my own story,—of course with the popular feature that Pumblechook was my earliest benefactor and the founder of my fortunes.

"Do you know the young man?" said I.

"Know him!" repeated the landlord. "Ever since he was—no height at all."

"Does he ever come back to this neighborhood?"

"Ay, he comes back," said the landlord, "to his great friends, now and again, and gives the cold shoulder to the man that made him."

"What man is that?"

"Him that I speak of," said the landlord. "Mr. Pumblechook."

"Is he ungrateful to no one else?"

"No doubt he would be, if he could," returned the landlord, "but he can't. And why? Because Pumblechook done everything for him."

"Does Pumblechook say so?"

"Say so!" replied the landlord. "He han't no call to say so."

"But does he say so?"

"It would turn a man's blood to white wine winegar to hear him tell of it, sir," said the landlord.

I thought, "Yet Joe, dear Joe, you never tell of it. Long-suffering and loving Joe, you never complain. Nor you, sweet-tempered Biddy!"

"Your appetite's been touched like by your accident," said the landlord, glancing at the bandaged arm under my coat. "Try a tenderer bit."

"No, thank you," I replied, turning from the table to brood over the fire. "I can eat no more. Please take it away."

I had never been struck at so keenly, for my thanklessness to Joe, as through the brazen impostor Pumblechook. The falser he, the truer Joe; the meaner he, the nobler Joe.

My heart was deeply and most deservedly humbled as I mused over the fire for an hour or more. The striking of the clock aroused me, but not from my dejection or remorse, and I got up and had my coat fastened round my neck, and went out. I had previously sought in my pockets for the letter, that I might refer to it again; but I could not find it, and was uneasy to think that it must have been dropped in the straw of the coach. I knew very well, however, that the appointed place was the little sluice-house by the limekiln on the marshes, and the hour nine. Towards the marshes I now went straight, having no time to spare.

CHAPTER LIII

It was a dark night, though the full moon rose as I left the enclosed lands, and passed out upon the marshes. Beyond their dark line there was a ribbon of clear sky, hardly broad enough to hold the red large moon. In a few minutes she had ascended out of that clear field, in among the piled mountains of cloud.

There was a melancholy wind, and the marshes were very dismal. A stranger would have found them insupportable, and even to me they were so oppressive that I hesitated, half inclined to go back. But I knew them well, and could have found my way on a far darker night, and had no excuse for returning, being there. So, having come there against my inclination, I went on against it.

The direction that I took was not that in which my old home lay, nor that in which we had pursued the convicts. My back was turned towards the distant Hulks as I walked on, and, though I could see the old lights away on the spits of sand, I saw them over my shoulder. I knew the limekiln as well as I knew the old Battery, but they were miles apart; so that, if a light had been burning at each point that night, there would have been a long strip of the blank horizon between the two bright specks.

At first, I had to shut some gates after me, and now and then to stand still while the cattle that were lying in the banked-up pathway arose and blundered down among the grass and reeds. But after a little while I seemed to have the whole flats to myself.

It was another half-hour before I drew near to the kiln. The lime was burning with a sluggish stifling smell, but the fires were made up and left, and no workmen were visible. Hard by was a small stone-quarry. It lay directly in my way, and had been worked that day, as I saw by the tools and barrows that were lying about.

Coming up again to the marsh level out of this excavation,—for the rude path lay through it,—I saw a light in the old sluice-house. I quickened my pace, and knocked at the door with my hand. Waiting for some reply, I looked about me, noticing how the sluice was abandoned and broken, and how the house—of wood with a tiled roof—would not be proof against the weather much longer, if it were so even now, and how the mud and ooze were coated with lime, and how the choking vapor of the kiln crept in a ghostly way towards me. Still there was no answer, and I knocked again. No answer still, and I tried the latch.

It rose under my hand, and the door yielded. Looking in, I saw a lighted candle on a table, a bench, and a mattress on a truckle bedstead. As there was a loft above, I called, "Is there any one here?" but no voice answered. Then I looked at my watch, and, finding that it was past nine, called again, "Is there any one here?" There being still no answer, I went out at the door, irresolute what to do.

It was beginning to rain fast. Seeing nothing save what I had seen already, I turned back into the house, and stood just within the shelter of the doorway, looking out into the night. While I was considering that some one must have been there lately and must soon be coming back, or the candle would not be burning, it came into my head to look if the wick were long. I turned round to do so, and had taken up the candle in my hand, when it was extinguished by some violent shock; and the next thing I comprehended was, that I had been caught in a strong running noose, thrown over my head from behind.

"Now," said a suppressed voice with an oath, "I've got you!"

"What is this?" I cried, struggling. "Who is it? Help, help, help!"

Not only were my arms pulled close to my sides, but the pressure on my bad arm caused me exquisite pain. Sometimes, a strong man's hand, sometimes a strong man's breast, was set against my mouth to deaden my cries, and with a hot breath always close to me, I struggled ineffectually in the dark, while I was fastened tight to the wall. "And now," said the suppressed voice with another oath, "call out again, and I'll make short work of you!"

Faint and sick with the pain of my injured arm, bewildered by the surprise, and yet conscious how easily this threat could be put in execution, I desisted, and tried to ease my arm were it ever so little. But, it was bound too tight for that. I felt as if, having been burnt before, it were now being boiled.

The sudden exclusion of the night, and the substitution of black darkness in its place, warned me that the man had closed a shutter. After groping about for a little, he found the flint and steel he wanted, and began to strike a light. I strained my sight upon the sparks that fell among the tinder, and upon which he breathed and breathed, match in hand, but I could only see his lips, and the blue point of the match; even those but fitfully. The tinder was damp,—no wonder there,—and one after another the sparks died out.

The man was in no hurry, and struck again with the flint and steel. As the sparks fell thick and bright about him, I could see his hands, and touches of his face, and could make out that he was seated and bending over the table; but nothing more. Presently I saw his blue lips again, breathing on the tinder, and then a flare of light flashed up, and showed me Orlick.

Whom I had looked for, I don't know. I had not looked for him. Seeing him, I felt that I was in a dangerous strait indeed, and I kept my eyes upon him.

He lighted the candle from the flaring match with great deliberation, and dropped the match, and trod it out. Then he put the candle away from him on the table, so that he could see me, and sat with his arms folded on the table and looked at me. I made out that I was fastened to a stout perpendicular ladder a few inches from the wall,—a fixture there,—the means of ascent to the loft above.

"Now," said he, when we had surveyed one another for some time, "I've got you."

"Unbind me. Let me go!"

"Ah!" he returned, "I'll let you go. I'll let you go to the moon, I'll let you go to the stars. All in good time."

"Why have you lured me here?"

"Don't you know?" said he, with a deadly look.

"Why have you set upon me in the dark?"

"Because I mean to do it all myself. One keeps a secret better than two. O you enemy, you enemy!"

His enjoyment of the spectacle I furnished, as he sat with his arms folded on the table, shaking his head at me and hugging himself, had a malignity in it that made me tremble. As I watched him in silence, he put his hand into the corner at his side, and took up a gun with a brass-bound stock.

"Do you know this?" said he, making as if he would take aim at me. "Do you know where you saw it afore? Speak, wolf!"

"Yes," I answered.

"You cost me that place. You did. Speak!"

"What else could I do?"

"You did that, and that would be enough, without more. How dared you to come betwixt me and a young woman I liked?"

"When did I?"

"When didn't you? It was you as always give Old Orlick a bad name to her."

"You gave it to yourself; you gained it for yourself. I could have done you no harm, if you had done yourself none."

"You're a liar. And you'll take any pains, and spend any money, to drive me out of this country, will you?" said he, repeating my words to Biddy in the last interview I had with her. "Now, I'll tell you a piece of information. It was never so well worth your while to get me out of this country as it is to-night. Ah! If it was all your money twenty times told, to the last brass farden!" As he shook his heavy hand at me, with his mouth snarling like a tiger's, I felt that it was true.

"What are you going to do to me?"

"I'm a going," said he, bringing his fist down upon the table with a heavy blow, and rising as the blow fell to give it greater force,—"I'm a going to have your life!"

He leaned forward staring at me, slowly unclenched his hand and drew it across his mouth as if his mouth watered for me, and sat down again.

"You was always in Old Orlick's way since ever you was a child. You goes out of his way this present night. He'll have no more on you. You're dead."

I felt that I had come to the brink of my grave. For a moment I looked wildly round my trap for any chance of escape; but there was none.

"More than that," said he, folding his arms on the table again, "I won't have a rag of you, I won't have a bone of you, left on earth. I'll put your body in the kiln,—I'd carry two such to it, on my Shoulders,—and, let people suppose what they may of you, they shall never know nothing."

My mind, with inconceivable rapidity followed out all the consequences of such a death. Estella's father would believe I had deserted him, would be taken, would die accusing me; even Herbert would doubt me, when he compared the letter I had left for him with the fact that I had called at Miss Havisham's gate for only a moment; Joe and Biddy would never know how sorry I had been that night, none would ever know what I had suffered, how true I had meant to be, what an agony I had passed through. The death close before me was terrible, but far more terrible than death was the dread of being misremembered after death. And so quick were my thoughts, that I saw myself despised by unborn generations,—Estella's children, and their children,—while the wretch's words were yet on his lips.

"Now, wolf," said he, "afore I kill you like any other beast,—which is wot I mean to do and wot I have tied you up for,—I'll have a good look at you and a good goad at you. O you enemy!"

It had passed through my thoughts to cry out for help again; though few could know better than I, the solitary nature of the spot, and the hopelessness of aid. But as he sat gloating over me, I was supported by a scornful detestation of him that sealed my lips. Above all things, I resolved that I would not entreat him, and that I would die making some last poor resistance to him. Softened as my thoughts of all the rest of men were in that dire extremity; humbly beseeching pardon, as I did, of Heaven; melted at heart, as I was, by the thought that I had taken no farewell, and never now could take farewell of those who were dear to me, or could explain myself to them, or ask for their compassion on my miserable errors,—still, if I could have killed him, even in dying, I would have done it.

He had been drinking, and his eyes were red and bloodshot. Around his neck was slung a tin bottle, as I had often seen his meat and drink slung about him in other days. He brought the bottle to his lips, and took a fiery drink from it; and I smelt the strong spirits that I saw flash into his face.

"Wolf!" said he, folding his arms again, "Old Orlick's a going to tell you somethink. It was you as did for your shrew sister."

Again my mind, with its former inconceivable rapidity, had exhausted the whole subject of the attack upon my sister, her illness, and her death, before his slow and hesitating speech had formed these words.

"It was you, villain," said I.

"I tell you it was your doing,—I tell you it was done through you," he retorted, catching up the gun, and making a blow with the stock at the vacant air between us. "I come upon her from behind, as I come upon you to-night. I giv' it her! I left her for dead, and if there had been a limekiln as nigh her as there is now nigh you, she shouldn't have come to life again. But it warn't Old Orlick as did it; it was you. You was favored, and he was bullied and beat. Old Orlick bullied and beat, eh? Now you pays for it. You done it; now you pays for it."

He drank again, and became more ferocious. I saw by his tilting of the bottle that there was no great quantity left in it. I distinctly understood that he was working himself up with its contents to make an end of me. I knew that every drop it held was a drop of my life. I knew that when I was changed into a part of the vapor that had crept towards me but a little while before, like my own warning ghost, he would do as he had done in my sister's case,—make all haste to the town, and be seen slouching about there drinking at the alehouses. My rapid mind pursued him to the town, made a picture of the street with him in it, and contrasted its lights and life with the lonely marsh and the white vapor creeping over it, into which I should have dissolved.

It was not only that I could have summed up years and years and years while he said a dozen words, but that what he did say presented pictures to me, and not mere words. In the excited and exalted state of my brain, I could not think of a place without seeing it, or of persons without seeing them. It is impossible to overstate the vividness of these images, and yet I was so intent, all the time, upon him himself,—who would not be intent on the tiger crouching to spring!—that I knew of the slightest action of his fingers.

When he had drunk this second time, he rose from the bench on which he sat, and pushed the table aside. Then, he took up the candle, and, shading it with his murderous hand so as to throw its light on me, stood before me, looking at me and enjoying the sight.

"Wolf, I'll tell you something more. It was Old Orlick as you tumbled over on your stairs that night."

I saw the staircase with its extinguished lamps. I saw the shadows of the heavy stair-rails, thrown by the watchman's lantern on the wall. I saw the rooms that I was never to see again; here, a door half open; there, a door closed; all the articles of furniture around.

"And why was Old Orlick there? I'll tell you something more, wolf. You and her have pretty well hunted me out of this country, so far as getting a easy living in it goes, and I've took up with new companions, and new masters. Some of 'em writes my letters when I wants 'em wrote,—do you mind?—writes my letters, wolf! They writes fifty hands; they're not like sneaking you, as writes but one. I've had a firm mind and a firm will to have your life, since you was down here at your sister's burying. I han't seen a way to get you safe, and I've looked arter you to know your ins and outs. For, says Old Orlick to himself, 'Somehow or another I'll have him!' What! When I looks for you, I finds your uncle Provis, eh?"

Mill Pond Bank, and Chinks's Basin, and the Old Green Copper Ropewalk, all so clear and plain! Provis in his rooms, the signal whose use was over, pretty Clara, the good motherly woman, old Bill Barley on his back, all drifting by, as on the swift stream of my life fast running out to sea!

"You with a uncle too! Why, I know'd you at Gargery's when you was so small a wolf that I could have took your weazen betwixt this finger and thumb and chucked you away dead (as I'd thoughts o' doing, odd times, when I see you loitering amongst the pollards on a Sunday), and you hadn't found no uncles then. No, not you! But when Old Orlick come for to hear that your uncle Provis had most like wore the leg-iron wot Old Orlick had picked up, filed asunder, on these meshes ever so many year ago, and wot he kep by him till he dropped your sister with it, like a bullock, as he means to drop you—hey?—when he come for to hear that—hey?"

In his savage taunting, he flared the candle so close at me that I turned my face aside to save it from the flame.

"Ah!" he cried, laughing, after doing it again, "the burnt child dreads the fire! Old Orlick knowed you was burnt, Old Orlick knowed you was smuggling your uncle Provis away, Old Orlick's a match for you and know'd you'd come to-night! Now I'll tell you something more, wolf, and this ends it. There's them that's as good a match for your uncle Provis as Old Orlick has been for you. Let him 'ware them, when he's lost his nevvy! Let him 'ware them, when no man can't find a rag of his dear relation's clothes, nor yet a bone of his body. There's them that can't and that won't have Magwitch,—yes, I know the name!—alive in the same land with them, and that's had such sure information of him when he was alive in another land, as that he couldn't and shouldn't leave it unbeknown and put them in danger. P'raps it's them that writes fifty hands, and that's not like sneaking you as writes but one. 'Ware Compeyson, Magwitch, and the gallows!"

He flared the candle at me again, smoking my face and hair, and for an instant blinding me, and turned his powerful back as he replaced the light on the table. I had thought a prayer, and had been with Joe and Biddy and Herbert, before he turned towards me again.

There was a clear space of a few feet between the table and the opposite wall. Within this space, he now slouched backwards and forwards. His great strength seemed to sit stronger upon him than ever before, as he did this with his hands hanging loose and heavy at his sides, and with his eyes scowling at me. I had no grain of hope left. Wild as my inward hurry was, and wonderful the force of the pictures that rushed by me instead of thoughts, I could yet clearly understand that, unless he had resolved that I was within a few moments of surely perishing out of all human knowledge, he would never have told me what he had told.

Of a sudden, he stopped, took the cork out of his bottle, and tossed it away. Light as it was, I heard it fall like a plummet. He swallowed slowly, tilting up the bottle by little and little, and now he looked at me no more. The last few drops of liquor he poured into the palm of his hand, and licked up. Then, with a sudden hurry of violence and swearing horribly, he threw the bottle from him, and stooped; and I saw in his hand a stone-hammer with a long heavy handle.

The resolution I had made did not desert me, for, without uttering one vain word of appeal to him, I shouted out with all my might, and struggled with all my might. It was only my head and my legs that I could move, but to that extent I struggled with all the force, until then unknown, that was within me. In the same instant I heard responsive shouts, saw figures and a gleam of light dash in at the door, heard voices and tumult, and saw Orlick emerge from a struggle of men, as if it were tumbling water, clear the table at a leap, and fly out into the night.

After a blank, I found that I was lying unbound, on the floor, in the same place, with my head on some one's knee. My eyes were fixed on the ladder against the wall, when I came to myself,—had opened on it before my mind saw it,—and thus as I recovered consciousness, I knew that I was in the place where I had lost it.

Too indifferent at first, even to look round and ascertain who supported me, I was lying looking at the ladder, when there came between me and it a face. The face of Trabb's boy!

"I think he's all right!" said Trabb's boy, in a sober voice; "but ain't he just pale though!"

At these words, the face of him who supported me looked over into mine, and I saw my supporter to be—

"Herbert! Great Heaven!"

"Softly," said Herbert. "Gently, Handel. Don't be too eager."

"And our old comrade, Startop!" I cried, as he too bent over me.

"Remember what he is going to assist us in," said Herbert, "and be calm."

The allusion made me spring up; though I dropped again from the pain in my arm. "The time has not gone by, Herbert, has it? What night is to-night? How long have I been here?" For, I had a strange and strong misgiving that I had been lying there a long time—a day and a night,—two days and nights,—more.

"The time has not gone by. It is still Monday night."

"Thank God!"

"And you have all to-morrow, Tuesday, to rest in," said Herbert. "But you can't help groaning, my dear Handel. What hurt have you got? Can you stand?"

"Yes, yes," said I, "I can walk. I have no hurt but in this throbbing arm."

They laid it bare, and did what they could. It was violently swollen and inflamed, and I could scarcely endure to have it touched. But, they tore up their handkerchiefs to make fresh bandages, and carefully replaced it in the sling, until we could get to the town and obtain some cooling lotion to put upon it. In a little while we had shut the door of the dark and empty sluice-house, and were passing through the quarry on our way back. Trabb's boy—Trabb's overgrown young man now—went before us with a lantern, which was the light I had seen come in at the door. But, the moon was a good two hours higher than when I had last seen the sky, and the night, though rainy, was much lighter. The white vapor of the kiln was passing from us as we went by, and as I had thought a prayer before, I thought a thanksgiving now.

Entreating Herbert to tell me how he had come to my rescue,—which at first he had flatly refused to do, but had insisted on my remaining quiet,—I learnt that I had in my hurry dropped the letter, open, in our chambers, where he, coming home to bring with him Startop whom he had met in the street on his way to me, found it, very soon after I was gone. Its tone made him uneasy, and the more so because of the inconsistency between it and the hasty letter I had left for him. His uneasiness increasing instead of subsiding, after a quarter of an hour's consideration, he set off for the coach-office with Startop, who volunteered his company, to make inquiry when the next coach went down. Finding that the afternoon coach was gone, and finding that his uneasiness grew into positive alarm, as obstacles came in his way, he resolved to follow in a post-chaise. So he and Startop arrived at the Blue Boar, fully expecting there to find me, or tidings of me; but, finding neither, went on to Miss Havisham's, where they lost me. Hereupon they went back to the hotel (doubtless at about the time when I was hearing the popular local version of my own story) to refresh themselves and to get some one to guide them out upon the marshes. Among the loungers under the Boar's archway happened to be Trabb's Boy,—true to his ancient habit of happening to be everywhere where he had no business,—and Trabb's boy had seen me passing from Miss Havisham's in the direction of my dining-place. Thus Trabb's boy became their guide, and with him they went out to the sluice-house, though by the town way to the marshes, which I had avoided. Now, as they went along, Herbert reflected, that I might, after all, have been brought there on some genuine and serviceable errand tending to Provis's safety, and, bethinking himself that in that case interruption must be mischievous, left his guide and Startop on the edge of the quarry, and went on by himself, and stole round the house two or three times, endeavouring to ascertain whether all was right within. As he could hear nothing but indistinct sounds of one deep rough voice (this was while my mind was so busy), he even at last began to doubt whether I was there, when suddenly I cried out loudly, and he answered the cries, and rushed in, closely followed by the other two.

When I told Herbert what had passed within the house, he was for our immediately going before a magistrate in the town, late at night as it was, and getting out a warrant. But, I had already considered that such a course, by detaining us there, or binding us to come back, might be fatal to Provis. There was no gainsaying this difficulty, and we relinquished all thoughts of pursuing Orlick at that time. For the present, under the circumstances, we deemed it prudent to make rather light of the matter to Trabb's boy; who, I am convinced, would have been much affected by disappointment, if he had known that his intervention saved me from the limekiln. Not that Trabb's boy was of a malignant nature, but that he had too much spare vivacity, and that it was in his constitution to want variety and excitement at anybody's expense. When we parted, I presented him with two guineas (which seemed to meet his views), and told him that I was sorry ever to have had an ill opinion of him (which made no impression on him at all).

Wednesday being so close upon us, we determined to go back to London that night, three in the post-chaise; the rather, as we should then be clear away before the night's adventure began to be talked of. Herbert got a large bottle of stuff for my arm; and by dint of having this stuff dropped over it all the night through, I was just able to bear its pain on the journey. It was daylight when we reached the Temple, and I went at once to bed, and lay in bed all day.

My terror, as I lay there, of falling ill, and being unfitted for tomorrow, was so besetting, that I wonder it did not disable me of itself. It would have done so, pretty surely, in conjunction with the mental wear and tear I had suffered, but for the unnatural strain upon me that to-morrow was. So anxiously looked forward to, charged with such consequences, its results so impenetrably hidden, though so near.

No precaution could have been more obvious than our refraining from communication with him that day; yet this again increased my restlessness. I started at every footstep and every sound, believing that he was discovered and taken, and this was the messenger to tell me so. I persuaded myself that I knew he was taken; that there was something more upon my mind than a fear or a presentiment; that the fact had occurred, and I had a mysterious knowledge of it. As the days wore on, and no ill news came, as the day closed in and darkness fell, my overshadowing dread of being disabled by illness before to-morrow morning altogether mastered me. My burning arm throbbed, and my burning head throbbed, and I fancied I was beginning to wander. I counted up to high numbers, to make sure of myself, and repeated passages that I knew in prose and verse. It happened sometimes that in the mere escape of a fatigued mind, I dozed for some moments or forgot; then I would say to myself with a start, "Now it has come, and I am turning delirious!"

They kept me very quiet all day, and kept my arm constantly dressed, and gave me cooling drinks. Whenever I fell asleep, I awoke with the notion I had had in the sluice-house, that a long time had elapsed and the opportunity to save him was gone. About midnight I got out of bed and went to Herbert, with the conviction that I had been asleep for four-and-twenty hours, and that Wednesday was past. It was the last self-exhausting effort of my fretfulness, for after that I slept soundly.

Wednesday morning was dawning when I looked out of window. The winking lights upon the bridges were already pale, the coming sun was like a marsh of fire on the horizon. The river, still dark and mysterious, was spanned by bridges that were turning coldly gray, with here and there at top a warm touch from the burning in the sky. As I looked along the clustered roofs, with church-towers and spires shooting into the unusually clear air, the sun rose up, and a veil seemed to be drawn from the river, and millions of sparkles burst out upon its waters. From me too, a veil seemed to be drawn, and I felt strong and well.

Herbert lay asleep in his bed, and our old fellow-student lay asleep on the sofa. I could not dress myself without help; but I made up the fire, which was still burning, and got some coffee ready for them. In good time they too started up strong and well, and we admitted the sharp morning air at the windows, and looked at the tide that was still flowing towards us.

"When it turns at nine o'clock," said Herbert, cheerfully, "look out for us, and stand ready, you over there at Mill Pond Bank!"

CHAPTER LIV

It was one of those March days when the sun shines hot and the wind blows cold: when it is summer in the light, and winter in the shade. We had out pea-coats with us, and I took a bag. Of all my worldly possessions I took no more than the few necessaries that filled the bag. Where I might go, what I might do, or when I might return, were questions utterly unknown to me; nor did I vex my mind with them, for it was wholly set on Provis's safety. I only wondered for the passing moment, as I stopped at the door and looked back, under what altered circumstances I should next see those rooms, if ever.

We loitered down to the Temple stairs, and stood loitering there, as if we were not quite decided to go upon the water at all. Of course, I had taken care that the boat should be ready and everything in order. After a little show of indecision, which there were none to see but the two or three amphibious creatures belonging to our Temple stairs, we went on board and cast off; Herbert in the bow, I steering. It was then about high-water,—half-past eight.

Our plan was this. The tide, beginning to run down at nine, and being with us until three, we intended still to creep on after it had turned, and row against it until dark. We should then be well in those long reaches below Gravesend, between Kent and Essex, where the river is broad and solitary, where the water-side inhabitants are very few, and where lone public-houses are scattered here and there, of which we could choose one for a resting-place. There, we meant to lie by all night. The steamer for Hamburg and the steamer for Rotterdam would start from London at about nine on Thursday morning. We should know at what time to expect them, according to where we were, and would hail the first; so that, if by any accident we were not taken abroad, we should have another chance. We knew the distinguishing marks of each vessel.

The relief of being at last engaged in the execution of the purpose was so great to me that I felt it difficult to realize the condition in which I had been a few hours before. The crisp air, the sunlight, the movement on the river, and the moving river itself,—the road that ran with us, seeming to sympathize with us, animate us, and encourage us on,—freshened me with new hope. I felt mortified to be of so little use in the boat; but, there were few better oarsmen than my two friends, and they rowed with a steady stroke that was to last all day.

At that time, the steam-traffic on the Thames was far below its present extent, and watermen's boats were far more numerous. Of barges, sailing colliers, and coasting-traders, there were perhaps, as many as now; but of steam-ships, great and small, not a tithe or a twentieth part so many. Early as it was, there were plenty of scullers going here and there that morning, and plenty of barges dropping down with the tide; the navigation of the river between bridges, in an open boat, was a much easier and commoner matter in those days than it is in these; and we went ahead among many skiffs and wherries briskly.

Old London Bridge was soon passed, and old Billingsgate Market with its oyster-boats and Dutchmen, and the White Tower and Traitor's Gate, and we were in among the tiers of shipping. Here were the Leith, Aberdeen, and Glasgow steamers, loading and unloading goods, and looking immensely high out of the water as we passed alongside; here, were colliers by the score and score, with the coal-whippers plunging off stages on deck, as counterweights to measures of coal swinging up, which were then rattled over the side into barges; here, at her moorings was to-morrow's steamer for Rotterdam, of which we took good notice; and here to-morrow's for Hamburg, under whose bowsprit we crossed. And now I, sitting in the stern, could see, with a faster beating heart, Mill Pond Bank and Mill Pond stairs.

"Is he there?" said Herbert.

"Not yet."

"Right! He was not to come down till he saw us. Can you see his signal?"

"Not well from here; but I think I see it.—Now I see him! Pull both. Easy, Herbert. Oars!"

We touched the stairs lightly for a single moment, and he was on board, and we were off again. He had a boat-cloak with him, and a black canvas bag; and he looked as like a river-pilot as my heart could have wished.

"Dear boy!" he said, putting his arm on my shoulder, as he took his seat. "Faithful dear boy, well done. Thankye, thankye!"

Again among the tiers of shipping, in and out, avoiding rusty chain-cables frayed hempen hawsers and bobbing buoys, sinking for the moment floating broken baskets, scattering floating chips of wood and shaving, cleaving floating scum of coal, in and out, under the figure-head of the John of Sunderland making a speech to the winds (as is done by many Johns), and the Betsy of Yarmouth with a firm formality of bosom and her knobby eyes starting two inches out of her head; in and out, hammers going in ship-builders' yards, saws going at timber, clashing engines going at things unknown, pumps going in leaky ships, capstans going, ships going out to sea, and unintelligible sea-creatures roaring curses over the bulwarks at respondent lightermen, in and out,—out at last upon the clearer river, where the ships' boys might take their fenders in, no longer fishing in troubled waters with them over the side, and where the festooned sails might fly out to the wind.

At the Stairs where we had taken him abroad, and ever since, I had looked warily for any token of our being suspected. I had seen none. We certainly had not been, and at that time as certainly we were not either attended or followed by any boat. If we had been waited on by any boat, I should have run in to shore, and have obliged her to go on, or to make her purpose evident. But we held our own without any appearance of molestation.

He had his boat-cloak on him, and looked, as I have said, a natural part of the scene. It was remarkable (but perhaps the wretched life he had led accounted for it) that he was the least anxious of any of us. He was not indifferent, for he told me that he hoped to live to see his gentleman one of the best of gentlemen in a foreign country; he was not disposed to be passive or resigned, as I understood it; but he had no notion of meeting danger half way. When it came upon him, he confronted it, but it must come before he troubled himself.

"If you knowed, dear boy," he said to me, "what it is to sit here alonger my dear boy and have my smoke, arter having been day by day betwixt four walls, you'd envy me. But you don't know what it is."

"I think I know the delights of freedom," I answered.

"Ah," said he, shaking his head gravely. "But you don't know it equal to me. You must have been under lock and key, dear boy, to know it equal to me,—but I ain't a going to be low."

It occurred to me as inconsistent, that, for any mastering idea, he should have endangered his freedom, and even his life. But I reflected that perhaps freedom without danger was too much apart from all the habit of his existence to be to him what it would be to another man. I was not far out, since he said, after smoking a little:—

"You see, dear boy, when I was over yonder, t'other side the world, I was always a looking to this side; and it come flat to be there, for all I was a growing rich. Everybody knowed Magwitch, and Magwitch could come, and Magwitch could go, and nobody's head would be troubled about him. They ain't so easy concerning me here, dear boy,—wouldn't be, leastwise, if they knowed where I was."

"If all goes well," said I, "you will be perfectly free and safe again within a few hours."

"Well," he returned, drawing a long breath, "I hope so."

"And think so?"

He dipped his hand in the water over the boat's gunwale, and said, smiling with that softened air upon him which was not new to me:—

"Ay, I s'pose I think so, dear boy. We'd be puzzled to be more quiet and easy-going than we are at present. But—it's a flowing so soft and pleasant through the water, p'raps, as makes me think it—I was a thinking through my smoke just then, that we can no more see to the bottom of the next few hours than we can see to the bottom of this river what I catches hold of. Nor yet we can't no more hold their tide than I can hold this. And it's run through my fingers and gone, you see!" holding up his dripping hand.

"But for your face I should think you were a little despondent," said I.

"Not a bit on it, dear boy! It comes of flowing on so quiet, and of that there rippling at the boat's head making a sort of a Sunday tune. Maybe I'm a growing a trifle old besides."

He put his pipe back in his mouth with an undisturbed expression of face, and sat as composed and contented as if we were already out of England. Yet he was as submissive to a word of advice as if he had been in constant terror; for, when we ran ashore to get some bottles of beer into the boat, and he was stepping out, I hinted that I thought he would be safest where he was, and he said. "Do you, dear boy?" and quietly sat down again.

The air felt cold upon the river, but it was a bright day, and the sunshine was very cheering. The tide ran strong, I took care to lose none of it, and our steady stroke carried us on thoroughly well. By imperceptible degrees, as the tide ran out, we lost more and more of the nearer woods and hills, and dropped lower and lower between the muddy banks, but the tide was yet with us when we were off Gravesend. As our charge was wrapped in his cloak, I purposely passed within a boat or two's length of the floating Custom House, and so out to catch the stream, alongside of two emigrant ships, and under the bows of a large transport with troops on the forecastle looking down at us. And soon the tide began to slacken, and the craft lying at anchor to swing, and presently they had all swung round, and the ships that were taking advantage of the new tide to get up to the Pool began to crowd upon us in a fleet, and we kept under the shore, as much out of the strength of the tide now as we could, standing carefully off from low shallows and mudbanks.

Our oarsmen were so fresh, by dint of having occasionally let her drive with the tide for a minute or two, that a quarter of an hour's rest proved full as much as they wanted. We got ashore among some slippery stones while we ate and drank what we had with us, and looked about. It was like my own marsh country, flat and monotonous, and with a dim horizon; while the winding river turned and turned, and the great floating buoys upon it turned and turned, and everything else seemed stranded and still. For now the last of the fleet of ships was round the last low point we had headed; and the last green barge, straw-laden, with a brown sail, had followed; and some ballast-lighters, shaped like a child's first rude imitation of a boat, lay low in the mud; and a little squat shoal-lighthouse on open piles stood crippled in the mud on stilts and crutches; and slimy stakes stuck out of the mud, and slimy stones stuck out of the mud, and red landmarks and tidemarks stuck out of the mud, and an old landing-stage and an old roofless building slipped into the mud, and all about us was stagnation and mud.

We pushed off again, and made what way we could. It was much harder work now, but Herbert and Startop persevered, and rowed and rowed and rowed until the sun went down. By that time the river had lifted us a little, so that we could see above the bank. There was the red sun, on the low level of the shore, in a purple haze, fast deepening into black; and there was the solitary flat marsh; and far away there were the rising grounds, between which and us there seemed to be no life, save here and there in the foreground a melancholy gull.

As the night was fast falling, and as the moon, being past the full, would not rise early, we held a little council; a short one, for clearly our course was to lie by at the first lonely tavern we could find. So, they plied their oars once more, and I looked out for anything like a house. Thus we held on, speaking little, for four or five dull miles. It was very cold, and, a collier coming by us, with her galley-fire smoking and flaring, looked like a comfortable home. The night was as dark by this time as it would be until morning; and what light we had, seemed to come more from the river than the sky, as the oars in their dipping struck at a few reflected stars.

At this dismal time we were evidently all possessed by the idea that we were followed. As the tide made, it flapped heavily at irregular intervals against the shore; and whenever such a sound came, one or other of us was sure to start, and look in that direction. Here and there, the set of the current had worn down the bank into a little creek, and we were all suspicious of such places, and eyed them nervously. Sometimes, "What was that ripple?" one of us would say in a low voice. Or another, "Is that a boat yonder?" And afterwards we would fall into a dead silence, and I would sit impatiently thinking with what an unusual amount of noise the oars worked in the thowels.

At length we descried a light and a roof, and presently afterwards ran alongside a little causeway made of stones that had been picked up hard by. Leaving the rest in the boat, I stepped ashore, and found the light to be in a window of a public-house. It was a dirty place enough, and I dare say not unknown to smuggling adventurers; but there was a good fire in the kitchen, and there were eggs and bacon to eat, and various liquors to drink. Also, there were two double-bedded rooms,—"such as they were," the landlord said. No other company was in the house than the landlord, his wife, and a grizzled male creature, the "Jack" of the little causeway, who was as slimy and smeary as if he had been low-water mark too.

With this assistant, I went down to the boat again, and we all came ashore, and brought out the oars, and rudder and boat-hook, and all else, and hauled her up for the night. We made a very good meal by the kitchen fire, and then apportioned the bedrooms: Herbert and Startop were to occupy one; I and our charge the other. We found the air as carefully excluded from both, as if air were fatal to life; and there were more dirty clothes and bandboxes under the beds than I should have thought the family possessed. But we considered ourselves well off, notwithstanding, for a more solitary place we could not have found.

While we were comforting ourselves by the fire after our meal, the Jack—who was sitting in a corner, and who had a bloated pair of shoes on, which he had exhibited while we were eating our eggs and bacon, as interesting relics that he had taken a few days ago from the feet of a drowned seaman washed ashore—asked me if we had seen a four-oared galley going up with the tide? When I told him No, he said she must have gone down then, and yet she "took up too," when she left there.

"They must ha' thought better on't for some reason or another," said the Jack, "and gone down."

"A four-oared galley, did you say?" said I.

"A four," said the Jack, "and two sitters."

"Did they come ashore here?"

"They put in with a stone two-gallon jar for some beer. I'd ha' been glad to pison the beer myself," said the Jack, "or put some rattling physic in it."

"Why?"

"I know why," said the Jack. He spoke in a slushy voice, as if much mud had washed into his throat.

"He thinks," said the landlord, a weakly meditative man with a pale eye, who seemed to rely greatly on his Jack,—"he thinks they was, what they wasn't."

"I knows what I thinks," observed the Jack.

"You thinks Custum 'Us, Jack?" said the landlord.

"I do," said the Jack.

"Then you're wrong, Jack."

"AM I!"

In the infinite meaning of his reply and his boundless confidence in his views, the Jack took one of his bloated shoes off, looked into it, knocked a few stones out of it on the kitchen floor, and put it on again. He did this with the air of a Jack who was so right that he could afford to do anything.

"Why, what do you make out that they done with their buttons then, Jack?" asked the landlord, vacillating weakly.

"Done with their buttons?" returned the Jack. "Chucked 'em overboard. Swallered 'em. Sowed 'em, to come up small salad. Done with their buttons!"

"Don't be cheeky, Jack," remonstrated the landlord, in a melancholy and pathetic way.

"A Custum 'Us officer knows what to do with his Buttons," said the Jack, repeating the obnoxious word with the greatest contempt, "when they comes betwixt him and his own light. A four and two sitters don't go hanging and hovering, up with one tide and down with another, and both with and against another, without there being Custum 'Us at the bottom of it." Saying which he went out in disdain; and the landlord, having no one to reply upon, found it impracticable to pursue the subject.

This dialogue made us all uneasy, and me very uneasy. The dismal wind was muttering round the house, the tide was flapping at the shore, and I had a feeling that we were caged and threatened. A four-oared galley hovering about in so unusual a way as to attract this notice was an ugly circumstance that I could not get rid of. When I had induced Provis to go up to bed, I went outside with my two companions (Startop by this time knew the state of the case), and held another council. Whether we should remain at the house until near the steamer's time, which would be about one in the afternoon, or whether we should put off early in the morning, was the question we discussed. On the whole we deemed it the better course to lie where we were, until within an hour or so of the steamer's time, and then to get out in her track, and drift easily with the tide. Having settled to do this, we returned into the house and went to bed.

I lay down with the greater part of my clothes on, and slept well for a few hours. When I awoke, the wind had risen, and the sign of the house (the Ship) was creaking and banging about, with noises that startled me. Rising softly, for my charge lay fast asleep, I looked out of the window. It commanded the causeway where we had hauled up our boat, and, as my eyes adapted themselves to the light of the clouded moon, I saw two men looking into her. They passed by under the window, looking at nothing else, and they did not go down to the landing-place which I could discern to be empty, but struck across the marsh in the direction of the Nore.

My first impulse was to call up Herbert, and show him the two men going away. But reflecting, before I got into his room, which was at the back of the house and adjoined mine, that he and Startop had had a harder day than I, and were fatigued, I forbore. Going back to my window, I could see the two men moving over the marsh. In that light, however, I soon lost them, and, feeling very cold, lay down to think of the matter, and fell asleep again.

We were up early. As we walked to and fro, all four together, before breakfast, I deemed it right to recount what I had seen. Again our charge was the least anxious of the party. It was very likely that the men belonged to the Custom House, he said quietly, and that they had no thought of us. I tried to persuade myself that it was so,—as, indeed, it might easily be. However, I proposed that he and I should walk away together to a distant point we could see, and that the boat should take us aboard there, or as near there as might prove feasible, at about noon. This being considered a good precaution, soon after breakfast he and I set forth, without saying anything at the tavern.

He smoked his pipe as we went along, and sometimes stopped to clap me on the shoulder. One would have supposed that it was I who was in danger, not he, and that he was reassuring me. We spoke very little. As we approached the point, I begged him to remain in a sheltered place, while I went on to reconnoitre; for it was towards it that the men had passed in the night. He complied, and I went on alone. There was no boat off the point, nor any boat drawn up anywhere near it, nor were there any signs of the men having embarked there. But, to be sure, the tide was high, and there might have been some footpints under water.

When he looked out from his shelter in the distance, and saw that I waved my hat to him to come up, he rejoined me, and there we waited; sometimes lying on the bank, wrapped in our coats, and sometimes moving about to warm ourselves, until we saw our boat coming round. We got aboard easily, and rowed out into the track of the steamer. By that time it wanted but ten minutes of one o'clock, and we began to look out for her smoke.

But, it was half-past one before we saw her smoke, and soon afterwards we saw behind it the smoke of another steamer. As they were coming on at full speed, we got the two bags ready, and took that opportunity of saying good by to Herbert and Startop. We had all shaken hands cordially, and neither Herbert's eyes nor mine were quite dry, when I saw a four-oared galley shoot out from under the bank but a little way ahead of us, and row out into the same track.

A stretch of shore had been as yet between us and the steamer's smoke, by reason of the bend and wind of the river; but now she was visible, coming head on. I called to Herbert and Startop to keep before the tide, that she might see us lying by for her, and I adjured Provis to sit quite still, wrapped in his cloak. He answered cheerily, "Trust to me, dear boy," and sat like a statue. Meantime the galley, which was very skilfully handled, had crossed us, let us come up with her, and fallen alongside. Leaving just room enough for the play of the oars, she kept alongside, drifting when we drifted, and pulling a stroke or two when we pulled. Of the two sitters one held the rudder-lines, and looked at us attentively,—as did all the rowers; the other sitter was wrapped up, much as Provis was, and seemed to shrink, and whisper some instruction to the steerer as he looked at us. Not a word was spoken in either boat.

Startop could make out, after a few minutes, which steamer was first, and gave me the word "Hamburg," in a low voice, as we sat face to face. She was nearing us very fast, and the beating of her peddles grew louder and louder. I felt as if her shadow were absolutely upon us, when the galley hailed us. I answered.

"You have a returned Transport there," said the man who held the lines. "That's the man, wrapped in the cloak. His name is Abel Magwitch, otherwise Provis. I apprehend that man, and call upon him to surrender, and you to assist."

At the same moment, without giving any audible direction to his crew, he ran the galley abroad of us. They had pulled one sudden stroke ahead, had got their oars in, had run athwart us, and were holding on to our gunwale, before we knew what they were doing. This caused great confusion on board the steamer, and I heard them calling to us, and heard the order given to stop the paddles, and heard them stop, but felt her driving down upon us irresistibly. In the same moment, I saw the steersman of the galley lay his hand on his prisoner's shoulder, and saw that both boats were swinging round with the force of the tide, and saw that all hands on board the steamer were running forward quite frantically. Still, in the same moment, I saw the prisoner start up, lean across his captor, and pull the cloak from the neck of the shrinking sitter in the galley. Still in the same moment, I saw that the face disclosed, was the face of the other convict of long ago. Still, in the same moment, I saw the face tilt backward with a white terror on it that I shall never forget, and heard a great cry on board the steamer, and a loud splash in the water, and felt the boat sink from under me.

It was but for an instant that I seemed to struggle with a thousand mill-weirs and a thousand flashes of light; that instant past, I was taken on board the galley. Herbert was there, and Startop was there; but our boat was gone, and the two convicts were gone.

What with the cries aboard the steamer, and the furious blowing off of her steam, and her driving on, and our driving on, I could not at first distinguish sky from water or shore from shore; but the crew of the galley righted her with great speed, and, pulling certain swift strong strokes ahead, lay upon their oars, every man looking silently and eagerly at the water astern. Presently a dark object was seen in it, bearing towards us on the tide. No man spoke, but the steersman held up his hand, and all softly backed water, and kept the boat straight and true before it. As it came nearer, I saw it to be Magwitch, swimming, but not swimming freely. He was taken on board, and instantly manacled at the wrists and ankles.

The galley was kept steady, and the silent, eager look-out at the water was resumed. But, the Rotterdam steamer now came up, and apparently not understanding what had happened, came on at speed. By the time she had been hailed and stopped, both steamers were drifting away from us, and we were rising and falling in a troubled wake of water. The look-out was kept, long after all was still again and the two steamers were gone; but everybody knew that it was hopeless now.

At length we gave it up, and pulled under the shore towards the tavern we had lately left, where we were received with no little surprise. Here I was able to get some comforts for Magwitch,—Provis no longer,—who had received some very severe injury in the Chest, and a deep cut in the head.

He told me that he believed himself to have gone under the keel of the steamer, and to have been struck on the head in rising. The injury to his chest (which rendered his breathing extremely painful) he thought he had received against the side of the galley. He added that he did not pretend to say what he might or might not have done to Compeyson, but that, in the moment of his laying his hand on his cloak to identify him, that villain had staggered up and staggered back, and they had both gone overboard together, when the sudden wrenching of him (Magwitch) out of our boat, and the endeavor of his captor to keep him in it, had capsized us. He told me in a whisper that they had gone down fiercely locked in each other's arms, and that there had been a struggle under water, and that he had disengaged himself, struck out, and swum away.

I never had any reason to doubt the exact truth of what he thus told me. The officer who steered the galley gave the same account of their going overboard.

When I asked this officer's permission to change the prisoner's wet clothes by purchasing any spare garments I could get at the public-house, he gave it readily: merely observing that he must take charge of everything his prisoner had about him. So the pocket-book which had once been in my hands passed into the officer's. He further gave me leave to accompany the prisoner to London; but declined to accord that grace to my two friends.

The Jack at the Ship was instructed where the drowned man had gone down, and undertook to search for the body in the places where it was likeliest to come ashore. His interest in its recovery seemed to me to be much heightened when he heard that it had stockings on. Probably, it took about a dozen drowned men to fit him out completely; and that may have been the reason why the different articles of his dress were in various stages of decay.

We remained at the public-house until the tide turned, and then Magwitch was carried down to the galley and put on board. Herbert and Startop were to get to London by land, as soon as they could. We had a doleful parting, and when I took my place by Magwitch's side, I felt that that was my place henceforth while he lived.

For now, my repugnance to him had all melted away; and in the Hunted, wounded, shackled creature who held my hand in his, I only saw a man who had meant to be my benefactor, and who had felt affectionately, gratefully, and generously, towards me with great constancy through a series of years. I only saw in him a much better man than I had been to Joe.

His breathing became more difficult and painful as the night drew on, and often he could not repress a groan. I tried to rest him on the arm I could use, in any easy position; but it was dreadful to think that I could not be sorry at heart for his being badly hurt, since it was unquestionably best that he should die. That there were, still living, people enough who were able and willing to identify him, I could not doubt. That he would be leniently treated, I could not hope. He who had been presented in the worst light at his trial, who had since broken prison and had been tried again, who had returned from transportation under a life sentence, and who had occasioned the death of the man who was the cause of his arrest.

As we returned towards the setting sun we had yesterday left behind us, and as the stream of our hopes seemed all running back, I told him how grieved I was to think that he had come home for my sake.

"Dear boy," he answered, "I'm quite content to take my chance. I've seen my boy, and he can be a gentleman without me."

No. I had thought about that, while we had been there side by side. No. Apart from any inclinations of my own, I understood Wemmick's hint now. I foresaw that, being convicted, his possessions would be forfeited to the Crown.

"Lookee here, dear boy," said he "It's best as a gentleman should not be knowed to belong to me now. Only come to see me as if you come by chance alonger Wemmick. Sit where I can see you when I am swore to, for the last o' many times, and I don't ask no more."

"I will never stir from your side," said I, "when I am suffered to be near you. Please God, I will be as true to you as you have been to me!"

I felt his hand tremble as it held mine, and he turned his face away as he lay in the bottom of the boat, and I heard that old sound in his throat,—softened now, like all the rest of him. It was a good thing that he had touched this point, for it put into my mind what I might not otherwise have thought of until too late,—that he need never know how his hopes of enriching me had perished.

CHAPTER LV

He was taken to the Police Court next day, and would have been immediately committed for trial, but that it was necessary to send down for an old officer of the prison-ship from which he had once escaped, to speak to his identity. Nobody doubted it; but Compeyson, who had meant to depose to it, was tumbling on the tides, dead, and it happened that there was not at that time any prison officer in London who could give the required evidence. I had gone direct to Mr. Jaggers at his private house, on my arrival over night, to retain his assistance, and Mr. Jaggers on the prisoner's behalf would admit nothing. It was the sole resource; for he told me that the case must be over in five minutes when the witness was there, and that no power on earth could prevent its going against us.

I imparted to Mr. Jaggers my design of keeping him in ignorance of the fate of his wealth. Mr. Jaggers was querulous and angry with me for having "let it slip through my fingers," and said we must memorialize by and by, and try at all events for some of it. But he did not conceal from me that, although there might be many cases in which the forfeiture would not be exacted, there were no circumstances in this case to make it one of them. I understood that very well. I was not related to the outlaw, or connected with him by any recognizable tie; he had put his hand to no writing or settlement in my favor before his apprehension, and to do so now would be idle. I had no claim, and I finally resolved, and ever afterwards abided by the resolution, that my heart should never be sickened with the hopeless task of attempting to establish one.

There appeared to be reason for supposing that the drowned informer had hoped for a reward out of this forfeiture, and had obtained some accurate knowledge of Magwitch's affairs. When his body was found, many miles from the scene of his death, and so horribly disfigured that he was only recognizable by the contents of his pockets, notes were still legible, folded in a case he carried. Among these were the name of a banking-house in New South Wales, where a sum of money was, and the designation of certain lands of considerable value. Both these heads of information were in a list that Magwitch, while in prison, gave to Mr. Jaggers, of the possessions he supposed I should inherit. His ignorance, poor fellow, at last served him; he never mistrusted but that my inheritance was quite safe, with Mr. Jaggers's aid.

After three days' delay, during which the crown prosecution stood over for the production of the witness from the prison-ship, the witness came, and completed the easy case. He was committed to take his trial at the next Sessions, which would come on in a month.

It was at this dark time of my life that Herbert returned home one evening, a good deal cast down, and said,—

"My dear Handel, I fear I shall soon have to leave you."

His partner having prepared me for that, I was less surprised than he thought.

"We shall lose a fine opportunity if I put off going to Cairo, and I am very much afraid I must go, Handel, when you most need me."

"Herbert, I shall always need you, because I shall always love you; but my need is no greater now than at another time."

"You will be so lonely."

"I have not leisure to think of that," said I. "You know that I am always with him to the full extent of the time allowed, and that I should be with him all day long, if I could. And when I come away from him, you know that my thoughts are with him."

The dreadful condition to which he was brought, was so appalling to both of us, that we could not refer to it in plainer words.

"My dear fellow," said Herbert, "let the near prospect of our separation—for, it is very near—be my justification for troubling you about yourself. Have you thought of your future?"

"No, for I have been afraid to think of any future."

"But yours cannot be dismissed; indeed, my dear dear Handel, it must not be dismissed. I wish you would enter on it now, as far as a few friendly words go, with me."

"I will," said I.

"In this branch house of ours, Handel, we must have a—"

I saw that his delicacy was avoiding the right word, so I said, "A clerk."

"A clerk. And I hope it is not at all unlikely that he may expand (as a clerk of your acquaintance has expanded) into a partner. Now, Handel,—in short, my dear boy, will you come to me?"

There was something charmingly cordial and engaging in the manner in which after saying "Now, Handel," as if it were the grave beginning of a portentous business exordium, he had suddenly given up that tone, stretched out his honest hand, and spoken like a schoolboy.

"Clara and I have talked about it again and again," Herbert pursued, "and the dear little thing begged me only this evening, with tears in her eyes, to say to you that, if you will live with us when we come together, she will do her best to make you happy, and to convince her husband's friend that he is her friend too. We should get on so well, Handel!"

I thanked her heartily, and I thanked him heartily, but said I could not yet make sure of joining him as he so kindly offered. Firstly, my mind was too preoccupied to be able to take in the subject clearly. Secondly,—Yes! Secondly, there was a vague something lingering in my thoughts that will come out very near the end of this slight narrative.

"But if you thought, Herbert, that you could, without doing any injury to your business, leave the question open for a little while—"

"For any while," cried Herbert. "Six months, a year!"

"Not so long as that," said I. "Two or three months at most."

Herbert was highly delighted when we shook hands on this arrangement, and said he could now take courage to tell me that he believed he must go away at the end of the week.

"And Clara?" said I.

"The dear little thing," returned Herbert, "holds dutifully to her father as long as he lasts; but he won't last long. Mrs. Whimple confides to me that he is certainly going."

"Not to say an unfeeling thing," said I, "he cannot do better than go."

"I am afraid that must be admitted," said Herbert; "and then I shall come back for the dear little thing, and the dear little thing and I will walk quietly into the nearest church. Remember! The blessed darling comes of no family, my dear Handel, and never looked into the red book, and hasn't a notion about her grandpapa. What a fortune for the son of my mother!"

On the Saturday in that same week, I took my leave of Herbert,—full of bright hope, but sad and sorry to leave me,—as he sat on one of the seaport mail coaches. I went into a coffee-house to write a little note to Clara, telling her he had gone off, sending his love to her over and over again, and then went to my lonely home,—if it deserved the name; for it was now no home to me, and I had no home anywhere.

On the stairs I encountered Wemmick, who was coming down, after an unsuccessful application of his knuckles to my door. I had not seen him alone since the disastrous issue of the attempted flight; and he had come, in his private and personal capacity, to say a few words of explanation in reference to that failure.

"The late Compeyson," said Wemmick, "had by little and little got at the bottom of half of the regular business now transacted; and it was from the talk of some of his people in trouble (some of his people being always in trouble) that I heard what I did. I kept my ears open, seeming to have them shut, until I heard that he was absent, and I thought that would be the best time for making the attempt. I can only suppose now, that it was a part of his policy, as a very clever man, habitually to deceive his own instruments. You don't blame me, I hope, Mr. Pip? I am sure I tried to serve you, with all my heart."

"I am as sure of that, Wemmick, as you can be, and I thank you most earnestly for all your interest and friendship."

"Thank you, thank you very much. It's a bad job," said Wemmick, scratching his head, "and I assure you I haven't been so cut up for a long time. What I look at is the sacrifice of so much portable property. Dear me!"

"What I think of, Wemmick, is the poor owner of the property."

"Yes, to be sure," said Wemmick. "Of course, there can be no objection to your being sorry for him, and I'd put down a five-pound note myself to get him out of it. But what I look at is this. The late Compeyson having been beforehand with him in intelligence of his return, and being so determined to bring him to book, I do not think he could have been saved. Whereas, the portable property certainly could have been saved. That's the difference between the property and the owner, don't you see?"

I invited Wemmick to come up stairs, and refresh himself with a glass of grog before walking to Walworth. He accepted the invitation. While he was drinking his moderate allowance, he said, with nothing to lead up to it, and after having appeared rather fidgety,—

"What do you think of my meaning to take a holiday on Monday, Mr. Pip?"

"Why, I suppose you have not done such a thing these twelve months."

"These twelve years, more likely," said Wemmick. "Yes. I'm going to take a holiday. More than that; I'm going to take a walk. More than that; I'm going to ask you to take a walk with me."

I was about to excuse myself, as being but a bad companion just then, when Wemmick anticipated me.

"I know your engagements," said he, "and I know you are out of sorts, Mr. Pip. But if you could oblige me, I should take it as a kindness. It ain't a long walk, and it's an early one. Say it might occupy you (including breakfast on the walk) from eight to twelve. Couldn't you stretch a point and manage it?"

He had done so much for me at various times, that this was very little to do for him. I said I could manage it,—would manage it,—and he was so very much pleased by my acquiescence, that I was pleased too. At his particular request, I appointed to call for him at the Castle at half past eight on Monday morning, and so we parted for the time.

Punctual to my appointment, I rang at the Castle gate on the Monday morning, and was received by Wemmick himself, who struck me as looking tighter than usual, and having a sleeker hat on. Within, there were two glasses of rum and milk prepared, and two biscuits. The Aged must have been stirring with the lark, for, glancing into the perspective of his bedroom, I observed that his bed was empty.

When we had fortified ourselves with the rum and milk and biscuits, and were going out for the walk with that training preparation on us, I was considerably surprised to see Wemmick take up a fishing-rod, and put it over his shoulder. "Why, we are not going fishing!" said I. "No," returned Wemmick, "but I like to walk with one."

I thought this odd; however, I said nothing, and we set off. We went towards Camberwell Green, and when we were thereabouts, Wemmick said suddenly,—

"Halloa! Here's a church!"

There was nothing very surprising in that; but again, I was rather surprised, when he said, as if he were animated by a brilliant idea,—

"Let's go in!"

We went in, Wemmick leaving his fishing-rod in the porch, and looked all round. In the mean time, Wemmick was diving into his coat-pockets, and getting something out of paper there.

"Halloa!" said he. "Here's a couple of pair of gloves! Let's put 'em on!"

As the gloves were white kid gloves, and as the post-office was widened to its utmost extent, I now began to have my strong suspicions. They were strengthened into certainty when I beheld the Aged enter at a side door, escorting a lady.

"Halloa!" said Wemmick. "Here's Miss Skiffins! Let's have a wedding."

That discreet damsel was attired as usual, except that she was now engaged in substituting for her green kid gloves a pair of white. The Aged was likewise occupied in preparing a similar sacrifice for the altar of Hymen. The old gentleman, however, experienced so much difficulty in getting his gloves on, that Wemmick found it necessary to put him with his back against a pillar, and then to get behind the pillar himself and pull away at them, while I for my part held the old gentleman round the waist, that he might present and equal and safe resistance. By dint of this ingenious scheme, his gloves were got on to perfection.

The clerk and clergyman then appearing, we were ranged in order at those fatal rails. True to his notion of seeming to do it all without preparation, I heard Wemmick say to himself, as he took something out of his waistcoat-pocket before the service began, "Halloa! Here's a ring!"

I acted in the capacity of backer, or best-man, to the bridegroom; while a little limp pew-opener in a soft bonnet like a baby's, made a feint of being the bosom friend of Miss Skiffins. The responsibility of giving the lady away devolved upon the Aged, which led to the clergyman's being unintentionally scandalized, and it happened thus. When he said, "Who giveth this woman to be married to this man?" the old gentlemen, not in the least knowing what point of the ceremony we had arrived at, stood most amiably beaming at the ten commandments. Upon which, the clergyman said again, "WHO giveth this woman to be married to this man?" The old gentleman being still in a state of most estimable unconsciousness, the bridegroom cried out in his accustomed voice, "Now Aged P. you know; who giveth?" To which the Aged replied with great briskness, before saying that he gave, "All right, John, all right, my boy!" And the clergyman came to so gloomy a pause upon it, that I had doubts for the moment whether we should get completely married that day.

It was completely done, however, and when we were going out of church Wemmick took the cover off the font, and put his white gloves in it, and put the cover on again. Mrs. Wemmick, more heedful of the future, put her white gloves in her pocket and assumed her green. "Now, Mr. Pip," said Wemmick, triumphantly shouldering the fishing-rod as we came out, "let me ask you whether anybody would suppose this to be a wedding-party!"

Breakfast had been ordered at a pleasant little tavern, a mile or so away upon the rising ground beyond the green; and there was a bagatelle board in the room, in case we should desire to unbend our minds after the solemnity. It was pleasant to observe that Mrs. Wemmick no longer unwound Wemmick's arm when it adapted itself to her figure, but sat in a high-backed chair against the wall, like a violoncello in its case, and submitted to be embraced as that melodious instrument might have done.

We had an excellent breakfast, and when any one declined anything on table, Wemmick said, "Provided by contract, you know; don't be afraid of it!" I drank to the new couple, drank to the Aged, drank to the Castle, saluted the bride at parting, and made myself as agreeable as I could.

Wemmick came down to the door with me, and I again shook hands with him, and wished him joy.

"Thankee!" said Wemmick, rubbing his hands. "She's such a manager of fowls, you have no idea. You shall have some eggs, and judge for yourself. I say, Mr. Pip!" calling me back, and speaking low. "This is altogether a Walworth sentiment, please."

"I understand. Not to be mentioned in Little Britain," said I.

Wemmick nodded. "After what you let out the other day, Mr. Jaggers may as well not know of it. He might think my brain was softening, or something of the kind."

CHAPTER LVI

He lay in prison very ill, during the whole interval between his committal for trial and the coming round of the Sessions. He had broken two ribs, they had wounded one of his lungs, and he breathed with great pain and difficulty, which increased daily. It was a consequence of his hurt that he spoke so low as to be scarcely audible; therefore he spoke very little. But he was ever ready to listen to me; and it became the first duty of my life to say to him, and read to him, what I knew he ought to hear.

Being far too ill to remain in the common prison, he was removed, after the first day or so, into the infirmary. This gave me opportunities of being with him that I could not otherwise have had. And but for his illness he would have been put in irons, for he was regarded as a determined prison-breaker, and I know not what else.

Although I saw him every day, it was for only a short time; hence, the regularly recurring spaces of our separation were long enough to record on his face any slight changes that occurred in his physical state. I do not recollect that I once saw any change in it for the better; he wasted, and became slowly weaker and worse, day by day, from the day when the prison door closed upon him.

The kind of submission or resignation that he showed was that of a man who was tired out. I sometimes derived an impression, from his manner or from a whispered word or two which escaped him, that he pondered over the question whether he might have been a better man under better circumstances. But he never justified himself by a hint tending that way, or tried to bend the past out of its eternal shape.

It happened on two or three occasions in my presence, that his desperate reputation was alluded to by one or other of the people in attendance on him. A smile crossed his face then, and he turned his eyes on me with a trustful look, as if he were confident that I had seen some small redeeming touch in him, even so long ago as when I was a little child. As to all the rest, he was humble and contrite, and I never knew him complain.

When the Sessions came round, Mr. Jaggers caused an application to be made for the postponement of his trial until the following Sessions. It was obviously made with the assurance that he could not live so long, and was refused. The trial came on at once, and, when he was put to the bar, he was seated in a chair. No objection was made to my getting close to the dock, on the outside of it, and holding the hand that he stretched forth to me.

The trial was very short and very clear. Such things as could be said for him were said,—how he had taken to industrious habits, and had thriven lawfully and reputably. But nothing could unsay the fact that he had returned, and was there in presence of the Judge and Jury. It was impossible to try him for that, and do otherwise than find him guilty.

At that time, it was the custom (as I learnt from my terrible experience of that Sessions) to devote a concluding day to the passing of Sentences, and to make a finishing effect with the Sentence of Death. But for the indelible picture that my remembrance now holds before me, I could scarcely believe, even as I write these words, that I saw two-and-thirty men and women put before the Judge to receive that sentence together. Foremost among the two-and-thirty was he; seated, that he might get breath enough to keep life in him.

The whole scene starts out again in the vivid colors of the moment, down to the drops of April rain on the windows of the court, glittering in the rays of April sun. Penned in the dock, as I again stood outside it at the corner with his hand in mine, were the two-and-thirty men and women; some defiant, some stricken with terror, some sobbing and weeping, some covering their faces, some staring gloomily about. There had been shrieks from among the women convicts; but they had been stilled, and a hush had succeeded. The sheriffs with their great chains and nosegays, other civic gewgaws and monsters, criers, ushers, a great gallery full of people,—a large theatrical audience,—looked on, as the two-and-thirty and the Judge were solemnly confronted. Then the Judge addressed them. Among the wretched creatures before him whom he must single out for special address was one who almost from his infancy had been an offender against the laws; who, after repeated imprisonments and punishments, had been at length sentenced to exile for a term of years; and who, under circumstances of great violence and daring, had made his escape and been re-sentenced to exile for life. That miserable man would seem for a time to have become convinced of his errors, when far removed from the scenes of his old offences, and to have lived a peaceable and honest life. But in a fatal moment, yielding to those propensities and passions, the indulgence of which had so long rendered him a scourge to society, he had quitted his haven of rest and repentance, and had come back to the country where he was proscribed. Being here presently denounced, he had for a time succeeded in evading the officers of Justice, but being at length seized while in the act of flight, he had resisted them, and had—he best knew whether by express design, or in the blindness of his hardihood—caused the death of his denouncer, to whom his whole career was known. The appointed punishment for his return to the land that had cast him out, being Death, and his case being this aggravated case, he must prepare himself to Die.

The sun was striking in at the great windows of the court, through the glittering drops of rain upon the glass, and it made a broad shaft of light between the two-and-thirty and the Judge, linking both together, and perhaps reminding some among the audience how both were passing on, with absolute equality, to the greater Judgment that knoweth all things, and cannot err. Rising for a moment, a distinct speck of face in this way of light, the prisoner said, "My Lord, I have received my sentence of Death from the Almighty, but I bow to yours," and sat down again. There was some hushing, and the Judge went on with what he had to say to the rest. Then they were all formally doomed, and some of them were supported out, and some of them sauntered out with a haggard look of bravery, and a few nodded to the gallery, and two or three shook hands, and others went out chewing the fragments of herb they had taken from the sweet herbs lying about. He went last of all, because of having to be helped from his chair, and to go very slowly; and he held my hand while all the others were removed, and while the audience got up (putting their dresses right, as they might at church or elsewhere), and pointed down at this criminal or at that, and most of all at him and me.

I earnestly hoped and prayed that he might die before the Recorder's Report was made; but, in the dread of his lingering on, I began that night to write out a petition to the Home Secretary of State, setting forth my knowledge of him, and how it was that he had come back for my sake. I wrote it as fervently and pathetically as I could; and when I had finished it and sent it in, I wrote out other petitions to such men in authority as I hoped were the most merciful, and drew up one to the Crown itself. For several days and nights after he was sentenced I took no rest except when I fell asleep in my chair, but was wholly absorbed in these appeals. And after I had sent them in, I could not keep away from the places where they were, but felt as if they were more hopeful and less desperate when I was near them. In this unreasonable restlessness and pain of mind I would roam the streets of an evening, wandering by those offices and houses where I had left the petitions. To the present hour, the weary western streets of London on a cold, dusty spring night, with their ranges of stern, shut-up mansions, and their long rows of lamps, are melancholy to me from this association.

The daily visits I could make him were shortened now, and he was more strictly kept. Seeing, or fancying, that I was suspected of an intention of carrying poison to him, I asked to be searched before I sat down at his bedside, and told the officer who was always there, that I was willing to do anything that would assure him of the singleness of my designs. Nobody was hard with him or with me. There was duty to be done, and it was done, but not harshly. The officer always gave me the assurance that he was worse, and some other sick prisoners in the room, and some other prisoners who attended on them as sick nurses, (malefactors, but not incapable of kindness, God be thanked!) always joined in the same report.

As the days went on, I noticed more and more that he would lie placidly looking at the white ceiling, with an absence of light in his face until some word of mine brightened it for an instant, and then it would subside again. Sometimes he was almost or quite unable to speak, then he would answer me with slight pressures on my hand, and I grew to understand his meaning very well.

The number of the days had risen to ten, when I saw a greater change in him than I had seen yet. His eyes were turned towards the door, and lighted up as I entered.

"Dear boy," he said, as I sat down by his bed: "I thought you was late. But I knowed you couldn't be that."

"It is just the time," said I. "I waited for it at the gate."

"You always waits at the gate; don't you, dear boy?"

"Yes. Not to lose a moment of the time."

"Thank'ee dear boy, thank'ee. God bless you! You've never deserted me, dear boy."

I pressed his hand in silence, for I could not forget that I had once meant to desert him.

"And what's the best of all," he said, "you've been more comfortable alonger me, since I was under a dark cloud, than when the sun shone. That's best of all."

He lay on his back, breathing with great difficulty. Do what he would, and love me though he did, the light left his face ever and again, and a film came over the placid look at the white ceiling.

"Are you in much pain to-day?"

"I don't complain of none, dear boy."

"You never do complain."

He had spoken his last words. He smiled, and I understood his touch to mean that he wished to lift my hand, and lay it on his breast. I laid it there, and he smiled again, and put both his hands upon it.

The allotted time ran out, while we were thus; but, looking round, I found the governor of the prison standing near me, and he whispered, "You needn't go yet." I thanked him gratefully, and asked, "Might I speak to him, if he can hear me?"

The governor stepped aside, and beckoned the officer away. The change, though it was made without noise, drew back the film from the placid look at the white ceiling, and he looked most affectionately at me.

"Dear Magwitch, I must tell you now, at last. You understand what I say?"

A gentle pressure on my hand.

"You had a child once, whom you loved and lost."

A stronger pressure on my hand.

"She lived, and found powerful friends. She is living now. She is a lady and very beautiful. And I love her!"

With a last faint effort, which would have been powerless but for my yielding to it and assisting it, he raised my hand to his lips. Then, he gently let it sink upon his breast again, with his own hands lying on it. The placid look at the white ceiling came back, and passed away, and his head dropped quietly on his breast.

Mindful, then, of what we had read together, I thought of the two men who went up into the Temple to pray, and I knew there were no better words that I could say beside his bed, than "O Lord, be merciful to him a sinner!"

CHAPTER LVII

Now that I was left wholly to myself, I gave notice of my intention to quit the chambers in the Temple as soon as my tenancy could legally determine, and in the meanwhile to underlet them. At once I put bills up in the windows; for, I was in debt, and had scarcely any money, and began to be seriously alarmed by the state of my affairs. I ought rather to write that I should have been alarmed if I had had energy and concentration enough to help me to the clear perception of any truth beyond the fact that I was falling very ill. The late stress upon me had enabled me to put off illness, but not to put it away; I knew that it was coming on me now, and I knew very little else, and was even careless as to that.

For a day or two, I lay on the sofa, or on the floor,—anywhere, according as I happened to sink down,—with a heavy head and aching limbs, and no purpose, and no power. Then there came, one night which appeared of great duration, and which teemed with anxiety and horror; and when in the morning I tried to sit up in my bed and think of it, I found I could not do so.

Whether I really had been down in Garden Court in the dead of the night, groping about for the boat that I supposed to be there; whether I had two or three times come to myself on the staircase with great terror, not knowing how I had got out of bed; whether I had found myself lighting the lamp, possessed by the idea that he was coming up the stairs, and that the lights were blown out; whether I had been inexpressibly harassed by the distracted talking, laughing, and groaning of some one, and had half suspected those sounds to be of my own making; whether there had been a closed iron furnace in a dark corner of the room, and a voice had called out, over and over again, that Miss Havisham was consuming within it,—these were things that I tried to settle with myself and get into some order, as I lay that morning on my bed. But the vapor of a limekiln would come between me and them, disordering them all, and it was through the vapor at last that I saw two men looking at me.

"What do you want?" I asked, starting; "I don't know you."

"Well, sir," returned one of them, bending down and touching me on the shoulder, "this is a matter that you'll soon arrange, I dare say, but you're arrested."

"What is the debt?"

"Hundred and twenty-three pound, fifteen, six. Jeweller's account, I think."

"What is to be done?"

"You had better come to my house," said the man. "I keep a very nice house."

I made some attempt to get up and dress myself. When I next attended to them, they were standing a little off from the bed, looking at me. I still lay there.

"You see my state," said I. "I would come with you if I could; but indeed I am quite unable. If you take me from here, I think I shall die by the way."

Perhaps they replied, or argued the point, or tried to encourage me to believe that I was better than I thought. Forasmuch as they hang in my memory by only this one slender thread, I don't know what they did, except that they forbore to remove me.

That I had a fever and was avoided, that I suffered greatly, that I often lost my reason, that the time seemed interminable, that I confounded impossible existences with my own identity; that I was a brick in the house-wall, and yet entreating to be released from the giddy place where the builders had set me; that I was a steel beam of a vast engine, clashing and whirling over a gulf, and yet that I implored in my own person to have the engine stopped, and my part in it hammered off; that I passed through these phases of disease, I know of my own remembrance, and did in some sort know at the time. That I sometimes struggled with real people, in the belief that they were murderers, and that I would all at once comprehend that they meant to do me good, and would then sink exhausted in their arms, and suffer them to lay me down, I also knew at the time. But, above all, I knew that there was a constant tendency in all these people,—who, when I was very ill, would present all kinds of extraordinary transformations of the human face, and would be much dilated in size,—above all, I say, I knew that there was an extraordinary tendency in all these people, sooner or later, to settle down into the likeness of Joe.

After I had turned the worst point of my illness, I began to notice that while all its other features changed, this one consistent feature did not change. Whoever came about me, still settled down into Joe. I opened my eyes in the night, and I saw, in the great chair at the bedside, Joe. I opened my eyes in the day, and, sitting on the window-seat, smoking his pipe in the shaded open window, still I saw Joe. I asked for cooling drink, and the dear hand that gave it me was Joe's. I sank back on my pillow after drinking, and the face that looked so hopefully and tenderly upon me was the face of Joe.

At last, one day, I took courage, and said, "Is it Joe?"

And the dear old home-voice answered, "Which it air, old chap."

"O Joe, you break my heart! Look angry at me, Joe. Strike me, Joe. Tell me of my ingratitude. Don't be so good to me!"

For Joe had actually laid his head down on the pillow at my side, and put his arm round my neck, in his joy that I knew him.

"Which dear old Pip, old chap," said Joe, "you and me was ever friends. And when you're well enough to go out for a ride—what larks!"

After which, Joe withdrew to the window, and stood with his back towards me, wiping his eyes. And as my extreme weakness prevented me from getting up and going to him, I lay there, penitently whispering, "O God bless him! O God bless this gentle Christian man!"

Joe's eyes were red when I next found him beside me; but I was holding his hand, and we both felt happy.

"How long, dear Joe?"

"Which you meantersay, Pip, how long have your illness lasted, dear old chap?"

"Yes, Joe."

"It's the end of May, Pip. To-morrow is the first of June."

"And have you been here all that time, dear Joe?"

"Pretty nigh, old chap. For, as I says to Biddy when the news of your being ill were brought by letter, which it were brought by the post, and being formerly single he is now married though underpaid for a deal of walking and shoe-leather, but wealth were not a object on his part, and marriage were the great wish of his hart—"

"It is so delightful to hear you, Joe! But I interrupt you in what you said to Biddy."

"Which it were," said Joe, "that how you might be amongst strangers, and that how you and me having been ever friends, a wisit at such a moment might not prove unacceptabobble. And Biddy, her word were, 'Go to him, without loss of time.' That," said Joe, summing up with his judicial air, "were the word of Biddy. 'Go to him,' Biddy say, 'without loss of time.' In short, I shouldn't greatly deceive you," Joe added, after a little grave reflection, "if I represented to you that the word of that young woman were, 'without a minute's loss of time.'"

There Joe cut himself short, and informed me that I was to be talked to in great moderation, and that I was to take a little nourishment at stated frequent times, whether I felt inclined for it or not, and that I was to submit myself to all his orders. So I kissed his hand, and lay quiet, while he proceeded to indite a note to Biddy, with my love in it.

Evidently Biddy had taught Joe to write. As I lay in bed looking at him, it made me, in my weak state, cry again with pleasure to see the pride with which he set about his letter. My bedstead, divested of its curtains, had been removed, with me upon it, into the sitting-room, as the airiest and largest, and the carpet had been taken away, and the room kept always fresh and wholesome night and day. At my own writing-table, pushed into a corner and cumbered with little bottles, Joe now sat down to his great work, first choosing a pen from the pen-tray as if it were a chest of large tools, and tucking up his sleeves as if he were going to wield a crow-bar or sledgehammer. It was necessary for Joe to hold on heavily to the table with his left elbow, and to get his right leg well out behind him, before he could begin; and when he did begin he made every down-stroke so slowly that it might have been six feet long, while at every up-stroke I could hear his pen spluttering extensively. He had a curious idea that the inkstand was on the side of him where it was not, and constantly dipped his pen into space, and seemed quite satisfied with the result. Occasionally, he was tripped up by some orthographical stumbling-block; but on the whole he got on very well indeed; and when he had signed his name, and had removed a finishing blot from the paper to the crown of his head with his two forefingers, he got up and hovered about the table, trying the effect of his performance from various points of view, as it lay there, with unbounded satisfaction.

Not to make Joe uneasy by talking too much, even if I had been able to talk much, I deferred asking him about Miss Havisham until next day. He shook his head when I then asked him if she had recovered.

"Is she dead, Joe?"

"Why you see, old chap," said Joe, in a tone of remonstrance, and by way of getting at it by degrees, "I wouldn't go so far as to say that, for that's a deal to say; but she ain't—"

"Living, Joe?"

"That's nigher where it is," said Joe; "she ain't living."

"Did she linger long, Joe?"

"Arter you was took ill, pretty much about what you might call (if you was put to it) a week," said Joe; still determined, on my account, to come at everything by degrees.

"Dear Joe, have you heard what becomes of her property?"

"Well, old chap," said Joe, "it do appear that she had settled the most of it, which I meantersay tied it up, on Miss Estella. But she had wrote out a little coddleshell in her own hand a day or two afore the accident, leaving a cool four thousand to Mr. Matthew Pocket. And why, do you suppose, above all things, Pip, she left that cool four thousand unto him? 'Because of Pip's account of him, the said Matthew.' I am told by Biddy, that air the writing," said Joe, repeating the legal turn as if it did him infinite good, 'account of him the said Matthew.' And a cool four thousand, Pip!"

I never discovered from whom Joe derived the conventional temperature of the four thousand pounds; but it appeared to make the sum of money more to him, and he had a manifest relish in insisting on its being cool.

This account gave me great joy, as it perfected the only good thing I had done. I asked Joe whether he had heard if any of the other relations had any legacies?

"Miss Sarah," said Joe, "she have twenty-five pound perannium fur to buy pills, on account of being bilious. Miss Georgiana, she have twenty pound down. Mrs.— what's the name of them wild beasts with humps, old chap?"

"Camels?" said I, wondering why he could possibly want to know.

Joe nodded. "Mrs. Camels," by which I presently understood he meant Camilla, "she have five pound fur to buy rushlights to put her in spirits when she wake up in the night."

The accuracy of these recitals was sufficiently obvious to me, to give me great confidence in Joe's information. "And now," said Joe, "you ain't that strong yet, old chap, that you can take in more nor one additional shovelful to-day. Old Orlick he's been a bustin' open a dwelling-ouse."

"Whose?" said I.

"Not, I grant you, but what his manners is given to blusterous," said Joe, apologetically; "still, a Englishman's ouse is his Castle, and castles must not be busted 'cept when done in war time. And wotsume'er the failings on his part, he were a corn and seedsman in his hart."

"Is it Pumblechook's house that has been broken into, then?"

"That's it, Pip," said Joe; "and they took his till, and they took his cash-box, and they drinked his wine, and they partook of his wittles, and they slapped his face, and they pulled his nose, and they tied him up to his bedpust, and they giv' him a dozen, and they stuffed his mouth full of flowering annuals to prewent his crying out. But he knowed Orlick, and Orlick's in the county jail."

By these approaches we arrived at unrestricted conversation. I was slow to gain strength, but I did slowly and surely become less weak, and Joe stayed with me, and I fancied I was little Pip again.

For the tenderness of Joe was so beautifully proportioned to my need, that I was like a child in his hands. He would sit and talk to me in the old confidence, and with the old simplicity, and in the old unassertive protecting way, so that I would half believe that all my life since the days of the old kitchen was one of the mental troubles of the fever that was gone. He did everything for me except the household work, for which he had engaged a very decent woman, after paying off the laundress on his first arrival. "Which I do assure you, Pip," he would often say, in explanation of that liberty; "I found her a tapping the spare bed, like a cask of beer, and drawing off the feathers in a bucket, for sale. Which she would have tapped yourn next, and draw'd it off with you a laying on it, and was then a carrying away the coals gradiwally in the soup-tureen and wegetable-dishes, and the wine and spirits in your Wellington boots."

We looked forward to the day when I should go out for a ride, as we had once looked forward to the day of my apprenticeship. And when the day came, and an open carriage was got into the Lane, Joe wrapped me up, took me in his arms, carried me down to it, and put me in, as if I were still the small helpless creature to whom he had so abundantly given of the wealth of his great nature.

And Joe got in beside me, and we drove away together into the country, where the rich summer growth was already on the trees and on the grass, and sweet summer scents filled all the air. The day happened to be Sunday, and when I looked on the loveliness around me, and thought how it had grown and changed, and how the little wild-flowers had been forming, and the voices of the birds had been strengthening, by day and by night, under the sun and under the stars, while poor I lay burning and tossing on my bed, the mere remembrance of having burned and tossed there came like a check upon my peace. But when I heard the Sunday bells, and looked around a little more upon the outspread beauty, I felt that I was not nearly thankful enough,— that I was too weak yet to be even that,—and I laid my head on Joe's shoulder, as I had laid it long ago when he had taken me to the Fair or where not, and it was too much for my young senses.

More composure came to me after a while, and we talked as we used to talk, lying on the grass at the old Battery. There was no change whatever in Joe. Exactly what he had been in my eyes then, he was in my eyes still; just as simply faithful, and as simply right.

When we got back again, and he lifted me out, and carried me—so easily!—across the court and up the stairs, I thought of that eventful Christmas Day when he had carried me over the marshes. We had not yet made any allusion to my change of fortune, nor did I know how much of my late history he was acquainted with. I was so doubtful of myself now, and put so much trust in him, that I could not satisfy myself whether I ought to refer to it when he did not.

"Have you heard, Joe," I asked him that evening, upon further consideration, as he smoked his pipe at the window, "who my patron was?"

"I heerd," returned Joe, "as it were not Miss Havisham, old chap."

"Did you hear who it was, Joe?"

"Well! I heerd as it were a person what sent the person what giv' you the bank-notes at the Jolly Bargemen, Pip."

"So it was."

"Astonishing!" said Joe, in the placidest way.

"Did you hear that he was dead, Joe?" I presently asked, with increasing diffidence.

"Which? Him as sent the bank-notes, Pip?"

"Yes."

"I think," said Joe, after meditating a long time, and looking rather evasively at the window-seat, "as I did hear tell that how he were something or another in a general way in that direction."

"Did you hear anything of his circumstances, Joe?"

"Not partickler, Pip."

"If you would like to hear, Joe—" I was beginning, when Joe got up and came to my sofa.

"Lookee here, old chap," said Joe, bending over me. "Ever the best of friends; ain't us, Pip?"

I was ashamed to answer him.

"Wery good, then," said Joe, as if I had answered; "that's all right; that's agreed upon. Then why go into subjects, old chap, which as betwixt two sech must be for ever onnecessary? There's subjects enough as betwixt two sech, without onnecessary ones. Lord! To think of your poor sister and her Rampages! And don't you remember Tickler?"

"I do indeed, Joe."

"Lookee here, old chap," said Joe. "I done what I could to keep you and Tickler in sunders, but my power were not always fully equal to my inclinations. For when your poor sister had a mind to drop into you, it were not so much," said Joe, in his favorite argumentative way, "that she dropped into me too, if I put myself in opposition to her, but that she dropped into you always heavier for it. I noticed that. It ain't a grab at a man's whisker, not yet a shake or two of a man (to which your sister was quite welcome), that 'ud put a man off from getting a little child out of punishment. But when that little child is dropped into heavier for that grab of whisker or shaking, then that man naterally up and says to himself, 'Where is the good as you are a doing? I grant you I see the 'arm,' says the man, 'but I don't see the good. I call upon you, sir, therefore, to pint out the good.'"

"The man says?" I observed, as Joe waited for me to speak.

"The man says," Joe assented. "Is he right, that man?"

"Dear Joe, he is always right."

"Well, old chap," said Joe, "then abide by your words. If he's always right (which in general he's more likely wrong), he's right when he says this: Supposing ever you kep any little matter to yourself, when you was a little child, you kep it mostly because you know'd as J. Gargery's power to part you and Tickler in sunders were not fully equal to his inclinations. Theerfore, think no more of it as betwixt two sech, and do not let us pass remarks upon onnecessary subjects. Biddy giv' herself a deal o' trouble with me afore I left (for I am almost awful dull), as I should view it in this light, and, viewing it in this light, as I should so put it. Both of which," said Joe, quite charmed with his logical arrangement, "being done, now this to you a true friend, say. Namely. You mustn't go a overdoing on it, but you must have your supper and your wine and water, and you must be put betwixt the sheets."

The delicacy with which Joe dismissed this theme, and the sweet tact and kindness with which Biddy—who with her woman's wit had found me out so soon—had prepared him for it, made a deep impression on my mind. But whether Joe knew how poor I was, and how my great expectations had all dissolved, like our own marsh mists before the sun, I could not understand.

Another thing in Joe that I could not understand when it first began to develop itself, but which I soon arrived at a sorrowful comprehension of, was this: As I became stronger and better, Joe became a little less easy with me. In my weakness and entire dependence on him, the dear fellow had fallen into the old tone, and called me by the old names, the dear "old Pip, old chap," that now were music in my ears. I too had fallen into the old ways, only happy and thankful that he let me. But, imperceptibly, though I held by them fast, Joe's hold upon them began to slacken; and whereas I wondered at this, at first, I soon began to understand that the cause of it was in me, and that the fault of it was all mine.

Ah! Had I given Joe no reason to doubt my constancy, and to think that in prosperity I should grow cold to him and cast him off? Had I given Joe's innocent heart no cause to feel instinctively that as I got stronger, his hold upon me would be weaker, and that he had better loosen it in time and let me go, before I plucked myself away?

It was on the third or fourth occasion of my going out walking in the Temple Gardens leaning on Joe's arm, that I saw this change in him very plainly. We had been sitting in the bright warm sunlight, looking at the river, and I chanced to say as we got up,—

"See, Joe! I can walk quite strongly. Now, you shall see me walk back by myself."

"Which do not overdo it, Pip," said Joe; "but I shall be happy fur to see you able, sir."

The last word grated on me; but how could I remonstrate! I walked no further than the gate of the gardens, and then pretended to be weaker than I was, and asked Joe for his arm. Joe gave it me, but was thoughtful.

I, for my part, was thoughtful too; for, how best to check this growing change in Joe was a great perplexity to my remorseful thoughts. That I was ashamed to tell him exactly how I was placed, and what I had come down to, I do not seek to conceal; but I hope my reluctance was not quite an unworthy one. He would want to help me out of his little savings, I knew, and I knew that he ought not to help me, and that I must not suffer him to do it.

It was a thoughtful evening with both of us. But, before we went to bed, I had resolved that I would wait over to-morrow,—to-morrow being Sunday,—and would begin my new course with the new week. On Monday morning I would speak to Joe about this change, I would lay aside this last vestige of reserve, I would tell him what I had in my thoughts (that Secondly, not yet arrived at), and why I had not decided to go out to Herbert, and then the change would be conquered for ever. As I cleared, Joe cleared, and it seemed as though he had sympathetically arrived at a resolution too.

We had a quiet day on the Sunday, and we rode out into the country, and then walked in the fields.

"I feel thankful that I have been ill, Joe," I said.

"Dear old Pip, old chap, you're a'most come round, sir."

"It has been a memorable time for me, Joe."

"Likeways for myself, sir," Joe returned.

"We have had a time together, Joe, that I can never forget. There were days once, I know, that I did for a while forget; but I never shall forget these."

"Pip," said Joe, appearing a little hurried and troubled, "there has been larks. And, dear sir, what have been betwixt us—have been."

At night, when I had gone to bed, Joe came into my room, as he had done all through my recovery. He asked me if I felt sure that I was as well as in the morning?

"Yes, dear Joe, quite."

"And are always a getting stronger, old chap?"

"Yes, dear Joe, steadily."

Joe patted the coverlet on my shoulder with his great good hand, and said, in what I thought a husky voice, "Good night!"

When I got up in the morning, refreshed and stronger yet, I was full of my resolution to tell Joe all, without delay. I would tell him before breakfast. I would dress at once and go to his room and surprise him; for, it was the first day I had been up early. I went to his room, and he was not there. Not only was he not there, but his box was gone.

I hurried then to the breakfast-table, and on it found a letter. These were its brief contents:—

"Not wishful to intrude I have departured fur you are well again dear Pip and will do better without JO.

"P.S. Ever the best of friends."

Enclosed in the letter was a receipt for the debt and costs on which I had been arrested. Down to that moment, I had vainly supposed that my creditor had withdrawn, or suspended proceedings until I should be quite recovered. I had never dreamed of Joe's having paid the money; but Joe had paid it, and the receipt was in his name.

What remained for me now, but to follow him to the dear old forge, and there to have out my disclosure to him, and my penitent remonstrance with him, and there to relieve my mind and heart of that reserved Secondly, which had begun as a vague something lingering in my thoughts, and had formed into a settled purpose?

The purpose was, that I would go to Biddy, that I would show her how humbled and repentant I came back, that I would tell her how I had lost all I once hoped for, that I would remind her of our old confidences in my first unhappy time. Then I would say to her, "Biddy, I think you once liked me very well, when my errant heart, even while it strayed away from you, was quieter and better with you than it ever has been since. If you can like me only half as well once more, if you can take me with all my faults and disappointments on my head, if you can receive me like a forgiven child (and indeed I am as sorry, Biddy, and have as much need of a hushing voice and a soothing hand), I hope I am a little worthier of you that I was,—not much, but a little. And, Biddy, it shall rest with you to say whether I shall work at the forge with Joe, or whether I shall try for any different occupation down in this country, or whether we shall go away to a distant place where an opportunity awaits me which I set aside, when it was offered, until I knew your answer. And now, dear Biddy, if you can tell me that you will go through the world with me, you will surely make it a better world for me, and me a better man for it, and I will try hard to make it a better world for you."

Such was my purpose. After three days more of recovery, I went down to the old place to put it in execution. And how I sped in it is all I have left to tell.

CHAPTER LVIII

The tidings of my high fortunes having had a heavy fall had got down to my native place and its neighborhood before I got there. I found the Blue Boar in possession of the intelligence, and I found that it made a great change in the Boar's demeanour. Whereas the Boar had cultivated my good opinion with warm assiduity when I was coming into property, the Boar was exceedingly cool on the subject now that I was going out of property.

It was evening when I arrived, much fatigued by the journey I had so often made so easily. The Boar could not put me into my usual bedroom, which was engaged (probably by some one who had expectations), and could only assign me a very indifferent chamber among the pigeons and post-chaises up the yard. But I had as sound a sleep in that lodging as in the most superior accommodation the Boar could have given me, and the quality of my dreams was about the same as in the best bedroom.

Early in the morning, while my breakfast was getting ready, I strolled round by Satis House. There were printed bills on the gate and on bits of carpet hanging out of the windows, announcing a sale by auction of the Household Furniture and Effects, next week. The House itself was to be sold as old building materials, and pulled down. LOT 1 was marked in whitewashed knock-knee letters on the brew house; LOT 2 on that part of the main building which had been so long shut up. Other lots were marked off on other parts of the structure, and the ivy had been torn down to make room for the inscriptions, and much of it trailed low in the dust and was withered already. Stepping in for a moment at the open gate, and looking around me with the uncomfortable air of a stranger who had no business there, I saw the auctioneer's clerk walking on the casks and telling them off for the information of a catalogue-compiler, pen in hand, who made a temporary desk of the wheeled chair I had so often pushed along to the tune of Old Clem.

When I got back to my breakfast in the Boar's coffee-room, I found Mr. Pumblechook conversing with the landlord. Mr. Pumblechook (not improved in appearance by his late nocturnal adventure) was waiting for me, and addressed me in the following terms:—

"Young man, I am sorry to see you brought low. But what else could be expected! what else could be expected!"

As he extended his hand with a magnificently forgiving air, and as I was broken by illness and unfit to quarrel, I took it.

"William," said Mr. Pumblechook to the waiter, "put a muffin on table. And has it come to this! Has it come to this!"

I frowningly sat down to my breakfast. Mr. Pumblechook stood over me and poured out my tea—before I could touch the teapot—with the air of a benefactor who was resolved to be true to the last.

"William," said Mr. Pumblechook, mournfully, "put the salt on. In happier times," addressing me, "I think you took sugar? And did you take milk? You did. Sugar and milk. William, bring a watercress."

"Thank you," said I, shortly, "but I don't eat watercresses."

"You don't eat 'em," returned Mr. Pumblechook, sighing and nodding his head several times, as if he might have expected that, and as if abstinence from watercresses were consistent with my downfall. "True. The simple fruits of the earth. No. You needn't bring any, William."

I went on with my breakfast, and Mr. Pumblechook continued to stand over me, staring fishily and breathing noisily, as he always did.

"Little more than skin and bone!" mused Mr. Pumblechook, aloud. "And yet when he went from here (I may say with my blessing), and I spread afore him my humble store, like the Bee, he was as plump as a Peach!"

This reminded me of the wonderful difference between the servile manner in which he had offered his hand in my new prosperity, saying, "May I?" and the ostentatious clemency with which he had just now exhibited the same fat five fingers.

"Hah!" he went on, handing me the bread and butter. "And air you a going to Joseph?"

"In heaven's name," said I, firing in spite of myself, "what does it matter to you where I am going? Leave that teapot alone."

It was the worst course I could have taken, because it gave Pumblechook the opportunity he wanted.

"Yes, young man," said he, releasing the handle of the article in question, retiring a step or two from my table, and speaking for the behoof of the landlord and waiter at the door, "I will leave that teapot alone. You are right, young man. For once you are right. I forgit myself when I take such an interest in your breakfast, as to wish your frame, exhausted by the debilitating effects of prodigygality, to be stimilated by the 'olesome nourishment of your forefathers. And yet," said Pumblechook, turning to the landlord and waiter, and pointing me out at arm's length, "this is him as I ever sported with in his days of happy infancy! Tell me not it cannot be; I tell you this is him!"

A low murmur from the two replied. The waiter appeared to be particularly affected.

"This is him," said Pumblechook, "as I have rode in my shay-cart. This is him as I have seen brought up by hand. This is him untoe the sister of which I was uncle by marriage, as her name was Georgiana M'ria from her own mother, let him deny it if he can!"

The waiter seemed convinced that I could not deny it, and that it gave the case a black look.

"Young man," said Pumblechook, screwing his head at me in the old fashion, "you air a going to Joseph. What does it matter to me, you ask me, where you air a going? I say to you, Sir, you air a going to Joseph."

The waiter coughed, as if he modestly invited me to get over that.

"Now," said Pumblechook, and all this with a most exasperating air of saying in the cause of virtue what was perfectly convincing and conclusive, "I will tell you what to say to Joseph. Here is Squires of the Boar present, known and respected in this town, and here is William, which his father's name was Potkins if I do not deceive myself."

"You do not, sir," said William.

"In their presence," pursued Pumblechook, "I will tell you, young man, what to say to Joseph. Says you, "Joseph, I have this day seen my earliest benefactor and the founder of my fortun's. I will name no names, Joseph, but so they are pleased to call him up town, and I have seen that man.""

"I swear I don't see him here," said I.

"Say that likewise," retorted Pumblechook. "Say you said that, and even Joseph will probably betray surprise."

"There you quite mistake him," said I. "I know better."

"Says you," Pumblechook went on, "'Joseph, I have seen that man, and that man bears you no malice and bears me no malice. He knows your character, Joseph, and is well acquainted with your pig-headedness and ignorance; and he knows my character, Joseph, and he knows my want of gratitoode. Yes, Joseph,' says you," here Pumblechook shook his head and hand at me, "'he knows my total deficiency of common human gratitoode. He knows it, Joseph, as none can. You do not know it, Joseph, having no call to know it, but that man do.'"

Windy donkey as he was, it really amazed me that he could have the face to talk thus to mine.

"Says you, 'Joseph, he gave me a little message, which I will now repeat. It was that, in my being brought low, he saw the finger of Providence. He knowed that finger when he saw Joseph, and he saw it plain. It pinted out this writing, Joseph. Reward of ingratitoode to his earliest benefactor, and founder of fortun's. But that man said he did not repent of what he had done, Joseph. Not at all. It was right to do it, it was kind to do it, it was benevolent to do it, and he would do it again.'"

"It's pity," said I, scornfully, as I finished my interrupted breakfast, "that the man did not say what he had done and would do again."

"Squires of the Boar!" Pumblechook was now addressing the landlord, "and William! I have no objections to your mentioning, either up town or down town, if such should be your wishes, that it was right to do it, kind to do it, benevolent to do it, and that I would do it again."

With those words the Impostor shook them both by the hand, with an air, and left the house; leaving me much more astonished than delighted by the virtues of that same indefinite "it." I was not long after him in leaving the house too, and when I went down the High Street I saw him holding forth (no doubt to the same effect) at his shop door to a select group, who honored me with very unfavorable glances as I passed on the opposite side of the way.

But, it was only the pleasanter to turn to Biddy and to Joe, whose great forbearance shone more brightly than before, if that could be, contrasted with this brazen pretender. I went towards them slowly, for my limbs were weak, but with a sense of increasing relief as I drew nearer to them, and a sense of leaving arrogance and untruthfulness further and further behind.

The June weather was delicious. The sky was blue, the larks were soaring high over the green corn, I thought all that countryside more beautiful and peaceful by far than I had ever known it to be yet. Many pleasant pictures of the life that I would lead there, and of the change for the better that would come over my character when I had a guiding spirit at my side whose simple faith and clear home wisdom I had proved, beguiled my way. They awakened a tender emotion in me; for my heart was softened by my return, and such a change had come to pass, that I felt like one who was toiling home barefoot from distant travel, and whose wanderings had lasted many years.

The schoolhouse where Biddy was mistress I had never seen; but, the little roundabout lane by which I entered the village, for quietness' sake, took me past it. I was disappointed to find that the day was a holiday; no children were there, and Biddy's house was closed. Some hopeful notion of seeing her, busily engaged in her daily duties, before she saw me, had been in my mind and was defeated.

But the forge was a very short distance off, and I went towards it under the sweet green limes, listening for the clink of Joe's hammer. Long after I ought to have heard it, and long after I had fancied I heard it and found it but a fancy, all was still. The limes were there, and the white thorns were there, and the chestnut-trees were there, and their leaves rustled harmoniously when I stopped to listen; but, the clink of Joe's hammer was not in the midsummer wind.

Almost fearing, without knowing why, to come in view of the forge, I saw it at last, and saw that it was closed. No gleam of fire, no glittering shower of sparks, no roar of bellows; all shut up, and still.

But the house was not deserted, and the best parlor seemed to be in use, for there were white curtains fluttering in its window, and the window was open and gay with flowers. I went softly towards it, meaning to peep over the flowers, when Joe and Biddy stood before me, arm in arm.

At first Biddy gave a cry, as if she thought it was my apparition, but in another moment she was in my embrace. I wept to see her, and she wept to see me; I, because she looked so fresh and pleasant; she, because I looked so worn and white.

"But dear Biddy, how smart you are!"

"Yes, dear Pip."

"And Joe, how smart you are!"

"Yes, dear old Pip, old chap."

I looked at both of them, from one to the other, and then—

"It's my wedding-day!" cried Biddy, in a burst of happiness, "and I am married to Joe!"

They had taken me into the kitchen, and I had laid my head down on the old deal table. Biddy held one of my hands to her lips, and Joe's restoring touch was on my shoulder. "Which he warn't strong enough, my dear, fur to be surprised," said Joe. And Biddy said, "I ought to have thought of it, dear Joe, but I was too happy." They were both so overjoyed to see me, so proud to see me, so touched by my coming to them, so delighted that I should have come by accident to make their day complete!

My first thought was one of great thankfulness that I had never breathed this last baffled hope to Joe. How often, while he was with me in my illness, had it risen to my lips! How irrevocable would have been his knowledge of it, if he had remained with me but another hour!

"Dear Biddy," said I, "you have the best husband in the whole world, and if you could have seen him by my bed you would have—But no, you couldn't love him better than you do."

"No, I couldn't indeed," said Biddy.

"And, dear Joe, you have the best wife in the whole world, and she will make you as happy as even you deserve to be, you dear, good, noble Joe!"

Joe looked at me with a quivering lip, and fairly put his sleeve before his eyes.

"And Joe and Biddy both, as you have been to church to-day, and are in charity and love with all mankind, receive my humble thanks for all you have done for me, and all I have so ill repaid! And when I say that I am going away within the hour, for I am soon going abroad, and that I shall never rest until I have worked for the money with which you have kept me out of prison, and have sent it to you, don't think, dear Joe and Biddy, that if I could repay it a thousand times over, I suppose I could cancel a farthing of the debt I owe you, or that I would do so if I could!"

They were both melted by these words, and both entreated me to say no more.

"But I must say more. Dear Joe, I hope you will have children to love, and that some little fellow will sit in this chimney-corner of a winter night, who may remind you of another little fellow gone out of it for ever. Don't tell him, Joe, that I was thankless; don't tell him, Biddy, that I was ungenerous and unjust; only tell him that I honored you both, because you were both so good and true, and that, as your child, I said it would be natural to him to grow up a much better man than I did."

"I ain't a going," said Joe, from behind his sleeve, "to tell him nothink o' that natur, Pip. Nor Biddy ain't. Nor yet no one ain't."

"And now, though I know you have already done it in your own kind hearts, pray tell me, both, that you forgive me! Pray let me hear you say the words, that I may carry the sound of them away with me, and then I shall be able to believe that you can trust me, and think better of me, in the time to come!"

"O dear old Pip, old chap," said Joe. "God knows as I forgive you, if I have anythink to forgive!"

"Amen! And God knows I do!" echoed Biddy.

"Now let me go up and look at my old little room, and rest there a few minutes by myself. And then, when I have eaten and drunk with you, go with me as far as the finger-post, dear Joe and Biddy, before we say goode by!"

I sold all I had, and put aside as much as I could, for a composition with my creditors,—who gave me ample time to pay them in full,—and I went out and joined Herbert. Within a month, I had quitted England, and within two months I was clerk to Clarriker and Co., and within four months I assumed my first undivided responsibility. For the beam across the parlor ceiling at Mill Pond Bank had then ceased to tremble under old Bill Barley's growls and was at peace, and Herbert had gone away to marry Clara, and I was left in sole charge of the Eastern Branch until he brought her back.

Many a year went round before I was a partner in the House; but I lived happily with Herbert and his wife, and lived frugally, and paid my debts, and maintained a constant correspondence with Biddy and Joe. It was not until I became third in the Firm, that Clarriker betrayed me to Herbert; but he then declared that the secret of Herbert's partnership had been long enough upon his conscience, and he must tell it. So he told it, and Herbert was as much moved as amazed, and the dear fellow and I were not the worse friends for the long concealment. I must not leave it to be supposed that we were ever a great House, or that we made mints of money. We were not in a grand way of business, but we had a good name, and worked for our profits, and did very well. We owed so much to Herbert's ever cheerful industry and readiness, that I often wondered how I had conceived that old idea of his inaptitude, until I was one day enlightened by the reflection, that perhaps the inaptitude had never been in him at all, but had been in me.

CHAPTER LIX

For eleven years, I had not seen Joe nor Biddy with my bodily Eyes,—though they had both been often before my fancy in the East,—when, upon an evening in December, an hour or two after dark, I laid my hand softly on the latch of the old kitchen door. I touched it so softly that I was not heard, and looked in unseen. There, smoking his pipe in the old place by the kitchen firelight, as hale and as strong as ever, though a little gray, sat Joe; and there, fenced into the corner with Joe's leg, and sitting on my own little stool looking at the fire, was—I again!

"We giv' him the name of Pip for your sake, dear old chap," said Joe, delighted, when I took another stool by the child's side (but I did not rumple his hair), "and we hoped he might grow a little bit like you, and we think he do."

I thought so too, and I took him out for a walk next morning, and we talked immensely, understanding one another to perfection. And I took him down to the churchyard, and set him on a certain tombstone there, and he showed me from that elevation which stone was sacred to the memory of Philip Pirrip, late of this Parish, and Also Georgiana, Wife of the Above.

"Biddy," said I, when I talked with her after dinner, as her little girl lay sleeping in her lap, "you must give Pip to me one of these days; or lend him, at all events."

"No, no," said Biddy, gently. "You must marry."

"So Herbert and Clara say, but I don't think I shall, Biddy. I have so settled down in their home, that it's not at all likely. I am already quite an old bachelor."

Biddy looked down at her child, and put its little hand to her lips, and then put the good matronly hand with which she had touched it into mine. There was something in the action, and in the light pressure of Biddy's wedding-ring, that had a very pretty eloquence in it.

"Dear Pip," said Biddy, "you are sure you don't fret for her?"

"O no,—I think not, Biddy."

"Tell me as an old, old friend. Have you quite forgotten her?"

"My dear Biddy, I have forgotten nothing in my life that ever had a foremost place there, and little that ever had any place there. But that poor dream, as I once used to call it, has all gone by, Biddy,—all gone by!"

Nevertheless, I knew, while I said those words, that I secretly intended to revisit the site of the old house that evening, alone, for her sake. Yes, even so. For Estella's sake.

I had heard of her as leading a most unhappy life, and as being separated from her husband, who had used her with great cruelty, and who had become quite renowned as a compound of pride, avarice, brutality, and meanness. And I had heard of the death of her husband, from an accident consequent on his ill-treatment of a horse. This release had befallen her some two years before; for anything I knew, she was married again.

The early dinner hour at Joe's, left me abundance of time, without hurrying my talk with Biddy, to walk over to the old spot before dark. But, what with loitering on the way to look at old objects and to think of old times, the day had quite declined when I came to the place.

There was no house now, no brewery, no building whatever left, but the wall of the old garden. The cleared space had been enclosed with a rough fence, and looking over it, I saw that some of the old ivy had struck root anew, and was growing green on low quiet mounds of ruin. A gate in the fence standing ajar, I pushed it open, and went in.

A cold silvery mist had veiled the afternoon, and the moon was not yet up to scatter it. But, the stars were shining beyond the mist, and the moon was coming, and the evening was not dark. I could trace out where every part of the old house had been, and where the brewery had been, and where the gates, and where the casks. I had done so, and was looking along the desolate garden walk, when I beheld a solitary figure in it.

The figure showed itself aware of me, as I advanced. It had been moving towards me, but it stood still. As I drew nearer, I saw it to be the figure of a woman. As I drew nearer yet, it was about to turn away, when it stopped, and let me come up with it. Then, it faltered, as if much surprised, and uttered my name, and I cried out,—

"Estella!"

"I am greatly changed. I wonder you know me."

The freshness of her beauty was indeed gone, but its indescribable majesty and its indescribable charm remained. Those attractions in it, I had seen before; what I had never seen before, was the saddened, softened light of the once proud eyes; what I had never felt before was the friendly touch of the once insensible hand.

We sat down on a bench that was near, and I said, "After so many years, it is strange that we should thus meet again, Estella, here where our first meeting was! Do you often come back?"

"I have never been here since."

"Nor I."

The moon began to rise, and I thought of the placid look at the white ceiling, which had passed away. The moon began to rise, and I thought of the pressure on my hand when I had spoken the last words he had heard on earth.

Estella was the next to break the silence that ensued between us.

"I have very often hoped and intended to come back, but have been prevented by many circumstances. Poor, poor old place!"

The silvery mist was touched with the first rays of the moonlight, and the same rays touched the tears that dropped from her eyes. Not knowing that I saw them, and setting herself to get the better of them, she said quietly,—

"Were you wondering, as you walked along, how it came to be left in this condition?"

"Yes, Estella."

"The ground belongs to me. It is the only possession I have not relinquished. Everything else has gone from me, little by little, but I have kept this. It was the subject of the only determined resistance I made in all the wretched years."

"Is it to be built on?"

"At last, it is. I came here to take leave of it before its change. And you," she said, in a voice of touching interest to a wanderer,—"you live abroad still?"

"Still."

"And do well, I am sure?"

"I work pretty hard for a sufficient living, and therefore—yes, I do well."

"I have often thought of you," said Estella.

"Have you?"

"Of late, very often. There was a long hard time when I kept far from me the remembrance of what I had thrown away when I was quite ignorant of its worth. But since my duty has not been incompatible with the admission of that remembrance, I have given it a place in my heart."

"You have always held your place in my heart," I answered.

And we were silent again until she spoke.

"I little thought," said Estella, "that I should take leave of you in taking leave of this spot. I am very glad to do so."

"Glad to part again, Estella? To me, parting is a painful thing. To me, the remembrance of our last parting has been ever mournful and painful."

"But you said to me," returned Estella, very earnestly, "'God bless you, God forgive you!' And if you could say that to me then, you will not hesitate to say that to me now,—now, when suffering has been stronger than all other teaching, and has taught me to understand what your heart used to be. I have been bent and broken, but—I hope—into a better shape. Be as considerate and good to me as you were, and tell me we are friends."

"We are friends," said I, rising and bending over her, as she rose from the bench.

"And will continue friends apart," said Estella.

I took her hand in mine, and we went out of the ruined place; and, as the morning mists had risen long ago when I first left the forge, so the evening mists were rising now, and in all the broad expanse of tranquil light they showed to me, I saw no shadow of another parting from her.